U0039450

CHINESE

ENGLISH

現代

漢英

詞典

王存柏 ■ 編

王雪丙 ■ 原校訂

臺灣商務印書館

第二次改訂四角號碼檢字法　　　王雲五發明

第一條　　筆畫分為十種,各以號碼代表之如下:

號碼	筆名	筆形	舉例	說明	注意
0	頭	亠	言主广疒	獨立之點與獨立之橫相結合	0456789各種均由數筆合為一複筆。檢查時遇單筆與複筆並列,應儘量取複筆;如一應作0不作3,寸應作4不作2,厂應作7不作2,心應作8不作32,小應作9不作33。
1	橫	一乚乚	天土地江元風	包括橫,刁與右鈎	
2	垂	丨丿丨	山月千則	包括直,撇和左鈎	
3	點	丶丶	宀衤一厶之衣	包括點與捺	
4	乂	十乂	草杏皮刈大尌	兩筆相交	
5	插	扌	扌戈申史	一筆通過兩筆以上	
6	方	口	國鳴目四甲由	四邊齊整之形	
7	角	刁丿コ𠃌一	羽門辰陰雪衣學宰	橫與垂的鋒端相接處	
8	八	八丷人一	分頁羊余災永疋午	八字形與其變形	
9	小	小灬龸忄	尖糸舞㬎惟	小字形與其變形	

第二條　　每字祇取四角之筆。其順序:
(一)左上角　(二)右上角　(三)左下角　(四)右下角

（例）

```
 (一)左上角          (二)右上角
             端
 (三)左下角          (四)右下角
```

檢查時按四角之筆形及順序。每字得四碼:

（例）頏 = 0128　　截 = 4325　　睬 = 6789

第三條　　字之上部或下部,祇有一筆或一複筆時,無論在何地位,均作左角,其右角作0。

（例）宣　直　首　冬　軍　宗　母

每筆用過後,如再充他角,亦作0。

（例）干　之　持　掛　大　十　車　時

第四條　　由整個口門閂所成之字,其下角取內部之筆,但上下左右有他筆時,不在此例。

（例）因 = 6043　閒 = 7724　鬥 = 7712　茵 = 4460　瀾 = 3712

附　則

I 字體均照楷書如下表

正	住[0] 匕[1] 反 衤[3] 戶[3] 安 心[3] 卜[3] 斤[3] 刃[3] 业[23] 亦[4] 草[4] 真 執[4] 禺[7] 衣[3]
誤	住[3] 匕[2] 反[2] 衤 戶[1] 安 心[1] 卜 斤[1] 刃[2] 业[3] 亦[1] 草[1] 真[1] 執[5] 禺[2] 衣[4]

II 取筆時應注意之點

(1) 宀戶等字, 凡點下之橫, 右方與他筆相連者, 均作 3, 不作 0。

(2) 尸皿門等字, 方形之筆端延長於外者, 均作 7, 不作 6。

(3) 角筆之兩端, 不作 7, 如 乛[2]。

(4) 交义之筆, 不作 8, 如 美。

(5) 业 小 中有二筆, 水 小 旁有二筆, 均不作小形。

III 取角時應注意之點

(1) 獨立或平行之筆, 不問高低, 概以最左或最右者為角。

（例）　非　倬　疾　浦　帝

(2) 最左或最右之筆, 有他筆蓋於其上或承於其下時, 取蓋於上者為上角, 承於下者為下角。

（例）　宗　幸　寧　共

(3) 有兩複筆可取時, 在上角應取較高之複筆, 在下角應取較低之複筆。

（例）　功　盛　頤　鴨　奄

(4) 撇為他筆所承時, 取他筆為下角。

（例）　春　奎　碓　衣

(5) 左上之撇作左角, 其右角取右筆。

（例）　勾　鈎　俾　鳴

IV 四角同碼字較多時, 以右下角上方最貼近而露鋒芒之一筆為附角; 如該筆業已用過, 則附角作 0。

（例）　芒 = 4471[0]　元[1]　洋[1]　是[1]　疝[2]　歃[2]　畜[3]　殘[3]　主[4]　難[4]　霖[4]
　　　　毯[5]　拼[6]　蠻[6]　覽[7]　功[7]　郭[7]　癥[8]　愁[8]　金[9]　速[9]　仁[0]　見[0]

附角仍有同碼字時, 得按各該字所含橫筆(即第一種筆形, 包括橫刁及右鈎)之數順序排列:

例如「市」「帝」二字之四角及附角均同, 但市字含有二橫, 帝字含有三橫, 故市字在前帝字在後, 餘照此類推。

序

　　民國92年（2003年），我承廣東中山市市政府之邀請，參加了第四屆世界中山同鄉懇親大會及 國父孫中山先生136歲誕辰。大會中，有一記者來訪問我是否為多年前重慶商務印書館出版《現代漢英詞典》之編者。我問她是如何知道的？她說是由電腦中看到一檔案，謂當年毛澤東常使用這本王雲五校訂，王學哲編輯的《現代漢英詞典》。我問她有無確實證據。次日，她帶來一篇文章給我，這文章名叫〈毛澤東學英語〉，作者為林克，摘自中央文獻出版社2001年5月出版之《老一代革命家的讀書生活》。

　　該文作者林克是在1954年秋到毛澤東辦公室擔任他的國際問題秘書，前後有十二年。除了秘書工作外，大部分時間幫助他學習英語，茲擇要該文如下：

「毛澤東歷來十分重視中國語言和外國語言的學習，並主張把學習本國語言和學習外國語言結合起來。在70年代，他還提倡六十歲以下的『同志』要學習英語。1954年，我到他身邊工作時，他那時熟悉的單詞還不很多。他的湖南口音很重，有些英語單詞發音不準，他就讓我領讀。有時，他自己再練習幾遍，請我聽他的發音是否合乎標準。他身邊經常放著兩本字典，一部英漢字典、一部漢英字典，備他經常查閱，《現代漢英詞典》就是其中之一。」

　　上文可見當年毛澤東是相當注重英語，目前兩岸三地對外交流日繁，學習英語者日增，且開始學習英語者也愈來愈年輕，學習英語之工具如「英漢」及「漢英」詞典亦成為一件必需品。

　　這本《現代漢英詞典》是我在民國33年（1944年），大學四年級時開始編輯，經過兩年之工作，當我大學畢業後在重慶商務印書館編輯部服務時完成。當年「漢英詞典」非常缺少，且從來沒有用「四角號碼」編排者，所以出版後流行尚廣。惟當年所能收集之詞語僅約有三萬。直至民國40年（1951年）改由台北之華國出版社出版，為增進原書之效用，更就當時最流行之詞語盡量蒐集，得一千餘詞語，列為該詞典之附錄，離今不覺又是五十餘年。

　　我承臺灣商務印書館股東之愛護及支持，被選為該館之董事長。幸而公司組織健全，全體同仁工作努力。同時，我又從在美經營將近五十年之保險業退休。因此我有些空閒的時間，決定重編這本《現代漢英詞典》。回想當年，我是在四川成都市攻讀大學，民國33年我畢業後，到重慶工作。那時抗日戰爭尚未結束，經過八年抗戰的大後方，物資非常缺乏，沒有打字機更沒有今日的電腦，全是由我獨自用筆記簿紙，剪成今日的卡片，把收集之資料抄寫在紙片上，再用四角號碼排列。次序排成後，再抄寫在當時的筆記本上，約有一百本之多。再送呈先父王雲五先生校正。

民國 93 年（2004 年）初，我在檀香山時即開始重編這詞典，最初請了在「凱撒高中」（Kaiser High School）工讀的幾位華裔女學生協助我，把收集的資料剪貼在卡片上。我再選擇編寫，由原來約有三萬詞語增加爲五萬餘詞語。我仍採用原有之四角號碼排列，另加索引兩種，一爲部首筆劃，另一是用國語注音排列，因此本詞典可以採用三種系統來查索。

編寫完成後即寄回台北市財團法人王雲五圖書館基金會，聘請數位工讀生把資料放在電腦中，又請了侯儀玲和陳惠文兩位女士協助編寫與校對之工作。這過程都是相當的煩雜，需要一位主持者來統籌計劃，幸而得有王雲五基金會的館長趙佩芳女士來主持這件重大的責任。當年詞典之校訂，是由先父王王雲五先生親自校訂，現今先父已仙逝二十多年，我已不可能再得到他的教導了。幸而得有今日台灣商務印書館的總編輯方鵬程博士來擔任這件校訂的重任。我要在這裡向上述各位致謝。

最後，我想把這本重編的《現代漢英詞典》貢獻給與我「同舟共濟，共嘗甘苦」與我結爲夫妻已有六十年的呂慧貞女士。

王學哲於台北

0

0010₄

主 〔**Chu**〕 *n.* owner, proprietor, lord, master, chief, ruler, host, landlord, sovereign. *v.* rule, manage, play host to, stay with, *adj.* principal, leading, chief, main, important, prominent.

00-- 產物	staple product.
-- 席	*n.* chairman, president, speaker, host at dinner, toastmaster. *v.* preside, take the chair, be in chair.
-- 席團	presidium.
-- 意	sentiment, intention, will, decision.
-- 文	text, main body, decree, operative part of judgment.
01-- 語	subject.
04-- 計長	comptroller, pay master, accountant.
-- 計處	office of the comptroller general.
-- 謀	chief plotter, chief instigator, mastermind.
05-- 講	*n.* lecturer, *v.* deliver a lecture.
06-- 課	main subject, major course.
08-- 旋律	(in music) theme.
10-- 要	*n.* importance, essence, *adj.* important, essential, principal, main, chief, leading, major.
-- 要敵人	archenemy.
-- 要科目	major subject.
-- 要環節	key link.
-- 要矛盾	principal contradiction.
-- 要標誌	outstanding feature.
-- 要的	main, principal, chief, primary.
-- 要目標	main objective.
-- 要目的	superobjective.
11-- 張	*n.* advocacy, assertion, pretension, contention, assertion, maintenance. *v.* advocate, assert, maintain, hold, insist, contend, bear in mind.
12-- 形	archetype.
-- 刑	principal punishment, major penalty.
17-- 子	boss, master.
18-- 攻	main attack, major in.
20-- 位	host's seat, subject case.
-- 辭	subject.
21-- 旨	keynote, theme.
-- 旨鮮明	main idea is clear.
22-- 任	chief, head, superintendent, director, *v.* be in charge of, *adj.* in charge, in chief.
23-- 編	chief editor.
24-- 動	*n.* motive power, prime mover, *v.* take the leading part, *adj.* active, driving.
-- 動者	mover, promoter.
-- 動力	agency, action.
-- 動權	initiative.
-- 科	major subject.
-- 使	*n.* instigation, *v.* instigate.
27-- 角	hero, leading character.
將	chief commander.
30-- 宰	*n.* arbiter, *v.* dictate, overrule
-- 賓話別	both the host and guest bid adieu.
31-- 顧	customer, patron, client.
-- 顧常臨	customers constantly make calls.
33-- 治醫生	a physician-in-charge, chief physician
-- 演	play the leading part.
34-- 流	main stream, main current.
37-- 潮	main current.
38-- 導	leading, dominant, guiding
-- 導思想	dominant idea.
40-- 力	main force, stamina.
-- 力線	main line.
-- 力軍	main force, regular forces.
-- 力艦	capital ship.
-- 力戰	main operation.
42-- 婚	to preside over a wedding ceremony.

44-- 考 chief examiner.
-- 權 sovereignty, supreme power.
-- 權國家 sovereign state.
46-- 觀 n. subjectivity, subjective view, v. take a subjective view, adj. subjective.
-- 觀主義 subjectivism.
-- 觀認識 subjective view.
-- 觀論 subjectivism.
-- 觀願望 subjective wish.
-- 觀性 subjectivity.
47-- 犯 principal offense, principal offender.
-- 婦 lady, mistress, hostess, matron, landlady, goodwife.
-- 格 n. nominative, subject, adj. subjective.
-- 教 n. bishop, primate, cardinal, pontiff, hierarch, adj. episcopal.
-- 幹 n. superintendent, head, chief, v. superintend, manage.
50-- 事務所 principal office.
54-- 持 act as master, hold the reins.
-- 持正義 uphold justice.
-- 持人 anchor, host.
-- 持會議 preside over a meeting.
60-- 日 Sunday, Sabbath day, Lord's day.
-- 日學校 Sunday school.
-- 見 point of view.
-- 因 primary cause, principal factor.
61-- 題 principal theme, subject.
63-- 戰 vote of war, to advocate war.
-- 戰派 War Party.
75-- 體 main body, main part, principal part.
80-- 人 host, master, owner, head of the family, ruler of the roast.
-- 人翁 master, hero, heroine.
-- 義 principle, theory, doctrine, dogma, platform, ism.
-- 食 staple food, principal food.

88-- 筆 chief editor, editor in chief, managing editor.
-- 管 n. authority, management, administration, v. manage, have charge of.
-- 管機關 office in charge, administration.

童 〔Tong〕 n. child, lad, kid, youngster, boy, virgin, adj. childish, boyish, young, youthful, pure, bald.
01-- 顏 youthful countenance, boyish features, childlike features.
02-- 話 fairy tale, fable, juvenile story.
07-- 謠 juvenile song, nursery rime.
10-- 工 child labor, child laborer.
17-- 子 child, minor.
-- 子軍 boy scout.
21-- 貞 chastity, maidenhood.
24-- 裝 boy's dress, children's wear.
77-- 叟不欺 no imposition on old or young, neither young nor old cheated here.
80-- 年 childhood, youthful age.

壅 〔Yeong〕 v. stop, obstruct, block up.
30-- 塞 obstruct, block.
-- 塞窒息 block and suffocated.
37-- 閉 block up, congest.
-- 閉不通 obstructed, constipated.

0010₈
立 〔Li〕 n. liter, v. stand, set up, fix, erect, found, establish, draw up, make stand, put up, institute, arrange, stand on end, get on one's feet, adj. established, fixed, upright.
00-- 方 cube, hexahedron, adj. cubic, cubical.
-- 方碼 cubic yard.
-- 方寸 cubic inch.
-- 方根 cubic root.
-- 方體 cube, cubic.
-- 方體戰 three-dimensional warfare.
-- 方尺 cubic foot.
-- 方米 cubic meter.
-- 意 n. decision, volition, v. decide, resolve, make up one's

	mind, form an opinion, determine, fix one's resolution, propose.
-- 交橋	overpass, flyover.
02-- 刻	adj. instant, immediate, adv. instantly, directly, immediately, at once, in a second.
-- 新功	win fresh merit.
-- 證	n. proof, v. verify, prove, establish proof, bear testimony, mate out.
08-- 論	n. argument, proposition, position, v. argue, reason, lay down a proposition, make a point.
10-- 正	n. attention, v. draw oneself up, stand at attention.
-- 夏	beginning of summer, commencement of summer.
14-- 功	establish one's merit, win one's spurs.
22-- 穩	stand firm.
27-- 冬	beginning of winter, commencement of winter.
-- 身	rise in the world, establish oneself.
-- 約	conclude an agreement, enter bonds, bind to, contract, make agreement.
-- 約人	covenanter, promisor.
29-- 秋	beginning of autumn, commencement of autumn.
30-- 憲	n. constitution, v. establish a constitution.
-- 憲政體	constitutional form of government.
-- 憲制度	constitutional system.
-- 定	stay, set in, halt, make a stand.
-- 案	n. registration, v. put on record, register in a governmental office, charter.
34-- 法	n. legislation, enactment, law making, making of law, v. enact, legislate, make a law.

-- 法權	legislative power.
-- 法委員	legislator, member of the Legislative Yuan.
-- 法機關	legislature, legislative organ.
-- 法者	law maker, law giver, Solon.
-- 法院	The Legislative Yuan.
-- 法院長	President of the Legislative Yuan.
35-- 遺囑	make a will.
40-- 志	n. determination, v. decide, determine, resolve, make up one's mind.
41-- 櫃	cloth closet, wardrobe, hanging cupboard.
46-- 場	position, ground, footing, situation, stand point, point of view.
47-- 起	stand up, rise, rise to one's feet.
50-- 春	beginning of spring, commencement of spring.
52-- 誓	take oath, make a vow, swear, give one's word of honor.
60-- 國	n. foundation of a state, v. found a state.
-- 界	n. delimitation, v. delimit.
-- 足地	footing, foothold, station.
67-- 嗣	n. adoption, v. adopt, adopt an heir.
75-- 體	n. solid, cube, adj. solid, cubic.
-- 體音樂	stereo system.
-- 體幾何	solid geometry.
77-- 即交貨	prompt delivery, immediate delivery, spot delivery.

0011₁

症 〔Cheng〕 n. disease, malady.

23-- 狀	symptoms of a disease.

痙 〔Ching〕 n. cramp, v. cramp, be cramp, be contracted.

22-- 攣	n. convulsive fit, convulsions, spasm, cramp, v. be convulsed, be cramp, jerk,

twitch.

疵〔Tsy〕*n.* flaw, fault, scab, mole, defect.

17-- 瑕   flaw, defect, fault, blemish.

瘧〔Yaw〕*n.* malaria.

00-- 疾   malaria.

51-- 蚊   anopheles mosquito.

0011_4

痊〔Chyuan〕*v.* recover, get well, be cured, be restored to health, return to health, *adj.* cured, convalescent, well.

00-- 癒   recover.

疣〔You〕*n.* tumor, wart.

17-- 子   wart.

癱〔Tan〕*n.* palsy, paralysis, *v.* paralyze.

00-- 瘓   paralysis, paralytic, paralyzed.

17-- 子   palsied person, paralytic.

77-- 腳   paralyzed in the legs.

0011_7

疤〔Ba〕*n.* scar, scab, birthmark.

00-- 痕   scar.

瘟〔Wen〕*n.* epidemic, plague.

00-- 病   pestilence.

-- 疫   contagion, pestilence, infection, plague.

瘋〔Feng〕*n.* insanity, lunacy, *adj.* insane, lunatic, wild.

00-- 癲   *n.* insanity, lunacy, craziness, *v.* crack one's brain, *adj.* insane, out of one's right mind.

-- 癱   palsy.

17-- 子   madman, lunatic.

41-- 狂   insane, off one's rocker.

47-- 狗   mad dog.

80-- 人   mad man, maniac, lunatic, bedlamite.

-- 人院   madhouse, lunatic asylum.

0011_8

痘〔Dow〕*n.* smallpox, variola.

00-- 疤   smallpox scabs.

-- 瘡   smallpox.

44-- 苗   vaccine.

0012_0

痢〔Li〕*n.* dysentery, diarrhea.

00-- 疾   dysentery, diarrhea.

0012_1

疔〔Ding〕*n.* boil, carbuncle.

0012_2

疹〔Jeen〕*n.* skin disease, a kind of rash, pock.

17-- 子   measles, rash, pimple.

0012_7

病〔Bing〕*n.* illness, sickness, disease, disorder, complaint, abnormality, v. become ill, ail, catch a disease, lie ill, be in ill health, *adj.* ill, sick, being in ill health, out of order.

00-- 痊   *v.* recover from one's illness, get well, come round, be cured, *adj.* cured, recovered.

-- 魔   demon of ill health, disease, curse of a disease, malady.

-- 癒   *n.* recovery, *v.* recover from a disease, *adj.* recovered.

-- 死   *n.* death from disease, v. die of an illness, succumb to a disease, die in one's bed.

-- 理   pathology.

-- 弱   *n.* feebleness, *v.* have a weak constitution, *adj.* sickly, weak, infirm, invalid.

21-- 態   *n.* morbidity, *adj.* morbid.

22-- 例   case of a disease.

-- 倒   fall ill.

-- 後   *n.* convalescence, *adj.* convalescent.

23-- 狀   symptoms of a disease.

24-- 牀   sickbed.

休   sick leave.

27-- 假   sick leave, leave on sickness.

28-- 徵   symptoms of a disease.

-- 從口入   food is the source of all di-

	seases, more die by food than famine, disease comes in from the mouth.
30-- 室	sick room, ward, infirmary.
-- 房	ward.
-- 害蟲	plant diseases and insect pests.
-- 害蟲控制	pest control.
31-- 源	cause of a complaint, pathogeny.
44-- 菌	germs causing a disease.
47-- 根	old complaint, the lingering effect of a chronic disease.
48-- 故	die of illness.
50-- 蟲害	plant disease and insect pests.
50-- 毒	virus.
60-- 因	cause of a complaint.
61-- 號	sick personnel, patient.
71-- 歷	case history.
73-- 院	hospital, infirmary, nursing home.
80-- 人	sick man, patient, invalid.
94-- 灶	focus of disease.

瘖 〔Lau〕 *n.* consumption, decay, tuberculosis.

00-- 病	tuberculosis, consumption, phthisis.

痛 〔Tong〕 *n.* pain, ache, painfulness, trouble, grief, anguish, pang, agony, *v.* complain of a pain, be painful, grieve, *adj.* painful, sore.

00-- 言	bitter criticism, cutting remarks.
08-- 論	discuss with heat, express oneself strongly.
10-- 不欲生	grieve to the event of wishing to die.
-- 不可忍	unbearably painful.
18-- 改前非	reform thoroughly.
21-- 處	sore spot, tender spot.
26-- 自悔改	show deep repentance.
33-- 心	*n.* grief, distress, wound. *v.* grieve, be grieved, cut one to the heart, *adj.* brokenhearted.
-- 心疾首	feel extremely bitter about something.
-- 心切齒	burn with anger.
44-- 苦	*n.* pain, pang, torment, throe, agony, distress, affliction, suffering, misery, *v.* scarify, smite, wring, *adj.* bitter, grievous, painful, sore.
50-- 責	*n.* scotch blessing, *v.* knock one into the middle of next week, lay on the jack, exclaim against.
51-- 打	*n.* severe blow, sound thrashing, *v.* curry one's skin coat, strike hard, dust one's jacket.
53-- 感	fell keenly.
57-- 擊	batter, trounce.
60-- 罵	*n.* condemnation, abuse, scathing sarcasm, bit of one's mind, *v.* condemn, denounce, abuse, inveigh against, revile, blow up, give one's fits, taunt, rail at.
66-- 哭	cry bitterly, lament, moan, cry one's heart out, cry one's eyes out.
-- 哭失聲	cry bitterly.
-- 哭流涕	crying bitterly.
72-- 斥	denounce, scold severely, trounce.
87-- 飲	deep drinking, riotous drinking, revels. binge drinking.
-- 飲黃龍	drink for triumph over the enemy.
94-- 惜	regret deeply, be very sorry for.
95-- 快	highly delighted, delightful, outspoken, frank.
97-- 恨	*n.* bitter hatred, deep mortification, great regret, bitterness, *v.* hate bitterly, hate, detest, *adj.* virulent.
-- 恨在心	*n.* hatred in the mind, *v.* cherish bitter.
98-- 悔	*n.* bitter repentance, re-

morse, *v.* resent oneself, *adj.* contrite, remorseful.

瘍〔Yung〕*n.* ulcer, sore.
72-- 腫　　　sore, swollen up.

瘠〔Chi〕*v.* become lean, lose flesh, grow gaunt, fall out of flesh, *adj.* lean, thin, slender, slim, meager, skinny, fat as a hen's forehead.
00-- 瘦　　　lean, thin, emaciated
44-- 地　　　barren land.
-- 薄　　　sterile, unproductive.

癘〔Li〕*n.* dangerous disease.
00-- 疾　　　leprosy, leper.
-- 疫　　　plague, pestilence.

0012₈
疥〔Chie〕*n.* itch, itching.
00-- 癬　　　ringworm, itch, scab, mange.
-- 瘡　　　itch sores, scabies.

0012₉
痧〔Sha〕*n.* cholera.
17-- 子　　　measles.
67-- 眼　　　trachoma.

0013₁
痣〔Chih〕*n.* mole, spot, heat spot, mother's mark, blue mark.

0013₂
痕〔Hen〕*n.* scar, mark, cicatrice, trace, print, impression, ripples, wrinkles.
60-- 跡　　　scar of wound, marks, signs, evidence, trace.

癒〔Yuh〕*n.* cure, heal, treat successfully, be healed of.
80-- 合　　　consolidate.

癢〔Yang〕*n.* itch, *v.* itch, be itchy, *adj.* itchy, itching.
10-- 而不痛　　itching but not painful.
26-- 得難熬　　too itchy to endure.

0013₃
疼〔Tering〕*n.* pain, ache, rawness, smart, pang, sore, *v.* ache, sting, tingle, pain, feel a pain, *adj.* sore, painful.
00-- 痛　　　soreness, ache, pain.
20-- 愛　　　love tenderly, be very fond of.

0013₄
疾〔Chi〕*n.* sickness, disease, quickness, haste, *v.* dislike, hate, envy, *adj.* quick, hasty.
00-- 言　　　clatter.
-- 病　　　disease, illness, ailment.
-- 病保險　　sick insurance, health insurance.
-- 病津貼（福利）
　　　　　　sick benefit.
-- 病叢生　　be infested with all diseases.
10-- 惡　　　hate evil, hate evil doers.
12-- 飛　　　flit, swift-winged.
21-- 行　　　fly, trip, go like a streak, run like anything.
35-- 速　　　*n.* rapidity, swiftness, *adj.* speedy.
36-- 視　　　look at angrily.
40-- 奔　　　scour, scurry.
-- 走　　　*n.* running fast, *v.* run fast, walk fast, scour, trot, out strip the wind.
-- 走如飛　　run fast like flying.
44-- 苦　　　suffering.
60-- 足先登　　he who acts fast will succeed first.
62-- 呼　　　*n.* cry havoc, urging, *v.* shout, yell, call out, screech, urge.
71-- 厲　　　severe.
74-- 馳如風　　go like the wind.
77-- 風　　　gale, strong breeze, strong wind.
80-- 首痛心　　be enraged and feel pain at heart.

0013₇
癮〔Yin〕*n.* addiction, habit, craving.
11-- 頭　　　craving, addiction.
17-- 君子　　besotted opium-smoker.

0014₁
癖〔Pi〕*n.* addiction, vice, habit way, peculiarity, propensity.
95-- 性　　　inclination, propensity.
-- 性難改　　one's propensity is hard to

change.
47-- 好　　　　　*n.* passion, *adj.* given, fancied.

痔 〔**Chih**〕 *n.* piles, hemorrhoids.
00-- 瘡　　　　piles, hemorrhoids.
-- 瘡出血　　　piles bleeding, hemorrhoid bleeding.

0014₆
瘴 〔**Jang**〕 *n.* miasma, plague, epidemic caused by miasma.
00-- 癘　　　　plague, epidemic caused by miasma.
80-- 氣　　　　maisma, pestilential vapor.

0014₇
疫 〔**Yih**〕 *n.* epidemic, plague, pest, pestilence.
00-- 病　　　　epidemic, plague, pestilence.
44-- 苗　　　　vaccine.

疲 〔**Pi**〕 *n.* fatigue, weariness, exhaustion, *v.* be tired, get tired, be exhausted, grow weary, *adj.* wearisome, tiresome.
06-- 竭　　　　exhausted.
08-- 於　　　　be tired with.
-- 於奔命　　　tired from running around.
20-- 乏　　　　tired, fatigued, exhausted.
-- 乏無力　　　fatigued and weak.
29-- 倦　　　　*n.* fatigue, weariness, jade, *v.* tire, jade, fatigue, get tired.
-- 倦至極　　　being fatigued to the extreme.
99-- 勞審問　　persistent cross-examination.
-- 勞過度　　　excessive fatigue.
99-- 勞轟炸　　long and tedious harangue.

瘦 〔**Shou**〕 *n.* leanness, thinness, lankness, tire, *v.* become thin, lose flesh, become peaky, *adj.* skinny, lean, meager, slightly built, slight in build.
17-- 弱　　　　lean and weak, lank.
-- 子　　　　lean person.
40-- 肉　　　　lean meat.

71-- 長　　　　lanky.
90-- 小　　　　thin and weak, emaciated.
92-- 削　　　　gaunt, emaciated.

0014₈
癈 〔**Fey**〕 *adj.* chronic, incurable, *v.* abolish, disable.
72-- 兵　　　　disabled soldier.

癥 〔**Jeng**〕 *n.* disease of abdomen.

0015₁
癬 〔**Shean**〕 *n.* ringworm, tetter.

0016₁
瘖 〔**In**〕 *n.* dumb, mute, deaf and dumb.

0016₂
瘤 〔**Liou**〕 *n.* tumor, lump, wen, hunch, swelling.

0016₇
瘡 〔**Chuang**〕 *n.* sore, ulcer, wound.
00-- 疤　　　　scab, scar.
60-- 口　　　　open sore.

0017₂
疝 〔**Shan**〕 *n.* lumbago, hernia, swelling of the testicles.

癌 〔**Yen**〕 *n.* cancer, carcinoma.

0017₅
疳 〔**Gan**〕 *n.* venereal sore.

0018₁
癡 〔**Chih**〕 *n.* foolishness, stupidity, folly, *adj.* foolish, crazy, dull, stupid, silly, off at the nail, short of a sheet.
01-- 語　　　　drivel.
17-- 子　　　　madman, idiot.
23-- 獃　　　　stupid.
33-- 心妄想　　daydream, covet after something.
46-- 想　　　　vain-thought.
80-- 人說夢　　talk fantastic nonsense.
88-- 笑　　　　*n.* giggle, simper, horse laugh, *v.* simper.
95-- 情　　　　infatuation, blind love, passion of love.

0018₆
癩 〔**Lay**〕 *n.* skin disease, itch, scab, leprosy, *adj.* leprous.
00-- 瘡　　　　scabies.

-- 癬　ringworm, spreading scab.
-- 痢頭　scabby head.
40-- 皮狗　mangy dog, scabby dog.
58-- 蛤蟆　toad.

癲 〔Tien〕 n. madness, convulsions, v. go mad, have one's head turn, adj. mad, infatuated, bereft of reason.
00-- 癎　epilepsy.
41-- 狂　n. madness, mania, craziness, lunacy, insanity, v. be crazy, be crazed, go mad, run mad, have one's garret unfurnished, have rats, adj. crazy, lunatic, mad, loony, insane, off one's head, short of a sheet.
80-- 人　mad man, insane person, lunatic.
-- 人院　insane asylum, dark house, mad house.

0018₇
疚 〔Jiow〕 n. distress, shame, prolonged illness.

0018₉
痰 〔Tan〕 n. mucus, sputum, phlegm, expectoration.
10-- 盂　spittoon, cuspidor, spit box.

0019₄
痲 〔Ma〕 n. measles, chicken-pox, leprosy, pockmark.
00-- 瘋　leprosy.
-- 疹　measles.
10-- 面　pockmarked face.

0019₆
療 〔Liao〕 n. recuperation, restoration, v. cure, heal, restore, treat.
00-- 癒　cured, convalescent.
08-- 效　curative effect.
26-- 程　course of treatment.
33-- 治　cure, heal, treat.
34-- 法　therapy, cure.
80-- 養　medical treatment, recuperation, v. be under medical treatment, recruit one's health, recuperate, conva-

lesce.
-- 養院　convalescent hospital, infirmary, sanatorium.

0020₁
亭 〔Ting〕 n. pavilion, shed, arbor, kiosk.
00-- 亭　straight and erect.
-- 亭玉立　standing gracefully.
17-- 子　arbor, bower.
-- 子間　garret.
-- 台樓閣　pavilions, terraces and towers.

0021₁
庇 〔Pi〕 n. penthouse, v. cover, shelter, protect, shield, shade, harbor, take under one's wing.
04-- 護　n. protection, favor, shelter, harbor, v. protect, shield, harbor, hide.
24-- 佑　protection and support, divine protection and aid.

鹿 〔Lo〕 n. deer, stag, hind.
27-- 角　buckhorns, deer's horn, antler.
40-- 肉　venison.
-- 皮　deerskin.
44-- 茸　deer's young antlers.

靡 〔Mi〕 v. give in one's submission, do harm, bend to, yield to, submit to, destroy, adj. unable to stand, small, fine, extravagant.
55-- 費　extravagant.

龐 〔Pang〕 n. lofty house, adj. huge, gigantic, confused.
00-- 雜　disorder.
40-- 大　enormous, colossal, gigantic, huge, prodigious.

0021₂
庖 〔Pao〕 n. kitchen, cook-house.
00-- 廚房　kitchen.
10-- 丁　cook.
17-- 刀　kitchen knife, chopping knife.
-- 丁職務　perform the duties of another person.
23-- 代　substitute.

0021₃

充 〔Chong〕v. fill, fulfill, act as, apply, serve as, act in place of.

10-- 電	recharge.
-- 耳不聞	turn a deaf ear to.
27-- 血	n. congestion, determination of blood, adj. engorged.
30-- 塞	v. stuff, fill up, block up, adj. crowded, chock-full.
-- 實	n. replenishment, completion, fullness, fulfillment, v. complete, perfect, substantiate, improve, develop more fully, bulk out.
34-- 滿	n. fullness, suffusion, v. fill, be filled with, be full, be replete with. adj. full, plenty, abundant, crowded.
-- 滿人情	full of the milk of human kindness.
37-- 軍	n. exile, banishment, liability to labor as a camp-follower, v. banish, be exiled lag.
38-- 裕	ample, abundant.
-- 裕國庫	abundantly fill the national treasury.
44-- 填	stuff, stow.
-- 其量	at best.
60-- 足	n. sufficiency, competence, plenitude, adj. adequate, enough, sufficient, fertile, sound, ample, no lack.
-- 足的證據	abundant proof.
-- 足的資本	abundant capital.
72-- 斥	glut, flood, congest.
-- 斥市場	glut the market.
80-- 公	n. confiscation, v. confiscate, become public property.
-- 分	full, ample, sufficient.
-- 分利用	make full use of
-- 分供應	in amply supply.
-- 分就業	full employment.

87-- 飢	satisfy hunger, stay the stomach.
90-- 當	act for, serve as.

魔 〔Mo〕n. devil, demon, Satan, the enemy of man.

21-- 術	magic, black art, witchery, witchcraft, white magic.
-- 術家	magician, wizard, enchanter, wise man.
26-- 鬼	devil, demon, Satan.
40-- 力	magical power, fascination, power to charm, glamour, adj. fascinating, bewitching, attractive.
72-- 爪	claws of the evil one.
90-- 掌	clutches of the devil.

0021₄

雍 〔Iong〕v. block up, adj. harmonious, concordant.

26-- 和	n. peace, harmonious.
30-- 容華貴	graceful and poised, adj. regal.
-- 容自得	poised, imposing.

座 〔Tso〕n.seat, throne, stand, bench, foundation, cockpit.

09-- 談	talk, discuss.
-- 談會	forum, symposium, discussion meeting.
20-- 位	seat, chair.
40-- 右銘	motto, maxim.
41-- 標	(in math) coordinates.
80-- 無虛席	there is standing room only.

產 〔Chan〕n. childbirth, maternity, estate, property, confinement, lying-in, v. bear, produce, give birth, be confined, be in labor, become a mother, bring forth.

17-- 子	give birth to a son, bring forth the young.
22-- 出價值	value of output.
24-- 值	value of output.
-- 科	obstetrics.
-- 科醫生	obstetrician.
-- 科醫院	maternity hospital.
-- 科學校	school of obstetrics.

25-- 生	n. production, generation, bearing, breeding, creation. v. produce, yield, bring forth, generate, give birth to, see the light.
27-- 假	maternity leave.
31-- 額	output, the quantity of output.
32-- 業	n. property, estate, industry.
-- 業效果	industry effect, adj. industrial.
-- 業工人	industrial worker.
-- 業改組	industrial reorganization.
-- 業集團	industrial group.
-- 業利潤	industrial profits.
-- 業投資	industrial investment.
-- 業界	industrial circles.
-- 業戰	industrial war.
34-- 婆	midwife, maternity nurse.
35-- 油國	oil producing country.
44-- 地	place of production.
-- 地證明書	certificate of origin.
-- 地國	state of origin.
47-- 婦	woman in childbed, laying-in woman.
60-- 品	n. product, production, v. produce.
-- 品交換	exchange of product.
-- 品設計	product design.
-- 品說明	description of products.
-- 品說明書	catalogue.
-- 品種類	range of products.
-- 品測試	products testing.
-- 品壽命	product life.
-- 品中心	product center.
-- 品成本	product cost.
-- 品規格	product standard.
-- 品目錄	catalogue.
-- 品品種	product line.
-- 品質量	quality of products.
-- 品陳列	product display.
-- 品分配	product distribution.
-- 品銷售	sales of finished products.
-- 品性能	functions of products.
-- 量	yield, output, production.
-- 量統計	output, statistics.

71-- 區	producing district.
73-- 院	maternity home.
77-- 兒	newly-born baby.
89-- 銷	production and marketing.

麾 〔Hui〕 n. banner, colors, standard, flag, v. signalize, make signals, motion, wave, point.

塵 〔Chern〕 n. dust, dirt, rubbish, garbage, that which obscures the mind, adj. carnal.

25-- 積	v. begrime, adj. dusty, rusty-fusty-dusty.
30-- 寰	the world.
40-- 土	dust, ash.
-- 土嗆人	the dust is choking.
42-- 垢	dirt.

0021₆

庵 〔An〕 n. convent, religious house.

竟 〔Jing〕 n. end, close, utmost, extremity, somewhat to one's surprise, v. finish, go through to the end, adv. accomplish, adj. at an end, actually, finally, at last.

18-- 敢	have the courage to.
23-- 然如此	v. be so, adj. somewhat to one's surprise.
40-- 有	unexpectedly.
-- 有此事	everyone's surprise.

競 〔Ching〕 n. bout, contest, v. compete, strive, contend, struggle.

08-- 敵	rival.
20-- 爭	n. competition, contest, contention, warfare, conflict, bout, strife, v. compete, contend with, strive with, measure sword, play against.
-- 爭市場	competitive market.
-- 爭對手	competitor.
-- 爭者	contender, competitor rival.
-- 爭壓力	pressure of competition.
27-- 舟	boat race.
30-- 賽	contest, race, competition.
37-- 選	election campaign.
40-- 走	n. race, running match,

dash, v. run a race, run a match, run prizes.
54-- 技　　match, contest, race.
-- 技場　　arena, prize ring, circus.
60-- 買　　bid.
71-- 馬　　horse-racing.
　　馬師　　jockey, knight of the pig-skin.

0021₇

亢 〔Kang〕 v. uplift, adj. overbearing, strong.
60-- 旱　　drought.
-- 旱不雨　　drought.

亮 〔Liang〕 n. light, brightness,brilliancy, v. display, adj. light, clear, bright, brilliant, open, transparent.
00-- 度　　the intensity of a light.
90-- 光　　light.

廬 〔Lu〕 n. cottage, mat hut.
80-- 舍　　lodge.

贏 〔Ying〕 n. surplus, overplus, adj. full, abundant.
22-- 利　　profit, gain.
26-- 得　　win, gain, score, obtain.
88-- 餘　　excess, surplus, profit.

羸 〔Lei〕 adj. thin, emaciated, weak, lean.

0022₀

廁 〔Tsu〕 n. lavatory, toilet, closet, water closet, v. put in a row, insert.

0022₁

廝 〔Ssu〕 n. menial, servant, attendant, v. split, forage.
47-- 殺　　slay.

0022₂

序 〔Shiuh〕 n. preface, order, series.
00-- 言　　preface, foreward, prelude, introduction.
12-- 列　　order, sequence.

37-- 次　　order, sequence.
44-- 幕　　prelude, prologue.
55-- 曲　　prelude, overture.
58-- 數　　ordinal numbers.

0022₃

齊 〔Chyi〕 v. arrange, regulate, set in order, adj. orderly, level, even, equal.
20-- 集　　assemble.
-- 集一堂　　assemble in one place.
24-- 備　　all prepared, completed, ready, all arranged.
30-- 家治國　　regulate the family and rule the state.
33-- 心　　unanimous, of one mind, with one accord.
-- 心合力　　pull together.
47-- 聲　　with one voice.
58-- 整　　n. orderliness, v. clear up, adj. orderly, neat, well arranged, even.
60-- 唱　　sing in chorus.
80-- 全　　complete.

齋 〔Jai〕 n. vegetable food, fasting, study, library, v. fast, abstain from meat diet, respect.
41-- 期　　fast-day.
53-- 戒　　abstinence, fasting, purification, v. fast, practice abstinence, be in a state of abstinence.

0022₇

方 〔Fang〕 n. s4quare, rectangular, method, prescription, recipe, region, place, direction, way, means, adj. square, quadrangular.
00-- 言　　dialect, idiom, provincialism.
10-- 正　　square, upright, good, right, excellent, up the pole, of high moral character.
-- 面　　direction, position, section, region, side, part, sector,

square face, phase, aspect.

20-- 位　situation, direction, aspect, trend.

21-- 便　*n.* expediency, convenience, *adj.* expedient, convenient.

-- 便食品　convenience foods, fast foods.

26-- 程式　equation.

27-- 向　direction, course, trend, aspect, bearing, prospect.

-- 向盤　steering-wheel.

-- 纔　just, just then, now, just a while ago, a moment, only then.

30-- 案　plan, scheme, proposal.

34-- 法　method, ways, plan, measures, process, procedure, manner, scheme, mode, wise.

-- 法論　methodology.

40-- 才　just then, just now.

43-- 式　formula, formality, method, form, system, process, legal form, line and level, system.

47-- 根　square root.

50-- 丈　abbe, abbot, chief priest, prior.

52-- 括弧　square brackets.

60-- 里　square li.

-- 圓　square and round, surface area of a land.

67-- 略　policy, plan, scheme, tactics, mode of action, means, stratagem.

-- 陣　square, matrix.

80-- 今　at present.

84-- 針　direction, course, policy, purpose, aim, keynote, way, line.

市〔Shyh〕*n.* city, town, municipality, market place, fair, trade, mart, *adj.* city, civic, municipal, urban.

00-- 立　municipal.

-- 立學校　municipal school.

-- 廳　municipal hall, town house,

municipal building, municipal council.

07-- 郊　the suburbs.

08-- 議會　city council, municipal council.

-- 議員　city councilor, member of city council.

10-- 面　market, state of trade, area of business.

面蕭條　business is slim.

18-- 政　municipal administration, municipal work.

-- 政廳　municipal hall, town house.

-- 政府　municipal government, city government.

20-- 委　the Municipal Party Committee.

-- 集　fair, market.

21-- 街　street.

-- 價　market price, exchange value, extrinsic value.

26-- 自治　municipal self-government.

28-- 儈　crafty businessman.

30-- 容　the appearance of the city.

46-- 場　market, market place, fair forum, market hall.

60-- 邑　township, borough.

71-- 區　urban district, downtown, borough.

-- 長　mayor.

77-- 民　townsfolk, townspeople, citizen, people of a city, freeman, townsman.

-- 民大會　mass meeting of the city.

81-- 鎮　towns and cities.

帝〔Dih〕*n.* emperor, monarch, the throne, the supreme ruler on earth.

10-- 王　*n.* king, emperor, monarch, crowned head, *adj.* monarchic, imperial.

18-- 政　imperialism.

20-- 位　emperorship, throne, crown.

22-- 制　imperialism.

30-- 室　the royal family.

32-- 樂　the reign of an emperor.

60-- 國　*n.* empire, *adj.* imperial.

-- 國主義	imperialism.	
-- 國的	imperial.	
61-- 號	the appellation of an emperor.	
80-- 命	imperial order.	

腐 〔Fu〕 *n.* corruption, putridity, *v.* rot, go bad, spoil, turn sour, decompose, *adj.* spoiled, rotten, corrupt, putrid.

22-- 乳	soured bean-curd.
24-- 化	*n.* deterioration, decomposition, *v.* corrupt, demoralize.
-- 化分子	degenerate, corrupted element.
26-- 臭	*v.* taint, stink, putrefy, *adj.* fetid.
41-- 朽	decay.
68-- 敗	*n.* decomposition, rot, spoilage, corruption, decay, taint, *v.* be spoiled, rot, go bad, decompose, decay, *adj.* depraved, corrupt, rotten, decomposed.
85-- 蝕	*n.* corrosion, etching, canker, rot, *v.* corrode, rot, cauterize, erobe, rust, eat, bite in, burn into, give fire.
-- 蝕劑	caustic, corrodent, corrosive agent.
-- 蝕損壞	corrosion damage.
91-- 儒	pedants.
97-- 爛	*n.* decomposition, putridity, putrefaction, rot, corruption, *v.* decompose, decay, corrupt, putrefy, fester, *adj.* rotten, spoilt.

旁 〔Pang〕 *n.* the side, *adj.* side, lateral, *prep.* by, by the side of, beside.

00-- 註	interlinear explanation, marginal note, gloss.
01-- 證	circumstantial evidence.
14-- 聽生	listener, auditor.
-- 聽席	visitors' seat.
36-- 邊	the side.
46-- 觀	*v.* look on by the side, *adj.* indifferent.
-- 觀者	bystander, spectator, beholder.
80-- 人	bystander, outsider, looker-on, others.

席 〔Hsi〕 *n.* mat, table, feast, banquet. *v.* cover with mats, spread out.

20-- 位	seat, position.
59-- 捲	engulf, sweep over.

鷹 〔Chih〕 *n.* kind of animal.

育 〔Yu〕 *v.* bear children, bring forth, rear, support, raise, educate in virtue.

22-- 種	seed cultivation, breeding of seed.
66-- 嬰院	orphanage, nursery, foundling hospital.
80-- 養成人	bring up to manhood.

商 〔Shang〕 *n.* merchant, dealer, tradesman, trade, commerce, *v.* trade, carry on commerce, consult, deliberate, arrange, devise.

00-- 店	shops, stores.
08-- 議	*n.* deliberation, consultation, negotiation, *v.* discuss, confer, consult, negotiate, lay heads together, be closeted with.
-- 議大計	talk over the great scheme.
09-- 談	negotiate, exchange views.
10-- 賈	dealer, merchant.
17-- 務	commercial affairs, business affairs.
-- 務參贊	commercial counsellor.
-- 務代表	trade representative, commercial agent.
-- 務代表團	commercial mission.
21-- 行	firm, company.
27-- 船	merchant ship, mercantile marine, freighter.
30-- 定	agree upon.
32-- 業	commerce, trade.
-- 業部	the Ministry of Commerce.
-- 業大街	business street.
-- 業機密	trade secret.
-- 業網	trade network.
-- 業地理	commercial geography.

-- 業中心	business center, commercial center.
-- 業區	commercial district, downtown.
-- 業學校	commercial school.
-- 業公所	the bureau of commerce.
-- 業銀行	commercial bank.
34-- 法	commercial law, mercantile law, business law.
41-- 標	trademark, brand.
-- 標註冊	trademark registration.
-- 標權	trademark right.
46-- 場	market, bazaar.
47-- 埠	commercial port, treaty port.
60-- 界	commercial world.
-- 量	consult, talk over.
-- 團	trade corps.
-- 品	goods, commodity, ware, merchandise.
-- 品交流	interflow of commodities.
-- 品交易	commodity transaction.
-- 品糧	commodity grain.
-- 品制度	commodity system.
-- 品陳列所	show room, bazaar.
-- 品檢驗局	commodity inspection bureau.
-- 品展覽	commodity show, trade show.
61-- 號	trade name, business entity, firm name.
71-- 區	downtown, business quarter.
-- 學院	business college, business school.
-- 譽	good will, image, business reputation.
80-- 人	merchant, trader, businessman, son of trade.
-- 會	chamber of commerce.
-- 情	market (business) condition.

廊 〔Long〕 n. porch, corridor, veranda, colonnade.

10-- 下	veranda.

高 〔Kao〕 adj. high, tall, lofty, honorable, advanced, excellent, good in quality, noble.

00-- 度	height, altitude, elevation.
-- 產	high yield.
-- 音喇叭	loud speaker.
08-- 於	above, higher than.
-- 效	high efficiency.
09-- 談	brag, talk wild.
-- 工資	high wage.
11-- 麗	Korea.
-- 麗人	Korean.
12-- 水位	high water level.
-- 飛	soar.
20-- 位	dignity, precedence.
21-- 價	n. better price, high price, long figure, adj. costly.
-- 處	high place, high position.
-- 頻	high frequency.
22-- 低	height, high and low.
-- 低不平	uneven, rugged.
-- 利	usury.
-- 利貸	usury, high interest rate.
-- 利貸者	loan shark.
-- 峯	pinnacle, summit, peak.
-- 山	high mountain.
24-- 射砲	antiaircraft gun.
-- 估	overestimate, up-valuation.
-- 科技產品	high-tech products.
-- 升	be promoted, raise high.
27-- 血壓	hypertension, high blood pressure.
-- 級	high grade, high, superior.
-- 級商品	quality merchandise.
-- 級工程師	senior engineer.
-- 級職員	senior executive, officials.
-- 級的	advanced, high level.
-- 級材料	high-grade materials.
-- 級專家	high qualified specialist.
-- 級品	high quality goods.
-- 級會計師	senior accountant .
-- 級管理人員	high-ranking management personnel.
-- 級副官	adjutant general.
28-- 傲	n. mighty, arrogant, v. carry the head high, adj. high, high-minded, high-souled,

	lofty, haughty.
-- 收入	high income.
-- 稅率	high tariff .
-- 齡	aged, advanced age, in fullness of age.
-- 聳	surmount.
31-- 漲	v. upsurge, run high.
35-- 速	high-speed.
-- 速計算機	high-speed accounting machine.
-- 速公路	express highway, throughway.
36-- 溫	high temperature.
37-- 過	above.
-- 粱	kaoliang, sorghum.
-- 潮	high tide, climax, upsurge.
-- 消費	high mass consumption.
40-- 才生	advanced student.
-- 大	big, great, lofty.
-- 校	an institution of higher learning.
44-- 地	upland, highland, uplands altitude, high lying land.
-- 薪	high salary.
-- 薪階層	high-salaried stratum.
46-- 架鐵路	overhead railway.
47-- 聲	loud voice, high-tone, at the top of one's voice, in full cry.
-- 欄	high hurdles.
-- 檔	high-class, high-grade.
-- 檔貨	high-class goods.
50-- 中	senior school.
-- 貴	n. nobility, rank, distinction, adj. dignified, great, noble, grand, honorable, worshipful.
54-- 技術	hi-tech, high technology.
-- 技術產品	high-tech products.
-- 技術公司	high-tech firm.
60-- 昂價格	fancy price.
62-- 呼	shout, hail.
64-- 蹺	stilt.
67-- 明	wise, superior, excellent, bright, intelligent.
71-- 壓	high pressure, high-handed.
-- 壓手段	high-handed measures.

-- 壓線	high-tension wire.
-- 原	highland, upland, plateau.
77-- 舉	lift, uplift, rise to high honors.
-- 舉雙手	with both hands raised.
-- 層建築	high-rise building.
-- 層公寓	high-rise apartment.
-- 興	pleased, cheerful, pleasant, high-spirits, in merry pin, in high feather.
80-- 年	aged, senior.
-- 年生	senior student.
-- 分子	high polymer.
82-- 矮	tall and short, high and low, stature.
88-- 等	advanced, high of degree, in advance of, above all praise.
-- 等動物	higher animal.
-- 等法院	the high court.
-- 等考試	the Higher Civil Examination in the country.
-- 等教育	higher education.
-- 等會計	advanced accounting.
90-- 尚	high-principled, highminded, noble, aristocratic, magnanimous.
-- 尚華貴	elegant and majestic.
91-- 爐	blast furnace.
95-- 情曲	ode.

裔 〔Yih〕n. descendants, posterity, offspring, the skirt of a robe, border, frontier.

庸 〔Yong〕n. merit, service, v. employ, use, adj. ordinary, common, usual, foolish, stupid.

28-- 俗	vulgar, philistine.
40-- 才	mediocre person, ordinary talents, mediocre ability.
71-- 醫	quack doctor, gipsy.
80-- 人	insignificant person, simpleton.
-- 人自擾	ignorant people disturb themselves.
91-- 懦	dastard, craven.
-- 懦無能	indolent, timid and inca-

pable.

廓〔**Kuo**〕*v*. enlarge, expand, *adj*. wide, extensive, great, empty, open.

35-- 清 sweep away, clean up.

膺〔**Ying**〕*n*. breast, ornaments on the breast of a horse, *v*. bear, sustain, undertake, receive, oppose, stand up against, attack.

22-- 任 undertake.

廟〔**Miao**〕*n*. temple, shrine.

30-- 宇 temple.

80-- 會 temple fair.

90-- 堂文 court literature.

膏〔**Kao**〕*n*. fat, grease, lard, *v*. fatten, enrich, *adj*. rich, fertile, sweet.

35-- 油 lard.

37-- 梁 rich fare, good food.

40-- 壤 rich soil.

44-- 藥 plaster, ointment.

71-- 脂 grease, fat.

90-- 火 lamp oil.

0023_0

卞〔**Pien**〕*adj*. hurried.

0023_1

庶〔**Shu**〕*n*. people, mass, multitude, *adj*. numerous, various, all.

17-- 子 concubine's son.

17-- 務 general affairs, business.

-- 務員 one who attends to general affairs.

22-- 幾 almost, probably, nearly.

30-- 室 concubine.

77-- 民 people, masses, commons, crowd.

-- 母 father's concubine.

廡〔**Wu**〕*n*. veranda, passage, corridor, porch.

應〔**Ying**〕*n*. answer, response, echo, effect, *v*. should, must, ought, answer, respond, reply.

00-- 該 ought to, behoove.

08-- 許 promise.

10-- 否 whether it should be or not.

12-- 酬 *n*. social intercourse, *v*. entertain.

17-- 承 accept.

22-- 繼分 succession portions.

23-- 允 consent, comply with, assent to.

24-- 付 deal with, cope with, give and take.

26-- 得 *n*. merit, *v*. deserve, earn.

27-- 急 meet the exigence.

28-- 徵 be enlisted.

34-- 對 reply, answer.

38-- 邀 at the invitation of.

47-- 聲蟲 parrot.

50-- 接 receive.

-- 接不暇 not able to attend to all, very busy.

-- 接日 at-home day.

51-- 援 come to the rescue, go to one's aid.

63-- 戰 accept a battle, take the glove.

64-- 時 seasonable, fashionable.

77-- 用 *v*. use, apply, meet one's want, come into play, *adj*. applied, practical.

-- 用科學 applied science.

-- 用物品 various articles required.

78-- 驗 be confirmed, be verified.

90-- 當 proper, fitting, worthy of.

廕〔**Yin**〕*v*. shelter, protect, shade.

廳〔**Ting**〕*n*. hall, parlor, saloon, court, sub-prefecture.

90-- 堂 hall.

0023_2

康〔**Kang**〕*n*. peace, repose, happiness, *adj*. healthy, delightful.

22-- 樂 *n*. happiness, delight, joyfulness, mirth, *adj*. healthy, delightful.

25-- 健 healthy, vigorous.

30-- 寧 repose.

44-- 莊大道 broad thoroughfare.

80-- 年 abundant year, plentiful year.

豪〔**Hao**〕*adj*. eminent, excellent, superior, brave, heroic, martial.

00-- 商	merchant prince.
08-- 放	unrestrained, carefree, open-minded.
-- 放不羈	vigorous and unrestrained.
14-- 豬	porcupine.
24-- 俠	*n.* chivalry, *adj.* heroic, chivalrous, high-minded, high-spirited.
25-- 傑	hero.
30-- 富	millionaire.
-- 宴	sumptuous banquet.
34-- 邁	great, high, elevated, lofty, exalted, large-hearted.
40-- 爽	liberal, straightforward.
-- 奪巧取	take by force and by treachery.
44-- 華	luxurious.
-- 華商店	expensive shops.
-- 華旅館	luxury hotel.
50-- 貴	aristocratic.
64-- 賭	unrestrained gambling.
71-- 臣	powerful miniser.
77-- 舉	heroic movement.
80-- 氣	heroism, exhilaration.
-- 氣未除	one's spirit of chivalry still exists.
87-- 飲	drink a lot, revel.
90-- 光	dazzling light.
95-- 情	enthusiasm.

0023₇

庚〔Keng〕*n.* age, year.

廉〔Lien〕*n.* corner, angle, *adj.* frugal, honest, pure, incorrupt, cheap.

13-- 恥	modest, sense of honor.
21-- 價	cheap at the price, cheap, low price, dirt-cheap, dog-cheap, cheap as dirt.
-- 價商店	discount shop, store, bazar.
-- 價市場	bargain market or center.
-- 價部	bargain counter.
-- 價品	bargain, cheap goods, distress merchandise.
28-- 儉	frugal and clean.
37-- 潔	honest, cleanhanded, pure, upright.

0023₉

麼〔Mo〕*adj.* small, minute, delicate.

0024₀

府〔Fu〕*n.* mansion, residence, prefecture, storehouse.

| 00-- 庫 | treasury. |

廚〔Chu〕*n.* kitchen, cookhouse, wardrobe.

10-- 工	cook.
17-- 刀	chopper.
-- 子	cook.
30-- 房	kitchen, cookroom.
41-- 櫃	cupboard.
43-- 娘	kitchenmaid.

0024₁

庭〔Ting〕*n.* courtyard, court of justice, hall.

02-- 訓	instructions of one's father.
23-- 外和解	settle out of court.
73-- 院	courtyard.

麝〔She〕*n.* musk, deer, civet.

| 20-- 香 | musk. |
| -- 香牛 | musk ox. |

0024₂

底〔Ti〕*n.* bottom, base, rough draft. *v.* stop, reach, come to, *adj.* low, menial, *prep.* below, underneath.

10-- 下	under, underneath, below.
-- 面	the under-surface.
20-- 稿	draft, first copy, manuscript.
21-- 價	base price, minimum price.
22-- 片	negative of a photograph.
26-- 細	details.
-- 薪	base salary, base wage.
44-- 蘊	essence, true facts.
77-- 層	basement, ground floor.

0024₇

夜〔Yeh〕*n.* night, darkness.

00-- 夜	nightly, every night.
-- 市	night markets.
-- 市繁榮	the night markets are prosperous.
-- 盲症	night blindness.
01-- 襲	night attack, night raid.
10-- 工	night work.

-- 不安枕	toss about in bed.
11-- 班	night shift.
21-- 行	travel by night.
22-- 出	appear by night and hide by day.
28-- 以繼日	day and night.
27-- 色	vast darkness of the night.
37-- 深	late at night.
-- 深人靜	in the depth of night.
40-- 來香	tuberose.
-- 校	night school, evening school.
44-- 禁條例	regulation prohibiting going out late at night.
46-- 場	evening show, night show.
52-- 靜人稀	the night is quiet with few people.
60-- 景畫	nocturne.
-- 景美麗	the night scenes are beautiful.
63-- 戰	night fighting, night battle.
-- 賊	burglar.
67-- 晚	night, at night.
70-- 防	watch at night.
71-- 長夢多	the night is long and there are numerous dream.
77-- 間飛行	night flight.
-- 間演習	night exercise.
80-- 會服	evening dress.
82-- 飯	supper, dinner.
90-- 光錶	glow watch.
-- 半	midnight.
-- 半更深	late at night.
99-- 鶯	nightingale.

度 〔 **To** 〕 *n.* measure, capacity, limit, degree, rule, *v.* spend, pass, cross over, estimate, guess, calculate.

23-- 外	beyond the estimate.
37-- 過	spend (the days), pass.
-- 過難關	turn the corner, tide over a difficulty.
58-- 數	degrees, reading a measuring instrument.
60-- 日	live, spend the day, make a living.
-- 量	measure, capacity.

-- 量工具	measuring instruments.
-- 量衡	measure, capacity and weight.
-- 量衡制	system of weights and measures.
-- 量單位	unit of measurement.

慶 〔 **Ching** 〕 *n.* blessing, happiness, welfare, felicity, joy, *v.* bless, congratulate, reward, *adj.* good, blessed, lucky, happy, excellent, joyful.

14-- 功	triumph.
36-- 祝	celebrate, congratulate.
-- 祝勝利	celebrate a victory.
-- 祝會	celebration party.
40-- 幸	rejoice.
46-- 賀	*n.* congratulation, *v.* congratulate, hail.
-- 賀會	celebration party.
55-- 典	jubilee, congratulatory state usages.

廈 〔 **Sha** 〕 *n.* mansion.

廢 〔 **Fei** 〕 *v.* throw aside, put away, discontinue, do away with, abandon, abolish, give up, *adj.* spoiled, destoryed, ruined, discarded, useless, worthless, waste.

00-- 棄	abandon, cast-away, throw aside, fling to the winds, cast to the dog, throw overboard.
02-- 話	nonsense, idle talk.
10-- 票	cancelled cheque, cancelled ticket.
-- 而不用	stop using.
12-- 水	waste water.
-- 水利用	reclamation of waste water.
14-- 弛	neglect.
17-- 君	*n.* deposed emperor, *v.* dethrone.
21-- 止	annul, repeal, undo.
22-- 紙	waste paper.
-- 紙箱	waste-paper box.
25-- 件	spoiled work.
27-- 物	useless thing, refuse, rubbish, waste, chaff and dust.
-- 物處理	waste treatment, waste dis-

posal.

-- 物利用　utilization of waste material, make good use of waste material.

41-- 墟　demolitions, ruins.

44-- 熱　waste heal.

50-- 事　waste one's efforts.

60-- 品　waste products.

62-- 時　waste time, kill time, consume time, waste the precious hour, burn daylight.

-- 時傷財　waste time and money.

78-- 除　annul, abolish, revoke, repeal, abrogate, declare null and void, cancel.

-- 除軍備　de-militarize.

80-- 人　cripples, disabled persons.

-- 金屬　scrap metal.

-- 氣　waste gas, exhaust.

83-- 鐵　scrap iron.

87-- 鋼　scrap steel.

94-- 料　rejected material, rubbish, waste and scrap.

-- 料價格　scrap price.

0024₈

廠〔Chang〕n. factory, plant, mill, workshop, foundry.

00-- 主　owner of a factory, manufacturer.

10-- 礦企業　industrial and mining enterprises.

30-- 房　factory building.

71-- 長　director of a factory.

0025₂

摩〔Mo〕v. feel, touch, rub with the hand, polish, rub against each other.

10-- 天　heaven-kissing.

-- 天樓　sky-scrapper.

-- 弄　handle playfully, feel about and play with.

30-- 肩　rub shoulder.

52-- 托化　motorization.

-- 托車　motorcycle.

53-- 擦　friction.

-- 擦力　friction force.

0025₆

庫〔Kuh〕n. storehouse, depot, treasury, granary.

30-- 房　storeroom.

-- 空如洗　the treasury is empty as though washed.

40-- 存　stock, reserve.

-- 存商品　merchandise inventory.

-- 存現金　cash in hand.

-- 存貨物　warehouse goods.

-- 存量　storage on hand.

44-- 藏　repository.

0026₀

廂〔Hsing〕n. side room.

30-- 房　sideroom.

0026₁

店〔Tien〕n. shop, store, inn, tavern.

00-- 主　shopkeeper, innkeeper, storekeeper.

10-- 面　store front.

-- 面廣告　point-of-purchase advertising.

17-- 務繁雜　the shop-work is intricate.

-- 務管理　shop keeping.

29-- 伙計　shop boy.

30-- 客　guest, lodger.

40-- 內廣告　in-store advertising.

50-- 東　the proprietor of a shop

60-- 員　shopman, clerk, salesman, shop assistant.

67-- 夥　tradesman, counterjumper.

83-- 鋪　shop, store.

磨〔Mo〕n. mill, v. grind, rub, sharpen.

00-- 床　grinding machine.

10-- 平　planish.

11-- 礪　discipline.

17-- 刀　grind a knife.

-- 刀石　hone, whetstone, grindstone.

22-- 利　sharpen, edge.

24-- 牀　grinder, grinding machine.

33-- 滅　obliterate.

40-- 坊　mill.

-- 難　affliction, sufferings, difficulties.

53--	擦	n. friction, v. chafe, brush.
56--	損	wear, tear and wear, wear away.
60--	墨	grind the Chinese ink.
88--	銳	sharpen.
90--	光	polish.
95--	快	sharpen.
--	煉	train, discipline, temper.

0026₇

唐〔Tang〕n. path to a hall, adj. rude, hasty, wild, boastful.

04--	詩	poems of the Tang dynasty.
30--	突	rude, rough, rash, obtrusive.
--	塞	allege, advance as truth.

0028₆

廣〔Kwang〕n. breadth, width, v. enlarge, broaden, extend, adj. wide, extensive, spacious, vast, ample, enlarged, broad.

00--	度	dimension.
--	廈	spacious mansion.
24--	佈	widespread.
--	告	n. advertisement, v. advertise.
--	告商	advertising agent.
--	告商品	door buster.
--	告部	advertising department.
--	告調查	advertising research.
--	告設計	advertising design.
--	告設計員	advertising designer.
--	告效果	advertising effectiveness.
--	告面	display face.
--	告頁	advertising page.
--	告預算	advertising budget.
--	告稿	advertising copy.
--	告價格	advertising rates.
--	告片	advertising film.
--	告社	advertising agency.
--	告傳真	ad-fax.
--	告牌	billboard, hanger.
--	告郵件	advertising post.
--	告業	advertising industry.
--	告費	advertising cost (fee, rates, expenses).
--	告圖樣	design for advertisement.
--	告員	advertising manager.

--	告戰	advertising war.
--	告贈品	stuffer.
--	告印刷品	advertising printed matter.
--	告人	advertiser.
--	告公司	advertising company.
--	告方法	publicity.
--	告求職	advertise for a job.
--	告欄	advertisement column, ad column.
--	告畫	poster, poster painting.
32--	泛	extensive, comprehensive.
--	泛支持	extensive supporter.
40--	大	vast, broad, capacious.
--	大眼光	widen one's vision.
--	大無邊	boundless.
43--	博	extensive.
46--	場	square.
52--	播	broadcast.
--	播電臺	broadcasting station.
--	播稿	broadcast message.
--	播送話器	microphone.
--	播媒介	broadcast media.
--	播員	announcer.
77--	闊	n. breadth, width. broad, wide, extensive, vast.
	闊天地	wide prospect.
80--	義	in a broad sense, general meaning, general sense.
89--	銷	widen sale.

0029₄

麻〔Ma〕n. hemp, adj. pock-marked.

00--	痺	palsy, paralysis.
10--	醉	dope, anesthetize, narcotize.
--	醉劑	narcotic.
--	醉師	anaesthetist.
--	醉品	narcotics, anaesthetic.
17--	子	pockmark.
20--	紡廠	flax mill, hemp mill.
23--	織品	linen fabrics.
--	袋	hemp bag, gunny-bag.
26--	線	linen thread.
27--	繩	hemp rope.
29--	紗	yarn of flax and ramie.
35--	油	sesame oil.
40--	布	linen, hempen fabrics.

-- 木		*n.* numbness, *v.* benumb, numb, *adj.* paralyzed, unfeeling, torpid.
44-- 藥		anaesthetic.
61-- 點		pit.
90-- 雀		sparrow.
-- 雀牌		Mah-jong.
91-- 煩		cumbersome.

廩〔Ling〕 *n.* granary.

0032_7

鷹〔Ying〕 *n.* eagle, kite, falcon, hawk, king of birds.

26-- 鼻	aquiline nose.
43--犬	falcons and dogs.

0033_0

亦〔I〕 *adv.* also, too, likewise, moreover, further, besides, as well.

10-- 可	also possible, may be all right.
10-- 工亦農	be engaged in both industry and agriculture.
11-- 非	nor.
-- 非過言	it is not too much to say that.
-- 非全壞	not altogether bad.
23-- 然	also, thus, as well.
47-- 好	it will do too, also good.

0033_1

忘〔Wang〕 *v.* forget, escape the mind, neglect, disregard, put out of one's head.

07-- 記	*n.* forgetfulness, lapse of memory, oblivion, obliteration of the past, decay of memory, failure of memory, *v.* forget, lose the memory of, think no more of, put out of one's head, *adj.* forgotten, out of mind, bygone, past recollection.
12-- 形	forget oneself, forget one's manner.
23-- 我	*v.* forget oneself, *adj.* selfless, self-forgetful.
47-- 却	forget.
50-- 本	forget one's origin.
60-- 恩	*v.* forget favors, *adj.* ungrateful.
80-- 八	villain, rascal.

0033_2

烹〔Peng〕 *v.* boil, cook, decoct.

07-- 調	*n.* cooking, *v.* cook.
30-- 宰	boiling and killing, the work of a cook.
82-- 飪	cook, cooking.
-- 飪法	cookery.

0033_6

意〔I〕 *n.* thought, idea, opinion, sentiment, intention, inclination, motive, purpose, meaning.

03-- 識	consciousness, sense, mind, judgement.
-- 識形態	ideology, ideological situation.
-- 識到	discern, perceive, be conscious of.
-- 識流	stream of consciousness.
06-- 譯	free translation.
10-- 不相投	disagree, hold different views, clash in opinion.
21-- 旨	view, motive, spirit, drift, tenor, bearing.
23-- 外	unexpected, accidental, beyond all hope, unthought of, unhoped-for.
-- 外保險	accident insurance.
-- 外事件	accident, casualty.
27-- 向	intention, object, inclination, frame of mind.
40-- 志	intention, will, purpose, volition.
-- 大利	Italy.
-- 大利人	Italian.
50-- 中人	lover, sweetheart, lady of one's heart.
60-- 見	idea, opinion, view, notion, way of thinking.
-- 見一致	consensus, agreement.
-- 見不同	dissent, disagreement, discord, discordance, difference of opinion, diversity

of opinion.

-- 見書   memorandum.

-- 思   meaning, expression, sense, purport, signification.

-- 思一致   meeting of minds.

80-- 義   sense, meaning, purpose, significance.

-- 氣   emotion, personal grudges.

-- 氣相投   be attracted to each other by common thought and taste.

-- 會   understand by insight.

87-- 欲   wish, intend, be inclined to, have an intention of, have a mind to.

94-- 料   guess, suppose, conjecture.

-- 料之中   expected.

-- 料之外   unexpected.

0040₀

文 〔Wen〕 n. the written language, writing, literature, dispatch, streaks, lines, adj. refined, elegant, genteel, stylish, scholarly, accomplished, classical, literary

00-- 章   essay, literary composition.

-- 言   literary language.

-- 言文   classical Chinese language.

-- 言小說   a novel written in literary language.

-- 盲   illiterate.

11-- 工團   art troupe, cultural troupe.

13-- 職   civil service, civil post.

-- 武   literary and military, civilian and military.

-- 武全才   versed in both literary and military arts.

16-- 理   phraseology, arrangement of ideas in writing.

20-- 集   collection of works.

-- 稿   manuscript.

23-- 獻   literature, documents.

24-- 化   culture, civilization.

-- 化交流   cultural exchange.

-- 化課   cultural course, literacy class.

-- 化侵略   cultural exploitation.

-- 化復興   cultural renaissance.

-- 化流氓   cultural villain.

-- 化運動   cultural movement.

-- 化協定   cultural pact.

-- 化界   cultural circles.

-- 化領域   sphere of culture.

-- 化館   cultural center.

-- 告   statement, proclamation.

-- 科   liberal arts, department of arts, department of literature.

-- 科碩士   Master of Arts.

-- 科學士   Bachelor of Arts.

25-- 件   documents, dispatch, scrip, papers.

-- 件框   file.

-- 件夾   portfolio.

27-- 物   cultural relics or objects.

30-- 字   writings, written characters, black and white.

-- 字改革   reform of the written language.

-- 字源流   derivation of words.

-- 官   civil officer, civil servant.

-- 官制度   system of civil service.

-- 官考試   civil service examination.

34-- 法   grammer, rules of composition.

37-- 選   anthology.

40-- 壇   literary world.

-- 真   to speak the truth.

44-- 藝   writings, the literal arts.

-- 藝復興   renaissance.

50-- 書   document, paper.

67-- 明   n. civilization, civility, adj. civilized, enlightened.

70-- 雅   genteel, graceful, well-bred, polite, elegant.

77-- 學   literature, letters.

-- 學博士   doctor of literature.

-- 學界   men of letters, literary world.

-- 具   stationery.

80-- 人   literati, man of letters, man of learning, literary man.

-- 氣   context.

0040₁

辛〔Hsin〕 *adj.* bitter, sad, grievous, suffering, toilsome.

05-- 辣	acrid, peppery, poignant, strong taste.
44-- 勤	industrious, diligent.
-- 苦	*n.* toilsome, suffering, *adj.* sweat of one's brow.
99-- 勞	pains, troubles.

0040₃

率 〔Shuai〕 *n.* pattern, example, guide, rate, *v.* lead, guide, command, follow, obey, observe, act in accordance to.

23-- 然	suddenly, hastily.
24-- 先	take the lead.
28-- 從	*v.* follow.
40-- 直	frank, candid, straightforward.
-- 直而言	speak straightforwardly.
-- 真	speak the truth.
72-- 兵	lead troop.
81-- 領	lead, head.
95-- 性	follow one's fancies, allow to indulge in unreasonable conduct.
-- 性正直	one's natural disposition is upright.

0040₄

妄 〔Wang〕 *adj.* erroneous, false, perfidious, wrong, absurd, wild, thoughtless, disorderly.

00-- 言	*n.* lie, falsehood, *v.* tell a lie, prattle.
-- 言妄動	speak or act recklessly.
01-- 語	lie, jargon.
-- 語虛詞	wild talks and vain words.
02-- 證	false witness.
-- 誕	fabulous, incoherent.
09-- 談	vain and foolish talk, nonsense.
17-- 取	misappropriate, squeeze.
20-- 信	delusion.
22-- 斷	*n.* misjudgement, *v.* jump to a conclusion, rush to a conclusion.

24-- 動	move rapidly and rashly, rush headlong.
-- 動輕舉	take an ill-considered action.
26-- 自尊大	arrogant, haughty.
28-- 作妄為	act recklessly.
32-- 測	run away with a notion, run away with an idea, jump to a conclusion.
46-- 想	*n.* illusion, imagination, *v.* indulge in vain hopes, give play to the imagination, give play to the fancy, be in the cloud, have a bee in the head.
47-- 殺	give no quarters.
50-- 事推測	make wild predictions.
55-- 費	waste, lavish.
60-- 口巴舌	absurd wild talk.
-- 圖	attempt vainly, make a vain attempt.
77-- 開	separate, put apart, hold off, keep away.
-- 用	abuse.
-- 問	stir up division, come between.
80-- 人	crazy fellow.
-- 合	wild intercourse.

妾 〔Chieh〕 *n.* concubine, secondary wife.

0040₆

章 〔Chang〕 *n.* essay, chapter, section, *v.* exhibit, show, *adj.* clear, beautiful, variegated.

26-- 程	regulation, rule, by law.
程草稿	a draft of rules.
27-- 魚	cuttle fish, octopus.
-- 句	paragraphs and sentences.
34-- 法	style, phraseology.
60-- 回小說	a serial novel.
88-- 節	chapters and sections.

0040₇

享 〔Hsiang〕 *v.* enjoy, receive, offer up with thanks.

20-- 受	*n.* enjoyment, *v.* enjoy, receive, indulge oneself in.

22-- 樂	*n.* enjoyment, *v.* enjoy.
-- 樂主義	self-indulgence, hedonism.
31-- 福	enjoy happiness.
35-- 清福	enjoy the happiness of leisure.
40-- 有	enjoy, possess.
-- 壽	enjoy long life.
77-- 用	enjoy, enjoy the use of.

0040₈

交 〔 **Chiao** 〕 *n.* friendship, intimacy, acquaintance, intercourse, *v.* join, unite, pay to, deliver up, hand over, commit to, communicate, exchange, copulate.

00-- 雜	interlace, intertwine, interlink, cross, intermix, intersect.
02-- 託	deliver in trust, commit to the care of.
03-- 誼	friendship.
-- 誼會	party.
09-- 談	speak to.
10-- 惡	mutually disliking.
-- 妥	complete a transaction.
11-- 班	change shift.
20-- 安	complete a transaction.
-- 集於心	bill and coo, whisper.
21-- 價	pay the price of goods.
22-- 出	deliver out.
-- 出錢來	fork out your money.
23-- 代	hand over to a successor in office.
-- 織	weave.
24-- 付	deliver, convey, trust, commit to the hand of.
-- 付現金	cash payment.
-- 付定金	down payment.
-- 結	keep company with, associate with.
-- 貨	deliver goods.
-- 貨收據	delivery receipt.
-- 貨日	delivery day.
-- 貨人	consignor.
-- 貨合約	contract of delivery.
27-- 響樂	symphony.
-- 爭	strive, struggle.

30-- 流	exchange, interflow.
-- 流電	alternative current.
31-- 涉	negotiate with.
-- 涉員	diplomatic officer.
-- 割日	settlement day.
33-- 心	heart-to-heart talk.
-- 淺言深	have a hearty talk with a recent acquaintance.
36-- 還	return, give back.
37-- 通	*n.* communication, traffic, intercourse, *v.* communicate.
-- 通部	The Ministry of Communication.
-- 通部長	The Minister of Communication.
-- 通工具	means of transportation.
-- 通工程	traffic engineering.
-- 通要道	vital communication lines.
-- 通線	lines of communication.
-- 通斷絕	communications cut off.
-- 通網	network of communication.
-- 通費	traffic allowance.
-- 通規則	traffic rules.
-- 通圖	traffic map.
-- 通阻塞	traffic holdup, traffic jam.
-- 通銀行	The Bank of Communication.
-- 通管制	traffic control.
-- 通燈	traffic light.
38-- 遊	*n.* friends, acquaintance. associate with, make friends with.
-- 遊廣闊	have a wide circle of friends.
40-- 叉	intersect, cross.
-- 友	make friend with.
-- 友宜慎	one must be careful in making friends with others.
41-- 帳	turn over the account.
42-- 婚	intermarriage.
45-- 媾	sexual intercourse, copulation.
47-- 切	*n.* intersection, *v.* intersect.
-- 好	*n.* cordiality, friendship, *adj.* cordial, friendly.

-- 款處	paying counter, paying office.
50-- 接	*n.* intercourse, *v.* receive.
53-- 感神經系	sympathetic system.
55-- 替	*n.* alternation, substitution, *v.* alternate, substitute, take the place of.
57-- 換	exchange, substitute, reciprocate.
-- 換意見	exchange views.
-- 換台	switchboard.
-- 換貨幣	money of exchange.
-- 換教授	exchange professor.
60-- 口稱讚	praise somebody or something unanimously.
-- 易	*n.* exchange, barter, trade, commercial transaction, *v.* exchange, trade.
-- 易者	negotiator.
-- 易協定	business agreement.
-- 易所	stock exchange, bourse.
-- 界	*n.* border, boundary, frontier, *v.* border on.
61-- 賬	turn over the account.
-- 點	point of intersection.
63-- 戰	join battle, engage in battle, bear arms against, fight, war.
-- 戰國	belligerent.
70-- 臂	with folded arms.
74-- 際	*n.* intercourse, connection, *v.* socialize.
-- 際花	belle of society.
-- 際費	entertaining expenses.
-- 際會	social meeting.
77-- 尾	copulate, have sexual intercourse.
-- 叉	cross.
80-- 合	copulate, have sexual intercourse.
84-- 錯	crossed.
87-- 鋒	engage in battle, cross swords.
-- 卸	vacate, lay down.
95-- 情	friendship, mutual affection, good graces.

卒〔**Tsu**〕*n.* soldier, private, *v.* conclude, finish, die, come to an end.

00-- 亡	die.
23-- 然	in haste, in a great hurry.
-- 然宣戰	declare war suddenly.
29-- 償素願	have one's wishes fulfilled at long last.
32-- 業	graduate, finish the course of study.
-- 業證書	diploma, leaving certificate.
-- 業生	graduate.
44-- 其學業	finish his scholastic studies.

0041₄

離〔**Li**〕*v.* separate, depart, leave.

00-- 座	leave one's seat.
-- 席	get up from the table.
-- 棄	abandon.
13-- 職	off duty.
17-- 子	ion.
-- 岸的	offshore.
27-- 鄉	leave one's village.
30-- 家	leave one's home.
33-- 心力	centrifugal force.
40-- 奇	wonderful, quaint, curious.
-- 去	depart, stay away, evacuate, be absent, keep away, withdraw, go away.
-- 校	leave school.
42-- 婚	divorce.
44-- 世	die.
48-- 散	dispersed, scattered.
61-- 題	digress from the subject.
62-- 別	say good-bye to, bid farewell, part from, take leave of.
77-- 開	separate, put apart, hold off, keep away, go farther off, remain at a distance.
-- 間	stir up division, come between.
80-- 合	partings and meetings.

0044₁

辨〔**Pien**〕*v.* distinguish between, discriminate.

00-- 音力	auditory discrimination.

02-- 證   dialectics.
07-- 認   recognize, distinguish, identify.
26-- 白   explanation.
27-- 色   distinguish color.
40-- 士   pence.
62-- 別   distinguish between, discriminate.
-- 別力   power of discrimination.
-- 別是非   discriminate between right and wrong.
67-- 明   identify, call to account.

辦 〔 **Pan** 〕 *v.* manage, perform, attend to.
10-- 不到   impracticable, cannot do.
16-- 理   deal, transact, take in hand, set about.
-- 理付款   effect payment.
-- 理保險   effect on insurance.
20-- 妥   manage satisfactorily.
24-- 貨   buy goods.
26-- 得好   well done!
30-- 案   deal with lawsuits.
34-- 法   plan, means, measure, step.
40-- 校   run a school.
47-- 報   run a newspaper.
50-- 事   transact business.
-- 事處   office.
-- 事員   clerk, staffer.
-- 事得當   do a thing properly.
60-- 罪   punish.
80-- 公   do office work, transact official duties.
-- 公設備   office equipments.
-- 公室經理   office manager.
-- 公費   office expenses.
-- 公時間   office hours, business hours.
-- 公用品   office supplies.
-- 公室   office.
-- 公廳   office.

瓣 〔 **Pan** 〕 *n.* petals.
辮 〔 **Pien** 〕 *n.* plait, braid, intertwine.
17-- 子   braid, queue.
辯 〔 **Pien** 〕 *v.* argue, dispute, debate, discuss.

02-- 證   *n.* dialetics, *v.* dialetical.
-- 證法   dialectics.
04-- 護   defend, plead, support, speak out, stand up for, say in defense, bear out.
-- 護士   lawyer, barrister, apologist.
08-- 論   debate, argue, dispute.
-- 論員   debater.
-- 論會   debating society or club, debate lyceum.
26-- 白   explain, allege.
27-- 解   justify, cover with excuse, palliate.
40-- 才   eloquence.
67-- 明   explain clearly.
74-- 駁   argue, criticize, contradict, rebut, dispute.

0050_2
牽 〔 **Chien** 〕 *v.* pull, drag, haul, induce, connect with, lead, implicate.
12-- 引   pull, draw, lead, drag.
-- 引力   pull, tractive power.
13-- 強   *adj.* forced, unnatural, *adv.* unnaturally, arbitrarily.
20-- 纏   detain, be unwilling to let go.
22-- 制   restrain, check, embarrass, involve in trouble.
-- 制戰   containing action, holding action.
24-- 動大局   upset the general situation
25-- 牛   lead an ox or a cow.
-- 牛花   morning-glory.
31-- 涉   be dragged into the matter, entangle, implicate.
35-- 連   involve, draw into, implicate.
53-- 掛   in suspense, be in anxiety, be worried.
57-- 挽   pull one along by the hand.
60-- 累   be entangled with.
0060_1
言 〔 **Yen** 〕 *n.* word, sentence, discourse, speech, *v.* say, talk, address.
01-- 語   words, talk, speech, locution, parlance.

--	語支離	speak diffusively.
--	語尖刻	bitterness of speech.
--	語學	philology.
07--	詞辯論	confrontation of litigants at a court.
--	詞鋒利	speak daggers.
08--	論	discourse, discussion, expression of opinion.
--	論自由	freedom of speech.
--	論激烈	give extreme views.
09--	談	conversation, speech, talk.
10--	不符實	the statement does not tally with the fact.
20--	辭矛盾	be contradictory in a statement.
21--	行	words and actions.
--	行一致	suit one's action to one's word.
--	行失檢	let oneself loose, misbehave oneself.
--	行錄	biography.
27--	歸於好	kiss and make up, reconcile.
--	歸正傳	return to our mutton.
30--	之過甚	exaggerated statement.
--	之過早	too early to say, premature to say.
--	之有理	it stands to reason, sensibly said.
--	官	censor.
37--	過其實	exaggerate, overstate.
50--	盡於此	have nothing more to say.
88--	符其實	doesn't make a mountain out of a molehill.

音〔Yin〕n. sound, musical note.

06--	譯注	transliterate.
--	韻	rime, rhyme.
--	韻學	phonology.
07--	調	pitch, tone, melody.
--	訊	news, information, message.
20--	信	news, message, tidings.
22--	樂	music.
--	樂廳	music hall, concert hall.
--	樂家	musician.
--	樂隊	band, orchestra.
--	樂學校	musical school, conservatory.
--	樂會	concert.
25--	律	cadence.
26--	程	interval.
27--	響	audio, sound, acoustics.
--	響學	acoustics.
--	色	timbre of a sound or voice.
35--	速	sonic speed.
41--	標	phonetic sign, phonetic symbol.
43--	域	(in music) compass.
60--	量	sound volume, voice volume.
71--	階	musical scale.
88--	節	syllable.
--	符	phonogram.

盲〔Manag〕adj. blind, dark, deceived.

24--	動主義	adventurism.
28--	從	implicat obedience, follow blindly.
30--	進	go it blind, run amuck.
60--	目	n. blindness, adj. blind, blind as a bat, adv. blindly.
--	目崇拜	worship blindly.
--	目性	blindness, rashness.
61--	啞院	blind and dumb asylum.
--	啞學校	school of blind and dumb.
76--	腸炎	typhlitis.
80--	人	blind, blind person.

0060₃

畜〔Chu〕n. domestic animals, v. feed, raise, rear, nourish, domesticate.

00--	產	husbandry products.
--	產品	animal products.
25--	生	animals, brute.
28--	牧	pasture, graze, rear domestic animals.
--	牧業	animal husbandry.
--	牧場	livestock farm.
--	牧時代	age of pasture.
--	牧學	zootechny.
80--	養	feed, raise, rear.
90--	糞	dung, animal droppings.

91-- 類   animal.

0060₄
吝 〔**Lin**〕 v. grudge, spare, adj. stingy, covetous, sordid, close-fisted, niggardly.

40-- 嗇	niggardly, close-fisted, stingy, penurious, miserly, shabby, scrubby.
-- 嗇漢	miser, stingy fellow.
94-- 惜	v. grudge, be stingy about, adj. close-fisted.
-- 惜財物	be sparing of money and goods, not willing to spend.

0061₄
註 〔**Chu**〕 n. note, annotation, explanation, commentary, v. explain, annotate, define.

07-- 記	take note of, keep a record.
26-- 釋	comment, explain, annotate, illustrate.
-- 釋者	commentator.
27-- 解	n. note, annotation, commentary, v. unfold, expound, comment upon.
44-- 者	annotator.
77-- 冊	registration, register.
-- 冊主任	chief registrar.
-- 冊商標	registered trademark.
-- 冊處	registry office.
-- 冊公司	registered corporation.
89-- 銷	cancel.

誰 〔**Shui**〕 pron. who, whom, whose.

06-- 謂	who says ?
10-- 不	who would not ?
18-- 敢	who dares ?
21-- 能	who can ?
27-- 的	whose ?
30-- 家	of what family ?
46-- 想	who would have thought so ?
60-- 是誰非	who is right and who is wrong ?
86-- 知	who knows ?

0062₂
諺 〔**Yen**〕 n. proverb, common saying.

0062₇
訪 〔**Fang**〕 v. visit, inquire for a friend, inquire to, ask advice of, consult.

40-- 友	visit a friend.
-- 古	search for ancient ruin.
-- 查	search, find out.
50-- 事	find out an affair.
60-- 員	reporter, correspondent.
77-- 問	inquire of, ask, call, see, look up, interview, call on, look round, give a call.
-- 問團	mission.

諦 〔**Ti**〕 n. truth, v. inquire into, examine, investigate.

| 36-- 視 | scrutinize, examine closely. |

謫 〔**Tse**〕 n. fault, error, v. blame, reproach, scold, punish, banish.

| 41-- 奸 | condemn wicked deeds. |
| 60-- 罰 | punish by fine. |

謗 〔**Pang**〕 v. slander, defame, detract, backbite, speak against.

| 50-- 書 | scurrilous letter. |
| 77-- 毀 | slander, defame, vilify, detract. |

譹 〔**Ho**〕 v. bawl, roar, slander, vilify.

| 66-- 躁 | vicious, cruel. |

0063₁
譙 〔**Chiao**〕 v. blame, scold, ridicule.

| 45-- 樓 | watchtower. |
| 50-- 責 | blame, scold. |

0063₂
讓 〔**Yang**〕 v. yield, give away, adj. humble, retiring, courteous, polite.

20-- 位	abdicate, give away, make room, give place.
21-- 步	give in, yield a step, give ground to, make allowance.
30-- 渡	transfer, convey, assign.
44-- 權	yield one's right.
67-- 路	yield the path.
77-- 與	cede to, yield, surrender.

0064₇
諄 〔**Chun**〕 v. teach with care, impress upon, reiterate, adj. carefully, ear-

nestly.
67-- 囑　　　repeat one's order.

0064₈

誶 〔Sui〕 v. rail at, abuse, vilify, accuse, reproach.
01-- 語　　　blame, reprimand.
60-- 罵　　　scold, abuse, reproach, rail at.

0066₁

諳 〔An〕 adj. versed in, acquainted with, skilled in, accustomed to.
07-- 誦　　　recite, chant.
17-- 習　　　have expert knowledge.
25-- 練　　　experienced, skilled, proficient, good at.

0068₂

該 〔Kai〕 adj. proper, right, fit, necessary, v. owe, deserve.
10-- 死　　　deserving death.
21-- 處　　　the place in question.
24-- 備　　　prepared, ready.
43-- 博　　　of wide knowledge, well read.
60-- 罰　　　deserve punishment.
90-- 當　　　ought to, should be, be bound to.

0069₆

諒 〔Liang〕 v. excuse, pardon, believe, have faith in, adj. sincere, faithful.
27-- 解　　　understand, come to understand.

0071₀

亡 〔Wang〕 v. lose, perish die, escape, run away, abscond, adj. ruined, destroyed, lost, gone, extinct, dead.
48-- 故　　　n. dead, v. die.
60-- 國　　　subjugated state, ruin of a country, national extinction.
-- 國之音　　　decadent music, presaging fall of the country.
-- 國滅種　　　ruin the state and destroy the race.
-- 國奴　　　slaves under foreign conquerors.
80-- 人　　　exile, fugitive, runaway.

-- 羊歧路　　　lost horse at a cross roads
-- 羊補牢　　　lock the stable door after the sheep has been stolen.
-- 命　　　desperado, fugitive, refugee.
-- 命之徒　　　desperado, fugitive.

0071₄

毫 〔Hao〕 n. long soft hair, Chinese writing brush, adj. trifling, minute, petty.
10-- 不　　　not in the least, not at all.
-- 不讓步　　　not to bate a jot of one's demands.
-- 不費力　　　without more ado, without effort.
-- 不留情　　　absolutely without consideration for others.
24-- 升　　　millilitre.
29-- 秒　　　millisecond.
40-- 克　　　milligram.
50-- 末　　　very minute.
58-- 釐　　　very little, mere fraction.
-- 釐不差　　　having not the least error.
-- 釐千里　　　a miss is as good as a mile.
72-- 髮　　　minute thing, hair.
80-- 無　　　none, not a bit, not an ace.
-- 無誠意　　　have no sincerity at all.
-- 無可取　　　totally worthless.
-- 無生氣　　　lifeless.
-- 無疑義　　　no doubt, without the least doubt.
-- 無希望　　　hopeless.
-- 無根據　　　groundless.
-- 無所得　　　without any results.
-- 無限制　　　no hold barred.
-- 無阻礙　　　without let or hindrance.
-- 無關係　　　not to give a damn.
90-- 米　　　millimeter.

雍 〔Yung〕 adj. harmonious.

0071₇

甕 〔Weng〕 n. urn, earthen jar.
50-- 中之鱉　　　rat in a hole.

0073₂

衣 〔I〕 n. clothes, garments, coat, dress, v. put on clothes, wear, dress.

10--	不稱身	the garments do not fit the body.
23--	袋	pocket.
32--	衫襤褸	threatbare, tattered, in rags.
34--	襟	lapel of a coat.
35--	袖	sleeve.
36--	邊	hem.
37--	冠	hat and clothes, the gentry.
40--	夾	clothes-peg, clothes-pin.
41--	櫃	wardrobe, chest of drawers, clothes press.
46--	架	clothes-horse.
47--	帽間	cloak room, check room.
72--	刷	clothes-brush.
77--	服	clothes, dress, garments, gowns.
80--	食	back and belly.
--	食住	clothing, food and house.
81--	領	collar.
88--	飾	caparison.
95--	料	material for clothing, drapery.

玄 〔**Hsuan**〕 *adj.* dark, black, dim, somber, still, quiet, deep, profound.

12--	孫	great-great grandson.
49--	妙	mysterious, abstruse, profound.
77--	學	metaphysics.

0073₂

哀 〔**Ai**〕 *n.* sorrow, grief, pity, commiseration, lament, *v.* grieve for, compassionate, feel for, sympathize, *adj.* sorrowful, distressing.

00--	痛	mourning.
17--	歌	elegy, dirge.
22--	樂	grief and joy.
24--	告	*n.* entreaty, *v.* make a piteous report.
27--	懇	implore.
--	的美敦書	ultimatum.
38--	啓	obituary.
43--	求	*n.* supplication, *v.* appeal to one's feeling.
64--	嘆	sigh, lament.
66--	哭	wail, weep bitterly.
67--	鳴	whine.

91--	悼	lament, deplore, bewail.
95--	情	feeling.
99--	憐	*v.* pity, feel for other's woes, sympathize, have pity, show pity, *adj.* compassionate.

衷 〔**Chung**〕 *n.* heart, mind, feeling, sincerity.

33--	心	*adj.* heartfelt, wholehearted, whole heartedly.
--	心佩服	*adv.* admire from the heart.
55--	曲	inner feeling, inner thought.
90--	懷	mind, feeling.
95--	情	feeling, mind.

衰 〔**Shui**〕 *n.* mourning dress, *adj.* wearing away, declining, decaying, fading, growing old.

00--	亡	wither away, fall into decay
17--	弱	*n.* decline, falling off, decadence, *adj.* weak, feeble, decayed with age, sickly, unhealthy.
21--	頹	failing, decay, on one's last legs.
28--	微	*n.* diminution, decay, *v.* die out, reduce to nothing, fall into decay, *adj.* dwindled away, *adv.* behindhand.
37--	運	decayed fortune, misfortune.
--	退	decline, be in depression.
44--	落	decline, fade, languish, decay, descend, ebb, retire into the shade, run low, crumble.
--	落中	declining, on the wane.
--	萎	wither, languish.
--	老	old and feeble, decayed, declining, second childhood.
--	世	age of decline.
68--	敗	*n.* debasement, decrease, wane, ebb, *v.* be worse, be deteriorated, degenerate, go down, decline, be at a low ebb, *adj.* falling, declining, worn-out, spoiling.

褒 〔**Pao**〕 *v.* praise, admire, extol, laud.

27--	奬	*n.* honorable mention, *v.* praise, extol.
62--	貶	praise and blame, give one a good or bad character.

裹 〔**Kuo**〕 *v.* wrap, envelop, wind around.

28--	傷口	dress a wound.
60--	足	bind feet, stop.

裏 〔**Li**〕 *adj.* inside, internal, inner.

00--	衣	underwear.
10--	面	interior, inside, within.
17--	子	lining of a dress.
23--	外	inside and outside.
--	外受敵	encounter enemy within and without.

褻 〔**Hsieh**〕 *n.* undress, dishabille, *v.* dishonor, treat irreverently, *adj.* dirty, filthy.

21--	穢	dirty, filthy.
34--	瀆	profane, blaspheme, violate, desecrate.

襄 〔**Hsiang**〕 *v.* help, assit.

16--	理	assistant manager.
--	理職務	assistant manager duties.
74--	助	assist, help.
77--	同	take part in, assist.

0080₀

六 〔**Liu**〕 *adj.* six, sixth.

06--	親無靠	having nobody to turn to.
10--	弦琴	guitar.
20--	倍	six times.
36--	邊形	hexagon.
37--	次	six times.
40--	十	sixty.
52--	折	forty percent discount.
77--	月	June.
80--	合	the universe.

0090₃

紊 〔**Wen**〕 *adj.* confused, raveled, disordered.

22--	亂	confused, chaotic, in confusion, at sixes and sevens.
--	亂不堪	utterly confused.

0090₄

棄 〔**Chi**〕 *v.* reject, abandon, desert, cast aside, give up, throw off, forgo.

00--	市	be executed in public.
--	文就武	quit civilian life and join the military.
13--	職	abandon one's post.
17--	取	be accepted or rejected.
20--	信背義	discard faith and reject righteousness.
27--	物	refuse, garbage, waste matter.
--	絕	relinquish entirely, annul, renounce, cast to the wind, cast away, throw to the dogs.
30--	之可惜	it is a waste to discard it.
32--	業	abandon one's property, leave one's occupation.
40--	去	give up.
44--	舊戀新	reject the old and love the new.
--	舊迎新	replace the old with the new.
--	舊換新	change the old for the new.
--	權	abstain, relinquish a right, renounce a right.
50--	妻	abandon a wife.
60--	暗投明	give oneself up to the authorities.
--	置不用	discard.
77--	邪	depart from evil, forsake evil.
--	邪歸正	mend one's way, change from bad to good, leave the heterodox and come back to the orthodox, turn over a new leaf.
80--	人於危	leave a man in the lurch.
81--	短取長	forget someone's shortcoming and make use of his strong points.

稟 〔**Bing**〕 *n.* petition, nature, *v.* obey, report.

0090₆

京 〔**Ching**〕 *n.* capital, metropolis.

43--	城	capital city.

47-- 都   capital city.

0091₄

雜 〔**Tsa**〕 *adj.* various, mixed, mingled, promiscuous, miscellaneous, confused

00-- 文   essay.

-- 交   hybridaization, crossbreed.

04-- 誌   magazine, journal, periodical.

07-- 記   sketch, miscellaneous record.

17-- 務   miscellaneous business.

22-- 亂   *n.* disorder, *adj.* confused, out of order, messy.

-- 種   crossbreed, variety, diverse.

-- 種兒   half-blood, half-breed, half-caste.

24-- 貨   miscellaneous goods, general cargo.

-- 貨店   grocery, general store.

27-- 役   servant.

-- 物   miscellaneous articles, sundries.

-- 色   multicolored, parti-colored, motley.

44-- 草   weeds.

50-- 事   miscellaneous affairs, odd jobs.

54-- 技   acrobatics.

-- 技團   acrobatic troupe.

55-- 曲   medley.

-- 費   sundry expenses.

72-- 質   impurity, heterogeneity.

96-- 糧   coarse cereals.

98-- 燴   chop-suey, hodgepodge.

0110₄

壠 〔**Lung**〕 *n.* barrow, grave. *v.* monopolize goods.

22-- 斷   forestall, engross goods, monopolize goods.

-- 斷市場   corner the market.

-- 斷居奇   hoard goods and sell them at high prices.

-- 斷價格   monopoly.

-- 斷資產階級   monopoly bourgeoisie.

-- 斷資本家   monopoly capitalist.

0116₁

站 〔**Chan**〕 *n.* station, *v.* stand up, stand still, stop.

11-- 班   stand in a row.

-- 住   stop, halt.

22-- 崗   be at post, stand sentry, stand guard.

-- 出來   step forward.

-- 穩   stand firmly.

23-- 台   station.

47-- 起   stand up.

71-- 長   station master.

0118₆

顫 〔**Chan**〕 *v.* shiver, tremble, *adj.* shivering, trembling.

00-- 音   trill.

22-- 動   tremble, quiver, vibrate.

54-- 抖   shiver, tremble.

0121₁

龍 〔**Lung**〕 *n.* dragon.

11-- 頭   faucet, tap, leader of a gang.

20-- 爭虎鬥   fierce battle between giants.

27-- 舟   dragon boat.

-- 舟競賽   dragon boat race.

37-- 袍   imperial robes.

57-- 蝦   lobster.

59-- 捲風   tornado, twister.

-- 眼   longan.

73-- 鬚菜   asparagus.

77-- 骨   keel.

80-- 舞   dragon dance.

82-- 鍾   tottering.

-- 鍾老者   old man, decrepit man.

-- 鍾老態   signs of senility.

0124₇

敲 〔**Chiao**〕 *v.* strike, beat, knock, tap.

08-- 詐   extort, blackmail.

10-- 碎   break in pieces.

44-- 鼓   beat a drum.

51-- 打   knock, beat.

77-- 門   knock at the door.

-- 門磚   stepping-stone.

80-- 鐘   strike a bell, knoll, sound the alarm.

86-- 鑼   beat a gong.

0128₆

顏 〔Yen〕 n. face, countenance, color.
10-- 面　　　countenance.
27-- 色　　　color.
30-- 容　　　countenance, face, features.
71-- 厚　　　thick-skinned, shameless,
　　　　　　unprincipled, immodest.
94-- 料　　　dyeing materials, dye stuff.

0140₁

聾 〔Lung〕 n. deafness, adj. deaf, hard
of hearing.
17-- 子　　　deaf man.
61-- 啞　　　deaf and dumb.
-- 啞者　　　deaf-mute.

0160₁

礱 〔Long〕 n. mill, v. grind.
80-- 穀　　　hull grain.

0161₀

訌 〔Hung〕 n. rout, disorder, confusion,
quarrel.
21-- 亂　　　in disorder, rebellious.

0161₁

誆 〔Kuang〕 v. swindle, cheat,deceive.
証 〔Ching〕 v. witness, prove, confront.
51-- 據　　　proof, evidence.
67-- 明　　　prove, certify.
80-- 人　　　witness.
誹 〔Fei〕 v. slander, backbite, defame.
00-- 謗　　　libel, speak evil of, speak
　　　　　　with ill language, say evil
　　　　　　things of , decry, defame,
　　　　　　slander.
-- 謗行爲　　act of libel or slander.
01-- 譖　　　revile, defame, slander, li-
　　　　　　bel.
08-- 議　　　malicious talk.
77-- 譽　　　slander and praise.
譃 〔Niueh〕 v. joke, jest, jeer, mock at,
laugh at, make sport of, ridicule.

0161₄

誑 〔Kuang〕 n. lie, falsehood, v.
deceive,delude, impose upon.
00-- 言　　　lies, falsehood, cock-and-
　　　　　　bull story, traveller's tale.
-- 言妄語　　wild tales and lies.

02-- 誕無稽　　absurd and unfounded.
73-- 騙　　　deceive, impose upon.

0161₆

謳 〔Ou〕 n. local ditties, v. sing, chant.
17-- 歌　　　local ditties.
68-- 吟　　　sing.

0161₇

詎 〔Chu〕 conj. but, however.
11-- 非　　　is it so?

0161₈

誣 〔Wu〕 v. make a false accusation,
inculpate falsely.
01-- 證　　　false witness.
24-- 告　　　charge falsely, accuse
　　　　　　falsely.
44-- 蔑　　　smear, slander, malign.
57-- 賴　　　implicate falsely, involve
　　　　　　others by false charge.
-- 捏　　　charge a crime on.
77-- 陷　　　ruin by slander.

0162₀

訂 〔Ting〕 v. arrange, adjust, settle,
conclude, examine, compare, edit,
revise.
00-- 立　　　draw up.
-- 立契約　　enter into a contract.
04-- 計劃　　make a plan.
10-- 正　　　revise, edit, rectify.
21-- 價　　　pricing.
27-- 約　　　contract, covenant, agree
　　　　　　for, engage, conclude a
　　　　　　treaty.
30-- 定　　　settle, close with, conclude.
-- 戶　　　subscriber.
34-- 貨通知　　order notify.
-- 貨量　　　quantity of order.
-- 貨合同　　contract job.
-- 貨付現　　cash in order.
-- 貨處　　　order desk.
-- 貨　　　place order, order goods.
42-- 婚　　　n. engagement, betrothal,
　　　　　　v. engage, betroth.
47-- 期　　　fix a date, fix a time, make
　　　　　　an appointment.
65-- 購　　　order, place an order.

-- 購量	order quantity.	

-- 購量　order quantity.
-- 購單　order form.
66-- 單　order, indent.
67-- 盟　make peace, form an alliance with.
80-- 合同　contract, settle a bargain.

訶〔Ho〕v. blame, upbraid.
43-- 求　find fault.
50-- 責　blame, upbraid.

0163_2
詠〔Cho〕v. accuse, vilify, report against.
07-- 謠　slander, defame.

0164_0
訐〔Chieh〕v. disclose people's secret, seize hold on people's fault.

訝〔Ya〕v. express surprise at, wonder at.

0164_6
譚〔Tan〕v. talk, discuss, boast.

0164_9
評〔Ping〕v. discuss, deliberate upon, criticize, comment on.
00-- 註　commentary and notes.
08-- 論　discuss, debate, view, criticize, comment upon.
-- 論是非　discuss the right and wrong of a matter.
-- 論員　commentator.
-- 議　deliberate, criticize, talk over.
-- 議員　member of a committee.
-- 議會　committee, advisory council.
11-- 比　compare, appraise.
12-- 價　estimate, appraise, valuate.
16-- 理　judge, discuss.
22-- 斷　decide.
24-- 估　appraisal, comment.
27-- 獎　the granting of awards through discussions.
30-- 定　judge, decide.
-- 定稅額　assess a tax.
80-- 介　comment and introduce.
-- 分　grading, marks given by a judge.
92-- 判　n. review, criticism, critique, v. criticize, review.
-- 判員　judge, umpire.

譹〔Hu〕v. call out, cry, scream.

0166_1
詣〔I〕n. achievement. v. reach, go to, repair to.
06-- 謁　pay a visit.

語〔Yu〕n. language, words, speech, expressions, conversation, discourse, v. talk with, speak with, tell, inform.
00-- 文　language.
-- 言　language, words, speech.
-- 言學　philology.
-- 言學家　linguist, philologist.
-- 音　articulation, speech sound.
-- 音學　phonetics, phonology.
-- 音學家　phonetician.
07-- 調　tone, intonation.
20-- 系　stock of a language.
21-- 態　articulation, voice (in grammar).
27-- 句　phrases and sentences.
34-- 法　grammer, phraseology, wording.
47-- 根　radix, base (in grammar).
45-- 勢　emphasis.
80-- 氣　wording, address, tone, mood, diction.
87-- 錄　written record of lectures.

譖〔Tsan〕v. slander, defame, vilify.
77-- 毀　injure by slander.

0166_2
諧〔Hsieh〕n. harmony, v. harmonize, accord with, agree upon, joke, laugh at.
00-- 音　chime.
01-- 謔　jest, joke.
07-- 調　(in music) harmony.
26-- 和　harmony, consonance.
47-- 聲　harmonious, symphonious.

0168_9
詼〔Hui〕v. joke, jest, ridicule, play

with.

01-- 諧	*v.* joke, jest, humor, *adj.* funny, laughable, humorous.
88-- 笑	make fun of, make sport of.

0173_2

襲 〔Hsi〕 *v.* inherit, invade, make a surprise attack, attack, assail, set on.

01-- 雜	mixed, confused.
57-- 擊	attack, beat up, press upon, be down upon.
99-- 營	surprise a camp.

0211_4

氈 〔Chan〕 *n.* carpet, felt, rug, blanket.

17-- 子	rug, carpet, felt.
29-- 毯	felt rug.
31-- 褥	felt mattress.
44-- 鞋	felt shoes.
46-- 帽	felt hat.

0212_7

端 〔Tuan〕 *n.* beginning, origin, head, end, extermity, piece, cause, *adj.* correct, *proper*, upright, modest, sober, grave, decent.

08-- 詳	*v.* look at carefully, *adj.* minutely, in detail.
10-- 正	upright, correct.
20-- 重	grave, sedate.
27-- 倪	clues.
30-- 容	grave countenance, sober mien.
44-- 莊	decent-looking, dignified.
58-- 整	orderly, proper, neat.
66-- 嚴	serious, dignified, grave, sober.
80-- 午節	the Dragon-boat Festival.
81-- 飯	serve a meal.

0220_0

刻 〔Ke〕 *n.* a quarter of an hour, *v.* carve, sculpture, engrave, chisel, cut out.

00-- 意求工	do one's very best to achieve perfection.
10-- 工	sculptor, carver.
-- 下	now, presently.

-- 石	engrave on a stone.
-- 不容緩	imminent, pressing.
17-- 己待人	practice self-denial in service to fellowmen.
21-- 版	cut blocks.
30-- 字	engrave characters.
-- 花	engrave figures.
-- 薄	*v.* ill-treat, oppress, ill-use, bully, domineer, maltreat, *adj.* iron-hearted, inexorable.
44-- 苦	*v.* mortify, suffer hardship, *adj.* painstaking, hardworking.
-- 苦耐勞	work hard without complaint.
-- 苦自勵	suffer hardship and incite self-effort.
-- 苦用功	work hard at studies.
50-- 毒	malicious.
60-- 日決戰	fight a decisive battle at an early date.
77-- 骨銘心	inscribe the debt of gratitude in one's mind.
85-- 鏤	inlay.
92-- 削百姓	exploit the masses.

剷 〔Chan〕 *v.* spade, raze, pare down.

10-- 平	raze.
17-- 子	spade, shovel.
78-- 除	obliterate.

劑 〔Chi〕 *n.* dose, *v.* trim, adjust.

0242_2

彰 〔Chang〕 *v.* manifest, display, show, exhibit, make known to, *adj.* distinguished, manifested.

61-- 顯	manifested, evident, apparent.
67-- 明＝彰顯	
80-- 善	encourage virture, make publicity of good deeds.

0260_0

剖 〔Pou〕 *v.* cut open, divide, split up, lay open, disclose, anatomize.

22-- 斷	give judgement, sentence.
26-- 白	exonerate, maintain one's

innocence.

-- 白良心　exonerate one's conscience.
27-- 解　dissect, anatomize, cut up.
42-- 析　solve.
67-- 明　expound.
77-- 屍　dissect a dead body.
-- 開　rip, cut open.

訓〔Hsun〕*n.* instruction, advice, precept, *v.* teach, instruct, caution, admonish, discipline.

00-- 育　discipline.
02-- 話　instructive speech.
04-- 詁　*n.* commentary, explanation, *v.* explain, comment.
08-- 諭　order, injunction.
-- 誨　instruct, correct, correct and train.
10-- 示　instruction, direction.
18-- 政時期　the period of political tutelage.
20-- 辭　instruction.
25-- 練　drill, train, educate.
-- 練營　training camp.
53-- 戒　*n.* admonition, *v.* admonish, warn, caution.
80-- 令　instruction, injunction, mandate, letter of instruction.

0261₄

託〔To〕entrust to, charge, commission, trust to, rely on, commit to the care of.

00-- 病　plead illness.
-- 庇　under your protection, by your auspices.
20-- 辭　excuse, pretext.
24-- 付　deliver in charge, entrust.
48-- 故　make an excuse, give a pretext.
77-- 兒所　day care, nursery school.
95-- 情　engage another's influence, ask favor.

0261₈

證〔Cheng〕*n.* evidence, proof, testimony, *v.* witness, prove by evidence, confront, testify.

00-- 章　badge.
-- 言　testimony.
07-- 詞　testimony, attestation.
27-- 物　evidence.
30-- 實　confirm, prove, ascertain, verify.
50-- 書　certificate, scrip.
51-- 據　proof, evidence, testimony, verification, warrant, certificate.
-- 據確實　valid evidence.
67-- 明　*n.* prove, evidence, *v.* testify, certify, *adj.* certified, proven.
-- 明有罪　convict, be proved guilty.
-- 明書　certificate, voucher.
80-- 人　witness.
90-- 券　stock.
-- 券交易所　stock exchange.

0262₁

訢〔Hsin〕*adj.* happy, pleasant.

0262₇

誘〔Yiu〕*v.* lead on, tempt, allure, entice, seduce.

08-- 敵　draw out the enemy, lure the enemy, make a diversion.
24-- 供　entrap one into making a confession.
27-- 物　bait, decoy, inducement.
32-- 逃　induce one to run away.
38-- 導　induce, influence, lead.
40-- 姦　seduce, lay siege to a woman's honesty.
53-- 惑　allure, tempt, fascinate. attract, entice, captivate.
56-- 拐　kidnap, convey away, carry of.
73-- 騙　inveigle, cajole.
77-- 陷　decoy, betray, lure, delude.
81-- 餌　decoy, lure, bait.

0263₁

訴〔Su〕*v.* inform, tell, plead, state, complain.

04-- 諸武力　resort to violence.
-- 諸公論　appeal to public opinion.

05-- 請	appeal to.
08-- 訟	*n.* accusation, charge, lawsuit, legal action, *v.* make an accusation, charge.
-- 訟主體	subject of the action.
-- 訟委任	mandate in litigation.
-- 訟代理人	legal representative.
-- 訟程序	legal procedure.
-- 訟當事人	parties in action.
23-- 狀	plaint, indictment.
44-- 苦	make complaint, tell one's grievance, state one's wrongs.
-- 苦會	accusation meeting.
71-- 願	petition.

0264₀
詆 〔 **Ti** 〕 *v.* defame, slander, vilify, speak against.

00-- 謗	slander, defame, detract, run down, carry down.
-- 謗官司	libel case.
77-- 毀	defame, slander.

0264₁
誕 〔 **Tan** 〕 *v.* boast, brag, deceive, bear children.

00-- 育	nourish, bring up.
25-- 生	*n.* birth, *v.* be born, give birth to, bear.
-- 生地	birthplace.
71-- 辰	birthday.

0264₄
諉 〔 **Wei** 〕 *v.* lay blame on others, shirk, evade.

| 02-- 託 | shift on to other's shoulder. |
| 04-- 謝 | decline politely. |

0264₇
諼 〔 **Hsuan** 〕 *v.* impose on, cheat, forget

0265₃
譏 〔 **Chi** 〕 *v.* ridicule, mock at, joke, jeer, slander, satirize, blame.

07-- 諷	satirize.
09-- 誚	ridicule, jeer, gird.
88-- 笑	ridicule, mock at, jeer, flout at, satirize, sneer at.

0265₇
諍 〔 **Cheng** 〕 *v.* remonstrate with, ex-

postulate with.

05-- 諫	persuade strongly, remonstrate.
08-- 訟	litigation.
-- 議	debate, dispute.

0266₁
詬 〔 **Kou** 〕 *v.* abuse, insult, put to shame.

| 00-- 病 | *n.* shame, mortification, *v.* blame, insult, disagree. |
| 60-- 罵 | abuse, curse, revile, rail at. |

話 〔 **Hua** 〕 *n.* speech, words, discourse, talk, conversation, *v.* talk, tell, narrate.

21-- 劇	modern drama.
-- 劇團	modern drama troupe.
41-- 柄	topic of conversation.
44-- 舊	talk over old times.
61-- 題	topic, theme.
62-- 別	say good-bye, bid farewell.
71-- 匣子	phonograph, talkative fellow, chatterbox.
88-- 筒	microphone.

0267₀
訕 〔 **Shan** 〕 *v.* slander, vilify, backbite, speak evil of.

| 00-- 謗 | slander, vilify, backbite. |
| 88-- 笑 | laugh at, mock at. |

訩 〔 **Hsiung** 〕 *adj.* disorder.

0267₇
諂 〔 **Tao** 〕 *adj.* doubtful, uncertain.

0292₁
新 〔 **Hsin** 〕 *v.* renew, restore, *adj.* new, fresh, modern, late, recent, just made.

00-- 產品	new product.
-- 高	new climax, new high tide.
-- 文化	new culture.
-- 衣	new clothes.
04-- 詩	modern poetry.
10-- 黴素	neomycin.
12-- 型	new pattern, new type.
14-- 功	fresh merit.
-- 殖民主義	neo-colonialism.
17-- 習慣	new habit.
18-- 政	New Deal.
-- 政策	new policy.

20-- 手	new hand, inexperienced person.	
21-- 穎	up-to-date.	
22-- 任	newly appointed, new incumbent.	
-- 任務	new task, new job.	
24-- 動向	new trend.	
-- 貨	new goods.	
25-- 生	new born, new life, new student.	
-- 生活運動	New Life Movement.	
-- 生力量	new forces.	
-- 秩序	new order.	
27-- 貌	new looks.	
-- 的	new, fresh, newly-made.	
-- 約	New Testament.	
-- 紀元	new epoch.	
28-- 鮮	fresh, fresh as rose, fresh as a daisy.	
-- 鮮經驗	new experience.	
-- 鮮空氣	fresh air.	
30-- 房	the chamber of the newly married couple.	
32-- 近	recently, of late, lately.	
34-- 法	new method.	
-- 造	newly-built, newly-made.	
37-- 軍	modern army.	
-- 郎	bridegroom.	
39-- 沙皇	new tsar (or czar).	
40-- 奇	novel, strange.	
-- 來者	newcomer.	
42-- 婚	marriage, newlywed.	
43-- 娘	bride.	
-- 式	new style, latest fashion.	
44-- 舊	new and old.	
-- 舊交替	the transition from the old to the new.	
48-- 教	Protestantism.	
50-- 事物	new things, novel things.	
-- 書包紙	jacket.	
60-- 思想	new ideology, modern thinking.	
-- 四軍	the New Fourth Army.	
64-- 時代	new era, modern times.	
71-- 階段	new stage.	
-- 曆	new calendar, Gregorian	

Calendar.

72-- 兵	recruit.
75-- 陳代謝	metabolism.
77-- 風俗	new custom.
-- 月	new moon.
-- 聞	news, intelligence, piece of information.
-- 聞廣播	newscast.
-- 聞記者	newspaperman, journalist.
-- 聞記錄片	newsreel, news film.
-- 聞處	office of the press attache.
-- 聞紙	newspaper, the press.
-- 聞界	fourth estate.
-- 聞公報	press communique.
-- 聞學	journalism.
-- 民主主義	new democracy.
-- 興	newly emerging.
80-- 人	bride, newly wed, new employee.
-- 人新事	new people and new things.
-- 年	new year.
-- 會員	new member.
-- 氣象	fresh spirit, new atmosphere.

0312₁
苧 〔**Chu**〕 v. stand for a longtime, wait for, expect.

00-- 立	stand for a long time.
07-- 望	look forward to with anxiety, expect.
63-- 眺	look over.

0314₇
竣 〔**Chun**〕 v. stop work, complete a task, stand still, adj. completed, finished, done.

10-- 工	finish work, complete a task.
50-- 事＝竣工	

0332₇
鷲 〔**Chiu**〕 n. eagle, hawk, vulture.

0342₇
犏 〔**Pan**〕 adj. variegated.

0344₀
斌 〔**Bin**〕 n. ornament and plainness properly mixed.

0360₀

訃〔Fu〕 *n.* announcement of death.

77-- 聞 obituary, message announcing a death.

0361₄

詫〔Cha〕 *v.* be astonished, boast, brag, deceive, exaggerate.

60-- 異 be surprised, be amazed.

0361₆

諠〔Hsuan〕 *v.* brawl, forget.

64-- 嘩 *n.* uproar, clamor, *adj.* noisy.

0361₇

誼〔I〕 *n.* friendship, relations.

77-- 同手足 brotherly relationship.

0362₇

諞〔Pien〕 *v.* talk artfully and deceitfully.

諞〔Shan〕 *v.* seduce, impose upon, excite, instigate.

52-- 惑人心 deceive and stir up people's mind.

0363₂

詠〔Yung〕 *v.* sing, hum, chant, intone.

04-- 詩 chant verses.
17-- 歌 sing.

0363₄

讞〔Yen〕 *n.* sentence, judgement, *v.* sentence, decide a case, pronounce judgement.

24-- 牘 records of criminal cases.
43-- 獄 sentence.

0364₀

試〔Shih〕 *v.* try, attempt, test, examine, experiment

00-- 亦無妨 there is no harm in trying.
-- 亦無用 there is no use in trying.
-- 辦 introduce provisionally.
02-- 劑 reagent.
12-- 飛 *n.* test flight, *v.* test fly.
20-- 航 trial trip.
21-- 行 try, test.
-- 行和解 attempting for compromise.
22-- 製 trial-produce, trial manufacture.
33-- 演 practise, try.
40-- 賣 trial sales.
48-- 樣 *n.* sample, *v.* take a sample.
50-- 車 *n.* trial run, *v.* test the working of a machine, test-drive.
57-- 探 explore, feel for, sound out.
60-- 圖 attempt, intend.
61-- 點 experiments made at selected points
65-- 味 taste.
77-- 用 *n.* probation, *v.* employ on trial, test one's fitness.
78-- 驗 test, experiment, examine, verify, put to trial, make trial of, bring to test, make an experiment, put one's facing.
-- 驗紙 test paper.
-- 驗結婚 companionate marriage.
-- 驗室 laboratory.
-- 驗場 testing ground.
-- 驗田 experimental farm plot.
-- 驗錯誤法 a trial and error method.
-- 驗管 test tube.
80-- 金石 touchstone.
90-- 卷 examination paper.

0365₀

誠〔Cheng〕 *adj,* sincere, honest, guileless, *adv.* really, indeed, truly, certainly.

00-- 意 sincerity, earnestness, cordiality, *adj.* earnest, cordial, from the bottom of one's heart, *adv.* heartily.
20-- 信 good faith.
-- 信價格 bona fide price.
-- 信原則 principal of good faith.
23-- 然 quite, indeed, in fact, in truth, in reality, exactly.
27-- 懇 honest, cordial.
-- 懇待人 treat others with sincerity.
30-- 實 honest, sincere, true, faithful, frank-hearted.
-- 實可靠 honest and reliable.
33-- 心＝誠意
48-- 敬 sincere and reverent.

誡 〔Chieh〕 *n.* rule of conduct, commandment, precept, in junction, *v.* warn, prohibit.

28-- 條	rules of conduct.

識 〔Shih〕 *n.* knowledge. *v.* know, understand, recognize.

14-- 破	detect, see through, be fully aware of.
24-- 貨	know the quality of goods.
30-- 字	be able to read, literate.
-- 字班	literacy class.
-- 字本	reading primer.
60-- 見	experience, insight.
62-- 別	distinguish, discern.

讖 〔Chan〕 *n.* prophecy, omen, *adj.* prognostic.

0366₀

詒 〔I〕 *v.* present, bequeath, hand down

06-- 誤	cause any delay to business, throw hindrance in the way of.
25-- 傳	bequeath, hand down.
68-- 贈	give to, present with, donate.

0391₄

就 〔Chiu〕 *v.* go to, approach, complete, finish. adv. then, just now, immediately, presently, forthwith, thereupon.

00-- 座	take a seat, take one's seat.
13-- 職	*n.* inauguration, *v.* take office, take up one's office.
-- 職儀式	inauguration, installment.
-- 職宣言	inaugural address.
20-- 位＝就座	
22-- 任	inauguration.
23-- 我所知	to the best of my knowledge, as far as I know.
24-- 緒	be completed, be arranged.
27-- 將	soon, at once.
30-- 寢	go to bed, sleep.
32-- 近	take a short cut, avoid going far.
-- 業	*n.* employment, *v.* get employed.
-- 業率	employment rate.
-- 業訓練中心	employment training center.
-- 業咨詢	employment counseling.
-- 業機會	employment opportunity, job opening.
-- 業人數	number of persons employed, total employed.
35-- 逮	under arrest.
38-- 道	set out on a journey, start.
40-- 來	coming, come at once.
-- 去	go at once.
44-- 地	on the spot.
-- 地正法	execute summarily, summary execution, carry out a death sentence on the spot.
-- 地取材	obtain material locally.
-- 地解決	solve a problem right on the spot.
-- 地辦理	settle a case on the spot.
50-- 事	take up some work, take up one's duty.
-- 事論事	take the matter on its merits.
60-- 是	namely, exactly, that is.
77-- 醫	see a doctor, go to the doctor.
80-- 義從容	die for a righteous cause without any fuss.

0410₄

塾 〔Shu〕 *n.* anteroom, vestibule, domestic schoolroom, family school.

21-- 師	private tutor.

0422₇

劾 〔He〕 *v.* prosecute, accuse, impeach.

0428₁

麒 〔Chi〕 *n.* unicorn, monoceros.

09-- 麟	unicorn, monoceros.

0433₁

熟 〔Shu〕 *adj.* ripe, mature, cooked, well-acquainted with, familiar.

00-- 諳	make oneself master of.
03-- 識	acquainted, familiar, intimate, hand and glove.
04-- 計	*n.* matured plan, *v.* delib-

erate.

-- 讀		read thoroughly, get by heart, have by heart, learn by heart, repeat by rote.
07-- 記		commit in memory, learn by heart.
17-- 習		*n.* skillfulness, dexterity, expertness, competence, *v.* be skillful in, be familiar with, have full and ready knowledge of, *adj.* skillful, expert.
20-- 悉＝熟習		
-- 悉情形		get the run of things.
-- 手		expert, old hand, experienced, man, practised hand, experienced hand.
21-- 能生巧		practice makes perfect, practice brings perfection.
-- 慮		*n.* mature consideration, *v.* ponder, deliberate, think carefully.
-- 慮其後		consider maturely of the consequence.
24-- 貨		manufactured articles.
25-- 練		skilled, skillful, expert.
36-- 視		look at carefully.
-- 視無睹		ignore, be indifferent to.
60-- 思		deliberate, ponder over, revolve in the mind.
62-- 睡		*n.* deep sleep, sound sleep, *v.* sleep soundly, sleep like a dog.
80-- 人		acquaintance, one who is familiar.
-- 食		cooked food.
83-- 鐵		wrought iron.
91-- 煙		prepared tobacco.

0441₇

孰 〔Shu〕 *pron.* who? whom?

21-- 能當之		who is worthy of such responsibility?
60-- 是孰非		which is right and which is wrong?

0442₇

効 〔Hsiao〕 *n.* merit, result, effect, *v.* toil, labor at, imitate.

34-- 法		imitate examples.
40-- 力		render one's service to.
77-- 用		function.
78-- 驗		result, effect.
80-- 命疆場		defend the territory with one's life.
99-- 勞		serve, offer one's services.

0460₀

計 〔Chi〕 *n.* plan, scheme, device, plot, trick, *v.* plan, count, calculate, plot, scheme, reckon.

04-- 謀		plan, plot, scheme.
08-- 議		consider, think over.
21-- 上心來		come across one's mind.
25-- 件價格		piece price.
-- 件計酬		pay by the piece.
-- 件合同		agreement by piece.
-- 件工作		piece work.
-- 件工人		piece worker.
30-- 窮		at the end of one's resources.
50-- 畫		*n.* plan, scheme, program, design, arrangement, *v.* plan, design, arrange, lay out.
52-- 劃＝計畫		
-- 劃經濟		planned economy.
-- 劃專家		planning analyst.
-- 劃者		planner.
-- 劃預算		planning budget.
-- 劃行動		program action.
-- 劃銷售		planned selling.
-- 劃投資		intended investment.
-- 劃市場		planned market.
-- 劃草案		rough plan.
50-- 較		take into consideration, dispute.
55-- 費時間		chargeable time.
58-- 數		count.
60-- 日工作		day-wage work.
-- 日工資		daily wage.
-- 日工		day man, day laborer.
-- 量單位		measure unit.
64-- 時員		time keeper.

--時器	timer, timing meter.
--時卡	time card.
--時工作	time work.
--時費用	time charges.
--時成本	hour cost.
--時	time keeping.
88--算	n. calculation, v. calculate, reckon, count, cast in the mind.
--算值	calculated value.
--算誤差	calculation error.
--算機	computer.
--算機網	computer network.
--算機軟件	software.
--算表	calculating table.
--算者	counter, calculator.
--算尺	slide rule.
--算器	computer.
--策	plan, stratagem, project.

討 〔Tao〕 v. ask for, demand, make war on, impose military sanction on.

08--論	discuss, argue, debate, confer, talk over, deal with a subject.
--論會	conference, discussion session.
21--便宜	seek for one's own benefit, take one's advantage of.
--價還價	bargain, haggle.
22--亂	suppress rebellions.
23--伐	make war on, impose military sanction on, take punitive action against.
25--債	demand a debt, dun.
--債者	dun.
40--索	demand for, claim for.
47--好	please, flatter, get over a person.
63--賊	exterminate rebels.
71--厭	v. displease, take offense, adj. odious, troublesome.
81--飯	n. beggar, v. beg for food.
84--饒	seek forgiveness.

謝 〔Hsieh〕 v. thank, express gratitude, decline, refuse, fade.

00--意	thanks, gratitude.
04--謝	many thanks, thank you!
27--絕	refuse, decline, reject.
--絕參觀	no visitors allowed.
30--客	decline seeing visitors.
44--幕	curtain call.
44--世	die, pass away.
60--罪	beg pardon, apologize, offer apology, confess one's fault.
--恩	return thanks for kindness received.
80--乞	beg for.
81--飯	beg for food.

0461_0

訛 〔Er〕 n. false, erroneous, fallacious, v. extort, move.

00--言	lie.
08--詐	blackmail, extort.
25--傳	misinform.

0461_1

詾 〔Hsin〕 v. ask, inquire, inform, notify.

謊 〔Hoang〕 n. lie, falsehood.

00--言	lie, falsehood.
01--語者	liar.
02--話	lie falsehood.
47--報	misstatement.
--報財產	false declaration of assets.
--報稅額	false declaration.
73--騙	cheat, impose upon.

譁 〔Shen〕 v. believe. adj. sincere.

0461_4

謹 〔Chin〕 adj. careful, cautious, attentive, respectful, speak carefully.

00--言	speak carefully.
07--記	carefully remember, have in thought, have in mind, hold in thought.
20--重	careful and attentive.
30--守	guard carefully.
53--戒	especially guard against.
66--嚴	serious, stern, precise.
70--防	be on one's guard against.
--防假冒	beware of imitation!
--防扒手	beware of pickpockets!
80--領	receive with respect.

94-- 慎　　　　cautious, careful, watchful.

讙 〔Huan〕 n. clamor, noise, voice of joy.

77-- 鬧　　　　clamor, noise.
98-- 悅　　　　shout of joy.

0462₇

謁 〔Yeh〕 v. visit, see, call upon.

60-- 見　　　　visit, interview, have an audience.
-- 見上司　　see a superior.

訥 〔Noh〕 v. speak cautiously, stammer.

60-- 口　　　　stammer, stutter, hesitate, falter, hammer, hum.

誇 〔Kua〕 v. boast, brag, bluster, exaggerate, take pride in, pride one's self on, boast of, be proud of, glory in.

01-- 語　　　　big words, bombast.
10-- 示　　　　flaunt.
11-- 張　　　　v. talk big, blow one's own trumpet, exaggerate, overstate, adj. high-sounding, pompous, big-sounding, high-flown, tumid, bombastic.
-- 張法　　　hyperbole.
21-- 能　　　　boast of one's ability.
27-- 獎　　　　praise, extol.
40-- 大　　　　v. boast, brag, show off, puff up, make much of, swagger, adj. boasting, flaming.
-- 大狂　　　megalomania.
60-- 口　　　　boastful.
97-- 耀　　　　show off, make display.

0463₁

誌 〔Chih〕 n. history, annals, record v. remember, record, express, show.

00-- 哀　　　　express one's grief, condole.
40-- 書　　　　annals, records.
87-- 銘　　　　carve an inscription on stone, epitaph.

讌 〔Yen〕 v. assemble at a banquet.

80-- 會　　　　banquet, feast, entertainment.

0463₄

謨 〔Mo〕 n. plan, scheme, well-organized plan.

0464₁

詩 〔Shih〕 n. poem, poetry, verse.

00-- 文　　　　poems and essays, poetry and prose.
06-- 韻　　　　rhyme of poetry, rhyme of verses.
20-- 集　　　　collection of poems, anthology.
27-- 句　　　　verses.
40-- 才　　　　poetic faculty, richness of imagination.
77-- 學　　　　poetry, poetics.
80-- 人　　　　poet, poetess, bard.
88-- 節　　　　verses.

譸 〔Choo〕 v. deceive, delude.

0464₇

詖 〔Pi〕 adj. improper, unreasonable.

護 〔Hu〕 v. protect, guard, escort, help, aid, save, deliver.

00-- 庇　　　　shelter, protect, shade.
16-- 理　　　　n. nursing, v. nurse, look after.
20-- 航隊　　　convoy.
21-- 衛　　　　guard, escort, defend.
-- 衛兵　　　guard, escort, military guard.
27-- 身符　　　protective talisman, charm for protection.
-- 身甲　　　armour, cuirass.
38-- 送　　　　escort, convoy.
40-- 士　　　　nurse.
43-- 城河　　　city moat.
44-- 林　　　　forest protection.
67-- 路　　　　n. maintenance of a road, v. maintain a road.
-- 照　　　　passport.
77-- 胸甲　　　breast plate.
-- 短　　　　screen one's faults, side with one who is wrong.

0465₄

譁 〔Hua〕 n. noise, clamor, tumult.

22-- 變　　　　mutiny.
23-- 然　　　　adj. noisy, clmorously.

0465_6

諱 〔Hui〕 v. avoid, deny, hide, conceal.

0466_0

詁 〔Ku〕 n. explanation, commentary, v. explain, expound.

諸 〔Cho〕 adj. all, many, every.
20-- 位   you, ladies and gentlemen.
27-- 侯   feudal princes.
-- 般   all sorts, every variety.
-- 多   many.
-- 色   all kinds.
46-- 如此類   and so on, and so forth, etcetera (etc.).

0466_1

詰 〔Chi〕 v. ask, interrogate, investigate, question, examine.
30-- 究   scruntinize narrowly.
47-- 朝   tomorrow morning.
50-- 責   hold up to execration, hold up to reprobation.
60-- 口供   demand a confession.
77-- 問   examine, question, ask with authority.

誥 〔Kao〕 n. imperial declaration, v. order, command.
03-- 誡   enjoin solemnly.
52-- 授   confer a title of honor.
80-- 命   an imperial patent conferring title of honor.

0466_4

諾 〔No〕 v. answer, promise, give one's word.
00-- 言   promise.

0468_6

讀 〔Tuh〕 n. clause,short sentence. v. read, study, recite.
00-- 音   pronunciation.
-- 音統一   unification of the spoken language.
10-- 一遍   read over.
-- 不起書   unable to afford an education.
20-- 稿   read proofs.
27-- 物   reading material.
30-- 完   read through, finish reading.

34-- 法   methods of reading.
44-- 者   reader, reading public.
50-- 本   reader, reading book.
-- 書   study, read, learn.
-- 書界   reading public, reading circle.

讚 〔Tsan〕 n. eulogy, eulogium, commendation, v. commend, praise, eulogize, extol.
00-- 文   written eulogium.
01-- 語   good word, eulogium.
10-- 不絕口   praise again and again.
27-- 歌   sing the praises of.
56-- 揚   praise, commend, eulogize.
80-- 美   praise, admire, commend.
-- 善   praise the virtuous.
81-- 頌   sing the praise of.
90-- 賞   n. commendation, good, v. commend and reward.

0469_4

謀 〔Mou〕 v. plot, plan, devise, deliberate, ponder, consult with.
13-- 職   seek employment, apply for a job.
22-- 利   contrive after gain, make a profit.
-- 利益   work in the interest of.
-- 私利   v. seek personal interest, adj. selfish.
25-- 生   make a living, work for one's living, live.
-- 生手段   means of life, means of earning a living.
30-- 害   plot against
40-- 士   adviser, counselor, strategist.
43-- 求   n. pursuit of, v. pursue, seek.
47-- 殺   murder, plot a murder, premeditated murder.
50-- 畫   scheme, plan, design, frame, contrive.
64-- 財   scheme after others' money.
-- 財害命   murder for money.
67-- 略   strategy, plot, stratagem.
72-- 反   plot, treason, plan rebellion, plot and rebel.

諜 〔Tieh〕 n. spy, detective, spying, espionage.
04-- 諜　talkative, garrulous.
47-- 報　intelligence, espionage, spy's report.
-- 報敵情　spy and report on the enemy's conditions.

0512_7
靖 〔Ching〕 v. tranquilize, pacify, keep in order.
38-- 逆　suppress rebels, put down rebellion.
60-- 國　restore order in the country.

0519_6
竦 〔Sung〕 v. be afraid, dread, fear, respect.
23-- 然　terrified, frightened.
24-- 動　agitated, excited, aroused.
48-- 敬　respect.
91-- 慄　tremble, shudder.
96-- 懼　terrified, horror-stricken.

0549_6
辣 〔La〕 adj. hot, acrid, pungent, piquant.
07-- 詞　poignant words.
20-- 手　cruel, violent hand.
44-- 苦　acrid and bitter.
47-- 醬　piquant sauce.
-- 醬油　chilli sauce.
-- 椒　capsicum.
65-- 味　hot, peppery taste, piquancy.

0562_7
請 〔Ching〕 v. invite, request, beg, engage, beg leave, ask permission.
02-- 託　ask favor of, requst a person to do something.
10-- 示　request instruction, ask for instruction.
27-- 假　ask for leave.
30-- 進來　come in please.
-- 安　give one's best regards, present one's compliments.
-- 客　invite guest, give a spread, stand treat, give a feast.
41-- 帖　invitation card.

43-- 求　ask, beg, request, apply, pray, make a request.
-- 求權　right of claim.
48-- 教　take counsel, take advice with, consult.
-- 救兵　requisition for reinforcement.
60-- 罪　apologize, ask for pardon, confess a fault.
71-- 願　n. application, solicitation, petition. v. make application.
-- 願書　petition.
-- 原諒　excuse me, I beg your pardon.
77-- 問　ask respectfully, please tell me.
-- 醫　send for a doctor.
80-- 命　request orders.
88-- 坐　please take a seat.

0563_0
訣 〔Jyue〕 n. rule, art, trick, secrets of any craft, v. say good-bye, bid farewell, take leave.
30-- 竅　secret, knack, trick.
62-- 別　bid farewell, say good-bye, take leave.

訣 〔Tieh〕 v. forget.

0563_7
譴 〔Chin〕 v. blame, scold, reprimand, find fault with, question sternly.
50-- 責　blame, condemn, rebuke.

0564_5
講 〔Chiang〕 v. speak, talk, converse, discuss, preach, explain, discourse.
00-- 座　lectureship.
02-- 話　talk, speak.
16-- 理　reason, appeal to reason.
17-- 習　practise, study.
-- 習班　study group, seminar.
21-- 衛生　attach importance to hygiene.
-- 價　haggle over prices.
-- 師　lecturer, instructor, speaker.
-- 師團　lecturers' group.
23-- 台　platform, pulpit.
26-- 和　negotiate peace, put up the sword.

27-- 解   *n.* explanation, *v.* explain.
30-- 究   *v.* devote to particular, care to, *adj.* elegant.
33-- 演   lecture, give an address, make a speech.
-- 述   relate, tell, describe, recite.
38-- 道   preach.
40-- 壇   rostrum.
50-- 書   explain books.
60-- 員   lecturer.
67-- 明白   fully explained, clearly stated.
80-- 義   lecture, lecture sheets.
90-- 堂   lecture hall, class room.
95-- 情   make an appeal.

0568₆
讀 〔 Hui 〕 *v.* stop.

0569₀
誅 〔 Chu 〕 *v.* kill, punish, put to death, reprove, censure, clear away.
13-- 戮   kill, slay, behead, execute.
33-- 滅   exterminate utterly.
60-- 罰   punish.
-- 暴   put the violent to death.
78-- 除奸雄   exterminate an able scoundrel.

誄 〔 Lei 〕 *n.* obituary, funeral oration.

0569₆
諫 〔 Chien 〕 *n.* advice, counsel, expostulation, *v.* admonish, advise, remonstrate.
21-- 止   urge one to desist.

0612₇
竭 〔 Chieh 〕 *v.* exhaust, use up, put forth to the utmost, carry to the utmost point, *adj.* exhausted, finished, used up, wanting.
03-- 誠   with all one's heart, most heartily, most sincerely.
40-- 力   do one's best, exhaust one's full energy, exhaust one's full strength, put the best foot forward.
50-- 盡   exhausted.
61-- 蹶   *v.* stagger, totter.

0662₇

謁 〔 Yeh 〕 *v.* visit, call on.
60-- 見   visit, interview, wait on, have an audience.
-- 見室   audience chamber.

謂 〔 Wei 〕 *n.* meaning, *v.* address, call, say, inform, tell, speak of.
01-- 語   (in grammar) predicate.

諤 〔 E 〕 *v.* speak plainly, *adj.* blunt, honest.

0663₄
誤 〔 Wu 〕 *v.* mistake, fail, delay, *adj.* erroneous, fallacious.
00-- 言   say wrong.
06-- 譯   misinterpret, mistranslate.
07-- 記   remember incorrectly.
-- 認   *n.* mistaken recognition, *v.* recognize wrong, mistake for.
-- 認爲   mistake for, recognize by mistake.
10-- 工   loss of working time.
12-- 刊   misprint, printer's error.
20-- 信   *n.* mistaken confidence, *v.* misbelieve.
22-- 斷   misjudge, misestimate, misconjuncture, misconceive.
25-- 傳   misinform, misreport, give erroneous information.
27-- 解   *n.* misapprehension, *v.* mistake, misunderstand, misinterpret, put a false construction.
28-- 傷   accidental injury.
30-- 寫   wrongly written.
-- 寫日子   misdate, date erroneously.
47-- 期   delay, be in arrears, fall behind schedule.
38-- 導   mislead.
47-- 殺   *n.* homicide by misadventure, manslaughter, *v.* kill in mistake.
50-- 事   spoil an affair.
53-- 捕   mis-arrest, get the wrong sow by the ear.
77-- 用   misuse, misapply.
80-- 人   lead astray.

-- 人子弟　mislead and cause harm to the young people.
-- 入歧途　deviate, go astray.
-- 差　error, mistake, defect.
-- 會　*n.* misconception, *v.* misunderstand, misapprehend.
-- 公　delay public business.
88-- 算　miscalculate, miscount.

0664₁
譯〔I〕*v.* translate, interpret.
00-- 文　translation, translated version.
-- 音　transliteration.
17-- 務　translation work.
22-- 製　(in movie) to dub, dubbing.
27-- 解　decipher.
44-- 者　translator, interpreter.
50-- 本　version of translation.
53-- 成密碼　encode.
60-- 員＝譯者

0664₇
謾〔Man〕*v.* insult, deceive, disdain, scorn.
00-- 言　lie.
60-- 罵　abuse, scold scornfully.

0668₁
諟〔Shih〕*n.* reason, *v.* examine, *adj.* right, *proper.*

0668₆
韻〔Yun〕*n.* rime, riming, tone, harmony of sound, *adj.* refined, polished, elegant.
00-- 文　poem, rhyme.
25-- 律　rhythm, cadence.
50-- 事　romantic incident.

0669₄
課〔Ke〕*n.* lesson, course, taxes, *v.* teach, tax, levy, impose upon.
00-- 文　text, lesson.
21-- 桌　student's desk.
26-- 程　curriculum, course of study.
-- 程表　curriculum, class schedule.
28-- 稅　*n.* taxation, *v.* tax.
-- 稅過重　overtax.
30-- 室　classroom.
47-- 期　session.
50-- 本　textbook.
90-- 堂　classroom, schoolroom.
-- 堂討論　seminar.

譟〔Sao〕*n.* noise, clamor, disturbance, *v.* abuse, slander.
51-- 擾　excite and disturb.

0691₀
親〔Chin〕*n.* parents, relative, kindred, relationship, *v.* love, kiss, be attached *adj.* near, intimate, dear, personal close.
08-- 族　kinsmen.
10-- 王　prince.
-- 疏　near and distant relationshp.
20-- 信　*n.* confidant, righthand man, *adj.* trusted.
-- 愛　*v.* love dearly, *adj.* dear, beloved, intimate.
-- 手　of one's own hand.
21-- 征　imperial expedition.
25-- 生　of one's own begetting.
26-- 自　personally, in person.
27-- 身＝親自
30-- 家　relatives by marriage.
-- 密　familiar, close, intimate, hand and glove.
32-- 近＝親密
40-- 友　relatives and friends.
44-- 熱　warm, cordial.
47-- 切　cordial, intimate, warm and sincere.
53-- 戚　relatives, relations, kindred.
50-- 事已定　already engaged.
61-- 暱　intimate, close, cheek by jowl.
-- 嘴　kiss.
64-- 睦　*v.* get on with, keep on terms with, *adj.* on good term, on good friendly term, on good footing, on good cordial footing.
67-- 眼　with one's own eyes.
71-- 歷其境　experience something personally.
74-- 隨　personal attendant.

77-- 屬　　relatives, kinsmen, kindred, folk ,blood relatives.
-- 屬法　　Law of Domestic Relation.
80-- 人　　kinsman , dear one.
-- 善　　goodwill, friendly, arm in arm.
88-- 筆　　n. one's own handwriting, autograph, adj. written by one's own hand.
-- 筆簽名　　autograph.
90-- 眷　　relatives.

0710₄

望〔Wang〕 n. hope, expectation, v. hope, expect, look for, look up, watch, gaze at.
00-- 塵莫及　　be left far behind.
07-- 望然　　ashamed at a loss.
08-- 族　　respected family.
10-- 而生畏　　be awe-stricken by.
23-- 台　　lookout, signal station.
34-- 遠　　take a distant view.
-- 遠鏡　　telescope.
60-- 見　　see.
67-- 眼欲穿　　aspire earnestly.
71-- 長久遠　　long time.

0711₀

颯〔Sa〕 n. sound of blowing wind, adj. suddenly, for a moment.
07-- 颯　　soughing.
-- 爽　　lively, strong and speedy.

0722₇

鷓〔Che〕 n. partridge.

0724₇

毅〔I〕 n. fortitude, resolution, adj. firm, resolute, intrepid.
17-- 勇　　brave, bold, courageous.
23-- 然　　adj. resolute, adv. resolutly.
-- 然決然　　resolutely and determindly.
-- 然振作　　brace up resolutely.
40-- 力　　firmness of mind, will-power, endurance, stamina, unwearied effort, grit.

0742₇

郊〔Chiao〕 n. suburb, country, out-skirts, borders, frontier, waste land.
23-- 外　　suburb, country.
38-- 遊　　picnic.
71-- 區　　suburbs of a city.

郭〔Kuo〕 n. suburb, outer wall of a city
23-- 外　　beyond the outer wall.

鶉〔Chun〕 n. quail.

0761₀

訊〔Sin〕 n. trial, judicial examination, tidings, v. examine, interrogate.
17-- 取口供　　question (a suspect) for oral testimony.
60-- 罪　　examine a criminal.
77-- 問　　try, investigate, inquire into, interrogate.

詛〔Chu〕 v. curse, imprecate.
60-- 罵　　curse, rail at, revile.

諷〔Feng〕 n. satire, irony. v. satirize, ridicule, recite.
01-- 語　　irony, satire.
05-- 諫　　reprove by satire, remonstrate ironically.
52-- 刺　　satirize, ridicule, grin, skit.
-- 刺詩　　parody.
-- 刺家　　satirist.
-- 刺畫　　caricature, cartoon.

0761₁

讄〔Se〕 v. stammer, stutter, falter.

0761₂

詭〔Kuei〕 v. deceive, cheat, defraund. adj. cunning, odd, strange.
00-- 辯　　n. sophistry, v. quibble, chop logic, prevaricate.
-- 辯家　　sophist.
-- 辯學派　　the school of sophism.
-- 辯學者　　sophist.
04-- 計　　trick, wile, intrigue.
-- 計多端　　full of cunning tricks, very cunning, very crafty.
-- 謀　　treacherous schemes.
08-- 詐　　treacherous, cunning, craft, double-faced, double-handed.
-- 詐者　　fox, sly boot.
60-- 異　　strange, odd, uncommon.

73-- 騙	play one a trick.	

讒 〔Chan〕 v. slander, defame, detract.

00-- 言	slanderous words, false charge, obloquy, calumny.	
-- 謗	slander, vilify.	

0761₇

記 〔Chi〕 n. record, register, mark, memory, v. remember, recollect, keep in memory, record, take note, register.

10-- 工具	work-point recorder.
-- 工簿	work-point registration book.
14-- 功	v. record merits, give merits.
23-- 住	memorize, commit to memory.
26-- 得	come to remembrance, call to memory.
-- 名	sign, put down one's name.
27-- 名支票	check to order.
33-- 述	narrate.
37-- 過	mark demerit, record demerits.
41-- 帳	keep account, charge in account.
-- 帳員	book keeper.
43-- 載	record, put down in record, make record.
44-- 者	reporter, journalist, correspondent.
47-- 起	remember, redeem from oblivion.
50-- 事	make a memorandum of events.
-- 事文	narration.
-- 書冊	notebook, scrapbook, pocketbook.
61-- 號	sign, mark, indication.
-- 號法	notation.
-- 賬	charge to an account.
-- 賬員	tally man.
80-- 入	inscribe.
-- 分	point.
-- 分員	scorer.

-- 念	remember, keep in mind.
-- 念物	reminder, keepsake, token of remembrance.
-- 念週	weekly assembly.
-- 念會	commemoration.
87-- 錄	n. record, memorandum, v. record, take notes, take an account, register, make a note of, commit to paper.
-- 錄片	documentary film, news reel, documentary.
-- 錄處	enrollment, registry.
-- 錄保存	records retention.
90-- 憶	n. memory, v. remember, recollect, retain in memory, memorize, bear in mind, keep in mind.
-- 憶力	memory, power of memory, retention.

0762₀

詢 〔Hsun〕 v. ask, inquire about, consult, deliberate, interrogate.

67-- 明	find out by inquiry.
77-- 問	ask, inquire of.
-- 問處	inquiry office, information desk.

詡 〔Hsu〕 v. boast, brag, adj. proud.

詞 〔Tzu〕 n. word, phrases, expression, terms.

00-- 意	meaning, import.
-- 章	writings, composition.
11-- 頭	prefix.
27-- 句	sentence.
-- 組	expressions, phrases, word groups.
-- 彙	vocabulary, dictionary.
34-- 法	morphology.
44-- 藻	figures of speech, elegant expressions.
55-- 典	dictionary.
-- 典編纂	process of compiling a dictionary.
91-- 類	parts of speech.

讕 〔Lan〕 v. abuse, revile.

00--	言	slander, abusive remark.
調	〔Tiao〕	*n.* tune, rime, air, *v.* mix, blend, adjust, temper, regulate, harmonize, make peace, move, transfer, ridicule, mock at.
00--	度	arrange, move, adjust, re-arrange.
--	度員	dispatcher.
--	音	tune, chime, harmonize, put in tune.
01--	劑	regulate, adjust, prepare drugs.
10--	工作	transfer.
--	弄	make fun with, play joke upon.
13--	職	transfer.
--	職旅費	travel expenses on transfer.
16--	理	regulate, recuperate.
17--	子	tone, melody.
--	配	allot, distribute.
20--	停	mediate, reconcile, intercede, interpose, settle difference.
21--	處	mediate.
--	經	regulate the menses.
22--	任	transfer from one post to another.
--	出	swing on.
23--	戲	flirt, dally with, insult.
24--	動	transfer, shift.
26--	和	compromise, reconcile, mix, blend, make peace, harmonize.
--	和折衷	compromise.
27--	解	mediate.
--	解人	mediator.
--	勻	attemper.
--	色	adjust color.
--	色版	palette.
40--	查	*n.* investigation, examination, *v.* investigate, examine, inquire into, search for.
--	查組	reporting panel.
--	查員	investigator.
--	查委員會	investigation committee.
--	查記錄	record of investigation.
--	查表	questionnaire, inquiry schedule. letter of reference.
--	查會	fact-finding meeting.
--	皮	naughty.
48--	幹部	transfer cadres.
51--	攝	recuperate, recover health.
52--	撥	*n.* allocation, *v.* sow discord.
57--	換	exchange, change, replace.
58--	整	*n.* adjustment, coordination, *v.* adjust, regulate.
60--	味	season food.
--	味品	seasoning, spice.
70--	防	transfer garrison.
72--	兵	move troops.
--	入	swing-in.
80--	羹	spoon.
--	養	recruit one's health, take care of one's health.
--	養地	health resort.
--	養身體	nurse oneself.
--	合	mix, compound.
88--	笑	ridicule, mock.
--	節	regulate, adjust.
95--	情	flirt.

0762₂

謬	〔Miu〕	*n.* error, mistake, falsehood, *adj.* misleading, fallacious, untrue.
00--	妄	absurd, erratic, untrue.
06--	誤	error, mistake, fallacy.
08--	說	nonsense, fallacious discourse.
--	論	fallacious reason, fallacious argument.
60--	見	mistaken notion.

0762₇

部	〔Pu〕	*n.* department, ministry, class, section, copy.
10--	下	subordinates.
20--	位	locality, location.
44--	落	tribe, clan.
60--	署	disposition, deployment, arrangement.
71--	長	minister, head of a department.
77--	屬	subordinate.
--	門	department, branch.

78-- 隊　　　army, troops, units of armed forces.
80-- 分　　　portion, part, section.

誦〔Sung〕v. chant, sing, intone, recite, hum over.
04-- 詩　　　recite poetry.
-- 讀　　　read, chant, go over.
21-- 經　　　chant the liturgy.

諏〔Tsou〕v. joke, jest, ridicule, talk at random.

譎〔Chueh〕adj. crafty, wily, intriguing.
05-- 諫　　　advise in an indirect way.
08-- 詐　　　deceiving.
97-- 怪　　　deceitful, crafty, strange.
0763₂

認〔Jen〕v. know, recognize, acknowledge, confess.
02-- 證謄本　certified copy.
03-- 識　　　recognize, know.
-- 識論　　theory of knowledge, epistemology.
-- 識到　　realize.
10-- 可　　　consent, approve, recognize, affirm.
22-- 出　　　identify, recognize.
25-- 債　　　admission of liability.
30-- 爲　　　deem, consider.
35-- 清　　　know clearly, take cognizance, grasp.
40-- 真　　　serious, conscientious, in earnest.
41-- 帳　　　acknowledge a debt.
56-- 捐　　　subscribe.
58-- 輸　　　admit defeat, yield to the victor, give in, acknowledge defeat.
60-- 罪　　　confess, apologize, acknowledge guilt.
67-- 明　　　know clearly.
77-- 股　　　subscription for shares.
80-- 人支票　check to order.
84-- 錯　　　confess to a fault, acknowledge one's fault.
86-- 知　　　recognition, perception.
0763₇

諛〔Ye〕v. flatter, adulate, toady.
00-- 言　　　flattering words.
44-- 墓　　　flattering epitaph.
0764₇

設〔Sheh〕v. set up, establish, arrange, suppose, institute.
00-- 立　　　establish, set up, erect, institute.
-- 席　　　lay the table, lay the cloth.
04-- 計　　　design, project, lay a plot, make measures.
-- 計工作　design work.
-- 計師　　designer, architect.
-- 計草圖　rough plan.
-- 計者　　designer, contriver.
-- 計教學法　the project method of education.
-- 計圖　　blueprint, construction plan.
08-- 施　　　plan, program, measures.
24-- 備　　　n. equipment, facilities, accommodation, v. furnish, equip.
-- 備完整　completely equipped.
-- 備折舊　depreciation of equipment.
-- 備維修　maintenance of equipment.
30-- 宴　　　give a feast, give a dinner party.
-- 宴歡迎　give a welcome party.
34-- 法　　　plan, devise, take measure.
46-- 想　　　n. plan, scheme, v. assume, suppose, imagine, presume.
48-- 教　　　found a religion, preach.
60-- 圈套　　set a trap, lay a snare.
70-- 防　　　fortify.
0765₆

諢〔Hum〕v. joke, jest.
27-- 名　　　nickname.
0766₁

讇〔Chan〕v. become delirious, adj. talkative, nonsensical.
00-- 妄　　　delirium.
01-- 語　　　jargon, incoherent talk.
0766₂

詔〔Chao〕v. decree, announce, proclaim, teach, instruct.

21--	旨	imperial decree.
24--	告	announce, proclaim.

韶 〔Shaur〕 *adj.* fine, good, beautiful, excellent.

44--	華	prime of one's life.

0766₈

諮 〔Tzu〕 *v.* consult, deliberate.

07--	詢	consult, inquire of, take advice.
--	詢委員會	consultative committee.
--	詢機關	advisory organ.
08--	議	discuss, take consult.

0767₂

謠 〔Yao〕 *n.* rumor, false report, *v.* sing.

00--	言	rumor, false report.
25--	傳	spread a false report.

0767₇

諂 〔Chan〕 *v.* flatter, cajole, toady, fawn upon.

00--	言	flattering words.
47--	媚	*n.* fair tongue, flattery, blandishments, *v.* flatter, cajole, pay compliment to, *adj,* fawning.
88--	笑	flatter and giggle.

0768₀

畝 〔Mu〕 *n.* Chinese acre.

00--	產量	per-mu yield.

0768₂

歆 〔Hsin〕 *v.* enjoy, move, excite.

00--	享	enjoy.

0774₇

氓 〔Meng〕 *n.* people, mass, vagabonds.

0821₂

施 〔Shih〕 *v.* give, bestow, spread, do, act, carryout, execute, enforce, distribute.

00--	主	benefactor, donor.
10--	工	work, construct.
--	工圖	working drawing, working plan.
--	工人員	builder, constructor.
--	工計劃	work schedule.
--	工管理	supervision of works.
18--	政	*n.* administration, *v.* administer.
20--	手術	*n.* operation, *v.* operate.
21--	行	enforce, carry out, put into force, carry into effect.
34--	洗	baptize.
35--	禮	pay respect to.
48--	救	save, relieve, give help.
58--	捨	give help, give alms.
60--	恩	show kindness, do a pleasure, bestow favor, confer benefit.
77--	肥	fertilize, manure, apply fertilizer.
--	展	spread out, show, manifest, launch forth, give full play.
80--	食	give food to the poor.

0821₄

旌 〔Ching〕 *n.* banner.

08--	旗	flags, banners.

旄 〔Mao〕 *n.* banner, *v.* waving of a banner.

0822₁

旖 〔Yi〕 *v.* waving a banner.

0822₇

膂 〔Lu〕 *n.* backbone.

40--	力	strength.

0823₂

旅 〔Lu〕 *n.* brigade, troops, forces, *v.* travel.

00--	店	hotel, inn, boarding house, tavern, public house.
21--	行	n. travel, trip, v. travel, tour, trip, journey.
--	行社	travel agency, tourist bureau, tourist agency.
--	行支票	traveler's check.
--	行指南	travel guide book.
26--	程	journey, route, itinerary.
29--	伴	fellow traveler.
30--	客	traveler, passenger.
38--	途	during travel.
--	遊業	tourist industry.

-- 遊團	tourist party.
-- 遊收入	tourist income.
-- 遊勝地	sightseeing resort.
-- 遊簽證	tourist visa.
55-- 費	lodging expenses, travelling expenses.
71-- 長	brigadier general.
83-- 館	hotel, inn.
-- 館賬單	hotel bill.
-- 館業	hotel industry.
-- 館管理	hotel management.
-- 館服務	room service.

0823₃

於 〔**Yu**〕 *prep.* in, on, at, by, from, with, through.

16-- 理不合	illogical.
-- 理甚當	very reasonable.
21-- 此	here, in this place.
34-- 法無效	invalid in point of law.
50-- 事無補	it doesn't help the situation.
60-- 是	then, thereupon, accordingly, consequently.
80-- 義不同	different in meaning.

0823₄

族 〔**Tsu**〕 *n.* family, clan, tribe, kindred, race.

08-- 譜	ancestry, lineage, genelogy of a clan.
71-- 長	head of a clan.
80-- 人	clansmen.
91-- 類	tribe, clan.

0824₀

放 〔**Fang**〕 *v.* set free, loosen, release, let off, let go, liberate, lay down, settle, put, place, set.

00-- 高利貸	practice usury.
-- 言高論	give a free and boastful talk.
-- 棄	abandon, renounce, give up, throw over, relinguish.
-- 棄權利	waive the right.
10-- 下	put down, lay down.
-- 工	quit work.
-- 電影	show a film.
-- 不下手	cannot stop doing something.
-- 不下心	cannot stop worrying.
12-- 水	discharge water, let the other side win purposely.
17-- 砲	fire a cannon, discharge a gun.
-- 砲示敬	fire cannons in salute.
20-- 手	let go one's hand, give a free hand to.
-- 手去做	act without considering consequences or difficulties.
21-- 行	give customs clearance, pass, let go.
22-- 任	release, let alone, indulge, indulge oneself in.
-- 任主義	the policy of interfering as little as possible.
-- 任的	laissez-faire.
24-- 射	shoot, discharge, emit, radiate.
-- 射微粒	fallout.
-- 射性	radioactivity.
-- 射性元素	radioactive element.
25-- 牛娃	cowherd.
-- 債	lend money, make loans to others.
26-- 釋	release, set free, clear the skirts of.
27-- 血	bleed, let blood.
-- 假	give a holiday.
-- 包	lay down the burden.
28-- 牧	graze.
-- 縱	allow to run wild, give the reins to, give loose to, have full swing.
30-- 寬	widen, loosen.
-- 寬胸懷	be relaxed, be broadminded.
-- 寬條件	soften the terms.
31-- 逐	deport, banish, exile.
-- 逐遠方	be exiled to a considerable distance.
-- 逐權	right of exclusion.
33-- 心	feel safe be at ease, ease oneself, set one's heart at rest.
35-- 禮炮	fire a salute.
37-- 恣	indulgence, intemperance,

	sensuality, high-living.
38-- 汽	blow a whistle.
-- 洋	put to sea, go abroad.
40-- 大	enlarge, magnify.
-- 大鏡	magnifier, magnifying glass.
-- 大機	enlarger (in photography).
-- 大業務	enlarge business.
-- 大眼光	broaden one's vision.
-- 大照片	enlarge a photo.
-- 在心裏	keep in mind.
-- 走	let one escape, release, let go.
41-- 鞭炮	let off firecracker.
44-- 蕩	v. set adrift, indulge, shake a loose leg, adj.unrestrained, luxurious, wild, extravagant, profligate.
-- 蕩度日	pass the day recklessly.
-- 蕩不羈	dissipated and unrestrained.
47-- 款	lend, make loans.
-- 款人	money-lender.
-- 款利息	interest upon loans.
-- 聲	give forth the voice.
48-- 槍	fire, shoot.
50-- 毒	spread poison.
60-- 置	set down, place, put, lay.
-- 暗箭	stab one in the back.
65-- 映	project (a motion picture).
-- 映機	projector.
69-- 哨	be on sentry-go.
-- 哨防守	place soldiers on sentry.
72-- 鬆	relax, loosen, slacken.
75-- 肆	n. shabbiness, villainy, v. relax, relax loosen, run wild, indulge, run riot.
-- 肆行爲	disorderly and rude behavior.
77-- 屁	break wind, fart, cut the cheese.
-- 風箏	fly a kite.
-- 膽	pluck up courage.
-- 學	go home after school, break up school.
-- 闊	widen.
-- 開手	release one's hold.
80-- 入	let in, put in.

88-- 箭	shoot an arrow.
90-- 火	n. arson, v. set fire.
-- 光	shine, gleam, emit light.
97-- 炮	fire an artillery piece, set off firecracker.

敵 〔Ti〕 n. enemy, foe, opponent, adversary, antagonist

00-- 意	hostility, animosity.
20-- 手	rival, adversary, opponent, antagonist.
21-- 僑	alien enemy.
22-- 後	behind the enemy lines.
24-- 僞軍	the enemy and puppet troops.
28-- 艦	hostile ship.
34-- 對	hostile, antagonistic.
-- 對行爲	hostile action.
36-- 視	be hostile toward.
37-- 軍	hostile army.
60-- 國	enemy state, enemy's country, hostile country.
75-- 陣	enemy's position.
80-- 人	enemy, foe.
95-- 情	enemy's situation.

0828₁

旋 〔Hsuan〕 v. turn, revolve, return, turn around, come back, rotate, twirl wheel, wheel.

25-- 律	melody.
37-- 渦	whirlpool, eddy, vortex.
55-- 轉	turn, revolve, rotate, roll, spin, turn round, wheel, twirl, trundle, bowl.
58-- 輪	revolve, trundle.
60-- 暈	giddy, dizzy.
77-- 風	whirlwind, cyclone.

旗 〔Chi〕 n. flag, banner, ensign.

20-- 手	standard-bearer, ensign bearer.
28-- 艦	flagship.
41-- 杆	flagstaff.
43-- 幟	flag, banner.
61-- 號	signal flag.
77-- 開得勝	win in the first battle.

0844₀

效 〔**Hsiao**〕 *n.* effect, result, efficacy, consequence, *v.* copy, imitate, devote, present, offer, learn, *adj.* effective, efficacious.

00--	率	efficiency.
21--	能	efficiency, potential.
34--	法	pattern after, follow the example, imitate, follow in the step.
40--	力	*n.* efficacy, power, potency, *v.* render one's service to.
43--	尤	follow an evil action.
50--	忠於	be loyal to, be faithful to.
60--	果	result, effect.
77--	用	potency, utility.
--	用甚微	avail one little.
78--	驗	result, effect.
80--	命疆場	serve on the battlefield.
99--	勞	render one's service.

敦 〔**Duen**〕 *v.* esteem, urge, impel, strengthen, regard as important, *adj.* honest, simple, sincere, generous, firm, solid.

05--	請	invite sincerely, employ.
26--	促	urge, hasten.
60--	品力學	upright in character and diligent in the pursuit of knowledge.
64--	睦	friendly, cordial.
--	睦鄰邦	be cordial and friendly to neighboring country.
71--	厚	honest, sincere.
--	厚長者	honest elder.

0861₁

詐 〔**Jah**〕 *v.* deceive, impose upon, defraud, cheat, pretend, feign, *adj.* cunning, artful, false, deceitful.

00--	病	feign sickness.
--	癲	feign madness.
04--	謀	scheme.
10--	醉	feign drunkenness.
17--	取	swindle, defraud.
--	取金錢	obtain money by fraud.
21--	術	juggle.
47--	欺	deceive, feign.
62--	睡	pretend to sleep.

66--	哭	crocodile tears.
73--	騙	defraud, swindle.
--	騙犯	swindler.

0861₄

詮 〔**Chuan**〕 *n.* truth, *v.* explain, discuss upon.

02--	證	explain by facts.
08--	論	discourse on, comment on.
26--	釋	explain, annotate, expound.

0861₆

說 〔**Shuo**〕 *n.* words, speech, sayings, theory, doctrine, a school of thought *v.* say, speak, talk, tell, explain, narrate.

02--	話	*n.* words, saying, *v.* talk, speak, discourse.
04--	謊	*v.* lie, tell lies, give lurch.
--	謊者	liar.
10--	不盡	untold, unable to finish telling.
12--	到	mention, speak of.
--	到底	in the final analysis.
16--	理	*n.* argument, reasoning, *v.* argue, reason.
22--	出	tell, speak, utter, let out, blab.
24--	動	*n.* persuasion, *v.* persuade.
26--	得好	well-said.
30--	空話	empty talk, talk nonsense.
--	完	finish speaking.
--	穿了	put it bluntly, in plain language.
--	客	spokesman, lobbyist, persuasive politician.
34--	法	version, way of speaking.
40--	大話	boast, brag.
44--	夢話	talk in one's dream, talk nonsense.
--	老實話	be frank, tell the truth.
48--	教	preach, lecture.
67--	明	*n.* illustration, explanation, exposition, *v.* explain, expound, clear up, show.
--	明書	specification, synopsis.
77--	服	convince, overcome, bring round, persuade, prevail on,

　　　pin one down.
-- 服力　persuasion, persuasiveness.
84-- 錯　have a slip of the tongue.
88-- 笑話　joke, jest.
95-- 情　apologize, intercede, solicit a favor.

0861_7

訖 [Chi] *adj.* finished, ended, done *prep.* up to, till, until.
80-- 今　up to the present, until now.

0862_1

諭 [Yu] *n.* order, edict, *v.* order, command, instruct, advise, know, understand.
21-- 旨　imperial decree.

0862_2

診 [Chen] *v.* examine, diagnose.
00-- 療室　medical consultation room.
22-- 斷　diagnosis.
-- 斷書　medical certificate.
72-- 所　doctor's office.
-- 脈　feel the pulse.

0862_7

論 [Lun] *v.* discuss, argue, evaluate, consult, debate, consider, criticize, discourse upon.
00-- 文　thesis, essay, theme, treatise, article, paper.
-- 辯　debate, discuss.
02-- 證　proof, demonstration.
07-- 調　tone of argument.
08-- 說　essay, treatise, discourse.
14-- 功行賞　decide awards on the basis of merits.
16-- 理學　logic.
-- 理學家　logician.
17-- 及　*v.* talk about, *prep.* inasmuch as, upon the subject of, in regard to, with reference to.
21-- 價　bargain.
22-- 斷　*n.* assertion, *v.* assert, conclude.
-- 件　by the piece of works.
25-- 件計酬　payment by the piece.

33-- 述　*n.* argumentation, *v.* deal with, treat.
51-- 據　data, basic argument.
61-- 點　thesis, proposition.
-- 題　topic, theme, subject, thesis.
63-- 戰　polemic.

0863_2

訟 [Sung] *n.* litigation, contention, lawsuit, dispute, *v.* litigate, demand justice, contend, dispute.
00-- 庭　law court.
07-- 詞　indictment.
21-- 師　pettifogger, litigation master.
50-- 事　litigation.

0863_7

謙 [Chien] *adj.* humble, modest, lowly.
00-- 讓　*n.* courtesy, *v.* yield, give way to others.
21-- 虛　humble, modest.
26-- 和　agreeable, modest and mild.
32-- 遜　humble, yielding, condescending.
37-- 退　retiring.
44-- 恭　respectful, polite.
-- 恭有禮　respectful and polite.

0864_0

許 [Hsu] *v.* allow, permit, consent, promise, grant.
04-- 諾　promise.
10-- 可　*n.* approval, permission, sanction, *v.* approve, permit, concede, endorse, ratify.
-- 可證　permit, licence, charter.
27-- 多　many, much, a great many, a good deal of.
-- 久　for a long time.
-- 久以前　a long time ago.
27-- 身救國　vow to save the country.
71-- 願　make a vow, bind oneself, commit oneself.

0865_1

詳 [Hsiang] *n.* detail, *v.* explain in de-

tail *adv*. carefully, fully.
00-- 文　　　　full report, full context.
08-- 說　　　　*n*. description, account, statement, *v*. tell in detail, make a clear breast of.
　-- 論　　　　discuss fully, enlarge upon a subject.
　-- 議　　　　consider in detail.
09-- 談　　　　tell in detail.
20-- 悉　　　　clearly, explicitly.
26-- 細　　　　in detail, detailed, part by part, circumstantial, by particulars.
　-- 細註解　　amplification.
　-- 細說明　　expound in detail, enter into particulars, enter into detail, detail.
　-- 細情形　　situation in detail, ins and outs.
27-- 解　　　　*n*. detailed explanation, *v*. explain clearly.
30-- 究　　　　deal with minutely.
33-- 述　　　　go into the details, enter into particulars, detail.
40-- 查　　　　examine carefully, scrutinize.
47-- 報　　　　detailed report.
77-- 問　　　　ask for the detail, inquire into fully.
95-- 情　　　　particulars, full information.

0865₃
議〔**I**〕*n*. discussion, deliberation, *v*. discuss, deliberate, blame, consult, talk about, criticize, find fault with.
08-- 論　　　　discuss, talk about.
26-- 和　　　　negotiate peace.
27-- 約　　　　negotiate.
30-- 定　　　　decide, agree, come to terms.
　-- 定書　　　protocol.
　-- 案　　　　bill, proposal for discussion, recommendation.
35-- 決　　　　resolve, resolution, pass a resolution.
　-- 決案　　　resolution.
50-- 事廳　　　assembly hall.

　-- 事日程　　agenda, programme for a meeting.
60-- 員　　　　congressman, senator, councillor, legislator, member of the parliament, assemblyman.
61-- 題　　　　subject for discussion.
71-- 長　　　　speaker, chairman, president.
73-- 院　　　　congress, parliament, chamber, legislature.
80-- 會＝議院

0865₇
誨〔**Hui**〕*v*. teach, instruct, educate, admonish, advise, induce.

0866₁
譜〔**Pu**〕*n*. record of something, music-book, genealogy, *v*. compose, record, list, register.
20-- 系學者　　student of genealogy.
55-- 曲　　　　set to music, compose a song.

0925₉
麟〔**Lin**〕*n*. female unicorn.

0962₇
誚〔**Chiao**〕*v*. blame, reprehend, scold, censure, ridicule, mock, satirize.

0963₁
讜〔**Tang**〕*n*. straightforward, speech, honest advice.

0968₉
謎〔**Mi**〕*n*. riddle, puzzle, enigma.
01-- 語　　　　riddle, conundrum, nut to crack.

0968₉
談〔**Tan**〕*n*. conversation, talk, *v*. talk, chat, converse.
02-- 話　　　　*n*. conversation, *v*. talk, converse, engage in conversation.
08-- 論　　　　*n*. discussion, discourse, *v*. discuss, talk about, converse, hold conference, hold intercourse.
12-- 到　　　　mention, speak of.

17-- 及	talk about, touch on.
18-- 政	talk about politics.
33-- 心	familiar talk, heart-to-heart talk.
72-- 兵	discuss military affairs.
88-- 笑	talk and laugh.
92-- 判	*n.* negotiation, *v.* negotiate, parley.

1

1000₀

一 〔Ⅰ〕 *n.* unit, union, *v.* unite into one, unify, *adj.* one, a, an, first.

00-- 病不起	die of illness.
-- 塵不染	perfectly clean.
-- 齊	all at once, uniformity, any and every, all of a heap.
-- 方	whole locality, one side.
-- 方面	one side, on the one hand.
-- 方行爲	unilateral act.
-- 方之寄	take a government position which carries considerable authority.
-- 文	cash.
-- 文不值	not with a penny, worthless.
-- 旁	one side, on the sideline.
-- 應俱全	complete with everything.
-- 夜成名	become famous overnight.
-- 夜不臥	go without sleep the whole night.
-- 章	chapter (of a book).
-- 度	once, at one time.
-- 度已足	once is enough for a man.
-- 言爲定	I give you word of honor. (It's a deal).
01-- 語道破	hit the nail on the head, pinpoint directly.
02-- 端	one end, one aspect.
-- 劑藥	dose of medicine.
-- 刻	quarter of an hour, short time.
-- 刻不停	never to stop for a moment.
-- 新耳目	present a new appearance.
03-- 就	no sooner than, at once.
04-- 諾千金	solemn promise, they keep

	a solemn promise.
06-- 誤再誤	commit one mistake after another.
07-- 望而知	know all at a sight glance.
-- 部	section, portion.
-- 部份	part, portion.
-- 部無效	void in part.
08-- 說	according to one version (theory), brief explanation.
-- 說便知	once said it becomes clear.
10-- 一	one by one.
-- 元論	monism.
-- 元化領導	centralized leadership.
-- 下	at one stroke, at a break.
-- 下子	at a blow, all at once.
-- 兩天	a day or two.
-- 天	whole day, one day.
-- 再	repeatedly, once and again.
-- 面	one side.
-- 面倒	at the thought of, excessively dependent upon something or somebody.
-- 面之交	have met once.
-- 面之詞	an one-sided story.
-- 百	hundred.
-- 百週年	centenary, centennial.
-- 頁	one page.
11-- 班	class (of student), squad (of foot soldiers).
-- 項	section.
-- 張	piece, sheet.
-- 頂	a (hat, cap or sedan chair).
-- 輩	generation.
-- 輩子	throughout one's life, as long as one lives, lifetime.
12-- 發難收	once started it can hardly stop.
-- 副	pair, suit, set.
17-- 刀兩斷	sever relations by one stroke.
-- 疋	roll (of cloth about 100 feet in length).
18-- 致	*n.* unification, consistency, coincidence, *v.* coincide, agree, accord, *adv.* unitedly, with one consent, with one shoulder, one and all, on

		all hands.
	-- 致性	coincidence, identity.
	-- 群	flock, herd, crown, group.
20--	千	thousand.
	-- 千年	thousand year, millenium.
	-- 季	season, one quarter (of the year).
	-- 雙	pair, couple.
	-- 手包辦	handle alone.
	-- 手扶植	protect and support personally.
	-- 番	kind, type, style, once.
	-- 毛	hair, one dime or ten cents, insignificant thing.
	-- 毛不拔	parsimonious.
	-- 看到	at the sight of.
	-- 系列	series of.
	-- 秉至公	perfectly just.
	-- 統	*n.* unification, unity, *v.* unify.
21--	些	some, little, few.
	-- 步	pace, step.
	-- 行	row, line, single file.
	-- 桌	a banquet or feast of 8 to 12 people.
	-- 片	piece, slice.
	-- 片焦土	with everything burned down and lying in ruins, scorched earth.
	-- 片汪洋	vast body of water, great ocean.
	-- 片丹心	utter loyalty.
22--	絲不掛	naked, unclothed, in a state of nature.
	-- 絲希望	little hope.
	-- 種	sort of, kind of.
	-- 紙	a (letter), a (document).
23--	代	generation.
24--	動	*n.* move, jerk, jolt, *v.* move once.
	-- 升	pint.
25--	生	life time, all one's born day, from the cradle to the grave.
	-- 件	article, piece.
	-- 律	uniformly, equably, without exception.
26--	個	one, a, an.
	-- 得一失	whatever one gains in one

		respect, one loses in another.
	-- 息尚存	as long as one is alive.
	-- 綑	bundle.
	-- 線	thread, ray.
	-- 線生機	feeble thread of life.
	-- 線希望	a hope against hope.
27--	身	suit, the whole body, all over, solitary person.
	-- 身臭汗	stink with perspiration.
	-- 身是病	be afflicted by several ailments or diseased.
	-- 向	always, consistently.
	-- 般	general common.
	-- 般化	*n.* generalization, *v.* generalize.
	-- 般模樣	look alike.
	-- 般無二	completely the same.
	-- 般性	generality, common quality.
	-- 句話	in a nutshell, sentence.
	-- 包	parcel, pack.
	-- 齣戲	act, play.
	-- 餐	meal.
	-- 組	group of, suite of.
	-- 網打盡	capture all in only one casting of net.
	-- 盤散沙	lacking spirit of cooperation.
28--	份	share, copy.
	-- 併	all, wholly, at the same time, together with.
	-- 併帶走	take it along with others.
	-- 條心	of one mind.
29--	伙	gang of, band of.
30--	定	no doubt, certainly, surely.
	-- 滴	drop.
	-- 窩蜂	(to do something) in a confused manner like a swarm of bees.
	-- 家	family.
	-- 竅不通	completely ignorant, utterly stupid, very poor (writing).
	-- 字千金	a single word is worth a thousand pieces of gold.
	-- 字之差	the change of one word (would make a great deal of difference).

-- 客	person's share (of food).		41-- 帖藥	herbal medicines list in a prescription for a particular ailment.
-- 定	certainly, surely.			
-- 定程序	degree of a measure of.		-- 幅	piece (of painting).
32-- 派	school (of thought, etc.), faction, group of people sharing the same ideals or interest.		-- 概	all, entirely, altogether, the whole of.
			-- 概而論	regard all in the same manner.
-- 派胡言	complete nonsense.		-- 概不准	all forbidden.
33-- 心	with all one's heart, heartily, with the whole heart, very earnestly.		-- 杯	cup, glassful.
			42-- 剎那	in a moment.
-- 心一意	one mindedly, whole heartedly.		43-- 截	section, length.
			44-- 封	a (letter).
-- 心一德	single-minded, of one mind.		-- 鼓而下	conquer in an over-powering attack.
-- 心要	set one's mind on, be bent on.		-- 鼓作氣	muster up one's courage all at once.
34-- 對	couple, pair, brace.		-- 落千丈	(said of prestige, fortune, etc.) nose-dive, decline drastically.
-- 流	first-rate, of the same class.			
-- 流人物	first-rate figure.			
35-- 清二白	completely clear.		-- 幫	gang, clique, group of people devoted to a common cause.
-- 決雌雄	compete for championship, fight a duel.			
-- 神教	monotheism.		-- 幕	one act (of play).
-- 連	successively, consecutively, in a row, company (of foot soldiers).		-- 世	lifetime, age, epoch.
			-- 世紀	century.
			-- 萬	ten thousand, myriad.
-- 連串	series of, string of.		-- 帶	all along, in the neighborhood of.
36-- 邊	on one side, by the side.			
-- 邊倒	fall on one side, side with somebody without reservation, predominate, enjoy overpowering superiority, leaning to one side.		-- 共	altogether, totally, in all.
			-- 模一樣	exactly the same, identical.
			-- 枝	a (flower, pen, cigarette, etc.), piece of, branch.
			45-- 株	a (tree, weed, flower, etc.)
-- 視同仁	treat all alike without discrimination, impartial.		44-- 夢	merely dream.
			46-- 塊	piece.
37-- 週	circle, round, week.		-- 塊兒	together.
38-- 道	together, on the same path, a (problem, etc.)		-- 場	performance, a (long period of association), a (dream).
-- 道菜	course, dish.		-- 場空	all in vain, futile.
40-- 大堆	lot of, conglomeration of.		-- 塌糊塗	in a muddle.
-- 直	straight (ahead), right (on), always, constantly.		-- 廂情願	wishful thinking.
			-- 棵	a (tree), a head (of cabbage).
-- 堆	pile, heap.		47-- 切	all, wholly.
-- 去不回	leave for good.		-- 切從緩	go slow in everything.
-- 套	set, suit.		-- 切成空	all in vain.
-- 來	on the one hand, as soon as (someone) arrives.			

-- 切眾生	all living things.
-- 帆風順	may you have favorable winds in your sails!
-- 朝	in one day, once.
-- 起	in the same place, together, in company.
48-- 樣	same, alike, identical, in the same manner, of the same sort.
-- 枚	a (coin, medal, etc.).
50-- 事無成	without a single accomplishment.
-- 串	string.
-- 本	copy, volume.
-- 本正經	serious, solemn, sanctimonious.
-- 本萬利	gain enormous profit with small investment, make handsome profits with a small capital.
-- 夫一妻制	monogamy.
-- 夫多妻	polygamy.
-- 夫二妻制	bigamy.
-- 妻多夫制	polyandry.
-- 表人才	with the appearance of a talent, very handsome.
-- 束	bundle, sheaf.
51-- 排	range, rank, platoon.
-- 批	batch, lot, group.
-- 打	dozen.
-- 輛	a (car, truck, carriage, etc.).
-- 頓	pause (in reading), a (meal).
52-- 折	90 percent discount, one fold.
53-- 盞	a (lamp), a (cup).
-- 成	10 percent.
-- 成不變	invariable, changeless, unchangeable.
54-- 技之長	useful in some kind of work, professional skill, specialty.
55-- 曲	song.
56-- 捆	bundle.
57-- 抱	armful.
-- 把	handful, bundle, bunch.
-- 把手	good hand, expert.
-- 掃而光	make a clean sweep of.
-- 掬	handful.
58-- 整套	the whole set of.
60-- 口	mouthful.
-- 口咬定	accuse definitely accuse categorically.
-- 口氣	in one breath, at a stretch, at a sitting.
-- 口答應	promise without hesitation.
-- 日	day.
-- 日千里	fast improvement, progress by leaps and bounds.
-- 星期	one week.
-- 旦	once, at some time or other, suddenly, in a moment.
-- 目了然	(said of clarity in presentation) to understand fully at a glance.
-- 見	at first sight.
-- 見傾心	fall in love at first sight.
-- 見難忘	once seen never forgotten.
-- 見如故	be good friends at the first meeting, become intimate at first sight.
-- 見鍾情	fall in love at first sight.
-- 吊	string (of coins).
-- 團	lump, body.
-- 團和氣	prevailing mood of harmony.
-- 團糟	in a mess, in utter chaos.
-- 回	once, occasion, round (in boxing).
-- 回事	one and the same (thing), one thing.
-- 圈	circle, one round (in mahjong game).
61-- 點	little, dot, point.
-- 點一滴	every drop, every little bit.
-- 點不	not a bit, by no means, not at all.
-- 點兒	little, bit.
-- 顆	piece (of candy), a (heart, seal, diamond, mole, etc.)
62-- 瞬間	at lightning speed, in a minute, in a wink.
-- 則	firstly.
64-- 時	sometimes, temporarily, for a while.

-- 時疏忽	oversight at the time.
-- 時之氣	in a moment of anger.
67-- 呎	foot.
-- 鳴驚人	become famous overnight, achieve enormous success at the very first try.
-- 眼看去	at first glance.
-- 躍千里	go a long distance in one jump.
-- 路	all the way, through the journey, go the same way, take the same route, single file.
-- 路平安	bon voyage! have a good journey.
-- 路上	all the way.
-- 路順風	may you have favorable winds on the way.
-- 夥	group, gang.
68-- 敗塗地	crashing defeat.
70-- 臂之力	(to give) a helping hand.
-- 臂之助	lend a hand.
71-- 馬當先	be the first to take on the enemy or do a job.
72-- 所	a (school, charity institute, etc.).
-- 髮千鈞	hang by a thread, sleep on a volcano.
73-- 院制	single house system, unicameral system.
75-- 陣	sudden gust (of wind, laughter, etc.).
77-- 月	January, one month.
-- 同	together, altogether.
-- 周	week, circle, round, cycle.
-- 腳	kick, take part in something (offer unsolicited).
-- 腳踢開	kick aside.
-- 局	game (of chess), (baseball) an inning.
-- 服	dose (of medicine).
-- 股	one share (in stock-holding.), hand (of bandits), a (strong smell), full of spirit, zest, etc.
-- 段	section, section one.

-- 層	one story or floor (of a multi-story building).
-- 冊	copy, volume.
-- 開始	from the very beginning, from the start.
-- 舉一動	every movement.
-- 舉兩得	kill two birds with one stone.
-- 門	course in a curriculum, family (of patriotic people, heroes, etc.).
-- 門忠烈	family of loyalty and patriotism.
-- 閃	glance.
-- 貫	consistently, from beginning to end.
-- 貫作風	consistent way of doing things.
78-- 覽	general survey.
-- 覽表	list, table, schedule.
-- 隊	group of, company.
80-- 盆	plate or tray (of food), pot (of flower), basin (of water).
-- 介書生	plain scholar.
-- 分爲二	divide one thing into two.
-- 念之差	the error of one thought.
-- 無所有	penniless, destitute.
-- 無所獲	have gained nothing.
-- 無所長	have no special ability, own nothing at all.
-- 無所知	know nothing at all, completely unaware, be absolutely ignorant of.
-- 年	one year, annual.
-- 年到頭	all (the) year round.
-- 年半載	in a year or so.
-- 年一度	once a year.
-- 會兒	soon, while, few moment.
-- 氣	n. without stop, at a stretch, v. get angry.
83-- 錢不值	not worth a penny, completely worthless, mere trash.
84-- 針見血	point out precisely, exactly right, to the point.
86-- 知半解	know superficially, half-baked knowledge.

88-- 箭雙雕	kill two birds with an arrow.
-- 等	top-notch, first class, first rate.
-- 筆勾銷	wipe out, annul all at once.
-- 節	section or passage (of a written work).
90-- 小撮	tiny group (or flock).
-- 堂	in the same hall, under the same roof.
-- 黨專政	one-party dictatorship.
-- 半	half.
-- 掌	slap.
-- 卷	scroll.
99-- 勞永逸	once for all, a stick in time saves nine.

1010₀

二 〔Erh〕 *adj.* two, second, both.

00-- 度梅	married for the second time, second marriage.
10-- 三其德	of changeable character.
-- 元論	dualism.
-- 元論者	dualist.
12-- 副	the second mate (officer), second deputy.
20-- 重	double, duplication.
-- 重奏	duet.
20-- 倍	double, twofold, two times, twice.
33-- 心	unfaithful, double minded.
-- 遍苦	second dose of suffering.
34-- 流子	loafer, lounger.
37-- 次	twice, second, two times.
-- 次大戰	Second World War.
40-- 十	twenty, score, twentieth.
44-- 地主	sub-landlord.
-- 者	both, secondly.
45-- 樓	second floor.
47-- 胡	two-stringed Chinese fiddle (Chinese violin).
60-- 星期	fortnight.
-- 國同盟	Dual Alliance.
62-- 則	secondly.
73-- 院	both houses.
77-- 月	February.
-- 層樓	second story.
80-- 八弘規	the full regulations.

-- 八佳人	budding beauty of sixteen.
-- 八美女	sixteen-year old beauty.
-- 八年華	sweet sixteen.
-- 分之一	half.
88-- 等	second class.
-- 等艙	tourist class.

工 〔Kung〕 *n.* work, job, service, duty, *v.* work, labor, *adj.* delicate, find.

00-- 序	working process.
-- 商部	Department of Trade and Industry.
-- 商業	industrial and commercial enterprises, industry and commerce.
-- 商業稅	business tax, industrial and commercial tax.
-- 商業者	industrialists and businessmen.
-- 商法規	commercial and industrial law and regulations.
-- 商界	business circles, business world, industrial and commercial circles, world of industry and commerce.
-- 商界人士	commercial and industrial figures.
-- 商局	bureau of commerce and industry.
-- 廠	factory, plant, workhouse, mill, works, workshop.
-- 廠產品	factory products.
-- 廠設備	plant equipment.
-- 廠生產能力	factory capacity, plant capacity.
-- 廠檢驗	factory inspection.
-- 廠成本	factory cost.
-- 廠法	factory law.
-- 廠管理	the factory management, plant management, shop management.
08-- 效	work efficiency.
11-- 班	gang of workman.
-- 頭	foreman, boss, overseer, task-master, headman.
17-- 務局	the bureau of public works.
21-- 價	wages, prices, prices of

	work.
22-- 種	branch of work, kind of work.
24-- 裝褲	overalls.
25-- 件	work piece.
26-- 程	construction work, engineering, project.
-- 程計畫	program of works.
-- 程設計	engineering design.
-- 程部	engineering department.
-- 程師	engineer.
-- 程條件	engineering specifications.
-- 程完工期限	completion date of a project.
-- 程進度	job schedule.
-- 程顧問	engineering adviser.
-- 程諮詢師	consulting engineers.
-- 程諮詢公司	engineering consultant firm.
-- 程概算	budgetary estimates of projects.
-- 程機械	engineering machinery.
-- 程勘測	engineering surveying.
-- 程技術	hard technology.
-- 程費用	works expenses.
-- 程量	volume of works.
-- 程器材	engineering goods.
-- 程質量	quality of works.
-- 程師	engineer.
-- 程隊	engineer corps.
28-- 作	n. work, job, task, v. work, operate, toil.
-- 作證	identity card.
-- 作文件	working document, working paper.
-- 作計劃	work plan, working program, working scheme.
-- 作設計	work design.
-- 作效率	work efficiency, working efficiency.
-- 作許可	work permit.
-- 作研究	working study.
-- 作手冊	work book.
-- 作能力	ability to work, capacity for labor, capacity for work, operation capacity, productive capacity.

-- 作強度	working strength.
-- 作台	work bench.
-- 作負擔	working load.
-- 作流程	flow of work.
-- 作組	working team.
-- 作作風	the style of work.
-- 作進程	progress of work.
-- 作福利	work fare.
-- 作業績	work performance.
-- 作道德	work ethics.
-- 作機會均等	equal employment opportunity.
-- 作者	worker, operator.
-- 作考績	assessment performance.
-- 作模型	working model.
-- 作規程	working regulation.
-- 作規則	work rules.
-- 作導引	operational guidance.
-- 作日	working day, work day.
-- 作圖	work map.
-- 作量	amount of work, operation capacity, quantity of work, volume of work, work amount, work volume, work load.
-- 作最忙時期	peak workload period.
-- 作時間	work time.
-- 作時間卡	job time card, job time ticket.
-- 作時數	productive hours.
-- 作單位	unit of work.
-- 作質量	performance quality.
-- 作周	work week.
-- 作周期	length of working cycle, work period.
-- 作母機	machine tool.
-- 作聯繫	working relationship.
-- 作服	working clothes.
-- 作隊	political work force.
-- 作人員	staff, functionary.
-- 作人口	working population.
-- 作等級	class of work.
-- 作簡化	work simplification.
-- 傷害事故	industrial accident.
-- 傷責任	liability for injury.
-- 齡	working years, length of

	the time employed, working age.
32-- 業	industry.
-- 業主義	industrialism.
-- 業產品	manufactured products, industrial output.
-- 業競爭	industrial competition.
-- 業廢水	industrial effluent, industrial liquid waste, industrial waste water.
-- 業廢料	industrial wastes.
-- 業計劃	industrial planning.
-- 業設計	industrial design.
-- 業設備	industrial equipment.
-- 業效能	industrial efficiency.
-- 業工程	industrial engineering.
-- 業項目	industrial project.
-- 業港口	industrial port.
-- 業政策	industrial policy, policy for industry.
-- 業經濟學	industrial economics.
-- 業化	v. industrialize, n. industrialization.
-- 業生產	industrial production.
-- 業生產能力	industrial capacity, industrial production capacity.
-- 業生產額	industrial output.
-- 業復興	industrial recovery, industrial rehabilitation.
-- 業進步	industrial progress, industry progress.
-- 業污水	industrial sewage, trade effluent.
-- 業污染	industrial pollution.
-- 業潛力	industrial potential.
-- 業大國	industrial power.
-- 業機器人	industrial robot.
-- 業博覽會	industrial fair.
-- 業城市	industrial city.
-- 業基地	industrial base.
-- 業化學	industrial chemistry.
-- 業制度	industrialism, industrial system.
-- 業資本	industrial capital.
-- 業資本家	factory capitalist.
-- 業革命	the industrial revolution.
-- 業中心	hub of industry, industrial center (centre).
-- 業專利	industrial patent.
-- 業國	industrial country, industrial nation, industrial state.
-- 業園	industrial park.
-- 業團體	industrial group.
-- 業品	industrial products, industrial goods, manufacture goods.
-- 業品出口	industrial exports.
-- 業品進口	industrial imports.
-- 業時代	industrial age, industrial stage.
-- 業區	industrial district, industrial area, industrial occupancy, industrial quarter, industrial region, industrial section.
-- 業用地	industrial estate, industrial land occupancy.
-- 業局	bureau of industry, Industrial Bureau.
-- 業展覽館	industrial museum.
-- 業展覽會	industrial (trade) show (fair).
-- 業原料	industrial raw materials.
-- 業間諜	industrial espionage.
-- 業企業	industrial enterprise, industrial undertaking.
-- 業分布	industrial dispersion.
-- 業合作	industrial cooperation.
-- 業管理	industrial control, industrial management.
-- 業學校	technical school, industrial school.
37-- 資	wage, pay, salary, emolument.
-- 資率	rate of pay, rate of wage.
-- 資調整	wage adjustment, wage regulation.
-- 資水平	wage level.
-- 資改革	wage reform.
-- 資委員會	wage board.
-- 資統計	wage statistics.
-- 資上升	wages hike.
-- 資上漲	wage raise.

-- 資制度	wage system.
-- 資袋	wage packet, pay envelope, pay pocket.
-- 資等級	the wage scale.
-- 資總額	amount of wages, gross wages, gross payroll, total payroll.
-- 資穩定	wages stabilization.
-- 資收入	wage earnings, wage income.
-- 資稅	payroll taxes, salary tax, wage tax.
-- 資凍結	wage freeze, pay freeze.
-- 資淨額	net pay.
-- 資支票	pay check.
-- 資標本	wage standard, wage scale.
-- 資增加	wage hike.
-- 資表	pay list, wage sheet.
-- 資指數	index number of wage, wage index number.
-- 資成本	wage cost.
-- 資扣除	wage deduction.
-- 資賬戶	payroll account.
-- 資單	pay bill, pay sheet, wage sheet, payroll, pay list.
-- 資單位	wage unit.
-- 資照發	receive full pay.
-- 資冊	salary roll.
-- 資差別	wage differential, wage disparity.
-- 資分析	payroll analysis.
-- 資會計	payroll accounting.
-- 資等級	scale of payment, scale of wages, wage category.
-- 資管理	salary-and-wage administration.
-- 資管理員	payroll clerk.
-- 資削減	pay cut.
44-- 地辦公室	field office.
-- 地	construction-site, work site.
-- 地管理	field management, site management.
-- 藝	craft, industrial art, technology, workmanship.
-- 藝要求	technological requirements.
-- 藝研究	process study.
-- 藝品	arts and crafts.

-- 藝品館	Hall of Arts and Crafts.
-- 藝學	technology.
-- 藝學校	technological school.
-- 藝美術師	industrial artist.
-- 藝驚湛	fine workmanship.
-- 薪總額	payroll.
-- 薪稅	payroll tax.
-- 薪扣款	payroll deduction.
-- 薪管理	wage and salary control.
46-- 場	workshop, yard, shop.
47-- 期	term of works.
50-- 事	field work, defense works.
-- 夫	time or effort put into a piece of work.
55-- 農聯盟	the alliance of workers and peasants.
-- 農兵	workers, peasants and soldiers.
-- 農兵學員	worker-peasant-soldier students.
60-- 團主義	syndicalism.
-- 團社會主義	guild socialism.
-- 具	tool, instrument.
-- 具袋	tool bag.
-- 具箱	tool box.
61-- 號	job code.
63-- 賊	scab-person who does not join the labor union.
64-- 時	work hour, working hour, hour of labor, labor hour, man-hour.
-- 時卡	time card, clock card.
71-- 匠	craftsman, artisan, skilled worker, mechanic.
-- 長	foreman, master worker, section chief.
72-- 兵	engineering corps, sapper.
-- 兵學	military engineering.
77-- 學院	engineering institute.
-- 段長	section chief.
80-- 人	worker, workman, laborer.
-- 人運動	labor movement.
-- 人階級	working class.
-- 分	work-point.
-- 會	trade union, labor union,

	會費	worker's organization.
--	會費	trade union contributions.
--	會會員	unionist.
90--	黨	Labor Party.
94--	料	labor and material.

1010₁

三 〔Ⅰ〕 *adj.* three, third, *adv.* thrice.

00--	文治	sandwich.
04--	讀	the third reading of a bill in a legislative session.
07--	部曲	trilogy.
--	部合奏	trio.
10--	三制	three-three system (three years for junior high and three years for senior high school), work in three shifts.
--	更半夜	late at night.
--	百六十行	all trades and professions.
--	不管	district not within the jurisdiction of any of the neighboring magistrates.
11--	班制	three-shift work day system.
--	頭政治	the triumvirate.
12--	聯單	three-sectional tax form, triplicate forms, bill in three parts.
20--	倍	threefold, triple.
--	位一體	the Trinity, three-in-one.
--	隻手	pickpocket.
23--	絃琴	Chinese musical instrument with three strings played by fingers, trichord.
--	代	three generations, the three ancient Chinese Dynasties-Hsia, Shang and Chou.
--	代同堂	three generations living under the same roof.
24--	峽	the three gorges of the Yangtze River on the border of Szchuan and Hupei.
--	稜鏡	prism.
--	結合	three-in-one, combination.
25--	生有幸	*v.* have the good fortune of three lives, (to make friends with worthy persons or marry a virtuous and beautiful wife, etc.), *adj.* lucky indeed, very fortunate.
26--	和土	concrete.
27--	角	triangle, triangular, trigonometry.
--	角形	triangle.
--	角戀愛	love triangle.
--	角洲	delta.
--	角測量	triangulation.
--	角板	set square.
--	角學	trigonometry.
--	角尺	angle gauge.
--	角鐵	(construction) angle iron.
--	色	the three primary colors --yellow, blue and red.
--	色版	(printing) a three color halftone.
--	餐	three meals--breakfast, lunch and supper.
--	級跳遠	hop, skip and jump.
30--	字經	the Three-Character Classic or the Trimetrical classic, formerly the first primer in school.
33--	心二意	*v.* change one's mind, *adj.* hesitating, irresolute, halfhearted.
36--	溫暖	sauna bath.
37--	次	thrice, three times.
--	次程式	equation of the third degree or a cubic equation.
--	軍	the armed forces, the fighting services, tri-service.
40--	十	thirty.
--	十六行	all trades and professions.
--	十二開	thirty-two mo. (32mo).
--	叉路口	junction where three roads meet, tri-junction.
--	大洋	the three big oceans--the Pacific Ocean, the Atlantic Ocean, and the Indian Ocean.
--	寸丁	dwarf.
--	夾板	plywood, three-ply board.

44-- 權分立 separation of the legislative, executive and judicial functions of a government.

58-- 輪汽車 tricar, three-wheeler.

-- 輪車 pedicab, trishaw.

60-- 思而行 look before you leap, think thrice before you act.

-- 圍 the vital statistics or the three measurements of a woman.

-- 足凳 trivet.

61-- 點裝 bikini suit.

63-- 戰兩勝 the best of three games.

67-- 明治=三文治

71-- 長兩短 unforeseen disasters or accidents (usually referring to death).

77-- 胞胎 triplets.

-- 月 March.

-- 腳架 tripod.

-- 民主義 The Three Principles of the People.

-- 民主義青年團 Three Principles Youth Corps.

-- 段論法 syllogism.

80-- 八主義 the three "8" system under which a 24-hour day is divided into 8 hours of work, 8 hours of recreation and 8 hours of sleep.

-- 八婦女節 Women's Day on March the 8th.

-- 分之一 one third.

-- 合土 plaster concrete, mortar.

-- 合板 three-ply board, plywood.

-- 合會 the Triad Society (a secret society during the Ching Dynasty dedicated to the overthrow of the Manchus and the restoration of the Ming Dynasty).

-- 岔路 crossroads, tri-junction.

88-- 等 three grades or classes, the third grade, inferior.

正 〔Cheng〕 *n.* chief, head, *v.* correct, rectify, govern adjust, *adj.* proper, right, regular, true, principal, upright, straight, exact, correct, *adv.* just, exactly, directly, truly, really.

00-- 方形 square, four-square.

-- 文 original text, text.

01-- 顏屬色 in a serious manner.

10-- 面 front, the positive side, affirmation, the right sight.

-- 面攻擊 frontal attack.

-- 面人物 positive character, virtuous person.

-- 電 positive electricity.

-- 弦 (in math) sine.

-- 要 on the point of.

11-- 巧 by chance, in good time.

12-- 副 principal and secondary.

13-- 確 exact, right, accurate, true.

-- 確方針 correct policy.

-- 確對待 adopt a correct attitude towards.

-- 確路線 correct line of action.

-- 確性 accuracy, correctness.

20-- 統 traditional, orthodox.

21-- 比例 direct proportion.

-- 街 high street, main street.

24-- 告 warn sternly, tell in all seriousness.

27-- 色屬言 with a severe countenance and a harsh voice.

-- 餐 main meals of the day.

-- 負 positive and negative.

32-- 派 honest, decent.

-- 割 secant.

33-- 心 regulate the mind.

34-- 法 *n.* execution, *v.* execute.

36-- 視 face squarely.

38-- 道 the right way, the orthodox way.

40-- 大 upright, great and generous.

-- 大光明 fair and frank.

-- 直 *n.* uprightness, integrity, probity, rectitude, *adj.* upright, honest, straight, fair and square.

41-- 極 the positive pole.

43-- 式 formal, official, formally, cut and dried.

-- 式演說	formal oration.
-- 式聲明	official statement.
-- 式授職	inaugurate.
-- 式契約	formal contract.
-- 式開會	call to order.
46-- 如	exactly as, just as.
-- 相反	on the contrary.
47-- 好	proper, just right.
-- 切	tangent.
50-- 本	original.
-- 中	right in the middle.
-- 中下懷	exactly as one wishes or hopes for.
56-- 規	normal, regular.
-- 規軍	normal troop.
-- 規化	regularization.
-- 規戰	regular warfare.
58-- 數	positive number, plus.
60-- 因為	just because.
-- 是	exactly, just.
-- 是如此	that is the ticket.
61-- 號	plus, positive sign "+".
77-- 月	January.
-- 門	front door, the main gate.
80-- 人君子	gentleman.
-- 午	noon, high noon, midday.
-- 義	upright, justice.
-- 義感	sense of righteousness or justice.
-- 合我意	it's exactly what I am hoping for.
90-- 常	*adj.* normal, *adv.* normally.
-- 常出路	the normal path of discharge, the normal way of getting employed.
-- 常化	normalization.
-- 當	right, proper, true.
-- 當防禦	legal defense.

歪 〔Wai〕 *adj.* awry, bad, evil, wicked, slant.

10-- 面	awry face.
11-- 頭	awry neck.
20-- 毛兒	mischievous child.
33-- 心	evil-hearted, wicked, bad.
55-- 曲	distort, misrepresent, give an oblique view of.

-- 曲報道	the report has been mis-represent.
-- 曲事實	distort a story or fact.
68-- 路	wrong course, oblique way.
77-- 風	ill wind, noxious influence.
-- 風邪氣	perverse trends.
84-- 斜	*adj.* oblique, *adv.* aslant.

1010₃

玉 〔Yu〕 *n.* jade, gem, *adj.* precious, valuable, beautiful.

01-- 顏	beautiful face.
44-- 帶	jade belt.
-- 蘭花	magnolia.
53-- 成	help to accomplish.
60-- 蜀黍	indian corn.
-- 器	jade ware, jade articles.
90-- 米	corn, maize.
-- 米粉	cornflour.

璽 〔Shii〕 *n.* imperial seal.

1010₄

王 〔Wang〕 *n.* king, ruler, prince, *adj.* royal, princely, regal.

00-- 府	royal palace.
17-- 子	prince.
20-- 位	throne, royalty, crown, kingship.
-- 牌	trump, trump-card.
27-- 侯	princes and nobles.
30-- 室	royal family.
-- 宮	palace.
37-- 冠	crown.
38-- 道	the rule of right.
40-- 太后	queen dowager.
44-- 權	royalty, crown.
47-- 妃	royal concubine.
-- 朝	dynasty.
60-- 國	kingdom, realm, monarchy.
90-- 黨	royalist.

至 〔Chih〕 *v.* reach, go to, arrive at, *adj.* best, greatest, most, *prep.* to, at, up to, till.

00-- 高	highest.
-- 交	very intimate friend.
03-- 誠	most sincere.
06-- 親	nearest relative.

08-- 於 with regard to, with respect to, as for, upon the subject of.
10-- 要 most important.
16-- 聖 the great sage.
-- 理名言 famous dictum, axiom.
21-- 上 highest, supreme.
22-- 低 minimum.
27-- 多 at most, maximum.
30-- 寶 the most precious asset.
40-- 大 greatest, supreme.
-- 友 most intimate friend, bosom friend.
77-- 關緊要 of most importance.
80-- 今 now, still, hitherto, until now.
-- 尊 *n.* sovereign, *adj.* supreme.
-- 公無私 be absolutely just and have no prejudice.
-- 善 ultimate good.
90-- 少 least, at least.

亟 〔Chi〕 *adj.* urgent, hurry, hasty, pressing.
1010₇
五 〔Wu〕 *adj.* five, fifth.
00-- 方雜處 inhabited by people from all regions.
-- 方人士 people from all regions.
01-- 顏六色 varicolored.
10-- 一國際勞動節 May-Day, International Labor Day.
-- 零四散 all dispersed.
-- 百年 five hundred years.
11-- 項運動 pentathlon (in sport).
20-- 倍 five fold, quintuple.
-- 倍子 gallnut.
21-- 行八作 all walks of life, all trades.
22-- 彩 multicolored.
-- 彩片 color-film.
23-- 代同堂 five generations living together.
26-- 線譜 staff, musical score.
27-- 角大樓 the Pentagon.
-- 角星 five-pointed star.
30-- 官 the five sense organs.
-- 官端正 well-formed features.
31-- 福臨門 the five blessings descend upon the house.
34-- 斗櫃 five-drawer chest.
36-- 邊形 pentagon.
40-- 十 fifty.
-- 十年代 the fifties.
44-- 花八門 various, multifarious.
-- 權憲法 Five Power Constitution.
47-- 穀 crops, grain.
-- 穀豐登 have good harvests.
60-- 里霧中 lost in impenetrable fog or mystery.
65-- 味 the five flavors--sweet, sour, bitter, hot and salty.
-- 味瓶架 cruet stand.
75-- 體投地 stoop to complete prostration.
77-- 月 May.
80-- 金 metals.
-- 金廠 metal products plant, hardware factory.
-- 金匠 smith.
-- 分之一 one fifth.
-- 分四裂 divided into five and split into four--in total disunity.
-- 年計劃 five year plan.
90-- 光十色 resplendent with variegated coloration.

亙 〔Keng〕 *n.* extreme limit, *v.* fill *everywhere*, *adj.* universal, lasting.
40-- 古 from ancient time.
互 〔Hu〕 *adj.* mutual, reciprocal, *pron.* each other.
00-- 市 commerce.
06-- 讓 meet half way.
08-- 議 consult together.
09-- 談心曲 chat with each other on their deep feelings.
10-- 不侵犯 reciprocal non-aggression.
20-- 爭雄長 fight for leadership or hegemony.
22-- 利 mutual benefit, mutual advantage.
-- 聯網 internet, internetwork, interconnection network.
32-- 派大使 exchange of ambassadors.

33-- 補	complementary repercussions.	
-- 補商品	complementary goods.	
34-- 爲因果	interact as both cause and effect.	
37-- 選	mutual election.	
-- 通情報	exchange of information.	
46-- 相	each other, one another, mutual, reciprocal.	
-- 相牽連	tie up each other.	
-- 相讓步	split the difference.	
-- 相誤解	at cross purpose.	
-- 相平等	be on a plane with each other.	
-- 相聯繫	n. correlation, adj. interconnected, interlocking.	
-- 相殘殺	be involved in mutual slaughter.	
-- 相配合	coordinate.	
-- 相攻擊	attack each other.	
-- 相依賴	n. interdependence, adj. interdependent.	
-- 相愛慕	love and admire each other.	
-- 相爭論	spar at each other.	
-- 相爭奪	contend with each other.	
-- 相傾軋	fight each other for power.	
-- 相衝突	conflict with each other, come into collision with.	
-- 相角逐	contend with each other, collision with.	
-- 相勾結	collude with each other.	
-- 相遷就	make a compromise.	
-- 相爲力	mutual help.	
-- 相標榜	mutual praising.	
-- 相切磋	improve each other by active discussion.	
-- 相推諉	mutually making excuses.	
-- 相抵觸	contradict each other.	
-- 相呼應	take concerted action.	
-- 相影響	interaction, mutual influence.	
-- 相印證	corroborate each other.	
-- 相緊抱	be locked in each other's arm, hug, embrace.	
-- 相監督	mutual supervision.	
-- 相抵銷	cancel each other, mutual cancel out.	
50-- 惠	n. mutual advantage, mutual benefit, reciprocity, adj. reciprocal, mutually beneficial.	
-- 惠條約	reciprocal treaty.	
-- 惠關稅	reciprocal duties.	
-- 惠交易	reciprocity transaction.	
-- 惠待遇	reciprocal favorable treatment, reciprocal treatment.	
-- 惠協定	reciprocal agreement.	
-- 惠貿易	n. reciprocity, reciprocal trade, fair trade, commercial.	
-- 惠合作	mutual benefit and collaboration.	
-- 惠合同	reciprocal contract.	
-- 撞	n. collision, v. collide.	
57-- 換	exchange, interchange.	
65-- 購	counter-purchase, mutual purchasing, reciprocal buying.	
74-- 助	n. mutual help, mutual aid, fraternal insurance, reciprocal aid, v. help each other.	
-- 助組	mutual-aid team.	
-- 助保險	mutual insurance.	
-- 助基金	mutual fund, open-end fund.	
-- 助儲蓄銀行	mutual savings bank.	
-- 助資金公司	mutual fund company.	
77-- 毆	exchange blows.	

孟 〔Yu〕 n. basin, spittoon, cuspidor.
亞 〔Ya〕 adj. second, junior, inferior, next to.

00-- 麻	flax.	
-- 麻布	linen, cambric.	
10-- 于他人	be inferior to others.	
11-- 非利加洲	Africa.	
16-- 聖孟子	the second sage--Mencius.	
26-- 細亞洲	Asia.	
32-- 洲	Asia.	
-- 洲人	Asian.	
36-- 溫帶	subtropics, the subtemperate regions.	
37-- 軍	runner-up.	
44-- 熱帶	subtropics.	
80-- 美利加	America.	

87-- 鉛　　　zinc.

1010₈

巫〔WU〕 n. witch, enchantress.

21--術　　　black art, witchcraft.
34--婆　　　witch.
77--醫　　　wizards and quack doctors.

豆〔Tou〕 n. bean, legume, pea.

00--腐　　　bean curd, tofu.
--腐花　　　bean-curd jelly.
--腐乾　　　bean-curd cake.
--瓣醬　　　bean paste.
27--漿　　　bean juice, soybean milk.
35--油　　　bean oil, soybean oil.
39--沙　　　bean puree, mashed beans.
44--莖　　　bean stalk.
--芽　　　bean sprout.
--莢　　　bean pods.
72--質　　　legumin.
88--餅　　　bean cake.
--箕　　　bean stalk.
98--粉　　　bean flour.

靈〔Ling〕 n. spirit, soul, adj. spiritual, intelligent, effective, mysterious, divine, supernatural, handy, skillful.

11--巧　　　handy, skillful, ingenious.
--巧用品　gadgets.
16--魂　　　spirit, soul.
20--位　　　ancestral tablet.
32--活　　　active, nimble.
--活度　　　flexibility, flexible nature.
--活資金　liquid fund.
53--感　　　inspiration.
78--驗　　　effective, efficacious.
88--敏　　　smart, bright, intelligent, keen, acute, quick, sensitive.
--敏度　　　sensitivity.
95--性　　　spirituality.

1010₉

丕〔Pei〕 adj. first, unequaled, distinguished, great, magnificent.

1011₁

霏〔Fei〕 n. snowfall.

1011₃

琳〔Lin〕 n. precious stone, adj. glazed, bright.

10--璃　　　glossy stone, glass, glazed thing.
--璃瓦　　　glazed tiles.
13--球　　　Loochoo Island, Ryukyu Islands.

疏〔Su〕 v. clear out, spread, adj. far, open, wide apart, remiss, careless.

27--忽　　　negligent, careless, remiss, unwary, off one's guard.
34--遠　　　v. keep at arm's length, make a stranger of, turn a cold shoulder, adj. distant, estranged, alienated, distant.
37--通　　　clear out, enlighten, straighten out, channel.
47--嬾　　　lazy, idle.
48--散　　　evacuate, disperse, scatter.
97--懈　　　heedless, careless.
--懶　　　lazy, indolent.

1012₇

霈〔Pei〕 n. copious rain, adj. raining.

璃〔Li〕 n. glass, glazed thing, adj. bright, glazed.

1013₂

瓖〔Hsiang〕 n. ornaments on a horse, v. inlay, emboss, encase.

1014₁

矗〔Nieh〕 v. whisper, close.

1014₆

璋〔Chang〕 n. jade, scepter.

1016₄

露〔Lu〕 n. dew, v. disclose, expose, show through, exhibit, manifest. adj. disclosed, exposed, naked.

10--天　　　in the open air, open to the sky, exposed to the air.
--天礦　　　opencast mine, opencut mine.
--天市場　open-air market.
--面　　　show the face, make an appearance, appear in public.
12--水　　　dew.
--形　　　expose one's point.

15--	珠	dewdrops.
22--	出	disclose, expose, let out, open up.
--	出破綻	show one's slip.
--	出馬腳	show the cloven hoof, disclose the hidden secret, lay bare the hidden reality.
23--	台	porch.
30--	宿	sleep in the wild.
77--	骨	openly.
90--	光時間	exposure.
99--	營	camping.
--	營地	camp ground.

1017₇

雪 〔**Hsueh**〕 *n.* snow, *v.* snow, make clean, wipe out, avenge, *adj.* snowy.

00--	亮	bright.
13--	球	snowball.
--	恥	wipe away a disgrace, bring back the ashes, avenge an insult.
--	恥報仇	wipe away a disgrace and avenge a grievance.
22--	片	snowflakes.
--	片紛飛	snowflakes flutter about.
--	崩	snowslide, snowslip, avalanche of snow.
--	山	snow-capped mountain.
26--	白	snow-white.
27--	鳥	snowbird.
30--	冤	prove one's innocence, redress wrongs.
40--	堆	snowslip, snowbank, snowdrift.
42--	橇	sledge.
44--	花	snowflake, snow crystals.
--	花膏	cream.
--	地冰天	frozen land.
--	茄煙	cigar.
--	鞋	snowshoes.
50--	車	sledge.
--	青	purple color.
60--	景	snow scenery.
71--	原	snow field.
80--	人	snowman.
97--	恨	avenge, take one's revenge.

1019₄

霂 〔**Mu**〕 *n.* drizzle.

1020₀

丁 〔**Ting**〕 *n.* adult, workman, servant, individual, attendant.

10--	憂	be in mourning for parents.
20--	香	cloves.
--	香花	lilac, mace.
24--	壯	adults, youth, robust.
27--	役	services for one's country, compulsory labor service.
29--	稅	poll tax, capitation.
30--	寧	give repeated injunctions, direct with urgency.
--	寧再三	give injunction again and again.
--	字形	T-shape.
--	字尺	T-square.
--	字鐵	T-beam, T-bar.
56--	螺	snail.
60--	口	people, population.
--	口甚旺	men and women are on the increase.
--	男	male adult.
63--	賦	poll tax.
64--	財兩旺	prosperous both in the size of family and in wealth.

1020₇

歹 〔**Tai**〕 *adj.* bad, wicked, evil, malicious, depraved.

00--	意	bad intention, malicious intent.
80--	人	bad man, wicked person.

丐 〔**Kai**〕 *n.* beggar, mendicant, *v.* beg, request, ask alms.

11--	頭	chief of beggars.
43--	求	beg, request.

1021₀

兀 〔**Wu**〕 *v.* cut off the feet, *adj.* firm, stable, decided.

00--	立	standing, erect.
60--	日	unlucky day.

1021₁

元 〔**Yuan**〕 *n.* yuan, dollar, origin, cause, head, beginning, commencement, *adj.* original, primary, first, eldest, principal.

00--	音	vowel.
10--	元本本	from the very beginning.
24--	帥	marshal, generalissimo, commander-in-chief.
25--	件	element in a machine.
30--	宵節	the Lantern Festival.
43--	始	origin, beginning.
44--	老	elder statesman.
--	老執政	the aged directs the state affairs.
--	老院	senate.
--	老院議員	senator.
50--	素	element.
60--	旦	new year's day.
77--	月	January.
80--	首	head, ruler, supreme ruler, head of state.
--	氣	vigor, health, spirit.
--	氣大傷	one's constitution is greatly injured.
--	氣回復	restoration of one's vigor.
--	氣旺盛	be full of vigor.

霹 〔**Li**〕 *n.* thunder clap.
1021₂

死 〔**Si**〕 *n.* death, decease, demise, departure, fall, loss, debt of nature *v.* die, be dead, come to an end, lose one's breath, *adj.* dead, lifeless, departed, inanimate, out of the world.

00--	亡	*n.* death, breathlessness, *v.* die, pass away.
--	亡率	mortality.
--	亡證書	death certificate.
--	亡保險	life insurance.
--	亡通告	obituary.
--	亡甚多	great mortality.
--	亡表	necrology.
07--	記	learn by rote.
08--	於病	die of sickness.
--	於非命	*n.* premature death, *v.* die unnaturally.
--	敵	deadly enemy, diehard enemy.
11--	硬派	diehards.

12--	刑	capital punishment, death-penalty.
--	水	stagnant water, dead -water.
22--	後	after death, posthumous.
24--	結	hard knot.
--	仇	implacable enmity.
25--	生	death and life.
27--	物	inanimate.
28--	傷	toll of human lives, casualties.
--	傷數	casualty.
30--	守	defend to the last, hold fast till death, die in the last ditch.
33--	心眼	stubborn, obstinate.
40--	力爭扎	struggle to the last.
--	難	die for the country.
41--	板	rigid, punctilious.
44--	者	the dead, the deceased.
--	老虎	slain tiger.
47--	胡同	blind alley.
60--	罪	capital offence.
67--	路	road to destruction.
73--	胎	stillborn, stillbirth.
77--	尸	corpse.
--	鬥	mortal combat, war to the knife.
90--	光	death-ray.
--	黨	sworn followers.

1021₄
霍 〔**Ho**〕 *n.* speed, *adv.* suddenly, quickly.

22--	亂	cholera.
23--	然	suddenly.

霾 〔**Mai**〕 *n.* sand storm, *adj.* misty, foggy.
1021₇
霓 〔**I**〕 *n.* rainbow, *adj.* colored, variegated.

51--	虹	neon.
--	虹燈	neon light.
--	虹招牌	neon sign.

1022₇
丙 〔**Ping**〕 *adj.* third.

00--	夜	midnight.

而〔**Erh**〕*conj.* and, also, but, yet.

17--己	that's all.
22--後	afterwards, henceforth.
77--且	more-over, also, besides, furthermore.
80--今	now, the present time.

兩〔**Liang**〕*n.* pair, couple, ounce, tael, *adj.* two, double, both, *adv.* twice, again.

10--下	both side, the two parties.
--可	alternative, ambiguous.
--面	double-faced.
--面討好	please both sides.
--面受敵	between fires, be attacked on both sides.
--面手法	double-faced game.
--面作戰	fight on two fronts.
--面派	double-dealer.
--面夾攻	attack from both sides, hem in, pincer movement.
--面性	dual character.
--可	ambiguous.
--不誤	without neglecting either.
--不相涉	give no concern to each other.
11--班制	double day-shift system, double shift.
--頭落空	fall between two stools.
20--重人格	double personality.
--重國籍	dual nationality, dual citizenship.
--重性	dual nature.
--倍	double, twofold.
33--心相許	have tacit promise to marry each other.
--心相悅	the two hearts are mutually delighted.
35--袖清風	having not a cent, out at elbows.
36--邊討好	please both sides, run with the hare and hunt with the hounds.
--邊倒	sit on the fence.
37--次	twice, two times, once again.
40--難	dilemma.
--難之間	between two difficulties.
41--極性	polarity.
44--權分立	political system under which the legislative and executive branches are independent of each other.
45--棲動物	amphibian animal.
48--樣	different.
46--相	mutually.
--相對立	be opposed to each other.
--相情願	mutual consent.
60--星期	fortnight.
68--敗俱傷	both sides are defeated and wounded.
73--院制	the two-chamber system, bicameral system.
77--月刊	bimonthly.
--用詞	participle.
--腳規	compasses.
--層火車	double-decker train.
80--全其美	benefit both parties.
--分	bisect.
--合公司	limited copartnership, joint company.
90--小無猜	both of them young and innocent.

雨〔**Yu**〕*n.* rain, shower, *v.* rain, *adj.* rainy.

00--衣	rain coat, waterproof coat.
10--天	rainy day, fine day for young ducks.
--雲	rain clouds, nimbus.
--雪	sleet.
--雪紛紛	confused falling of rain and snow.
--露	rainand dew.
12--水	rain water.
20--季	raining season.
37--過天晴	after the storm comes a calm.
40--布	water-proof cloth.
44--鞋	overshoes, galoshes.
46--帽	rain cap.
54--靴	rain boots.
60--量	rainfall, rain gauge.
--量計	rain gauge, udometer .

61-- 點   rain drop.

80-- 傘   umbrella.

需 〔**Hsu**〕 *n.* necessity, need. *v.* need, require, have occasion for, hesitate, wait.

10-- 要   *n.* need, necessity, *v.* need, lack, require, demand, want, claim, entail, call for, *adj.* needful, necessary, essential, indispensable.

40-- 索   extort, levy, exact.

43-- 求   require, need, want, have occasion for.

47-- 款   be in need of money.

55-- 費   cost, expenditure.

77-- 用品   necessity, requirement.

-- 用經費   necessary expenses, required funds.

爾 〔**Erh**〕 *pron.* you, your.

88-- 等   you, all of you.

霄 〔**Shiao**〕 *n.* heaven, sky

10-- 雲   fleecy clouds.

34-- 漢   the skies.

40-- 壤   heaven and earth.

-- 壤之別   great difference as that between heaven and earth.

霧 〔**Wu**〕 *n.* fog, mist, vapor,

20-- 季   season of fog.

80-- 氣   fog or mist.

1023₀

下 〔**Hsia**〕 *n.* bottom, lower portion, *v.* go down, descend, fall, lay, *adj.* inferior, poor in quality, mean, low, vulgar, next, *adv.* below, beneath, under.

00-- 廚   go to the kitchen, prepare food.

-- 意識   *n.* subconsciousness, *adj.* subconscious.

-- 文   the statement that follows, the orders that fellow, the words that follow, sequel, the case is not over.

06-- 課   class is over, class dismissed.

07-- 詔   issue imperial orders or instruction.

07-- 部   lower part.

08-- 放   send to lower level.

-- 放勞動   go down to do manual labor.

-- 議院   House of Commons, the Lower House.

10-- 一個   next.

-- 一級   the next lower level.

-- 工   leave when the work is over.

-- 工廠   go out to the factories.

-- 工夫   devote much time and energy to a task.

-- 元   the 15th day of the 10th month in the Chinese lunar calendar.

-- 雨   rain, rainfall.

-- 不了台   be nonplused.

-- 不爲例   this must not serve as a precedent.

-- 不去   go against, harass, cause someone to lose face.

-- 不來   cannot get down, be embarrassed.

-- 雪   *n.* snow, snowfall, *v.* snow.

11-- 班   off duty.

-- 頭   as follows, below, under.

-- 輩   the next generation, the younger generation of a family.

-- 輩子   the next life, the next incarnation.

12-- 水   *n.* down water, *v.* launch.

-- 水禮   the ceremony of launching a ship, ship launch ceremony.

-- 水道   sewer, sewerage, drain.

-- 列   as follow, what are listed below, pay attention to the following points.

-- 飛機   alight from a plane, deplane.

14-- 功夫   make effort.

15-- 聘   present betrothal gifts.

17-- 蛋   lay eggs.

20-- 垂   slouch, droop.

-- 手	begin, set to work, put one's hand to.	
21-- 處	lodging, hotel.	
-- 拜	bow.	
22-- 崗	come or go off sentry duty.	
-- 山	go down the hill.	
-- 種	sow seed.	
23-- 台	go off, quit a high position, give up office.	
24-- 牀	get up.	
-- 裝	take off one's costume (especially referring to performers).	
-- 結論	draw a conclusion, perorate.	
27-- 向	declination.	
-- 旬	the last ten days of a month.	
-- 級	inferior, junior, subordinate, lower level official or unit.	
-- 身	lower part of the body, the privates.	
-- 鄉	go to the countryside.	
-- 條子	send notes or memos to one's subordinates.	
-- 船	go ashore, disembark.	
30-- 注	put stake, stake a wager, wager.	
-- 房	the servants quarters.	
-- 定	sent betrothal gifts or money.	
-- 定義	define.	
-- 流	downstream, lower class.	
-- 流話	vulgar words, vulgarism.	
-- 流社會	low life, rabble.	
31-- 酒	go with wine or liquor.	
-- 逐客令	show a person the door.	
33-- 述	the flowing, the undermentioned.	
35-- 決心	make up one's mind.	
-- 連隊	go out to the army companies.	
36-- 邊	as follow, following, below, under.	
37-- 沉	sink.	
-- 次	coming, the next time.	
38-- 游	downstream, lower course of a river.	
-- 海	turn professional (usually referring to show business), go to sea.	
40-- 土	the earth, the world, the countryside.	
-- 女	maid.	
-- 去	go down, go on.	
-- 來	descend, come down.	
41-- 帖	send an invitation.	
-- 麵	cook noodles.	
43-- 獄	imprison, jail, cast into prison.	
-- 嫁	marry someone beneath her station.	
44-- 地	go to the fields, leave a sickbed.	
-- 地獄	go to hell.	
-- 坡	be on the downgrade, go down hill.	
-- 落	whereabouts.	
-- 落不明	whereabouts unknown.	
-- 棋	play chess.	
-- 藥	write a prescription, put in poison.	
45-- 樓	go downstairs.	
46-- 場	n. the conclusion, the end, v. get to playground to compete, play ball etc, exit on the stage .	
-- 榻	take up abode, stay.	
50-- 中農	lower-middle peasants.	
-- 車	alight, get off a vehicle.	
-- 毒	put poison in, envenom.	
-- 毒手	lay violent hand on some one.	
-- 書	deliver a letter.	
60-- 星期	next week.	
-- 田	work on farmland, cultivate the land.	
-- 界	the earth (in the eyes of supernatural beings who are supposed to dwell in heavens above), the world of mortals.	
-- 回	next time.	
61-- 顎	lower jaw, mandible.	
63-- 戰書	deliver a challenge in writing.	

-- 賤	mean, base, vile, rascally.
67-- 略	what follow is omitted.
-- 跪	kneel down.
-- 野	quit or resign from official posts for politics (referring to top-rank officials).
71-- 馬	dismount, alight.
-- 馬威	prompt reprisals, instant severity, initial show of power.
-- 脣	the lower lip.
73-- 院	lower chamber, House of Commons.
-- 膊	the lower arm.
74-- 墮	n. downfall, v. fall down.
-- 肢	lower limbs.
75-- 體	genitals, privates.
77-- 風	leeward, in an inferior position, at a disadvantage.
-- 月	next month.
-- 腳	n. residual raw materials, scraps, v. get a foothold, make a short stay.
-- 學	leave for home after school.
-- 學期	next term, the second term.
-- 屆	next (term, election, etc.).
-- 降	go down, descend, fall.
-- 層	subordinate level.
-- 層社會	lower class.
-- 屬	subordinates.
-- 巴	the chin, the lower jaw.
78-- 墜	fall.
80-- 人	servants, attendants, valet.
-- 令	give an order, command.
-- 午	afternoon.
81-- 頜	lower jaw.
83-- 舖	lower berth.
84-- 錨	cast anchor.
88-- 等	low-grade, mean, depraved.
-- 筆	set a pen to paper, begin writing.
-- 筆千言	write at a great speed.
-- 餘	remnant.
-- 策	the worst policy, bad policy.
90-- 懷	one's desire, one's concern,
-- 半夜	after midnight, the wee hours.

-- 半旗	fly a flag at half-mast.
-- 半場	the second half(of a game).
-- 半月	the last half month after the 15th of a month.
-- 半年	the latter half of the year.
-- 卷	the last volume.

1023₂
豕 〔Shih〕 n. pig, hog.
00-- 膏	pig's fat.
40-- 肉	pork.

汞 〔Gung〕 n. mercury.
10-- 礦	mercury ore.

弦 〔Hsien〕 n. string, chord, crescent.
40-- 索	stringed instrument.
22-- 樂器	string instrument.
-- 樂隊	string band.
77-- 兒	string.

震 〔Chen〕 n. terror, fear, vibration, v. shake, vibrate, shock, move, quiver, tremble, terrify.
01-- 顫	quake, quiver, shake.
10-- 耳	ring in the ear, thunder in the ear, ear-splitting.
24-- 動	shake, vibrate, move, agitate, tremble, quake, shiver, flutter.
-- 源	epicenter, seismic center.
47-- 怒	thunder, tremble with rage.
48-- 驚	startle, shock, strike with alarm.
53-- 感	strike with awe.
91-- 悼	be shocked with grief.
96-- 懼	tremble with fear, shake with fear.

1024₇
夏 〔Hsia〕 n. summer.
00-- 衣	summer dresses.
10-- 至	summer solstice.
-- 天	summer.
20-- 季	summer, the season of summer.
-- 季攻勢	summer offence.
28-- 收	summer harvest.
40-- 布	grass clothes, Chinese linen.

71--	曆	the lunar calendar.
80--	令=夏季	
--	令營	summer camping, summer camp.
88--	節	mid-summer festival.

憂 〔**Yu**〕 *n.* sorrow, grief, sickness, illness, *v.* mourn, sympathize with, *adj.* sorrowful, sad, downcast, depressed, grieved, sorry, mournful, melancholy.

10--	天憫人	worry about the destiny of mankind.
12--	形於色	look worried.
21--	慮	*n.* anxiety, care, solicitude, *v.* be anxious, worry oneself, be concerned about.
22--	樂同享	share joys and sorrows.
27--	色	long face.
--	急	sad and anxious.
28--	傷	grief, sadness, distress.
29--	愁	*n.* sadness, broken heart, distress, bitterness, sorrow, grief, *v.* have blue grief, eat one's heart out, *adj.* cast down, sorrowful, mournful, melancholy, dejected, heartsick, grieved, sad, distressed.
--	愁滿面	wear a mournful expression.
33--	心	anxiety, heavy heart, broken heart.
44--	鬱	out of spirits, heavy-hearted, down-hearted, lowspirited.
--	鬱成病	be ill with anxiety and melancholy.
50--	患	misery, distress.
--	患餘生	have gone through countless distress and misfortune.
77--	悶	sorry, grieved, spiritless, disappointed, cast down in mind.
80--	念	anxiety.
94--	怵	eat one's heart out.
99--	勞成疾	fall sick with worry and toil.

覆 〔**Fu**〕 *v.* overturn, upset, overthrow, topple, defeat, cover over, answer, reply, repeat.

00--	言	repeat in word.
--	亡	fallen, ruined, destroyed.
03--	試	second examination, re-examine.
20--	信	reply, reply in writing, reply a letter.
27--	舟	sunken ship.
30--	審	re-examine, re-trial.
33--	滅	defeated, sunk, routed, destruction, demolition, overthrow, ruin.
37--	沒	sink, be defeated and destroyed.
40--	土	cover with earth.
44--	蓋	cover, overlay, overcast.
58--	轍	lesson of a failure.
80--	命	report.

霞 〔**Hsia**〕 *n.* red clouds.

90--	光	golden sunlight.

1024₈

霰 〔**Hsien**〕 *n.* hail, sleet, snow and rain.

16--	彈	canister shot.

1030₇

零 〔**Ling**〕 *n.* drizzle, small rain, fraction, remainder, residue, zero, naught, *adj.* fractional, broken-up, withered, lonely.

00--	度	zero degree, zero point.
07--	部件	components and parts, accessories and repairs.
10--	工	seasonal worker, temporary worker.
--	丁	lonely, solitary.
--	下	below zero.
--	碎	fragments, broken pieces, odds and ends.
--	碎東西	odds and ends.
11--	頭	change, fraction, oddment.
20--	售	*n.* retail sales, *v.* retail, sell by retail.
--	售價	retail price.

-- 售商	retailer, retail dealer, retail merchant, retail trader.
-- 售店	retail shop, retail store.
-- 售市場	retail market.
-- 售總額	gross retail sales, total volume of retail sales.
-- 售銷路	retail outlet.
25-- 件	parts, accessory.
32-- 活	chores, odd jobs.
40-- 賣	retail, sell by retail.
-- 賣商	retailer.
44-- 落	ruined, scattered, withered down in the world.
-- 花錢	pocket money.
58-- 數	fractions, odd number, oddment, fractional amount.
60-- 頭	buy at retail.
-- 星	odds and ends, fragmentary, odd, small lot.
-- 星商品	miscellaneous commodities.
-- 星交易	job lot trading, odd lot, odd lot trading.
64-- 時	twelve o'clock.
77-- 用錢	pocket money, pin money, spending money.
80-- 食	refreshments, collation.
83-- 錢	small change, change, odd money, odd change.

1032₇

焉 〔Yen〕 *adj*. how? why? when? etc.

18-- 敢	how dare?
21-- 能	how can?
40-- 有此事	is there such a case?
86-- 知	how could one know?
-- 知非福	how do you know it is not a blessing?

1033₁

惡 〔Er, wu〕 *n*. evil, wickedness, sickness, illness, *v*. bad, wicked, vicious, unpleasant, ugly, awkward, disgust.

00-- 疾	noxious disease, incurable complaint.
-- 疾不治	the dreadful disease is incurable.
-- 意	ill will, bad intention, bad faith, malice.
-- 意行爲	malicious act.
-- 意動機	malicious motive.
-- 言	bad language, crosswords.
-- 魔	devil, wicked spirits, mother of mischief.
-- 霸	bully, local despot.
17-- 習	bad habit, abuse, vice, besetting sin.
-- 習難改	evil practices are difficult to reform.
21-- 行	misdeed, villainy.
24-- 化	*n*. corruption, aggravation, deterioration, *v*. aggravate, worsen, deteriorate.
-- 徒	villain, rowdies, roughs, bad characters.
26-- 鬼	devil.
27-- 名	ill fame, bad reputation.
28-- 作劇	*n*. practical joke, *v*. monkey.
-- 俗	bad custom.
33-- 心	nauseated.
34-- 漢	varlet, villain.
36-- 濁	unclean, foul, dirty.
37-- 運	misfortune, mischance.
40-- 有惡報	sow the wind and reap the whirlwind.
43-- 犬	fierce dog.
46-- 棍	villain, rogue, scoundrel.
47-- 報	ill recompense.
50-- 事	malpractice, black deed.
-- 毒	vicious, malicious.
-- 毒話	malicious language, pungent remark.
52-- 耗	bad news.
53-- 感	bad impression, bad blood.
60-- 果	disastrous results, serious consequences.
80-- 人	bad man, bad egg, child of the devil.
90-- 劣	bad, wicked,
-- 劣行爲	mischief, ill deeds.
95-- 性	malignant, malignity.
-- 性瘤	malignant tumor, cancer.
-- 性瘧	malignant malaria.
-- 性倒閉	fraudulent insolvency.

1033₃

忐 〔Te〕 *n.* disquiet of the mind, *adj.* nervous, uneasy, timid, timorous.

21-- 忑不安　　nervous and uneasy.

1040₀

干 〔Kan〕 *n.* shield, bank of a river, stem of a tree, *v.* seek for, try to obtain, provoke, oppose, interfere, offend against.

10-- 預	meddle with, interfere, intervene.
-- 預其事	interfere with the affair.
24-- 休	stop.
31-- 涉	interfere, intervene, meddle, have part in, tamper with, intermeddle, interpose, have a finger in the pie, have a hand in.
-- 涉內政	interfere in the internal affairs of another country.
47-- 犯	violate, offense.
51-- 擾	interfere with, jam.
53-- 戈	shield and spears, weapons, arms.
-- 戈相見	declare war on each other.

于 〔Yu〕 *v.* go, proceed, *prep.* in, at, to, through.

33-- 心何忍	how can you bear it in your heart?
60-- 是	thereupon, accordingly, consequently.
80-- 今	now, at present.

耳 〔Erh〕 *n.* ear, handle.

00-- 痛	earache.
01-- 語	whisper, take one aside for private conversation.
-- 聾	deaf, deafness, hard of hearing.
12-- 孔	auditory canal.
16-- 環	ear rings.
17-- 朵	ears.
20-- 垂	ear lobe.
24-- 科醫生	aurist, otologist.
26-- 鼻喉科	otolaryngology.
40-- 力	power of hearing.
-- 套	ear laps.
42-- 垢	ear wax.
-- 機	earphone.
44-- 鼓	ear drum.
-- 熱	have burning ears.
53-- 挖	ear pick.
60-- 目	ears and eyes.
-- 目一新	pleasant change of atmosphere or appearance of a place.
67-- 鳴	ringing in the ears, buzzing in the ears.
74-- 膜	ear drum.
77-- 聞	hearing.
78-- 墜	ear-drop.
90-- 炎	otitis.

1040₁

霆 〔Ting〕 *n.* thunder.

1040₄

耍 〔Shua〕 *n.* sport, play, joke, game.

01-- 語	jokes.
20-- 手腕	finesse, play politics (or tricks), manoeuvre.
23-- 戲法	juggle.
44-- 花招	play tricks.
53-- 威風	make a show of authority.
57-- 把戲	play a dirty game.
80-- 無	deliberately dishonest.
83-- 錢	gamble.
88-- 笑	insult, chaff.
90-- 拳	box.
-- 掌者	boxer.

要 〔Yao〕 *v.* want, need, require, desire, intend, be in want of, ask for, *adj.* important, necessary, essential.

00-- 言	important words.
02-- 端	important circumstance, essential part.
10-- 面子	desirous of not losing face.
-- 電即發	dispatch the urgent telegram at once.
-- 不然	otherwise.
-- 不得	undesirable, intolerable, no good.
13-- 職	dignity, influential post.

082

霎平 1040₉

17-- 務	important affairs.
20-- 信	urgent letter.
21-- 旨	important principle, main idea, key note, important point, sum and substance.
27-- 約	make an agreement, contract with.
30-- 害	the key of a position, strategic position.
-- 塞	fortress, stronghold, garrison.
-- 塞戰	siege warfare.
-- 害	vital part, key point, essential element.
-- 害受傷	fatal part of the body was wounded.
-- 害之地	place of importance.
38-- 道	important highway, main road, important doctrine.
43-- 求	demand, claim, request, lay claim to, run upon, demand for, call for, appeal to.
-- 求過高	make too high a demand.
47-- 犯	dangerous criminal.
50-- 事	important business, case of need, case of life and death, matter of necessity.
-- 素	essence, important elements, principle, constituent.
54-- 挾	coerce, force.
60-- 因	factor.
-- 略	synopsis.
61-- 點	high light.
77-- 緊	important, requisite, important and urgent, of consequence.
80-- 人	influential person, big bug, cock of the roost, great gun.
81-- 領	essential, sum and substance, important points.

霎〔Sha〕*n.* slight shower, passing rain, instant.

23-- 然	suddenly.
64-- 時	momentarily, for a short time, at a bow.
67-- 眼	wink.

1040₉
平〔**Ping**〕*n.* peace, tranquillity, *v.* tranquilize, pacify, conciliate, subdue, regulate, adjust, *adj.* even, level, flat, plain, smooth, equal, uniform, common, ordinary, peaceful, just, equitable, fair.

00-- 方	square (in math).
-- 方尺	square foot.
-- 方根	square root.
-- 方米	(in math) square meter.
-- 庸	commonplace, mean.
08-- 放	prostrate.
10-- 正	level, even, just.
-- 平穩穩	sure and steady.
-- 平安安	without any accident.
-- 面	plane.
-- 面三角	plane trigonometry.
-- 面幾何	plane geometry.
-- 面圖	plane chart, plane figure.
12-- 列	abreast.
20-- 信	ordinary mail.
21-- 行	parallel.
-- 行線	(in math) parallel lines.
-- 行透視	parallel perspective.
-- 行四邊形	parallelogram.
-- 衡	*n.* balance, equilibrium, *v.* balance, establish equality, restore equality.
-- 衡態	parity, balanced condition.
-- 價	parity, par, par value, parity price, parity value, at original price.
-- 價商店	fair price shop.
22-- 亂	reduce rebels.
-- 穩	steady, peaceable.
23-- 台	platform.
24-- 射炮	cannon.
25-- 生	during the whole life.
-- 生大事	big event in one's life.
26-- 息	quell, calm down, assuage.
30-- 房	bungalow, house of one story.
-- 安	safe, peaceful, on sure ground, out of woods.

--	安到達	safe arrival.
--	安康泰	enjoy peace and well-being.
--	安無事	safe and sound, in peace.
--	空	suddenly.
--	定	n. pacification, v. pacify, quell, suppress, tranquilize.
33--	心	with a calm mind, sober-minded, self-possessed.
--	心靜氣	calm, cool-headed, free of excitement, smooth.
37--	滑	level and smooth.
39--	淡	commonplace.
44--	地	flat, plain, open country.
--	權	equality of rights.
46--	坦	level, even, flat, plain.
47--	均	average, equable, on an average.
--	均主義	equalitarianism.
--	均市價	equilibrium.
--	均速度	average speed.
--	均運動	mean motion.
--	均壽命	average life expectancy, mean length of life, average life span, life expectancy.
--	均地權	equalization of land ownership.
--	均數	average amount, mean.
--	均計算	take the average.
--	均價格	average price, mean price, equilibrium price.
--	均值	average value, mean value.
--	均收入	average income.
--	均分配	equal division.
52--	靜	calm, peaceful, quiet, tranquil.
60--	日	usually, daily.
--	日之事	daily affairs.
--	日考試	text examination.
--	易近人	amiable, well-disposed.
64--	時	n. peace time, normal times, peace, adv. usually.
--	時編制	peace establishment.
--	時公法	international law for peace.
71--	反	rehabilitate, redress a wrong.
--	原	plain.
77--	局	draw, tie (of a game).

--	凡	common, ordinary, homely, plain.
--	服	bring down.
--	民	civilian, common people, commoner.
--	民政治	democracy.
--	民教育	mass education.
78--	臥	prostrate.
80--	分	n. equal share, equal distribution, bisection, v. divide equally.
88--	等	n. equality, equal rank, adv. on a par with, on a level with, on a footing with.
--	等互惠	reciprocal favored treatment.
--	等條約	treaty of equality.
--	等待遇	equal treatment, parity of treatment.
90--	常	ordinary, common, usual.
91--	爐	open-hearth furnace.

1043₀

天 〔Tien〕 n. sky, heaven, air, nature, day, god, adj. celestial.

00--	主	God.
--	主教	The Roman Catholic religion.
--	主教徒	Catholic.
--	主教皇	Pope.
--	主教堂	Catholic church.
--	亮	daybreak.
--	方夜譚	Arabian Nights.
--	意	act of God.
--	文	astronomy.
--	文台	observatory.
--	文家	astronomer.
--	文圖	map of stars.
--	文儀	analemma.
--	文學	astronomy.
--	文學家	astronomer.
--	高氣爽	the sky is high and weather fine.
--	意人緣	heaven's will and human affinity.
--	衣無縫	without a trace.
10--	王星	the planet Uranus .
--	下	under the heaven, under the

	sun, under the sky, world, empire.
-- 下一家	all under the heaven are of one family.
-- 下大亂	the whole nation is in disorder (chaos).
-- 下大勢	the general situation of the world.
-- 下太平	peace reigns over the land.
-- 下爲公	the world is for all people.
-- 下無雙	peerless in the whole world.
-- 下無敵	be invincible throughout the world.
-- 雨連綿	it rains continuously.
-- 平	balance, scales.
-- 天	everyday, day by day.
-- 不作美	the heaven does not act beautifully--bad weather hinders some scheduled activity.
-- 不從人	the heaven declines to comply with one's wish.
-- 不絕人	the heaven would not fail a man.
13-- 球	globe, celestial globe.
16-- 理不容	intolerable by natural law.
-- 理難測	the ways of heaven are inscrutable.
-- 理昭彰	God's justice is manifest.
-- 理人情	law of nature and feelings of man--reasonable.
17-- 子	The emperor.
20-- 香國色	heavenly fragrance and national beauty--a great beauty.
21-- 經地義	most appropriate, matter of course.
-- 秤	balance.
22-- 災	natural calamity, catastrophe.
-- 災人禍	natural disaster and human calamity.
-- 仙	fairy, angel.
23-- 然	natural, not artificial.
-- 然產物	things made by nature.
-- 然之理	evident principle.
-- 然淘汰	natural selection.
-- 然孳息	natural fruit.
-- 然氣	natural gas.
24-- 佑	divine favor.
25-- 生	natural, inborn.
-- 生才子	born great artist, genius.
-- 生麗質	born beauty.
-- 使	angel.
26-- 線	aerial, antennas.
-- 線杆	aerial mast.
27-- 鵝	swan.
-- 鵝絨	velvet.
-- 各一方	we are each in a different quarter.
-- 翻地覆	the sky turns and the earth collapses--in total disorder.
-- 色	color of the sky, the time of the day.
-- 色不早	it's getting late.
28-- 作之合	union made in heaven--ideal marriage.
-- 倫之樂	the happiness of a family.
-- 從人順	heaven complies with the wish of a person.
30-- 空	sky, air, heaven.
-- 之驕子	specially privileged person.
-- 安門	Tien An Men, Tiananmen.
-- 良	conscience.
-- 良喪盡	have lost all one's conscience.
-- 窗	sky-light, dormer window.
31-- 涯	world's end.
-- 涯海角	the ends of heaven and earth, any distant place.
-- 河	the milky way, the Galaxy.
33-- 演	evolution.
-- 演論	theory of evolution.
37-- 邊	the world's end, the horizon.
-- 朗氣清	the sky is bright and the air refreshing.
-- 資	genius, great abilities, sacred fire, natural gift, natural property.
-- 資聰穎	intelligent by nature.
38-- 道	ways of God.
40-- 壤之別	an immeasurably vast difference, a world of difference.

-- 才	genius, gift, sacred fire.
-- 真	natural, naive, innocent.
-- 真活潑	innocent and lively.
44-- 地	heaven and earth.
-- 地良心	from the bottom of my heart, tell the truth.
-- 地萬物	everything in the world.
-- 花	smallpox.
-- 花板	ceiling.
47-- 棚	awning.
55-- 井	court, yard, courtyard.
60-- 國	Kingdom of God.
-- 旱	drought, dry weather.
-- 罰	damnation.
63-- 賦	innate, inborn.
-- 賦人權	inherent human rights.
66-- 賜良機	godsend chance.
67-- 明	daybreak.
71-- 長地久	lasting as long as heaven and earth, everlasting.
72-- 昏地暗	gloomy above and below.
75-- 體	celestial body.
78-- 險	natural barrier, natural obstacle.
80-- 命	fate, chance, heaven's decree, the will of God.
-- 氣	weather, climate.
-- 氣預報	weather forecast.
-- 公地道	as fair as heaven and earth, absolutely fair.
90-- 堂	paradise, heaven, sky, throne of God.
-- 堂地獄	heaven and hell.
95-- 性	instinct, natural disposition.

1044₁

弄〔Lung〕*n.* alley, lane, *v.* play with, handle, perform, mock at, ridicule.

10-- 死	kill, put to death.
11-- 巧	affect to be clever.
-- 巧成拙	suffer from being too smart.
20-- 舌	tattle, jabber.
35-- 清	clarify.
-- 清是非	distinguish right from wrong.
40-- 壞	spoil, put out of order.
44-- 權	abuse one's power.

82-- 飯	cook rice.
84-- 錯	make a mistake.
90-- 堂	alley, lane.

1044₇

再〔Tsai〕*adv.* again, twice, second time, also, further.

00-- 病	get a relapse of sickness.
02-- 訴	second suit.
03-- 試	try again, make another attempt.
08-- 說	speak again, repeat, furthermore.
-- 說一遍	repeat what was said once more.
10-- 一次	once more, once again.
-- 三	repeatedly, time after time, again and again, over and over again.
-- 三敦請	extend a cordial invitation repeatedly.
-- 三再四	over and over again.
-- 三叮嚀	give repeated injunctions.
-- 再	redouble.
12-- 延期	put off again.
21-- 版	reprint, second edition.
-- 行延期	make further delay.
22-- 出	reissue.
25-- 生	reproduce, be born again.
-- 生產	*n.* reproduction, *v.* reproduce.
28-- 作	do over, resume.
34-- 造	reconstruct, born a second time.
-- 造之恩	the grace of giving a second birth.
30-- 審	re-trial.
-- 進	re-enter.
40-- 來一個	encore.
42-- 婚	remarriage.
44-- 者	furthermore, moreover.
47-- 犯	repeat an offence.
-- 犯不赦	repeated offenders are unpardonable.
48-- 教育	re-education.
-- 幹	make a fresh start.
50-- 接再厲	make unremitting efforts.

60-- 四思維　　think it over again and ag-
　　　　　　　　ain.
　-- 見　　　　farewell.
　-- 思　　　　think again.
　-- 思而行　　act after repeated consider-
　　　　　　　　ation.
77-- 開　　　　reopen.
78-- 驗　　　　re-inspect.
80-- 分　　　　subdivide.
　-- 會　　　　goodbye, so long, adieu.

1048₂

孩〔**Hai**〕*n.* child, baby, infant.
17-- 子　　　　child, children, kid, boy.
　-- 子氣　　　childish, boyish.
80-- 氣未除　　one's childishness still re-
　　　　　　　　mains.

1050₆

更〔**Keng**〕*n.* change, alteration, *v.*
change, repair, renew, act for substitute. *adv.* more, further, moreover,
still, again.
00-- 衣　　　　change clothes, wash.
　-- 衣室　　　dressing room, toilet.
01-- 訂　　　　revise, amend.
02-- 新　　　　*n.* renewal, replacement,*v.*
　　　　　　　　begin a new life, reform an
　　　　　　　　evil habit, renew, replace,
　　　　　　　　update.
10-- 正　　　　*n.* adjustment, revision, *v.*
　　　　　　　　correct, rectify, make right,
　　　　　　　　make correction, revise.
　-- 正條款　　amendment clause.
18-- 改　　　　*n.* alteration, *v.* change, al-
　　　　　　　　ter.
24-- 動　　　　make a turn.
25-- 生　　　　regeneration.
27-- 多　　　　more.
34-- 遠　　　　further.
35-- 迭　　　　by turns.
37-- 深人靜　　the night is late and people
　　　　　　　　are quiet.
40-- 大　　　　bigger, more.
44-- 壞　　　　worse.
　-- 甚　　　　further, farther.
46-- 加　　　　still, all the more.
47-- 好　　　　much better.

49-- 妙　　　　so much the better.
50-- 夫　　　　watchman.
57-- 換　　　　replace, substitute, change.
79-- 勝一籌　　even better.
90-- 少　　　　less.

1050₇

霉〔**Mei**〕*n.* mildew, mold, *adj.* moldy,
damp.
10-- 天　　　　dump weather.
26-- 臭　　　　frowzy.
40-- 壞　　　　spoiled by mold.
44-- 菌　　　　mold.
97-- 爛　　　　moldering away, rot, decay.

1052₇

霸〔**Pa**〕*n.* conqueror, tyrant, chief,
feudal lord, bully, oppression, *v.* rule
by force.
00-- 主　　　　tyrant.
10-- 王　　　　conqueror, overlord.
21-- 佔　　　　encroach upon, usurp, seize
　　　　　　　　by force.
38-- 道　　　　tyranny, the rule of might.
44-- 權　　　　mastery, hegemony.
　-- 權主義　　hegemonism.

1060₀

石〔**Shih**〕*n.* stone, rock.
00-- 膏　　　　gypsum.
　-- 膏像　　　plaster figure.
10-- 工　　　　mason, stonemason.
　-- 耳　　　　lichen.
16-- 碑　　　　stone tablet, gravestone.
17-- 子　　　　pebbles.
22-- 崖　　　　cliff, precipice.
　-- 片　　　　stone slabs.
　-- 炭　　　　mineral coal, coal.
23-- 絨　　　　rock-cork.
27-- 像　　　　stone statue.
35-- 油　　　　petroleum, oil, rock oil.
　-- 油產品　　petroleum products.
　-- 油化學　　petrochemistry.
　-- 油危機　　oil crisis.
　-- 油污染　　oil pollution.
　-- 油勘探　　oil prospecting.
　-- 油燃料　　oil fuel.
37-- 洞　　　　rock cave.
40-- 灰　　　　lime.

-- 灰岩	limestone.	
-- 女	barren woman.	
-- 堆	heap of stones.	
-- 柱	stone pillar.	
41-- 壩	stone dam.	
-- 板	slate, stone slab.	
42-- 橋	stone bridge.	
44-- 花菜	agar-agar.	
-- 英	quartz.	
-- 英鐘	quartz-clock.	
46-- 塊	stone, rock, fragments of stone.	
-- 棉	asbestos.	
-- 棉瓦	asbestos tiles.	
47-- 榴	pomegranate.	
50-- 青	dark-green.	
52-- 蠟	paraffin wax.	
60-- 墨	graphite.	
-- 田	barren fields.	
66-- 器	stoneware, stone implements.	
-- 器時代	stone age.	
67-- 路	stone-paved road.	
70-- 雕	stone sculpture.	
71-- 脂	clay.	
-- 匠=石工		
77-- 印	n. lithography, v. lithograph.	
88-- 竹	pink.	
-- 筆	slate pencil.	
-- 筍	stalagmite.	

百 〔Pai〕 n. hundred.

00-- 方	all means.	
10-- 工	all classed of artisans.	
12-- 列登森林會議	Bretton Woods conference.	
-- 發百中	every time a bull's eye, every shot told.	
20-- 倍	hundredfold.	
24-- 貨	general merchandise.	
-- 貨公司	department store, general merchandise store.	
-- 貨商店	department store.	
-- 科全書	encyclopedia.	
27-- 般	in every possible way.	
-- 物	all things.	
44-- 萬	million.	

-- 萬富翁	millionaire.	
-- 葉窗	shutter, blind, Venetian blind.	
45-- 姓	people, subject.	
52-- 折不撓	indomitable.	
-- 折不回	pushing forward despite repeated frustrations.	
60-- 日咳	whopping cough.	
-- 足	centipede.	
63-- 戰百勝	ever-victorious.	
80-- 分比	percentage, percent.	
-- 分率	percentage.	
-- 分點	percentage point.	
-- 分之一	hundredth.	
-- 無一失	you can't possibly go wrong.	
-- 無一長	good for nothing.	
-- 年	century.	
-- 年紀念	centenary.	
-- 合	lily.	
90-- 米賽跑	100-metre dash.	

西 〔Hsi〕 n.the west, adj. western, occidental.

00-- 方	west, westward, the West, the Occident.	
-- 方列強	Western Powers.	
-- 方人	westerner.	
10-- 貢	Saigon.	
11-- 北	northwest.	
-- 班牙	Spain.	
-- 班牙人	Spaniard.	
21-- 經	west longitude.	
-- 紅柿	tomato.	
38-- 洋景	peep shows.	
40-- 南	southwest.	
43-- 式	western style.	
44-- 藏	Tibet.	
-- 藏的	Tibetan.	
72-- 瓜	watermelon.	
77-- 風	west wind.	
-- 半球	the western Hemisphere.	

面 〔Mien〕 n. face, countenance, surface, plane, side, direction, v. face, confront, meet, adv. personally.

00-- 交	hand over personally.	
02-- 訴	complain verbally.	
03-- 試	oral examination, interview.	

04-- 詰	question personally.
05-- 講	request personally.
07-- 部	face.
09-- 談	discuss verbally, talk over in person.
10-- 面俱到	well considered in every respect.
12-- 孔	one's face or feature.
17-- 子	face, honor.
21-- 紅	blush, flush.
24-- 值	par value, face value, nominal value.
25-- 積	area.
26-- 貌	looks, appearance, countenance, feature.
-- 貌一新	take on a new look.
27-- 向	face.
-- 角	facial angle.
-- 色	complexion, countenance, facial expression.
29-- 紗	veil.
31-- 額	face value, face amount, denomination.
34-- 對	face, confront, envisage.
-- 對面	face to face.
38-- 洽	personal contact, discuss with somebody face to face.
40-- 巾	towel.
-- 布	face-cloth.
-- 有愁色	pull a long face, anxious countenance.
41-- 頰	check.
46-- 相	physiognomy.
50-- 責	reproach personally.
60-- 目	appearance, features.
-- 罩	veil.
70-- 壁	face the wall.
78-- 臨	be faced with, be confronted with.
80-- 盆	basin.
-- 盆架	wash basin stand.
-- 前	in the presence of.
-- 無人色	look blank, look aghast.

1060_1
吾 〔**Wu**〕 *pron.* I, me, my, we, our, us.
| 00-- 亦能之 | I can do it as well. |

| 40-- 力所不及 | beyond my power, above my strength. |
| 80-- 人 | we, us. |

晉 〔**Chin**〕 *n.* Tsin Dynasty, Shansi Province, *v.* increase, grow, flourish, proceed, forward.
| 06-- 謁 | have an interview. |
| 27-- 級 | promoted in rank. |

1060_3
雷 〔**Lei**〕 *n.* thunder, mine.
10-- 雨	thunder shower, thunderstorm.
-- 電	thunderbolt.
-- 霆	thunder, fury.
34-- 達	radar.
35-- 神	the God of thunder.
47-- 聲	thunderclaps.
51-- 打	thunderstruck.
57-- 擊	be struck by lightning.
67-- 鳴	thunder rolls.
77-- 同	similar, alike.
88-- 管	detonator.

1060_9
否 〔**Foul**〕 *adj.* negative, bad, wicked, evil, *adv.* no, nay, not, else, otherwise.
07-- 認	*v.* deny, repudiate, disavow, *adj.* denial, disavowal.
30-- 定	*n.* negation, *v.* negate, *adj.* negative.
-- 定語	negative expression.
35-- 決	veto, reject.
-- 決權	veto, veto power.
62-- 則	otherwise, or else.

1061_3
硫 〔**Liu**〕 *n.* sulphur, brimstone.
13-- 酸	sulphuric acid.
-- 酸銨	ammonium sulphate.
14-- 磺	sulphur, brimstone.
-- 磺泉	sulphur spring.
24-- 化	*n.* sulphurate, *adj.* sulphurous.

1062_0
可 〔**Ke**〕 *v.* can, may, be able, permit, tolerate, *adj.* worthy, fit, competent,

possible.

02-- 託	trustworthy.
06-- 親	amiable, agreeable, affable.
10-- 惡	disgustful, detestable, odi-ous.
-- 惡之至	utterly detestable.
-- 憂	sorrowful.
-- 可	cocoa, cacao.
-- 否	will it do or not?
11-- 巧	luckily, fortunately.
-- 悲	regrettable, lamentable.
12-- 型性	docility.
13-- 恥	shameful, disgraceful.
17-- 取	fit to be adopted.
-- 了不得	how wonderful !
-- 歌可泣	very moving, very touch-ing.
18-- 攻可守	equally valuable as a stepping-stone for offense or a strong point for de-fense.
20-- 信	credible, believable.
-- 信任的	accredited.
-- 愛	lovely, lovable, pleasant, winsome, amiable.
-- 乘之機	advantage, good chance.
21-- 能	n. possibility, v. be able, be possible, adv. possibly, by possibility.
-- 能性	possibility, chance.
-- 行	practicable, feasible.
-- 行性	feasibility.
-- 比	comparable.
22-- 樂	joyful, pleasant.
24-- 靠	reliable, trustworthy, true as steel.
-- 靠的	reliable, dependable.
-- 靠性	reliability.
-- 供數量	quantity available.
26-- 得	attainable, obtainable.
27-- 多可少	the amount doesn't matter.
-- 佩	admirable, respectable.
-- 疑	suspicious, doubtful, ques-tionable.
-- 獎	commendable.
-- 的松	cortisone.

28-- 以	v. may, can, might, adj. possible.
-- 以理解	understandable.
-- 以想像	conceivable, thinkable.
-- 以接受	acceptable, agreeable.
33-- 進可退	be free to go forward or back off.
-- 溶性	solubility.
34-- 達	accessible, within reach, within measurable distance.
-- 流通的	negotiable.
36-- 視電話	videophone.
37-- 追索	with recourse.
-- 資鑑戒	can serve as warning exam-ple.
40-- 大可小	the size is changeable.
-- 有可無	non-essential, dispensable.
-- 喜	joyful, welcome.
-- 喜可賀	be congratulated.
-- 嘉	worthy of praise, praise-worthy.
44-- 蘭經	Koran, Alkora .
-- 共患難	can be trusted in time of trouble.
46-- 觀	considerable, remarkable.
-- 想而知	you can imagine.
-- 賀	worthy of congratulation.
47-- 欺	can be bullied.
48-- 驚	appalling.
-- 敬	respectable, honorable.
-- 敬可嘉	be worthy of respect and praise.
50-- 貴	valuable, precious.
55-- 耕地	arable land.
56-- 操勝算	stand a good chance of vic-tory.
58-- 徹銷的	revocable, voidable.
60-- 口	tasty, delicious, please to taste, palatable.
-- 見	visible, evident, apparent.
-- 畏	fearful, dreadful.
-- 是	but, however.
64-- 嘆	sad, deplorable.
66-- 咒	accursed.
67-- 鄙	despicable, contemptible.
70-- 駭	appalling, impressing with fear.

71-- 厭	detestable, disgusting.
-- 原	excusable.
-- 長可短	the length is changeable.
77-- 用	usable.
-- 留則留	if you think you can stay on, then stay on.
80-- 分割的	divisible.
87-- 塑體	plastic.
-- 塑性	plasticity.
-- 欲	desirable, ridiculous.
88-- 笑	laughable.
93-- 燃性	inflammability.
94-- 惜	*adj.* piteous, *adv.* unfortunately. It is a pity.
-- 恃	dependable.
-- 怖	terrible, horrible, dreadful, tremendous.
96-- 怕=可怖	
97-- 怪	strange, wonderful.
-- 恨	hateful, abominable.
-- 憎	disgusting.
99-- 憐	pitiable, piteous, poor.
-- 憐相	pitiable look.
-- 憐虫	poor creature, poor fellow, wretch.

1062₁
哥 〔**Ke**〕 *n.* elder brother.

1062₇
磅 〔**Pang**〕 *n.* pound, pound sterling, sound of stone crashing.

| 14-- 礴 | vast, widespread, extensive, filling up all space. |
| 21-- 秤 | scale. |

靄 〔**Ai**〕 *n.* cloudy sky, *adj.* cloudy, obscured, kind.

1063₁
礁 〔**Chiao**〕 *n.* reef, shoal.

| 10-- 石 | reef, rock. |
| -- 石沈舟 | strike on a rock and sink. |

1063₂
釀 〔**Niang**〕 *v.* brew, ferment.

22-- 亂	excite rebellion, incite rebellion.
31-- 酒	ferment wine, brew wine.
34-- 造	brew.
-- 造所	brewery, distillery.
37-- 禍	create trouble, hatch mischief.
53-- 成	brew, cause, foment, bring about slowly.
-- 成巨禍	bring about a great calamity.
75-- 膿	maturation.
77-- 母	yeast.

1064₁
霹 〔**Pi**〕 *n.* thunderclap.

| 10-- 靂 | thunderbolt, thunderclap. |

1064₇
醇 〔**Chun**〕 *n.* strong wine, *adj.* generous, rich, good, pure, unmixed.

| 31-- 酒 | spirit, strong wine. |
| 71-- 厚 | pure-minded and honest. |

1064₈
醉 〔**Tsui**〕 *adj.* drunk, intoxicated, *v.* be drunk, be under the table, crook the elbow, be in one's cup.

00-- 意	drunken sign, slightly drunk.
10-- 死	dead-drunk.
16-- 醒	sobered.
22-- 倒	fall down drunk, be dead drunk.
25-- 生夢死	lead a befuddled life.
31-- 酒	drunk, tipsy, intoxicated.
33-- 心於	be infatuated with, be entranced in.
34-- 漢	drunkard, sot.

碎 〔**Shu**〕 *n.* small pieces, fragments. *v.* break to pieces, smash, pound.

10-- 玉	broken jade.
-- 石	macadam.
12-- 裂	break to pieces, take to pieces.
22-- 片	clip, fraction, fragments, shreds.
27-- 的	broken.
40-- 肉	minced meat.
-- 布	rags.
46-- 塊	scrap, shred, rag.
90-- 米	crushed rice.
94-- 煤	slack coal.

97-- 爛　broken.

礮〔Pao〕 n. cannon, gun, ordnance.

00-- 座　bulwark.

00-- 場　artillery park.

16-- 彈　cannon balls, shot, ammu-
　　　nition.

18-- 攻　cannonade.

20-- 手　gunner.

21-- 術　gunnery.

23-- 台　fort, fortress, castle.

24-- 塔　turret.

50-- 車　carriage.

-- 轟　bomb, shell.

60-- 口　embrasure.

63-- 戰　artillery duel.

72-- 兵　artillery man.

-- 兵輜重　artillery train.

-- 兵陣地　artillery position.

78-- 隊　battery.

90-- 火線　line of fire.

1066₁

磊〔Lei〕 n. heap of stones.

44-- 落　upright conduct, open-
　　　hearted.

-- 落光明　openhearted, unaffected.

1068₆

礦〔Kuang〕 n. mine, ore of metal.

00-- 產　minerals.

-- 產品　minerals, mineral produce.

-- 產儲蓄　mineral reserves.

-- 產資源　mineral resource.

10-- 工　miner, pitman.

-- 石　ore.

-- 石收音機　crystal set, crystal receiver.

-- 務　mining affairs.

19-- 砂　metallic ores, ore.

21-- 師　mining engineer.

22-- 山　mine.

26-- 泉　mineral spring.

-- 泉水　mineral water.

27-- 物　mineral.

-- 物油　mineral oil.

-- 物學　mineralogy.

32-- 業　mining industry.

35-- 油　mineral oil.

40-- 坑　mine-pit.

44-- 苗　mineral outcrop.

-- 藏　mineral deposits, mineral
　　　reserves.

-- 權　mineral rights.

55-- 井　shaft, pit.

72-- 脈　mineral vein.

77-- 學家　mineralogist.

1071₂

雹〔Pao〕 n. hail.

32-- 冰　hailstone.

1071₆

電〔Tien〕 n. electricity, lightning, adj.
electric.

00-- 療　electric-therapy, electrical
　　　treatment.

-- 療法　electric-therapy.

-- 廠　power plant.

01-- 站　power station.

02-- 話　telephone.

-- 話聽筒　ear-phone.

-- 話線　telephone wire.

-- 話機　telephone, telephone set.

-- 話接線生　telephone operator.

-- 話號碼　telephone number.

-- 話局　telephone office.

-- 話簿　telephone directory.

-- 話聯係　telephone communication.

-- 話中心　telephone centers.

-- 話推銷　telephone sale.

-- 話局　telephone office.

-- 話分機　extension.

07-- 訊設備　telecommunication equip-
　　　ment.

10-- 工　electrician.

-- 石　flint.

-- 覆　reply by telegram.

11-- 碼　telegraphic code.

17-- 子　electron.

-- 子商務　e-commerce.

-- 子工業　electronic industry.

-- 子計算機　electronic computer.

-- 子計算器　electronic calculator.

-- 子望遠鏡　electron telescope.

-- 子郵件	E-mail.	
-- 子顯微鏡	electronic microscope.	
-- 子信息產品	electronic information products.	
-- 子信息技術	electronic information technology.	
-- 子出版系統	electronic publishing system.	
-- 子付款系統	electronic payment system.	
-- 子和計算機工業	electronics and computer industry.	
-- 子收銀機	electronic cash register.	
-- 子通訊裝置	pager.	
-- 子數字計算機	electronic digital computer.	
-- 子時代	electronic age.	
-- 子購物	electronic shopping.	
-- 子貿易	electronic trade, e-trading.	
-- 子銀行業務	electronic banking.	
-- 子學	electronics.	
-- 子管	electron tube, radio tube.	
18-- 磁	electromagnet.	
20-- 信	telecommunication.	
-- 信員	electrician.	
-- 信局	telecommunications office.	
23-- 台	radio station.	
24-- 付	payment by wire.	
-- 動	electromotion.	
-- 動機	electric motor, electromotor.	
-- 動打字機	electric typewriter.	
25-- 傳	telex.	
-- 傳打字	teletype.	
-- 傳打字機	teletypewriter, teleprinter.	
-- 傳通訊網路	telecommunication network.	
26-- 線	wire, telegraph line.	
-- 線桿	telegraph pole.	
27-- 解	electrolysis.	
28-- 纜	electric-cable.	
-- 纜廠	electric wire and cable factory.	

30-- 扇	electric fan.
-- 容	condenser (in electricity), capacitor.
32-- 冰箱	electric refrigerator.
34-- 池	battery, cell.
-- 流	electric current.
-- 波	electric waves.
36-- 視	television.
-- 視廣播	televise, telecast.
-- 視廣告片	TV advertising film.
-- 視電話	picture phone, video telephone.
-- 視攝像機	telecamera, television camera.
-- 視機	television receiver, television set.
40-- 力	voltage, electric power, electricity.
-- 力網	electric power net, electric power grid.
-- 力表	wattmeter.
-- 力工業	electrical industry, electric-power, power industry.
-- 力公司	electric utilities.
-- 木	bakelite.
41-- 極	electrodes.
-- 杆	telephone poles.
42-- 機	dynamo, generator.
-- 機廠	electrical machinery plant.
44-- 荷	electric charge.
-- 熱	electric heat, electrothermal.
47-- 報	telegram, telegraph.
-- 報碼	cable code.
-- 報機	telegraph transmitter or receiver.
-- 報局	telegraph office.
-- 報通知	cable advice, cable notification.
-- 報費	cable charges.
-- 報匯票	telegraph money order.
-- 報公司	cable company.
48-- 警鈴	electric alarm.
-- 梯	elevator, lift.

50--	車	tram, electric tram, streetcar.
--	車站	tram stop.
55--	費	electricity expense.
62--	影	movies, motion picture, film.
--	影放映機	motion picture projector.
--	影劇本	screenplay, scenario.
--	影觀眾	movie-goers.
--	影攝影機	cinecamera.
--	影院	cinema.
66--	器廠	electrical appliance plant.
67--	路	circuit.
71--	匯	telegraphic transfer, cable transfer, remittance by telegraph, wire transfer.
--	匯票	cable draft.
--	匯款	telegraphic money.
--	匯單	telegraphic money order.
--	壓	voltage.
72--	腦	computer.
--	腦化會計	computerized accounting.
--	腦終端機	computer terminals.
--	腦技術	computer technology.
74--	熨斗	electric iron, electric flatiron.
77--	阻	resistance (in electricity).
--	學	electricity.
--	閃	lightning.
80--	鍍	electroplating.
--	氣	electricity.
--	氣設備	electrical equipment.
--	氣工程師	electrical engineer.
--	氣工程	electrical engineering.
--	氣化	electrify.
--	氣化學	electrochemistry.
--	氣感應	electro-induction.
--	氣分析	electroanalysis.
--	鐘	electric clock.
--	鍍	electroplate.
--	鍍廠	electroplating factory.
81--	瓶	battery.
85--	錶	electrometer, electric meter.
88--	鈴	electric bell, buzzer.
--	算化會計	electronic data processing accounting.
90--	光	electric spark.

91--	爐	electric stove, electric furnace.
92--	燈	electric lamp, electric light.
--	燈泡	bulb.
96--	焊	electric welding.
97--	烙鐵	electric soldering-iron.

1071₇

瓦〔**Wa**〕*n.* tile, pottery, earthenware, watt.

10--	工	tiler, bricklayer.
--	面	roof.
11--	頂	tiled roof.
12--	礫	rubble, broken pottery and tiling.
15--	磚	tile and brick.
22--	片	piece of tile.
24--	特	watt.
27--	解	*n.* disintegration, *v.* ruin, disintegrate, disorganize.
--	盤	earthen dish.
30--	房	tiled house.
--	窰	tile kiln.
42--	斯	gas.
66--	器	earthenware, pottery.
71--	匠	bricklayer, tile-maker.
77--	屋	tiled building.
--	屋頂	tiled roof.
84--	罐	earthen jar.
87--	鍋	earthen pot.

1073₁

云〔**Yun**〕*v.* say, speak.

10--	云	so and so, and so forth, and so on.

雲〔**Yun**〕*n.* clouds, *adj.* cloudy.

10--	霄	fleecy clouds.
--	霧	fog, mist, cloudy vapor.
--	霞	colorful clouds.
20--	集	gather together, assemble, swarm, gather like clouds.
22--	彩	clouds illuminated by the sun.
48--	梯	scaling ladder.
77--	層	banks of clouds.
--	母石	mica.
90--	雀	skylark.

1077₂

函〔Han〕n. letter, epistle, v. contain, envelop.
00-- 商	consult by letter.
02-- 託	request a favor by letter.
07-- 詢	inquire by letter.
10-- 覆	write a letter in reply.
-- 電	correspondence.
24-- 告	inform by letter, write something.
25-- 件	letter, correspondence.
52-- 授	correspondence instruction.
-- 授學校	correspondence school.
58-- 數	function (in math).
65-- 購	mail order, purchase by mail.

1080_6
頁〔Yeh〕n. page, sheet, folio.
22-- 岩	shale.
58-- 數	number of pages.

貢〔Kung〕n. tribute, revenue, v. present as tribute.
23-- 獻	present as tribute, offer contribute.
-- 獻者	contributor.
28-- 稅	taxes, revenue.
60-- 品	things offered as tribute.

賈〔Ku〕n. merchant, shopman.
00-- 市	market.

1090_0
不〔Bu〕adv. not, never, no.
00-- 高興	unhappy, unpleasant, ill humor.
-- 方便	n. inconvenience, adj. inconvenient.
-- 意之中	in a moment of carelessness.
-- 文法	unwritten law.
-- 言而喻	tell its own tale.
-- 言不語	keep silent.
-- 言可知	it goes without saying.
-- 言爲妙	better leave it unsaid.
03-- 誠實	dishonest.
-- 識字	illiterate.
-- 識事務	ignorant of the world.
04-- 計	no matter what, irrespective of.
-- 計名利	not mindful of fame or wealth.
-- 計其數	too numerous to be counted.
-- 計成敗	regardless of success or failure.
-- 計毀譽	disregard praise or criticism.
-- 計利息	free of interest, bearing no interest.
-- 計報酬	without consideration of salary, irrespective of pay.
-- 謀私利	unselfish.
-- 熟練	unskilled.
05-- 講理	unreasonable.
06-- 誤	without fail.
07-- 記名支票	check to bearer.
-- 設防城市	open city.
-- 設防區域	demilitarized zone.
-- 調	n. discord, adj. out of keeping.
08-- 放心	feel uneasy.
-- 論	no matter, apart from.
-- 論何處	anywhere, no matter where.
-- 論何時	anytime, no matter when.
-- 論何人	anyone.
-- 論睛雨	rain or shine.
-- 許	disallow, forbid.
10-- 一	not a few, unlike.
-- 一致	n. disagreement, adj. inconsistent.
-- 一定	uncertain, not sure.
-- 正	incorrect, awry.
-- 下	no less than.
-- 二價	no two prices, fixed prices, never quote two prices, one price only.
-- 正常	abnormal.
-- 正當公司	shady company.
-- 正當貿易	illicit trade.
-- 至於	not so as to.
-- 干預	non-intervention.
-- 干涉政策	hands-off policy.
-- 要緊	never mind, unimportant.
-- 要客氣	please feel at home.
-- 要見外	do not refuse my gift.

-- 要見怪	don't take it ill.
-- 平	uneven, unjust, on one side, indignant.
-- 平衡	unbalanced, out of balance.
-- 平的	uneven, rough.
-- 平等	inequality, unequal.
-- 平等條約	treaty of inequality.
-- 平等貿易	discriminative trade, unfair trade.
-- 平常	unusual, extraordinary.
-- 再	no longer, no more.
-- 再拘禮	without more ado.
-- 再有效	no longer valid.
-- 可	ought not, should not.
-- 可退貨	without return.
-- 可言傳	unspeakable.
-- 可磨滅	indelible.
-- 可計量	immeasurable.
-- 可調和	irreconcilable, uncompromising.
-- 可否認	undeniable.
-- 可不慎	great caution is necessary.
-- 可理喻	unreasonable.
-- 可信	beyond belief.
-- 可能	impossible.
-- 可任性	don't be wayward.
-- 可靠	unreliable.
-- 可靠的商人	fly-by-night trader.
-- 可動搖	unshakable.
-- 可忽視	not to be despised.
-- 可收拾	uncontrollable (situation), hopeless.
-- 可避免	unavoidable, inevitable.
-- 可逆料	unforeseeable.
-- 可克服	insurmountable.
-- 可想像	unimaginable, inconceivable.
-- 可救藥	incurable, beyond remedy, cureless.
-- 可抗拒	irresistible.
-- 可抗力	accidental force, force majeure, act of God.
-- 可捉摸	unpredictable.
-- 可思議	incomprehensible, inconceivable, unthinkable, mysterious.
-- 可戰勝	invincible.
-- 可勝言	indescribable, countless.
-- 可入性	impenetrability.
-- 可企及	incomparable.
-- 可勝數	innumerable, numberless, countless.
-- 可分割	inalienable, inseparable.
-- 可知論	agnosticism.
-- 可缺少	indispensable.
-- 可轉讓的	non-negotiable, non-transferable.
-- 可流通的	non-negotiable.
-- 可兌換的貨幣	non-convertible currency.
-- 可廢除條款	non cancellation clause.
-- 靈	inefficacious, unresponsive.
11-- 巧	unfortunately, by mischance.
-- 預先通知	without previous notice.
12-- 發達	underdeveloped.
-- 發達國家	underdeveloped countries (nations).
-- 發達地區	less-developed area, under-developed area.
-- 列顛聯邦	British Commonwealth.
-- 能晚於	not later than.
-- 能回收的	non-recoverable.
14-- 耐煩	impatient.
16-- 理	v. disregard, ignore, prep. despite.
-- 理解	not to understand.
-- 現實	unrealistic.
17-- 取分文	not to take a cent.
-- 了解	not to understand.
-- 及	out of reach, not in time, not up to.
-- 及格	below the mark, disqualified.
-- 及時	untimely.
-- 承認	deny, disavow, refuse assent, refuse to acknowledge.
-- 忍	impatient, out of patience, unbearable, cannot bear, cannot endure.
-- 忍爲之	unable to bring oneself to do it.
-- 予追究	let the matter pass.

-- 尋常尺寸	odd sizes.
-- 務正業	not engaged in proper work.
18-- 敢	dare not.
-- 敢後人	I must do my share.
-- 敢自信	dare not trust one's own opinion.
-- 敢作聲	dare not make any noise.
-- 敢啓齒	dare not mention.
-- 敢領教	too bad to be accepted.
20-- 重要	unimportant, of no importance, of no consequence.
-- 重視	dispose, neglect.
-- 停	incessant, ceaseless.
-- 信	disbelieve, doubt, distrust.
-- 信任	mistrust, discredit.
-- 信任投票	vote of non-confidence.
-- 信實	dishonest.
-- 悉內容	be outside the ropes.
-- 妥	unsafe.
-- 妥協	uncompromising.
-- 毛	barrenness, barren (land).
-- 毛之地	barren land.
21-- 便	inconvenience.
-- 能	cannot, unable, impossible.
-- 能忘情	unable to forget one's old sentiments.
-- 能勉強	cannot be forced.
-- 能自制	be out of one's skin.
-- 能容忍	n. intolerable, v. cannot tolerate.
-- 能遲延	admit of no delay.
-- 能領略	fall flat on one's ear.
-- 虛此行	the travel is not fruitless.
-- 行	impracticable, no good.
-- 肯	unwilling, reluctant.
-- 肯干休	refuse to stop a dispute.
-- 肯通融	not accommodating.
-- 經濟	uneconomical.
-- 經世故	inexperienced in worldly affairs.
22-- 倒翁	Chinese tumbler.
-- 亂	equal to the occasion.
-- 斷	continual, unbroken, uninterrupted, successive, perpetual.
-- 變	unchangeable, invariable.
-- 變價格	constant price, fixed price.

-- 出所料	just as expected.
-- 利	n. disadvantage, adj. disadvantageous.
-- 穩	unsafe, unstable, unsteady.
23-- 偏不倚	without fear or favor.
-- 然	on the contrary, if not, otherwise.
24-- 動	n. stillness, firm, adj. steadfast.
-- 動產	real estate, real asset, real property, fixed property.
-- 動產共有人	joint tenant.
-- 動產抵押	real estate mortgage.
-- 動產收入	income from real estate.
-- 動心	unaffected.
-- 動如山	immovable as a mountain.
-- 動聲色	v. remain in silence, adj. unmoved.
-- 動腦筋	without using one's brains.
-- 先不後	just at the right time.
-- 值一錢	worthless.
-- 值一笑	not worth even a laugh.
-- 值得提	not worth mentioning.
-- 值分文	not worth a penny.
-- 待思索	without stopping to think, self-evident.
-- 告而別	depart without saying goodbye.
-- 贊成	object, disapprove.
-- 結盟國家	non-aligned nation, non-aligned countries.
25-- 生產的	non-productive.
-- 健全	unsound.
-- 生效力	v. produce no effect, adj. ineffectual, invalid.
26-- 自量力	put a quart into a pint pot.
-- 自覺	unconscious.
-- 但如此	not only this.
-- 得意	disappointed.
-- 得不	be forced, be obliged, compelled.
-- 得了	terrible, my goodness!
-- 得而知	still unknown.
-- 得要領	unable to get the important.
-- 得翻身	have no chance to rise again or recover.
-- 得過問	not allowing any interfer-

	ence.
-- 得其法	unable to obtain the right way.
-- 得其所	be out of one's element.
-- 得人意	be in someone's black books.
-- 得善終	impossible to acquire a peaceful end.
-- 得退回	non-returnable.
-- 息	restless.
-- 和	unfriendly, discord, not on good terms, at enmity, in disagreement.
27-- 多	few, little, not much, not many.
-- 勻	uneven.
-- 像	unlike.
-- 侵犯協定	non-aggression pact, treaty of non-aggression.
-- 疑	make no doubt.
-- 疑有他	not to suspect other motives.
-- 名譽	dishonor, ignominious.
-- 名一錢	worthless, haven't a bean, not to pay a single cash.
-- 夠	insufficient, short, deficient.
-- 夠標準	not up to standard.
-- 久	soon, shortly, before long.
-- 久以前	short time ago.
-- 欠債	get even.
-- 負責	irresponsible, not responsible, unaccountable.
-- 負任何風險	assume no risk.
28-- 繳稅	passive resistance.
-- 以爲伍	refuse to associate with.
-- 以爲奇	not to consider as strange.
-- 以爲苦	not to regard as painful.
-- 作爲	negative act.
-- 作爲犯	crime of omission.
-- 收小費	no gratuities (tips) accepted.
-- 收服務費	no service charge accepted.
29-- 倦	untiring.
30-- 完善的	imperfect.
-- 流行	go out of fashion.
-- 准出售	sale forbidden.

-- 准動手	hands off.
-- 准進口	importation prohibited, importation forbidden.
-- 宣而戰	*n.* undeclared war, *v.* fight without declaration of war.
-- 宜如此	should not be like this.
-- 注意	*v.* pay no attention to, overlook, neglect, *adj.* careless.
-- 濟於事	be of no help to the matter.
-- 進則退	not to advance is to go back.
-- 適應	be unaccustomed to.
-- 適時宜	be out of season.
-- 適合	unsuitable, unfitting, inappropriate, inapplicable.
-- 適當	improper, unfitting.
-- 守信用	not to keep one's words.
-- 安	uneasy, uncomfortable, out of quiet, searching of heart.
-- 安定	unstable.
-- 客氣	impolite, you are welcome.
-- 容於世	be shut out of society.
-- 容辯解	allow of no excuse.
-- 良	bad.
-- 良記號	black mark.
-- 良於行	have difficulty with walking.
-- 良貸款	bad loan, non-performing loan, problem loan.
-- 定	uncertain, changeable.
-- 定的	uncertain, unstable.
-- 定收益	uncertain pay off.
-- 定期航行	tramp navigation.
-- 定期存款	irregular deposit.
-- 定期報告	non-periodical report.
31-- 顧	*v.* disregard, neglect, ignore, let pass, *prep.* notwithstanding.
-- 顧信用	abuse of trust.
-- 顧死活	take no choice of the serious consequences.
-- 顧後果	give no heed to the consequences.
-- 顧人情	divest oneself of humanity.
32-- 測	unforeseen.
-- 近人情	indifferent to others' feelings.
-- 透明	opaque.
-- 透水	water proof, water tight.

-- 透風	air tight, air proof.
33-- 必	needless, unnecessary, no need.
-- 必要	unnecessary.
34-- 對	wrong, incorrect, discontent.
-- 滿	dissatisfied, discontent.
-- 法	illegal, unlawful, lawless.
-- 法行爲	criminal act.
-- 法之徒	lawless elements.
-- 遠	not far, at hand.
-- 爲所動	be unmoved.
35-- 清不楚	not clear .
-- 清不白	not clear, not open.
-- 凍港	warm water port, ice free port.
-- 決	irresolute.
-- 遺餘力	leave no stone unturned, make the best of one's way.
-- 速之客	uninvited guest.
36-- 逞之徒	reckless fellows.
37-- 通行	no thoroughfare.
-- 遲於	not later than.
38-- 祥	unlucky, disastrous.
-- 道德	immoral, abandoned.
40-- 在	adj. absent. adv. away, out.
-- 在心上	not on one's mind.
-- 在其位	not in the position.
-- 幸	unfortunate, disastrous, unlucky, down on one's luck.
-- 幸事件	accident, mishap.
-- 友好	unfriendly.
-- 難	easy, not difficult.
-- 吉	sinister.
-- 吉兆	ill omen.
-- 喜	dislike.
-- 真	false.
41-- 枉此行	the trip is fruitful.
-- 朽	immortal.
-- 朽之作	imperishable work.
43-- 求名利	not to care for wealth or fame.
44-- 堪一擊	too weak to stand competition or attack.
-- 堪其苦	cannot bear the hardship.
-- 堪回首	too bitter to recall.
-- 堪入目	disgusting.
-- 考慮	take no account of, without consideration of.
-- 獲見諒	fail to have your sympathetic understanding.
-- 孝	disobedient.
-- 老實	dishonest.
-- 甘示弱	reluctant to show weakness.
-- 甘心	unwilling, not reconciled to.
-- 禁	can not help.
-- 禁失笑	can not help laughing.
46-- 相干	irrelevant.
-- 相往來	have no dealing with each other.
-- 相上下	match equally.
-- 相稱	disproportionate.
-- 相容	incompatible.
-- 相類似	not resembling one another.
47-- 好	bad, not good.
-- 好意思	embarrassing, embarrassed.
-- 切實際	impractical.
-- 期而遇	meet unexpectedly.
48-- 敬	disrespect.
50-- 中	miss.
-- 中用	v. be of no use, adj. useless.
-- 忠	disloyal.
-- 由自主	involuntary.
51-- 打自招	confess without beating.
52-- 折不扣	nothing short of.
-- 抵抗	n. nonresistance, v. offer no resistance.
53-- 成	fail, come short, fall through.
-- 成文法	unwritten law.
-- 成體統	behave very badly.
-- 成問題	it cannot be a problem.
54-- 軌之人	lawless person.
56-- 提	not to mention.
-- 規則	irregular, out of frame.
-- 規矩	misbehaved.
-- 擇手段	by hook or by crook.
-- 提爲妙	it is better not to mention it.
57-- 拘	anyway.
-- 拘形式	regardless of formalities.
-- 拘小節	not to mind trifle formalities.
60-- 日	not many days.
-- 見	out of sight.

-- 見經傳	not supported by historical fact.
-- 見下文	sequel unknown.
-- 見天日	in total darkness.
-- 易之論	sound or irrefutable statement.
-- 思飲食	be off one's feed.
-- 團結	disunity, disunion.
-- 男不女	neither a male nor a female (grotesque in appearance).
-- 只	not only, not merely.
-- 足	v. fall short, be unequal to, adj. insufficient, scant, short.
-- 足徵信	not credible.
-- 足以賴	broken reed.
-- 足爲奇	nothing strange.
-- 足道	not worth mentioning.
-- 足掛齒	not worthy to be mentioned.
-- 足額	balance due.
-- 足輕重	unimportant.
-- 足介意	not necessary to concern oneself with.
-- 是	fault, it is not right.
-- 景氣	depression, recession, bad times, slump.
-- 另行通知	without further notice.
62-- 別而行	take French leave.
64-- 時之需	that which may be needed any time.
67-- 明	obscure, not to know.
-- 明底細	ignorant of the true picture.
-- 明不白	not clear.
-- 明確	indefinite, unclear.
-- 明事故	not acquainted with the occasion of the trouble.
-- 明智	unwise, ill-advised.
68-- 賒欠	no credit charge.
-- 敗之地	undefeated position.
70-- 雅	ungraceful.
-- 雅觀	awkward, ugly.
71-- 願	unwilling, loath, reluctant.
-- 辱使命	have succeeded in carrying out an assignment.
-- 反對	have no objection.
75-- 體面	dishonorable, disgraceful.
77-- 堅定	unsteady.
-- 用	disuse, dispense with.

-- 用謝	not at all.
-- 用說	needless to say, not to mention.
-- 用心	inattentive.
-- 同	different, disagreeable, distinct, other than.
-- 同意	disagree.
-- 同的	different.
-- 凡	uncommon.
-- 覺	unconscious.
-- 覺失去	slip through one's fingers.
-- 履行	default, breach, fail to carry out, non-performance.
-- 服	disobey.
-- 服水土	not used to the climate.
-- 服從	v. disobey, adj. disobedient.
-- 留心	absent-minded.
-- 屈	inflexible, unbending, persistent.
-- 屈不撓	not to be cowed, not to give up.
-- 關心	indifferent.
-- 學而能	do something easily, naturally.
-- 學無術	have neither learning nor skill.
-- 問而知	know without asking.
-- 問好歹	no matter whether it is right or wrong.
-- 問情由	without first asking about what has happened.
-- 留餘力	spare no effort or energy.
-- 留餘地	leave no leeway.
-- 留情面	be very strict.
79-- 勝悲哀	be overcome with sorrow.
-- 勝其任	not fit for the position.
-- 勝其煩	too much bother (trouble).
-- 勝感激	I could never thank you enough.
-- 勝感愧	feel overwhelmed with shame.
-- 勝枚舉	innumerable, more than can be listed.
80-- 分高低	be equally matched.
-- 分彼此	make no distinction between one another.
-- 分晝夜	day and night.

--分勝負	run neck and neck.	--知自量	do something beyond one's ability.
--無可疑	not above suspicion.		
--無小補	it might be of some small help.	--知進退	not sure whether to advance or retreat.
--念舊惡	forget old grievance.	--知深淺	not to know the depth of things.
--義	treachery.		
--義之財	ill-gotten wealth.	--知道	not aware of, be ignorant of, have no idea.
--合	disagreeing, discordant, out of character.	--知去向	not to know the where-abouts.
--合理	unreasonable, illogical.	--知甘苦	not familiar with the sweet and bitter of life.
--合作	uncooperative.		
--合作運動	non-cooperative move-ment.	--知好歹	not able to discriminate be-tween good and bad.
--合適	unsuitable, unfit.	--知著落	not to know the where-abouts of someone.
--合邏輯	illogical.		
--合時宜	out of time, inopportune.	--知輕重	unable to tell the important from the unimportant.
--合格	unqualified, disqualified.		
--合算	not paying, not profitable.	--知所云	not realizing what one has said.
--善於	not good at.		
--含糊	unequivocal, explicit.	--知所以	have no idea why it is so.
--公	n. injustice, adj. unjust.	--知羞恥	have no sense of shame.
--公平	unfair, inequitable.	--知悔改	not repentant.
--銹鋼	stainless steel.	88--符事實	not in accord with facts.
--義之財	ill-gotten gains.	--等	unequal.
--合規格	fall short of specification, be not according to specifi-cation.	--等式	(math) inequality.
		--管	v. disregard, neglect, prep. despite, no matter, in spite of.
--公開公司	non-public company.		
84--錯	right, not bad.		
86--知	ignorant of.	90--少	not a few, considerable.
--知痛癢	not sensitive to pain or ir-ritation, unfeeling.	--少於	no less than.
		--肖	unworthy, degenerate.
--知底細	not to know the details, un-aware of the ins and outs.	--肖子弟	the depraved younger gen-eration.
--知死活	being not acquainted with life and death (ignorant of the danger involved).	--肖之徒	worthless fellow.
		--省人事	unconscious, be in a faint, delirious.
--知不覺	unconsciously, unknowing-ly.	--當	improper, unsuitable.
		--當利益	unjustified benefit, illegal profit.
--知可否	not to know whether it is right or not.		
		--當競爭	undue competition .
--知虛實	not to know whether it is true or false.	94--懷好意	with evil intention.
		--料	unexpectedly, contrary to expectation.
--知利害	not to know the real situ-ation.		
--知恥	shameless, dead to shame.	--慌	in no hurry, composed.
--知自愛	have no knowledge of self-		respect, misbehave oneself.

-- 慌不忙	with full composure.
-- 懂事	immature.
-- 懂人事	ignorant of the ways of the world.
-- 惜	not to spare, be ready to.
-- 惜一戰	be prepared to go to war.
-- 惜工本	be ready to go to extreme lengths.
-- 惜勞苦	spare no effort or pain.
95-- 情	unreasonable.
-- 情之請	my bold request.
-- 快於心	not pleased, displeased.
96-- 怕	fearless, not to be afraid of.
97-- 慣	unaccustomed.
98-- 愉快	unhappy.
-- 悔改	*v.* refuse to repent, *adj.* unrepentant.
99-- 勞而獲	get without any labor, gain without pain, something for nothing.

1090_1

示 〔Shi〕 *n.* notice, proclamation, manifestation, *v.* show, exhibit, make known, proclaim.

00-- 意	hint.
-- 意圖	diagram, sketch.
17-- 弱	show one's weakness.
30-- 寂	die (said of a monk or nun).
27-- 眾	make known to the public.
53-- 威	demonstrate, make a show of force, shake the fist at, awe.
-- 威運動	demonstration.
80-- 知	inform, notify.
88- 範	serve as a model, set an example, demonstrate.

票 〔Piao〕 *n.* ticket, bill, note, warrant.

60-- 面	the face (value) of a note, bond, etc.
-- 面值	face value.
17-- 子	ticket, bill.
21-- 價	fare, price of a ticket.
30-- 房	booking office, box office.
40-- 夾	wallet.
47-- 根	counterfoil, stub, stubs of a checkbook.

51-- 據	bills, certificate, voucher, note, negotiable instrument.
-- 據法	law of negotiable instrument.
58-- 數	number of vote.

1090_4

粟 〔Su〕 *n.* millet, grains.

90-- 米	Indian corn, maize.

栗 〔Lih〕 *n.* chestnut.

17-- 子	chestnut.
27-- 色	chestnut color.
44-- 樹	chestnut tree.

1096_3

霜 〔Shuang〕 *n.* frozen dew, hoarfrost.

30-- 害	damage caused by frost.
44-- 葉	leaves turning white.
47-- 期	frosty period.

1099_4

霖 〔Lin〕 *n.* continuous rain.

1110_1

韭 〔Wa〕 *n.* leeks, scallions.

44-- 菜	leeks, scallions.

1111_0

北 〔Peh〕 *n.* north, *adj.* northern, arctic.

00-- 方	northern regions, the North.
24-- 緯	north latitude.
33-- 冰洋	the Arctic Ocean.
34-- 斗	Charles' Wain, the Plough, Big Dipper.
40-- 極	the north pole.
-- 極星	the pole star, north star.
-- 極圈	arctic circle.
77-- 風	north wind.

1111_1

非 〔Fei〕 *n.* evil, wrong, *v.* blame, reproach, *adj.* bad, wrong, not right, unreal, false, *adv.* not.

00-- 主流	non-principal.
-- 交戰國	non-belligerent.
04-- 熟練工人	odd-job worker, unskilled worker.
08-- 議	criticize.
10-- 正式	unofficial, informal.
-- 正式契約	informal agreement.
-- 互惠原則	principle of non-reciprocity.

-- 正義	unjust.	
14-- 耐用物品	non-durable goods.	
30-- 官方	unofficial.	
32-- 洲	Africa.	
-- 洲人	African, African people.	
33-- 必需品	nonessentials.	
34-- 法	illegal, unlawful.	
-- 法交易	illegal dealing, illicit trading, unlawful trading.	
-- 法經商	unlawful trade.	
-- 法行為	illegal act, illegal practice.	
-- 法利潤	illegal profit.	
-- 法侵佔	illegal encroachment.	
-- 法翻印	piracy.	
-- 法翻印品	pirated products.	
-- 法收入	illegal income.	
-- 法雇用	illicit employment.	
-- 法罷工	illegal strike.	
-- 法貿易	illegal trade, illicit trade.	
-- 法合同	backdoor contract, illegal contract.	
35-- 禮	indecent, improper, impolite.	
38-- 導體	non-conductor.	
40-- 難	n. criticism, imputation, v. find fault, impute, censure, bring charge against.	
-- 賣品	not for sale.	
42-- 婚生子女	illegitimate children.	
44-- 禁品	non-contraband.	
48-- 故意的	inadvertent.	
53-- 掛牌証券	unlisted securities.	
63-- 戰主義	pacifism.	
-- 戰論	anti-war argument.	
-- 戰鬥員	non-combatant.	
-- 戰公約	Kellogg Pact, Anti-war pact.	
77-- 凡	uncommon, unusual, extraordinary.	
80-- 人生活	miserable life.	
-- 金屬	non-metal.	
-- 命	unnatural death.	
-- 會員國	non-member state.	
90-- 常	unusual, uncommon, over and above, out of common run.	
-- 常重視	make much account of.	

-- 常受益	abnormal gains.
-- 常稅	extraordinary tax.
-- 常支出	extraordinary expenditure, extraordinary disbursement.
-- 常損失	abnormal loss(es) .
-- 常時期	extraordinary period, time of emergency.
99-- 營利的	uncommercial, nonprofit.
-- 營利機構	nonprofit institutions, nonprofit organizations.
-- 營利公司	nonprofit corporation.
-- 營業收入	non-business income.

玩 〔**Wan**〕 v. play, enjoy, amuse oneself with, toy with.

10-- 耍	play, toy with, amuse with playing, flirt with.
-- 弄=玩耍	
27-- 忽	neglect, ignore.
34-- 法	disregard the law.
77-- 具	toy, plaything.
-- 具室	playhouse.
88-- 笑	n. fun, v. jest, joke, make fun with.
90-- 火	play with fire.
-- 賞	enjoy, find pleasure in.

1111₂

豇 〔**Jiang**〕 n. cowpea.

1111₄

班 〔**Pan**〕 n. class, company, rank, group, squad of soldiers, v. distribute, with draw.

21-- 師	withdraw troops.
27-- 組	shifts of work, teams.
37-- 次	class of student, designated number of a bus, a train, or plane in schedule.
38-- 導師	teacher in charge of a class.
58-- 輪	liner, liner ship, liner vessel, regular steamship service, schedule steamer.
71-- 長	captain of a squad, squad leader.

斑 〔**Pan**〕 n. spot, adj. striped, variegated.

00--	疹	eruption (on the body).
--	疹傷寒	typhus.
20--	紋	streaks, stripes, mottles.
26--	白	gray.
47--	鳩	cushat, turtledove.
61--	點	spots, mottle, speck, speckles.
71--	馬	zebra.

1111_6

疆〔Chiang〕 *n.* boundary, frontier, limit, border.

43--	域	territory.
46--	場	battlefield.
60--	界	boundary, frontier.

1111_7

琥〔Huu〕 *n.* amber.

甄〔Jen〕 *v.* examine, distinguish.

53--	拔	select from many.
62--	別	screen, grade, discern.

1112_0

珂〔Ke〕 *n.* jade-like stone.

21--	羅版	collotype.

1112_7

巧〔Chiao〕 *adj.* clever, skillful, talented.

00--	言	artful words.
01--	語花言	artificial phrases and flowery words.
04--	計	clever trick, clever device, artifice.
--	計良謀	clever plan and outstanding scheme.
10--	工	artisan.
20--	手	skilled workman, skillful hand.
30--	避	evade.
40--	奪天工	divine skill displayed in a work of art.
--	克力	chocolate.
48--	幹	work ingeniously, work resourcefully.
49--	妙	clever, skillful, ingenious, artful.
--	妙手段	ingenious or clever move.
--	妙之至	sharp or witty reply.
54--	捷	witty.
--	技	trick.
80--	合	coincidence.
--	合姻緣	match made by chance.

瑪〔Ma〕 *n.* cornelian, agate.

12--	瑙	cornelian, agate.

翡〔Fei〕 *n.* malachite.

17--	翠	emerald.

1113_2

琢〔Cho〕 *v.* carve, cut, work on gem.

00--	磨	polish, carve, cut, refine, think over.
10--	工	lapidary.

1113_6

蜚〔Fei〕 *v.* fly.

01--	語	rumor.

1116_0

玷〔Tien〕 *v.* stain, spot, blot.

31--	污	smear, soil.
71--	辱	disgrace, insult, be a disgrace.
--	辱祖宗	bring shame upon one's ancestors.
--	辱聲名	fall into discredit.

1118_6

項〔Hsiang〕 *n.* neck, funds, sum of money, sort, kind, item.

44--	帶	necktie.
60--	圈	necklace.
--	目	item, article point, heading.

頸〔Jing〕 *n.* neck.

11--	項	neck.
--	背	nape.
25--	鍊	necklace.
40--	巾	neckerchief, scarf, hood.

頭〔Tou〕 *n.* head, top, chief, leader, boss, two ends of something, *adj.* first, best, beginning.

00--	痛	headache.
06--	韻	alliteration.
10--	一回	the first time.
11--	頸	neck.
--	頂	top, pate, vertex.
21--	顱	skull, head.

-- 版	front page.
24-- 緒	clues, clews, leads.
26-- 繩	hair-lace.
40-- 巾	cap, kerchief, turban, head-dress.
-- 布	scarf.
-- 皮	scalp.
42-- 垢	dandruff.
44-- 蓋骨	cranium, skull.
60-- 目	head, leader, ringleader, chieftain, cock of the loft.
-- 暈	dizzy, giddy.
62-- 號	number one, principal.
72-- 腦	brains, head.
-- 腦清醒	sanity, clear-headed.
-- 腦冷靜	sober-minded, clear-headed, cool.
-- 腦簡單	simple-minded.
-- 髮	hair.
88-- 等	first class.
-- 等艙位	first class cabin.

1120₇

琴 〔Chin〕 *n.* piano, organ, lute.

| 20-- 弦 | strings of a stringed instrument. |
| 47-- 聲 | sound of a piano (or organ, lute). |

1121₁

麗 〔Li〕 *n.* beautiful, elegant, graceful, fair, handsome, pretty, splendid, fine, glorious.

60-- 日和風	bright sun and pleasant breezes.
72-- 質天生	natural beauty.
80-- 人	beauty.
-- 人如雲	beauties are numerous like clouds.

1121₆

殭 〔Chiang〕 *adj.* stiff, rigid, stolid.

| 77-- 屍 | rigid corpse. |

1122₇

彌 〔Mi〕 *v.* reach, extend to, spread, close up, stop, fill, complete, *adj.* distant, remote, full, universal.

| 10-- 天大罪 | great sin. |

24-- 佈	extend, spread.
27-- 縫	patch up, screen from, make good.
33-- 補	make up, indemnify, recoup, make good, patch up, retrieve.
-- 補損失	make good the loss.
-- 補過失	make up for a fault.
34-- 遠	still further.
36-- 漫	widespread, suffused, smoky.
58-- 撒	mass.

背 〔Pei〕 *n.* back, rear, opposite, reverse, back side, *v.* turn the back on, carry on the back, repeat, remember by rote, break, violate.

00-- 主	desert one's master.
-- 主忘恩	turn the back on a master, forgetting his kindness.
-- 痛	backache.
-- 離	deviate from.
07-- 部	back.
-- 誦	recite from memory.
11-- 脊	backbone.
20-- 信	treachery, perfidy, violation of trust, double cross.
-- 信棄義	faithless, treacherous.
22-- 後	behind the back.
24-- 倚	lie back.
-- 靠背	back to back.
27-- 包	pack, knapsack.
-- 約	break a promise, discard a verbal contract, break an agreement.
33-- 心	vest, waistcoat.
-- 泳式	backstroke.
44-- 地裏	in the back.
48-- 教	apostatize.
50-- 書	*n.* endorsement, *v.* recite from memory, endorse, indorse.
-- 書人	endorser.
60-- 景	background.
-- 景畫	scene painting.
91-- 叛	*n.* rebellion, *v.* revolt, rebel, betray, fall away.

脊〔Chi〕*n.* spine, backbone, ridge.
40-- 椎　　　vertebra, spine.
-- 椎動物　　vertebrates.
-- 柱倚斜　　spinal curvature.
74-- 髓　　　spinal marrow , spinal cord.
-- 髓炎　　　myelitis.
77-- 骨　　　spine, backbone.
1123_2
張〔Chang〕*n.* leaf, sheet, piece, *v.* extend, stretch, open, increase, enlarge, set out.
07-- 望　　　look around.
08-- 放　　　open, display, set out.
14-- 弛　　　tension and relaxation.
17-- 弓　　　draw a bow.
26-- 皇　　　panic-stricken, frightened.
27-- 移　　　set a net.
40-- 力　　　tension, tensile force.
-- 大　　　*n.* expansion, enlargement, *v.* enlarge, extend, stretch, open wide, make much of.
-- 大其詞　　boastful of one's words.
-- 大其事　　exaggerate an event.
44-- 幕　　　pitch a tent.
53-- 掛　　　hang up.
56-- 揚　　　proclaim, publicize.
60-- 羅　　　raise money, receive guests.
61-- 嘴　　　open the mouth, gape.
77-- 開　　　unfold, outspread, open, spread out.
1124_0
弭〔Mi〕*n.* end of a bow, *v.* stop, put an end to, eliminate.
00-- 謗　　　stop slander.
72-- 兵　　　peace, armistice.
-- 兵之戰　　war for armistice.
1128_6
頂〔Ting〕*n.* top, peak, summit, superior, utmost, *v.* offend, go against, wear on the head, substitute, *adj.* topmost, extreme.
00-- 高　　　highest.
21-- 上　　　best, topmost.
20-- 住　　　withstand, support with the head.
27-- 角　　　vertical angle, opposite to the base of a triangle.
40-- 大　　　largest.
44-- 壞　　　worst.
45-- 樓　　　attic.
47-- 好　　　best, excellent.
55-- 替　　　substitute.
60-- 回去　　rebuff.
61-- 嘴　　　talk back, retort.
-- 點　　　summit, top.
77-- 風　　　head wind, contrary wind.
84-- 針　　　thimble.
90-- 尖　　　apex, summit, top.
預〔Yu〕*v.* participate,*adj.* prepared *adv.* beforehand, previously, in advance.
00-- 言　　　*n.* prediction, prophecy, *v.* predict, foretell, prophesy, augur.
-- 言家　　prophet.
01-- 訂　　　pre-engage, subscribe.
03-- 試　　　preliminary examination.
04-- 謀　　　premeditate, scheme in advance.
-- 計　　　premeditate, anticipate.
10-- 示　　　presage, betoken.
21-- 行演習　preliminary drill.
24-- 付　　　*n.* advance, *v.* pay in advance.
-- 先　　　in advance, in anticipation, beforehand.
-- 估　　　estimate.
-- 科　　　preparatory class.
-- 備　　　prepare, get ready, take a step.
-- 備隊　　reserves.
-- 備會議　preparatory meeting.
-- 告　　　predict, foretell, advance notice.
27-- 約　　　*n.* advance subscription, *v.* subscribe, make an appointment.
30-- 定　　　*n.* reservation, *v.* settle before-hand, reserve, prede-

		termine, expect, anticipate.
--	賽	trial or preliminary contest
32--	測	forecast, prognosis.
--	兆	presage, omen, portent, augury, auspices.
37--	選	pre-election.
--	選會	primary.
46--	想	anticipate, preconceive.
47--	報	forecast.
--	期	*n.* anticipation, foresight, *v.* look forward.
53--	感	premonition.
60--	見	*n.* foresight, *v.* foresee.
70--	防	*n.* precaution, prevention, *v.* prevent.
--	防物	preventive.
--	防藥	preventive medicine.
--	防錯誤	obviate the possibility of a mistake.
77--	覺	presage, presentiment.
86--	知	foreknowledge, premonition.
88--	算	budget.
--	算案	budget bill.
--	算書	budget statement.
-	算表	budget.
94--	料	anticipate, predict, surmise.
--	料不到	unexpected, unforeseen.

頑 〔**Wan**〕 *v.* play, *adj.* stupid, dull, doltish, obstinate, naughty, ignorant.

00--	童	mischievous boy, naughty child, urchin.
13--	強	stubborn, unyielding, tenacious.
40--	皮	naughty, mischievous.
50--	抗	recalcitrant, show a bold front.
60--	固	obstinate, stiff-necked, stubborn.
--	固派	die-hards, obstinate.
--	固分子	the die-hards.
85--	鈍	stupid, dull, stubborn.
90--	劣	stupid and stubborn.

1133_1

悲 〔**Bei**〕 *n.* sad, grief, sympathy, *v.* commiserate, be sad, grieve, lament, sympathize, *adj.* grievous, doleful.

00--	痛	*n.* grief, *adj.* heartbreaking.
--	哀	sorrowful, sad, mournful.
10--	不自勝	abandon oneself in grief.
17--	歌	monody, threnody, dirge.
22--	劇	tragedy.
--	劇重演	repeat a tragedy.
28--	傷	*v.* mourn, bewail, lament, deplore, *adj.* sad, sorrowful, mournful.
29--	愁	broken-hearted.
30--	泣	*n.* wailing, *v.* wail.
40--	喜交集	intermingling of sorrow and joy.
46--	觀	pessimism.
--	觀主義	pessimism.
--	觀者	pessimist.
60--	啼	cry bitterly.
64--	嘆	lament continually.
93--	慘	sad, miserable.
94--	慟終日	be mournful for the whole day.
--	憤	grievous and indignant.
--	憤交集	sadness and anger coming together.

瑟 〔**Se**〕 *n.* lute, harp.
1140_0
斐 〔**Fei**〕 *n.* streaks, veins, *adj.* graceful, elegant, adorned.
1142_7
孺 〔**Ju**〕 *n.* child, suckling, young child.

17--	子	suckling.
--	子牛	suckling ox.
--	子可教	the young man is worthy to be taught.

1150_6
輩 〔**Bei**〕 *n.* generation, class, kind, sort.

22--	出	appear in succession.

1161_0
砒 〔**Pi**〕 *n.* arsenic.

10--	霜	arsenic compound.
13--	酸	arsenic acid.

1161_2
砸 〔**Tzar**〕 *v.* smash.

10--	碎	break to pieces.

97-- 爛　　　　　smash.

1162₇

碼 〔 **Ma** 〕 *n.* yard, numerals, numbers.

11-- 頭　　　　　wharf, dock, jetty, pier, water, terminal, quay.

-- 頭工人　　　docker, dock hand, harbor worker.

-- 頭稅　　　　wharfage.

77-- 尺　　　　　yardstick, yard-measure.

1164₀

研 〔 **Yen** 〕 *v.* rub, grind, triturate, powder, study, examine, investigate.

10-- 碎　　　　　grind to powder.

26-- 細　　　　　grind fine.

30-- 究　　　　　study, investigate, research.

-- 究科　　　　post-graduate course.

-- 究生　　　　post-graduate student, research student.

-- 究員　　　　research member (or fellow).

-- 究院　　　　academy, research institute.

-- 究所　　　　graduate school.

-- 究津貼　　　fellowship.

矵 〔 **Yah** 〕 *v.* grind, roll.

1164₆

硬 〔 **Ying** 〕 *n.* hardness, stiffness, *adj.* hard, solid, stiff, firm, rigid, powerful, strong.

00-- 席　　　　　hard seats, wooden seats.

-- 度　　　　　hardness, temper.

10-- 要　　　　　insist, importune, be determined to have.

11-- 頸　　　　　stiff-necked.

12-- 水　　　　　hard water.

24-- 化　　　　　*v.* harden, *adj.* hardening.

25-- 仗　　　　　stiff fight, desperate combat.

31-- 逼　　　　　compel.

33-- 心　　　　　coldhearted.

-- 心之人　　　hardhearted man.

34-- 漢　　　　　man of fortitude.

40-- 套　　　　　apply arbitrarily.

-- 木　　　　　hardwood.

47-- 殼　　　　　hard shell.

-- 殼蟲　　　　beetle.

88-- 鉛筆　　　hard-pencil.

95-- 性　　　　　hardness, stiffness, obstinacy.

-- 性規定　　　rigid regulation.

98-- 幣　　　　　coin, hard cash.

1164₉

砰 〔 **Peng** 〕 *n.* crash a stone, sound of drum-beats.

19-- 磅　　　　　with a bang.

1166₀

砧 〔 **Chuo** 〕 *n.* block, anvil, block of wood or stone.

41-- 板　　　　　chopping board, block of wood.

1168₆

碩 〔 **Shuo** 〕 *adj.* great, eminent, ripe.

00-- 言　　　　　high-sounding words.

21-- 儒　　　　　eminent scholar.

40-- 士　　　　　master, master's degree, holder of the master's degree.

-- 大　　　　　prodigious.

60-- 量　　　　　broad mind, liberality.

77-- 學　　　　　great learning, great scholar.

80-- 人　　　　　pretty woman.

1171₁

琵 〔 **Pi** 〕 *n.* lute.

11-- 琶　　　　　lute, Chinese guitar, balloon-guitar.

1173₂

裴 〔 **Pei** 〕 *adv.* to and fro.

1180₁

冀 〔 **Chi** 〕 *v.* desire, hope, expect.

07-- 望　　　　　hope, expect.

1210₀

剄 〔 **Ching** 〕 *n.* cutting throat.

到 〔 **Tao** 〕 *v.* reach, arrive at, attain to, come to, *prep.* to, at, up to, till, until.

00-- 底　　　　　after all, finally, in the long run, finally, at last, in the end.

-- 底如何　　　how will it turn out after all?

17-- 那時　　　by that time.

20-- 手　　　　　receive, come to hand, fall

		into one's hand.
21--	此	come here.
	-- 處	everywhere, in every quarter, in all quarter, in all directions, far and wide, on every side.
	-- 處一樣	everywhere is the same.
	-- 處爲家	everywhere may be one's home.
22--	任	arrive at one's post.
	-- 岸重量	landed weight, landing weight, arrival weight.
	-- 岸價格	cost, insurance & freight, CIF price.
24--	貨	arrival of the goods.
	-- 貨通知	advice of arrival, cargo arrival notice.
30--	案	appear in court.
34--	達	reach, arrive, come to hand, come at.
	-- 達站	destination station, destination.
	-- 達通知單	notice of arrival.
	-- 達時間	arrival time.
	-- 達口期	date of arrival.
	-- 達港	port of arrival, port of destination.
	-- 港船	arrival vessel.
43--	來	approach, arrive.
46--	場	be present.
47--	期	*n.* maturity, in due time, at maturity, *v.* fall due, come due, mature, become due.
	-- 期日	date of maturity, maturity date, date due, day of maturity, due date, in due time.
	-- 期票據	matured bills (notes).
	-- 期價值	maturity value.
	-- 期催單	reminder of due date, in due time.
	-- 期利息	interest due.
	-- 期付款	payable at maturity, payment at maturity.
	-- 期支票	matured check (cheque).
	-- 期金額	maturity amount.
60--	目前爲止	so far, by now.
64--	時再說	speak again in due course.

80--	今	until now, up to the present.

1210_4

型 〔Hsing〕 *n.* mould, model, pattern, form, style, type.

83--	鐵	section iron, profile iron.
87--	鋼	shaped steel, structural steel.
	-- 鋼管	shaped steel pipe.

1210_8

登 〔Tent〕 *v.* ascend, mount, step up, advance, go up, attain, place on paper, record, note, register, climb up.

00--	高	mount, ascend, climb mountain.
	-- 廣告	advertise, advertise for something.
	-- 廣告徵求	advertise for.
07--	記	*n.* enrollment, registration, *v.* enroll, register, book, enlist.
	-- 記商標	registered trade mark.
	-- 記處	registry, booking office.
	-- 記員	registrar.
	-- 記簿	register, register book.
	-- 記手續	registration formality.
	-- 記註冊	register.
	-- 記標準	listing standard.
	-- 記表	registry form.
	-- 記日	record date.
	-- 記費 (註冊費)	registration fee.
10--	天	ascend to heaven.
20--	位	accession.
22--	岸	land , go ashore.
	-- 峯造極	reach the summit of achievement.
	-- 山	ascend a mountain.
	-- 山隊	mountaineering team.
	-- 山隊員	mountaineer.
23--	台	go up to the platform, appear in the stage, take up a high position.
	-- 台演說	deliver a speech from a platform.
41--	極	enthrone, come to the throne.

43-- 載	publish, carry (a news).
44-- 基	ascend the throne (coronation).
46-- 場	n. appearance, v. come up the stage.
47-- 報	advertise in a newspaper, put it in the paper.
-- 報聲明	clarify or announce by a newspaper advertisement.
61-- 賬	enter in the account.
74-- 陸	n. landing, v. land, proceed overland.
-- 陸部隊	landing forces, beach party.
-- 陸艇	landing ship, landing craft.
87-- 錄	register.

1212₇

瑞 〔Jui〕 n. happy omen, jade tablet, adj. lucky, felicitous, auspicious.

10-- 雪	auspicious snow, seasonable snow.
40-- 士	Switzerland.
55-- 典	Sweden.

1217₂

聯 〔Lien〕 n. alliance, league, v. unite, combine with, make alliance with, join, adj. connected, joined, united, associated.

00-- 席會議	joint conference, joint meeting.
20-- 繫	contact, coalition, relation.
-- 繫人	contact person.
24-- 結	n. union, v. be united with.
26-- 保	mutual security.
27-- 絡	relate, communicate, contact.
-- 絡處	liaison office.
-- 絡官	contact officer.
-- 絡員	liaison officer, liaison man.
-- 絡兵	connecting file.
-- 絡參謀	liaison officer.
-- 名	n. joint signatures, v. sign together.
-- 名請願	send a petition in joint signatures.
30-- 賽	league tournament.

37-- 運	through transportation.
-- 軍	allies, allied forces.
42-- 婚	marry, couple, tie the nuptial knot.
46-- 想	n. association, connection, v. remind, bring to one's mind.
-- 姻	alliance marriage.
47-- 歡	hold a party.
-- 歡節	festival.
57-- 邦	federated states, federation.
-- 邦預算	federal budget.
-- 邦主義	federalism.
-- 邦主義者	federalist.
-- 邦政府	federal government.
-- 邦制	federal system.
-- 邦派	federalist.
-- 邦國	confederation of states.
-- 邦同盟	federal union.
-- 邦調查局	the (U.S.) Federal Bureau of Investigation (FBI).
-- 邦所得稅	federal income tax.
-- 繫	link, contact.
-- 繫人	link.
67-- 盟	n. union, v. ally, league, adv. in alliance, with confederacy.
78-- 隊	regiment.
80-- 合	n. union, unification, combination, junction, embodiment, v. combine, unite, joint, associate.
-- 合主義	unionism.
-- 合聲明	joint statement.
-- 合國	United Nations.
-- 合國大會	General Assembly of the United Nations.
-- 合國善後救濟總署	United Nations Relief and Rehabilitation Administration.
-- 合企業	combine.
-- 合會	union, association.
89-- 鎖商店	chain stores, multiple shop, multiple store.
99-- 營	affiliation, combination, jointly run business, pool-

ing, joint venture.

-- 營公司　associated company, allied company, affiliated company, affiliated corporation, related company .

1220₀

列 〔 **Lieh** 〕 *n.* rank, series, file, row, line *v.* set in order, arrange, set forth.

00-- 席	sit, attend.
-- 席旁聽	attend the meeting as an observer.
-- 席代表	observer.
13-- 強	The Great Powers, the powerful nations, world powers.
22-- 後	as following.
30-- 寧主義	Leninism.
-- 祖列宗	array of ancestors, all the ancestors.
50-- 車	train.
-- 車員	conductor.
-- 表	list, make a list, tabulate.
75-- 陣	in battery.
77-- 舉	enumerate.
78-- 隊	dress ranks.
80-- 入	include, fall under.

引 〔 **Yin** 〕 *n.* preface, introduction, *v.* lead, guide, conduct, introduce, quote, recommend, retire, bring in, draw out, stretch, tempt, seduce.

00-- 文	quotation.
-- 言	introduction, foreword, preface.
02-- 證	quote, cite, adduce, confirm by quotation.
-- 誘	entice, seduce, tempt, lure, bring on.
08-- 論	introduction.
11-- 張	strain.
12-- 水	channel water, divert water.
21-- 例	give an example, produce an instance, cite a case.
-- 經據典	quote authoritative works.
22-- 出	elicit, lead out, bring out.
26-- 線	fuse, guide, spy.

27-- 向	lead to.
-- 句號	inverted commas.
28-- 以爲誇	boast of.
-- 以爲慰	take comfort in.
-- 以爲榮	take pride in.
-- 咎辭職	take the blame and resign.
30-- 進	introduce.
-- 渡	*n.* extradition , *v.* extradite.
37-- 退	retire.
38-- 導	lead, guide, usher, conduct, conduce, instruct.
40-- 力	attraction, gravitation.
42-- 橋	the approach span of a bridge.
47-- 起	lead to, induce, draw upon, cause, open the door to.
-- 起爭論	controversial.
-- 起注意	attract attention.
-- 起暴動	raise a riot.
48-- 擎	engine.
50-- 申	amplify, extend (the meaning).
60-- 見	introduce to a superior.
61-- 號	quotation mark.
67-- 路	lead the way.
71-- 長	prolong.
77-- 用	quote, cite.
-- 用語	quotation.
-- 用私人	employ one's favorite.
-- 用良才	employ a talented person.
80-- 入	led in, usher in, bring in.
-- 入歧途	led astray.
-- 人注意	catch the attention of other people.
-- 人注目	noticeable, conspicuous.
-- 人發笑	make one laugh.
-- 人入勝	fascinating, attractive, alluring.
90-- 火	light, set fire, strike a light, kindle a fire.
-- 火物	lighter, igniter.

1221₇

凳 〔 **Teng** 〕 *n.* bench, stool.

1223₀

水 〔 **Shui** 〕 *n.* water, stream, fluid, liquid,

flood, inundation, *adj.* watery.

00--	痘	chicken pox.
--	療法	hydropathy, hydrotherapy.
--	產	marine products, aquatic products.
--	底	bed, seabed, seafloor.
--	庫	reservoir.
--	文	hydrology.
--	文站	hydrographic station.
--	文工作者	hydrologist.
--	文地理	hydrography.
--	甕	pitcher.
01--	龍頭	faucet, tap, fire engines.
--	龍帶	hose.
08--	族	aquatic tribes.
--	族館	aquarium.
10--	下	underwater, submarine.
--	泵	pump.
--	平	level, standard.
--	平面	horizontal plane, water level.
--	平線	level, horizontal line.
--	平儀	level, leveling instrument.
--	雷	torpedo, mine.
--	雷艇	minelayer.
--	面	water level.
--	電站	hydro-power station.
13--	球	water polo.
20--	手	sailor, seaman, crew, mariners, navigator.
--	位	water level.
21--	上飛機	sea-craft, seaplane.
--	上運動	aquatic sports.
--	上警察	water police.
--	上人家	boat dwellers.
--	師	marine troops.
22--	利	water beneficial to agriculture, watering irrigation, water conservancy.
--	利化	bring all farmland under irrigation.
--	利局	conservancy bureau.
--	彩	watercolor.
--	彩畫	watercolor painting.
--	仙	narcissus, daffodil.
--	災	flood, inundation.
--	稻	paddy rice.
25--	牛	buffalo.
--	生植物	aquatic plants.
26--	線	water line.
26--	程	voyage.
27--	鳥	water bird, waterfowl.
30--	流	water current.
--	流量	discharge of water.
--	牢	water cell.
31--	漲	tide flows, inundate.
--	源	source of water.
--	渠	irrigation canal.
34--	池	pool, basin, pond.
--	波	wave, ripples.
35--	溝	drain, ditch.
--	沫	foam, froth.
--	漬	stained by water, water stains.
36--	邊	waterside.
37--	泡	blister, bubble.
--	泥	cement.
--	泥廠	cement works (or plant).
--	運	water transport.
38--	道	waterway, watercourse.
40--	力	hydropower, waterpower.
--	力發電機	water-motor.
--	力學	hydraulics.
40--	壺	pitcher, jug, kettle.
41--	壩	dam.
44--	塔	water tower.
--	芹菜	cress.
--	蒸氣	steam, water vapor.
--	草	aquatic plants.
45--	槽	gutter, cistern.
47--	獺	otter, beaver.
--	桶	bucket, pail.
48--	松	yew.
50--	車	water wheel, water mill.
51--	蛭	leech.
53--	蛇	water snake.
60--	田	paddy field, irrigated land.
--	星	planet Mercury.
--	墨畫	Chinese monochrome.
--	晶	crystal.
--	果	fruit.
67--	路	waterway, watercourse.
71--	壓機	hydraulic press.
72--	腫	dropsy.

74-- 陸交通	land and water communications.
-- 陸作戰部隊	amphibious forces.
-- 陸兩用	amphibious.
77-- 閘	flood gate, dam.
78-- 險	marine insurance.
80-- 盆	basin.
-- 分	moisture, humidity.
-- 餃	ravioli, dumping.
81-- 缸	water jar.
87-- 銀	mercury, quicksilver.
-- 銀柱	mercury column.
-- 銀燈	mercury lamp.
88-- 管	water-pipe.
91-- 煙筒	water pipe.
95-- 性楊花	fickle and lascivious.

弧 〔Hu〕 n. wooden bow, arc.

00-- 度	radian.
10-- 三角	spherical trigonometry.
12-- 形	bow-shaped, spherical.
90-- 光	arc light.
-- 光燈	arc light lamp.

1223₄

殀 〔Yao〕 v. die prematurely.

1224₇

發 〔Fa〕 v. send forth, throw out, issue forth, spring up, utter, ferment, rise, begin, start, express, pay out, proceed.

00-- 麻	be numbed.
-- 瘋	go mad.
-- 病	fall ill.
-- 病率	rate of incidence of diseases.
-- 癲	become mad.
-- 亮	polished, shining.
-- 育	grow, bloom.
-- 育心理學	genetic psychology.
-- 育障礙	arrested development.
-- 高燒	have a high fever.
-- 音	pronounce.
-- 音法	pronunciation.
-- 音學	phonetics.
-- 言	speak, utter, deliver, break silence.
-- 言權	voice, say, the right to speak.
-- 言人	spokesman.
-- 市	have customers, get customers, begin business.
02-- 端	n. outset, beginning, v. rise, originate.
08-- 議	bring up proposals.
-- 放證件	issue certificate.
-- 放貸款	offer loans, extend a loan.
10-- 工資	issue pay, pay salaries (wages).
-- 霉	mould, grow mouldy, mildew, go moldy.
-- 電	generate electricity, power generation, cable, wire, telegraph.
-- 電廠	power plant, power house.
-- 電設備	generating equipment.
-- 電站	power station.
-- 電機	electric generator, dynamo.
-- 電報	cable, telegraph.
-- 電量	electricity output, generating capacity.
-- 電所	generating station.
-- 票	bill of sales, invoice, receipt, bill.
-- 票地	place of issue.
-- 票人	drawer.
-- 票價格	invoice price.
-- 票金額	amount of invoice, invoice amount, invoiced value.
-- 票存根	invoice stub.
-- 票日期	date of draft, date of invoice, invoice date.
-- 票號	invoice number, invoice No.
-- 票簿	invoice book.
-- 不義之財	become wealthy by illegal and dishonest methods.
12-- 刊詞	introduction, preface, prologue.
-- 球	serve a ball.
14-- 酵	fermentation.
16-- 現	discover, appear, turn up, lay bare, crop out.
20-- 信	dispatch a letter, send out

		a letter.
-- 信人	sender of a letter.
-- 售	sell, put on sale.
21-- 行	publish, issue, wholesale.
-- 行者	publisher.
-- 行所	head office, main office, sales office.
-- 行證券	float securities.
-- 行日	date of issue.
-- 行股票	stock issue, capital issue, issue of shares, issue shares.
22-- 出	issue, proceed, send out, send forth.
-- 出訂單	place (placing) an order.
-- 出招標	put out to tender.
23-- 獃	become stupefied.
24-- 動	move, mobilize, launch, set on foot, stir, press the button.
--動機	engine, motor.
-- 射	shoot, launch.
-- 射台	launching pad.
-- 射場	launching site.
-- 佈	proclaim, issue.
-- 貨	issue goods, dispatch goods, deliver goods, send out goods, consign.
-- 貨站	shipping center.
-- 貨室	shipping room.
-- 貨通知	consignment note, notice of. shipment goods, shipping order, letter of advice.
-- 貨通知單	advice of dispatch.
-- 貨日期	date of dispatch.
-- 貨單	dispatch list.
-- 貨人	consignor, shipper, sender.
25-- 生	happen, generate, breed, bring on, take place, come to pass.
-- 生器	generator.
-- 生學	embryology.
27-- 急	get excited.
-- 包	awarding contract, issuing contract.
-- 包工程	contracting construction.
28-- 作	break out.
-- 條	coiled spring.

-- 給	give, issue.
-- 給証明	issue a certificate.
-- 給證明單	issue a certificate.
-- 給簽証	issue a visa.
29-- 愁	worry, feel sad.
30-- 牢騷	complain, grumble.
31-- 汗	sweat, perspire.
-- 源地	fountainhead, cradle, place of origin.
-- 福	become fat.
34-- 泄	vent.
-- 達	develop, get ahead, prosper.
-- 達經濟	advanced economy.
-- 達的	developed, flourishing.
-- 達國家	developed countries, developed nations .
35-- 津貼	give allowances.
-- 洩	let out, pour forth, express, vent.
36-- 還	return.
38-- 送數量	quantity originated.
40-- 奮	strive, exert one's energy.
-- 大財	make a killing.
41-- 狂	get mad, go crazy, become insane, lose one's wit, be beside oneself.
44-- 落	dispose.
-- 芽	sprout, bud, germinate.
-- 薪日	pay day.
45-- 熱	n. fever, v. feel feverish.
47-- 怒	anger, rage, get one's back up, lose one's temper.
-- 起	promote, sponsor, originate, initiate.
-- 起國	sponsoring country, founding nation.
-- 起人	promoter, sponsor, initiator, founder, organizer, original founder.
50-- 表	reveal, express, bring forth, notify, publish.
52-- 誓	take oath, vow, make a vow.
53-- 威	bristle up, get one's back up.
54-- 抖	shiver, shudder, tremble.
56-- 揚民主	promote democracy.
-- 揚光大	promote, enhance.
57-- 揮	exert, develop, explicate,

	給play to.	give play to.
-- 揮作用	produce a marked effect.
-- 掘	excavate, uncover.
60-- 見	discover, make to light.
-- 暈	get giddy.
61-- 嘑	laugh.
64-- 財	*n.* prosper by becoming wealthy, *v.* make money, make fortune, get rich, take in the dough.
67-- 明	invent, bring to light.
-- 明家	inventor.
-- 明人	inventor.
-- 明人證單	inventor's certificate.
-- 明專利權	patent for invention.
72-- 昏	faint, fall into a swoon, be giddy.
76-- 脾氣	lose one's temper, become angry.
77-- 覺	find out, be discovered, come to light.
-- 展	*n.* development, *v.* grow, expand, develop.
-- 展項目	development project.
-- 展階段	development stage.
-- 展經費	development expense.
-- 展中國家	developing countries.
-- 問	question.
-- 悶	feel gloomy.
80-- 令	give command, order.
88-- 笑	laugh, bring about a laugh.
90-- 光	enlighten, radiate, shine.
-- 光體	shiner, luminous body.
-- 火	get angry.
-- 炎	inflammation.
94-- 慌	be upset, become confused.
-- 燒	have a fever.
-- 憤	make great efforts, shake one's self together.

1233₀

烈 〔 **Lieh** 〕 *adj.* burning, fiery, energetic, high-principled.

40-- 士	hero, patriot, martyr.
-- 女	virtuous woman, woman of strong character.
60-- 日	blazing sun.
71-- 馬	spirited horse.
77-- 風	hurricane, violent wind.
-- 屬	family of a martyr.
90-- 火	very hot fire, raging fire.
95-- 性	violent temper.
-- 性酒	spirits, strong wine.

1240₀

刊 〔 **Kan** 〕 *v.* publish, cut, chop, hew, carve.

21-- 行	*n.* publication, *v.* publish.
27-- 物	journal, periodical, publication.
40-- 布	set forth, give to the world, publish.
-- 本	edition.
43-- 載	carry, publish.
77-- 印	print, publish.

刑 〔 **Hsing** 〕 *n.* punishment, penalty, torture.

00-- 庭	criminal court.
07-- 訊	put to the torture, third degree, exact confession through torture.
27-- 網難逃	hard to escape the meshes of law.
34-- 法	penal law, criminal law, penal code.
-- 法學	penology.
46-- 場	execution ground.
47-- 期	term or penalty.
50-- 事	criminal case.
-- 事訴訟	criminal action.
-- 事訴訟法	the law of criminal procedure.
-- 事案	criminal case.
-- 事裁判	criminal trial.
-- 事裁判所	criminal court.
-- 事裁判權	power of criminal trial.
-- 事訴訟法	code of criminal procedure.
-- 事犯	criminal.
60-- 罰	penalty, punishment pains and penalties.
-- 罰學	penology.

1240₁

廷 〔 **Ting** 〕 *n.* court, palace.

00-- 議	court discussion.

延 〔 **Yen** 〕 *v.* delay, postpone, protract, defer, extend, prolong, lengthen, invite, bring.

05-- 請	invite.
06-- 誤	delay.
15-- 聘	invite the service of, engage.
22-- 緩	delay, put off, fall behind, hold over.
-- 緩爆炸彈	delayed-action bomb.
25-- 伸	extend.
37-- 遲=延緩	
47-- 期	postpone, delay, lie over, defer.
-- 期償付	moratorium, delay payment.
57-- 擱	detain, defer, stay, lay aside.
58-- 攬人才	employ talents.
60-- 見	give audience to, grant an interview with.
71-- 長	prolong, protract, extend, spin out.
74-- 髓	medulla oblongata.
80-- 年益壽	lengthen one's life.

1241_0

孔 〔 **Kung** 〕 *n.* hole, orifice, pore, opening, os.

17-- 子	Confucius.
30-- 穴	hole, aperture, opening.
48-- 教	Confucianism.
90-- 雀	peacock.

1241_3

飛 〔 **Fei** 〕 *v.* fly, *adj.* speedy, fast, high, hanging in the air.

14-- 碟	flying saucer.
16-- 彈	missile.
20-- 往	fly to.
21-- 步	tearing pace.
-- 行	*n.* flight, aviation, *v.* fly.
-- 行術	aviation.
-- 行險	flight risk.
-- 行家	aviator, airman, flying man.
-- 行甲板	flight deck.
-- 行員	pilot, flyer, aviator.
-- 行場	airfield, flying field.
-- 行列車	fly train.
-- 行堡壘	flying fortress.
-- 行人員	air-crew.
22-- 艇	flying boat, airship.
27-- 魚	flying fish.
-- 船	airship.
32-- 漲	go up with a rush, rocket, soar, skyrocket, skyrocketing.
33-- 濺	sputter.
39-- 沙	blown sand.
40-- 奔	hurry, scudding.
-- 去	fly away.
42-- 機	plane, airplane, flying machine.
-- 機失事	aircraft accident, plane crash.
-- 機場	airfield, airport.
-- 機棚	hanger.
-- 機跑道	runway.
-- 機隊	squadron of air forces.
53-- 蛾	moth.
58-- 蟻	flying ant.
67-- 跑	run quickly.
-- 躍	leap forward, advance quickly.
87-- 翔	hover, soar.
95-- 快	at top speed.
99-- 螢	firefly.

1242_2

形 〔 **Hsing** 〕 *n.* form, shape, figure, appearance, condition, situation, *v.* describe, show, compare.

10-- 而上學	metaphysics.
21-- 形色色	of all shapes and colors.
21-- 態	manner, status.
-- 態學	morphology.
23-- 狀	shape, form, figure.
26-- 貌醜陋	be ugly in appearance.
27-- 像	shape, form, phase, image.
27-- 色倉皇	appear in a big hurry as a fugitive.
28-- 似	resemble, look like.
30-- 容	*n.* description, *v.* modify, describe.
-- 容詞	adjective phrase.

-- 容字　　adjective.
-- 容憔悴　sorrowful and worn-out look.
43-- 式　　form, shape model, condition.
-- 式主義　formalism.
44-- 勢　　situation, state, condition, circumstances.
-- 勢惡劣　things look bad.
-- 勢漸佳　things begin to look brighter.
-- 勢甚好　the situation is very good.
53-- 成　　form, make shape.
60-- 跡　　trace.
-- 跡可疑　behavior or manner that arouse suspicion.
63-- 影不離　inseparable like a person and his shadow.
-- 影相隨　follow someone like his shadow.
68-- 蹤詭秘　secretive in movement.
75-- 體　　body, substance, materiality.

1243₀ 孤〔Ku〕n. orphan, single, adj. alone, solitary.

00-- 立　　v. isolate, adj. unassisted, single-handed, alone, deserted.
-- 立主義　isolationism.
-- 立派　　isolationists.
17-- 子　　orphan.
20-- 僻　　v. keep to oneself, adj. eccentric.
27-- 身　　single, alone.
28-- 伶　　desolate, forlorn.
-- 傲　　aloof and arrogant.
30-- 注　　wager.
-- 注一擲　stake everything on one act.
-- 寂　　n. solitude, adj. lonely, lonesome.
44-- 苦零丁　alone and helpless, aloof from the world.
-- 枕獨眠　sleep alone on a single pillow.
46-- 獨　　alone, single, solitary, deso-

late.
77-- 兒　　orphan.
-- 兒院　　orphanage, orphan asylum.

1249₃ 孫〔Sun〕n. grandson, grandchild.
17-- 子　　grandson.
40-- 女　　grand-daughter.

1260₀ 酬〔Chou〕v. entertain, requite, repay, reward, toast.
04-- 謝　　return thanks, requite a favor.
47-- 報　　wage, reward, retribution.
80-- 金　　earning, reward, gratuity, remuneration, recompense, emolument .
-- 金菲薄　something given in return for service is pittance.
88-- 答　　repay, requite, give something in return.
99-- 勞　　reward, salary.
-- 勞獎金　reward bonus.

副〔Fu〕n. assistant, deputy, v. aid, assist, second, adj. vice, second.
00-- 主席　　vice chairman.
-- 主教　　archdeacon.
-- 產品　　by-product, accessory product, accessory substance, co-product, residual and waste product, secondary product, side-product, subsidiary products.
04-- 讀　　adverbial clause.
07-- 詞　　adverb, adverbial phrase.
-- 部長　　vice minister.
17-- 飛行員　co-pilot.
20-- 手　　assistant.
21-- 經理　　assistant director, assistant manager, deputy manager, sub-manager.
26-- 總裁　　assistant president, deputy managing director.
-- 總理　　vice-premier.
-- 總統　　vice-president.
-- 總經理　deputy managing director,

deputy general manager, assistant general manager.
-- 總編輯　　associate editor.
27-- 條件　　side conditions.
28-- 作用　　side effect, deleterious effect.
-- 業　　sideline production, subsidiary production, subsidiary business, side occupation.
-- 業產品　　sideline product.
30-- 字　　adverb.
-- 官　　aid-decamp.
32-- 業　　side line, part-time job.
40-- 本　　duplicate.
-- 本單據　　duplicate documents, the second copy.
48-- 教授　　assistant professor.
50-- 本　　copy, counterpart, duplicate.
60-- 署　　counter sign.
-- 署簽名　　countersign, countersignature.
80-- 食品　　non-staple food (food stuff), subsidiary foodstuffs.
81-- 領事　　vice consul.

1262₁
斫〔Che〕v. chop, cut, hew off.

1263₁
醺〔Shiun〕adj. drunk, intoxicated.
12-- 醺　　drunk, intoxicated.

1264₀
砥〔Chib〕n. grindstone, v. discipline, polish.
11-- 礪　　discipline, polish, smooth a difficulty.
40-- 柱　　mainstay.

1267₀
酗〔Shiuh〕v. indulge in wine, lose temper when drunk.
31-- 酒　　drink hard.

1268₉
碳〔Tann〕n. carbon.
13-- 酸　　carbonic acid.
-- 酸鈉　　soda.

24-- 化　　carbonize, carbonate.
87-- 鋼　　carbon steel.

1269₃
沓〔Tah〕v. join, connect, adj. repeated, numerous, crowded.
00-- 離　　crowded and mixed.
12-- 沓　　sluggish, talkative, running fast.

1269₄
酥〔Su〕n. curd, cheese.
35-- 油　　butter.
88-- 餅　　shortcake.
90-- 糖　　sugar cake.

礫〔Li〕n. gravel, pebble, small stones.
22-- 岩　　conglomerate.

1273₂
裂〔Lieh〕v. crack, split, rend, break, tear, rip open.
00-- 痕　　fissure, chasm.
20-- 紋　　crack.
22-- 片　　splinter.
27-- 縫　　fissure, breach.
60-- 口　　gap, crack.
77-- 開　　split open.

1290₀
剁〔To〕v. chop, cut fine, mince.
10-- 碎　　mince, chop to pieces.
40-- 肉　　mince meat.

剽〔Piao〕v. cut, stab, pierce, puncture.
30-- 竊　　plagiarize, copy.
-- 竊者　　plagiarist, copyist.
50-- 掠　　rob, plunder.

1293₀
瓢〔Piao〕n. calabash vessel, gourd, ladle.

1310₀
恥〔Chih〕n. shame, humiliation, chagrin, v. feel ashamed, blush, insult, disgrace, adj. ashamed, disgraced, humbled.
71-- 辱　　dishonor, disgrace, shame.
77-- 與爲伍　　feel ashamed to be associated with someone.
88-- 笑　　laugh at, ridicule.

1311₂

豌 〔Wan〕 *n.* garden pea.
1313_2

球 〔Chiu〕 *n.* ball, sphere, globe.
02-- 證	ball empire.
10-- 面幾何學	spherical geometry.
12-- 形	*n.* globes, *adj.* round, spherical.
39-- 迷	ball-game fan.
44-- 莖	corm, bulk.
45-- 棒	bat.
46-- 棍	bat.
-- 場	football ground, ball park.
56-- 拍	racket, bat.
60-- 員	player.
75-- 體	globe, sphere.
77-- 門	goal.
78-- 隊	team of ball players.

1314_0

武 〔Wu〕 *adj.* military, warlike, brave, fierce.
14-- 功	martial art, military merit.
-- 功隊	armed working team.
22-- 斷	*n.* arbitrary decision, *adj.* dogmatic.
24-- 備	armaments.
-- 備限制	limitation of armaments.
-- 俠	knightly, chivalrous.
-- 裝	armed, under arms.
-- 裝部隊	armed forces.
-- 裝衝突	armed conflicts.
-- 裝和平	armed peace.
-- 裝侵略	armed aggression.
-- 裝中立	armed neutrality.
30-- 官	military attache, military officer.
40-- 力	force, force of arms.
-- 力干涉	interfere by force.
-- 力解決	arbitrament of the sword, solve a problem by force, solution through the use of force.
-- 力壓制	dragoon.
-- 士	*n.* cavalier, samurai, heroic fighter, chivalrousness, warrior, knight.
-- 士制度	chivalry.
-- 士氣概	chivalry.
44-- 藝	military arts.
-- 藝超群	excellent in martial arts.
66-- 器	arms, weapons.
-- 器競爭	arms race.
-- 器庫	arsenal, armory.
77-- 鬥	wage a struggle by force.

玳 〔Day〕 *n.* the tortoise shell.
16-- 瑁	hawksbill turtle.

1315_0

職 〔Chih〕 *n.* duty, position, post, office, service, occupation, title.
10-- 工	staff and workers.
-- 工組合	trade union.
17-- 務	duty, work, office, service, business.
20-- 位	situation, office, post, appointment, official rank.
21-- 能	functional authority.
22-- 任＝職務	
30-- 官	government officials.
32-- 業	occupation, employment, profession, vocation.
-- 業病	occupational disease, professional sickness.
-- 業外交家	career diplomat.
-- 業的	professional.
-- 業學生	professional students.
-- 業學校	vocational school.
-- 業介紹	labor exchange.
-- 業介紹所	employment office, employment agency.
44-- 權	obligation and right, functions and powers.
-- 權處分	disposal by official right.
-- 權範圍	limits of one's functions and powers.
-- 責	responsibility.
-- 責所在	duty-bound.
60-- 員	clerk, staff, officials, functionary.

1320_2

弘 〔Hung〕 *adj.* large, great, vast.
40-- 大	huge, very large.
60-- 量	liberal-minded.

1323₆

強 〔Chiang〕 *n.* compel, strengthen, force, *adj.* strong, powerful, forcible, violent.

00--	度	intensity, strength.
--	辯	argue arbitrarily, argue willfully, face it out.
07--	記	*n.* weary memory, *v.* try hard to remember.
--	調	emphasize, stress.
08--	敵	formidable enemy.
10--	霸	take by force.
11--	硬	thick-ribbed, stubborn, rigid.
12--	烈	violent, intense.
17--	弱	strong and weak.
21--	佔	seize, usurp, take by force, occupy by force.
22--	制	oblige, force, coerce.
--	制處分	subject to a forcible measure, compulsory execution.
--	制執行	execute forcibly.
24--	壯	strong and healthy, stout, full of life.
25--	健	healthy, strong, robust, vigorous of good health.
30--	渡	forced crossing, force-cross a river.
33--	心針	heart stimulant.
36--	迫	*n.* compulsion, coercion, *v.* compel, force, press, constrain.
--	迫教育	compulsory education.
--	迫降落	emergency landing, forced landing.
37--	盜	robber, highway-man, bandit, brigand.
40--	大	powerful, mighty.
--	有力	strong, vigorous.
--	姦	rape, violate, ravish, commit a rape.
--	姦罪	violation of woman, rape.
43--	求	demand urgently, importune.
44--	權	brute force.
--	橫	violent.
46--	加	impose upon, force.
53--	盛	strong and prosperous.
58--	搶	snatch, rob.
60--	國	powerful country.
--	暴	*v.* rape, *adj.* violent, overbearing, outrageous.
71--	壓	oppress.
77--	風	gale.
80--	入	break into.
96--	悍	impetuous.

1325₀

戮 〔Lu〕 *v.* slay, kill, slaughter.

40--	力	by one effort, with great effort.
77--	民	oppress the people.

戳 〔Cho〕 *n.* stamp, seal, *v.* stab, pierce, punch, oppress, kill, massacre, slaughter.

28--	傷	wounded by stabbing.
40--	力	join forces.

殲 〔Chien〕 *v.* kill, exterminate, destroy, extirpate.

00--	敵	destroy the enemy.
33--	滅	annihilate, exterminate, extirpate.
--	滅戰	war of annihilation.
57--	擊機	fighter plane.

1325₃

殘 〔Tsan〕 *n.* remainder, leftover, *v.* injure, spoil, destroy, ruin, damage, kill, *adj.* spoiled, useless, cruel, ruined, crippled.

00--	廢	*n.* deformity, *adj.* disabled, crippled.
--	廢院	asylum for the disabled.
--	廢償金	disability benefit.
--	廢補助金	disability pension.
--	廢險	disability insurance.
10--	而不廢	disabled but useful.
--	疾	deformed, maimed.
14--	酷	cruel, harsh, merciless, ruthless.
17--	忍	cruel, harsh, hardhearted, inhuman.
--	忍刻薄	cruel and cold-hearted.

13-- 戮無辜　　ruthless slaughter of the innocent.
25-- 生何望　　what can I hope in my closing years?
27-- 物　　　　remainder, relics.
30-- 害　　　　injure, destroy, damage.
34-- 渣　　　　dregs and remnants.
44-- 枝　　　　stump.
　 -- 花　　　　withered flower.
47-- 殺　　　　slay, butcher, slaughter, massacre.
60-- 暴　　　　atrocious, brutal, violent.
62-- 喘苟延　　the last breath is delayed.
72-- 兵敗將　　the remnants of a defeated army.
76-- 陽山落　　the setting sun falls behind the hill.
80-- 年　　　　old age, declining years.
　 -- 年多病　　be prone to illness in the failing years.
85-- 缺　　　　imperfect, deficient, incomplete.
　 -- 缺不全　　incomplete.
88-- 餘　　　　remainder, remnant, residue.
　 -- 餘消滅　　the remnants were annihilated.

1326₀
殆 〔Tai〕 adj. dangerous, perilous, tired, adv. perhaps, probably, almost, nearly.
10-- 至一載　　nearly a year.
　 -- 不可能　　that is scarcely possible.
17-- 及　　　　nearly.
80-- 無價值　　it has but little value.

1328₆
殯 〔Pin〕 n. burial, funeral, v. carry to burial, put a corpse in the coffin.
18-- 殮遺骸　　dress and prepare the remains for a coffin.
28-- 儀館　　　funeral parlor.
44-- 葬　　　　bury, inter.

1361₂
碗 〔Wan〕 n. bowl.
41-- 櫃　　　　cupboard.
88-- 筷　　　　bowls and chopsticks.

1364₇
酸 〔Suan〕 n. acid. adj. sour, painful, sad, grieved, aching, jealous, envious.
00-- 辛　　　　bitter, miserable.
05-- 辣湯　　　sour-pepper soup.
14-- 醋　　　　vinegar.
24-- 甜苦辣　　all the sweet and bitter experiences of life.
33-- 心　　　　sick at heart.
44-- 黃瓜　　　sour cucumber.
　 -- 菜　　　　pickles.
60-- 果　　　　pickles.
65-- 味　　　　sour, acidity.
　 -- 味飲料　　sour or acid drinks.
95-- 性　　　　acid, acidity.

1365₀
硪 〔Er〕 n. stone-pounded.
17-- 子　　　　stone-pounded.

1368₁
碇 〔Ting〕 v. come to anchor.
36-- 泊　　　　come to anchor, take a berth.

1411₂
耽 〔Dan〕 v. love, revel, delay, be addicted to.
06-- 誤　　　　delay, lose time.
08-- 於享樂　　surrender oneself to pleasure.
　 -- 於惡習　　surrender oneself to a bad habit.
　 -- 於奢侈　　repose in the lap of luxury.
　 -- 於思慮　　be sunk in thoughts.
22-- 樂　　　　indulge in pleasure.
37-- 溺　　　　revel, be addicted.
57-- 擱　　　　delay, linger.

1412₁
琦 〔Chi〕 n. valuable gem.

1412₇
功 〔Kung〕 n. merit, achievement, efficacy, accomplishment, honor, adj. meritorious.
00-- 率　　　　power (in mechanics).
　 -- 率曲線　　power curve.
06-- 課　　　　lesson, work, task, school

		work.
	-- 課表	time table.
08--	效	effect, efficacy.
	-- 效如神	as effective as a god.
10--	不可沒	the contribution cannot be left unrecognized.
	-- 不補過	demerits outweigh merits.
21--	能	function.
	-- 能報酬	functional return.
22--	利主義	the political and moral theory of utilitarian, utilitarianism.
	-- 利主義者	utilitarian.
24--	德	virtuous deeds.
	-- 德無量	the merits are beyond bounds.
	-- 勳	meritorious deeds.
25--	績	achievements.
	-- 績獎金	merit bonus.
27--	名	honor, rank, degree, official rank.
	-- 名富貴	fame, wealth and honor.
37--	過	merits and faults.
	-- 過相抵	merits equal demerits.
50--	夫	martial arts, work, service, ability, effort.
53--	成身退	retire after having made one's mark.
	-- 成名就	achieve success and acquire fame.
71--	臣	meritorious statesman.
77--	用	use, effect, function.
99--	勞	merit, credit, achievement.

勁〔**Ching**〕*n.* energy, strength. *adj.* strong, powerful, stiff, hard.

08--	敵	powerful foes.
11--	頭	energy, strength, zeal.
	-- 頭足	with great zeal.
40--	力	strength, energy.

1413₁

聽〔**Ting**〕*v.* hear, listen to, obey, comply, allow, wait, manage, govern, let, allow.

02--	話	obey.
05--	講	attend a lecture.
06--	課	attend a lecture, attend class.
08--	說	hearsay, it is said that.
	-- 診器	stethoscope.
10--	而不聞	hear but pay no attention.
	-- 不清	unable to hear clearly.
	-- 天由命	resign to one's fate or God's will, be fatalistic.
12--	到	hear.
17--	取	hear.
20--	信讒言	hear and believe slanders.
22--	任	leave, allow, let.
26--	得入神	completely absorbed.
27--	眾	audience.
	-- 候	wait for.
	-- 候佳音	waiting for good news.
28--	從	obey, comply, agree with, listen to.
44--	者	auditor, hearer.
51--	指揮	obey orders.
77--	覺	sense of hearing, auditory faculty.
80--	差	attendant.
	-- 命	obey, do one's bidding.
88--	管	receiver (of a telephone).

琺〔**Fah**〕*n.* enamel, enamelware.

13--	琅	enamel.

1413₄

瑛〔**Ying**〕*n.* lustre of a gem.

1414₇

玻〔**Po**〕*n.* glass.

10--	璃	glass.
	-- 璃珠	glass beads.
	-- 璃紙	cellophane.
	-- 璃片	window glass, glass plate.
	-- 璃板	plate-glass.
	-- 璃匠	glass blower.
	-- 璃光	glaze.
	-- 璃杯	glass cup, glass, tumbler.
	-- 璃器皿	glassware.
	-- 璃管	glass tube.
	-- 璃工業	glass industry.

豉〔**Shih**〕*n.* salted bean.

35--	油	soy sauce.

1419₀

琳〔**Lin**〕*n.* valuable jade.

13--	琅	fine pieces of jade.

| -- 琅滿目 | very array of beautiful and fine things. |

1420_0

耐〔**Nai**〕 v. bear, stand, endure, suffer, forbear, last, adj. patient.

27-- 久	v. last, endure, stand, wear, well, lasting long, adj. durable.
-- 久的	durable.
-- 久力	durability.
30-- 穿	durable to wear.
-- 寒	able to endure cold.
33-- 心	patience.
-- 心等候	wait for with great patience.
-- 心探究	having patience to make a thorough investigation.
40-- 力	endurance.
44-- 苦	hardy.
77-- 用	durable.
90-- 火	fireproof.
-- 火磚	firebrick.
-- 火材料	refractories, fire-resistant material, flame resistant materials.
91-- 煩	be patient.
99-- 勞	able to endure hardship.
-- 勞刻苦	able to toil for a long time and to suffer hardship.

1421_2

弛〔**Shih**〕 v. relax, slacken, loose, lax, unstring a bow.

08-- 放	relax, loosen, let go.
27-- 解管束	loosen the control.
40-- 力	relax one's strength.

1421_7

殖〔**Chih**〕 v. produce, grow, cultivate, plant, prosper, flourish, thrive.

77-- 民	colonize, settle.
-- 民主義	colonialism.
-- 民主義者	colonialist.
-- 民統治	colonial rule.
-- 民的	colonial.
-- 民地	colony, settlement.
-- 民地化	colonization.
-- 民政策	colonial policy.
-- 民教育	colonial education.

1426_0

豬〔**Chu**〕 n. pig, hog.

20-- 毛	hog's bristle.
35-- 油	lard.
40-- 肉	pork.
47-- 欄	pigsty.
62-- 叫	grunt.

1461_2

酖〔**Chen**〕 adj. given to drink, fond of the bottle.

1461_4

確〔**Chueh**〕 adj. hard, solid, firm, certain, sure, adv. really, truly, certainly, indeed.

00-- 立	build up.
-- 言	assure.
02-- 證	infallible proofs, firmly established evidence.
07-- 認	n. identification, affirmation, v. affirm.
20-- 信	firmly believe, rest assured, be sure of, be certain of.
23-- 然	certain, sure, sure as fate, for certain.
26-- 保	assure, guarantee.
30-- 實	true, certain, actual, accurate, exact, surely, indeed, really, actually, truly.
-- 定	v. decide, determine, make sure, fix, adj. firm, definite.
40-- 有其事	it actually happened.
-- 有其人	there is indeed such a person.
47-- 切	certain, definite, exact.
86-- 知	be fully assured of.

1461_6

醃〔**Yen**〕 v. salt, cure, pickle, adj. salted, pickled.

27-- 魚	salted fish.
40-- 肉	bacon, salted meat.
44-- 菜	pickles, pickled vegetables.

1461_7

磕〔**Ko**〕 v. knock, bump.

| 11-- 頭 | kowtow. |
| -- 頭行禮 | perform the ceremony of |

kowtowing.

1463_1

砝 〔Fa〕 *n.* steelyard weight.

11--	碼	steelyard weight, weight.

1464_7

破 〔Po〕 *v.* break, split, ruin, defeat, conquer, lay bare, *adj.* broken, ruined, injured, destroyed.

00--	產	*n.* bankruptcy, *v.* bankrupt, to overrun the constable, become impoverished, go bankrupt, go to pot, go to smash, play smash, ruin.
--	產法	law of bankruptcy, bankrupt law, insolvent law.
--	產者	bankrupt.
07--	記錄	break record.
--	記錄者	record breaker.
10--	天荒	unprecedented.
--	碎	broken into pieces, fracture, breakage.
12--	裂	*v.* break, burst, rupture, *adj.* cracked, broken.
22--	例	break a rule, make an exception.
23--	綻	rent, flaw, weak point.
27--	身	be deflowered, be raped.
--	約	*n.* rejection, *v.* break an engagement.
--	包	packing torn, torn bags.
--	船	shipwreck.
28--	傷風	tetanus.
30--	案	clear up a case, solve a criminal case.
32--	冰船	icebreaker, ice cutter.
33--	滅	wreck, vanish, come to nothing.
40--	土	break ground.
--	布	rags.
--	壞	destroy, violate, demolish, sabotage.
--	壞秩序	violation of social order.
--	壞力	destructive power.
44--	落戶	decayed family, declining family.
--	獲	discover a criminal case

		and make arrests.
--	舊	worn out.
47--	格	break the rule, make an exception.
52--	折號	dash (—)(-).
55--	費	spend money, squander.
56--	損	breakage, wreck, damaged from crushing.
60--	口	abuse, rebuke.
64--	財	lose property, lose money.
--	曉	daybreak, dawn.
77--	開	split open, break open.
--	屋	ruined house.
78--	除	break away, do away with.
80--	釜沈舟	burn one's boat, burn one's bridge.
97--	爛	ragged, tattered, broken.
--	爛貨	rubbish, useless thing.

酵 〔Shiao〕 *n.* yeast, leaven.

50--	素	ferment, yeast.
77--	母	yeast, ferment.

1466_1

酷 〔Ku〕 *adj.* cruel, tyrannical, oppressive, brutal, *adv.* extremely, very.

12--	刑	torture.
20--	愛	very fond of, devoted to, ardent love.
21--	虐	harsh, tyrannical, cruel.
28--	似	be much like, as like as two peas.
44--	熱	scorching, sultry.
60--	暑	extremely hot.
--	暑迫人	the hot summer is intolerable.
90--	肖	very similar.

醋 〔Tsu〕 *n.* vinegar.

00--	意熾烈	burning with jealousy.
13--	酸	acetic acid.
38--	海生波	disturbance due to jealousy.

1467_0

酣 〔Han〕 *v.* enjoy drinking, *adj.* merry from wine.

10--	醉	drunk, tipsy, intoxicated.
17--	歌	sing in a tipsy way, sing happily after drinking.

62-- 睡 sleep soundly.

87-- 飲 drink to intoxication, drink much.

1468_1

礎 〔Chu〕 n. base, foundation, basis.

1468_6

磺 〔Hwang〕 n. sulphur, brimstone.

13-- 酸 sulfonic acid.

-- 酸藥品 sulfa drug.

1469_4

碟 〔Tieh〕 n. dish, plate, saucer.

17-- 子 plate, dish, saucer.

46-- 架 plate rack.

1512_7

聘 〔Pin〕 v. engage, invite with, pay a visit.

05-- 請 invite, employ, engage.

22-- 任 appoint to position.

30-- 定 engaged.

50-- 書 contract for employment.

77-- 用單 appointment letter, letter of appointment, letter of engagement.

80-- 金 money paid at a betrothal.

1519_0

珠 〔Chu〕 n. pearl, bead.

17-- 子 pearl, bead.

30-- 寶 gems, jewelry.

-- 寶商 jeweler.

-- 寶店 jeweler's shop.

-- 寶箱 coffer.

31-- 江 the Pearl River.

44-- 花 flower of pearls.

50-- 串 string of pearls.

1519_4

臻 〔Jen〕 n. the highest degree, best, utmost, v. reach, arrive at.

1523_0

殃 〔Yang〕 n. misfortune, calamity, accident, adj. calamitous.

17-- 及池魚 bring disaster to the fish in the moat--cause trouble to the innocent.

-- 及無辜 involve innocent people in trouble.

77-- 民禍國 injure the masses and bring disaster to the country.

1523_6

融 〔Jung〕 v. melt, dissolve, compromise, harmonize.

24-- 化 dissolve, melt, thaw.

26-- 和 compromise, harmonize.

38-- 洽 accord, harmonize, understand fully, blend with.

1529_0

殊 〔Shu〕 v. kill, exterminate, extinguish, slaughter, v. define, mark of, distinguish, adj. different, unlike, adv. really, very, extremely.

10-- 死戰 fight to the death, last ditch battle.

-- 不可解 really difficult to understand.

14-- 功 special merit.

28-- 俗 strange custom.

34-- 爲可惜 that is too bad.

37-- 深 extremely.

38-- 途同歸 all roads lead to Rome.

44-- 堪嘉尙 really deserving commendation.

-- 甚 extremely, very much.

53-- 感欣慰 feel much satisfied.

99-- 榮 special honor.

1540_0

建 〔Chien〕 v. establish, build, set up, found, construct, organize, constitute, suggest.

00-- 立 build, erect, found, establish.

-- 立功勳 do a meritorious deed.

-- 立信心 build confidence.

-- 立信用 created credit.

-- 交 establish diplomatic relations.

07-- 設 n. construction, v. construct, constitute, organize.

-- 設性 constructiveness.

08-- 議 propose, suggest, offer for consideration.

--議單	recommendation.
30 --房貸款	housing loan.
34-- 造	building, architecture.
44-- 材	building materials.
37-- 軍節	Army Day.
47-- 都	found a capital.
60-- 國	*n.* national reconstruction, *v.* found a state.
-- 國方略	Plan of National Reconstruction.
-- 國大綱	Fundamentals of National Reconstruction.
88-- 築	build, construct, erect, raise, set up.
-- 築設備	construction equipment.
-- 築工程	construction engineering, construction project, construction works.
-- 築工業	construction industry, building industry.
-- 築工人	building worker, construction worker.
-- 築貸款	building loan.
-- 築物	building, structure.
-- 築業	building industry, construction business, construction building industry.
-- 築師	architect.
-- 築學	architecture.
-- 築經費	building expenses.
-- 築材料	building materials, housing materials, construction building materials, materials of construction.
-- 築用地	building lot, building plot.
-- 築公司	building company.

1560₀

砷 〔**Shen**〕 *n.* arsenic.

13-- 酸	arsenic acid.
50-- 中毒	arsenical poisoning.

1564₃

磚 〔**Chuan**〕 *n.* brick.

00-- 廠	brickyard, brickkiln.
10-- 瓦	brick and tiles.
-- 瓦廠	brick and tile plant, brickyard.
11-- 頭	bricks.
30-- 窯	brickkiln.
40-- 土	brick-clay.
44-- 茶	brick tea.

1568₁

碘 〔**Tien**〕 *n.* iodine.

31-- 酒	tincture of iodine.

1568₆

磧 〔**Chi**〕 *n.* rocks and gravel under water.

1569₀

硃 〔**Chu**〕 *n.* vermilion.

19-- 砂	cinnabar.

1610₀

珀 〔**Po**〕 *n.* amber.

1610₄

聖 〔**Sheng**〕 *n.* sage, wisdom, *adj.* holy, sacred, divine, perfect.

02-- 誕節	Christmas.
-- 誕老人	Santa Claus.
04-- 詩	carol, hymn.
10-- 靈	holy soul, holy spirit.
17-- 歌	psalm, hymn.
21-- 旨	imperial edict, imperial decree.
-- 經	Bible, God's book, holy writ.
-- 經賢傳	sacred classics.
24-- 徒	apostle.
27-- 餐	sacrament, holy communion.
37-- 潔	sanctity.
44-- 地	holy land, sacred place.
52-- 哲	sage.
65-- 蹟	miracle, relics of a sage.
77-- 母	The Virgin, queen of grace.
-- 賢	sage.
80-- 人	saint, sage.

1611₀

現 〔**Hsien**〕 *n.* cash, *v.* manifest, appear, display, show, *adv.* now, at present, at once.

21-- 行	in force.
-- 行語	living language.
-- 行法	operative law.

22-- 出	reveal, expose, manifest.
23-- 代	modern, up-to-date, present generation.
-- 代主義	modernism.
-- 代劇	modern play.
-- 代化	modernize, make up-to-date, update.
-- 代派	modernism, modernist school.
-- 代史	modern history, contemporary history.
-- 代人	modern people.
24-- 付	cash payment.
-- 貨供應	off the shelf.
27-- 象	phenomenon.
-- 役	actual service (militias), active service (standing armies).
-- 役軍人	service man, soldier in active service, serviceman.
30-- 實	n. reality, adj. actual, real.
-- 實主義	realism.
-- 實意義	practical importance.
-- 實性	actuality.
40-- 在	now, present, actual, current, for the time being.
-- 在式	the present tense.
-- 存	on hand, in stock.
-- 有	on hand, available.
46-- 場	on-the-spot.
-- 場表演	live show, reenactment of a crime by the criminal at the same scene.
53-- 成	ready-made, prepared, at hand.
-- 成衣服	ready-made clothes.
-- 成貨	ready-made goods.
60-- 買現賣	sell something right after it is bought.
64-- 時	at present, just now, nowadays.
71-- 原形	show one's true colors, reveal one's true character or features.
80-- 金	cash, ready money.
-- 金買賣	business transaction in cash.
-- 今	nowadays, at present.
83-- 錢	hard cash, real money.
-- 錢交易	bargain for cash, real money trade.

1611₃

瑰 〔**Guei**〕 n. stone less valuable than jade, adj. precious and rare.

11-- 麗	extraordinarily beautiful.

1611₄

理 〔**Li**〕 n. law, doctrine, theory, principle, reason, v. arrange, regulate, govern, manage, look after, pay attention.

08-- 論	n. theory, v. debate, discuss
-- 論家	theorist.
24-- 科	science subject, faculty of science, department of natural sciences.
-- 化	physics and chemistry.
27-- 解	understand, comprehend, realize.
-- 解力	intellect, understanding, the faculty of understanding.
46-- 想	idea, imagination, aspiration, the mind's eye.
-- 想化	idealize.
-- 想家	idealist, thinker.
-- 想主義	idealism.
-- 想世界	ideal world, utopia.
-- 想產品	ideal product.
50-- 由	reason, argument, cause, consideration.
-- 事	member of the Executive Committee, director, manager.
-- 事會	Executive Committee, board of directors, board of management, board of governors, directorate, governing board.
60-- 賠	n. satisfaction of a claim, v. meet a claim, satisfy a claim, comply with a claim, settle a claim.

62--	睬	make notice of, pay attention.
64--	財	finance, financing.
--	財之道	the way of managing financial affairs.
--	財方法	financing method.
72--	髮	*n.* barber, hairdressing, haircut, *v.* dress the hair.
--	髮店	barber's shop, barbershop.
--	髮軋	hair-clippers.
--	髮剪	hair scissors.
--	髮匠	barber, hairdresser.
--	所當然	as a matter of course.
77--	學院	college of science.
80--	會	notice, attend to.
86--	智	intelligence, reason, wit.
90--	當	right, proper.
95--	性	*n.* reason, senses, rationality, *adj.* reasonable, rational.
--	性論	rationalism.

1613₀

聰 〔**Tsung**〕 *n.* cleverness, wisdom. *adj.* clever, bright, sharp-witted.

67--	明	clever, bright, intelligent.
--	明自誤	be ruined by one's own cleverness.
--	明絕頂	extremely clever or intelligent.
--	明活潑	clever and active, smart and lively.

1613₂

環 〔**Huan**〕 *n.* ring, bracelet, circlet, *v.* surround, go around, encircle.

08--	旋	revolve, go around.
10--	天線	frame aerial.
13--	球	round the whole world.
--	球航行	round-the-world trip.
20--	航	circumnavigate.
21--	行	go around, encircle.
24--	繞	environ, encircle, encompass, surround.
--	顧左右	look to the left and the right.
--	顧四週	look around.
26--	保項目	environmental protection project.
36--	視	look around.
38--	遊	travel around, tour.
--	遊世界	take a round-the-world tour.
40--	境	environment, surrounding.
--	境惡化	environmental degradation.
--	境破壞	environmental damage.
--	境政策	environmental policy.
--	境改良	environmental reform.
--	境衛生	environmental hygiene, environmental sanitation.
--	境保護	environmental conservation, environment protection, environmental protection.
--	境保持	environment conservation.
--	境學家	environmentalist.
88--	節	segment, link.

1616₀

瑁 〔**Mei**〕 *v.* sceptre, tortoiseshell.

1625₆

殫 〔**Tan**〕 *v.* do the utmost.

彈 〔**Tan**〕 *n.* bullet, ball, shot, pellet, shell, *v.* shoot, impeach.

04--	劾	impeach.
11--	琴	play piano.
--	琴娛賓	amuse the guest by playing the harp.
12--	孔	shot-hole.
17--	子	bullet, ball, pellet.
--	子房	billiard-room.
--	子枱	billiard table.
--	弓	crossbow.
22--	片	splinter.
40--	力	elasticity, elastic force.
--	坑	shell crater.
44--	幕	barrage.
--	藥	munitions, ammunition.
--	藥庫	ammunition depot.
46--	棉花	bow cotton.
47--	殼	cartridge-case.
50--	丸	bullet, ball, shot.
--	奏	play.
60--	回	rebound.
66--	唱	play and sing.

71--	壓	repress, quell, put down.
87--	鋼琴	play the piano.
88--	簧	spring.
--簧秤		spring-balance.
--簧鎖		spring lock.
95--	性	elasticity, elastic.

1628_6
殞 〔Yeun〕 v. die, perish.

| 80-- | 命 | n. death, v. die. |

1660_0
砳 〔Nao〕 n. sal ammoniac.

1660_1
碧 〔Bih〕 n. blue jade, adj. green, blue.

10--	玉	blue jade.
27--	綠	bright green.
--	血	dark blood.
38--	海	blue sea.

1661_0
硯 〔Yen〕 n. ink-stone.

靦 〔Tean〕 adj. ashamed, shy, bashful.

| 01-- | 顏事仇 | shamelessly collaborate with the enemy. |

1661_3
醜 〔Chou〕 adj. ugly, awkward, shameful, disgraceful.

02--	話	ugly language.
10--	惡	ugly, hideous, repulsive.
21--	行	shameful conduct. infamous act.
--	態	unseemly manner, disgraceful behavior.
--	態百出	behave in a revolting manner.
24--	化	defame, tarnish.
27--	名	infamy, notoriety.
--	名遠播	the bad reputation is widespread.
47--	婦	hag.
50--	事	disgraceful affair, scandal.
71--	陋	inelegant, ugly, deformed.

1661_4
醒 〔Hsing〕 v. awaken, rouse up, stir up.

| 00-- | 言 | awakening words. |
| 40-- | 來 | awake, come to oneself. |

44--	世之言	good advice that cautions the world.
60--	目	catching the eye, attracting one's notice.
76--	脾	refresh one's mind, entertaining.
91--	悟	awaken, realize, become aware, become conscious of.

1661_7
醞 〔Yun〕 v. brew liqueur.

| 10-- | 釀 | brew wine, agitate secretly, work underhand. |
| 30-- | 戶 | brewers. |

1664_4
碑 〔Bei〕 n. monument, tombstone.

00--	文	epitaph, inscription on a tablet.
16--	碣	stone tablet.
41--	帖	rubbings from tablet.

1664_8
礦 〔Yan〕 v. strong (beverage).

1671_3
魂 〔Hun〕 n. soul, spirit.

| 10-- | 不附體 | greatly frightened. |
| 26-- | 魄 | soul, manes. |

1710_3
丞 〔Cheng〕 n. assistant, deputy, v. aid, second.

| 46-- | 相 | prime minister. |

1710_5
丑 〔Chou〕 n. clown, jester, buffoon.

| 27-- | 角 | buffoon, clown, jester, comedian. |

1710_7
孟 〔Meng〕 adj. eldest, senior, rude, rough.

17--	子	Mencius.
33--	浪	unrestrained, rough, rude.
60--	買	Bombay.

盈 〔Ying〕 n. abundance, excess, v. exceed, fill, be full, adj. full, abundant, overflowing.

| 21-- | 虧 | gain and loss, profit and loss, wax and wane. |

34-- 滿　　　　full, self-satisfied.
38-- 溢　　　　excessive, overflowing, superabundant.
57-- 握　　　　handful.
88-- 餘價值　　surplus value.
-- 餘滾存　　　accumulated or cumulative surplus.
-- 餘　　　　　profit, gain, surplus.

1710_8

翌 〔 **I** 〕 *n*. tomorrow, next day.
47-- 朝　　　　tomorrow morning.
60-- 日　　　　tomorrow, next day.
80-- 年　　　　next year.

1711_0

虱 〔 **Shih** 〕 *n*. lice, louse, flea, bug.

1712_0

刁 〔 **Tiao** 〕 *adj*. wicked, artful, cunning, crafty, perverse.
02-- 話　　　　violent words, cunning expression.
08-- 詐兇悍　　knavish and violent.
10-- 惡　　　　wicked, depraved, outrageous.
11-- 頑　　　　rascally, reckless.
22-- 蠻　　　　barbarous, savage, unruly.
34-- 斗森嚴　　strict army discipline.
37-- 滑　　　　vicious, cunning, crafty, deceitful.
40-- 狡　　　　vicious, cunning, knavish.
-- 難　　　　　obstruct.
57-- 賴　　　　deny artfully.
84-- 鑽古怪　　perverse and grotesque.
96-- 悍　　　　knavish and violent.
-- 悍之徒　　　cunning and shrewish rascals.

羽 〔 **Yu** 〕 *n*. feather, plume.
17-- 翼　　　　wings, assistants.
20-- 毛　　　　feather, plume.
-- 毛球　　　　badminton.
29-- 紗　　　　camlet, bombasine.
30-- 扇　　　　feather fans.
40-- 士　　　　Taoist priests.
90-- 黨　　　　accomplices.

聊 〔 **Liao** 〕 *v*. rely, depend, *adv*. merely
10-- 天　　　　chat.

28-- 以自娛　　with a view to amusing oneself.
-- 以自慰　　　merely comfort oneself.
79-- 勝於無　　only better than nothing.

1712_7

耶 〔 **Yeh** 〕 *n*. father.
42-- 穌　　　　Jesus Christ.
-- 穌聖誕　　　Christmas.
-- 穌教　　　　Christianity.
-- 穌門徒　　　disciples of Jesus.
43-- 娘　　　　father and mother.

弱 〔 **Ruoh** 〕 *n*. weakness, *adj*. weak, feeble, soft, young, tender.
10-- 不勝衣　　so fragile as to lack even the strength to bear the weight of clothing.
40-- 肉強食　　the weak is to serve as a prey to the strong.
44-- 者　　　　weak fellow.
60-- 國　　　　weak nation.
61-- 點　　　　weak point, weak side.
72-- 質　　　　feeble constitution.
90-- 小　　　　small and weak, puny.
-- 小民族　　　weak nation.

鵡 〔 **Wu** 〕 *n*. parrot, cockatoo.

1713_6

蛋 〔 **Dan** 〕 *n*. egg.
26-- 白　　　　albumen, egg white .
-- 白質　　　　protein, albumen.
44-- 黃　　　　yolk.
47-- 殼　　　　eggshell.
98-- 糕　　　　cake.

蝨 〔 **Shih** 〕 *n*. flea, lice, louse, bug.

1714_0

取 〔 **Chu** 〕 *v*. take, lay hold on, receive, choose, select.
10-- 而代之　　replace.
11-- 巧　　　　be clever, take advantage, manipulate things for selfish purpose.
18-- 攻勢　　　be the attacking party, take the offensive.
20-- 信於人　　establish credibility among others.
-- 締　　　　　repress, suppress, ban, out-

		law.
22--	出	take out, bring out.
--	利	derive interest, make stock of.
--	樂	pursue pleasure.
--	樂縱情	run after pleasure and give rein to the passion.
23--	代	*n.* replacement, *v.* replace.
26--	得	get, gain, obtain.
--	得進展	get ahead, gain ground.
--	得時效	acquisitive prescription.
27--	名	name, take a name.
28--	作比譬	take it for example.
--	給於民	demand supply from the people.
30--	之不盡	inexhaustible.
34--	法	take example from.
35--	決於	depend on, be contingent.
38--	道	follow the patch.
39--	消	annul, nullify, cancel, withdraw, take back, call off.
--	消資格	disqualify.
--	消前約	countermand an agreement.
--	消限制	decontrol.
40--	去	deprive of, take away.
--	來	bring, fetch.
44--	材上乘	use material of high quality.
47--	款	draw on an account, draw money.
--	款人	remittee.
58--	捨不決	undecided about whether to accept or to refuse.
62--	暖	warm oneself.
71--	長補短	make up for each other's deficiencies.
77--	鬧	cause a row.
79--	勝	win, come over.
80--	人之長	suck a person's brains.
87--	錄	take in, accept, pass.
88--	笑	ridicule, laugh, mock at, make fun with.
--	笑挖苦	ridicule sarcastically.
90--	火	make fire, strike fire.
95--	快一時	for a moment's pleasure.
92--	媛	warm, bask.
98--	悅於世	please the world.

1714_5

珊 〔**Shan**〕 *n.* coral.

17--	瑚	coral, madrepore.
--	瑚礁	coral reef.
--	瑚島	coral island.

1714_7

瑕 〔**Hsia**〕 *n.* error, fault.

00--	疵	weak point, defect, blemish.
--	病	flaw, blemish.

瓊 〔**Chiung**〕 *n.* fine jade, *adj.* excellent, pretty, brilliant.

10--	玉	valuable-jade.
17--	瑤	beautiful jade.
27--	漿	nectar, fine wine.
44--	花	rare flower.
71--	脂	agar-agar.

1717_2

瑤 〔**Yao**〕 *n.* precious jade.

1718_0

玖 〔**Chiu**〕 *n.* black jade, *adj.* nine.

1719_4

琛 〔**Chen**〕 *n.* jewelry, rarity.

璨 〔**Tsan**〕 *n.* beautiful stone.

1720_2

予 〔**Yu**〕 *v.* give, confer, bestow, grant *pron.* I, me.

17--	取予求	take as one desires, take and demand freely.
--	假	grant leave.
28--	以	give, grant.
--	以解釋	throw some light on.

1720_7

了 〔**Liao**〕 *v.* understand, complete, finish, *adj.* finished, concluded, intelligent, *adv.* very, fully, wholly.

10--	不得	exceedingly, extraordinarily, startling, wonderful, excellent.
--	不起	remarkable, marvelous.
--	不長進	cannot make any progress.
17--	了	clear, distinct, intelligent, bright.
21--	此一生	end this life.
--	此殘生	end this miserable life.
--	此心願	fulfill this wish.

23-- 然　understand.
-- 然明白　understand fully.
24-- 結　finish, end, settle, have completed, be through with, have done with, bring to an end.
27-- 解　understand, apprehend, know.
35-- 清　settle completely.
50-- 事　finish up the matter, settle a matter.
77-- 局　end of a matter.
80-- 無長進　having made no progress or improvement in the least.

弓〔Kung〕n. bow, archery, adj. bow shaped, arched, curved.
10-- 弦　bowstring, chord.
12-- 形　segment.
20-- 手　archer, bowman.
80-- 矢　bow and arrow.

1721₀
殂〔Tsu〕v. die.
44-- 落　fall and die.

1722₀
刀〔Tau〕n. knife, sword.
10-- 豆　French bean.
11-- 背　back of a knife.
22-- 片　razor blade.
27-- 魚　mullet.
28-- 傷　knife-cut.
40-- 叉　knife and fork.
-- 套　scabbard, sheath.
41-- 柄　handle of knife.
49-- 鞘　sheath, scabbard.
60-- 口　blade, edge.
-- 具　cutting tool.
87-- 鋒極快　the knife is very sharp.

殉〔Hsun〕v. be buried with the dead, comply with, die for.
13-- 職　die a martyr at one's post
38-- 道精神　martyrdom.
40-- 難　die for one's country.
-- 難者　martyr.
44-- 葬者　funerary object, sacrificial object.

48-- 教　religious martyrdom.
60-- 國　die for one's country.
80-- 義　martyrdom.
95-- 情　die for love.

1722₂
矛〔Mao〕n. spear, lance.
11-- 頭　spearhead.
72-- 盾　contradiction, discordance.
-- 盾律　law of contradiction.

1722₇
乃〔Nai〕v. to be, adj. that, those, your, adv. but, however, more over.

甬〔Yeong〕v. road flanked by walls, corridor.

鷸〔Yuh〕n. snipe.

務〔Wu〕n. business, affair, concern, function, v. attend to, strive after.
21-- 須容忍　you must be tolerant.
25-- 使　ensure.
30-- 實　emphasize practical matters.
33-- 必　must, have to.
-- 必請早　come as soon as possible.
-- 必小心　must be careful.
43-- 求　must, by all means.
55-- 農　attend to agriculture.

帚〔Chou〕n. broom.
60-- 星　comet.

胥〔Hsu〕v. wait, help, adj. distant.
27-- 役　runners.
50-- 吏　clerk.

粥〔Chou〕n. porridge, gruel, congee.

1723₂
承〔Cheng〕v. undertake, contract for, acknowledge, confess, accept, take a charge, succeed, inherit.
00-- 辦　undertake, go at.
-- 辦商(承辦人) undertaker.
01-- 襲　inherit.
04-- 諾　acceptance, promise to undertake.
-- 諾單　letter of undertaking(L/U), letter commitment, written acknowledgment.

-- 諾人	acceptor.
07-- 認	*n.* recognition, consent, *v.* confess, acknowledge, admit, accept.
12-- 發人	process-server.
20-- 受	undertake, take up, underwrite.
22-- 繼	inherit, succeed.
-- 繼權	heirship, reversion.
-- 繼人	successor, inheritor, heir.
23-- 允	promise, agree to.
24-- 付期	acceptance period.
26-- 保	underwrite, cover, accept insurance.
-- 保單	cover note, insurance policy.
-- 保人	underwriter, undertaker.
27-- 租	rent.
-- 租人	renter, tenantry, tenant.
-- 包工程	contract work.
-- 包業	contracting business.
-- 包人(包商)	contractor, labor contractor.
-- 包合同	contract, work contract.
37-- 運	accept for carriage, acceptance for carriage.
-- 運人	transport contractor, carrier.
50-- 惠	receive kindness.
57-- 擔	*n.* assumption, *v.* undertake, assume.
-- 擔工程	undertake works.
-- 擔業務	assume obligations.
-- 擔責任	bear the responsibility, keep one's commitments, assume liabilities, undertake responsibility.
-- 擔費用	assume charge.
-- 擔風險	take a risk, risk-taking, assumption of risk.
-- 擔人	person assuming the debt.
58-- 攬	undertake.
60-- 實	contract for purchase.
80-- 兌	*n.* acceptance *v.* honor, accept to pay.
-- 兌費	accepting charge.
-- 兌日期	date of acceptance.
-- 兌人	acceptor.

-- 兌合同	acceptance contract.
-- 兌銀行	acceptance bank.
89-- 銷	consignment in, consignment inward.
-- 銷品	consigned goods, goods on consignment-in.
-- 銷人	consignee, underwriter.

聚〔**Chu**〕*v.* assemble, gather, collect, bring together.

08-- 議	meet for discussion.
20-- 集	collect, assemble, bring together, get together.
27-- 餐	mess, Dutch treat.
64-- 賭	assemble for gambling.
77-- 居	live in compact communities.
80-- 合	unite, aggregate, gather.
-- 首	gathering of friends, gather.
-- 會	meeting, gathering.
90-- 光燈	spotlight.

豫〔**Yu**〕*adj.* easy, contented, peaceful, happy.

00-- 言	prophecy.
24-- 備	prepare, prearrange.
30-- 審	preliminary examination.
-- 定	fixed beforehand.
32-- 兆	presage.
70-- 防	prepare against.
88-- 算	budget.

1724₇

及〔**Jyi**〕*v.* reach to, attain, extend to, *conj.* and, as well as, *prep.* to, until, till, with.

47-- 格	up to standard, pass an examination, be qualified.
60-- 早	early, promptly, while it is early.
-- 早回顧	turn back as soon as possible.
64-- 時	seasonable, in time, in good time, timely.
-- 時行樂	enjoy life whenever possible.
-- 時趕到	get under the wire.
-- 時努力	work hard whenever pos-

	sible.
-- 時付款	payment in due course.
-- 時性	timeliness.

歿〔Muo〕 n. death, the dead, v. perish, die.

44-- 也不忘	never forget.
-- 世不忘	shall never forget.

1732₀

刃〔Jen〕 n. blade, edge of a knife, v. kill.

28-- 傷事主	cut and injure the victim.
60-- 具	cutlery.
-- 具廠	cutting instrument plant.

1733₁

忌〔Chi〕 n. antipathy, dislike, death anniversary of one's parents or grandparents, v. dread, fear, shun, shirk, avoid, dislike, envy, adv. perhaps, probably.

04-- 諱	regard as taboo.
30-- 避	avoid, shun.
33-- 心	jealous feeling.
60-- 日	day of death.
80-- 食	avoid eating, abstain from eating.
96-- 憚	fear, dread.

恐〔Kung〕 n. terror, fear, fright, alarm, v. fear, doubt, threaten, scare.

01-- 龍	dinosaur.
64-- 嚇	threaten, scare, frighten, terrify, intimidate.
94-- 慌	horror, scare, panic, terrified, frightened, panicky.
-- 怖	n. terror, fear, fright, horror, adj. dreadful.
-- 怖主義	terrorism.
-- 怖政策	policy of terror.
-- 怖時代	reign of terror, age of terror.
-- 怖分子	terrorists.
96-- 惶	frightened, alarmed, terrified.
-- 怕	v. be afraid of, fear, adv. probably, perhaps.
-- 懼	terror, tremor, fear, fright, dread.

1733₂

忍〔Jen〕 n. patience, endurance, fortitude, forbearance, v. endure, bear, forbear, be indulgent to, put up with, be able to sustain, adj. harsh, hardhearted, severe, cruel, merciless. adv. patiently.

00-- 痛	bear pain.
-- 讓	n. forbearance, v. forbear.
10-- 不住	cannot stand it.
14-- 耐	endure, bear, put up with.
20-- 住	restrain by will power.
-- 受	bear, suffer, endure, stand, sustain.
33-- 心	cruel, hard-hearted.
-- 心害理	ruthless and devoid of human feelings.
-- 淚	restrain one's tears.
71-- 辱	digest an insult, endure contempt.
80-- 無可忍	cannot stand it any longer.
-- 氣吞聲	swallow one's anger and pride.
82-- 饑	stay the stomach.
-- 饑挨餓	suffer hunger.
88-- 笑	repress laughter, keep one's countenance.
95-- 性	patient, disposition.
-- 情	repress one's emotion.

1734₁

尋〔Hsun〕 v. search for, look for, seek.

00-- 訪	make inquiry about.
10-- 死	try to kill one's self, commit suicide, seek one's own death.
12-- 到	find out.
20-- 覓	look for, search.
22-- 樂	seek for amusement.
-- 出	find out, trace out, make out, hunt out, fish out, root out.
43-- 求	look for, seek, hunt after.
44-- 花問柳	visit brothels.
-- 藉口	find an excuse.
47-- 歡作樂	pursue sensual pleasures.

-- 根問底	investigate thoroughly, examine into the bottom.
50-- 事	interfere, meddle with.
-- 事生非	find fault and make trouble.
-- 東西	look for something.
53-- 找	seek, look for.
60-- 思	reflect, consider.
67-- 路	find one's way.
80-- 人	look for someone.
-- 常	usual, ordinary, common.

1740₄

娶 〔**Chu**〕 n. marriage, v. marry, take a wife.

00-- 妾	take a concubine.
50-- 妻	marry, lead a woman to the altar.

1740₇

孑 〔**Chieh**〕 adj. only, alone, single.

00-- 立無依	stand alone with no one to rely on.
23-- 然獨立	be left alone.
-- 然一身	be alone completely.
27-- 身赴會	attend the meeting alone.
62-- 影孤單	left alone with one's shadow.

子 〔**Tzu**〕 n. son, heir, boy, lad, teacher, master, seed.

00-- 夜	midnight.
-- 音	consonant.
12-- 孫	children, offspring, descendants.
-- 孫滿堂	sons and grandsons fill the hall.
16-- 彈	bullet, ball, shell, cartridge, shot.
-- 彈帶	bandolier, cartridge belt, ammunition belt.
20-- 爵	viscount.
26-- 細胞	daughter cell.
27-- 句	clause.
30-- 宮	womb, uterus.
-- 宮癌	cancer of the uterus or womb.
30-- 宮核	ovary.
-- 房	ovary, pericarp.

-- 實	seed.
40-- 女	children, sons and daughters.
-- 女相愛	the children love one another.
44 --葉	seed leaf.
60-- 口稅	transit dues.
80-- 弟	children, young people.
-- 弟兵	troops who are the sons and brothers of a general.
-- 午線	meridian.

孕 〔**Yun**〕 n. pregnancy, v. conceive, be pregnant, adj. conceived, pregnant.

00-- 育	give birth.
-- 育成才	nourish one to become a talent.
47-- 婦	pregnant woman, expectant mother.
-- 婦臨盆	parturition of a pregnant woman.
73-- 胎	pregnant womb.

1740₈

翠 〔**Tsui**〕 n. bluish, green, emerald, green jade.

27-- 鳥	kingfisher.
-- 色	bluish green.
-- 綠	verdure, verdant.

1741₃

兔 〔**Tu**〕 n. rabbit.

1742₇

勇 〔**Yung**〕 n. bravery, courage, adj. fearless, daring, brave, courageous, bold.

08-- 於戰爭	fight bravely, act a good part in war.
10-- 而無謀	be brave but have no plans.
13-- 武	martial, warlike.
18-- 敢	n. courage, bravery, boldness, v. dare, be courageous, venture, front danger, adj. courageous, brave, valorous, spirited, high-spirited, martial, warlike.

-- 敢善戰	brave and resourceful in battle.
20-- 往直前	go forward courageously, go ahead boldly.
27-- 將	brave general.
40-- 士	brave man.
44-- 者不懼	bravery admits no fear.
47-- 猛	fearless, fierce.
-- 猛無比	be unparalleled in valor.
-- 猛精進	make progress fearlessly and skillfully.
80-- 氣	bravery, brave spirit, high blood, stout heart, courage, vigor, valor.

1750₁

羣 〔Chun〕 *n.* group, flock, crowd, herd, company, multitude.

20-- 集	gather, together, crowd, swarm, cluster together.
26-- 侶	friends, companions.
27-- 島	archipelago, islands.
44-- 英會	meeting of heroes.
27-- 眾	mass, crowd, mob.
-- 眾運動	mass movement.
-- 眾大會	mass meeting (or rally).
-- 眾路線	mass line.
77-- 居	live as a group.

1750₆

鞏 〔Kung〕 *v.* guard, strengthen, secure, tie or bind with thongs.

60-- 固	*v.* guard, strengthen, stabilize, *adj.* stable, firm.
-- 固防線	strengthen the line of defense.

1752₇

弔 〔Tiao〕 *v.* condole, console, mourn, hang, suspend.

10-- 死	hang, hang oneself to death.
11-- 頸	hang by the neck.
-- 頸自盡	commit suicide by hanging.
12-- 水	draw water.
30-- 床	hammock.
-- 渡犯人	extradite a criminal.
40-- 喪慰問	condole with one in one's bereavement.
42-- 橋	drawbridge, suspension bridge.
44-- 孝	condole.
47-- 起	raise, hang up.
-- 桶	bucket.
50-- 車	crane.
51-- 打	hang up and flog.
60-- 唁	condole with.
67-- 嗓子	train the voice.
74-- 慰	console, sympathize.

那 〔Na〕 *pron.* who, which, what, that, those, *adv.* how.

00-- 麼	then.
-- 麼多	that much, so much.
-- 裏	where?
21-- 些	those.
26-- 個	which? that.
-- 邊走	that way.
64-- 時	at that time, then.
77-- 兒	there.
80-- 人	which person? that man.
80-- 年	which year? that year.

1760₂

召 〔Chao〕 *v.* call, summon.

05-- 請	invite, send for.
20-- 集	call, convene, summon, assemble, convoke.
27-- 租	advertise a house to let, to let.
30-- 之即來	report for duty at a moment's call.
44-- 募	enlist, conscript.
60-- 見	summon to an interview, grant an audience.
-- 回	recall.
67-- 喚	summon, call, send for.
77-- 開	convoke.

習 〔Hsi〕 *n.* custom, usage, habit, *v.* learn, practice, *adj.* intimate, familiar, accustomed, skilled.

01-- 語	idiomatic phrase, phrase.
08-- 於	accustom to.
28-- 俗	habit and custom.
-- 以為常	become accustomed to.
-- 俗	custom, convention.
30-- 字帖	copybook, learn penma-

nship.

34-- 染　　corrupted.
60-- 見　　have often seen.
61-- 題　　exercises.
77-- 聞　　often heard of.
80-- 氣　　habit, habitual practice.
97-- 慣　　habit, custom, usage.
-- 慣法　　customary law, common law.

1760_7
君 〔**Chun**〕 *n.* king, ruler, sovereign, prince, sir, Mr, *pron.* you.

00-- 主　　king, monarch.
-- 主主義　　monarchism.
-- 主立憲　　constitutional monarchy.
-- 主政體　　monarchy.
-- 主專制　　absolute monarch.
-- 主國　　monarchy.
10-- 王　　king, lord, monarch, ruler.
17-- 子　　gentleman, man of honor.
-- 子協定　　gentleman's agreement.
-- 子自重　　the worthy should respect himself.
-- 子之交　　the friendship of worthies.
44-- 權　　sovereignty.
77-- 民同慶　　both the sovereign and people celebrate together.

1761_2
砲=礮 〔**Pao**〕

1761_7
配 〔**Pei**〕 *n.* mate, equal, *v.* mate, unite, match, fit, compound, dispense.

00-- 方　　dispense prescriptions.
-- 音　　*v.* dub, *adj.* dubbed.
02-- 劑處　　dispensary.
-- 劑學　　pharmacology.
10-- 不上　　unsuitable, unable to match.
21-- 上　　match.
22-- 製　　mix drugs, make up a prescription.
-- 種　　artificial insemination.
24-- 備　　equip, furnish, provide.
25-- 件　　accessories, service parts.
26-- 偶　　couple, match, pair, spouse, mate.

27-- 角　　minor role, supporting actor or actress.
-- 色　　match colors.
28-- 給　　rationing.
-- 給證　　coupon.
-- 給制　　ration system.
31-- 額　　quota, allocation.
34-- 對　　couple, mate.
40-- 套　　manufacture complete sets, form a complete set.
42-- 婚　　consummate a marriage.
44-- 藥　　compound or prepare medicine.
77-- 尼西林　　penicillin.
80-- 合　　*v.* assimilate, fit, suit, conjugate, match, *adj.* in coordination with, in harmony with.

1762_0
司 〔**Ssu**〕 *n.* department. *v.* control, manage, preside over, attend to, have charge of.

28-- 儀員　　marshal, master of ceremonies.
30-- 空見慣　　common things.
34-- 法　　*n.* judicature, *adj.* judicial.
-- 法權　　jurisdiction, judicial power, judicial authority, sound of justice.
-- 法部　　Ministry of Justice.
-- 法部長　　Minister of Justice.
-- 法手續　　judicial process.
-- 法行政　　judicial administration.
-- 法的　　judicial.
-- 法機關　　judicial organizations.
-- 法警察　　judicial police.
42-- 機　　locomotive engineer, chauffeur, drive.
50-- 事　　manager.
71-- 長　　head of a department, department chief.
77-- 閽者　　doorkeeper.
80-- 令　　commander.
-- 令部　　headquarter.
-- 令官　　commander, commanding

		general.
--	令員	commander.

酌 〔Cho〕 *v.* pour out wine, consider, consult, drink.

08--	議	deliberate, consult.
30--	定	deliberate and decide upon.
33--	減	propose to reduce.
60--	量	consider, deliberate, weigh.
--	量情形	allow for the circumstances.
95--	情	considering the circumstances.
--	情處理	deal with on the merits of each case.

碉 〔Tiao〕 *n.* blockhouse.

| 26-- | 堡 | blockhouse, fortress, stone house. |

矽 〔Shih〕 *n.* silicon.

80--	谷	Silicon Valley.
87--	鋼	silicon steel.
--	鋼片	iron silicon alloys.

砌 〔Chih〕 *v.* pave, lay, build.

07--	詞誣告	heap up charges and accuse falsely.
15--	磚	brick, lay bricks.
24--	牆	build a wall.

硼 〔Peng〕 *n.* natural borax.

13--	酸	boric acid.
--	酸鹽	borate.
19--	砂	natural borax.

1762₇

郡 〔Chun〕 *n.* prefecture, district, county.

00--	主	daughter of a prince.
30--	守	prefect.
43--	城	county town.
62--	縣	district.

1763₂

碌 〔Lu〕 *n.* green, jasper. *adj.* rough, uneven, incapable, busy, laborious.

| 17-- | 碌 | common, ordinary, busy, toilsome, laborious. |

碾 〔Nien〕 *n.* stone roller, *v.* roll, triturate, grind.

10--	碎	pulverize, triturate.
30--	房	mill room.
58--	輪	roller.
90--	米	husk rice, hull rice.
--	米廠	rice-hulling mill.
--	米機	rice machine.

1766₄

酪 〔Lao〕 *n.* cream, cheese.

酩 〔Ming〕 *adj.* tipsy, intoxicated.

| 11-- | 酊 | tipsy, intoxicated. |
| -- | 酊大醉 | dead drunk. |

1768₁

礙 〔Ai〕 *n.* hindrance, impediment, obstacle, block, objection, *v.* hinder, retard, impede, check, prevent, restrain.

| 20-- | 手礙腳 | stand in the way. |
| 67-- | 眼 | not pleasing to the eye. |

1768₂

砍 〔Kan〕 *v.* cut, chop, fell, cut off, hew.

10--	下	cut down, chop off.
17--	刀	chopper.
11--	頭	behead.
21--	柴	chop wood.
22--	斷	cut in two, chop off.
23--	伐	fell a tree, hew.
28--	傷	wound by cutting.
44--	樹	fell a tree.
51--	掉	chop off.
77--	開	split open.

歌 〔Ko〕 *v.* song, ballad, carol, praise, *v.* sing, carol.

03--	詠	sing.
--	詠隊	choir.
04--	詩	sing a poem.
07--	謠	pastoral, ballad, folk song.
--	誦	carol, sing praises.
--	調	tune, strain.
--	詞	song, verses of a song.
14--	功頌德	glorify a ruler's character and accomplishments.
22--	劇	opera, lyric drama.
--	劇院	opera house.
40--	女	singing girl.
44--	妓	prostitute songsters.

--	者	songster, singer.
47--	聲	the sound of singing.
50--	本	song book.
55--	曲	song, tune, chant.
66--	唱	sing, chant.
--	唱家	singer, vocalist.
80--	舞	song and dance.
--	舞團	song and dance ensemble.
--	舞昇平	n. life in time of peace, v. celebrate peace.
81--	頌	carol, sing praise, eulogize.

1771_0

乙 〔I〕adj. number two, curved, bent, secondary.

10--	醇	alcohol, ethyl alcohol.
19--	醚	ether.
88--	等	class II, grade B.
95--	炔	acetylene.

1771_7

己 〔Chi〕pron. I, myself, self, oneself.

27--	身難保	it is hard to protect one's own self.

已 〔I〕adv. already, too.

00--	廢的	defunct.
20--	往	the past, ancient, bygone.
21--	經	already.
27--	久	long since, long time.
35--	決囚	condemned criminals.
60--	畢	already finished.
86--	知數	known number.

1780_1

疋 〔Pi〕n. piece, bale, roll.

11--	頭	piece goods.
--	頭舖	piece-goods store, dry goods shop.
40--	布	piece of cloth.

翼 〔I〕n. wing, fins, flank of an army, v. help.

24--	贊	help, assists.

1780_6

負 〔Fu〕n. defeat, loss, lose, bear, carry, defeat, adj. ungrateful, negative.

10--	電	negative electricity
20--	重忍辱	bear a heavy burden and disgrace with patience.
25--	債	be in debt, owe, run in debt.
--	債國	debtor country.
27--	約	break a promise.
28--	傷	injured, hurt, wounded.
--	咎引退	bear the consequence of something and tender one's resignation.
33--	心	ungrateful.
44--	荷	bear.
50--	責	be in duties, be responsible.
--	責人	the person in charge.
--	責管理	take charge of.
57--	擔	n. burn, v. bear.
58--	數	negative number, minus, quantity.
60--	累	pressure.
--	恩	ungrateful of one's favors.
61--	販	peddler, hawker.
--	號	minus, negative sign (-).
80--	義	ingratitude.

1790_4

柔 〔Jou〕adj. soft, flexible, tender, delicate, amiable, pliable.

17--	弱	feeble, tender.
21--	順	tame, yielding, submissive.
--	術	Japanese boxing, jujitsu.
--	能克剛	gentleness can overcome strength.
26--	和	mild, gentle, tender.
--	和婉順	gentle and agreeable.
47--	媚	charming, attractive.
57--	韌	pliable.
--	軟	soft, mild, tender.
--	軟體操	physical exercise.
76--	腸寸斷	broken-hearted.

1791_0

飄 〔Piao〕v. whirl, blow, waft, adj. floating.

10--	雪	whirling snow.
24--	動	flutter, wave.
32--	浮	waft, be afloat.
34--	流	drift, float.
36--	泊	v. draft, wander, have no fixed abode, adj. wandering.

39--	渺	obscure, misty, dim.
44--	蕩	waft, drift, float.
56--	揚	wave, fly, flutter.

1812₂

珍 〔Chen〕 *n.* curiosities, rarities, jewel, treasure, *v.* prize, esteem, value, *adj.* precious, valuable, scarce, excellent, beautiful, delicate, delicious.

15--	珠	pearls.
--	珠貝	pearl-oyster.
20--	愛	prize, love.
--	重	take care of , value, prize.
27--	物	gem, precious thing.
30--	寶	precious thing, jewels.
36--	視	prize, cherish, valuable.
40--	奇	scarce, dear.
44--	藏	*n.* collection of precious thing, *v.* treasure.
50--	貴	rare, precious, valuable.
--	本	rare book (or copy).
60--	品	curiosities, precious objects.
88--	飾	jewelry.
94--	惜	treasure and value.
--	惜分陰	improve oneself every moment.

1813₇

玲 〔Ling〕 *adj.* finely carved, smart, fine.

11--	瓏	elegant, smart, witty, tinkling of jade pendants.

聆 〔Ling〕 *v.* listen, hear, pay attention to.

20--	悉	hear, learn.
48--	教	listen to one's instructions.
79--	勝於無	half a loaf is better than no bread.

1814₀

攻 〔Kung〕 *v.* attack, assault.

04--	讀	study hard.
10--	下	batter down.
14--	破	carry by assault.
17--	取	take, capture.
21--	佔	occupy.
30--	守	offensive and defensive.
--	守同盟	offensive and defensive alliance.
33--	心爲主	psychological offense is the best of tactics.
40--	克	overcome, conquer.
43--	城	assault a city.
--	城砲	siege gun.
50--	撞	*n.* collision, *v.* collide.
51--	打	fight, engage in battle, attack.
57--	擊	*n.* offensive, *v.* attack, fall upon, pitch into.
--	擊線	line of attack.
--	擊點	point of attack.
60--	圍	lay siege to, be siege.
77--	聯計劃	key projects program.
80--	入	incursion.
--	無不克	all-conquering.

玫 〔Mei〕 *n.* sparkling red gem.

16--	瑰	rose.
--	瑰園	rose gardens, rosary.

政 〔Cheng〕 *n.* politics, administration, government.

00--	府	government, administration.
--	府黨	party in power.
--	府訓令	government instruction.
--	府機關	government organization.
08--	論家	publicist, political commentator.
17--	務	government affairs, political affairs.
20--	委	political commissar.
22--	變	revolution, coup, coup d'etat.
27--	綱	platform, policy, political platform.
30--	客	politicians.
33--	治	politics.
--	治立場	political standpoint.
--	治部	Ministry of Political Training, political department.
--	治面目	political features.
--	治家	statesman.
--	治地理	political geography.
--	治犯	political offender, political

		prisoner, political criminal.
--	治表演	political showing.
--	治眼光	political judgement.
--	治戰	political warfare.
--	治歷史	political history.
--	治學	political science.
--	治覺悟	political consciousness.
--	治局	Political Bureau, Politburo.
--	治性	political nature.
44--	權	ruling power, regime.
50--	事	politics.
60--	見	political views.
--	界	political circles.
75--	體	political form of government, government system.
--	體共和	the form of the government is that of a republic.
77--	局	political situation.
80--	令	government orders.
--	令不行	the government's orders aren't obeyed.
88--	策	policy, platform.
90--	黨	party, political party.
--	黨領袖	leader of a political party.

致 〔**Che**〕 n. one's interest, principle, etc. v. cause, originate, bring about, render, carry out, send, give.

00--	意	regard, salute, give one's compliments.
04--	謝	convey thanks, thank.
07--	詞	address, make a speech.
10--	死	cause death.
17--	函	write to.
20--	辭	address.
27--	候	n. compliment, v. pay respect.
28--	傷	cause a wound, cause an injury.
30--	富	get rich, make a pile.
40--	力	endeavor.
46--	賀	convey congratulations.
48--	敬	salute, show courtesy, pay respect.
--	敬意	pay respect.
--	敬電	message of salutation.
79--	勝	win.

80--	命	fatal, mortal, deadly.
--	命傷	fatal wound.
--	命打擊	mortal blow.
88--	答詞	make a reply speech.

敢 〔**Kan**〕 v. dare, venture on, presume, adj. bold, daring, intrepid.

00--	言	speak boldly.
08--	於	dare to.
--	說	dare to say.
10--	死隊	dare-to-die, suicide squad, commando.
28--	作敢爲	not afraid to do what should be done.
34--	爲	dare to do, bell the cat.
46--	想	have the courage to think.
48--	幹	dare to do.
51--	打	dare to fight.
53--	拚	dare to risk all.
77--	闖	have the courage to break through.

1821₁

尬 〔**Gan**〕 adj. embarrassed.

48--	尬	awkward, embarrassing, embarrassed .

1822₇

殤 〔**Shang**〕 n. premature death, v. die young.

矜 〔**Jin**〕 n. widower. v. pity, commiserate with, boast, brag, adj. dignified.

04--	誇	brag, boast.
08--	矜	cautious.
30--	寡孤獨	widower, widow, orphan and childless.
54--	持	austere, solemn, dignified, reserved.
97--	恤	sympathize with.
99--	憐	pity.

1828₆

殮 〔**Lien**〕 v. shroud.

00--	衣	shroud.
16--	埋	shroud and bury.

1832₇

鶩 〔**Wuh**〕 n. duck.

1833₄

憨 〔**Han**〕 adj. foolish, silly.

1844_0

孜 〔Tsu〕 *adj.* strenuous, diligent.

18-- 孜	diligently.
-- 孜不倦	industrious, with assiduity.

1861_1

磋 〔Tso〕 *v.* rub, polish, work at, grate.

00-- 商	*n.* consultation, *v.* consult with, confer with, discuss with, discourse with, drive a bargain.
-- 商大計	discuss a great scheme.
-- 磨	polish, rub.

1863_2

磁 〔Tzu〕 *n.* chinaware, crockery, porcelain.

10-- 石	magnet, loadstone.
-- 電	electro-magnetism.
35-- 油	glaze (on porcelain).
40-- 力	magnetic force.
-- 力性	magnetic-curves.
-- 土	porcelain clay.
41-- 極	magnetic poles.
44-- 帶錄音	tape-recording.
-- 帶機	magnetic tape unit.
-- 帶錄音機	tape recorder.
46-- 場	magnetic field.
66-- 器	porcelain ware.
77-- 學	magnetism.
80-- 氣赤道	magnetic equator.
-- 氣感應	magnetic induction.
83-- 鐵	magnet, magnetic iron.
84-- 針	magnetic needle.
95-- 性	magnetism, magnetic properties, *adj.* magnetic.
-- 性水雷	magnetic mine.
-- 性體	magnetic body.

1874_0

改 〔Kai〕 *v.* change, alter, amend, reform, correct.

01-- 訂	revise.
10-- 正	*n.* correction, amendment, *v.* correct, amend.
-- 惡從善	remove the evil and follow the good.
-- 天換地	transform heaven and earth, remake nature.
-- 不過來	cannot change.
11-- 頭換面	disguise, change one's looks.
15-- 建	*n.* alteration, *v.* rebuild, carry out reconstruction, reconstruct.
-- 建費用	reconstruction expenses.
17-- 邪歸正	reform oneself, give up heresy and return to the truth, give up evil and return to virtue.
18-- 攻爲守	defend instead of offend.
21-- 行	change one's occupation, reform one's conduct.
22-- 變	change, vary, alter.
-- 變主意	change one's mind.
-- 變政策	shuffle the policy.
-- 變局面	turn the tables, change the situation.
23-- 編	*n.* revision, re-organization, *v.* reorganize, revise, remodel.
24-- 裝	remodel, refit, disguise, repacking.
-- 動	*n.* alteration, modification *v.* change, modify.
-- 造	rebuild, reconstruct, remold, reform, transform.
27-- 組	*n.* restructure, reorganization, *v.* reorganize, reshuffle.
-- 名	change one's name.
-- 名換姓	change one's whole name.
28-- 作	make over, lick into shape.
30-- 寫	rewrite, adapt (a story, etc.).
-- 進	improve.
-- 良	*n.* betterment, improvement, *v.* improve, reclaim, mend, better, make better.
-- 良主義	reformism.
-- 良主義者	reformist.
-- 良費用	improvement expense.
-- 寄	redirect.
37-- 過	reform, correct one's error.
-- 過自新	turn over a new leaf.

-- 過遷善	correct evil doings and revert to good deeds.
-- 過所	reformatory.
-- 選	re-elect.
38-- 道	change course.
44-- 革	reform.
-- 革者	reformer.
-- 革家	reformer.
47-- 期	postpone, alter the date, stand over.
48-- 樣	convert into another form.
57-- 換	change, convert, exchange.
80-- 善	*n.* improvement, *v.* improve, better, mend, make better.
-- 善觀	meliorism.
-- 善環境	environmental enhancement.
-- 善服務	improve the service.
-- 善生活條件	improve the living conditions.
98-- 悔	regret, repent.

1918₀

耿 〔Geng〕 *adj.* bright, upright, honest, worried.

19-- 耿	honest, upright,disquieted.
40-- 直	straightforward, upright.
80-- 介	uptight, honest.

1918₆

瑣 〔So〕 *adj.* fragmentary, fine, small, petty, trifling.

10-- 碎	trifling, trivial and varied.
26-- 細	trivial.
-- 細之事	unimportant, nothing to speak of.
-- 細事務	odd job.
27-- 物	trinket.
50-- 事	trifle.

1962₀

砂 〔Sha〕 *n.* sand, gravel.

10-- 石	sandstone.
22-- 紙	emery paper.
40-- 布	emery cloth.
57-- 鍋	casserole.
58-- 輪	grinding wheel, emery wheel.
90-- 粒	gravel, pebbles.

-- 糖	granulated sugar.

1962₇

硝 〔Hsiao〕 *n.* niter, saltpeter. *v.* tan leather.

10-- 石	niter, saltpeter.
13-- 酸	nitric acid.
-- 酸廠	nitric acid plant.
40-- 皮	tannery.

1965₉

磷 〔Lin〕 *n.* phosphorus.

10-- 礦	phosphorus ore.
13-- 酸	phosphoric acid.
24-- 化物	phosphide.
77-- 肥	phosphate fertilizer.
90-- 光	phosphorescence.

2

2010₄

垂 〔Chui〕 *v.* suspend, hang down, drop, hand down, condescend, bend down, bow, *adj.* suspended, hanging.

10-- 下	hang, drop.
-- 死	at death's door.
11-- 頭	hang down the head, drop the head.
-- 頭喪氣	downcast, dejected.
27-- 危	in great danger.
32-- 涎	long for.
40-- 直	perpendicular.
-- 直線	perpendicular line.
44-- 老	growing old, in declining years.
47-- 柳	weeping willow.
58-- 擺	dangle.
80-- 念	think of, favor with a consideration.

重 〔Chung〕 *adj.* heavy, weighty, important, grave, violent, severe.

00-- 音	accent.
-- 率	specific gravity.
01-- 訂租約	release, renew a lease.
-- 訂合同	renew a contract.
02-- 新	anew, afresh.
-- 新訂貨	reorder.

-- 新評價	reappraisal.
-- 新調整	readjustment.
-- 新談判	renegotiate .
-- 新估價	reassess, revalue.
-- 新安排	reschedule, rearrange.
-- 新考慮	reconsider.
04-- 讀	repeat, stress.
08-- 說	reiterate.
10-- 工業	heavy industry, staple industry.
-- 要	importance, consequence, significance.
-- 覆訂貨	repeat order.
-- 覆試驗	repeated trial.
-- 覆計算	double counting.
-- 覆調查	repeated survey.
12-- 孫	great-grandson.
-- 刊	reprint.
14-- 聽	deaf.
15-- 建	n. reorganization, reconstruction, v. re-establish, reorganize, reconstruct.
16-- 現	reappear.
17-- 聚	reassemble.
-- 砲	heavy gun.
-- 負	heavy burden.
20-- 位	important post.
21-- 版	reprint.
22-- 任	great responsibility.
-- 製	make over.
-- 利	usury.
24-- 估價	revaluation.
25-- 生	regenerate.
27-- 包工者	cub contractor.
-- 租	underlease.
28-- 稅	heavy taxes.
-- 做	do over.
-- 傷	heavy wound.
30-- 寫	rewrite.
33-- 心	center of gravity.
-- 演	repeat a performance, recurrence.
35-- 油	heavy oil.
36-- 視	regard, make account of , esteem, value, care for.
38-- 複	n. repetition, v. repeat, adj. double, duplicate.
40-- 力	gravity.
-- 大	grave, important, serious.
-- 大過失	gross negligence.
-- 大事件	matter of consequence.
-- 大損失	heavy losses.
42-- 婚	bigamy.
51-- 打	beat severely, thump.
57-- 擊	blow.
58-- 整	n. reorganization, v. reorganize.
60-- 量	weight.
-- 量超過	over weight.
-- 罪	felony.
-- 累	n. burden, fardel, v. encumber.
-- 置	n. replacement, v. replace.
-- 置準備	reserve for replacement.
61-- 點產品	major products.
-- 點工程	major project, priority project.
62-- 踏	stamp.
65-- 購	repurchase.
71-- 壓	oppress, weight down.
80-- 金屬	heavy metal.
88-- 算	recount.
-- 簽合同	re-contract.

2011₁
乖 〔**Kuai**〕adj. perverse, obstinate, cunning, artful, crafty, wily, strange, odd.

01-- 語	perverse.
11-- 巧	ingenious, artful.
20-- 僻	perverse.

2011₄
雌 〔**Tzu**〕adj. female, weak, inferior.

40-- 雄異體	gonochorism.
44-- 芯	pistil.
-- 老虎	tigress, loud-mouthed shrew.

2013₂
黍 〔**Shu**〕n. millet, sorghum.

17-- 子	variety of millet.
90-- 米	millet grain.

2021₄

住 〔**Chu**〕 *v.* live in, dwell, halt, stop, cease, detain.

20-- 手	stop, halt, hold, stop an action.
21-- 步	halt.
-- 處	residence, dwelling.
30-- 房	dwelling chamber, housing, lodgings.
-- 宿	lodge, stay over night.
-- 宿費用	lodging expense.
-- 戶	resident family.
-- 宅	house, residence, dwelling house.
-- 宅建設	housing building, residential building, construction, dwelling construction.
-- 宅稅	inhabited house duty.
-- 宅區	residential district, quarter.
32-- 近	live close to.
41-- 址	address.
54-- 持	abbot.
60-- 口	stop talking, ceases to speak.
72-- 所	domicile, abode.
73-- 院	be hospitalized.
-- 院醫生	resident.
77-- 民	inhabitant, resident.

往 〔**Woang**〕 *v.* proceed, depart, go, *prep* to, *adj.* toward, past, *adv.* formerly.

12-- 返票價	return fare.
40-- 來文件	correspondence, communications.

隹 〔**Chui**〕 *n.* short-tailed birds, as pigeons.

僮 〔**Tung**〕 *n.* slave boy.

23-- 僕	slave boy, foot boy, errand boy.

讎 〔**Chou**〕 *n.* enemy, foe, match. *v.* collate, revise.

08-- 敵	enemy, foe, adversary, opponent.
40-- 校	collate books.

2021₆

覓 〔**Mi**〕 *v.* look for, seek, hunt for.

17-- 尋	search for, look for, hunt for.
26-- 得	find.
-- 保	find, offer securities.
40-- 索	seek, search for.
67-- 路	seek the right road.
80-- 食	seek food.

2021₇

伉 〔**Kang**〕 *n.* pair, couple.

21-- 儷	pair, couple, husband and wife.

禿 〔**Tu**〕 *n.* bald head, *adj.* bald, hairless, bare.

00-- 瘡	scald.
11-- 頂	bald.
-- 頭	hairless.
17-- 子	baldhead, baldpate.
22-- 山	bare hill.
72-- 髮	alopecia.
88-- 筆	blunt pencil, blunt writing brush.

2021₈

位 〔**Wei**〕 *n.* seat, place, position, situation, post, throne.

08-- 於	located at, situated at.
17-- 子	seat.
37-- 次	order, series, sequence.
60-- 置	position, situation.
80-- 分	one's social status.

2022₁

停 〔**Ting**〕 *v.* stop, cease, discontinue, hold, pause, hold up, stand still, rest, delay.

00-- 產	stop production, shutdown.
-- 辦	suspend, stop handling.
06-- 課	suspend class.
07-- 訊	stop judicial procedure.
08-- 放	park, place.
10-- 工	rest, knock off, cease work, stop work, shut down.
-- 電	power failure, cut off power.
12-- 水	cut off water.
-- 刊	suspend publication.
20-- 妥	have been park in proper place, properly parked.

21-- 止　cease, stop, give over, hold up, discontinue, desist from doing something, stop doing something.

-- 止交易　close account.

-- 止公權　suspension of civil right.

-- 經期　menopause.

24-- 付　stop payment, payment stopped.

-- 靠　stop, berth.

32-- 業　stop doing business, business closed, go out of business, termination of business, close down.

34-- 滯　n. standstill, sluggishness, v. delay, obstruct, stagnate.

36-- 泊　anchor, moor, call at a port, lie at anchor in a harbor.

44-- 薪　suspend payment to an employee.

50-- 車　stop a cart.

-- 車場　car park.

51-- 頓　run down, come to standstill.

63-- 戰　n. truce, cessation of arms, v. stop war.

-- 戰協定　truce, armistice.

77-- 用　lay down.

-- 學　rustication, suspension.

-- 留　stop, stay, remain.

2022₇

仿〔Fang〕v. imitate, adj. similar, resembling.

00-- 辦　adopt similar measures.

22-- 製　manufacture an imitation.

-- 製品　imitation, copy, replica, imitation production.

28-- 作　replication.

34-- 造　imitate.

40-- 古　imitate the ancient style.

67-- 照　do according to, pattern after.

仿〔Fang〕adj. undecided, unclear.

25-- 彿　similar, like, resembling, doubtful.

26-- 徨　adj. undecided, irresolute.

don't know what to do.

秀〔Hsiu〕adj. prosperous, luxuriant, beautiful, fair, refined, elegant.

10-- 雅　elegant, refined, graceful.

11-- 麗　beautiful, handsome, fair.

22-- 出　outstanding.

40-- 才　accomplished scholar, bachelor of literature.

80-- 美　elegant, graceful, beautiful.

-- 氣　elegant manners.

傍〔Pang〕n. side, prep. by side of, near.

10-- 面　lateral.

26-- 徨　v. wander about, hover, adj. irresolute, undecided.

46-- 觀者　third person, onlooker, bystander.

67-- 晚　dusk, twilight, nightfall.

80-- 午　near noon time, short before noon, shortly before noon.

喬〔Chiao〕adj. high, stately, lofty, crooked, curved.

24-- 裝　disguise.

31-- 遷　remove, move to a new house.

40-- 麥　buck wheat.

-- 木　tall tree, large tree.

雋〔Chuan〕adj. fat, fleshy, strange, heroic, valiant.

53-- 拔　outstandingly talented.

77-- 譽　reputation.

傭〔Yung〕v. hire, engage, serve.

10-- 工　hire laborer, work as a laborer.

27-- 役　hired servant.

47-- 婦　woman servants.

72-- 兵　mercenaries.

80-- 人　servants.

2023₁

僬〔Chiao〕n. pigmy, dwarf.

24-- 僥　pigmy, dwarf.

2023₂

依〔I〕v. rely on, trust to, conform to, comply with, prep. according to, in accordance with.

00--	序	in order, according to rank, in succession, one by one.
02--	託	trust, depend on.
20--	依不捨	unwilling to part with.
22--	例	according to rules.
--	戀	attach.
23--	然	as usual, as before.
--	然如故	remain as before.
24--	靠	rely on, depend upon, hang on.
27--	約	follow tradition, in accordance with the promise.
28--	從	in conformity to, in agreement with, in obedience to, in compliance with.
31--	憑	rely on, depend on.
32--	近	near by, close by.
34--	法	according to law.
37--	次=依序	
44--	舊	as used, as before.
47--	期	in due time, at fixed time, at stated period.
51--	據	base on.
57--	賴	depend on.
--	賴性	habit of relying upon others.
67--	照	in accordance with, in obedience to, according to.
74--	附	adhere to, agree with.

2023_6

億 〔I〕 *v.* guess, calculate, *adj.* hundred thousand, billion.

00--	度	guess, calculate.
12--	兆	vast number, innumerable.
44--	萬	vast number, innumerable.
--	萬富翁	billionaire.

2024_0

俯 〔Fu〕 *v.* bend down, stoop, condescend, bow, look down.

03--	就	condescend.
21--	拜	obeisance.
--	衝	dive.
--	衝轟炸	dive bombing.
--	衝轟炸機	dive bomber.
23--	伏	fall, prostrate, bow and kneel, cast oneself at one's feet.

--	允	condescend, grant gracious permission.
27--	仰	look up and down.
28--	從	obey, give into.
30--	准	permit graciously.
36--	視	overlook, look down.
80--	念	take into consideration.
--	首	stop, bow.

2024_1

僻 〔Pi〕 *adj.* private, secluded, obscured, prejudiced, partial.

21--	處	live in seclusion.
34--	遠	distant and out of the way.
38--	道	seldom-traveled road.
44--	地	solitude.
--	巷	side lane, private alley.
52--	靜	secluded, out-of-the -way.
60--	見	partial view.
71--	陋	rustic, clownish, out of the way place.

辭 〔Tzu〕 *n.* words, speech, expression, phrase, *v.* refuse, decline, take leave, retire, depart.

04--	謝	decline with thanks.
10--	工	resign from manual work.
13--	職	*n.* resignation, *v.* resign, retire, deliver up, leave office, hand in one's resignation.
21--	行	take a farewell.
27--	句	expression.
--	彙	vocabulary.
37--	退	turn away, leave a post, dismiss, discharge.
55--	典	dictionary, encyclopedia.
62--	別	take leave, bid farewell, say good-bye.
87--	卻	reject, decline.

2024_4

佞 〔Ning〕 *n.* eloquence, flattery, *adj.* eloquent.

47--	婦	glib-tongued woman.
60--	口	oily-mouthed, eloquent.
80--	人	deceitful person.
90--	黨	clique of traitors.

2024_7

愛 〔Ai〕 *n.* love, kindness, regard, *v.*

love, dote on, like, be fond of ,wish, desire, covet.

04-- 護	care for, look after.
10-- 面子	be sensitive about one's reputation.
17-- 己主義	egoism.
18-- 群	love for all.
22-- 戀	in love.
24-- 他主義	altruism.
27-- 物	favorite.
31-- 酒	be fond of drinking.
35-- 神	the blind deity, Cupid.
38-- 滋病	AIDS (acquired immune deficiency syndrome).
40-- 力	affinity.
44-- 慕	take a real liking, be fond of.
47-- 好	care for, affect, like, cling to, fancy, prefer, take to.
50-- 妻	wife of one's bosom.
60-- 國	n. patriotism, public virtue, v. love one's country, be patriotic.
-- 國主義	patriotism.
-- 國心	patriotism, public spirit.
-- 國運動	patriotic movement.
-- 國者	patriot.
-- 國公債	government bonds.
64-- 財	fond of money.
77-- 用	love to use, prefer to use.
80-- 人	lover, sweetheart, darling, favorite, beloved.
94-- 惜	spare, prize, value, cherished.
-- 情	love.
99-- 憐	show love for.

2026₁

倍〔Pei〕v. double, adj. double, twofold.

00-- 率	percentage.
22-- 利	double profit.
58-- 數	multiple.

信〔Hsin〕n. faith, sincerity, confidence, trust, letter, epistle, note, v. trust, believe, have faith in.

02-- 託	trust, entrust, confide, charge.
-- 託公司	trust company (corporation), safe company.
-- 託人	trustee (trustor).
10-- 不過	have no trust in.
17-- 砲	signal gun.
20-- 稿	draft of a letter.
22-- 任	trust, confide in, believe in, put one's trust in, believe, credit, give credit to.
-- 任狀	credentials.
-- 任投票	the vote of confidence.
23-- 貸	credit.
24-- 紙	letter paper.
-- 徒	follower, believer, disciple.
26-- 得過	can be believed.
-- 息	news, information, message.
-- 息服務	information service.
-- 息庫	information bank.
-- 息網路	information network.
27-- 仰	n. faith, belief, v. believe.
-- 條	creed, code, dogma, precept.
28-- 從	trust and follow.
30-- 守	abide by, keep promise.
-- 實	good faith, honesty, reliability.
33-- 心	faith, credence.
40-- 女	female believer.
42-- 札	letter, note, correspondence.
44-- 封	envelope.
46-- 加	double.
48-- 教	believe in a religion.
50-- 奉	believe in.
57-- 賴	depend, fall back on.
61-- 號	signals.
-- 號彈	signal shot, flare.
-- 號手	signaler.
-- 號燈	signal light.
77-- 風	trade wind, seasonal wind.
-- 用	credit, trust, trustworthiness.
-- 用交易	credit transaction.
-- 用卡	credit card, access card.
-- 用評級	credit rating.
-- 用借款	open credit, fiduciary loan.

-- 用狀	letter of credit.
-- 用欠款	debt of honor.
-- 用組合	credit association.
-- 局	post office.
-- 服	trust, accept in faith, believe in, be convinced, admire.
-- 譽	credit and reputation, good reputation, goodwill, credit worthiness, reputation.
80-- 差	messenger.
-- 念	belief, conviction.
-- 義	honesty.
87-- 鴿	carrier pigeon.
88-- 箱	letter box, mail box, post box.

2030₇
乏 〔Fa〕 adj. defective, deficient, wanting, lacking, insufficient, empty, exhausted, poor, weary, fatigued, worn out, tired.

47-- 趣	lacking in interest.
65-- 味	monotony, dull, tasteless.

2033₁
焦 〔Chiao〕 adj. scorched, burned, dried up, anxious, harassed.

06-- 竭	worried.
11-- 頭爛額	in bad shape, in great trouble.
21-- 慮	worried, be on the rack.
27-- 急	v. disquiet, adj. anxious, crazy.
33-- 心	n. agony of mind, adj. distressed.
40-- 土	scorched earth.
-- 土抗戰	adopt a scorched earth policy in fighting.
61-- 點	focus.
94-- 煤	coke.
97-- 灼	vexed, harassed.

熏 〔Hsun〕 n. vapor, fog, smoke, fumes, v. smoke, heat.

10-- 死	suffocated to death.
-- 天	overwhelming.
17-- 烝	steamy vapor.
20-- 香	kind of incense.

27-- 魚	smoked fish.
-- 灸	cauterize.
40-- 肉	smoke meat.
45-- 熱	burning heat.
48-- 乾	dry at the fire.
60-- 黑	blackened by smoke.
66-- 躁	anxious and getting impatient.
91-- 爐	baker, bake pan.

2033₉
悉 〔Hsi〕 v. know, understand, comprehend, adj. all, entire, total, adv. altogether, entirely, wholly, fully.

33-- 心	with one's entire mind, with whole heart.
40-- 力	with all one's strength, with might and main.
58-- 數	n. whole lot, v. tell the whole story.

2034₈
鮫 〔Chiao〕 n. large shark.
2039₆
鯨 〔Ching〕 n. whale.

10-- 吞	gulp down.
34-- 波	huge waves.
35-- 油	whale oil.
87-- 飲	swill, guzzle.

2040₀
千 〔Chien〕 adj. thousand.

00-- 言萬語	innumerable words.
-- 方百計	in all possible ways, by all means.
10-- 瓦	kilowatt.
40-- 古	ancient times.
-- 克	kilogram.
60-- 里	thousand li--long distance.
-- 里鏡	telescope.
87-- 鈞一髮	hang by a thread.
90-- 米	kilometer.

2040₄
妥 〔To〕 adj. secure, safe, stable, firm, settled, fixed, ready.

00-- 辦	transact satisfactorily.
38-- 洽	safe, secure.
44-- 協	compromise, be compatible, come to terms.

-- 協份子	appeaser.
61-- 貼	for the best, properly fitting.
80-- 善	proper, satisfactory.
90-- 當	appropriate, ready, secure.

委 〔Wei〕 v. confide to, put in charge of, commit, delegate.

00-- 辦	commission.
-- 棄	give up, abandon.
02-- 託	n. consignment, v. intrust, entrust, commit, give in charge, assign.
-- 託商行	commission house.
-- 託寄賣	commission sales.
-- 託書	power of attorney, proxy statement, warrant of attorney.
-- 託人	client.
18-- 政	deputize a minister.
22-- 任	n. nomination, v. appoint, delegate, trust, commission.
-- 任統治	mandatory administration.
-- 任狀	commission, credential, letter of attorney, power of attorney (P.O.A.), power of procuration.
-- 任單	letter of appointment.
27-- 身	devote, dedicate, fall to, be taken up with.
30-- 實	really, indeed.
32-- 派	attach, accredit, depute, appoint, send, commission.
40-- 查	appoint to inquire.
55-- 曲	complicated, perplexed, circuitous.
60-- 員	deputy, delegate, special commissioner.
-- 員會	commission.
77-- 屈	grievance, complaints.
80-- 命	leave oneself to fate.

2040₇

受 〔Shou〕 v. receive, accept, bear, sustain, suffer, inherit, succeed to.

00-- 主	receiver.
-- 讓人	transferee, endorsee, assignee, grantee.
02-- 訓	receive training.
-- 託	be entrusted with.
07-- 訊	face trial in court.
10-- 不了	cannot stand it, cannot take it.
12-- 刑	receive punishment, be punished.
15-- 聘	accept a job offer.
16-- 理	accept and hear a case.
-- 理案件	assume jurisdiction.
17-- 孕	n. pregnancy, v. conceive, be pregnant.
22-- 制	under restraint.
24-- 貨人	recipient of goods, consignee.
26-- 保人	insurant.
28-- 傷	be wounded.
30-- 涼	catch cold, catch chill.
-- 寒	catch cold.
-- 審	stand trial.
-- 害	be injured.
-- 害人	victim.
31-- 逼	lie under, be compelled to.
34-- 洗	be baptized.
35-- 禮	receive a gift.
40-- 難	suffer disaster, be in distress.
44-- 封	be appointed with a title.
-- 苦	suffer, agonize.
47-- 款人	beneficiary payee.
48-- 驚	get a fright, be frightened.
50-- 惠	be benefited.
-- 惠國	benefit country, beneficiary, preference receiving country.
52-- 託人	bailee, trustee, referee, consignee.
-- 託管理人	custodian trustee.
56-- 損	sustain damage, damaged.
-- 押人	pledgee, mortgagee.
58-- 挫	be defeated, suffer a set back.
60-- 罪	suffer hardship, have a bad time.
-- 恩	receive favors.
-- 罰	be punished, pay the forfeit,

	be fined.
-- 困	obsession.
-- 累	be involved, get involved in a trouble.
64-- 賄	be bribed, receive, (take, accept) bribes.
71-- 壓迫	suffer oppression.
-- 辱	be insulted, be disgraced.
73-- 騙	be deceived, be fooled.
77-- 降	accept the surrender.
-- 屈	be wronged.
80-- 益	benefit, be benefited, be the better for..., benefit from.
-- 益方	beneficiary party, benefited party.
-- 益人	beneficiary, in favor of (F/O).
-- 命	be ordered, on the order of, accepted an order.
-- 氣	suffer indignation.
90-- 賞	receive a reward.
95-- 精	fertilization.
-- 精卵	zygote.

季 〔**Chi**〕 *n.* season, quarter.

00-- 度產量	quarterly production.
-- 度收益	quarterly returns.
10-- 票	season ticket.
12-- 刊	quarterly.
27-- 候	season.
-- 候風	monsoon and any other seasonal wind.
37-- 軍	second runner-up, third prize winner.
47-- 報	quarterly report, seasonal report.
50-- 末銷售	end-of-season sale.
77-- 風	the monsoon.
-- 月	last month of a season.
88-- 節	season.
-- 節性	seasonal.
-- 節工	seasonal labor, laborer, worker.
-- 節因素	seasonal factor.
-- 節性工業	seasonal industry.
-- 節性工作	seasonal work.

| -- 節性供應 | seasonal supply. |
| -- 節性供求 | seasonal demand and supply. |

隻 〔**Chih**〕 *adj.* one, single.

00-- 立	stand alone.
20-- 手	single-handed.
27-- 身	alone, by oneself.
30-- 字	single word or character.
-- 字片言	very brief note or letter.
62-- 影	all alone, all by oneself.
67-- 眼	one-eyed, original idea, fresh view.

雙 〔**Shuang**〕 *n.* pair, couple, brace, *adj.* two, both, double, even.

00-- 方	both sides, both parties.
-- 方同意	mutual consent.
-- 亡	both are dead.
06-- 親	parents.
10-- 下巴	double chin.
-- 面	two-sided, double-edged, double faced.
12-- 飛	fly in pair.
17-- 子葉	dicotyledon.
20-- 重	double, dual, twofold.
-- 重標準	double standard.
-- 重國籍	dual nationality.
-- 重人格	dual personality.
-- 倍	*adj.* double, twofold, *adv.* two times, twice.
-- 倍收費	double charge.
-- 手	both hands.
25-- 生	twin.
27-- 峰駝	double-humped camel, Bactrian camel.
-- 向交通	two-way traffic.
-- 名	given name consisting of two character.
30-- 肩	both shoulders.
36-- 邊貿易	bilateral trade, two way trade.
-- 邊合伙	bilateral partners.
-- 邊合同、雙邊契約	bilateral contract.
37-- 週刊	biweekly, fortnightly.
40-- 十節	Double Tenth festival
41-- 幅	double standard width (fab-

	rics or piece goods).	
-- 頰	both cheeks.	
44-- 薪家庭	two-paycheck families.	
45-- 姓	family name consisting of two character.	
-- 棲	live together as man and wife.	
47-- 殺	double play (tennis).	
51-- 打	play in double (tennis).	
53-- 掛號	registered mail with return receipt.	
54-- 軌	double-tracked.	
-- 軌制	double tracked system (education).	
55-- 曲線	hyperbola (mathematics).	
58-- 數	dual, even number.	
60-- 日	even days.	
-- 目失明	be blind in both eyes.	
61-- 號	even number.	
77-- 月刊	bimonthly.	
-- 腳	both feet, two feet.	
-- 胞胎	twins.	
-- 層	double layers, double decks.	
-- 層床	double-decked bunk.	
80-- 人床	double bed.	
-- 人房	double room, twin room.	
-- 人舞	dance for two people.	
-- 全	both (parents) alive.	
-- 氧水	hydrogen peroxide.	
88-- 管齊下	do two things simultaneously.	
-- 簧	kind of variety show featuring two performers, two-person standup comedy.	
94-- 料	articles or products built with added strength.	

2041₄

雞 〔Chi〕 *n.* cock, fowl, chicken.

17-- 蛋	egg.
-- 蛋黃	yolk.
-- 蛋糕	sponge cake.
20-- 毛帚	chicken feather duster.
30-- 窩	chicken coop.
33-- 心	jewel shaped like a chicken's heart.
34-- 汁	chicken broth.
36-- 湯	chicken soup.
37-- 冠	cockscomb.
-- 冠花	cockscomb (botany).
40-- 皮	shriveled skin of the aged.
-- 姦	sodomy, bugger.
43-- 犬不寧	not even the chicken and dogs are left in peace--great disturbance.
60-- 啼	crowing of cocks, cock crow.
67-- 鳴	cock crows.
77-- 腿	drumstick, chicken leg.
-- 胸	chicken breast.
88-- 籠	basket for fowls, fowl coop.

雛 〔Chu〕 *n.* chicken.

12-- 形	embryo, fledgling.
27-- 鳥	very young bird.
40-- 女	young girl.
44-- 妓	very young prostitute.
-- 菊	daisy.

2041₇

航 〔Hang〕 *v.* navigate, sail.

10-- 天工業	space industry, aerospace industry.
-- 天飛機	space shuttle.
20-- 信	aerial mail, air mail.
21-- 行	navigate, sail, fly.
-- 行者	voyager.
26-- 線	marine routes, aerial line.
-- 程	distance of an air or a sea trip, voyage, passage.
27-- 向	course (of a ship or plane).
-- 船	liner.
30-- 空	aviation, aeronautics.
-- 空站	air station, air field.
-- 空部	air ministry.
-- 空工業	aircraft industry.
-- 空信	airmail, airmail letter, air letter.
-- 空委員會	Commission of Aeronautical Affairs, Commission of Air Force.
-- 空貨運	airfreight.
-- 空貨運站	cargo air terminal.

-- 空郵件	airmail.	
-- 空郵包	air post parcel.	
-- 空急件傳送	air express.	
-- 空術	aviation.	
-- 空網	network of air routes.	
-- 空運輸	carriage by air, air transport.	
-- 空運輸公司	air transport company.	
-- 空掛號	registered airmail.	
-- 空圖	aerial chart.	
-- 空員	airman, aviator.	
-- 空學校	aviation school.	
-- 空母艦	aircraft carrier.	
-- 空服務	air service.	
-- 空公司	airline company, air line, airways.	
32-- 業	shipping business.	
-- 業公司	shipping company.	
37-- 運	shipping, aerial transportation.	
38-- 海	navigate, voyage, sail on the seas.	
-- 海術	art of navigation.	
-- 海家	navigator, seafarer.	
-- 海業	shipping industry.	
-- 海圖	marine chart, nautical chart, sea-chart.	
-- 海權	sea power.	
-- 海學	maritime navigation.	
-- 道	navigation route, water way.	
44-- 權	right of navigation.	
67-- 路	line, ocean lane, shipping route.	

2042₇

舫 〔Fang〕 n. large boat.

2043₀

夭 〔Yao〕 adj. young, tender.

00-- 亡	die young, die prematurely, come to an untimely end.
52-- 折	early death.

2043₂

舷 〔Hsien〕 n. gunwales, the side of a ship.

48-- 梯	accommodation ladder.
77-- 門	gunway.

2050₀

手 〔Shou〕 n. hand, arm, handful.

00-- 底下	one's subordinates.	
-- 癢	itch on one's hand.	
01-- 語	dactylology, sign language.	
05-- 辣	ruthless.	
07-- 詔	personally handwritten imperial decree.	
10-- 工	handicraft, handiwork.	
-- 工業	manual trade, handicraft industry, craft industry.	
-- 工業品	handmade goods.	
-- 工藝	handicrafts, handiwork.	
-- 工藝品	handicrafts, handicraft articles, articles of handicraft, fancy works.	
-- 下	subordinates, under the leadership of, under control.	
-- 電筒	flashlight, electric torch.	
-- 不釋卷	studying constantly.	
-- 工勞動	hand labor, manual labor.	
11-- 巧	skillful.	
-- 頭	on hand, at hand, in hand.	
-- 頭緊	short of cash, closefisted.	
-- 頭鬆	liberal in spending.	
13-- 球	hand ball.	
20-- 重	heavy-handed, with too much force.	
-- 稿	manuscript.	
-- 紋	lines of the hand.	
-- 術	operation, manipulation.	
-- 術刀	scalpel.	
-- 術室	operation room.	
-- 術台	operation table.	
21-- 上	in one's hand.	
22-- 製	handmade.	
-- 紙	toilet paper.	
24-- 動機器	hand-operated machine.	
-- 續	proceeding, process, procedure, step, formality.	
-- 續費	procedure fee, service charge, commission, commission charge, costs of formalities, handling expenses.	
27-- 縫	sew by hand, space between the fingers.	
28-- 煞車	hand brake.	

32-- 淫	self-abuse, self-pollution, masturbation.
33-- 心	palm of the hand.
34-- 法	workmanship, skill, artistry.
36-- 邊	at hand, handy.
40-- 巾	handkerchief.
-- 套	gloves.
42-- 札	personal handwritten letter.
-- 機關鎗	submachine gun.
44-- 勢	gesture, sign.
-- 藝	workmanship, craft, the useful art, craftsmanship.
-- 藝人	handicraftsman.
-- 植	personally planted.
-- 模	finger print.
45-- 杖	stick, cane.
46-- 帕	handkerchief.
-- 相	telling one's fortune, palmistry, palm reading.
47-- 榴彈	grenade, hand grenade.
50-- 車	barrow.
-- 推車	handcart, wheelbarrow.
-- 拉手	hand in hand.
51-- 輕	light-handed.
-- 指	finger.
-- 指頭	fingertip.
54-- 技	art, manual skill, jugglery.
56-- 提	v. carry with a hand, adj. portable.
-- 提包	bag, handbag.
-- 提箱	suitcase, attachécase.
57-- 摺	account book.
-- 軟	hesitate to inflict punishment from pity.
59-- 抄	copy by hand.
-- 抄本	hand-copied copy, manuscript.
60-- 甲	nail.
-- 圈	bracelet.
-- 足	brothers.
-- 足之情	brotherly affection.
67-- 眼快	quick in action, nimble.
70-- 臂	arm from the wrist up.
72-- 鬆	spending money freely, liberal, generous, freehanded.
73-- 腕	wrist, ability, trick, skill, tact.

77-- 風琴	accordion.
-- 段	measure, means.
-- 冊	manual, handbook.
-- 印	impression of the thumb.
-- 緊	short cash, thrifty, reluctant to spend money.
80-- 令	personally handwritten order.
-- 拿	hold in hand, take by hand.
-- 氣	luck (in gambling).
84-- 銬	handcuff, manacles.
-- 鉗	pincers.
85-- 錶	wristwatch.
86-- 鐲	circlet, bracelet.
-- 鎗	pistol, revolver, gun, hand gun.
-- 筆	autograph, handwriting.
90-- 忙腳亂	be in a flurry, be very busy.
-- 掌	palm.
-- 卷	scroll.
91-- 爐	portable charcoal stove.
95-- 快	quick in action, nimble.
96-- 慢	slow in action, slow moving.

2050₇
爭 [Cheng] v. contest, contend, strive, quarrel, fall out, come to blows, measure swords.

00-- 產	fight for inheritance.
-- 席	contend for a seat.
-- 辯	debate, argue, dispute.
-- 競	compete.
02-- 端	cause of a quarrel, bone of contention, subject of dispute.
08-- 論	dispute, rebut, debate, quarrel, argue, contest.
-- 訟	go to law, dispute through a lawsuit.
-- 議	engage in controversy, dispute, argue.
10-- 霸	contend for hegemony, scramble for supremacy.
-- 霸戰	struggle for power.
-- 面子	try to win for the sake of

face.

13-- 強		struggle for supremacy.
14-- 功		contend for merit.
17-- 取		try to get, win over, strive for, compete for.
-- 取時間		avoid waste of time, act quickly.
24-- 先恐後		anxious to be ahead of others.
26-- 得		win.
27-- 名		compete for honor.
-- 名奪利		struggle for fame and wealth.
40-- 雄		struggle for supremacy.
-- 奪		struggle for, fight for, contend for.
-- 奪戰		battle over a city or others.
44-- 地		quarrel over land.
-- 執		fall out, take issue, be contentious.
61-- 嘴		argue in self-defense.
-- 點		point of contention.
67-- 鳴		contend.
69-- 吵		quarrel, wrangle.
77-- 鬧		snub, throw a stone, have words with.
-- 鬥		struggle, contend, conflict, come to blows, do battle with, measure strength.
79-- 勝		strive for mastery.
80-- 氣		don't let down, try to win credit for.
90-- 光		win glory.

2060₁

售〔**Shou**〕v. sell, dispose of, trade.

00-- 主		seller.
10-- 票		sell tickets.
-- 票處		booking office, box office, ticket office.
-- 票員		ticket seller, conductor.
21-- 價		price, sale price, selling price.
22-- 出		sell, dispose of.
24-- 貨店		retail store.
-- 貨機		vending machine.
-- 貨員		salesman, shop assistant,

salesclerk.

30-- 完		sell out of something, run out of stock, run out of something.
40-- 賣		selling, sale.
47-- 罄		completely sold out, sell out.
60-- 品		goods.

2060₃

吞〔**Tun**〕v. swallow, devour, bolt, gorge, gulp, absorb, seize, merge, squeeze.

10-- 下		swallow, swallow down, take down, gulp.
-- 雲吐霧		smoke.
21-- 佔		usurp, take possession of land illegally.
28-- 併		annex, merger, take possession of.
33-- 滅		devour, swallow up, conquer and annex.
37-- 沒		take possession of, engulf.
-- 沒公款		n. embezzlement, v. embezzle public funds.
47-- 聲		suppress complaints.
64-- 吐		v. swallow and spit, gorge and disgorge, adv. hesitatingly.
-- 吐量		volume of goods handled at a seaport.
68-- 噬		swallow or devour.
80-- 入		engulf.
-- 公款		embezzle public funds.
-- 食		swallow, devour.

2060₄

舌〔**She**〕n. tongue, red flannel.

00-- 音		lingual sound.
11-- 頭		tongue.
47-- 根		root of the tongue.
63-- 戰		argue, dispute, debate.
87-- 鋒		eloquence.
90-- 尖		tip of the tongue.
-- 尖音		apical sound.

看〔**Kan**〕v. look at, see, observe, guard, watch over, visit, look after.

00-- 病	attend to a patient, see a doctor.
-- 齊	follow the example of.
04-- 護	*n.* nurse, *v.* take care of, pay attention to, look after
07-- 望	visit, call on.
10-- 面子	for the sake of.
-- 不出	unable to perceive (detect, foresee, etc).
-- 不得	should not see.
-- 不起	look down upon, despise.
-- 不慣	detest, disdain.
12-- 到	catch sight of, see.
14-- 破	see through a thing.
17-- 取	let's see.
20-- 重	respect, esteem.
21-- 上	favor, be satisfied with, choose.
22-- 出	make out, see.
23-- 戲	see a performance, go to a theater.
-- 台	stand for spectators, bleachers.
24-- 待	treat.
26-- 得起	think highly of, have a high opinion of, respect.
28-- 作	regard as, consider to be, treat as.
30-- 穿	see through.
-- 守	watch, look after, shepherd, have an eye on.
-- 守費	watchman's expenses.
-- 守人	keeper, warden.
32-- 透	see through, be resigned to what is inevitable.
34-- 法	opinion, viewpoint.
35-- 清楚	see clearly.
40-- 來	it looks as if.
42-- 機會	look for a chance, watch for an opportunity.
45-- 熱鬧	go where the crowds are.
46-- 相	visit a fortune-teller.
-- 相家	physiognomist.
48-- 樣子	it seems, it looks as if.
50-- 中	feel satisfied with, favor, choose, settle on, prefer to.
-- 書	read.

51-- 輕	slight, look down upon.
60-- 見	see, catch sight of.
77-- 門人	doorkeeper, gatekeeper.
-- 醫生	consult a doctor.
80-- 人	visit someone.
84-- 錯	bark up the wrong tree.
88-- 管人	custodian.
95-- 情形	depending on circumstances.
97-- 慣	be used to seeing.

2060₉

香 〔Hsiang〕 *n.* incense, perfume, fragrance. *adj.* fragrant, scented, sweet-smelling.

12-- 水	perfume.
22-- 片	jasmine tea.
-- 甜	sweet, delicious.
30-- 客	pilgrims.
34-- 港	Hong Kong.
35-- 油	aromatic oil.
40-- 肉	dog meat.
43-- 檳酒	champagne.
44-- 蕉	banana.
-- 菇	mushroom.
-- 菌	mushroom.
-- 菜	parsley.
65-- 昧	perfume, savor.
72-- 瓜	muskmelon, cantaloupe.
76-- 腸	sausage.
77-- 閨	lady's chamber.
80-- 氣	flavor, fragrance.
91-- 爐	censer.
-- 煙	cigarettes.
92-- 燈	incense sticks and lamps.
94-- 料	spices.
98-- 粉	cosmetic.

番 〔Fan〕 *n.* barbarians, savage, turns.

10-- 石榴	guava.
44-- 地	strange land, foreign land.
-- 茄	tomato.
-- 茄醬	tomato ketchup.
-- 茄汁	tomato juice.
-- 薯	potato.
57-- 邦	barbarian state.
80-- 人	savages, aborigines, barbarians.

2064₈
皎〔Chiao〕n. white moon, adj. splendid, pure.
17-- 潔　　clear and pure.
26-- 白　　brightly white.
60-- 日　　bight daylight.
71-- 厲　　proud.

2071₄
毛〔Mao〕n. hair, fur, feathers.
00-- 病　　fault, flaw, defect, disease.
-- 衣　　woolen sweater.
02-- 氈　　carpet, felt, rug.
10-- 豆　　green soybeans.
11-- 瑟鎗　　Mauser.
-- 頭　　youngster, child.
12-- 孔　　pores of the skin.
14-- 玻璃　　frosted glass.
20-- 毛雨　　drizzle.
-- 紡廠　　woolen textile mill.
22-- 利　　gross earning, gross profit.
23-- 織物　　tweeds, woolen cloth.
26-- 細管　　capillary tube.
-- 線　　woolen yarn.
-- 線衣　　knitted woolen garment, sweater, wool.
29-- 毯　　woolen blanket.
30-- 褲　　long woolen underwear.
40-- 巾　　towel.
-- 布　　sackcloth.
-- 皮　　fur, pelt.
50-- 蟲　　caterpillar.
66-- 躁　　irritable, rash and restless.
88-- 管　　quill.
-- 筆　　Chinese pencil, hair pencil, writing brush.
-- 筆畫　　drawing done with a writing brush.
94-- 料　　woolen material.

2073₁
丟〔Tiu〕v. cast away, throw aside, rid, leave, lose.
00-- 棄　　cast off, throw away, reject, abandon.
10-- 下　　lay down, leave behind.
16-- 醜　　disgrace oneself.
25-- 失　　lose.
40-- 去　　get rid of, cast away.
51-- 掉　　lose, cast away, throw away.
77-- 開　　put aside, leave it off, not to mention.
78-- 臉　　lose face, be disgraced.

2074₆
嶂〔Chang〕n. steep cliff, range of peaks.

爵〔Chueh〕n. rank, wine, cup.
20-- 位　　noble rank, peerage.
37-- 祿　　degree and emolument of nobility.
40-- 士　　knight.
-- 士音樂　　jazz music.
-- 士樂隊　　jazz band.

2090₁
乘〔Cheng〕v. ride, mount, avail oneself of, take advantage of, multiply.
21-- 便　　take advantage of the chance, at your convenience.
27-- 船　　take a ship, take a boat, embark.
30-- 涼　　take an airing, enjoy the cool air.
-- 空　　do something while one has plenty of time on hand.
-- 客　　passenger.
34-- 法　　multiplication.
42-- 機　　seize the right time, snatch the opportunity, lose no time, embrace an opportunity.
42-- 機漁利　　profiteering.
44-- 勢　　take advantages of circumstances.
50-- 車　　take carriage, ride.
58-- 數　　multiplier, multiplicator.
-- 數表　　multiplication table.
61-- 號　　sign of multiplication.
71-- 馬　　ride a horse, take a ride.
77-- 風破浪　　ride the wind and weather the storm--great ambition.
-- 興　　on the spur of the moment.
78-- 除　　multiplication and division.

2090₃
系〔Hsi〕n. connection, succession,

system, connecting link.

00--	主任	head or chairman of a department.
08--	族	family lineage.
--	譜	genealogy.
12--	列	series, row, set.
--	孫	distant, descendants.
20--	統	system.
--	統化	n. systematization, v. systematize.
--	統軟件	system software.
--	統設計	system design.
--	統學	phylogenetic.
58--	數	coefficient.

2090₄

禾 〔 **Ho** 〕 *n.* corn, crop, growing grain.

20--	黍	millet.
26--	稈	straw, stalk of a rice plant.
50--	虫	harvest bug.
60--	田	grain field, corn land.
90--	米	paddy.

采 〔 **Tsai** 〕 *n.* bright colors, *v.* pluck, gather, choose, *adj.* variegated, brilliant, adorned, gay-colored.

00--	辦	select and purchase.
20--	集	gather, collect.
47--	聲	applause, cheer.

集 〔 **Chi** 〕 *n.* market, fair, literary works, *v.* flock together, gather, assemble, bring together, collect, mix, blend.

00--	市	fair, market.
--	市場所	fair ground.
--	市日	market day.
--	市貿易	rural bazaars, country markets, market fairs, open markets, village fair trade.
02--	訓	camp training.
08--	議	assemble for discussion.
12--	刊	collect papers.
17--	聚	collect, gather together.
--	子	collection, collect work, anthology.
24--	裝箱	container, lift van.
--	裝箱船	container ship, container-carrying vessel.
--	裝箱吊車	container crane.

27--	郵	stamp collection, philately.
--	郵家	stamp collector, philatelist.
--	郵簿	stamp album.
30--	注	focus.
37--	資	*n.* funds raising, capital raising, equity financing, pool funds, money raising, pool resources, *v.* collect money, collect funds, call for funds, raise capital, raise money.
44--	權	concentration of power, centralized power.
48--	散地	port of distribution.
50--	中	*n.* concentration, *v.* concentrate, centralize.
--	中計劃	plan of concentration.
--	中處理	centralized processing.
--	中資本	centralization of capital.
--	中地點	point of concentration.
--	中火力	concentrated fire.
--	中採購	centralized purchasing.
--	中營	concentration camp.
60--	團	combination, group, bloc, clique, ring.
--	團結婚	mass marriage, mass wedding.
--	團軍	army group, group army.
--	團公司	consortium company, group company.
75--	體	collective.
--	體旅行	party travel.
--	體生產	collective production.
--	體健康保險	group health insurance.
--	體保險	collective insurance.
--	體保險費	group insurance premium.
--	體收入	collective income.
--	體決定	group decision.
--	體協定	collective agreement.
--	體責任	collective liability, collective responsibility.
--	體耕作	collective farming.
--	體管理	group management, mass management.
--	體經濟	collective economy.
--	體安全	collective security.
--	體農場	collective farm.
77--	股	collect capital.

80-- 合	assemble, aggregate, collect, gather, congregate.
-- 合名詞	collective noun.
-- 合犯	collective offense.
-- 合體	aggregate.
-- 會	*n.* meeting, congress, aggregation, conference , *v.* meet, gather together, assemble.
-- 會自由	freedom of assembly.

2090₇

秉 〔 **Ping** 〕 *v.* hold, grasp, seize.

18-- 政	hold the political power.
40-- 直	frank and honest.
54-- 持	hold on to, hold in hand.
80-- 公	with justice, justly.
-- 公辦理	act strictly according to official procedures, handle a matter impartially.
95-- 性	disposition.

2091₃

統 〔 **Tung** 〕 *v.* rule, control, command, lead, *adj.* total, whole, entire.

00-- 率	command, lead.
04-- 計	statistics.
-- 計處	bureau of statistics.
-- 計資料	statistical data.
-- 計表	table of figures, statistical returns.
-- 計圖	statistical chart, diagrammatic map.
-- 計學	statistics, science of statistics.
-- 計學家	statist, statistician.
-- 計局	statistical bureau.
-- 計概要	statistical summary.
10-- 一	*n.* unity, consolidation, unification, *v.* unify, integrate.
-- 一天下	unify the whole country.
-- 一市場	single market, uniform market.
-- 一發票	uniform invoice.
-- 一黨	unionist party.
-- 一價	flat yield.
-- 一經營	centralized management.
-- 一化	unification.

20-- 系	system.
22-- 制	control, rule.
-- 制經濟	planned economy.
-- 稱	known together as.
24-- 帥	generalissimo, supreme commander.
-- 帥部	supreme headquarter.
-- 帥權	right of supreme command.
27-- 御	reign, rule control.
28-- 艙	steering.
33-- 治	*n.* sovereignty, *v.* reign, rule, dominate.
-- 治權	sovereignty, supreme authority.
-- 治階級	ruling class.
-- 治者	ruler.
44-- 共	total, whole.
51-- 括	all included, all encompassing.
53-- 轄	rule, govern, control.
65-- 購	unified purchase, centralized purchase.
-- 購統銷	state purchasing and selling.
72-- 兵	lead troops.
81-- 領	commanding officer.
88-- 籌	plan as a whole, overall arrangement, unified planning.
89-- 銷	sell jointly, joint marketing, planned distributing.

2091₄

稚 〔 **Chih** 〕 *adj.* tender, young, small, delicate, immature.

17-- 弱	tender and delicate.
-- 子	child, lad.
21-- 齒	young people, children.
28-- 齡	tender age.
40-- 女	young girl.
80-- 氣	childish.

維 〔 **Wei** 〕 *n.* fiber, *v.* tie, hold together, connect.

02-- 新	reform, modernize.
-- 新政治	reform politics, political reformation.
-- 新黨	reformers.

04-- 護　　　safeguard, uphold, pre-
　　　　　　serve, protect.
10-- 吾爾　　the Uygur tribe in Sinkiang
　　　　　　（Xinjiang）.
24-- 他命　　vitamin.
27-- 修　　　*n.* maintenance, *v.* keep in
　　　　　　repair, service, maintain,
　　　　　　repair.
　-- 修費　　maintenance expenses.
47-- 艱　　　very hard or difficult.
54-- 持　　　keep, maintain, support,
　　　　　　sustain, upkeep, preserve,
　　　　　　stand, bear out.
　-- 持市面　regulate market.
　-- 持現狀　maintain the status quo,
　　　　　　maintain the present con-
　　　　　　dition.
　-- 持秩序　call to order, keep order.
　-- 持治安　maintain public order.
　-- 持世界和平　preserve or maintain world
　　　　　　peace.
　-- 持費　　maintenance charges (costs).
57-- 繫　　　hold together, maintain,
　　　　　　tie up.

纏〔**Chan**〕*v.* bind up, entwine, cling
to, implicate, involve, bother.
00-- 裹　　　wrap up, cover tightly.
08-- 訟　　　be involved in a tangled
　　　　　　lawsuit.
11-- 頭　　　turban.
20-- 住　　　entangled, entwined, wrap
　　　　　　tightly, wind around.
24-- 繞　　　wind round and round, en-
　　　　　　circle.
26-- 綿　　　affectionate, inseparable.
27-- 身　　　be delayed, be held up by
　　　　　　something.
51-- 擾　　　bother persistently.
60-- 累　　　implicate.
　-- 足　　　bind up the feet.
77-- 緊　　　bind tightly.
2092₇
紡〔**Fang**〕*v.* spin, reel, twist.
22-- 絲　　　reel silk.
　-- 絲機　　filature.
23-- 織　　　spin and weave.

-- 織產品　　textile products.
-- 織工業　　textile industry.
-- 織廠　　　textile mill.
-- 織工人　　spinner, textile worker, tex-
　　　　　　tile factory worker.
-- 業　　　　textile industry.
-- 織機　　　looms, spinning and wea-
　　　　　　ving machine.
-- 織娘　　　kind of grasshopper.
-- 織品　　　cotton textile, textiles.
-- 織品市場　piece market.
-- 織原料　　textile materials.
-- 織公司　　textile company.
27-- 綢　　　pongee.
29-- 紗　　　spin cotton into yarn.
　-- 紗廠　　spinning mill.
　-- 紗機　　spinning jenny.
50-- 車　　　spinning wheel.
82-- 錘　　　spindle.

締〔**Ti**〕*n.* spin, reel, twist.
00-- 交　　　contract friendship, estab-
　　　　　　lish diplomatic ties.
24-- 結　　　contract, conclude, estab-
　　　　　　lish.
　-- 結合同　negotiate a contract.
27-- 約　　　conclude a treaty, enter a
　　　　　　contract, enter into a treaty.
　-- 約雙方　both contracting parties.
　-- 約國　　treaty powers, contracting
　　　　　　country, state.
34-- 造　　　construct, compose, build,
　　　　　　found, create.
46-- 姻　　　be united in wedlock.
67-- 盟　　　form an alliance.

縞〔**Kao**〕*n.* plain white silk.
00-- 衣　　　thin white silk, mourning
　　　　　　dress.
50-- 素　　　mourning dress.

稿〔**Kao**〕*n.* manuscript.
00-- 底　　　rough draft.
12-- 酬　　　fees paid to a writer.
17-- 子　　　draft, manuscripts
22-- 紙　　　manuscript or draft paper.
25-- 件　　　manuscripts, sketch, rough
　　　　　　draft.
50-- 本　　　manuscript, draft.

55-- 費　contribution fee, payment to a writer.

2093₂

絃 〔Hsien〕 *n.* string.

17-- 弓　fiddle bow.
-- 子　kind of three stringed musical instrument.
22-- 樂　string music.
-- 樂器　stringed instruments.
-- 樂隊　stringed band.
26-- 線　fiddle string.
40-- 索　stringed instrument.
71-- 馬　bridge of a violin.

2094₀

紋 〔Wen〕 *n.* figures, marks lines, traces.

00-- 章　armorial bearing.
16-- 理　lines, strips, veins, grain.
27-- 身　tattoo.
87-- 銀　horseshoe-shaped silver.

2094₈

絞 〔Chiao〕 *v.* twist, strangle.

00-- 痛　acute pain.
10-- 死　*n.* death by strangling, *v.* hang.
12-- 刑　death by hanging.
23-- 台　gibbet.
27-- 盤　windlass, capstan.
28-- 纜　twist ropes.
35-- 決　execution by hanging.
47-- 犯　strangle a criminal.
60-- 罪　penalty of strangulation.
77-- 緊　twist tight.

2095₃

縴 〔Chian〕 *v.* tow.

27-- 繩　towrope, towline.
50-- 夫　boat tower.

2104₇

版 〔Pan〕 *n.* board, prank.

10-- 面　space of a whole page, layout.
28-- 稅　royalty, copyright royalty
-- 稅收益　income from royalties.
37-- 次　edition.
44-- 權　copyright, literary property.

-- 權保護　copyright protection.
-- 權侵犯　copyright infringement.
-- 權法　copyright law.
-- 權費　copyright fee.
-- 權所有　all rights reserved, copyright reserved, copyrighted.
-- 權合同　copyright contract.
50-- 本　edition.
-- 畫　print, picture printed.
60-- 圖　territory, census and maps.
88-- 籍　census.

2108₆

順 〔Shun〕 *v.* accord with, follow, agree to, obey, comply with, *adj.* obedient, filial, compliant, agreeable.

00-- 序　order, order in turn, series, course, sequence.
-- 序編號　sequence number.
16-- 理　reasonable, logical.
21-- 便　at one's convenience, in passing.
22-- 利　easy, smooth, prosperous, flourishing.
28-- 從　obey, comply with.
30-- 流　with the stream, with the tide.
-- 適　at ease, smoothly.
33-- 心　satisfactorily, gratifying.
37-- 次　in turn, on the cards.
38-- 道　obey good reason, do something on the way.
50-- 事　matters that make one leap with joy.
56-- 暢　smooth, be in luck.
67-- 路　by the way.
77-- 風　down the wind, downwind.
-- 風耳　well-informed person.
-- 民　loyal people, people surrendering to foreign conquerors.
80-- 命　obey order, resigned to one's fate.
-- 差　favorable balance, surplus.

2110₀

上 〔Shang〕 *n.* superiors, emperor, *v.* go up, ascend, mount, *adj.* upper, high, superior, excellent, *adv.* up, upward, above, *prep.* on above, upon.

00--	癮	become addicted to.
--	座	seat of honor.
--	帝	God, Lord, Heaven, The Absolute, The Supreme Being.
--	方	place above, celestial realm.
--	床	go to bed.
--	文	preceding part (context).
--	衣	upper garments, jackets.
--	市	hit the stand, come into the market, appear on the market.
--	市股票	listed stock.
--	市公司	listed (quoted) companies.
02--	訴	appeal.
--	訴權	right of appeal.
04--	計	best plan.
06--	課	attend class, go to class, begin the school.
07--	部	upper portion, first part.
08--	議院	The Upper House, Upper Chamber, Senate.
10--	工	begin work.
--	下	up and down, above and below, rise and fall.
--	面	upper surface, top, above, higher authorities.
--	不去	cannot go up.
11--	班	go to office, go on duty, go on shift.
--	班時間	office hours.
--	頭	top, above up, the authorities.
--	輩	earlier generation, one's senior.
12--	水	sail against the current, add water.
--	發條	wind a (watch or clock).
--	列	above listed (mentioned).
17--	弔	commit suicide by hanging, hang oneself.
--	司	superior officials.
20--	位	top seat.
21--	街	go shopping, go into the street.
22--	任	proceed to one's post.
--	岸	land, go shore.
--	山	go up the mountain, go uphill.
23--	代	previous generation.
--	台	go on stage, assume office.
24--	升	ascend, rise, increase in production, upswing.
--	告	appeal.
--	裝	dress up, make up.
27--	將	full general (陸空軍), admiral (海軍).
--	身	upper part of the body.
--	旬	first ten days of a month.
--	級	superior, higher, lighter level.
--	船	board, embark.
28--	稅	pay tax.
30--	空	in the sky, overhead.
--	流	upper stream.
--	流社會	the upper class, high society.
--	進	make progress, advance.
--	賓	distinguished guests.
31--	漲	rise, harden, run high, firm up, swing up, go up, be running up.
32--	浮	floating upward, float upward.
33--	演	perform, stage.
--	述	aforesaid, aforementioned.
35--	油	apply lubricant.
37--	次	last time.
--	週	last week.
38--	海	Shanghai.
--	游	upper reaches.
40--	士	first sergeant.
--	古	antiquity, pristine.
--	去	go up, ascend.
--	榜	have one's name listed as a successful candidate of an examination.
--	校	colonel.
--	來	come up, come out.
44--	坡	climb a slope.
--	坡路	uphill road, ascending road,

-- 墳	upward slope.
	visit somebody's grave.
-- 世	primeval times, prehistoric times.
-- 菜	best dishes, place dishes on the table.
45-- 樓	go upstairs.
46-- 場	go on stage, enter the field, listing.
-- 枷	pillory.
47-- 報	published in newspaper, report to one's boss.
-- 期	previous period.
50-- 車	mount a carriage, get in a car, bus, or taxi.
-- 書	present a petition.
54-- 軌道	get on the right track.
60-- 品	superior quality.
61-- 賬	put a purchase on credit.
65-- 映	show.
67-- 路	start a journey.
-- 略	proceeding part omitted.
70-- 臂	upper arm.
71-- 馬	mount a horse.
73-- 院=上議院	
74-- 尉	captain (陸軍), lieutenant (海軍).
-- 肢	upper limbs.
75-- 陣	go to battle, pitch into the work.
77-- 風	upper hand, advantage, windward.
-- 月	last month.
-- 屆	previous term.
-- 層	upper layer or level.
-- 學	go to school.
-- 門	visit, call.
80-- 鏡頭	photogenic, appear in a movie.
-- 前	come forward.
-- 午	forenoon, morning.
-- 年紀	getting on in years.
83-- 鋪	upper berth.
88-- 等	first class, first rate, best quality, superior.
-- 等貨	choice goods, prime quality, super cargo, real stuff, real

	thing.
-- 等社會	the upper class, upper circles, high life.
-- 算	economical.
-- 策	best stratagem, best plan.
89-- 鎖	lock.
90-- 半夜	before midnight, first half of the night.
-- 半天	morning, forenoon.
-- 半身	upper part of a body, above the waist.
-- 半場	first half of (a game).
-- 半月	first of a month.
-- 當	cheated, imposed upon.
-- 火車	board a train.

止 〔Chih〕 v. stop, cease, desist, halt, remain.

00-- 痛	stop pain, allay pain.
-- 痛藥	painkiller, anodyne.
-- 癢	stop itching.
08-- 於	stop at, this far and no further.
20-- 住	stop, halt, desist.
21-- 步	n. standstill, v. halt.
24-- 付	stop payment.
27-- 血	n. restringent, hemostasis, v. stop bleeding.
-- 血藥	styptic, restringent.
33-- 瀉	stop diarrhea.
36-- 渴	quench thirst.
47-- 怒	stop anger.
60-- 咳	stop coughing.
61-- 點	stopping point.
87-- 飢	appease one's hunger.

2110₁

些 〔Hsieh〕 adj. little, some, few, adv. rather, somewhat, slightly.

28-- 微	slightly.
90-- 少	any, a bit of.

2111₀

此 〔Tsu〕 adj. this, the.

02-- 刻	now, at this moment.
11-- 輩	such people, people of this type.
20-- 番	this time.
21-- 處	here.

22--	後	hereafter, from now on, henceforth.
23--	外	besides, in addition to, furthermore.
25--	生	this life.
44--	地	this place, here.
50--	事	this matter.
60--	日	this day.
64--	時此地	here and now.
67--	路不通	no thoroughfare.
77--	間	this place, within this.
--	舉	this action, this undertaking, this move.
80--	人	this man.
88--	等	this kind, this type, such.

2116₀

黏 〔**Nien**〕 *adj.* sticky, viscid, gluey, glutinous.

20--	住	stick, adhere.
30--	液	mucus.
35--	油	sticky oil, heavy oil.
40--	力	adhesion.
--	土	clay.
44--	著	stick, cohere, cling.
--	著性	tenacity.
47--	韌	tenacious, tough, strong, resisting.
74--	附	stick like wax, stick close.
--	膜	mucous membrane.
80--	合	cohere, adhere, stick, cling, hold, clasp.
--	合劑	adhesives.
90--	米	glutinous rice.

2120₁

步 〔**Pu**〕 *n.* pace, step, *v.* walk slowly.

07--	調	marching order.
17--	子	step, pace.
21--	步	step by step, steadily.
--	步高陞	get promoted step by step.
--	行	walk, pace, march, step, tread, walk on foot.
22--	後塵	follow the footstep of others.
23--	伐	step, paces.
34--	法	walk, gait.
48--	槍	rifle.
69--	哨	sentry, outguard.

72--	兵	infantry.
77--	驟	procedure, steps taken.
78--	隊	troops, army.

2121₀

仁 〔**Jen**〕 *n.* humanity, mercy, kindness, charity, kernel, *adj.* kind, humane, benevolent, merciful, tender, charitable.

18--	政	good administration.
20--	愛	*n.* humanity, kindness, *adj.* humane, kind.
33--	心	kind heart.
44--	者	man of benevolent character.
--	慈	kind, humane, gracious.
80--	人君子	kind-hearted gentleman, good people.
--	義	benevolence and justice.

2121₁

征 〔**Cheng**〕 *n.* attack, invade, impose (tax).

04--	討	punitive expedition.
23--	伐	attack, bring war upon.
28--	收	impose, levy, collect, levy and collect.
--	收所得稅	tax income.
--	稅	*n.* tax levy, taxation, tax collection, *v.* impose tax, raise tax.
38--	途	journey of a traveler.
63--	戰	fight in battle.
65--	購	requisitioned purchase, wanted to purchase.
77--	服	conquer, beat, vanquish.
--	服者	conqueror.
--	屬	family of a soldier.
--	用	requisition.
--	用土地	requisition of the land.

徑 〔**Ching**〕 *n.* byway, footpath, diameter.

30--	賽	track events (sport).
40--	直	straight, directly.
67--	路	byway, narrow path.
77--	尺	caliber ruler.

徘 〔**Pai**〕 *v.* walk about, wander.

26--	徊	*v.* walk to and fro, *adj.* ir-

| | resolute, hesitating, unde-cided. |
| -- 徊歧途 | linger around the wrong path. |

虐〔Nueh〕*n.* cruelty, harshness, cala-mities, *v.* oppress, maltreat, *adj.* har-sh, cruel, fierce, tyrannical, oppres-sive.

18-- 政	tyrannical government, iron rule.
24-- 待	maltreat, give hard mea-sure, be hard upon, bear a heavy hand on, be down upon, ill-treat.
-- 待狂	sadist, sadism.

能〔Neng〕*n.* ability, talent, capacity, *v.* can be, may be, be able, *adj.* skil-lful, talented, capable, able, com-petent, possible.

00-- 率	power.
-- 言	eloquent.
10-- 否	whether it is possible or not.
14-- 耐	skill, capability, ability.
20-- 手	good hand at, expert.
27-- 夠	able to, capable of, can.
28-- 做	able to do, capable of doing.
30-- 力	ability, capacity.
31-- 源	source of energy, power so-urces, energy resource.
-- 源計劃	energy program.
-- 源工業	energy industry.
-- 源需求	energy needs.
-- 源危機	energy crisis.
-- 源發展	energy development.
-- 源科學	energy science.
-- 源資源	energy resources.
-- 源節約	energy conservation.
-- 源管理	energy control.
40-- 士	capable person.
-- 力	ability.
44-- 者多勞	the capable are usually the busy ones.
48-- 幹	talent, ability.
-- 幹者	man of ability, capable man.
60-- 量	energy, capability.
-- 見度	visibility.

| 77-- 屈能伸 | adaptable, flexible. |
| 80-- 人 | talented person. |

2121₆

傴〔Yu〕*adj.* hunchbacked, hump-backed.

| 25-- 僂 | hunchbacked, crooked back, hum-back. |

僵〔Chiang〕*adj.* stiffened, dead-lock.

00-- 立	stand rigidly.
10-- 死	dead, ossified.
11-- 硬	rigid, stiff.
23-- 仆	fall down unconsciously.
54-- 持	come to a deadlock, be at a stalemate.
77-- 屍	stiff corpse.
-- 局	deadlock, stalemate, im-passe.

軀〔Chu〕*n.* body.

47-- 殼	body.
48-- 幹	trunk.
75-- 體	body.

2121₇

伍〔Wu〕*n.* file, squad, company, com-rade, *v.* associate with, keep com-pany with.

| 71-- 長 | corporal. |

虎〔Hu〕*n.* tiger.

28-- 政	cruel government.
27-- 將	brave general.
30-- 穴	tiger's cave.
40-- 皮	tiger skin.
53-- 威	majestic.
60-- 口	dangerous spot.
90-- 掌	poisonous plant.

虛〔Hsu〕*n.* vacancy, *adj.* empty, va-cant, false, untrue, unreal, weak, vain.

00-- 度	idle away time.
-- 言	lie, airy talk.
04-- 誇	*v.* rant, *adj.* high-sounding, inflated.
17-- 弱	weak.
21-- 價	overcharge, nominal price
22-- 偽	deceitful, dishonest, faith-less, erroneous, untrue, false, unreal

30-- 字	particles
32-- 浮	unsubstantial, airy, vain, flashy.
34-- 造	cook up.
35-- 禮	artificial manner, dead forms, company manner.
45-- 構	n. fiction, v. create, devise, invent.
46-- 想	n. imagination, fancy, v. image, fancy, conceive, dream.
47-- 報	fraudulent decla. ration, make a false report.
-- 報賬目	cook accounts, falsify the accounts, cook the books.
80-- 無主義	nihilism.
88-- 飾	pretension, disguise.
99-- 榮	vanity.

2122₀

何〔Ho〕pron. who? which? what? adv. why? how?

10-- 不	why not?
18-- 敢	how dare?
21-- 止	far more than.
-- 處	where?
-- 須	why is necessary?
22-- 樂不爲	why not do it gladly?
28-- 以	why? wherefore?
33-- 必	why must? why need?
36-- 況	let alone, much less, not to mention.
40-- 在	where is?
-- 妨	there is no harm.
-- 去何從	what course to follow?
44-- 者	which?
-- 苦	why take the trouble?
-- 地	where?
48-- 故	why? for what reason?
64-- 時	when? what time?
77-- 用	of what use?
80-- 人	who? whom?
88-- 等	how? what sort of? what kind of?

2122₁

行〔Hsing〕n. row, line, series, firm, store, trade, path, road, conduct, behavior, action, v. walk, move, do, act, perform.

00-- 商	traveling traders.
08-- 旅	travelers.
10-- 不得	cannot be done.
-- 不通	block, unable to pass, won't do.
12-- 列	array, line, procession.
-- 刑	execute, torture.
-- 刑場	execution ground.
18-- 政	administration.
-- 政處分	disciplinary measures taken against an official.
-- 政官	administrative officer.
-- 政法	administrative law.
-- 政法院	administrative court.
-- 政權	executive power.
-- 政機構	administrative machinery, (organization, authorities).
-- 政長官	top administrator.
-- 政院	Executive Yuan.
-- 政費	administrative (organizational) cost.
-- 政人員	administrator.
-- 政管理	administrative management, management engineering.
21-- 步	walk, pace.
-- 伍	rank, army.
-- 徑	path, trail, one's conducts.
22-- 兇	commit killing or murder.
-- 樂	amuse, enjoy.
24-- 動	action, movement.
-- 動電話	cellular telephone.
-- 動自由	freedom of action.
-- 裝	kit, baggage, luggage.
25-- 使	exercise, employ, perform.
-- 使權	right to exercise powers.
-- 使權利	enforcement of rights, enjoyment of right, exercise one's right.
26-- 程	journey.
30-- 宮	abode of emperor on a tour.
32-- 業	practice, occupation.
-- 業種類	business, business line, line of business, line, trade.
-- 業壟斷	trade monopolies.

--	業調查	industry survey.
--	業類別	industrial classification.
34--	爲	conduct, action, behavior, performance.
--	爲不端	misconduct.
35--	禮	salute, make one's act, do one's manner.
37--	軍	march.
--	軍床	cot.
40--	李	baggage, luggage.
--	李票	baggage check, luggage check, luggage ticket.
--	李房	baggage room.
--	李車	luggage train, baggage car, luggage van.
--	李托運	luggage transportation.
--	李費	bag money, baggage fee.
--	走	walk, go, tread.
47--	期	date of departure.
50--	車	drive a vehicle.
--	車執照	driver's license.
--	車時間表	schedule of train or bus.
--	書	cursive hand.
--	囊	wallet.
52--	刺	assassinate.
54--	轅	headquarter, temporary office.
60--	星	planet.
64--	賄	bribe, corrupt, offer a bribe.
67--	路	travel, walk on the road.
--	路人	passer-by, passerby. pedestrian.
68--	蹤	tracks, whereabouts.
71--	騙	cheat, deceive, swindle.
75--	駛	sail, drive.
80--	人	traveler, pedestrian.
--	人道	pavement, sidewalk.
--	乞	beg, be a beggar.
83--	館	temporary dwelling place of a high official.
89--	銷	sell, effect sales.
90--	當	profession, trade.
95--	情	current price, market conditions, quotation.
--	情上漲	market is rising, strong, be in the upward tendency.
--	情猛漲	soaring market.
--	情猛跌	market falls sharply.

衍〔**Yen**〕 v. overflow, extend, spread, adj. abundant, numerous, beautiful, elegant.

22--	變	develop and change, evolve.
25--	生	derive from.
32--	沃	fertile plains.

術〔**Shu**〕 n. art, way, plan, device, method.

01--	語	technical term, terminology, term.
--	語學	terminology.
40--	士	magician, juggler, conjurer
58--	數	astrology.

銜〔**Hsien**〕 n. title, name.

11--	頭	title.
50--	接	adjoin, lie next to, connect, link up.
80--	命	follow an order.
97--	恨	harbor grudges.

街〔**Chieh**〕 n. street, avenue, thoroughfare.

00--	市	market, shopping streets.
11--	頭	street corners.
21--	上	on the street.
38--	道	street, road.
40--	坊	neighbor.
44--	巷	streets and lanes.
57--	招	circulars.
92--	燈	street light (lamp).

衙〔**Ya**〕 n. government office, court.

77--	門	yamen, court, government office.

衡〔**Heng**〕 n. balance, scale, v. weigh.

10--	平	weigh and consider in order to uphold justice.
36--	視	look horizontally.
60--	量	weigh, measure, consider, judge, estimate.
--	量平法	law of equity.
--	量單位	unit of measurement.
66--	器	weighing apparatus.
95--	情	consider the actual condition.

衝 〔**Chung**〕 *n.* path, thoroughfare, *v.* rush against, move toward.

10--	要	strategic point, important junction.
14--	勁	aggressiveness, drive.
--	破	break through, breach, smash.
22--	出	rush out, cut one's way through.
--	倒	upset, overthrow.
24--	動	impulse.
30--	進	burst in, rush in.
--	突	*n.* conflict, contradiction, collision, *v.* conflict, encounter, dash against, run foul of.
40--	力	momentum, impulsive forces.
47--	殺	charge, rush ahead.
48--	散	scatter, put to flight.
50--	撞	rush against, smash.
57--	擊	strike against, pound against, charge.
--	擊力	force of thrust.
80--	入	interruption, incursion.
87--	鋒	break through.
--	鋒隊	storm troops.
--	鋒鎗	tommy gun, submachine gun.

衛 〔**Wei**〕 *n.* military station, *v.* escort, guard, protect, defend.

25--	生	sanitation, hygiene, health.
--	生衣	kind of tight cotton underwear, long Johns, thermals.
--	生設備	sanitary facilities.
--	生部門	sanitary authorities.
--	生處	department of public health.
--	生組織	sanitary organization.
--	生紙	toilet paper, tissue paper.
--	生棉	sanitary napkin.
--	生檢疫	health quarantine.
--	生家	hygienist.
--	生措施	sanitary measures.
--	生局	health office, Health Service.
--	生所	public health clinic.
--	生院	hospital.
--	生學	hygiene.
--	生隊	sanitary troops.
40--	士	guard, bodyguard.
53--	戍	garrison.
--	戍司令	garrison commander.
60--	星	satellite.
--	星通訊	communication by satellite, satellite telecommunications.
--	星轉播站	satellite earth station.
--	星國家	satellite nations.
72--	兵	bodyguard, guard.
78--	隊	guard.

2122₇

倆 〔**Liang**〕 *adj.* two, double, *adv.* twice.

60--	口子	husband and wife.
77--	月	couple of month.
80--	人	two persons.

儒 〔**Ju**〕 *n.* scholar, men of letters.

30--	家	Confucianist, the Confucian school.
44--	者	Confucian Scholar, man of letters.
48--	教	Confucianism.
70--	雅	scholarly and refined, elegant style.
77--	風	style of Confucian scholar.

肯 〔**Ken**〕 *v.* assent, permit, allow, consent, *adj.* willing, voluntary.

10--	不肯	are you willing or not?
30--	定	positive, affirmative, positive reply.
48--	幹	willing to put in hard work.

虜 〔**Lu**〕 *n.* prisoner, captive, *v.* seize, capture.

44--	獲	capture.
50--	掠	seize, plunder, capture.

膚 〔**Fu**〕 *n.* skin, surface, *adj.* great, large, beautiful, admirable.

14--	功	great merit.
33--	淺	superficial.
72--	髮	skin and hair.

虧 〔**Kuei**〕 *n.* failure, deficiency, defect,

loss, *v.* injure, fail, lose in trade.

24-- 待	treat shabbily, maltreat.
26-- 得	fortunately, luckily, thanks to.
27-- 負	be ungrateful to, lose.
-- 欠	in debt, in arrears, be in arrears, have a deficit.
30-- 空	*n.* deficit, bankruptcy, debt, *v.* be in debt, go into red ink, make a hole in.
33-- 心	*v.* go against one's conscience, *adj.* ungrateful, discreditable.
-- 心事	matter of remorse.
50-- 本	*n.* loss on a capital, deterioration of profit, *v.* lose money, fail in business, lose one's capital.
52-- 折	loss, deficit.
-- 耗	loss.
56-- 損	*n.* deficit, operation loss, loss, deficiency, in the red, *v.* deplete.
-- 損額	total value of loss, amount of loss.
58-- 數	number of deficiency.
60-- 累	unable to make both ends meet, be in debt.
81-- 短	short, lacking.
85-- 蝕	eclipse, deficit.

2123₁

卡 〔**Ka**〕 *n.* card, guardhouse, station, custom's barrier.

22-- 片	card.
30-- 賓槍	carbine.
37-- 通	cartoon.
43-- 式	cassette.
44-- 帶	cassette tape.
50-- 車	freight car, truck.
-- 車工業	trucking industry.
67-- 路里	calorie.
77-- 門	toll gate.

2123₄

虞 〔**Yu**〕 *n.* accident, emergency, danger, *v.* expect, be anxious.

2123₆

慮 〔**Lu**〕 *n.* anxiety, suspicion, doubt. *v.* be anxious, be concerned, plan, devise, *adj.* anxious, suspicious, doubtful, thoughtful.

2124₀

虔 〔**Chien**〕 *v.* respect, seize, take by force, kill, *adj.* devout, pious, sincere, respectful.

03-- 誠	sincere, devout.
24-- 告	pray respectfully.
33-- 心	devout, pious.
37-- 潔	pure, clean, spotless.
48-- 敬	piety.

2124₁

處 〔**Chu**〕 *n.* place, position, state, condition, *v.* deal, treat, mete out.

00-- 方	prescribe.
10-- 死	punish with death.
12-- 刑	inflict punishment, punish.
16-- 理	treat, get along, manipulate, bear through.
-- 理效果	treatment effect.
-- 理業務	deal with business.
-- 理爭端	adjudicate a dispute.
21-- 處	here and there.
22-- 斷	decide, determine, resolve.
27-- 身	behave.
33-- 治	execute, operate, perform, act.
35-- 決	decide, resolve, execute.
40-- 境	position, situation.
-- 境困難	be in a tough spot, be in tight corner.
-- 女	maid, virgin, damsel.
-- 女作	maiden effort.
-- 女地	virgin land.
-- 女航	maiden voyage.
-- 女膜	hymen, maidenhead.
44-- 世	attend to the affairs of the world, lead a life, run a race, play a game.
50-- 事	execute, perform.
60-- 置	manage, settle, carry on.
-- 罰	punish, mete out.
71-- 長	section chief, head of a department or office.

80-- 分　　　deal with, punish.

2124₆

便〔**Pien**〕*adj.* convenient, handy, expedient, advantageous, ordinary, common.

00-- 衣　　　ordinary dress.
-- 衣隊　　　plain-clothes troops.
08-- 於　　　easy to, convenient for.
17-- 函　　　memorandum, note.
21-- 步　　　walk at ease.
22-- 利　　　advantageous, convenient.
-- 利品　　　convenience goods.
27-- 餐　　　ordinary meal.
-- 條　　　note.
30-- 宜貨　　cheap article, bargain, junk, good buy.
-- 宜的　　　cheap, economical.
33-- 祕　　　constipation.
40-- 壺　　　chamber pot.
44-- 鞋　　　slipper, cloth shoes.
47-- 帽　　　cap.
-- 桶　　　container for stool.
55-- 捷　　　easy and convenient.
66-- 器　　　stool.
67-- 路　　　shortcut, bypath.
72-- 所　　　toilet, lavatory, rest room.
77-- 服　　　ordinary clothing, everyday dress, informal dress.
-- 門　　　side door.
81-- 飯　　　ordinary meal, simple food.
90-- 當　　　*n.* box lunch, adj. convenient.

2124₇

優〔**Yu**〕*n.* actor, performer, player, *adj.* abundant, excessive, overmuch, distinguished, excellent, superior.

08-- 於　　　better than.
20-- 秀　　　remarkable, outstanding.
-- 秀份子　　elite.
24-- 先　　　priority.
-- 先權　　　prerogative, preference right, precedence, priority, right of priority, preference.
-- 先股　　　preference stocks, preferred share (stock), prior

stock, privileged share.

24-- 待　　　do honor, make much of, do the handsome thing, give preferential treatment.
-- 待券　　　complimentary ticket, discount ticket.
25-- 生學　　　eugenics.
27-- 獎　　　ample reward.
28-- 伶　　　actor, player.
30-- 良　　　fine, good.
36-- 遇　　　treat well.
38-- 游　　　carefree.
-- 裕　　　well-to-do, wealthy, comfortable.
43-- 越　　　superiority, excellence, distinction.
44-- 勢　　　supremacy, superiority, advantage, upper hand.
50-- 惠　　　preferential, favorable.
-- 惠待遇　　preferential treatment, favorable treatment.
-- 惠稅率　　import tariff from a favored nation.
-- 惠期　　　days of grace.
-- 惠國　　　favored nation.
61-- 點　　　merit, worth.
70-- 雅　　　fair, polite.
71-- 厚　　　favorable, liberal.
72-- 質　　　fine quality, high quality, high grade.
77-- 閑　　　*n.* leisure, *adj.* carefree, free and content.
79-- 勝　　　championship, superiority, predominance.
-- 勝旗　　　champion flag.
-- 勝獎　　　winning prize.
-- 勝者　　　winner, champion.
-- 勝杯　　　champion cup.
-- 勝劣敗　　the survival of the fittest.
80-- 美　　　nice, excellent, admirable, refine, fine, good.
88-- 等　　　excellent grade, first rate, best class, high-class, superior.
90-- 劣　　　good and bad, bright and dull, fit and unfit.

2125₃

歲 〔Sui〕 *n*. year, age.

22--	出	annual expenditure.
25--	俸	annuity, annual income.
27--	夕	New Year's Eve.
28--	收	annual income.
--	終	end of the year.
58--	數	age.
77--	月	time, time and season.
--	月如流	time flies.
80--	入	revenue, annual income.
--	首	beginning of a year.

2126₀

佔 〔Chan〕 *v*. usurp, seize by force, occupy, arrogate, assume.

21--	上風	have the upper hand.
--	便宜	be in advantageous position, take advantage.
24--	先	presume, lead, forestall.
26--	線	the line is busy.
40--	有	own, occupy, possess, hold.
--	有者	occupant.
51--	據	occupy by force.
81--	領	occupy, capture, seize other's land.
--	領軍	occupation troops.
--	領區域	occupied area.

2126₁

僭 〔Chien〕 *v*. assume, arrogate, usurp.

00--	主	tyrant.
20--	位	usurp the throne, aspire to the throne.
30--	竊	usurp.
43--	越	arrogate, overstep.
44--	權	usurp one's power.

2126₂

偕 〔Chieh〕 *v*. accompany, *adv*. jointly, together.

21--	行	walk together.
44--	老	grow old together as man and wife.
77--	同	with, together.

2128₁

徙 〔Hsi〕 *v*. move, shift, remove.

22--	任	be transferred to another job.
27--	移	move.
77--	居	change one's house, move one's abode.
--	貫	move one's residence.

2128₆

偵 〔Cheng〕 *n*. spy, scout, detective, *v*. spy out, detect, explore.

07--	詢	examine a suspect.
14--	破	bust a crime, crack a criminal case.
--	聽	intercept, monitor.
26--	緝	search out, investigate.
30--	察	*n*. reconnaissance, *v*. investigate.
--	察敵情	gather intelligence about the enemy.
--	察機	scout plane, reconnaissance plane.
40--	查	*n*. inquisition, *v*. investigate.
57--	探	*n*. detective, spy , *v*. detect, espy.
--	探小說	detective story.

須 〔Hsu〕 *v*. ought, must, should be, *adj*. necessary, needful, serviceable.

10--	要	have to, must.
24--	待	have to wait, expect, look forward to.
26--	得	must have, should have.
77--	用	need.
86--	知	should know.
90--	當	must.

傾 〔Ching〕 *v*. overturn, pour out, turn upside down.

09--	談	have a good heart-to-heart talk.
10--	覆	overturn, overset, upset, subvert.
14--	聽	hear out, listen, give an ear to.
22--	側	inclined.
--	倒	tumble, dump, fall for.
27--	危	mean, treacherous, precarious.
--	向	*n*. inclination, tendency,

		disposition, *v.* incline, trend, bend, dip.
	-- 角	inclination.
30--	注	pour.
	-- 家蕩產	exhaust one's wealth, dissipate one's fortune.
33--	心	be all for, admire wholeheartedly.
	-- 瀉	come down in torrents.
38--	溢	run over.
41--	杯	drink up, empty the glass.
65--	跌	fall.
68--	敗	beaten, defeated.
80--	盆大雨	pouring rain.
84--	斜	obliquity, declivity.
89--	銷	dumping, cutthroat sale.
	-- 銷市場	dumping ground (market).
	-- 銷商品	dumping goods.

頻 〔 Pin 〕 *adv.* frequently, often, repeatedly.

00--	率	frequency.
38--	道	channel (television) .
58--	數	repeatedly, incessantly.
91--	煩	frequent, incessant, busy.

價 〔 Chia 〕 *n.* price, value, cost, worth.

00--	高	dear, expensive.
	-- 廉	cheap, at low price.
	-- 廉物美	excellent quality at low price, good bargain, be of fine quality and price, cheaper and better goods, low price and fine wares.
24--	值	value, worth.
	-- 值証明書	certificate of value.
	-- 值要素	element of value.
	-- 值升高	rise in value.
	-- 值連城	invaluable, priceless.
	-- 值標準	standard of value.
	-- 值穩定	stability of value.
	-- 值減少	shrinking in value.
31--	漲	price advancing.
47--	格	rate, price.
	-- 格競爭	aggregate (price) competition.
	-- 格調整	monetary correction, price adjustment.

	-- 格飛漲	price has shot up, rapid rise in price.
	-- 格系統	pricing system.
	-- 格上漲	increase in the prices, price rises, prices are up, jump high in price, price hikes, rise in the price.
	-- 格穩定	aggregate stability, price-stabilizing, price steadiness, stability of price, stabilization of price.
	-- 格漲落	price fluctuations.
	-- 格凍結	price freeze.
	-- 格清單	schedule of prices.
	-- 格過高	excessive price, extravagant price.
	-- 格表	price list.
	-- 格趨勢	price tendency.
	-- 格回落	fall back.
	-- 格暴漲	price bulge, spurt in price.
	-- 格戰	price war.
	-- 格跌落	recede, slide in prices.
	-- 格風險	price risk.
	-- 格公道	at fair price, reasonable price.
60--	目	price, quotation.
	-- 目單	price list.
	-- 目表	price catalogue (P/C), price list, price bulletin, quotation table, rate sheet, table of price.
80--	差	variance in price, spread price difference (differential).

頹 〔 Tui 〕 *v.* collapse, fall, flow down, *adj.* ruined, fallen.

00--	廢	ruined, destroyed.
	-- 廢主義	decadentism.
37--	運	declining fortune.
40--	喪	beaten, ruined, discouraged.
45--	勢	declining tendency.
68--	敗	degenerating, decadent, depraved.
77--	風	decadent custom, corruptive practices.

2131₆

鱷〔Eh〕 *n.* crocodile, alligator.
2133₁

熊〔Hsiung〕 *n.* bear.
24-- 貓　　　　panda.
77-- 膽　　　　gall secretion of a bear.
90-- 掌　　　　palms of a bear.

態〔Tai〕 *n.* manner, attitude, figure, form, bearing.
00-- 度　　　　manner, attitude.
-- 度和平　　　friendly, peaceful attitude.
-- 度壞　　　　ill-mannered, impolite.
-- 度好　　　　well-mannered, well be-haved.
2140₆

卓〔Cho〕 *adj.* high, tall, lofty, upright.
00-- 立　　　　stand alone, stand out.
03-- 識　　　　lofty ideas, elevated view.
27-- 絕　　　　super-eminent, outstanding.
43-- 越　　　　excellence, greatness, re-markable.
44-- 著　　　　prominent, eminent.
60-- 見　　　　brilliant idea or view.
2144₀

鼾〔Han〕 *n.* snore, *v.* snore.
47-- 聲　　　　snoring.
62-- 睡　　　　heavy sleep with snoring.
2155₀

拜〔Pai〕 *v.* bow, worship, visit, honor, salute.
00-- 訪　　　　visit, give a call.
02-- 託　　　　request, beg.
04-- 謝　　　　express one's thanks.
06-- 謁　　　　pay one's respect to.
20-- 辭　　　　take leave, say goodbye.
25-- 佛　　　　worship Buddha.
27-- 候　　　　visit, call on.
30-- 客　　　　make a call.
35-- 神　　　　worship gods.
37-- 祖　　　　worship ancestor.
40-- 壽　　　　congratulate one on his bir-thday.
62-- 別　　　　take leave, say good-by.
77-- 服　　　　admire.
80-- 金主義　　mammonism, bullionism, money worship.
-- 年　　　　pay New Year's call.
81-- 領　　　　accept with thanks.
2160₀

占〔Chan〕 *v.* occupy, take possession, divine, foretell.
21-- 優勢　　　predominate.
23-- 卜　　　　*n.* sooth-saying, *v.* divine, cast lots.
24-- 先　　　　*n.* anticipation, *v.* precede.
40-- 有　　　　*n.* possession, *v.* possess, own, take possession of.
-- 有物　　　　possession.
-- 有權　　　　possession, right of pos-session.
51-- 據　　　　occupy, take possession of
81-- 領　　　　occupation.

鹵〔Lu〕 *v.* plunder, rob, *adj.* stupid, dull, rude, insolent.
12-- 水　　　　alkaline, saline ground wat-er.
44-- 莽　　　　rash, careless, remiss, rude.
-- 獲文件　　　captured document.
50-- 掠　　　　plunder, seize, capture.
65-- 味　　　　salty taste, pot-stewed fowl or meat.
2160₁

旨〔Chih〕 *n.* decree, order, meaning, sense, intention, purpose.
00-- 意　　　　will, intention, imperial de-cree.
47-- 趣　　　　objective and interest.
2160₂

皆〔Chieh〕 *adj.* all, *adv.* altogether.
10-- 可　　　　all will do.
40-- 大歡喜　　everybody is satisfied.
60-- 因　　　　only because, all because.
-- 是　　　　all are.
86-- 知　　　　known to all.
2171₀

匕〔Pi〕 *n.* spoon, ladle.
80-- 首　　　　dagger.

比〔Pi〕 *v.* compare, classify, sort.
00-- 方　　　　for instance.
-- 率　　　　ratio, proportion.

13-- 武　compare strength.

20-- 重　specific gravity.

21-- 價　comparative price, parity rate, price relations, price rations, rate of exchange.

22-- 例　proportion.

-- 例尺　scale.

-- 例分攤　prorate distribution.

30-- 肩　shoulder to shoulder, side by side.

-- 肩作戰　fight side by side.

-- 賽　*n.* competition, match, contest, *v.* compete, contest.

44-- 熱　specific heat.

50-- 較　compare, draw a parallel of.

-- 較要素　element of comparison.

-- 較成本　comparison costs.

57-- 擬　in comparison with.

2171₆

崛 〔Chu〕 *adj.* rugged, mountainous.

24-- 崎　rocky, rugged, uneven.

2172₇

師 〔Shih〕 *n.* division, army, master, teacher.

24-- 徒　master and his student.

25-- 生　teacher and student.

37-- 資　qualifications of a teacher.

44-- 姑　nun.

45-- 妹　younger female fellow student.

50-- 表　model worthy of emulation.

77-- 母　wife of one's tutor.

71-- 長　teacher, divisional commander.

80-- 父　tutor, master, teacher.

88-- 範　*n.* master, tutor, *v.* imitate, emulate.

-- 範生　student of a normal school.

-- 範教育　normal-education.

-- 範學校　normal school.

2177₂

齒 〔Che〕 *n.* teeth.

00-- 痛　toothache.

-- 音　dental sound.

24-- 科　dentistry.

47-- 根　root of a tooth.

54-- 軌　rack railway.

58-- 輪　gear wheel.

72-- 質　dentine.

73-- 腔　gum of the tooth.

2178₆

頃 〔Ching〕 *n.* a land measure of one hundred mu（hectare）.

02-- 刻　in a moment, in a twinkling.

21-- 步　half a step.

77-- 間　just, recently, of late.

-- 聞　just heart, recently reported.

2180₆

貞 〔Chen〕 *n.* virginity, maidenhood, *adj.* chaste, pure, virtuous.

12-- 烈　honesty, courage and virtue.

26-- 白　chastity, integrity.

40-- 女　virgin.

47-- 婦　chaste woman.

52-- 靜　modesty.

56-- 操　virtue.

60-- 固　stick to righteousness and virtue.

88-- 節　chastity, purity, virtue.

2190₃

紫 〔Tzu〕 *adj.* purple, brown.

17-- 翠玉　alexandrite.

21-- 紅　purple.

23-- 外線　ultraviolet rays.

27-- 色　purple, violet.

44-- 菜　laver.

-- 藥水　gentian violet solution.

2190₄

桌 〔Cho〕 *n.* table, desk.

10-- 面　table top.

13-- 球　table tennis, ping-pong.

17-- 子　table, desk.

40-- 布　tablecloth.

-- 帷　table cover.

柴 〔Chai〕 *n.* fire wood, brushwood, fuel, faggot.

11-- 頭　knotty stick.

21-- 行　shop where firewood is sold.

40-- 堆　stack of fuel.

50-- 車　crude carriage.

57-- 把　bundle of firewood.

77-- 門　　　　door of brushwood.
90-- 火　　　　fuel, wood.
　-- 米　　　　fuel and rice--the household needs.

2191₀

紅 〔**Hung**〕 *n*. red color, *adj*. rosy, red, ruddy, fiery.

00-- 衣主教　cardinal.
　-- 痢　　　dysentery, red flux.
05-- 辣椒　　pimiento, red chili pepper.
10-- 豆　　　scarlet bean, red bean.
11-- 頭文件　red tape, internal official document.
22-- 衛兵　　red guard.
　-- 利　　　bonus, dividend.
　-- 利股　　bonus dividend, bonus stock, bonus share.
　-- 利分配　profit sharing.
23-- 外線　　infrared rays.
27-- 色　　　red, blush.
　-- 包　　　red paper bag containing money, bribe, kickback.
　-- 血球　　red corpuscle.
　-- 綠燈　　traffic light.
30-- 寶石　　ruby.
37-- 軍　　　Red Army.
38-- 海　　　Red Sea.
40-- 十字　　Red Cross.
　-- 十字會　Red Cross Society.
　-- 木　　　red wood.
44-- 茶　　　black tea.
　-- 葉　　　red leaves.
　-- 藥水　　mercurochrome.
　-- 蘿蔔　　carrots, radish.
50-- 棗　　　red dates .
60-- 墨水　　red ink.
77-- 股　　　bonus.
78-- 臉　　　blushed face, reddened face.
90-- 糖　　　brown sugar.
92-- 燈　　　red light, red traffic light.

2191₁

經 〔**Ching**〕 *n*. classics, Bible, menses, monthly courses, *v*. manage, regulate, pass through.

00-- 度　　　longitude.
　-- 商　　　trade, carry on business, do business, be in business, go into business, carry on business.
12-- 水　　　the menses, the monthly courses.
16-- 理　　　*n*. manager, commission agent, director, *v*. manage, direct, execute.
20-- 手　　　handle, deal with, through the agency of.
　-- 手人　　one who is responsible for.
　-- 售　　　sell, deal in.
25-- 練　　　experienced, keen and sharp.
26-- 線　　　longitude.
27-- 紀　　　*n*. broker, agent, brokerage, manager, *v*. manage.
　-- 紀費　　brokerage, brokerage charges.
　-- 紀人　　broker, agent, commission broker, middleman.
30-- 濟　　　economy.
　-- 濟主義　economism.
　-- 濟方針　economic guidelines.
　-- 濟部　　Ministry of Economic Affairs.
　-- 濟集團　economic bloc.
　-- 濟建設　economic construction.
　-- 濟政策　economic policy.
　-- 濟不景氣　business depression, economic distress.
　-- 濟研究　economic studies.
　-- 濟研究所　economic research institute, Institute of Economics.
　-- 濟發展　economic development, economic advance.
　-- 濟建設　economic construction.
　-- 濟環境　economic circumstances (environment).
　-- 濟集團　economic bloc (group).
　-- 濟制度　economic system.
　-- 濟制裁　economic sanction, punitive economic measure.
　-- 濟崩潰　bust, economic bust breakdown, economic disinteg-

ration.

-- 濟參事	economic counselor.
-- 濟特區	special economic zone (SEZ), economic special region.
-- 濟負擔	economic burden.
-- 濟侵略	economic penetration (aggression).
-- 濟穩定	economic stability (stabilization), stable economy.
-- 濟復興	business recovery (revival) economic rehabilitation (recovery).
-- 濟危機	economic Dunkirk, economic crisis.
-- 濟絕交	severance of economic relation.
-- 濟作戰部	Ministry of Economic Warfare.
-- 濟艙	economy class, tourist class.
-- 濟收益	economic yield.
-- 濟潛力	economic potential.
-- 濟福利	economic welfare.
-- 濟混亂	economic chaos.
-- 濟大國	economic big power.
-- 濟基礎	economic basis.
-- 濟革命	economic revolution.
-- 濟封鎖	economic blockade.
-- 濟蕭條	slump, economic (business) depression.
-- 濟獨立	economic independence, independence in economy.
-- 濟犯罪	economic crime.
-- 濟好轉	upturn in the economy.
-- 濟趨勢	economic trend.
-- 濟增長	economic gain (growth).
-- 濟擴張	economic expansion.
-- 濟回升	business uptrend (upturn, upswing, pick-up).
-- 濟史	history of economy.
-- 濟援助	economic aid.
-- 濟提攜	economic assistance.
-- 濟戰	economic warfare.
-- 濟困難	financial difficulties.
-- 濟顧問	economic adviser (advisor, counselor).
-- 濟學	economics.

-- 濟學家	economist.
-- 濟情況	economic condition, state of business.
37-- 過	pass through, pass, pass over, go across, go over.
47-- 期	the time of menses, period of menstruation.
55-- 費	expenses, fund, expenditure, spending.
-- 典	classical allusions, classics.
60-- 界	boundary marking on the farmland.
78-- 驗	experience.
-- 驗豐富	well-experienced.
89-- 銷	*n.* distribution, *v.* handle distribution, sell on commission.
90-- 常	*adj.* regular, constant, *adv.* frequently, often, constantly.
-- 常費	routine outlays, overhead charges, current expenditure, regular expenses, standing expense.
99-- 營	*n.* operation, *v.* practice, prosecute, bear through, carry on, operate, ply, handle, deal in, trade in, be engaged in, manage, be in the line.
-- 營效率	business efficiency, efficiency of operation, operating efficiency.
-- 營項目	lines of business.
-- 營業績	operating performance.
-- 營管理	management control, operating management.

2191₆

繮 〔Chiang〕 *n.* bridle, rein, halter.

27-- 繩	rein.

2194₆

綽 〔Cho〕 *adj.* ample, wide, spacious, liberal, generous.

27-- 約	gentle and modest.
38-- 裕	liberal, generous.
61-- 號	nickname.

2194₇

稱 〔Cheng〕 *n.* name, style, steelyard. *v.* call, designate, praise, admire, say, remark, state, *adj.* suitable, fit.

00-- 意	agreeable, gratifying, satisfactory.
04-- 讚	praise, admire, uphold, command, appreciate.
-- 謝	thank.
08-- 許	praise, approve, compliment, esteem, value, honor, command.
13-- 職	well qualified, competent.
27-- 身	fit perfectly.
33-- 心	satisfaction.
-- 心如意	very gratifying and satisfactory, happy and content.
60-- 量	weigh.
-- 量費	weighing charges.
61-- 號	title, designation.
62-- 呼	call, name, style.
71-- 願	just as one wishes.
81-- 頌	do credit to.

2194₉

秤 〔Cheng〕 *n.* balance, scales, steelyard.

41-- 杆	bean of a steelyard.
82-- 錘	weight used with a steelyard.

2195₃

穢 〔Hui〕 *v.* debauch, defile. *adj.* dirty, filthy, unclean, mean, vile, indecent, obscene, detestable.

00-- 言	dirty word, foul language, indecent talk.
21-- 行	bad behavior.
22-- 亂	debauch, defile.
26-- 臭	stinking, bad smelling.
27-- 名	bad name.
31-- 污	dirty, foul, filthy, unclean, impure.
40-- 土	dirty earth.
50-- 事	dirty affair, improper doing, disgraceful affair.
80-- 氣	foul air.

2200₀

川 〔Chuan〕 *n.* river, stream, running water.

34-- 流不息	constant flow, continuous.
37-- 資	travelling expenses.
44-- 菜	Szechwan style of cooking.
60-- 貝	fritillaria (Chinese medicine).

2202₁

片 〔Pien〕 *n.* strip, leaf, slip, slice, sheet, chip, flake, piece.

00-- 言	few words.
02-- 刻	instantly, in a moment.
10-- 面	one side.
-- 面之交	casual acquaintance.
17-- 子	visiting card.
27-- 租	film rent.
64-- 時	moment.
71-- 長	length of a motion picture.
77-- 段	parcel, fragment.

2210₀

剝 〔Po〕 *v.* split, tear, peel, strip, extort.

40-- 皮	peel, flay, skin, extort, fleece.
-- 奪	deprive, strip, take away.
-- 奪公權	deprivation of civil right, civil death.
-- 奪權利	abridge one's rights.
92-- 削	oppress, squeeze, undermine.

2210₈

豈 〔Chi〕 *adv.* how?

10-- 可	how can?
-- 不	wouldn't it be?
18-- 敢	how dare?
21-- 能	how can?
40-- 有此理	how can there be such a principle?

豐 〔Feng〕 *adj.* abundant, plentiful, copious, fertile, fruitful.

28-- 收	abundant harvest.
30-- 富	*n.* rich, wealthy, plenty, *adj.* abundant and fertile, bountiful, copious.
38-- 裕	abundance, plentiful.
53-- 盛	plentiful, abundant, pros-

	perous.
60-- 足	affluent, wealthy, abundant.
71-- 厚	plentiful, rich.
80-- 年	year of abundance, plentiful year.
84-- 饒	fertile, fruitful.

2213₆

蠻 〔**Man**〕*n.* barbarians, *adj.* savage, barbarous, brutal, unreasonable.

10-- 不講理	rude, brutal, savage.
17-- 勇	dare-devil.
-- 子	barbarians.
40-- 力	brute force.
48-- 幹	go ahead without considering the consequence.
50-- 夷	barbarian.
95-- 性	barbarous disposition.

2220₀

刎 〔**Wen**〕*v.* cut crosswise.

11-- 頸	kill oneself.
-- 頸之交	David and Jonathan.

俐 〔**Li**〕*adj.* clever, intelligent.

例 〔**Li**〕*n.* rules, bylaw, custom, usage.

00-- 言	direction.
17-- 子	example, instance.
21-- 行公事	official routine, routine.
23-- 外	exception.
27-- 假	statutory holiday, legal holiday.
30-- 案	precedent.
46-- 如	for example, for instance.
80-- 會	regular meeting.

制 〔**Chih**〕*n.* rule, law, system, *v.* regulate, govern, make, invent, hinder, prevent.

00-- 度	system, rules, regulation, policy.
21-- 止	withhold, suppress, inhibit.
30-- 定	enact, set down.
-- 空權	command of the air.
38-- 海權	command of the sea.
77-- 服	*n.* uniform, suppression, control, *v.* put down, suppress, bring under control.

79-- 勝	conquer, overcome, gain the day.

倒 〔**Dao**〕*v.* fall over, tumble down, turn over.

00-- 立	stand upside down.
10-- 下	fall down.
21-- 片	rewind (a film or movie) .
34-- 流	flow backward.
37-- 退	retire, withdraw, reverse.
-- 運	be out of luck, unlucky.
40-- 臺	fall from power.
44-- 填日期	dating backward.
50-- 車	back up a car.
53-- 戈	mutiny, desert to the enemy.
55-- 轉	turn the other way.
57-- 換	rotate, take turn, exchange, substitute.
58-- 數	count from bottom to top, count backward.
-- 數時間	count down.
60-- 是	actually, really.
61-- 賬	bad debts, insolvency, become bankrupt.
71-- 反	unexpectedly.
77-- 閉	*n.* failure, *v.* bust, close down, close down a shop, go bankrupt.
-- 閣	resignation of the cabinet.
98-- 斃	fall dead.

側 〔**Tse**〕*n.* side, *v.* incline, turn toward, *adj.* lateral, in clining.

10-- 面	lateral face.
-- 面圖	profile.
18-- 攻	flank attack.
21-- 衛	flank guard.
57-- 擊	flank attack.
60-- 目	squint.
62-- 影	silhouette, profile.
73-- 臥	sleep on one side.
77-- 門	side door.
-- 聞	overhear.

劇 〔**Chu**〕*n.* play, act, *adj.* annoying, distressing, *adv.* extremely, seriously.

00-- 痛	torture, pang.
01-- 評	review of a play.

08--	論	strong argument.
12--	烈	sharp, acute, sore, grave, hard, cruel.
--	烈競爭	cut-throat competition.
27--	終	end, curtain fall.
28--	作家	playwright, dramatist.
--	減	steep decline.
37--	盜	notorious robber.
46--	場	play house, theater.
50--	中人	character in a play.
--	本	play, drama.
--	毒	deadly poison.
60--	團	theatrical group, troupe.
--	員	actor.
73--	院	stage, theater.
95--	情	plot.

2220₇
彎 〔**Wan**〕 *v.* bend, *adj.* curved, crooked, arched, bend.

10--	下	decline.
17--	弓	bend the bow.
--	子	curve, bend.
55--	曲	*v.* crook, lean, bend, *adj.* crooked, curved.
67--	路	crooked road, tortuous path.

2221₀
亂 〔**luan**〕 *n.* chaos, anarchy, confusion, distraction, rebellion, revolt, *v.* confuse, confound, throw into disorder.

00--	言	babble, talk wild.
08--	說	lie, say what should be said.
01--	語	sputter.
12--	斫	slash.
17--	子	disturbance, trouble.
22--	衝	rush.
28--	倫	incest.
34--	流	turbulent flow.
40--	堆	lumber.
--	來	act foolishly or recklessly.
44--	世	troublesome time, stirring period.
47--	殺	slaughter, carnage.
51--	打	bang about.
60--	罰	mete out unjustified punishment.

--	嚷	clamor.
68--	吃	eat without caution.
72--	兵	rebels, soldiers on the rampage.
77--	風	degenerate social customs.
--	民	mob，rebels.
90--	黨	rebels.
95--	性	upset the presence of mind.

2221₄
任 〔**Jen**〕 *n.* office, responsibility, duty, trust, *v.* bear, sustain, undertake, be responsible for.

00--	意	have one's own way, have a will of one's own.
13--	職	discharge an office.
17--	務	role, duty, responsibility.
21--	何	what? whatever?
--	何物	anything.
--	何人	anyone.
--	便	at discretion, at one's convenience.
27--	免	hiring and firing, employment and discharge.
47--	期	term of office, term.
77--	用	employ, hire, engage.
80--	人	let people do.
--	命	*n.* appointment, designation, *v.* appoint.
--	命書	certificate of appointment.
95--	性	have one's own way.

催 〔**Tsui**〕 *v.* urge, press, hasten, importune.

00--	辦	press somebody to do something.
04--	討	press for repayment.
05--	請	urge.
17--	函	reminder letter.
24--	化	catalysis (chemistry).
--	化劑	catalyst (chemistry).
--	付款	press for a payment.
25--	生	hasten the birth of a child.
--	生針	pituitary extract.
--	債	dun, press for payment of debt.
26--	促	urge, hurry, hasten.

-- 促付款	demand for payment.	
27-- 租	press for rent.	
28-- 收貸款	call in a loan.	
31-- 逼	quicken, urge, put on.	
33-- 淚彈	tear shell.	
66-- 單	reminder.	
67-- 眠劑	opiate.	
-- 眠	hypnotism.	
-- 眠歌	lullaby.	
77-- 問	urging for a reply.	

崖 〔Yai〕 *n.* cliff, rock, precipice.

10-- 石	cliff, ledge, precipice.
22-- 岸	haughty.
70-- 壁	precipice.
80-- 谷	valley between precipices.

2221₇

兇 〔Hsiung〕 *adj.* barbarous, hardhearted, brutal, cruel, fierce, savage.

10-- 惡	furious, devilish.
11-- 頑	cruel, brutal.
20-- 手	murderer, cutthroat.
24-- 徒	ruffian.
44-- 橫	furious, vicious.
47-- 猛	fierce, furious.
56-- 悍	grumpy, surly.
60-- 暴	fierce, savage.
66-- 器	weapon.

凭 〔Ping〕 *v.* leanon, trust.

2222₁

鼎 〔Ting〕 tripod vessel with two ears.

2222₇

崗 〔Kang〕 *n.* ridge, mound, post.

17-- 子	mound, ridge.
20-- 位	post, station.
48-- 警	policeman who performs his duties at a fixed post.
69-- 哨	lookout post, sentry, sentinel.

僑 〔Chiao〕 *v.* emigrate, sojourn.

17-- 務	affairs concerning nationals living abroad.
-- 務委員會	Overseas Chinese Affairs Commission.

25-- 生	overseas Chinese student.
37-- 資	overseas Chinese capital.
40-- 校	schools run for oversea Chinese.
71-- 匯	remittance sent back home by emigrants, overseas Chinese remittance, overseas remittance, immigrant remittance.
77-- 胞	oversea Chinese.
-- 居	reside in a country other than his own.
-- 民	emigrant.
81-- 領	leaders of oversea Chinese.
90-- 眷	dependents of oversea Chinese, relatives of nationals living abroad.

崩 〔Peng〕 *v.* collapse, fall in ruin.

12-- 裂	break open, fall in.
35-- 潰	collapse, breakdown, beruined.
44-- 壞	rack and ruin.
48-- 散	fall asunder.

2223₄

僕 〔Pu〕 *n.* servant.

27-- 役	servant, servitor.
80-- 人	servant.

嶽 〔Yueh〕 *n.* lofty summit, high mountain peak.

2224₀

低 〔Ti〕 *v.* bend down, incline, lower, droop, *adj.* low, down, humble, base.

00-- 產	low yield, short crop, low-yielding.
-- 產出	low returns.
-- 率、廉價	cheap rate.
-- 廉	cheap, low.
-- 音	bass.
07-- 調	lowkey.
08-- 效率	inefficiency, low-level, poor efficiency.
10-- 下	low.
-- 工資	low wage, moderate salary.
-- 於標準	below the mark (standard).

-- 於成本	below cost.
11-- 頭	bow one's head, lower one's head.
21-- 能	back ward.
-- 能兒	mentally retarded child.
-- 價	cheap (easy, competitive, at a low price), low in (cheap, keen) price.
-- 價住房	low cost housing.
-- 價貨	low priced good.
22-- 利	low interest.
-- 利率	low interest rate, cost of money.
-- 利政策	low interest policy.
24-- 估	*n.* undervaluation, underestimation, *v.* underestimate, undervalue, underrate.
25-- 生活水平	low standard of living.
26-- 息貸款	cheap credit, low-interest-credit, loan.
27-- 血糖	hypoglycemia.
-- 級	elementary, vulgar, low.
-- 級的	low class (grade).
-- 級品	low quality.
28-- 收入	low income.
-- 收入家庭	low-income family.
-- 收入等級	low income bracket.
30-- 空	atmosphere near the earth, low altitude.
36-- 濕	low and moist.
-- 溫	low temperature.
37-- 潮	low tide.
41-- 標價	low bid.
44-- 地	low land.
-- 落	low, downcast.
47-- 聲	under one's breath, below one's breath.
-- 欄	low hurdles.
72-- 值貨	inferior quality goods.
80-- 氣壓	low atmospheric pressure.
88-- 等動物	lower animal.
-- 等級	inferior grade.
90-- 劣	poor in quality.
98-- 檔商品	inferior goods.

2224₁

岸 〔An〕 *n.* shore, bank, beach.

21--上	on the bank, ashore.

2224₄

倭 〔Wo〕 *n.* Japan.

30-- 寇	Japanese invaders.

2224₇

後 〔Hou〕 *adj.* hind, posterior, subsequent, late, last, *adv.* afterwards, at last, at length, in the end, finally, subsequently, in future, *prep.* behind, after, at the back of.

00-- 序	epilogue.
-- 方	in the rear.
-- 方勤務	logistics.
-- 方勤務部	Board of Military Transportation and Supplies, Logistics Department.
-- 裔	descendant, heir, offspring, successor.
-- 部	posterior, behind, the back of.
08-- 效	future performance.
10-- 天	day after tomorrow.
-- 面	back.
11-- 輩	juniors, inferiors, descendants.
21-- 衛	rear guard.
-- 街	back street.
22-- 任	successor.
23-- 代	descendants, future generations.
24-- 備兵	*n.* reservist, *v.* reserve force.
-- 備隊	reserve army.
30-- 進	juniors, rising generation.
-- 宮	harem, seraglio.
31-- 福	blessing to follow, good days to come.
33-- 補	make amends, replenish.
-- 述	as follow.
35-- 遺症	sequela, after-effect.
37-- 退	retreat.
40-- 來	afterwards, at last, subsequently, finally.
-- 臺	backstage, backer.
43-- 娘	stepmother.

44-- 勤	logistic service.
-- 者	the latter.
-- 世	descendants.
47-- 期	behind schedule, latter part of a period.
48-- 梯	back stair.
50-- 事	consequence, funeral ceremony.
-- 夫	second husband.
-- 患	lurking dangers.
-- 妻	second wife.
-- 奏曲	epilogue, postlude.
51-- 排	backrow.
52-- 援	reinforcement, backing.
60-- 日	day after tomorrow.
-- 果	consequence.
67-- 嗣	heir.
-- 路	rear of an army, road of retreat.
-- 跟	heel.
72-- 盾	support, supporter, backing.
-- 腦	hind brain.
73-- 院	backyard.
77-- 段	latter part.
-- 學	students of younger generation.
-- 母	stepmother.
-- 門	back entrance.
80-- 人	n. descendants, v. be behind others.
-- 年	year after next.
90-- 半部	latter portion.
-- 半天	latter half of a day.
-- 半生	latter half of one's life.
98-- 悔	regret, repent.

俘 〔Fu〕 n. prisoner of war, captive. v. capture alive.

21-- 虜	prisoner, captive.
-- 虜營	concentration camp.
24-- 獲	captivate.

變 〔Pien〕 n. change, transformation, alteration, revolution, v. change, transform, alter, adj. changeable, versatile.

00-- 方向	change direction, alter one's course.
-- 度	variation.
-- 產	realize property.
07-- 調	change a tune or melody.
10-- 更	alter, change.
-- 更航程	change of voyage.
12-- 形	transfigure, transform.
-- 形蟲	amoeba.
16-- 現能力	liquidity.
18-- 政	reform of government.
20-- 位	displacement.
21-- 態	metamorphosis, transformation.
-- 態心理學	abnormal psychology.
22-- 亂	rebellion, revolt, upheaval, chaos.
-- 種	mutation.
23-- 戲法	conjuring, juggle, sleight of hand.
24-- 動	n. fluctuation, v. change, alter, fluctuate, adj. fluctuating.
-- 化	variation, change, transformation.
27-- 色	change color, turn color.
-- 約	alter an agreement.
23-- 心	change one's mind.
34-- 法	revise the law.
-- 為	become, be converted into.
37-- 通	be flexible.
40-- 壞	spoil, go bad, change for the worst.
-- 賣	sell off, turn into money, realize.
-- 賣財產	realize property.
46-- 相	change form.
-- 相傾銷	disguised dumping.
47-- 好	become fine or good, reform.
48-- 故	calamity, misfortune.
-- 樣	change in design.
53-- 成	become, change into, be converted into, turn to.
57-- 換	vary, convert, change,

		switch.
58--	數	variable.
60--	易	variation, mutation.
71--	壓器	transformer.
77--	局	critical situation.
95--	性	transmute.

2224₈

嚴 〔Yen〕 n. cliff, precipice.

10--	石	rock.
37--	洞	mountain cave.

2226₄

循 〔Hsun〕 v. follow, comply with, accord, proceed in order.

16--	理	in accordance with reason.
--	環	n. circulation, cycle, rotation, v. circulate, revolve.
22--	例	in accordance with precedents, according to rules.
67--	照	according to.

2227₀

仙 〔Hsien〕 n. fairy, immortal.

37--	姿	fairylike look.
40--	女	fairy, angel.
--	境	fairyland.
77--	丹	divine pill, cure-all, panacea.
80--	人	immortal, very beautiful woman, faerie.
--	人掌	cactus.

2228₉

炭 〔Tan〕 n. carbon, charcoal.

12--	水化合物	carbohydrate.
13--	酸	carbonic acid.
24--	化	carbonization.
--	化作用	carbonization.
--	化物	carbides.
50--	畫	charcoal drawing.
71--	灰	ashes.
80--	氣	carbonic gas.
88--	筆	charcoal for drawing.
90--	火	charcoal fire.
91--	爐	brazier.

2229₃

係 〔Hsi〕 n. concern, consequence, v. bind, belong to, attach to, connect with.

22--	戀	bound in love.
58--	數	coefficient(mathematical).
60--	累	bound up with.
77--	屬	connected with, belonging to.

2232₇

鸞 〔Luan〕 n. fabulous bird.

2233₉

戀 〔Luan〕 v. long after, dote on, lust after, feel attachment for.

17--	歌	love song.
20--	愛	n. romance, the gentle passion, v. fall in love, lose one's heart.
44--	慕	have a tender feeling towards.
--	舊	yearn for the past.
80--	念	long after.
--	人	sweetheart.
95--	情	love between man and woman.

2238₆

嶺 〔Ling〕 n. ridge, mountain range.

2240₇

孿 〔Luan〕 n. twin.

25--	生	twin.

2241₀

乳 〔Ju〕 n. milk, breast, nipple, teat.

11--	頭	nipple, pap, teat.
13--	酸	lactic acid.
17--	酪	cream, cheese.
20--	毛	plume.
22--	製品	dairy products.
24--	化劑	emulsifier.
25--	牛	dairy cattle, milk cow, milker.
--	牛場	dairy farm.
26--	白	milk white.
27--	名	pet name given to a child.
30--	房	breast.
60--	罩	brassiere, bra.
--	品業	dairy husbandry.
63--	哺	feed with milk.
71--	脂	butter.

76-- 腺　mammary gland.
77-- 母　nurse, wet nurse, foster-dam.

2244₁

艇〔Ting〕 *n.* boat, canoe, barge, punt.
71-- 長　skipper.

2245₃

幾〔Chi〕 *adv.* almost, nearly, about, rather, somewhat.
17-- 及　approach.
20-- 乎　nearly, almost, at the point of.
21-- 何　how much?
-- 何學　geometry.
26-- 個　several.
27-- 多　how many? how much?
80-- 分　some, somewhat.

2247₀

舢〔Shan〕 *n.* canoe, barge.
41-- 板　sampan.

2250₂

掣〔Che〕 *v.* obstruct, hinder, embarrass, drag, pull.
10-- 電　as fast as lighting.
74-- 肘　*n.* hindrance, *v.* impede the elbow, be rendered powerless.

2250₄

峯〔Feng〕 *n.* peak, summit.
22-- 嶺　mountain ranges.

2260₀

刮〔Kua〕 *v.* pare, scrape off, plane off, shave, rub, raze, brush away.
00-- 磨　rub off, scrape off.
10-- 平　raze, level down.
14-- 破　cut, hurt.
17-- 刀　scraper.
72-- 鬚　shave beard.
78-- 臉刀　razor.

2264₀

舐〔Shih〕 *v.* lick, lap.
00-- 音　lapping.
50-- 盡　lick up.

2270₀

刨〔Pao〕 *n.* plane, *v.* plane, smooth, level, dig, excavate.
40-- 坑　dig a hole.
44-- 花　shavings.
-- 地　dig the ground.
53-- 挖　dig, excavate.

2271₁

崑〔Kun〕 *n.* high mountain.

2272₁

斷〔Tuan〕 *v.* break off, sever, cut off, interrupt, stop, decide, determine, settle, judge, *adv.* certainly, decidedly, positively, absolutely.
00-- 言　assert, declare.
-- 交　cut off friendly relation.
10-- 面　section.
-- 電　power failure, blackout.
-- 不　certainly not, by no means.
11-- 頭台　guillotine.
12-- 水　cut off water supply.
22-- 後　cover a retreat, have no offspring.
-- 乳　wean.
-- 片　segment, fragment.
26-- 線　disconnection.
27-- 句　puncturate.
-- 絕　cease, cut off, discontinue, stop entirely, break off, sever.
-- 絕外交　break off diplomatic relations.
-- 絕關係　sever relation.
30-- 定　decide, determine, settle
-- 案　close a legal case.
31-- 酒　abstain from alcohol.
47-- 奶　wean.
-- 根　be cured completely.
52-- 折　break off.
60-- 口　fracture.
67-- 路　block up the way.
76-- 腸　heart-broken.
77-- 層　fault.
78-- 除　exterminate, get rid off.
80-- 命　die.
-- 食　starve to death voluntarily.

| -- 氣 | breathe one's last. |
| 96-- 糧 | run out of food supply. |

2273₂

製 〔**Chih**〕 *v.* make, form, manufacture.

28-- 作	prepare.
34-- 法	receipt.
-- 造	produce, manufacture, construct, turn out.
-- 造法	workmanship.
-- 造廠	factory, manufactory.
-- 造業	manufacturing industry.
-- 造品	manufactured goods.
44-- 革所	tan yard.
53-- 成	manufactured.
60-- 圖	chart.
90-- 糖廠	sugar refinery.
95-- 煉場	smelter.

2277₀

山 〔**Shan**〕 *n.* mountain, hill, range.

11-- 頂	mountaintop, summit.
-- 脊	ridge.
12-- 水	landscape.
17-- 砲	mountain gun.
20-- 系	mountain system.
22-- 崩	landslide.
-- 峯	peak.
24-- 峽	ravine.
37-- 洞	cave.
44-- 坡	slope.
-- 地	hilly country.
-- 地戰	mountain warfare.
-- 茶	wild tea, camellia.
-- 林	forest.
63-- 賊	brigand.
72-- 脈	mountain range.
80-- 羊	goat.
-- 谷	valley, ravine.

凶 〔**Hsiung**〕 *adj.* cruel, fierce, evil, unfortunate, unlucky, unhappy.

10-- 惡	evil, cruel, fierce.
20-- 信	bad news.
-- 手	murderer.
32-- 兆	bad omen, evil-boding.
44-- 荒	famine.
50-- 事	unlucky affair.

-- 毒	malignancy.
60-- 日	black day.
-- 暴	*n.* violence, *adj.* violent, cruel, malignant.
66-- 器	arm of offense.
78-- 險	hazard.
80-- 年	bad year.
90-- 黨	rebels, ruffians.

幽 〔**You**〕 *adj.* dark, gloomy, dim, obscure, mysterious, lonely, solitary, secret.

10-- 靈	specter, spirits, devil.
16-- 魂	ghost, the soul.
52-- 靜	lonesome.
60-- 囚	confine, imprison, shut up in prison.
63-- 默	humor.
70-- 雅	graceful.
77-- 閉	imprison.
80-- 谷	dark gorge.

2277₂

出 〔**Chu**〕 *v.* go out, go forth, proceed, from, issue, appear, beget, produce, pay, spend.

00-- 主意	plan.
-- 產	production, yield, output.
-- 產地	place of origin, country of origin.
-- 產量	quantity of output.
-- 席	*n.* attendance, *v.* attend, be, present.
-- 庭	attend the court.
-- 高價	bid a high price.
-- 廠價格	ex factory price, factory gate price, ex-mill price.
-- 廠日期	release date.
-- 讓者	transferor.
08-- 於誠意	in good faith.
10-- 票	draw a bill.
-- 票日期	date of draft.
-- 票人	biller, drawer.
12-- 發	start.
-- 發港	port of departure, port of sailing.
13-- 殯	funeral procession.
16-- 現	appear, come to light, be

		visible, present to view.
	-- 醜	incur disgrace.
20--	售	sell, bring to market, sell out, vend.
	-- 售價格	offering price.
	-- 售物	offering.
	-- 售過多	oversell.
	-- 售中	on the market.
	-- 航	sail.
21--	價	bid, make a bid, make an offer, offer.
	-- 版	*n.* publication, *v.* publish, put out.
	-- 版物	print, publication.
	-- 版物廣告	publication advertising.
	-- 版家	publisher.
	-- 征	go to the front.
	-- 行	leave, depart.
	-- 版權	publishing right.
	-- 版費	publishing cost.
	-- 勤時間	attendance time.
22--	低價	bid a low price.
23--	外	go out.
24--	納	*n.* cashier, teller, *v.* receive and pay out money or bills.
	-- 納主任	general cashier, head teller, chief cashier.
	-- 納科	cashiers department, cashiers division.
	-- 納室	treasury office.
	-- 納櫃	cashiers counter.
	-- 納機	cash register, teller's machine.
	-- 納帳	cash-book.
	-- 納員	cashier, teller, pay clerk, paymaster, purser.
	-- 借	lend to, on loan.
	-- 貨單	delivery order (D/O).
25--	使	be sent on a mission, go on an embassy.
26--	自	out of.
27--	血	bleed.
	-- 租	let, rent, put out to lease, hire, hire out, for rent.
	-- 租率(旅館)	occupancy rate.
	-- 租面積	rentable area space.

	-- 租業務	leasing.
	-- 租汽車	hired car.
	-- 租人	leaser, lessor.
30--	家	become a monk, priest, or nun.
31--	汗	sweat.
34--	港	clear a port.
	-- 港許可	clearance permit.
	-- 港引水費	outward pilotage.
	-- 港費	port charges, outward, clearing fee.
35--	清	liquidation.
	-- 清存貨	clear out one's holding, clearing stock.
37--	資比例	investment proportion.
	-- 沒	in and out.
38--	洋	go abroad.
40--	境旅客	outward passengers.
	-- 境簽証	exit visa.
	-- 力	exert one's strength, make an effort, drive at, take the trouble.
	-- 賣	sell, be in market, betray.
43--	嫁	marry.
46--	場	appear on stage.
47--	超	excess of exports, export surplus, overbalance of export, trade surplus.
50--	事地點	scene of action.
54--	軌	off the rails, derail, be unfaithful.
60--	口	*n.* exit, way out, exportation, *v.* export, sail out of harbor.
	-- 口產品	products for export, exports.
	-- 口市場	export market.
	-- 口商	export distributor, export trader, exporter.
	-- 口商協會	exports association.
	-- 口商品	export commodities.
	-- 口商品交易會	export commodities fair.
	-- 口商品目錄	export list, list of export commodities.
	-- 口商品展銷會	export bazaar.
	-- 口證明單	certificate of exportation, export certificate.

-- 口訂單	export order.
-- 口設備	export of equipment.
-- 口許可證	export license, license of export, export permit.
-- 口項目	export item.
-- 口登記	export entry.
-- 口盈餘	export surplus.
-- 口信用證	export letter of credit, export credit.
-- 口手續	process of export, export-formalities.
-- 口行	export house.
-- 口價格	export price.
-- 口傾銷	export dumping.
-- 口經銷商	export distributor.
-- 口外匯	export exchange.
-- 口貸款	credit export.
-- 口供應	export supply.
-- 口特許證	special permission export.
-- 口自由	freedom of export.
-- 口總值	gross export value, total export value.
-- 口條例	export regulation.
-- 口配額	export quota.
-- 口包裝	export packing, packing suitable for export.
-- 口貨物	exports, outward cargo.
-- 口免稅	free export.
-- 口收入	export earnings proceeds.
-- 口稅	export duty tax.
-- 口稅率	export rate.
-- 口額	amount of export.
-- 口業務	export business.
-- 口港	port of exit, port of export.
-- 口清單	shipping bills.
-- 口津貼	bounty on exportation.
-- 口運費	outward freight.
-- 口限額	export quota.
-- 口支出	export debit.
-- 口基地	export bases.
-- 口地點	point of exportation.
-- 口加工區	export processing zone.
-- 口報單	export entry, declaration for exportation.
-- 口檢疫	export quarantine.
-- 口檢驗	export inspection.
-- 口檢驗證	certificate for export, export

	inspection certificate.
-- 口申請	notice of export.
-- 口推銷	export drive.
-- 口技術	export technique.
-- 口投資	export investment.
-- 口口岸	outlet for export produce.
-- 口量	export quantum, volume of exports.
-- 口國	exporting country.
-- 口品種	variety of the products for export.
-- 口單據	export documents.
-- 口限制	export restriction.
-- 口貿易	export trade.
-- 口貿易額	export trade volume.
67-- 賬	charge off.
77-- 風頭	make a figure, cut a cash.
80-- 入境手續	entry and exit procedures.
-- 入權	right of access.
-- 差	mission assignment, on business trip.
-- 差旅行	travel on official business.
-- 差津貼	travelling allowance, travel pay, per diem.
83-- 錢	provide money, put one's hand to one's pocket.
88-- 籍	expatriate oneself.

2278_2

嵌 〔Chien〕 v. inlay, insert.

2280_6

賃 〔Renn〕 v. rent, lease, hire, charter.

22-- 出	let, lease.
80-- 入	hire.

2280_9

災 〔Tsai〕 n. calamity, misery, misfortune, danger, conflagration.

00-- 病	pestilence.
15-- 殃	misery, affliction.
30-- 害	distress.
-- 害保險	accident insurance.
37-- 禍	affliction, misery, ill, evil.
40-- 難	calamity, disaster, suffering.

2288_6

巔 〔Tien〕 n. mountain top.

2290_0

利〔**Li**〕*n.* gains, profit, advantage, interest, *v.* benefit, *adj.* sharp, acute, advantageous, beneficial, useful.

00-- 市	prosperous trade, good market.
-- 率	rate of interest, interest rate.
21-- 便	*v.* accommodate, facilitate, smooth the way, *adj.* convenient, handy, advantageous.
24-- 他主義	altruism.
26-- 得	gains.
-- 得稅	profit tax.
-- 息	interest, cost of money.
-- 息券	coupon.
27-- 己	*v.* benefit oneself, *adj.* egoistic.
-- 己主義	egoism.
30-- 害	*n.* advantages and disadvantages, bright and dark, *adj.* severe, serious.
31-- 源	resources.
37-- 潤	profit, gain, profit return.
-- 潤率	margin of income, percentage of profit, profit margin, profit rate, profit ratio, rate of profit.
44-- 薄	little profit.
-- 權	right and privileges.
66-- 器	arms, edge-tool, useful tool.
77-- 用	utilize, avail, use, turn to account, make the best of.
-- 用主義	utilitarianism.
-- 與弊	pros and cons.
80-- 益	advantage, benefit, utility, profit, interest.

糾〔**Chiu**〕*v.* correct, examine, connect, join, combine, associate.

04-- 劾	impeach.
10-- 正	correct, put right, redress.
28-- 紛	complication, dispute.
30-- 察	examine, investigate.
-- 察長	master-at-arms.

剿〔**Chao**〕*v.* attack, destroy, extirpate, exterminate, put down.

71-- 匪	*n.* bandit suppression, *v.* put down bandits.

剩〔**Sheng**〕*n.* overplus, remainder, leavings.

10-- 下	remain over, left over.
24-- 貨	remnants, leavings.
88-- 餘	*n.* overplus, surplus, *v.* remain.
-- 餘產品	surplus product.

2290₁

崇〔**Chung**〕*v.* honor, respect, worship, *adj.* high, lofty, noble, dignified, honorable.

21-- 拜	worship, adore, honor, glorify.
-- 拜偶像	idol-worship.
-- 拜英雄	hero-worship.
48-- 敬	respect, look up to.
90-- 尚	adore.

2290₃

糸〔**Mi**〕*n.* silk, fine floss.

2290₄

梨〔**Li**〕*n.* pear.

00-- 膏	pear jam.
12-- 形	pear-shaped.

巢〔**Chaur**〕*n.* nest.

彎〔**Luan**〕*n.* bladder tree.

樂〔**Leh**〕*n.* music, joy, pleasure, delight, mirth, ecstasy, *v.* enjoy, take pleasure, be pleased with, rejoice in, *adj.* happy, cheerful, joyful, delightful, pleased.

00-- 意	willingly, voluntarily.
-- 音	music.
08-- 譜	fugue, score.
10-- 而忘返	abandon oneself to pleasure.
40-- 土	heaven, fairly land.
-- 境	paradise, bed of roses.
46-- 觀	*n.* optimism, *v.* look on the sunny side of things, hope for the best, *adj.* optimistic.
-- 觀主義	optimism.
55-- 曲	music.
66-- 器	musical instrument.
78-- 隊	band, orchestra.

2291_3

繼〔**Chi**〕*v.* continue, succeed to, follow, adopt, take the place of.

10-- 電器	relay(for electricity).
17-- 承	succeed to, accede to.
-- 承稅	succession duties, inheritance tax.
-- 承法	law of succession, law of inheritance, succession law.
-- 承遺志	carry on the unfinished lifework of the deceased.
-- 承權	right of succession, right of inheritance.
-- 承人	successor, heir, successor.
-- 承財產	heirloom.
-- 承的遺產	estate of inheritance.
-- 子	adopted heir.
20-- 位	succeed to the throne.
22-- 任	succeed to an office.
24-- 續	continue, remain, keep.
-- 續進行	continue the process, go on, keep going.
-- 續犯	continuing crime.
-- 續供應	go on with the delivery.
-- 續有效	keep effective, remain in force.
-- 續合作	continued cooporation.
40-- 志	continue the pursuit of the deceased.
47-- 起	succeeded to, follow the foot step.
77-- 母	stepmother.
80-- 父	stepfather.

2291_4

種〔**Chung**〕*n.* seed, kernel, germ, race, tribe, sort, kind, variety, *v.* plant, sow, cultivate.

00-- 痘	vaccinate.
-- 畜	stud stocks.
08-- 族	tribe, race.
-- 族歧視	racial discrimination.
-- 族革命	racial revolution.
-- 族原則	Ethnographica Principle.
17-- 子	seed, germ.
-- 子隊	seeded team(in sports).
22-- 種	all descriptions.

37-- 禍	sow the seed of calamity or misfortune.
44-- 地	farm, cultivate the land.
-- 花	raise flowers.
-- 菜	plant vegetables.
-- 植	plant.
-- 植面積	planted area.
-- 植園	plantation farm.
60-- 田	cultivate, till fields.
62-- 別	classification.
91-- 類	kind, class, sort, species, description.

2292_2

彩〔**Tsai**〕*n.* prize, bright colors, *adj.* brilliant, gay, ornamented, variegated.

10-- 雲	clouds of many hues.
-- 票	lottery.
11-- 頭	good luck, lucky.
27-- 色	colored, variegated.
-- 色版	chromolithograph printing.
-- 色電視	color television.
-- 色軟片	color film.
-- 色畫	colored painting.
-- 色印刷	chromolithograph, color lithography.
44-- 帶	colored ribbon.
50-- 車	float.
51-- 虹	rainbow.
80-- 氣	good luck or fortune.
88-- 筆	color crayons.
-- 飾	adorn, ornament.

2293_0

私〔**Ssu**〕*adj.* private, personal, secret, selfish, partial.

00-- 產	personal property, personal estate.
-- 立	established and operated by private funds, privately run, private.
-- 立學校	private school.
-- 交	personal friendship.
-- 章	personal seal.
02-- 話	personal words or talk, confidential talk.
05-- 塾	village school supported

		by private means.
07-- 設		established without authorization.
09-- 談		talk in private.
10-- 下		privately, secretly.
12-- 刑		mob law, illegal punishment.
20-- 吞		misappropriation.
21-- 處		private parts.
22-- 利		private interest, personal gains.
24-- 仇		personal grudge.
-- 德		personal virtue, personal morals.
-- 貨		smuggled goods.
25-- 生		be born on the wrong side of the blanket.
-- 生子		bastard, natural child, love child.
-- 生活		private life.
-- 債		personal debts.
26-- 自		secret, private, personally, privately, without permission.
27-- 怨		personal grudge.
30-- 家偵探		private detective.
-- 家車		private car.
-- 宅		private residence.
32-- 逃		escape, elope, abscond.
33-- 心		selfishness, selfish motive.
34-- 法		private law.
37-- 通		criminal connection, love affairs.
-- 運		smuggle.
40-- 有		privately owned.
-- 有土地		privately owned land.
-- 有財產		private property.
-- 奔		elope, runaway.
-- 賣		illicit sale.
44-- 藏		private collection.
46-- 娼		unlicensed prostitutes or brothels.
50-- 事		private affairs, private business.
60-- 田		privately owned farm land.
61-- 販		dealers in contraband goods, smugglers.

71-- 願		personal wish.
77-- 用		for one's own private use, personal use.
80-- 人		personal, private.
-- 人祕書		private secretary.
-- 人財產		personal assets(estate, property, wealth), private property.
-- 人企業		private enterprises.
95-- 情		private feeling, illicit love.
98-- 弊		dishonest practice, irregularities.
99-- 營		privately operated.
-- 營企業		privately-run enterprise, free (private) enterprise, private business, private undertaking.

2293_7

穩〔**Wen**〕 *adj.* firm, stable, steady, immovable, safe.

20-- 重		careful.
-- 住		hold stable.
-- 妥		proper and secure.
21-- 便		safe and convenient.
-- 步		steady.
25-- 健		sound, firm and steady.
-- 健的		firm, steady.
-- 健派		moderates.
30-- 定		*n.* stability, stabilization, *adj.* stabilized, stable, steady *adv.* steadily.
-- 定市場		stabilize the market.
-- 定平衡		stable equilibrium(physics).
-- 定物價		*n.* stable price, price stabilization, *v.* stabilize commodity prices, stabilize the price of goods.
60-- 固		*v.* fix, *adj.* strong, firm.
62-- 睡		sleep soundly.
90-- 當		proper and secure, safe and sound.

2294_0

紙〔**Chih**〕 *n.* paper.

11-- 張		sheet of paper.
12-- 型		paper matrices.
21-- 版＝紙型		

22-- 片	tag, card.	
23-- 袋	paper bag.	
26-- 牌	playing cards, poker.	
27-- 漿	paper pulp.	
-- 條	slip of paper.	
30-- 扇	paper fan.	
32-- 業	paper industry.	
-- 業公司	pulp and paper company.	
40-- 夾	clip.	
-- 巾	tissue paper.	
41-- 板	cardboard, paper board.	
-- 板箱	carton.	
43-- 鳶	kites.	
54-- 袂	portfolio.	
80-- 盒	cardboard box.	
-- 傘	paper umbrella.	
91-- 煙	cigarette.	
98-- 幣	paper money, paper currency, note.	

2294₄

綏〔Sui〕v. soothe, comfort, tranquilize, adj. pacify, restore peace.

05-- 靖	pacify, restore peace and order.
-- 靖主任	Pacification Director-general.
58-- 撫	pacify, soothe, tranquilize.

2294₇

緩〔Huan〕v. delay, postpone, retard, adj. slow, tardy, dilatory, adv. gradually, slowly, gently.

08-- 議	defer the discussion.
12-- 刑	reprieve, delay the punishment.
21-- 步	n. small pace, jog, trot, v. walk slowly.
-- 行	at a foot's pace.
-- 衝	serve as a buffer.
-- 衝地帶	buffer zone.
-- 衝國	buffer state.
26-- 和	v. soften, temper, pacify. adj. moderate.
27-- 役	draft deferment.
-- 急	degrees of urgency.
28-- 徵	defer the draft of.
35-- 決	stay the execution.

37-- 追債項	stall a debt.
47-- 期	postpone a deadline, suspend, grace.
72-- 兵之計	scheme to gain time.
77-- 限	put off the deadline, extend the time limit.
96-- 慢衰退	mild recession.

2296₉

繙〔Fan〕v. translate, interpret.

06-- 譯	translate, turn in to.
-- 譯員	translator, interpreter.

2297₇

稻〔Tao〕n. paddy.

25-- 秧	rice seeding, rice shoots.
44-- 草	straw.
-- 草紙	straw paper.
-- 草褥	straw mattress.
-- 草人	scarecrow, jack of straw.
46-- 場	yard for sunning unhulled rice.
47-- 穀	paddy.
60-- 田	corn field, rice field.
90-- 米	rice, paddy.

2299₃

絲〔Ssu〕n. silk, fibers, threads, wire.

00-- 商	silk merchant.
-- 廠	silk mill.
-- 毫	tiniest, slightest, least bit.
23-- 織品	silk fabrics, silk goods, wrought silk.
26-- 線	silk thread.
-- 綿	silk batting.
27-- 緞	satin.
-- 綢	silk, silk cloth.
-- 綢之路	Silk Road.
-- 綢工業	silk industry.
34-- 襪	silk stockings.
44-- 帶	silk ribbons.
46-- 帕	silk handkerchief.
72-- 瓜	towel gourd.

2300₀

卜〔Pu〕v. divine, foretell.

43-- 卦	divine by the Eight Diagrams.
77-- 居	take up one's abode.

2305₃

牋〔Chien〕 *n.* letter, notepaper.

2313₄

獃〔Tai〕 *adj.* foolish, silly, simple.
02-- 話　　　nonsense.
17-- 子　　　fool, simpleton.
20-- 住了　　dumbfounded.
46-- 相　　　silly look.
80-- 氣　　　stupidity.
88-- 笑　　　silly laugh.

2320₀

仆〔Pu〕 *v.* fall to the ground.
22-- 倒　　　fall down.

外〔Wai〕 *adv.* out, outside, *prep.* without, beyond, outside.
00-- 商　　　foreign business.
-- 文　　　foreign language.
-- 交　　　diplomacy.
-- 交部　　Foreign Office, Foreign Ministry.
-- 交部長　Minister of Foreign Affairs.
-- 交政策　foreign policy.
-- 交家　　skillful diplomat.
-- 交官　　diplomat.
-- 交團　　diplomatic body.
-- 衣　　　overcoat, dress.
07-- 部　　　exterior, external.
-- 調　　　transfer to other places, transfer to other localities.
08-- 放　　　send an official for an oversea assignment.
-- 敵　　　foreign enemy.
10-- 面　　　surface, outside.
11-- 頭　　　outside.
12-- 形　　　feature, outline, outside, appearance, external form.
-- 孫　　　son of one's daughter.
17-- 務　　　foreign affairs.
21-- 行　　　layman, new hand.
-- 行話　　layman's language.
-- 版書　　books not published by the shop selling them.
22-- 出　　　go out.
-- 出血　　external hemorrhage.
-- 僑、僑民　foreign residents, alien population.
24-- 科　　　surgery.
-- 科醫生　surgeon, operator.
25-- 債　　　foreign loan foreign debt, external debt, obligation to foreign government.
26-- 甥　　　nephew.
-- 甥女　　niece.
-- 貌　　　outward appearance, appearance, countenance.
27-- 向　　　turn outward.
-- 角　　　external angle.
-- 鄉　　　another part of the country.
-- 鄉人　　strangers, people from other lands.
28-- 侮　　　foreign aggression.
-- 傷　　　external injuries.
30-- 室　　　mistress living outside one's own house.
-- 家　　　parental home of a married woman.
-- 宿　　　stay outside overnight.
-- 客　　　stranger.
-- 賓　　　foreign visitors.
32-- 逃　　　flee.
34-- 流　　　flow outward.
-- 婆　　　maternal grandmother.
36-- 邊　　　outside.
-- 遇　　　have extra-marital affairs.
37-- 祖　　　maternal grandfather.
-- 資　　　foreign capital.
-- 資投資　foreign capital investment, investment of foreign capital.
38-- 洋　　　foreign, abroad.
40-- 力　　　foreign influence.
-- 太空　　outer space.
-- 在　　　external, extrinsic.
-- 來　　　outside, external, foreign.
-- 來語　　foreign term, foreign language.
-- 套　　　overcoat, cloak, robe.
-- 觀　　　outward appearance.
44-- 地　　　parts of the country other than where one is located.
-- 勤　　　work done outside the office.

-- 帶	carryout.
-- 蒙古	Outer Mongolia.
46-- 加	besides.
-- 觀	aspect, outward appearance.
47-- 埠	cities outside of one's own.
-- 殼	outer covering, shell, case.
50-- 表	appearance, outward appearance, exterior.
-- 事局	Bureau of Foreign Affairs.
-- 患	foreign invasion.
52-- 援	foreign grants, foreign aid, external assistance.
60-- 國	foreign country.
-- 國語	foreign language.
-- 國貨	imported goods, goods of foreign made, goods of foreign origin.
-- 國資本	foreign capital.
-- 國人	foreigner, alien.
-- 星人	E. T. (extraterrestrial), alien.
-- 界	outsiders.
-- 圍	perimeter.
61-- 號	nickname.
-- 因	extraneous cause.
67-- 野	outfield(baseball).
-- 野手	outfielder.
-- 路人	outsider, stranger.
71-- 匯	foreign exchange.
-- 匯市場	foreign exchange market.
-- 匯交易	foreign exchange transactions.
-- 匯統制	exchange control.
-- 匯處	exchange office.
-- 匯牌價	foreign exchange quotations, exchange rate quotation.
-- 匯匯率	rate of foreign exchange.
-- 匯局	exchange office.
-- 匯管理	foreign exchange management.
-- 匯管理局	state administration of foreign exchange control.
-- 匯管制	exchange control.
77-- 用	external use.

-- 貿	foreign trade, external trade.
-- 貿順差	foreign trade surplus.
-- 貿協會	China External Trade Development Council (現改爲 TAITRA).
80-- 人	outsiders, strangers, foreigners.
-- 分泌	exocrine, external secretion.
-- 公	maternal grandfather.
-- 企	foreign company.
88-- 籍	foreign nationality.
-- 籍人士	foreigners, aliens.
89-- 銷	export, export sales, export trade.
-- 銷貨	export goods.
90-- 省	other provinces.
-- 省人	persons from another province.
95-- 快	extra income.
98-- 幣	foreign currency, exchange currency, currency.
-- 幣準備	foreign money reserve.
-- 幣兌換	foreign currency exchange.

2320₂

参〔San〕v. participate, take part in, blend, mix, counsel, advise, consult with.

00-- 雜	mixed, blended, confused.
04-- 謀	staff officers.
-- 謀部	general staff.
-- 謀部長	chief of the general staff.
08-- 議	consult.
-- 議員	senator.
-- 議院	senate.
10-- 天	reach the sky.
18-- 政	take part in politics.
-- 政員	member of the People's Political Council.
-- 政權	public right.
-- 政會	People's Political Council.
-- 攷書	reference book.
20-- 看	refer to, quod vide.
-- 看上文	vide supra.

24--	贊	councilor, attaché.
37--	軍	*n.* military staff officer, *v.* join the army.
--	軍長	presidential chief military aide.
44--	考	refer, look up.
46--	加	participate.
--	加費	initial charge, participation fees.
--	加商號	participating house.
--	加證書	participation certificate.
--	加保險	participating insurance.
--	加展覽會	participate in an exhibition.
--	觀	visit, take a view of.
50--	事	councilor.
60--	見	call on, visit.
--	見下文	vide infra.
63--	戰	participate in a war, enter a war.
--	戰國	belligerent state.
67--	照	refer.
77--	閱	see and consult, examine and compare.
--	與	participation.
--	股	equity participation.
--	股者	equity participant.
--	與計劃	participation program.
--	與管理	participatory management.
80--	差	irregular.

2321_0
允〔**Yun**〕*v.* promise, permit, consent, assent, accede to, allow, grant, agree.

04--	諾	accept, assent.
08--	許	permit, allow, grant, admit, promise, go with.
24--	納	accede.
28--	從	acknowledge, give consent, give into, follow.
30--	准	permission.
38--	洽	proper, fair, well, settled.
90--	當	advisable, appropriate, suitable, fit.

2321_1
倥〔**Kung**〕*adj.* ignorant, rude, rough, sudden.

27--	侗	ignorant.
--	傯	under great pressure of time, suddenly.

2321_4
僱〔**Ku**〕*v.* hire, engage.

00--	主	employer.
10--	工	engage workman.
20--	傭	person employed by another.
30--	定	contract the employment of.
60--	員	employee.
77--	用	employ, hire, engage.

2322_1
佇〔**Chu**〕*v.* stand and wait, long for.

00--	立	stand and wait.
--	立以待	on tiptoe.
20--	看	gaze at, stare at.
27--	候	stand and wait.

2322_7
偏〔**Pien**〕*adj.* selfish, partial, prejudiced, leaning, deflected, bent on, inclined to.

00--	疼	undue partiality.
--	離	deviate, diverge.
04--	護	*v.* favor, *adj.* in favor of, upon the side of.
10--	要	positively choose.
11--	頭痛	migraine.
20--	重	be partial to.
--	僻	out of the way.
--	愛	partiality, leaning.
22--	私	selfish, partial.
24--	倚	lean on.
27--	角	declination.
--	向	deflect, lean, be inclined toward.
33--	心	partiality, bias.
34--	遠	remote, far away.
36--	祖	partial, in favor of.
45--	執	obstinate.
60--	見	prejudice, one-sided view.
80--	差	declination, deviation.
84--	斜	slant.
99--	勞	let one person take on the

work.

徧 〔Pien〕 v. go around, pervade, adv. everywhere, all round.

17--	及	all over, have reached everywhere.
21--	處	everywhere, in every direction, far and wide.
27--	身	whole body.
40--	布	spread far and wide.
44--	地	everywhere, all places.
57--	搜	search everywhere.

2323₂

傢 〔Chia〕 n. belonging to the family.

22--	私	furniture.
29--	伙	character, jerk, fellow, guy.

2323₄

伏 〔Fu〕 v. hide, conceal, keep hidden, subject, suppress.

22--	倒	lay down on the ground.
24--	特	volt (electricity).
--	特計	voltmeter.
34--	法	suffer decapitation.
57--	擊	attack from ambush.
58--	輸	concede.
60--	罪	admit guilt.
72--	兵	ambush.
80--	氣	yield willingly.

狀 〔Chuang〕 n. form, appearance, shape, certificate.

07--	詞	contents of an accusation.
21--	態	appearance, state, status, phase.
--	態惡劣	in bad condition.
--	態良好	in good condition.
22--	紙	official form for filing a lawsuit.
26--	貌	look, appearance.
36--	況	circumstance.

獻 〔Hsien〕 v. offer, present, contribute to.

04--	計	give advice.
07--	詞	dedication.
08--	旗	present flags.
16--	醜	expose one's defects.
27--	身	offer oneself.

--	祭	sacrifice.
30--	寶	present a treasure.
31--	酒	offer wine.
35--	禮	present a gift.
44--	花	present flowers, lay a wreath.
--	藝	perform, exhibit one's skill.
47--	媚	curry favor.
54--	技	display one's feat.
80--	金	subscribe, contribute to.
--	金運動	"offer gold to the state" movement.
88--	策	offer a plan, advise.

俟 〔Ssu〕 v. wait, expect, look, prep. till, until.

27--	候	wait for.
64--	時	wait for an opportunity.

2324₀

代 〔Tai〕 n. generation, dynasty, reign, v. substitute, take the place of, change, alter, prep. in place of, instead of, as a substitute for.

00--	辦	n. commission agent, charge d'affaires, v. act for, manage for another.
--	辦商	commission merchant.
--	辦行	commission house.
--	辦律師	attorney.
--	辦人	commission agent.
--	辦公使	charge d'affaires.
--	言	be a spokesman, speak in behalf of.
--	言人	spokesman.
06--	課	teach on behalf of another teacher.
08--	議政府	representative government
10--	工製造	sub-contract manufacturing
16--	理	n. agent, v. act for, take the place of, do duty for another.
--	理商	business agent.
--	理證書	letter of attorney.
--	理處	agency.
--	理行	agency house.
--	理經理	acting manager.
--	理總經理	acting general manager.

-- 理總裁	acting president.
-- 理佣金	agent commission.
-- 理業務	agent service, agency service(business).
-- 理協定	agency agreement.
-- 理權	attorneyship, power of attorney, proxy.
-- 理中間人	agent middleman.
-- 理費	agency charge, agency fee, agent fee, commission fee.
-- 理貿易	commission agency.
-- 理聯係	agent relation.
-- 理人	agent, procurator, proxy.
-- 理合同	agency contract.
-- 理公使	charge d'affaires.
-- 理領事	acting consul.
-- 理銀行	agent bank.
-- 理簽字	signature by procuration.
21-- 價	price, expense, cost, at the cost (expense)of.
-- 步	means of transportation.
24-- 付	pay for another.
27-- 名字	pronoun.
28-- 收銀行	collecting bank.
45-- 墊	advance money for another.
50-- 表	n. representative, delegate, representation, deputy, v. represent, stand for.
-- 表廠商	representative firm.
-- 表大會	representative assembly.
-- 表權	proxy, representation, power of attorney, right of representation.
-- 表團	delegation, deputation.
-- 表人	representative.
-- 表作	representative works.
-- 表性樣品	representative sample.
55-- 替	n. substitution, v. substitute, replace, represent, stand for, take the place of.
57-- 換	replace.
58-- 數學	algebra.
61-- 號	code name.
-- 號表	code table.
65-- 購	buy on behalf of somebody.
-- 購代銷點	purchasing and marketing

agency, supply and marketing center.

77-- 用	substitute for something.
-- 用品	substitute, substitute articles, substitute goods.
-- 用卷	token.
88-- 筆	write for another, be a ghost writer.
-- 管	manage or govern on behalf of another, held in trust.
89-- 銷	n. sale by agent, sale by proxy, v. sell on consignment, sell goods on a commission basis.
-- 銷店	outlet store.
-- 銷商品	merchandise on consignment.
-- 銷貨	consigned goods.
-- 銷人	retail distributor.
98-- 幣	token money, token.
99-- 勞	labor on behalf of another.

2324₂

傅 〔Fu〕 n. tutor, teacher, v. assist, guide, support.

2324₇

俊 〔Chun〕 adj. superior, eminent, remarkable, refined.

20-- 秀	graceful.
24-- 偉	superior and great.
25-- 傑	brave and superiorperson, person of extraordinary talent.
29-- 俏	elegant.
-- 士	fine scholar.
50-- 才	talented person.
80-- 美	charming, handsome, good-looking.

2325₀

伐 〔Fa〕 v. invade, attack, cut down, brag, boast.

40-- 木	fell trees, cut down trees.
-- 木工人	lumberman.
-- 木業	logging, lumbering.
-- 木者	lumberer, lumberjack.
60-- 罪	punish an offense.

戕〔Chiang〕*n.* spear, lance, *v.* kill, wound.
30-- 害　　　wound.
63-- 賊　　　destroy, ruin.

侔〔Mou〕*adj.* equal, alike.

臧〔Tsang〕*n.* servant, *adj.* good, virtuous.
10-- 否　　　comment, criticize.
44-- 獲　　　servants, slaves.

戲〔Hsi〕*n.* play, game, sport, amusement. *v.* play, sport, jest, ridicule, joke, make fun of, play a trick on.
00-- 文　　　theatrical writing, drama.
-- 言　　　joke.
01-- 譃　　　play practical jokes, make sport of.
07-- 詞　　　words of an actor's part, actor's lines.
10-- 弄　　　play a trick on, make fun of, make a fool of.
-- 票　　　admission ticket.
11-- 玩　　　disport, play trick.
-- 班　　　dramatic troupe.
12-- 水　　　play with water.
17-- 子　　　actor, actress, player.
22-- 劇　　　drama.
-- 劇化　　　dramatize.
-- 劇家　　　playwright, dramatist.
-- 劇界　　　dramatic circles.
23-- 台　　　stage.
24-- 裝　　　theatrical costume.
34-- 法　　　magic, conjuring.
39-- 迷　　　drama fan.
40-- 本子　　　script, text for a play.
44-- 嬉　　　play, frolic.
46-- 場　　　theater.
55-- 曲　　　drama, play.
60-- 園=戲場
-- 目　　　theatrical program.
-- 具　　　theatrical appurtenances, stage properties, stage prop.
66-- 單　　　bill of the play, program of acts, playbill.
73-- 院　　　theater, playhouse.

俄〔E〕*n.* Russia, *adv.* suddenly, momentarily.
00-- 文　　　Russian.
01-- 語　　　Russian.
60-- 國　　　Russia.
-- 羅斯社會主義共和國
　　　　　　Soviet Russia, U.S.S.R., Soviet Union.
80-- 人　　　Russian.
2328₆

儐〔Pin〕*v.* entertain.
46-- 相　　　master of ceremonies.
2331₁

鴕〔To〕*n.* ostrich.
2333₁

黛〔Tai〕*n.* black dye, *adj.* umberblack.
22-- 絲　　　beauty in full dress.
77-- 眉　　　blacken the eyebrow.
2333₂

然〔Jan〕*adv.* yet, so, thus, *conj.* but, however, though, although.
04-- 諾　　　promise, give one's word.
10-- 而　　　however, but, though, although, nevertheless, on the other hand.
22-- 後　　　then, afterwards.
62-- 則　　　but, but then, in that case.
2333₆

怠〔Tai〕*adj.* careless, heedless, lazy, indolent.
00-- 廢　　　idle.
10-- 工　　　sabotage, go-slow-strike, strike on the job, labor slowdown, go-slow tactics, slowdown, go-slow, lazy strike.
22-- 緩　　　idle and lax, procrastination.
29-- 倦　　　lazy, idle, indolent, remiss.
94-- 惰　　　idle and lazy.
96-- 慢　　　negligent, disrespectful.
2341₁

舵〔To〕*n.* rudder, helm.
10-- 工　　　helmsman.
-- 工長　　　quartermaster.

20-- 手		helmsman.
50-- 夫		pilot.

2344_0 弁 〔Bin〕 n. hat.

00-- 言		preface, foreword.

2350_0 牟 〔Mou〕 v. usurp, encroach upon.

17-- 取		seek, obtain, try to gain.
22-- 利		n. money-making, v. make money.

2355_0 我 〔Wo〕 pron. I, me, my.

00-- 方		our side, we.
11-- 輩		we, us.
26-- 自己		my self.
27-- 們		we, us.
-- 們的		our, ours.
30-- 家		my home, my house.
37-- 軍		our troops, our army.
60-- 國		our country.

2360_0 台 〔Tai〕 n. terrace.

01-- 端		your good self.
07-- 詞		stage dialogue.
13-- 球		billiard.
21-- 秤		platform scale.
32-- 灣		Taiwan.
37-- 資		capital from Taiwan.
40-- 布		table-cloth.
-- 柱		important actor, important person.
41-- 楷		step.
77-- 風		stage manners.

2365_0 鹹 〔Hsien〕 adj. salt, saltish.

12-- 水		saline water, salt water.
-- 水魚		salt water fish.
13-- 酸		saltish-sour.
17-- 蛋		salt egg.
27-- 魚		salt fish.
37-- 鹼		salt lakes.
40-- 肉		bacon, salted meat.
44-- 菜		salt vegetable.
65-- 味		salty taste.

67-- 鴨蛋		salted duck's egg.

2373_2 袋 〔Tai〕 n. bag, sack, pocket, purse, pouch, case.

17-- 子		bag, sack, pocket.
24-- 裝貨		bag cargo, bagged cargo, cargo in bag.
27-- 鼠		kangaroo.
61-- 號		bag number.

2374_7 峻 〔Chun〕 adj. high, lofty, steep, stern, severe.

22-- 嶺		lofty range.
27-- 急		intolerant and impatient.
29-- 峭		high and steep.

2375_0 峨 〔Eh〕 adj. high, lofty.

27-- 嵋山		Mount Omi.

2380_6 貸 〔Tai〕 v. lend, release, pardon.

00-- 方		lender, creditor, creditor side.
22-- 出		lend to, lending.
24-- 借		borrow.
28-- 給		credit.
47-- 款		n. loan, v. extend credit to, loan, grant advances, grant a loan, make loans.
-- 款承諾		loan commitment.
-- 款經理人		lending broker, loan agent.
-- 款利率		loan interest rate, price of money.
-- 款條件		conditions for loans, terms of credit, terms of loan.
-- 款佣金		loan commission.
-- 款收入		income from loans.
-- 款額		loan volume.
-- 款業務		lending activities, lending operations, loan business, loan services.
-- 款協定		finance agreement, loan agreement.
-- 款期限		length of maturity, loan time limit, period of credit.
-- 款損失		lending loss.

-- 款擔保	loan guarantee.
-- 款數量	size of the loan.
-- 款拖欠	loan delinquency.
-- 款銀行	lending bank.
-- 款合同	money lending contract.
-- 款人	accommodator.
80-- 入	borrow, ask for a loan.
-- 金	loan.
88-- 餘	credit balance.

2390₀

秘 〔**Mi**〕 *adj.* private, secret, personal.

20-- 信	confidential letter.
27-- 魯	Peru.
30-- 密	secret.
-- 密通信	confidential correspondence.
-- 密會議	conclave, chamber-council.
50-- 書	secretary.
-- 書處	secretary office, secretariat.
-- 書長	chief secretary, secretary general, general secretary.

2392₇

編 〔**Pien**〕 *v.* arrange, weave, connect with a cord, edit.

01-- 訂	revise and correct.
06-- 譯	edit and translate.
-- 譯所	editorial department.
-- 譯員	editor, compiler.
-- 譯館	institute for compilation and translation.
10-- 工	plaiting.
11-- 預算	prepare budget.
12-- 列	list, arrange systematically, arrange in order.
22-- 制	formation, composition, constitution.
-- 劇	dramatize.
-- 劇者	dramatist, playwright.
23-- 織	knit, weave.
-- 織匠	weaver.
-- 織機	knitting machine.
24-- 結	tie, bind.
25-- 練	organize and train.
27-- 組	organize into groups.
-- 組手冊	organization manual.
-- 修	compile, edit.

30-- 戶	families entered in household registers.
-- 寫	compile, write.
-- 審	edit and screen.
-- 審委員會	editing and screening committee.
32-- 派	libel, vilify.
33-- 述	arrange and narrate.
37-- 造	form, fabricate.
-- 選	select and edit.
38-- 導	*n.* director, *v.* write and direct.
44-- 著	compile and write.
47-- 報表	prepare statement.
50-- 書	edit and compile books.
51-- 排	arrange.
56-- 輯	*n.* editor, compiler, *v.* edit, compile.
-- 輯部	editorial department.
60-- 目	cataloguing.
61-- 號	number.
78-- 隊	*n.* formation, *v.* organize into group.
80-- 入	enroll, enlist, include.
-- 年	*n.* annals, yearbook, *v.* compile annals, prepare a chronological record.
-- 年史	chronicle.
88-- 纂＝編輯	
91-- 類	arrange into categories.

2393₂

稼 〔**Chia**〕 *n.* farming, *v.* plant, farm, cultivate.

24-- 穡	*n.* farming, agriculture, *v.* sow and reap.

2394₂

縛 〔**Fu**〕 *v.* tie up, bind.

20-- 住	tie up, bind up.
-- 手縛腳	too many constraints.
44-- 帶	fasten up a girdle.
50-- 束	bind, tie.
77-- 緊	tie or bind tightly.

2395₀

絨 〔**Jung**〕 *n.* wool, floss.

02-- 氈	blanket.
20-- 毛	wool.

26-- 線　　　woolen thread.
-- 線衫　　　woolen sweater.
29-- 毯　　　woolen blanket.
40-- 布　　　woolen cloth, flannel.

緘〔Chien〕v. seal up, close, bind up.
30-- 密　　　sealed up secret.
42-- 札　　　letter.
44-- 封　　　seal up.
60-- 口　　　keep the mouth shut.
63-- 默　　　keep silence, hold one's peace, hold the tongue.

織〔Chih〕v. weave.
10-- 工　　　weaver.
20-- 紋　　　woven pattern.
27-- 物　　　woven goods.
33-- 補　　　darn, mend, patch up.
40-- 布　　　weave cloth.
-- 布廠　　　weaving mill.
-- 女　　　spinning damsel.
42-- 機　　　loom.
60-- 品　　　drapery.
86-- 錦　　　brocade.

纖〔Hsien〕adj. small, fine, delicate.
00-- 疵　　　little fault.
-- 瘦　　　delicate and slender.
-- 毫　　　very little.
11-- 巧　　　skillful.
17-- 弱　　　fragile, delicate.
20-- 手　　　delicate hand.
-- 維　　　fiber, staple.
-- 維工業　　textile industry.
-- 維素　　　cellulose.
-- 維質　　　fiber, filament.
-- 毛　　　cilia.
26-- 細　　　minute, fine, delicate.
41-- 妍　　　slim and pretty.
2395₃

綫〔Hsien〕n. cord, thread, line.
00-- 麻　　　hemp, flax.
40-- 索　　　clue.
2396₁

縮〔So〕v. condense, abridge, contract, shrink, shrivel.
30-- 寫　　　shorthand, abbreviate.
33-- 減　　　rescue, lessen, decrease, curtail, cut down.
50-- 本　　　pocket size or abridged edition.
60-- 回　　　retract.
-- 圖器　　　pantograph.
81-- 短　　　shorten, abridge.
90-- 小　　　reduce, diminish.
-- 小範圍　　reduce the scope.

稽〔Chi〕v. inspect, examine, investigate, search for.
12-- 延　　　delay, procrastinate.
40-- 查　　　examine, inspect, search for, check for smuggling and tax evasion.
-- 查員　　　inspector.
-- 核　　　audit, examine, inspect and audit, check.
-- 核所　　　audit department.
44-- 考　　　n. reference, v. examine, verify.
77-- 留　　　detain.
2397₇

縉〔Wan〕v. string together, run through, tie up, connect.
2398₁

綻〔Chan〕n. slit, seam, rent, v. open, rip, rend, split.
10-- 露　　　reveal a matter.
12-- 裂　　　split or rip open.
2398₆

繽〔Ping〕n. brilliancy, adj. mixed, crowded.
22-- 亂　　　confused, disordered.
28-- 紛　　　brilliancy of colors.
2399₁

綜〔Tsung〕v. collect, sum up, gather up.
16-- 理　　　arrange or manage everything, be in overall charge.
46-- 觀　　　view the whole situation.
52-- 括　　　sum up, recapitulate, encompass.
78-- 覽　　　view generally.
80-- 合　　　generalization, synthesis.
-- 合雜誌　　catchall magazine, maga-

	zine of general interest.
-- 合報導	comprehensive dispatch.
-- 合報告	comprehensive report, general report, summary reports.
-- 合報表	comprehensive statement.
-- 合所得稅	consolidated income tax.
-- 合費用	general expenses.
-- 合規劃	comprehensive planning.
-- 合公司	conglomerate company.
88-- 算	sum up, total up, strike a balance.
-- 管	be in overall charge.

2408₆
牘 〔**Tu**〕 *n.* document, book, note, letter.

2409₄
牒 〔**Tieh**〕 *v.* document, dispatch.
| 00-- 文 | official dispatch. |

2411₁
靠 〔**Kao**〕 *v.* rely on, depend on, lean upon.
10-- 不住	unreliable, untrustworthy.
11-- 背	back of a chair.
-- 背椅	chair with a high back.
22-- 岸	*v.* pull into shore, draw alongside, *adv.* alongside.
26-- 自己	rely on oneself.
-- 得住	trustful, reliable.
32-- 近	near.
44-- 椅	easy chair, lounge chair.
45-- 墊	cushion.
51-- 攏	shorten the distance, shift allegiance.
-- 攏分子	turncoat, tergiversator.
90-- 火	keep near to the fire.

2411₇
豔 〔**Yen**〕 *v.* admire, desire, *adj,* beautiful, handsome.
11-- 麗	radiantly beautiful, charming, gorgeous.
27-- 色	beauty.
31-- 福	good fortune in love affairs.
47-- 婦	beautiful woman.
50-- 史	love affairs, romantic adventures.
-- 事	erotic affairs.
80-- 羨	admire, long for.
-- 舞	striptease, entice dances.
77-- 服	beautiful dress.

2412₇
動 〔**Tung**〕 *n.* motion, movement, momentum, action, conduct, behavior, *v.* move, affect, excite, influence, act, *adj.* movable, restless.
00-- 產	movable property, personal estate, personality, mobile property, movable estate, personal property.
07-- 詞	verb.
08-- 議	propose, make a motion.
10-- 工	begin work, commence work.
-- 電	dynamical electricity.
-- 電學	electric-dynamics.
12-- 刑	apply torture, torture.
13-- 武	use force, start a fight.
14-- 聽	appealing to the ear.
16-- 彈	budge, move, stir.
20-- 手	begin, start, lift a hand.
-- 手術	operate on a patient, have an operation.
21-- 能	kinetic energy.
-- 態	development.
22-- 亂	disturbance, disorder, unrest, commotion, upheaval.
27-- 向	trends, general directions.
-- 身	start.
-- 物	animal.
-- 物園	zoo, zoological garden.
-- 物界	animal kingdom.
-- 物學	zoology.
-- 物膠	gelatin.
28-- 作	*n.* action, motion, operation, *v.* act, move, work.
30-- 字	verb.
33-- 心	be moved mentally, show interest.
40-- 力	impetus, motive power.
-- 力資源	power resources.
-- 力學	dynamics.
-- 土	break ground, start construction.

42--	機	motive, cause.
44--	蕩	n. unrest, adj. uneasy, un-stable.
--	植物檢疫	quarantine of animals and plants.
47--	怒	anger, enrage.
52--	搖	waver, shake, be in com-motion.
57--	靜	in motion or at rest.
60--	量	momentum.
--	員	n. mobilization, v. mobilize, call to the color.
--	員令	mobilization order.
72--	兵	go to war, take up arms.
--	脈	artery.
--	脈硬化症	arteriosclerosis.
--	腦筋	think, try to get some covet-ed thing.
77--	用	use, employ.
--	用公款	use public money.
80--	人	charming, touching, pa-thetic.
--	氣	take offense, get angry.
88--	筆	start writing, put pen to pa-per.
90--	火	get angry, lose temper.
95--	情	excite passion.
97--	粗	resort to violence.
99--	憐	pity, touch, move, excite to compassion, raise pity.

2414₇
歧 〔Chi〕 adj. forked, diverging.

06--	誤	mistake.
36--	視	n. discrimination, v. dis-criminate against.
38--	途	wrong way, road of evil.
60--	見	different opinions, conflic-ting ideas.
--	異	conflicting, divergent.
67--	路	diverging roads.
80--	念	evil thoughts.

2420₀
什 〔Shih〕 adj. sundry, miscellaneous.

00--	麼	what?
27--	物	things, miscellaneous goods.
86--	錦	assorted, multiple ingredi-ents.

付 〔Fu〕 v. pay, give to, send, transfer, deliver over to another.

00--	高價	pay heavy price, pay high.
02--	託	confide, charge one with trust.
08--	訖	paid in full, pay already.
10--	工資	pay the workmen.
12--	刊	be published, send to the press.
16--	現	pay cash, pay in cash, pay ment by cash, payment in cash.
--	現錢	pay in cash.
22--	出	pay, give, expend.
--	出利息	interest paid.
26--	保證金	advance security.
--	息	pay interest, payment of in-terest.
27--	郵	mail.
28--	給	pay, deliver.
30--	定錢	advance money on a con-tract, pay earnest money.
35--	清	pay in full, clear off an ac-count, account paid, full paid, paid, paid off.
41--	帳	clear one's account.
47--	款	n. payment, v. pay money, make payment, pay.
--	款承諾	promise to pay.
--	款處	pay office.
--	款代理人	pay agent, payable agent.
--	款給抬頭人	pay to order.
--	款憑證	evidences of payment, pay-ment voucher.
--	款地點	place of payment.
--	款期	time of payment.
--	款單	letter of payment.
--	款日	account day, cash day.
--	款人	payer, drawee.
60--	足	paid up.
61--	賬	pay a bill, pay one's score, settle.
77--	印	turn over to the printing

		shop, send to the press.
-- 關稅		pay tariff.
88-- 管		entrust.

豺 〔Chai〕 *n.* jackal.

21-- 虎	jackals and tigers.
43-- 狼	jackal and wolf.

射 〔Sheh〕 *v.* shoot out, dart, spurt.

10-- 死	be killed by an arrow, shot dead.
13-- 球	kick or shoot the ball.
16-- 彈	projectile.
20-- 手	archer, shooter.
21-- 術	archery.
22-- 出	shoot, emanate.
26-- 線	ray (physics).
-- 程	range.
27-- 角	angle of fire.
50-- 中	shoot at the mark.
57-- 擊	shoot, fire.
-- 擊場	shooting range.
62-- 影	projection.
-- 門	kick the ball toward the goal (soccer etc.).
88-- 箭	shoot an arrow.
90-- 光	radiation.
95-- 精	ejaculation.

2421$_0$

化 〔Hua〕 *n.* change, alternation, transformation, mutation, *v.* change, alter, transform, reform, convert, transmute, civilize, melt.

10-- 工	chemical engineering, chemical industry.
-- 工品	chemicals.
-- 石	fossils.
17-- 子	beggar.
24-- 裝室	dressing room, parlor.
-- 裝表演	pageantry.
-- 裝品	cosmetics, toilet article.
-- 裝舞會	masquerade.
27-- 身	personification.
-- 解	settle, bring reconciliation.
-- 名	assumed name.
-- 緣	solicit alms.
35-- 油器	carburetor.
55-- 費	expenditure.

77-- 肥	chemical fertilizer.
-- 學	chemistry.
-- 學方程式	chemical equation.
-- 學記號	chemical symbol.
-- 學工業	chemical industry.
-- 學教授	professor of chemistry.
-- 學成分	chemical composition.
-- 學引力	chemical attraction.
-- 學平衡	chemical equilibrium.
-- 學武器	chemical weapon.
-- 學變化	chemical change.
-- 學纖維	synthetic fiber.
-- 學家	chemist.
-- 學戰	chemical warfare.
-- 學反應	chemical reaction.
-- 學肥料	chemical fertilizer.
-- 學分解	chemical decomposition.
-- 學分析	chemical analysis.
-- 學作用	chemical action.
-- 學性	chemical property.
-- 開	spread out after diluted.
78-- 除	dissolve to nothing, dispel, remove.
-- 驗	test, chemical examination.
-- 驗室	laboratory, assay office.
-- 驗報告	analysis report.
80-- 合	chemical combination.
-- 合物	compound.
-- 合量	combining weight.
90-- 糞池	septic tank, cesspit.

仕 〔Shih〕 *v.* serve the government.

30-- 宦	officials.
38-- 途	political career.
40-- 女	young men and women.

壯 〔Chuang〕 *v.* encourage, strengthen, *adj.* strong, stout, robust, healthy, hardy.

10-- 丁	adult, all-able man.
11-- 麗	splendid, noble, great and glorious.
25-- 健	healthy, blooming, stout, in fine feather.
40-- 士	brave soldier.
77-- 膽	encourage, keep up courage.
80-- 年	*n.* youth, manhood, *adj.*

| | full-grown. |
| -- 氣 | high spirit. |

魁〔**Kuei**〕*n.* chief, head, best, *adj.* great, eminent.

24-- 偉	stalwart.
40-- 士	eminent scholar.
80-- 首	chief.

2421₁

先〔**Hsien**〕*n.* ancients, *adj.* first, previous, former, part, late, *adv.* before, formerly, past, early, ahead, in front.

03-- 試	foretaste.
10-- 天	inherent, congenital, innate.
-- 天不足	inborn deficiency, inherited weakness.
11-- 頭	ahead, in front, in advance.
-- 頭部隊	advance detachment, vanguard.
-- 輩	senior, predecessor.
12-- 烈	martyrs.
21-- 佔	preoccupy.
22-- 例	precedent.
-- 後	before and after, first and last.
25-- 生	teacher, master, mister, sir.
28-- 修班	preparatory class.
30-- 進	senior, predecessor.
-- 進國	advanced nations, developed powers, civilized nations.
-- 進國家	advanced country.
-- 進技術	advanced technology, sophisticated technology.
-- 進設備	sophisticated equipment.
32-- 兆	omen, prognostic.
35-- 決條件	prerequisite, precondition, prior condition.
38-- 導	*n.* mentor, model, guide, forerunner, *v.* lead the way.
40-- 來先得	first come, first served.
47-- 期	before, already.
50-- 夫	my late husband.
60-- 見	foresee, forecast.
-- 見者	foreseer.
71-- 驅	forerunner, pioneer, harbinger.
-- 驅工業	pioneer industry.
77-- 覺	prophet.
-- 民	ancient, former men.
-- 母	my late mother.
80-- 前	before, previously.
-- 父	my late father.
-- 令	shilling.
86-- 知	prophet.
-- 知先覺	ahead of the age.
87-- 鋒	forerunner, vanguard.
-- 鋒隊	vanguard, storm troop.

佐〔**Tso**〕*n.* assistant, deputy, *v.* assist, second.

| 01-- 証 | evidence. |
| 10-- 理 | assist. |

佬〔**Lao**〕*n.* man, adult.

僥〔**Chiao**〕*adj.* lucky, fortunate.

| 24-- 倖 | luckily, by chance. |

2421₂

他〔**Ta**〕*pron.* he, she, it, *adj.* another, other.

00-- 方	the other party, other places.
-- 意	another intention.
11-- 項	other item.
20-- 往	go away, go to another place.
21-- 處	elsewhere.
24-- 動字	transitive verb.
26-- 自己	himself, herself.
27-- 物	anything else.
-- 的	his, her.
-- 鄉	another place.
-- 們	they, them.
-- 們的	their, theirs.
31-- 顧	look away.
33-- 心	dishonesty, insincerity, unfaithfulness.
50-- 事	anything else.
60-- 日	other day.
-- 國	other country.
80-- 人	other, other people, somebody else, another person.

紽〔**Tan**〕*v.* delay, obstruct, hinder.

| 06-- 誤 | delay, hinder, retard. |
| 08-- 於 | devote, indulge in, give |

one's selfup.

| 33-- 心 | be worried, be apprehensive. |

2421₄

佳〔Chia〕*adj.* beautiful, pretty, fine, splendid, excellent, nice, good, superior, handsome, fair.

00-- 音	good news, fine voice.
-- 言	good words.
02-- 話	fine story.
07-- 調	melody.
11-- 麗	handsome, beautiful.
26-- 偶	fine pair.
28-- 作	fine composition.
30-- 賓	distinguished or honored guest.
40-- 肴	delicacy.
47-- 期	wedding or nuptial day.
49-- 妙	pretty, excellent, fine.
60-- 景	beautiful scenery.
80-- 人	beauty, pretty woman.
88-- 節	festival.

僅〔Chin〕*adj.* only, merely, simply, just, barely.

10-- 可	barely enough to.
21-- 能	just able to.
24-- 僅	barely.
27-- 夠	barely enough.
40-- 有	have only, here is only.
60-- 足	just enough.

2421₆

俺〔An〕*pron.* I, me.

2421₇

仇〔Chou〕*n.* enemy, foe, opponent, rival, adversary.

08-- 敵	enemy, opponent.
30-- 家	personal enemy.
36-- 視	hate.
47-- 殺	murder committed out of grudge.
80-- 人	foe, enemy, rival, opponent, adversary.
97-- 恨	hatred, enmity, hostility, spite.

值〔Chih〕*v.* cost, incur, meet, happen.

11-- 班	on duty.
26-- 得	be worthy of, deserve.
60-- 日	be on duty for the day.
-- 日官	orderly officer, officer of the day.
-- 日生	student on duty.
83-- 錢	valuable, expensive.

2422₁

倚〔I〕*v.* rely on, depend upon, trust in, lean against.

20-- 重	entrust.
24-- 靠	lean back, rely on, trust to.
25-- 仗	presume on.
45-- 勢	rely on authority.
-- 勢凌人	take advantage of one's position to bully people.
52-- 托	rely on, depend on.
57-- 賴	*n.* trust, reliance, *v.* trust, rely on.

2422₇

佈〔Pu〕*v.* extend, spread, diffuse.

08-- 施	give money or material to the poor.
10-- 雷	lay mine.
22-- 崗	post sentries, mount guards.
24-- 告	*n.* notice, *v.* announce, declare, publish.
34-- 滿	be covered with.
38-- 道	preach the gospel.
60-- 置	arrange, set, bring into order.
-- 景	scene.
70-- 防	organize the defense.
75-- 陣	lay a trap.
77-- 開	scatter.

僞〔Wei〕*adj.* false, unreal, pretended, hypocritical.

00-- 言	lie, misrepresentation.
-- 充	pretend to be.
02-- 託	under the cloak of.
-- 證	perjury.
08-- 說	perjury.
17-- 君子	hypocrite, fox in lamb's skin.
18-- 政府	puppet government.
21-- 態	mockery.

24--	裝	camouflage.
27--	組織	quisling government.
34--	造	n. forgery, v. invent, fabricate, trump up, cook, counterfeit, falsify, forge.
--	造文書	forgery, counterfeit documents.
--	造賬目	falsify accounts.
--	造印章	falsification of seal.
60--	國	illegal state.
80--	善	hypocritical.
89--	鈔票	forged banknote.
98--	幣	counterfeit money, spurious coin, counterfeit bank note, false coin, queer money.

劬 〔Chin〕 n. catty.

備 〔Pei〕 v. prepare, make ready, provide, adj. ready, prepared, complete, entire, all.

00--	忘錄	memorandum, note.
--	辦	prepare, provide, get thing ready.
--	註	remarks, footnote.
24--	貨	prepare the goods.
25--	件	spare parts.
30--	案	keep on record, for the record.
40--	查	for reference.
44--	考	for reference.
63--	戰	prepare for action.
71--	馬	saddle a horse.
73--	胎	spare tire.
77--	用	reserve, spare, alternate.
--	用現金	till cash, till money, vault cash.
--	用零件	replacement parts.
--	用袋	spare bag.

2423_1

德 〔Te〕 n. virtue, morality, goodness, favor, kindness .

00--	育	moral education.
--	文	the German language, German.
18--	政	benevolent administration or government.
21--	行	virtue, morality.
60--	國	Germany.

--	國語	German.
--	國人	German.
95--	性	morality.

2423_8

俠 〔Chia〕 adj. heroic, chivalric, generous, noble-minded.

12--	烈	chivalrous.
30--	客	knight.
80--	義	chivalric.
--	氣	heroism.

2424_0

妝 〔Chuang〕 v. adorn, decorate, beautify, disguise, feign, pretend.

00--	病	sham illness, pretend to be sick.
27--	假	pretend, make believe.
40--	奩	dowry.
58--	扮	decorate, dress.
61--	點	dress up, adorn, apply make up.
73--	腔	affect, pretend.
88--	飾	adorn, dress up.

2424_1

侍 〔Shih〕 v. serve, attend, wait on, accompany.

00--	立	attendance.
21--	衛	bodyguard.
27--	候	serve, wait on.
--	役	waiter, servant.
28--	從	attendants, servants.
--	從室	generalissimo's headquarter.
--	從武官	aide-de-camp to the president.
40--	女	maid, maidservant.
44--	者	attendants, waiters.

待 〔Tai〕 v. wait, expect, treat.

00--	辦	yet to be taken care of, due out.
--	交貨	goods awaiting delivery.
08--	敵	wait for the enemy.
12--	到	wait until.
--	發	ready to depart.
15--	聘	wait for employment, position wanted.
20--	售	for sale.

24-- 付款	obligation.
-- 裝	be ready for shipment.
28-- 收	due in.
30-- 客	receive a guest, entertain guests.
-- 客周到	treat a guest properly.
32-- 業	job-waiting, unemployment.
36-- 遇	*n.* salary, remuneration, treatment, *v.* treat.
-- 遇優厚	excellent pay and conditions.
-- 遇菲薄	shabby treatment.
40-- 查	yet to be investigated.
42-- 機	await the opportune moment.
60-- 見	wait to be received.
-- 罪	wait for punishment.
63-- 哺	wait for feeding.
64-- 時	wait for the suitable time.
80-- 命	await order.
81-- 領	wait for a claimant.
98-- 斃	await death.

倖 〔Hsing〕 *adj.* fortunate, lucky, *adv.* luckily, fortunately, by chance.

27-- 免	escape by mere luck.
40-- 存	survive by good luck.
44-- 獲	obtain by mere luck.

儔 〔Chou〕 *n.* comrade, mate, fellow, friend, company, party, class.

71-- 匹	companion.
91-- 類	class.

2424_7

伎 〔Chi〕 *n.* talent, ability, cleverness.

11-- 巧	cleverness.
21-- 能	talent, art.
44-- 藝	mechanical arts, expert skill.

彼 〔Pei〕 *pron.* he, she, it, *adj.* that.

00-- 方	other party, other side.
11-- 輩	those people.
21-- 此	this and that, you and I.
-- 此之間	between you and me.
-- 此互利	mutually beneficial.
-- 處	there, yonder, in that place.
22-- 岸	other side.
64-- 時	at that time.

80-- 人	that person.
88-- 等	those people.

2425_6

偉 〔Wei〕 *adj.* great, gigantic, powerful, strong, mightily, admirable.

25-- 績	great achievements.
32-- 業	great achievement.
40-- 大	great, gigantic.
80-- 人	great man, hero.

2426_0

估 〔ku〕 *v.* estimate, reckon, guess, think, consider.

00-- 產	appraise the assets, estimate the yield.
-- 計市場	estimated market value.
-- 計利潤	estimated profit.
-- 計過高	overvalue, overrate.
-- 衣	second hand clothes.
-- 衣鋪	outfitter's shop.
04-- 計	estimate, reckon, suppose, conjecture.
20-- 重	estimated weight.
21-- 價	estimate, estimate price, appraise, set a price on, evaluate.
-- 價證書	certificate of appraisal.
-- 價單	list of cost estimate, estimate sheet, bill of estimate, value bill.
-- 價人	appraiser, assessor, valuator.
24-- 值	assessment, estimated value, value of assessment.
30-- 定價格	estimated price.
-- 定損失	assessment of loss, loss assessment.
60-- 量	consider, guess.
88-- 算利息	calculated interest.
-- 算法	technique of estimation.

佑 〔Yu〕 *v.* aid, assist, help, protect.

74-- 助	help, aid, assist.

貓 〔Mao〕 *n.* cat.

11-- 頭鷹	owl.
21-- 熊	panda.
62-- 叫	meowing of a cat.

儲 〔Chu〕 *v.* hoard, store.

00--	庫	storehouse.
24--	備	savings, reserves, store for future use, lay in.
--	備率	stocking rate.
--	備資金	reserve capital.
--	備基金	reserve funds, nest egg.
--	備銀行	reserve bank.
25--	積	accumulate, hoard, store up.
--	積金	accumulated fund.
30--	戶	depositor.
35--	油	oil storage.
40--	存	*n.* storage, saving, *v.* store, stockpile, lay up.
44--	蓄	*n.* deposit, saving, savings deposit, *v.* save, lay away.
--	蓄率	saving ratio.
--	蓄銀行	savings bank.
--	蓄存款	saving deposit, savings.
--	蓄存款利率	saving deposit rate.
--	蓄債券	saving certificate.
--	蓄機構	thrift intermediary, thrift institution.
--	蓄賬戶	thrift account, savings account (S. A.)
--	蓄金	saving deposits.
--	蓄公債	saving bond.
--	藏	accumulate, store up.
--	藏費	warehousing charge.
--	藏礦量	possible ore, inferred ore.
--	藏室	store room, repository.
--	存期	storage period.
--	存品	stores.
47--	款	save money.
60--	量	reserves.
66--	單	bill of store.
80--	金	savings.
--	倉庫	warehousing storage.

2426₁

佶〔**Chi**〕*adj.* strong, stout.

借〔**Chieh**〕*v.* lend, borrow.

00--	主	creditor.
--	意	metaphorically.
--	方	debit, debit side.
04--	讀	study at a school on a temporary basis.
07--	調	temporary transfer.

20--	重	rely on, seek the assistance.
--	住	stay in another's house.
22--	出	loan.
--	出者	lender.
23--	貸	credit and debit.
--	貸聯係	creditor-debtor relation, debtor-creditor relationship.
25--	債	borrow money.
27--	條	I owe you (IOU).
30--	宿	ask for lodging.
47--	款	*n.* loan, *v.* borrow money, ask for a loan.
--	款申請書	loan application.
--	款契約	loan agreement.
--	款人	borrower.
48--	故	find a excuse.
50--	書証	library card.
51--	據	IOU (I owe you), evidence of debt, receipt for a loan, receipt for borrowed money, debit note.
68--	喻	for instance.
74--	助	have the aid of.
77--	用	borrow.
--	與	lend.
80--	入	borrow.
83--	錢	borrow money.
88--	鑑	benefit by another person's past experiences.

牆〔**Chiang**〕*n.* wall.

37--	洞	loophole.
70--	壁	wall.

2426₄

偌〔**Jo**〕*adj.* such, *adv.* thus, so.

2426₅

僖〔**Hsi**〕*adj.* joyful.

2428₁

供〔**Kung**〕*v.* supply, provide with, offer to, present to, contribute, confess.

00--	應	supply, accommodate.
--	應充足	in abundant (ample, plentiful) supply.
--	應部	supply department, ministry of supply.

--	應站	supply station.
--	應證	ration book.
--	應計劃	plan of supply.
--	應下降	shortfall of supply.
--	應不足	failure of supply, scarcity of supplies, short supply, undersupply.
--	應能力	supply capacity.
--	應線	supply line, supply routes, supporting line.
--	應稀少	in scarce supply.
--	應總額	total supply.
--	應條件	conditions of supply.
--	應過剩	oversupply, excess supply.
--	應者	supplier.
--	應量大	in free supply.
--	應量小	in light supply.
--	應困難	supply bottleneck.
--	應點	supply center.
--	應限制	supply restriction, supply constraints.
--	應短缺	short supply.
--	應管道	supply pipeline.
--	應情況	supply position.
07--	認	confess, own a crime, own the soft impeachment.
--	詞	*n.* confession, depositions, *v.* statement.
10--	電	power supply.
--	不應求	supply is unable to meet the demand.
--	不應求的市場	tight market.
--	需平衡	coordination of supply and demand, balance of supply and demand.
--	需總量	total supply and demand.
13--	職	hold the office.
20--	出售的	for sale.
22--	出租	for hire.
23--	獻	*n.* offering, consecration, dedication, *v.* present, dedicate.
--	獻物	offering, oblation, sacrifice.
--	參考	for reference, for your reference.
24--	貨商	supplier.
--	貨充裕	favorable supply situation.

28--	給	supply, provide, afford, equip, fit out.
--	給市場	supply market.
--	給價格	supply aggregate.
--	給過多	overstock, oversupply.
--	給表	supply schedule.
--	給與需要	supply and demand.
33--	述=供詞	
37--	過於求	excessive supply, supply in excess of demand, excess of supply, over demand, supply exceeds demand.
40--	存查	for files.
43--	求	supply and demand.
--	求平衡	equation of demand and supply, balance, equilibrium of supply and demand, supply-demand balance.
50--	奉	offer, sacrifice.
80--	養制度	supply system.
89--	銷	offer for sale, supply and marketing.

徒 〔**Tu**〕 *n.* foot soldier, follower, pupil, disciple, *adv.* in vain.

12--	刑	penal servitude.
20--	手	bare hand, unarmed.
--	手運動	free gymnastics.
21--	步	walk on foot, go afoot.
23--	然	in vain.
80--	弟	pupil, apprentice, follower.
99--	勞	make a vain attempt, beat the air, bark at the moon.

2429₀

休 〔**Hsiu**〕 *v.* rest, stop, cease, pause, take rest.

21--	止	stop.
26--	息	rest, take rest.
--	息室	drawing room, refreshment room.
--	息日	holiday, off day.
27--	假	*n.* leave of absence, *v.* have vacation, go on a vacation, have.(take) a holiday, go on a holiday.
32--	業	suspend business.
63--	戰	armistice, truce.

77--	閑	leisure, relaxation, ease.
--	閑服	casual wear, sport wear.
--	學	leave of absence.
80--	會	adjourn a meeting.
--	養	rest, recuperate.

牀 〔Chung〕 *n.* bed, couch.
31--	褥	coverlet, bed-quilt.
40--	布	bedspread.
46--	架	bedstead.

2429₆
僚 〔Liao〕 *n.* colleague, companion.
40--	友	comrade.
77--	屬	staff.

2432₀
勳 〔Hsun〕 *n.* meritorious effort, merit.
00--	章	decoration, achievement insignia, medal, chest hardware.
14--	功	meritorious services.
32--	業	meritorious achievements or contribution.
99--	勞	merits, meritorious contributions.

2433₂
憊 〔Bei〕 *n.* fatigue, weariness, *adj.* weary, tired, fatigued, exhausted, worn-out.

2436₁
鰭 〔Chi〕 *n.* fin, gill.

2440₀
升 〔Sheng〕 *n.* pint, *v.* advance, rise, ascend, hoist.
00--	高	lift, heighten.
08--	旗	hoist a flag.
10--	天	ascent to heaven.
24--	值	*n.* appreciation, revaluation, *v.* appreciate, revalue.
27--	級	promoted to an upper class (rank), promotion.
--	級考試	promotion examination.
31--	遷	*n.* promotion, *v.* get transferred to higher position.
47--	起	rise.
--	格	promote, upgrade, elevate.
77--	降	ascend and descend.

--	降機	elevator, lift.
--	學	enter or advance to higher school.
--	學考試	entrance examination for a higher school.
90--	堂	appear in court to conduct a trial.

2441₂
勉 〔Mien〕 *v.* endeavor, try, encourage, stimulate, use effort.
13--	強	*n.* reluctance, *adj.* forced, compelled, constrained, urged, pressed, reluctant.
34--	爲其難	force oneself to do a hard task.
40--	力	diligent, strenuous.
74--	勵	encourage, stimulate, energize, excite, give energy.

2444₇
皺 〔Chou〕 *adj.* wrinkle, furrow.
00--	痕	crease, wrinkle.
10--	面	shrivelled surface.
20--	紋	wrinkles, crease, folds, rumples.
57--	摺	creases, folds.
77--	眉	frown, scowl.

2451₀
牝 〔Pin〕 *n.* female.
00--	鹿	doe.
25--	牛	cow.
71--	馬	mare.

牡 〔Mu〕 *n.* male.
00--	鹿	buck, stag.
25--	牛	bull, ox.
71--	馬	horse.
77--	丹	peony.

2454₁
特 〔Te〕 *adj.* special, single, prominent, eminent, *adv.* specially, particularly.
00--	產	special or unique products, special product, special local product, speciality.
--	效	special efficiency.
08--	效藥	most effective medicine, potent medicine, wonder

-- 許	n. patent, privilege, concession, special permission v. patent.	-- 約記者	special correspondent.
		-- 約撰稿人	special contributor.
		-- 約醫院	hospitalexclusively engaged by an organization.
-- 許証	charter, permit, charter of concession, chartered concession.	-- 級	special class or grade.
		-- 級上將	five star general.
-- 許的	chartered.	28-- 徵	characteristics, attribute, feature, speciality point.
-- 許權	patent, chartered right, franchise, right of special permission.	-- 稅	extra duties, special assessment.
-- 許專賣	monopoly.	30-- 准	special permit.
10-- 工	special service.	-- 家新聞	exclusive report (news), scoop.
-- 需	special procurement.	-- 寫	feature story.
12-- 刊	extra edition.	-- 定	specially designed, specific, specified.
15-- 殊	n. peculiarity, distinction, adj. special, particular.	-- 定關稅	differential duties.
-- 殊份子	special members.	32-- 派	specially dispatched.
17-- 務	secret service.	-- 派記者	special correspondent.
-- 務人員	secret agent.	-- 派員	correspondent.
18-- 攻隊	commando units, rangers.	35-- 遣隊	task force.
21-- 價	specially reduced price, special offer, special price, bargain price.	37-- 選	select specially.
		40-- 大	extra large, exceptionally big.
-- 優	excellent, extraordinary.	-- 大號	king size, extra large size, oversize.
22-- 任	special appointment rank.	-- 有	peculiar.
-- 任官	official of highest rank, official of cabinet rank.	-- 支費	special allowance.
-- 例	special case.	44-- 權	privilege, prerogative, franchise, liberty, special privilege.
-- 製	manufactured for a specific purpose.		
-- 出	outstanding, distinguished, prominent.	-- 權階級	privileged class.
-- 種	special kind, special type, particular kind.	48-- 赦	special pardon, act of grace.
		-- 赦權	power to grant amnesty.
-- 種兵	special troops.	50-- 惠	special preference.
-- 種營業	special business operations.	-- 惠關稅	preferential tariffs.
-- 稱	special description.	54-- 技	special skill, stunts.
25-- 使	special envoy.	60-- 異	singularity.
27-- 色	speciality, feature, special character, characteristics.	61-- 點	trait, distinctive or special feature.
		62-- 別	special, uncommon.
-- 免	dispensation.	-- 別市	special municipality.
-- 急	special urgency.	-- 別工作小組	task force.
-- 獎	special or grand prize.	-- 別要求	ad hoc request.
-- 約	special contract, engage by special arrangement.	-- 別手續	special procedure.
		-- 別待遇	special treatment.
-- 約商店	appointed store.	-- 別紅利	extra dividend, special bo-

nus.

-- 別代理人	special agent.	
-- 別的	extraordinary.	
-- 別收益	special earning.	
-- 別法	special law.	
-- 別法庭	special court.	
-- 別權	privileges, special power.	
-- 別費	extraordinary or special expenses.	
-- 別費用	special charge-off, special charges, special expenses, particular charges.	
-- 別規定	special provisions.	
-- 別區域	special administrative district.	
-- 別開支	special expenses.	
-- 別會議	special meeting.	
-- 別快	ultra-rapid, urgent.	
-- 別快車	express train.	
71-- 長	strong point.	
72-- 質	special qualities, peculiarities.	
80-- 命全權大使	ambassador extraordinary and plenipotentiary.	
88-- 等	special class or grade.	
-- 等艙	stateroom.	
95-- 性	character, nature, attribute, trait, special character.	

2458₆

犢 〔Tu〕 *n.* calf.

2460₁

告 〔Kao〕 *n.* announce, inform, tell, proclaim, notify, impeach, accuse, charge.

02-- 訴	accuse.
03-- 誡	warn, enjoin on.
10-- 示	notice, proclamation.
12-- 發	accuse, indict.
20-- 辭	take leave, say good-bye, bid farewell.
23-- 狀	accusation, indictment.
-- 貸	ask for a loan.
26-- 白	notice, advertisement, placard.
27-- 假	ask for leave.
-- 急	critical, in danger, urgent

need of help.

30-- 密	give confidential information, give a tip.
37-- 退	resign, withdraw, leave the scene.
48-- 警	alert, issue a distress call.
53-- 成	be completed.
55-- 捷	triumph, win a victory.
60-- 罪	admit a mistake, announce the crimes.
62-- 別	say good-bye, bid adieu, bid farewell to, take leave.
-- 別詞	farewell message.
86-- 知	tell, inform, notify.

2466₁

皓 〔Hao〕 *adj.* bright, luminous, pure, white.

10-- 天	summer sky.
77-- 月	brilliant moon.

2467₀

甜 〔Tien〕 *adj.* sweet.

11-- 頭	sweet taste, good benefit.
20-- 香	sweet and fragrant.
30-- 密	sweet, fond, happy.
33-- 心	sweetheart.
44-- 菜	beet.
61-- 點	sweet, dessert.
62-- 睡	sound sleep.
65-- 味	sweet taste.
72-- 瓜	sweet melon.
80-- 美	sweet, pleasant, refreshing.
-- 食	sweet food.

2472₁

崎 〔Chi〕 *adj.* rugged, uneven.

21-- 嶇	rugged, uneven.

2472₇

幼 〔Yu〕 *n.* youth. *adj.* youthful, immature, delicate, tender.

00-- 主	youthful monarch.
-- 童	boy, kid, lad, child.
-- 童軍	cub scout.
17-- 弱	young and delicate.
20-- 稚	infant, immature, naive.
-- 稚教育	preschool education.

-- 稚園	kindergarden.
26-- 細	delicate, fine.
40-- 女	young girl.
44-- 芽	young buds.
-- 苗	tender seedling.
47-- 根	rootlet.
48-- 嫩	young and tender, delicate.
50-- 虫	larva, caterpillar.
77-- 兒	infant, baby.
-- 兒期	infancy.
80-- 年	infancy, childhood.
90-- 小	young and small, infantile, in the cradle, in long clothes.

帥 〔Shuai〕 *n.* marshal, commander-in-chief.

77-- 印	seal of a commander-in-chief.
80-- 令	order of the commander.
81-- 領	command.

2473₂

裝 〔Chuang〕 *n.* baggage, luggage, fashion, style, costume, *v.* dress, decorate, adorn, load, contain, pack, pretend, affect.

00-- 癡	pretend madness, make an ass of oneself.
-- 病	feign illness, pretend illness.
-- 病者	malingerer.
07-- 設	be equipped with, install.
10-- 死	play dead, feign death.
-- 醉	pretend to be drunk.
14-- 璜	*n.* decoration. *v.* decorate.
17-- 子彈	load a gun.
-- 配	assemble, fit together, assembling.
-- 配廠	assembly plant.
-- 配工具	assembly tools.
-- 配過程	assembling process.
-- 配線	assembly line.
24-- 備	equipment, outfit.
-- 貨	load or pack goods, loading, ship the cargo.
-- 貨清單	loading list.
-- 貨機	loading machines.

-- 貨單	shipping list, shipping order (S/O).
27-- 假	disguise, pretend.
-- 船	load cargo aboard a freighter, loading on board, shipment.
28-- 艙	stowage of cargo.
-- 作	pretend, feign.
-- 修	decorate and repair, refurbish, fit up.
34-- 滿	fill up.
-- 潢	decoration.
37-- 運	transport, ship.
43-- 載	*n.* loading, stowage, *v.* load, charge, take load up.
-- 載過重	overload.
44-- 模作樣	pose, strike air.
50-- 車	load on a truck, vehicle etc.
-- 束	apparel.
-- 束入時	fashionable dress.
58-- 扮	*n.* dressing, *v.* dress up, disguise, play at.
60-- 置	*n.* equipment, installation, *v.* equip, install.
-- 置員	equipment officer.
-- 睡	pretend to be asleep.
-- 甲	steel-clad, deck armor.
-- 甲部隊	armored troop.
-- 甲列車	armored train.
-- 甲汽車	armored car.
-- 甲師團	armored division.
61-- 點	decorate, dress.
73-- 腔作勢	give oneself air.
81-- 釘	*n.* binding, *v.* bind.
-- 釘廠	plant for binding books.
87-- 卸	load and unload.
-- 卸工人	stevedore.
88-- 飾	adorn, embellish, decorate, ornament, beautify.
-- 飾品	ornament, adornment, decoration.
-- 箱	pack, box up, pack a box.
-- 箱費	crating charge.
-- 筐機	crate packer.

2473₈

峽 〔Hsia〕 *n.* gorge, canyon.

30-- 灣	fiord.

60-- 口	pass, defile.	
80-- 谷	gorge, valley, canyon.	

2474₁

峙 〔Chih〕 *n.* peak. *v.* pileup, heap.

00-- 立	stand firm.

2474₇

岐 〔Chi〕 *n.* branch road, *adj.* precipitous, divergent.

36-- 視	discriminate against.

崚 〔Ling〕 *n.* steeply, abrupt.

2480₆

貨 〔Huo〕 *n.* goods, ware, merchandise, commodities, money, wealth.

00-- 主	owner of goods.
12-- 到付款	cash on arrival, cash on delivery, cash against delivery, payment against arrival, pay on delivery.
-- 到收款	collect on delivery(C.O.D.).
21-- 價	price of goods.
27-- 物	goods, ware, merchandise, cargo, commodities, goods.
-- 物單	list of goods, invoice.
-- 物發送	delivery of goods.
-- 物重量	cargo weight.
-- 物集裝箱	cargo container.
-- 物保險	cargo insurance.
-- 物運輸	cargo transportation.
-- 物托運	consignment of goods.
-- 物原產國	country of origin.
-- 色	kind, stock of trade, stuff.
-- 色齊全	goods of every description are available.
-- 船	merchant vessel, cargo boat, carrier, freighter, ship, vessel.
28-- 艙	the hold of a ship, cargo bay(airplane), cargo compartment, cargo hold.
30-- 客兩用船	cargo-passenger ship.
31-- 源	source of goods, supply of goods, merchandise resources.
37-- 運	shipment of commodities, transportation service, cargo traffic, carriage of cargo, goods traffic, freight transport.
-- 運站	freight station, freight terminal, goods depot, goods station.
-- 運飛機	air freighter, air truck.
-- 運價值	shipping value.
-- 運業務	cargo service.
-- 運港	cargo port.
-- 運機場	cargo airport.
-- 運量	freight traffic, volume of freight traffic, volume of goods transported, volume of freight.
-- 運距離	distance of freight carried.
-- 運單	shipping list, bill of freight.
-- 運單位	shipping unit.
-- 運單據	shipping document, waybill, cargo documents.
-- 運服務	freight service.
-- 運公司	forwarding company.
41-- 櫃	container.
-- 櫃運輸	container shipment.
-- 櫃船	van ship, container ship.
43-- 棧	warehouse, storehouse, stores.
47-- 款	payment for goods.
48-- 樣	sample, sample goods, specimen.
50-- 車	truck, wagon, freight car, goods car.
-- 攤	stall.
58-- 輪	cargo, vessel, steamer, boat, carrier, freighter, ship, tanker.
60-- 品	goods, commodities.
66-- 單	list of goods, cargo certificate, waybill manifest, shipping list.
80-- 倉	warehouse, storehouse.
-- 倉部	store department.
88-- 箱	packing box.
98-- 幣	money, coin, currency.
-- 幣市場	currency market.
-- 幣交換	exchange through money.
-- 幣交換商 (處)	money changer.
-- 幣交易	monetary operations.

-- 幣不穩定　currency disturbance.
-- 幣需求　money demand.
-- 幣預算　monetary budget.
-- 幣發行　issuance of currency, issuance of paper money, monetary issue, issue paper money, currency issue.
-- 幣政策　monetary policy.
-- 幣改革　currency reform, monetary reform.
-- 幣價值　monetary value, money value, value of money.
-- 幣體系 (制度) monetary system.
-- 幣統一　currency unification.
-- 幣利率　money rate of interest.
-- 幣貸款　money advance.
-- 幣動蕩　monetary disturbances, monetary unrest.
-- 幣儲蓄　currency reserve.
-- 幣危機　monetary crisis.
-- 幣準備　monetary reserves .
-- 幣流通　circulation of money, currency circulation, monetary process, money circulation.
-- 幣匯率　monetary exchange rate.
-- 幣波動　monetary fluctuations .
-- 幣周轉　money turnover.
-- 幣本位　monetary standard.
-- 幣報酬　monetary payoff.
-- 幣增值　appreciation of currency.
-- 幣貶值　currency devaluation, depreciation of money, devaluation of currency.
-- 幣兌換　monetary convertibility.
-- 幣兌換商　money changer.
-- 幣管制　currency control, money management, currency management.

贊 〔Tsan〕 v. assist, help, second, praise, admire.
08-- 襄　aid, help.
-- 許　approve of.
47-- 歎　exclaim in praise.
53-- 成　second, approve, consent, go in for.
56-- 揚　acclaim.

74-- 助　assist, help, support, second, patronize, back up.
-- 助者　patron, supporter.
77-- 同　agree, consent, approve of.
80-- 美　praise, exalt, glorify.
90-- 賞　praise, admire.

2490_0
科 〔Ko〕 n. class, series, order, section.
11-- 研補助金　research grant.
-- 研人材　scientific manpower.
21-- 征　levy tax.
54-- 技　science and technology.
60-- 目　subject of study, curriculum.
-- 罰　inflict punishment.
-- 員　sectional staff, section member, member of an administrative section.
71-- 長　sectional chief, section chief.
77-- 學　science.
-- 學工業園區 Science Industrial District, science-based industrial park.
-- 學家　scientist.
-- 學方法　scientific methods.
-- 學協會　scientific institution.
-- 學化　scientism.
-- 學儀器　scientific instruments.
-- 學教育　science education.
-- 學知識　scientific knowledge.
-- 學管理　scientific management.
-- 舉　competitive examination for old Chinese civil service.

2491_1
繞 〔Jao〕 v. wind round, compass, surround, coil up.
20-- 航　n. deviation, v. deviate.
21-- 行　detour, revolve, go round about, orbit.
-- 纏　entangle.
30-- 避　avoid, evade.
32-- 灣　go round a corner.
37-- 過　pass over.

60-- 圈子　go round and round.
67-- 路　make a detour.

2491₇

紈〔**Wan**〕*n.* white silk.
34-- 子　dandy, son of rich family.

2492₁

綺〔**Chi**〕*n.* kind of silk with cross figures.
11-- 麗　pretty, beautiful.
46-- 想　beautiful thought.
80-- 年　youth.
95-- 情　tender feeling.

2492₇

納〔**Na**〕*n.* insert, enter, admit, receive, pay.
00-- 妾　take a concubine.
-- 交　make friends with, befriend.
10-- 貢　tributary.
28-- 稅　pay duties, pay tax.
-- 稅申報單　tax return.
-- 稅過重　overtax.
-- 稅人　taxpayer, rate payer, tax bearer, contributory tax payer.
-- 稅義務　obligation to pay taxes.
47-- 款　pay money.
64-- 賄　offer bribes.
80-- 入　bring into.
90-- 粹　Nazi.
-- 粹主義　Nazism.
-- 粹黨　Nazi party.

稀〔**Hsi**〕*adj.* few, scarce, rare, sparse.
10-- 疏　scattered, sparse.
-- 硫酸　diluted sulphuric acid.
37-- 罕　curious, rare.
40-- 有　rare.
-- 有金屬　rare metals, scarce metals.
-- 奇=稀罕
44-- 薄　thin.
-- 世　extremely rare.
48-- 散　sparse.
81-- 飯　congee, gruel, porridge.
90-- 少　rare, scarce, very few.
97-- 爛　completely mashed, smashed to pieces.

2493₀

紘〔**Hung**〕*n.* cord, string.

2494₇

稜〔**Leng**〕*n.* corner, angle.
17-- 子　angle, right angle, corner.
27-- 角　corner, angle.
80-- 錐體　pyramid.
-- 鏡　prism.
90-- 光　diffracted light.

紼〔**Fu**〕*n.* large rope.

綾〔**Ling**〕*n.* sarcenet.
26-- 絹　silk gauze.
30-- 空　silk brocades.

穫〔**Huo**〕*n.* reaping, harvest, *v.* crop, reap, harvest.

2495₆

緯〔**Wei**〕*n.* woof, latitude.
00-- 度　degrees of latitude.
26-- 線　latitude.

2496₀

緒〔**Hsu**〕*n.* clue, beginning.
08-- 論　introduction, preface, forward.
32-- 業　business, calling.
88-- 餘　surplus, remainder.

2496₁

結〔**Chieh**〕*n.* knot, skein, button, bond, engagement, *v.* connect, tie, knit, wind up, conclude, close, settle, unite, congeal.
00-- 交　make friend, form acquaintance, contract friendship, associate.
-- 辮　braid.
-- 疤　heal, skin over, scab over.
03-- 識　make acquaintance.
06-- 親　contract a marriage.
08-- 論　conclusion.
17-- 子　bear fruit.
20-- 集　concentrate.
22-- 綵　festoon.
24-- 仇　breed enmity, contract hatred.
27-- 繩　tie knot.
-- 怨　arouse ill will, incur hatred.
29-- 伴　accompany.

30-- 實	durable, lasting, firm.	
-- 案	wind up a case.	
32-- 冰	freeze.	
-- 冰點	freezing point.	
-- 業	graduate.	
-- 業典禮	commencement, graduation ceremony.	
34-- 社	form a union.	
35-- 清	n. settlement, v. pay up a bill, settle, settle a debt, square up, square accounts.	
-- 清賬目	close (settle, square) accounts, get one's account square.	
40-- 存	credit balance.	
-- 核	tubercle.	
-- 核病	tuberculosis.	
42-- 婚	n. marriage, wedding, nuptials, v. marry, wed, tie the nuptial knot.	
-- 婚証書	marriage certificate.	
-- 婚年齡	the age of consent.	
-- 紮	ligation (medicine).	
45-- 構	construction, structure, framework, fabric.	
47-- 好	befriend, be intimated with, win favor from.	
50-- 束	wind up, close, put an end.	
60-- 晶	crystallization.	
-- 晶體	crystal.	
-- 果	n. outcome, result, effect, consequence, end, fruit, crop, harvest, v. bear fruit.	
61-- 賬	pay up an account, close book, reckon account, strike a balance, settle a bill, settle an account, square account, balance an account.	
-- 賬日期	closing date, settlement date.	
67-- 盟	form an alliance, ally with.	
-- 夥	form a band, collude, band together.	
71-- 匯	foreign exchange settlement, settlement of exchange, surrender of exchange, convert foreign ex-	

	change.	
74-- 膜	conjunctiva.	
-- 膜炎	conjunctivitis.	
77-- 局	conclusion, end, outcome, result, upshot, final stroke.	
-- 關港口	port of clearance.	
78-- 隊	group.	
80-- 合	join, associate, combine, ally.	
-- 合力	affinity.	
88-- 算	balance an account, settle, settle an account, close an account, balance accounts, final estimate.	
-- 算表	settlement sheet.	
-- 餘	surplus, balance.	
-- 節	knot.	
90-- 黨	band together, join together.	

稽〔Seh〕n. grain ready to be reaped, husbandry.

50-- 夫	farmer, husbandman.	
-- 事	harvest, reaping.	

2498_6

續〔Hsu〕v. continue, keep on, connect, join on, add to, follow, succeed to.

00-- 言	add.	
15-- 聘	continue to employ.	
20-- 絃	marry again.	
-- 集	sequel.	
21-- 版	reprint.	
23-- 編	sequel.	
24-- 借	renew.	
26-- 保	n. renewal of insurance, renewal, v. renew.	
27-- 假	extend leave.	
-- 約	supplementary treaty.	
32-- 添	add to, supplement.	
88-- 篇	sequel, continuation.	

2500_0

牛〔Niu〕n. cattle, cow, ox, bull.

00-- 瘟	cattle disease.	
-- 痘	vaccine, cowpox.	
14-- 勁	great strength.	
17-- 刀	butcher knife.	
-- 酪	butter and cheese, yogurt.	

22-- 乳	milk.
-- 乳油	butter.
-- 乳皮	cream.
-- 乳餅	cheese.
27-- 角	horns of cattle.
-- 仔	cowboy.
-- 仔褲	blue jeans, Jeans.
35-- 油	butter.
-- 津大學	Oxford University.
40-- 肉	beef.
-- 肉麵	noodles served with stewed beef.
-- 肉汁	beef extract.
-- 肉湯	beef soup.
-- 肉乾	dried roast beef, beef jerky.
-- 皮	hides.
-- 皮紙	brown paper, kraft paper.
47-- 奶=牛乳	
-- 奶場	dairy.
-- 奶公司	dairy company.
-- 棚	dairy.
50-- 車	ox cart.
51-- 排	beefsteak.
71-- 馬	cattle and horses.
-- 馬生活	life of drudgery.
76-- 脾氣	stubbornness, obstinacy.
88-- 筋	cattle tendon.
90-- 糞	cow dung.
95-- 性	stubbornness.

2503₀

失 〔 **Shih** 〕 *n.* loss, omission, fault, mistake, failure, *v.* lose, miss, omit, leave behind, slip, fail, disregard, neglect.

00-- 主	loser.
-- 意	disappointed, despaired, displeased.
-- 言	make a slip of the tongue.
04-- 計	miscalculation, poor planning.
06-- 誤	mistake, blunder, fault, miss.
07-- 望	*n.* disappointment, hopelessness, *v.* disappoint, despair, lose all hope, cast down.
-- 調	disorder, out of tune, dis-location, imbalance, maladjustment.
08-- 效	lose effect, come to naught.
10-- 面子	lose face.
13-- 職	*n.* delinquent, defection, negligence of duty, *v.* neglect duty, lose place, be out of collar, *adj.* negligent in the performance of duties.
18-- 政	misrule, bad government.
20-- 信	*v.* break faith, betray a trust, forfeit one's word, *adj.* unfaithful.
-- 手	lose grasp, make slip.
21-- 態	misbehave.
22-- 戀	lost of love, shot down in flames.
-- 利	suffer a defeat, lose.
24-- 德	lost of virtue.
26-- 和	be on bad terms.
27-- 血	lose blood.
-- 物	lost property.
-- 色	become pale, lost of color.
-- 約	*n.* breach of contract, *v.* break promise, fail in an engagement, fail to keep an appointment.
30-- 守	be defeated, lose a city, fall into the hand of an enemy.
-- 寵	lose favor, fall in disgrace.
-- 察	*v.* be careless, neglect, overlook, *adj.* negligent, absent-minded.
-- 竊	be stolen, have something stolen, suffer loss by theft.
32-- 業	unemployed, out of employment.
-- 業率	percentage of unemployment, rate of unemployment, unemployment rate, jobless rate.
-- 業補助	unemployment benefit, unemployment compensation.
-- 業者	jobless person.
-- 業救濟	unemployment benefit, unemployment relief, unem-

ployment compensation.

35--	神	v. lose wit, *adj.* absent-minded, careless, abstracted.
	-- 禮	v. be rude to, *adj.* disrespectful.
37--	盜	be robbed, be burglarized.
39--	迷	get lost.
42--	機會	miss an opportunity, lose the chance.
44--	落	n. loss, v. lose.
	-- 地	territory occupied by enemy force.
45--	勢	lose one's position.
47--	聲	lose one's voice.
	-- 款	lose money.
48--	敬	being disrespectful.
	-- 散	loose and scattered.
	-- 檢	indiscretion, careless in personal conduct.
50--	事	accident.
51--	掉	lose.
53--	控	out of control, run away.
60--	口	escape one's lips, slip of the tongue.
	-- 足	slip, miss one's step, run awry.
63--	踪	disappear.
64--	時	out of season, day after the fair.
67--	明	lose eyesight, become blind
	-- 眠	lose sleep, have a restless night.
	-- 眼症	insomnia.
	-- 路	lose way.
68--	敗	n. failure, collapse, v. fall, fail, fall to the ground, break down.
	-- 敗主義	defeatism.
72--	所	out of place.
75--	體	out of character.
77--	覺	forget.
	-- 學	lack formal schooling, neglect to learn.
	-- 民心	lose the support of the people.
88--	笑	cannot help laughing.

	-- 算	miscalculate.
	-- 策	mistake, blunder.
90--	火	catch fire.
	-- 常	out of order, not in proper condition.
	-- 當	n. impropriety, adj. improper.
91--	慎	careless.

2510₀

生 〔 **Sheng** 〕 *n.* life, vitality, birth, livelihood, *v.* bear, bring forth, produce, beget, live, grow.

00--	病	fall ill, get sick.
	-- 瘡	get an ulcer.
	-- 產	n. production, birth, bearing, manufacture, v. produce, bear, bring forth, give birth to, adj. manufacturing.
	-- 產率	production rate, output rate, productive rate, productivity, rate of output.
	-- 產計劃	production plan.
	-- 產部	productive department.
	-- 產部門	production department.
	-- 產工具	instrument of production.
	-- 產工人	production labor, production worker.
	-- 產要素	element of production, essential factors of production, production factors, productive factors.
	-- 產線	production line.
	-- 產能力	capacity, manufacturing capacity, output capability (capacity), producing capacity, production potentiality.
	-- 產過剩	over production, surplus production.
	-- 產過程	production process, procedure in production, process of production, production run.
	-- 產力	productivity, productive forces.
	-- 產機關	production organization.

-- 產者	producer.	
-- 產中心	production center.	
-- 產成本	cost of production, cost of manufacture, output cost, production cost, fabrication cost, manufacturing cost.	
-- 產技術	production technique, production engineering, production technology.	
-- 產量	productive output, production volume, quantity of production.	
-- 產局	board of production.	
-- 產管理	production management, administration of production, production control.	
-- 育	beget, get, generate, give birth to.	
-- 育限制	birth control.	
-- 意	business trade.	
-- 意經	businessmen's talk.	
-- 意興隆	boom business, brisk business, business prospering, roaring trade, trade is brisk.	
04-- 計	livelihood, living, one's daily bread.	
08-- 效	go into effect.	
10-- 死	life and death.	
-- 平	the whole life.	
-- 疏	strange.	
14-- 殖	reproduction, generation.	
-- 殖力	fecundity.	
-- 殖細胞	generative cell.	
-- 殖作用	reproduction.	
-- 殖器	generative organ, genitals.	
16-- 理	physiological functions.	
-- 理學	physiology.	
20-- 手	beginner, novice, raw hand, green horn.	
-- 番	savages, barbarians.	
21-- 態學	ecology.	
-- 態環境	ecological environment.	
22-- 利	bring in profit.	
24-- 動	vivid, lifelike, lively.	
26-- 息	bear interest.	
27-- 物	creature, animal, life.	
-- 物工程	bioengineering.	

-- 物化學	biochemistry.
-- 物技術	biotechnology.
-- 物學	biology.
-- 物學家	biologist, naturalist.
-- 疑	throw doubt upon, raise a question, cause a doubt.
-- 色	add color, add splendor.
30-- 字	new words, unfamiliar word.
-- 客	new guest.
31-- 涯	career.
32-- 活	*n.* living, life, way of life, *v.* subsist, go in and out.
-- 活方法	method of life.
-- 活富裕	be well off.
-- 活力	vitality.
-- 活必需品	necessities of life, daily necessaries, necessaries of life, primary wants.
-- 活水平	level of living, scale of living.
-- 活程度	standard of living.
-- 活標準	standard of living, living standard.
-- 活機能	vital function.
-- 活素質	quality of life.
-- 活指數	index of living cost.
-- 活費	cost of living, subsistence money, alimony, subsistence cost, subsistence expenses, living expense.
-- 活費津貼	cost of living allowance, subsistence allowance.
-- 活問題	problems of livelihood.
35-- 油	uncooked edible oil.
36-- 還	come back alive, survive.
-- 還者	survivor.
40-- 力軍	reinforcement, fresh troop.
-- 皮	raw hide, untanned hide.
-- 來	since one's birth.
-- 存	*n.* existence, life, being, living, survival, *v.* exist, live, come to being, keep alive.
-- 存競爭	struggle for existence.
-- 存空間	living sphere.
-- 存權	right to life.

42-- 機	vitality, animation.	
44-- 菜	salad.	
47-- 根	take root.	
50-- 事	create trouble.	
58-- 擒	catch alive.	
60-- 日	birthday.	
-- 界	biological world.	
64-- 財	furniture and office equipment.	
66-- 啤酒	draught beer.	
67-- 路	way to make a living, way to survive.	
68-- 吃	eat raw, eat without cooking	
71-- 厭	become bored, tired of something.	
-- 長	n. growth, v. grow up.	
-- 長激素	growth hormone.	
72-- 髮油	hair tonic, ointment.	
80-- 人	living person, stranger.	
-- 前	before death, while one was alive.	
-- 父	real father.	
-- 命	life, heart's blood.	
-- 命保險	life insurance.	
-- 命保險公司	life insurance company.	
-- 命線	lifeline, lifeblood.	
-- 命力	vitality.	
-- 命帶	life belt, life preserver.	
-- 命權	right of life.	
-- 氣	vitality, liveliness, animation.	
82-- 銹	rust.	
83-- 鐵	pig iron.	
90-- 火	kindle a fire.	
94-- 料	raw material.	

2520₀

仗〔**Chang**〕v. rely on, depend on, look up to.

80-- 義	rely on a sense of justice.
-- 氣	rely on emotion.
94-- 恃	rely on.

件〔**Chien**〕n. article, item, subject.

10-- 工	piece-work.
25-- 件	everything.
58-- 數	number of things, number of packages.
61-- 號	package number, piece number.

2520₆

仲〔**Chung**〕n. the middle one.

00-- 立人	broker, middle man.
43-- 裁	n. arbitrage, arbitration, v. arbitrate, interpose, intermediate.
-- 裁法	arbitration law, arbitration act.
-- 裁費	arbitration fees, fees for arbitration.

伸〔**Shen**〕v. extend, stretch, straighten out.

02-- 訴	complain, make a statement, submit a grievance.
11-- 張	expand, enlarge, widen, extend, increase, spread.
20-- 手	stretch out the hand.
22-- 出	stretch out.
23-- 縮性	extensibility, flexibility, elasticity.
37-- 冤	clear up a case, bring to justice.
40-- 直	straighten.
71-- 長	lengthen.
77-- 展	spread, stretch, extend.
-- 開	stretch out, extend, spread.

使〔**Shih**〕n. messenger, envoy, v. send, commission, employ, use, expend, order, command, cause, effect.

14-- 勁	exert strength.
22-- 出	exert.
24-- 徒	apostle.
26-- 得	all right, can be done.
40-- 女	maid servant.
44-- 者	messenger.
60-- 團	diplomatic corps.
67-- 喚	use.
77-- 用	use, employ, make use of, press into service.
-- 用說明	direction for use, instructions.
-- 用權	right to use, right of use.
-- 用期限	lifetime, time limit for use.
83-- 館	legation, embassy.

88--	節	envoy, official mission.

2520₇

律〔**Lu**〕 *n.* rule, regulation, law, code, statute.

00--	度	laws and institutions.
21--	師	lawyer, attorney, solicitor, barrister .
--	師費	attorney fee.
--	師事務所	lawyer's office.
--	師公會	bar association.
22--	例	statute, canon.
55--	典	code.
80--	令	laws and regulations, order given according to law.

2521₇

儘〔**Chin**〕 *adj.* utmost, extreme, all, *adv.* totally, entirely, completely.

10--	可能	as far as possible, to the best of one's ability.
24--	先	very first.
27--	夠	quite enough.
60--	量	as much as possible, as soon as possible.
--	早	as early as possible.
88--	管	in spite of , even if, no matter.

2521₉

魅〔**Mei**〕 *n.* devil.

40--	力	glamor, sexiness, attractiveness, charm.
53--	惑	*n.* bedevil, bewitch, *adj.* captive.

2522₇

佛〔**Fu**〕 *n.* Buddha.

20--	手	bergamot, citron.
21--	經	the religious book of Buddha, Buddhist scriptures.
24--	徒	Buddhist disciple.
30--	家	Buddhist, Buddhist followers.
34--	法	Buddhist doctrines.
40--	寺	Buddhist temple.
48--	教	Buddhism.
77--	學	Buddhistic study.
--	門	Buddhism, Buddhist faith.
90--	堂	Buddhist sanctuary.

彿〔**Fu**〕 *adv.* similarly, as if.

倩〔**Chien**〕 *adj.* pretty, comely, witty, charming.

62--	影	beautiful image of a woman.
90--	粧	beautiful make-up and becoming clothes.

2523₀

佚〔**I**〕 *n.* ease, rest, repose, retirement, *adj.* idle, leisure.

2524₀

健〔**Chien**〕 *v.* strengthen, invigorate, *adj.* strong, vigorous, robust, stout.

00--	康	health.
--	康產品	health product.
--	康証	health certificate.
--	康證明書	certificate of health, medical certificate.
--	康保險	health insurance.
--	康保險費	health insurance expense.
--	康教育	health education.
--	康檢查	health examination.
--	康檢驗證書	inspection certificate of health.
--	康食品	health food.
--	忘	forgetful.
--	忘症	amnesia.
--	全	sound, perfect.
09--	談	brilliant conversation.
21--	步	walk fast, capable of walking a long way.
--	行	hiking.
24--	壯	healthy and robust, strong and vigorous.
27--	身房	gymnasium.
--	身操	exercise, fitness exercise.
--	將	one who plays a leading role.
40--	在	be in good health.
80--	全	all right, perfect, in good condition.
--	美	healthy and handsome, healthy and pretty.

2524₃

傳〔**Chuan**〕 *n.* record, biography, *v.*

hand down, perpetuate, transmit, interpret, explain, spread, carry forward.

00--	言	n. rumor, v. bring word, send a verbal message.
02--	話	n. interpreter, v. interpret, pass on a message.
--	證	summon witness.
07--	記	biography, memoir, life.
--	訊	summon.
08--	說	it is said, as the story goes, legend.
10--	下	hand down, descend, bequeath.
--	示	give notice, send word.
--	票	summons.
17--	習	teach and learn.
--	習所	school, institute.
20--	信	message.
--	信鴿	homing pigeon.
--	統	tradition, convention.
--	統產品	traditional products.
--	統商品	traditional commodities.
--	統食品	traditional food.
22--	種	propagate species.
23--	代	hand on from generation to generation.
28--	給	import.
30--	家寶	heirloom.
--	案	summon.
32--	遞	forward, hand over, convey, send, pass, transmit, pass on.
34--	達	n. transmission, v. communicate, herald.
--	達室	reception office.
--	達者	herald.
--	染	infect, taint.
--	染病	infection, plague, contagion.
--	染病毒	virus.
38--	道	preach.
--	道會	commission.
--	導	conduct.
--	導體	conductor.
--	送	convey, deliver.

40--	布	spread, announce, blow off, let out, propagate.
--	真	facsimile, transmit photo.
--	真設備	facsimile equipment.
--	真發送	facsimile transmission.
--	真機	fax or facsimile machine.
--	奇	storybook, legend, saga.
45--	熱	n. heat conduction, communicate heat.
46--	觀	pass on.
47--	聲筒	megaphone.
48--	教	propagate or preach a religion.
--	教師	preacher, missionary.
52--	授	instruct, teach, impart knowledge to.
--	播	spread, propagate, circulate.
--	播媒體	news medium, mass medium, mass media.
--	播體	media, journalistic circles.
58--	輸通道	transmission channel.
--	輸媒介	transmission medium.
--	輸成本	transmission cost.
56--	揚	expose, extend.
62--	呼電話機	paging telephone set.
--	呼系統	paging system.
--	呼機	pager.
66--	單	handbill, circulars, flyers.
67--	喚	summon.
77--	聞	hearsay, unconfirmed report.
--	閱	be circulated.
80--	令	deliver or give orders.
--	令嘉獎	citation.
--	令兵	messenger, orderly runner.
--	令鴿	carrier-pigeon.
95--	情	flirt, play at love.

2524₄

僂 〔Lou〕 adj. hunchbacked, humpbacked.

27-- 佝   deformed, short and ugly.

2525₃

俸 〔Feng〕 n. salary, remuneration, allowance, wage, income, emolument.

37-- 祿   salary, income, emolument.

80-- 金　salary.

2528₆
債〔Chai〕n. debt, obligation.
00-- 主　creditor.
10-- 票　bond, bill of debt.
17-- 務　debt, obligation, liability, indebtedness.
-- 務額　amount of debt.
-- 務人　debtor.
30-- 戶　debtor.
44-- 權　right to recover debt, creditor right, financial claim, obligation right, right of credit.
-- 權人　creditor, claimer.
90-- 券　bond, bond certificate, debenture, debenture certificate, loan bond.

2529₀
侏〔Chu〕n. dwarf, pigmy.
21-- 儒　pigmy, dwarf.

2529₄
傑〔Chieh〕n. hero. adj. heroic.
22-- 出　eminent.
28-- 作　masterpiece.

2529₆
㑛〔Su〕adj. trembling, frightened.

2531₇
魨〔Tun〕n. freshwater porpoise.

2532₂
鯖〔Ching〕n. mackerel.

2540₀
肄〔I〕v. learn, practice.
17-- 習　practice, get skillful.
32-- 業　study, learn a profession.

2551₀
牲〔Sheng〕n. victims, v. sacrifice.
00-- 畜　livestock.
60-- 口　livestock.

2571₄
毽〔Chien〕n. shuttle-cock.

2590₀
朱〔Chu〕n. red, vermilion.
00-- 衣　red robe.

19-- 砂　cinnabar.
21-- 紅　scarlet, red, vermilion.
40-- 古力　chocolate.
60-- 墨　red ink.
-- 愚　stupid, ignorant.

2590₄
桀〔Chieh〕n. hen-roost, adj. cruel, savage, tyrannical.

2590₆
紳〔Shen〕n. the gentry, the literati, officials. v. bind, girdle.
40-- 士　gentleman.
-- 士協約　gentlemen's agreement.
緤〔Shieh〕n. bridle, bonds, fetter, v. tie up, secure, fetter.
60-- 羈　n. bridle, v. curb, restrain.

2591₇
純〔Chun〕adj. pure, unmixed, uniform, simple, honest, sincere, find, best, adv. entirely, wholly.
00-- 產品　net product, straight product.
-- 文學　pure literature.
04-- 熟　proficient, very skillful.
10-- 一　sincere, simple, uniform, pure, homogenous.
-- 正　upright.
16-- 理論　theory.
-- 現值　present net worth.
20-- 毛　all wool.
22-- 利　net profits.
-- 利率　net profit ratio, net rate, pure interest rate, rate of net profit.
-- 利息　net interest.
-- 利益　net return.
-- 種　pure-bred, thoroughbred.
25-- 生產額　net produce (product).
26-- 白　pure white.
27-- 色　of one color, pure color.
28-- 收入　income net, net income, net return, net revenue.
-- 收益　yield net.
30-- 良　good, kind, honest.
32-- 淨　pure, unmixed.
-- 淨重　net weight.

-- 淨的	fine, net, clean.
37-- 潔	fine, pure and clean.
-- 資本	net capital, pure capital.
40-- 直	unaffected.
42-- 樸	simple and sincere.
44-- 孝	truly filial.
53-- 成本	flat cost.
56-- 損	net loss, dead loss.
57-- 投資	true investment.
60-- 品	of the purest quality, completely unmixed.
71-- 厚	sincere, honest.
72-- 質	unadulterated substance.
80-- 金	pure gold, fine gold.
83-- 鐵	pure iron.
87-- 銀	fine silver, pure silver.
90-- 粹	pure, absolute.

2592_7

繡〔**Hsiu**〕 *v.* embroider, *adj.* variegated, embellished.

10-- 工	embroidery.
13-- 球	ball of rolled silk.
-- 球花	hydrangea.
26-- 線	embroidery thread.
44-- 花	embroider.
-- 花鞋	embroidered shoes.
-- 花針	embroidery needle.
50-- 畫	embroidered pictures.
71-- 匠	embroiderer.

2593_0

秩〔**Chih**〕 *n.* order, rank, series.

00-- 序	order, series, sequence.
-- 序大亂	total disorder.
-- 序井然	perfect order.
-- 序單	program.

秧〔**Yang**〕 *n.* young plant, fry.

17-- 子	shoots, sprouts.
-- 歌	songs sung by farmers when transplanting rice.
20-- 禾	rice shoots, paddy sprouts.
44-- 苗	young shoots.
60-- 田	water field.

2593_3

穗〔**Sui**〕 *n.* ear of a grain, tassel.

2594_4

縷〔**Lu**〕 *n.* thread, yarn, *adj.* ragged, shabby.

27-- 解	explain in detail.

2598_6

積〔**Chi**〕 *n.* product, *v.* gather together, collect, accumulate, hoard, store up, pile up, heap up.

08-- 效考核	performance appraisal.
-- 效考核制度（考績制）	merit system.
10-- 雪	accumulated snow.
12-- 水	accumulate water.
17-- 聚	accumulate, amass.
-- 習	deep-rooted practice, old habit.
27-- 怨	accumulated malice or hatred.
-- 欠	accumulated debts, arrears, account in arrears, have one's debts, piling up, run up a score.
-- 久	for a long time.
32-- 冰	ice which exists for a long time, pack ice, ice accretion, ice accumulation, external ice, black ice (on roads).
40-- 存	save, store, store up, lay up.
-- 木	building blocks, wooden blocks.
41-- 極	positive.
-- 極主張	agitate.
-- 極主義	positivism.
-- 極手段	positive means.
-- 極行為	positive act.
-- 極態度	active attitude.
-- 極抵抗	active resistance.
-- 極分子	activist, enthusiast, radical.
-- 極合伙人	working partner.
44-- 蓄	save, store, treasure, heap up.
60-- 累	accumulation.
-- 累資金	accumulate funds.
71-- 壓	accumulate and hold up.
-- 壓文件	backlog document.
-- 壓物資	arrear of stock, overstock-

	ing of goods.
-- 壓資金	let funds lie idle.
80-- 分	accumulated points, integral calculus.
-- 善	accumulate virtue.
98-- 弊	deep-rooted evils.
99-- 勞成疾	fall sick from overwork.

績〔**Chi**〕*n.* merit, *v.* twist, wind silk, spin.

00-- 麻	spin hemp.
08-- 效	results, effects, achievements.
-- 效預算	performance budgeting.
20-- 紡	spin.
40-- 女	spinster.
53-- 成	achievements.

2599₀

秣〔**Mo**〕*n.* ration, fodder, *v.* feed.

71-- 馬	feed horse.

2599₆

練〔**Lien**〕*v.* practice, train, drill.

13-- 球	practice a ball game.
-- 武	train oneself in martial arts.
14-- 功	do exercise, practices kill.
17-- 勇	militiaman.
-- 習	*n.* exercise, *v.* practice, train, drill.
-- 習生	trainee, apprentice.
-- 習所	training school.
-- 習艦	training ship.
-- 習題	exercise.
-- 習簿	exercise book.
-- 習體操	drill exercise.
72-- 兵	drill troops.
90-- 拳	practice boxing.

2600₀

白〔**Pai**〕*v.* make clear, state, express, manifest, *adj.* white, snowy, bright, clear, pure, fair, *adv.* in vain.

00-- 衣	white clothes.
-- 衣天使	nurses.
02-- 話	local dialect.
-- 話文	writing in vernacular Chinese.
08-- 說	talk in vain.
10-- 天	day-time, open-day.
-- 雲	white clouds.
11-- 斑	white specks, white spots.
12-- 水	plain water.
17-- 刃	naked blade, sharp knife.
-- 刃戰	close battle.
22-- 種人	white people, Caucasians.
24-- 牡丹	white peony.
27-- 血球	leukocytes, white blood cell.
-- 色	white color.
30-- 字	misused words ,wrong written characters.
-- 宮	White House.
31-- 酒	white spirits.
36-- 濁	gonorrhea.
37-- 軍	white army.
38-- 送	give away.
40-- 布	plain white cloth.
-- 內障	cataract.
-- 皮書	white paper.
-- 木耳	white colored edible fungus.
44-- 帶	white flow, leucorrhea (medicine).
-- 花	white flowers.
-- 蘭地	brandy.
-- 菜	Chinese cabbage.
46-- 楊	abele, poplar.
50-- 晝	full daylight, light of day, open day.
55-- 費	use up without profit, waste.
58-- 蟻	white ant, termite.
60-- 日	daytime, daylight, sun.
-- 墨	chalk.
-- 果	ginkgo nut.
67-- 喉	diphtheria.
72-- 髮	*n.* grey hair, *adj.* grey headed.
77-- 開水	boiled water.
80-- 金	platinum.
-- 食	free meal.
81-- 飯	cooked white rice.
-- 領工人	white collar, white collar worker.
-- 領階級	white-collar class.
87-- 鴿	pigeon.

90-- 米	white polished rice.
-- 糖	white sugar, refined sugar.
98-- 粉	chalk.

囱 〔Chung〕 *n.* window flue, sky light.

自 〔Tzu〕 *pron.* oneself, self, *adv.* naturally, personally, spontaneously, *prep.* from, since.

00-- 主	*n.* liberty, one's own man, *v.* stand one's ground, on one's own.
-- 主權	right of self-government, decision-making power, power to make decisions, freedom of action.
-- 主國	sovereign state, independent state.
-- 立	*n.* self-support, *v.* stand on one's own bottom, support oneself, stand on one's legs, *adj.* independent.
-- 產	self-production.
-- 立門戶	keep house.
-- 豪	boast.
-- 序	author's own preface.
-- 言自語	soliloquy.
02-- 新	be born again.
04-- 誇	boast, brag, plume oneself.
-- 謀出路	find one's own means of livelihood, seek jobs on one's own.
06-- 謂	in one's own conceit.
-- 誤	forfeit one's own chances.
07-- 認	acknowledge, confess, profess.
08-- 謙	humble, modest.
13-- 強	fortify oneself.
17-- 習課	homework.
-- 取	of one's own doing.
-- 己	oneself, self.
-- 己人	persons closely related with each other.
-- 負	*n.* vanity, self-conceit, egotism, self-importance, *v.* feel one's oats, think oneself wise, plume oneself.
20-- 重	*n.* self-esteem, *v.* hold one's

	hand high, be true to one's self.
-- 信	*v.* flatter oneself, *n.* self-confidence.
-- 愛	self-love, self-respect.
21-- 此	from then on, henceforth.
-- 行	personally, individually.
-- 行車	bicycle.
-- 衛	self-defense, self-protection.
-- 衛權	right of self-defense.
-- 便	as one wishes.
22-- 後	henceforth, hereafter.
-- 任	appoint oneself, assume control personally.
-- 制	*n.* self control, self-command, self-restraint, self-government, *v.* forbear, hold in.
-- 製	self made, self-manufactured.
-- 私	selfish.
-- 私自利	self-concern.
-- 稱	call oneself, claim.
23-- 然	*n.* nature, *adj.* natural, *adv.* of course, at ease, no doubt, assuredly.
-- 然主義	naturalism.
-- 然療法	natural way of healing, naturopathy.
-- 然災害	natural calamity, natural hazard, act of nature.
-- 然現象	natural phenomenon.
-- 然科學	natural science.
-- 然律	natural law.
-- 然法	natural law.
-- 然淘汰	natural selection.
-- 然資源	natural resources, nature resources.
-- 然壽命	natural life.
-- 然哲學	natural philosophy.
-- 然力	natural power.
-- 然界	natural world.
-- 然人	natural person, physical person.
-- 然美	natural beauty, beauty of nature.

-- 我批評	self-criticism.
-- 我檢討	self-examination.
24-- 動	*n.* automatic motion, self action, *adj.* voluntary.
-- 動電話	automatic telephone.
-- 動取款機	automatic teller machine, cashomat.
-- 動售貨機	auto mat, automatic vending machine, vending machine.
-- 動的	automatic.
-- 動步槍	automatic rifle.
-- 動化	automation.
-- 動力	automatic power.
-- 動梯	moving staircase.
-- 動車	automotive vehicles.
-- 動櫃員機	automatic teller machine (ATM).
-- 動提款機	automated teller machine.
-- 動販賣機	vending machine.
-- 動開關	automatic switch.
-- 動鉛筆	mechanical pencil.
-- 備	self-provided.
25-- 傳	autobiography, memoir.
26-- 得	content with oneself.
-- 卑感	inferiority complex.
-- 保	self-insurance.
27-- 身	oneself.
-- 身難保	unable even to protect oneself.
-- 負	have a very high opinion of oneself, conceited.
28-- 修	self-study, self-education.
-- 從	since, ever since.
-- 作孽	make one's own bed.
-- 作自受	take the consequences of one's own deeds, reap the fruits of one's action.
-- 縊	hang oneself.
-- 給	self-supply.
-- 給自足	*n.* self-sufficiency, autarky, *adj.* self-sufficient.
30-- 害	hurt oneself, pull about one's ear.
33-- 治	self-government, autonomy.
-- 治市	municipal borough.
-- 治行政	self-government.
-- 治區	autonomous region, dominion.
-- 治團體	self-governing body, autonomous body.
-- 治會	student government of a school.
-- 治領	dominion.
-- 必	naturally, unavoidably, certainly, surely.
-- 述	narrate one's own story.
34-- 滿	be satisfied with oneself.
-- 瀆	self-abuse, masturbation.
37-- 選商店 (自助商店)	self-service store.
40-- 大	*v.* assume great airs, magnify oneself, get on the high horse, *adj.* proud, conceited, self-important.
-- 力更生	self reliance, rely on one's own efforts, self-dependence.
-- 在	comfortable, at ease.
-- 來水	running water, tap water.
-- 來水廠	waterworks.
-- 來水筆	fountain pen, self feeding pen.
-- 來火	safety match, gas light.
-- 古至今	from old until now, in all ages.
43-- 始至終	from beginning to end, from top to bottom, all along.
46-- 相殘殺	internecine warfare.
-- 相矛盾	self-contradiction.
47-- 殺	*n.* suicide, self-murder, self-destruction, *v.* commit suicide, destroy oneself, kill oneself.
48-- 救	rescue oneself.
50-- 由	*n.* liberty, freedom, *v.* be free, be at ease, feel at home, *adj.* free, independent, loose.
-- 由主義	liberalism.
-- 由競爭	free competition, laissez-faire.
-- 由意志	free will.

-- 由職業	professions that do not require fixed office hours, liberal profession.
-- 由行動	freedom of action.
-- 由經濟	free economy.
-- 由戀愛	free love.
-- 由之戰	war of freedom.
-- 由港	free port, free dock, optional port.
-- 由式	freestyle (swimming).
-- 由權	liberty.
-- 由民	free people, yeoman.
-- 由區	free zone, free area, free district.
-- 由貿易	free trade, unrestricted trade.
-- 由鐘	liberty bell.
-- 由兌換	free convertibility.
-- 由黨	liberal party.
-- 由黨員	whigs.
-- 由勞動	free in labor.
-- 畫像	self-portrait.
-- 責	blame oneself.
54-- 持	restrain or discipline oneself.
55-- 轉	*n.* rotation, *v.* revolve on its own.
-- 費	at one's own charge (expense), self-supported, self-supporting, self-financed.
-- 費生	self-supported student.
56-- 招	confess.
60-- 量	measure oneself, make a self assessment.
-- 署	sign one's name, autograph.
-- 足	self-sufficient, complacency.
-- 暴自棄	abandon oneself.
67-- 鳴鐘	striking clock.
71-- 願	voluntary, of one's own accord.
-- 願兵	volunteer, volunteer soldier.
-- 願捐助	voluntary contribution.
74-- 助	self help, help oneself.
-- 助洗衣店	launderette, laundromat.
-- 助餐	buffet.
-- 助餐室	cafeteria.

77-- 覺	self-consciousness.
-- 用	for personal or private use.
-- 用物品	personal belongings.
-- 問	ask oneself, search one's own soul.
80-- 今	from now on, henceforth.
-- 尊	self-respect, self-esteem.
-- 首	deliver oneself up to justice, turn oneself in.
-- 命	pretension.
89-- 銷	self-sale, sell through one's own channels.
90-- 省	introspection.
98-- 斃	destroy oneself.

2604_0

牌 〔**Pai**〕 *n.* tablet, board, shield, signboard, card.

10-- 示	notification, notice to the public.
17-- 子	label, tag, bulletin board.
20-- 位	ancestral tablet.
40-- 九	Chinese dominoes.
-- 坊	monument, arch.
45-- 樓	ceremonial arch.
61-- 號	store name appearing on the signboard.
67-- 照	license plate.
77-- 局	gambling game.

2610_4

堡 〔**Pao**〕 *n.* earthwork, bulwark.

60-- 壘	fortress, stronghold, castle, bulwark.
70-- 障	defense, rampart.

皇 〔**Huang**〕 *n.* sovereign, emperor, ruler.

00-- 帝	emperor.
08-- 族	royal blood, prince of the blood.
17-- 子	prince.
21-- 上	His Majesty.
24-- 儲	crown prince.
30-- 宮	imperial palace.
-- 家	imperial family.
37-- 冠	imperial crown.
40-- 太子	crown prince.
-- 太后	empress dowager.

60-- 恩	imperial favor or kindness.
72-- 后	empress, queen.
74-- 陵	imperial mausoleum.

2611₀

覿 〔Chi〕 v. long for.

2612₇

甥 〔Sheng〕 n. nephew.

40-- 女	niece.
77-- 兒	nephew.

2620₀

佃 〔Tien〕 v. plow, till.

27-- 租	land rent.
30-- 戶	farmer on tenancy, tenant.
55-- 農	tenant farmer.

伯 〔Pai〕 n. uncle, senior uncle.

20-- 爵	count, earl.
-- 爵夫人	countess.
77-- 母	aunt.
80-- 父	uncle, senior uncle.

伽 〔Chia〕 n. Buddhist.

個 〔Ke〕 n. individuality, unit.

17-- 子	physical size of a person, build.
62-- 別	particular, individual.
-- 別合同	specific contract.
-- 別品牌	individual brand.
75-- 體	individual.
-- 體戶	individual business or shop.
-- 體商店	individually-run shop.
-- 體經營	individual operation.
80-- 人	personal, individual.
-- 人主義	individualism.
-- 人計算機	personal computer.
-- 人工資	individual wage.
-- 人需要	individual demand.
-- 人行李	personal luggage (effects).
-- 人儲蓄	personal savings, individual savings.
-- 人稅	personal tax.
-- 人收入	individual income, personal income, personal revenue.
-- 人資格	individual capacity.
-- 人資本	individual capital, personal capital.
-- 人支票	individual check.

-- 人支出	personal outlays.
-- 人存款	personal savings.
-- 人責任	individual liability, private responsibility, sole responsibility.
-- 人擔保	personal guarantee, personal security.
-- 人投資	personal investment.
-- 人投機	individual speculation.
-- 人賬戶	personal account.
-- 人財富	individual wealth, personal wealth.
-- 人財產	personal effects (goods), personal possessions, personal property, personal wealth, individual wealth.
-- 人險	personal risk.
95-- 性	personality, individuality.

徊 〔Hui〕 v. walk to and fro, wander about, adj. forward and backward.

2620₇

粤 〔Yueh〕 n. Kwangtung.

80-- 人	Cantonese.

2621₀

但 〔Tan〕 adv. only, merely, simply. conj. but, still, yet, however, nevertheless.

60-- 是	but, however, yet.
71-- 願	wish, hope.

侃 〔Kan〕 adj. faithful, upright, straightforward.

2621₁

貔 〔Pi〕 n. white fox, a kind of tiger.

2621₃

鬼 〔Kuei〕 n. ghost, devil, spirit.

00-- 魔	evil spirit, demons.
02-- 話	lies, nonsense, false word.
16-- 魂	spirit, ghost.
22-- 祟	misfortunes brought by evil spirit.
78-- 臉	grimace.
97-- 怪	ghost, devil.

傀 〔Kuei〕 adj. vast, huge, big, strange.

26-- 儡	puppet, doll, tool.
-- 儡戲	puppet show.

-- 儡政府　puppet government.
-- 儡國　puppet state.

2621₄

俚 〔**Li**〕 *adj.* vulgar, rustic, rude, rough.
01-- 語　slang.
17-- 歌　rustic songs.
28-- 俗　vulgar, rustic, rude, rough.

貍 〔**Li**〕 *n.* wild cat.

徨 〔**Huang**〕 *adj.* confused, doubtful.

2622₇

帛 〔**Po**〕 *n.* silk, fabrics, taffeta.

偶 〔**Ou**〕 *n.* image, idol, puppet, statue, pair, couple, match, companion, comrade, *v.* marry, pair, harmonize, *adv.* unexpectedly, accidentally, suddenly.
23-- 然　unexpectedly, accidentally, by chance, by accident.
27-- 像　idol, statue.
36-- 遇　happen, come upon.
60-- 見　come across.

觸 〔**Chu**〕 *v.* touch, excite, offend, oppose, hit against.
27-- 角　tentacle.
47-- 犯　offend, affront.
-- 怒　enrage, exasperate, irritate, excite one's anger.
60-- 目　catch the eye, strike the eye.
-- 目驚心　strike the eye and rouse the mind.
72-- 鬚　tentacle.
77-- 覺　the sense of touch.

2623₂

泉 〔**Chuan**〕 *n.* spring, fountain.
12-- 水　spring water.
31---源　spring.

2624₀

俾 〔**Pi**〕 *v.* cause, effect, enable.
26-- 得　so as to, in order that.

2624₁

得 〔**Te**〕 *v.* get, secure, obtain, gain, possess, acquire, come by, come into possession.
00-- 主　possessor, gainer.
-- 病　get ill, become sick.
-- 意　*v.* satisfy one's desire, *adj.* satisfied.
20-- 手　obtain, succeed.
21-- 便　at convenience.
22-- 利　profit, reap profit, make money.
25-- 失　gain and loss.
28-- 以　in order that, so that.
30-- 寵　win favor, be in one's book.
34-- 法　have got the way of doing anything, successful.
-- 達　reachable, accessible.
40-- 寸進尺　give him an inch and he will take an ell.
-- 力人手　seasoned hand.
41-- 標、中標　acceptance of bid.
44-- 勢　in power.
48-- 救　be saved.
58-- 數　answer.
60-- 罪　offend, displease.
77-- 閒　at leisure.
79-- 勝　win, be victorious.
80-- 益　profit, reap the benefit.

2624₇

傻 〔**Sha**〕 *adj.* foolish, stupid, silly.
02-- 話　nonsense.
17-- 子　simpleton, fool.
80-- 笑　simper.

2624₈

儼 〔**Yen**〕 *adj.* stern.
23-- 然　dignified, stately.

2626₀

侶 〔**Lu**〕 *n.* companion, mate, comrade, *v.* associate with, keep company with, mate together.
29-- 伴　comrade, companion.

倡 〔**Chang**〕 *n.* leader, guide, prostitute, *v.* introduce, promote, lead, start.
00-- 率　lead.
-- 言　advocate.
08-- 議　make a motion.
38-- 導　lead, promote.
41-- 狂　profligate.
43-- 始　initiate, originate.

儡 〔**Lei**〕 *n.* puppet.

2628₁

促 〔Tzu〕 *adj.* urgent, hurried, near, close, shortened, contracted.

25-- 使	impel, urge.	
-- 使價格上升	drive prices up.	
30-- 進	*n.* facilitation, promotion, acceleration, *v.* stimulate, promote, set forward, facilitate, acceleration.	
-- 進者	promoter.	
-- 進出口	export promotion.	
-- 進進口	import promotion.	
-- 進貿易	give a impetus to trade.	
-- 進生產	promoting production.	
-- 進投資	investment promotion.	
-- 進業務	promote business.	
-- 進因素	stimulus factors.	
-- 進友好關係	contribute to the growth of friendship.	
36-- 迫	urge, press, hurry on.	
44-- 狹	narrow, narrow-minded.	
53-- 成	precipitate.	
89-- 銷	sales promotion, promote the sale of.	
-- 銷措施	sales promotion measures.	
-- 銷定價	promotional pricing.	
-- 銷方法	sale approach.	
-- 銷服務	services of sales promotion.	
-- 銷途徑	channel promotion.	
-- 銷運動	marketing campaign.	
90-- 忙	in a hurry.	

2629₄

保 〔Pao〕 *n.* guardian, protector, guarantee, *v.* protect, guard, defend, warrant, guarantee, secure, keep safe, insure.

00-- 育	raise.
-- 育院	nursery, orphanage.
02-- 證	guarantee, warrant, assure, certify.
-- 證退款	money back guarantee.
-- 證書	warrant, letter of guarantee, warranty.
-- 證人	guarantee, sponsor, guarantor, surety warrantor.
-- 證金	security money, security, cash deposit or collateral, cash guarantee, cash security, guaranty money, margin, earned money, marginal deposit, security money, security deposit, warrant money.
04-- 護	protect, guard, defend, take under one's protection.
-- 護主義	protectionism.
-- 護色	protective color.
-- 護政策	protective policy.
-- 護性關稅	protective duties.
-- 護條款	protective provisions, safeguard clause.
-- 護民生	livelihood protection.
-- 護者	protector, preserver.
-- 護權	protectorate.
-- 護區	protected area.
-- 護國	protectorate.
-- 護貿易	protective trade, protective of trade and commerce, protective trade.
-- 護人	guardian.
10-- 不住	cannot be defended, most likely, may well.
12-- 水險	marine insurance.
20-- 重	take care of oneself.
21-- 衛	defend, guard against.
24-- 佑	bless.
-- 值	preserve the value of, maintain value.
25-- 健	health protection, health care.
-- 健站	health station.
-- 健工作	public health work.
-- 健品	health care products.
-- 健津貼	health allowance.
-- 健費	healthy subsidies, subsidies for health.
-- 健箱	medical kit.
26-- 釋	release on bail.
-- 釋金	bail.
27-- 修	guarantee to keep something in good repair.
28-- 齡球	bowling.
-- 齡球場	bowling alley.
30-- 守	*v.* conserve, keep, stand

	fast, *adj*. conservative.
-- 守黨	conservative party.
-- 守主義	conservatism.
-- 安	ensure local security.
-- 安措施	security measures.
-- 安隊	national guard, territorial guard.
-- 安人員	security personnel.
-- 密	keep the secret.
-- 密防諜	keep the secret and prevent espionage.
-- 密通信	secret communication.
31-- 額	insured amount.
36-- 溫	preserve heat, keep hot.
-- 溫杯	thermos cup.
-- 溫材料	thermal insulation material.
38-- 送	send a student to a school or college without an entrance examination.
40-- 存	preserve, keep.
-- 有	possession.
-- 壽險	insure against death.
44-- 藏	conserve, preserve.
-- 藏所	repository.
47-- 姆	nurse.
50-- 本	break even.
-- 本投資	break even investment.
54-- 持	reserve, keep, retain.
-- 持原樣	keep intact.
-- 持涼爽	keep cool.
-- 持接觸	keep in contact with.
-- 持乾燥	keep dry.
66-- 單	insurance policy, document of guaranty, affirmative, covenant, guaranteed warranty, guarantee slip, insurance policy.
70-- 障	defense.
-- 防工作	security measures.
71-- 長	constable.
77-- 舉	recommend.
-- 留	retain, reserve, preserve, hold back.
-- 留地	reservation.
-- 留權利	reservation of right, rights reserved.
-- 留份額	reserved quota.

78-- 險	*n.* insurance, assurance, *v.* insure, assure, warrant.
-- 險庫	strong room.
-- 險不足	underinsured.
-- 險客戶	policyholder.
-- 險行	insurance firm.
-- 險價值	insurance value, insured value, value of insurance.
-- 險集團	insurance pool.
-- 險絲	fuse wire.
-- 險代理行	insurance agency.
-- 險儲蓄	insurance saving.
-- 險線	safety wire.
-- 險經紀人	insurance broker, insurance agent, canvasser.
-- 險額	amount insured, coverage.
-- 險套	condom, sheath.
-- 險槓	bumper.
-- 險推銷員	insurance man, insurance canvasser.
-- 險期	insurance period, term of guaranteed service.
-- 險申請書	application for insurance.
-- 險申請人	insurance applicant.
-- 險單	insurance policy, insurance certificate, insurance slip.
-- 險帶	safety belt.
-- 險費	premium, insurance premium.
-- 險費用	insurance expense.
-- 險費率	premium rate, rate of premium.
-- 險開關	cut-out switch.
-- 險人	insurer, underwriter, assurer.
-- 險金額	amount insured, insured amount, amount covered, sum insured, sum of insurance.
-- 險公司	insurance company, assurance company, insurance society.
-- 險剃刀	safety razor.
-- 險業	insurance industry.
-- 險箱	strong box, safe.
80-- 人	guarantor, sponsor.
-- 全	assure the safety of.

-- 養		*n.* maintenance, *v.* take care, maintain, keep in good repair.
-- 養費		maintenance cost, upkeep.
-- 全公司		security company.
81-- 鏢		bodyguard, armed escort.
88-- 管		keep, have custody of.
-- 管室		storeroom.
-- 管庫		safe custody vault.
-- 管權		custody.
-- 管費		storage charges, custodian fee, safe custody charges, safe keeping fee, storage fee.
-- 管責任		custodial responsibility.
-- 管人		custodian.
90-- 火險		fire insurance, insured against fire.

2631₄
鯉 〔**Li**〕 *n.* carp.

2633₀
息 〔**Hsi**〕 *n.* respiration, gasp, interest, *v.* breathe, respire, rest, stop, suspend.

10-- 票		interest coupon, coupon, certificate of interest.
21-- 止		cease, stop.
47-- 怒		appease anger.
80-- 金		interest.
92-- 燈		blow out the lamp.

鰓 〔**Sai**〕 *n.* gills of a fish.

2633₃
鰥 〔**Kuan**〕 *n.* widower, unmarried man, bachelor.

50-- 夫		widower, bachelor.
77-- 居		live alone.

2640₀
卑 〔**Pei**〕 *adj.* low, base, vulgar, mean, inferior, humble, yielding.

00-- 讓		defer, yield with respect.
11-- 輩		inferiors.
24-- 幼		junior.
28-- 微		lowly, humble.
31-- 污		filthy, base, mean.
63-- 賤		vulgar, mean, vile.
67-- 鄙		base, low, mean, crooked.

-- 鄙手段		dirty tricks.
71-- 陋		low, crude, vulgar, inferior.
90-- 小		junior.
-- 劣		inferiority.

舶 〔**Po**〕 *n.* ocean-going ship.

40-- 來品		imported goods, foreign goods.

2640₁
睪 〔**Kao**〕 *n.* testis.

40-- 丸		testis.

2641₀
魏 〔**Wei**〕 *n.* Wei (a family name), *adj.* high, lofty, elevated.

2643₀
吳 〔**Wu**〕 *n.* Wu (a family name). *v.* bawl.

臭 〔**Chou**〕 *n.* strong smell, stench.

10-- 豆腐		fermented bean curd.
27-- 名		ill-fame, bad reputation.
35-- 溝		stinking ditch, gutter.
44-- 藥水		carbonic acid.
50-- 虫		bedbug.
-- 事		scandal.
60-- 罵		scold soundly.
65-- 味		strong smell, bad smell.
80-- 氣		stink, ozone, reek.
-- 氧		ozone.

2644₆
鼻 〔**Pi**〕 *n.* nose.

00-- 音		nasal sounds, snuffle.
12-- 孔		nostril.
27-- 血		nosebleed.
30-- 塞		have a stuffy nose, nasal congestion.
37-- 梁		bridge of the nose.
38-- 涕		mucus, snivel.
73-- 腔		nasal cavity.
77-- 骨		nasal bone.
88-- 管		nasal duct.
90-- 尖		tip of the nose.
-- 炎		nasal catarrh.
91-- 煙		snuff.
-- 煙壺		snuff box.

2661₃

魄 〔Po〕 *n.* soul, figure, form, shape.
2675_0

岬 〔Chia〕 *n.* promontory, headland, cape.
2690_0

和 〔Hu〕 *n.* harmony, union, concord, agreement, peace, *v.* harmonize, unite, mix, compound, make peace, *adj.* peaceful, harmonious, amiable.

00--	音	diapason.
01--	諧	*n.* harmony, concord, *adj.* compatible. harmonious, in harmony.
08--	議	peace accord or agreement.
09--	談	peace talks.
10--	平	*n.* peace, *adj.* peaceful, calm, tranquil, temperate.
--	平主義	pacifism.
--	平解決	amiable settlement, peaceful solution.
--	平條件	peace term.
--	平會議	peace conference.
--	靄	amiable.
22--	緩	relaxation.
27--	解	*n.* compromise, conciliation, pacification, reconciliation, *v.* compromise, conciliate, make peace, become reconciled.
--	解政策	appeasement policy.
--	解解決	compromise solution, settle by compromise.
--	解法案	compromise bill.
--	解協定	deed of arrangement.
--	解契約	contract of compromise.
--	約	peace treaty.
40--	姦	fornication, amour, intrigue.
44--	協	cooperate harmoniously.
--	菜	fixed menu in a restaurant.
47--	好	reconcile, agree, be on good terms.
--	好如初	become reconciled, make up with.
--	聲	harmony.
50--	事者	peacemaker, mediator.
62--	暖	mild and warm.
64--	睦	have friendly ties, be on friendly terms.
74--	陸	*n.* harmony, reconciliation, *adj.* on good terms.
77--	服	(Japanese) kimono.
--	局	tie, draw (said of a contest).
80--	善	kind and gentle, grace, agreeable.
--	會	peace conference.
--	氣	kind, agreeable, affable.
90--	尚	monk.
98--	悅	pleasant.

細 〔Hsi〕 *adj.* fine, small, thin, delicate, pretty, *adv.* carefully, minutely, closely.

01--	語	low and tender talk.
04--	讀	read carefully, peruse.
05--	講	explain in detail.
07--	部	details, minute parts.
09--	談	talk over, talk in detail.
10--	工	fine and delicate work or craftsmanship.
--	雨	drizzle, fine rain.
17--	弱	weak, slight.
19--	瑣	petty, trifles.
20--	毛	fine hair.
--	看	look at carefully, examine in detail.
22--	絲	fine thread.
27--	繩	string.
28--	微	small, minute.
30--	流	small stream.
--	字	fine print.
--	密	fine and delicate, careful, cautious.
--	察	examine thoroughly.
33--	心	careful, attentive, heedful.
37--	瓷	fine porcelain.
39--	沙	fine sand.
40--	查	investigate thoroughly.
--	索	cords.
44--	菌	bacteria, micro-organism.
--	菌戰	bacterial warfare.
--	學	bacteriology.
--	枝	slender twig.
46--	想	think over carefully, ponder.

47--	聲	very low voice.
48--	故	trifling matter.
50--	事	trifle, small matter.
58--	數	net amount.
60--	目	detail, particularity, detailed catalogue, specific item.
61--	賬	detail account, itemized account.
62--	則	by-laws, regulation, detailed rules and regulations, minor regulations.
67--	呢	broad cloth.
--	路	narrow path.
71--	長	slender.
77--	胞	cell.
--	胞組織	cellular tissue.
--	胞膜	cell membrane.
--	胞核	cell nucleus.
--	胞質	cell-wall membrane.
--	胞體	cell-body.
--	胞學	cytology.
--	胞分裂	cell-division.
--	問	question in detail.
80--	分	detailed final sorting.
88--	節	minor points, trifles, detail, particulars.
90--	小	tiny, little, thin, petty.
--	粒	granule.
91--	類	subgroup.

2691_4

程〔**Cheng**〕*n.* rule, pattern, limit, *v.* measure, estimate.

00--	序	order, sequence, procedure.
--	序設計	program composition, programming.
--	序手冊	procedure manual.
--	序法	procedural law.
--	序控制	procedure control.
--	序圖	procedure chart.
--	度	point, degree, extent.
--	度不等	varying extent, in smaller or lesser degree.
27--	租船	voyage charter, trip charter.
38--	途	journey, course.
43--	式	example, pattern, formula.

2692_2

穆〔**Mu**〕*adj.* amicable, accordant, complaisant, *v.* admire, love.

2692_7

綿〔**Mien**〕*n.* cotton.

12--	延	continuance.
26--	線	cotton thread.
29--	紗	cotton yarn.
40--	力	my limited power.
--	布	cotton cloth.
44--	薄	limited power, poor abilities.
57--	軟	soft, weak.
80--	羊	sheep.

絹〔**Chuan**〕*n.* taffeta, handkerchief, kind of thick, loosely woven raw silk fabric.

2693_0

總〔**Tsung**〕*v.* collect, unite, sum up, manage, control.

00--	主筆	chief editorial writer.
--	產量	gross product, gross output, sum total of production, total output.
--	商會	general chamber of commerce.
--	廠	general factory.
--	辦	manager, directors.
--	辦事處 (總公司) general office.
04--	計	in all, all in all, total, in total, in the aggregate, lump sum, major total, sum total.
07--	部	headquarters.
08--	論	general discussion, summary, introduction.
10--	工會	federation of labor unions, general labor union.
--	工程師	chief engineer.
--	平均	overall average.
--	要	should always.
--	需求	aggregate demand, total demand.
11--	預算	general budget.
12--	發行所	head office, main office.
16--	理	prime minister, president, general manager, managing

director.

17-- 司令	commander-in-chief.
-- 司令部	general headquarters.
-- 承包	general contract.
-- 承包人	prime contractor, general contractor.
-- 務	general affairs.
-- 務部	general affairs department.
18-- 攻擊令	orders for the general offensive.
20-- 統	president.
-- 統府	president's office.
-- 統制	political system under which the president is the chief executive.
-- 統候選人	presidential candidate.
-- 統當選人	president-elect.
-- 集	complete works.
21-- 行 (店)	head office, parent bank, main office.
-- 價	gross price, total price.
-- 經理	general manager, managing director, general management executive, top executive, top manager.
-- 經銷	exclusive distribution.
-- 經銷商	sole distributor.
22-- 稱	general term.
-- 利潤	gross profit, total profit.
23-- 代理	general agency, general agent, managing agent.
-- 代理人	general agent, free agent.
-- 編輯	editor-in-chief.
24-- 動員	general mobilization.
-- 值	total value, global value, gross value.
-- 結	summation, conclusion.
-- 付	lump-sum payment.
26-- 得	have to, somehow.
27-- 督	governor, governor-general, viceroy.
-- 網	general principles.
-- 負責人	person in overall charge.
28-- 稅務司	inspector-general.
-- 收入	gross earnings, gross income, total income, total revenue.

30-- 之	in short, in conclusion.
31-- 額	total amount, gross sum.
32-- 業績	overall performance.
35-- 決算	general final accounts, general summary of accounts, final accounts.
37-- 選舉	general election.
-- 資本	aggregate capital.
40-- 支出	total disbursement, total expenditure, total expenses.
41-- 帳	ledger.
42-- 機	telephone switchboard.
43-- 裁(總經理)	president, managing director.
44-- 共	in all, altogether.
48-- 幹事	chief secretary.
-- 教官	chief instructor.
50-- 表	summary statement.
-- 事務所	head office.
51-- 批發	general wholesale distribution.
-- 批發商	general distributor.
-- 指揮	commander-in-chief.
52-- 括	sum up, summarize.
57-- 投資	gross investment, total investment .
58-- 數	sum, amount.
60-- 量	total amount.
-- 目	general index.
-- 罷工	general strike.
-- 是	always, without exception.
61-- 賬	general account, general ledger.
62-- 則	general rule.
71-- 長	state secretary, minister.
75-- 體戰	all-out war, total war.
77-- 局	head office, headquarter.
-- 貿易	general trade.
-- 貿易額	total value of trade.
78-- 監	inspector general, director general.
80-- 人口	total population.
-- 合	assemblage.
-- 會	association, club, assemblage, central committee.
-- 公司	head office, controlling company, home office.

81-- 領事	consul-general, general consul.	
-- 領事館	consulate-general.	
88-- 算	on the whole, all things considered.	
-- 管	superintendent, supervisor, director.	
-- 管理處	general administration division.	

2693_2

線 〔Hsien〕 *n.* thread, cord, wire, fuse, clue, trace.

11-- 頭	end of a thread, beginning of things.
24-- 裝本	book bound in the traditional Chinese style.
40-- 索	clue.
55-- 軸	spool.
67-- 路	circuit, narrow path.

纏 〔Huan〕 *v.* bind, tie round, strangle.

80-- 首	strangle.

2694_0

稗 〔Pai〕 *n.* grass, weed, *adj.* small, minor.

30-- 官	petty officials, story-writer.
50-- 史	fictitious history.

2694_1

稈 〔Gan〕 *n.* straw, stalk.

17-- 子	stalk of a rice plant.

釋 〔Shih〕 *v.* release, free, liberate, explain.

08-- 放	release, liberate, let go, set free.
20-- 手	part from.
27-- 疑	dispel doubt.
48-- 嫌	dispel suspicion, dispel.
80-- 義	*n.* definition, *v.* explain the meaning.

緝 〔Chi〕 *v.* catch, pursue, come after.

22-- 私	*n.* preventive service, *v.* seize smugglers or smuggled goods.
-- 私船	ships of preventive service, anti-smuggling patrol boat, coast guard vessel, revenue cutter.
-- 私隊	preventive service.
-- 私人員	coast guard, anti-contraband personnel.
44-- 獲	catch, seize, arrest.

繹 〔I〕 *v.* unfold, explain, *adj.* continuous, unceasing.

2694_4

纓 〔Ying〕 *n.* fringe, tassel.

2694_7

稷 〔Chi〕 *n.* millet.

縵 〔Man〕 *n.* plain silk.

2699_3

緤 〔Lei〕 *n.* black rope, fetter.

2710_0

血 〔Hsueh〕 *n.* blood.

00-- 庫	blood bank.
-- 癌	leukemia.
06-- 親	blood relatives, blood relation.
08-- 族	blood relation.
12-- 型	blood type, blood group.
13-- 球	blood cells, corpuscle.
-- 球素	globin, hemoglobin.
20-- 統	bloodline, lineage, parentage, blood relationship.
21-- 紅	sanguine.
27-- 緣	blood relationship, strain.
30-- 液	blood.
-- 液學	hematology.
-- 案	murder case, bloody incident.
31-- 污	bloody, bloodstained.
-- 汗	blood and sweat.
-- 汗錢	hard-earned money.
33-- 淚	tears and blood.
35-- 清	serum.
37-- 凝	blood coagulation.
40-- 赤素	hemoglobin.
50-- 本	net cost, rock-bottom cost, original capital.
60-- 量	blood volume.
-- 跡	bloodstains.
63-- 戰	bloody war, war to the knife.

67--	吸虫	blood fluke.
71--	壓	blood pressure.
--	壓高	high blood pressure, hyper-tension.
--	壓計	blood pressure monitor.
--	壓低	low blood pressure, hypo-tension.
72--	脈	blood vessels, blood rela-tionship.
76--	腥	bloody.
80--	氣	animal spirit.
88--	管	blood vessel.
--	管硬化	hardening of blood vessel, vascular sclerosis.
90--	糖	blood sugar, blood glucose.
95--	性	enthusiasm, strong sense of righteousness.

2710_4

墾 〔Ken〕 v. plow, exploit, break land, develop new land.

14--	殖	plow and sow, colonize by cultivation of land.
22--	種	plow and sow.
44--	荒	develop barren land.

壑 〔Ho〕 n. ravine, valley, pit, pool, pond.

2710_7

盌 〔Wan〕 n. bowl, cup.

盤 〔Pan〕 n. dish, plate, basin, vessel, v. coil up, twist, wind, examine.

08--	旋	n. convolution, circulation, v. go round.
17--	子	tray, plate, dish.
24--	繞	coil, curl.
--	貨	take stock, make an inven-tory, make an inventory of stock, make an inventory of stock on hand, take in-ventory, take stock.
40--	查	question, cross-examine.
--	存	take an inventory of.
51--	據	occupy and hold a place.
55--	費	travelling expenses.
--	曲	n. wave, undulation, twist, v. coil up, wind, wave, twirl.
60--	足	cross one's legs.

61--	點	check, make an inventory of.
--	賬	examine the account, audit accounts, check accounts.
77--	問	n. inquisition, v. inquire, interrogate.
--	尼西林	penicillin.
88--	算	calculate, figure.

2711_0

凱 〔Kai〕 n. victory, triumph.

08--	旋	return in triumph.
--	旋門	Triumphal Arch.
22--	樂	music of triumph.
17--	歌	song of victory.

2711_7

龜 〔Kuei〕 n. tortoise, turtle.

11--	頭	penis, glans.
47--	殼	tortoise's carapace.
60--	貝	tortoise shell.
--	甲	tortoise shell.

2712_0

勻 〔Yun〕 v. divide equally, adj. equal, even.

07--	調	even, balance.
22--	稱	symmetry.
58--	整	neat, even and orderly.
80--	分	distribute equally.

卹 〔Hsu〕 v. feel for, pity, sympathize, compassionate, be sorry for.

80--	金	compensation, indemnity.
--	養	raise, aid in the sustenance of.

2712_7

郵 〔Yu〕 n. postal service, mail, adj. postal, mail.

10--	票	postal stamp, post stamp, postage stamp, stamp.
--	電	postal and cable service.
17--	務司	postmaster.
--	務局	post office.
--	務局長	postmaster.
18--	政	postal service, postal and telecommunication.
--	政信箱	post-office box (P.O.B.).
--	政總局	general post office.
--	政局	post office.

-- 政局長	postmaster.
-- 政儲蓄	postal savings.
-- 政儲金	postal savings.
23-- 袋	mail bag.
25-- 件	mail, mail matters, post matters, postal items.
27-- 包	postal parcel.
-- 船	passenger liner.
30-- 寄	send by mail.
-- 寄名單	mailing list.
32-- 遞	send by mail, mail service.
-- 遞區號	zip code.
37-- 資	postage, postal charge.
-- 運	deliver by mail, mail transportation.
47-- 期	mail day.
50-- 車	postal car.
55-- 費=郵資	
-- 費不足	insufficient postage.
-- 費已付	postpaid.
65-- 購	mail order, purchase of goods by post.
-- 購公司	mail order firm.
68-- 輪	mail steamer (M/S).
71-- 匯	remit by post, send money by mail, postal money order.
-- 區	postal district.
73-- 戳	post mark.
77-- 局	post office.
-- 局職員	postal clerk.
80-- 差	post man, messenger.
88-- 筒	post box, mail box, mail drop.
-- 簡	air letter.

歸〔**Kuei**〕 *v.* return, go back, revert, send back, restore.

00-- 主	return to the Lord.
08-- 於	belong to, be attributed to, result in, ascribe.
10-- 正	return to the right path.
-- 天	pass away.
14-- 功	give credit to.
21-- 順	submit, surrender.
22-- 僑	returned oversea Chinese.
24-- 告	blame.

-- 結	end, sum up, put in a nutshell.
-- 化	naturalize.
-- 納	generalize, induct.
-- 納法	inductive method.
-- 納推理	inductive reference.
26-- 程	homeward journey.
27-- 向	turn toward, incline to.
28-- 併	merge into, unite, combine, amalgamate.
-- 咎	lay blame on, impute.
30-- 家	return home.
-- 案	arrest a criminal and bring him to court, bring to justice.
33-- 心	homesick, idea of returning home.
36-- 還	*n.* restitution, *v.* return, restore, revert.
38-- 途	on the way home, homeward journey.
44-- 老	retire.
47-- 期	returning date.
49-- 檔	return back to file, file away.
60-- 罪	blame, charge.
-- 國	return to fatherland.
74-- 附	follow, pledge allegiance to.
77-- 屬	attach.
78-- 隊	go back to the unit, return to the ranks.
80-- 入	classify, include.
91-- 類	assort, classify.

2713₂

黎〔**Li**〕 *n.* black color.

67-- 明	daybreak, peep of day, dawn.
77-- 民	people.

2713₆

蟹〔**Hsieh**〕 *n.* crab.

44-- 黃	crab spawn.
47-- 殼	crab shell.
88-- 箝	nippers of a crab.

2720₀

夕〔**Hsi**〕 *n.* evening, sunset, twilight.

76-- 陽　　　　setting sun.

2720₇

多 〔**To**〕 *n.* plenty, great number, *adj.* many, numerous, plentiful, *adv.* often, mostly.

00-- 病　　　　sickly.
-- 病者　　　martyr of disease.
-- 方　　　　by all means, in every way.
-- 麼　　　　how, what.
-- 言　　　　talkative, loquacious.
02-- 端　　　　in many respects.
04-- 謝　　　　many thanks, thank you very much.
10-- 至　　　　as many as, as much as.
-- 元論　　　pluralism.
-- 面形　　　polyhedron.
-- 面角　　　polyhedral angle.
-- 雲　　　　cloudy.
11-- 班制　　　multi-shift operation.
-- 頭　　　　taking a long position (stock exchange).
-- 頭政治　　polyarchy.
22-- 變　　　　changeable, varied.
-- 種產品　　multiple product.
-- 種價值　　multi values.
-- 種經營　　engage in diverse economic undertakings.
-- 種用途的　multi-purpose.
24-- 付　　　　*n.* overpayment, *v.* overpay.
27-- 久　　　　how long?
-- 角形　　　polygon.
-- 疑　　　　suspicious.
28-- 收　　　　overcharge.
29-- 愁　　　　afflicted.
33-- 心　　　　suspicious.
35-- 禮　　　　very polite, over courteous.
-- 神教　　　polytheism.
36-- 邊　　　　multilateral.
-- 邊形　　　polygon.
-- 邊交易　　multilateral transaction.
-- 邊協定　　multilateral agreement.
-- 邊貿易　　multilateral trade.
-- 邊會談　　multilateral talks.
37-- 次　　　　many times, often.
-- 過　　　　above, over.
-- 退少補　　refund for any overpayment

or a supplemental payment for any deficiency.

40-- 大　　　　how big?
-- 有　　　　mostly.
48-- 樣化投資　diversified investment.
50-- 事　　　　officious, meddlesome, eventful.
58-- 數　　　　majority, bulk, plural number.
60-- 國公司　　multinational firm, multinational corporation.
71-- 長　　　　how long?
80-- 年　　　　many years.
-- 年生莖　　perennial stem.
-- 年生植物　perennial plant.
-- 年生根　　perennial root.
-- 食　　　　surfeit, glut.
88-- 餘　　　　too much, unnecessary, superfluous, redundant.
90-- 半　　　　for the most part.
-- 少　　　　how many? more or less, some what.
95-- 情　　　　passionate, affectionate.

2721₀

佩 〔**Pei**〕 *n.* pendant, *v.* wear, hang, gird on, carry, respect.

10-- 玉　　　　jade ornament.
17-- 刀　　　　saber, hanger.
24-- 勳章　　　wear medals.
44-- 帶　　　　wear, carry.
77-- 服　　　　respect, admire, appreciate.

徂 〔**Tsu**〕 *v.* go to.

04-- 謝　　　　wither, fade, die.
44-- 落　　　　pass away, die.

2721₂

危 〔**Wei**〕 *n.* peril, danger, hazard. *adj.* dangerous, hazardous, risky, perilous.

00-- 症　　　　dangerous disease.
-- 亡　　　　in great danger.
27-- 急　　　　hanging by a thread.
30-- 害　　　　endanger, harm, injure, jeopardize.
-- 害治安　　jeopardize public security.
36-- 迫　　　　dangerous and pressing.
38-- 途　　　　dangerous road.

40-- 難	in peril, in danger.	
42-- 機	crisis, critical point.	
77-- 局	dangerous or critical condition.	
78-- 險	*n.* danger, risk, hazard, peril, *adj.* dangerous.	
-- 險職業	dangerous occupation.	
-- 險物	dangerous goods.	
-- 險地界	dangerous zone.	
-- 險份子	dangerous elements.	
-- 險品	hazardous substances, dangerous articles, hazardous articles.	

2721₇

貌 〔**Mao**〕*n.* appearance, countenance, form, figure, face.

16-- 醜	ugly, ill looking, ill-made.
28-- 似	seem, look like.
46-- 相	judge someone by his appearance only.
80-- 美	beautiful.

鳧 〔**Fu**〕*n.* wild duck.

2722₀

勿 〔**Wu**〕*adv.* not, never.

00-- 言	don't speak.
08-- 論	regardless of, let alone.
10-- 要	need not.
12-- 延	without delay.
24-- 動	don't touch, don't move.
25-- 失	do not let (a chance) slip away.
77-- 用	not necessary, not to use.
80-- 念	do not worry.

豹 〔**Baw**〕*n.* leopard, panther.

仰 〔**Yang**〕*v.* look up, expect.

07-- 望	expect, hope.
10-- 天	look up to heaven.
11-- 頭	raise the head.
21-- 止	admiration.
33-- 泳	backstroke.
44-- 慕	admire.
65-- 跌	fall with the face upward.
78-- 臥	lie on one's back.

向 〔**Hsiang**〕*n.* intention, object, *adj.* facing, opposite to, *adv.* formerly, hither to, before, previously, *prep.* toward, to.

10-- 下	downward.
-- 西	westward.
11-- 北	northward.
12-- 水性	hydrotropism.
21-- 上	upward.
22-- 後	backward.
-- 例	according to custom.
23-- 外	outward, turn around.
-- 外性	extroversion.
33-- 心力	centripetal force.
40-- 內	inward.
-- 內性	introversion.
-- 左	to the left.
-- 右	to the right.
-- 南	southward.
-- 來	hitherto, until now, always.
44-- 著	toward, face.
50-- 東	eastward.
60-- 日葵	sunflower.
80-- 前	forth, onward, forward.

伺 〔**Ssu**〕*v.* wait upon, serve, watch, detect.

27-- 候	attend, wait upon.
57-- 探	spy, detect.

匍 〔**Pu**〕*v.* crawl, creep.

21-- 行	crawl, creep, scramble.

佣 〔**Yong**〕*n.* commission.

80-- 金	commission.

御 〔**Yu**〕*n.* charioteer, *v.* drive a chariot, control, manage, *adj.* imperial, royal.

00-- 座	throne.
21-- 旨	imperial decree.
44-- 者	driver.
-- 花園	imperial garden, emperor's garden.
77-- 醫	emperor's physician.
-- 用	used by the emperor, for the use of the emperor.
88-- 筆	handwriting of the emperor.

夠 〔**Kou**〕*adj.* sufficient, enough, satisfied.

00-- 意思	generous, really kind.
20-- 受	unbearable, intolerable.

47-- 格　　　be qualified.

90-- 忙　　　enough work to keep one busy, have one's hand full.

們 〔**Men**〕 *n.* a word signifying plural number.

徇 〔**Hsun**〕 *v.* follow, greed for.

徇 〔**Hsun**〕 *v.* comply with, follow after, accord with.

00-- 庇　　　protect, harbor.

22-- 私　　　selfish, profit oneself.

95-- 情　　　favoritism.

2722_2

修 〔**Hsiu**〕 *v.* repair, adjust, mend, rebuild, adorn, decorate.

01-- 訂　　　revise.

-- 訂版　　revision, revised edition.

-- 訂章程　revision of by-laws.

10-- 正　　　*n.* revision, amendment, *v.* revise, rectify.

-- 正案　　amendment.

15-- 建　　　repair and build.

16-- 理　　　repair, mend, regulate.

-- 理部門　repair department.

-- 理者　　repairer.

-- 理時間　repair time.

-- 理費　　repairing charges.

18-- 改　　　correct, alter, mend, revise.

-- 改合同　amendment of contract, modification of contract.

20-- 辭學　　rhetoric.

28-- 復　　　complete a repair job.

32-- 業證書　certificate of attendance.

33-- 補　　　repair, mend.

-- 治　　　repair and adjust.

38-- 道　　　cultivate according to a religious doctrine.

-- 道院　　monastery, cloister, convent.

40-- 士　　　sister, nun.

47-- 好　　　amity.

52-- 指　　　manicure.

58-- 整　　　repair and maintain.

67-- 路　　　repair roads.

-- 路機　　steamroller, road roller.

80-- 剪　　　trim, cut, clip, prune.

88-- 飾　　　adorn, decorate, embellish,

beautify.

-- 飾品　　cosmetic, decoration, ornament.

2722_7

仍 〔**Jeng**〕 *adv.* as before, still, just so, thus, in like manner.

18-- 敢　　　still dare.

23-- 然　　　still, the same as before.

-- 然如是　it remains the same.

-- 然有效　remain in effect.

40-- 在　　　still in existence.

44-- 舊　　　as of old, as usual, as formerly.

50-- 未完成　remain unfinished, remain unfulfilled.

-- 未執行　remain unperformed.

侈 〔**Chih**〕 *adj.* luxurious, wasteful, profuse, extravagant, prodigal.

00-- 言　　　wild talk, exaggeration.

08-- 論　　　exaggerated talk.

侷 〔**Chu**〕 *adj.* narrow, cramped, confined.

26-- 促　　　cramped, hobbled.

角 〔**Chiao**〕 *n.* horn, corner, angle.

00-- 度　　　angle.

27-- 色　　　actor, role, character.

31-- 逐　　　contest.

40-- 力　　　wrestle, try a fall.

-- 力家　　wrestler.

44-- 落　　　corner, nook.

躬 〔**Kung**〕 *n.* body, *adv.* personally, in person.

06-- 親　　　in person, personally.

21-- 行　　　do personally.

27-- 身　　　bow, bend the body in respect.

78-- 臨　　　be present personally, attend in person.

2723_2

偬 〔**Tsung**〕 *adj.* urgent.

彖 〔**Tuan**〕 *n.* hedgehog.

象 〔**Hsiang**〕 *n.* elephant.

12-- 形文字　hieroglyphic, pictograph.

26-- 鼻　　　elephant's trunk.

28--	徵	symbolize , symbol.
--	徵性	as a token, symbolic.
40--	皮紙	kind of thick and strong paper for drawing.
44--	棋	Chinese chess.
71--	牙	ivory.

像〔Hsiang〕*n.* figure, portrait, statue, idol, image, *adj.* like, similar, resembling.

22--	片	personal photograph.
27--	貌	figure, form, countenance, personal look.
28--	似	*v.* resemble, look like, *adj.* resembling, similar to.
48--	樣	proper in appearance, presentable, decent.
60--	是	look like, seem.

很〔Heng〕*adj.* disobedient, cruel, fierce, harsh, stern, *adv.* very, rather.

27--	多	very much.
33--	心	harsh, hard-hearted.
40--	大訂貨	order of considerable.
--	大改進	much improvement.
--	大的代價	fat price.
47--	好	very good.
95--	快賣掉	sell like hot cakes.

漿〔Chiang〕*n.* juice, congee, thick fluid.

00--	衣服	starch clothes.
34--	汁	juice.
--	洗	wash and starch.
--	洗店	laundry.
37--	泥	mire.
60--	果	berry.
97--	糊	paste.

2723_4
篌〔Shu〕*adv.* suddenly, quickly.
侯〔Hou〕*n.* marquis.

20--	爵	marquis.

候〔Hou〕*v.* wait for, await, expect, inquire after.

07--	訊	await examination.
27--	鳥	migratory bird.
30--	審	await trial.
33--	補	expectant.

--	補名單	waiting list.
--	補人	candidate.
37--	選人	candidate.
50--	車室	waiting room.

2724_0
將〔Chiang〕*n.* general, *v.* will, shall, be going to, intend.

03--	就	make the best of an unsatisfactory situation.
10--	死	on the point of death, about to die, almost dead.
--	要	going to, about to.
12--	到	near at hand, about to come.
24--	帥	marshal.
30--	官	general officer.
32--	近	close to, nearly, hardly.
37--	軍	general, admiral.
40--	士	military officers and soldiers.
--	來	future, day to come.
--	來值	future value.

2724_7
仔〔Tzu〕*v.* undertake, bear, *adj.* careful.

26--	細	careful, attentive.

役〔I〕*n.* servant, battle, *v.* serve, employ.

00--	卒	runners.
25--	使	employ, enslave.
28--	齡	enlisted age.
50--	夫	laborer, servant.

侵〔Chin〕*v.* invade, aggress, entrench, encroach upon.

01--	襲	attack, raid.
20--	吞	*n.* embezzlement. *v.* misappropriate, embezzle, take by illegal means.
--	吞公款	graft, embezzle public funds.
21--	佔	invade, occupy, overrun, encroach.
--	佔罪	offense of misappropriation, embezzlement.
30--	害	aggression, injury.
40--	奪	seize upon by violence.
47--	犯	*n.* offence, aggression, in

vasion, v. invade, offend, aggress.

-- 犯權利　infringement of right.
50-- 掠　invade, harass and loot.
51-- 擾　disturb, trespass.
67-- 略　invasion, aggression.
-- 略主義　jingoism.
-- 略者　aggressor, invader.
-- 略戰　offensive war, aggressive war.
80-- 入　intrude, invade.
85-- 蝕　erosion, encroach.

假〔Jea〕 n. holiday, v. pretend, borrow, adj. false, unreal, feigned, hypocritical.

00-- 充　pretend to be.
-- 意　false-hearted, false intent.
-- 文件、假証件 false papers.
01-- 証件　false certificate.
-- 証據　false witness.
02-- 話　lie, falsehood.
-- 託　excuse, pretext.
07-- 設　postulate, hypothesis.
-- 設成本　hypothetical cost.
08-- 說　hypothesis.
10-- 面具　mask.
-- 正經　hypocritical.
-- 死　play dead, feign death, sham death.
20-- 手　do something by means of others.
21-- 處分　provisional disposition.
22-- 山　artificial hill.
24-- 裝　pretend, feign, disguise.
-- 借　borrow.
25-- 使　if, in case, supposing .
26-- 釋　parole, free on probation.
27-- 名　assumed name, fictitious name.
30-- 寐　fox sleep, dog sleep.
-- 定　assume, suppose, presume, postulate.
-- 定價格　hypothetical price, presumed value.
-- 定成本　assumed cost, hypothetical cost.

33-- 淚　crocodile tears.
34-- 造　forge, counterfeit.
40-- 支票　counterfeit check, forged check.
44-- 花　artificial flower.
46-- 想　imagination, hypothesis, supposition.
-- 想敵　imaginary enemy.
-- 如　supposing, in case, if.
47-- 期　vacation, leave of absence.
52-- 托　pretense, dissimulation.
58-- 扮　disguise, make believe.
60-- 日　holiday, festival.
-- 日工資　holiday pay, vacation pay.
-- 日獎金　holiday premium pay.
-- 冒　counterfeit, false pretense, sham.
61-- 賬　false account.
66-- 單証 (假票據) factitious paper.
71-- 牙　false teeth, denture.
72-- 髮　wig.
80-- 公濟私　jobbery, promote one's private interests under the guise of serving the public.
89-- 鈔票　forged note, query, counterfeit note, forged banknote, the queer, funny money.

殷〔Yen〕 adj. flourishing, abundant, many.

00-- 商　prosperous merchants.
30-- 實　substantial, rich, well-to-do.
44-- 勤　diligent and attentive.
53-- 盛　thriving, flourishing, prosperous, abundant.

2725₂
解〔Chie〕 v. explain, make clear, understand, release, extricate, loosen, untie.

00-- 痛　relieve the pain.
-- 離　dissociation.
-- 衣　disrobe, strip, undress, remove one's clothes.
02-- 剖　dissect, analyze.
-- 剖刀　dissecting knife.
-- 剖室　dissecting room.
-- 剖學　anatomy.

08-- 放	n. emancipation, v. liberate, free, unbind, set free, emancipate.
-- 放區	liberated area.
-- 說	explain, make clear.
09-- 謎	put the ax in the helve.
10-- 憂	relieve worries.
13-- 職	relieve someone of his duties, dismiss from office.
15-- 聘	relieve one of his duties, dismiss, discharge.
20-- 手	wash one's hand, go to W. C., relieve oneself.
26-- 釋	n. explanation, interpretation, solution, v. explain, illustrate, resolve, define, expound, interpret.
-- 和	resolve a dispute, mediate.
27-- 約	close a contract, cancel a contract, terminate an agreement.
-- 危	head off danger.
28-- 紛	resolve a dispute, disentangle.
30-- 雇	n. dismissal, termination of employment, v. discontinue the employment, dismiss, dismiss from office, discharge, discharge from employment, boot, relieve somebody of his post.
-- 雇率	layoff rate.
-- 雇費	dismissal wage, severance pay.
35-- 決	n. solution, v. solve, dispose of, finish off.
-- 決爭議	settle dispute.
-- 凍 (銀行存款)	release (of bank accounts), unfreeze.
36-- 渴	quench thirst, slake.
38-- 送	deliver to.
42-- 析	analysis.
-- 析幾何	analytical geometry.
44-- 禁	lift the bar.
47-- 款	transfer of fund, pay in (into).
48-- 散	n. dissolution, v. dismiss,

	dissolve, disband, disorganize.
-- 散軍隊	disband soldiers.
-- 散國會	dissolve parliament.
-- 救	rescue, extricate.
50-- 囊	open one's purse.
-- 毒	counteract poison, neutralize poison, antidote.
-- 毒劑	antidote.
56-- 扣	unbutton.
60-- 圍	raise a siege.
61-- 題	answer to a problem.
67-- 明	explain.
75-- 體	disintegration, dissolution.
77-- 開	disentangle, untie, unbind, loosen.
78-- 脫	avoid, escape, free, extricate.
-- 除	release, exempt, discharge, remove, relieve.
-- 除條約	cancellation of treaty.
-- 除武裝	unarm, disarm.
-- 除婚約	renounce an engagement.
-- 除警報	clear out, all clear.
-- 除封鎖	raise a blockade, unblock.
-- 除禁運	lift embargo.
-- 除責任	absolve.
-- 除業務	relieve from obligations.
-- 除合同	terminate a contract .
87-- 鈕	unbutton.
88-- 答	key, answer.

2725₇

伊〔**I**〕*pron.* he, she, it.

37-- 朗	Iran.
42-- 斯蘭	Islam.
-- 斯蘭教徒	Moslem.
50-- 拉克	Iraq.

2726₁

詹〔**Chan**〕*v.* reach, manage, *adj.* talkative.

2726₂

貂〔**Tiao**〕*n.* sable.

43-- 裘	sable robe.

2726₄

貉〔**He**〕*n.* badger.

倨 〔**Chu**〕 *adj.* bold, imperious.
28-- 傲　　　haughty, overhearing.
2727_2
倔 〔**Chueh**〕 *adj.* obstinate, stubborn.
13-- 強　　　stubborn.
47-- 起　　　rise suddenly.
2728_1
俱 〔**Chu**〕 *adj.* all, whole, both, *adv.* altogether.
22-- 樂部　　club.
24-- 備　　　everything ready.
40-- 在　　　all present.
80-- 全　　　all are complete.
2729_2
你 〔**Ni**〕 *pron.* you.
26-- 自己　　yourself.
27-- 們　　　you.
-- 們的　　your, yours.
-- 的　　　your, yours.
2729_4
條 〔**Tiao**〕 *n.* branch, twig, clause, article, item, section, law, rule.
00-- 文　　　provision.
16-- 理　　　order, system, sequence.
17-- 子　　　note, chit.
20-- 紋　　　bar, streak.
25-- 件　　　condition, terms.
27-- 約　　　treaty.
47-- 款　　　terms, provision, clause, article, item.
60-- 目　　　schedule.
躲 〔**To**〕 *v.* hide, avoid.
10-- 雨　　　take shelter from the rain.
-- 不了　　unavoidable, inescapable.
25-- 債　　　avoid one's creditors, evade paying debts, run away from one's creditor.
30-- 避　　　hide, avoid, dodge, shun, ward off, escape from.
-- 避法律　evade the law.
44-- 藏　　　conceal one's self, hide.
77-- 開　　　get out of the way, run away from.

-- 閃　　　dodge, ward off.
97-- 懶　　　shirk work.
2730_3
冬 〔**Tung**〕 *n.* winter.
10-- 至　　　winter solstice.
-- 天　　　winter.
20-- 季　　　winter.
-- 季攻勢　winter offense.
-- 季大減價　winter sales.
24-- 裝　　　winter dress.
44-- 菇　　　mushroom.
67-- 眠　　　hibernate.
70-- 防　　　winter curfew.
72-- 瓜　　　pumpkin, wax gourd, white gourd.
88-- 筍　　　winter sprouts of bamboo.
2731_2
鮑 〔**Pao**〕 *n.* pickled fish, dried fish.
27-- 魚　　　abalone.
2732_0
勺 〔**Shao**〕 *n.* spoon, ladle, *adj.* spoonful.
17-- 子　　　ladle, spoon, scoop.
鯽 〔**Chi**〕 *n.* crucian carp.
2732_7
烏 〔**Wu**〕 *n.* crow, raven. *adj.* black, dark.
01-- 龍茶　　oolong tea.
10-- 雲　　　black cloud.
-- 豆　　　black beans.
27-- 龜　　　tortoise.
-- 魚　　　black mullet.
40-- 有　　　nothing, naught.
-- 木　　　ebony.
52-- 托邦　　Utopia.
63-- 烏賊　　cuttlefish.
72-- 髮　　　dark hair.
80-- 合之眾　rabble.
鳥 〔**Niao**〕 *n.* bird.
17-- 蛋　　　bird's egg.
22-- 巢　　　nest, aviary.
60-- 園　　　aviary.
67-- 喙　　　beak.
68-- 瞰　　　bird's eye view.
88-- 鎗　　　shot-gun, fowling piece.

-- 籠	cage, birdcage.
90-- 糞	bird droppings.
91-- 類	fowl, birds.
-- 類學	ornithology.

鴛〔Yuan〕 n. the drake of the mandarin duck.

26-- 侶	spouse.
50-- 鴦	mandarin duck.

2733₁

怨〔Yuan〕 n. ill will, resentment, hatred, malice, wrong, v. hate, dislike, blame, adj. dissatisfied, murmuring.

00-- 言	spiteful words.
47-- 聲	whine, murmur.
80-- 命	blame one's life.
-- 忿	grudge, bitterness, animus.
95-- 情	resentment.
97-- 恨	hate, dislike.

2733₂

忽〔Hu〕 v. disregard, slight, overlook, neglect, forget, adj. sudden, careless, negligent, adv. suddenly, unexpectedly, all at once.

23-- 然	suddenly, on a blow, on a sudden, all at once.
36-- 視	disregard, overlook, neglect, give a cold shoulder.
60-- 見	see suddenly.
67-- 略	v. disregard, neglect, slight, overlook, adj. careless, negligent, forgetful.
77-- 聞	hear suddenly, learn of something unexpectedly.

2733₃

懇〔Ken〕 v. beg, implore, importune, solicit, adv. truly, earnestly, eagerly.

02-- 託	make a sincere request.
05-- 請	beg, plead, solicit, entreat, request earnestly.
06-- 親會	PTA (parent-teacher association).
09-- 談	have a sincere talk.
20-- 辭	decline earnestly.
30-- 准	ask permission.
43-- 求=懇請	

47-- 切	very sincere, earnest, eager, zealous.
60-- 恩	beg a favor.

2733₄

慇〔Yin〕 adj. sad, mournful, sorrowful.

44-- 勤	polite, attentive, courteous, affable, complaisant.

2733₆

魚〔Yu〕 n. fish.

00-- 市	fish market.
10-- 雷	torpedo.
-- 雷艇	torpedo boat.
17-- 子	fry, fish roe.
-- 子醬	caviar.
22-- 片	fillets of fish, slices of fish meat.
24-- 鰭	fins.
25-- 生	raw fish in fine cuts, sashimi.
27-- 網	fishing net.
29-- 鱗	fish scales.
34-- 池	fish pool.
40-- 塘	fish pond.
-- 肉	fish and meat.
47-- 翅	shark's fin, fish's fin.
71-- 肝油	cod-liver oil.
74-- 肚	fish maws.
77-- 叉	fish spear, harpoon.
-- 骨	fish bones.
81-- 缸	fish globe, fishbowl.
87-- 鈎	fish hook.
88-- 竿	fishing rod, fish pole.
91-- 類學	ichthyology.

2733₇

急〔Chi〕 v. hurry, hasten, adj. hasty, hurried, impatient, anxious, earnest, urgent, necessary, fast, quick, rapid, swift.

00-- 病	emergency, sudden illness, acute disease.
-- 辯	retort.
-- 言	hasty words.
08-- 診	emergency case, emergency treatment.
10-- 需	n. crying want, imperious

	need, *v.* need urgently.
-- 需資金	much-needed funds .
-- 需品	spot needs.
-- 電	urgent telegram or cable.
-- 雨	driving rain, shower.
17-- 務	pressing and urgent business.
21-- 行	hasten, hurry on, make a dash, push on, hurry forward.
-- 行軍	forced march, rapid march.
22-- 劇上漲	drastic increase.
-- 劇降低 (大幅度削減) drastic reduction.
-- 變	crisis, emergency, quick turn of event.
-- 彎	sharp turn.
25-- 件	urgent document or dispatch, hot jobs.
26-- 促	hasty, hurried.
28-- 煞車	brake a car abruptly.
30-- 流	torrent, swift currents.
-- 進	make rapid progress, forge ahead vigorously.
-- 進主義	radicalism.
-- 進份子	radical.
35-- 速	quick, fast, swift, urgent.
36-- 迫	urged, forced, impelled, urgent, pressing, in haste, in a hurry.
40-- 走	hurry.
-- 難	emergency.
47-- 切	*adj.* urgent, pressing, eager, *adv.* anxiously.
48-- 救	first-aid.
-- 救箱	first-aid kit.
50-- 事	urgent matter.
66-- 躁	irritable, passionate.
77-- 降	quick dive.
-- 用	urgent use or need.
86-- 智	quick-witted.
90-- 忙=急促	
95-- 性	acute case.

2734₁

鱘 〔Hsun〕 *n.* sturgeon.
2740₀

身 〔Shen〕 *n.* body, trunk.

00-- 亡	die.
-- 高	height, stature.
17-- 子	body, trunk.
-- 孕	pregnancy.
20-- 手	ability, artistic skill.
21-- 價	one's social position or prestige.
22-- 後	after death.
-- 後名	posthumous fame.
28-- 份證	identification card, identity card, ID card.
-- 份證明書	identity certificate.
30-- 家	family background, ancestry.
33-- 心	body and mind.
44-- 材	figure, physical build, physique.
48-- 故	die.
71-- 長	length, height.
75-- 體	body, trunk.
-- 體檢查	physical examination, check up.
77-- 段	physique, figure, postures.
80-- 分	status, state, position.

2740₇

阜 〔Fu〕 *n.* mound.
2741₅

免 〔Mien〕 *v.* get off, evade, escape, avoid, elude, free from.

00-- 疫	immunity.
09-- 談	not necessary to discuss.
10-- 票	free pass, free ticket, free of charge.
-- 不了	unavoidable.
12-- 刑	remission, exempt from punishment.
13-- 職	dismiss.
26-- 得	avoid, save.
27-- 役	exemption from military service.
28-- 稅	duty exemption, duty free, free of duty, tax-free, tax exemption, free of tax, exempt from taxes.

-- 稅商店	duty-free shop.
-- 稅物品	duty-free articles.
-- 稅收益	tax exempt income.
-- 稅品	goods exempt from taxation.
-- 繳	exempt from payment.
35-- 禮	forego formalities.
55-- 費	free of charge, free charge, free of cost, no charge, not charged, without charge.
-- 費商品	gratuitous goods.
-- 費試用	free trial.
-- 費參觀	admission free.
-- 費送貨	delivery free, free delivery.
-- 費樣品	free sample.
-- 費服務	free service, gratis service, gratuitous service.
60-- 罪	pardon, forget an offense, be acquitted, exonerate.
-- 罰	impunity.
78-- 除	*n.* free, immunity, exemption, remission, *v.* excuse, prevent, avoid, release, remit, *adj.* immune.
-- 驗	exempt from examination, forego inspection.

2742₇

芻〔Chu〕*n.* hay, straw, fodder.

鴇〔Pao〕*n.* bustard.

47-- 婦	procuress, brothel keeper.

鄒〔Tsou〕*n.* name of a small ancient state.

鷄〔Chi〕*n.* chicken, fowl, cock.

13-- 蛋	egg.
36-- 湯	chicken soup.
40-- 姦	sodomy.
67-- 眼	corn.
77-- 母	hen.
-- 尾酒	cocktail.
-- 尾酒會	cocktail party.

鶵〔Chu〕*n.* brood.

2743₀

奐〔Huan〕*adj.* bright, elegant, brilliant.

奧〔Ao〕*adj.* mysterious, marvelous, obscure.

33-- 祕	subtle, hidden.
44-- 地利	Austria.
-- 林匹亞運動會	Olympic Games.
49-- 妙	wonderful, marvelous, mysterious.
80-- 義	hidden meaning.

獎〔Chiang〕*n.* prize, reward, *v.* praise, encourage, laud, extol.

00-- 章	medal.
23-- 狀	citation of meritorious service.
26-- 牌	medal.
28-- 懲	award and punishment, rewards and punishments.
-- 懲規定	provisions for award and punishment.
30-- 進	encourage to advance further.
41-- 杯	cup.
60-- 品	reward, prize, trophy.
74-- 勵（獎賞）	*n.* prize, *v.* encourage, encourage and reward, reward, clap on the shoulders.
-- 勵辦法	award method.
-- 勵工資	premium wages, wage incentive, premium wages.
-- 勵制度	incentive system, system of bonus.
-- 勵津貼	incentive pay.
-- 勵金	bounty, premium.
77-- 學金	scholarship, fellowship.
80-- 金=獎勵金	
-- 金制度	incentive plan, incentive system.
90-- 券	lottery , lottery tickets.
-- 賞	awards, rewards, commend and reward.

2744₀

舟〔Chou〕*n.* boat, vessel, junk.

17-- 子	boatman, waterman, ferryman.
55-- 費	boat fare.
71-- 長	captain.

2744₇

般〔Pan〕*n.* class, sort.

艘〔Sao〕*n.* number of boats.

2746₁

船〔Chuan〕*n.* boat, ship, vessel, junk.

00-- 主	captain, owner, shipowner.
-- 廠	dockyard, shipyard.
10-- 面	deck.
-- 票	passage ticket.
11-- 頭	bow.
20-- 舷	broadside.
-- 位	shipping space, freight space, berth.
21-- 上交貨價	F.O.B. (free on board).
25-- 失事	shipwreck, wreck of a ship.
26-- 舶	crafts, vessels, ships.
-- 舶工程	marine engineering.
-- 舶容量	capacity of vessel.
-- 舶噸	vessel ton.
-- 舶吃水	draught (draft).
-- 舶公司	shipping firm.
27-- 身	hull, hulk.
-- 級	ship's class (classification).
-- 租	charter hire.
28-- 艙	cabin.
30-- 客	passengers.
36-- 邊	shipside.
37-- 資	fare.
-- 運	transport by ship.
41-- 板	deck.
47-- 塢	shipyard, dock, shipbuilding yard, building yard.
-- 期	shipping schedule.
-- 桅	mast.
50-- 夫	sailor, waterman, boatman.
55-- 費	freight, fare, passage money.
60-- 員	crew, sailor.
-- 員室	forecastle.
71-- 長	captain, commander, master, sea-captain, shipmaster.
-- 長室	captain's cabin.
77-- 尾	stern.
78-- 隊	fleet, flotilla.
80-- 公司	shipping company.
88-- 篷	coverings of a boat.
-- 籍	register of flag, nationality of ship.

2748₁

疑〔I〕*n.* suspicion, doubt, mistrust, *v.* doubt, suspect, *adj.* doubtful, suspicious.

17-- 忌	suspicious, jealous.
22-- 兇	suspected murderer.
30-- 案	unsettled case, uncertain case.
33-- 心	suspicion, doubt.
-- 心病	skepticism, hypochondria.
47-- 犯	criminal suspect.
43-- 獄	doubtful case.
53-- 惑	suspect, mistrust, doubt about.
61-- 點	doubtful or questionable point.
77-- 問	*n.* question, problem, interrogation, *v.* ask, query.
-- 問詞	interrogative mark, question mark.
-- 問句	interrogation.
-- 問號	question mark.
80-- 義	dubious interpretation.

2750₂

犁〔Li〕*n.* plow, *v.* plow.

2752₀

物〔Wu〕*n.* thing, matter, article, substance, goods.

00-- 主	possessor, owner.
-- 產	production, products, produce.
16-- 理學家	physicist.
-- 理學	physics.
-- 理變化	physical change.
21-- 價	price, value.
-- 價穩定	stability of commodities, prices remain stable, stable prices, price stabilization, price stability.
-- 價管理	price administration.
-- 價管制	price control.
22-- 種	species.
25-- 件	thing, substance, article, goods.
32-- 業稅	property tax.
37-- 資	goods and materials.

44-- 權	real right.
60-- 品	article.
72-- 質	substance, matter.
-- 質文明	material civilization.
75-- 體	body, matter, object.
80-- 美價廉	low prices and fine quality, (something) of high quality and inexpensive, attractive and reasonably priced.
94-- 料	material, substance.

2752₇
邦 〔Pang〕 *n.* state, country, nation.
| 00-- 交 | diplomatic, relations. |
| 60-- 國 | states, nations. |

鵝 〔O〕 *n.* goose.

2760₀
名 〔Ming〕 *n.* name, title, fame, honor, reputation, *v.* name, designate, *adj.* famous, well-known, noted, renowned.
00-- 產	famous product, staple.
07-- 望	fame, reputation.
-- 詞	term, noun.
20-- 垂不朽	name handed down forever.
22-- 稱	name, term, style.
-- 片	visiting card, calling card.
-- 利	fame and profit, wealth and fame.
26-- 牌	famous-brand, name brand, name plate, popular brand.
27-- 將	illustrious general.
30-- 流	man of fashion.
-- 字	name, noun.
-- 家	great master, great author
42-- 媛	lady.
47-- 聲	reputation, honor.
50-- 貴	valuable.
61-- 號	denomination, epithet.
66-- 單	list.
77-- 冊	roll, list of name.
-- 譽	honor, credit, fame, renown, reputation, feather in one's cap.
-- 譽職	honorary.
-- 譽教授	emeritus professor, professor emeritus.
-- 譽博士	honorary doctor.
-- 譽學位	honorary degree.
-- 譽會員	honorary member.
79-- 勝	celebrated place, famous place of scenery.
80-- 人	famous man, man of mark, people of distinction, great man.
-- 人錄	roll of fame.
-- 分	obligation.
-- 義	nominal.

2760₁
醬 〔Chiang〕 *n.* soy, sauce, condiment.
| 35-- 油 | soy sauce. soy. |

響 〔Hsiang〕 *n.* noise, echo. *adj.* noisy. *v.* incline to, guide, approach, *prep.* toward, near.
00-- 應	echo, respond.
20-- 往	aspire, long for, look forward to.
38-- 導	guide, courier.

2760₃
魯 〔Lu〕 *adj.* stupid, vulgar, blunt, common, simple.
| 44-- 莽 | vulgar, hand over head. |
| 85-- 鈍 | dull, stupid, gross-headed, weak-headed. |

2760₄
各 〔Ko〕 *adj.* each, every, all, separate, various.
21-- 處	everywhere.
22-- 種	every sort, different kinds.
-- 種津貼	miscellaneous allowances.
-- 種款式	various styles.
-- 種尺寸	assorted sizes.
23-- 方代表	representatives from various quarters.
24-- 種貨物	goods of all descriptions.
26-- 自	by oneself.
-- 自付帳	go dutch.
-- 個擊破	divide and conquer, defeat in detail.
27-- 級政府	all levels of governments.

-- 色　　　　　of all kinds, of every de-scription.
44-- 地　　　　everywhere.
50-- 盡所能　　from each according to his ability, to each according to his work.
60-- 界（行各業）all walks of life.
-- 國　　　　　every country, every quarter.
80-- 人　　　　every one.
91-- 類　　　　each kind.

督 〔Tu〕 v. direct, rule, lead, command.
00-- 率　　　　lead, take the direction.
-- 辦　　　　　n. director-general, v. over-see, supervise.
22-- 催　　　　urge on.
30-- 察　　　　n. inspector, supervisor, v. superintend, supervise, overlook.
50-- 責　　　　reprove.

2762_0
句 〔Chu〕 n. sentence, clause, phrase.
04-- 讀　　　　sentence.
34-- 法　　　　syntax.
61-- 點　　　　punctuation.

旬 〔Hsun〕 n. a period of ten days.
60-- 日　　　　ten days.

甸 〔Tien〕 n. the imperial domain, v. rule, hunt.

的 〔Ti〕 n. the bull's-eye of a target, adj. bright, clear, distinct, evident, actual, real, true, adv. clearly, obviously, evidently.
13-- 確　　　　real, actual.
30-- 準　　　　accurate, exact.
90-- 當　　　　properly, rightly.

翻 〔Fan〕 v. turn over, upset, revise, fly to and fro, flutter about.
02-- 新改造　　retrofit.
06-- 譯　　　　translate, interpret.
-- 譯社　　　　translation bureau.
-- 譯員　　　　translator, interpreter.
27-- 身　　　　turn turtle.
28-- 修　　　　facelift, rebuild.
-- 船　　　　　overturning of vessel, cap-

size.
30-- 案　　　　reopen a closed case.
55-- 轉　　　　upturn, turned round, wrong side up.
-- 轉權　　　　flip flop option.
77-- 印　　　　reproduce, reprint.
78-- 臉　　　　get angry.

匐 〔Fu〕 v. creep.
2762_7
鵠 〔Hu〕 n. swan. 〔Ku〕 bull's eye.
2771_2
包 〔Pao〕 n. bundle, parcel, bale, wrapper, v. wrap up, put up, envelop, contain, hold, embrace, include, undertake, contract, insure.
00-- 庇　　　　harbor, shelter, shield.
-- 裹　　　　　n. parcel, bundle, v. wrap up.
-- 裹郵費　　　parcel postage.
-- 裹運費率　　parcel rates.
-- 裹車　　　　package car.
-- 裹袋　　　　parcel bag.
-- 廂　　　　　box.
-- 辦　　　　　undertake, undertake completely, assume full responsibility.
-- 辦酒席　　　contract for feast.
10-- 工　　　　contract labor, contract for job, contract for work, job work, by contract.
-- 工制　　　　labor contract system, system of fixed responsibility for a specified job.
-- 票　　　　　guaranty, certificate of guarantee.
11-- 頭　　　　fillet, headband.
15-- 建　　　　be built by contract.
21-- 價　　　　contract price.
22-- 出去　　　put out to contract.
24-- 裝　　　　n. packing, package, v. pack.
-- 裝計劃　　　packing design.
-- 裝工人　　　wrapper.
-- 裝不良　　　improper packing, insufficient packing.
-- 裝裝潢　　　package and presentation, packing and presentation.

-- 裝物	packing article.	
-- 裝業	packing service.	
-- 裝機	packing machine, sack filler.	
-- 裝成本	packing cost.	
-- 裝費	packing expense, packing charge, wrapping expense.	
-- 裝清單	packing list.	
-- 裝用品	packing supplies.	
-- 裝箱	packing box.	
27-- 租	charter, charter hire.	
-- 租費	charter fee.	
-- 租合同	charter contract.	
-- 修	guarantee the repair of something.	
-- 船	chartered vessel.	
30-- 准	guarantee.	
33-- 治	guarantee a cure.	
-- 袱	wrapper, burden, liability.	
-- 心菜	cabbage.	
36-- 還包退	guarantee to exchange if returned or unsuitable, on approval.	
37-- 運	transportation.	
40-- 皮	prepuce, tare, wrapper, foreskin.	
42-- 紮	bundle.	
-- 機	chartered airplane, air charter, charter plane.	
44-- 封	enclosure.	
50-- 車	chartered bus.	
52-- 括	include, involve, embrace, cover.	
57-- 換	guarantee replacement.	
58-- 攬	monopolize, take on everything.	
60-- 圍	n. encirclement, embrace, siege, v. enclose, surround, invest, environ.	
-- 賠	guarantee to compensate.	
64-- 賭	protect illegal gambling casinos.	
68-- 賺	guarantee profits, profits assured.	
77-- 用	guarantee a thing to be suitable.	

80-- 含	contain, include, involve, comprise, take in.	
81-- 飯	board, eat meals on a monthly payment basis, contract to supply meal at a fixed price.	
88-- 管	guarantee, assure.	
89-- 銷	assume the responsibility for the sale, exclusive sales, have exclusive selling rights, under write.	
-- 銷人	sale agent.	

2771_4

齷 〔Wo〕 adj. petty, narrow-minded.
26-- 齪 dirty, nasty.

2771_7

色 〔Se〕 n. color, countenance, looks, beauty.
00-- 盲	color blindness.
-- 衰	lose color.
07-- 調	tone, shade of color.
22-- 彩	color, tint, hue, tint.
26-- 鬼	satyr, lecher.
39-- 迷	given up to lust.
40-- 喜	showing pleasure, looking pleased.
44-- 藝	beauty and accomplishments.
50-- 素	pigment.
-- 素細胞	chromatophore.
77-- 覺	sensation of color.
87-- 慾	lust, sexual desire, venery.
95-- 情	sexual passion, lust, amorousness.
-- 情狂	sexual insanity.

2772_0

勾 〔Kou〕 n. hook, v. make of, cancel, reject.
12-- 引	entice, seduce, allure.
16-- 魂	bewitch, fascinate.
17-- 子	hook.
37-- 通	in league with.
39-- 消	liquidate, strike out, cancel.
50-- 串	conspire with, gang up.
54-- 搭	have illegitimate relations, conspire with, seduce, en-

tice.

89-- 銷　　　　cancel, write off, liquidate, strike off.

匈〔Hsiung〕 n. breast, bosom.
47-- 奴　　　　The Huns.

幻〔Huan〕 adj. unreal, magic.
21-- 術　　　　magic.
27-- 象　　　　illusion, phantasm.
40-- 境　　　　airy.
44-- 夢　　　　daydream, fantasy.
46-- 想　　　　n. imagination, fancy, airy, v. fancy, dream, image.
-- 想曲　　　　fantasy.
60-- 景　　　　mirage.
62-- 影　　　　illusion, phantasm.
77-- 覺　　　　hallucination, illusion.
92-- 燈　　　　magic lantern.
-- 燈廣告　　　slide advertising.
-- 燈電影　　　slide-film.
-- 燈片　　　　slide.
-- 燈機　　　　slide projector.
2772₇

島〔Tao〕 n. island, isle.
27-- 嶼　　　　islet, island.
60-- 國　　　　island nation.
77-- 民　　　　islander.

鄉〔Hsiang〕 v. village, country.
00-- 音　　　　native accent, local accent.
06-- 親　　　　fellow countryman.
10-- 下　　　　countryside, rural area.
-- 下人　　　　villagers, country bumpkins.
44-- 村　　　　village.
-- 村音樂　　　country music.
65-- 味　　　　food from one's native place.
67-- 野　　　　country.
71-- 長　　　　chief of a village.
77-- 間　　　　in the country, in the rural area.
80-- 人　　　　villager, countryman, rustic.
-- 公所　　　　public office in charge of the administration of a group of villages.
84-- 鎮　　　　small town, rural village.

鷂〔Yao〕 n. kite, sparrow hawk.
17-- 子　　　　kite.
2773₂

餐〔Tsan〕 n. meal, food.
00-- 廳　　　　restaurant, dining hall, mess hall.
21-- 桌　　　　board, dining table.
40-- 巾　　　　napkin.
50-- 車　　　　buffet car.
55-- 費　　　　boarding expense, food bill.
77-- 具　　　　dinner set, dinner-service.
83-- 館　　　　restaurant, eating house.
87-- 飲業　　　restaurant business.
90-- 券　　　　meal coupon, meal ticket.

饗〔Hsiang〕 v. give a feast, enjoy.
2777₂

崛〔Chueh〕 v. rise abruptly.
24-- 崎　　　　steep.
47-- 起　　　　upstart, rise abruptly.
2778₁

嶼〔Yu〕 n. island, islet.
2780₀

久〔Chiu〕 adj. long, lasting, permanent.
04-- 計　　　　long-range plan.
17-- 已　　　　long, since, for a long time.
22-- 後　　　　afterwards.
27-- 候　　　　wait for a long time.
34-- 遠　　　　long ago, in the distant past.
62-- 別　　　　long separated.
71-- 長　　　　long, of long standing.
77-- 留　　　　stay for a long time.
2780₂

欠〔Chien〕 v. owe, be short of, lack, be wanting in, adj. deficient, insufficient, wanting, lacking.
00-- 交稅款　　back duty.
10-- 票　　　　promissory note, debit-note.
20-- 妥　　　　not very proper, not satisfactory.
24-- 佳　　　　not satisfactory.
-- 付工資　　　back pay, back salary.
25-- 債　　　　n. debt, obligation, liability,

	v. owe.
-- 債人	debtor.
28-- 繳	have not paid.
-- 稅	tax arrears.
30-- 戶	debtor.
41-- 帳	outstanding accounts.
44-- 薪	back pay.
47-- 款	debts, liabilities, arrears, balance due, debt.
51-- 據	I.O.U. note.
66-- 單=欠票	
83-- 錢	owe money.
85-- 缺	wanting, lacking, deficient.

2780₉

灸〔Jeou〕*v.* cauterize.

33-- 治	treat by moxa cautery.
52-- 刺	cautery and acupuncture.

炙〔Chih〕*v.* roast flesh, toast, cauterize.

48-- 乾	dry by applying heat.
99-- 炒	broil.

2790₁

祭〔Chi〕*n.* sacrifice, offering, *v.* sacrifice, worship.

00-- 文	prayer, sacrificial writing.
17-- 司	priest.
23-- 獻	offer sacrifice.
27-- 物	sacrifices.
37-- 祖	perform rites in honor of ancestors.
40-- 壇	altar.
55-- 典	services or ceremonies of offering sacrifice.
60-- 品	sacrifice, offering.
-- 日	high day.

禦〔Yu〕*v.* resist, oppose, withstand, prevent, stop, hinder.

08-- 敵	resist enemy, withstand enemy.
21-- 止	prevent.
28-- 侮	resist insult.
30-- 寒	keep out of cold, protect from cold.
87-- 飢	appease hunger.

2790₄

粲〔Tsan〕*adj.* bright, clear.

11-- 麗	elegant, luxurious.

槳〔Chiang〕*n.* oar, paddle.

20-- 手	oarsman.

梟〔Hsiao〕*n.* owl, *adj.* brave, heroic, strong, wicked.

74-- 騎	brave horseman.

2791₀

租〔Tsu〕*n.* rent, tax, duty, excise, *v.* rent, lease.

20-- 售	rent or sale.
21-- 價	rent.
22-- 出	let, rent.
-- 賃	rent, let, lease, tenancy.
-- 賃契約	lease contract.
24-- 借	lease, rent, hire.
-- 借法案	Lease-Lend Act.
-- 借協定	Lease-Lend Agreement.
27-- 約	lease, lease agreement, lease bond.
28-- 稅	tax, excise, tribute.
30-- 戶	lease, tenant, lessee.
44-- 地法	tenure.
47-- 期	lease term.
55-- 費	royalties, rent charge, rental payment, rental.
57-- 契	lease.
60-- 界	concession, settlement, foreign settlement.
77-- 屋人	tenant.
-- 用	rent for use, rent from others.
80-- 金	rent, rental, charter money, hire charge, lease rent, rental charges.

組〔Tsu〕*n.* girdle, silk band, *v.* organize.

02-- 訓	organize and train.
23-- 織	*n.* organization, texture, system, *v.* organize, construct, arrange.
-- 織化	systematize.
-- 織法	organic law, organization.
-- 織學	histology.
25-- 件	components, package.

53-- 成		*n.* composition, *v.* compose, constitute, form.
71-- 長		department chief.
77-- 閣		form a cabinet.
80-- 合		corporation, partnership, combination.

2791₅

紐 〔**Niu**〕 *n.* cord, knot, ribbon, button.

24-- 結	fasten.
27-- 約	New York.
44-- 芬蘭	Newfoundland.

2791₆

統 〔**Wen**〕 *n.* mourning clothes.

77-- 服	mourning apparel.

2791₇

紀 〔**Chi**〕 *n.* order, rule, age, century, record, *v.* arrange, record, write down.

10-- 元	epoch, era.
-- 元後	A.D. (Anno Domini), C.E. (Common Era).
-- 元前	B.C. (Before Christ), B.C.E.(Before Common Era).
-- 要	summary, recording of important facts.
14-- 功	record merit.
-- 功坊	triumphal arch.
25-- 律	discipline, morale.
-- 律嚴整	be under perfect discipline.
27-- 綱	rule and regulation.
30-- 實	record the facts.
33-- 述	objective reporting , recording of facts.
43-- 載	record, write down.
50-- 事	memorandum.
80-- 念	*n.* commemoration, *v.* remember, commemorate.
-- 念章	commemoration medal.
-- 念碑	monument, memorial.
-- 念物	token, monument.
-- 念郵票	commemorative stamp.
-- 念郵戳	commemoration postmark.
-- 念週	weekly assembly.
-- 念日	memorial day, celebrated day, high-day.

-- 念會	commemoration, memorial service, celebration.
-- 念館	memorial hall, museum.
-- 念幣	commemorative coin.
87-- 錄	record, minutes.
-- 錄片	documentary film.
-- 錄者	recorder.
-- 錄簿	register.

絕 〔**Chueh**〕 *v.* exterminate, renounce. *adj.* cut off, interrupted, *adv.* very, most, decidedly.

00-- 交	breach, cut off, fall out, break off intercourse.
-- 症	incurable disease.
07-- 望	hopeless, desperate, despairing, in despair.
10-- 不	never.
11-- 頂	*n.* summit, *adj.* extremely, very.
21-- 版	out of print.
22-- 崖	cliff, precipice.
-- 種	commit genocide, exterminate, become extinct, die out.
-- 後	heirless, without posterity.
23-- 代	matchless.
27-- 緣體	insulator.
-- 色	stunning beauty.
34-- 對	absolute.
-- 對論	absolutism.
-- 對價值	absolute value.
-- 對溫度	absolute temperature.
-- 對權	absolute right.
-- 對勝利	decisive victory.
40-- 才	incomparable talent.
44-- 世佳人	goddess.
46-- 好	extremely good.
49-- 妙	extremely wonderful.
54-- 技	feat, stunt.
60-- 品	exquisite articles, goods of the highest quality or value.
67-- 跡	vanish, cease.
-- 嗣=絕後	
-- 路	dead end, impasse.
80-- 命	*n.* death, *v.* die, breathe one's last.

-- 命書	last writing.	
-- 無	nothing, never, absolutely negative.	
-- 食	stop eating, fast.	
96-- 糧	run out of food.	

繩〔Sheng〕n. cord, string, strand, rope, twine, v. correct, rectify, continue.

00-- 床	hammock, rope bed.
17-- 子	rope, string, cord.
40-- 索	rope, riggings.
42-- 橋	suspension bridge.
48-- 梯	rope ladder.

2792₀

約〔Yueh〕n. compact, treaty, contract, agreement, v. bond, cord up, restrict, restrain, be bound, adj. brief, condensed, straitened, adv. nearly, about.

00-- 章	treaty.
05-- 請	invite.
30-- 定	fix, engage by agreement, make an agreement, make an appointment.
-- 定地點	appointed place.
-- 定期限	stipulated duration.
-- 定時間	appointed time.
34-- 法	provisional constitution.
47-- 款	articles of agreement.
50-- 束	restrain, restrict, hold, suppress, limit, bond.
67-- 明	with the understanding.
-- 略	n. outline, adj. brief, condensed.
77-- 同	make an appointment, agree to do something together.
80-- 會	engagement, appointment.
-- 會地點	place to meet.

紉〔Jen〕v. thread, sew, stitch.

綱〔Kang〕n. law, bond, tie, subject, general principle, v. regulate, control.

10-- 要	element, outline.
27-- 紀	principle, discipline, law, order.
81-- 領	general idea, summary.

網〔Wang〕n. web, net, network.

13-- 球	tennis.
-- 球場	tennis court.
-- 球拍	tennis racket.
17-- 子	net.
27-- 魚	catch fish.
-- 絡	network.
-- 結構	network configuration.
-- 絡軟件	network software.
32-- 衫	net jacket.
60-- 羅	net, entrap.
67-- 路	network.
-- 眼	meshes of a net.

繃〔Peng〕v. tie, fasten.

44-- 帶	bandage.

綢〔Chou〕n. pongee, thin silk.

00-- 衣	silk garments.
27-- 緞	silk and satin

稠〔Chou〕adj. close, dense, crowded, thick.

30-- 密	thick, crowded, dense.

2792₂

紓〔Shu〕v. relax, free from.

22-- 緩	little by little.

繆〔Miu〕v. twist, strangle, adj. wrong, misleading.

08-- 論	absurd language.

2792₇

移〔I〕v. remove, shift, emigrate, transmit, change, displace.

00-- 交	transfer, hand over, turn over.
07-- 調	transposition.
10-- 靈	move a corpse to a funeral parlor.
14-- 殖	naturalize.
20-- 住	immigrate.
-- 往	remove to.
24-- 動	remove, move, shift.
32-- 近	move nearer.
40-- 去	move away.
44-- 植	transplant.
55-- 轉	shift, transfer.
60-- 置	move, displace.

77-- 居　　immigrate.
-- 民　　*n.* immigration, immigrant, *v.* immigrate, emigrate.
-- 民勞工　immigrant labor.
-- 民政策　policy of immigration.
-- 民法　immigration laws.
-- 民區　settlement, colony.
-- 民問題　colonial problems.
-- 民局　immigration office.
-- 民船　emigrant ship.
-- 開　move aside.

綁〔**Pang**〕*v.* tie, bond, take up.
10-- 票　kidnap for ransom, kidnapping.
47-- 起來　tie up.
71-- 匪　kidnaper.
77-- 腿　leggings.
-- 緊　bind tight.

綢〔**Chou**〕*n.* crape, crepe, fine linen, *v.* shrink, contract, *adj.* wrinkled, shrunk.
00-- 痕　pucker.
20-- 紋　crape, rumple.
27-- 綢　crepe silk, crape silk.
29-- 紗　crape, crepe.
40-- 布　crepe, crape.
77-- 眉　bend the brow, frown.
78-- 臉　drawn face.

2793₂
緣〔**Yuan**〕*n.* side, margin, edge.
34-- 法　follow the old law.
36-- 邊　hem, margin, edge, border.
47-- 起　origins, preface, forward.
48-- 故　cause, reason.
50-- 由　cause, reason.
60-- 因　reason, the why and wherefore.
80-- 分　relationship fate.

綠〔**Lu**〕*n.* green.
10-- 豆　green beans, green bean sprouts.
-- 豆糕　small cakes made with green- bean flour.
30-- 寶石　emerald.
44-- 林　greenwood, the adventur-

ers' stronghold.
92-- 燈　green light.

2793₃
終〔**Chung**〕*n.* end, *v.* last, die, *adj.* whole, all, entire, *adv.* finally, at last, at length.
00-- 竟　finally.
-- 夜　through the night.
01-- 站　terminal stop.
02-- 端　terminal.
08-- 於　in the end, finally, at last.
10-- 天　forever.
21-- 止　close, stop, cease, come to an end.
-- 止協議　terminate an agreement.
-- 止日期　expiry date.
-- 止合同　terminate a contract.
-- 止營業　wind up operation.
24-- 結　conclude, be at an end.
25-- 生　whole life.
-- 生年金　life annuity.
27-- 身　for life, lifelong, throughout one's life.
-- 身職　lifetime job.
-- 身大事　great event affecting whole life (marriage).
-- 身人壽保險　whole life insurance.
-- 久　after all, in the end, in the long run.
-- 歸　conclusion, finally, after all.
44-- 老　until death, through one's life.
46-- 場　end of a show.
60-- 日　all day long, as the day is long.
61-- 點　end, terminus, terminal.
-- 點站　terminal, terminal station.
77-- 局　conclusion, end, result, outcome.
80-- 年　through the whole year, all the year round.

2793₄
縫〔**Feng**〕*v.* patch, sew, stitch.
00-- 衣　sew clothes.
10-- 工　tailor, sewing worker, seamstress.

27-- 紉　　　　stitch.
-- 紉機　　　　sewing machine.
-- 紉婦　　　　needlewoman.
33-- 補　　　　mend and patch.
80-- 合　　　　join by sewing (medicine).
-- 合線　　　　suture.

2794_0

叔〔Shu〕 n. uncle.
28-- 伯　　　　paternal uncle.
41-- 姪　　　　uncles and nephews.
77-- 母　　　　wife of father's younger brother.
80-- 父　　　　father's younger brother.
-- 公　　　　granduncle.

2794_7

級〔Chi〕 n. class, grade, rank, step.
22-- 任　　　　class tutor.
-- 任導師　　　homeroom teacher.
58-- 數　　　　progression, series.
71-- 長　　　　monitor, class leader, prefect.
80-- 會　　　　class association.
-- 差稅率　　　graded tariff.

綴〔Chui〕 v. stop, sew together.
30-- 字　　　　spell.
-- 字法　　　　spelling.

緞〔Duan〕 n. satin.

2796_4

絡〔Lo〕 n. vein, blood vessel, v. bind, tie up, join, embrace.

2810_0

以〔I〕 v. use, do, consider, regard as, prep. by, with, by means of, in order to, so as to, because of, on account of, conj. because, that.
04-- 計取勝　　outwit.
10-- 下　　　　below.
-- 至　　　　up to.
17-- 及　　　　and, including, as well as.
20-- 往　　　　in the past, formerly.
21-- 上　　　　above.
-- 便　　　　for the convenience of , in order to.
-- 此　　　　thus, in order to.
22-- 後　　　　later, after, hence, after-

ward.
23-- 外　　　　besides, beyond, other than.
24-- 備　　　　be ready for.
27-- 身作則　　set an example.
-- 免　　　　in order to avoid.
34-- 爲　　　　regard as, take to be.
40-- 內　　　　within.
-- 太　　　　ether.
-- 來　　　　since.
80-- 前　　　　before, formerly.

2820_0

似〔Ssu〕 v. seem, resemble, adj. like, similar, resembling, seeming.
11-- 非　　　　apparently not.
20-- 乎　　　　seeming, appearing.
40-- 有　　　　probably.
60-- 是　　　　plausibly.
-- 是而非　　　seemingly correct but really incorrect, paradoxical.

2821_1

作〔Tso〕 n. operation, work, workmanship, v. make, do, act, become, write ,compose.
00-- 主　　　　take the responsibility, rule the roast.
-- 痛　　　　be painful.
-- 廢　　　　cancel, recall, nullify.
-- 廢支票　　　voided check.
-- 文　　　　n. composition, v. compose, write an essay.
02-- 證　　　　bear witness, give evidence, testify, witness.
04-- 詩　　　　compose verse, write poem.
-- 計劃　　　　planning making, plan-making.
10-- 工　　　　work.
-- 惡　　　　do violence, do harm.
-- 弄　　　　tease, make a fool of.
20-- 秀　　　　appear in a show.
22-- 出評定　　pass a judgement on.
-- 樂　　　　make merry, play music.
-- 亂　　　　rebel.
26-- 保　　　　guarantee, vouch for, by somebody's guarantor.
27-- 假　　　　pretend, cheat, falsify.
-- 物　　　　crops, literary composi-

tions.
29-- 伴　　keep company.
30-- 家　　author, writer.
-- 完　　finish , get through.
32-- 業　　student's homework, job of a person.
34-- 爲　　doings, acts.
-- 法　　way of doing things, course of action.
44-- 者　　writer, author.
50-- 事　　work.
53-- 成　　complete, finish, accomplish.
55-- 曲　　compose.
-- 曲家　　composer.
60-- 圖　　plot.
-- 品　　composition, work.
63-- 戰　　fight, war.
70-- 陪　　accompany, escort.
71-- 反　　rebel, rise up in revolt.
73-- 成交易　　conclude the deal, close business.
-- 成判決　　enter a judgement.
77-- 用　　function, operation.
-- 風　　style, one's way of doing things.
97-- 怪　　v. make trouble, adj. mischievous.
98-- 弊　　cheat.

2822₇
偷〔**Tou**〕v. steal, pilfer, adv. secretly.
01-- 襲　　attack by surprise.
10-- 工　　scamper work.
-- 工減料　　use inferior materials and turn out substandard products, jerry-build, scamp work.
11-- 巧　　finesse, take a shortcut.
14-- 聽　　overhear, eavesdrop.
20-- 看　　peep at, steal a glance, cast a sheep's eye.
28-- 稅　　smuggle, tax evasion, evade tax.
-- 稅人　　tax dodger.
30-- 空　　snatch a moment, take time off.

-- 竊　　steal, thieve.
-- 渡　　steal into another country, stealing a crossing.
-- 渡者　　stowaway.
37-- 運　　smuggle.
-- 盜　　steal, pilfer.
-- 盜保險　　burglary insurance.
50-- 東西　　steal things.
95-- 情　　make love, carry on a clandestine love affair.
97-- 懶　　be lazy, loaf on a job.

份〔**Fen**〕n. part, portion, share.
31-- 額　　quota, share, portion, lot.

倫〔**Lun**〕n. relationship, kinship, affinity.
08-- 敦　　London.
16-- 理　　moral principles, ethics.
-- 理學　　ethics.
-- 理學家　　moralist.
37-- 次　　series.
90-- 常　　human relationship.

傷〔**Shang**〕n. wound, injury, harm, v. injure, hurt, wound, harm, grieve, distress, mourn.
00-- 痕　　bruise, scar of a wound.
-- 疤　　scar.
-- 痛　　mourn.
-- 亡　　die of wound.
13-- 殘　　wounded and disabled.
27-- 身　　be injurious to health.
30-- 寒病　　typhoid.
-- 害　　injure, harm, hurt.
33-- 心　　sorrow, broken heart.
35-- 神　　nerve-racking, overtax one's nerve.
44-- 勢　　condition of a wound.
53-- 感情　　hurt the feeling.
56-- 損　　damage.
60-- 口　　stab, wound.
64-- 財　　lose money, waste money.
72-- 兵　　wounded soldier.
-- 腦筋　　beat one's brain, have a nut to crack.
77-- 風　　catch cold.
-- 風化　　breach of morality.

80-- 人　　　　hurt people, harmful to health.

觴〔Shang〕*n.* cup, goblet.

2823₇

伶〔Ling〕*n.* actor, musician, *adj.* clever, skillful, lonely, sole.

11-- 巧　　　　skillful.
21-- 仃　　　　lonely.
22-- 利　　　　clever, smart.
40-- 女　　　　actress.
80-- 人　　　　actor.

2824₀

攸〔Yu〕*v.* start suddenly, find a home.

仵〔Wu〕*n.* pair, equal in rank.

28-- 作　　　　coroner.

傚〔Hsiao〕*v.* imitate, follow, pattern after.

倣〔Fang〕*v.* imitate, model, copy after, take after.

28-- 傚　　　　imitate, model after, tread upon one's heel, tread in the steps of.
34-- 造　　　　pattern, make according to.
40-- 本　　　　copy book.
67-- 照　　　　according to.

做〔Tso〕*v.* do, act, perform.

00-- 主　　　　take charge of, decide.
　-- 文章　　　write an essay.
04-- 謀　　　　go between.
10-- 工　　　　work.
　-- 弄　　　　make fun of, play jokes upon.
20-- 手腳　　　tamper something with the intention to cheat.
　-- 愛　　　　make love.
25-- 生日　　　give a birthday party.
27-- 假　　　　cheat.
30-- 官　　　　become an official, join government service.
　-- 客　　　　be a guest.
32-- 活　　　　earn a living.
35-- 禮拜　　　go to church.
47-- 好事　　　do a good deed, help the needy.

　-- 聲　　　　make a sound.
50-- 事　　　　handle affairs, act.
53-- 成　　　　complete, finish, accomplish.
80-- 人　　　　act as a man.
　-- 人情　　　do something as a favor, do someone a favor.

傲〔Ao〕*n.* pride, *adj.* proud, arrogant, overbearing.

36-- 視　　　　turn one's nose at.
77-- 骨　　　　self-esteem, lofty character.
80-- 氣　　　　pride, haughtiness.
95-- 性　　　　proud temperament.
96-- 慢　　　　arrogant, impudent.

微〔Wei〕*adj.* small, slight, minute, mean, trifle, petty.

00-- 意　　　　token of gratitude.
10-- 雨　　　　light rain, drizzle.
　-- 電腦　　　microcomputer.
17-- 弱　　　　feeble.
22-- 利　　　　narrow margin of profit, meager profit.
25-- 生物　　　microbe.
　-- 生蟲　　　bacteria, germs.
　-- 積分　　　calculus.
　-- 積分學　　differential and integral calculus.
26-- 細　　　　trifle, very small.
27-- 血管　　　capillaries.
28-- 傷　　　　slightly injured.
34-- 波　　　　microwaves.
　-- 波爐　　　microwave oven.
44-- 薄　　　　low, mean, thin, little, trifling.
　-- 茫　　　　obscure, unclear, uncertain.
49-- 妙　　　　subtle, delicate, occult.
60-- 量　　　　trace, micro.
62-- 睡　　　　slumber.
77-- 風　　　　slight breeze.
80-- 恙　　　　slight indisposition.
88-- 管　　　　capillary.
　-- 笑　　　　smile.
90-- 小　　　　very small, minute.
　-- 光　　　　gleam.

徽〔Hui〕*n.* flag, pennant.

00-- 章　　　　badge, ensign, medal, in-

signia, mark, symbol.
80-- 美　　　　excellent.

徹〔Che〕 v. remove, penetrate, prep. through.
00-- 底　　　　thorough.
40-- 去　　　　remove.

徵〔Cheng〕 v. summon, call, collect, levy.
00-- 文　　　　collect writings publicly.
07-- 調　　　　conscript, call out.
-- 詢　　　　solicit opinions.
15-- 聘　　　　solicit a competent person for a vacancy.
20-- 集　　　　collect , levy.
27-- 象　　　　v. indicate, n. indication.
28-- 收　　　　collect, take on.
-- 收官　　　collector.
-- 稅　　　　levy tax.
43-- 求　　　　ask, seek, want, canvass.
-- 求會員　　recruit members.
44-- 募　　　　recruit, enlist.
72-- 兵　　　　conscript, recruit.
-- 兵制　　　conscription system.
77-- 用　　　　requisition, conscript, take over for use.

傲〔Chiao〕 adv. luckily, happily.
徼〔Yao〕 n. boundary, frontier, v. take a turn, beg, demand.
24-- 倖　　　　luckily, by chance.
49-- 妙　　　　mysterious, occult.

儌〔Ching〕 v. warn, caution.
2824₁
併〔Ping〕 v. unite, annex, concur, absorb.
20-- 吞　　　　absorb.
2824₇
復〔Fu〕 v. return, recover, restore, report, reply, answer, adv. again, repeatedly, over and over.
00-- 交　　　　reestablish diplomatic relations, resume friendship.
02-- 新　　　　make new.
04-- 課　　　　resume classes.
08-- 診　　　　repeat visiting a doctor.
10-- 元　　　　n. recovery, restoration, v.

refresh, take a fresh lease of life.
-- 工　　　　go back to work, start operations again.
-- 電　　　　cable back, cable a reply.
12-- 發　　　　relapse.
-- 刊　　　　resume publication.
13-- 職　　　　rehabilitation.
16-- 現　　　　reappear.
17-- 習　　　　review lessons.
20-- 位　　　　reinstate.
22-- 任　　　　return to a former office.
-- 製　　　　reproduce, make a copy of.
-- 製品　　　replica, reproduction.
-- 出口　　　re-export.
24-- 仇　　　　take revenge, wreak vengeance, avenge.
25-- 生　　　　become alive again.
-- 健　　　　rehabilitation.
-- 健中心　　rehabilitation center.
26-- 得　　　　regain.
28-- 稅　　　　compound duty, double imposition.
30-- 審　　　　reexamine or retrial.
31-- 返　　　　return.
32-- 活　　　　n. resurrection, v. revive, come to life again, rise from the dead.
-- 活節　　　Easter.
-- 業　　　　return or resume to business.
40-- 古　　　　revive old customs.
-- 核　　　　review, reexamine, adjust accounts, recheck, counter check.
-- 校　　　　reactivate a school.
-- 查　　　　re-examine, re-check.
60-- 員　　　　demobilization.
-- 員令　　　demobilization orders.
70-- 辟　　　　restoration of a monarchy.
71-- 原　　　　recovery, recuperation.
77-- 興　　　　restoration, revival.
-- 學　　　　go back to school, resume studies.
78-- 驗　　　　reinspect.
70-- 命　　　　report to.

2825₁

佯 〔Yang〕 n. pretend, feign, simulate, affect.

00-- 病	pretend to be ill.
10-- 死	feign death, pretend to be dead.
34-- 爲	disguise, assume, make believe, make as if.
88-- 笑	pretend to laugh.

徉 〔Yang〕 adj. roving, going to and fro.

2825₃

儀 〔I〕 n. ceremony, rite, manner, style, aspect.

00-- 文	manner, style.
12-- 型	paragon.
21-- 態	bearing, appearance.
25-- 仗隊	guard of honor.
30-- 容	fashion.
43-- 式	form, ceremony.
50-- 表	appearance, personal look.
66-- 器	apparatus.
78-- 隊	honor guard.

2825₇

侮 〔Wu〕 v. insult, despise, ridicule, scorn.

10-- 弄	mock at, make a fool of.
44-- 蔑	disgrace, slight.
60-- 罵	insult with words.
71-- 辱	disgrace, insult.
96-- 慢	insult, scorn, slight.

2826₆

僧 〔Seng〕 n. monk, Buddhist.

26-- 侶	monk.
37-- 袍	frock.
40-- 寺	Buddhist temple.
71-- 長	prior.
77-- 尼	Buddhist monks and nuns.
73-- 院	cloister, monastery.
80-- 人	monk.

儈 〔Kuai〕 n. broker, middleman.

2826₇

傖 〔Tsang〕 n. mean fellow.

50-- 夫	lubber.

2826₈

俗 〔Ssu〕 n. custom, usage, adj. vulgar, boorish, common, unrefined.

00-- 諺	common saying.
01-- 語	colloquial, proverb, idiom.
02-- 話	common saying, proverb.
18-- 務	chores, routines.
22-- 稱	commonly called, commonly known as.
40-- 套	social conventions.
50-- 事	everyday matters, daily affairs.
80-- 人	layman, vulgarian.
-- 氣	vulgar, in poor taste.

2828₁

從 〔Tsung〕 v. fellow, accompany, pursue, agree with, prep. from, by, through.

00-- 旁	from outside.
10-- 不	never.
18-- 政	enter politics.
21-- 此	henceforth.
-- 此以後	from now on, from this moment on.
22-- 緩	postpone.
28-- 俗	conform to custom, swim with the tide.
30-- 容	feel at home.
-- 寬	leniently.
32-- 業者	practitioner.
35-- 速	without delay.
-- 速辦理	prompt attention.
37-- 軍	enlist, become a soldier.
40-- 來	ever since, from the beginning.
47-- 犯	accessory, principal in the second degree.
50-- 事	engage in, put the hand to, employ oneself, be taken up.
-- 事研究工作	be engaged in research.
-- 中	in the process, from the inside, in the middle.
-- 未	never, at no time.
53-- 戎	join the army.
66-- 嚴	severely, strictly.
67-- 略	forgo, the text is omitted.
80-- 前	before now, formerly, be-

fore, once upon a time.
-- 命	obey a command.
-- 公	manage official affairs.
-- 今天起生效	take effect as from today.
88-- 簡	be simple.
90-- 小	from one's childhood, since one was very young.

2828₆
儉〔Chien〕*adj.* moderate, temperate, economical.
00-- 吝	miserly, parsimonious.
27-- 約	thrifty and temperate, straiten oneself, use economy.
42-- 樸	be thrifty, simple in dressing.
44-- 薄	sordid.
90-- 省	frugal, economical.

2829₄
徐〔Hsu〕*adj.* slow, steady, tardy, *adv.* slowly, steadily.
21-- 步	walk slowly.
22-- 緩	slowly, unhurriedly.

2833₄
悠〔Yu〕*adj.* far, distant, remote, far-reaching.
34-- 遠	far-off, long distance.

煞〔Sha〕*v.* kill, murder, *adj.* baleful, *adv.* very, extremely.
80-- 氣	noxious influence.

懲〔Cheng〕*n.* warning, cautious, punishment, *v.* punish, repress, curb.
00-- 辦	take disciplinary action against.
21-- 處	penalize, punish.
27-- 役	hard-labor punishment.
33-- 治	remedy by punishment.
53-- 戒	punish, correct.
60-- 罰	punish, chastise.
-- 罰稅	penalty duty.

2835₁
鮮〔Hsien〕*adj.* fresh, new, pure, clean, bright, few, rare.
21-- 紅	bright red.
24-- 豔	beautiful as flowers.
-- 甜	fresh and sweet.
-- 貨	live cargo.
27-- 血	fresh blood.
-- 魚	fresh fish.
40-- 肉	fresh meat.
44-- 花	fresh cut flower.
-- 菜	fresh vegetable.
60-- 果	fresh fruit.
65-- 味	fresh favor.
67-- 明	sharp, distinct, bright-colored.
80-- 美	fresh and delicious.
90-- 少	few.

2836₁
鱔〔Shan〕*n.* eel.

2840₁
聳〔Sung〕*v.* urge, excite, stimulate, incite, *adj.* high, elevated.
00-- 立	tower aloft, rise up steeply.
17-- 恿	urge on, agitate.
24-- 動	stir up, incite, egg on.
30-- 肩	shrug shoulders.
47-- 起	stick up.
80-- 人聽聞	sensational, alarming talk.
96-- 惕	tremble.

2841₇
艦〔Chien〕*n.* ship, battleship, war vessel, man-of-war.
71-- 長	captain, skipper.
78-- 隊	fleet, navy, squadron.
-- 隊司令	fleet commander.

2846₇
艙〔Tsang〕*n.* cabin, hold.
00-- 底	bottom of the hold.
10-- 面	deck.
21-- 位	cabin, berth.
-- 位租用	space charter.
24-- 貨	hold cargo.
30-- 房	cabins.
60-- 口	hatchway.
66-- 單	manifest of cargo, inward manifest.

2846₈
谿〔Chi〕*n.* brook, stream.

2854₁
牧〔Mu〕*n.* shepherd, cowherd, *v.* tend

	cattle, pasture.	
00-- 童	cow boy.	
-- 畜	stock farming.	
17-- 歌	pastoral song, shepherd song.	
21-- 師	preacher, clergyman, church man, pastor, minister.	
25-- 牛	keep cow.	
44-- 地	pasture.	
46-- 場	field, ranch, pasture, green land.	
71-- 馬	pasture horse.	
-- 區	pasturing area.	
80-- 人	herdsman.	
-- 羊人	shepherd.	
-- 羊犬	shepherd dog, collie.	

2855₃

犧 〔Hsi〕 *n.* victims.

25-- 牲	sacrifice.
-- 牲生命	sacrifice one's life.
-- 牲者	prey, victims.
-- 牲財產	give up one's property.

2860₄

咎 〔Chiu〕 *n.* fault, vice, defect, mistake, *v.* blame, censure, reproach.

2864₇

馥 〔Fu〕 *n.* fragrance.

2868₆

鹼 〔Chien〕 *n.* alkali, salt.

00-- 度	basicity.
10-- 石灰	soda-lime.
12-- 水	salt water, alkaline water.
24-- 化	saponification.
95-- 性	alkalinity.

2871₀

嵯 〔Tso〕 *adj.* high and steeply, irregular.

2871₇

屹 〔Yi〕 *n.* isolated mountain.

2873₇

齡 〔Ling〕 *n.* age, one's year.

2874₀

收 〔Shou〕 *n.* receive, collect, gather, close, reap, harvest.

00-- 音機	radio receiving set.
-- 市	closing.
-- 市價	closing price, close price, closing rate.
08-- 效	result, reap, bear fruit, yield results.
-- 訖	payment received, received in full.
10-- 工	stop work, end the day's work, knock off.
-- 下	accept, receive.
-- 票員	check-taker, ticket collector.
12-- 到	received.
-- 發	receive and send out.
-- 發室	office through which correspondence is received or sent out.
-- 發區	receiving and delivering bay.
18-- 殮	prepare a corpse for burial.
20-- 受	receive, take in, accept.
-- 受者	receiver.
-- 看	watch.
-- 集	gather, collect, call, bring together.
23-- 縮	shrink, contract, straiten.
24-- 納	accept.
-- 貨	receive delivered goods, take delivery, take delivery of goods.
-- 貨人	cargo receiver.
-- 貨部	receiving department.
-- 貨單	receiving note.
25-- 件人	addressee, consignee, recipient.
-- 債	collect debt.
27-- 盤	closing quotation.
-- 歸國有	nationalize.
-- 租	collect rent.
-- 條	receipt.
28-- 復失地	recover lost territories.
-- 稅	collect taxes, receive tax, tax collection.
-- 稅員	collector, tax collector.
-- 稅單	tax form.
-- 繳	take over, capture.

30-- 容	give shelter, harbor.
-- 容所	asylum.
32-- 割	reap, harvest.
-- 割機	reaping machine.
33-- 心	concentrate attention.
35-- 禮	accept a gift.
37-- 沒	confiscate.
40-- 支	income and expenditure, revenue and expenditure, expenses and receipts, receipt and payment.
-- 支平衡	the accounts are balanced.
-- 支員	cashier.
-- 存	receive for keep.
41-- 帳	collect debts.
-- 帳人	bill collector.
44-- 藏	keep, store up.
-- 穫	crop, reap, harvest, get in the harvest.
-- 穫者	reaper, collector.
46-- 場	conclude, come to an end.
-- 埋	collect and bury.
47-- 款	make collections.
-- 款處	cash desk.
-- 款人	recipient, payee, collector, receiver.
-- 款員	receiving teller.
51-- 據=收條	
53-- 成	harvest.
55-- 費	collect fee, collect charge, charge for.
-- 費處	tollhouse.
-- 費橋	toll bridge.
-- 費公路	toll highway, toll road, tollway.
58-- 拾	repair, put in order, muster up.
60-- 回	n. repossession, v. recall, get back, receive again, repossess, withdraw, recover, take back.
-- 回成命	call back.
-- 口	closure of a wound.
-- 買	redeem, buy up, bribe.
-- 羅	collect, gather, enlist.
61-- 賬	collection.
64-- 賄	accept bribe.

-- 贖	redeem, get out of pawn.
65-- 購	buy up, purchase.
77-- 留	harbor, give shelter.
80-- 入	income.
-- 益	n. earnings, return, v. get benefit, profit, gain.
-- 養	adoption.
-- 報人	addressee.
83-- 錢	collect payment.
87-- 斂	improve, mend ways.
-- 錄	employ, enter, enroll, recruit.
-- 銀機	cash register.
88-- 管	take over, charge of.

2891₆

稅 〔Shui〕 n. duties, taxes, revenue.

00-- 率	tariff, rate of tax, rate of taxation, tax rates, rate of duty.
17-- 務	taxation.
-- 務司	commissioner of customs.
-- 務機	tax offices.
-- 務員	tax collector.
-- 務局	tax bureau, tax office, revenue office.
22-- 制	tax system, taxation system.
-- 種	type of tax, items of taxation, categories of taxes.
28-- 收	tax revenue, tax receipts.
-- 收員	collector of taxes.
31-- 額	taxation, amount of tax to be paid.
-- 源	tax fund, tax revenue sources, source of taxation.
34-- 法	tax law, law of tax.
47-- 款	tax money, tax payment, taxation, tax.
50-- 吏	tax-collector, tax-gatherer.
56-- 捐	duties.
60-- 目	tax designation, category of tax, items of duty, tax items.
62-- 則	tax code, tariff schedule, tax regulations.
66-- 單	tax form, tax invoice, duty memo, tax roll.

77--	關	customs-house.
--	印	tax seal.
80--	金	tax and duty.

纜〔Lan〕*n.* rope, cable.

40--	索	rope, rigging.
50--	車	peak-tram, cable car, gondola.
--	車道	cable railroad.

2891₇

紇〔Ho〕*n.* tassel.

縊〔I〕*v.* hang, strangle.

10--	死	strangle.
11--	頸	hang.

2892₇

紛〔Fen〕*adj.* confused, reveled, numerous.

00--	雜	mixed up, in great confusion.
12--	飛	fly all over.
20--	爭	dispute, quarrel.
22--	亂	disorderly, confused, chaotic.
24--	岐	discrepancy, difference.
51--	擾	*n.* turmoil, *v.* lose one's presence of mind, confuse.

綸〔Lun〕*n.* silk, cords.

2893₂

稔〔Jen〕*n.* harvest, ripe, grain, *v.* store, accumulate, *adj.* familiar.

05--	熟	good harvest.
20--	悉	know thoroughly.
40--	友	bosom friend.
86--	知	know well, familiar.

2894₀

繳〔Chiao〕*v.* bind, wind around, surrender, deliver, hand over, send in, pay, return, give back.

00--	交	deliver up, hand up, turn in.
--	庫	pay into the treasure, pay into the treasury.
24--	納	pay.
--	納稅款	tax payment.
--	納罰款	pay the penalty.
27--	解	forward.
28--	稅	pay tax.

36--	還	return.
43--	械	disarm, unarm.
47--	款	make payment.
--	款通知	payment notice.
55--	費	pay fees.
60--	罰款	pay forfeit money.
--	回	hand back, refund.
--	呈	submit to a superior.
78--	驗	submit to examination.
80--	入資本	capital paid-in.
90--	卷	hand in one's examination paper.

緻〔Chih〕*adj.* delicate, softy, fine.

30--	密	dense, thick.

2896₁

給〔Kei〕*v.* give, afford, offer, supply, provide, issue.

12--	發	issue, grant.
--	水	water supply.
17--	予	confer.
--	予折扣	allow a discount, discount granted.
27--	假	give a holiday, grant in leave.
--	獎	award prizes.
28--	以	give.
60--	足	sufficiency, affluence.
77--	與	give to, allow, accord.
80--	養	ration.
--	養船	maintenance ship.
--	人承包	put out to contract.

2896₅

繕〔Shan〕*v.* copy, write out, prepare.

10--	正	make a fair copy, copy neatly.
30--	寫	write out.
59--	抄	copy, transcribe.
--	圖員	draftsman.

2896₆

繪〔Hui〕*v.* draw, paint, embroider.

27--	像	paint portrait.
50--	畫	paint, draw.
--	畫術	art of painting.
60--	圖	draw a picture.
--	圖員	draftsman.

2898₁

縱 〔Tsung〕 *v.* allow, tolerate, overlook, let go, indulge in, *conj.* although, even if.

09--	談	speak freely.
12--	列	column.
23--	然	however.
30--	容	connive at.
32--	淫	debauchery.
37--	恣	licentious.
--	觀	take a free look, take a sweeping look.
47--	聲	shout at the top of one's voice.
77--	貫	run north-south（railroad, road）.
78--	隊	column.
87--	慾	debauch.
--	慾者	man of pleasure.
--	飲	indulge in drinking.
90--	火	set fire.
--	火者	firebrand, arsonist.

2921₂

倦 〔Chuan〕 *adj.* tired, fatigued, weary, worn out.

99--	勞	tiresome.

2922₇

俏 〔Chiao〕 *adj.* elegant, pretty, handsome, beautiful.

11--	麗	beautiful, pretty.
40--	皮	winsome, attractive.

倘 〔Tang〕 *conj.* if, supposing that, on condition that, in case that.

18--	敢	if dare.
21--	能	if possible.
40--	有	in case of, in the event of.
44--	若	if, in case that, supposing that.

躺 〔Tang〕 *v.* lie down.

10--	下	lie down.
44--	椅	couch, deck chair, reclining chair.

2923₁

儻 〔Tang〕 *adj.* free, unrestrained.

40--	來	obtain expectedly.

2925₀

伴 〔Pan〕 *n.* companion, comrade, associate, partner, *v.* accompany, associate.

26--	侶	companion, partner, comrade.
28--	從	accompany.
37--	郎	best man.
43--	娘	bridesmaid.
50--	奏	accompany.

2928₀

伙 〔Huo〕 *n.* comrade, companion.

29--	伴	comrade, partner, companion.
80--	食	food.
--	食房	pantry.

2928₆

償 〔Chang〕 *n.* compensation, reward, *v.* compensate, pay back, indemnify, recompense, reward.

24--	付債務	payment of debts.
35--	清	extinguish.
--	清貸款	extinguish loan.
36--	還	*n.* redemption, reimbursement, repayment, restitution, *v.* reimburse, repay, compensate, pay, refund.
--	還債務	redemption of debt, repayment of debt, meet one's liabilities, service debt.
--	還日	redemption date.
--	還公債	redemption of public loan.
80--	金	indemnity.
--	命	forfeit one's life.

2933₈

愁 〔Chou〕 *adj.* sad, sorry, mournful, melancholy.

30--	容	sad look, long face.
44--	苦	grieved, distressed, broken-hearted.
77--	悶	grieved.

2935₉

鱗 〔Lin〕 *n.* scale.

2971₈

毯 〔Tan〕 *n.* carpet, blanket.

2972₇

峭 〔Chiao〕 *n*. abrupt hill, *adj*. steep, abrupt, precipitous.
40-- 直	stern, strict.
70-- 壁	precipice.

2992₀
秒 〔Miao〕 *n*. second, floss, mite.
80-- 針	second hand.
85-- 錶	stop watch.

紗 〔Sha〕 *n*. thin silk, yarn, gauze.
00-- 廠	cotton mill, textile mill.
30-- 窗	gauze window, screen window.
40-- 布	bandage, gauze.
41-- 帳	mosquito net.
83-- 錠	spindle.
88-- 籠	sarong.
92-- 燈	gauze lantern.

2992₇
稍 〔Shao〕 *adj*. small, little, *adv*. gradually, slightly.
10-- 可	tolerable, well enough.
22-- 後	later, shortly afterward.
-- 緩	little slower, not so fast.
26-- 息	rest on one's arms.
27-- 候	wait for a while.
28-- 微	somewhat, slightly.
35-- 濃	a little too thick.
47-- 好	a little better.

綃 〔Hsiao〕 *n*. raw silk, fabric made of raw silk.

2995₀
絆 〔Pan〕 *v*. stumble, entangle, stub, trip up.
20-- 住	detained, prevented.
22-- 倒	trip and fall, stumble.
57-- 拘	restrain, keep under control.
77-- 腳	hinder, fettered.
-- 腳石	stumbling block.

2998₀
秋 〔Chiu〕 *n*. autumn, fall.
00-- 意	cool and a little chilly.
10-- 天	autumn, fall.
-- 雨	autumn rain.
20-- 千	swing.
-- 季	autumn.
27-- 色	autumn scene.
28-- 收	harvest, crop.
30-- 涼	autumn chill.
34-- 波	bewitching eye, soft glance.
38-- 海棠	begonia.
44-- 老虎	scorching heat in early autumn.
77-- 風	autumn wind.

3

3010₁
空 〔Kung〕 *n*. hole, sky, space, spare time, leisure, vacancy, blank, *v*. deplete, exhaust, leave blank, *adj*. empty, vacant, void, leisure, unemployed, exhausted, poor, useless, wanting, deficient, *adv*. in vain, in no purpose.
01-- 襲	air-raid.
-- 襲預防法	air-raid precautions.
-- 襲警報	alert.
-- 襲警報器	siren.
-- 話	empty talk, babble.
07-- 調器	air-conditioner.
08-- 論者	closet strategist.
09-- 談	mere words, empty talk, bosh, foolish talk.
11-- 頭	short position, oversold position, short, bear.
-- 頭支票	dishonored cheque, empty promise, bad cheque, rubber cheque.
-- 頭人情	offer lip-service.
20-- 手	empty-handed, empty hands.
-- 位	vacancy, empty space, unoccupied seat.
-- 乏	wanting, empty.
21-- 虛	empty, void, vain, unreal.
-- 虛無物	empty, containing nothing.
-- 處	space.
26-- 白	blank, white space.
-- 白支票	blank cheque (check).
-- 白表格	blank form, spacing chart.
-- 白點	blank.
27-- 名	mere name, in name only.
-- 的	empty, devoid, vacant.

30-- 房	empty room.
31-- 額	vacancy.
37-- 軍	air force.
-- 軍參謀	air staff.
-- 軍基地	air base.
-- 洞	hollow, cave.
-- 運	airlift, air transport, air freight, delivery by air, *adj.* airborne.
-- 運師	airlift division.
-- 運費	airfreight.
-- 運隊	ferry command, airlift command.
44-- 地	open ground, vacant spot.
46-- 想	*n.* imagination, phantasy, fantasy, fancy, illusion, castle in the air, *v.* wish for in vain.
-- 想主義	utopianism.
-- 想家	dreamer.
-- 場	field.
50-- 中	in the sky.
-- 中列車	aerial train.
-- 中堡壘	Flying Fortress.
-- 中走廊	air corridor.
-- 中樓閣	cloud castle, castle in the air.
-- 中攝影	aerophotography.
-- 中爆炸	air burst.
57-- 投	air-drop.
60-- 曠	wide, open.
63-- 戰	aerial fight, air warfare, air fight.
-- 喊	empty clamor.
70-- 防	air defence.
77-- 閑	leisure, idle, free.
-- 間	space, room.
-- 屋	empty house.
-- 降師	airborne division.
79-- 隙	clearance, interval, crevice.
80-- 前	break the record, unprecedented, all-time, unheard-of.
-- 前紀錄	all-time record.
-- 前絕後	unprecedented and unrepeatable.
-- 無所有	completely empty.
-- 氣	atmosphere, air.

-- 氣調節	air conditioning.
-- 氣污染	air pollution.
-- 氣傳染	air-borne infection.
-- 氣流通	good air ventilation.
-- 氣浴	air bath.
85-- 缺	vacancy.
90-- 忙	fruitless effort.
98-- 炸	bomb.
-- 炸點	point of burst.

3010₄

室〔**Shih**〕*n.* room, house, home, family, chamber, dwelling, mansion, apartment.

23-- 外	outdoor, outside the house, in the open.
36-- 溫	room temperature.
40-- 內	indoor.
-- 內遊戲	indoor games.

窒〔**Chih**〕*v.* stop, obstruct.

17-- 礙	*n.* obstacle, *v.* stop, close up.
26-- 息	smother, suffocate.
30-- 塞	stop up.
77-- 悶	smother.

塞〔**Sai**〕*n.* cork, stopper, pass, frontier, *v.* stop up, block, cork, close, fill up, hinder, obstruct.

17-- 子	cork, plug, stopper.
20-- 住	stop up, close, plug, block up, fill up, cork up, shut up.
23-- 外	beyond the frontier.
30-- 實	filled.
-- 進	stuff.
34-- 滿	fill up, stuff full.
38-- 道	block up a road.
50-- 責	evade responsibility, avoid responsibility.
60-- 口	stop a hole.
80-- 入	crowd.

3010₆

宣〔**Hsuan**〕*v.* proclaim, declare, notify, announce, promulgate, publish, make known.

00-- 言	*n.* declaration, manifesto, statement, *v.* declare, predict.

04--	讀	read out in public.
05--	講	preach.
10--	露	disclose, let out.
24--	佈	post, declare, announce, proclaim.
--	佈戒嚴	proclaim martial law.
--	告	declare, announce, proclaim.
--	告破產	declared bankruptcy, adjudication of bankruptcy.
--	告罪狀	condemnation.
25--	傳	*n.* propaganda, publicity, *v.* promulgate, propagate.
--	傳部	Ministry of Information, publicity department.
--	傳網	propaganda network.
--	傳機關	propaganda organization.
--	傳畫	propaganda poster.
--	傳費	propaganda expense.
--	傳品	propaganda material, introductory offer.
--	傳員	propagandist.
--	傳戰	war of propaganda.
--	傳局	Publicity Bureau.
--	傳隊	Propaganda Corps.
35--	洩	let out, leak out, drain off.
40--	布	notify, proclaim, announce, predicate, indicate.
52--	誓	vow, take oath, call heaven to witness.
--	誓就職	be sworn in.
--	誓書	affidavit.
56--	揚	make known, advocate, advertise.
63--	戰	declare war, hang out the red flag.
92--	判	sentence, pass judgement.

3010₇

宜 〔 I 〕 *adj.* fit, proper, suitable, accordant.

08--	於	be fitted to, suitable to.
--	於攝影	photogenic.

3011₃

窕 〔 Tiao 〕 *adj.* profound.

30--	窈	modest and refined.

流 〔 Liu 〕 *n.* fluid, stream, rivers, *v.* flow, circulate, spread, pass, drift, move about, diffuse, *adj.* flowing, drifting, moving, shifting.

00--	產	*n.* abortion, abnormal birth, miscarriage, *v.* miscarry, cast young.
--	言	rumor.
--	離	homeless, wandering.
--	亡	fugitive, exile.
07--	氓	rascal, vagabonds, hooligan.
10--	露	appear, reveal, show.
12--	水	running water, living water.
--	水帳	current account, day book, day-to-day account.
--	刑	banishment.
16--	彈	spent ball, stray bullet.
21--	行	*v.* prevail, circulate, have a run, *adj.* prevalent, current, fashionable, popular.
--	行症	epidemic.
--	行貨	articles in great demand.
--	行性感冒	influenza.
22--	利	fluent, easy.
--	出	outflow.
24--	動	*n.* flow, run, drift, *adj.* mobile.
--	動工人	migrant labor, migrant worker.
--	動資本	floating capital, circulating capital, liquid funds, working capital.
--	動人口	floating population, fluid population.
--	動性	fluidity.
25--	傳	spread, diffuse, hand down.
--	傳後世	hand down to future generations.
26--	線型	streamlined.
27--	血	bleed, shed blood.
30--	寇	brigand, bandit.
31--	汗	perspire, sweat.
32--	涎	slaver, drivel.
33--	淚	weep, shed tears.
--	淚彈	lachrymatory shell, tear-gas shell.
--	浪	wander, stray.

-- 浪者	wanderer.
36-- 涸	drain.
37-- 通	*n.* currency, circulation, negotiation, *v.* circulate, negotiate.
-- 運票據	negotiable bill (documents, instruments, papers), straight paper.
38-- 溢	flow over.
39-- 沙	quicksand.
40-- 布	diffuse.
43-- 域	valley, basin.
44-- 落異鄉	be left behind in a strange village.
50-- 毒	harmful influence, ill effect.
56-- 暢	fluent, running smoothly.
60-- 星	meteor.
-- 量	run-off, volume of flow.
72-- 質	fluid, liquid.
80-- 入	influx, inflow.
98-- 弊	current corruption, corrupt practice.

3011₄

注〔Chu〕*n.* comment, note, *v.* pour, pay attention to, comment, explain.

00-- 意	attend, take notice, pay attention to.
-- 意力	attention.
-- 意情報	warning.
-- 音	phonetic annotation.
20-- 重	concentrate on, lay stress upon, emphasize.
24-- 射	inject, transfuse, inoculate.
-- 射劑	injection.
-- 射預防針	vaccinate.
-- 射器	injector, syringe.
27-- 解	explanation, note, annotation.
30-- 定	be doomed to.
36-- 視	regard, gaze, stare, look, behold.
60-- 目	watch, fix the eyes upon, gaze at.
77-- 冊	*n.* registration, register, entering to the register.
-- 冊商標	register trademarks.
-- 冊證書	registered certificate.

-- 冊處	register office, registration office.
-- 冊會計師	certified public accountant, registered accountant.
80-- 入	inject, infuse, transfuse.
89-- 銷	*n.* cancellation, *v.* cancel, withdraw.

准〔Chun〕*n.* license, promise, permission, *v.* allow, permit, grant, consent, approve.

08-- 許	allow, permit, authorize.
-- 許狀	permit.
10-- 票	warrant.
27-- 將	brigadier-general.
-- 假	leave of absence, grant a leave.
74-- 尉	warrant officer.
80-- 入	admit.

准〔Huai〕*n.* the Huai river.

窪〔Wa〕*n.* pit, hollow, swamp, bog.

44-- 地	low ground, hollow.

潼〔Tung〕*n.* the Tung river.

灘〔Tan〕*n.* beach, shoal.

11-- 頭堡	beachhead.

3011₇

瀛〔Ying〕*n.* ocean.

32-- 洲	fairyland.

3011₈

泣〔Chi〕*v.* weep, shed tears.

47-- 歎	lament.
66-- 哭	weep, cry.

3012₃

濟〔Chi〕*v.* help, aid, relieve.

22-- 私	serve one's own ends.
27-- 急	relieve one's necessities.
30-- 良所	house of refuge.
80-- 人	be helpful to others.
-- 貧	relieve the poor.
-- 貧法	poor law, poor relief law.
-- 貧院	almshouse.
96-- 糧	give alms of grain.

3012₇

沛〔Pei〕*adj.* copious, super-abundant.

滂〔Pang〕*n.* heavy rain, *adj.* extensive,

torrential.
33-- 沱　　　torrential.
-- 沱大雨　　heavy shower.
38-- 洋　　　vast, extensive.

滴〔Ti〕 *n.* drop, *v.* drop, drip.
10-- 下　　　drop, drip.
22-- 出　　　drip out.
80-- 入　　　instill.
88--管　　　pipette.

3013₀

汴〔Pien〕 *n.* the Pien river.

3013₂

滾〔Kun〕 *v.* roll, boil, rotate, *adj.* boiling, bubbling.
12-- 水　　　boiling water.
13-- 球軸承　ball-bearing.
17-- 子　　　roller.
24-- 動　　　trundle, wheel, roll over.
36-- 邊　　　embroider a border.
40-- 存盈餘　accumulated surplus.
-- 存利益　accumulated profit.
-- 存費用　deferred charge.
55-- 轉　　　roll.
77-- 開　　　begone! get away!
88-- 筒機　　rotary, rotary printing machine.

濠〔Hao〕 *n.* moat, ditch, trench, dyke.
35-- 溝　　　ditch.

3013₆

蜜〔Mi〕 *n.* honey, nectar.
01-- 語　　　sweet talk.
50-- 棗　　　candied date.
57-- 蜂　　　bee, honey bee.
72-- 蠟　　　beeswax.
77-- 月　　　honeymoon.
-- 月旅行　　honeymoon trip.
83-- 餞　　　preserves, sweetmeats.
90-- 糖　　　honey.

3014₀

汶〔Wen〕 *n.* the Wen river.

3014₇

液〔Yeh〕 *n.* liquid, fluid, saliva.
21-- 態　　　liquidity, fluidity, liquid state.
24-- 化　　　liquefaction.

75-- 體　　　liquid, fluid.
-- 體燃料　　liquid fuel.

渡〔Tu〕 *n.* ferry, ford, *v.* cross, ferry over, ford.
11-- 頭　　　ferry.
27-- 船　　　ferry, ferryboat.
31-- 江　　　cross a river.
-- 河　　　cross a river.
37-- 過　　　pass, bridge over.
-- 過難關　　turn the corner, tide over difficulties.
42-- 橋　　　ferry bridge.
50-- 夫　　　ferryman.
60-- 口　　　ferry, ferry crossing.
77-- 難關　　get over difficulties.

淳〔Chun〕 *adj.* simple.

3014₈

淬〔Tsui〕 *v.* temper, dye, come into contact with.
24-- 勉　　　strive, arouse to action, persuade.
87-- 鋼　　　tempered steel.
90-- 火　　　quench (iron or steel) to temper.

3016₇

溏〔Tang〕 *n.* pool.

3019₄

凜〔Ling〕 *adj.* cold, wintry, frosty.
30-- 凜　　　awe-inspiring, stern, severe.
32-- 冽　　　piercing cold, intense cold.
44-- 若冰霜　cold as ice and frost.

3019₆

涼〔Liang〕 *adj.* cold, cool, refreshing.
00-- 亭　　　pavilion, garden house.
10-- 天　　　cold day.
12-- 水　　　cold water.
40-- 爽　　　cold as a cucumber, refreshing.
44-- 茶　　　cold tea.
-- 鞋　　　sandals.
46-- 帽　　　summer hat, straw hat.
47-- 棚　　　awning.
77-- 風　　　cool breeze.
95-- 快　　　cool and pleasant.

3020₁

寧〔Ning〕 *v.* would rather, had better,

prefer, *adj.* tranquil, peaceful.

10--	可	would rather, preferably.
--	死不去	would rather die than go.
--	死不辱	prefer death to disgrace.
--	死不屈	would rather die than surrender.
21--	肯	would rather.
52--	靜	peaceful, quiet, tranquil.
71--	願	prefer, would rather.

3020_2
寥 〔**Liao**〕*adj.* empty, void, vacant, vast, wide, solitary.

30--	寥	very few.
44--	落	deserted.

3020_7
穹 〔**Chiung**〕*n.* heaven, sky, *v.* stop up, *adj.* lofty, high, deep, empty, spacious, vast, eminent.

30--	窿	vault, arched firmament.
80--	谷	deep valley.

3021_1
完 〔**Wan**〕*v.* finish, complete, conclude, *adj.* complete, perfect, finished, used up, gone.

10--	工	finish a job.
17--	了	finished, completed.
24--	結	concluded, settled, finished.
--	備	complete, all ready, fully prepared, perfect, well-prepared.
34--	滿	satisfaction.
35--	清債務	pay all debts.
42--	婚	get married.
46--	場	drop the curtain.
47--	好	perfect, in good condition.
--	好無損	intact.
50--	事	finish, bring the matter to an end.
53--	成	finish, complete, achieve, perfect, accomplish.
--	成使命	complete one's mission.
58--	整	complete, perfect, round.
--	整領土	territorial integrity.
60--	足	in full, complete, in all.
--	畢	accomplish, conclude, finish, complete.

80--	人	perfect man.
--	全	*adj.* full, complete, perfect, entire, *adv.* altogether, absolutely, all in all.
--	全對	quite right, perfectly right.
--	全同意	see eye to eye.
--	美	perfect, faultless.

窄 〔**Chai**〕*adj.* narrow, strait, tight, contracted.

27--	縫	chink.
38--	道	narrow path.
44--	狹	confined, closely hemmed.
54--	軌	narrow gauge.
67--	路	narrow path, narrow lane.
77--	胸	narrow-minded.
78--	險	defile.
--	隘	defile, narrow pass.
90--	小	narrow and small.

扉 〔**Fei**〕*n.* door.

寵 〔**Chung**〕*v.* love, confer, favor.

20--	愛	favor, love, delight in.
77--	兒	favorite.

3021_2
宛 〔**Wan**〕*conj.* as if, same as.

12--	延	winding.
23--	然	*adj.* seeming, *adv.* seemingly.
44--	者	same as.
46--	如	seemingly as if, as though, the same as.
55--	轉	*adj.* roundabout, *adv.* tactfully.

3021_3
寬 〔**Kuan**〕*n.* width, breadth, *v.* widen, enlarge, loosen, take off, *adj.* wide, broad, gentle, kind, liberal.

00--	度	width, breadth.
--	廣	wide, vast.
--	廣博大	vast and extensive.
--	衣服	undress.
12--	延	postpone.
14--	弛	slacken.
24--	待	treat generously.
26--	和	kind.
30--	窄	extent, width, breadth.
--	宏大量	generous, magnanimous.

-- 容　　　　*n.* forbearance, *v.* tolerate.
-- 容待人　　be lenient in treating others.
38-- 裕　　　abundant, well-to-do.
40-- 大　　　spacious, liberal, lenient, generous.
-- 大處理　　lenient treatment.
46-- 恕　　　pardon, forgive.
71-- 厚　　　generous, lenient.
72-- 鬆　　　free.
74-- 慰　　　comfort.
77-- 限　　　*n.* grace, *v.* extend the limit of time.
-- 限期　　　grace period.
-- 緊帶　　　elastic braid.
87-- 舒　　　relaxation.
-- 銀幕　　　wide screen (for movie).
98-- 敞　　　spacious.
-- 敞舒適　　spacious and comfortable.

3021₄

寇〔**Kou**〕*n.* bandits, robber, thieves, highwayman, enemy, *v.* rob, plunder, invade.

雇〔**Ku**〕*v.* engage, hire, employ.
00-- 主　　　employer.
10-- 工　　　*n.* hired hands, *v.* hire laborers.
-- 工合同　　contract of hire of labour and services.
27-- 佣關係　　employer-employee relationship.
-- 佣勞動　　hired labor.
-- 佣船　　　hire a boat.
60-- 員　　　staff, employee, clerk.
-- 員名單　　employment roll.
77-- 用　　　engage, employ.
-- 用者　　　employer.
-- 用合同　　employment contract (agreement).

窿〔**Lung**〕*n.* hole, cavity.
47-- 起　　　protuberance.

3022₇

宵〔**Hsiao**〕*n.* night, *adj.* dark, small.
44-- 禁　　　curfew.

房〔**Fang**〕*n.* house, building, apartment, room.
00-- 主　　　landlord.

-- 產　　　　estate, house property.
-- 產經紀人　house agent, real-estate agent, realtor.
-- 產稅　　　house tax, real-estate tax, property tax.
-- 市　　　　housing market.
11-- 頂　　　roof.
17-- 子　　　house, building.
27-- 租　　　rent.
-- 租津貼　　rental allowance, lodging allowance.
30-- 客　　　tenant.
44-- 地產　　　real estate, real property, housing and land.
-- 地產市場　real estate market.
-- 地產註冊　property register.
-- 地產投資　real estate investment.
-- 地產公司　real estate company.
-- 地產管理　management of properties.
-- 地契　　　real estate title deeds.
-- 荒　　　　housing shortage.
50-- 東　　　house owner, landlord.
77-- 屋　　　house.
-- 屋出租　　house for rent.
-- 屋裝修　　house improvement and betterment.
-- 屋租約　　house lease.
-- 屋稅　　　house tax.
-- 屋管理人　house keeper, housing manager, property manager.
83-- 錢　　　house rent.

扁〔**Pien**〕*n.* tablet, signboard, *adj.* flat, thin, low, mean.
10-- 平　　　flat.

宥〔**Yu**〕*v.* excuse, pardon, forgive.
23-- 貸其罪　　forgive his crime.

肩〔**Chien**〕*n.* shoulder, *v.* shoulder, carry on shoulder.
00-- 章　　　shoulder-straps, epaulets.
40-- 巾　　　shawl.
44-- 帶　　　shoulder-girdles.
52-- 挑　　　carry on shoulder.
70-- 膀　　　shoulder.
76-- 胛　　　shoulder blade, scapula.
80-- 並肩　　shoulder to shoulder, side by side.

甯 〔Ning〕 v. prefer, rest.

10-- 死	rather die.
-- 可	better to, much rather.
-- 不	rather not.
21-- 肯	would rather.

扇 〔Shan〕 n. fan, leaf of a door.

12-- 形	sector.

窩 〔Wo〕 n. nest, den, nook, hollow, lair, v. harbor, receive secretly.

30-- 家	house where stolen goods are hidden.
33-- 心	annoyed, insulted, heart-warming.
44-- 藏	harbor, receive secretly, conceal, shelter.
47-- 棚	shelter, booth.
63-- 贓	conceal plunder.

寡 〔Kua〕 n. widow, adj. few, little, single, friendless, solitary, alone.

00-- 言	n. reticence, adj. reticent, taciturn.
10-- 不敵眾	be outnumbered.
11-- 頭	oligarch.
-- 頭政治	oligarchy.
47-- 婦	widow.
60-- 見	of little experience.
77-- 居	live in widowhood.
-- 聞	ill-informed, not well-informed.
90-- 少	rare, short.

窮 〔Chiung〕 n. poverty, extremity, v. investigate thoroughly, search out.

20-- 乏	poverty, need, want, lack, necessity, distress, difficulty.
22-- 兇極惡	extremely ferocious.
27-- 鄉	poor village.
30-- 究	examine thoroughly.
34-- 漢	poor man.
36-- 迫	drive to the wall, pursue everywhere.
37-- 追	follow up, drive to the wall, pursue everywhere.
41-- 極	very poor.
44-- 苦	miserable, wretched.

-- 巷	blind alley.
46-- 相	miserable appearance, distressed looks.
50-- 盡	n. end, extremity, adj. exhausted.
60-- 困	poverty, poor, distressed, straitened.
80-- 人	poor person, pauper, have-nots.
90-- 光蛋	penniless vagrant.

3023₂

永 〔Yung〕 adj. permanent, perpetual, eternal, far-reaching, everlasting.

10-- 不	never.
25-- 生	n. eternal life, adj. immortal, deathless.
27-- 久	everlasting, eternal, perpetual.
-- 久性	perpetuity, permanence.
-- 久租契	lease in perpetuity.
34-- 遠	forever, eternally.
40-- 存	everlasting.
44-- 世不忘	will never forget.
62-- 別	part forever, die.
91-- 恆	eternal, everlasting.

家 〔Chia〕 n. home, house, family, household.

00-- 主	housemaster, goodman.
-- 產	estate.
-- 廟	ancestral temple.
-- 庭	family, home, fireside, hearth.
-- 庭旅館	family hotel.
-- 庭工業	house industry, home industry.
-- 庭手工業	cottage industry.
-- 庭經營	family operation, household management.
-- 庭生產	household production.
-- 庭收支	family income and expenditure.
-- 庭收入	household income.
-- 庭津貼	family allowance.
-- 庭消費	household consumption.
-- 庭教師	tutor.
-- 庭教育	home education.

-- 庭用品	household goods (articles).
-- 庭服務業	domestic services.
-- 庭醫生	family doctor.
-- 庭企業	family business (enterprise).
-- 產	family property (possessions) .
-- 畜	cattle, livestock, domestic animals.
04-- 計	family budget, household budget.
08-- 族	family clan.
-- 族制度	family system.
-- 族合伙	family partnership.
-- 譜	genealogy.
14-- 破	rack and ruin.
-- 破人亡	the family is ruined and its members are dead.
17-- 務	housework, family affairs.
18-- 政	domestic economy, home economics.
-- 政學系	department of domestic science.
20-- 系	lineage, ancestry.
22-- 私	furniture.
25-- 傳物	heirloom.
26-- 俱	furniture.
27-- 鄉	motherland, homeland.
-- 佣	domestic servant.
34-- 法	home rules.
38-- 道	family condition.
44-- 世	descent, ancestry, birth.
48-- 教	home education, tutor, manners.
50-- 事	family affairs, house work, household, household duties.
-- 史	family history.
71-- 長	patriarch, head of the family.
-- 長政治	paternalism.
77-- 屬	household.
-- 用電器	home appliances.
-- 用物品	household effects.
-- 具	furniture.
-- 具店	furniture store.
80-- 禽	poultry.
90-- 常	homely, common.
-- 常便飯	homely meal.
-- 眷	family.

3023₄

戾 〔Li〕 *n.* sin, crime, guilt, *adj.* crooked, distorted, perverse, rebellious, ungovernable, *v.* come to, stop, settle, oppose.

| 21-- 止 | come, arrive. |

3024₁

穿 〔Chuan〕 *v.* wear, dress, put on, penetrate, pierce through, string, dig, bore, perforate, chisel.

00-- 衣	dress, wear, put on.
-- 衣鏡	cheval glass.
12-- 孔	punch, perforate, pierce.
22-- 出	go through.
26-- 線	thread.
32-- 透	penetrate, pierce.
37-- 洞	dig a hole.
-- 過	go through , perforate, cross.
44-- 孝	wear mourning.
-- 鞋	wear shoes.
-- 舊	worn-out, threadbare.
52-- 刺	prick.
80-- 入	enter, dig, penetrate, pierce.
-- 著=穿衣	
84-- 針	thread a needle.

3024₇

戽 〔Hu〕 *n.* baling ladle.

| 34-- 斗 | scoop. |

寢 〔Chin〕 *n.* rest, repose, chamber, dwelling house.

00-- 衣	night clothes, nightgown.
30-- 室	bedroom, dormitory, bed chamber.
46-- 帽	night cap.
77-- 具	bedding.
80-- 食不安	have no peace of mind day and night.
-- 食難忘	constantly in one's mind.

3024₈

竅 〔Chiao〕 *n.* opening, hollow, hole, orifice, pore, point.

| 61-- 點 | point. |
| 67-- 眼 | intelligence. |

3025₀

褲 〔Ku〕 *n.* trousers, breeches, pantaloons, pants.

39--	襠	the seat of trousers.
44--	帶	waist-belt.
71--	腰	top of trousers.
77--	腿	legs of trousers.

3026₁

宿 〔Su〕 v. lodge, sojourn, stay at, keep, remain.

00--	疾	inveterate disease.
24--	仇	feud, old grudge.
27--	將	old mustache, veteran.
--	怨	old grievance.
71--	願	long-cherished desire.
80--	舍	dormitory, lodging house.
--	命論	fatalism.
99--	營	camp.
--	營地	quartering area.

寤 〔Wu〕 v. awake.

3027₂

窟 〔Ku〕 n. hole, opening, den, cavity, cave, cavern.

30--	室	underground chamber, cellar.
--	窿	hole, opening.
--	穴	hole, opening.

3027₇

戶 〔Hu〕 n. gate, door, family.

00--	主	head of a house.
23--	外	open air, outdoor.
--	外廣告	outdoor advertising.
--	外運動	outdoor sport.
60--	口	population.
--	口調查	census.
--	口登記	household registration.
88--	籍	census registration, domicile.

3029₄

寐 〔Mei〕 v. sleep, doze, drowse, slumber.

3030₁

進 〔Chin〕 n. advance, progress, promotion, entrance, entry, v. advance, proceed, enter, offer, recommend, introduce.

00--	度	rate of progress.
--	度表	progress chart, progress sheet, (report).
10--	一步	further, go a step further.
--	貢	send tribute.
11--	項	income.
17--	取	advance.
--	取心	spirit of enterprise, aggressiveness.
18--	攻	invade, attack, assault.
--	攻運輸	attack transport.
20--	香	worship.
--	香客	palmer, pilgrim.
21--	行	proceed, advance, march, progress, carry on, get on.
--	行曲	marching song.
--	步	n. progress, improvement, advance, v. improve, progress, advance, get along, get ahead, gain ground.
--	步黨	Progressive Party.
--	步性	progressiveness.
22--	出口	imports and exports.
--	出口商	import and export merchant.
--	出口稅	import and export dutiess.
--	出口銀行	export and import bank.
--	剿	advance and exterminate.
24--	化	n. evolution, v. evolve, develop.
--	化論	theory of evolution.
--	化論者	evolutionist.
--	貨	purchase, stock with goods.
--	貨過多	overstock.
--	貨成本	purchase cost.
26--	程	progress.
37--	退	advance or draw back, movement.
--	退兩難	dilemma, between a rock and a hard place.
--	退維谷	be in the cart.
--	軍	march troops to war.
--	軍號	clarion call for advance.
47--	款	income, revenue.
--	犯	n. invasion, v. invade.
60--	口	importation.
--	口商	importer, import merchant.
--	口許可	licensing of import.

-- 口價格	import price.
-- 口經紀人	import broker.
-- 口貨	imports, import commodities.
-- 口稅	import duties (tax, levy).
-- 口港	import port.
-- 口運費	inward freight.
-- 口量	volume of imports.
-- 口貿易	import trade.
72-- 兵	advance of troops.
77-- 展	progress, advancement.
78-- 膳	dine.
80-- 入	enter.
88-- 等	promotion of ranks.

3030₂

適〔Shih〕 *v.* suit, hit off, go to, reach, *adj.* comfortable, agreeable, *adv.* just, now, suddenly.

00-- 度	moderately, within measure.
-- 應	*n.* adjustment, adaptation, *v.* adjust, fit, arrange.
-- 應性	adaptability.
-- 意	in accordance with one's wishes, comfortable.
08-- 於	good for.
10-- 可而止	do not overdo a thing, play it just right, enough is enough.
24-- 值其時	happen at the right time, favorable time.
26-- 得其反	just on the contrary.
28-- 齡	be of age.
30-- 宜	*v.* fit, agree, suit, *adj.* suitable, agreeable.
37-- 逢	it so happens that, accidentally.
-- 逢其會	come just at the right time.
40-- 才	just now.
44-- 者生存	survival of the fittest.
60-- 口	palatable.
64-- 時	opportune , timely, seasonable.
77-- 用	*v.* apply, answer, hold true for, *adj.* applicable.
-- 用範圍	scope of application.
80-- 合	*n.* accommodation, fitness, adaptation, *v.* suit, meet, fit, befit, accommodate, *adj.* suitable.
-- 合用處	just what one needs.
90-- 當	appropriate, proper, well, suitable.

3030₃

迹〔Chi〕 *n.* footmark, trace, track, clue, *v.* trace, follow.

遮〔Che〕 *v.* cover, hide, screen, shade, obstruct.

04-- 護	protect, shade, shelter.
16-- 醜	hide one's shame.
20-- 住	cover, shade, shut.
44-- 蓋	cover, cloak, keep secret.
-- 蔽	screen, shade.
-- 藏	conceal, hide.
54-- 掩	conceal.
59-- 擋	parry, impede, block.
64-- 瞞	conceal.
76-- 陽	parasol, sunshade.
-- 陽篷	shade, sunshade.
80-- 羞	cover up one's shame, hide one's shame.
-- 羞布	mask, fig leaf.
88-- 飾	disguise.

寒〔Han〕 *adj.* cold, chilly, frigid, shivering, trembling, poor.

00-- 衣	winter clothes.
10-- 天	cold weather.
-- 不可支	unbearably cold.
27-- 假	winter vacation.
30-- 流	cold current, cold wave.
33-- 心	frightened, afraid, heart-breaking.
38-- 冷	cold, chill.
44-- 熱	fever, cold and fever.
-- 帶	frigid zones.
60-- 暑	cold and heat.
-- 暑表	thermometer.
77-- 風	chill wind.
80-- 氣	coldness.

3030₄

避〔Pi〕 *v.* avoid, evade, free from, keep away.

00-- 讓　give way to.
10-- 雷針　lightning rod, lightning conductor.
-- 不見面　avoid meeting someone.
17-- 孕　avoid conception, contraception.
25-- 債　avoid the creditor.
27-- 免　avoid, get off, get clear off.
-- 免赴會　give the party a miss.
28-- 稅　evade payment of duty, tax avoidance, tax shelter.
40-- 難　seek refuge, avoid trouble.
-- 難港　refuge harbor.
-- 難權　right of asylum.
-- 難所　asylum.
48-- 嫌　avoid suspicion.
60-- 暑　avoid the heat.
-- 暑地　summer resort.
-- 罪　avoid punishment.
63-- 戰　refuse battle.
71-- 匿　abscond.
77-- 風港　port of refuge.
-- 開　avoid, evade, hand off.
90-- 光　keep in a dark place.

3030₆

這 〔**Che**〕 adj. this, adv. here, now.
00-- 裏　here, in this place.
-- 麼　thus, in this way.
-- 麼一來　in this way, as a result.
21-- 些　these.
22-- 種　such a, this kind of.
25-- 件事　this affair, this matter.
26-- 個　this.
36-- 邊　this side, on this side, here.
44-- 地　here.
48-- 樣　in this way.
60-- 回　this time.
64-- 時　now, at the present time.
80-- 人　this man.

3030₇

之 〔**Chih**〕 v. go to, pron. he, she, it, this, that, prep. of, for.
23-- 外　besides, in addition.

3032₇

寫 〔**Hsieh**〕 v. write, compose, copy, draw, sketch.
10-- 下　write down, take down.
20-- 信　write a letter.
25-- 生　paint natural objects.
-- 作　n. writing, v. write, compose.
30-- 字　write, write character.
-- 字桌　desk.
-- 字紙　writing paper.
-- 字間　office.
-- 實　realistic.
-- 實主義　realism.
-- 實主義者　realist.
-- 實體　realistic style.
40-- 真術　photography.
-- 真器　camera.
67-- 明　write plainly.
-- 照　portrayal, description.
84-- 錯　erratum, slip of the pen.

騫 〔**Chien**〕 v. fly, adj. injured, broken.

3033₁

窯 〔**Yau**〕 n. kiln, cave.
17-- 子　brothel, prostitute.
37-- 洞　cave-dwelling, cave-residence.

3033₆

憲 〔**Hsien**〕 n. law, regulation, constitution.
00-- 章　constitutional provisions, charter.
18-- 政　constitutional government.
-- 政時期　period of Constitutional Government.
34-- 法　constitution.
-- 法起草委員會　committee to draft a constitution.
72-- 兵　gendarme, military police.
-- 兵學校　constabulary college.

3034₂

守 〔**Shou**〕 v. keep, maintain, hold, protect, guard, defend, watch, supervise, attend to.
00-- 夜　watch, keep watch at night.
04-- 護　protect, guard.
07-- 望　keep watch, look out.
17-- 已　self-control.

-- 已安分	be law-abiding, act properly according to one's status.
20-- 住	hold out, keep.
-- 信	keep one's word.
21-- 衛	watch, stand for, defend.
-- 貞	celibacy, singleness.
24-- 備隊	garrison.
27-- 約	keep one's word, keep faith, keep an appointment.
-- 候	wait for.
-- 紀律	uphold discipline.
33-- 祕密	keep secret.
34-- 法	*n.* law abiding, *v.* abide by the law, obey the law.
35-- 禮	keep one's feet.
44-- 舊	conservative, behind the time.
-- 舊派	old school.
-- 勢	defensive.
-- 其本分	stick to one's lot.
53-- 成不變	hold to existing custom.
60-- 口如瓶	tight-lipped.
63-- 戰	defensive war.
64-- 時	keep time.
-- 財奴	miser, screw, scrooge.
77-- 門員	goal-keeper, goal-tender.
88-- 節	chastity.
91-- 恆	conservation.

3040₁

宇〔**Yu**〕*n.* universe, *v.* cover, shelter.

30-- 宙	universe, cosmos.
-- 宙論	cosmology.
-- 宙飛行員	cosmonaut, astronaut, spaceman, taikonaut.
-- 宙飛船	spaceship.
-- 宙航空學	astronautics.
-- 宙線	cosmic rays.
-- 宙空間	cosmic space, outer space.
-- 宙觀	world outlook, world -view.

宰〔**Tsai**〕*n.* ruler, *v.* govern, rule.

32-- 割	cut up.
46-- 相	prime minister.
47-- 殺	slaughter, kill, butcher.

準〔**Chun**〕*n.* level, standard, criterion, scale, *v.* prepare, mark, would be, to be, *adj.* criterial, exact, true, right.

00-- 度	criterion.
10-- 死	civil death.
13-- 確	accurate, exact, correct, strict.
-- 確說明	explain in exact terms, definite explanation.
21-- 占人	quasi-possessor.
24-- 備	prepare, get ready, arrange, fit up.
-- 備齊全	everything is ready.
-- 備基金	reserve fund.
-- 備萬一	keep your powder dry.
-- 備時期	preparatory period.
-- 備金	emergency fund, reserve fund.
-- 備好	get ready, fix up.
27-- 繩	standard, marking line.
35-- 決賽	semi-final.
62-- 則	principle, rule, standard, guiding principle.
64-- 時	in time, on time, punctual, on schedule.

3040₄

安〔**An**〕*v.* tranquilize, pacify, place, settle, lay down, *adj.* still, quiet, calm, peaceful, comfortable, safe, contented, easy in mind.

00-- 康	peaceful and healthy.
05-- 靖	peace and quiet.
07-- 設	establish.
08-- 放	lay, put.
22-- 樂	comfortable, ease and happiness.
-- 樂度日	pass the days happily.
-- 樂椅	armchair, easy chair.
-- 穩	steady, secure, stable.
24-- 裝	fix, install.
-- 裝工程	installation works.
-- 裝地點	installation site.
-- 裝費	installation cost, cost of erection.
26-- 息	rest peacefully.
-- 息日	Sabbath day, Sunday.
27-- 危	safe or in danger.
28-- 份守己	keep one's duty and have self-control.
30-- 寧	peace, tranquility.

--家	support the family.
--定	at rest, tranquilly.
--定人心	quiet the public sentiment.
--適	n. feel at home, breathe freely, adj. comfortable.
33--心	breathe freely, put one's mind at rest.
37--逸	at ease, relaxed, easy.
44--枕	sound sleep.
--葬	bury.
51--排	n. adjustment, arrangement, v. compose, set, arrange, set in order.
--排面談	call for interview.
--排安當	arrange everything properly.
--頓	settle.
52--靜	n. repose, v. keep silence, adj. peaceful, quiet.
60--置	settle, fix, put off, place, plant.
62--睡	n. placid sleep, v. sleep peacefully .
67--眠藥	sleeping pills, sleeping draught.
74--慰	comfort, console, soothe, set at ease.
77--居	settle.
--居樂業	be well settled down and do one's work happily.
80--全	n. safety, assurance, adj. safe.
--全計劃	safety program.
--全理事會	Security Council.
--全行車	safe driving.
--全網	safety net.
--全帽	safety helmet.
--全抵達	safe arrival.
--全第一	safety first.
--全規則	safety rules.
--全界	zone of safety.
--全防火	fire safety.
--全用具	safety appliance.
--全管理	safety management, security management.
--全火柴	safety match.
--分	contend with one's lot, take

	things as theycome.
宴〔Yen〕	n. feast, banquet, v. entertain, feast.
05--請	treat, entertain.
22--樂	happiness.
30--客	banquet, give a party.
80--會	party, feast, banquet.
87--飲	feast, regale.
寠〔Chu〕	adj. sordid, poor, in want.
80--人	indigent man.
--貧	indigent.

3040₇

字〔Tzu〕	n. letter, character, word.
00--音	pronunciation.
--裏行間	between the lines.
11--碼	figure, character code.
20--傍	radical.
22--紙籠	wastebasket.
27--彙	vocabulary, glossary.
31--源	etymology, derivation.
41--帖	copybook.
44--幕	caption (in a movie), subtitle.
50--畫	stroke.
52--據	bill, written evidence.
55--典	dictionary.
60--跡	handwriting.
67--眼	term, expression, wording.
75--體	script, type.
77--母	letter.
80--首	prefix.
--義	meaning of a word.
91--類	part of speech.

3041₃

宛 見 3741₃

3041₇

究〔Chiu〕	n. consequence, conclusion, end, v. examine, investigate, search out, inquire, adv. after all, at last, in the end, finally.
00--竟	finally, at last, after all.
--辦	punish, investigate and deal with.
40--查	investigate, probe.
77--問	examine in court, inquire into.

3042₇

寓〔Yu〕*n.* residence, dwelling, lodging, *v.* lodge, live in, dwell in.

00-- 言	fable, parable, metaphor.
-- 意	moral of tale.
30-- 客	lodger.
72-- 所	lodging, dwelling, residence, abode.

3043₀

宏〔Hung〕*adj.* ample, wide, spacious, great, large, vast.

00-- 亮	sonorous.
-- 廣	widely.
11-- 麗	magnificent, grand, fine, spacious, rich.
24-- 壯	magnificent, splendid.
-- 偉	splendid, grand, magnificent.
34-- 遠	widespread, far-reaching.
40-- 大	vast, splendid, spacious, great.
46-- 觀經理學	macroeconomics.
71-- 願	ambition, great aspiration, great vow.

突〔Tu〕*n.* chimney, *v.* rush out, run against, offend, penetrate, *adv.* abruptly, suddenly, unexpectedly.

12-- 發	break forth.
14-- 破	breach, make a breaking-through.
-- 破口	breach, gap.
22-- 出	*v.* protrude, project, fly out, stick out, *adj.* outstanding, prominent.
-- 變	mutation, sudden change.
23-- 然	suddenly, abruptly, at a blow, all at once.
30-- 進	dash, rush, plunge.
47-- 起	protuberance.
57-- 擊	attack suddenly, make a clash, rush the enemy.
-- 擊手	shock worker, member of a shock brigade.
-- 擊檢查	make a search without prior notice.
-- 擊隊	shock brigade, storm troops.

60-- 圍	break through, break a siege.

3043₆

寞〔Mo〕*adj.* silent, solitary, still, lonesome, quiet.

3050₂

牢〔Lao〕*n.* jail, prison, pen, stable, cage, *adj.* strong, firm, secure.

07-- 記	bear in mind, commit to memory, learn by heart, get by heart, keep firmly in mind.
10-- 不可破	indestructible.
24-- 靠	reliable, secure.
43-- 獄	jail, prison, black flower of civilized society.
47-- 犯	prison.
60-- 固	strong, firm, durable.
77-- 騷	*n.* grievance, *adj.* complaint.
88-- 籠	cage, prison.

3051₆

窺〔Kuei〕*v.* watch, spy, peep, pry, watch in secret.

20-- 看	watch, peep.
30-- 察	pry into, observe.
32-- 測	observe in secret, spy out.
36-- 視	look into, peep at.
57-- 探	spy, pry, detect.

3055₈

穽〔Chin〕*n.* pitfall, snare, pit.

3060₁

窖〔Chiao〕*n.* cellar, cavern, pit, vault.

44-- 藏	store up in a cellar.

害〔Hai〕*n.* harm, injury, evil, danger, calamity, *v.* injure, hurt, damage, harm, wound, *adj.* injurious, harmful.

00-- 病	suffer from sickness, get ill.
10-- 死	murder.
17-- 己	ruin oneself.
18-- 群之馬	the black sheep of a flock.
21-- 處	evil, injury, harm, disadvantage.
27-- 鳥	pernicious bird, pest bird.
28-- 傷	hurt, injure, wound.
47-- 殺	kill.

50-- 蟲 | insect vermin, pest insect.
60-- 國殃民 | do harm to the country and the people.
80-- 人 | ruin a person, cook one's goose, do one harm.
-- 羞 | bashful, shy.
-- 羞面紅 | blush because of bashfulness.
-- 命 | murder, take a life.
-- 命謀財 | take someone's life in order to acquire his wealth.
94-- 怕 | v. fear, be afraid of, adj. frightened, terrified.

3060₂

窗 〔**Chuang**〕 n. window, light, shutter, skylight.

23-- 台 | elbowboard, windowsill.
30-- 帘 | window curtain, window blind.
-- 戶 | window.
-- 扉 | casement.
41-- 框 | sash.
-- 板 | window shutter.
88-- 簾 | curtain.

3060₄

客 〔**Ko**〕 n. guest, visitor, stranger, customer.

00-- 廳 | parlor, reception room, drawing room.
-- 商 | traveling merchant.
-- 店 | inn, hotel, lodging house.
24-- 貨船 | cargo and passenger ship, mixed boat.
28-- 艙 | the cabin of a plane or a ship.
30-- 室 | salon, drawing room.
34-- 滿 | full house.
37-- 運 | passenger service.
40-- 套 | conventional greetings.
42-- 機 | passenger plane.
43-- 棧 | hotel, inn, rest-house.
46-- 觀 | objective.
-- 觀主義 | objectivism.
-- 觀存在 | objective reality.
-- 觀規則 | objective law.
50-- 串 | amateur player.

-- 車 | passenger train or bus.
58-- 輪 | passenger ship.
75-- 體 | object.
80-- 人 | guest, visitor.
氣 | polite, courteous, formal.
90-- 堂=客室

3060₅

宙 〔**Chou**〕 n. universe, all ages, eternity.

3060₆

宮 〔**Kung**〕 n. palace, temple, mansion, castration.

00-- 主 | princess.
12-- 刑 | castration.
-- 廷 | royal court.
-- 延政變 | palace coup.
30-- 室 | mansion.
40-- 女 | maids-of-honor, court lady.
77-- 殿 | palace.
92-- 燈 | palace lantern.

富 〔**Fu**〕 adj. rich, wealthy, abundant.

00-- 豪 | great haves.
11-- 麗 | splendid, luxurious.
-- 麗堂皇 | beautiful and majestic.
13-- 強 | rich and powerful, prosperous and strong.
30-- 家子弟 | sons of rich families.
31-- 源 | resources of wealth.
38-- 裕 | be well off, be well-to-do, wealthy.
40-- 有 | rich, in abundance.
50-- 貴 | rich and noble.
-- 貴人家 | rich and political influential family.
-- 貴榮華 | wealth and worldly glory.
55-- 農 | rich peasant.
60-- 國 | rich country.
-- 國強兵 | make the country rich and strong.
-- 甲天下 | the richest in the world.
80-- 人 | rich man, capitalist.
-- 翁 | millionaire, rich man, billionaire.
84-- 饒 | opulent, rich.

3060₇

窮 〔**Chiung**〕 n. poverty, v. harass, distress, trouble, *adj.* distressed, straitened, persecuted, afflicted, harassed.

27-- 急	in the utmost need.
30-- 窮	misery, poor.
36-- 迫	distressed, harassed, embarrassed.
40-- 境	in straitened circumstances.
60-- 困	miserably poor.
71-- 辱	insulted.

3060₈
容〔Jung〕*n.* countenance, figure, manner, *v.* contain, hold, tolerate, permit.

08-- 許	*n.* permission, allowance, *v.* permit, let, allow, admit.
17-- 忍	endure, tolerate, bear.
24-- 納	accept, hold, embrace, take in, admit.
25-- 積	volume, capacity, cubic content.
27-- 貌	countenance, feature, face, look, expression, manner.
46-- 恕	pardon, forgive.
50-- 接嘉賓	entertain honorable guest.
-- 表非凡	uncommon in looks and manners.
60-- 量	capacity, volume.
-- 易	easy, at ease.
-- 易解決	easy to settle.
66-- 器	receptacle, container.
72-- 隱過失	tolerate and conceal faults.

3060₉
審〔Shen〕*n.* trial, *v.* examine, discriminate, discern, try, judge, know, be cautious.

00-- 度	deliberate upon, ponder.
04-- 計	audit.
-- 計主任	auditor in charge.
-- 計處	auditing department.
-- 計員	auditor.
07-- 訊	*n.* inquest, *v.* interrogate, try.
08-- 議	deliberate.
16-- 理	try, hear.
22-- 斷	sentence.
30-- 定	authorize, examine and approve.

-- 察	investigate.
-- 案	trial.
40-- 查	inspect, review, examine, go over, investigate.
-- 查者	investigator.
-- 核	examine and make a decision.
48-- 幹	examine the personal records of cadres.
77-- 問	try, examine.
-- 閱	examine, check.
80-- 美觀念	esthetic sense or notion.
92-- 判	judge, try, bring to trial.
-- 判廳	court of justice.
-- 判員	judge.
-- 判長	chief judge.
94-- 慎	deliberation.

3062₁
寄〔Chi〕*v.* send, transmit, remit, deposit, post.

00-- 交	send by post.
01-- 語	send word.
02-- 託	commission, entrust, commit in charge.
08-- 放	deposit.
12-- 發	send forth, mail, forward.
17-- 子	adopted son.
20-- 信	send a letter.
-- 售	consigned for sale, sale on consignment.
-- 售商品	sell goods on commission.
-- 售協議	consignment agreement.
-- 售人	consignor.
25-- 生	parasitic growth.
-- 生蟲	parasite.
30-- 宿	lodge, sojourn, board at a place.
-- 宿舍	dormitory, boarding house.
-- 宿學校	boarding school.
36-- 泊港	port of call.
40-- 存	in deposit.
-- 存行李處	left-luggage office, cloakroom, baggage room.
-- 存單據	depositary receipt.
48-- 樣品	send a sample.
-- 賣	commission sale.

--賣行	commission shop, second-hand shop.
52--托	entrust to the care of.
55--費	postage.
78--膳	board.
80--人籬下	depend on another person for support.
--父	adopted father.
--養	board-out, consign (a child) to someone's care.
83--錢	n. remittance, v. remit.
89--銷	consignment.
--銷收益	consignment profit.
--銷費用	consignment expenses.

3071₄

宅 〔Chai〕 n. house, dwelling, residence.

44--地	homestead.
80--舍	house.

它 〔Ta〕 pron. it.

26--自己	itself.
27--們	they, them.
--的	its.

3071₇

宦 〔Huan〕 n. officer, official, eunuch.

30--官	eunuch.

竄 〔Tsuan〕 v. escape, hide, run away, flee, expel, exile.

18--改	change, tamper with.
30--竊	steal, pilfer.
32--逃	sneak off, escape.
47--犯	invade.

竈 〔Tsao〕 n. cooking stove, fireside, oven.

3072₇

窈 〔Yao〕 adj. profound, deep, extensive, distant.

30--窕	modest and refined.

3073₂

良 〔Liang〕 adj. good, excellent, virtuous, gentle, fine.

21--能	instinct.
--師	mentor.
22--種	picked seeds, good strains.
--種繁育	seed-breeding.
27--久	for a very long time.
33--心	conscience.
--心發現	be stung by conscience.
--心有愧	have a guilty conscience.
40--友	good friend.
42--機勿失	don't let the good chance slip.
44--藥	good medicine.
47--好	fine, pretty, good.
71--辰美景	pleasant day coupled with a fine landscape.
77--民	good citizen, law-abiding people.
--朋益友	worthy friends.
80--善	respectable, virtuous, good virtue.
86--知	intuition, intuitive knowledge.
88--策	good device, good scheme.
95--性瘤	benign tumour.

寰 〔Huan〕 adj. vast, extensive.

13--球	the world.

3077₂

密 〔Mi〕 n. secret, adj. mysterious, thick, dense, tight, hidden, secret, intimate, friendly, adv. close together.

00--度	density.
--交	intimate friendship.
--言	secret, private talk.
01--語	whisper.
04--計	plot.
--謀	secret plot.
08--議起事	have a secret discussion on uprising.
09--談	talk with one in private, private talk.
10--函告知	inform one by means of confidential letters.
11--碼	cipher, secret code.
--碼通訊	communicate with code telegrams.
20--集	thick, dense, cluster together.
--集區	congested district.

-- 紋唱片	long-playing record.
25-- 使	emissary.
27-- 約	secret treaty, secret agreement, secret date.
30-- 室	private room.
40-- 布	cover.
-- 友	intimate friend.
-- 查	secret inquiry.
44-- 封	seal up, air-proof.
-- 植	densely-planted.
47-- 切	intimate, close.
50-- 事	private affair.
57-- 探	*n.* secret service, detectives, *v.* spy out.

3077₇

官〔**Kuan**〕*n.* officer, official, authorities, government.

00-- 立學校	governmental school.
-- 方	official, the authorities.
-- 方註冊	official register.
-- 方身份	official capacity.
-- 方統計	official statistics.
-- 方消息	official information.
-- 辦企業	government enterprise.
02-- 話	mandarin.
13-- 職	rank.
17-- 司	lawsuit.
21-- 銜	official title.
-- 能	organ, sense, physical faculty.
-- 價	official fixed price, official rate (price).
24-- 僚	fellow officials, bureaucrat.
-- 僚主義	bureaucratism.
-- 僚政治	bureaucracy.
-- 僚作風	officialism.
-- 僚資本	bureaucrat-capital.
30-- 定價格	official price.
44-- 地	state land.
46-- 場	official circles.
47-- 報	gazette.
48-- 樣文章	red tape, official formalities.
50-- 吏	officer.
55-- 費	at government expense.
-- 費學生	government supported student.
60-- 員	official.
72-- 兵	officers and soldiers.
80-- 氣	official airs.

3080₁

定〔**Ting**〕*v.* fix, settle, determine, decide, arrange, *adj.* tranquil, secure, fixed, firm, stable, steady, *adv.* really, absolutely, surely, certainly.

00-- 座	reserve seat, book seat.
-- 音鼓	timpani.
07-- 調子	set the tune.
08-- 論	conclusion.
16-- 理	theory, proposition.
20-- 稿	draft in final form, final draft.
21-- 價	*n.* valuation, listed price, *v.* settle the price, fix a price.
-- 價低	undercharge.
-- 價偏低	under-price.
-- 價貨目表	priced catalogue.
-- 價過高	overprice, overvalue.
-- 價表	pricing schedule.
22-- 製	made to order.
-- 製品	articles made to order.
24-- 貨	order goods.
-- 貨單	order bill, order form.
25-- 律	theory, canon, law.
27-- 約	covenant, contract.
-- 向	direction.
28-- 做	made-to-order, custom-made.
30-- 案	*n.* decision on a case, *v.* pass judgement.
31-- 額	quota, flat rate.
-- 額計酬	payment on the basis of fixed quotas.
-- 額收入	determinable income, fixed income.
-- 額津貼	flat rate allowance.
-- 額資本	given capital.
42-- 婚	engage, betroth.
43-- 式	formula.
47-- 期	periodically, at stated times.
-- 期交貨	deliver on term, time delivery, regular delivery.

-- 期交易	time bargain.	
-- 期班機	regular air service.	
-- 期航班	regular line vessel, regular liner, scheduled flight.	
-- 期航線	regular line, regular shipping lines.	
-- 期維修	routine maintenance.	
-- 期刊物	periodical.	
-- 期貸款	term loan, time loan, fixed loan.	
-- 期付款	periodic payment.	
-- 期收入	periodic income.	
-- 期存款	fixed deposits, time deposit, term deposit.	
-- 期支付	time payment.	
-- 期報表	periodic statement.	
-- 期檢修	period repair.	
-- 期檢查	periodic check-up (inspection, review), routine test.	
-- 期匯票	time draft.	
-- 期合同	fixed term contract.	
57-- 數	fatality.	
60-- 量	quantitative, ration, fixed quantity.	
-- 量試驗	quantitative test.	
-- 量配合	ration.	
-- 量供應	put on rations.	
-- 量分析	quantitative analysis.	
-- 罪	sentence, convict.	
-- 界說	define.	
62-- 則	regulation, principle.	
64-- 時炸彈	time bomb.	
65-- 購	book.	
-- 購貨品	goods on order.	
66-- 單	order for goods, order form.	
77-- 局	foregone conclusion, end to the matter.	
-- 居	settle down.	
80-- 金	earnest money, down payment.	
-- 義	definition.	
83-- 錢	bargain money, deposit.	
88-- 等級	class, rate.	
95-- 性	qualitative.	
-- 性分析	qualitative analysis.	
3080₂		

穴 〔 Hsueh 〕 n. cave, hole, cavity, opening, nest, den.

22-- 巢	nest, den.	
38-- 道	vital point or a nerve center in the body, tunnel.	
77-- 居	cave dwelling, live in the cave, troglodytism.	
-- 居人	troglodyte.	
3080₆		

賓 〔 Pin 〕 n. visitor, guest.

00-- 主	guest and host.	
20-- 位	predicate.	
30-- 客	guest, visitor.	
83-- 館	guest house, guesthouse.	

實 〔 Shih 〕 n. solidity, fruit, seed, fact, reality, v. fill, true, stuff, solid, hard, adj. real, true, actual, solid, hard, sincere.

02-- 話	truth.	
-- 話實說	tell the truth.	
-- 證論	positivism.	
08-- 施	n. implementation, v. enforce, implement, take effect, carry into execution, go into operation.	
-- 效	actual effect, practical results.	
10-- 不相瞞	to tell the truth.	
-- 不知情	really have no knowledge of the matter.	
16-- 現	n. realization, v. realize, fulfill, materialize, come true.	
-- 彈	live shell, live ammunition.	
-- 彈射擊	ball firing.	
-- 彈演習	target practice.	
17-- 習	exercise, practise.	
-- 習醫生	intern.	
21-- 行	put into action, carry out, practice, put into effect, give effect, put in force, carry out, execute, perform.	
-- 行家	realist, man of action.	
-- 行封鎖	enforce a blockade.	
-- 行制裁	impose sanction.	

-- 價	net cost, actual price.
22-- 例	example, instance, case, concrete example.
-- 利	utility, actual profit, net profit.
-- 利主義	utilitarianism.
24-- 值	actual worth.
27-- 物	object, physical goods.
32-- 業	industry.
-- 業計劃	plans for industrial development.
-- 業部	the Ministry of Industry.
-- 業部長	the minister of industry.
-- 業家	industrialist.
-- 業革命	industrial revolution.
-- 業界	industrial circle, business quarter.
-- 業巨頭	tycoon.
-- 業學校	industrial school.
33-- 心實意	sincerely.
37-- 深感謝	be truly grateful.
40-- 力	actual strength.
-- 在	n. reality, adj. real, true, net, adv. really, truly, exactly, verily, in fact, indeed.
-- 在論	realism.
-- 有其事	it is a fact.
-- 存	actual balance.
44-- 地	on the spot.
-- 地應用	practical application.
-- 權	actual power.
47-- 報實銷	report expenses honestly, be reimbursed for what one spends.
48-- 幹	work energetically.
50-- 事求是	work in a practical way, seek truth from facts.
58-- 數	real number.
63-- 踐	practice.
-- 踐性	practicality.
72-- 質	material, reality, essence.
-- 質上	virtually, in essence.
-- 質相同	substantially the same.
75-- 體	substance, entity.
77-- 用	n. utility, adj. practical, useful.

-- 用主義	pragmatism.
-- 際	n. reality, adv. practically, actually, as a matter of fact.
-- 際上	practically, actually.
-- 際經驗	practical experience.
78-- 驗	experiment.
-- 驗室	laboratory.
-- 驗的	experimental.
-- 驗農場	experimentation farm, pilot farm.
89-- 銷利潤	profit to net sales.
95-- 情	the fact.

賽 〔Sai〕 n. race, tournament, v. race, strive, compete, contest, rival, contend for.

13-- 球	ball game.
27-- 船	boat race.
37-- 過	surpass, excel.
67-- 跑	race.
71-- 馬	horse race.
-- 馬場	race course.
80-- 會	exhibition, display, carnival, procession.

寶 〔Pao〕 n. jewel, gem, adj. precious, valuable, honorable, noble.

00-- 庫	treasury, treasure house.
10-- 石	gem, jewel, precious stone.
44-- 塔	pagoda.
-- 藏	treasure house, treasury.
50-- 貴	precious, valuable.
-- 貴光陰	valuable time not to be wasted.
60-- 貝	n. jewel, treasure, adj. costly, precious, valuable.

3090₁

宗 〔Tsung〕 n. ancestors, family, clan, kindred, sort.

00-- 廟	ancestral temple.
08-- 族	clan, family, kindred.
-- 族觀念	ancestral idea.
-- 譜	pedigree, lineage record.
21-- 旨	purpose, aim, principle, objective.
32-- 派	sect, faction, clique.
-- 派主義	sectarianism.
34-- 法	social rules within a clan.

37--	祠	ancestral temple.
48--	教	religion.
--	教改革	reformation, religious reform.
--	教自由	religious freedom.
--	教法典	canon law.
--	教革命	religious revolution.
--	教學	theology, science of religion.
71--	原	origin, source.

察 〔 **Cha** 〕 *v.* examine, inspect, observe, inquire into.

20--	看	examine, look into, survey.
30--	究	investigate.
77--	問	enquire.

3090₄

案 〔 **An** 〕 *n.* table, desk, case, record, register, *v.* scrutinize, examine, investigate, observe.

00--	訪	detect, investigate.
17--	子	law suit.
20--	看	inspect.
22--	例	case.
--	例法	case law.
25--	件	case.
--	件繁多	cases are numerous.
77--	覺	find, discover.
90--	卷	archive, records, files.
95--	情	details of a case.
--	情複雜	case is complicated.
--	情大白	riddle of a puzzling case has been completely unraveled.

宋 〔 **Sung** 〕 *n.* the Sung dynasty.

寨 〔 **Chai** 〕 *n.* stockade, bulwark, palisade.

窠 〔 **Ko** 〕 *n.* nest, den, hole.

3090₆

寮 〔 **Liao** 〕 *n.* hut, small house, cottage.

3092₇

竊 〔 **Chieh** 〕 *v.* steal, pilfer, usurp.

14--	聽	overhear, eavesdrop.
--	聽器	bug, tapping device.
17--	取	steal, usurp.
20--	位	usurp the throne.

--	看	steal a glance at.
32--	逃	escape.
37--	盜	burglar, theft, burglary.
--	盜罪	larceny.
51--	據	occupy illegally.
63--	賊	thief, burglar.
88--	笑	laugh in one's sleeves, laugh in secret.

3094₇

寂 〔 **Chi** 〕 *adj.* silent, solitary, still, lonesome.

23--	然無聲	quiet and noiseless.
30--	寞	solitude, lonesome.
--	寥	silence, lonely, deserted.
33--	滅	death of a Buddhist high monk or nun.
52--	靜	silent, quiet.

3111₀

江 〔 **Chiang** 〕 *n.* river, water.

10--	西	Kiangsi Province.
12--	水	river water.
22--	山	the country, territory.
32--	灣	estuary.
33--	心	the middle of a river.
36--	邊	riverside, water-front, river bank.
37--	湖	rivers and lakes, the world.
58--	輪	river steamer.
44--	蘇	Kiangsu Province.

3111₁

沅 〔 **Yuan** 〕 *n.* the Yuan river.

涇 〔 **Ching** 〕 *n.* the Ching river, *adj.* flowing.

瀝 〔 **Li** 〕 *n.* remaining drops of liquids, *v.* drop, trickle, strain liquids.

50--	青	asphalt, pitch.
--	青紙	tar paper.
--	青鈾礦	pitchblende.

滙 〔 **Hui** 〕 *n.* whirling water, *v.* remit money.

10--	票	draft, bill of exchange.
47--	款	*n.* remittance, draft, *v.* remit.
55--	費	remittance fee.

灑 〔 **Sa** 〕 *v.* sprinkle.

12--	水	sprinkle water.
--	水車	watering-cart, sprinkler.
57--	掃	sprinkle and sweep.

3111_4

汪 〔Wang〕 adj. vast and deep.

38--	洋	wide ocean, vast ocean, open sea.

涯 〔Yia〕 n. bank, limit, shore, water front, water line, margin of a river.

湮 〔Yian〕 v. sink, fall, soak, bury, block.

38--	沒	be drowned, be sunk, be buried.

溉 〔Kai〕 v. irrigate, water, wash.

溼 〔Shih〕 adj. wet, damp, moist, low-lying.

00--	度	humidity.
--	度表	hydrometer.
32--	透	wet through.
44--	地	wet ground.

3111_6

漚 〔Ou〕 v. soak.

77--	肥	make compost.

3111_7

瀘 〔Lu〕 n. the Lu river.

3112_0

汀 〔Ting〕 n. beach, shore, narrow strip of land.

河 〔Ho〕 n. river, stream.

00--	底	river bed.
22--	岸	bank, riverside.
--	山	territory of a country.
30--	流	stream, flow, water way.
31--	源	source.
36--	邊	riverside.
37--	運	river transport.
38--	道	course, waterway.
46--	堤	dyke, bank.
60--	口	estuary.
--	口港	estuary port.
67--	路運輸	inland water transportation.
71--	馬	hippopotamus.
--	豚	globefish.
80--	岔	branches of a river.

3112_1

涉 〔She〕 v. ford, wade, pass through, concern, intervene.

12--	水	wade across.
17--	及	concern, refer to.
--	及細微	enter into details.
--	及全體	over the length and breadth of something.
44--	世未深	inexperienced in the world.

3112_7

污 〔Wu〕 v. stain, insult, defile, slander, adj. dirty, foul, filthy, impure, unclean, muddy, corrupt, depraved.

12--	水	dirty water, sewage, water borne wastes.
--	水處理	sewage disposal, sewage treatment.
--	水管	sewer.
21--	穢	dirty, foul, filthy, unclean.
27--	名	bad name.
--	物	filth, dirt.
34--	瀆	abuse, profane.
--	染	pollution, contamination.
36--	濁	thick, muddy, dirty, filthy.
37--	泥	muddy.
44--	蔑	smear, slander, malign.
56--	損	v. defile, slander, adj. stained.
61--	點	stain, spot, blot, taint.
71--	辱	defile, insult, defame, stain.

馮 〔Feng〕 n. Feng (a family name) v. gallop.

濡 〔Ju〕 v. soak in, adj. fresh, moist, damp.

34--	滯	detained.
--	染	be influenced.
37--	溺	immersed.

瀰 〔Mi〕 adj. full, overflowing.

36--	漫戰	war in the fourth dimension.

3113_2

涿 〔Cho〕 n. the Cho river.

漲 〔Chang〕 n. inundation, v. overflow, expand, rise.

12--	水	swell, rise.
14--	破	burst through expansion.

21-- 價 advance, increase, advance in price, market up, rise in price.
23-- 縮 elasticity.
37-- 潮 flowing tide, flood-tide.
38-- 溢 overflow, inundate.
40-- 大 extend, enlarge, swell.
44-- 落 fluctuation.
65-- 跌 highs and lows.
77-- 風 bullish tone, upward trend of price.

3113_6

瀘 〔Lu〕 v. filter, purify, cleanse, strain.
12-- 水池 filter bed.
22-- 紙 filter.
37-- 過 filter, percolate.
66-- 器 strainer, percolator.
90-- 光鏡 filter (in a camera).

3114_0

汙＝污

汗 〔Han〕 n. sweat, perspiration.
30-- 滴 beads of sweat.
-- 流滿面 perspire all over one's face.
-- 褲 drawers.
32-- 衫 sweater, underwear.
46-- 如雨下 sweat profusely.

3114_3

溽 〔Ju〕 n. sultry.

3114_6

淖 〔Nao〕 n. mud, mire, slush.
潭 〔Tan〕 n. deep pool, big pond.

3116_0

沾 〔Chan〕 v. moisten, tinge, wet.
00-- 病 catch a disease.
31-- 污 stain, smear.
34-- 染 be affected by, stain, corrupt.
-- 染惡習 slide into bad habits.
90-- 光 gain some advantage from another.

洒 〔Sa〕 v. sprinkle, dash, scatter.
12-- 水 sprinkle water.
44-- 花 sprinkle water on flowers.
57-- 掃 mop, sprinkle and sweep.

滷 〔Lu〕 n. brine, rock-salt.
34-- 汁 brine.

酒 〔Chiu〕 n. wine, liquor, alcoholic drink.
00-- 店 public house, saloon, tavern.
-- 癮 addiction to alcohol.
-- 席 feast, banquet.
10-- 醉 drunken, intoxicated.
24-- 徒 drunkard, intemperate man.
27-- 色 woman and wine.
-- 色之徒 debauchee.
28-- 稅 alcohol tax.
30-- 家 public house.
-- 宴 banquet.
-- 窩 dimples.
40-- 友 bottle companion.
-- 肉朋友 friends only for wining and dining together, not in one's need.
41-- 杯 wine cup, goblet, tumbler.
50-- 盅 wine cup.
51-- 排間 bar.
60-- 量 ability to drink, capacity for drinking.
67-- 吧 bar, pub.
83-- 錢 tip.
-- 館 restaurant, tavern.
86-- 罎 flagon.
95-- 精 alcohol.
-- 精廠 alcohol plant.

3116_1

潛 〔Chien〕 n. hide, swim, ford, pass across.
00-- 意識 subconscious mind.
12-- 水 dive.
-- 水員 diver.
21-- 行軍 secret march.
22-- 艇 submarine.
23-- 伏 conceal, hide.
-- 伏期 period of incubation, latent period.
32-- 逃 elope, abscond.
40-- 力 potential, energy, latent power.

-- 在	latent, potential.	
44-- 熱	latent heat.	
-- 勢力	potentiality.	
80-- 入	enter secretly, sneak into, creep in.	

3117₂

涵〔**Han**〕v. submerge, contain, bear, treat leniently, *adj.* capacious, vast.

44-- 蓄	reserved.
80-- 養	cherish, be patient.
-- 養功夫	deep culture, especially shown in restraint, forbearance.

3118₆

瀕〔**Pin**〕*n.* beach, bank.

12-- 死	at the last gasp.
27-- 危之際	be on the verge of danger.
78-- 臨	approach, close to, near.

3119₁

漂〔**Piao**〕v. float, drift, bleach, blanch, *adj.* beautiful, pretty, bright, smart, brilliant.

00-- 亮	smart, pretty, beautiful.
26-- 白	bleach.
-- 白粉	chloride of lime, bleaching powder.
30-- 流	drift, float.
-- 流無定	drift about.
32-- 浮	*n.* floatage, *v.* float about.
36-- 泊	wander, stray, rove.
-- 泊者	wanderer, rover, vagrant.
38-- 洋過海	sail across an ocean.
40-- 布	bleach cloth.
44-- 蕩	adrift.

3119₄

溧〔**Li**〕*adj.* frigid, bleak.

3119₆

源〔**Yuan**〕*n.* source, spring, origin.

11-- 頭	source.
20-- 委	beginning of something, detail of something.
26-- 泉	spring, fountain, source.
30-- 流	source and history, fountainhead.

31-- 源不絕	continue without end.
-- 源本本	from beginning to end.

3121₀

祉〔**Chi**〕*n.* blessedness, happiness, joy.

3124₃

褥〔**Ju**〕*n.* cushion, mattress, mat, bedding.

17-- 子	mattress, cushion.
44-- 墊	mattress.
66-- 單	sheet.

3126₆

福〔**Fu**〕*n.* prosperity, felicity, happiness, good fortune, good luck.

00-- 音	gospel, evangel, good news.
15-- 建	Fukien Province.
22-- 利	welfare, material benefits, fringe benefit.
-- 利設施	welfare facilities.
-- 利效果	welfare effect.
-- 利制度	benefit system.
-- 利補貼	welfare allowances.
-- 利基金	welfare fund.
-- 利費	welfare expenses.
-- 利事業	welfare work, welfare projects.
32-- 州	Foochow.
40-- 壽	happiness and longevity.
60-- 星	felicitous star, luck star.
80-- 氣	felicity, good luck.

3128₆

禎〔**Cheng**〕*adj.* lucky, felicitous, auspicious.

顧〔**Ku**〕v. attend to, observe, take care, regard, care for, mind, look after, reflect on, look back, turn the head around and look.

00-- 主	customer, client, patron.
10-- 面子	care for one's face or reputation.
17-- 及	consider, regard, take into account.
-- 忌	fear, concern.
21-- 慮	consider, worry.

30-- 客	customer, shopper.	
-- 客滿意	customer satisfaction.	
-- 客服務台	customer service desk.	
-- 家	care for the home.	
40-- 大局	take the whole situation into consideration.	
77-- 問	adviser, counsellor.	
-- 問工程師	consultant engineer.	
-- 問公司	consultant firm.	
80-- 全大局	take overall interest into account.	
-- 念	consider, regard, allow for.	
99-- 憐	pity.	

3130₁

逕 〔Ching〕 *n.* path, passage, byway, *v.* reach, pass by, *adv.* directly.

21-- 行	directly, do directly.
43-- 赴	go directly towards.
67-- 路	path, course.

逛 〔Kuang〕 *v.* ramble, stroll, walk about.

10-- 一逛	take a stroll, take a walk.
21-- 街	stroll down the street.
40-- 來逛去	stroll aimlessly.

逗 〔Tou〕 *v.* stay, delay, tarry.

61-- 點	comma.
77-- 留	delay, stay, tarry.

遷 〔Chien〕 *v.* remove, move, shift, change, transpose.

03-- 就	make a compromise, accommodate, appease.
07-- 調費用	relocation cost.
12-- 延	delay, postpone, linger.
21-- 徙=遷移	
27-- 移	remove, immigrate, change one's quarter.
-- 移費	moving expenses.
77-- 居=遷移	

3130₂

邇 〔Erh〕 *adj.* near, close, lately, recently.

40-- 來	recently, lately, hitherto.

3130₃

逐 〔Chu〕 *v.* drive, expel, chase, pursue, compete, contest, follow, *adv.* one by one, in succession.

10-- 一	one by one.
21-- 步	step by step, bit by bit, by degree.
-- 步到位	phase in, phased implementation.
-- 步推廣	gradual popularization.
22-- 出	cast off, drive out, expel.
28-- 條	item by item, point by point.
30-- 字逐句	literally, word by word.
-- 戶推銷	house-to-house selling.
32-- 漸	gradually, by degrees, by inches, little by little, step by step.
60-- 日	day by day, daily.
-- 回	repulse, drive back.
77-- 層	in succession, layer by layer.
80-- 年	year by year.

遽 〔Chu〕 *n.* stage-coach, *v.* tremble. *adj.* hurried, agitated, urgently, scared, *adv.* suddenly, quickly.

3130₄

迂 〔Yu〕 *v.* distort, *adj.* winding, roundabout, impractical, unrealistic, *adj.* far, distant, wide.

00-- 腐	doltish, pedantic.
22-- 緩誤事	sluggishness causes trouble.
27-- 久	long time.
34-- 遠	far, wide, impractical, absurd.
37-- 迴	circuitous, roundabout.
44-- 執	obstinate.

迓 〔Ya〕 *v.* meet, greet, welcome.

返 〔Fan〕 *v.* return, go back, revert, come back.

10-- 工	remake, rework.
20-- 航	return to base, homeward voyage.
-- 航船	homebound vessel.
26-- 程	return journey.
27-- 租	leaseback, sale and leaseback.
30-- 家	return home.

44-- 老還童　　second youth, regain youth.
60-- 國　　　return to one's own country.
-- 回　　　return, go back, come back.
67-- 照　　　reflect.
89-- 銷　　　buy back.

3130_6

逼〔**Pi**〕*v.* compel, force, press upon, constrain, oblige.

10-- 不得已　be compelled against one's will, be forced to.
24-- 供　　　extort a confession.
25-- 使　　　force, compel.
-- 債　　　press for the payment of a debt.
30-- 良爲娼　force a good family girl into prostitution.
32-- 近　　　crowd on, draw near, approach.
36-- 迫　　　force, compel, oppress, press.
40-- 真　　　lifelike.
-- 索　　　extort.
44-- 勒　　　constrain, compel.
71-- 壓　　　oppress.
80-- 人　　　overawe.
-- 人太甚　be relentless, be merciless in forcing demands, push one too hard.

3133_2

憑〔**Ping**〕*n.* proof, evidence, diploma, *v.* lean on, trust to, rely on, depend on.

02-- 證　　　proof, evidence, certificate.
25-- 仗勢力　lean on one's influential power.
30-- 空　　　without proof, groundlessly.
-- 良心說　be fair.
44-- 藉　　　lie on, sit on, lean on, stand on.
-- 熱情　　be guided by enthusiasm.
-- 藉　　　by virtue of, resort to.
50-- 推測　　by guess.
51-- 據　　　evidence, proof, ground.
-- 據充足　the proof is sufficient.
66-- 單　　　bill, certificate, receipt.

3168_6

額〔**Er**〕*n.* forehead, front, brow, limited number.

23-- 外　　　*n.* excess, *adj.* exceptional, additional, extra.
-- 外工資　extra wage.
-- 外利潤　extra profit.
-- 外收入　additional income, surplus receipts.
-- 外津貼　extra allowance.
-- 外資金　additional finance.
-- 外費用　extra charge, additional expenses.
-- 外損失　extraneous loss.
-- 外投資　extra investment.
-- 外風險　extraneous risks.
-- 外股利　dividend extra.
-- 外開支　additional outlay, extra cost (expenses).
27-- 角　　　temples, corners of the forehead.
58-- 數　　　fixed number.
72-- 髮　　　forelock.

3190_4

渠〔**Chu**〕*n.* drain, gutter, ditch, *adj.* large, great.

24-- 魁　　　chief, leader.
38-- 道　　　drain, canal.

3200_0

州〔**Chou**〕*n.* state, province, region, country, prefecture.

71-- 長　　　governor.

3210_0

洲〔**Chou**〕*n.* continent, islet.

冽〔**Lieh**〕*n.* chill, cold air.

32-- 冽　　　chilly, bleak.

測〔**Tse**〕*v.* measure, survey, estimate, *adj.* sharp, pure, clear.

00-- 度　　　measure, estimate, calculate.
-- 度空間　measure space.
-- 度深淺　fathom.
-- 音器　　sound locator.

03--	試標準	test criteria.
04--	謊器	lie detector.
10--	雷器	mine detector.
27--	角器	goniometer.
28--	繪	draw a map, surveying and drawing, survey and map.
30--	定	determine by survey.
48--	檢程序	test（detect）routine.
52--	揆	infer, guess.
60--	量	measure, survey.
--	量記錄	record of measurement.
--	量員	surveyor.
--	量單位	measuring unit.
--	量局	survey office.
--	量學	surveying.
--	圓器	cyclometer.
71--	驗	test.
--	驗設備	test equipment.

淵 〔Yuan〕*n.* whirlpool, gulf, abyss, *adj.* deep.

31--	源	source.
43--	博	wide, broad, learned, extensive.

瀏 〔Liu〕*n.* clear water.

78--	覽	glance, pore over.

3211_2

洮 〔Tao〕*v.* wash.

3211_3

兆 〔Chao〕*n.* omen, sign, million, trillion.

11--	頭	omen, sign.
77--	周	megacycle.

3211_4

淫 〔Yin〕*n.* sexual desire, sexual misconduct, *v.* debauch, commit adultery, soak, *adj.* lewd, licentious, obscene, immoral, excessive.

00--	意	lewd idea.
17--	邪	immodesty, grossness, obscenity.
--	歌	licentious song.
21--	穢	obscene, dirty, indecent, indelicate.
22--	亂	*n.* debauchery, *adj.* lewd.
25--	佚	dissolution.
40--	女	wanton woman, harlot.
--	奔	elope.
44--	蕩	debauched, lecherous.
--	蕩無恥	licentious and shameless.
46--	猥	indecent, obscene.
47--	婦	lewd woman, adulteress, lady of easy virtue.
50--	夫	lewd man, adulterer.
--	夫淫婦	the lovers who are not legally married.
--	書	obscene books.
--	畫	pornography.
53--	威	brute force, excessive use of one's power.
87--	慾	debauchery, immorality, carnal desire, lust.

3211_8

澄 〔Cheng〕*v.* settle, purify, *adj.* clear, pure, transparent.

35--	清	*v.* clarify, purify, *adj.* clear, clean, pure.

3212_1

沂 〔Yi〕*n.* the Yi river.

浙 〔Che〕*v.* bent, scour rice.

31--	江	Chekiang Province.

淅 〔Hsi〕*n.* water for washing rice. *v.* wash rice.

31--	瀝	pattering of a river.

漸 〔Chien〕*v.* advance by degree, flow, penetrate, reach, *adv.* gradually, little by little, by degree, slowly.

00--	瘥	recover gradually, be on the mending hand.
22--	變	gradual change.
30--	進	advance gradually, progress step by step.
32--	漸	gradually, slowly, little by little, step by step, by degrees.
33--	減	tailing-off.
37--	次	gradually, step by step.
44--	老	advance in life.
48--	增	increase slowly.

3212_2

澎 〔Peng〕*n.* rushing of water, roaring

of waves, boom.

3212₇

湍 〔 Tuan 〕 *n.* rapid current.
30-- 流　　　rapid current.

灣 〔 Wan 〕 *n.* bay, gulf, cove, winding shore, *v.* anchor, moor.
55-- 曲　　　crooked, winding, curved.

3213₀

冰 〔 Bing 〕 *n.* ice.
00-- 庫　　　icehouse.
10-- 天雪地　frozen and snow-covered land.
　-- 雹　　　hailstones.
12-- 水　　　ice water.
13-- 球　　　ice hockey.
22-- 山　　　iceberg.
　-- 川　　　glacier.
23-- 袋　　　ice bag.
27-- 島　　　ice land .
31-- 河時代　glacial epoch, ice age.
34-- 淇淋　　ice cream.
35-- 凍　　　*n.* refrigeration, *v.* freeze.
38-- 冷　　　ice-cold.
39-- 消瓦解　dissolve like ice.
40-- 柱　　　icicle.
44-- 鞋　　　skate.
45-- 棒　　　frozen sucker, popsicle.
47-- 期　　　ice period.
61-- 點　　　freezing point.
88-- 箱　　　refrigeration, icebox.
90-- 糖　　　sugar-candy, crystallized sugar, rock candy.

3213₂

派 〔 Pai 〕 *n.* branch, sect, clan, tribe, *v.* distribute, appoint, send, depute.
22-- 出　　　detach.
　-- 出所　　police substation.
25-- 生　　　derivation.
　-- 生詞　　derivative word.
30-- 定　　　assign.
35-- 遣　　　send, dispatch, delegate.
62-- 別　　　factions, groups, sects, clan.
72-- 兵　　　dispatch troop.
　-- 兵遣將　dispatch troops and generals.

80-- 人　　　send a person.
　-- 差　　　appoint.
95-- 性　　　factionalism.

3213₃

添 〔 Tien 〕 *v.* add, increase, annex, replenish.
07-- 設　　　establish more.
10-- 丁　　　have a son.
　-- 丁發財　may you have an increase in your family and be prosperous.
27-- 多　　　increase.
　-- 多減少　increase or decrease.
31-- 福添壽　add to your happiness and longevity.
33-- 補　　　recruit, replenish.
　-- 補不足　add in order to make up a deficiency.
35-- 油加醋　play up, blow up (a story).
72-- 兵　　　re-enforce.

3213₄

沃 〔 Wo 〕 *v.* water, irrigate, drain, enrich, cleanse, *adj.* rich, fertile, fat.
40-- 土　　　rich soil, fertile land.

溪 〔 Chi 〕 *n.* brook, stream, ravine, creek.
12-- 水　　　brook water.
30-- 流　　　mountain stream.
80-- 谷　　　valley, dale.

3213₇

泛 〔 Fan 〕 *v.* float, drift, sail, *adj.* impractical, general.
00-- 言　　　vague talk, speak in general terms.
04-- 讀　　　read widely.
27-- 舟　　　row a boat.
38-- 濫　　　inundation.
　-- 游　　　wander about.
51-- 指　　　vague reference.
78-- 覽　　　read extensively.

3214₁

涎 〔 Yen 〕 *n.* saliva, slaver, spittle.
35-- 沫　　　saliva, spittle.
40-- 巾　　　pinafore.
76-- 腺　　　salivary gland.

3214₇

浮 〔**Fu**〕 v. float, drift, waft, exceed, overflow, adj. superficial, insubstantial, unreal.

00--	言	reckless talk, groundless talk.
04--	誇	exaggerate, vaunt, boast.
10--	面	external.
--	雲	cloud-drift, floating clouds.
22--	出	emerge.
--	佻	frivolous.
24--	動	v. float, adj. floating, mobility.
--	動碼頭	floating pier.
28--	船塢	floating dock .
31--	額	overplus.
32--	泛	swim.
--	冰	floe.
37--	沉	sink and swim, floating and sinking.
38--	溢	flood.
40--	力	buoyancy.
41--	標	buoy.
42--	橋	flying bridge, pontoon-bridge.
44--	華	vanity, pompousness.
--	萍	duckweed.
47--	起	float up, buoy up.
--	塢	floating dock.
--	報	give inflated figures in a report.
60--	吊	floating crane.
64--	財	movable property.
66--	躁	reckless, impatient, restless, fidgety.
70--	雕	relief.
72--	腫	dropsy, swollen, swelling.
77--	屠	pagoda.
88--	筒	buoy.

潑 〔**Po**〕 v. splash, spatter, spill, pour off water, adj. fierce, ferocious.

05--	辣	pungent, saucy.
12--	水	splash water.
33--	濺	dash, spatter.
38--	冷水	discourage, dishearten, throw cold water on.

47--	婦	termagant, shrew.

叢 〔**Tsung**〕 n. bushy place, copse, adj. crowd, thick, dense.

25--	生	overgrow.
44--	林	thick wood, jungle.
--	林戰	bush fighting, jungle warfare.
50--	書	series, collection of books.

3215₇

淨 〔**Chin**〕 adj. neat, pure, clean, undefiled, v. cleanse, purify, wash.

12--	水	pure water.
17--	盈餘	net surplus.
20--	重	net weight, actual weight.
21--	價	net price, net cost.
22--	利	net profit, net gain, net income.
24--	化	purification, purgation.
--	值	net worth, net value.
28--	收益	net earnings, net income, net yield.
31--	額	net amount.
56--	損失	net loss.
60--	量	net weight.
89--	銷售額	net sales.

3216₄

活 〔**Huo**〕 n. livelihood, living, v. live, survive, save, work, adj. living, lively, active, movable, running.

00--	該	serve one right.
04--	計	woman's work, job.
10--	下去	live on.
--	頁	loose-leaf.
--	頁地址簿	loose-leaf address book.
--	頁賬夾	loose-leaf binder.
12--	水	living water, running water.
24--	動	n. activity, operation, adj. active, movable.
--	動電影	motion picture.
--	動房屋	mobile home.
--	動力	energy, vitality.
--	動存款	active deposit, current deposit.
--	動財產	active assets.
--	動分子	activist.

-- 動餘地	room for activity.
-- 結	hitch, slip-knot.
25-- 生生	living, vivid.
30-- 塞	piston.
-- 字	type.
32-- 潑	*n.* activity, liveliness, life, *adj.* alive, bright, active, vivacious.
40-- 力	vitality, vigor.
-- 力論	vitalism.
44-- 著	be alive.
-- 葉的	loose-leaf.
46-- 埋	bury alive.
47-- 期存款	current deposit.
-- 報劇	living newspaper drama, poster drama.
56-- 捉	catch alive.
67-- 躍	active, lively.

3216_9
潘〔**Pan**〕*n.* Pan (a family name).

3217_0
汕〔**Shan**〕*n.* the Shan river, fishing.

11-- 頭	Swatow.

3217_7
滔〔**Tao**〕*n.* rushing water, flood, *v.* flow, overpass.

10-- 不絕	talk one's self out of breach.
-- 天大罪	flagrant crime, sin which is like foaming billows dashing to the skies--a great sin.
32-- 滔	rushing (water), fluent (speech).
-- 滔不絕	incessant talk.

3218_7
浜〔**Peng**〕*n.* ditch, creek.

3220_0
剜〔**Wan**〕*v.* scoop out, cut out, excavate, gouge.

22-- 出	excavate, gouge.
33-- 心待人	be absolutely sincere in treating people.
-- 補	cut out a part and patch up the other.

3221_4

衽〔**Jen**〕*n.* breast of a coat, mat.

3221_7
褫〔**Chih**〕*v.* deprive, take off, strip off.

40-- 奪	deprive of, strip off.
-- 奪公權	*n.* deprivation of civil rights,*v.* disfranchise.
78-- 脫	strip off, disrobe.

3222_1
祈〔**Chi**〕*v.* request, beg, offer a sacrifice, pray, supplicate, implore.

07-- 望	hope, expect.
25-- 使句	imperative sentence.
31-- 福	bless.
34-- 禱	pray, invoke, bless.
43-- 求	request, beg, beseech, implore, entreat.

3222_2
衫〔**Shan**〕*n.* skirt, coat, jacket.

3224_0
祗〔**Chih**〕*n.* respect, veneration, reverence, *v.* revere, venerate, *adv.* only, merely.

40-- 有	simply.

3230_1
逃〔**Tao**〕*v.* run away, escape, flee, abscond, evade, get away.

00-- 亡	flee, run off, cut one's luck.
-- 亡者	fugitive.
22-- 出重圍	break out from a heavy siege.
25-- 生	run for one's life.
-- 債	dodge a creditor, evade paying debts.
28-- 稅	tax evasion, evade payment of duty, tax cheating, tax dodging.
30-- 避	get away, escape, evade, shirk.
-- 避現實	bury one's head in the sand.
-- 避現實者	escapist.
-- 避責任	shirk one's responsibility.
32-- 遁	flee, escape.
37-- 逸	escape.

40-- 去　　　　　get away, flee.
-- 奔　　　　　elope, flight.
-- 走　　　　　escape,flee, run away, cut and run.
-- 難　　　　　flee for one's life.
44-- 荒　　　　　escape the famine.
47-- 犯　　　　　fugitive from justice.
48-- 散　　　　　flee and disperse.
71-- 匿無蹤　　skulk without a trace.
72-- 兵　　　　　deserter.
77-- 學　　　　　play truant, run away from school.
78-- 脫　　　　　break loose, make free, make one's escape.
80-- 命=逃生

遞〔**Ti**〕*v.* transmit, send, exchange, give, hand, present.
00-- 稟　　　　　petition.
-- 交　　　　　present to forward.
10-- 更　　　　　exchange.
12-- 延收益　　deferred income.
20-- 信　　　　　deliver a letter.
27-- 解出境　　escort someone to leave the country, expel someone, deport.
33-- 減　　　　　continuously decreasing, decrease by degrees.
-- 補　　　　　vacancies in the proper order.
38-- 送　　　　　deliver.
-- 送公文　　send official documents.
48-- 增　　　　　continuously increasing, progressive increase.

3230₂

近〔**Chin**〕*v.* draw near, approach, *adj.* near, close to, *adv.* nearby, recently, lately, soon, at the door.
06-- 親　　　　　near relatives.
07-- 郊　　　　　suburb, purlieu.
20-- 乎　　　　　approximately, nearly, almost.
23-- 代　　　　　modern.
28-- 似　　　　　similar, approximate, resembling, close, near.
36-- 視　　　　　short-sighted, near-sighted.
38-- 海　　　　　near the sea.

-- 海地區　　offshore areas.
40-- 在眼前　　right under one's nose.
-- 來　　　　　recently, lately.
44-- 地　　　　　vicinity.
60-- 日　　　　　recently, lately, these days.
-- 因　　　　　proximate cause.
61-- 距離　　　short range.
63-- 戰　　　　　close-range fighting.
80-- 年　　　　　in recent years.
95-- 情近理　　acceptable to reason.
97-- 鄰　　　　　neighborhood.

逝〔**Shih**〕*v.* die, part, go, pass away.
44-- 世　　　　　die, pass away.

透〔**Tou**〕*v.* pass through, penetrate, comprehend, understand, *adj.* clear, thoroughly, completely.
10-- 露　　　　　reveal, disclose.
12-- 水　　　　　water percolation.
28-- 徹　　　　　thoroughly, to the back bone.
36-- 視　　　　　*n.* perspective, *v.* have an X-ray taken, see through.
37-- 過　　　　　penetrate, permeate, through, by means of.
40-- 支　　　　　overdraw, overdraft.
-- 支額　　　overdraft.
-- 支薪水　　anticipate one's pay.
44-- 熱　　　　　pervious to heat.
67-- 明　　　　　transparent.
-- 明度　　　transparency.
-- 明體　　　transparent body.
77-- 風　　　　　ventilate.
80-- 入　　　　　penetrate.
-- 鏡　　　　　lenses.
-- 氣　　　　　let the air in or out, ventilate.

遄〔**Chuan**〕*v.* come and go rapidly.

3230₃

巡〔**Hsun**〕*v.* cruise, patrol.
00-- 夜　　　　　night watchman.
10-- 丁　　　　　watchman.
21-- 行　　　　　ambulation.
30-- 官　　　　　police officer.
-- 察　　　　　patrol.
36-- 邏　　　　　patrol.

-- 邏隊	patrol, patrol team.	
-- 視	make the rounds, tour of inspection.	
37-- 迴	circulation.	
-- 迴演出	tour of performances.	
-- 迴法院	court of assize, circuit court.	
38-- 洋艦	cruiser.	
-- 游	tour.	
40-- 查	inspect, reconnoiter.	
48-- 警	policeman, constable.	
53-- 捕=巡警		
-- 捕房	police station.	
69-- 哨	sentry-go.	

3230₆
遁 〔Tun〕 v. run away, retire, hide away, conceal, vanish, avoid.

20-- 辭	evasive words, excuse.
40-- 去	run away.

3230₉
遜 〔Hsun〕 v. give up, accord with, withdraw, escape, adj. humble, modest.

00-- 讓	cede, yield.
20-- 位	abdicate.
-- 位與人	abdicate the crown in someone's favor.

3260₀
割 〔Ko〕 v. cut, wound, injure, divide, deduct.

00-- 讓	n. cession, v. cede.
12-- 裂	separate, isolate.
20-- 愛	cut off affection, part with a beloved object.
-- 禾	reap.
-- 禾者	reaper.
21-- 價	reduce the price.
22-- 斷	sever, cut apart.
-- 稻	cut rice.
28-- 傷	cut, wound.
40-- 麥	cut wheat.
44-- 地	partition, cede territory.
-- 草	mow, cut grass.
-- 草機	mower, mowing machine.
47-- 切線	secant line.
51-- 據	occupy and rule a region of a nation.

77-- 開	rip open, cut asunder.
-- 與	cede to.

3290₄
業 〔Yeh〕 n. employment, profession, business, occupation, calling, industry, property, estate, patrimony.

00-- 主	proprietor, owner, property owner.
-- 主權利	rights of the owner of property.
17-- 務	vocation, trade, service, occupation, profession.
-- 務主任	managing director.
-- 務主管	operating officer.
-- 務往來	business transaction, business contact.
-- 務經理	office manager.
-- 務行爲	execution of proper occupation.
-- 務指南	business guide.
-- 務量	volume of business.
-- 已	already.
21-- 師	one's tutor, one's teacher.
25-- 績報告	performance report.
88-- 餘	amateur, spare time.
95-- 精於勤	efficiency comes from diligence.

3300₀
心 〔Hsin〕 n. heart, mind, middle, center, bosom, desire, will, sense.

00-- 痛	heartache, love deeply.
-- 底裡	from the bottom of one's heart.
-- 意	mind, intention.
-- 裏好過	feel good.
04-- 計毒辣	cruel schemes.
10-- 靈	spirit, soul, intellect, inspiration.
-- 下不安	feel uneasy.
-- 平氣和	be in a calm mood, calm, tranquil.
-- 碎	heart broken, heart-rending.
-- 電感應	telepathy.
-- 不自主	unable to control the mind.
-- 不在焉	absent-minded, inattentive.

-- 不由主	lose self-control.	-- 境	sentiment, frame of mind.
11-- 硬	hard-hearted.	-- 灰	discouraged, disheartened.
-- 硬如石	extremely hard-hearted.	-- 志	will.
13-- 酸	sad, grief.	-- 有不安	be ill at ease.
16-- 理	mentality, psychology.	42-- 機	wit, ingenuity, craftiness.
-- 理上	psychologically, mentally.	44-- 地善良	good-natured.
-- 理變態	mental abnormities.	-- 地光明	open-minded.
-- 理作用	mental reaction.	-- 花怒放	be brimming with joy.
-- 理戰	psychological warfare.	-- 甘情願	willingly.
-- 理學	psychology.	46-- 如刀割	heart-stricken.
-- 理分析	psycho-analysis.	47-- 狠手辣	callous and cruel.
20-- 愛	beloved.	48-- 驚膽破	heart startled and gall blad-
-- 焦	vexed, anxious, worried.		der broken--terrified to de-
-- 焦萬分	be worried to the greatest		ath.
	degree.	50-- 事	care, worry, concern, anx-
-- 手相應	mind and hand in accord.		iety, heart's burden.
21-- 虛	afraid of being found out.	-- 中不安	feel ill at ease.
-- 虛膽怯	apprehensive and cowardly.	-- 中了然	understand in one's mind.
22-- 亂	confused, perplexed.	57-- 投意合	be in perfect agreement.
24-- 緒不寧	be disturbed in mind.	60-- 思	thought, idea, design.
25-- 生一計	hit upon an idea.	-- 曠神怡	be carefree and happy.
26-- 得	comprehension, idea obta-	-- 目中	in one's mind, in one's eyes.
	ined.	-- 黑辣	black-hearted and cruel.
27-- 血	heart's blood, painstaking	-- 回意轉	change one's mind.
	effort.	62-- 跳	beating of heart, palpitation
-- 血來潮	suddenly to think of a thing.		of heart.
-- 像	image.	67-- 眼明亮	lay all one's cards on the
30-- 室	ventricles of the heart.		table.
-- 房	atrium of the heart.	-- 明如鏡	the mind is as clear as a
-- 安理得	have nothing on one's con-		mirror.
	science.	71-- 願	hope, desire, wish.
33-- 心相印	complete understanding be-	-- 灰意冷	be discouraged, be dishe-
	tween two minds.		artened, be disappointed.
34-- 滿意足	*n.* satisfaction, *v.* be satis-	74-- 臟	heart.
	fied, *adj.* content.	-- 病	heart disease, anxiety.
35-- 神	the mind.	-- 學	cardiology.
-- 神不寧	not peaceful in mind.	77-- 肌	cardiac muscle.
-- 神不定	be agitated, be restless in	-- 胸狹窄	be narrow-minded.
	mind.	-- 胸開闊	be broad-minded.
-- 神顛倒	utterly confused, unable to	-- 服口服	admit somebody's superi-
	think straight.		ority.
-- 神舒暢	relaxed and cheerful.	78-- 腹	intimate, confidential.
40-- 力	vigor, mental strength.	-- 腹話	confidential talk.
-- 力交瘁	be worn-out in both body	-- 腹之交	bosom friend.
	and mind.	-- 腹之話	heart-to-heart talk.
-- 直口快	be blunt and outspoken.	80-- 氣	temper.

81-- 領神會　appreciate, understand without being told.
88-- 算　mental arithmetic.
91-- 煩意亂　be worried and confused.
94-- 怯　timid, shy.
-- 慌意亂　be scared and confused.
95-- 情　mood, mind, state of mind, affection.
-- 情舒暢　be light-hearted, be at ease of mind.

必〔Pi〕v. be certain, be necessary, adj. necessary, requisite, adv. certainly, surely, must.
10-- 需　v. require, need, put in requisition, adj, essential, necessary.
-- 需品　requirement, necessity.
-- 死之心　with one's back to the wall.
-- 要　n. necessity, adj. necessary.
-- 要手續　necessary formality.
-- 要條件　essential condition, necessary condition.
-- 要消費品　necessary consumer goods.
-- 要費用　necessary expenses.
-- 要時　if necessary, in time of need, in case of necessity.
-- 要條件　prerequisite.
-- 要小心　take every caution against error.
-- 不可免　unavoidable.
-- 不得已　if it cannot be helped.
21-- 須　must, of necessity, ought to.
23-- 然　certainly, by all means, necessarily.
-- 然性　inevitability.
-- 然之事　matter of certainty.
27-- 修課　requirement.
30-- 定　certainly, without fail, at all events.
44-- 恭必敬　show great respect.
3310_0
沁〔Chin〕v. immerse, soak.
80--入　soak into.
泌〔Pi〕v. secrete, gush forth, bubble out.

30-- 液　urinary secretion.
77-- 尿　urinary.
-- 尿器　urinary organ.
泓〔Hung〕adj. deep, clear.
3311_1
沱〔To〕n. affluent, heavy rain.
浣〔Huan〕v. wash and cleanse.
3311_4
窪〔Wa〕n. clear water.
44-- 地　low land.
3311_7
滬〔Hu〕n. the Hu river, Shanghai.
22-- 劇　Shanghai opera.
31-- 江　Shanghai.
3312_1
濘〔Ning〕adj. miry.
3312_2
滲〔Shen〕v. soak, leak, permeate, percolate, infiltrate.
22-- 出　ooze, seep.
32-- 透　percolate, permeate, infiltrate, penetrate.
-- 透作用　the function of osmosis.
39-- 淡　dismal.
80-- 入　infiltrate.
3312_7
浦〔Pu〕n. river bank, area around an estuary.
瀉〔Hsieh〕n. purging, diarrhea, flux, dysentery, v. purge, ooze, leak, let off water.
00-- 痢　dysentery, flux.
35-- 清　purge.
44-- 藥　laxative, purgative.
74-- 肚　diarrhea, loose bowels.
78-- 鹽　Epsom salts.
3313_2
泳〔Yung〕v. swim.
浪〔Lang〕n. wave, billow, surge, adj. dissolute.
11-- 頭　crest of a wave.
17-- 子　prodigal, squanderer.
36-- 漫　romantic.

-- 漫主義　　　romanticism.
-- 漫派　　　　romantic school.
44-- 花　　　　spray, foam.
55-- 費　　　　waste, squander, dissipate.
80-- 人　　　　rascal, ronin.

3313₄

淚〔Lei〕 *n.* tear, beads of sorrow.
00-- 痕　　　　traces of tears.
-- 痕滿面　　　the face is covered with traces of tears.
12-- 水　　　　tears.
15-- 珠　　　　teardrops.
30-- 容滿面　　tearful look.
46-- 如雨下　　burst into a flood of tears
67-- 眼　　　　swimming eyes, weeping eyes.

3314₁

滓〔Tzu〕 *n.* dreg, sentiment.

3314₂

溥〔Pu〕 *adj.* vast, extensive, universal.

3314₇

浚〔Chun〕 *v.* deepen, dredge.

3315₀

滅〔Mieh〕 *v.* destroy, perish, overthrow, extinguish, quench, exterminate, put out.
00-- 亡　　　　*n.* extinction, death, extermination, *adj.* ruined, exterminated.
11-- 頂　　　　drowned in water.
22-- 種　　　　destroy a race, genocide.
27-- 絕　　　　exterminate, extinguish, quench, stamp out, put out, run out.
60-- 跡　　　　destroy all the evidence, obliterate.
-- 國　　　　destroy a state.
90-- 火　　　　put out a fire.
-- 火器　　　fire hydrant, fire extinguisher.
92-- 燈　　　　put out a light.
96-- 熄　　　　quench.

減〔Chien〕 *v.* subtract, decrease, diminish, reduce, deduct, cut down.
00-- 讓　　　　make allowance for, give in.

-- 產　　　　decrease in output, drop in production.
-- 衣縮食　　practise austerity, be economical.
12-- 刑　　　　*n.* commutation of punishment, *v.* mitigate a punishment.
17-- 弱　　　　weaken.
21-- 價　　　　*n.* abatement, depreciation, *v.* reduce the price, undersell, cut under.
-- 價商店　　cut-price shop, discount store.
-- 價出售　　sell at a discount.
22-- 低　　　　lower, reduce, cut.
-- 低價格　　deflate price.
23-- 縮　　　　abbreviate.
24-- 值　　　　decrease in value.
34-- 法　　　　subtraction.
35-- 速　　　　retard.
37-- 資　　　　reduce capital.
40-- 去　　　　take away, deduct from.
44-- 薪　　　　reduction of wages, salary reduction.
51-- 輕　　　　*n.* relief, *v.* relax, ease, mitigate, diminish, extenuate.
56-- 損　　　　degradation.
58-- 數　　　　subtraction.
60-- 罪　　　　mitigate a crime.
-- 員　　　　reducing staff, cut down the size of staff, downsize, reduction in force.
61-- 號　　　　the minus sign (-).
78-- 除　　　　abate.
-- 除成本　　deductible costs.
81-- 短　　　　shorten.
88-- 筆　　　　abbreviation.
90-- 少　　　　diminish, descend, decrease, lessen, reduce, retrench, abridge, take down.
-- 少工時　　reduce work hours.
-- 少供給　　reduce supplies.
-- 少存貨　　inventory cutting.
-- 少費用　　reduce expenses.
-- 牛　　　　reduce to one half.
94-- 料　　　　lessen the quantity of ma-

terial.

3315₃

淺〔Chien〕*adj.* shallow, light, superficial, simple.

10--	而易見	easily understood.
12--	水	shallow water.
26--	白言之	talk in a simple way.
27--	色	light color, tint.
30--	灘	beach, bank.
32--	近	simple, easy to learn.
35--	漕	trough.
44--	薄	superficial, mean.
71--	陋不堪	very shallow and detestable.
77--	學之士	superficial scholar.
87--	鍋	pan.

濺〔Chien〕*n.* swift-flowing water, *v.* spatter against, splash, spurt.

3316₀

冶〔Yeh〕*v.* fuse, melt, smelt, *adj.* fascinating, enticing, charming, bewitching.

10--	工	smelter.
27--	艷	fascinating, charming, bewitching.
71--	匠	founder.
80--	金學	metallurgy.
--	金學家	metallurgist.
--	金工業	metallurgical industry.
95--	煉	smelt.
--	煉廠	metallurgical plant.
--	煉爐	furnace, blast furnace.

治〔Chih〕*v.* govern, rule, manage, punish, regulate, cure, remedy, treat.

00--	病	cure a disease.
--	病救人	cure the sickness to save the patient.
--	療	cure, heal, remedy.
--	療法	treatment cure.
12--	水	water control.
16--	理	govern, manage.
--	理者	governor.
22--	亂	suppress a revolt, deal with disorder.
23--	外法權	extraterritorial rights.
30--	安	public order, public security.

31--	河	harness a river, tame a river.
34--	洪	flood control.
40--	喪	arrange a funeral.
47--	好	cured.
60--	罪	punish, condemn.
--	國	govern a country.
80--	愈	heal, cure, be cured.

3316₈

溶〔Jung〕*v.* dissolve, melt.

00--	度	solubility.
02--	劑	solvent.
24--	化	melt, dissolve.
27--	解	*v.* dissolve, melt, *adj.* soluble.
--	解度	solubility.
--	解於水	be dissolved in water.
30--	液	solution.

3316₉

瀋〔Shen〕*n.* juice, broth.

3318₁

淀〔Tien〕*n.* shallow water.

3318₆

演〔Yen〕*v.* practise, act, perform, exhibit, exercise.

05--	講	speak, lecture, give a lecture.
--	講術	oratory, elocution.
--	講家	orator, excellent speaker.
--	講員	lecturer.
--	講會	lyceum.
08--	說	*v.* discourse, speak, deliver a speech, address, *n.* oration, speech, address.
--	說家	orator.
--	說台	rostrum.
--	說者	speaker.
13--	武場	drill ground.
17--	習	practise, drill, learn, military manoeuvres, war game.
--	習射擊	dry-shoot.
22--	變	development, variation.
--	出	stage, perform, play.
--	出者	performer, player.
--	出節目	program, repertoire.
23--	戲	perform, act.

24-- 化	*n.* evolution, *v.* evolve.
26-- 繹	deduce.
-- 繹法	deduction.
50-- 奏	performance, musical performance.
-- 奏者	musical performer, musical player.
54-- 技	acting skills.
60-- 員	actor, player.
-- 員表	cast of a film or performance.
66-- 唱	sing on stage.
80-- 義	historical novel.
88-- 算	mathematical exercise.

濱〔**Pin**〕*n.* coast, shore, bank, beach.

38-- 海	seashore.
78-- 臨大海	on the brink of sea.

3320_0

祕〔**Mi**〕*adj.* secret, private, mysterious.

00-- 方	nostrum.
04-- 計	intrigue, underhand trick.
05-- 訣	wrinkle.
25-- 傳	hand down privately.
30-- 密	secret, secrecy.
-- 密話	secret words.
-- 密偵探	private detective.
-- 密室	private room, romance room.
-- 密消息	confidential.
-- 密警察	gestapo.
-- 密會議	secret conference, conclave.
50-- 事	mystery.
-- 書	secretary.
-- 書處	secretariat.
-- 書長	secretary general.
57-- 探	detective.

褂〔**Kua**〕*n.* jacket, overcoat, robe, gown.

3322_7

補〔**Pu**〕*v.* repair, mend, patch, fill up, help, aid, assist.

00-- 衣	patch clothes.
-- 充	supply, replace.
-- 充語	complement.
-- 充站	depot.
-- 充存貨	replenish the stock of goods.
-- 充投資	additional investment, secondary investment.
-- 充人力	replenish manpower.
-- 交稅款	pay taxes in arrears, pay an overdue tax.
02-- 訓	replacement and training.
-- 訓處	replacement and training center.
06-- 課	make up missed lessons.
10-- 牙	fill a tooth.
17-- 習	continuation study, cram school.
-- 習學校	continuation school, supplementary school.
22-- 片	patch.
28-- 給	replenish, supply.
29-- 償	*n.* compensation, indemnity, *v.* mend, redress, offset, make up for.
-- 償制度	back off system.
-- 償收入	off-setting receipt.
-- 償報酬	compensatory payment.
-- 償損失	make good the loss, compensating for loss or damage.
-- 償金	compensating payment, compensatory payment.
30-- 空	cover, bear covering .
35-- 遣	supplement.
44-- 考	supplementary examination.
-- 藥	tonic medicine.
47-- 報	make a report after the event, make a supplementary report.
48-- 救	save, redress, recover, remedy, repair.
60-- 足	fill up, replenish.
61-- 貼	*n.* subsidy, *v.* subsidize, cover deficit by state subsidies.
74-- 助	help, assist, subsidize,

benefit.
-- 助計劃　　grant program.
-- 助津貼　　compensatory allowance.
-- 助金　　　subsidy, financial aid, sup-
　　　　　　plementary benefit.
81-- 釘　　　patch.
85-- 缺　　　fill up a vacancy.

褊 〔Pien〕 adj. narrow, small.
30-- 窄　　　narrow.
33-- 淺　　　shallow, narrow-minded.
90-- 小　　　small, narrow, mean.
3323₄

袚 〔Fu〕 n. wrapper.
3323₆

襁 〔Chiang〕 n. swaddling clothes.
3324₄

祓 〔Fo〕 v. drive off, wash away, cleanse.
3330₂

遍 〔Pien〕 n. time, v. go round, make
a circuit, adv. everywhere,through-
out, whole, entire.
17-- 尋　　　ransack.
21-- 處　　　everywhere.
34-- 達　　　run through.
40-- 走　　　go everywhere.
44-- 地=遍處
57-- 搜　　　ransack, search every-
　　　　　　where.
67-- 跑　　　run about.
3330₆

迨 〔Tai〕 v. come up to, reach, conj.
till, until, when.
22-- 後　　　till, afterwards.
3330₉

述 〔Shu〕 v. narrate, state, tell, relate,
explain, follow, continue.
17-- 及　　　mention.
28-- 作　　　write, compose.
3390₄

梁 〔Liang〕 n. bridge, beam, plank,
ridge.
21-- 上君子　thief, burglar, stealer.
40-- 木　　　beams of a house.

粱 〔Liang〕 n. millet.
3400₀

斗 〔Tou〕 n. measurement, Chinese
peck,container for wine.
30-- 室　　　small room.
77-- 膽　　　great boldness.
88-- 篷　　　mantle,cloak, blouse.
-- 笠　　　leaf hat.
3402₇

爲 〔Wei〕 v. act, do, perform, make,
play the part of, manage, attend to,
conj. for, because, for the sake of,
on behalf of, phr. on account of, for
the sake of.
00-- 主　　　predominate.
-- 誰　　　for whom.
02-- 證　　　as a witness, as an evidence.
10-- 惡　　　do evil.
11-- 非　　　do wrong.
-- 非作惡　do evil.
17-- 己　　　selfish, for oneself.
-- 了　　　for, to, so that.
21-- 何　　　why? for what reason?
24-- 什麼　　why?
30-- 害　　　injure.
40-- 難　　　embarrass, place in diffi-
　　　　　　culty.
60-- 國效命　give one's life to the coun-
　　　　　　try.
-- 國增光　struggle for the glory of the
　　　　　　country.
-- 國盡力　serve one's country.
-- 國捐軀　die for one's country.
-- 時已晚　day after the fair, too late.
-- 時過早　premature, too early.
77-- 民除害　remove evils for the people.
-- 民前鋒　be the vanguard of the pe-
　　　　　　ople.
80-- 人　　　for other's sake.
-- 人恥笑　commit a blazing indiscre-
　　　　　　tion.
-- 人師表　be a model of virtue for
　　　　　　others.
-- 人表率　be a model for others.
-- 人厚重　be kind and generous.
-- 人所知　put on the map, be known.

--	人民服務	serve the people.
--	首	led by, headed by.
--	善	do good.
--	公爲私	for public or for personal interests.
90--	小失大	sell one's birthright for a pottage of lentils.

3410₀

汁 〔**Chih**〕 *n.* juice, sap, fluid.

30--	液	juice, fluid, sap.

對 〔**Tui**〕 *n.* pair, opponent, couple. *v.* front, correspond to, suit, answer, reply, respond, *adj.* correct, right, consistent with, agreeing.

00--	立	contrary, stand opposed to.
--	立面	the opposite side.
--	立物	things in opposition.
--	立統一規律	the law of the unity of opposites.
--	症下藥	prescribe medicine according to the disease.
--	方	the opposite side, the other party (side).
--	應	correspond.
02--	證	eye-witness, personal evidence.
--	話	dialogue.
07--	調	exchange.
08--	敵	*n.* enemy, foe, opponent, *v.* antagonize, oppose, kick against.
--	於	in regard to, as to.
10--	面	opposite to, face to face.
--	不起	excuse me, I am sorry, beg your pardon.
11--	頭	opponent, enemy.
--	頂角	vertical angle.
12--	聯	parallel sentences, scroll, chinese couplets.
17--	了	that is right.
20--	手	rival, competitor, opponent.
21--	比	contrast with, contrast.
22--	稱	symmetry.
--	岸	on the opposite bank of the river.
23--	外交易	foreign transaction.
--	外政策	foreign policy.
--	外經濟技術合作	foreign economic and technological cooperation .
--	外出口	export abroad.
--	外關係	foreign relations (policy).
--	外貿易	external trade, foreign trade.
--	外貿易政策	external trade policy.
--	外貿易順差	favorable balance of trade, foreign trade surplus.
--	外貿易商	foreign trader.
--	外貿易商會	chamber of foreign commerce.
--	外貿易區	foreign trade zone.
24--	付	deal with, cope with, serve.
--	待	treat, deal with.
--	峙	stand opposite to each other.
--	峙而立	standing opposite each other.
26--	白	dialogue.
27--	向	opposite.
--	角線	diagonal.
--	象	object, sweetheart.
--	句	antithesis.
30--	流	convection.
--	準	aim at.
--	內對外	internal and external.
50--	抗	*n.* confrontation, antagonism, *v.* confront, oppose.
--	抗性	antagonism.
51--	打	fight with, fight against each other.
58--	數	logarithm.
--	數表	logarithm table.
60--	日勝利日	V-J Day (Victory-in-Japan Day).
61--	號	counter mark, check mark, check the number.
67--	照	contrast, counterview.
--	照表	balance sheet, synopsis.
71--	歐勝利日	V-E Day (Victory-in-Europe Day).
72--	質	*n.* confrontation, *v.* confront each other with questions.

77-- 門	the opposite door, facing the door.	
88-- 答	*n.* dialogue, *v.* answer, reply.	
-- 答如流	give fluent replies.	
-- 簿公庭	confront each other in the court.	
-- 等	*n.* equity, *adj.* equal, reciprocal.	
-- 等待遇	reciprocal treatment.	
-- 策	countermeasure.	
89-- 銷	offset.	
90-- 半	fifty-fifty.	
-- 當	opposition.	

3411₁
洗 〔Hsi〕 *v.* wash, clean, bathe, purify, rinse, vindicate.

00-- 衣	wash cloth.
-- 衣店	laundry.
-- 衣板	washboard.
-- 衣機	washing machine.
-- 衣刷	fuller brush.
10-- 面	wash face.
-- 面架	washstand.
-- 面盆	washbasin.
11-- 頭	shampoo.
13-- 恥	wash off disgrace.
-- 恥報仇	wipe out a disgrace and have revenge.
20-- 手	wash hands.
32-- 淨	clean, cleanse, wash down.
33-- 心改過	cleanse the heart from sin.
35-- 清	purify.
-- 禮	*n.* baptism, *v.* baptize, christen.
-- 禮名	Christen name.
36-- 澡	take a bath, wash, bathe.
-- 澡盆	bathtub.
37-- 濯	wash, dip.
-- 濯店	wash house.
38-- 浴=洗澡	
-- 滌	rinse, wash.
-- 滌劑	wash, detergent.
51-- 掉	wash off.
72-- 刷	wash and scrub.

74-- 熨	launder.
78-- 臉	wash face.
-- 臉盆	washbasin.

澆 〔Chiao〕 *v.* water, irrigate, moisten, sprinkle, pour, cast, *adj.* ungrateful, perfidious.

12-- 水	water.
-- 水壺	water-can.
30-- 字	typecasting.
34-- 灌	irrigate.
44-- 花	sprinkle flower.
84-- 鑄	cast (a type, statue, etc).

3411₂
沈 〔Chen〕 *v.* sink, immerse, droop, submerge, drown, plunge, suppress, *adj.* deep, sound, very, hidden, profound.

00-- 痛	acute pain, great grief, deep sorrow.
07-- 毅	presence of mind.
10-- 下	sink, subside.
-- 醉	dead drunk, be intoxicated.
20-- 重	very heavy, sedate, serious.
26-- 得住氣	retain one's composure.
27-- 船	shipwreck.
37-- 沒	sink, subside.
-- 澱	subside.
-- 澱物	sediment, settlement, precipitate.
-- 溺	drown, be drowned, indulge, sunk in, infatuated.
39-- 迷	be infatuated.
-- 迷不醒	in a coma, deeply addicted to something.
-- 迷不悟	be lost in evil, be stuck with wrong ideas.
52-- 靜	stillness, quiet.
60-- 思	*n.* deep thinking, *v.* ponder, think deeply, speculate, contemplate.
62-- 睡	*n.* sound sleep, *v.* sleep soundly.
63-- 默	reserved, discreet.
77-- 悶	closeness, depressed, dull,

tedious.

80-- 入　merge in.

-- 著　composed, sedate.

-- 著應付　handle something impassively.

池〔Chih〕*n.* pond, pool, moat.

12-- 水　pond water.

40-- 塘　pond.

3411₄

灌〔Kuan〕*n.* irrigation, watering, *v.* irrigate, water, pour, make a libation.

10-- 醉　make a person drunk.

30-- 注　flow into, pour in.

31-- 溉　irrigate, water.

-- 溉渠　irrigation canal.

40-- 木　shrub, bushes, underbrush.

58-- 輸　instill, indoctrinate, nourish, transmit.

76-- 腸　give an enema or clyster.

3411₆

渣〔Cha〕*n.* dreg, sediment, dross, refuse, slag.

33-- 滓　dregs, refuse, dross, sediment.

淹〔Yen〕*v.* overflow, immerse, soak, saturate.

10-- 死　drowned.

34-- 滯　hindered, detained.

37-- 沒　overflow, deluge.

3411₇

泄〔Hsieh〕*v.* scatter, disperse, leak, divulge, vent, *adj.* slow, lax.

12-- 水閘　gated spillway.

10-- 露　become known, come out.

30-- 密　disclose a secret.

37-- 漏　*n.* revelation, *v.* disclose, reveal, divulge, leak out.

80-- 氣　be disappointed, despond, lose one's spirit.

94-- 憤　vent one's spite.

港〔Kang〕*n.* harbor, port, seaport, anchorage.

17-- 務局 (處)　harbor bureau.

-- 務局長　harbormaster.

28-- 稅　port dues.

32-- 灣　bay.

37-- 澳同胞　compatriots from Hongkong and Macao.

60-- 口　harbor, port, seaport.

-- 口交貨　delivered at harbor.

-- 口設備　harbor facility.

-- 口稅　port due (tax).

-- 口拖船　harbor tug.

71-- 區　port area.

3411₈

湛〔Chan〕*adj.* deep, clear.

60-- 恩　great kindness.

3412₁

漪〔I〕*n.* ripples.

3412₇

滿〔Man〕*n.* fullness, pride, Manchus, *v.* fill, complete, abound, replenish, *adj.* full, replete, sufficient, enough, entire, whole, complete.

00-- 座　full house.

-- 意　contented, satisfied.

-- 意之至　satisfied to the utmost degree.

10-- 面笑容　smiling all over.

-- 面春風　beaming with joy.

27-- 身　whole body, all over the body.

32-- 州　Manchuria.

38-- 溢　overflow.

43-- 載　full load (cargo), capacity load.

44-- 地　all over the ground.

47-- 期　*n.* full time, maturity, expiry, termination of term, *v.* expire.

-- 期通知　expiration notice.

-- 期日　day of maturity.

58-- 數　complement.

60-- 口應承　promise with great readiness.

-- 足　content, satisfy, fulfill.

-- 足於　be content with.

-- 足要求　meet demand.

72-- 腦子　with one's head crammed with.

77--	月	full moon.
80--	分	full mark.
90--	懷信心	with full confidence.

淆〔Yao〕 adj. confused and mixed.

22--	亂視聽	mislead the public.
36--	混本末	confound the means with the end.

瀟〔Hsiao〕 n. driving wine and rain, sound of beating rain and wind, roar of strong wind.

31--	洒	lighted-hearted, unconventional, casual and elegant.

滯〔Jih〕 v. stagnate, be detained, adj. stagnant, blocked, impeded.

25--	積不銷	overstocked and unsellable.
30--	塞不通	obstructed, impeded.
77--	留	stagnate, hold up.
98--	銷	dull of sale, poor market, slow sale, sluggish sales.
--	銷貨	unsellable goods, dead stock, slow-moving items.

3413_0

汰〔Tai〕 v. wash out, clean, rinse, adj. excessive.

3413_1

法〔Fa〕 n. law, statute, rule, regulation, ways, means, method, France, French, v. imitate, emulate.

00--	庭	court, tribunal.
--	庭書記員	tribunal clerk.
--	庭費	court fees.
--	文	French language, legal text.
--	度	means, way, law and institution.
--	辦	be dealt with according to law.
01--	語	French language.
10--	西斯主義	Fascism.
11--	碼	standard weight.
16--	理	principle of law.
--	理學	jurisprudence.
17--	子	method, way, process.
20--	系	genealogy of law.
21--	術	magic, black art.
--	價	standard legal price.
22--	制	legislation, legal system.
24--	貨	legal tender.
25--	律	law, code, statute jurisprudence.
--	律文件	legal document.
--	律訴訟	action at law.
--	律效力	force of law, legal effect.
--	律手續	legal formalities.
--	律行爲	act of law, legal act.
--	律制裁	legal sanction.
--	律保護	legal protection.
--	律程序	legal procedure, process of law.
--	律條文	articles of law.
--	律修正	law amendment.
--	律顧問	legal counsellor (adviser).
--	律衝突	conflict of law.
--	律機構	legal body.
--	律事務所	law firm (offices).
--	律專家	legal expert.
--	律費	legal fee.
--	律責任	legal obligation (liability).
--	律規定	legal rules, statutory provisions.
27--	紀	law and discipline.
--	網難逃	it is difficult to escape from the meshes of the law.
30--	官	judge, justice.
--	家	legalist, jurist.
--	定	legal, statutory.
--	定文件	statutory document (instruments).
--	定職業	legal occupation.
--	定手續	due process of law.
--	定平價	par of exchange.
--	定承繼人	heir at law, legal heir.
--	定價格	official price, legal price.
--	定利率	legal interest.
--	定代表	legal representative.
--	定休假日	legal holiday.
--	定貨幣	lawful money.
--	定保護人 (監護人)	legal guardian.
--	定準備基金	legal reserve fund.
--	定資產	legal assets.
--	定資本	legal capital.

--定資格	statutory qualification.
--定權利	statutory authority (right).
--定權力	statutory power.
--定責任	statutory duty.
--定規則	statutory provisions, prescriptive rules.
--定時效	statutory limitation, legal limits of time.
--定人數	quorum.
--定年齡	lawful age, legal age.
--定義務	legal duty.
--寶	effective weapon.
--案	law case, bill, the act of congress.
31--源	origin of law.
33--治	rule by law, rule of law.
--治國	legal state.
37--郎	franc.
44--蘭絨	flannel.
--權	jurisdiction.
46--場	execution ground.
55--典	code, statute, canon, body of laws.
56--規	rules and regulations.
60--國	France.
--國梧桐	plane tree.
62--則	laws, rules.
73--院	court, forum, court of justice.
--院的管轄	jurisdiction.
--院裁決	court decision.
77--學	jurisprudence.
--學家	jurist.
--學士	bachelor of law.
--學院	college of law.
80--人	juridical person, corporate person, fictitious person, legal entity.
--令	law and bylaws, statutes.
--令嚴峻	the laws are austere.
98--幣	legal money.

3413_2

漆 〔Chi〕 v. paint, varnish, lacquer, adj. pitch black.

10--工	painter, varnisher.
60--黑	jet black.
66--器	lacquerware.

3413_4

漠 〔Mo〕 n. desert, adj. indifferent, cool, careless.

10--不相干	no concern of.
--不關心	n. indifference, adj. apathetic.
23--然	careless, indifferent, nonchalant, cold.
36--視	neglect, disregard, take no heed to.

漢 〔Han〕 n. man, Chinese, Han Dynasty.

00--文	the Chinese written language.
01--語	the Chinese spoken language.
--語拼音	Chinese phonetic alphabet.
17--子	fellow, man.
30--字	Chinese ideograph, Chinese character.
41--奸	traitor to China, Chinese traitor.
44--英字典	Chinese-English dictionary.
47--朝	the Han Dynasty.
60--口	Hankow.
77--學	sinology.
80--人	Chinese people.

3414_0

汝 〔Ju〕 pron. you.

3414_1

濤 〔Tao〕 n. surges, billows, large waves.

3414_7

波 〔Po〕 n. waves, surge, billows, ripples, v. influence.

00--音公司	Boeing.
10--平浪靜	the sea is calm.
17--及	involve, implicate.
20--紋	ripple.
24--動	wave, surge, fluctuate.
--動匯率	fluctuating exchange rate, floating rate.

33--	浪	wave, billows.
42--	斯	Persia, Persian.
--	斯文	Persian language.
--	斯人	Persian.
44--	蘭	Poland.
--	人	Polish.
60--	羅	pine apple.
71--	長	wave-length.

凌 〔Ling〕 v. insult, abuse, disrespect, rise, ride.

10--	雲	soaring.
--	雲壯志	strong resolution to ride the clouds (great ambition).
22--	亂	n. disorder, adj. disorderly.
--	亂無序	confused and disordered.
46--	駕他人	excel others.
60--	罵	taunt.
71--	辱	abuse, insult, maltreat.
--	厲	maltreat, ill-treat.

凌 〔Ling〕 v. pass over, travel across.

3416₀

沽 〔Ku〕 v. buy, sell.

31--	酒	buy wine.

3416₁

浩 〔Hao〕 adj. great, extensive, immense, vast, numerous, many.

34--	浩蕩蕩	grand, magnificent, overwhelming.
38--	瀚	vast, in huge quantities.
40--	大	very great, extensive vast.
44--	劫	great calamity, great disaster, catastrophe.
46--	如海	as vast as a misty ocean.
88--	繁	numerous, voluminous.

3418₁

洪 〔Hung〕 adj. vast, extensive, n. flood, inundation.

00--	亮	loud, sonorous.
12--	水	flood, deluge, inundation.
--	水保險	flood insurance.
27--	峰	flood peak, the high point of a flood.
30--	流	powerful current, giant torrent.
40--	大	immense, huge.
--	才	great mind with great sche-

		me, military talent.

3418₆

瀆 〔Tu〕 n. ditch, gutter, river, v. profane, offend, annoy.

13--	職	malfeasance in office.
35--	神	blasphemy.

3419₀

沐 〔Mu〕 v. wash, bathe, clean, rinse, receive, take a leave, have a holiday.

38--	浴	bathe, take a bath.
60--	日	holiday.
--	恩	receive favors.

淋 〔Lin〕 n. gonorrhea, v. drop, drip, moisten, pour water over, soak with water.

00--	病	gonorrhea.
30--	漓	dripping, dropping.
32--	透	be dripping wet, be soaked.
36--	濕	be drenched with rain.
38--	浴	shower bath.
--	浴室	shower room.
77--	巴	lymph.
--	巴腺	lymphatic glands.

3419₆

潦 〔Lao〕 n. flood, great rain, v. flood, overflow, adj. careless, neglectful, disheartened.

22--	倒	unlucky in life.
44--	草	v. scribe over, adj. careless, illegible, negligent.

3421₀

社 〔She〕 n. association, society, company, village.

00--	交	social contact, social intercourse.
--	交應酬	social functions.
--	交場所	social clubs.
--	交場合	social life.
--	交公開	open social intercourse between male and female.
--	交性	sociability.
08--	論	editorial.
27--	約論	doctrine of social contract.
60--	員	member, partner.
--	員大會	general convention of an association.

-- 團	association, society, clubs, organizations.
-- 團法人	association.
71-- 長	president of a society, director of a company.
-- 區服務	community service.
80-- 會	society, community.
-- 會主義	socialism.
-- 會主義者	socialist.
-- 會主義建設	social construction.
-- 會主義革命	social revolution.
-- 會帝國主義	social-imperialism.
-- 會新聞	human interest stories, crime stories.
-- 會工作者	social worker.
-- 會現象	social phenomena.
-- 會政策	social policies.
-- 會改良	social reform.
-- 會制裁	social sanction.
-- 會科學	social science.
-- 會生活	community life, social life.
-- 會保險	social security (insurance).
-- 會保險制	social security.
-- 會名流	well-known persons, fashionable society.
-- 會組織	social organization.
-- 會進化	social evolution.
-- 會心理	social psychology.
-- 會福利工作	social service (work).
-- 會地位	social position.
-- 會教育	social education.
-- 會事業	social work, social service.
-- 會階級	social stratum.
-- 會學	sociology.
-- 會學者	sociologist.
-- 會問題	social problems.
-- 會賢達	community leaders.
-- 會人士	prominent public figures.
-- 會性	social nature, social character.

3422₇
袴〔Ku〕n. trousers, breeches, drawers.

3424₁
禱〔Dao〕v. pray, supplicate.

24-- 告	pray.
-- 告文	prayer.
36-- 祝平安	pray for someone's safety.

3424₇
被〔Pei〕n. bedclothes, coverlet, quilt, v. cover, extend to, clothe, wear, suffer.

01-- 誣	be falsely charged.
17-- 子	bedding.
20-- 乘數	multiplicand.
21-- 處罰	forfeit.
22-- 俘	be taken prisoner.
24-- 告	defendant.
-- 動	passive.
26-- 保證人	warrantee.
-- 保險人	the assured.
27-- 解僱	laid off, unemployed, get the axe.
30-- 害	be injured.
-- 害者	injured party.
31-- 褥	bedding, coverlet, mattress, quilt.
-- 逼	be compelled.
33-- 減數	minuend.
37-- 選舉權	right of being elected, eligibility.
47-- 殺	be killed.
-- 欺	be cheated.
53-- 控	be accused.
56-- 提名人	nominee.
57-- 拘留者	internee.
58-- 搶	be robbed.
66-- 單	sheet, bedspread.
77-- 服廠	clothing factory.
78-- 除數	dividend.

3425₃
襪〔Wa〕n. stocking, socks, hose.

17-- 子	stocking, socks.
44-- 帶	garter.

3426₀
祜〔Yu〕n. divine care, heavenly protection.

褚〔Chu〕n. bag, satchel, cotton, v. store.

3426₅
禧〔Hsi〕n. joy, good luck, blessing, favor.

00-- 慶   felicitous, occasion.
80-- 年   happy new year.

3428₁
祺 〔 Chi 〕 *adj.* fortunate, lucky, happy, felicitous.

3429₁
襟 〔 Chin 〕 *n.* lapel of a coat.
90-- 懷   bosom, feeling, ambition.
-- 懷寬大   generous, magnanimous, charitable, tolerant.

3430₁
逵 〔 Kuei 〕 *n.* thoroughfare.
遶 〔 Jao 〕 *v.* surround, compass.
21-- 纏   encircle, bind.
30-- 灣   go around a corner.
38-- 道   make a detour.

3430₂
邁 〔 Mai 〕 *v.* surpass, pass, *adj.* old, aged, vigorously, heroically.
21-- 步   walk vigorously, stride.
-- 步前行   take a step and go forward.

3430₃
遠 〔 Yuan 〕 *adj.* distant, remote, far, long in time, deep, profound, *v.* keep away, estrange.
00-- 方   distant country, remote place.
-- 離   keep at distance, stand aloof, remain at a distance, keep away, stand away.
04-- 謀   farsighted in planning.
06-- 親   distant relative.
21-- 征   expedition.
-- 征軍   expedition army, expeditionary force.
-- 慮   *n.* foresight, prescience, *adj.* farsighted.
-- 處   distance, distant place.
26-- 程   long-range.
-- 程火箭   long-range rocket.
30-- 避   hold off, keep at a distance.
32-- 近   far and near.
33-- 心力   centrifugal force.
36-- 視   far-sighted.
-- 視眼   hypermetropia.

38-- 洋輪   ocean liner, sea-going vessel.
40-- 大理想   great and far-reaching ideal.
-- 大眼光   farsightedness, prescience.
50-- 東   Far East.
60-- 見   farsightedness, prescience.
-- 因   remote cause.
-- 足   excursion.
-- 景   perspective, distant view.
-- 景規劃   long-term plan.
61-- 距離   long-distance.
71-- 隔   far-separated.

3430₄
達 〔 Ta 〕 *v.* reach, arrive at, achieve, express, inform, tell, make way to, *adj.* prominent, understanding, intelligent, wise.
00-- 意   talk, express.
10-- 不到   out of reach.
12-- 到   reach, arrive, achieve, gain, accomplish.
-- 到新水平   reach a new height, reach a new level.
30-- 官   high officer.
46-- 觀   wise, open-minded, oblivious of adversity.
47-- 姆彈   dumdum bullet.
53-- 成   reach, arrive at, come to.
-- 成交易   come to business, conclude a transaction close a deal.
-- 成和解   reach an amicable settlement.
-- 成協議   reach agreement.
80-- 人   philosopher, wise person.

違 〔 Wei 〕 *n.* evil, fault, *v.* disobey, oppose, defy, depart from, leave, avoid.
00-- 章   disregard regulations, breach of regulation.
11-- 背   break, disobey, act against.
-- 背良心   go against one's conscience.
-- 背國際公法   breach of the international law.
16-- 理   contrary to principle, unreasonable.
27-- 約   breach of contract, break a

	promise, default.
30-- 憲	violation of constitution, unconstitutionality.
34-- 法	n. illegality, v. break the law, violate the law, adj. illegal, unlawful.
-- 法行為	offense.
-- 法者	transgressor, law-breaker.
-- 法之舉	illegal act.
40-- 難	take refuge.
44-- 禁	violate a ban.
-- 禁品	contrabands, prohibited products.
-- 禁貨物	contraband goods.
-- 禁販酒者	bootlegger.
47-- 犯	violate, disobey, break.
50-- 抗	act contrary to, defy.
-- 抗命令	disobey orders.
56-- 規	disobey regulation.
71-- 反	disobey, violate, run counter to, infringe.
-- 反軍紀	breach of military discipline.
-- 反合同	breach of contract.
80-- 令	disobey orders.

3430₆
造 〔Tsao〕 n. party in a lawsuit, v. make, do, act, build, construct, create, institute, accomplish.

01-- 詣	attainment, achievement.
02-- 端	beginning.
03-- 就	accomplish, complete, train, bring up.
-- 就人才	make useful citizens through education.
07-- 謠	invent false report, start a rumour.
-- 謠生事	cause trouble by spreading rumors.
12-- 型	modeling, moulding.
-- 型藝術	plastic arts.
21-- 價	cost of a building.
22-- 紙廠	paper mill.
-- 紙工業	paper-making industry.
24-- 化	nature, luck, fortune, creation.

27-- 假	draw up false accounts.
-- 句	make a sentence.
-- 句法	construction, syntax.
-- 船	shipbuilding.
-- 船廠	dockyard, shipyard.
-- 船工業	shipbuilding industry.
31-- 酒	brewing.
-- 福人群	benefit all people.
42-- 橋	construct a bridge.
44-- 孽	commit sins, do evil things.
-- 林	afforest.
-- 林區	afforested area.
47-- 聲勢	create a spirited atmosphere.
50-- 表	make a list, compile a table.
53-- 成	create, produce, compose, constitute.
71-- 反	rebel, revolt.
-- 反精神	rebellious spirit.
77-- 屋	build a house.
-- 冊	tabulate.
98-- 幣	coinage.
-- 幣廠	mint.

3430₉
遼 〔Liao〕 adj. distant, far off, remote.

34-- 遠	remote, far, distant.
77-- 闊	vast, wide, extensive.

3440₄
婆 〔Po〕 n. grandmother, old woman, husband's mother.

30-- 家	husband's family.
34-- 婆	mother-in-law.
60-- 羅門教	Brahmanism.

3490₄
柒 =七
染 〔Jan〕 v. dye, tinge, stain, taint, infect, affect.

00-- 病	catch a disease, catch an infection, take a disease.
-- 廠	dye-works.
10-- 工	dyer.
27-- 色	dye, color.
-- 色體	chromosome.
31-- 污	v. be infected, pollute, defile, taint, adj. defiled, polluted, soiled.

40-- 布	dye clothe.
-- 坊	dye-house.
51-- 指	have a finger in the pie, put one's finger in.
81-- 缸	dyeing vat.
94-- 料	dye-stuff.

3510₆

沖 〔Chung〕 v. soar, shoot up, wash away, rush at, dash against, strike against, collide, mix, pour in.

00-- 床	punch, punching machine.
10-- 天	rise up to the sky.
14-- 破	burst open, break through.
-- 破圍基	enclosing base was burst over by floods.
24-- 動	shake.
34-- 洗	wash with running water.
-- 洗底片	(in photography) develop negatives.
39-- 淡	dilute with water.
40-- 走	wash away.
44-- 茶	infuse tea.
48-- 散	scatter.
57-- 擊市場	raid the market.
72-- 刷	scrub and wash.
77-- 毀堤岸	the embankment was destroyed by the rush of water.
89-- 銷	abatement .

洩=泄 3411₇

3510₇

津 〔Chin〕 n. ferry, ford, creek, sap, juice, saliva, important path, v. overflow, moisten.

10-- 要固守	places of importance must be guarded carefully.
35-- 津樂道	talk with great relish.
-- 津有味	interesting, tasteful.
60-- 口	ferry.
61-- 貼	gratuity, allowance, subsidy, grant, bounty.

3511₇

沌 〔Tun〕 n. chaos.

3512₇

沸 〔Fei〕 v. boil, bubble up, adj. boiling.

12-- 水	boiling water.
38-- 溢	boil over.
61-- 點	boiling-point.
79-- 騰	boiling.

清 〔Ching〕 n. the Ching Dynasty, v. clear out, cleanse, purify, settle, adj. pure, clear, clean, quiet.

00-- 廉	n. integrity, gold proof, adj. incorruptible, honest, not covetous.
-- 高	lofty and pure of mind, virtuous.
09-- 談	feast of reason.
10-- 雅	elegant.
-- 平世界	peaceful and orderly world.
12-- 水	clean water.
16-- 理	n. settlement, clearance, arrangement, check up, clear up, tidy up.
-- 醒	v. get sober, come to one's sense, adj. sane, clearminded.
20-- 秀	graceful, pretty.
-- 秀眉目	handsome features.
-- 香	fragrant.
22-- 幽	secluded.
-- 幽雅緻	secluded and refined.
26-- 白	pure, clean, innocent, fair, unblemished.
-- 白廉	pure and honest.
-- 白人家	decent family.
29-- 償	pay off all debts, discharge.
30-- 涼	cool, refreshing.
32-- 淨	pure, clean.
33-- 心	purify one's mind.
34-- 漆	varnish.
36-- 湯	clear soup, light soup, consommé.
37-- 朗	broad.
-- 潔	clean, neat, pure.
-- 潔工	cleaner.
-- 潔隊	cleaning squad.
38-- 冷飲料	soft drinks.
-- 澈	clean and clear.
-- 道	clear the street.
-- 道夫	street sweeper, scavenger.
40-- 查	investigate, check, take

	stock of.
-- 真寺	mosque.
41-- 帳	clear off an account, balance an account, make up account.
44-- 楚	clear, plain, distinct, settled.
-- 苦好學	being poverty-stricken and given to study.
48-- 樣	fair copy.
50-- 毒	disinfect.
52-- 靜	quiet, calm.
57-- 掃戰場	mop up enemy remnants on the battlefield.
60-- 晨	early morning, dawn, daybreak.
-- 早	very early, at dawn.
61-- 點	count, check up, sort and count.
-- 點存貨	take an account of stock.
62-- 晰	clear-cut.
-- 晰可辨	clear and distinguishable.
-- 晰程度	visibility.
66-- 單	list, statement of accounts, detailed account.
67-- 明節	Tomb Sweeping Day.
77-- 風	fresh breeze.
-- 風亮節	integrity, high moral character.
-- 風徐來	the soothing breezes slowly blow this way.
-- 風明月	the soothing wind and the bright moon.
77-- 閑	leisurely, undisturbed.
78-- 除	weed out, clear out.
80-- 貧	honest poverty.
-- 貧家境	of a poor and honest family.
88-- 算	liquidation.
-- 算人	liquidator.
90-- 黨	purge.

3513_0

漣 〔Lian〕 *n*. ripples.

決 〔Chueh〕 *v*. determine, decide, settle, judge, break, pass sentence, *adj*. certain, sure.

00-- 意	determine, resolve, decide, make up one's mind.
08-- 議	*n*. resolution, decision, *v*. resolve, decide.
-- 議案	resolution.
10-- 不	by no means, never, on no account.
-- 不投降	nail one's own colors to the mast.
11-- 非	certainly not.
12-- 裂	*n*. breach, division, *v*. break off relation, split, rupture.
23-- 然	unquestionably, certainly, surely.
22-- 斷	decide finally, give judgement.
30-- 定	determine, decide, set down, fix, make a decision.
-- 定權	powers of decision.
-- 定因素	decisive factor.
-- 賽	decisive battle, play-off.
-- 賽選手	finalist.
33-- 心	determination, keep up one's mind.
-- 心書	pledge.
40-- 志	resolution.
41-- 標	award of bid.
60-- 口	breach, opening.
63-- 戰	decisive battle.
77-- 鬥	duel, affair of honor.
88-- 算	settle an account, final account, balance sheet.
-- 算期	period of settlement.
-- 算表	final statement.
-- 算書	final report.
-- 策	decision-making, policy decision.
-- 策者	policy-maker, decision maker.

3513_2

濃 〔Nung〕 *adj*. thick, strong, heavy, rich, dense, dark.

00-- 度	density, thickness, concentration.
23-- 縮	concentration.
-- 縮鈾	enriched uranium.
30-- 密	close.
36-- 湯	thick soup, rich soup.

39-- 淡	strong and weak.
44-- 茶	strong tea.
71-- 厚	thick, deep, strong.
91-- 煙	thick smoke, dark smoke.

3513₄

湊 〔Tsou〕 v. collect, gather, put together.

11-- 巧	by chance, happen to.
-- 巧之事	coincident.
40-- 在一起	put together.
47-- 款	subscription.
53-- 成	make up.
-- 成整數	make up an even amount.
80-- 合	collect together, assemble, put together.

3514₄

淒 〔Chi〕 adj. cloudy and rainy, bleak, cold, shivering, freezing, sorrowful, desolate.

30-- 涼	cold, frigid, bleak, lonely.
35-- 淒	sorrowful, sad, melancholy.
-- 淒涼涼	lonely, forlorn.
-- 淒切切	mournful, plaintive.
-- 淒慘慘	heartbreaking.
47-- 切動人	sadly moving.
93-- 慘	sad, sorrowful, tragic, melancholy.

3515₅

溝 〔Kou〕 n. ditch, trench, gutter, furrow, drain, channel, dyke, v. communicate, exchange ideas.

12-- 水	ditch-water.
31-- 渠	ditch, drain.
35-- 漕	groove.
37-- 通	intercourse, communication.
-- 通感情	promote friendly relations.

3516₀

油 〔Yu〕 n. oil, fat, grease, ointment, adj. oily, greasy, sleek, luxuriant, flourishing.

00-- 膏	ointment.
-- 商	oil man.
-- 廠	oil refinery.
-- 庫	oil depot, fuel depot.
20-- 毛氈	asphalt felt.

22-- 紙	oil paper.
23-- 然	copious, flourishing, abundantly.
27-- 船	tanker, oiler, tank-ship.
31-- 污染	oil pollution (contamination).
34-- 漆	n. paints, varnishes, v. paint, varnish.
-- 漆廠	paint factory.
-- 漆匠	painter.
35-- 漬	oil stain.
40-- 布	oil-cloth, oil-skin, tarpaulin.
44-- 菜	rape (a plant).
-- 菜子	rapeseeds.
47-- 桶	oil tank.
50-- 畫	canvas, oil painting.
-- 畫顏料	oil-colors.
55-- 井	oil-well, oil-spring.
58-- 輪	oil carrier (ship, tanker, streamer).
60-- 田	oilfield.
71-- 脂	grease, fat.
-- 灰	putty.
73-- 膩	greasy.
77-- 印機	mimeograph.
80-- 煎	fry.
88-- 箱	fuel tank.
-- 餅	oil-cake.
-- 管	oil-pipeline.
91-- 煙	soot.
94-- 料作物	oil-bearing crops.

3516₆

漕 〔Tsao〕 n. canal, channel, water, transportation.

3518₆

潰 〔Kui〕 v. overflow, rush through, break up, defeat, scatter, rot, adj. confused, defeated, scattered, broken.

00-- 瘍	ulcer.
08-- 敵	make the enemy fly in all directions.
22-- 亂	in disorder, in confusion.
32-- 逃	flee in disorder.
35-- 決	overflow the bank.
37-- 退	retreat in disorder.

40-- 走　　　rout, flight.
48-- 散　　　rout, scatter in defeat.
68-- 敗　　　defeated, beaten, destroyed, routed.
97-- 爛　　　ulcerate, rot, fester.

漬〔Tzu〕v. soak, steep, dye, stain.
00-- 痕　　　spot, stain.
3519₀

沫〔Mo〕n. foam, froth, saaliva, bubble.
3519₆

凍〔Tung〕v. cool, freeze, adj. cold, icy, freezing.
00-- 瘡　　　kibe, chilblain.
10-- 死　　　die of cold, freeze to death.
-- 豆腐　　　frozen bean curd.
12-- 冰　　　freeze.
20-- 手 aq 凍腳　freezing cold.
21-- 僵　　　numb with cold.
24-- 結　　　freeze, block.
-- 結工資　　freeze wage.
-- 結物價　　price freeze.
-- 結爲冰　　frozen into ice.
-- 結資產　　block assets, frozen assets.
-- 結存款　　block deposits, frozen deposits.
27-- 的　　　frozen, icy.
28-- 傷　　　frost-bite, frost bitten.
40-- 土　　　frozen soil.
-- 肉　　　frozen meat.
82-- 餒　　　cold and starvation.
3520₆

神〔Shen〕n. god, divinity, spirit, deity, spirit, energy. adj. wonderful, supernatural, mysterious, marvelous, wondrous.
00-- 童　　　infant prodigy, precocious boy.
-- 意　　　oracle.
01-- 話　　　myth, fairy-tale.
-- 話學　　　mythology.
09-- 效　　　wonderful efficacy, divine efficacy.
-- 諭　　　oracle.
16-- 聖　　　holy, sacred, divine.
-- 聖同盟　　holy alliance.
-- 魂　　　the soul.

21-- 經　　　nerve.
-- 經病　　　neuropathy, insanity, nervous disease, hysteria.
-- 經病人　　neurotic.
-- 經痛　　　neuritis, neuralgia.
-- 經衰弱　　nervous prostration, neurasthenia.
-- 經過敏　　nervous, over-sensitive.
-- 經戰　　　war of nerves.
-- 經胚胎　　neuro-blast.
-- 經質　　　nervousness.
-- 經學　　　neurology.
-- 經錯亂　　be beside oneself, be out of one's mind.
22-- 仙　　　angel, fairy, genie.
24-- 佑　　　providence.
27-- 色　　　appearance, look.
-- 色不變　　not to turn a hair.
-- 約　　　testament.
33-- 祕　　　mysterious, mystery.
-- 祕主義　　mysticism.
35-- 速　　　wonderfully prompt, unusually quick.
37-- 通廣大　　extremely resourceful, omnipotent.
40-- 壇　　　shrine.
-- 奇　　　marvelous, miraculous.
-- 奇變化　　miraculous changes.
44-- 權　　　divine right, divine power.
48-- 槍手　　　sharpshooter, marksman.
53-- 甫　　　priest.
67-- 明　　　deity.
77-- 學　　　theology, divinity.
-- 學家　　　theologist.
-- 學院　　　seminary.
80-- 龕　　　shrine.
-- 父　　　father, missionary, friar.
-- 氣　　　spirit, overweening pride.
95-- 性　　　divine nature.
-- 情　　　air, manner.
97-- 怪　　　gods and spirits.
3521₈

禮〔Li〕n. ceremony, rite, propriety, etiquette, courtesy.
00-- 讓　　　courteousness, modesty, condescension.

07--	記	The Book of Rites.
10--	礉	military salute.
21--	拜	worship, church service.
--	拜六	Saturday.
--	拜一	Monday.
--	拜二	Tuesday.
--	拜三	Wednesday.
--	拜五	Friday.
--	拜日	Sunday.
--	拜四	Thursday.
--	拜堂	church, House of God.
26--	貌	manner, courtesy, civility.
27--	物	present, gift.
28--	儀	ceremony , etiquette, good breeding.
30--	賓司	Office of Protocol, Protocol Department.
46--	帽	high hat.
48--	教	culture, ethical education.
60--	品	gift, present.
--	品店	gift shop.
--	品包裝	gift packaging.
77--	服	full dress, ceremonious dress, ritual coat, frock.
88--	節	formality, etiquette.
90--	堂	hall, auditorium.
--	券	gift certificate (cheque), present ticket.
97--	炮	gun salutes.

3523₂
裱 〔Piao〕 v. mount, paste.

97--	糊	papering.

3524₄
褸 〔Lu〕 adj. ragged, shabby.

3526₀
袖 〔Hsiu〕 n. sleeve.

00--	章	sleeve, badge.
11--	頭	cuff.
17--	子	sleeve.
18--	珍	pocket (edition).
--	珍本	pocket book, manual, hand book, pocket edition.
--	珍艦隊	pocket battleship.
20--	手旁觀	look on with folded arms.
60--	口	cuff, wristband.

3529₀
袜 〔Moh〕 n. sock.

3530₀
連 〔Lien〕 n. company of soldiers, v. join, connect, continue, succeed, unite, link, adj. continuous, connected, successive.

00--	夜	night after night.
16--	環	n. concatenation, connecting links, v. link,
--	環信	chair letter.
--	環圖	pictorial storybook, serial pictures.
21--	比例	continued proportion.
22--	任	renew the term of office.
24--	續	v. continue, chain, adj. continuous, continual, in series.
--	續性	continuity.
--	續不斷	continuous, in endless succession.
26--	保	joint security.
--	綿	continuous.
27--	絡	keep in touch with, make connection, communicate.
32--	衫裙	one-piece dress.
34--	襟	husbands of sisters.
42--	婚	allied by marriage.
44--	帶責任	jointly liability (responsibility, obligation).
47--	起來	connect, join together.
--	根拔除	uproot.
50--	接	n. connection, joint, v. connect, join, adjoin, meet, mix.
--	接語	connective (in grammar).
--	接詞	conjunction (in grammar).
--	接不斷	continuously.
--	本帶利	both the principal and the interest.
54--	拱壩	multiple-arch dam.
60--	日	consecutive days, for several days in a row.
--	累	implicate, involve.
71--	長	company commander, captain.

75--	體雙生	Siamese twins.
77--	貫	coherent.
78--	隊	company (of soldiers).
80--	合	n. connection, union, combination, v. unite, combine.
--	年	series of years, for years.
--	分數	continuedfraction.
88--	坐	joint responsibility.
89--	鎖	interlock, in a chain.
--	鎖商店	chain stores.
--	鎖反應	chain reaction.
90--	忙	at once, promptly, hurriedly.

3530_3

迭 〔 **Tieh** 〕 v. change alternate, adv. alternately, repeatly, reciprocally, by turns.

37--	次	repeatedly, over and over again.

逮 〔 **Tai** 〕 v. arrest, seize, catch, reach, chase, pursue.

08--	於今日	up to now.
33--	補	arrest, take into custody.
53--	捕	n. warrant of arrest, v. arrest.

3530_6

迪 〔 **Ti** 〕 v. advance, lead, educate.

遭 〔 **Tsao** 〕 n. time, turn, v. suffer, meet with, encounter.

10--	到	encounter, come up against.
15--	殃	meet with disaster (or calamity).
20--	受	suffer, be afflicted.
36--	遇	n. experience,ocuurrence, chance, v. incur, happen, undergo,meet with.
--	遇戰	encounter battle.
40--	難	experience calamity, difficulty.
60--	累	be involved.

3530_7

遣 〔 **Chien** 〕 v. exile, dismiss, banish, expel, dispel, send, despatch, depute.

25--	使	send an envoy.
31--	返	repatriate.
--	逐	expel, drive off.
32--	派	despatch, send, depute.
38--	送	send, despatch.
40--	去	dismiss, discharge.
48--	散	disband, disorganize.
--	散費	separation pay, compensation for termination.

3530_8

遺 〔 **I** 〕 v. lose, miss, omit, leave, remain, give, will, forget.

00--	產	legacy, bequest, inheritance.
--	產繼承人	heir to property.
--	產稅	death duty, probate duty, estate tax, inheritance tax.
--	產分析	partition of inheritance.
--	產管理	administration of estate.
--	忘	forget.
--	棄	discard, abandon, forsake.
--	棄罪	offense of abandonment.
02--	訓	dying instructions.
10--	下	remain.
25--	傳	n. heredity, inheritance, v. descend, transmit, run in the blood.
--	傳工程	genetic engineering.
--	傳學	genetics.
--	傳性	heredity.
25--	失	lose, mislay, misplace.
--	失物	lost thing.
--	失招領	lost and found.
27--	像	portrait of the dead.
--	物	relics, things left behind.
36--	澤	beneficence of the dead.
37--	漏	n. omission, v. omit.
60--	跡	trace, historical ruin, vestige.
67--	囑	will, testament, dying words.
68--	贈	bequeath.
75--	體	remains, corpse.
77--	留	remain, leave behind.
78--	腹子	posthumous son.
93--	憾	regret, be sorry.
95--	精	spermatorrhea, nocturnal emission.

3530_9

速〔Su〕adj. quick, rapid, speedy, hasty, swift.

00-- 度	speed, quickness, velocity.
-- 度表	tachometer.
-- 率	velocity, rate of speed.
07-- 記	shorthand, stenography.
-- 記員	stenographer.
08-- 效	quick results.
21-- 行	put the best foot forward.
30-- 寫	shorthand, sketch.
-- 進	advance quickly.
33-- 溶咖啡	instant coffee.
35-- 決	quick decision.
-- 決戰	war of quick decision.
40-- 去	go quick.
-- 來	come quickly.
63-- 戰速決	prompt military decision.
79-- 勝論	theory of quick victory.

3610₀

泅〔Hsin〕v. swim, float.

12-- 水	swimming, swim.

泊〔Po〕n. lakelet,swamp,marsh, v. anchor, moor.

20-- 位費	berth charge.
22-- 岸	disembark.
27-- 船	anchor, come alongside.

涸〔Ke〕v. dry up, adj. dried up, exhausted.

湘〔Hsiang〕n. the Hsiang river.

3610₇

盪〔Tang〕v. move, shove,cleanse, wash, rock, swing, adj. moved, agitated.

38-- 滌	cleanse, wash.
-- 激	swash about.
60-- 口	rinse the mouth.

3611₀

況〔Kuang〕n. circumstance, condition, plight, v. compare, adj. then, more, further.

60-- 味	the situation and the experience of it.
77-- 且	still more, moreover, furthermore, besides.

3611₁

混〔Hun〕v. dawdle, mix, mingle, adj. mingled, mixed, confused, disorderly, muddy, blended.

00-- 雜	v. mingle, mix up, intermingle, adj. mixed up, blended, half-and-half.
10-- 不下去	cannot stay on the job any longer.
-- 不過去	unable to fool others.
12-- 水	muddly water.
-- 水摸魚	fish in troubled waters.
17-- 蛋	blackguard,bloody fool.
22-- 亂	n. confusion, disorder, chaos, v. mix up, confuse, adj. in disorder.
26-- 和	combination, mixing.
34-- 淆	v. confuse, adj. confused.
-- 淆視聽	confuse the public opinion.
36-- 濁	muddy, turbid.
37-- 凝土	concrete.
40-- 土	puddle.
41-- 帳	nonsense.
60-- 日子	dawdle, idle.
63-- 戰	free fight, dogfight, pell-mell.
80-- 入	infiltrate, sneak into.
-- 合	mix, blend, mingle, interlace.
-- 合物	mixture.
-- 合爲一	blended into one.
-- 合成本	hybrid cost, mixed cost.
-- 合賬戶	mixed account.

3611₄

浬〔Li〕n. nautical mile, knot.

3611₇

溫〔Wen〕v. warm, heat, review, adj. warm, temperate, mild, gentle, kind.

00-- 度	temperature.
-- 度表	thermometer.
-- 文	gentle.
-- 文爾雅	gentle and graceful.
06-- 主課	review lessons.
10-- 雅	graceful.
12-- 水	warm water.
-- 水浴	hot bath.
17-- 柔	gentle, mild, soft, tender,

affable.

-- 柔敦厚 tender and gentle.

-- 習 review, study, go over.

21-- 順 meekness.

24-- 牀 hot bed.

26-- 泉 hot spring, spa.

-- 和 kind, mild, moderate, gentle.

-- 和態度 amiable attitude.

30-- 室 greenhouse, hothouse.

32-- 州 Wenchow.

-- 良 grace, benign.

44-- 帶 temperate zone.

-- 熱 lukewarm.

62-- 暖 warm.

87-- 飽 have enough to eat and wear.

95-- 情主義 paternalism.

3612₇

涓 〔Chuan〕 n. brook, small stream, adj. pure, clear, clean.

30-- 滴 dribble, trickle.

-- 滴歸公 every cent goes to public.

36-- 涓 water flowing.

渴 〔Ke〕 n. thirst, adj. thirsty, dry, desirous of, longing.

07-- 望 n. craving, v. long for, aspire after, adj. thirsty, eager, open-eyed.

44-- 慕 yearn for.

46-- 想 longing for, thirsty, anxious.

80-- 念之 how I have thought of.

湯 〔Tang〕 n. soup, hot water.

27-- 盤 soup plate.

34-- 婆子 hot-water bottle.

41-- 麵 noodles in soup.

60-- 團 dumpling.

61-- 匙 spoon.

濁 〔Cho〕 n. gonorrhea, adj. muddy, impure, turbid, evil, corrupt.

12-- 水 muddy water.

30-- 流 turbid stream.

80-- 氣 foul smell.

3613₂

瀑 〔Pu〕 n. waterfall.

40-- 布 waterfall, cataract, cascade.

-- 布飛泉 waterfalls and flying streams.

3613₃

濕 〔Shih〕 adj. wet, moist, humid, damp.

00-- 度 humidity.

-- 度調查儀 hydrostat.

-- 度表 hydrometer.

-- 疹 eczema.

32-- 透 wet through, be drenched wet as a drowned rat.

-- 透欲滴 be dripping wet.

37-- 潮 wet, moisten.

44-- 地 swamp.

80-- 氣 moisture, dampness, damp air.

3613₄

溴 〔Hsiu〕 n. bromine.

3614₁

澤 〔Tse〕 n. marsh, bog, fen, benefit, favor, grace, v. enrich, benefit, adj. glossy, smooth, bright.

44-- 地 moorland, marsh, swamp.

60-- 國 inundated land, flooded region.

3614₇

漫 〔Man〕 v. overflow, set loose, flood, adj. vast, endless, diffused, spreading.

02-- 話 empty talk.

08-- 論 ramble.

10-- 天雪 whirling snow.

21-- 步 wander, ramble.

22-- 出 overflow.

36-- 漫 extending endlessly.

38-- 遊 roam, ramble, rove.

50-- 畫 cartoon, caricature.

-- 畫家 cartoonist, caricaturist.

71-- 長 long, living.

3619₄

澡 〔Tsao〕 v. take a bath, wash.

80-- 盆 bathtub.

90-- 堂 bath room, public bath.

3620₀

裀 〔Yin〕 *n.* shirt, underclothes, mattress.
31-- 褥　mattress.
3621_0

祝 〔Chu〕 *v.* pray, invoke, celebrate, congratulate.
00-- 文　prayer.
07-- 詞　congratulatory, address.
15-- 融　god of fire.
20-- 辭　complimentary address.
24-- 告　pray, invoke, implore.
31-- 福　blessing, benediction.
46-- 賀　congratulate, hail, felicitate.
55-- 捷　celebrate victory.
71-- 願　wish.

袒 〔Tan〕 *v.* bare the arm, strip, protect improperly, side with.
04-- 護　side with, protect improperly, screen.
10-- 露　bare, naked.
26-- 白　plain, above board.
36-- 裸　bared, naked.

視 〔Shih〕 *v.* see, look at, observe, watch, regard as, compare, manage.
10-- 死如歸　take death calmly.
26-- 線　sight, visual line.
27-- 網膜　retina.
28-- 作　regard as.
30-- 察　inspect, visit, survey.
-- 察員　inspector.
-- 官　the organ of sight.
35-- 神經　optical nerves.
40-- 力　power of vision, sight, eyesight.
-- 力檢定表　test type, eye chart.
43-- 域　sight, range of vision.
50-- 事　attend to affairs.
67-- 野　range of vision.
77-- 覺　visual sensation.
-- 覺器材　video equipment.
-- 同兒戲　take it lightly.

襯 〔Chen〕 *n.* inner garment, underclothing, *v.* line, lie beneath.
00-- 衣　inner robe, underclothes, shirt.
-- 裏　lining.

30-- 褲　drawers, underpants.
32-- 衫　shirt, undershirt.
34-- 袴　drawers.
37-- 裙　petticoat.
44-- 墊　pad, padding.
52-- 托　foil, embellish.
3622_7

褐 〔Ho〕 *n.* coarse cloth, brown.
27-- 色　dark brown.
40-- 土　drab soil.
50-- 夫　poor man.
3623_0

昶 〔Chan〕 *n.* a long day.
3624_0

裨 〔Pei〕 *n.* advantage, benefit, *v.* assist, aid, supply, *adj.* small, little.
80-- 益　benefit, advantage.
3629_4

褓 〔Pao〕 *n.* swaddling cloth.

裸 〔Lo〕 *v.* strip, bare, *adj.* naked, bare, nude.
40-- 麥　rye.
60-- 足　barefoot.
75-- 體　naked, in a state of nature.
-- 體主義者　nudist.
-- 體生活主義　nudism.
-- 體像　nude picture.
67-- 野　field of vision.
3630_0

迫 〔Po〕 *v.* compel, coerce, press, force, urge, press upon, *adj.* pressing, urgent, imminent, narrow, embarrassed.
08-- 於形勢　compelled by circumstance.
25-- 使　force, compel, coerce.
26-- 得如此　forced to be like this.
-- 促　urge, compel.
28-- 從　enforce compliance.
30-- 害　persecute, outrage.
32-- 近　draw near, imminent, close, near.
47-- 切　anxious, urgent, imminent.
57-- 擊砲　mortar.
77-- 降　forced landing.

迴 〔Hui〕 *v.* curve, bend, return, go back, *adj.* crooked, winding.

08-- 旋飛行　circular flight.
-- 旋加速器　cyclotron.
-- 環　surround, enclose.
30-- 避　avoid, retire aside, stand back, keep away from.
-- 流　eddy.
46-- 想　recollect, recall, call up, trace back, recall to mind.
55-- 轉門　revolving door.
77-- 風　whirlwind.

3630₁

逞 〔Cheng〕 v. use up, show off, exhaust, free from, be free, get loose, adj. gratified.

13-- 強　use violence, be fierce, use vigorous effort, act tough.
21-- 能　boast.
22-- 凶　use violence, be audacious.
44-- 勢　rely on one's power.

徨 〔Huang〕 n. leisure, adj. leisurely, in a hurry, anxious.

27-- 急　in a hurry.

暹 〔Hsien〕 n. the sun rising higher and brighter.

60-- 羅　Siam.
-- 羅人　Siamese.

邏 〔Lo〕 v. patrol, watch, inspect.

00-- 卒　patrol.
56-- 輯　logic.

3630₂

遏 〔O〕 v. stop, curb, check, cut, put an end to, exterminate, stand still.

21-- 止　stop, cease, curb, check.
22-- 制　restrain, repress, curb, put down.
27-- 絕　cut off.
44-- 禁　prevent, prohibit.
87-- 慾　curb lust, curb one's passion.

遇 〔Yu〕 n. luck, opportunity, v. meet, fall in with, happen, occur, entertain, receive.

08-- 敵　encounter the enemy.
10-- 雨　be caught in the rain.
12-- 到　meet, encounter.
40-- 難　meet with death, meet with misfortunes, encounter difficulties.
60-- 見　meet, come across.
78-- 險　encounter danger.
-- 險信號　distress call, distress-signal.
80-- 著　fall in with, meet, hit.

邊 〔Pien〕 n. side, edge, margin, bank, border, boundary.

11-- 疆　frontier, border.
27-- 緣　margin, edge, brink.
40-- 境　borderland, frontier.
-- 境檢查站　frontier checkpoint.
44-- 地　outskirts.
60-- 界　border, limit, national boundary.
70-- 防　frontier defense.
-- 防站　frontier defense station.
-- 防要塞　strategic point on the border.
-- 防軍　frontier forces.
71-- 區　border region.
77-- 際　edge, margin.
-- 門　side door.

3630₃

還 〔Huan〕 v. return, come back, recompense, repay, revolve, rotate, adv. still, furthermore, even.

10-- 元　return to original state, restoration.
-- 不　still not enough.
-- 不錯　well enough, good enough.
20-- 手　return a blow, retaliate.
21-- 價　give a price, make an offer for, beat down, abate a price.
23-- 我河山　let's restore our lost land !
25-- 債　clean off debts, repay a debt, get out of debt.
28-- 俗　go back to lay life.
30-- 家　go home, return home.
35-- 清　pay up, pay off.
-- 清舊帳　pay off old scores.
37-- 沒有　not yet.
40-- 有　there is still some, furthermore.
-- 本　repayment of principal.

-- 本付息	pay principal and interest.
41-- 帳	pay a debt, foot a bill.
47-- 好	not bad.
-- 報	make a recompense, repay.
57-- 擊	counterattack, strike back.
60-- 早	still early.
-- 是	still, again.
71-- 願	redeem a vow.
-- 原	restore.
83-- 錢	repay, refund.
88-- 答	answer.

3680₉

燙 〔**Tang**〕 v. scald, burn, warm, iron, smooth.

00-- 痛	sore of a burn.
-- 衣服	iron clothes.
10-- 平	ironing.
22-- 出泡	blister.
28-- 傷	scald, burn.
34-- 斗	flatiron.

3710₇

盜 〔**Tao**〕 n. thief, robber, burglar, footpad, bandit, pirate, brigand, v. steal, rob, filch, embezzle.

17-- 取	rob, plunder.
21-- 版	pirate.
30-- 案	case of robbery.
-- 竊	n. stealing, robbery, v. steal, thieve, rob.
-- 竊保險	burglary insurance.
-- 竊犯	burglar, embezzler.
31-- 汗	night-sweats.
32-- 淫	deflower.
40-- 賣	sell fraudulently.
47-- 劫保險	robbery insurance.
63-- 賊	thief, robber, pirate, highwayman.
71-- 匪	bandits, robbers.
77-- 用	embezzle, usurp.
-- 用公款	embezzle public funds, defalcate.

3710₉

鑿 〔**Tsao**〕 n. chisel, punch, v. dig, chip, chisel, adj. certain, sure, true.

10-- 石	quarry.
17-- 子	chisel.
30-- 穿	chisel through.
40-- 木	chisel wood.
55-- 井	make a well.
80-- 入	chisel into.

3711₀

汎 〔**Fan**〕 v. float, sail, be driven by winds and waves, adj. wide, extensive, universal.

10-- 理論	panlogism.
20-- 愛	universal love.
22-- 愛主義	philanthropism.
31-- 灑	sprinkle everywhere.
33-- 心論	panpsychism.
35-- 神論	pantheism.
38-- 濫	overflow, excessive.
80-- 美主義	Pan-Americanism.
-- 美會議	Pan-American Conference.

汛 〔**Hsun**〕 n. high water.

47-- 期	high-water season.

洫 〔**Hsu**〕 n. ditch, gutter.

沮 〔**Chu**〕 v. stop, quash, prohibit, injure, spoil, ruin, destroy, frighten.

21-- 止	stop.
40-- 喪	v. gloom, cast down, languish, adj. melancholy, dejected, downcast, depressed, discouraged, disheartened.

3711₁

泥 〔**Ni**〕 n. mud, clay, mire, soil, mixed fine particles, paste, plaster earth, adj. muddy, miry.

12-- 水匠	mason, bricklayer.
17-- 刀	trowel.
22-- 炭	n. peat, turf, adj. miry, muddy.
24-- 牆	mud-wall.
29-- 鰍	mudfish, loach.
33-- 濘	n. muddiness, adj. muddy.
39-- 沙	clay and sand.
40-- 土	earth, soil, mud.
-- 坑	mire.
46-- 塊	lump of mud, clod.
67-- 路	muddy road.
77-- 屋	mud-house.
-- 肥	mud fertilizer.

80-- 人   doll, clay figurine.
87-- 塑   clay model.
94-- 煤   peat.

涅〔Nieh〕n. black mud.

澀〔Se〕adj. rough, acrid, bitter, harsh, difficult to understand, slow of tongue.
60-- 味   acerbity, rough taste.

3711_2

氾〔Fan〕n. flood, overflowing, v. overflow, flood, inundate, adj. unsettled, wide, extensive.
08-- 論   general discussion.
27-- 祭   disperse sacrifices widely.
37-- 氾   floating about, unsettled.
38-- 濫   inundate, overflow, flood.
43-- 博   wide, extensive.

泡〔Pao〕n. foam, froth, bubble, suds, v. soak, dip, infuse.
35-- 沫   froth, foam, bubble.
44-- 茶   make tea, infuse tea.
62-- 影   bubble and shadow, unreal thing.
-- 影夢   unreal and visionary.
87-- 塑料   foam plastics.

3711_4

渥〔Wo〕v. steep, soak, water, moisten, tinge.

濯〔Cho〕v. wash, cleanse, dip.
37-- 濯   bright, treeless.
60-- 足   wash feet.

3712_0

汐〔Hsi〕n. evening-tide, night-tide.

澗〔Jian〕n. mountain stream, rivulet.

洶〔Hsiung〕n. uproar, clamor, excitement, noise of water. adj. clamorous, tumultuous, forcible, violent.
24-- 動   unquiet, excited.
37-- 洶   clamorous, tumultuous, excited, bawling, noise of rushing water.
-- 湧   surging, dashing of waves, rush of torrent.

洶〔Hsun〕adv. really.

洞〔Tung〕n. cave, hole, den, cavity, opening.
00-- 底   bottom of a hole.
20-- 悉   understand thoroughly.
30-- 房   bridal chamber.
-- 察   v. perceive, investigate thoroughly, adj. fully convinced.
-- 穴   cave, cavity, hole.
96-- 燭   know clearly.

淘〔Tao〕v. wash rice, sift, scour, search for.
19-- 砂揀金   wash the sand for gold.
34-- 汰   n. natural selection, v. eliminate the inferior, washout, sift and reduce in number.
-- 汰競爭   elimination contest.
-- 汰出去   clean it out.
39-- 沙   sift sand.
55-- 井   cleanse a well, scour a well.
80-- 氣   mischievous, irritated.
90-- 米   wash rice, scour rice.

凋〔Tiao〕v. fade, become withered, be exhausted, adj. fading, withered, declined.
04-- 謝   wither, fall into decay, decay.
10-- 零   declined, fallen, fall and scatter.
-- 零殘敗   fallen and destroyed.
13-- 殘   declining, fading, destitute.
44-- 萎   fade, go off, wither, decay.
98-- 敝不堪   so destitute that it is unbearable.

溯〔Su〕v. go against a stream, trace up a source.
17-- 及   go back to.
-- 及效力   retroactivity.
31-- 源   derive, trace something to its source.
43-- 求權   right of recourse.
50-- 本求源   go back to the source or origin.

湖〔Hu〕n. lake, water.

11-- 北	Hupeh Province.	
12-- 水	lake water.	
36-- 泊港	lake harbor.	
40-- 南	Hunan Province.	
90-- 光山色	the natural beauty of lakes and mountains.	

潤 〔Jun〕 *v.* moisten, enrich, fatten, *adj.* moist, rich, sleek, glossy.

27-- 色	embellish, put the finishing touch on.
35-- 清	smooth, slippery.
36-- 澤	*v.* moisten, *adj.* smooth, glossy.
37-- 滑	*n.* lubrication, *v.* lubricate.
-- 滑劑	lubricant.
-- 滑油	lubricating oil.

潮 〔Chao〕 *n.* tide, damp, *adj.* moist, damp, humid.

12-- 水	tide.
30-- 流	tidal current, tide, tendency, trend.
36-- 濕	moist, damp, rainy.
37-- 汐	tide.
-- 汛	tides.
80-- 氣	moisture.

瀾 〔Lan〕 *n.* billow, vast expanse of water, *adj.* overflowing.

36-- 漫	overflowing, carefree.

沏 〔Chi〕 *v.* infuse.

44-- 茶	make tea, infuse tea.

3712₇

涌 〔Yung〕 *v.* gush forth, rise up, rush on.

12-- 到	flood to.
16-- 現	come forward, come to the fore.
21-- 上心來	well up in the mind.
22-- 出	gush out, spout out.
26-- 泉	spring, bubbling fountain.

漏 〔Lou〕 *n.* leak, slip, neglect, *v.* leak, drip, disclose, let out, lose, omit.

10-- 電	leak of electricity.
12-- 水	leak of water, leaking.
22-- 出	leak out.
27-- 網	escape from the net.
-- 船	leaky ship.
28-- 稅	*n.* tax evasion, smuggling, *v.* evade taxes.
34-- 斗	funnel, hopper.
37-- 洞	loophole, flaw.
51-- 掉	leave out, miss out.
77-- 屋	leaking house.

湧 〔Yung〕 *v.* flow rapidly, gush out, bubble out, run out, rush on.

22-- 出	gush, pour, roll.
26-- 泉	bubbling fountain.
30-- 進	rush into.

渦 〔Wo〕 *n.* whirlpool, eddy.

30-- 流	eddy, vortex.
58-- 輪	turbine.
-- 輪發電機	turbo-generator.

滑 〔Hua〕 *v.* slip, slide, *adj.* smooth, slippery, glassy, polished, cunning, crafty, sharp.

10-- 石	soapstone, talc.
-- 雪	ski.
-- 下去	slide further away.
11-- 頭	crafty, tricky, shrewd.
22-- 倒	slip down, lose one's footing.
23-- 稽	*n.* humor, joke, *adj.* humorous, jesting, comical, funny.
-- 稽文	burlesque.
-- 稽戲	farce.
-- 稽家	humorist.
24-- 動	slip, glide, slide.
32-- 冰	skating, skate.
-- 冰者	skater.
-- 冰鞋	skate.
-- 冰場	skating-rink, rink.
37-- 潤	*v.* lubricate, *adj.* oily, greasy.
-- 油	lubricant.
-- 溜	slippery.
-- 過	glide by.
40-- 走	slide.
44-- 落	slip off.
48-- 梯	slide (in a playground).
58-- 輪	pulley.
75-- 跌	slip down.
67-- 路	slippery road.
77-- 膩	greasy, oily.

| 87-- | 翔 | glide in the air. |
| -- | 翔機 | glider. |

鴻 〔**Hung**〕 *n.* wild swan, letters, *adj.* huge, great, large, huge.

20--	毛	swan's feather, very light thing.
35--	溝	gulf, gap.
44--	荒	chaos.
47--	鵠	wild swan.
60--	恩	great mercy.
--	圖	big plan.
71--	雁	wild goose, swan, refugees.

溺 〔**Ni**〕 *n.* urine, *v.* sink, drown, pass urine.

10--	死	be drowned.
13--	職	neglect one's duty.
20--	愛	dote on, be fond of, make much of.
--	愛子女	dote on one's children.
66--	器	chamber pot.

澳 〔**Ao**〕 *n.* bank, bay, cove, harbor.

| 40-- | 大利亞 | Australia. |
| 77-- | 門 | Macao. |

渙 〔**Huan**〕 *v.* disperse, scatter, spread out.

| 48-- | 散 | disorganization. |

3713_6

漁 〔**Yu**〕 *n.* fishing, *v.* fish, pursue improperly.

00--	產	aquatic products.
24--	穫量	catch.
27--	網	fishing-net.
--	船	fishing boat, trawler.
32--	業	fishery, fishing.
37--	汛期	fishing season.
44--	權	piscary, fishing rights.
46--	場	fishing ground.
71--	區	fishing area.
77--	民	fisherman.
--	具	fishing-tackle, fishing-gear.
80--	人	fishingman.
88--	竿	fishing rod.

3714_0

淑 〔**Shu**〕 *adj.* virtuous, pure, beautiful, uncorrupted, clear.

20--	秀	virtuous, modest.
24--	德	female virtues.
40--	女	virgin, pure and graceful woman, virtuous woman.
80--	善君子	gentleman.

3714_1

潯 〔**Hsun**〕 *n.* water frontage.

3714_7

汲 〔**Chi**〕 *v.* draw liquid, lead, drag.

| 12-- | 水 | draw water. |

沒 〔**Mo**〕 *v.* die, perish, sink, drown, immerge, bury, hide, disappear, vanish, confiscate, eliminate, destroy, *adj.* dead, gone, exhausted, sunk, finished, *adv.* no, not, not yet.

28--	收	*n.* confiscation, forfeiture, *v.* confiscate, expropriate.
--	收物	forfeit.
35--	禮貌	*n.* bad manner, *adj.* impolite.
40--	有	not, without, lack of, have not, none, there is not.
--	有的話	it can be.
--	有的事	it's impossible.
--	有誠意	insincere.
--	有理由	unreasonable.
--	有系統	unsystematic, desultory.
--	有資格	unqualified, incompetent.
--	有根據	groundless.
--	有把握	not sure, not confident.
--	有是非	do not get involved in disputes, there is no justice.
--	有原則	unprincipled.
--	有前例	unprecedented.
--	有銷路	unsellable, go begging.
44--	落	decline.
--	世不忘	I shall never forget in my life.
46--	趕上	miss (a train, a bus, etc)
65--	味道	tasteless, insipid.
77--	用	useless, good-for-nothing, futile.
--	關係	never mind, not at all.
80--	人	none, nobody, no one.
84--	錯	nothing wrong.

泯 〔**Min**〕 *v.* destroy, eliminate, vanish, *adj.* exhausted.

33-- 滅　　　annihilate, eliminate.

浸 〔Chin〕 v. immerse, soak, dip, plunge.
10-- 死　　　drowned.
12-- 水　　　drench, soak in water.
22-- 種　　　soak seeds.
30-- 液　　　dip.
32-- 透　　　drench through, thoroughly soaked.
35-- 禮　　　baptism, immersion.
36-- 濕　　　soaked.
37-- 沒　　　immersion.
40-- 在水中　submerge in water.
80-- 入　　　immerse, dip into.

澱 〔Tien〕 n. dreg, sediment.
98-- 粉　　　starch.

潺 〔Chan〕 n. water flowing, sound of water.

3715_6

渾 〔Hun〕 adj. muddy, dirty, chaotic, mixed, confused.
27-- 身　　　the whole body.
-- 身是膽　　very daring.
35-- 沌　　　confuse, disordered, chaotic.

3716_1

沿 〔Yen〕 v. follow, follow along, go along, prep. along the river.
22-- 岸　　　alongshore, coastal area.
31-- 江　　　along the river.
-- 河　　　along the river.
36-- 邊　　　alongside.
38-- 海　　　alongshore, along the coast.
-- 海工業　　industry in the coastal regions.
-- 海港口　　coastal harbor.
-- 海漁場　　in-shore, fishery.
-- 海貿易　　coastwise trade.
44-- 革　　　successive change.
67-- 路　　　along the way, on the way.

澹 〔Tan〕 adj. tranquil, placid.
3716_2

沼 〔Chao〕 n. pool, pond, marsh.
36-- 澤　　　marsh, fen, swamp.
80-- 氣　　　marsh gas, firedamp.

溜 〔Liu〕 v. float, slide, slop, flow gen-tly, go away secretly, adj. smooth, slippery, tricky.
32-- 冰　　　skating.
-- 冰場　　　skating rink.
40-- 走　　　slip away, sneak away.

3716_4

洛 〔Lo〕 n. the Lo river.
3716_7

湄 〔Mei〕 n. bank, water front.
3718_0

溟 〔Ming〕 n. drizzling rain.
3718_1

凝 〔Ning〕 v. freeze, congeal, concrete, concentrate, consolidate.
17-- 聚　　　n. cohesion, v. curdle.
-- 聚精神　　concentrate one's attention.
23-- 縮　　　concentrate.
24-- 結　　　n. congelation, concretion, condensation, v. solidify, condense, freeze.
-- 結力　　　chemical affinity.
32-- 冰　　　freeze.
34-- 滯　　　hang on.
35-- 神　　　concentrate.
36-- 視　　　gaze, stare, regard.
60-- 固　　　n. solidification, v. solidify, concrete, consolidate.
-- 固汽油彈　napalm bomb.
-- 思　　　meditate, contemplate, be lost in thought.
61-- 點　　　freezing point.

3718_2

次 〔Tzu〕 n. order, turns, position, post, time, the next, the second, adj. second, next, subordinate, inferior.
00-- 序　　　order, series, sequence.
-- 序顛倒　　in reverse order.
-- 序排好　　the order was arranged.
08-- 於　　　second to, inferior to.
10-- 要　　　secondary, of secondary importance.
-- 要收益　　second income.
-- 要作用　　secondary function.
-- 要問題　　secondary question.
14-- 殖民地　semi-colonial state.
17-- 子　　　second son.

24-- 貨	inferior materials, low quality goods.
37-- 次獲勝	win the victory every time.
58-- 數	number of times.
60-- 日	next day, following day.
-- 日交貨	next day delivery.
-- 品	seconds, second-raters, faulty goods (items), defective goods.
-- 品率	defective rate.
71-- 長	vice-minister.
88-- 等	second-class, second-grade.
-- 第	order, turns.

漱 〔Shu〕 v. rinse, gargle.
60-- 口   gargle, rinse the mouth.

3718₆
瀨 〔Lai〕 n. torrent.

3719₃
潔 〔Chieh〕 v. purify, clean, adj. clean, pure, neat, tidy.
26-- 白   pure white.
27-- 身自愛   lead an honest and clean life.
-- 身自好   well-behaved.
32-- 淨   clean, pure.

3719₄
滌 〔Ti〕 v. wash, cleanse, sweep.
32-- 淨   clean.

深 〔Shen〕 n. depth, adj. deep, profound, long (time), adv. very, extremely.
00-- 度   depth.
-- 交   intimacy, intimate friendship.
-- 夜   dead hours, midnight, the dead of night.
-- 意   deep meaning.
01-- 刻   penetrating, keen, strong, far-reaching.
-- 刻印象   having a deep impression.
04-- 謀   deep design.
-- 謀遠慮   think and plan far ahead.
10-- 惡   hate.
-- 惡痛絕   hate strongly.
-- 更半夜   deep in the night.
-- 不可測   extremely abstruse, unfathomable.
12-- 水   deep water.
-- 水炸彈   depth bomb.
20-- 信   believe firmly, have faith in, deeply convinced.
-- 信不疑   believe without a shadow of doubt.
21-- 紅   dark red.
22-- 山   deep in the mountain.
24-- 仇   rancor.
27-- 奧   deep, profound, abstract, mysterious.
-- 色   deep colors, dark colors.
28-- 以爲非   condemn strongly.
-- 以爲恥   feel deeply ashamed of.
-- 以爲憾   feel deep regret over.
-- 微奧妙   profound and mysterious.
30-- 究   make a thorough investigation, deep-research.
32-- 淵   abyss.
33-- 淺   deep and shallow, depth.
-- 淺不知   ignorant, inexperienced.
34-- 遠   far, distant, remote, far-reaching.
-- 爲感動   be deeply moved.
-- 染惡習   deeply imbued with evil practices.
37-- 通   be well versed in.
40-- 坑   deep pit.
46-- 加研究   make a penetrating research.
47-- 切   intensely, deeply profoundly.
-- 切厭惡   dislike strongly.
-- 切體會   feel intensely.
-- 根蒂固   deeply rooted.
49-- 妙   profound, subtle.
50-- 表同情   be very sympathetic.
53-- 感   affect deeply, feel deeply.
55-- 耕   deep ploughing.
60-- 思   deep thinking, contemplation, deep thought.
-- 思熟慮   careful consideration.
62-- 呼吸   deep breath.
-- 睡   deep sleep.
67-- 明大義   know clearly the right things to do and the prin-

	ciples to follow.
71-- 願	with sincerely.
-- 厚	profound, strong (affection).
77-- 居簡出	live in seclusion with few social contacts.
80-- 入	enter into, penetrate deep into, study thoroughly.
-- 入研究	in-depth study.
-- 入淺出	at once simple and profound.
-- 入人心	deeply rooted in the heart of the people.
86-- 知	be well aware of, know well.
95-- 情	deep feeling, strong affection.
-- 情似海	strong love.
-- 情厚誼	long and close friendship.
97-- 恨	deep hatred.

3721₀

祖 〔Tsu〕 *n.* ancestor, grandfather, forefathers, founder, originator.

00-- 廟	ancestral temple.
12-- 孫	ancestry and posterity, grandparents and grandchildren.
24-- 先	ancestor, progenitor.
25-- 傳	handed down from one's ancestor.
60-- 國	mother country, fatherland.
77-- 母	grandmother.
80-- 父	grandfather.
-- 父母	grandparent.

3721₂

袍 〔Pao〕 *n.* robe, gown, long garment.

| 36-- 澤 | colleagues, comrades-in-arms. |

3721₄

冠 〔Kuan〕 *n.* cap, hat, crown, bonnet, *v.* wear a cap.

07-- 詞	article (in grammar).
30-- 字	article.
37-- 軍	champion.
44-- 蓋雲集	gathering of dignitaries.
-- 帶齊全	in full dress.

3721₇

冗 〔Jung〕 *n.* business, affairs, occupation, *adj.* busy, extra, superfluous, disorderly.

00-- 雜	confused, mixed.
55-- 費至巨	the unnecessary expense is great.
60-- 員停薪	stop paying supernumeraries.
71-- 長	prolix, verbose.

祀 〔Ssu〕 *n.* sacrifice year, *v.* sacrifice.

35-- 神	make offering to gods.
37-- 祖	worship ancestors.
55-- 典	sacrificial.

3722₀

初 〔Chu〕 *adj.* first, beginning, early, original, *adv.* originally, at first.

00-- 交	the beginning of friendship.
-- 度良晨	the lucky moment of the first born.
03-- 試	first trial.
-- 試啼聲	the first cry of a newborn infant.
10-- 露頭角	make a first show of one's ability, debut.
16-- 現	open to the view.
21-- 步	*n.* first step, *adj.* elementary, preliminary, initiative.
-- 步試驗	preliminary trial.
-- 步計劃	preliminary plan.
-- 步預算	preliminary budget.
-- 步研究	preliminary study.
-- 步估計	preliminary estimate.
-- 步審查	initial examination.
-- 步協議	preliminary agreement.
-- 步檢查	preliminary review.
-- 步檢驗	preliminary inspection, initial survey.
-- 步分析	preliminary analysis.
-- 步繁榮	initial prosperity.
-- 版	first edition.
-- 歲元祚	in the first year of the reign.
22-- 出茅廬	be wet behind the ears.
24-- 值	initial value.
25-- 生	the first growth, first born.
27-- 級	primary, elementary.

--級產業	primary industry.
--級教練	primary training.
--級中學	junior high school.
--級會計員	junior accountant.
37-- 次	first time.
--次訂單	initial order.
--次出售	first sale.
40-- 校	first revisal.
42-- 婚	newly-married, first marriage.
43-- 始費用	initial cost.
47-- 犯	first offence, first crime.
--期	infancy, initial stage.
--期儲備	initial reserves.
--期存貨	initial stock.
--期協議	initial treaty.
60-- 見成效	initial success.
77-- 學	n. elementary instruction, v. begin study.
--學者	beginner.
80-- 入世途	start in life.
88-- 等	primary, elementary.
--等代數	elementary algebra.
--等教育	elementary education.
--等學校	elementary school.
--等小學校	primary school.

祠〔Tzu〕n. temple, shrine, sacrifice, offering, v. offer sacrifices, worship.
| 90-- 堂 | family temple, ancestral temple. |

翩〔Pien〕n. flutter to and fro, fly about, v. flutter, fly quickly, hover.

3722_7
祁〔Chi〕adv. very, adj. much, more, numerous, large.

禍〔Huo〕n. evil, calamity, injury, woe, misfortune, adversity, v. harm, injure, bring disaster upon.
12-- 水	apple of discord.
22-- 亂	disturbance.
30-- 害	damage, injury, evil, harm.
31-- 福	weal and woe, good and evil.
33-- 心	malicious design, evil intention.
47-- 根	root of evil, source of disaster.
50-- 患	misfortune, woe, calamity, evil.
80-- 首	ringleader, principal criminal.

3723_2
冢〔Chung〕n. grave, tomb, peak, mound.

祿〔Lu〕n. prosperity, happiness, income, emolument.
| 25-- 俸 | salary, official pay. |

3723_3
褪〔Tun〕v. disrobe, with, fade.
| 20-- 毛 | cast the feather. |
| 27-- 色 | discolor, fade. |

3723_4
襖〔Ao〕n. jacket, coat, short garment.

3726_2
摺〔Tieh〕n. plait, pleat, lined coat, riding jacket, v. plait.
| 17-- 子 | plaits, pleats. |
| 37-- 裙 | pleated skirt. |

3726_7
裙〔Chun〕n. skirt, petticoat.
| 17-- 子 | skirt, petticoat. |
| 37-- 褶 | flouncing, plaits on each side of a petticoat. |

3730_1
迅〔Hsun〕adj. swift, quick, fast, rapid, speedy.
10-- 雷	sudden clap of thunder.
35-- 速	rapid, quick, swift, speedy.
55-- 捷	prompt, speedy.

逸〔I〕n. extravagance, ease, idleness, hermit, recluse, fault, mistake, v. exceed, go to excess, set free, release, run away, adj. ease, quick, rapid, outstanding, superior.
40-- 士	recluse, hermit.
50-- 事	anecdote.
77-- 居	live at leisure.

3730_2
迎〔Ying〕v. welcome, receive, meet.
| 06-- 親 | go to meet a bride. |
| 10-- 面 | head-on, coming towards |

		one.
11--	頭痛擊	deal a telling blow.
--	頭趕上	try to catch up with.
30--	賓	receive a guest.
50--	接	welcome, meet, greet, receive.
--	春花	the yellow jasmine.
57--	擊	repulse.
--	擊敵人	attack an advancing enemy face to face.
63--	戰	accept a battle, intercept.
80--	合	cater to, please, agree to.
--	合人意	fall in with the wishes of other persons.

迴 〔Chiung〕 *adj.* distant, remote, far-off.

23--	然	apparently.
60--	異	very different.
71--	隔	far separated.

通 〔Tung〕 *v.* communicate, pervade, go through , understand thoroughly, communicate, lead to, reach, *adj.* fluent, smooth.

00--	商	commercial intercourse.
--	商口岸	treaty ports.
--	病	common failing.
02--	訊	correspond, communicate.
--	訊網絡	communication network.
--	訊社	news agency, press service.
--	訊報導	reportage, reports.
--	訊員	correspondent, reporter.
--	訊兵	signalman.
--	訊兵團	signal corps.
--	訊所	signal station, message center.
--	訊隊	signal units, the service of communication.
--	訊錄	address book.
08--	敵	*n.* treason, *v.* collaborate (collude, conspire) with the enemy.
--	論	generalization.
10--	電	circular telegram, electrify.
--	電話	telephone, dial, ring up.
--	不過	impassable, unable to get through, not to passed.

15--	融	accommodate, compromise, act of grace.
17--	函	circular letters.
20--	信	*n.* correspondence, *v.* communicate, correspond.
--	信聯絡	intercommunication.
--	信處	one's address.
--	信社	news agency.
--	信網	communicative net, network of communications.
--	信袋	message net.
--	信員	correspondent.
--	信兵	signal corps, signal man.
--	航	accessible by navigation, open to navigation.
21--	行	current, prevailing, travel through.
--	行證	pass, safe-conduct, traveling permit.
--	行權	right of way.
--	行費	toll.
--	行無阻	accessible to the public.
22--	例	usage, custom.
--	稱	general designation, commonly called.
24--	告	*n.* notice, announcement, *v.* announce, notify.
--	貨	currency, current money.
--	貨貶值	devaluation of the currency.
--	貨膨脹	inflation.
--	貨緊縮	deflation.
26--	緝	order the arrest of.
27--	盤計劃	overall plan.
--	郵	accessible by personal communication, accessible by postal communication.
28--	俗	popular, common.
--	俗教育	popular education.
30--	宵	overnight, all night.
33--	心粉	macaroni.
37--	過	pass, go through, approve.
40--	姦	illicit intercourse, adultery.
47--	報	information.
50--	車	open traffic.
--	事	interpreter.
62--	則	principle.
64--	曉	understand thoroughly, well

		versed in.
67--	路	passage, open road.
77--	用	currency, in common use.
--	風	n. ventilation, v. ventilate, adj. airily, ventilating.
--	風設備	ventilation system.
--	風艙	ventilate compartment.
--	學生	day student.
78--	脫	unrestrained.
80--	氣	ventilate.
86--	知	notify, advertise, inform, communicate.
--	知書	notice, communication, letter of advice, letter of information.
--	知日	declaration date.
--	知單	advice note.
90--	常	general, accustomed, as a rule, for the most part, ordinary, average.
95--	性	generality.

週 〔**Chou**〕 n. week, period, revolution, v. return, receive, go around, revolve.

10--	工資	weekly wage.
12--	刊	weekly, periodical.
--	到	thoroughly.
21--	行	revolve, go around.
38--	遊	travel all over, ambulate.
47--	報	weekly statement (report).
--	期	period, periodic, cycle.
--	期律	periodic law.
--	期表	periodic table.
--	期性	periodicity.
50--	末	weekend.
55--	轉	circulation, turnover.
--	轉率	turnover rate.
--	轉不靈	have insufficient fund to meet all the needs.
--	轉現金	working cash.
--	轉期	turnover period.
80--	年	anniversary.
86--	知	make known to the public.

過 〔**Kuo**〕 n. error, fault, mistake, v. pass, go by, pass over, exceed, adv. too much, prep. over, above, beyond.

00--	度	too much, excessive, im-
		moderate, beyond the limit.
--	度供求	oversupply.
--	度估計	overestimate.
--	度興奮	hyperirritable, hyper.
--	高估計	overestimate.
--	高價格	exorbitant price, excessive price, outrageous price.
--	高要價	overcharge.
--	高要求	steep demand.
--	高利潤	exorbitant profit.
--	夜	stay overnight.
08--	於	over, above, too much.
10--	磅	weigh.
--	不下去	unable to live on.
20--	重	overweight.
--	重行李費	excess baggage charges.
21--	慮	overanxious.
22--	低估計	underestimate, underrate.
--	剩	surplus, excess.
--	剩需求	excessive demand.
--	繼	n. adoption, v. adopt.
25--	失	defect, error, blame, fault.
--	失致死	manslaughter.
--	失責任	liability for fault.
26--	得去	passable, not too bad.
--	得慣	feel at home.
--	程	process.
27--	多	excessive, too much, too many.
--	獎	overpraise.
28--	份	excessive.
30--	渡	n. transition, v. cross a river by ferry.
--	渡時期	transitional stage.
--	戶	transfer ownership, transfer of names.
--	戶手續費	transfer charge.
--	戶代理人	transfer agent.
--	戶單	transfer.
--	渡期	interim period.
31--	河	cross river.
--	濾	filter.
32--	活	live on.
37--	遲	too late, day after the fair.
40--	大需求	excessive demand.
--	境通行	transit passage.
--	境站	transit station.

-- 境手續	transit formalities.	
-- 境便利	passage facility.	
-- 境費用	transit expenses.	
-- 境簽証	transit visa.	
42-- 橋費	toll thorough.	
-- 去	v. pass, go by, pass away, adj. past, gone.	
47-- 期	n. past due date, v. expire, exceed the time limit, adj. overdue.	
-- 期票據	overdue bill (note).	
-- 期利息	overdue interest.	
-- 期支票	overdue check.	
-- 期賬款	past due account.	
60-- 日子	live, get along.	
-- 目	glance at, take a glance.	
-- 目不忘	be gifted with an extraordinarily retentive memory.	
-- 早	too early.	
64-- 時	behind times, past time, out of date, out of fashion, obsolete.	
-- 時產品	obsolescent product.	
-- 時設備	obsolete equipment.	
-- 時的	outdated, out of date, obsolete.	
-- 時式樣	outdated fashion.	
67-- 路人	passer-by.	
77-- 問	interfere, inquire into.	
-- 關	pass a test, pass a barrier.	
80-- 分	overmuch, immoderate.	
84-- 錯	fault, error, mistake.	
88-- 敏	allergic.	
90-- 半	more than half.	
-- 半數	majority.	
-- 火	go too far.	
99-- 勞	overwork.	

遍 〔Yu〕 v. follow, adj. wrong, incorrect.
3730₃

退 〔Tui〕 v. decline, reject, withdraw, draw back, retire, retreat, go down.

00-- 讓	yield, give away, knock under, give ground, cede.
10-- 票	dishonour.
13-- 職	resign, dismiss.
-- 職金	retirement pay, retiring

benefit, dismissal pay.

20-- 位	abdicate.
21-- 伍軍人	ex-servicemen, veteran.
-- 伍兵	discharged soldier.
-- 步	withdraw, degenerate, retrograde.
22-- 後	draw back, drop astern.
-- 出	withdraw from.
23-- 縮	shrink back, hold back, cut out.
24-- 化	degenerate, retrograde.
-- 休收入	retirement income.
-- 休法	retirement plan.
-- 休費	retirement cost.
-- 休金	retired pay, retirement allowance (benefit, pension).
-- 休年金	retirement annuity.
-- 貨	goods rejected, returned goods.
26-- 保	return premium.
27-- 役	out of commission.
-- 役軍人	ex-serviceman.
-- 租	throw a lease.
-- 約	withdraw from an engagement.
28-- 稅	tax refund, back tax, tax reimbursement, tax rebate.
29-- 伙	retirement of a partner.
30-- 避	withdraw from, shun, retreat.
47-- 款	refund.
-- 款單	refund order.
60-- 回	return, send back.
69-- 哨	come off sentry.
72-- 兵	retreat, beat a retreat.
-- 隱	retire, seclude.
77-- 股	withdraw shares.
80-- 會	secede.
90-- 堂	dismiss a court.

3730₄

遐 〔Hsia〕 adj. distant, remote, far-off.

邂 〔Hsieh〕 v. meet by chance.

32-- 逅	meet unexpectedly.

逢 〔Feng〕 v. meet, come across, happen.

37-- 迎　　　　　meet, welcome.

遲〔Chih〕v. delay, wait for, walk slowly, adj. slow, late, tardy, dilatory.

06-- 誤失事　　　spoil a matter by delay.
12-- 到　　　　　be late, come late.
-- 延　　　　　delay, protraction.
-- 延交付　　　delay deliverance.
22-- 緩　　　　　v. retard, relax, slacken. adj. slow, tardy, dilatory.
24-- 付　　　　　delay in payment.
27-- 疑　　　　　hesitating, in doubt, irresolute.
-- 疑不決　　　cannot make up one's mind.
34-- 滯　　　　　delay.
37-- 遲　　　　　slowly, tardy.
60-- 早　　　　　sooner or later.
-- 回　　　　　hesitating, irresolutely.
85-- 鈍　　　　　dull, blunt, heavy in hand.
-- 鈍不靈　　　obtuse and unintelligent.

運〔Yun〕v. move, revolve, transport, make use, turn around.

22-- 出　　　　　export.
24-- 動　　　　　n. movement, athletics, physical exercise, v. exercise, move, work upon.
-- 動家　　　　sportsman, athlete.
-- 動衫　　　　sport-shirt.
-- 動場　　　　field, playground, recreation ground.
-- 動員　　　　sportsman, athlete.
-- 動戰　　　　mobile warfare.
-- 動會　　　　sports, athletic meeting.
-- 貨　　　　　transport goods, cargo transport.
-- 貨員　　　　shipper.
-- 貨單　　　　waybill.
31-- 河　　　　　canal.
38-- 送　　　　　convey, carry.
-- 送契約　　　contract for carriage.
-- 送人　　　　carrier, common carrier.
42-- 載工具　　　means of delivery.
55-- 轉　　　　　operate, revolve, function, work.
-- 費　　　　　freight, carriage, postage, shipping freight, transport charge.

58-- 輸　　　　　n. transportation, conveyance, carriage, v. transport, freight, convey.
-- 輸設備　　　transportation facility.
-- 輸行　　　　forwarding agent.
-- 輸統制局　　Board of Transportation Control.
-- 輸線　　　　supply line.
-- 輸網　　　　transport network.
-- 輸業　　　　transport business.
-- 輸途中　　　in transit.
-- 輸機　　　　military transport, cargo plane.
-- 輸費用　　　traffic expense, transportation charges (expenses).
-- 輸量　　　　traffic capacity (volume, amount).
-- 輸局　　　　shipping office.
-- 輸公司　　　transportation company.
77-- 用　　　　　operate, apply, make use, put in action, bring into play.
-- 用資產　　　working assets.
-- 用資本　　　working capital.
80-- 入　　　　　import.
-- 命　　　　　fate, lot.
-- 氣　　　　　fortune, luck, fate.
88-- 算　　　　　(in math) operation.
-- 籌學　　　　operational research.

3730₆
迢〔Tiao〕adj. distant, remote, faraway.

37-- 迢　　　　　distant, remote, faraway.

遛〔Liu〕v. walk about.

71-- 馬　　　　　walk a horse.

3730₇
追〔Chui〕v. follow, pursue, chase, trace, run after, escort.

07-- 認　　　　　subsequent confirmation.
17-- 及　　　　　overtake, catch up with, come up with.
-- 尋　　　　　follow up, trace, pursue, hunt down.
21-- 上　　　　　overtake, catch up.
25-- 債　　　　　recover debts, dun for debt.
29-- 償　　　　　recovery.

30-- 究	investigate, trace, scrutinize, search into.
-- 究禍原	investigate the origin of the misfortune.
31-- 逐	pursue, hound, run after.
-- 逼	press, force.
37-- 溯	retrace, derive, date back to.
-- 溯既往	trace the origin of the bygone.
-- 過	overrun.
40-- 查責任	find out where the responsibility lies.
-- 索積欠	demand repayment of a past debt.
42-- 獵	hunt, chase.
43-- 求	run after, hunt for, pursue, seek, chase.
-- 求真理	pursuit of truth.
46-- 趕	chase.
-- 加	add supplementary.
-- 加預算	pass an addition to the budget.
-- 趕	chase, pursue.
47-- 根問底	raise one question after another.
53-- 捕	hunt down.
57-- 擊	attack, give chase to, follow up a victory.
-- 擊戰	running fight.
60-- 回	recover.
63-- 踪	trace, follow up.
-- 贓	recover booty.
72-- 兵	soldiers in pursuit.
74-- 隨	follow, pursue, follow behind.
-- 隨左右	follow someone, accompany someone.
77-- 肥	additional manuring, top-dressing of fertilizer.
-- 問	inquire into.
90-- 憶	remember, recollect, recall.
91-- 悼	commemorate the dead.
-- 悼會	memorial service.
98-- 悔	regret.
-- 悔莫及	too late for repentance.

遙 〔Yao〕 adj. distant, far, remote, far away.

00-- 夜	long night.
07-- 望	look from afar.
34-- 遠	distant, remote, far-off.
37-- 遙無期	be put off to an indefinite date, hopeless.
-- 遙在先	be home free at, be far ahead.
53-- 控	remote control, distant control.
71-- 隔	in the distance, far separated.

3730₈

選 〔Hsuan〕 n. selection, choice, v. choose, select, elect.

10-- 礦	dress ore, ore dressing.
-- 票	ballot-paper.
17-- 取	n. selection, election, v. select, pick and choose.
20-- 手	contestant, champion, competitor.
-- 集	n. anthology, selected works.
22-- 任	appoint, elect someone to a post.
-- 出	pick out, choose.
-- 種	select seeds.
-- 種機	selector, selecting machine.
24-- 科	elective course.
30-- 定	be elected, designate.
32-- 派	select and appoint.
48-- 樣	sample.
53-- 拔	select, pick out.
56-- 擇	choose, select, pick out.
-- 擇錯誤	be wrong in one's choice, make a bad choice.
65-- 購	selective purchasing.
71-- 區	constituency.
77-- 民	constituency, voters, electorate.
-- 民證	voter's card, elector's certificate.
-- 舉	elect, vote, select.
-- 舉票	ballot.
-- 舉法	electoral law.
-- 舉運動	elective campaign.
-- 舉權	right of election, right to

vote, suffrage, elective franchise.

-- 舉區　　　elective district.

-- 舉人　　　voter, elector.

3733_8

恣〔Tsu〕 *n*. dissipation, lust, levity, *v*. dissipate, discard all restraints, throw off restraint, *adj*. licentious, loose.

00--意　　　without restraint, unrestrained, do as one likes.

-- 意任性　　do as one feels like it.

-- 意妄爲　　act as one pleases.

-- 意所欲　　give rein to vehement desire.

21-- 行無忌　act recklessly without fear.

28-- 縱　　　give up the reins.

95-- 情縱慾　indulge in passion and run wild.

3740_1

罕〔Han〕 *adj*. scarce, rare, seldom, few.

27-- 物　　　curiosity.

40-- 有　　　rare, seldom, few.

-- 奇　　　strange.

60-- 見　　　rarely seen, seldom seen, rare.

3740_4

姿〔Tzu〕 *n*. manner, looks, style, gesture.

27-- 色　　　beauty, looks.

-- 色平常　　be common in appearance.

41-- 態　　　manner, figure, demeanour, carriage.

-- 態端莊　　graceful in carriage.

30-- 容　　　figure.

44-- 勢　　　attitude, gesture, pose, posture.

72-- 質聰穎　clever in mutual disposition.

3741_3

冤〔Juan〕 *n*. wrong, grievance.

24-- 仇深結　the enmity is deeply tied.

30-- 家　　　enemy, foe.

41-- 枉　　　*n*. wrong, injustice, *v*. wrong.

-- 枉好人　　have wronged a good person.

77-- 屈難伸　grievance is difficult to redress.

3750_6

軍〔Chun〕 *n*. army, troop, armed forces, military, soldiers, corp.

01-- 語　　　military terms.

02-- 訓　　　military training.

-- 訓部　　　Board of Military Training.

-- 氈　　　blanket.

07-- 部　　　corps headquarters.

08-- 旗　　　colors, banner, army flag.

10-- 工　　　war industry, armament industry, ordnance.

-- 需　　　military requirements (contribution, supplies).

-- 需官　　　paymaster, quartermaster.

-- 需品　　　war materials (equipment, supply), defense goods.

17-- 歌　　　military song.

18-- 政　　　military administration.

-- 政府　　　military government.

20-- 委會　　Military Commission.

21-- 銜　　　military rank.

-- 銜制　　　system of military rank.

22-- 樂　　　military band.

-- 種　　　armed services, branch of the armed forces.

23-- 代表　　army representative.

-- 縮　　　disarmament.

-- 縮會議　　disarmament conference.

24-- 備　　　armament.

25-- 律　　　articles of war.

27-- 郵處　　postal section.

-- 紀　　　military discipline.

28-- 艦　　　warship.

30-- 官　　　military officer.

33-- 心　　　moral of the troops.

34-- 港　　　naval port.

-- 法　　　martial law .

35-- 禮　　　military courtesy, salute.

40-- 力　　　military power, military strength.

-- 校　　　military academy.

-- 校生　　　cadet.

43-- 械　　　arms, weapons, ordnance.

-- 械庫	armory, ammunition depot.	
-- 械局	arsenal armory.	
44-- 鞋	shoes for servicemen.	
-- 權	military power.	
46-- 帽	service hat.	
50-- 事	military affairs.	
-- 事訓練	military drill.	
-- 事工程	military project.	
-- 事委員會	Military Affairs Committee.	
-- 事行動	action, operation.	
-- 事衝突	military clash.	
-- 事偵探	military spy.	
-- 事代表團	military mission.	
-- 事顧問	military adviser.	
-- 事化	militarize, be place on a military footing.	
-- 事家	strategist, military expert.	
-- 事演習	military manoeuvres.	
-- 事法庭	court martial.	
-- 事通訊員	military correspondent.	
-- 事力量	military power.	
-- 事基地	military base.	
-- 事協定	military alliance.	
-- 事封鎖	military blockade.	
-- 事專家	military expert.	
-- 事援助	military aid (assistance).	
-- 事費用	military expenses.	
-- 事目標	military objective.	
-- 事會議	council of war, military conference.	
-- 事常識	soldiery.	
-- 事當局	military authority.	
55-- 曹	sergeant.	
-- 費	military expense (expenditures, spending).	
60-- 團	army, corps, regiment.	
-- 國主義	militarism.	
-- 國大事	affairs of national defense and administration.	
61-- 號	trumpet, bugle.	
71-- 長	army commander.	
-- 區	military area, military district.	
77-- 用病院	military hospital.	
-- 用電話	military telephone service.	
-- 用包	field bag.	

-- 用物質	defense materials, war materials.	
-- 用地圖	battle map.	
-- 用車	military vehicle.	
-- 用品	munition, field equipment.	
-- 用機	military plane, war craft, warplane.	
-- 用無線電話	military radiotelephone service.	
-- 閥	warlord.	
-- 屬	dependents of the troops.	
-- 服	uniform.	
-- 醫	surgeon.	
-- 醫院	military hospital.	
-- 醫長	chief surgeon.	
78-- 隊	army, military, troop, force, corps.	
80-- 人	soldier, man-at-arms, serviceman.	
-- 人精神	military spirit.	
-- 分區	military sub-area, military subdistrict.	
-- 令	military order.	
-- 令部	Board of Military Operation.	
-- 令會	Military Control Commission.	
87-- 餉	military provision.	
88-- 管區	army area.	
90-- 火	ammunition, arms and ammunition.	
-- 火商	munitions dealers, arms merchants (dealer), merchants of death.	
-- 火走私	gun running.	
96-- 糧	food for the army, MRE（meals ready to eat）.	

3760₈

咨〔Tzu〕v. deliberate, plan, consult about.

00-- 文	official message, official note.	
-- 訪高見	inquire about one's opinion.	
07-- 詢	deliberate, consult about, seek advice, inquire about.	
-- 詢專家	consultancy expert, expert consultant.	

-- 詢費	consulting fee.
-- 詢服務	advisory services, consultant service, consultancy.
-- 詢公司	consulting firm.
-- 調卷宗	request the transfer of a file.
10-- 覆來文	reply to a communication.

3771₇
瓷 〔Tzu〕 *n.* crockery, porcelain, chinaware.

15-- 磚	porcelain tiles.
40-- 土	porcelain-clay.
66-- 器	china, porcelain, chinaware.

3772₀
朗 〔Lang〕 *adj.* clear, bright.

| 07-- 誦 | read distinctly. |

3772₇
郎 〔Lang〕 *n.* man, gentleman, young man, husband.

| 17-- 君 | husband. |
| 40-- 才女貌 | perfect match between a man and a woman. |

3780₀
冥 〔Ming〕 *adj.* gloomy, dim, dark dusk.

00-- 府	Hades, hell.
10-- 王星	Pluto (in astronomy).
11-- 悲	contemplation.
37-- 冥之中	in the unseen world.
46-- 想	*n.* contemplation, *v.* meditate, muse.
60-- 思出神	be in a brown study.
67-- 眼	long sleep.

3780₆
資 〔Tzu〕 *n.* wealth, property, stock, capital, money, natural endowment, gift, *v.* supply, depend on, avail of, use.

00-- 產	assets, property.
-- 產淨值	net assets value (worth).
-- 產表	statement of assets.
-- 產階級	monied classes, bourgeoisie.
-- 方	those representing capital.
07-- 望	reputation.
08-- 敵	supply the enemy.
25-- 俸	salary.
31-- 源	resource, natural resources.
-- 源豐富	abundant resources.
40-- 力富厚	solid financial strength.
47-- 格	qualification.
50-- 本	capital.
-- 本主義	capitalism.
-- 本重估	recapitalization.
-- 本集中	concentration of capital.
-- 本外流	capital outflow, emigration of capital.
-- 本總額	total capital, capital sum.
-- 本家	capitalist.
-- 本投資	capital investment.
-- 本回流	reflux of capital.
71-- 歷	seniority, work record, order of seniority.
72-- 質	nature, gift, talents.
74-- 助	aid, help, subsidize, contribute funds.
80-- 金	funds, capital, financial resources.
-- 金需要	demand for funds, fund requirement (demand).
-- 金積累	accumulation of funds.
-- 金運用	application of fund, fund operation.
-- 金來源	capital source, fund source, financial source.
-- 金雄厚	abundant financial resources.
-- 金周轉	turnover of capital.
-- 金缺乏	lack of capital, fund shortage.
-- 斧	traveling expenses.
94-- 料	material, data , means.
-- 料庫	data bank, information bank.

3810₄
塗 〔Tu〕 *v.* plaster, smear, blot out, erase, daub.

18-- 改	blot out, alter.
22-- 炭生靈	bring great suffering to the people.
31-- 污	smear, daub.
35-- 油	oil.
39-- 消	cancel.
51-- 掉	strike out, blot out.
55-- 抹	rub out, erase, wipe off.

71--	脂抹粉	make up, apply rough and powder.
88--	飾	adorn.
89--	銷	cancel.

3811₇

汽 〔Chi〕 n. steam, gas, vapor.

12--	水	soda water, soda pop, aerated water.
22--	艇	motorboat, steam launch.
24--	化	vaporization.
27--	船	steamer, steamship, steamboat.
35--	油	gasoline, petrol.
--	油庫	petrol dump.
--	油站	gas station, filling station, petrol pump.
--	油彈	gasoline bomb.
42--	機	steam engine, locomotive.
48--	槍	air gun.
50--	車	automobile, motor car, car.
--	車方向盤	steering wheel.
--	車廠	automobile factory.
--	車行	garage.
--	車保險	automobile insurance, motor car insurance, car insurance.
--	車夫	driver.
--	車胎	automobile tire.
--	車間	garage.
58--	輪機	steam turbine.
--	輪發電機	turbo-generator.
77--	門	steam valve.
81--	缸	cylinders.
87--	鍋	steam boiler.
88--	笛	siren, steam-whistle.
--	管	steam pipe.
91--	爐	steam radiator.

溢 〔I〕 v. overflow, inundate, spread, flow out, adj. excessive, abundant.

12--	水管	overflow pipe.
21--	價	at a premium, premium price.
22--	出	n. effusion, overflow, v. flow out, flow over.
--	額	overage, surplus.
34--	滿	full, abundant.
--	洪道	spillway, flood diversion.

濫 〔Lan〕 v. overflow, flood, exceed, abuse, adj. reckless, unrestrained, extravagant, excessive, lawless, irregular, make friends freely.

00--	交	make friends recklessly.
--	言	be too lavish of one's tongue.
07--	調	stock argument, platitude.
21--	征稅	abuse of taxation.
30--	寫	scribble.
40--	支	lavish expenditure.
55--	費	waste.
77--	用	misuse, abuse, waste, lavish.
--	用職權	misuse one's power.
--	用威權	abuse one's authority.
--	用無度	use without limit.
--	用公款	irregularities in use of public funds.
98--	炸	wanton bombing.

3812₁

渝 〔Yu〕 v. change, alter, change mind, n. Chungking.

27--	約	retreat from an engagement.

3812₇

汾 〔Fen〕 n. the Fen river.

涕 〔Ti〕 n. tear, snivel, v. weep.

10--	零如雨	tears streaming down like rain drops.
30--	泣	weep.
33--	淚	tear.
36--	泗交流	tears and snivel fall down at the same time.

淪 〔Lun〕 n. ripple, v. sink, fall, be ruined, adj. submerged, engulfed.

30--	為	be reduced to.
40--	喪	ruined, lost, destroyed.
44--	落	fall.
--	落異鄉	be left alone in a foreign land.
77--	陷	be occupied.
--	陷區	occupied area.

3813₀

淞 〔Sung〕 n. the Woosung river.

3813_2

滋〔**Tzu**〕*n.* taste, savor, flavor, juice, sap, *v.* sprout, breed, grow, increase, nourish.

25--	生	sprout, multiply.
33--	補	*n.* tonic, *v.* nourish, strengthen.
--	補藥	tonic.
51--	擾	*n.* nuisance, *v.* disturb, annoy.
65--	味	taste, savor, flavor, relish.
71--	長	grow and spread, spring up.
80--	養	nourish, nurture.
--	養物	nurture, aliment.
--	養品	nourishment, nutriment.

飡〔**Tsan**〕*n.* meal.

漾〔**Yan**〕*n.* water in commotion, *v.* ripple, overflow.

3813_3

淤〔**Yu**〕*n.* sediment, mud, *v.* silt up, *adj.* muddy, blocked.

25--	積	deposition of mud, silt up.
27--	血	stagnant blood, blood clot.
30--	塞	silt up, blocked by silt.
31--	漑禾田	irrigate paddy fields with muddy water.
37--	泥	silt, sediment.

3813_7

冷〔**Leng**〕*v.* cool, chill, *adj.* cold, chilly, frigid, icy, indifferent.

00--	言冷語	sarcastic remarks.
10--	天	cold weather.
--	不防	unexpectedly.
--	霜	cold cream.
12--	水	cold water.
--	水浴	cold bath.
14--	酷	chilly, harsh, grim.
27--	血	cold-blooded.
--	盤	cold dish.
34--	漠無情	sternly cool and unmoved person.
35--	清	lonely, deserted and quiet.
--	凍	freeze.
--	凍食品	frozen foods.
39--	淡	cool, indifferent, cold-hearted.
--	淡待人	treat a person coldly.
44--	落	lonesome, receive coldly.
--	藏	refrigerate, cold storage.
--	藏庫	cold storage, refrigerating chamber (warehouse, compartment).
--	藏設備	cold storage equipment.
--	藏貨	refrigerated goods.
--	藏車	refrigerator car (van), chill car.
--	若冰霜	cold as ice.
52--	軋	cold rolling (in machine).
--	靜	quiet, calm, dispassionate.
63--	戰	cold war.
67--	嘲	sneer, scoff.
--	嘲熱諷	alternately taunt and jeer at someone.
--	眼旁觀	look coldly from the sidelines.
77--	風	cold wind.
80--	氣	air condition.
--	氣設備	air-conditioning.
87--	卻	cool, cooling.
88--	箭傷人	injure a person with hidden arrows.
--	笑	cold laugh, cynical smile.

3814_0

激〔**Chi**〕*v.* rouse, excite, arouse, encourage, *adj.* indignant, vexed, drastic, radical, unusual, *adv.* drastically, speedily.

12--	烈	exasperated, violent, acute, fierce, radical.
--	烈競爭	keen (sharp) competition, fierce rivalry, tug of war.
--	發	evoke, arouse to action.
22--	變	revulsion.
24--	動	excite, incite, inflame, work up.
--	動人心	soul-stirring.
--	化	intensify.
30--	流	torrent.
--	進措施	radical measures.
31--	漲	sharp rise, steep rise.

47-- 怒　irritate, provoke, anger, enrage, annoy, exasperate, aggravate.
-- 怒於人　tread on one's toes.
-- 起　arouse, stir up.
48-- 增　sudden increase, drastic increase, shoot up, soar.
50-- 素　hormone.
60-- 昂　*n.* excitement, *v.* run high, *adj.* fervent and excited.
-- 昂慷慨　tremendously excited.
63-- 戰　fierce battle.
65-- 跌　sharp fall.
71-- 厲　arouse, stimulate.
74-- 勵　encourage, spur.
90-- 光　laser.
95-- 情　strong emotion.

澈〔Che〕*n.* clear water, *v.* search out, excite, stimulate, stir up.
00-- 底　thoroughly, completely.
40-- 查　make a thorough investigation, search out.

3814₇
游〔Yu〕*v.* travel, wander, roam, swim, float, drift.
08-- 說　stump, lobby, sell the idea.
20-- 手　idler, loafer.
-- 手好閑　loitering about and doing nothing.
22-- 艇　yacht, barge.
-- 山玩水　enjoy sightseeing.
-- 絲　hairspring.
23-- 戲　*n.* amusement, recreation, play, *v.* play, sport.
27-- 移　hesitate, waver.
28-- 牧　nomadic.
-- 牧生活　nomadism, nomadic life.
33-- 泳　swim, bathe.
-- 泳衣　swimming suit.
-- 泳褲　swimming trunks.
-- 泳池　swimming pool.
-- 泳帽　bathing cap.
37-- 資　idle funds (capital), floating capital (fund), loose fund.
42-- 獵　hunting.
44-- 蕩　wandering, rambling.

57-- 擊戰　guerilla warfare.
-- 擊隊　guerrilla forces, flying army.
-- 擊隊員　guerillas.
71-- 歷　tour, travel.
77-- 民　idler, vagrant.
78-- 覽　sightseeing, excursion.
-- 覽車　tourist coach (bus).
-- 覽圖　tourist map.

3815₁
洋〔Yang〕*n.* ocean, *adj.* vast, wide, extensive, foreign, imported.
00-- 文　foreign language.
21-- 行　foreign firm.
24-- 裝　foreign costume.
-- 貨　foreign goods.
38-- 溢　overflow.
44-- 葱　onion.
-- 菜　agar-agar.
47-- 奴　foreigner's slave, flunkey of imperialism.
77-- 服　foreign dress.
80-- 人　foreigner.
-- 鎬　pickax, pick.
-- 傘　umbrella.

3815₇
海〔Hai〕*n.* sea, marine, *adj.* marine, maritime, vast, boundless.
00-- 產　marine product, sea products.
-- 商　marine commerce.
-- 商法　marine law.
-- 鷹　sea-eagle.
-- 底　seabed, bottom of the sea.
-- 底電線　marine cable, submarine cable.
-- 底電報　cable, marine dispatch, cablegram.
-- 底油田　seabed oilfield.
-- 底資源　seabed resources.
10-- 王星　the planet Neptune.
-- 面　sea level, surface of the sea.
12-- 水浴　sea-bathing.
14-- 豬　sea-hog.
20-- 航　navigation.
21-- 上　marine, maritime, at sea, on the sea.

-- 上飛機	sea-drome, sea plane.	-- 運	maritime transportation, sea transportation.
-- 上航道	seaway.		
-- 上保險	marine insurance.	-- 運費	ocean freight.
-- 上沉沒	foundering at sea.	-- 軍	navy, fleet, naval forces.
-- 上封鎖	naval blockade.	-- 軍部	Naval Department, admiralty, Ministry of Navy.
-- 上事故	marine accident, maritime casualty.		
		-- 軍部長	Minister of Navy.
-- 上風險	perils (risks) of the sea.	-- 軍元帥	Admiral of the Fleet.
-- 上貿易	marine trade, maritime commerce (trade).	-- 軍司令部	Naval Command.
		-- 軍上將	admiral.
22-- 岸	coast, seashore.	-- 軍總司令	Commander-in-chief of the Navy.
-- 岸線	coastline.		
23-- 外	oversea, abroad.	-- 軍次長	vice-minister of the navy.
-- 外市場	overseas market.	-- 軍大臣	First Lord of the Admiralty.
-- 外交易	overseas trade (transaction).	-- 軍封鎖	naval blockade.
-- 外旅行	overseas trip.	-- 軍根據地	naval base.
-- 外顧客	overseas customer.	-- 軍中將	vice admiral.
-- 外資產	overseas assets.	-- 軍戰術	naval tactics.
-- 外資金	offshore funds.	-- 軍陸戰隊	marines, marine corps.
-- 外華僑	overseas Chinese.	-- 軍學校	naval academy.
-- 外事業	overseas business.	-- 軍少將	rear admiral.
-- 外子公司	affiliate company incorporated abroad.	38-- 洋	ocean, sea, the deep.
		-- 洋工程	oceanographic engineering.
-- 外供貨商	supplier abroad.	-- 洋動物	marine animal.
-- 外投資	overseas investment.	-- 洋法	law of the sea.
-- 外貿易	overseas trade, ocean commerce.	-- 洋國	maritime state.
		-- 洋性氣候	maritime climate.
-- 外合同	overseas contract.	40-- 內無雙	unequaled or peerless in the whole country.
-- 外公司	overseas company.		
-- 參	sea slug, sea cucumber.	-- 難	casualty shipping, maritime perils, sea perils.
24-- 峽	strait, channel.		
-- 峽問題	strait question, Taiwan Strait issue.	41-- 獅	sea-lion.
		44-- 藻	seaweed.
26-- 程	sea voyage.	-- 帶	edible seaweed, kelp, sea tangle.
-- 綿	sponge.		
27-- 龜	sea turtle.	-- 燕	petrel.
-- 角	headland.	-- 權	sea power.
-- 角天涯	the corners of the world.	-- 禁大開	open the country to foreign trade.
-- 豹	seal.		
-- 島	island.	47-- 報	poster.
-- 船	sea-going vessel.	52-- 蜇	jellyfish.
32-- 灣	bay, gulf.	-- 誓山盟	lover's pledge of eternal loyalty.
33-- 濱	seacoast, seashore.		
34-- 港	sea port, harbor.	53-- 拔	elevation, above sea level.
37-- 盜	pirate, rover.	58-- 輪	sea-going vessel, harbor.
-- 盜行為	piracy.	60-- 口	seaport.
-- 潮	ocean tide.	-- 里	knot, nautical mile, sea mile.

-- 員	seaman, sailor, mariner.	00-- 衣	bathrobe.
-- 員俱樂部	seamen's club.	30-- 室	bathroom.
-- 景悅目	the seascape pleases the eyes.	80-- 盆	bathtub.

3818₁

漩〔Hsuan〕*n.* whirlpool, eddy.

63-- 戰	naval battle, naval warfare, naval action.
65-- 味	seafood, marine delicacy.
-- 味山珍	delicacies from the sea and mountains--rare and delicate food.
67-- 路	sea route, seaway.
70-- 防	coastal defense.
-- 防鞏固	the coastal defense is strong.
71-- 豚	dolphin.
-- 馬	sea horse.
74-- 陸空軍	the fighting services.
-- 陸運輸	sea and land transport.
77-- 風	sea breeze.
-- 鷗	seagull.
-- 關	customs, customs house (office).
-- 關經紀人	customs-house broker.
-- 關緝私船	customs guard vessel.
-- 關稅	custom duty.
-- 關稅率	tariff, customs duty rate.
-- 關法	customs code (law).
-- 關稅務司	commissioner of custom.
-- 關查驗	customs examination.
-- 關協定	customs agreement.
-- 關封條	customs seal.
-- 關檢查站	customs inspection post.
-- 關扣留	customs detention.
-- 關監督	superintendent of customs.
-- 關人員	customs house officer, collector of customs.
78-- 險	sea risk.

37-- 渦　　　whirlpool.

3819₄

涂〔Tu〕*n.* road, way.

3821₇

檻〔Lan〕*adj.* ragged, tattered, shabby.

35-- 褸　　　ragged, shabby, in rags.

3824₇

複〔Fu〕*v.* double, *adj.* overlapping, complex, complicated.

00-- 雜	complex, complicated, intricate.
17-- 習	review.
21-- 比例	compound proportion.
22-- 利	compound interest.
-- 製	reproduce.
27-- 句	complex sentence.
30-- 寫	duplicate copies of writing.
-- 寫紙	carbon paper.
-- 賽	semifinal.
33-- 述	rehearse.
35-- 決權	referendum, power of referendum.
37-- 選	indirect vote.
43-- 式簿記	double entry.
44-- 葉	compound leaf.
45-- 姓	double surname.
50-- 本	duplicate copies.
-- 本位	double standard.
58-- 數	plural number.
80-- 合	compound.
-- 合語	compound (in grammar).
-- 合國	composite states.

3816₁

洽〔Chia〕*v.* harmonize.

00-- 商	make arrangements with, talk over with.
90-- 當	suitable, proper.

3816₇

滄〔Tsang〕*adj.* cold, wintry.

3816₈

浴〔Yu〕*n.* bath, *v.* bathe, wash, take a bath.

3825₁

祥〔Hsiang〕*n.* happiness, good luck, felicity.

32-- 兆　　　auspicious omen.

3826₈

裕〔Yu〕*adj.* rich, abundant, plentiful, affluent, sufficient, generous, liberal, indulgent.

60-- 足		sufficient, ample.

3830_1

迄〔Chi〕 *adv.* until, finally, at length. *prep.* till, up to.

50-- 末		not yet.
80-- 今		till now, up to now, up to date.

迤〔Yi〕 *v.* move awry, *adj.* connected.

31-- 邐		tortuous, winding.
38-- 迤		continuous extending.

3830_2

逾〔Yu〕 *v.* pass over, exceed, surpass, pass over, cross.

31-- 額		go beyond the given number.
43-- 越		overstep.
-- 越權限		exceed one's power.
47-- 期		exceed the time limit, overdue, past due.
64-- 時		pass the time.
77-- 限		overpass the mark.

3830_3

遂〔Sui〕 *v.* complete, realize, succeed, have one's will, *adv.* hereby, therefore, as a result.

00-- 意		agreeable to one's wishes.
40-- 志		carry out one's purpose.
71-- 願		attain one's end, carry out one's purpose, gratify one's desire.

送〔Sung〕 *v.* present, give, send, forward, dispatch, see off, send off.

00-- 交		hand over, forward to, deliver.
10-- 電		power transmission.
20-- 信		deliver a letter.
21-- 行		see a person off, see one off, send one off.
22-- 出		send off.
24-- 貨		deliver goods.
-- 貨員		delivery man.
-- 貨單		invoice.
34-- 達		delivery.
35-- 禮		*n.* present, gift, *v.* send a present, give a present.
40-- 喪		attend a funeral.

-- 來		send here, bring here.
44-- 葬		attend a funeral ceremony.
60-- 回		return, send back.
62-- 別		see off.
80-- 公糧		deliver the grain tax in kind.

3830_4

遊〔Yu〕 *v.* travel, ramble, wander, roam, saunter, study, befriend, wield freely.

07-- 記		travel, travelogue.
08-- 說		take the stump.
-- 說家		stump orator.
20-- 手好閑		be a lazy good-for-nothing.
21-- 行		*n.* parade, demonstration, *v.* parade.
-- 行示威		demonstrate in protest.
-- 街		take a walk.
23-- 戲		sport, game, play, amusement.
-- 戲者		player.
27-- 船		dumb barge.
28-- 牧		nomadic.
30-- 客		tourist, visitors, travelers.
42-- 獵		hunt.
44-- 蕩		dissipate, wander.
57-- 擊戰術		tactics of guerrilla warfare.
60-- 園會		garden party.
71-- 歷		travel, go on a tour.
77-- 民		gipsy, vagabonds.
78-- 覽		excursion, sightseeing.

遨〔Ao〕 *v.* ramble, roam, travel for pleasure.

38-- 遊		roam.

邀〔Yao〕 *v.* intercept, invite, send for, ask, request.

05-- 請		invite, ask, send an invitation to.
30-- 客		invite guests.

遵〔Tsun〕 *v.* follow, obey, comply with, abide.

21-- 行		carry out obediently.
22-- 循		act upon, abide by.
28-- 從		obedience to, according to, follow, obey.
-- 從法令		act in accordance with the law.

30-- 守	obey, keep, observe, conform to, abide by.
-- 守諾言	keep one's words, stick to one's words.
-- 守合約	observe the agreement, abide by contract.
34-- 法	obey law.
-- 法施行	obey the law and to put something into operation.
67-- 照	in compliance with, in accordance with, according.
80-- 命	obey an order, in compliance with an order.
-- 命辦理	handle according to an instruction.

逆 〔Ni〕 v. oppose, disobey, resist, receive, go against, oppose, adj. rebellious, adverse, contrary, beforehand, in advance.

10-- 耳	grate on the ear.
12-- 水	backset, against the current.
-- 水行舟	sail against the current.
17-- 子	unfilial son, undutiful son.
30-- 流	against the stream, up stream, counter-current, adverse current.
-- 流而上	go upstream, run counter to the current of the times.
40-- 境	adversity.
77-- 風	adverse wind, head wind.
80-- 差	deficit, trade deficit, unfavorable balance.
90-- 黨	band of rebels.
94-- 料	predict, conjecture.

3830_6

道 〔Tao〕 n. road, way, path, method, principle, doctrine, v. state, speak, say.

04-- 謝	express thanks.
16-- 理	principle, doctrine, reason.
24-- 德	morality, virtue.
-- 德重整運動	moral rearmament movement.
-- 德觀	moral outlook.
27-- 候	pay one's compliment.
40-- 士	Taoist priest.

-- 喜	congratulate.
44-- 地貨	real thing.
-- 林紙	wood-free paper.
48-- 教	Taoism.
67-- 路	road, path, way.
77-- 具	stage properties, props.
80-- 義	morality, moral, rectitude.
-- 岔	sidetrack, turnout.
87-- 歉	apologize.

3830_9

途 〔Tu〕 n. road, way, path.

21-- 徑	course, road, channel.
26-- 程	journey.
50-- 中	on the way, en route.
52-- 耗	ullage.

3834_3

導 〔Tao〕 v. lead, guide, direct.

00-- 言	introduction, conduct.
12-- 引	conduct, lead.
16-- 彈	missile, guided missile.
18-- 致	result in, give rise to.
20-- 航	navigate, pilot.
21-- 師	tutor, teacher.
-- 師制	the tutorial system.
27-- 向	conduct to, lead to.
33-- 演	director.
75-- 體	conductor, electric conductor.
88-- 管	pipe, duct, meatus.
90-- 火線	fuse, direct cause of an event.

3850_7

肇 〔Chao〕 v. commence, initiate, begin, found.

02-- 端	initiate, inaugurate.
22-- 亂	stir trouble.
24-- 緒	clue of a thing.
50-- 事	stir up trouble.
77-- 興	found.

3860_4

啓 〔Chi〕 v. open, explain, unclose, break, inform.

10-- 示	disclose, discover, reveal.
12-- 發	develop, enlighten, awaken.
-- 發式	teaching by suggestion.
21-- 行	start, put off.

26-- 程   start a journey, set out, set
                  sail.
44-- 蒙   enlightenment, teach chil-
                  dren.
50-- 事   notice, announcement.
77-- 開   open.

3866₈
豁 〔Huo〕 n. open valley, v. split, break,
open up, exempt from.
23-- 然   thoroughly.
27-- 免   exempt from, release, abate,
                  forgive.
-- 免區   exempt zone.
34-- 達   generous, liberal, broad-
                  minded.

3911₁
洸 〔Kuang〕 n. martial appearance.

3911₃
瀅 〔Ying〕 n. clear water.

3912₀
沙 〔Sha〕 n. sand, ravel.
00-- 文主義   chauvinism.
01-- 龍   salon.
10-- 丁魚   sardine.
-- 石   sandstone.
12-- 發椅   sofa.
17-- 子   sand.
22-- 紙   sandpaper.
23-- 袋   sandbag.
26-- 皇   tsar, czar.
27-- 盤演習   sand table exercise.
-- 魚   shark.
30-- 灘   sandbank, beach.
31-- 濾水   filtrated water.
-- 濾器   sand filter.
32-- 州   shoal, sandbank.
34-- 漠   desert.
40-- 土   sandy soil.
-- 士汽水   sarsaparilla.
44-- 地   sands.
61-- 啞   hoarse.
67-- 眼病   trachoma.
72-- 丘   sandhill.

渺 〔Miao〕 adj. small, tiny, boundless,
far, vague.

10-- 不足道   too small to mention.
39-- 渺   tiny and far away.
44-- 茫   vague, doubtful.
-- 茫得很   completely at sea, uncer-
                  tain.
90-- 小   tiny, negligible.

3912₇
消 〔Hsiao〕 v. melt, dissolve, exhaust,
evaporate, digest, dispel, disappear,
vanish, eliminate, abate, diminish.
00-- 瘦   lost flesh, become thin,
                  lean, thin.
-- 磨   spend, pass, use up.
-- 亡   wither away, die out.
11-- 弭   quell, smooth, pacify.
16-- 魂   be fascinated, be spell-
                  bound.
20-- 售   for sale.
24-- 化   n. digestion, v. digest.
-- 化不良   indigestion.
-- 化作用   digestion.
-- 化液   digestive juice, digesting
                  fluid.
-- 化道   alimentary canal.
-- 化藥   peptic.
-- 化器官   digestive organ.
-- 化腺   digestive gland.
25-- 失   melt, flee, disappear, van-
                  ish, evaporate.
26-- 息   news , information, intel-
                  ligence, message, reports,
                  communication, word.
-- 息靈通   well-informed.
-- 釋   melt away.
29-- 愁解悶   disencumber one's mind
                  from care.
32-- 逝   elapse.
33-- 滅   vanish, disappear, annihi-
                  late, eradicate, extinguish,
                  wipe out.
35-- 遣   n. amusement, pastime, di-
                  version, v. employ time,
                  play away, kill time, fill up
                  the time.
-- 遣時光   kill time.
37-- 沉   depression, downhearted.

-- 遙自在	enjoying complete freedom from care.
-- 遙法外	go free, be at large.
40-- 去	cancel, write off.
41-- 極	negative, passive, inactive.
-- 極主義	negativism, pessimism.
-- 極手段	negative means.
-- 極行爲	negative act.
-- 極怠工	sabotage, sit down strike.
-- 極抵抗	passive resistance.
-- 極因素	negative factor.
48-- 散	dissolve, disappear.
50-- 毒	disinfection, sterilize.
-- 毒作用	disinfection.
-- 毒藥	disinfectant, disinfector.
52-- 耗	consume, waste, exhaust, consume.
-- 耗者	consumer.
-- 耗量	wastage, consumption.
-- 耗品	expendables, expendable goods.
-- 耗戰	consumption warfare, war of attrition.
55-- 費	*n.* consumption, *v.* spend, consume, waste, make away with.
-- 費稅	excise, consumption tax.
-- 費者	consumers.
-- 費品	consumption goods, consumable.
-- 費財	consumers' goods.
-- 費合作社	cooperative store.
70-- 防	fire prevention, fire-control.
-- 防隊	fire brigade, fire company.
78-- 除	abolish, eliminate, remove, clear away.
-- 除惡念	eliminate evil thought.
-- 除災難	eliminate disasters.
-- 除戰力	eliminate the war capability.
90-- 火機	fire engine.
-- 火器	fire extinguisher.
-- 炎片	sulfaguanidine tablets.

浉 〔Tang〕 *v.* drop, drip.
10-- 下	trickle down.
31-- 汗	perspire.

60-- 口水	dribble.
67-- 眼	shed tears .

澇 〔Lao〕 *v.* flood.
3915₀

泮 〔Pan〕 *v.* melt, scatter.
3918₉

淡 〔Tan〕 *adj.* fresh, weak, light, tasteless, dull, insipid, light, disinterested, indifferent.
00-- 市	bear market.
10-- 而無味	tasteless, insipid.
12-- 水	fresh water.
20-- 季	slack season (in business), dull season, dead season, slow season.
-- 季票價	slack season fare, low season fare.
23-- 然置之	take it easy.
27-- 色	light color.
34-- 漠	look at it nonchalantly.
36-- 泊	plain, without worldly desires.
-- 泊生涯	plain living.
-- 泊名利	indifferent to fame and wealth.
39-- 淡相逢	meet friends insipidly.
44-- 薄	indifferent, diluted, weak.
60-- 日	dull day.
80-- 食粗衣	simple food and coarse clothing.

3926₆
襠 〔Dang〕 *n.* seat of trousers.
3930₂
逍 〔Hsiao〕 *v.* ramble, roam, loiter.
37-- 遙	*v.* ramble, wander about, saunter, be at leisure, stroll, *adj.* at ease.
-- 遙自在	free and unrestrained, be at ease.
-- 遙法外	get away with crime.

3930₅
遴 〔Lin〕 *v.* choose, select, *adj.* difficult to do, misery.
37-- 選	choose carefully, select carefully.

3930₉

迷 〔Mi〕 *v.* confuse, deceive, delude, go astray, *adj.* deceived, deluded, intoxicated, mad of.

00--	離	indistinct, blurred, vague.
20--	信	superstition.
--	住	*v.* fascinate, charm, *adj.* fascinated, charmed.
22--	亂	bewilder, confound.
--	戀	be infatuated with.
25--	失	*v.* lose one's self, lose one's head, go astray, *adj.* bewildered, fascinated.
44--	夢	illusion, fond dream.
53--	惑	bewitch, bewilder, enchant.
67--	路	lose way, lose oneself, be lost, stray, lose one's way.
80--	人	charming.
--	人心竅	captivate, charm, fascinate.
97--	糊	be confused, muddle-headed.

3933₆

鯊 〔Sha〕 *n.* shark.

27--	魚	shark.
40--	皮革	shagreen.

3973₇

裟 〔Sha〕 *n.* dress of a monk.

4000₀

叉 〔Cha〕 *n.* fork, crotch, *v.* fork, cross the arms, fold the hands.

12--	形	furcate.
17--	子	fork.
44--	枝	forked branch.
67--	路	crossing, a fork in the road.

十 〔Shih〕 *adj.* ten, tenth.

00--	六	sixteen, sixteenth.
--	六開本	sixteenmo (16mo).
03--	誡	the ten commandments.
10--	一	eleven, eleventh.
--	一月	November.
--	二	twelve, twelfth.
--	二指腸	duodenum.
--	二月	December.
--	三	thirteen, thirteenth.
--	五	fifteen, fifteenth.
--	惡不赦	beyond redemption.
--	不得一	get not even one out of ten.
--	面體	decahedron.
20--	倍	tenfold, ten times.
--	億	billion, milliard.
27--	角形	decagon.
30--	字街	crossway, crossroads.
--	字軍	Crusade.
--	字架	cross.
--	字路口	crossing, crossroads.
--	之八九	in nine cases out of ten.
--	進法	the decimal system.
40--	七	seventeen, seventeenth.
--	九	nineteen, nineteenth.
--	有九敗	fail in nine out of ten cases.
--	有八九	eight or nine out of ten cases.
43--	式起重車	forklift truck.
44--	萬	hundred thousand.
--	萬火急	extremely urgent .
50--	車	fork, forklift.
53--	成成功	one hundred percent successful.
60--	四	fourteen .
--	足	complete, perfect.
77--	月	October.
--	月革命	the October Revolution.
80--	八	eighteen, eighteenth.
--	全十美	perfect in every way.
--	分	full, perfect, not less than.
--	分之一	one tenth.
--	分滿意	be perfectly satisfied.
--	無其一	not even one in ten.
--	年	decade.
--	年樹木	it takes ten years to grow a tree.
--	拿九穩	ninety percent sure.

4001₁

左 〔Tso〕 *n.* the left-hand side, *v.* degrade, verify, prove, go against, *adj.* left, improper, wrong.

02-- 證	n. evidence, v. prove.
17-- 翼	left wing.
18-- 改右改	make changes over and over again.
20-- 手	left hand .
-- 舷	port of a ship.
21-- 傾	left deviation.
22-- 派	the Left.
36-- 祖	take sides.
-- 邊	left, left hand.
40-- 右	right and left, near to, about, around.
-- 右手	assistant.
-- 右爲難	be in a dilemma.
-- 右兩難	caught in two difficulties or danger.
-- 右相稱	the left and the right fit each other.
58-- 輪槍	revolver.
60-- 思右想	ponder, consider carefully.
97-- 鄰右舍	with neighbors both on the left and the right.

4001₄

雄 〔**Hsiung**〕 *n.* male, hero, chief, leader, *adj.* male, masculine, heroic, brave.

00-- 鹿	stag.
-- 鷹	tercel.
-- 辯	eloquence, declamation.
-- 辯者	debater, orator, eloquent debater.
20-- 雞	cock.
21-- 虎	tiger.
-- 師	crack troops.
24-- 壯	strong, burly, powerful.
-- 偉	grand, imposing, magnificent.
33-- 心	ambition, lofty aspiration.
40-- 才大略	of outstanding ability.
41-- 獅	lion.
44-- 豬	boar.
60-- 圖大略	great design and a big plan.
67-- 鴨	drake.
80-- 羊	ram.

4001₇

九 〔**Chiu**〕 *adj.* nine, ninth.

10-- 一八事件	the Mukden incident.
-- 死一生	a hair-breath escape, ten percent chance to survive.
20-- 倍	ninefold, nine times.
26-- 泉	hell, the Hades.
27-- 角形	nonagon.
40-- 十	ninety, ninetieth.
-- 九表	multiplication table.
53-- 折	ten percent discount.
60-- 國公約	nine-power pact.
77-- 月	September.

丸 〔**Wan**〕 *n.* pill, ball, small ball.

| 44-- 藥 | pill. |
| 48-- 散 | pill and powder. |

4002₇

力 〔**Li**〕 *n.* strength, power, force, energy, spirit, vigor, might, *adj.* energetic, zealous, vigorous.

00-- 衰	weak, feeble, languid.
-- 辨	argue strongly.
06-- 竭	strength exhausted, be exhausted.
10-- 不從心	bite off more than one can chew.
-- 不勝任	one's strength is not equal to one's duties.
13-- 強	strong.
17-- 弱	weak.
20-- 爭	struggle hard.
21-- 行	practice energetically.
-- 行不怠	do something persistently without a cessation.
24-- 壯	robust.
30-- 之所及	the best of one's power, within one's power.
-- 守城池	defend the city vigorously.
-- 守成規	strive hard to observe the rules.
40-- 大	powerful.
-- 大無比	without match in physical prowess.
-- 索	demand strongly.
43-- 求	require earnestly, strive for, try hard to.
-- 求上進	strive vigorously to improve oneself.

-- 求名利	seek fame and wealth vigorously.		-- 言欺人	exaggerate.
-- 求獨立	strive after independence.		-- 衣	cloak, outer garment, overcoat.
44-- 薄	weak.		-- 雜燴	hodge-podge, hotchpotch.
50-- 推	thrust.		02-- 話	bragging, boast.
-- 拉	tug.		-- 話連天	a lot of big talk.
-- 盡筋疲	be tired and exhausted.		-- 謊話	gross lie.
-- 持鎮定	try to keep calm.		05-- 講	talk a great deal about.
60-- 量	strength, force, power.		-- 講堂	auditorium, hall.
-- 量對比	balance of force.		07-- 謬	blunder.
-- 圖自強	earnestly strive for self-reliance.		-- 詞書	encyclopedia.
61-- 點	point of force.		-- 部	principally.
72-- 所不及	beyond one's reach.		-- 部分	most of, the major part of.
-- 所能及	within one's power.		07-- 調整	extensive readjustment.
77-- 學	dynamics, mechanics.		08-- 敵當前	be confronted with a strong opponent.
-- 與願違	be unable to do what one wishes.		-- 論戰	great polemic.
80-- 氣	physical strength.		10-- 工業	large-scale industry.
90-- 小	flaccid.		-- 豆	soybean.

4003_0

大 〔Ta〕 *v.* enlarge, grow large, magnify, *adj.* great, large, big, huge, gigantic, enormous, important, *adv.* largely, greatly, highly, very, extremely.

00-- 主教	archbishop.		-- 雨	heavy rain, downpour.
-- 方	generous, liberal.		-- 元帥	generalissimo.
-- 方向	general orientation.		-- 而無當	big but useless.
-- 廳	hall, main hall.		-- 雪	heavy snow.
-- 廈	palace, mansion, edifice, large building.		-- 雪紛飛	snow is falling thick and fast.
-- 庭廣眾	public, in broad daylight and in front of everybody.		-- 百貨公司	emporium.
-- 麻	hemp, marijuana, pot, cannabis.		-- 面積	large area.
-- 廉價	bargain sale.		-- 西洋	Atlantic Ocean.
-- 意	general meaning, general idea, careless, negligent.		-- 可一試	it is worth trying.
			-- 可不必	it is not all worth it.
-- 意不差	not wrong in general.		-- 不如前	have deteriorated or declined a great deal.
-- 率相等	be equal on the whole.		-- 不相同	entirely or totally different.
-- 亨	tycoon.		-- 哥	eldest brother.
-- 辯論	great debate.		-- 醉	have a brick in one's hat.
-- 言	*n.* bluster, boast, brag, big words, *v.* boast, brag, talk big.		-- 不列顛	Great Britain.
			11-- 頭菜	the turnip.
-- 言不慚	boast without shame.		12-- 水	flood.
			-- 水連天	the flood reaches the horizon.
			-- 發雷霆	be in a blaze of anger.
			-- 發牢騷	dissipate one's grievance extensively.
			-- 發展	rapid development.
			-- 副	the chief mate (or officer).
			-- 型工程	major engineering work.

-- 型工業	large-scale industry.
-- 型卡車	large truck, transporter.
-- 型超級市場	hypermarket.
14-- 功	extraordinary merit, great achievement.
-- 功告成	the achievement of a great meritorious service.
-- 破	destroy in a big way, defeat utterly.
16-- 理石	marble.
17-- 刀	big knife.
-- 砲	cannon, artillery.
18-- 致	in general.
-- 致平均	on a rough average.
-- 改組	large-scale reshuffle, shake-up.
21-- 步	stride.
-- 街	main street.
-- 街小巷	big streets and small lanes, in every street and lane.
-- 便	go to stool, shit, excrement.
-- 熊貓	giant panda.
-- 師	great master, master, high monk.
22-- 豐收	bumper harvest.
-- 倒退	great retrogression.
-- 傻瓜	big fool.
-- 後方	great rear area.
-- 變動	great change.
-- 災難	catastrophe, disaster.
23-- 代數	higher algebra.
24-- 動盪	great upheaval.
-- 動脈	aorta.
25-- 使	ambassador.
-- 使館	embassy.
-- 失敗	end in nothing.
-- 失所望	be greatly disappointed.
26-- 自然	nature.
-- 白菜	Chinese cabbage.
-- 總統	president.
27-- 血戰	great sanguinary battle.
-- 綱	outline.
-- 約	probably, generally, perhaps, around, nearly, likely.
-- 約費用	probable cost.
-- 多數	majority of, most of.
-- 包	bale.
-- 將	general.
-- 名鼎鼎	famous, well-known.
-- 修	capital repair, major overhaul.
-- 修計劃	plan of major repair.
-- 修理	heavy repair.
28-- 作	monumental work.
30-- 家	all of us, everybody.
-- 家閨秀	young lady of a noble family.
-- 戶人家	wealthy and influential family.
-- 寒	severe cold.
-- 寫	capital letter.
-- 憲章	great charter, Magna Charta.
-- 宴會	carnival, grand banquet.
-- 字報	big character poster.
-- 字標題	headline.
-- 富	of great wealth.
-- 富翁	millionaire, billionaire.
-- 客廳	saloon.
-- 宗	large amount, staple.
-- 宗商品	bulk commodity.
-- 宗貨物	bulk goods, lot cargo.
-- 宗包裹	bulky parcel.
-- 宗銷售	bulk sale.
31-- 漲價	huge price increase, heavy advance.
-- 漲大落	fluctuate violently.
32-- 業告成	have accomplished the great task.
33-- 浪	billows.
-- 減價	cheap sale, grand sale.
34-- 為震怒	fly into rage.
35-- 禮服	frock coat.
36-- 瀑布	big waterfall, cataract.
37-- 禍臨門	disaster befalls.
-- 選	general election.
-- 軍	great army, large forces.
38-- 海	sea.
-- 海撈針	dredge a needle in the ocean, find a needle in a haystack, find a needle in a meadow.

-- 洋	ocean.		-- 草原	prairie.
-- 道	highway.		-- 權在握	hold great power.
-- 道理	great truth, major principles.		-- 蒜	garlic.
			-- 堤	main dike.
40-- 力士	giant, man of unusual strength, Herculean man.		47-- 聲	thunder, roar.
-- 力讚賞	sing the praises.		-- 聲高呼	shout from the house-top.
-- 大地	greatly, largely.		-- 聲急呼	give a clarion call, awaken the public.
-- 大生氣	hit the ceiling, very angry.		-- 怒	in a great rage, in great anger.
-- 麥	barley.			
-- 才小用	great talent employed in a petty way.		48-- 驚	great surprise.
-- 有可爲	very hopeful.		-- 赦	amnesty.
-- 有可觀	very considerable.		-- 教堂	cathedral.
-- 有來頭	very influential socially or politically.		-- 檢修	general overhaul, major overhaul.
-- 有分別	entirely different.		-- 檢查	large-scale inspection.
-- 難臨頭	imminent catastrophe or disaster.		50-- 本營	headquarter.
-- 喜	gladness, joy, bliss.		-- 丈夫	man of honour.
-- 喜欲狂	go crazy with joy.		-- 事	landmark, great event.
-- 吉大利	be auspicious and prosperous.		-- 事記	chronicle of events.
			-- 事宣傳	ballyhoo.
-- 木桶	barrel.		-- 事年表	chronology.
41-- 概	in general, mainly, for the most part, probably, generally.		-- 事鋪張	make an extravagant show.
			-- 車	cart.
-- 概如此	that's about the size of it.		51-- 批	great numbers, large run.
-- 幅度	large extent.		-- 批交易	extensive transaction.
-- 幅度增長	substantial increase.		-- 批訂貨	extensive order, large order.
43-- 城市	metropolis.		-- 批出售	sell in bulk.
-- 協作	large-scale cooperation.		-- 批生產	high-run production.
44-- 考	final examination.		-- 批裁員	mass sacking.
-- 勢	the force of circumstance.		-- 批銷售	mass sale.
-- 勢已去	the situation is beyond salvation, it is irretrievable.		-- 批判	mass criticism.
-- 勢所趨	be dictated by the general trend.		-- 打出手	get into a brawl, get into a free-for-all.
-- 地	good earth.		52-- 抵如此	in general it is thus.
-- 地主	lord of broad acres, big landlord.		-- 折扣	heavy discount.
			53-- 成問題	very doubtful.
-- 地產	large estate.		55-- 捷	major victory.
-- 地回春	the great earth returns to spring.		56-- 規模	on a large scale, extensive, massive.
-- 蕭條	great depression.		-- 規模投機	heavy speculation.
-- 熱	n. sultriness, adj.sultry.		-- 規模購買力	mass purchasing power.
-- 熱天	scorching day.		-- 規模銷售	mass marketing.
			-- 提琴	cello, violoncello.
			-- 拍賣	sell at a bargain.
			57-- 拇指	thumb.
			-- 掃除	general cleaning.

-- 都市	big city.	
58-- 數	great number, large number.	
60-- 量	mass, large quantity.	
-- 量發行	mass circulation.	
-- 量市場	mass market.	
-- 量需求	heavy demand.	
-- 量訂購	place a large order, huge order.	
-- 量供應	free supply, liberal supply.	
-- 量消費	heavy consumption.	
-- 量生產	mass production.	
-- 罪	serious crime, enormity.	
-- 暴露	major exposure.	
-- 暴跌	big slump.	
-- 國	great powers, powerful country.	
-- 旱	drought.	
-- 暑	dog day.	
-- 買主	heavy buyer.	
-- 眾	public, general, masses.	
-- 眾意見	the opinion of the people.	
-- 眾化	n. popularization, v. popularize.	
-- 眾化價格	popular price.	
-- 眾傳播	mass communication.	
-- 眾消費品	large-scale goods.	
-- 眾媒介	mass media.	
-- 眾捷運系統	mass rapid transit system.	
62-- 呼	clamor, cry, lift up the voice.	
-- 踏步	in great strides, in full stride.	
-- 叫	cry.	
-- 喊大叫	raise a great hue and cry.	
63-- 戰	decisive battle, major engagement, large-scale warfare.	
-- 戰犯	arch war criminal.	
64-- 財主	millionaire.	
65-- 跌	crash, heavy decline.	
-- 跌價	collapse of price, heavy fall.	
66-- 罵	violent abuse.	
-- 哭	wail.	
67-- 略	roughly.	
-- 躍進	the Big Leap Forward.	
67-- 路	highway, high street.	

68-- 敗	beat all to sticks, bite the dust, complete defeat.	
69-- 吵大鬧	roughhouse.	
71-- 反覆	great reversal.	
-- 反攻	general counter-offensive.	
-- 臣	minister, secretary, high official.	
-- 牙	tusk.	
72-- 腦	cerebrum.	
-- 兵團	army corps.	
73-- 騙局	pure swindle.	
74-- 陸	continent, mainland.	
-- 陸政策	continental policy.	
-- 陸性	continental.	
75-- 體上	in the main, generally.	
-- 體同意	agree in principle.	
-- 肆吵鬧	create a rumpus.	
76-- 腸	the large intestine.	
77-- 門	street door, front door.	
-- 膽	bold, brave, daring.	
-- 風	gale, typhoon, high wind.	
-- 風雪	blizzard.	
-- 用戶	large user, bulk user.	
-- 同主義	cosmopolitanism.	
-- 同世界	a world where harmony, equality and justice prevail, a world of universal brotherhood.	
-- 同小異	be alike with minor difference, be more or less the same.	
-- 局	the general prospect, overall situation.	
-- 局危險	the general situation is critical.	
-- 展身手	fully show one's capability.	
-- 腿	the thigh.	
-- 股東	large stockholder, big stockholder, major stockholder.	
-- 膽	bold, daring, venturous.	
-- 學校	university, college.	
-- 學生	college student.	
-- 學校長	college president, chancellor, president of a university.	
-- 民主	mass democracy.	

--門	gate, main entrance, portico.
--興土木	build many new building.
78--隊	regiment, battalion.
--除夕	New Year's Eve.
79--勝	smashing victory.
80--人	adult, grown-up .
--人物	great man, great gun.
--企業	big business, enterprise on a large scale.
--企業家	tycoon.
--前提	the major premise.
--分化	great division.
--無畏精神	undaunted spirit, utterly fearless.
--慈大悲	all loving and merciful.
--義滅親	uphold justice and righteousness even at the sacrifice of blood relations.
--合唱	chorus.
--會	mass meeting, general meeting, conference.
--公無私	selfless, unselfish.
--氣	atmosphere.
--氣污染	atmospheric pollution.
--氣層	atmospheric layer.
--氣壓	atmospheric pressure.
84--錯	terrible mistake, terrible blunder.
87--飲	swig.
88--笑	hearty laugh, good laugh, horselaugh.
--筆款項	heavy money, important money.
--節	matters of principle.
90--小	size, extent, dimension, magnitude.
--牛	largely, chiefly, mostly.
--半輩子	in most of one's life.
--火	conflagration.
--米	rice .
--快人心	cheer the people's heart greatly.
97--炮	cannon, artillery.
98--氅	cloak.
--悅	overjoy, enchant.

太 〔Tai〕 adj. very, too, excessively, extremely.

00--高	too high.
10--平	peace, tranquillity.
--平洋	Pacific ocean.
--平洋學會	the Institute of Pacific Ocean.
--平洋盆地	Pacific Basin.
--平洋會議	the Pacific Conference.
--平盛世	reign of peace, order and prosperity.
--平景象	atmosphere of peace.
--平門	emergency door.
--平年月	peaceful times.
17--子	crown prince.
21--上皇	overlord, the emperor's father.
26--息	sigh.
27--多	too much, too many.
30--空	ether, outer space.
37--遲	too late, a day after the fair.
--過	adj. excessive, exorbitant, adv. excessively.
--淡	too quiet (in color), too thin (in wine, soup etc.)
40--大	too large.
--古	too old, great antiquity.
41--極拳	Tai-Chi boxing, Tai Chi Chuan.
50--貴	too expensive.
60--早	too early.
76--陽	sun.
--陽系	the solar system .
--陽能	solar energy.
--陽能電池	solar battery.
--陽能發電	power generation with solar energy.
--陽穴	temples of human beings.
--陽眼鏡	sunglasses.
78--監	eunuch.
90--小	too small.
--忙	too busy.

4003₄

爽 〔Shuang〕 n. dawn, daybreak, v. fail, miss, lose, adj. clear, happy, cheerful, light-hearted.

00--	言	fail in one's promise.
27--	身粉	talcum powder.
--	約	break an appointment, fail to keep an engagement.
37--	朗	open-minded, open-hearted, clear.
40--	直	candid, downright, straightforward.
80--	氣	racy, accommodating.
95--	快	refreshing, pleasant, happy, cheerful, frank.

4003₈

夾〔**Chia**〕*n.* clip, clamp, folder, pincer, *v.* press, succor, squeeze, *adj.* double, lined.

00--	衣	double garment.
--	裏	lining.
--	雜	mix.
17--	子	clamp, clip, pincer movement.
18--	攻	attack from both sides, included angle.
27--	角	included angle.
41--	板	plywood, splint.
44--	帶	smuggling, bring secretly.
74--	肢窩	armpit.
77--	緊	press rightly.
--	針	hairpin .
--	鉗	pincers.

4004₇

友〔**Yu**〕*n.* friend, companion, comrade, brotherly love, *adj.* friendly, cordial, kind.

03--	誼	friendship, fellowship.
--	誼賽	friendly match (or game).
--	誼深厚	deep friendship.
10--	于之愛	brotherly love.
20--	愛	friendliness, friendship, amity.
37--	軍	friendly troop.
47--	好	friendly, on good terms.
--	好調解	amicable composition.
--	好解決	amicable settlement.
--	好往來	friendly intercourse.
--	好協定	friendship pact.
--	好關係	friendly relations.
57--	邦	ally.

80--	人	friend, acquaintance.
--	善	kind, friendly, familiar.
--	善相處	be on friendly terms and live together harmoniously.

4010₀

土〔**Tu**〕*n.* earth, ground, soil, land, mud, region, territory, *adj.* native, local.

00--	產	native product, native goods.
--	產商店	native products shop.
--	音	brogue, local accent.
--	豪	demagogue, local tyrant, local despot.
--	豪劣紳	local bullies and bad gentry.
--	豪辦法	indigenous method.
01--	語	local dialect.
02--	話	dialect, patois.
07--	設備	indigenous equipment.
10--	工	earth work.
--	豆	potatoes.
--	耳其	Turkey.
--	耳其人	Turkish.
17--	司	chieftain of a tribe.
18--	改	land reform, agrarian reform.
20--	番	aborigines.
24--	化肥	indigenous chemical fertilizer.
--	特產	local special products.
--	貨	native goods, domestic products.
25--	生土長	be born and grow up in the local community.
28--	黴素	terramycin.
30--	窖	cellar.
40--	壤	soil .
--	布	hand-woven cloth.
--	木工程	civil-engineering, civil work.
--	木材料	engineering materials.
41--	壩	earth dam.
44--	著	natives, aborigines.
--	地	land, territory, country, earth, ground.
--	地證	title deed, land certificate.
--	地改革	land reform.
--	地徵用	expropriation of land.
--	地法	land law.

-- 地所有人	landholder.
45-- 塊	clod.
46-- 棍	ruffian.
60-- 星	the planet Saturn.
66-- 器	earthenware.
71-- 匪	bandits.
80-- 人	natives.

士 〔Shih〕 *n.* scholar, learned man, soldier, gentleman, official.

00-- 卒	soldier.
30-- 官	non-commissioned officer.
-- 大夫	scholar-bureaucrat.
72-- 兵	soldier.
80-- 人	scholar.
-- 氣	martial spirit, morale of the armed forces.

4010₄

圭 〔Kuei〕 *n.* gem.

奎 〔Kuei〕 *n.* the Kuei star.

30-- 寧	quinine.

臺 〔Tai〕 *n.* tower, terrace, stand, stage, platform, observatory, check, look into.

32-- 灣	Formosa, Taiwan.
71-- 階	steps.

4010₆

查 〔Cha〕 *v.* examine into, search into, inquire into, investigate, check, look into.

00-- 辦	examine, investigate.
01-- 證	investigate and verify.
07-- 詞典	consult a dictionary.
-- 詢台	information desk, inquiry desk.
-- 詢表格	question, blank, inquiry form.
-- 詢費	enquiry fee.
-- 詢	investigate, search.
08-- 訖	check off.
22-- 出	discover, find out, seek out.
28-- 收	receive accordingly.
-- 稅	tax inspection.
30-- 究	try, examine, investigate, inquire into.
-- 究辦理	investigate and act accord-

	ingly.
-- 究實情	look into the actual state of affairs.
34-- 對	check up.
-- 對帳目	check the account.
40-- 核存貨	check the stock.
41-- 帳	audit.
-- 帳員	auditor, controller.
44-- 勘	survey .
-- 封財產	seal up and confiscate property, attachment on one's property.
-- 封	seal up, close down.
-- 禁走私	prevention of smuggling.
61-- 賬	audit.
-- 賬報告	auditor's report.
-- 賬員	auditor, auditing officer.
-- 點財產	inspection of property.
67-- 明	ascertain.
-- 照辦理	please consider and act accordingly.
-- 閱	consult, look up.
77-- 問	investigate, inquire about, look into, question, examine.
-- 驗	examine, scrutinize.
-- 無實據	it has been found that the report is not sustained by facts.

4010₇

直 〔Chih〕 *v.* straighten, *adj.* straight, upright, outspoken, exact, honest, sincere, firsthand.

00-- 立	*v.* stand up, erect, *adj.* vertical, upright.
-- 率	frank, candid, open, plain.
-- 言	speak plainly, speak frankly.
-- 譯	literal translation.
07-- 認	confess frankly, avow.
-- 說=直言	
-- 說法	indicative mood.
10-- 至	until, directly to, heading to.
12-- 到	until, till, up to.
20-- 系親屬	lineal relatives.
21-- 上	straight upward.
-- 徑	diameter.
-- 行	advance straight forward.

26--	線	straight line.
27--	角	right angle.
30--	流電	direct current (D.C.).
34--	達	reach directly, nonstop, through.
--	達車	through train, through traffic train, express train.
40--	爽	frank, outspoken, straight forward, candid.
--	去直來	go and return without undue delay.
50--	接	direct, at first hand.
--	接交涉	direct negotiation.
--	接交易	direct transaction.
--	接政治	direct government.
--	接稅	direct tax.
--	接通商	direct transaction in business.
--	接成本	direst cost, prime cost.
--	接教授法	direct method.
--	接影響	direct impact.
--	接原因	immediate cause.
--	接匯兌	direct exchange.
--	接銷售	direct selling (placement).
53--	轄	direct control.
--	轄市	municipality directly under the central authority.
60--	昇飛機	helicopter.
76--	腸	rectum.
77--	覺	intuition.
--	尺	straightedge, ruler.
80--	入	go straight in.
89--	銷	direct marketing, door to door sale.

壺 〔Hu〕 n. pot, jug, kettle.

44--	蓋	cover, lid.
61--	嘴	spout.

4010₈

壹 〔I〕 v. join into one, adj. one, uniform alike.

47--	切	the whole of.

4011₄

堆 〔Tui〕 n. heap, mass, pile, stack, mound, v. heap up, pile, store, accumulate.

08--	放	pile, heap up.
10--	石	pile up stones.
--	石成山	gather stones into a heap.
17--	砌	pile up.
25--	積	heap, pile, accumulate.
--	積如山	lie in a large heap.
30--	塞	block up.
43--	棧	storehouse, warehouse.
77--	肥	stock manure, compost.

4011₆

境 〔Ching〕 n. region, district, limit, boundary, border.

36--	遇	situation, circumstance.
--	遇不佳	be in bad circumstances.
--	況	situation, plight, circumstances.
40--	內	within the boundary.
44--	地	situation.
60--	界	boundary, limit, frontier.

壇 〔Tan〕 n. stage, altar, platform for ceremonies.

41--	坫	place for important meeting, place for the gathering of literary men.
46--	坊	altar in the open air.

4011₇

坑 〔Keng〕 n. pit, ditch, trench, hole, hollow, v. throw into a pit, entrap, involve.

30--	害	injure.
31--	渠	drain.
38--	道	tunnel, ditch.
--	道戰	tunnel warfare, underground warfare.
47--	坎	pit.
77--	陷	entrap.
80--	谷	valley.

矗 〔Chu〕 v. rise up high, adj. upright, lofty.

00--	立	tower over.
23--	然	straight, upright.

4011₈

垃 〔La〕 n. rubbish, dust.

47--	圾	rubbish, dust.
--	圾堆	dump, garbage heap, dirtheap.

-- 圾車	dirt-wagon, dust cart, garbage truck.
-- 圾夫	dustman, garbage man, garbage collector.
-- 圾箱	garbage can, garbage container .

4012₇

坊 〔**Fang**〕 *n.* lane, alley, store, workshop, monument.

| 00-- 市 | market place. |

4013₂

壕 〔**Hao**〕 *n.* ditch, moat, entrenchment.

| 35-- 溝 | ditch, moat, trench. |

壤 〔**Jang**〕 *n.* soil, earth.

| 40-- 土 | soil, earth. |

壞 〔**Huai**〕 *n.* ruin, spoil, injure, perish, destroy, *adj.* spoiled, corrupted, bad, rotten, evil, malicious.

00-- 意	malice.
-- 疽	gangrene.
10-- 死	necrosis.
17-- 蛋	bad egg, rotten egg, scoundrel.
-- 了	spoiled, out of order, go wrong.
21-- 處	defect.
27-- 名	bad reputation.
-- 的	rotten, spoiled, bad.
-- 船	wreck.
32-- 透了	downright bad, too bad.
33-- 心眼	evil-hearted, malicious.
37-- 運氣	bad luck.
50-- 事	mischief, evil, bad thing.
61-- 賬	bad debt (account), uncollectible debt.
-- 賬準備	reserve for bad loan (uncollectible accounts).
77-- 脾氣	ill nature, ill-tempered, bad tempered.
80-- 人	evil-doer, villain.
-- 分子	bad element.

4016₁

培 〔**Pei**〕 *v.* cultivate, nourish, nurse, foster.

| 00-- 育 | cherish, breed, nourish, |

	rear.
-- 育人才	nourish people of ability.
02-- 訓	training.
-- 訓班	training courses.
-- 訓津貼	training benefit (allowance).
-- 訓期	training period.
-- 訓中心	training center.
14-- 殖	nourish.
44-- 植	support, cultivate.
80-- 養	cultivate, nourish, bring up, educate.
-- 養人才	train people for professions.

4016₇

塘 〔**Tang**〕 *n.* pool, pound, dike, embankment.

4018₂

垓 〔**Kai**〕 *n.* far distance, boundary, billion.

4020₀

才 〔**Tsai**〕 *n.* ability, talent, faculty, gift, natural ability, mental faculty.

17-- 子	genius.
-- 子佳人	handsome scholar and a pretty girl.
21-- 能	talent, ability, capacity.
27-- 貌	talent and personage.
-- 色兼備	have both wit and beauty.
40-- 力	talent, mental faculty, intelligence.
-- 力過人	exceed others in ability.
44-- 藝	capacity, ability, talent.
48-- 幹	ability, capability, gift.
77-- 學	learning scholarship.

4020₇

麥 〔**Mai**〕 *n.* wheat, barley, oat.

22-- 片	oatmeal.
24-- 秸	stalk or straw of wheat.
25-- 穗	ears of wheat.
31-- 酒	beer, ale.
40-- 克風	microphone.
44-- 芽	wheat sprout, malt.
-- 芒	awn of wheat.
-- 芽糖	malt sugar.
87-- 麩	mash.
88-- 餅	bannock.

98-- 粉　　　　flour.

夸〔**Kua**〕*adj.* prodigious, conceited.
4021₁

堯〔**Yao**〕*n.* Emperor Yao (an ancient emperor of China).
4021₄

在〔**Tsai**〕*v.* be it, lie in, belong to, rest on, consist in, live, be alive, *prep.* in, on, at, within.

00-- 座　　　　be present.
-- 旁　　　　by, alongside.
-- 意　　　　notice, bear in mind, be attentive, mind, care.
07-- 望　　　　be in sight, be within sight.
08-- 於　　　　lie in, rest with, consist in.
10-- 下　　　　beneath, below, under, down.
-- 下文　　　hereinafter, hereinbelow.
13-- 職　　　　in office.
-- 職人員　　in-service staff.
15-- 建工程　　construction work in process.
17-- 那裡　　　be here.
20-- 乎各人　　depend on each individual.
-- 手邊　　　be at hand .
-- 手　　　　on hand, in stock.
21-- 上　　　　above, over.
22-- 後　　　　after, behind.
-- 製品　　　work-in-process.
23-- 外　　　　outside, without.
24-- 先　　　　before, previous to, in front of.
27-- 危險中　　be at stake, be in danger.
-- 假期中　　during the vacation.
-- 船上　　　be on board.
30-- 家　　　　be at home.
-- 這裡　　　be here.
-- 案　　　　on record.
34-- 遠處　　　be in the distance.
38-- 途中　　　be on the way, in transit.
40-- 內　　　　within, inside in, among.
44-- 幕後　　　be behind the curtain, be behind the scenes.
-- 世　　　　in the world, in life, alive.
-- 某處　　　be at a certain place.
46-- 場　　　　presence, be on the spot,

be present.
47-- 朝黨　　　party in power, the government power, ruling party.
50-- 中間　　　in the middle.
62-- 別處　　　be elsewhere .
67-- 野黨　　　party out of office, opposition party.
-- 眼前　　　be in sight.
72-- 所不能　　impossible to do.
-- 所不免　　cannot be avoided.
-- 所不惜　　regardless of the cost or sacrifice.
77-- 學　　　　be at school.
80-- 前　　　　before, in front of, ahead.

帷〔**Wei**〕*n.* curtain, drape, hanging screen, canopy, tent.
41-- 帳　　　　curtain.
46-- 幔　　　　drapery.
90-- 裳　　　　apron.
4021₆

克〔**Ke**〕*v.* can, be able to, sustain, overcome, conquer, repress, control.
08-- 敵　　　　conquer the enemy .
-- 敵致勝　　defeat the enemy and win a victory.
17-- 己　　　　deny oneself, be master of oneself, be one's own man, self-control.
22-- 山病　　　the Keshan disease.
-- 制　　　　overpower, restrain, check, overcome, conquer.
28-- 復　　　　recapture, recover.
50-- 拉　　　　carat.
77-- 服　　　　overpower, overcome, overmaster.

4022₇

巾〔**Chin**〕*n.* handkerchief, napkin, towel.
46-- 幗英雄　　heroine.
-- 幗鬚眉　　women who act and talk like men, mannish women, masculine women.

內〔**Nei**〕*adj.* inner, inside, internal, interior, *prep.* within, in, among, in the midst of.

00--	應	betray, inside man.
--	衣	underwear.
--	應外合	treachery within and without.
01--	訌	internal dissension.
07--	部	inside, interior, internal.
10--	需	domestic needs.
--	憂外患	internal revolt and foreign invasion.
17--	務	civil affairs.
18--	政	internal affairs, civil affairs.
--	政部	Home Department, Home Office, Ministry of Interior.
--	政部長	Minister Interior, Home Minister.
21--	行	expert, old hand.
22--	亂	internecine war, civil war, internal strife.
--	出血	internal hemorrhage.
23--	外	internal and external.
24--	科	medicine, general medicine.
--	科醫生	physician.
25--	件	contents.
--	債	internal debts.
27--	爭	internecine warfare.
28--	傷	internal injury, lesion.
30--	容	contents, substance.
31--	河	inland waterway.
--	河運輸	river transport, inland water transport.
33--	心	heart, at heart.
--	心自忖	think within oneself .
--	資	domestic capital.
38--	海	enclosed sea.
41--	奸	traitor.
44--	地	inland, back country, interior.
--	幕	behind the scenes, inside story, inside knowledge.
50--	中	inner, inside, within, among.
60--	因	internal cause.
63--	戰	civil war.
74--	助	wife, helpmate.
--	臟	intestines, internal organs.
77--	服	for internal use (said of medicine).
--	閣	cabinet.
--	閣總理	prime minister.
80--	分泌	internal secretion.
--	弟	brother-in-law, younger brother of one's wife.
89--	銷	domestic sales.
93--	燃機	internal combustion engine.

肉 〔 **Jou** 〕 *n.* meat, flesh.

00--	瘤	sarcoma, fleshy tumor.
10--	丁	cubed meat, diced meat.
12--	刑	corporal punishment.
22--	片	chop, broken meat, meat slices.
16--	彈	human bullet.
22--	絲	shredded meat, sliced meat.
27--	色	flesh-color, quality of the meat.
34--	汁	gravy.
35--	凍	meat jelly.
36--	湯	broth, meat-soup.
37--	冠	the comb (of a bird).
40--	丸	meat balls.
44--	桂	cinnamon.
50--	末	mince, minced meat.
53--	搏	fight hand to hand, come to close quarter.
--	感	sensual, sexy, buxom.
--	戰	hand to hand warfare.
73--	鬆	dried fluffy meat, shredded dried meat.
75--	體	body, flesh.
80--	食	animal food, meat.
--	食動物	meat eating animal, carnivorous animal.
83--	鋪	butchers' shop, meat market.
87--	慾	carnal, sexual appetite.
91--	類	meats.

布 〔 **Pu** 〕 *n.* cloth, *v.* spread, arrange, scatter, announce.

00--	店	drapery store.
--	商	draper, mercer.
--	衣	simple-dressed.
08--	施	charity, giving.
10--	丁	pudding.

--	爾什維克	Bolshevik.
17--	疋	stuff, piece goods.
22--	片	rag.
24--	告	*n.* announcement, proclamation, declaration, *v.* announce, proclaim, declare.
--	告天下	proclaim throughout the country.
--	告牌	notice-board, bulletin board.
27--	條	strap.
41--	帳	curtain, screen.
44--	帶	belt.
47--	穀鳥	cuckoo.
48--	散	*n.* distribution. *v.* spread, distribute about.
60--	置	arrange, array.
--	置得宜	arrange suitably.
--	置展覽	arrange exhibits.
--	置堂皇	the stage-scenery is grand.
71--	匹	drapery, piece-goods.
77--	局	layout, overall arrangement.

希〔Hsi〕*v.* hope, expect, wish, desire, *adj.* few, scarce, rare, strange, precious, *adv.* seldom, rarely.

07--	望	hope, expect, prospect, wish, desire.
37--	罕	uncommon, rare, scarce.
40--	奇	curious, strange.
44--	世之寶	extremely rare treasure.
72--	臘	*n.* Greece, *adj.* Greek.
--	臘文	the Greek language.
95--	少	rare, few, seldom, rarely.

有〔Yu〕*v.* have, possess, exist, attain, get.

00--	意	purposely, intentionally, on purpose.
--	意義	meaningful.
--	病	sick, ill.
--	產階級	the bourgeoisie, the capitalist class.
--	文化	cultured.
04--	計劃	have a plan to, according to the plan.
07--	望	hopeful.

08--	效	*v.* remain in effect, hold good, adj, effective.
--	效射程	effective range.
--	效期	effective term, period of validity.
--	效期限	time of effect.
10--	需求	be in demand.
12--	形	visible, concrete.
14--	功	meritorious.
16--	理	reasonable.
--	現款	be in cash.
17--	矛盾	be at variance.
21--	些	somewhat, certain, some.
--	步驟	methodically, step by step.
--	能力	capable, able.
--	價值	valuable, worthy.
--	價證券	negotiable note, valuable papers (securities).
22--	出息	promising.
--	利	beneficial, profitable, favorable, advantageous.
--	利可圖	lucrative.
--	利條件	favorable condition.
--	利投資	good investment, lucrative.
24--	仇	be at enmity with someone, have a hatred for someone.
--	待於	need, require.
25--	生之年	for the rest of one's life.
--	生以來	since one's birth .
27--	色人種	man of color.
--	色金屬	non-ferrous metal.
--	名	famous, celebrated, well known, renowned.
--	名無實	nominal, titular.
--	獎公債	lottery bond.
--	獎儲蓄	premium saving.
--	組織	in an organized way.
--	紀律	disciplined.
--	條件	conditioned.
30--	空	at leisure, unoccupied.
--	害	detrimental, injurious, harmful, noxious.
33--	心	intentionally, on purpose.
34--	遠見	far-sighted.
35--	禮	polite, courteous.
37--	資格	qualified, competent, eligible.

40-- 力	powerful, forcible, forceful.
-- 才能	gifted.
-- 存貨	in stock.
-- 希望	hopeful, promising.
-- 志氣	have noble aspirations.
42-- 機	organic.
-- 機玻璃	organic glass, plexiglas.
-- 機化學	organic chemistry.
-- 機物	organic matter.
-- 機物廢料	organic wastes.
-- 機物資	organic.
-- 機體	organic body, organism.
-- 機肥料	organic fertilizer.
44-- 勢力	influential, mighty, powerful.
-- 權	have a right to.
47-- 趣	interesting, funny.
-- 起色	be picking up, be getting better.
-- 期徒刑	penal servitude for a definite period.
-- 根據	well-founded, well-grounded.
50-- 事	occupied, engaged, employed.
-- 史以來	since the existence of human record, since history began, since the annals of time.
-- 夫之婦	married woman.
-- 毒	poisonous, noxious, venomous.
53-- 成效	efficacious.
57-- 把握	with confidence, be certain of.
-- 賴於	depend on.
60-- 罪	guilty.
62-- 影響	influential.
64-- 時	sometimes, in some case, occasionally, at times.
67-- 眼光	far-seeing, far-sighted, sagacious.
-- 路子	have friends in high places.
74-- 助於	contributory to.
77-- 用	useful.
-- 限	limited, finite.
-- 限責任	limited liability.

-- 限戰爭	limited war.
-- 限公司	limited company, incorporated company.
-- 膽	brave, bold.
-- 關	relevant, relative, related.
-- 關方面	parties concerned, interested parties.
-- 關證件	relevant documents.
-- 關當局	the proper authorities.
80-- 益	beneficial.
81-- 領導	with leadership.
83-- 錢	rich.
88-- 節奏	rhythmic, rhythmical.
91-- 恆心	having constancy, with perseverance.
95-- 情	sentimental.

肴〔Yao〕*n.* viands, fine food, dainties.
| 87-- 饌 | fine dishes, nice food. |

南〔Nan〕*adj.* south, southern, austral.
00-- 京	Nanking.
-- 方	the south.
-- 方人	southerner.
11-- 北	north and south.
24-- 緯	south latitude.
32-- 冰洋	the Antarctic Ocean.
38-- 洋	Southern China, south sea.
41-- 極	south pole.
-- 極圈	the Antarctic Circle.
-- 極光	aurora australis.
72-- 瓜	pumpkin.
77-- 風	south wind, wind blowing from the south.
80-- 美洲	South America.
90-- 半球	southern hemisphere.

脅〔Hsieh〕*n.* ribs, flank, *v.* coerce, intimidate, reprimand, reprove, force.
10-- 下	armpit.
28-- 從者	accomplice under duress.
36-- 迫	threaten, force, coerce, compel.
77-- 骨	ribs.

4024₆
幢〔Chang〕*n.* silk screen.
4024₇
皮〔Pi〕*n.* skin, leather, fur, surface,

hide, bark, *adj.* naughty.

00--	商	furriers.
--	衣	fur dress.
10--	下注射	hypodermic injection.
13--	球	ball, rubber ball.
17--	蛋	preserved egg.
20--	手套	leather gloves.
--	毛	superficial.
21--	膚	skin.
--	膚病	skin disease.
--	膚科	dermatology.
22--	紙	parchment.
23--	袋	leather bag.
24--	貨	furs, leather articles.
--	貨商	furriery.
27--	色	one's complexion.
--	包	bag, hand bag.
--	條	strips of leather.
35--	油	tallow.
36--	襖	fur coat.
40--	大衣	fur coat.
--	肉	skin and flesh.
--	夾子	wallet.
44--	帶	leather belt.
--	帶輪	pulley.
--	革	leather, hide.
--	鞋	leather shoes.
--	靴	leather boot.
46--	帽	fur cap.
--	棉	ginned cotton.
71--	匠	leather-worker, dresser of leather.
77--	尺	tape measure.
81--	領	fur collar.
88--	箱	leather box, trunk.

存 〔 **Tsun** 〕 *v.* preserve, maintain, retain, keep, store, deposit, remain, exist, *adj.* alive, existing.

00--	亡	survival or extinction, alive or dead.
07--	記在心	keep in mind.
08--	放	deposit, put down.
--	放處	depository.
24--	儲	storage.
--	儲基金	non-expendable fund.
--	儲計劃	stock planning.

--	貨	stock in trade, stock of goods, inventory.
--	貨充足	adequate stock, be well stocked with.
--	貨市價	market value of inventory.
--	貨記錄	inventory record.
--	貨調整	inventory adjustment.
--	貨不足	short supply of stock, understock.
--	貨制度	inventory system.
--	貨估值	stock evaluation.
--	貨審查	inventory audit.
--	貨清單	inventory.
--	貨過多	overstock.
--	貨過少	understock.
--	貨資產	inventory assets.
--	貨地點	stock point.
--	貨增加	increase in stocks.
--	貨表	inventory sheet.
--	貨目錄	stock inventory.
--	貨週轉	inventory turnover.
--	貨會計	inventory accounting.
--	貨管理	store control.
--	貨管理人	stock keeper.
30--	戶	depositor.
--	案	keep on record.
--	案備查	file for further reference.
33--	心	have the mind, set on, take into one's head, intend to.
--	心不良	cherish an evil intention, harbor evil intensions.
40--	在	*n.* existence, subsistence. *v.* exist, subsist.
47--	款	deposit, save.
--	款利息	deposit interest.
--	款準備金	reserve against deposit.
--	款人	depositor.
--	款銀行	deposit bank.
--	根	counterfoil, receipt.
50--	車處	cycle-stand, a place for keeping bicycles or motor-cycle.
57--	摺	bankbook.
--	單	certificate of deposit.
80--	入	deposit.
--	金	gold stock.
--	倉	deposit in godown, storage.

83-- 錢　　　saving.

4024_8

狡 〔**Chiao**〕 *adj.* crafty, cunning.

00-- 童　　　handsome lad.
-- 辯　　　quibble.
04-- 計　　　crafty trick, trick.
08-- 詐　　　deceitful, swindling, cunning, treacherous.
24-- 徒　　　smart fellow.
47-- 猾　　　crafty, artful, cunning, wily, sly.
-- 猾手段　artful means.
57-- 賴　　　prevaricate.
73-- 騙　　　cheat, deceive, circumvent.

猝 〔**Tsu**〕 *adj.* sudden, abrupt.

23-- 然　　　abruptly, suddenly, unexpectedly.

4030_0

寸 〔**Tsun**〕 *n.* inch, *adj.* short, small, little.

21-- 步不讓　not to yield a single step.
-- 步不離　not to move a step away from.
-- 步難行　difficult to move.
30-- 進　　　small progress.
40-- 土之地　an inch of land.
-- 地千金　an inch of land is worth a thousand pieces of gold.
44-- 草不生　not even a blade of grass grows.

4033_1

赤 〔**Chih**〕 *adj.* red, naked, bare, poor, barren, sincere, loyal.

00-- 痢　　　dysentery.
17-- 子　　　infant.
20-- 手　　　empty-handed.
24-- 化　　　reddened, inclined, communize.
27-- 血球　red corpuscle.
30-- 字　　　deficit, loss, in the red.
-- 字財政　deficit finance.
33-- 心　　　sincerity.
36-- 裸　　　naked, bare, nude.
38-- 道　　　equator.
44-- 地　　　barren land.
73-- 膊　　　half-naked.

77-- 腳　　　barefoot.
-- 腳醫生　barefoot doctor.
80-- 金　　　solid gold, pure gold.
-- 貧　　　poor, destitute.
90-- 米　　　coarse rice.
94-- 忱　　　sincerity.

志 〔**Chih**〕 *n.* aim, will, intention, inclination.

00-- 高　　　ambitious.
-- 意　　　will, purpose.
27-- 向　　　inclination, will, aim, intention.
-- 向遠大　have great aspirations.
40-- 士　　　man of determined will.
-- 在必得　be bent on getting.
47-- 趣　　　interest, ambition, inclination.
-- 趣相投　be of similar purpose and interest.
71-- 願　　　voluntary, willing.
-- 願兵　volunteer.
-- 願書　written consent.
77-- 同道合　be like-minded, be of one mind.
80-- 氣　　　spirit, noble aspiration, determination.
-- 氣消沉　be downcast.
-- 氣軒昂　aim high in life.

4033_6

熹 〔**Hsi**〕 *n.* twilight, *adj.* bright.

4034_1

寺 〔**Szu**〕 *n.* temple, monastery, abbey, convent.

73-- 院　　　monastery, temple.

奪 〔**To**〕 *v.* snatch, seize, grasp, carry off, lay hands on.

17-- 取　　　seize away, carry off.
21-- 佔　　　usurp.
22-- 彩　　　win the prize.
26-- 得　　　get, win, obtain.
36-- 還　　　recapture.
40-- 去　　　take away by force.
41-- 標　　　win the race.
44-- 權　　　seize power.
60-- 目　　　dazzling.
-- 回　　　recover, recapture.

4040_0

爻 〔**Yao**〕 *v.* mix, interweave, lay crosswise.

女 〔**Nu**〕 *n.* girl, maid, woman, female, the gentle sex, lady, daughter.

00--	童子軍	girl scout.
	主	mistress, hostess.
	主角	chief actress, actress in a leading role.
	廁所	woman's lavatory, lady's room .
	高音	soprano.
10--	工	needlework, woman worker.
	王	queen.
	巫	witch, sorceress.
	孩	girl.
12--	飛行員	aviatress.
20--	委員	committeewoman, woman member of a committee.
	售貨員	saleswoman, salesgirl.
22--	低音	alto.
23--	僕	maidservant.
	儐相	bridesmaid, maid of honor.
24--	裝店	dress shop.
25--	生	girl.
26--	皇	empress.
27--	兒	daughter.
	色	lust for woman, feminine attraction.
28--	伶	actress.
33--	演員	actress.
35--	神	goddess.
37--	運動員	sportswoman.
	郎	maiden.
40--	大當嫁	girls should get married upon reaching womanhood.
	校長	mistress, headmistress.
	士	miss, lady.
44--	英雄	heroine.
	權主義	feminism.
46--	帽	bonnet.
47--	聲	female voice.
	婿	son-in-law.
48--	教師	schoolmistress, lady teacher.

50--	丈夫	virago, amazon.
58--	扮男裝	woman disguised as a man.
60--	界	womanhood.
77--	服務員	stewardess, waitress.
	學生	school girl, girl student.
	學校	girl's school.
	醫生	lady doctor.
80--	人	woman, one's life.
	傘	parasol.
95--	性	womanhood, female, the gentle sex.
	性的	feminine.

4040_1

幸 〔**Hsing**〕 *n.* happiness, welfare, luck, good fortune, *adj.* fortunate, lucky, happy.

10--	而	luckily, fortunately.
17--	免	survive, have a narrow escape from.
21--	虧	luckily, fortunately, thanks to .
31--	福	fortune, welfare, happiness, felicity.
37--	運	luck, fortune, good luck.
	運兒	child of fortune.

辜 〔**Gu**〕 *n.* guilt, offence, crime.

27--	負	disappoint, be ungrateful, fall short of someone's expectation.
	負好意	be ungrateful for someone's good intention.

4040_7

支 〔**Chih**〕 *n.* branch, *v.* support, hold up, withstand, bear up, separate, pay, *adj.* divergent, branched.

00--	店	branch store.
	離	irrelevant, vague.
07--	部	branch headquarter .
10--	吾	make excuse, evade, falter, hesitating in speech.
	票	check, cheque, bill.
	票存根	check stub, counterfoil.
	票兌現	cash a check.
	票兌取	check collection.
	票簿	checkbook.

17-- 配	*n.* disposition, control, *v.* control, manage, govern, direct, arrange, manipulate, dominate.
--配權	power of control, right to dispose.
20-- 委會	branch committee.
22-- 出	expenditure, expenses, disburse.
24-- 付	pay, give, defray.
26-- 線	branch lines, feeder line.
27-- 解遺體	dismember the remain.
30-- 流	tributary, feeder.
32-- 派	tribe, branch.
40-- 柱	pillar, mainstay.
46-- 架	frame, support.
51-- 輻	pivot.
52-- 援	aid, assist.
54-- 持	support, uphold, bear up, carry through, sustain, maintain.
--持不住	unable to keep up effort.
--持價格	support price.
--持點	support point.
--持者	supporter, upholder, adherent.
--撑	support, prop up.
--撑危局	prop up a perilous situation.
61-- 點	fulcrum.
77-- 局	branch office.
78-- 隊	detachment, military detachment.
80-- 氣管	bronchi.
--氣管炎	bronchitis.
85-- 錢	pay money.

李 〔**Lee**〕 *n.* plum.

| 17-- 子 | plum. |
| 44-- 樹 | plum tree. |

4042₁
婷 〔**Ting**〕 *adj.* graceful, elegant.

4042₇
妨 〔**Fang**〕 *n.* hindrance, obstacle, obstruction, objection, *v.* hinder, obstruct, interfere, stand in the way.

| 17-- 礙 | *n.* difficulty, hindrance, obstruction, interruption, *v.* |

---

	hinder, obstruct.
21-- 止妥協	take precaution against a compromise.
30-- 害	obstruct, hamper, jeopardize.
--害商務	injurious to trade.
--害信用	offense against personal credit.
--害治安	jeopardize public security.
--害風化	undermine public morality.

嫡 〔**Ti**〕 *n.* proper wife, *adj.* principal, legitimate.

06-- 親	blood relative.
17-- 子	legitimate son.
20-- 系	legal branch of a family.
32-- 派親支	blood relation.
77-- 母	legitimate mother.

4043₄
嫉 〔**Chi**〕 *n.* envy, jealousy, *v.* dislike, hate, detest, *adj.* jealous, envious.

10-- 惡如仇	hate evil people as if they were one's deadly foes.
17-- 忌	dislike, hate.
43-- 妒	jealous, envious.

4044₀
卉 〔**Hui**〕 *n.* plants, herbs.

4044₄
奔 〔**Pen**〕 *v.* run, flee, run away, rush, dash.

27-- 向自由	seek freedom.
34-- 波	*v.* hurry, bustle, *adj.* disquieted.
--波勞碌	be busy and constantly on the move.
40-- 走	run, flee, go running around, scamper.
--走謀事	be busy looking for a job.
--走天涯	run to remote regions.
--走如飛	run like flying.
74-- 馳	gallop.
80-- 命	run for life.
90-- 忙	bustle about, fag, toil.
--忙勞碌	be busy and constantly on the run.

姦 〔**Chien**〕 *n.* adultery, rape, fornication, *v.* ravish, rape, violate, deflower, reduce, *adj.* cunning, artful.

10-- 惡狡猾	malicious and cunning.
17-- 邪	obscenity.
37-- 通	adultery.
-- 通罪	guilty of adultery.
47-- 婦	adulteress.
50-- 夫	adulterer, paramour.

4044₈

姣 〔**Chiao**〕 *adj.* handsome, pretty, beautiful, lewd.

00-- 童	handsome boy.
21-- 態	attractive.
40-- 女	pretty girl.
80-- 美	beautiful, fascinating.

4046₅

嘉 〔**Chia**〕 *v.* praise, commend, *adj.* good, fine, excellent.

00-- 慶	Chia Ching (a Manchu emperor).
08-- 許	praise, approve.
24-- 納	approbation, approval.
27-- 獎	praise, commend, praise and reward, cite.
30-- 賓	respected guest, honorable guest.
35-- 禮	wedding.
65-- 味	delicacy.

4050₆

韋 〔**Wei**〕 *n.* hide, leather.

4051₄

難 〔**Nan**〕 *n.* difficulty, trouble, distress, misfortune, *v.* distress, rebuke, reprimand, *adj.* difficult, hard, troublesome, grievous.

02-- 童	war-orphan.
-- 產	suffering of child birth, difficult delivery.
-- 忘	unforgettable.
-- 辦	difficult to manage.
-- 辦真偽	hard to distinguish between true and false.
-- 辦是非	difficult to discriminate between right and wrong.
17-- 忍	beyond endurance.
20-- 信	hard to believe, against all chances.
-- 住	be stumped.
-- 受	uncomfortable, hard to bear.
-- 看	ugly, repulsive.
21-- 上加難	most difficult.
-- 能可貴	exceptionally commendable.
-- 處	hard point, hard to handle, hard to get along with.
26-- 保	uncertain.
-- 得	hard to get, difficult to obtain, rare, scarce.
27-- 解	hard to understand.
-- 免	difficult to avoid, unavoidable.
28-- 做	difficult to do.
-- 以形容	indescribable, beyond words.
-- 以出口	difficult to speak out of one's mind.
-- 以估計	inestimable.
-- 以置信	unbelievable, incredible.
-- 作好人	difficult to be a good man.
32-- 逃法網	crime does not pay.
34-- 爲情	shy.
37-- 過	sad, sorrowful.
38-- 道	is it possible?
44-- 堪	unbearable, intolerable, embarrassed.
50-- 事	difficulty, difficult thing.
53-- 成	difficult matter to accomplish.
61-- 題	difficult question, hard problem, puzzle, knotty problem.
77-- 民	refugee.
-- 民營	refugee camp.
-- 學	difficult to learn.
-- 局	impasse, blind alley, difficult situation.
-- 關	impasse, barrier, dilemma.
-- 關重重	a lot of obstacles.
88-- 管	difficult to deal with, intractable.
94-- 懂	difficult to understand.
97-- 怪	no wonder.

4060₀

古 〔**Ku**〕*n*. antiquity. *adj*. ancient, primitive, old, old-fashioned, antique.

00--	文	ancient writing, classical writing, paleography.
11--	玩	curios, antiques.
--	玩店	curios store.
20--	今往來	in all history.
23--	代	antiquity, old times, ancient times.
24--	裝美人	beauty in ancient costume.
27--	物	antiques.
--	物商	frippers.
--	色古香	in graceful ancient style.
34--	爲今用	make the past serve the present.
41--	桓	conservative, bigoted .
43--	式	ancient-style.
--	城	ancient city.
44--	董=古玩	
--	老	old, ancient.
55--	典	classic.
--	典主義	classicism.
--	典主義者	classicist.
--	典音樂	classical music.
--	典的	classical.
60--	跡	old ruins, relics, historic spot, ancient relics.
--	跡廢墟	ancient remains and village ruins.
64--	時	in ancient times.
65--	蹟=古跡.	
77--	風	ancient practices.
80--	人	ancients.
--	今	ancient and modern.
87--	銅	bronze.
97--	怪	odd, quaint, queer, strange, peculiar.

右 〔**Yu**〕*n*. the right side, right hand, *adj*. right.

17--	翼	right wing.
20--	手	right hand, better hand.
21--	傾	right-leaning, right deviation.
--	傾思想	rightist ideas.
--	派	the Right.
--	派分子	Rightists.
--	邊	the right side, right-hand.

4060₁

吉 〔**Chi**〕*adj*. fortunate, luckily, good, happy, auspicious.

00--	慶	happiness.
21--	順	favorable.
22--	兇	the bright and the black side of thing.
--	凶未卜	cannot predict the outcome, good or bad.
--	利	auspicious.
24--	他	guitar.
32--	兆	lucky omen.
35--	神	good angel, lucky angel.
38--	祥	fortunate, auspicious.
--	祥如意	propitious as one wishes.
60--	日	lucky day, red-letter day.
--	星高照	the lucky star shines bright — have good luck.
80--	人天相	heaven helps a good man.
--	普車	jeep.

嗇 〔**Se**〕*adj*. stingy, mean, niggard, miserly.

50--	夫	farmer, miser.

奮 〔**Fen**〕*v*. rouse, excite, stir up, exert oneself, endeavor, invigorate, *adj*. courageous, zealous, violent.

10--	不顧身	do something at the risk of one's life.
12--	發	arouse, excite, stir up, exert oneself, brace oneself for.
--	發圖強	rejuvenate a nation by dedicated work.
17--	勇	energetically, courageous, pluck up courage.
24--	勉	strive, work hard.
38--	激	excite, stir up.
40--	力	effort.
--	力而爲	work like a brick, work hard.
--	志	enthusiasm.
47--	起	arouse, spring up.
--	起抵抗	rise in resistance.
63--	戰	fight courageously.

-- 鬥	strive, struggle.
-- 鬥到底	fling away the scabbard, struggle to the end.

4060₄

奢 〔She〕 *adj.* extravagant, prodigal, profuse, wasteful, luxurious.

07-- 望	extravagant hopes, wild wishes, wild hope, unusual great hope.
-- 望不多	have few extravagant hope.
27-- 侈	luxurious, extravagant, prodigal.
-- 侈過度	butter both sides of the bread.
-- 侈品	*n.* luxury, *adj.* luxurious.
-- 侈稅	tax on luxuries.
44-- 華	extravagant, luxurious.

4060₅

喜 〔Hsi〕 *n.* joy, delight, gladness, pleasure, happiness, *v.* be pleasure with, be fond of, rejoice, take delight in, *adj.* happy, joyous, glad, delighted, cheerful.

02-- 新厭舊	abandon the old for the new.
07-- 訊	good news, glad news.
-- 訊傳聞	the happy news spreads.
-- 不可言	inexpressibly joyful.
-- 不自禁	overwhelmed with joy.
-- 不自勝	unable to contain oneself for joy.
20-- 信	good news.
-- 愛	be fond of, love, enjoy, favor.
22-- 樂	joy, delight.
-- 劇	comedy.
-- 出望外	happy beyond expectations.
27-- 色	joyful countenance, look of pleasure.
28-- 從天降	a sudden unexpected happy event.
30-- 容	joyful countenance.
31-- 酒	wedding feast, wedding banquet.
35-- 禮	wedding ceremony.
41-- 極而泣	cry for joy.
43-- 娘	bridesmaid.

47-- 怒	joy and anger.
-- 怒哀樂	pleasure, anger, sorrow and happiness.
-- 怒無常	having an unpredictable temper.
-- 歡	like, be fond of.
50-- 事	marriage, wedding, joyous event.
80-- 氣洋溢	highly exhilarated, full of joy.
-- 氣洋洋	full of joy.
98-- 悅	*n.* pleasure, joy, delight, *adj.* cheerful, rejoicing, pleased, gratified.

4060₉

杏 〔Hsing〕 *adj.* apricot, almond.

21-- 仁	almond.
-- 仁油	almond oil.

杳 〔Miao〕 *adj.* obscure, dark, somber, deep and dark, quiet, silent.

37-- 冥	obscure, dark, cloudy.
40-- 杳無蹤	be gone without leaving a trace.
80-- 無音信	no news for a long time.

4062₁

奇 〔Chi〕 *adj.* strange, wonderful, rare, curious, peculiar, extraordinary.

01-- 襲	surprise attack.
10-- 零	odd, remainder.
11-- 巧	ingenious, curious, clever.
14-- 功	distinguished merit.
21-- 行	strange conduct.
24-- 特	peculiar.
-- 裝異服	outlandishly dressed.
36-- 遇	unusual good chance, adventure, strange encounter, chance encounter.
46-- 觀	spectacle, wonderful spectacle.
-- 想	imagination.
49-- 妙	marvelous.
50-- 事	miracle, adventure, wonder, strange thing.
58-- 數	odd number.
60-- 異	strange, remarkable, unusual, extraordinary, pecu-

	liar, fantastic.
65-- 蹟	miracle.
77-- 聞	strange news.
-- 聞逸事	strange news and extraordinary affairs.
80-- 人	strange personality.
85-- 缺	critical shortage of.
97-- 怪	strange, queer, curious, mysterious, wonderful.

4064₁
壽〔Shou〕*n.* longevity, long life, birthday, old age, life span.

00-- 衣	burial dress, shroud.
-- 高德重	of a long life and great virtue.
02-- 誕	birthday.
11-- 頭壽腦	stupid-looking.
21-- 比南山	many, many happy returns of the day.
27-- 終	die a natural death, die on one's bed, die in old age.
-- 終正寢	die peacefully in bed.
40-- 木	coffin.
71-- 辰	birthday.
-- 長	long-lived.
80-- 命	age, the span of one's life, life span.

4071₀
七〔Chi〕*adj.* seven, seventh.

00-- 言八語	all talking in confusion or offering different opinions.
10-- 弦琴	lyre.
-- 面體	heptahedron.
-- 巧圖	tangram.
20-- 倍	sevenfold.
27-- 角形	heptagon.
40-- 十	seventy.
-- 十年代	the seventies.
52-- 折	thirty percent discount.
77-- 月	July.

4071₆
奄〔Yen〕*v.* cover, remain, tarry, *adv.* hastily, quickly, forthwith.

| 77-- 留 | stay a long time, remain long. |
| 80-- 人 | eunuch. |

奩〔Lien〕*n.* dowry, trousseau, toilet box.

4073₁
去〔Chu〕*v.* go, leave, depart, quit, give up, do away with, get rid of, give up, go away from, *adj.* apart, off, away.

03-- 就之間	between going and staying.
10-- 惡從善	shun the evil and follow the good.
40-- 皮	pare, hull, skin.
42-- 垢	cleanse.
44-- 世	passed away, death.
-- 舊更新	do away with the old and changed it for the new.
47-- 殼	hull.
51-- 掉	do away with, get rid of.
67-- 路	exit.
77-- 留未決	whether to go or to stay is not yet decided.
80-- 年	last year.

套〔Tao〕*n.* case, wrapper, envelop, covering, suit, set, over all, *v.* encase, envelop, trap.

02-- 話	courteous conversation, polite greeting.
17-- 子	cover.
20-- 住	hitch, slip on, trap.
30-- 褲	leggings.
32-- 衫	pullover.
44-- 鞋	overshoes, galoshes.
71-- 匯	cross exchange, illegal remittance of foreign exchange.

4073₂
袁〔Yuan〕*n.* Yuan (a family name).
喪〔Sang〕*n.* mourning, funeral, death. *v.* lose, lament, mourn, die.

25-- 失	lose, fail, miss.
-- 失立場	lose one's stand.
-- 失信心	be disheartened.
-- 失信用	discredit.
-- 失權利	loss of rights, forfeit one's rights.
-- 失時機	miss a chance.
30-- 家狗	homeless dog, stray dog.

33-- 心	insane, bereft of reason, broken-hearted.	
35-- 禮	funeral rites.	
44-- 葬	funeral service and burial.	
50-- 事	funeral service.	
-- 盡天良	have no conscience .	
77-- 服	mourning clothes.	
-- 膽	lose heart, be disheartened, tremble with fear.	
80-- 鐘	death bell, knell.	
-- 命	die, lose one's life.	
-- 氣	downcast , in low spirit, disheartened.	

4080₁

走 〔**Tsou**〕 *v.* walk, run, go, flee, gallop.

00-- 廊	corridor, veranda, passage.
04-- 讀生	day student, day pupil, commuter.
21-- 上	step onto, embark on.
22-- 出	run out.
-- 出來	come out.
-- 彎路	make a detour, take a round-about route.
-- 後門	go in by the back door.
-- 私	*n.* smuggling, *v.* smuggle.
-- 私商	smugglers.
-- 私貨物	run goods, smuggled goods.
24-- 動	move about.
25-- 失	lose one's way, get lost, stray.
27-- 向前	walk forward.
30-- 進	enter, get into, come in .
32-- 近	come near, draw near, approach.
-- 近路	take a shortcut, take a bee-line for.
37-- 漏	disclose, leak out.
-- 過	walk by.
41-- 極端	go to extremes.
47-- 狗	hound, servile dependant, running dog.
48-- 樣	be out of shape, go astray.
55-- 捷徑	take a shortcut.
57-- 投無路	go down a dead alley.
60-- 累	over walk oneself.
63-- 獸	beast.

65-- 味	loss flavor.
67-- 路	walk, quit.
71-- 馬燈	lantern adorned with revolving circle of paper horses.
77-- 開	run away, get out, go away.
-- 邪路	go to the bad, go astray.
84-- 錯	go astray.
87-- 鋼線	wire-walking, tightrope walking.
90-- 火	go off, accidental discharge.

真 〔**Chen**〕 *n.* truth, *adj.* true, real, actual, sincere, pure, genuine.

00-- 諦	truth.
02-- 話	truth.
03-- 誠	*n.* sincerity, *adj.* sincere, earnest, cordial.
10-- 正	real, genuine, true.
-- 面目	true color, one's true self.
-- 不二價	never quote two prices.
15-- 珠	pearl.
16-- 理	truth, gospel.
17-- 刀真槍	genuine swords and spears.
24-- 貨	genuine goods.
27-- 假	real and false.
30-- 空	vacuum.
-- 空包裝	vacuum packing.
-- 空管	vacuum tube.
-- 實	true, real, actual, sincere, genuine.
-- 實情況	the fact of the case, the real situation.
31-- 憑實據	indisputable evidence.
33-- 心	sincerity, actual intention.
44-- 摯	earnest, sincere.
-- 材實料	genuine material and solid substance, real stuff.
46-- 相	real fact, real appearance, reality, true features.
-- 相大白	the case is entirely cleared up.
80-- 人真事	the characters are real and the story is true.

4080₆

賁 〔**Pen**〕 *adj.* bright, large, great.

賣 〔**Mai**〕 *v.* sell, betray.

00--	主	seller, vendor.
10--	弄	show off.
--	票	sell ticket.
--	票處	booking-office, ticketing office.
24--	貨攤	booth.
27--	身	sell one's bacon.
--	身契	indenture for selling somebody.
30--	空	sell short.
--	完	sell out.
32--	淫	*n.* prostitution, *v.* engage in prostitution.
40--	力	labor, effort.
44--	花姑娘	flower girl.
51--	據	bill of sale.
60--	國賊	traitor.

4090₀

木〔**Mu**〕*n.* tree, wood, lumber, timber.

00--	廠	timber yard.
02--	刻	woodcut.
10--	工	woodworks.
--	耳	fungus.
--	石心腸	flinty-hearted.
11--	頭	wood.
17--	乃伊	mummy.
21--	行	timber store.
22--	片	chip.
--	炭	charcoal.
--	製	wooden.
26--	偶	puppet, idol.
--	偶戲	puppet-show.
30--	塞	cork.
40--	梳	wooden comb.
41--	板	board, plank.
--	板箱	crate.
44--	材	tree, timber, lumber.
45--	槽	trough.
46--	架	wooden shelf.
--	棉	kapok.
47--	桶	tub, barrel.
--	柵	stockade.
--	槌	wooden mall.
--	欄	hurdle.
48--	栓	peg.
--	幹	trunk, stock.

60--	星	the planet Jupiter.
66--	器	wooden ware.
--	器場	wooden furniture factory.
71--	馬	trestle, wooden horse.
--	匠	carpenter.
72--	質	wood.
--	質部	xylem.
--	瓜	papaya.
77--	屐	clog, wooden shoes, pattens.
--	屋	log cabin.
--	屑	sawdust.
80--	盆	tub.
88--	箱	wooden box (case).
94--	料	timber, lumber.

4090₁

奈〔**Nai**〕*conj.* but, how.

21--	何	What should be done?

4090₃

索〔**So**〕*n.* rope, cord, *v.* search, demand, ask for, seek, *adj.* exhausted, used up, isolated, lonely, alone.

08--	詐	extort, black mail.
12--	引	index.
17--	尋	search, look for.
--	取	ask for, demand.
21--	價	charge, ask a price.
--	價過高	overcharge.
25--	債	dun for a debt.
--	債人	dunner.
29--	償	claim reimbursement.
42--	橋	cable bridge.
43--	求	importune.
--	款	reimburse.
55--	費	demand payment.
60--	回	reclaim.
--	思	think about.
--	賠	claim indemnity(compensation), make a claim.
95--	性	simply, flatly, might as well.

4090₈

來〔**Lai**〕*v.* come, arrive at, *adj.* future.

01--	龍去脈	the beginning and subsequent development of an incident, sequence of events.
10--	函敬悉	your letter was respectfully

	read.
-- 函	your letter.
-- 不及	be too late to .
11-- 頭不小	not to be taken lightly.
12-- 到	*n.* arrival. *v.* arrive, come.
20-- 往	social intercourse, come and go.
-- 往不絕	coming and going ceaselessly.
25-- 生	future life.
26-- 自	come from.
30-- 賓	guest, visitor.
-- 賓滿座	visitors are occupied all the seats, full house, guest-packed occasion.
31-- 源	source, origin.
-- 源可靠	from the horse's mouth, from a reliable source.
-- 福槍	rifle.
40-- 去	to and fro, come and go.
-- 去自如	come and go freely.
-- 去無定	coming and going without fixed time.
-- 來往往	coming and going in great number.
44-- 者不拒	all comers are welcome, zero reject.
60-- 日	coming day.
-- 日方長	the coming days will be long.
-- 日大難	difficult days are ahead.
-- 回	back and forth, come and go.
-- 回票	return ticket, round-trip ticket.
-- 回程	round voyage, round-trip.
71-- 歷	origin, background.
-- 歷不明	be of questionable source.
78-- 臨	befall, happen.
80-- 人	comer, bearer.
-- 年	next year.
94-- 料加工	process with customer's materials, process of imported materials.

4091_3
梳〔**Shu**〕*n.* comb, *v.* comb.

11-- 頭	comb the head.
17-- 子	comb.
24-- 裝	dress up.
-- 裝台	dresser.
72-- 刷	comb and brush.

4091_4
柱〔**Chu**〕*n.* pillar, post, support, column, *v.* uphold, support, sustain.

10-- 石	base of pillar.
17-- 子	pillar, post, column.

椎〔**Chui**〕*n.* mallet, beater, hammer, *v.* strike, beat, knock, kill.

44-- 鼓	beat a drum.
46-- 埋	kill and bury.
57-- 擊	beat.
77-- 骨	vertebra.

4091_6
檀〔**Tan**〕*n.* sandalwood.

20-- 香皂	sandalwood soap.
-- 香扇	sandalwood fan.

4091_7
杭〔**Hang**〕*n.* square.

32-- 州	Hangchow.

4092_7
柿〔**Shih**〕*n.* persimmon.

17-- 子	persimmon.
48-- 乾	dried persimmon.
88-- 餅	dried persimmon fruit.

榜〔**Pang**〕*n.* list, notice, *v.* beat.

10-- 示	notice.
48-- 樣	model, pattern, example.

槁〔**Kao**〕*adj.* dry, rotten, withered.

40-- 木	dry wood, rotten wood.

4093_1
樵〔**Chiao**〕*n.* woodcutter, fuel, firewood, *v.* gather firewood.

50-- 夫	woodman, woodcutter.

4094_0
櫥〔**Chu**〕*n.* case, chest, box, wardrobe, cabinet, cupboard.

17-- 子	cabinet.
30-- 窗	shop window, show-window.
-- 窗廣告	window advertising.
-- 窗佈置	window dressing.

-- 窗陳列　　　window display.

4094₁

梓〔**Tzu**〕*n.* Lindera, *v.* engrave characters on wood.

4094₆

樟〔**Chang**〕*n.* camphor tree.

44-- 樹　　　　camphor tree.
72-- 腦　　　　camphor.
-- 腦丸　　　　mothball, camphor ball.
-- 腦精　　　　camphor tincture.

4094₈

校〔**Hsiao**〕*n.* school, college, field grade (officers), *v.* compare, collate, revise, examine, proofread.

01-- 訂　　　　*n.* revision, *v.* revise.
10-- 正　　　　correct, revise.
-- 正版　　　　revised edition.
18-- 改　　　　real and correct proofs.
30-- 準　　　　adjust, calibrate.
34-- 對　　　　*n.* proofreading, *v.* revise, compare.
-- 對人　　　　proofreader.
40-- 友　　　　alumni.
-- 友會　　　　alumni meeting.
41-- 址　　　　location of a school.
44-- 勘　　　　collate.
48-- 樣　　　　proof-sheet, gallery proof.
65-- 園　　　　campus, school compound.
71-- 長　　　　principal, school-master, president.
77-- 閱　　　　review.
-- 閱人　　　　reviser.
-- 醫　　　　school doctor.
80-- 舍　　　　school house, school building, school premises.

4098₂

核〔**Ho**〕*n.* stone, kernel, nucleus, *v.* examine, inquire into, verify, check.

00-- 辦　　　　consider what to do.
-- 廢棄物　　　atomic waste.
01-- 壟斷　　　nuclear monopoly.
03-- 試驗　　　nuclear test.
04-- 訛詐　　　nuclear blackmail.
-- 計　　　　　check.
10-- 電子　　　nucleus electron.

12-- 發動機　　atomic engine.
13-- 武器　　　nuclear weapons.
16-- 彈　　　　nuclear bomb.
-- 彈頭　　　　nuclear warhead.
17-- 子　　　　nucleus, nucleon .
-- 子裝備　　　nuclear panoplies.
-- 子學　　　　nucleonics.
21-- 仁　　　　kernel, fruit-stone.
-- 能利用　　　nuclear energy uses.
-- 能源　　　　nuclear energy source.
-- 優勢　　　　nuclear superiority.
-- 保護　　　　nuclear protection.
24-- 裝置　　　nuclear installation.
30-- 准　　　　approve, permit, examine and approve.
-- 准賬目　　　approval of account.
-- 實　　　　　verify, confirm.
-- 實呈報　　　verify the reality and present a report.
-- 定　　　　　check and ratify.
-- 定預算　　　approval budget.
31-- 污染　　　nuclear pollution.
33-- 心　　　　core, nucleus.
34-- 對　　　　check, verify.
-- 對無誤　　　verified correct.
37-- 軍備　　　nuclear armament.
40-- 大國　　　nuclear power.
-- 力量　　　　nuclear capability.
-- 查　　　　　investigate.
-- 查制度　　　system of verification.
42-- 桃　　　　walnut.
44-- 基地　　　nuclear base.
50-- 擴散　　　nuclear proliferation.
63-- 戰爭　　　nuclear war.
70-- 防禦　　　nuclear defense.
88-- 算　　　　compute, adjust accounts.
-- 算員　　　　staff auditor.
96-- 爆炸　　　nuclear explosion.

4099₄

森〔**Sen**〕*adj.* dark, somber, severe, thick with trees.

44-- 林　　　　forest.
-- 林地帶　　　forest zone.
-- 林學　　　　forestry.
60-- 羅萬象　　all the phenomena of the universe.

66-- 嚴　　　　　stern, majestic, severe, in formidable array.

4108_6

頰〔Chia〕n. cheeks, jawbone.

4111_0

址〔Chih〕n. foundation, address.

4111_4

堰〔Yen〕n. embankment, dike, breakwater.

46-- 堤　　　　　dam.

4111_6

垣〔Yuan〕n. wall, city.

4111_7

墟〔Hsu〕n. market, fair, mound, ruined city or village, village fair.

4111_9

坯〔Pi〕n. unbaked earthenware.

40-- 布　　　　　grey cloth.
44-- 模　　　　　model, mould.

4112_7

壩〔Pa〕n. dike, embankment, breakwater.

4114_0

圩〔Gu〕n. dike, bank, lowland.

4114_7

坂〔Pan〕n. slope.

4114_9

坪〔Ping〕n. flat, plain, terrace, level place, an area of six feet square.

4121_4

狂〔Kuang〕adj. mad, insane, crazy, wild, eccentric, lunatic, reckless, violent.

00-- 病　　　　　madness.
-- 癲　　　　　foolish, crazy, out of one's sense.
-- 言　　　　　lying, nonsense, bluster.
-- 妄　　　　　eccentric, arrogant.
-- 妄自大　　　self-conceit, arrogant.
22-- 亂　　　　　frantic, frenzy.
24-- 徒　　　　　madman.
40-- 奔　　　　　run like mad, run riot.
-- 喜　　　　　frantic with joy, overjoyed.
43-- 犬病　　　　rabies.

44-- 熱　　　　　fanaticism, passion.
46-- 想　　　　　wild fancy.
-- 想曲　　　　fantasy, rhapsody.
47-- 歡　　　　　fury, wild cheer, raptures.
-- 歡節　　　　carnival.
-- 怒　　　　　fury.
60-- 暴　　　　　outrageous, violent.
63-- 喊　　　　　bawl.
65-- 跌　　　　　slump.
66-- 躁　　　　　tumultuous, eccentric.
75-- 肆　　　　　wild.
77-- 風　　　　　gust, gale, squall.
-- 飲　　　　　guzzle.

4122_7

獼〔Mi〕n. monkey.

47-- 猴　　　　　rhesus monkey.
63-- 吠　　　　　bark wildly.
80-- 人　　　　　madman.
88-- 笑　　　　　burst into foolish laughter.

獅〔Shih〕n. lion, king of beast, beast royal.

62-- 吼　　　　　the roar of a lion, preaching of the Buddha.

4123_2

帳〔Chang〕n. curtain, screen, tent, account, mosquito net.

17-- 子　　　　　curtain.
30-- 房　　　　　accounting office, accountant.
60-- 目　　　　　account.
66-- 單　　　　　bill.
87-- 鉤　　　　　curtain hook.
88-- 簿　　　　　account, passbook, account book.
-- 篷　　　　　tent, tabernacle.

4124_2

麵〔Mien〕n. wheat, flour.

27-- 包　　　　　bread, stuff of life.
-- 條　　　　　vermicelli, noodles .
46-- 棍　　　　　rolling-pin.
88-- 筋　　　　　wheat gluten.
-- 餅　　　　　wheat cake.
98-- 粉　　　　　flour, wheat flour.
-- 粉廠　　　　flour mill.

4126_0

帖 〔Tieh〕 *n.* copybook, document, card, invitation card.
17-- 子　invitation card.

4126₆

幅 〔Fu〕 *n.* roll, width of cloth.
00-- 度　extent, range, scope.
-- 度變動　amplitude variation.
60-- 員　the extent of a country, territory, area.

4128₂

獗 〔Chueh〕 *adj.* unruly, ferocious.

4128₆

幀 〔Cheng〕 *n.* roll (of picture).

頗 〔Po〕 *adj.* very, one-sided, partial, quite, inclined in one side, *adv.* exceedingly.
27-- 多　a great deal, very much, many many.
-- 久　very long.
47-- 好　pretty good, pretty well.

顴 〔Chuan〕 *n.* cheek bone.

4138₆

赬 〔Cheng〕 *adj.* red.

4141₀

妣 〔Pi〕 *n.* deceased mother.

4141₄

姪 〔Chih〕 *n.* nephew, nieces.
12-- 孫　grant-nephew.
-- 孫女　grant-niece.
17-- 子　nephew.
40-- 女　niece.

4141₆

姬 〔Chi〕 *n.* beautiful woman.
00-- 妾　concubine.

嫗 〔Yu〕 *n.* mother, old woman, dame.

4142₀

婀 〔E〕 *adj.* graceful, elegant.
47-- 娜　graceful.

4142₇

媽 〔Ma〕 *n.* mother, ma.
41-- 媽　mother, mamma.

嫣 〔Yen〕 *adj.* gracious, charming, beautiful, facinating.

21-- 紅　rich crimson.

4143₂

娠 〔Chen〕 *adj.* pregnant, conceived.
47-- 婦　pregnant woman.

4144₀

奷 〔Chien〕 *n.* traitor, *adj.* crafty, deceitful, traitorous, *v.* disturb, commit adultery, rape.
00-- 商　dishonest merchant.
04-- 計　wicked plot, crafty device, trick.
07-- 詭　artful.
08-- 詐　deceitful, cunning, double-dealing.
17-- 刁　knavish.
24-- 徒　rascal.
26-- 細　traitor, spy.
-- 污　rape.
47-- 猾　artful, deceptive, double-handed, double-hearted.
63-- 賊　knave, scoundrel.
71-- 臣　traitorous official.
77-- 邪　wicked.
80-- 人　artful villian.
90-- 黨　cabal.

妍 〔Yen〕 *adj.* elegant, pretty, handsome, beautiful.

4146₃

孀 〔Shuang〕 *n.* widow.

4149₁

嫖 〔Piao〕 *v.* whore, frequent a brothel.
30-- 客　whore master.
64-- 賭　whoring and gambling.

4151₆

韁 〔Chiang〕 *n.* bridle, reins.
27-- 繩　reins.

4153₁

韆 〔Chien〕 swing.

4154₆

鞭 〔Pien〕 *n.* whip, lash, *v.* flog, whip, lash.
17-- 子　whip, lash.
51-- 打　whip, lash.
54-- 撻　flog, lash.
71-- 長莫及　beyond one's control.

97-- 炮　　　firecrakers, crackers.

4180₄

赶〔Kan〕v. chase, pursue, hasten to.

00-- 市　　　hasten to market.
21-- 上　　　overtake, catch up.
43-- 赴　　　hasten to a place.
88-- 散　　　scatter.
56-- 車　　　drive a cart.
77-- 緊　　　make haste, hurry up .

4188₆

顛〔Tien〕n. top, apex, head, v. upset, overthrow, subvert, rock, fall, go mad.

10-- 覆　　　n. subversion, v. overturn, overthrow, subvert.
22-- 倒　　　upside down, reverse.
-- 倒是非　　confound right and wrong.
23-- 仆　　　fall.
41-- 狂　　　wild, mad, crazy.
62-- 躓　　　stumble.
88-- 簸　　　jolt, joggle.

4191₀

杠〔Kang〕n. crossbar, flagstaff.

37-- 樑　　　bridge.

枇〔Pi〕n. fruit, loquat.

47-- 杷　　　loquat.

4191₁

框〔Kuang〕n. frame, casing, door-sash.

17-- 子　　　frame.
46-- 架　　　framework.

4191₄

枉〔Wang〕n. wrong, injustice, oppression, v. do wrong, wrong, adj. oppressed, illegal, wrong, useless.

23-- 然　　　in vain, useless.
34-- 法　　　wrest the law.
55-- 費　　　spend to purpose, in vain, waste.
-- 費工夫　　waste time and energy.
-- 費心機　　flog a dead horse.

桎〔Chih〕n. fetters, shackles.

44-- 梏　　　shackles.

極〔Chi〕n. end, extremity, utmost point, v. exhaust, reach the end of,

adv. very, extremely, exceedingly.

00-- 高　　　topmost.
-- 度　　　utmost, extremity.
02-- 端　　　utmost, extreme, end.
21-- 便宜價格　dirt cheap price.
-- 上品　　　super-fine quality.
22-- 樂　　　paradise.
32-- 近　　　very close, within an ace of.
35-- 速　　　at full speed.
37-- 罕　　　very few.
40-- 大　　　greatest, largest, maximum.
-- 大值　　　maximum value.
-- 古　　　very old, old as a hill.
-- 力　　　with one's utmost strength, with the utmost strength, with might and main.
-- 力高呼　　cry at highest pitch of one's voice.
-- 力攻擊　　launch an all-out attack.
-- 力推薦　　recommend someone very highly.
-- 壞　　　worst, extremely bad.
-- 左　　　ultra-Left.
-- 右　　　ultra-Right.
44-- 其忙碌　　have one's hand full.
-- 權　　　totalitarian.
-- 權主義　　totalitarianism.
-- 權政治　　authoritarianism.
-- 權經濟　　totalitarian economy.
47-- 好　　　the best, extremely good.
60-- 品　　　highest rank, best quality.
61-- 點　　　extremity.
71-- 願　　　with all one's heart.
77-- 限　　　the limit, the maximum.
90-- 小　　　smallest, minimum.
-- 少　　　next to nothing.
-- 少數　　　very few, handful.
-- 光　　　aurora.
95-- 精致的　　super-fine.

概〔Kai〕n. summary, general outline, outline.

08-- 論　　　introduction, outline, sketch.
10-- 要　　　sketch, summary.
-- 而言之　　generally speaking.
-- 不賒欠　　no credit given.

26-- 貌　bird's eye view.
33-- 述　generalize.
36-- 況　general condition.
52-- 括　generalize, summarize.
　-- 括性　generality.
67-- 略　summary, outline.
80-- 念　conception, notion, idea, concept.
　-- 念化　generalize, put in abstract terms.
88-- 算　rough estimate, estimated budget, financial estimate.

4191₆

桓 〔Huang〕 adj. martial.

樞 〔Shu〕 n. axis, pivot, hinge, center.
10-- 要　the center of government, central part.
27-- 紐　pivot, cardinal point, hinge.
30-- 密　state affair.
55-- 軸　axis, pivot.

4191₇

柜 〔Chu〕 n. case.

椏 〔Ya〕 n. forking branch of a tree.

4191₈

柩 〔Chiu〕 n. coffin.
50-- 車　hearse.

櫃 〔Kuei〕 n. case, closet, chest, cupboard, cabinet, sandalwood.
17-- 子　cupboard, cabinet.
44-- 檯　counter, shopboard.
　-- 檯交易　over-the-counter.
97-- 桶　drawer.

4192₀

柯 〔Ko〕 v. ax-handle, stalk, branch.

4192₁

桁 〔Heng〕 n. wooden stopper, beam.

4192₇

朽 〔Hsiu〕 v. decay, spoil, adj. rotten, decayed, failing, worn-out.
40-- 木　rotten wood, decayed wood.
　-- 壞　spoiled, decayed, rotten.
97-- 爛　v. rot, adj. rotten, decayed.

柄 〔Ping〕 n. handle, grip, haft, power, authority.

4194₆

梗 〔Keng〕 n. stem, stalk, obstruction. v. obstruct, hinder, block.
30-- 塞　obstruct, block.
　-- 塞不通　obstruction to traffic.
40-- 直　upright, honest.
41-- 概　outline, general idea.

棹 〔Cho〕 n. table, oar.
13-- 球　billiard.
35-- 油　suet.
40-- 布　table cloth.

4194₇

板 〔Pan〕 n. board, plank.
12-- 凳　bench, stool.
27-- 條箱　crate.
70-- 壁　wooden partition.
72-- 刷　scrubbing-brush.

4196₀

柘 〔Che〕 n. cudrania triloba, sugarcane.

栖 〔Hsi〕 v. roost, perch, stay at, sojourn.

4196₁

梧 〔Wu〕 n. plane tree.

4196₂

楷 〔Kai〕 n. pattern, model.
44-- 模　model, pattern.
50-- 書　regular script （Chinese writing）.

4198₆

槓 〔Kang〕 n. pole, trunk.
17-- 子　pole.
46-- 桿　lever.

4199₀

杯 〔Bei〕 n. cup, glass, goblet, tumbler.
12-- 形　hollow.

4199₁

標 〔Piao〕 n. mark, signal, signboard, flag, banner, label, v. sign, mark, show.
00-- 高價格　price mark up.

01-- 語	watchword, motto, slogan.
03-- 識	emblem.
04-- 誌	symbol, mark, label.
07-- 記	mark.
10-- 示	mark.
20-- 售	selling tender.
21-- 價	labeled price, mark a price.
22-- 低價目	mark down.
27-- 的	target, object.
28-- 緻面貌	handsome face.
30-- 準	standard, criterion.
-- 準商標	standard brand.
-- 準工資	standard wage.
-- 準價格	standard price.
-- 準製品	standardized products.
-- 準貨幣	proof coin.
-- 準程序	standard program.
-- 準條款	model clauses.
-- 準業績	standard performance.
-- 準法	standard method (technique).
-- 準材料	standard materials.
-- 準成本	standard cost.
-- 準規格	standard specification.
-- 準量	standard volume.
-- 準圖	standard drawing.
-- 準品	standard products.
-- 準局	Bureau of Standard.
-- 準尺寸	standard size.
-- 準合同	standard contract.
-- 準時間	standard time .
-- 準化	*n.* standardization, *v.* standardize.
40-- 榜	advertise, brag.
48-- 槍	dart, javelin.
50-- 本	specimen, pattern, model, sample.
-- 本室	sample room.
61-- 點	punctuation.
-- 題	title, heading, topic.
67-- 購	buy at public bidding.
71-- 兵	pacesetter.
88-- 簽	label, tag.

4200₀

刈 〔I〕 *v.* mow, reap.

| 32-- 割 | reap, mow. |
| 44-- 草 | mow, cut grass. |

4212₁

圻 〔Chi〕 *n.* limit.

4212₂

彭 〔Peng〕 *n.* Peng (a family name).

4213₁

坼 〔Che〕 *v.* split, burst.

4216₁

垢 〔Kou〕 *adj.* dirty, filthy, disgraceful, shame.

4220₀

刳 〔Ku〕 *v.* open, rip, eat.

4221₀

剋 〔Ke〕 *v.* conquer, subdue, destroy, overcome limit.

22-- 制情感	restrain feeling.
56-- 扣	deduct, reduce, discount.
60-- 日	within a certain time.

4221₆

獵 〔Lieh〕 *n.* hunting, field sport, *v.* hunt, chase, seek, get.

00-- 鷹	falcon.
20-- 手	hunter, huntsman.
30-- 戶	huntsman.
43-- 犬	hound, hunting dog.
44-- 苑	park.
46-- 場	preserve.
80-- 人	hunter.
88-- 鎗	fowling-piece, hunting gun.

4223₀

狐 〔Hu〕 *n.* fox.

21-- 步舞	fox-trot.
22-- 仙	fairy fox.
27-- 疑	suspicious, hesitate, indecisive.
40-- 皮	fox fur.
43-- 裘	fox-fur coat, fox-fur robe.
46-- 狸	fox.
77-- 尾	foxtail, fox brush.

4225₇

猙 〔Cheng〕 *adj.* fierce.

| 43-- 獰 | fierce looking, hideous. |
| -- 獰面目 | appear like a mythical crea- |

ture--to have cruel and hideous look.

4226₉

幡 〔Fan〕 *n.* pennant, streamer, *adj* suddenly.

4229₃

猻 〔Sun〕 *n.* monkey.

4240₀

荆 〔Ching〕 *n.* bramble, thorn, briers.

| 47-- 婦 | my wife. |
| 55-- 棘 | *n.* thorn, *adj.* thorny, annoying, bramble, prickle. |

4241₂

姚 〔Yao〕 *n.* Yao (a family name), *adj.* handsome, good-looking.

4241₄

妊 〔Jen〕 *n.* pregnancy, *v.* conceive, become pregnant.

| 41-- 娠 | *n.* pregnancy, *v.* conceive, be with child, be pregnant. |
| 47-- 婦 | conceived woman, pregnant woman. |

4242₇

嬌 〔Chiao〕 *adj.* delicate, gracious, tender, lovely, charming.

11-- 麗	elegant.
17-- 弱	delicate, tender.
21-- 態	attractive, fascinating.
25-- 生慣養	be pampered.
27-- 艷	pretty, bright, lustrous.
47-- 聲嬌氣	speak in a seductive tone.
48-- 嫩	delicate.
-- 嫩細膩	pretty, delicate and glossy.
90-- 小玲瓏	dainty and cute.

4243₄

妖 〔Yao〕 *n.* phantom, fairy, monster, goblin, *adj.* bewitching, fascinating, magical, weird.

00-- 魔	goblin.
21-- 術	magic, black art.
34-- 法	enchantment, incantation.
44-- 嬈	beautiful, lovely, fascinating.
47-- 婦	witch, enchantress.
77-- 風	evil wind.

| 95-- 精 | goblin, phantom, elf. |

4244₇

媛 〔Yuan〕 *n.* beauty, lady.

4246₁

婚 〔Hun〕 *n.* marriage, wedding, *v.* marry, wed.

17-- 配	engage, contract marriage.
-- 娶	get married.
27-- 約	betrothal.
35-- 禮	wedding ceremony, wedlock.
43-- 嫁之事	the mater of marriage.
46-- 姻	marriage.
-- 姻法	Marriage Law.
47-- 期	wedding day.
50-- 書	contract of marriage.
88-- 筵	wedding-feast.

4252₁

靳 〔Chin〕 *adj.* stingy.

4260₂

皙 〔Hsi〕 *v.* distinguish.

晳 〔Hsi〕 *adj.* white.

4270₀

刦 〔Chieh〕 *v.* rob, plunder, snatch.

37-- 盜	robber, plunderer, highwayman.
50-- 掠	rob, plunder.
58-- 數	fate.

4280₀

赳 〔Chiu〕 *adj.* powerful, martial, warlike.

| 42-- 赳 | brave, valorous, valiant. |
| -- 赳武夫 | soldier of dauntless courage. |

4282₁

斯 〔Szu〕 *adj.* this, that, these, those.

00-- 文	gentle, scholarly.
64-- 時	at this time, presently.
80-- 人	this person.

4290₀

刹 〔Cha〕 *n.* a Buddist temple, abbey, monastery.

| 17-- 那 | a moment. |

4290₃

紮〔Cha〕*v.* tie, bind up, fasten, encamp, station.

00-- 裹	wrap, bind up, envelope.
27-- 綁	tie up, bind together.
44-- 帶	band.
77-- 緊	bind tight.
99-- 營	encamp, pitch one's tent.

4291₀

札〔Cha〕*n.* despatch, document, letter.

00-- 文	document.
07-- 記	*n.* notebook, *v.* note, outline.
20-- 委	despatch, appoint.

4291₁

檉〔Teng〕*n.* bench.

4291₃

桃〔Tao〕*n.* peach.

17-- 子	peach.
21-- 仁	peach kernel.
27-- 色	peach-color, pink.
-- 色新聞	news of illicit love.
-- 醬	peach jam.
31-- 源仙境	the peach orchard and the fairy land, Shangri-La.
40-- 李	peach and plums.
-- 李滿門	have many pupils.
-- 李滿天下	with students all over the world.
-- 核	peach stone.
44-- 花	peach blossoms.
-- 林	peach plantation.

4291₄

橇〔Chiao〕*n.* sledge.

4291₈

橙〔Cheng〕*n.* orange.

00-- 膏	marmalade.
10-- 露	orangeade.
17-- 子	orange.
21-- 紅色	orange pink.
27-- 色	orange-color.
34-- 汁	orange juice.

4292₁

析〔Hsi〕*v.* analyze, distinguish, divide, split, break apart, separate, explain.

22-- 出	separation.
80-- 義	explain the meaning of something.

4292₂

杉〔Shan〕*n.* fir, pine.

彬〔Bin〕*adj.* elegant and refined.

42-- 彬	with elegant manners.
-- 彬有禮	polite, courteous, good-mannered.

4292₇

橋〔Chiao〕*n.* bridge.

10-- 面	road surface of a bridge.
11-- 頭	either end of a bridge.
-- 頭堡	bridgehead.
26-- 牌	bridge (game).
30-- 洞	arches of a bridge.
37-- 梁	bridge.
-- 梁工程	bridge-work.
40-- 柱	pier, bridge posts.
44-- 塔	bridge-tower.
45-- 椿	piles of a bridge.
48-- 墩	foundation piers of a bridge.

4293₄

樸〔Pu〕*adj.* simple, plain, honest, sincere.

28-- 儉	frugal, thrifty.
30-- 實	simple-minded, plain honest, sincere.
50-- 素	simple, plain, naive.
-- 素大方	plain and dignified.

4294₀

柢〔Ti〕*n.* root of a tree, base, bottom.

4294₇

椶〔Tsung〕*n.* palm.

4295₃

機〔Chi〕*n.* machine, loom, chance, opportunity, *adj.* secret, hidden, clever, cunning.

00-- 床	machine tool.
-- 床廠	machine tool plant.
07-- 謀	artifice, stratagem.
10-- 靈	alert, shrewd.
-- 要	confidential.
-- 要文件	confidential document.
-- 電產品	machinery and electrical appliance.

--票	air ticket.
--不可失	golden opportunity not to be missed.
11--巧	cunning, crafty, ingenious, clever, skillful.
--巧善變	cunning and tactful.
21--能	function, faculty.
--師	artisan.
22--制	mechanism.
--變百出	with a thousand tricks up in the sleeves.
24--動	mobile, flexible.
--動三輪車	motor-tricycle.
--動權	maneuverability.
--動性	mobility, flexibility.
27--組人員	aircrew.
30--密	secret, private, confidential.
--密談話	confidential talk.
--密信件	confidential letter.
--密通知	confidential communication.
--密情報	confidential information.
--密檔案	confidential file.
43--械	machine, machinery, mechanical.
--械設備	mechanical installation.
--械效率	mechanical efficiency.
--械工程師	mechanical engineer.
--械工程學	mechanical engineering.
--械工具	mechanical devices.
--械功率	mechanical power.
--械製造	machine building.
--械製造者	machine maker.
--械論	theory of mechanism.
--械能	mechanical energy.
--械師	machinist.
--械化	n. mechanization, v. mechanize.
--械化部隊	mechanized unit.
--械化農業	mechanical farming.
--械自動化	mechanical automation.
--械運輸	mechanical transport.
--械加工	machine finishing.
--械操作	machine operation.
--械作用	mechanism.
--械學	mechanics.

45--構	institution, organization.
46--場	airport, airfield.
--場使用費	landing fee.
--場候機大樓	terminal building.
--場稅	airport tax.
--場海關	airport customs.
47--帆船	motorized junk.
48--警	alert, awake, keen, sharp, vigilant.
--警靈敏	sharp and ingenious.
--槍手	machine-gunner.
50--車	engine, motorcycle, locomotive.
66--器	machine, engine.
--器場	machinery plant.
--器製造	machine-made.
--器折舊	depreciation of machine.
--器腳踏車	motorcycle.
77--關	organ, organization, establishment, government office.
--關報	official newspaper.
--關鎗	machine gun.
80--會	opportunity, chance, turn, occasion.
--會主義	opportunism.
--會主義者	opportunist.
--會均等	equal opportunity.
--智	n. wit, quick-witted, adj. tactful, ingenious.
--智圓滑	tactful and accommodating.

4299_4

櫟 〔**Lih**〕n. the chestnut-leaved oak.

48--散	useless material.

4301_0

尤 〔**Yu**〕n. error, blunder, v. blame, murmur, reproach, adj. particularly, especially.

27--物	beautiful woman, rare beauty, uncommon thing.
--甚	still more.
--其	especially, particularly, in particular.
49--妙	still better.

4303_0

犬 〔**Chuan**〕n. dog, hound.

21-- 齒	canine tooth.
63-- 吠	bark, yelp.

4304_2

博 〔**Po**〕 *v.* game, gamble, *adj.* spacious, wide, extensive, universal, general, well-educated, learned.

00-- 奕	play chess.
10-- 而不精	extensive but shallow(in knowledge).
20-- 愛	universal love, charity.
-- 愛工程	love of humanity project.
-- 愛主義	the policy of love without distinction.
26-- 得	win.
-- 得名聲	gain a reputation.
-- 得好評	command a fine reputation.
27-- 物館	museum.
-- 大精深	broad and profound (in learning).
40-- 士	doctor, doctorate.
-- 古通今	master both ancient and modern learning.
77-- 學	well-educated, well read, learned.
-- 學之士	man of much learning.
-- 學家	walking library.
-- 學多才	be of great learning and great ability.
78-- 覽	well read.
-- 覽會	exposition, exhibition, trade fair.

4310_0

式 〔**Shih**〕 *n.* form, formula, fashion, example.

28-- 微	reduced to poverty, decline.
48-- 樣	example, model, fashion, pattern.
-- 樣依日	the pattern is as before.

4313_2

求 〔**Chiu**〕 *v.* ask, beg, implore, seek, search for, look for, request.

13-- 職	job application, job wanted.
-- 職者	job hunter, job applicant.
20-- 愛	make love to.
25-- 生	earn one's living, run for one's living.
26-- 和	seek peace.
29-- 償	reimburse oneself for, cover oneself for.
30-- 之不得	just what one wished for.
-- 宥	apologize.
37-- 過於供	the demand outstrips the supply.
42-- 婚	propose, court, suit, woo, make love to, sue for.
48-- 教	ask advice, take counsel.
-- 教於人	go to one for advice.
-- 救	ask one's help, ask for help, beg for help.
-- 救信號	signal of distress.
60-- 見	seek an interview.
64-- 財	seek wealth.
74-- 助	appeal for help.
77-- 學	learn, acquire knowledge.
78-- 降	hang out the white flag.
80-- 知心	curiosity.
95-- 情	ask for a favor, ask for mercy.

4313_4

埃 〔**Ai**〕 *n.* dust, dirt.

17-- 及	Egypt.

4315_0

城 〔**Cheng**〕 *n.* city, town.

00-- 市	city, town.
-- 市設施	urban facilities.
-- 市更新	urban renewal.
-- 市經濟	urban economy.
-- 市地區	urban area.
-- 市規劃	city layout, city planning.
-- 市財政	urban finance.
-- 裏	inside the city.
23-- 外	suburb, outside the city.
24-- 牆	city wall.
26-- 堡	castle, tower, bastion, citadel.
27-- 鄉	town and country, urban and rural.
-- 鄉計劃	town and country planning.
30-- 守	garrison.
45-- 樓	tower over a city gate.
77-- 門	city gate.
84-- 鎮	city or town.

域 〔Yu〕 *n*. frontier, border, region, land, country, district.

4322₁

獰 〔Ning〕 *n*. ferocious-looking, fierce appearance, *adj*. ferocious.

88-- 笑　　grim smile, grin, malignant laugh.

4323₂

狼 〔Lang〕 *n*. wolf.

33-- 心　　cruel, brutal.

44-- 藉　　scattered about, disorder, licentious.

46-- 狽　　*n*. embarrassment, *v*. be struck with dismay.

-- 狽爲奸　do evil in collusion.

47-- 狗　　wolf dog.

4323₄

獄 〔Yu〕 *n*. prison, jail, gaol.

00-- 卒　　gaoler.

50-- 吏　　jailer.

4324₂

狩 〔Shou〕 *n*. hunter, *v*. hunt, chase.

42-- 獵　　chase, hunt.

4325₀

截 〔Chieh〕 *v*. cut off, intercept, cut in two, stop, obstruct.

08-- 敵　　intercept the enemy.

10-- 面　　section.

13-- 球　　intercept a ball.

20-- 住　　stop, cut short, interrupt.

21-- 止　　stop, close, cut off, expire.

-- 止時間　deadline.

22-- 斷　　serve, part off, cut asunder, block, break.

23-- 然　　entirely, diametrically.

57-- 擊　　intercept.

-- 擊機　interceptor plane.

67-- 路　　cut off communication, intercept on the road.

74-- 肢　　amputate.

81-- 短　　clip.

幟 〔Chih〕 *n*. banner, flag.

4330₀

忒 〔Te〕 *n*. mistake, error, *v*. alter, change, *adv*. very, extremely.

4332₇

鳶 〔Yuan〕 *n*. kite.

4341₂

婉 〔Wan〕 *adj*. beautiful, graceful, pleasant, kindly, genial.

00-- 商　　dilatory discussion.

-- 言　　plead gently.

04-- 謝　　decline politely, refuse with thanks.

07-- 詞　　neatly mouthed, euphemism.

21-- 順　　yielding, accommodating, agreeable.

43-- 求　　entreat.

55-- 轉　　roundabout, tactfully.

4341₄

姹 〔Chah〕 *v*. boast, *adj*. charming, attractive.

4343₂

嫁 〔Chia〕 *v*. be married to.

17-- 娶　　marriage.

24-- 妝　　dowry, marriage portion.

37-- 禍於人　impute the blame to another.

40-- 女　　give one's daughter in marriage.

-- 奩　　dowry.

娘 〔Niang〕 *n*. girl, miss, young lady, mother.

17-- 子　　young lady, wife.

-- 子軍　female soldier, Amazon, Joan of Arc.

30-- 家　　wife's family.

45-- 姨　　woman servant.

4345₀

娥 〔E〕 *n*. imperial concubine, *adj*. beautiful.

77-- 眉　　arched eyebrows.

-- 眉月　crescent moon.

戟 〔Chi〕 *n*. lance.

4346₀

始 〔Shih〕 *n*. beginning, origin, commencement, *v*. start, begin.

27-- 終　　from first to last, from beginning to end, all along, constantly.

-- 終如一　consistent.
32-- 業式　inauguration.
37-- 祖　founder, first ancestor.
-- 初　beginning.
82-- 創　invent, initiate.

4346₉
嬸〔Shen〕*n.* aunt.

4347₇
妒〔Tu〕*v.* envy, be jealous of, *adj.* jealous, envious.
17-- 忌　envy, be jealous of.
33-- 心　jealous mind.
97-- 恨　grudge.

4348₆
嬪〔Pin〕*n.* handsome lady, maid of honor.

4354₄
鞍〔An〕*n.* saddle.
31-- 褥　saddlecloth.

4355₀
載〔Tsai〕*n.* year, load, *v.* contain, fill, record, carry, transport, convey.
20-- 重量　load, loading capacity.
24-- 貨　carry goods, cargo transport.
-- 貨重量　shipped weight.
-- 貨量　carrying capacity.
30-- 客　passenger transport, carry passenger.
34-- 滿　full-loaded.
37-- 運　transport, convey.
80-- 入　enter, record.

4373₂
裘〔Chiu〕*n.* fur, fur coat, fur garment.

4375₀
裁〔Tsai〕*n.* form, style, mode. *v.* cut, trim, reduce, diminish, cut off, measure, consider.
00-- 衣　cut out clothes, cutting.
-- 度　plan, decide.
07-- 設　install.
22-- 紙　cut paper.
24-- 備　*n.* equipment, *v.* equip.
-- 備良好　well-equipped.

27-- 縫　tailor.
33-- 減　reduce, curtail, diminish, cut down.
-- 減軍事預算　reduction of military budget.
35-- 決　ruling, arbitration award.
-- 決書　award.
-- 決人　arbitrator.
58-- 撤　abolish, do away with.
60-- 員　reduce the establishment, job displacement, personnel cut back *v.* lay off, downsize, *n.* layoff, dounsizing reduction in force.
92-- 判　judge, decide.
-- 判權　judicial power.
-- 判官　judge.
-- 判長　chief justice.
-- 判所　law court.

4380₀
赴〔Fu〕*v.* go to, proceed.
00-- 席　attend a banquet.
22-- 任　go to one's post, proceed to one's post.
27-- 約　fulfill an engagement.
30-- 宴　go to a feast.
36-- 湯蹈火　risk one's life.
80-- 會　attend a meeting.

貳〔Erh〕*n.* second, assistant, *v.* suspect, *adj.* two, second.

4380₅
越〔Yueh〕*v.* pass over, exceed, overstep, go across, go beyond, *adj.* far, remote, even more.
12-- 發　much more, ever more, all the more.
22-- 出　transgress, overstep, go beyond.
-- 出範圍　be beyond the scope.
27-- 多愈好　the more the better.
-- 級　skip grades, bypass the immediate leadership.
37-- 過　go beyond, go across, pass over.
40-- 境　pass beyond one's territory.

43--	獄	break prison, prison breach, break jail.
44--	權	exceed one's power, over-step one's authority.
--	權者	trespasser.
54--	軌	out of order, go astray, go out of the usual rut.
60--	早越好	the earlier the better.
67--	野	cross-country, cross the country.
95--	快越好	the quicker the better.

4385_0
戴 〔Tai〕 v. wear, put on.

46--	帽	put on a hat.

4391_1
榨 〔Cha〕 n. press machine, v. press, squeeze.

17--	取	n. exploitation, v. exploit, milk.
--	取暴利	milk the market.
22--	出	squeeze out, press out.
35--	油	press oil.
--	油廠	oil press plant.
--	油機	oil extracting machine.

4392_1
檸 〔Ning〕 n. lemon.

44--	檬	lemon.
--	檬酸	citric acid.
--	檬汁	lemonade, lemon juice.
--	檬汽水	lemonade.
--	檬糖	lemon drop.

4394_0
弑 〔Shih〕 v. kill one's elder.

06--	親罪	parricide.
17--	君	regicide.

4395_0
栽 〔Tsai〕 v. plant, cultivate, assist.

22--	種	plant and sow.
30--	定點	written verdict.
40--	培	cultivate, foster, patronize.
--	培人才	educate people, assist talented people.
44--	花	plant flowers.
--	花植木	plant flowers and trees.

械 〔Hsieh〕 n. weapon, arms, shackle, manacles, machinery.

77--	鬥	fight with weapons.

械 〔Chien〕 n. letter, envelope.

4395_3
棧 〔Chan〕 n. warehouse, storeroom, godown, hotel, inn.

27--	租	storage, godown charge.
30--	房	warehouse, storehouse, go-down.
38--	道	plank road.
55--	費	warehouse rent.
66--	單	delivery order, warehouse receipt (certificate).

4396_0
枱 〔Tai〕 n. table.

13--	球	billiard.

4396_8
榕 〔Rong〕 n. banyan.

4397_7
棺 〔Kuan〕 n. coffin.

4398_6
檳 〔Pin〕 n. betel-nut, areca-nut.

4399_1
棕 〔Tsung〕 n. coir palm.

27--	繩	coir rope.
--	色	brown.

4399_4
樑 〔Liang〕 n. ridge, beam.

40--	木	beam timber.

4400_0
卄 〔Nien〕 adj. twenty, score.

4400_5
卅 〔Sa〕 adj. thirty.

4402_7
協 〔Hsieh〕 n. agreement, concord, mutual help, v. agree with, be united with, aid, help, assist, harmonize.

00--	商	consult, confer, negotiate with, treat with, lay heads together.
--	辦	n. assistant, v. assist.
04--	謀	conspire.
07--	調	harmonize, coordinate,

	bring into line.
08-- 議	agreement.
-- 議書	letter of agreement.
16-- 理	assistant manager, assistant general manager.
26-- 和	harmony, union, compromise.
27-- 約	convention.
-- 約國	entente powers, allies.
28-- 作	n. coordination, v. collaborate.
30-- 定	concert, accord, agreement.
-- 定書	memorandum of agreement.
-- 定關稅	convention tariff.
-- 定稅率	conventional tariff.
40-- 力	n. cooperation, united effort, v. cooperate, take part with, join hand in hand.
-- 力同心	cooperate with one heart.
74-- 助	help, aid, assist, side with.
77-- 同	n. participation, v. join with another.
-- 同工作	team work, work together.
80-- 會	society, association, institute.

4410₀

封〔**Feng**〕n. envelop, v. seal, close, blockade, block, install as a feudal lord.

10-- 面	cover of a book.
-- 面女郎	front cover girl, cover girl.
15-- 建	feudal.
-- 建主義	feudalism.
-- 建制度	feudalism, feudal system.
-- 建地	fief.
-- 建勢力	feudalistic influence.
-- 建思想	anachronistic thinking.
-- 建時代	feudal age.
20-- 住	close up.
23-- 緘	enclose, seal up.
27-- 條	label, sealing tape.
34-- 港	blockade.
35-- 凍期	ice-bound season.
40-- 存	seal and store up, sterilize.
52-- 蠟	sealing.
60-- 口信件	sealed letter.

77-- 閉	seal up, close, bar.
-- 閉市場	closed market.
-- 閉港	closed port.
-- 閉工廠	lock-out.
-- 印	seal.
80-- 入	enclose, enfold.
89-- 鎖	blockade.
-- 鎖地區	blockade zone.
-- 鎖線	a line of blockade, cordon.

4410₁

莖〔**Ching**〕n. stem, stalk.

| 46-- 桿 | stalk. |

韮〔**Jean**〕n. leeks or scallions.

4410₄

基〔**Chi**〕n. foundation, basis, beginning, origin, v. found, base on.

07-- 調	keynote.
08-- 於理論	on theoretical ground.
10-- 石	cornerstone, foundation stone.
14-- 礎	foundation, base, ground.
-- 礎產業	basic industries.
-- 礎設施	parts of the infrastructure, projects of basic facilities.
-- 礎工程	foundation work.
-- 礎工業	key industries.
-- 礎課	foundation course, basic subject.
-- 建預算	construction budget.
21-- 價	base price.
27-- 督	Christ, prince of peace.
-- 督教	Christianity.
-- 督教徒	Christian.
30-- 準	basis, criterion.
41-- 址	foundation of a wall, basis.
44-- 地	base, bastion .
45-- 樁	foundation pi le.
50-- 本	fundamental, basic.
-- 本方向	cardinal points.
-- 本方針	basic policy.
-- 本商品	basic commodities.
-- 本證據	primary evidence.
-- 本設施	infrastructure.
-- 本工資	basic salaries (pay, wage).
-- 本需求	primary demand.

-- 本功　rudimentary training, essential skill.
-- 本建設　capital construction.
-- 本上　fundamentally, in the main, on the whole.
-- 本利率　prime interest rate.
-- 本生活工資　minimum wage for living.
-- 本客匯　prime borrowers.
-- 本消費　basic consumption.
-- 本材料　basic materials.
-- 本原理　basic principle, fundamental principle.
58-- 數　radix, cardinal number, basic figure.
60-- 因工程　genetic engineering.
61-- 點　basic point.
77-- 肥　base fertilizer.
-- 層　grassroot unit, primary unit.
-- 層幹部　basic-level cadre.
80-- 金　fund, endowment, foundation.
-- 金會　foundation.

董 〔**Tung**〕 n. committee, gentry, v. rule, direct, correct, supervise, oversee.
50-- 事　director, trustee.
-- 事費　director fees.
-- 事長　chairman of the Board of Directors, president of the Board of Director.
-- 事會　Board of Directors.
-- 事會會議　board of directors meeting.
-- 事會報告　director's report.

墓 〔**Mu**〕 n. grave, tomb, bed of dust.
04--誌銘　epitaph.
10-- 石　tombstone.
16-- 碑　tombstone, gravestone.
44-- 地　graveyard churchyard, cemetery, God's acre.

墊 〔**Tien**〕 n. cushion, v. place under, cushion, pay money for another in advance.
10-- 平　full up and make even.
17-- 子　pad, cushion.
24-- 付　advance payment.

-- 付款　funds advanced.
30-- 肩　shoulder padding .
31-- 褥　mattress.
41-- 板　pallet.
47-- 款　money advanced.
50-- 本　advance capital for.
77-- 腳石　stepping-stone.
4410_6
薑 〔**Chiang**〕 n. ginger.
44-- 黃　turmeric.
98-- 粉　ground ginger.
萱 〔**Hsuan**〕 n. a species of day lily with edible flowers.
44-- 草　day lily.
4410_7
蓋 〔**Kai**〕 n. cover, lid, covering, v. cover, hide, build, construct, surpass.
00-- 章　seal, stamp.
10-- 瓦　lay tiles.
-- 不住　cannot be covered.
17-- 子　lid, cover.
21-- 上　cover, lid.
23-- 然性　probability.
30-- 房子　build a house.
34-- 被子　cover with a quilt.
47-- 起來　cover.
77-- 印　seal, stamp on, imprint, affix a seal.

藍 〔**Lan**〕 adj. blue.
10-- 天　blue sky.
27-- 色　blue color.
30-- 寶石　sapphire.
40-- 布　blue cloth.
-- 皮書　blue book.
50-- 本　model-book, blueprint.
60-- 圖　blueprint.
4410_8
荳 〔**Tou**〕 n. bean, pea, legume.
00-- 腐　bean curd.
27-- 角　bean pod.
35-- 油　bean oil.
44-- 芽　bean sprout.
-- 蔻花　mace.
88-- 餅　bean cake.
98-- 粉　bean flour.

4411₀

茫〔**Mang**〕*adj.* vast, boundless, pensive, vague, uncertain.
23-- 然　　　puzzled, bewildered.
44-- 茫　　　vast.
80-- 無頭緒　be at a loss.

4411₁

菲〔**Fei**〕*n.* edible vegetable, *adj.* thin, poor, mean.
25-- 律賓　　Philippines.
44-- 薄　　　poor, small and mean, meager.

堪〔**Kan**〕*v.* sustain, able to, fit for, bear, *adj.* possible, capable.
22-- 任重職　be adequate for an important post.
27-- 負重任　be fit for the important task, stand the racket.
77-- 用　　　useful, serviceable, fit for use.
90-- 當　　　worthy of.

4411₂

地〔**Ti**〕*n.* ground, earth, land, place, field, space, soil, spot, region, position.
00-- 主　　　landlord, land owner, landholder.
-- 產　　　estate, property.
-- 產商　　realtor, real estate developer.
-- 產經理　estate manager.
-- 產經紀人 real estate agent (broker).
-- 產收益　estate income.
-- 產稅　　tax on property, property tax.
-- 產公司　real estate agency, land investment co.
-- 方　　　place, region, district, locality.
-- 方工業　local industry.
-- 方政府　local government.
-- 方戲　　local opera.
-- 方自治　local self-government, autonomy.
-- 方的　　local.
-- 方稅　　local taxes.

-- 方官　　local authorities.
-- 方法規　local law.
-- 方法院　the district court.
-- 方財政　local finance.
-- 方公司　local firm.
-- 方公益事業 local public utility.
-- 方銀行　local bank.
-- 方當局　local authorities.
-- 方分權　decentralization of political powers.
02-- 氈　　　carpet, rug.
04-- 誌　　　geography.
10-- 下　　　underground.
-- 下水　　subterranean water.
-- 下停車場 underground car park.
-- 下室　　cave shelter, dugout, cellar, basement.
-- 下軍　　underground army.
-- 下運動　underground movement.
-- 下鐵路　subway, underground railway.
-- 平線　　horizon.
-- 雷　　　mine, land mine.
-- 雷戰　　mine warfare.
-- 面　　　surface of the earth, ground, floor.
-- 震　　　earthquake.
-- 震保險　earthquake insurance.
12-- 形　　　topography, natural features.
-- 裂　　　land slide.
13-- 球　　　earth, world, globe.
-- 球物理學 geophysics.
-- 球儀　　globe.
16-- 理　　　geography.
-- 理學家　geographer.
20-- 位　　　position, situation, place.
-- 委　　　the Administrative Region Party Committee.
21-- 價　　　land price, price of land (lot).
-- 價稅　　assessment tax, land value tax.
-- 價成本　cost of floor space.
-- 價高漲　soaring estate.
22-- 利　　　geographical advantages.

24-- 峽	isthmus.
26-- 堡	blockhouse.
27-- 租	land rent, ground rent.
-- 角	cape.
-- 名	name of a place.
-- 名字典	gazetteer.
-- 租	land tax, rent.
28-- 稅	taxes on land.
30-- 牢	dungeon.
-- 窖	cellar, basement.
-- 穴	cave, hole on the ground.
33-- 心	earth nucleus.
-- 心吸力	gravity.
38-- 道	subway, tunnel.
-- 道戰	tunnel warfare.
40-- 力	fertility of the land.
-- 皮	plat (lot, site), land for building.
-- 皮交易	dealing in land.
-- 土	earth, territory, estate.
-- 大物博	vast territory and abundant resources.
-- 坑	pit.
41-- 址	address, location.
-- 板	floor.
43-- 域	region, district.
-- 獄	hell, bottomless pit, inferno.
44-- 基	foundation of a building.
-- 帶	zone, terrain.
-- 勢	physical feature.
-- 權	land ownership.
47-- 殼	earth crust.
50-- 中海	Mediterranean Sea.
-- 表	surface of the earth.
55-- 軸	earth axis.
57-- 契	title deeds, land contract.
60-- 圖	chart, map.
-- 界	boundary.
61-- 點	point, location.
71-- 區	region, district.
-- 區計劃	regional plan.
-- 區津貼	regional allowance.
-- 區經理	regional manager, zone manager.
-- 區開發	regional development.
72-- 瓜	sweet potato.
-- 質學	geology.

-- 質學家	geologist.
77-- 層	stratum.
83-- 鐵	subway, underground railroad.
-- 鐵廣告	underground railway advertising.
90-- 券	title deed.

范〔Fan〕*n.* plant, grass. 4411₃

蔬〔Shu〕*n.* vegetable, greens.
44-- 菜	vegetable, greens.
-- 菜園	market garden, vegetable garden.
80-- 食	vegetable diet.
4411₈

莅〔Li〕*v.* arrive, come to, enter upon.
21-- 止	arrive at.
22-- 任	accept office.
46-- 場	be present.
78-- 臨	attend, arrived, be present.
4412₇

坳〔Ao〕*n.* depression, cavity.

蒲〔Pu〕*n.* a kind of rush, calamus.
27-- 包	rush bag.
30-- 扇	rush fan.
60-- 團	rush mat, cushion.
80-- 公英	dandelion.

蕩〔Tang〕*v.* subvert, overturn, upset, rock, move to and fro, consume, wash away, *adj.* large, great, vast, extensive, licentious.
00-- 產	spend all the property, wipe out, quell.
10-- 平	overturn, subvert.
17-- 子	profligate, prodigal.
20-- 千秋	swing on a swing.
27-- 槳	row.
38-- 漾	glister, rock on the water.
47-- 婦	whore, loose woman.
50-- 盡	waste, exhaust, run out.

勤〔Chin〕*adj.* diligent, industrious.
17-- 務	service, duty.
-- 務兵	orderly.
-- 務員	servant, orderly.
24-- 勉	diligent, industrious.

28-- 以補拙　make up by diligence for one's want of ability.

-- 儉　*n.* industry and thrift, temperance, *adj.* diligent and frugal.

44-- 力　industrious.

77-- 學　*v.* study hard, *adj.* studious, assiduous in study, diligent.

95-- 快　hard-working.

99-- 勞　painstaking.

4412₉

莎〔So〕*n.* sedge, cyperus.

4413₂

藜〔Li〕*n.* goosefoot.

4414₂

薄〔Po〕*n.* peppermint, *v.* extend to, reach to, treat, reduce, diminish, slight, despise, *adj.* thin, poor, bad, slight, dilute, trifling, *adv.* coldly.

17-- 弱　weak, feeble.

22-- 片　slice , flake.

-- 利多銷　cut down the profit margin in order to sell more.

-- 紙　thin paper.

24-- 待　treat coldly, treat carelessly.

35-- 禮　little present, small gift.

41-- 板　sheet, thin board.

44-- 荷　peppermint, menthol.

-- 荷油　peppermint oil.

-- 荷糖　peppermint (candy).

-- 暮　evening, dusk, twilight, around sunset.

74-- 膜　membrane, film.

80-- 命　unfortunate life.

88-- 餅　pancake, wafer.

95-- 情　*n.* ingratitude, *adj.* ungrateful, cold.

4414₇

坡〔Po〕*n.* slope, hillside.

00-- 度　gradient of a slope.

77-- 兒　slope.

菠〔Po〕*n.* spinach.

44-- 菜　spinach.

-- 蘿　pineapple.

鼓〔Gu〕*n.* drum, *v.* beat a drum, rouse, vibrate, stir, bulge.

06-- 譟　mutiny.

20-- 手　drummer.

24-- 動　incite, arouse, agitate, excite.

-- 動人心　ferment agitation.

45-- 樓　drum tower.

47-- 起　plunk up (one's courage), bulge.

-- 槌　drum stick.

-- 聲　drumbeat.

66-- 噪　uproar, din.

67-- 吹　advocate, publicize.

74-- 勵　*v.* encourage, stimulate, promote, inspire, *adj.* incentive.

-- 勵獎金　incentive bonus.

-- 勵措施　incentive.

-- 勵投資　encouragement of investment.

-- 膜　eardrum.

77-- 風　blast furnace.

-- 風機　air blower.

80-- 舞　inspirit, excite, stir, pluck up.

-- 舞人心　encouraging, inspiring, exciting.

90-- 掌　clap hands, applaud.

4414₉

萍〔Ping〕*n.* duckweed.

12-- 水相逢　casual, temporary meeting, encounter.

4416₀

堵〔Tu〕*n.* stretch of wall, *v.* obstruct, stop, close, shut, block up.

10-- 死　smother to death.

20-- 住　close, stop, cork.

-- 住嘴　gag the mouth.

30-- 塞　block up, close against, choke up.

37-- 漏洞　stop a loophole.

43-- 截　cut off, intercept.

83-- 缺口　stop a dike breach.

4416₁

塔〔Ta〕*n.* tower, pagoda.

蓓 〔**Pei**〕 *n.* bud, flower-bud.
44-- 蕾　　　flower-bud.
4416₄

落 〔**Lo**〕 *n.* gathering place, village, *v.* come down, descend, sink, settle down, die.

10-- 下　　　fall, descend, go down, drop down, fall down.
　-- 雨　　　rainfall.
　-- 雪　　　snowfall.
11-- 班　　　relief.
12-- 水狗　　dog in the water, person who is down.
21-- 伍　　　*v.* fall behind, get behind. *adj.* behind the time.
22-- 後　　　*n.* backwardness, *v.* leave behind, fall behind, drop astern.
　-- 後國家　backward country.
　-- 空　　　come to naught.
　-- 戶　　　settle down.
　-- 實　　　fulfill, implement, carry out.
37-- 潮　　　falling tide, ebb tide.
　-- 選　　　fail in election.
40-- 難　　　encounter difficulty.
44-- 花生　　peanut.
　-- 葉　　　fallen leaves.
　-- 葉樹　　deciduous tree.
　-- 葉松　　larch.
51-- 拓　　　unrestrained, down on one's luck.
53-- 成　　　completion of a building.
　-- 成典禮　dedication ceremony of a building.
60-- 日　　　setting sun.
88-- 第　　　be plucked.
4416₉

藩 〔**Fan**〕 *n.* hedge, fence, boundary, frontier.
27-- 邦　　　feudatory state.
88-- 籬　　　defense.
4418₁

填 〔**Tien**〕 *v.* fill up, fill in, complete, stuff, supply enough.

00-- 充　　　fill the blanks.
10-- 平　　　full up, level off.
25-- 債　　　pay a debt.
30-- 塞　　　stop.
　-- 房　　　wife by second marriage.
　-- 寫　　　fill in (a blank, a form).
31-- 河　　　fill up a stream.
33-- 補　　　make good, make up for a deficiency.
34-- 滿　　　full up, stuff up.
35-- 溝　　　fill up a ditch.
37-- 遲日期　post date.
50-- 表格　　fill in a form.
60-- 早日期　antedate, predate, fore-date.
80-- 入　　　fill in.
4418₆

墳 〔**Fen**〕 *n.* grave, tomb, mound.
22-- 山　　　grave, low dwelling, one's long home.
44-- 墓　　　grave, tomb.
　-- 地　　　cemetery, graveyard.
47-- 起　　　swelling.
4419₄

藻 〔**Tsao**〕 *n.* algae, pond weed, aquatic plant.
91-- 類　　　algae.
4420₁

苧 〔**Chu**〕 *n.* China grass, ramie.
4420₇

考 〔**Kao**〕 *n.* examination, investigation, *v.* examine, question, test, study, investigate.

02-- 證　　　*n.* verification, *v.* verify.
03-- 試　　　examination, test.
　-- 試及格　pass an examination.
　-- 試院　　the Examination Yuan.
　-- 試院長　president of the Examination Yuan.
21-- 慮　　　deliberate, consider, discus, think over.
　-- 慮不周　ill-considered.
　-- 慮周到　well-contemplated.
30-- 究　　　*v.* investigate, inquire into, look over, *adj.* elegant, choosy.
　-- 察　　　examine, inspect, investi-

gate.

-- 察團	observation group, inspection group, investigation group.
40-- 查	inspect, investigate, inquire into.
-- 古家	antiquarian.
-- 核	assess, evaluation of one's performance.
-- 古學	archaeology.
44-- 勤	check work attendance.
47-- 期	date of examination.
78-- 驗	*n.* trial, *v.* test, try.

夢〔Meng〕*n.* dream.

02-- 話	somniloquy, talk in sleep, talk nonsense.
27-- 幻	visionary, illusory.
35-- 遺	nocturnal emissions.
38-- 遊	somnambulism, sleepwalk.
40-- 境	dream land.
46-- 想	*n.* dreaming, day dream, *v.* dream, fancy.
-- 想不到	far beyond one's expectation.
60-- 見	dream.
71-- 魘	nightmare.

萼〔O〕*n.* calyx, receptacle.
4421₁
荒〔Huang〕*n.* famine, wilderness, *v.* neglect, magnify, wild, waste, *adj.* wild, barren, waste, uncultivated.

00-- 廢	waste, ruin, desolate, neglect.
-- 唐	absurd, ridiculous.
02-- 誕	fabulous, fictitious, absurd.
07-- 謬	absurd, sheer nonsense.
30-- 涼	desolate, deserted.
32-- 淫	dissipated, profligate.
44-- 地	wilderness, barren land.
-- 蕪	wild, waste, desolate, uncultivated.
60-- 田	barren field.
67-- 野	wilds, desert, wilderness.
80-- 年	barren year, year of scarcity, lean year, year of bad harvests.

麓〔Lu〕*n.* the foot of a hill.
4421₂
苑〔Yuan〕*n.* park, pasture, garden.
4421₄
花〔Hua〕*n.* flower, blossom, *v.* spend, lay out, bloom.

00-- 瓣	petal.
13-- 球	bouquet, nosegay.
17-- 子	seed.
21-- 紅	bonus, premium.
22-- 崗石	granite.
25-- 生	peanut.
26-- 白	grey.
27-- 盤	flower pot.
-- 色	assortment, design and color.
-- 緞	brocade.
30-- 房	greenhouse.
35-- 神	Flora.
36-- 邊	lace, hemstitch.
37-- 冠	corolla.
-- 冤枉錢	pay for a dead horse, spend money to no avail.
40-- 壇	bed.
-- 布	print, printed cloth.
-- 卉	flowers and flowering herbs.
-- 柱	style of flower.
41-- 梗	peduncle.
44-- 莖	stem.
-- 落	blossoms falling off, falling of flowers.
-- 萼	calyx.
-- 花公子	beau, gilded youth, playboy.
-- 蒂	flower-stalk.
-- 蕊	pistil bud, flower bud.
-- 草	plants, flowers.
47-- 柳病	venereal disease, syphilis.
48-- 樣	pattern, style, variety.
50-- 束	bouquet.
52-- 托	torus.
55-- 費	expenditure.
57-- 招	tricks.
60-- 園	garden, park.

-- 圈	wreath, garland.
71-- 匠	gardener.
77-- 開	bloom.
-- 朵	flowers.
80-- 會	flower show.
-- 盆	flower pot.
81-- 瓶	vase.
88-- 籃	flower basket.
90-- 卷	steamed rolls.
98-- 粉	pollen.

莊〔Chuang〕*n.* village, country, store, shop , farm house, *adj.* serious, sedate, grave.

20-- 重	grave, solemn, serious, dignified.
23-- 稼	crops, grains.
-- 稼漢	field laborers.
30-- 容	grim-faced, long-faced, serious, sedate, grave.
60-- 園	manor.
66-- 嚴	serious, severe, rigorous, grave, solemn.

獾〔Huan〕*n.* boar, badger.

荏〔Jen〕*n.* Perilla, a kind of plant, *adj.* soft, weak.

17-- 弱	weak, soft, fragile.
44-- 苒	elapse gradually.

4421₆

兢〔Ching〕*v.* fear, *adj.* cautious, careful.

44-- 兢	fearful, terrified, cautious.

莧〔Hsian〕*n.* amaranth.

4421₇

犰〔Chiu〕*n.* armadillo.

梵〔Fan〕*n.* Sanskrit, Buddhist.

00-- 文	Sanskrit.
77-- 學	Buddhism.

藐〔Miao〕*v.* despise, disdain, look down, neglect, slight, *adj.* petty, small, slight.

34-- 法	in contempt of the law.
36-- 視	slight, despise, disdain, look down, scorn.
-- 視法律	set the law at defiance.

90-- 小	small, insignificant.

蘆〔Lu〕*n.* reeds, rushes , gourds.

00-- 席	rush mat.
21-- 柴	rush fagot.
44-- 葦	reed.
47-- 柵	rush hut.
88-- 笛	reed (musical instrument).

4422₁

芹〔Chin〕*n.* celery.

荷〔Ho〕*n.* lotus, water lily, *v.* bear, carry.

10-- 爾蒙	hormone.
27-- 包蛋	poached egg, fried egg.
44-- 花	lotus flowers, water lily.
-- 花池	lotus pond.
-- 蘭	Holland, Netherlands.
-- 蘭水	soda-water.
-- 蘭人	Dutch.
-- 葉	lotus leaf.

4422₂

茅〔Mao〕*n.* reed, thatch, rushes.

00-- 廁	earth-closet, latrine.
47-- 棚	thatched shed.
80-- 舍	cottage, cabin, hut.

4422₇

芬〔Fen〕*n.* fragrance, perfume of opening flowers, aroma.

44-- 芳	sweet, fragrant.
-- 蘭	Finland.
-- 蘭語	Finnish language.

芳〔Fang〕*adj.* fragrant, odoriferous, beautiful, fair, good, virtuous.

20-- 香	perfume, fragrance, aroma.
27-- 名	good reputation.
44-- 草	fragrant plant.
80-- 氣	sweet smell.

莠〔Yu〕*n.* weeds, foxtail, *adj.* bad, evil, wicked.

蒂〔Ti〕*n.* stem, stalk, base, peduncle.

60-- 固根深	deep-rooted.

帶〔Tai〕*n.* girdle, belt, tape, ribbon, zone, region, *v.* carry, bring, lead, conduct.

10-- 電	electric.
11-- 頭	take the lead.

17-- 子	girdle, belt.
20-- 信	carry letters.
27-- 魚	hairtail, ribbonfish.
40-- 去	take away.
-- 來	carry with.
44-- 薪休假	paid vacation.
-- 薪假期	leave with pay.
-- 薪假日	holiday with pay, pay holiday.
60-- 口信	send word.
-- 回	take back, bring back.
-- 累	involve others in.
67-- 路	act as a guide.
72-- 兵	lead troops.
80-- 入歧途	lead one up the garden path.
81-- 領	lead, guide.

蓆 〔**Hsi**〕 *n*. mat, straw mat.

17-- 子	mat, straw mat.
44-- 草	mat straw.

菁 〔**Ching**〕 *n*. flower of the leek.

44-- 華	essence.

蒨 〔**Chien**〕 *adj*. bright, fair, luxuriant.

葡 〔**Pu**〕 *n*. grape, vine.

44-- 萄	grape, grapevine.
-- 萄牙	Portugal.
-- 萄牙人	Portuguese.
-- 萄酒	grape wine, claret.
-- 萄汁	grape juice.
-- 萄樹	vine, grapevine.
-- 萄乾	raisin, plum.
-- 萄園	vine yard.
-- 萄糖	grape sugar.

幕 〔**Mu**〕 *n*. tent, curtain, screen, scene.

22-- 後	behind the scenes.
-- 後新聞	behind the scenes news.
-- 後操縱	wire-pulling.
-- 後人物	wire-puller.

薦 〔**Chien**〕 *n*. mat, *v*. introduce, recommend, offer.

11-- 頭行	employment agency.
12-- 引	introduce, bring in.
37-- 祖	worship ancestors.
50-- 書	letter of introduction.
77-- 舉	recommendation.

蒿 〔**Hao**〕 *n*. wormwood.

蕎 〔**Chiao**〕 *n*. buckwheat.

40-- 麥粉	buckwheat flour.

繭 〔**Chien**〕 *n*. cocoon.

17-- 子	cocoons.
27-- 綢	coarse pongee.
50-- 虫	pupa.

幫 〔**Pang**〕 *n*. party, clan, class, *v*. help, aid, assist.

00-- 辦	sub-manager, assistant superintendent.
04-- 護	protect, defend.
10-- 工	hired man.
20-- 手	assistant, supporter, helper.
22-- 兇	accomplice.
74-- 助	help, aid, assist, back up, take part, take a side.
90-- 忙	lend a helping hand, render a service, help, assist, aid.

蕭 〔**Hsiao**〕 *n*. artemisia, *adj*. lonely, desolate, quiet.

11-- 瑟	lonely, desolate.
27-- 條	depression, slump, desolate, solitary, poor.
-- 條地區	depressed area.
-- 條市場	flat market, sluggish market.

蘭 〔**Lan**〕 *n*. orchids.

勸 〔**Chuan**〕 *v*. advise, persuade, exhort, bring round.

02-- 語	persuade.
08-- 說	*n*. persuasion, *v*. persuade.
24-- 告	recommend, advise, counsel.
27-- 勉	exhort, inspire, persuade.
-- 解	make a compromise.
38-- 導	induce, give counsel and guidance.
56-- 捐	make a purse.
77-- 阻	dissuade, discourage.
-- 服	talk over, win over.

4422₈

芥 〔**Chieh**〕 *n*. mustard.

44-- 蒂	remorse, grudge.
-- 菜	mustard plant.

50-- 末　　　　　ground mustard.

4423₁

蔭〔Yin〕 *n.* shadow, shade, *v.* protect, shelter, overshadow.

00-- 庇　　　　　protect, shelter.
44-- 蔽　　　　　overshadow.

4423₂

蒙〔Meng〕 *v.* deceive, cover, hide, screen, impose upon, cheat, *adj.* ignorant, stupid, dull.

11-- 頭　　　　　over the head.
40-- 古　　　　　Mongolia.
 -- 古大夫　　　medical quack, quack doctor.
44-- 蔽　　　　　hide, screen, overshadow, deceive.
65-- 昧　　　　　stupid, ignorant.

猿〔Yuan〕 *n.* gibbon, ape.

80-- 人　　　　　ape man.

藤〔Teng〕 *n.* vines, rattan, creeping and climbing plant.

27-- 條　　　　　split rattan.
44-- 黃　　　　　gamboge.
 -- 椅　　　　　cane (or rattan) chair.
46-- 榻　　　　　cane (or rattan) bed.

4423₃

菸〔Yen〕 *n.* tobacco.

28-- 鹼　　　　　nicotine.

4423₄

茯〔Fu〕 *n.* Chinaroot, Tuckahoe.

苯〔Ben〕 *n.* benzene.

簇〔Tsu〕 *n.* collect, come together.

4423₇

蔗〔Che〕 *n.* sugarcane.

90-- 糖　　　　　cane sugar.

4423₈

狹〔Hsia〕 *adj.* narrow, strait, mean.

21-- 徑　　　　　small path.
30-- 窄　　　　　narrow, strait, close.
33-- 心　　　　　narrow-minded.
67-- 路　　　　　lane, alley, narrow path.
78-- 隘　　　　　narrow, narrow-minded.
80-- 義　　　　　restricted sense.
90-- 小　　　　　close, narrow.

4424₀

蔚〔Wei〕 *n.* a kind of odorous plant. *adj.* luxuriant.

44-- 藍　　　　　deep blue.

4424₁

芽〔Ya〕 *n.* bud, sprout.

44-- 菜　　　　　bean sprout.

4424₃

蓐〔Ju〕 *n.* mat.

4424₇

菱〔Ling〕 *n.* water chestnut.

獲〔Huo〕 *v.* catch, seize, arrest, get, obtain, chase, hit.

22-- 利　　　　　make money, make profit.
 -- 利出售　　　sell at a profit.
 -- 利者　　　　gainer.
26-- 得　　　　　get, obtain, acquire, gain, come into possession.
 -- 得利潤　　　earn a profit, pocket a profit.
 -- 得淨利　　　net profit.
60-- 暴利　　　　make a killing.
79-- 勝　　　　　gain a victory, win a victory.

蔣〔Chiang〕 *n.* Chiang (a family name).

4424₈

蔽〔Pi〕 *n.* brushwood, *v.* conceal, cover, hide, shade, shelter, keep out of view.

04-- 護　　　　　shelter, protect.
30-- 塞　　　　　screen, close up.
60-- 目　　　　　screen the eye, blindfold, cover the eyes.

4425₃

茂〔Mao〕 *adj.* flourishing, luxuriant, good, elegant, exuberant, excellent.

30-- 密　　　　　thick, dense.
44-- 林　　　　　thicket, grove, thick forest
53-- 盛　　　　　abundant, luxuriant.
80-- 年　　　　　youth, the green margin of one's life.

蔑〔Mieh〕 *v.* slight, despise, look down, discard, cast away.

36-- 視　　　　　despise, look down, defy, treat with contempt.

藏 〔Tsang〕 *n.* storage, warehouse, Tibet, *v.* hide, conceal, store up, lay by, hoard, accumulate.

23--	伏	hide, conceal.
41--	奸	harbor guile.
50--	書室	library.
52--	拙	conceal one's stupidity.
71--	匿	hide, conceal.
77--	民	Tibetans.
80--	入	tuck, hide.

4425₆

幃 〔Wei〕 *n.* curtain.

4426₀

豬 〔Chu〕 *n.* pig, hog, swine.

00--	瘟	hog cholera (or plague).
20--	毛	hog's bristle.
35--	油	lard.
40--	肉	pork.
47--	欄	pigsty , pigpen.
51--	排	pork chop.
72--	鬃	hog's bristle.
77--	尾巴	pigtail.
--	腳	pig knuckles, pig trotters.

貓 〔Mao〕 *n.* cat.

62--	叫	mew, meow.

4428₆

蘋 〔Pin〕 *n.* apple.

60--	果	apple.
--	果醬	apple jam.
--	果酒	cider.
--	果脯	dried apple.

4429₄

葆 〔Pao〕 *n.* cover, canopy, *v.* cover up, *adj.* bushy.

4429₆

獠 〔Liao〕 *n.* fierce man, *adj.* ferocious.

71--	牙	fang, bucktooth.

4430₅

蓬 〔Peng〕 *n.* a species of raspberry. *adj.* overgrown, tangled.

16--	頭	uncombed head.
44--	萊仙境	fairyland.
47--	勃	flourishing with vigor, full of vitality.
72--	鬆	disheveled, shaggy.

蓮 〔Lien〕 *n.* lotus, water lily.

17--	子	lotus seed.
40--	塘	lotus pond.
44--	花	lotus flower.
47--	馨花	primrose.
92--	燈	lantern shaped like a lotus flower.

4430₇

芝 〔Chih〕 *n.* a species of fungus.

44--	麻	sesame.
--	麻醬	sesame paste, sesame butter.
--	麻油	sesame oil.

苓 〔Ling〕 *n.* Chinaroot, Tuckahoe.

4432₇

芍 〔Shao〕 *n.* water chestnut.

驀 〔Mo〕 *v.* leap on a horse, mount a horse, leap over.

23--	然	suddenly.

4433₁

赫 〔Ho〕 *adj.* red hot, fiery, angry, red, bright, glorious.

44--	赫	glorious, fiery, hot, great, majestic.
47--	怒	angry, black in the face.

蒸 〔Cheng〕 *n.* steam, vapor, *v.* steam, boil, evaporate, distill, stew.

12--	發	vaporize, evaporate.
37--	溜	distill.
--	溜器	retort.
38--	汽	vapor, steam.
--	汽浴	vapor-bath, steam bath.
--	汽渦輪	steam turbine.
--	汽機	steam engine.
--	汽表	steam meter, steam gauge.
80--	氣	steam, vapor.
81--	飯	steam rice.
87--	鍋	saucepan, steamer.
--	餾	distill.
--	餾水	distilled water.

-- 餾器	distiller retort.
88-- 籠	steaming basket.

蕪〔Wu〕 *n.* rotten plant, *adj.* confused, mixed up.

00-- 雜	confused, mixed up.
44-- 菁	rape turnip.

蕉〔Chiao〕 *n.* banana.

熱〔Je〕 *n.* heat, fever, *v.* heat, *adj.* warm, hot, feverish.

00-- 病	fever.
-- 度	temperature.
-- 度針	thermometer.
03-- 誠	hearty, zealous, ardent, cordial, with heart and soul.
07-- 望	*n.* aspiration, ambition, *v.* hunger after, thirst after, run mad about.
10-- 天	hot day.
-- 電	thermoelectricity.
-- 電站	thermoelectric plant, thermal power station.
-- 電學	pyroelectricity.
12-- 烈	fiery, hot, zealous, warm, ardent, hearty.
-- 烈歡迎	warm welcome, ovation.
-- 水	hot water.
-- 水袋	hot-water bottle.
-- 水瓶	vacuum bottle, thermos, vacuum flask.
20-- 愛	devotion, ardent love.
21-- 處理	heat treatment.
22-- 戀	love.
26-- 線	hot line.
27-- 血	hot-blooded, fervent.
30-- 空氣	hot air.
31-- 河	Jehol province.
-- 漲	expansion by heat.
33-- 心	enthusiasm, zeal, ardency, warmth.
-- 心者	zealot, enthusiast.
37-- 潮	upsurge of interest in something.
40-- 力	heat power, thermal energy.
-- 核戰	thermonuclear war, nuclear war.
44-- 帶	torrid zone, tropics, tropi-

	cal.
47-- 切	enthusiasm.
50-- 中	be eager to, be highly interested in.
51-- 輻射	heat radiation.
60-- 量	calorific capacity, calories.
77-- 悶	sultry.
-- 門	in great demand, popular, hot.
-- 門貨	hot number, popular wares.
-- 鬧	busy, noisy.
95-- 情	passion, fervor.

燕〔Yen〕 *n.* swallow, *v.* rest, comfort.

01-- 語	swallow-twittering.
17-- 子	swallow.
30-- 窩	bird's nest.
-- 安	peaceful.
40-- 麥	oats.
77-- 尾	swallow tail.
-- 尾服	swallow-tailed coat.
87-- 飲	feast.

薰〔Hsun〕 *n.* perfume, fragrance, *v.* burn, cauterize.

77-- 陶	mold a person's character gradually.

4433₂

葱〔Tsung〕 *n.* onion, green onion, leek green.

11-- 頭	onion.
27-- 綠	light green.

4433₃

蕊〔Jui〕 *n.* pistil, stamen.

慕〔Mu〕 *n.* esteem, admire, long for, wish for.

27-- 仰	respect, admire.
-- 名而來	be attracted to a place by its reputation as scenic spot, etc.
-- 名求見	have respect for one's name and ask an interview.

蕙〔Hui〕 *n.* a species of fragrant grass.

33-- 心	pure heart.
44-- 蘭	a species of fragrant orchid.

4433₆

惹〔Je〕v. provoke, tease, rouse, excite, produce, attract, incur.

37-- 禍	incur mischief, induce calamity, bring evil.
47-- 怒	irritate.
-- 起	cause, induce, incur, stir.
48-- 嫌	provoke hatred.
50-- 事	provoke a fight, make trouble.
80-- 人笑	provoke laughter.
-- 人注目	stick out like a sore thumb, be much in evidence.

煮〔Chu〕v. cook, boil.

04-- 熟	cook thoroughly.
44-- 菜	cook food.
81-- 飯	boil rice, cook meal.

4433₈

恭〔Kong〕n. respect, reverence, v. respect, revere, venerate, adj. respectful, reverent, polite, courteous.

00-- 請	invite.
10-- 而有禮	modest and courteous.
20-- 維	praise, flatter.
27-- 候	await respectfully.
37-- 迎嘉賓	receive honored guest.
40-- 喜	congratulate.
46-- 賀	n. congratulation, v. congratulate.
48-- 敬	v. respect, venerate, adj. respectful, polite, courteous.

4433₉

懋〔Mao〕v. exert.

4435₁

蘚〔Hsien〕n. moss, lichen.

44-- 苔	moss, lichen.
91-- 類	moss.

4436₀

赭〔Che〕n. red earth, adj. red, reddish brown.

10-- 石	iron ore, ochre.
27-- 色	red, reddish brown.
40-- 土	umber.

4439₄

蘇〔Su〕v. revive, come to life again, cheer up.

15-- 醒	revive, come back to life.
20-- 維埃	Soviet.
40-- 木	Brazil-wood.
51-- 打	soda.

4440₀

艾〔Ai〕n. wormwood, mugwort, moxa, v. end, cease, stop.

23-- 絨	smashed dry moxa leaves.
27-- 灸	cauterize with moxa.
44-- 草	moxa.

4440₁

芋〔Yu〕n. taro.

11-- 頭	taro.

莘〔Hsin〕n. marsh, plant, adj. long.

茸〔Jung〕n. deer's horn, adj. soft, downy, confused, messy.

44-- 茸	soft and tender.

4440₄

婪〔Lan〕adj. greedy.

萎〔Wei〕v. wither, wilt, shrivel, be ill, decline weaken, adj. rotten, dying.

21-- 額	slack.
23-- 縮	shrink, wither.
27-- 絕	fade and wither.
51-- 頓	shrivel.

4440₆

草〔Tsao〕n. grass, weed, plants, adj. careless, rough.

00-- 席包	rush mat bale.
-- 章	draft copy of an agreement.
-- 率	careless.
20-- 稿	sketch, draft, rough draft, rough copy.
22-- 紙	cap paper, toilet paper.
23-- 袋	straw bag, rush bag.
-- 編製品	straw products.
27-- 繩	straw rope.
30-- 案	sketch, draft.
-- 字	writing in running hand, cursive writing, longhand.
40-- 堆	stack.
-- 皮	turf.
-- 木	plant and trees, vegetation.
41-- 坪	lawn, meadow, pasture.
44-- 墊	straw mattress.

-- 地	grass, lawn, meadow.
-- 席	straw mat.
-- 鞋	sandal.
-- 莓	strawberry.
-- 藥	herb or hay medicine.
46-- 帽	straw hat.
-- 場	meadow.
50-- 書	writing in cursive, writing in running hand.
57-- 擬	draft.
-- 擬合同	draw up a contract.
60-- 圖	rough map.
67-- 野	rustic.
71-- 原	meadow, grassland, pasture.
75-- 體	running hand.
77-- 屋	hut.
-- 肥	weed ferilizer.
80-- 人	scarecrow.
-- 舍	hut, shed.
82-- 創	originate, make a rough beginning.
94-- 料	hay, fodder.

鼙〔Pi〕n. war drum.
蕈〔Hsun〕n. mushroom, fungus.
44-- 菌 fungus.

4440₇
孝〔Hsiao〕adj. filial, obedient.
17-- 子 filial son.
21-- 順 dutiful, filial.
33-- 心 filial son.
48-- 敬 piety.

芟〔Shan〕n. scythe, v. mow, cut down.
蔓〔Man〕n. vines, tendril, v. spread, creep, adj. climbing, spreading.
12-- 延 overgrow, creep, spread.
25-- 生 overgrow.
44-- 蔓 adj. grassy, adv. extensively.
72-- 髮 tendrils.

孽〔Nieh〕n. retribution, misfortune, evils, sin, crime, son of a concubine.
22-- 種 bastard.

4440₈
萃〔Tsui〕adj. grassy.
20-- 集 collect together.

4441₁
姥〔Mu〕n. matron.
4441₂
她〔Ta〕pron. she, her.
26-- 自己 herself.
27-- 們 they, them.
-- 的 her, hers.
4441₄
娃〔Wa〕n. pretty girl, baby, beautiful woman.
44-- 娃 pretty girl, child.
蘺〔Li〕n. water grass.
44-- 藩 fence, hedge.
4441₇
執〔Chih〕v. hold, seize, maintain, keep, arrest, imprison.
00-- 意 maintain, hold, be determined to, be bent on.
18-- 政 n. administration, v. manage the government, be in power.
-- 政官 consul.
-- 政者 government authorities.
-- 政黨 party in power, ruling party.
21-- 行 n. execution, application, v. execute, take effect, perform.
-- 行委員會 executive committee.
-- 行任務 perform tasks.
-- 行官 administrative official.
-- 行機關 administrative organ.
-- 行權 executive power.
-- 行中止 respite.
-- 行人 operator, executive.
-- 行人員 law enforcement officials.
25-- 牛耳 be a dominant figure.
32-- 業 enter a profession.
34-- 法如山 uphold the law firmly.
-- 法機構 law enforcement agency.
40-- 有 in possession.
44-- 勤 do guard duty, keep guard.
50-- 事 manager.
54-- 持 keep, lay hold of.
-- 拗 obstinate, stubborn.
67-- 照 license, charter, permit, cer-

	tificate.	
-- 照持有者	licensee.	
-- 照費	license fee.	
88-- 筆	write.	
90-- 掌	manage, superintend, be in charge of.	

4442₇

荔 〔Li〕 n. lichee.

17-- 子	lichee.

勃 〔Po〕 adj. suddenly, abruptly, flourishing, prosperous.

12-- 發	storm.
23-- 然	suddenly.
-- 然變色	sudden change in countenance.
-- 然大怒	burst into great rage all at once.
38-- 豁	quarrel.
77-- 興	shoot up, happen suddenly.

媁 〔Wei〕 n. Wei(a family name).

萬 〔Wan〕 n. ten thousand, all, myriad.

10-- 一	in case of, if by any chance.
-- 靈藥	cure-all, panacea.
-- 惡	completely atrocious, altogether vicious, all vices.
20-- 應藥	panacea.
21-- 能	almighty, all-powerful, omnipotent.
-- 能卡	master card.
-- 歲	all hail! long live!
27-- 物	element, everything, all thing, the universe.
40-- 幸	very fortunately.
-- 古	forever, for immense ages.
44-- 花筒	kaleidoscope.
-- 世留芳	leave a good name.
-- 世師表	teacher for all ages.
50-- 事	everything.
-- 事通	jack-of-all-trades.
60-- 國	international, all nations.
-- 國郵政	international post.
-- 國運動會	international games.
-- 國博覽會	World's Fair, World Expo.
-- 國公法	international law.
-- 里長城	Great Wall of China.
80-- 分	extremely, utterly.

-- 年	ten thousand years, forever.	
-- 年青	Chinese evergreen.	
90-- 米	myriametre.	

勢 〔Shih〕 n. power, authority, influence, strength, state, condition, circumstance.

10-- 不兩立	irreconcilable, hostile, antagonistic.
-- 不可當	irresistible.
-- 不得已	the circumstances give one no other choice.
11-- 頭	situation.
-- 頭不對	the situation is unfavorable.
21-- 處兩難	be in a dilemma.
22-- 利	snobbish, snobbery.
-- 利之交	friendship based on worldly interests.
30-- 窮力竭	be in a deplorable plight and powerless.
33-- 必	be bound to.
40-- 力	strength, force, power, influence.
-- 力平均	balance of power.
-- 力範圍	sphere of influence.
46-- 如破竹	sweeping, irresistible.
47-- 均力敵	well matched, balanced in power.
72-- 所必至	be bound to come.
77-- 同水火	be incompatible like water and fire.

葯 〔Shuo〕 n. capsule.

募 〔Mu〕 n. enroll, v. enlist, collect, raise, call upon.

24-- 化	beg alms.
28-- 稅	levy taxes.
56-- 捐	n. subscription, v. raise funds, solicit subscription.
72-- 兵	enroll, enlist, recruit.

勱 〔Mai〕 n. exertion.

4443₀

樊 〔Fan〕 n. cage, railing, fence.

88-- 籬	fence, railing.
-- 籠	bird cage.

4443₁

葵 〔Kuei〕 n. sunflower.

44-- 花　　　　sunflower.

4443₆

莫 〔**Mo**〕*v.* do not.
11-- 非　　　most probably.
18-- 敵　　　nobody dares.
27-- 名其妙　　unintelligible, inexplicable, absurd.
38-- 逆之交　　friend with complete mutual understanding, close friendship.
40-- 大　　　greatest.
46-- 如　　　nothing like.

4443₈

莢 〔**Chia**〕*n.* pod, legume.

4444₁

葬 〔**Jang**〕*v.* bury, entomb, inter a coffin.
28-- 儀　　　last honor.
35-- 禮　　　funeral, rites, burial service.
38-- 送　　　bury, ruin.
44-- 地　　　burial ground.
50-- 事　　　burial, funeral.

4444₅

莽 〔**Mang**〕*n.* jungle, undergrowth, *adj.* rough, rude, rustic, reckless.
32-- 叢　　　jungle.
34-- 漢　　　rough fellow, blunderer.
50-- 撞　　　rude, rustic, reckless, intrusive.

4444₇

妓 〔**Chi**〕*n.* prostitution, whore, harlot.
40-- 女　　　whore, prostitute.
73-- 院　　　house of ill repute.

4445₆

韓 〔**Han**〕*n.* Han (a family name), Korea.

4446₀

姑 〔**Ku**〕*n.* aunt, mother-in-law, sister-in-law, father's sister.
26-- 息　　　appease, temporize, indulge.
43-- 娘　　　miss, girl, maiden, young lady.
47-- 嫂　　　sister-in-law.
50-- 丈　　　uncle.

77-- 且　　　granting that.
-- 且不談　　put aside for the time being.
-- 母　　　aunt.
80-- 父　　　uncle.

茄 〔**Chieh**〕*n.* eggplant, tomato.
17-- 子　　　eggplant.

茹 〔**Ju**〕*n.* eat, feed.
20-- 毛飲血　　eat the raw meat and drink the blood, live the life of a savage.

4446₄

菇 〔**Ku**〕*n.* mushroom, fungus.

4446₅

嬉 〔**Hsi**〕*n.* pleasure, amusement, sport, *v.* play with, sport, enjoy oneself, have fun.
23-- 戲　　　fun, pleasure, amusement.
40-- 皮笑臉　　funny-skinned and laughing-faced, sportive.
44-- 嬉　　　cheery.

4449₃

蓀 〔**Sun**〕*n.* sweet herb.

4449₄

媒 〔**Mei**〕*n.* matchmaker, marriage, go-between.
80-- 人　　　matchmaker, female go-between of marriage, middleman.
-- 介　　　medium, agent.
-- 介物　　inter-medium, medium.

4450₂

攀 〔**Pan**〕*v.* clamber, climb up, seize, grasp.
12-- 登　　　climb, clamber up.
24-- 繞植物　　climber(plant).

摹 〔**Mo**〕*v.* imitate, pattern after.
20-- 仿　　　imitate.
50-- 本　　　counterpart.

摯 〔**Chih**〕*adj.* earnest, brave, fierce.
20-- 愛　　　devotion.
40-- 友　　　intimate friend.

4450₄

華 〔**Hua**〕*n.* China, flower, powder, *adj.* glory, flowery, elegant, bril-

		liant, bright, charming, beautiful.
00--	裔	foreign citizen of Chinese origin.
10--	爾滋舞	waltz.
11--	麗	splendid, grand, beautiful, gorgeous.
22--	僑	overseas Chinese.
--	僑商人	overseas Chinese merchant.
50--	表	carved pillar.
--	貴	honorable, spendid.
72--	氏寒暑表	Fahrenheit thermometer.
77--	屋	mansion.
80--	美	beautiful.

4450₆

革〔Ke〕*n.* hide, skin, leather, *v.* change, alter, dismiss, abolish, remove, get rid of.

02--	新	*n.* innovation, *v.* renovate.
--	新能力	ability to innovate.
--	新者	innovator.
13--	職	depose, divest of office, dismiss from office.
--	職留任	dismiss but retain in office.
20--	委會	revolutionary committee.
37--	退	dismiss.
78--	除	abolish, eliminate, get rid of.
80--	命	*n.* revolution, *v.* revolutionize.
--	命化	revolutionize.
--	命家	revolutionary.
--	命運動	the revolutionary movement.
--	命路線	revolutionary line.
--	命黨	revolutionary party.
--	命黨人	revolutionist.

葦〔Wei〕*n.* rush, reed.
葷〔Hun〕*n.* meat, leek, onion, garlic.

4451₀

靴〔Hsueh〕*n.* boots.

17--	子	boots.

4451₄

鞋〔Hsieh〕*n.* shoes, slipper, footwear.

00--	底	sole of a shoe.
--	店	shoe shop, shoe store.
10--	面	instep, vamp.
17--	子	shoes.
35--	油	shoe-polish.
40--	套	over-shoe.
44--	帶	shoelace, shoestring.
67--	跟	heel of a shoe.
71--	匠	shoemaker.

4452₇

勒〔Leh〕*n.* bridle, rein, *v.* restrain, stop bind, strangle, curb, cease.

10--	死	strangle, throttle.
30--	住	restrain, check.
31--	逼	force, compel, molest.
40--	索	extort, black mail, pinch, squeeze, screw out.
56--	捐	force to subscribe.
71--	馬	bridle a horse.
80--	令	order.

4453₀

芙〔Fu〕*n.* hibiscus flower.

44--	蓉	hibiscus.
--	蓉鳥	rice-bird.

英〔Ying〕*n.* flower, able man, blossom, *adj.* superior, eminent, brave, heroic, English, British.

00--	文	English.
01--	語	the English language.
07--	畝	acre.
13--	武	brave, heroic.
17--	勇	heroic, brave, courage.
23--	俊	handsome, graceful, showing the freshness of youth.
40--	才	genius.
--	雄	hero, knight.
--	雄主義	heroism.
--	雄形象	heroic model.
--	雄本色	true color of a hero.
--	雄氣概	heroic spirit.
53--	威	dignified, commanding.
60--	國	England.
--	國人	English, Englishman.
--	里	mile.
67--	明	wise, sagacious, clever.
80--	鎊	pound sterling.
--	氣	bravery.

4460₀

茵 〔**Yin**〕 *n.* mat.

者 〔**Che**〕 *pron.* this, that, it, which, one.

菌 〔**Chun**〕 *n.* mushroom, fungus, mold, mildew.

44--	苗	vaccine.
77--	肥	bacterial fertilizer.
91--	類	fungi.
--	類學	mycology.

苗 〔**Miao**〕 *n.* sprout, shoot.

00--	裔	posterity, descendant.
17--	子	Miaotzu (native tribes residing in southwest China).
27--	條	graceful.
60--	圃	nursery, seeding nursery.

茴 〔**Hui**〕 *n.* fennel, thyme.

20--	香	fennel.

4460₁

昔 〔**Hsi**〕 *adj.* old, ancient, previous, *adv.* formerly, before, of old, in the past.

44--	者	formerly.
60--	日	formerly, in former days, on a previous day, aforetime.

茜 〔**Chien**〕 *n.* madder.

菩 〔**Pu**〕 *n.* fragrant herb, the sacred tree of Buddhism.

44--	薩	Budhisattva.
--	薩心腸	kind-hearted.
56--	提樹	linden tree, bo-tree.

礬 〔**Fan**〕 *n.* alum.

10--	石	alum stone, aluminite.
40--	土	alumina.

耆 〔**Chi**〕 *adj.* old, aged, decrepit.

蘠 〔**Chiang**〕 *n.* roses, marsh, smartweed.

44--	薇	rose.
--	薇色	rose-color, rosy.

4460₂

莦 〔**Tiao**〕 *n.* a plant much used for making brooms.

44--	莦	high, far away.

4460₃

苔 〔**Tai**〕 *n.* moss, lichen, algae, fungi.

44--	蘚	moss.
--	菜	algae.

蓄 〔**Hsu**〕 *v.* collect, save, store up, rear, bring up, lay up in store.

00--	意	premeditate, harbor some ideas.
--	音器	phonograph.
04--	謀	keep on plotting, consider a plan in secret.
10--	電池	battery, cell.
12--	水池	water reservoir.
25--	積	*n.* savings, accumulation, *v.* accumulate, hoard.
35--	洪區	water detention basin.
72--	鬚	feeler.
80--	養	foster, raise, rear.

暮 〔**Mu**〕 *n.* evening, sunset, dusk, ending, later.

00--	夜	evening.
80--	年	in old age, closing years of one's life, last days of one's life.
--	氣	spiritless, apathetic airs.

4460₄

若 〔**Jo**〕 *pron.* you, your, *v.* suppose, provided that, like, *adj.* comparable to, similiar to.

10--	干	some, how much? how many?
21--	何	how? what now?
41--	狂	*n.* frenzy *adj.* frantic.
60--	是	if, supposing.
67--	明若暗	ambiguous, unclear.

苦 〔**Ku**〕 *v.* dread, feel miserable about, toil, *adj.* bitter, painful, troublesome, unpleasant, pressing, urgent, hardship.

00--	痛	pain, suffering.
10--	工	hard labor, drudgery.
12--	刑	torture, severe punishment.
14--	功夫	pain, hard work.
21--	行	penance.
27--	役	hard labor, drudgery, slave labor.
33--	心	*v.* take pain, *adj.* painstak-

		ing.
	-- 心經營	elaboration.
40--	力	coolie.
	-- 志	miserable resolution.
	-- 難	misery, hardship.
44--	楚	*n.* distress, torture, *adj.* bitter, painful.
	-- 勸	press one hard.
48--	幹	painstaking, work hard.
	-- 幹者	painstaker.
60--	思	think hard, rack one's brain.
63--	戰	fight desperately, hard fighting, bitter struggle, fight one's back to the wall.
65--	味	bitterness, bitter taste.
72--	瓜	bitter melon, bitter gourd.
77--	膽	gall.
	-- 悶	be depressed, low-spirited.
	-- 學	study hard, plod at one's book.
80--	命	hard life, heavy fate.
	-- 著面	wear a troubled look.
88--	笑	forced smile.
92--	惱	trouble, annoyance, distress.

著 〔Chu〕 *v.* write, compose, edit, wear, make manifest, set forth, *adj.* clear, bright, conspicuous, obvious.

20--	手計劃	set a project afoot.
	-- 手進行	set out one's task.
27--	名	famous, reputed, marked, outstanding, illustrious, distinguished, great, well-known.
	-- 名人士	notables, celebrities.
28--	作	*n.* writing, work, *v.* write, compose.
	-- 作家	writer, author.
	-- 作權	copyright.
	-- 作人	author.
	-- 作物	literary works.
	-- 作等身	author with many works to his credit.
33--	述	write, edit.
44--	者	author, writer.
50--	書	write books.

薯 〔Shu〕 *n.* potato, Chinese yam.

瞽 〔Ku〕 *adj.* blind.

80--	人	blind man.
	-- 人院	asylum for the blind.

4460₇

茗 〔Ming〕 *n.* tea.

蒼 〔Tsang〕 *adj.* grey, deep-green, azure, hoary.

10--	天	blue sky, roof of the heaven, azure sky.
26--	白	pale, grey.
44--	老	old, hoary and old.
57--	蠅	fly.

4460₈

蓉 〔Jung〕 *n.* hibiscus.

4460₉

蕃 〔Fan〕 *v.* increase, multiply, breed, *adj.* luxuriant, flourishing, numerous, plentiful.

14--	殖	breed, multiply, propagate.
44--	茂	flourishing, luxuriant.
53--	盛	abundant, plentiful.

4461₇

葩 〔Pa〕 *n.* flower.

4462₁

苛 〔Ko〕 *v.* disturb, annoy, reprove. *adj.* severe, harsh, vexatious, petty, small.

00--	疾	dangerous illness.
	-- 癢	itch.
01--	評	hyper-criticism.
02--	刻	*v.* oppress grievously, bully, domineer, be hard upon, *adj.* severe, harsh, caustic.
	-- 刻條件	harsh condition (term), exacting terms.
18--	政	harsh government, oppressive government.
24--	待	treat unkindly, be hard upon.
43--	求	*n.* extortion, *v.* extort, put one in the screws, be too exacting.
50--	責	chide, denounce strongly.
56--	捐雜稅	extortive levies and mis-

cellaneus taxes.

60-- 暴　　　　violent.

95-- 性　　　　caustic (in chemistry).

4462_7

苟 〔Kou〕 adv. roughly, carelessly, conj. if, if only.

12-- 延　　　　prolong temporarily.

30-- 安　　　　be secure only for the time being, live with a false sense of security.

77-- 且　　　　careless, remiss, rude, rash.

-- 且了事　　　do a thing carelessly.

80-- 合　　　　illicit sexual intercourse.

荀 〔Hsun〕 n. Hsun (a family name).

萌 〔Meng〕 n. bud, sprout, shoot, germ, v. bud, germinate, shoot forth.

44-- 芽　　　　sprout, bud.

-- 芽時期　　　initial period.

葫 〔Hu〕 n. garlic, bottle-gourd.

44-- 蘆　　　　gourd, bottle-gourd, calabash.

蔔 〔Po〕 n. a kind of edible root.

藹 〔Ai〕 adj. luxuriant, flourishing, abundant, pleasing, agreeable.

4464_1

蒔 〔Shih〕 v. transplant, plant.

25-- 秧　　　　transplant, rice seeding.

4470_0

斟 〔Chen〕 v. pour into a cup, consider, deliberate.

17-- 酌　　　　n. consideration, v. consider, deliberate.

4471_0

芒 〔Mang〕 n. the sharp point of grass.

44-- 鞋　　　　sandals.

52-- 刺　　　　pricks, prickles.

60-- 果　　　　mango.

4471_1

老 〔Lau〕 v. respect, adj. old, aged, skilled, expert, experienced, ancient, venerable, worn-out, long time, adv. always, very, extremely.

00-- 主顧　　　regular customer.

02-- 話　　　　adage.

10-- 一輩　　　the old generation.

-- 一套　　　an old practice, the same old thing.

-- 百姓　　　people, the masses.

11-- 頭子　　　old man, old cock.

17-- 子　　　　father, Laotze.

-- 弱　　　　old and weak, senile.

20-- 手　　　　old hand, adept.

21-- 虎　　　　tiger.

-- 虎窗　　　dormer window.

-- 虎鉗　　　vices, vises.

-- 處女　　　old maid, spinster.

-- 師　　　　teacher.

-- 師傅　　　master worker.

23-- 傭農　　　old farmhand.

25-- 練　　　　skillful, experienced, seasoned, good hand at.

27-- 鴇　　　　procurer.

30-- 家　　　　native home.

-- 字號　　　firm of long standing.

-- 實　　　　honest, frank.

-- 實說　　　frankly speaking, tell the truth.

-- 實人　　　honest person.

34-- 邁　　　　n. senility, adj. aged, decrepit.

-- 婆　　　　wife.

40-- 大娘　　　grannie, granny.

-- 大爺　　　grandpa, uncle.

-- 友　　　　old friend, intimate.

43-- 式　　　　old fashion, old style.

44-- 花眼　　　presbyopia.

47-- 婦　　　　dame, old woman.

48-- 樣　　　　old fashion, same as before.

50-- 本　　　　original capital, principal.

53-- 成　　　　experienced.

55-- 農　　　　veteran peasant.

67-- 路　　　　beaten track.

-- 鴉　　　　crow.

72-- 兵　　　　veteran, campaigner.

77-- 闆　　　　boss.

-- 鼠　　　　rat, mouse.

80-- 人　　　　old man, aged person.

-- 人院　　　asylum for old man.

-- 爺　　　　lord.

-- 年　　　　old age, grey hair, evening of life, advancing age.

-- 年福利金	old age benefit.	
90-- 少	old and young.	
-- 光眼鏡	convex glasses.	

甚〔Shen〕*adj.* very, extremely, excessively, too.

00-- 麼	what.
10-- 至	even that.
27-- 多	a great deal, of very much.
-- 急	much excited.
34-- 遠	very far.
40-- 大	very large, very big.
47-- 好	very good, all right.
90-- 少	very few.

4471₂

也〔Yeh〕*adv.* also, too, besides, still, likewise, *conj.* as well as, and.

08-- 許	perhaps, probably, possibly, may be.
10-- 可	it may be done.
-- 可以去	you may also go.
-- 不	nor, neither.
-- 不一定	still it is not certain.
21-- 行	it may be done.
40-- 有此人	still there is such a man.
47-- 好	that will also do.
80-- 曾	already.
-- 曾試過	once he has tried it.

苞〔Pao〕*n.* bud, bract, *v.* wrap.

巷〔Hsiang〕*n.* alley, lane, street.

60-- 口	entrance to a lane.
63-- 戰	street fighting, street combat.

4471₆

菴〔An〕*n.* abbey, small temple.

4471₇

世〔Shih〕*n.* generation, world, age, period.

00-- 交	friendship of many generations.
01-- 襲	hereditary.
20-- 系	genealogy, pedigree.
21-- 上	world, in the world.
23-- 代	generation, age.
-- 代交替	alternation of generations.

-- 代相傳	hand down generation after generation.
-- 代書香	family of scholars for generations.
-- 外桃源	a peach orchard beyond this world (an ideal or idyllic place).
27-- 紀	century.
28-- 俗	secular.
38-- 道	worldliness, ways of the world.
48-- 故	sophisticated.
50-- 事	worldly concerns, worldly affairs.
60-- 界	world, earth.
-- 界主義	cosmopolitanism.
-- 界語	Esperanto.
-- 界和平	world peace.
-- 界經濟	world economy.
-- 界紀錄	world record.
-- 界潮流	tide of the world.
-- 界大勢	world situation.
-- 界大戰	world war.
-- 界大同	world of universal harmony.
-- 界觀	outlook on the world.
-- 界博覽會	international exhibition.
-- 界末日	doomsday, the last day, end of the world, the day of the last Judgement.
-- 界聞名	world-famous, world famed.
-- 界人	cosmopolitan.
-- 界範圍	worldwide.
77-- 風日下	the moral degeneration of the world is worse day by day.
-- 間	worldly, universal, under the sun.
80-- 人	mankind.
-- 無其匹	one's equal is not found on earth.
95-- 情	customs of the world.

芭〔Pa〕*n.* fragrant plant.

44-- 蕉	banana, plantain.
-- 蕉扇	palm-leaf fan.
-- 蕾舞	ballet.

4472₂

鬱〔Yu〕 v. hate, be depressed, adj. vexed, harassed, rooten, irritaed.
77-- 悶　depressed, gloomy.
80-- 金香　tulip.
4472₇
劫〔Chieh〕 n. robbery, plunder, v. rob, plunder.
22-- 後餘生　life after surviving a disaster.
37-- 盜　robber, knight of the road.
-- 奪　rob, take by force.
-- 奪者　bandits.
50-- 掠　rob, plunder, pillage.
54-- 持　seize, abduct, hold under duress.
萄〔Tao〕 n. grape.
葛〔Ko〕 n. hemp, creeper.
44-- 藤　creeper, complication.
勘〔Kan〕 v. compare, examine, try, collate.
06-- 誤表　corrigenda, errata.
30-- 究　examine.
-- 定界址　investigate and fix the boundary.
32-- 測　survey, reconnaissance.
34-- 對　compare, collate.
40-- 查　exmine.
-- 校　collate, correct errors.
57-- 探　prospect, explore.
4473₁
芸〔Yun〕 n. fragrant plant, v. weed.
20-- 香　rue.
藝〔I〕 n. art, craft, skill, ability, trade, bussiness, profession, adj. skillful, expert, cunning.
21-- 術　art, artistic.
-- 術設計　art layout.
-- 術片　feature film, story film.
-- 術家　artist.
-- 術標準　criterion of art.
-- 術品　work of art.
-- 術學校　art school.
-- 術性　artistry, artistic quality.
40-- 才　artistic genius, artistic talent.

80-- 人　performing artist.
4474₁
薛〔Hsueh〕 n. Hsueh (a family name).
4477₀
廿〔Nien〕 adj. twenty, score.
甘〔Kan〕 adj. sweet, delicious, pleasant, willing, voluntary.
00-- 言　sweet words.
10-- 霖　seasonable rain.
11-- 露　honeydew.
21-- 受　take up with.
24-- 休　be willing to let it go.
26-- 泉　fresh spring.
33-- 心　willing, pleased, be reconciled.
35-- 油　glycerin.
44-- 蔗　sugarcane.
-- 草　liquorice.
-- 薯　sweet potato.
-- 苦　sweet and bitter, prosperity and adversity.
50-- 肅　Kansu province.
71-- 願　be willing to.
80-- 美　delicious, luscious.
4477₂
茁〔Cho〕 adj. budding, growing, sprouting.
24-- 壯　sturdy, showing vigorous growth.
4477₇
舊〔Chiu〕 adj. old, past, ancient, secondhand, long-standing, former.
00-- 病復發　have a relapse.
-- 文化　old culture.
-- 衣服　old clothes.
17-- 習慣　old habits.
22-- 例　usage, practice.
-- 制度　ancient institution.
24-- 貨　secondhand goods, junk.
-- 貨店　junk shop (store), secondhand store.
-- 貨市場　junk market, rag fair, second-hand market.
27-- 的　ancient, old.
-- 約聖經　Old Testament.
30-- 家具　old furniture.

34-- 社會	old society.
43-- 式	old-fashioned, old style.
50-- 書	secondhand book.
60-- 跡	ruin.
-- 思想	old ideas.
71-- 曆	old calendar, lunar calender.
77-- 風俗	old custom.
-- 聞	old story.
-- 學校	old school or college.
80-- 年	last year.
-- 金山	San Francisco.

4480₁

共 〔**Kung**〕 *v.* share, partake, *adv.* all, altogether, whole, wholly, fully.

00-- 產主義	communism.
-- 產國際	the Communist International, Comintern.
-- 產黨	communist party.
-- 襄盛舉	cooperate for a great project.
-- 享	partake of enjoyment.
-- 享富貴	enjoy wealth and honor together.
03-- 識	consensus.
04-- 計	total, sum, in all, add up to, amount to.
-- 謀	conspire, lay heads together.
21-- 處	co-existence.
26-- 和	commonwealth, republic.
-- 和主義	republicanism.
-- 和國	republic, commonwealth.
-- 和黨	republican party.
-- 和黨員	republican.
26-- 總	altogether.
30-- 濟	co-action, co-operation.
-- 濟會	free masonry.
-- 寢	sleep together, share the bed.
32-- 通	reciprocal.
40-- 有	common ownership.
-- 有物	common property.
-- 有權	common right.
-- 有人	co-owner.
-- 存	co-existence.
43-- 赴國難	play the citizen's part together when the nation calls.
44-- 甘苦	share joys and sorrows.

45-- 棲	symbiosis.
47-- 犯	co-operation, accomplice.
50-- 事	work together, co-work.
-- 青團	the Communist Youth League.
-- 患難	go through hardships and tribulation together.
67-- 鳴	echo, share feeling, resonance.
74-- 助會	friendly society.
77-- 同	mutual, public, common, together, in common.
-- 同語言	common language.
-- 同市場	common market.
-- 同出資	joint contribution.
-- 同債務人	co-debtor.
-- 同保證	joint guaranty.
-- 同保險	coinsurance.
-- 同保險人	coinsurer.
-- 同資本	joint capital.
-- 同基金	common fund, mutual fund.
-- 同責任	solidarity.
-- 同投資	joint investment.
-- 同財產	common property, joint property.
-- 同管理	co-management.
-- 同被告	co-defendant.
-- 同點	common point, common ground.
80-- 命運	share the same lot.
95-- 性	general character.

其 〔**Chi**〕 *pron.* he, she, it, they, *adj.* this, that.

22-- 後	afterwards, hereafter, ever since.
-- 樂無窮	the joy is boundless.
24-- 他	other, another, every other, the rest.
30-- 實	in fact, indeed, truly, really, as a matter of fact.
37-- 次	next, more over.
50-- 中	therein, among, in the midst of.
-- 中之一	one of them.
80-- 人其事	the man and his deeds.
88-- 餘	the rest, for the rest, over and above.

95-- 情可憫　deserving sympathetic understanding.

楚〔Chu〕 *adj.* sharp, keen, painful, suffering, clear, distinct.

躉〔Tun〕 *n.* a whole number, a whole amount, whole sale.

24-- 貨　buy up goods.

27-- 船　hulk, pontoon, receiving ship.

40-- 賣　wholesale.

4480₆

黃〔Huang〕 *adj.* yellow.

00-- 疸病　jaundice.

-- 麻　jute.

10-- 豆　soybean.

22-- 種　yellow race.

27-- 色　yellow.

-- 色書　obscene books.

-- 魚　yellow croaker.

28-- 鱔　eel.

31-- 河　Yellow River.

-- 酒　yellow rice wine.

35-- 油　butter.

-- 連　Coptis Japonica.

38-- 海　Yellow Sea.

40-- 土　yellow soil, loess.

44-- 芽菜　Chinese cabbage, celery cabbage.

46-- 楊木　boxwood.

-- 楊樹　box tree.

57-- 蜂　wasp, hornet.

72-- 瓜　cucumber.

-- 昏　evening, twilight, dusk.

77-- 鼠狼　weasel.

80-- 金　gold.

-- 金市場　gold market.

-- 金證券　gold security (certificate).

-- 金價格　gold price.

-- 金債券　gold bonds (debenture).

-- 金官價　official gold price.

-- 金準備　gold reserves.

-- 金時代　golden age.

87-- 銅　brass.

99-- 鶯　oriole.

贄〔Chih〕 *n.* ceremonial present.

60-- 見　visit with a present.

4480₉

焚〔Fen〕 *v.* burn, fire, set on fire.

20-- 香　light incense.

77-- 毀　burn down, destroy by fire.

94-- 燒　burn fire, set fire.

-- 燒裝置　incinerator.

98-- 斃　be burned to death.

4490₀

村〔Tsun〕 *n.* village, hamlet.

17-- 子　village.

34-- 社牧場　common pasture.

44-- 落經濟　community economy.

-- 莊　hamlet, village.

47-- 婦　country woman.

50-- 夫　villager, countryman.

77-- 民　villager.

材〔Tsai〕 *n.* material, timber, wood, capacity.

21-- 能　capacity, ability.

40-- 木　timber, lumber.

94-- 料　material, stuff.

-- 料庫　material depot.

-- 料盤存　material inventory.

-- 料供應　material supplies.

-- 料清單　bill of material.

-- 料運輸　transportation of materials.

-- 料標準　material standard.

-- 料採購　material purchase.

-- 料規格　material specification.

-- 料庫　bill of material, material list.

-- 料分配　material allocation (allotment).

-- 料短缺　material shortage.

樹〔Shu〕 *n.* tree, plant, *v.* plant, erect, set up.

00-- 立　setup, erect, build up.

32-- 叢　bush, grove.

33-- 心　pitch.

40-- 皮　cortex, bark.

-- 雄心　have lofty ambition.

-- 木　tree.

-- 木參天　old trees that reach to the skies.

-- 木榜樣　set an example.

44-- 蔭　shade of a tree.

-- 苗	sapling.
-- 枝	branch, twig, bough.
-- 林	forest, woods.
-- 葉	leaf.
-- 杈	fork of a tree.
47-- 根	root.
49-- 幹	trunk, stock.
49-- 梢	topmost twig, tip of a tree, tree top.
77-- 膠	gum, resin.
80-- 人樹木	educate people and to plant trees.

4490₁

禁 〔Chin〕 n. prohibition, restriction, custody, detain, v. forbid, prohibit, prevent, imprison.

00-- 卒	jailer.
17-- 忌	ban, taboo.
20-- 航地區	prohibited area.
21-- 止	prohibit, forbid, prevent, forbear, stop.
-- 止設攤	no peddler.
-- 止停車	no parking.
-- 止倒垃圾	do not leave garbage here.
-- 止出口	lay an embargo, ban on export.
-- 止物	contraband.
-- 止進口	import embargo, prohibited importations.
-- 止招貼	post no bill!
-- 止輸出	embargo.
-- 止吸煙	no smoking!
-- 止入內	no entrance.
-- 止令	restraining order.
-- 衛	guardsman.
22-- 制	restrain, restrict, limit.
-- 制品	restricted cargo.
31-- 酒	abstinence from wine.
-- 酒令	prohibition of wine, dry law.
37-- 運	embargo.
-- 運品	prohibited goods (articles).
42-- 獵地	game preserve.
44-- 地	forbidden place.
53-- 戒	keep from, abstain.
64-- 賭	prohibit gambling.

67-- 鳴喇叭	no honking.
71-- 區	forbidden zone, restricted zone (area).
77-- 閉	confine, detain.
80-- 令	prohibition, injunction.
-- 食	fast, fasting.
86-- 錮	imprisonment.
91-- 煙	opium suppression, ban on smoking, smoking ban.

蔡 〔Tsai〕 n. Tsai (a family name).

4490₃

綦 〔Chi〕 n. shoe lace, ties.

4490₄

茶 〔Cha〕 n. tea.

00-- 商	tea dealer, tea merchant.
-- 廠	tea processing factory.
02-- 話會	tea party.
13-- 碗	tea cup.
14-- 碟	tea plate.
15-- 磚	brick tea, compressed tea.
27-- 盤	tea tray.
30-- 房	servant.
40-- 壺	tea-pot.
41-- 杯	tea cup.
44-- 花	camellia.
-- 樹	tea tree.
-- 葉	tea leaves.
-- 材	tea grove.
50-- 末	tea dust.
60-- 園	tea garden.
61-- 匙	tea spoon, teaspoon.
-- 點	refreshment.
-- 點室	refectory.
77-- 几	teapoy.
80-- 舞	tea dance.
-- 會	tea party.
81-- 缸	tea urn.
83-- 錢	tips.
-- 館	tea house, teahouse.

菜 〔Tsai〕 n. vegetable, food, greens, edible plants.

17-- 刀	chopper, kitchen knife.
-- 子	rape.
27-- 色	sickly color.
35-- 油	cabbage oil, rapeseed oil.
44-- 蔬	vegetable, greens.

46--	場	market.
50--	攤	green stall, vegetable stall.
60--	園	vegetable garden, kitchen garden.
66--	單	bill of fare, menu.
83--	館	restaurant.
97--	籽	rapeseed.

某〔**Mou**〕*pron.* certain person, *adj.* certain.

21--	些	some, certain.
--	處	certain place, somewhere.
27--	物	something, certain thing.
44--	某	so-and-so.
60--	日	certain day, someday, one day.
77--	月	certain month.
80--	人	certain person, someone.
--	年	certain year.

茉〔**Mo**〕*n.* jasmine.

44--	莉	jasmine.

茱〔**Chu**〕*n.* dogwood.

菓〔**Kuo**〕*n.* fruits.

22--	醬	jam.
30--	實	fruit.
34--	汁	fruit juice.
44--	樹	fruit tree.
60--	園	orchard.

蓁〔**Chen**〕*adj.* exuberant, luxuriant.

葉〔**Yeh**〕*n.* leaf, page, foliage, sheet.

17--	子	leaf.
--	子板	mudguard.
27--	綠素	chlorophyll.
41--	柄	leaf stalk.
77--	脈	the vein of a leaf.

藁〔**Kao**〕*n.* straw, stalk.

藥〔**Yao**〕*n.* medicine, recipe, drug, remedy.

00--	方	formula, prescription, recipe.
--	商	druggist.
--	膏	ointment.
--	店	pharmacy.
02--	劑	dose, medicine.
--	劑師	chemist, druggist, pharmacist.
08--	效	virtue of a drug.
12--	水	liquid medicine.
22--	片	tablet.
26--	皂	medicated soap.
27--	物	medicine, drug.
--	物學	pharmacology.
30--	房	dispensary, drugstore, pharmacy.
31--	酒	tincture, medicated wine.
40--	丸	pill, pilule.
44--	材	drug, doctor's stuff, medicinal materials.
55--	費	cost of medicine.
65--	味	taste of medicine.
81--	瓶	medicine bottle, phial.
95--	性	nature of a drug.
98--	粉	powder, medical powder.

4490₈

萊〔**Lai**〕*n.* fallow field, wild weeds, *adj.* grassy.

44--	菔	radish, turnip.

4491₀

杜〔**Tu**〕*v.* stop, restrict, shut out, plug, keep off, fabricate.

27--	絕	eliminate, cut off.
57--	撰	fabricate, invent.
67--	鵑	cuckoo.
--	鵑花	red azalea.

4491₁

椹〔**Shen**〕*n.* mulberry.

橈〔**Jao**〕*n.* oar, *v.* disperse, break. *adj.* crooked, distorted.

4491₂

枕〔**Chen**〕*n.* pillow, *v.* pillow, rest on.

11--	頭	pillow.
40--	套	pillow-slip, pillow-case.
--	木	railway sleeper, wooden sleeper, tie.

4491₄

桂〔**Kuei**〕*n.* cassia tree, laurel.

37--	冠	laurel wreath.
40--	皮	cassia bark.
44--	花	cassia flower, sweet osmanthus.
--	樹	laurel tree.

60-- 圓　　　　　dried longan.

榷〔Chueh〕*n.* plank over a stream, tax, government monopoly.

欙〔Tai〕*n.* table.
46-- 架　　　　　stage.
92-- 燈　　　　　table lamp.

蘿〔Lo〕*n.* creeping plant, radish, turnip.
44-- 蔔　　　　　turnip, radish.
48-- 蔔乾　　　　dried turnip, dried radish.

權〔Chuan〕*n.* power, authority, control, weight, scheme, expediency, *v.* weight, balance.
04-- 謀　　　　　scheme, stratagem.
21-- 能分開　　　the division of people's right and the powers of the government.
-- 衡　　　　　weight, measure, balance.
22-- 變　　　　　ready wit.
-- 利　　　　　right.
-- 利人　　　　obligee.
-- 變　　　　　versatile.
30-- 宜　　　　　temporary.
-- 宜之計　　　makeshift, measure of expediency.
40-- 力　　　　　power, authority, might.
44-- 勢　　　　　power, authority, influence.
50-- 貴之人　　　man of power and nobility.
53-- 威　　　　　authority.
-- 威人士　　　authority, authoritative person.
77-- 限　　　　　the limit of power.
-- 限不清　　　the limitation of authority is not distinct.

4491₆
楂〔Cha〕*n.* hawthorn.

4491₇
植〔Chih〕*n.* plant, vegetation, *v.* plant, set out, set up.
27-- 物　　　　　plant, vegetable, flora.
-- 物纖維　　　plant fibers.
-- 物保護　　　plant protection.
-- 物油　　　　vegetable oil.
-- 物黃油　　　margarine.
-- 物園　　　　botanical garden.

-- 物學　　　　botany, botanical.
-- 物學家　　　botanist.
40-- 皮　　　　　skin transplantation.
44-- 樹　　　　　plant trees, afforest.
-- 樹節　　　　Arbor Day — March 12.

蘊〔Yun〕*v.* collect, accumulate, heap, store up, hoard, *adj.* mysterious, secret.
44-- 藏　　　　　deposit.
-- 蓄　　　　　collect, accumulate.

4492₀
莉〔Li〕*n.* jasmine.

4492₁
椅〔I〕*n.* chair, couch, seat.
11-- 背　　　　　back of a chair.
17-- 子　　　　　chair.
40-- 套　　　　　tidy.
44-- 墊　　　　　cushion.

薪〔Hsin〕*n.* fuel, firewood, salary, pay.
10-- 工　　　　　wage.
12-- 水　　　　　salary, earning, pay, wage.
-- 水支票　　　paycheck.
25-- 俸　　　　　salary.
-- 俸稅　　　　salaries tax.
80-- 金支出　　　salaries expenses.

4492₇
菊〔Chu〕*n.* chrysanthemum.

葯=**藥**

橢〔To〕*adj.* elliptic, oval.
60-- 圓　　　　　ovalform, elliptic.
-- 圓形　　　　ellipse, oval.
-- 圓畫規　　　pair of elliptical compasses.

藕〔Ou〕*n.* lotus root.
98-- 粉　　　　　arrowroot powder, lotus-root powder.

4493₂
檬〔Meng〕*n.* lemon.

4493₄
模〔Mo〕*n.* mold, pattern, model, example, mould, form.
12-- 型　　　　　form, model.
-- 型地圖　　　relief map.
17-- 子　　　　　mould, form.
20-- 仿　　　　　imitate, ape, mimic.

24--	特兒	model.
34--	造	reproduce, imitate.
48--	樣	look, appearance, form, shape, style.
88--	範	standard, model, sample, example, pattern.
--	範軍	model army.
97--	糊	obscure, indistinct, dim, vague.
--	糊不清	blurred and indistinct.

4494₇

枝〔**Chi**〕*n.* branch, twig, bough, stick, limb.

44--	葉	branches and leaves.
48--	幹	trunk and branches.
67--	路	branch road.
88--	節叢生	branches and knots grow.
--	節問題	side issue, minor problem.

棱〔**Leng**〕*n.* corner, angle, angular.

4495₄

樺〔**Hua**〕*n.* birch.

4496₀

枯〔**Ku**〕*n.* rotten wood, dead tree, *adj.* rotten, putrid, decayed, dried up, withered, arid.

06--	竭	exhaust, drain.
41--	朽	rotten, putrid.
44--	萎	decay, wither.
--	草	rotten grass, withered grass.
--	樹	dead tree, rotten wood.
--	枝	dead branch.
55--	井	dried-up well.
77--	骨	old dried bones.
96--	燥	insipid, dry.
--	燥無味	as dry as a chip.

櫧〔**Chu**〕*n.* acorn.

4496₁

桔〔**Chieh**〕*n.* orange.

88--	餅	dried orange flattened like a cake.

梏〔**Ku**〕*n.* manacles, handcuff.

藉〔**Chieh**〕*n.* mat, cushion, pad, *v.* avail of, rely on, lean on.

21--	此	hereby, by means of this.
48--	故	avail oneself of an excuse.

60--	口	pretend, make a pretext.

4497₀

柑〔**Kan**〕*n.* mandarin, orange.

4498₁

棋〔**Chi**〕*n.* chess.

17--	子	chess.
20--	手	chess-player.
27--	盤	chessboard.
37--	逢敵手	good match, diamond cut diamond.

4498₆

橫〔**Heng**〕*v.* cross, go athwart, lie on, *adj.* crosswise, athwart, transverse.

10--	死	fatality, violent death.
17--	了心	become casehardened.
21--	徵暴斂	abuse of taxation.
--	行	walk sideways.
--	行霸道	lawlessness, ride roughshod over.
--	行不法	act illegally.
--	行無忌	act outrageously without scruple.
--	衝直撞	reckless, reckless action.
22--	蠻	brute.
--	斷	intersect.
--	斷面	cross-section.
25--	生支節	come upon unexpected difficulties.
--	生事端	incur unexpected trouble.
26--	線	cross-line, horizontal line.
27--	條	cross bar.
30--	度	cross (a river).
--	寫	write sideways .
33--	濱	Yokohama.
--	禍	accident.
--	禍飛來	coming of an unexpected calamity.
37--	過	cross, thwart.
41--	幅標語	banner, streamer.
43--	越	go across, go from side to side.
--	越大西洋班輪	transatlantic liner.
46--	加干預	thrust one's nose into other people affairs.
47--	樑	beams.

60-- 目	squint.
-- 暴	perverse and violent, un-reasonable and brutal.
64-- 財	windfall of wealth, unex-pected gain.
-- 財大	making a gross unexpected profit.
77-- 隔膜	diaphragm.
-- 豎	anyway, anyhow.
-- 貫	transversal, cross over.
78-- 隊	line formation.
88-- 笛	flute.

4499₀

林 〔Lin〕 n. forest, wood, grove.

00-- 立	numerous.
-- 產品	forest product.
32-- 業	forestry.
40-- 木	forest, woods.
44-- 蔭路	avenue.
71-- 區	forested area, forest region.
77-- 學	forestry.
-- 學院	forestry institute.

4499₁

蒜 〔Suan〕 n. garlic.

| 00-- 瓣 | quarters of garlic head. |
| 11-- 頭 | garlic bulb, garlic head. |

4510₆

坤 〔Kun〕 n. earth.

| 27-- 角 | actress. |

4522₇

狒 〔Fei〕 n. baboon.

猜 〔Tsai〕 v. guess, suspect, doubt, conjecture, surmise, adj. suspicious, cruel.

00-- 度	guess, surmise.
09-- 謎	guess a riddle.
17-- 忌	n. jealousy, adj. jealous.
27-- 疑	mistrust, suspect, doubt, suspicion.
32-- 測	guess, speculate.
46-- 想	imagine, surmise, presume, conjecture.
50-- 中	guess right.
90-- 拳	guess at fingers, rock, pa-per, scissors.

4541₀

姓 〔Hsing〕 n. name, family name, sur-name.

20-- 名	full name.
-- 名不祥	both the surname and the given name are unknown.
44-- 什麼	What is your name？

4542₇

姊 〔Chieh〕 n. sister, older sister, elder sister.

45-- 妹	sister.
-- 妹之情	the affection between sis-ters.
-- 妹公司	sister company.
50-- 夫	brother-in-law, husband of one's elder sister.

娉 〔Ping〕 adj. elegant, graceful.

4543₂

婊 〔Piao〕 n. prostitute.

姨 〔I〕 n. aunt, mother's sister, sister-in-law, wife's sister, concubine.

17-- 子	wife's sister.
41-- 媽	aunt, mother's sister.
50-- 丈	uncle.
77-- 母	aunt.
80-- 父	uncle, husband of one's ma-ternal aunt.

4544₇

媾 〔Kou〕 v. wed, marry, negotiate peace.

00-- 交	sexual intercourse.
26-- 和	make peace.
80-- 合	sexual intercourse.

4549₀

妹 〔Mei〕 n. younger sister.

| 50-- 夫 | brother-in-law, younger sis-ter's husband. |

姝 〔Shu〕 n. beautiful woman.

4553₀

鞅 〔Yang〕 n. martingale.

| 90-- 掌 | busy. |

4590₀

杖 〔Chang〕 n. stick, staff, cane, crutch, bamboo, v. beat, lean on, rely on, presume on.

4593_2

棣 〔**Ti**〕 *n*. wild plum tree, brother.

隸 〔**Li**〕 *n*. servant, slave, subordinate, *adj*. attached to, joined to, inferior, secondary.

77-- 屬　　belong to, attached to.

4594_4

棲 〔**Chi**〕 *v*. roost, perch, stay, sojourn, settle down.

21-- 止　　stop at.
27-- 身之所　　shelter.

樓 〔**Lou**〕 *n*. story, tower, floor, building of two or more stories.

00-- 座　　balcony, gallery.
10-- 下　　downstairs.
21-- 上　　upstairs.
30-- 房　　building with upper story.
40-- 臺　　tower.
48-- 梯　　staircase, stairway.
77-- 閣　　terrace.

4594_7

構 〔**Kou**〕 *v*. construct, build, plot, compose.

25-- 件　　member, element.
34-- 造　　*n*. construction, structure, frame, *v*. construct, build.
37-- 禍　　bring calamity.
　-- 禍自己　　bring disaster upon oneself.
53-- 成　　constitute, construct.
60-- 思　　meditate, design.
77-- 陷忠良　　implicate the loyal and good.

4595_3

棒 〔**Pang**〕 *n*. club, staff, stick.

13-- 球　　baseball, cricket.
32-- 冰　　ice sucker.
51-- 打　　cudgel.

4596_0

柚 〔**Yu**〕 *n*. grapefruit, pomelo, teak.

17-- 子　　pomelo, grapefruit.
40-- 木　　teak.

4596_3

椿 〔**Chun**〕 *n*. long-lived tree.

4596_6

槽 〔**Tsao**〕 *n*. trough, channel, fissure, groove, trench, ditch, furrow.

41-- 櫪　　stable.

4597_7

椿 〔**Chuang**〕 *n*. pile, post, stake.

17-- 子　　pile, stake.

4599_0

株 〔**Chu**〕 *n*. pole, trunk of trees.

00-- 主　　shareholder, stockholder.
43-- 式　　share, stock.
80-- 金　　share capital.
90-- 券　　share-certificate.

4599_4

榛 〔**Chen**〕 *n*. hazel, filbert.

17-- 子　　hazelnut, filbert.

4599_6

棟 〔**Tung**〕 *n*. beam, pillar.

30-- 宇　　mansion.
47-- 樑　　beam, main beam, ridge-pole.
　-- 樑之才　　man of tremendous promise.

4600_0

加 〔**Chia**〕 *n*. addition, enlargement, *v*. add to, increase, advance, promote, plus, *adj*. extra, additional.

00-- 高　　raise, heighten.
10-- 工　　extra work, processing.
　-- 工交易　　processing deal.
　-- 工工業　　process industry.
　-- 工能力　　process capacity.
　-- 工出口　　export processing.
　-- 工材料　　worked materials.
　-- 工技術　　processing technology.
　-- 工費用　　processing charges (fee), processed commodities.
　-- 工品　　finished goods, processed commodities.
　-- 工區　　manufacturing district.
　-- 工貿易　　processing trade.
11-- 班　　overtime work, extra work.
　-- 班工時　　overtime work hours, overtime hours.
　-- 班工作　　overtime work.
　-- 班工資　　overtime pay (wage).

-- 班津貼	overtime allowance (premium).	
-- 班費	overtime pay.	
12-- 強	strengthen, condense, reinforce.	
-- 刑	inflict punishment.	
20-- 倍	double.	
-- 倍小心	be twice as careful.	
21-- 上	plus, in addition to, besides.	
-- 征稅	tax for default.	
-- 價	advance in price.	
-- 銜	entitle.	
22-- 劇	aggravate.	
26-- 保	additional insurance.	
-- 保費	additional premium.	
-- 息	add-on interest.	
27-- 獎	award prize.	
-- 急電	urgent telegram.	
28-- 侖	gallon.	
-- 以	in addition to.	
32-- 添	increase.	
34-- 法	addition.	
35-- 油	oil, refuel, lubricate, cheer.	
-- 油站	filling station.	
-- 速	n. acceleration. v. accelerate, hasten, quicken.	
-- 速度	acceleration.	
-- 速發展	accelerated development.	
-- 速生產	speed up production.	
-- 速力	accelerated force.	
-- 速器	accelerator.	
-- 速原理	acceleration principle.	
37-- 冠	crown.	
-- 深	deepen.	
40-- 大	enlarge, increase.	
44-- 薪	increase salary.	
-- 熱	heat.	
48-- 增	add, increase.	
53-- 成	mark up.	
60-- 冕	coronation.	
61-- 號	plus sign (+).	
77-- 緊	intensify.	
80-- 入	join, enter, add, take part in, admit.	
-- 侖	gallon.	
-- 拿大	Canada.	
-- 拿大的	Canadian.	

-- 拿大人　Canadian.

4601_0
旭〔Hsu〕n. dawn, rising sun.
60-- 日　rising sun.

4611_0
坦〔Tan〕adj. level, plain, smooth, frank, quiet, open-minded.
00-- 率　frank, candid, open, outspoken.
-- 率無私　be frank without secrecy.
10-- 平　level, smooth.
23-- 然自承　own up.
26-- 白　frank, plain, broad, open, manifest, open, without reservation.
-- 白交代　confess, tell frankly.
-- 白直爽　open-hearted and straightforward.
38-- 道　broad way, level road.
-- 途　level road, bright future.
40-- 直　frank, plain, direct.
-- 克車　tank.
-- 克炮　tank gun, tank cannon.
77-- 胸露乳　go topless and bare the breast.

觀〔Chin〕v. have audience with.

4611_3
塊〔Kuai〕n. clod, piece, slice, fragment, lump.
44-- 莖　tuber.
47-- 根　tuberous root, root tuber.

4611_4
埋〔Mai〕v. bury, inter, conceal, hoard, lay low.
07-- 設伏兵　make an ambush.
11-- 頭　devote oneself to, be engrossed in.
-- 頭苦幹　bury oneself in work.
23-- 伏　ambush.
27-- 怨　murmur, complain, grumble.
-- 怨他人　blame others.
37-- 沒　hide, conceal.
-- 沒英雄　let a hero or genius lie unknown.
44-- 地雷　lay mines.
-- 藏　embed, hoard, lay up, bury

and conceal.

-- 葬   bury, inter, entomb, lay to rest.

4612$_7$

場 〔**Chang**〕 n. place, site, field, yard, court, open space.

40-- 內交易   pit trader.
-- 內商人   floor trader.
-- 內經紀人   floor broker, board broker.
44-- 地   site for a show or a game.
72-- 所   place, yard, site.
80-- 合   occasion, situation.

塲 〔**Ta**〕 v. collapse, cave.
00-- 方   cave, in.

4618$_1$

堤 〔**Ti**〕 n. dike, embankment, dam, bank.
22-- 岸   bank of a river.
41-- 壩   dam, embankment.

4620$_0$

帕 〔**Pa**〕 n. kerchief, handkerchief, veil.
幗 〔**Kuo**〕 n. woman's head dress.

4621$_0$

觀 〔**Kuan**〕 n. look, view, see, observe, inspect.
00-- 摩   compare notes, emulate.
07-- 望   look in, hesitate, wait and see.
-- 望不前   hesitate and make no move.
27-- 象台   observatory.
30-- 客   audience, spectator.
-- 察   n. observation, v. observe, survey.
-- 察對象   observation object.
-- 察者   observer.
-- 察員   observer.
-- 察點   standpoint, point of view.
-- 察所   observation post.
32-- 測   observe, survey.
35-- 禮   attend a ceremony, watch the parade.
-- 禮台   reviewing stand, rostrum.
37-- 潮派   those who take a wait-and-see attitude.
60-- 眾   audience, spectator.

61-- 點   point of view, viewpoint.
80-- 念   idea, concept, thought, conception.
-- 念論   idealism.
-- 念型態   ideology.
90-- 光   sightseeing, tour.
-- 光旅行   tour.
-- 光團   tourist group (party).
-- 賞   appreciate.

4621$_1$

幌 〔**Huang**〕 n. curtain, shop-sign, signboard.
17-- 子   shop-sign, label, pretext, signboard.

4621$_4$

狸 〔**Li**〕 n. fox, wild cat.
猩 〔**Hsing**〕 n. pongo, gorilla, chimpanzee.
21-- 紅   scarlet.
-- 紅熱   scarlet fever.
46-- 猩   gorilla, chimpanzee.

玀 〔**Lo**〕 n. the Lo tribe.

4622$_7$

狷 〔**Chuan**〕 adj. hasty, narrow-minded.
猬 〔**Wei**〕 n. hedgehog.
獨 〔**Tu**〕 adj. solitary, single, only, old and without a son, adv. alone.
00-- 立   n. independence, freedom, v. stand alone, be one's own master.
-- 立商店   independent store.
-- 立不移   standing alone unmoved.
-- 立自主   independence and initiative.
-- 立經商   independent economy.
-- 立經營   independent business operation, sole proprietary enterprises.
-- 立出口商   independent exporter.
-- 立自主政策 policy of independence and self-reliance.
-- 立機關   independent organ.
-- 立投資   autonomous investment.
-- 立國   independent state, sovereign state.
-- 立會計師   independent accountant.

-- 立性	independence.	
-- 立營業	do business for oneself.	
-- 立精神	spirit of independence.	
-- 立勞工黨	Independent Labour Party.	
01-- 語	talk to oneself.	
-- 一無二	unique, unmatched.	
-- 霸	dominate, exclusively.	
-- 到之處	special merits.	
17-- 子	only son.	
21-- 此一家	the only authentic brand.	
-- 占	n. monopoly, v. monopolize.	
-- 占者	monopolist.	
-- 占權	exclusive right, sole right.	
-- 處	live alone.	
22-- 斷	dogmatism, intolerance, independent judgement.	
24-- 特	specific, peculiar.	
26-- 白	monologue, soliloquy.	
-- 自	by oneself.	
27-- 身	n. single, bachelor, spinster, adj. unmarried.	
-- 身生活	single life.	
30-- 家新聞	scoop, exclusive news.	
-- 家許可證	sole licence.	
-- 家經濟	exclusive distribution.	
-- 家經銷商	exclusive distributor.	
-- 家經營	exclusive dealership (dealing).	
-- 家代理	sole agency, exclusive agency.	
-- 家代理商	sole agent, exclusive agent.	
-- 家特權	exclusive privilege.	
-- 家總代理	exclusive general correspondent, sole agent.	
-- 家經理	sole agency.	
37-- 資	sole proprietorship.	
-- 資公司	sole corporation.	
-- 資經營	sole ownership.	
-- 資經營者	sole proprietor.	
40-- 力	with one's own hand, single-hand.	
-- 木舟	canoe.	
-- 木橋	single-plank bridge.	
43-- 裁	n. dictatorship, adj. arbitrary, dictatorial.	
-- 裁主義	authoritarianism.	

-- 裁政治	autocracy.
-- 裁者	dictator.
44-- 幕劇	one-act play.
50-- 夫	individual, single man, autocrat.
-- 奏	recital.
58-- 輪車	wheelbarrow.
66-- 唱	solo.
77-- 居	live alone.
82-- 創	original, all created by oneself.

4623₂

猥 〔Wei〕 n. obscenity, lewdness, adj. humble.

00-- 褻罪	crime of misdemeanor.
26-- 細	petty, trifling.

4624₁

狴 = 悍 9604₁

4624₇

幔 〔Man〕 n. tent, curtain, screen.

4625₆

狎 〔Hsia〕 v. sport with, take liberties, be intimate with, adj. irreverent, disrespectful.

4626₀

猖 〔Chang〕 adj. mad, ravaging.

41-- 狂	mad, wild, frantic, frenzied, boisterous.
-- 獗	disturbing, notorious.

帽 〔Mao〕 n. hat, cap, bonnet.

00-- 店	hatter's shop.
17-- 子	cap, hat.
28-- 徽	cap insignia.
36-- 邊	brim.
46-- 架	hat-rack, hat stand.
80-- 盒	hat-box.

4628₀

狽 〔Pei〕 n. wolf.

4629₄

猓 〔Kuo〕 n. the Kuo tribe.

4632₇

駕 〔Chia〕 n. vehicles, inferior horse, v. ride, mount, ascend, drive.

22-- 崩	death of an emperor.
27-- 舟	sail a boat.

50-- 車	drive a car.
75-- 駛	drive, sail, navigate, steer, pilot.
-- 駛員	driver, pilot.
77-- 馭	rein, control, manage, hold in hand.
78-- 臨	your presence.

4633_0

恕 〔Shu〕 v. excuse, forgive, pardon, show mercy, adj. benevolent, humane, merciful, tender, considerate of.

10-- 不遠送	I am sorry I cannot escort you farther.
-- 不奉陪	I am sorry but I cannot keep you company.
17-- 己恕人	forgive others as you do yourself.
30-- 宥	forgive, excuse.
60-- 罪	forgive one's sin, excuse.

想 〔Hsiang〕 n. idea, conception, thought, v. think, consider, suppose, expect, hope, mind, meditate.

00-- 辦法	find a solution.
07-- 望	hope, expect.
10-- 一想	think it over.
-- 要	want, intend.
-- 不到	unforeseen, unthought-of.
-- 不通	be unable to comprehend or understand.
-- 不起來	unable to call to mind.
-- 不開	take things too hard.
11-- 頭	thought, hope, expectation, notion.
12-- 到	think of, anticipate, have in mind.
-- 出	reason out, figure.
27-- 像	n. imagine, fantasy, v. imagine, conceive, abstract, form an idea of, suppose.
-- 像不到	unthinkable, inconceivable.
-- 像力	power of imagination.
-- 像力強	strong in one's power of imagination, imaginative.
-- 家	think of home, homesick.
-- 家病	homesick.

34-- 法	idea, notion, view.
40-- 來想去	ponder.
47-- 起	recall, recollect, remember, call in mind, brush up the memory, come across the mind.
80-- 念	think of, think on, miss.
84-- 錯	mistake.
90-- 當然	jump to a conclusion, take for granted.

4640_0

如 〔Ju〕 adj. like, similar, resembling, comparable, as good as, conj. if, supposing, as if, as though.

00-- 意	as you wish, being contented.
-- 意算盤	counting one's chickens before they were hatched.
10-- 下	as follows, as below.
-- 雷灌耳	like thunders, piercing.
20-- 手如足	like brothers.
21-- 此	such, so, thus, like this.
-- 何	how？ why？
27-- 約	as agreed on.
40-- 有	if there is.
44-- 獲至寶	like acquiring a rare treasure.
47-- 期	on time, at time, in due time, punctually, at time appointed.
-- 期交貨	deliver the goods in time.
48-- 故	as formerly, as before.
60-- 日中天	like the midday sun--very influential.
-- 果	of, suppose, provided that, in the event of.
62-- 影隨形	as the shadow follows the form, inseparable.
71-- 願	n. satisfaction, v. fulfill one's wish.
77-- 同	resembling, as if.
-- 同身受	would regard it as a personal favor to me.
-- 同兒戲	be like a child's play.
78-- 臨大敵	be on one's guard for all possible dangers, be pre-

80-- 今	now, nowadays, at present, at this time.
90-- 常	as usual, as customary, according to routine.

姻 〔Yin〕 *n.* relationship by marriage.

06-- 親	relationship, relative by marriage.
22-- 緣	marriage affinity, bond between man and wife.
-- 緣註定	the fate that brings lovers together is destined.

4641₄

娌 〔Li〕 *n.* sister-in-law.

4641₇

媼 〔Wen〕 *n.* old woman, old dame.

4642₇

娟 〔Chuan〕 *adj.* beautiful, pretty, attractive, charming, elegant.

| 20-- 秀 | graceful, pretty, beautiful. |
| 47-- 媚 | attractive, beautiful. |

4643₀

媳 〔Hsi〕 *n.* daughter-in-law.

4643₄

娛 〔Yu〕 *n.* joy, pleasure, delight, amusement, enjoyment, *v.* amuse, please, rejoice, enjoy, entertain.

22-- 樂	*n.* amusement, entertainment, recreation, *v.* amuse, entertain.
-- 樂場	public house.
-- 樂稅	amusement tax, entertainment tax.
-- 樂業	entertainment industry, leisure industry.

4644₀

婢 〔Pi〕 *n.* maid servant, slave girl.

4645₆

嬋 〔Chan〕 *adj.* beautiful, graceful.

4646₀

娼 〔Chang〕 *n.* whore, prostitute, strumpet.

| 30-- 寮 | brothel, house of ill fame. |
| 44-- 妓 | whore, prostitute, woman |

of the town.

4651₀

靼 〔Ta〕 *n.* soft leather.

4661₀

覩 〔Tu〕 *v.* see, look, witness.

4673₂

袈 〔Chia〕 *n.* surplice.

4680₄

趕 〔Kan〕 *v.* chase, pursue, hasten, hurry.

00-- 市	go to market, drive.
-- 工時間	crush time.
10-- 下台	oust someone from office.
-- 不上	lag behind, fail to keep pace with, fail to catch up.
20-- 往	rush to, go to (a place) in a hurry.
-- 集	go to a fair.
21-- 上	catch up, overtake.
22-- 出	drive out.
26-- 得上	get there in time.
27-- 急	make haste, hurry, dash.
40-- 走	drive.
50-- 車	drive a cart, catch a bus or train.
67-- 路	hurry on, go faster.
95-- 快=趕急	

4680₆

賀 〔Ho〕 *v.* congratulate, felicitate.

07-- 詞	congratulatory address.
10-- 電	congratulatory telegram.
30-- 客	congratulator, well-wishers.
35-- 禮	present.
40-- 喜	congratulate.
80-- 年	wish one a happy new year.

4690₀

柏 〔Po〕 *n.* cypress.

35-- 油	tar, asphalt.
-- 油氈	tarred roofing felt.
-- 油路	asphalt road.

枷 〔Chia〕 *n.* pillory, cangue.

| 89-- 鎖 | lock, shackle, cangue. |

相 〔Hsiang〕 *n.* appearance, countenance, facial features, looks, prime minister, *v.* inspect, select, examine, look at, gaze, help, assist, *adj.* mutual, reciprocal, each other, one another.

00-- 應	correspond with each other, be in union with each other, be in harmony with each other.
-- 交	make friends with each other, have intercourse.
03-- 識	*n.* acquaintance, *v.* be acquainted.
09-- 談	confer with.
10-- 互	mutual, reciprocal, one another, each another.
-- 互依存	interdependence.
-- 互保險	mutual insurance.
-- 互保險公司	mutual insurance company.
-- 互校對	cross-check.
-- 互同意	mutual consent.
-- 互作用	interplay, interaction.
-- 互關係	interrelation.
-- 干	connected, concerned.
17-- 配	correspond.
20-- 依	interdepend.
-- 愛	love each other.
-- 爭	compete, quarrel.
-- 信	believe, trust.
21-- 術	physiognomy.
-- 比	compare.
22-- 片	photo, photograph.
-- 繼	one after another, in succession.
-- 稱	match each other, harmonize.
24-- 待	treat.
25-- 傳	hand down, transmit.
27-- 貌	countenance, appearance, facial features.
-- 向	opposite, face to face.
28-- 似	*v.* resemble, look like, *adj.* similar, alike.
29-- 伴	accompany, go along with.
30-- 宜	suitable, proper.
-- 安無事	be at peace with each other.
-- 容	compatible.
31-- 顧	mutual regard, look at each other.
32-- 近	near, close to, approximate.
34-- 對	oppose, relative, face to face.
-- 對論	theory of relativity, relativism.
-- 對價值	relative value.
-- 對性	relativity.
-- 法	physiognomy.
35-- 連	unite, join, connect.
36-- 遇	meet, encounter, come across.
47-- 聲	cross-talk, humorous dialogue.
50-- 撞	clash, collide, jostle.
51-- 打	fight, exchange blow.
52-- 抵	compensate, off set, counterbalance.
53-- 搏	buffet.
54-- 持	stalemated.
60-- 見	meet with.
-- 見恨晚	regret we did not meet sooner.
-- 思病	lovesickness.
-- 思鳥	robin.
-- 罵	quarrel.
-- 異	differ.
71-- 反	*n.* opposition, contrast, inversion, *v.* be opposed to each other.
74-- 助	help, aid, assist, bear a hand, mutual help.
77-- 同	identical, same, alike.
-- 關	*n.* connection, relation, *adj.* related, connected.
-- 間	alternation.
80-- 合	accord, correspond, join with, coincide.
-- 會	meet, fall in.
88-- 符	agreeing, corresponding, coincide with each other.
-- 等	equal, no better than.
90-- 當	suitable, corresponding, adequate.
-- 當數量	reasonable quantity.

4690₃

絮 〔Hsu〕 *n.* cotton, refuse silk, *adj.*

talkative, gossiping.

01-- 語	chattering.
91-- 煩	tired, weary.

4690₄

架〔Chia〕 *n.* frame, stand, shelf, rack, *v.* prop up, lay something on, build, fabricate.

17-- 子	frame, shelf.
26-- 線	lay wire.
27-- 床	bunk.
37-- 次	sortie.
42-- 橋	erect a bridge.

4691₁

棍〔Kun〕 *n.* stick, staff, club, rascal, villain.

13-- 球	baseball.
17-- 子	rod, stick.
24-- 徒	rascal, scoundrel, villain.
45-- 棒	club, cudgel.
73-- 騙	cheat, deceive, swindle.

4691₃

槐〔Huai〕 *n.* locust tree.

4692₇

枴〔Kuai〕 *n.* crutch, stick, old man.

45-- 杖	crutch, stick.

棉〔Mien〕 *n.* cotton.

00-- 衣	wadded cloth, cotton clothes.
17-- 子	cotton seed.
20-- 紡	cotton spinning.
-- 紡錠	cotton textile spindles.
-- 紡廠	cotton mill.
23-- 織品	cotton fabrics (textiles).
26-- 線	cotton thread.
29-- 紗	cotton yarn.
30-- 褲	cotton-wadded trousers.
34-- 被	cotton quilt.
36-- 襖	cotton-wadded coat.
37-- 袍	wadded coat.
40-- 布	cotton-cloth.
43-- 桃	cotton boll.
44-- 花	cotton.
-- 花田	cotton field.
-- 鞋	wadded shoes.

46-- 絮	cotton fibers.
51-- 蚜虫	cotton aphis.
57-- 籽	cotton-seed.

楊〔Yang〕 *n.* willow, poplar, aspen.

47-- 柳	willow.
48-- 梅	strawberry.

榻〔Ta〕 *n.* bed, sofa, couch.

4694₁

楫〔Chi〕 *n.* oar.

桿〔Gan〕 *n.* pole, rod, stick, staff.

4694₄

櫻〔Ying〕 *n.* cherry tree.

40-- 核	cherry stone.
42-- 桃	cherry.
44-- 花	cherry-blossoms.

4699₄

棵〔Ko〕 *n.* trunk of trees.

4702₇

鳩〔Chiu〕 *n.* turtle dove, pigeon.

4711₇

圯〔I〕 *n.* bridge.

4712₀

均〔Chun〕 *v.* equalize, blend, *adj.* equal, uniform, even, level, just, all, same.

10-- 一	uniform, homogenous.
-- 平	equal, equable, just.
21-- 衡	*n.* equilibrium, *v.* balance.
-- 衡論	the theory of equilibrium.
27-- 勻	uniform, even, equal.
44-- 勢	balance of power.
50-- 攤	share equally, contribute, allot equally.
80-- 分	divide equally, partake.
88-- 等	*n.* equality, *adj.* equal.

4712₇

壻〔Hsu〕 *n.* son-in-law.

堝〔Kuo〕 *n.* clay ware, melting pot.

塢〔Wu〕 *n.* dock, shipyard, village.

4713₂

垠〔Yin〕 *n.* beach, limit.

塚〔Chung〕 *n.* tomb, grave.

4713₈

懿 〔 I 〕 *adj.* nice, excellent.

4714₀

坍 〔 Tan 〕 *v.* fall, collapse, tumble down.
22-- 倒　fall, collapse.
23-- 台　disgraceful failure.

4714₇

圾 〔 Chi 〕 *n.* waste, *adj.* dangerous, hazardous.

埠 〔 Fu 〕 *n.* port, wharf, trading place.
11-- 頭　wharf, jetty, landing quay.

4718₁

堑 〔 Chu 〕 *n.* dike, embankment.

4718₂

坎 〔 Kan 〕 *n.* pit, hole.
41-- 坷　bad luck, hardship, ruggedness of a road.

4720₇

弩 〔 Nu 〕 *n.* crossbow.

4721₀

帆 〔 Fan 〕 *n.* sail, canvas.
27-- 船　sailing boat, sailboat.
40-- 布　canvas.
-- 布袋　canvas bag.
-- 布鞋　canvas-shoes.
88-- 篷　sail.

狙 〔 Chu 〕 *n.* ape, monkey, *v.* watch for, spy, ambush, snipe.
08-- 詐　tricky, treacherous.
57-- 擊　strike at, poke at, snipe.
-- 擊手　sniper.

4721₂

翘 〔 Chiao 〕 *n.* long tail feathers, talent, *v.* elevate, raise , lift, *adj.* high, elevated, dangerous, outstanding, eminent.
07-- 望　look for earnestly.
44-- 楚　eminent talent.
47-- 起　cock, raise.
60-- 足　stand on tiptoe.
80-- 首　raise the head.

犯 〔 Fan 〕 *n.* prisoner, criminal, *v.* offend, infringe,violate, invade, rush against, break, oppose, commit (a crime).

34-- 法　offend against law, break the laws, transgress.
-- 法者　transgressor.
56-- 規　break a rule, foul, commit a foul.
60-- 罪　commit a crime, offend, transgress.
64-- 禁　violate prohibition.
80-- 人　prisoner, criminal.
84-- 錯　make a mistake, commit error.

皰 〔 Pao 〕 *n.* pimples.

4721₄

幄 〔 Wo 〕 *n.* curtain, tent.

4721₇

猛 〔 Meng 〕 *adj.* severe, strict, stern, violent, strong, fierce, cruel, brave.
12-- 烈　strong, violent, ferocious, fierce.
-- 烈抨擊　attack fiercely, flay.
-- 烈炮火　drum-fire.
18-- 攻　*n.* fierce assault *v.* attack desperately, bombard, attack fiercely.
21-- 虎　fierce tiger.
23-- 然　suddenly.
30-- 進　radical reform.
31-- 漲　skyrocket, soar, sharp rise.
40-- 力　violent strength, full strength.
-- 士　brave man.
50-- 撞　drive, bounce.
52-- 撲　swoop down on, pounce upon.
57-- 擊　furious onslaught.
63-- 獸　fierce beast, fierce animal.
65-- 跌　nosedive.
80-- 禽　bird of prey.

4722₀

狗 〔 Kou 〕 *n.* dog.
21-- 熊　black bear.
30-- 窩　kennel.
60-- 咬　biting of a dog.
63-- 吠　*n.* bark of a dog, *v.* bark.
77-- 屎　dog's droppings.

猢 〔 Hu 〕 *n.* monkey.

4722₇

猾 〔Hua〕 *adj.* crafty, artful, cunning, wily.

11-- 頭　　　cunning, artful, treacherous.
41-- 奸　　　disloyal, treacherous.

鶴 〔Ho〕 *n.* crane, stork.

鸛 〔Kuan〕 *n.* heron, stork.

郁 〔Yu〕 *adj.* colorful, fragrant, beautiful, splendid, fine, refined, warm.

27-- 伊　　　melancholy.
47-- 郁　　　fragrant, colorful, ornamented.
-- 馨　　　sweet, scented.

4723₂

狠 〔Hen〕 *adj.* cruel, hard-hearted, atrocious.

33-- 心　　　hard-hearted, cruel, savage.
50-- 毒　　　cruel, malicious.
-- 毒心腸　　cruel hearted.
-- 鬥　　　fight relentlessly.

4723₄

猴 〔Hou〕 *n.* monkey, ape.

23-- 戲　　　monkey play.

4724₇

殼 〔Ke〕 *n.* shell, husk, covering, crust.

彀 〔Kou〕 *n.* bow drawn to its full stretch, *adj.* enough.

4728₂

歡 〔Huan〕 *v.* rejoice, gladden, be pleased, *adj.* jolly, glad, cheerful, merry, pleased, joyful, happy.

10--天喜地　extremely delighted, overjoyed.
17--聚一堂　happily gathered in a hall.
22--樂　　　*v.* rejoice, gladden, be pleased, *adj.* jolly, glad, cheerful, merry, pleased, joyful, happy.
30-- 容　　　happy face.
37-- 迎　　　welcome, greet, bid welcome.
-- 迎詞　　greeting, welcome speech.
-- 迎會　　reception, welcome party.
-- 送　　　send-off, see someone off.
-- 送詞　　farewell speech, valedictory speech.
-- 送會　　farewell party.
40-- 喜　　　joy, delight, happy, rejoicing, pleased.
62-- 呼　　　cheer, shout with joy, hail, applaud.
66-- 唱　　　sing cheerfully.
67-- 躍　　　dance with joy, frisk.
79-- 騰　　　go into raptures.
87-- 飲　　　crack a bottle.
88-- 笑　　　laugh with joy.
95-- 情　　　sensuality.
98-- 悅　　　happy.

4728₆

獺 〔Ta〕 *n.* otter.

40-- 皮　　　otter-fur.
-- 皮帽　　otter hat.
-- 皮領　　otter collar.

4729₄

猱 〔Nao〕 *n.* a species of monkey.

4733₄

怒 〔Nu〕 *n.* anger, fury, rage, *adj.* angry, out of temper, on fire.

00-- 言　　　angry, out of temper, on fire, vigorous.
27-- 色　　　angry face.
30-- 容　　　angry looks.
-- 容滿面　flush with fury.
36-- 視　　　look black at, give black looks.
37-- 潮　　　raging tide (of the sea).
56-- 視　　　look black upon, look with an evil eye.
60-- 目　　　flash eye.
-- 罵　　　abuse, scold, revile angrily.
61-- 號　　　scold, roar angrily.
72-- 斥　　　fulminate.
80-- 氣　　　anger, rage.
90--火沖天　in a surge of great fury.

4734₇

赧 〔Nan〕 *v.* blush, turn red.

4740₁

聲 〔Sheng〕 *n.* noise, voice, sound, music, harmony, reputation, celebrity, *v.* declare, make known.

00-- 音　　　sound, voice, noise.

-- 音字	phonetics, phonology.
-- 言	proclaim, announce.
04-- 討會	denunciation meeting.
05-- 請	apply, request.
-- 請學	application.
-- 請人	applicant.
06-- 韻	sound and echo.
07-- 調	tune, melody.
-- 望	reputation, prestige, popularity.
11-- 張	disclose, publicize.
21-- 頻	audio-frequency.
22-- 樂	vocal music.
-- 稱	state, declare.
27-- 名	fame, reputation.
-- 名掃地	fall into disrepute.
-- 響	noise.
33-- 浪	sound waves.
34-- 波	sound wave.
40-- 叉	tuning fork.
44-- 帶	vocal cord.
-- 勢	influence, prestige, power, display.
47-- 起	rise.
52-- 援	support.
67-- 明	*n.* statement, declaration, *v.* declare, affirm, make known.
77-- 譽	prestige, game, reputation.
88-- 管	vocal tube.

4740₂
翅〔Chi〕*n.* wing, fin.

| 70-- 膀 | wings. |

4741₀
姐〔Chieh〕*n.* elder sister.

45-- 妹	sister.
47-- 姐	elder sister.
59-- 夫	brother-in-law.

4741₁
妮〔Ni〕*n.* girl, maid, slave girl.
媲〔Pih〕*v.* match, be equal to.

| 80-- 美 | be on a par with. |

4741₄
娓〔Wei〕*adj.* complying, pleasant, unwearied, accommodating.

| 47-- 娓 | tireless, unwearied, pleasing, accommodating. |

4741₆
娩〔Wan〕*v.* bear a child.

4741₇
妃〔Fei〕*n.* imperial concubine.

| 43-- 嬪 | ladies in waiting, woman in palace. |

4742₀
妁〔Shuo〕*n.* match-maker, go-between.

朝〔Chao〕*n.* morning, day, dynasty, imperial court, *v.* have an audience with the emperor, face, go to court.

10-- 霞	sunglow.
23-- 代	dynasty, reign.
27-- 夕	morning and evening, early and late.
-- 夕不保	anything may happen any time.
28-- 鮮	Korea.
47-- 朝	every morning.
-- 報	morning post.
60-- 見	go to court.
71-- 臣	courtier.
76-- 陽	morning sun.
77-- 服	court dress.
80-- 前	forward, ahead.
-- 氣	vigor of youth, fresh spirit.
-- 氣蓬勃	vigorous, full of vigor and vitality.

嫻〔Hsian〕*adj.* gracious, refined, skilled.

04-- 熟	accomplished, skilled.
17-- 習	skilled in, skillful.
70-- 雅	refined, polished.

4742₇
奶〔Nai〕*v.* milk, nipple, breast of a woman.

11-- 頭	nipple, teat.
25-- 牛	milk cow.
27-- 名	pet name.
35-- 油	cream, butter.
41-- 媽	wet nurse.
46-- 場	dairy farm.

47--	奶	grandmother, granny.
90--	糖	toffee.
98--	粉	milk power.

努 〔Nu〕 v. strive, endeavor, exert oneself to the utmost.

40--	力	n. effort, endeavor, v. use endeavors, strive, make an effort.
--	力前進	work one's way, make one's way.

娜 〔No〕 adj. graceful.

媧 〔Wo〕 n. ancient empress.

婦 〔Fu〕 n. woman, lady, wife, female.

00--	產科	obstetrics and gynecology department of a hospital.
11--	孺皆知	known even to women and children.
12--	聯會	Chinese Women's Anticommunist League.
24--	科醫生	gynecologist.
40--	女	woman, lady, fair sex, womenfolk.
--	女運動	women's movement.
--	女會	sisterhood.
--	女協會	women's association.

嫋 〔Niao〕 adj. slender, feeble, delicate.

47--	嫋	delicate, soft and beautiful.

4744₀

奴 〔Nu〕 n. slave, servant, serf.

23--	僕	slave, servant.
27--	役	bondage, enslavement.
40--	才	flunkey, lackey.
45--	隸	slave, serf, bondman.
--	隸主	slave-owner, slaveholder.
--	隸廢止	abolitionism.
--	隸制	slavery.
--	隸解放	emancipation.
--	隸社會	slave society.
--	隸貿易	slave trade.
--	隸性	servility, slavishness.

4744₅

姍 〔Shan〕 v. laugh at, walk slowly, adj. god, beautiful.

47--	姍來遲	come late.

4744₇

好 〔Hao〕 v. live, be fond of, incline, wish for, adj. good, well, fine, nice, superior, excellent, dear, kind, friendly, adv. very, well, exceedingly.

00--	主意	good idea.
--	市	bull market, long market.
--	意	good will, kindness, well-intentioned.
--	高	ambitious.
01--	評	praise, appreciation, good opinion, good comments.
02--	話	persuasion, good words.
07--	望角	Cape of Good Hope.
10--	天	fine day.
--	歹	good and bad.
--	歹不知	not knowing the good and bad.
--	不高興	very excited, very displeased.
--	不容易	with great difficulty.
14--	聽	pleasant to listen, pleasing to the ear.
20--	看	beautiful, handsome, good looking, pretty.
--	手	adept, expert, master.
21--	價錢	good price.
--	處	advantage, profit, benefit.
22--	幾個	quite a few.
24--	動	active, sport-loving.
26--	得很	very well, very good.
27--	像	resemble, seem, look like, as if.
--	多	great number, very much, a great deal of.
--	色	sensual, lascivious, lustful, attached to the fair sex.
--	名譽	fair name, good reputation.
--	久	long while.
32--	兆頭	good omen.
33--	心	benevolence, kind intention.
34--	漢	hero.
37--	運	good fortune, good impression, good luck.
39--	消息	good news, welcome news.
40--	友	good friend.

-- 奇	curious, eager to know.
-- 奇心	curiosity.
41-- 極了	excellent.
42-- 機會	good chance.
50-- 事	fussy, good deed.
-- 事者	busybody.
-- 東西	good thing.
-- 表現	like to make a show of, show off.
52-- 靜	quiet, inactive.
53-- 感	good feeling, good impression.
-- 景	nice view.
55-- 轉	turn for the better.
63-- 戰	warlike, belligerent.
64-- 財	covetous, avaricious.
68-- 吃	delicious, palatable.
77-- 鬥	belligerent, pugnacious.
-- 學	studious, diligent.
-- 朋友	good friend.
-- 學不倦	be fond of learning and never get tired.
80-- 人	good man.
-- 人難做	it's difficult to please everybody.
-- 人好事	good people and exemplary deeds.
-- 年頭	favorable year.
-- 食	delicious, good to eat, very edible.
88-- 笑	laughable, ridiculous.
-- 管閒事	fond of meddling in other's business.

報〔Pao〕n. newspaper, report, v. report, declare, announce, inform, recompense, repay, compensate, return.

00-- 應	retribution.
-- 廢	scrap.
12-- 到	report for duty, announce.
-- 酬	n. reward, compensation, payment, remuneration, earning, v. reward, repay.
-- 酬率	rate of return.
-- 酬金	honorarium.
-- 刊	newspaper and magazine.
17-- 務員	operator.
20-- 信	inform, advise.
21-- 價單	quotation list.
22-- 紙	newspaper, press.
24-- 仇	revenge, avenge.
-- 仇雪恨	wreak vengeance.
-- 告	report, inform, tell of.
-- 告書	report, notice, herald.
-- 告人	reporter, informant.
27-- 名	register.
-- 名處	office of register.
28-- 復	n. retaliation, reprisal, v. retaliate, revenge, avenge.
-- 復行爲	reprisal.
-- 稅	declare dutiable goods.
29-- 償	compensation.
34-- 社	newspaper office.
38-- 道	report.
40-- 喜	report a good news.
44-- 幕員	announcer.
48-- 警	alarm, shake the bell.
50-- 攤	newsstand.
-- 表	report forms.
-- 表格式	statement form.
61-- 賬	render an account, apply for reimbursement.
66-- 單	declaration form.
77-- 關	declare at the custom.
-- 關單	bill of entry.
-- 關手續	custom entry.
83-- 館	newspaper office.
88-- 答	recompense, reward, reciprocate, repay, in return for.
89-- 銷	submit accounts for approval, send in account.
-- 銷旅費	submit traveling account.

嫂〔Sao〕n. sister-in-law, elder brother's wife.

4745₅

姆〔Mu〕n. nurse, woman tutor.

| 47-- 姆 | wife of one's husband's elder brother. |

4746₇

媚〔Mei〕v. flatter, fawn, cajole, seduce, adulate, adj. attracting, charming, bewitching, fascinating.

53-- 惑　　　　charming, fascinating.
67-- 眼　　　　bewitching eye.

4751₇

靶 〔Pa〕 *n.* target.
17-- 子場　　　rifle range.
33-- 心　　　　bull's eye.
46-- 場　　　　shooting range.

4752₀

韌 〔Jen〕 *adj.* elastic, tough, tenacious.
44-- 帶　　　　ligament.
95-- 性　　　　obstinate disposition, tenacity.

鞠 〔Chu〕 *n.* ball, *v.* bend, bear, raise, bring up.
27-- 躬　　　　bow, bend, incline, make one's best exertion.
-- 躬盡瘁　　　fag oneself to death, work oneself to death.

4753₂

艱 〔Chien〕 *adj.* hard, difficult, dangerous, distressful.
00-- 辛　　　　distressing, grievous.
40-- 難　　　　*n.* difficulties, *adj.* hard.
-- 難困苦　　　great difficulties or hardships.
44-- 苦　　　　hardship, trouble.
-- 苦奮鬥　　　arduous struggle.
77-- 阻　　　　seriously obstructed.
78-- 險　　　　difficult and dangerous.

4758₂

歎 〔Tan〕 *n.* moan, groan, sigh, admire, praise, applaud, extol.
20-- 辭　　　　interjection.
26-- 息　　　　moan, sigh, groan, regret.
94-- 惜　　　　regret, pity.

4759₄

鞣 〔Jou〕 *n.* leather.
13-- 酸　　　　tannic acid.
40-- 皮　　　　tanning.

4760₁

罄 〔Ching〕 *adj.* empty, exhausted.

4760₉

馨 〔Hsing〕 *n.* fragrance.
20-- 香　　　　sweet smell, fragrance.

4762₀

胡 〔Hu〕 *n.* Hu (a family name). *adv.* how？ why？
00-- 麻　　　　flax.
08-- 說　　　　talk nonsense.
11-- 琴　　　　fiddle.
22-- 亂　　　　confused, at random.
36-- 混　　　　loaf.
42-- 桃　　　　walnut.
44-- 蘿蔔　　　carrot.
47-- 椒　　　　pepper.
60-- 思亂想　　think confusedly.
77-- 鬧　　　　make a row, create disturbance.
-- 同　　　　lane.

4762₇

都 〔Tu〕 *n.* capital, metropolis, large city.
00-- 市　　　　city, town.
-- 市發展　　　urban development.
-- 市居民　　　townsfolk, townspeople.
27-- 督　　　　military governor.
47-- 好了　　　all's well, everything is ready.
80-- 會　　　　city, town.

鴣 〔Ku〕 *n.* partridge.

鵲 〔Chueh〕 *n.* magpie.

4772₀

切 〔Chieh〕 *v.* cut, carve, mince, slice, *adj.* urgent, eager, important.
00-- 音　　　　pronunciation.
07-- 記　　　　always remember.
-- 望　　　　eager, earnest, keen, burning.
10-- 碎　　　　cut into pieces.
-- 要　　　　very important.
-- 不要　　　on no account.
17-- 忌　　　　strictly forbidden, prohibited.
18-- 磋　　　　discuss.
21-- 齒　　　　gnash teeth.
22-- 片　　　　cut in slices.
-- 斷　　　　cut down, break.
26-- 線　　　　tangent line (in mathematics).
27-- 身　　　　one's own, personal.

30--	實	true, sincere, real, genius.
32--	割	incise.
40--	去	cut off.
44--	草機	silage cutter.
46--	想	longing.
61--	點	point of contact.
77--	開	cut apart, cut open, carve.
78--	腹	harakiri.

刧 〔 Chieh 〕 *n.* robbery, suffering, *v.* rob, plunder, snatch, take by violence.

30--	案	case of robbery.
37--	盜	robber, plunder, highwayman.
43--	獄	break open the jail.
50--	掠	rob, plunder.

4772_7

鵪 〔 An 〕 *n.* quail.

4777_4

罄 〔 Ching 〕 *v.* exhaust, use up, *adj.* empty, exhausted.

4780_1

起 〔 Chi 〕 *v.* stand up, rise, get up, being, start, commence, originate.

00--	立	stand up.
--	床	rise, get up.
02--	訴	sue one in court, sue, prosecute, indict, impeach, charge.
--	訴人	suitor.
--	端	origin, beginning.
10--	死復生	raise from the dead.
--	不來	unable to get up, unable to rise.
--	工	start work.
11--	頭	in the beginning.
--	碼	at least.
12--	飛	flying off, take off.
14--	勁	energetic, work enthusiastically.
20--	手	begin, start, commence.
--	重機	crane, derrick, jack.
--	稿	draft.
21--	價	raise the price, advance the price.
22--	岸費	landing charges (hire, expense).

23--	伏	ups and downs.
24--	牀號	reveille.
--	貨	discharge cargo.
--	貨單	bill of lading.
26--	程	begin a journey.
27--	身	improvement.
31--	源	beginning, origin, source.
37--	泡	raise blister.
--	初	initially, at first, in the beginning.
40--	來	raise, get up.
43--	始	originate, take rise.
44--	草	make a draft.
--	草計劃	draw up a plan.
--	草報告	draw up a report.
--	草人	drafter.
--	草合同	draw up a contract.
50--	事	uprising.
52--	誓	take oath.
60--	因	cause, reason.
--	早	get up early in the morning.
61--	點	starting point, beginning.
64--	哄	kick up a fuss, cause a disturbance.
71--	原	original cause.
77--	風	the wind rises.
--	居室	living room.
80--	義	*n.* insurrection, uprising, *v.* rise in revolt.
--	首	*v.* begin, start, *adj.* in the beginning.
--	火	catch fire, be on fire.

4780_2

趨 〔 Chu 〕 *v.* run, hasten, tend to.

72--	向	*n.* intention, *v.* head toward, be inclined to.
45--	赴	run toward.
44--	勢	tendency, trend.
50--	奉	attend.
64--	時	run after fashion.

4780_4

趣 〔 Chu 〕 *v.* proceed quickly, *adj.* interesting, amusing, pleasant.

02--	話	jest, pleasantry.
27--	向	direction, inclination, in-

		tention.
50--	事	interesting matters.
65--	味	interest.

4780_6

超 〔Chao〕 v. leap over, go before, surpass, excel, exceed, promote, raise.

00--	度	salvation.
--	產獎金	productivity bonus.
--	音速	supersonic speed.
--	高速客機	hypersonic transport.
10--	面值	above par.
16--	現值	excess present value.
17--	群	pre-eminence, transcendent.
20--	重	overweight, overload.
--	航	over carriage.
21--	價	overprice.
22--	出	beyond.
--	出預算	excess budget.
23--	然	stand aloof.
--	然派	neutral people.
24--	儲	overstock.
27--	級市場	supermarket.
--	級商店	superstore.
--	級油輪	supertanker.
--	級品	best line.
--	級公司	super-corporation.
--	級大國	superpower.
28--	齡	overage.
--	收	overcharge.
31--	額	above quota.
--	額利息	excess interest.
--	額利潤	excess earnings (profit), extra profit, exorbitant profit.
--	額供給	excess supply.
--	額條款	excess clause.
--	額收入	excess income.
--	額費用	excess charges.
35--	速	speeding.
37--	過	overrun, exceed, surpass, in excess of.
--	過限價	exceed a limit.
40--	支	over-expenditure, over spend, over draw.
43--	越	exceed, excel, transcend.

--	載	overload.
47--	聲波	supersonic wave.
64--	時	run after fashion.
71--	階級	transcending class.
77--	凡	remarkable, unusual, transcend worldly thing.
78--	脫	transcendence.
80--	人	superhuman.
81--	短褲	minipants.
--	短裙	miniskirt.
88--	等	super class.
89--	銷	oversell.

4782_0

期 〔Chi〕 n. time, date, year, period, time limit, appointed time, v. expect, hope, long for, make an appointment.

07--	望	look for, hope, expect.
10--	票	promissory note, time draft.
12--	刊	periodical.
24--	貨	future goods, futures.
--	貨交易	deal in futures, future trading.
--	待	await, expect, count on, hope for.
27--	約	appointment.
34--	滿	n. expiration, v. expire.
60--	日	time, date.
77--	限	term, limit of time.
--	間	time, term, period, duration.

4788_2

欺 〔Chi〕 v. deceive, cheat, insult, impose upon, bully.

08--	詐	n. cheat, deceit, humbug, adj. fraudulent.
10--	弄	insult.
27--	負	insult, oppress, bully.
71--	壓	oppress, ride roughshod over.
73--	騙	deceive, fool, swindle, impose upon, make a fool of.
--	騙手段	trick.
80--	人自欺	cheat oneself and others.
--	人太甚	it's really too much.
--	善怕惡	bully the good and fear the wicked.

4791_0

楓〔Feng〕*n.* maple.
44--葉   maple leaves.
--樹   maple.
4791₂
桅〔Wei〕*n.* mast.
41--杆   spar, mast.
91--燈   headlight of a boat.
枹〔Fu〕*n.* drumstick.
4791₇
杝〔Chi〕*n.* alder, birch.
杷〔Pa〕*n.* loquat, rake.
楹〔Ying〕*n.* pillar, column.
4792₀
杓〔Shao〕*n.* spoon, ladle.
17--子   ladle dipper.
柳〔Liu〕*n.* willow, willow twig.
44--葉   willow leaves.
--樹   willow tree.
--枝   willow stalk, willow branch.
46--絮   willow catkins.
桐〔Tung〕*n.* paulownia.
35--油   wood oil, tung oil.
--油布   oilcloth.
棚〔Peng〕*n.* shed, booth, mat awning, tent.
17--子   small tent.
30--戶   people who live in tent.
50--車   covered cart.
77--屋   shed.
欄〔Lan〕*n.* railing, balustrade, pen for animals.
4792₂
杼〔Chu〕*n.* shuttle.
4792₇
桶〔Tung〕*n.* bucket, cask, tub, bushel, barrel, pail.
00--底   bottom of a barrel.
44--蓋   lid of a barrel.
71--匠   cooper.
83--鋪   coopery.
桷〔Chueh〕*n.* rafter.
椰〔Yeh〕*n.* cocoa, cocoanut.

17--子   cocoanut.
--子汁   cocoanut milk.
--子油   cocoanut oil.
--子殼   cocoanut shell.
44--菜   cabbage, savoy.
橘〔Chu〕*n.* orange, tangerine.
17--子水   orangeade.
--子汁   orange juice.
--子醬   marmalade.
27--絡   orange-fibers.
40--皮   orange peel.
44--黃色   orange-tawny.
榔〔Lang〕*n.* betel palm, betel nut.
11--頭   hammer.
4793₂
椽〔Chuan〕*n.* beam, rafter.
根〔Ken〕*n.* root, bottom, foot, origin, source, foundation, basis, root of a number.
00--瘤   root tubercles.
--底   origin, cause and effect, basis.
20--毛   root hair.
30--究來歷   make a thorough investigation of the source.
31--源   source, origin, root cause.
--源何在   where lies the source?
33--治   effect a real cure, radical treatment.
37--深蒂固   deep-rooted.
40--查禍源   thoroughly look into the seeds of the trouble.
44--莖   root stock.
--基   foundation, base, bottom.
--基穩固   firmly-established.
--苗   sprout, origin.
50--本   root, base, origin, foundation.
--本上   fundamentally, basically.
--本解決   fundamental solution.
--本改革   radical reform.
--本觀念   radical conception.
--本問題   fundamental questions.
--本法   basic law.
--由   cause, reason.

51-- 據　　　　　*n.* ground, basis, *v.* base upon, rest upon, depend upon, repose upon, according to.
-- 據地　　　　base of operation, stronghold.
-- 據合同　　　in accordance with contract.
58-- 數　　　　root of a number (in math).
61-- 號　　　　radical.
78-- 除　　　　uproot, eradicate.

橡〔Hsiang〕*n.* rubber tree, oak.
30-- 實　　　　acorn.
40-- 皮　　　　rubber, eraser.
-- 皮膏　　　　plaster, adhesive.
-- 皮球　　　　rubber ball.
-- 皮線　　　　rubber cord.
-- 皮圖章　　　rubber stamp.
-- 皮艇　　　　rubber boat.
-- 皮胎　　　　rubber tire.
44-- 樹　　　　oak.
47-- 膠　　　　rubber.
77-- 膠廠　　　rubber-goods factory.
-- 膠園　　　　rubber plantation.

4793₄
楔〔Hsieh〕*n.* wedge.
17-- 子　　　　wedge, preface.

4793₇
槌〔Chui〕*n.* hammer, mallet, club.
13-- 球　　　　croquet.

4794₀
椒〔Chiao〕*n.* pepper.
50-- 末　　　　ground pepper.
90-- 粒　　　　pepper.
98-- 粉　　　　pepper.

4794₁
橞〔Hsun〕*n.* big tree.

4794₅
柵〔Cha〕*n.* barrier, fence, stockade, palisade.
17-- 子　　　　stockade.
41-- 極電路　　grid circuit (electricity).
47-- 欄　　　　fence, railing, barrier.
77-- 門　　　　fence-gate.

4794₇
殺〔Sha〕*v.* kill, slay, murder, put to death.
08-- 敵　　　　fight the enemy.
10-- 一儆百　　kill one to warn a hundred.
-- 死　　　　　kill, murder.
11-- 頭　　　　behead, decapitate.
13-- 球　　　　smash (in tennis).
-- 戮　　　　　slaughter, slay, kill.
20-- 手　　　　killer.
21-- 價　　　　reduce price, cut price.
27-- 身成仁　　die a martyr's death for a noble cause.
28-- 傷　　　　kill or wound.
30-- 害　　　　murder.
44-- 菌　　　　pasteurize, sterilize, disinfect, kill germs.
-- 菌藥　　　　bactericide, disinfectant.
-- 菌作用　　　sterilization.
50-- 蟲藥　　　insecticide, pesticide.
80-- 人　　　　kill a person, murder, homicide.
-- 人犯　　　　murderer.
-- 人不眨眼　　murder in cold blood.
-- 人者死　　　blood must atone for blood.
-- 人如麻　　　have killed many people.
-- 人罪　　　　homicide.
-- 氣衝天　　　death is in the air.
90-- 光　　　　kill all.

穀〔Ku〕*n.* corn, grain, cereals.
17-- 子　　　　millet.
22-- 種　　　　seed, seed-grains.
25-- 穗　　　　ear of corn.
27-- 物　　　　grain, cereals.
44-- 芒　　　　awn.
60-- 田　　　　cornfield, rice field.
80-- 倉　　　　barn, granary.
90-- 粒　　　　corn, grain.
91-- 類　　　　grain and corn, cereals.

4796₁
簷〔Yen〕*n.* eaves.

4796₂
榴〔Liu〕*n.* pomegranate.
10-- 霰彈　　　shrapnel.
16-- 彈　　　　high explosive shell.
-- 彈砲　　　　howitzer.

4796₃
櫓〔Lu〕*n.* oar, scull.

4796₄

格〔Ke〕n. pattern, model, form, standard, rule, v. correct, rectify.

00-- 言	precept, proverb, maxim, motto.
-- 度	one's moral character.
07-- 調	form, style, pattern.
08-- 於規定	be barred by regulations.
17-- 子	check, lattice, blank, trellis.
-- 子箱	crate, skeleton case.
22-- 紙	ruled paper.
23-- 外	extra, exceptional, especially, all the more, extraordinary.
-- 外開恩	pardon an offender.
-- 外留神	pay additional attention.
43-- 式	form, style, model, manner, fashion, lintel style.
47-- 殺勿論	execute summarily, kill on sight.
77-- 鬥	fisticuff.

4796₇

楣〔Mei〕n. lintel of a door.

4798₂

款〔Kuan〕n. money, fund, income, expanse, sum of money, article of a law or treaty, adj. sincere, honest, kind.

11-- 項	money, sum of money.
24-- 待	welcome, entertain, receive, treat.
30-- 客	entertain guest.
31-- 額	amount of money involved.
43-- 式	style, pattern, fashion, article.
-- 目	articles, clauses (of a law, treaty etc.).
-- 留	sincerely try to make a guest stay longer.

4801₂

尬〔Ka〕v. walk awry.

4801₃

尷〔Ka〕v. walk awry.

4814₀

救〔Chiu〕n. salvation, relief, v. save, deliver, rescue, relieve, assist.

00-- 主	savior, messiah.
-- 亡宣傳	salvation propaganda.
-- 亡圖存	save one's country so that it may survive.
-- 護	save and protect, relieve and nurse.
-- 護車	ambulance.
-- 護隊	first aid corps.
-- 護法	techniques of first aid.
-- 護站	aid station.
10-- 死	save one's life.
22-- 出	save, rescue, help out.
-- 災	provide disaster relief.
25-- 生	save, rescue.
-- 生衣	life jacket.
-- 生帶	life-belt, life-preserver.
-- 生圈	buoy.
-- 生艇	life boat.
30-- 濟	deliver, relieve, succor.
-- 濟方法	remedy.
-- 濟工作	relief work.
-- 濟貸款	relief loan.
-- 濟基金	fund for relief, relief fund (roll).
-- 濟貧民	aid the poors.
-- 濟物資	relief supplies.
-- 濟者	savior.
-- 濟院	reformatory, almshouse.
-- 濟金	relief funds (payment, dole).
44-- 世軍	salvation army.
-- 藥	remedy.
47-- 助	assist, help,
52-- 援	save, succor, give a helping hand.
60-- 星	savior, deliverer.
-- 國	save the country, national salvation.
-- 國公債	liberty bonds.
72-- 兵	reinforcements.
74-- 助	aid, relieve, help.
80-- 命	save life, help!
90-- 火	put out a fire, fight a fire, extinguish a fire.
-- 火皮帶	hose.
-- 火機	fire engine.
-- 火車	fire engine.
-- 火員	fireman.

-- 火局	fire department.
-- 火會	fire brigade.

墩 〔Tun〕 n. heap, mound, tumulus.
4816₆

增 〔Tseng〕 v. increase, add, augment.

00-- 產	increase production, production stimulation.
-- 產節約	increase production and practice economy.
-- 高	make higher, bring up, raise, heighten.
08-- 效	increase profit, heighten effect.
12-- 刊	supplementary issue, enlarged edition, supplement.
13-- 強	fortify, strengthen, reinforce.
-- 強警戒	heighten the vigilance.
14-- 殖	n. propagation, v. propagate.
21-- 價	increase the price, advance price, increment.
24-- 值	increase of value, appreciation.
-- 值稅	value added tax, appreciation tax.
27-- 多	multiplication.
28-- 稅	tax increase.
30-- 進	improve, advance, promote.
-- 進知識	increase one's knowledge.
32-- 添	increase.
33-- 減	increase and decrease.
-- 補	supplement.
37-- 資	increase capitalization.
40-- 大	enlarge, increase, augment.
46-- 加	n. addition, augmentation, v. increase, add, raise.
-- 加一倍	double.
-- 加值	value-added, added value.
-- 加生產	increase production.
52-- 援	reinforce.
71-- 長	increase and advances.
-- 長率	scale of increase, rate of increase.
-- 長知識	add to one's knowledge.
-- 厚兵力	increase the military strength.

72-- 刪	n. additions and deletion, v. amend, revise.
-- 刪條例	amend the regulation.
77-- 股	rights issue.
80-- 益	increase, profit, gain.
90-- 光	do honor, glorify, reflect credit on.

散 〔San〕 n. powder, v. disperse, distribute, scatter, diffuse, disseminate, break up, adj. loosened, separated, miscellaneous, in disorder.
4824₀

00-- 文	prose.
06-- 課	dismiss a class.
10-- 工	day labor, journey work, job work.
-- 頁	odd sheets.
12-- 發	circulate, distribute, give out.
21-- 步	walk, take a walk, stroll.
22-- 亂	disheveled.
24-- 佈	spread, diffuse.
-- 佈物	spreader.
-- 裝	in bulk, loose packed.
29-- 伙	dissolve partnership.
33-- 心	free oneself from anxiety, cheer up.
36-- 漫	sprawl, desultory.
40-- 去	drop away, disperse.
44-- 落	fall here and there, be scattered.
-- 熱	refrigeration (in medicine).
52-- 播	broadcast, strew, spread, scatter, give currency to.
72-- 兵	irregular soldier, loose order.
75-- 體詩	free verse.
-- 開	disperse, scatter.
80-- 會	dismiss a meeting, adjourn.
90-- 光	diffused light, astigmatism.

猶 〔Yu〕 adj. like, same, similar, equal to, adv. still, yet, no better than.
4826₁

17-- 豫	v. hesitate, falter, adj. doubtful, hesitating.
27-- 疑不決	be in two minds.

40-- 太　　　Jews.
-- 太教　　Judaism.
-- 太國　　Israel.
-- 太人　　Jews.
46-- 如　　as if.

4826₆

獪〔**Kuai**〕 *adj.* cunning, crafty.

4829₄

狳〔**Yu**〕 *n.* armadillo.

4832₇

驚〔**Ching**〕 *v.* terrify, frighten, startle, amaze, fear, surprise, astonish, *adj.* frightened, terrified, afraid, surprise, astonished.

01-- 訝　　wonder, amaze, surprise.
16-- 醒　　rouse.
17-- 恐　　alarm, frightened, scared.
24-- 動　　disturb, trouble, alarm.
33-- 心　　heartstricken, frightened.
-- 心動魄　terrifying, breathtaking.
40-- 奇　　be surprised.
51-- 擾　　disturb, cause trouble.
60-- 異　　marvel, surprise, be amazed.
62-- 呼　　howl in alarm.
64-- 嚇　　*n.* panic, fear, terror, *v.* scare, terrify, frighten.
-- 嘆　　admire, marvel.
70-- 駭　　frightened, terrified, afraid, astonished.
80-- 人　　surprising, astonishing, striking, shocking.
94-- 慌　　confusion, panic, alarm.
96-- 愕　　surprised, thunderstruck.

4834₀

赦〔**She**〕 *v.* excuse, forgive, pardon, remit, amnesty.

27-- 免　　excuse, forgive, pardon, let go.
-- 免法　　Act of Indemnity.
30-- 宥　　forgive.
60-- 罪　　remit, pardon, forgive sins.

4841₇

乾〔**Kan**〕 *adj.* dry, clean.

10-- 電池　　dry battery, cell.
17-- 酪　　cheese.
24-- 貨　　dry goods, dry cargo.
32-- 淨　　clean, neat, dry.
34-- 洗　　dry-clean.
36-- 渴　　thirsty.
-- 涸　　drain, dry up.
40-- 女　　adopted daughter.
41-- 杯　　toast, bottoms up!
43-- 娘　　adopted mother.
44-- 草　　hay.
-- 枯　　withered, dry.
45-- 坤　　universe, heaven and earth.
60-- 咳　　dry cough.
-- 旱　　drought.
-- 果　　dried fruit.
77-- 脆　　straightforward, downright.
96-- 糧　　ready-prepared food, trail ration, hard ration.
-- 糧袋　　dry ration bag.
-- 燥　　dry, parched, arid.
-- 燥劑　　dryer.

4842₇

翰〔**Han**〕 *n.* pencil, pen, *adj.* literary, *v.* soar.

30-- 墨　　literature and calligraphy.

4843₇

嫌〔**Hsian**〕 *v.* suspect, doubt, dislike, detest, mistrust, hate, have no sympathy with.

10-- 惡　　dislike, loathe, abhor.
27-- 疑　　*n.* suspicion, *v.* suspect, doubt.
-- 疑行爲　suspicious conduct.
-- 疑心重　be full of suspicion in mind.
-- 疑犯　　suspect.
71-- 厭　　hate.
79-- 隙　　disagreement, breach, grudge, misunderstanding.
90-- 少　　consider something insufficient.
91-- 煩　　dislike the trouble.

4844₀

教〔**Chiao**〕 *n.* religion, rule, *v.* teach, instruct, train up, incite, instigate.

00-- 主　　the master.

-- 育	*n.* education, instruction, culture, *v.* educate, teach, instruct.
-- 育廳	Department of Education.
-- 育部	Ministry of Education.
-- 育部長	Minister of Education.
-- 育經費	educational fund.
-- 育家	educator.
-- 育補助	education allowance.
-- 育補助金	education grant.
-- 育片	training film.
-- 育革命	revolution in education.
-- 育學	pedagogy.
02-- 訓	*n.* instruction, *v.* educate, lesson, instruct.
08-- 誨	instruct.
10-- 王	Pope, Pontiff.
11-- 研組	teaching research group.
16-- 理	doctrine.
17-- 務長	dean of studies.
-- 務處	the dean's office.
21-- 旨	doctrines.
-- 師	teacher, instructor, schoolmaster.
24-- 化	refine, cultivate, enlighten.
-- 科書	text book.
-- 徒	disciple, religious devotee or follower.
25-- 練	drill, train, coach.
26-- 皇	Pope.
-- 程	course of studies.
27-- 條	dogma.
30-- 室	classroom.
32-- 派	denomination, religious sect.
38-- 導	instruct, teach.
-- 導有方	skillful in teaching and providing guidance.
-- 導員	instructor.
40-- 士	priest, clergyman, pastor.
-- 友	fellow converts, fellow church member.
44-- 材	teaching material.
52-- 授	*n.* professor, *v.* teach, instruct.
-- 授法	teaching method.
60-- 員	instructor, teacher, master.

63-- 唆	incite, instigate.
-- 唆犯	abettor, fagin.
71-- 區	parish.
-- 長	prelate.
77-- 學	teach.
-- 學大綱	syllabus.
-- 門	door to Buddhism.
80-- 義	dogma, doctrine.
-- 會	church, mission.
-- 會學校	missionary school.
-- 養	bring up.
-- 養院	reformatory.
90-- 堂	church, temple, mosque.

嫩 〔Nen〕 *adj.* young, slender, tender, delicate.

44-- 芽	tender shoot.
-- 枝	twig, tender branch.
-- 葉	young leaves.

4844₁

姘 〔Pin〕 *n.* illicit intercourse.

03-- 識	cohabitation.
11-- 頭	lover, sweetheart.

幹 〔Kan〕 *n.* trunk, *adj.* capable, able.

07-- 部	fundamental officer.
40-- 才	ability.
50-- 事	officer.

4850₂

擎 〔Ching〕 *v.* raise, elevate, lift up.

47-- 起	raise high, lift up.

4860₁

警 〔Ching〕 *n.* police, alarm, urgency, *v.* warn, caution, admonish, guard, keep watch.

16-- 醒	awaken.
17-- 務	police affairs.
-- 務長	chief of police.
21-- 衛	guard, convoy.
-- 衛員	bodyguard.
-- 衛隊	guard, convoy.
24-- 備	vigilant, keep watch.
-- 備隊	garrison corps, police force.
-- 告	warn, caution, give warning.
-- 句	epigram.
30-- 官	police constable.
-- 察	police, constable.

-- 察所	police station.
-- 察署	police office.
-- 察派出所	police box.
40-- 士	policeman.
43-- 犬	police dog, patrol dog.
46-- 棍	billy.
47-- 報	alarm.
50-- 吏=警官	
53-- 戒	warn, caution, guard, take precaution, on the alert.
-- 戒線	cordon, danger line or mark.
-- 戒森嚴	be strictly on guard.
-- 戒地帶	outpost zone.
64-- 嚇	astonish.
78-- 監	police superintendent.
80-- 鐘	alarm bell.
88-- 笛	whistle.
96-- 惕	alert, vigilance.

4864_0
故〔Ku〕 n. cause, reason, v. die, pass away, adj. ancient, old, late, formerly, conj. therefore, so that.

00-- 意	intentionally, willingly, purposely.
-- 意謊報	fraudulent misrepresentation.
-- 意行爲	intentional act, willful action.
-- 意傷害	intentional injury.
-- 意違約	willful default.
27-- 鄉	native country, motherland.
40-- 友	old friend.
50-- 事	story, novel.
70-- 障排除	trouble shooting, troubleshooting.

敬〔Ching〕 v. respect, honor, worship, revere, adj. respectful, honorable, sedate.

00-- 意	regards, respect.
05-- 請	invite.
-- 請光臨	may I have the honor of your presence at.
20-- 重	respect, honor.
-- 愛	respect and love.
21-- 虔主義	pietism.
-- 拜	obeisance.
27-- 佩	admire.
-- 仰	revere, esteem.
31-- 酒	toast.
35-- 神	piety.
-- 禮	salute, greeting, reverence.
44-- 老院	home for the aged.
-- 慕	admire.
60-- 畏	in reverential fear of, revere.

4880_2
趁〔Chem〕 v. avail oneself of, take advantage of, follow.

21-- 便	take advantage of the opportunity.
60-- 早	take time by the forelock, as early possible.

4891_1
柞〔Tso〕 n. oak.

4891_4
栓〔Shuan〕 n. plug, pin, wooden peg.

4891_7
檻〔Chien〕 n. railing, cage, door-sill, threshold.

4892_1
榆〔Yu〕 n. elm.

4892_7
梯〔Ti〕 n. staircase, ladder, stairway.

12-- 形	trapezoid, trapezium.
17-- 子	ladder, staircase.
21-- 步	step.
22-- 山	clamber up a mountain.
27-- 級	steps of a ladder.
60-- 田	terraced field.

櫛〔Chieh〕 n. comb.

21-- 比	be close together like the teeth of a comb.

4893_2
松〔Sung〕 n. pine, evergreen.

13-- 球	pine cone.
17-- 子	fir seeds, pine seeds.
20-- 香	rosin.
-- 香油	rosin oil.
31-- 江	Sunkiang.
35-- 油	pine-tree oil.

40-- 木	pine, pine wood.
44-- 葉	pine needles.
-- 林	pine forest, pinery.
46-- 柏	pines and cypresses.
77-- 鼠	squirrel.
88-- 節油	turpentine.

樣〔**Yang**〕 *n.* kind, sort, manner, mode, way, style, form, shape, fashion, pattern, sample, model.

17-- 子	example, pattern, sample, form, style.
41-- 板	templet.
43-- 式	manner, fashion, style, form.
48-- 樣俱全	have all kinds of things.
-- 樣都會	can do everything.
50-- 本	specimen, sample, example.
60-- 品	sample, specimen, pattern.
-- 品陳列室	sample room.

4894₀

枚〔**Mei**〕 *n.* piece, *adj.* one, each.

58-- 數	count one by one.
77-- 舉	enumeration.

杵〔**Chu**〕 *n.* pestle.

77-- 臼	pestle and mortar.

橄〔**Gan**〕 *n.* olive, olive tree.

48-- 欖	olive.
-- 欖仁	olive seeds.
-- 欖油	olive oil.
-- 欖枝	olive branch.
-- 欖園	olive-orchard.

檄〔**Hsi**〕 *n.* official dispatch, official note.

00-- 文	summons to arm.

4895₅

梅〔**Mei**〕 *n.* plum, prune.

17-- 子	plums.
44-- 花	plum flowers.
50-- 毒	syphilis.
60-- 園	plum garden.

4896₇

槍〔**Chiang**〕 *n.* gun, lance, spear, pistol, rifle.

11-- 頭	head of a spear.
16-- 彈	ammunition, cartridge.
20-- 手	rifleman, spearman.
27-- 身	gun-barrel, barrel of a rifle.
34-- 法	art of fighting with a spear, marksmanship.
41-- 柄	spear-handle, steel.
46-- 架	stack for guns.
-- 桿	shaft of a spear, guns.
47-- 殺	shoot (to death), kill by shooting.
52-- 刺	bayonet.
60-- 口	muzzle of a rifle.
67-- 眼	loophole.
88-- 管	bore of a gun.
90-- 尖	spearhead, point of a spear.

4898₆

檢〔**Chien**〕 *v.* examine, investigate, inspect, restrict, control, revise, compare.

00-- 疫	quarantine.
-- 疫證書	health certificate, quarantine certificate.
-- 疫處理	quarantine treatment.
-- 疫官員	quarantine officer, health officer.
-- 疫機構	quarantine office.
-- 疫費	quarantine fee.
-- 疫所	quarantine office (station).
04-- 討	self-criticism.
-- 討書	statement of self-criticism.
27-- 修	overhaul, repair.
30-- 察	inspect, examine.
-- 察官	procurator, prosecutor.
-- 察長	attorney-general.
40-- 查	test, examine, search, censor, inspect, look up, see over.
-- 查證書	certificate of inspection.
-- 查試驗	test trial.
-- 查制度	censorship.
-- 查貨物	inspect the goods (cargo).
-- 查法	inspection method.
-- 查報告	inspection report.
-- 查費	inspection charges (expenses).
-- 查合格	passed examination.

-- 查員	censor, inspector.
-- 查所	examining, inspection bureau.
61-- 點	check, restrict.
77-- 閱	review, inspect, read through, go over.
-- 閱官	inspector-general, mustermaster.
-- 閱台	rostrum, reviewing stand.
-- 舉	inform the authorities of an unlawful act.
-- 舉信	letter of accusation.
78-- 驗	examine, test.
-- 驗主任	chief inspector.
-- 驗結果	results of tests.
-- 驗報告書	inspection report.
-- 驗日期	date of survey.
-- 驗員	surveyor.
-- 驗單	check list.

4928₀

狄 〔Ti〕 n. the Ti tribe (of North China).

4942₀

妙 〔Miao〕 adj. wonderful, perfect, splendid, interesting, ingenious, excellent, mysterious.

04-- 計	contrivance, clever device, ingenious scheme.
08-- 論	extraordinary argument.
20-- 手	expert, crack hand.
-- 手回春	bring back life to a patient.
46-- 想天開	some unheard of, fantastic idea.
80-- 年	youth, the prime of life.
88-- 策	tactics.

4942₇

嫦 〔Chang〕 n. fairy.

| 43-- 娥 | angel in the moon. |

4952₇

鞘 〔Chiao〕 n. sheath, scabbard.

4958₀

鞦 〔Chiu〕 n. crupper.

| 41-- 韆 | swing. |

4980₂

趙 〔Chao〕 n. Chu (a family name).

趟 〔Tang〕 n. times.

4992₇

梢 〔Shao〕 n. extreme end of a tree, paddle, oar.

4996₆

檔 〔Dang〕 n. wooden cross-piece, records, files.

| 30-- 案 | archives, files. |
| -- 案室 | archives. |

5

5000₀

丈 〔Chang〕 n. ten Chinese feet, father-in-law, elder, senior.

50-- 夫	husband.
-- 夫氣	manliness.
60-- 量	measure.
77-- 母	mother-in-law.
80-- 人	father-in-law.

5000₆

中 〔Chong〕 n. middle, center, heart, core, adj. inner, middle, medium, v. catch, hit (target), attain (a goal) prep. in the middle of, between, among, within.

00-- 立	n. neutrality, adj. neutral.
-- 立主義	neutralism.
-- 立國	neutral state, neutral country.
-- 產階級	the middle class, bourgeoisie.
-- 庸	n. golden mean, adj. moderate, mean, medium, temperate.
-- 庸主義	the doctrine of the mean.
-- 意	like, satisfied with.
-- 文	the Chinese language.
-- 計	fall into a trap.
01-- 站	transfer station.
07-- 部	n. central part, adj. central, middle.
10-- 正	right, just right.
-- 下等	below average.
-- 西合璧	good blending of Chinese and Western culture.
12-- 型	medium-sized.

-- 型工業	medium-scale industry.
16-- 彈	hit the bullet, be hit by a bullet.
17-- 子	neutron.
21-- 上等	better than average.
-- 止	suspend, stop, pause, discontinue, cease.
-- 肯	convincing, cogent, to the point.
22-- 斷	discontinue, suspend, interrupt.
23-- 外	China and foreign countries, at home and abroad.
-- 外馳名	celebrated both in China and abroad.
-- 外貿易	international trade, Chinese-foreigner trade.
26-- 和	neutralize.
-- 線	the median (of a triangle), center line.
27-- 將	lieutenant general (Army, Air Force), vice admiral (Navy).
-- 旬	the middle ten days of a month.
-- 餐	Chinese meal, Chinese food.
28-- 傷	vilify, undermine, defame.
29-- 秋節	the Mid-Autumn Festival, Moon Festival.
30-- 寒	catch cold.
33-- 心	center, core, nucleus, heart.
-- 心商場	shopping center.
-- 心商業區	central business district.
-- 心市場	central market.
-- 心供暖	central heating.
-- 心點	focus, central point.
-- 心區	central district.
-- 心問題	pivotal question.
34-- 波	medium wave (in radio).
38-- 游	middle reaches in the course of a river.
-- 途	midway, halfway.
-- 道而廢	stop halfway.
40-- 南海	Zhongnanhai.
-- 古	the middle age, medieval age.
-- 校	lieutenant-colonel.
41-- 標	win a bid (tender).
-- 樞	center.
-- 樞大員	high official of the central government.
44-- 草藥	herb-medicine, traditional Chinese medicine.
-- 華民族	the Chinese nation.
-- 華民國	The Republic of China.
-- 世紀	Middle Ages.
-- 藥	Chinese traditional medicine.
47-- 期	midterm, medium term.
49-- 檔	medium grade.
50-- 央	central, middle, center.
-- 央訓練團	central training corp.
-- 央計算機	central computer.
-- 央政府	central government.
-- 央集權	centralism, centralization.
-- 央社	Central News Agency.
-- 央軍校	Central Military Academy.
-- 央執行委員會	Central Executive Committee.
-- 央銀行	Central Bank.
-- 毒	*n.* intoxication, *v.* be poisoned.
-- 東	Middle East.
51-- 指	middle finger.
55-- 轉	change trains, transit shipment.
-- 農	middle-class peasant.
58-- 數	medium.
60-- 國	China.
-- 國貨	made in China goods.
-- 國的	Chinese, of China.
-- 國人	Chinese.
-- 暑	sunstroke.
61-- 號	medium size.
-- 層	middle level.
74-- 尉	lieutenant (Navy), first lieutenant (Army, Air Force).
77-- 堅	main body, backbone, mainstay.
-- 堅人物	key personnel, elite.
-- 風	apoplexy (in medicine), palsy, stroke.
-- 學校	middle school.

-- 學生	middle school student.
-- 學校長	principal of a middle school.
-- 間	middle, medium, intermediate, between, among.
-- 間商	jobber, go-between middleman.
-- 間派	middle-of-the-roader.
-- 堅分子	middle element.
-- 醫	doctor of Chinese medicine.
-- 興	renaissance, revival.
78-- 隊	detachment.
80-- 人	middle man, go-between, arbitrator, negotiator.
-- 介費	reward, middleman's fee.
-- 介國	intermediate nations.
-- 午	noon, midday.
-- 年	middle age.
82-- 飯	lunch.
87-- 鋒	center forward, center.
87-- 飽	embezzle.
88-- 等	*n.* average, *adj.* middle grade, middling, moderate.
-- 等身材	of medium height.
-- 等收入者	middle-income earners.
-- 等之才	medium or average talent.
-- 等社會	bourgeois.
-- 等城市	medium-sized town or city.
-- 等教育	secondary education.
-- 等學校	high school, middle school.
-- 等人才	ordinary or mediocre person.
-- 篇小說	novelette.
90-- 小企業	medium and small-sized business, small and medium-sized enterprises (SMEs).
95-- 性	neuter (in grammar), neutral (in chemistry).

史〔Shih〕*n.* history, story.

04-- 詩	epic.
27-- 的	historic, historical.
77-- 學	history, historical science.
-- 學家	historian.
80-- 前	pre-historic.
-- 無前例	unprecedented.
87-- 錄	record.

| 88-- 籍 | annals, chronicles. |

吏〔Li〕*n.* officer, government official.

申〔Shen〕*v.* extend, explain, stretch, prolong, report.

00-- 辯	defend, defend oneself.
-- 辦	bid for, apply permission to do.
02-- 訴	appeal.
04-- 謝	thank.
05-- 請	apply, demand, request.
-- 請註冊	application, request form.
-- 請延期	application for extension.
-- 請書	application.
-- 請表	application form.
-- 請專利	application for patent.
-- 請人	applicant.
08-- 說	declare.
33-- 述	state.
47-- 報	declare.
-- 報單	declaration form.
50-- 申	relaxed, at ease, again and again.
67-- 明	*n.* assertion, declaration, *v.* allege, assert, declare.
72-- 斥	reproach, reprove.
77-- 冤	redress an injustice, right a wrong.

曳〔I〕*v.* trail, tow, tug, draw, draft, drag, pull.

| 12-- 引 | *n.* traction, *v.* pull, tug. |
| 47-- 起 | hoist. |

串〔Chuan〕*n.* string, cluster, *v.* string together, connect, conspire, league together.

00-- 音	cross talk, overhearing.
12-- 聯	established ties, contact one by one.
35-- 連	get connected in a series, exchange experience with other.
37-- 通	collude, play booty.
-- 通舞弊	collusion.
47-- 起來	string together.
77-- 門	visit, call at one's home casually.

80-- 合　　　　league together.

車〔Che〕*n.* car, cart, carriage, vehicle.

00-- 廂　　　　car of a train, compartment.
-- 床　　　　lathe.
01-- 站　　　　station, bus stop.
10-- 工　　　　turner, lathe turner.
-- 票　　　　bus or train ticket.
12-- 水馬龍　　traffic is heavy.
24-- 牀　　　　lathe.
27-- 身　　　　body of a car.
-- 身廣告　　　dash sign.
30-- 房　　　　garage.
37-- 禍　　　　car accident.
-- 運費用　　　trucking expenses.
50-- 夫　　　　carter, driver, coachman, chauffeur.
51-- 輛　　　　vehicle, car, cart.
-- 輛登記　　　vehicle registration.
-- 輛稅　　　　vehicle taxes.
-- 輛載荷　　　carload.
-- 輛執照費　　car license fee.
54-- 技　　　　trick-cycling.
55-- 費　　　　fare.
58-- 轍　　　　rut.
-- 輪　　　　wheel.
67-- 照　　　　car license.
-- 馬費　　　　transportation allowance, (fee).
73-- 胎　　　　tire on vehicle wheels.
77-- 間　　　　workshop, machine shop.

丰〔Feng〕*adj.* graceful, fine.

20-- 秀　　　　plumb.
-- 采　　　　grace, fine manner.
-- 采依然　　　one's elegance remains as before.
-- 儀　　　　graceful, dignified.
37-- 姿　　　　elegance, charming appearance.
70-- 雅　　　　elegant, graceful.

5000₇

聿〔Yu〕*n.* pen, writing, instrument, *adv.* then, forthwith, at once.

事〔Shih〕*n.* affair, matter, case, work, serve, occupation, subject, theme, *v.* serve, attend, manage.

00-- 主　　　　client, prosecutor.
10-- 不如意　　the matter has gone wrong.
11-- 非得已　　there is no other choice.
-- 項　　　　affairs, matters.
12-- 到　　　　things having come to such a stage.
17-- 務　　　　affairs, matters, business.
-- 務員　　　　clerk.
-- 務所　　　　office, business premises.
-- 務管理　　　business management.
20-- 倍功半　　twice the work with half of the result — very inefficient.
21-- 例　　　　case, instance, example.
-- 態　　　　situation, state of things.
22-- 後　　　　after the event, later on, afterwards.
-- 後方知　　　be wise after the event, hindsight is always 20/20.
-- 變　　　　incident.
24-- 先　　　　beforehand, in advance.
-- 先定妥　　　arrange beforehand.
25-- 件　　　　event, incident, happening.
27-- 物　　　　thing, object.
30-- 實　　　　fact, matter, reality.
-- 實上　　　　in fact, as a matter of fact.
-- 實如此　　　such is the case.
-- 實俱在　　　there are all the facts.
32-- 業　　　　enterprise, occupation, vocation, calling.
37-- 過境遷　　things change after an affairs is over.
40-- 在人為　　human effort can achieve anything.
-- 有本末　　　there is a distinction of the basic essentials and the peripheries in everything.
-- 有始終　　　there is a sequence of beginning and end in everything.
44-- 權　　　　circumstance, current, of event, authority.
48-- 故　　　　accident, breakdown, cause.
-- 故保險　　　accident insurance.
50-- 事週到　　everything is fully done.
-- 事如意　　everything is as one wishes.

-- 奉	serve.	
-- 由	reason, cause.	
65-- 蹟	deeds.	
80-- 前	before the event, on the eve.	
90-- 尚未成	the matter is not yet settled.	
-- 半功倍	half the work with double result ─ very efficient.	
95-- 情	matter, affair, event.	

5001₁

轆 〔**Lu**〕 *n.* wheel and axle, roller, pulley.

51-- 轤	pulley, windlass, capstan.

5001₄

推 〔**Tui**〕 *v.* push, thrust, expel, infer, investigate.

00-- 度	inference, deduction.
-- 廣	*n.* publicity, *v.* popularize, spread.
-- 廣主任	chief of promotion.
02-- 諉	make an excuse.
-- 託	*n.* elusion, *v.* make an excuse.
08-- 論	infer, deduce, make advance.
-- 論法	inference.
20-- 重	hold in high esteem, admire.
-- 辭	refuse, decline.
22-- 斷	calculate, reckon.
-- 倒	push down.
-- 出	push out.
24-- 動	push, move, drive.
27-- 翻	overturn, overthrow, knock down, knock over.
-- 移	shuffle.
30-- 進	impulse, impel, propel.
-- 進機	propeller.
-- 定	conclude.
32-- 測	guess, suppose, deduce, infer, investigate, presume.
37-- 選	elect.
40-- 土機	bulldozer.
44-- 薦	recommend.
-- 薦書	letter of recommendation.
46-- 想	infer, think.
50-- 事	judge, magistrate.

77-- 開	push open, put off .
-- 舉	elect, recommend.
80-- 拿	massage.
88-- 算	calculate, reckon.
89-- 銷	sales promotion.
-- 銷計劃	sales program.
-- 銷費用	promotional cost (expenses).
-- 銷員	salesman, canvasser, promotion worker.
-- 銷術	salesmanship, sales technique.

撞 〔**Chuang**〕 *v.* strike, pound, knock against, collide with, come into conflict.

22-- 倒	pull down.
60-- 見	meet.
80-- 人	thrust into.

擁 〔**Yung**〕 *v.* embrace, press, clasp.

14-- 護	support, assert, stand for.
50-- 擠	*v.* overcrowd, congest, hustle, huddle, adj. overcrowded.
57-- 抱	embrace, clasp, infold.

攤 〔**Tan**〕 *n.* stall, booth, *v.* share, display, apportion, spread out, open out.

17-- 子	stall, stand.
20-- 位	stand.
-- 售	set up stalls along the street.
26-- 牌	showdown, show one's card.
32-- 派	contribute, apportion to each, allocate.
36-- 還	*n.* amortization, *v.* amortize.
61-- 販	street vendor, stall keeper.
77-- 開	open out, spread out.
80-- 分	divide up.

5001₆

擅 〔**Shan**〕 *v.* assume, presume, dare, usurp, *adj.* willful, arbitrary.

17-- 取	take unauthorized.
18-- 敢	venture to, dare to.
26-- 自	*v.* presume, assume, *adv.* arbitrarily.
-- 自離職	resign without permission.
30-- 進	enter without permission.

44-- 權　　　assume power, usurp power.
71-- 長　　　expert in, skilled in, versed in.

5001_7
抗〔Kang〕v. oppose, resist, withstand, rebel, reject, raise.

00-- 辯　　　argue, defend, remonstrate.
08-- 議　　　n. protest, remonstrance, v. object, protest against, exclaim against.
-- 敵　　　resist the enemy, fight against the enemy.
25-- 生素　　antibiotics.
27-- 爭　　　take opposite side, take issue.
38-- 逆　　　counter.
51-- 拒　　　n. opposition, antagonism, v. withstand, repel, resist, oppose, hold out.
60-- 旱　　　drought-resistance.
63-- 戰　　　resistance.
-- 戰到底　resist to the bitter end.
-- 戰建國　resistance and reconstruction.

5001_8
拉〔La〕v. pull, drag, tug, draw, bend.

10-- 丁　　　Latin.
-- 丁語　　Latin language.
-- 平　　　even up, bring to the same level.
20-- 手　　　shake hands.
-- 住　　　hold fast.
25-- 生意　　bring in business.
50-- 夫　　　press men into military service.
-- 車　　　draw a cart.
77-- 關係　　try to curry favor with, try to establish connection.

5002_3
擠〔Chi〕v. press, squeeze, crowd, push.

12-- 到　　　screw out, elbow out.
22-- 出　　　squeeze.
30-- 進　　　press in, squeeze in.
34-- 滿　　　overcrowded, packed, filled to capacity.

47-- 奶　　　milk a cow.
60-- 時間　　squeeze in every possible minute.
80-- 兌　　　squeeze, run on a bank.

5002_7
摘〔Chai〕v. pick, pull, pluck, expose, select, take of.

07-- 記　　　n. note, v. jot down.
10-- 下　　　pick off.
-- 要　　　n. digest, summary, epitome, v. abridge, abstract, summarize.
44-- 花　　　pluck flowers.
50-- 由　　　excerpt the most important point.
78-- 除　　　excise.
87-- 錄　　　make an extract, excerpt, take a passage.

5003_0
夫〔Fu〕n. husband, man, servant.

17-- 子　　　master.
27-- 役　　　porter, coolie.
44-- 權　　　authority of the husband.
-- 婦　　　man and wife, husband and wife, couple, mate.
-- 婦之道　the proper relations of husband and wife.
50-- 妻　　　husband and wife.
-- 妻店　　mom and pop store, convenience store.
66-- 唱婦隨　harmony between husband and wife.
80-- 人　　　wife, madam, mistress, lady.

央〔Yang〕n. center, middle, halfway, v. entreat, beg, request, press earnestly.

05-- 請　　　make a request.
43-- 求　　　beg, request, entreat, solicit.
-- 求宥諒　beg for forgiveness.

5003_1
摭〔Chih〕v. take up, gather together.

5003_2
夷〔I〕n. barbarian, v. exterminate, kill, annihilate, destroy, adj. even,

level.

10-- 平	level, raze to the ground.
33-- 滅	destroy, annihilate, exterminate.

攘 〔Jang〕 v. snatch, steal, snatch, reject, repel, shake.

| 40-- 奪 | seize, snatch, rob. |

5004₀

扠 〔Wen〕 v. wipe off.

5004₁

擗 〔Pi〕 v. open, cleave.

5004₃

摔 〔Shuai〕 v. throw down, dash down.

10-- 碎	smash into pieces.
22-- 倒	throw to the ground.
27-- 角	wrestling.
-- 角家	wrestler.

5004₄

接 〔Chieh〕 v. connect, join, unite, succeed to, follow on, associate with.

00-- 應	respond, supply, stand ready for assistance.
11-- 班	take over from, take one's turn on duty.
-- 班人	successor.
12-- 到	receive, come to hand.
13-- 球	catch a ball, return a served ball.
14-- 聽	respond.
20-- 手	take over, take charge of.
-- 受	accept, receive, take in.
-- 受訂貨	order acceptance, receive order.
-- 受委託	accept a commission.
-- 受外援	receive outside aid.
-- 受培訓	undergo training.
-- 受採訪	give an interview.
22-- 任	take up office.
-- 種	inoculate.
24-- 納	accept.
-- 待	receive, attend, entertain.
-- 待室	drawing room, reception-room, parlor.
-- 續	continue, connect.

-- 續字	conjunction.
25-- 生	midwife.
26-- 觸	touch, contact.
-- 線	wire, connect.
-- 線生	switchboard operator.
28-- 收	receive, take over, re-occupy.
30-- 濟	support, help, supply.
-- 客	receive guests.
32-- 近	close to, near, approaching.
35-- 連	connect, join, unite.
38-- 洽	contact, negotiate, consult with, arrange.
-- 送	receive and send off.
40-- 力賽跑	relay race.
44-- 樹	grafting.
-- 枝	graft, engraft.
60-- 見	receive, interview, give an audience.
67-- 吻	kiss.
88-- 管	take over.
-- 管令	receiving order.
90-- 合	join, unite, put together.

5004₇

掖 〔Yeh〕 v. help, support.

5004₈

捽 〔Tsu〕 v. clutch, seize with the hand.

較 〔Chiao〕 n. comparison, v. compare, compete, test, adj. rather, more.

27-- 多	more.
37-- 遲	behind time.
40-- 大	bigger, larger.
-- 壞	worse.
47-- 好	better.
60-- 量	n. trial of strength, v. compare by measurement, compare strength.
79-- 勝一籌	a little better, better by one degree.
90-- 少	less, minor.

5008₆

擴 〔Kuo〕 v. expand, stretch, enlarge, extend, magnify.

| 00-- 充 | expand, extend, enlarge. |
| -- 音器 | loudspeaker, microphone. |

11-- 張 | *n.* extension, expansion, *v.* develop, expand.
-- 張主義 | expansionism.
15-- 建 | expand.
37-- 軍 | expand armament.
40-- 大 | enlarge, expand.
-- 大貿易 | encourage business.
-- 大生產 | expand production, increase production.
-- 大營業 | enlarge (broaden, extend, widen) business.
-- 大會議 | enlarged conference.
47-- 聲器 | loudspeaker.
48-- 散 | spread, diffuse.
77-- 展 | expand, extend.

5009₆
掠 〔Lueh〕 *v.* rob, plunder.
02-- 誘 | kidnap.
40-- 奪 | rob, plunder, ravage, prey.
-- 奪性 | predatory character.

5010₆
晝 〔Chou〕 *n.* day time, day light.
00-- 夜 | day and night.
-- 夜不停 | round-the-clock.
-- 夜不息 | day and night without rest.
-- 夜服務 | day-and-night service.

畫 〔Hua〕 *n.* picture, drawing, painting, stroke, *v.* draw, paint, picture.
00-- 廊 | gallery.
10-- 一 | uniformity.
-- 面 | surface of a picture.
20-- 稿 | draft.
26-- 線 | draw a line.
27-- 像 | portrait.
30-- 室 | painting-room, studio.
-- 家 | painter, artist.
40-- 皮 | disguise.
41-- 板 | drawing board.
46-- 架 | easel.
47-- 報 | pictorial.
60-- 圖 | draw a picture.
-- 圖紙 | drawing-paper.
77-- 眉 | thrush.
80-- 分 | divide, delimit.
88-- 筆 | paint-brush.

5010₇
盅 〔Chung〕 *n.* glass, bowl, goblet, covered cup.
盎 〔Ang〕 *n.* tub, basin, dish.
17-- 司 | ounce.
盡 〔Chin〕 *n.* utmost, last, end, extremity, *v.* finish, exhaust, fulfill, complete, end, use up, be devoted, *adj.* all, exhausted, empty, finished, *adv.* fully, wholly, entirely, extremely.
00-- 棄 | all wasted, all in vain.
10-- 可能 | as possible.
11-- 頭 | the very end, the extremity.
13-- 職 | fulfill one's duty, perform one's duty.
33-- 心 | do the best, devote oneself to.
40-- 力 | make an effort, do the utmost, do one's best, make an exertion.
44-- 孝 | do one's filial duty.
50-- 忠 | show the highest degree of one's loyalty.
-- 責 | fulfill one's duty, pay one's way, be dutiful.
60-- 量 | utmost, fully, to the full extent.
77-- 興 | enjoy to one's heart's content.
80-- 義務 | fulfill one's duty.
-- 善盡美 | perfect, excellent.
95-- 性 | fulfill one's nature.
-- 情 | to one's heart's content.

蠱 〔Ku〕 *n.* internal worm, poison, venom.
50-- 毒 | poison.
53-- 惑 | bewitch, delude, fascinate.

5011₄
蛀 〔Chu〕 *adj.* eaten by insects.
21-- 齒 | decayed tooth.
30-- 空 | eat hollow.
37-- 洞 | cavity in a decayed tooth.
50-- 虫 | clothes moths, bookworm.
71-- 牙 | decayed tooth.

5012₇

螃〔Pang〕n. crab.

5013₂

泰〔Tai〕adj. great, grant, large, calm, peace, adv. largely, greatly, extensively.

10-- 平	peace.
22-- 山	Taishan, Mt. Tai in Shantung, Tarzan.
34-- 斗	star.
60-- 日	in the days of peace.

蠔〔Hao〕n. oyster.

| 35-- 油 | oyster sauce, oyster oil. |

5013₆

蠢〔Chun〕n. insect, worm.

00-- 腐	worm-eaten.
22-- 災	insect damage.
30-- 害	insect pests, damage caused by insect.
-- 害損失	damage by worm or vermin.
50-- 蛀	worm-eaten.
-- 蛀損失	moth damage.

蠢〔Chun〕v. wriggle, creep, adj. stupid, foolish, silly.

02-- 話	ignorant talk, babble.
24-- 動	itch for action.
34-- 漢	blockhead, donkey.
40-- 才	stupid person.
50-- 事	folly.
80-- 人	fool, idiot, blockhead.

5014₀

蚊〔Wen〕n. mosquito, gnat.

17-- 子	mosquito, gnat.
20-- 香	mosquito incense.
41-- 帳	mosquito net, curtain.
60-- 咬	mosquito bite.

5014₃

蟀〔Shuai〕n. cricket.

5014₆

蟑〔Chang〕n. cockroach.

5014₈

蛟〔Chiao〕n. scaly dragon.

5022₇

青〔Ching〕adj. green, blue, black, bamboo skin, young, youthful.

10-- 工	young worker.
-- 豆	green peas.
-- 霉素	penicillin.
17-- 翠	n. verdure, adj. verdant.
26-- 稞	barley.
27-- 魚	herring, mackerel.
-- 色	green color, blue.
-- 島	Tsingtao.
38-- 海	Tsinghai province.
44-- 草	green grass.
-- 苗	sprouts, rice seedlings.
-- 苔	green moss, lichen.
-- 菜	greens, vegetables.
45-- 樓	brothel, house of ill fame, house of prostitute.
50-- 春	young, youthful, prime of life.
-- 春期	puberty, adolescence.
54-- 蛙	frog.
60-- 果	fresh fruits, olive.
81-- 年	youth, young people, prime of life.
-- 年團	youth corp.
-- 年會	Young Men's Christian Association.
-- 年節	Chinese Youth Day (March 29).
87-- 銅	bronze.
90-- 少年	junior, teenager, juvenile.
-- 光眼	glaucoma.

胄〔Chou〕n. helmet.

| 60-- 甲 | armor. |

肅〔Su〕adj. respectful, solemn, serious, quiet, adv. gravely.

23-- 然	reverentially, solemnly.
35-- 清	liquidate, eliminate, eradicate, wipe out, tranquillize.
48-- 敬	respectful.
52-- 靜	dead silence.
71-- 反	suppression of a revolt.

5023₀

本〔Pen〕n. root, origin, beginning, foundation, source, capital, principal, copy, volume, base, capital (in business), adj. essential, radical, original, natural, proper.

00--	意	original intention.
--	文	text.
07--	部	headquarter.
10--	票	banker's cheque, cashiers check.
17--	子	book.
20--	位	standard.
--	位主義	departmentalism.
21--	能	instinct, inborn ability.
--	行	one's trade.
--	價	original price.
22--	利	principal and interest.
26--	息	principal and interest.
27--	身	itself.
--	色	natural color, true colors, true characteristics.
31--	源	derivation.
33--	心	original intention.
37--	週	this week.
40--	來	original.
--	來面目	the natural form, original look.
44--	地	local, native.
--	地市場	local market.
--	地貿易	local trade.
--	地銷售	local distribution.
--	地人	native.
47--	埠=本地	
--	期	current issue (period).
--	期投資	current investment.
--	期產量	production of current period.
--	期預算	current budget.
--	期盈餘	current surplus.
50--	事	ability, skill, talent.
--	末	beginning and end, essential and non-essential.
60--	日	today, the same day.
--	國	motherland, this country.
--	國語	mother tongue.
--	國工業	native industry.
--	國船舶	domestic ship.
--	國公司	domestic corporation.
--	國貨	native goods.
71--	原	origin, beginning.
72--	質	quality, essence.

75--	體	substance.
77--	月	this month.
--	月有效	good this month.
80--	金=本錢	
--	分	duty, obligation.
--	年	this year.
--	年淨利	net profit for the year.
--	義	original meaning, real meaning.
81--	領	capacity, ability, faculty.
83--	錢	capital, principal.
88--	籍	original domicile.
90--	當	ought to, should.
95--	性	nature, attribute.
--	性難移	one's nature cannot be altered.

5032₇
鴦〔Yang〕 n. the hen of the mandarin duck.

5033₃
惠〔Hui〕 n. benevolence, humanity, kindness, benefit, grace, mercy, favor, v. give in charity, bestow, adj. benevolent, gracious, kind, liberal.

20--	愛	benevolence, kindness.
31--	顧	patronage, kind attention.
66--	賜	bestow graciously.

5033₆
忠〔Chung〕 n. loyalty, devotion, adj. loyal, devoted, patriotic, sincere, faithful, honest, upright.

03--	誠	loyal and sincere.
--	誠可靠	faithful and trustworthy.
08--	於	be loyal to, be faithful to.
--	於職守	faithful to one's duties.
--	於國家	be faithful to one's fatherland.
12--	烈	patriotism, martyrdom.
--	烈祠	martyr's shrine.
17--	勇	loyal and brave.
--	勇無匹	be unsurpassed in valor and patriotism.
20--	信	faithful.
21--	貞之士	man of loyalty and chastity.
24--	告	n. advice, v. advise, admonish.

30-- 實	n. honesty, adj. faithful, devoted, loyal.
-- 實可靠	faithful and reliable.
-- 實同志	faithful comrade.
33-- 心	loyalty, faithfulness.
-- 心耿耿	firmly faithful.
44-- 孝	loyal and filial.
71-- 厚	honest.
-- 厚待人	treat others with honesty.

患 〔Huan〕 n. evil, grief, affliction, distress, misfortune, trouble, adversity, worry, v. suffer, grieve, be worried about.

00-- 病	be ill, suffer from, fall sick.
40-- 難	misfortune, adversity, trouble, hardship.
-- 難之交	friend in need.

5034₃

專 〔Chuan〕 v. monopolize, concentrate, adj. special, particular, exclusive, single.

10-- 一	concentration.
12-- 刊	special issue (of a publication).
18-- 攻	study exclusively, specialize in.
-- 政	dictatorship.
22-- 制	n. absolution, tyranny, adj. absolute, autocratic, despotic, arbitrary.
-- 制主義	absolutism, despotism.
-- 制政治	absolutism.
-- 制君主	tyrant.
-- 制政府	autocracy.
-- 制國	despotic state.
-- 斷	arbitrary decision.
-- 利	n. monopoly, patent, v. monopolize, have one's self.
-- 利證	patent.
-- 利法	patent law.
-- 利權	patent right.
-- 利品	patent product.
-- 利局	patent office.
24-- 科	special course of study, technical course.
-- 科學校	college, junior college.

-- 科醫生	medical specialist.
25-- 使	special envoy, envoy extraordinary, special commissioner.
30-- 注	fix one's attention on.
-- 家	specialist, expert.
-- 案管理	project management.
-- 案	specialized case.
-- 案組	special group for the examination of a case.
32-- 業	specialized job, profession, specialty.
-- 業知識	professional knowledge.
-- 業化	specialization.
-- 業隊伍	specialized personnel.
-- 業人員	professional staff.
-- 業分工	specialization and division of labor.
33-- 心	n. concentration, devotion, v. concentrate, devote, be absorbed, adj. with all the heart.
38-- 送	express delivery.
40-- 有	sole-ownership, sole, exclusive.
-- 有名詞	proper noun.
-- 有權	exclusive right.
-- 賣	monopoly, franchise.
-- 賣權	monopoly.
-- 賣品	monopolized thing.
-- 賣局	monopoly bureau.
42-- 機	chartered plane, special plane.
44-- 權	arbitrary power.
-- 橫	domineer, lay down the law, tyranny, despotic.
47-- 款	special fund.
-- 欄	column, special column.
-- 欄作家	columnist.
50-- 車	special train.
-- 擅	arbitrarily.
60-- 員	senior clerk, administrative superintendent.
61-- 賬	separate account.
-- 題論文	monograph, thesis.
71-- 區	special administrative re-

	gion, special zone.
-- 長	specialty, expert in.
77-- 用	use exclusively, devote, be appropriated.
-- 用工具	specific purpose tool.
-- 用資金	special purpose fund.
-- 用線	private line (of telephone), special railway.
-- 門	special, professional, technical, specific, particular.
-- 門語	technical terms.
-- 門化	specialize.
-- 門名詞	technical term.
-- 門家	specialist.
-- 門技能	specialized technique.
-- 門學校	college, academy, professional school.
-- 門人才	professionals, special talent.
80-- 人	special person.
-- 差	special messenger.
99-- 營	specialize in.

5040_4
妻 〔 **Chi** 〕 *n.* wife, better half.

5043_0
奏 〔 **Tsou** 〕 *v.* play music, function, report to the throne.

08-- 效	take effect, be effective, be successful.
22-- 樂	play music.
27-- 凱	sing the song of triumph.
67-- 鳴曲	sonata (in music).

5044_7
冉 〔 **Jan** 〕 *n.*Yan (a family name), *adj.* gradually.

5050_3
奉 〔 **Feng** 〕 *v.* receive respectfully, accept, offer, deliver, serve, wait.

02-- 託	request.
08-- 諭	receive command.
17-- 承	attend, flatter, receive respectfully.
-- 承話	flattery.
21-- 行	carry out, follow.
23-- 獻	dedicate, offer, consecrate.

| 80-- 命 | receive order, by order. |
| -- 公守法 | carry out official duties and observe the laws. |

5050_5
毒 〔 **Tu** 〕 *n.* poison, virus, toxin, *adj.* poisonous, virulent, noxious.

00-- 瘡	malignant ulcer.
-- 瘤	malignant tumor.
04-- 計	malice, insidious scheme.
05-- 辣	vicious.
10-- 死	poison to death.
20-- 手	malicious hand, atrocious act.
27-- 物	venomous thing.
-- 物學	toxicology.
30-- 害	poison, pernicious.
44-- 草	noxious herb.
-- 菌	mildew, poisonous mushrooms, poisonous germs.
-- 藥	poison, poisonous drug.
50-- 蟲	noxious insects.
-- 素	toxin, poisonous element.
51-- 打	beat cruelly.
53-- 蛇	viper, poisonous snake.
60-- 罵	call one a hard name.
-- 品	narcotic, drugs.
-- 品濫用	drug abuse.
-- 品走私販	drug dealer (trafficker).
71-- 牙	venom-fang of a snake.
80-- 氣	poison gas.
-- 氣彈	gas bomb.
-- 氣戰	toxic warfare.
88-- 箭	poisoned arrow.
95-- 性	toxicity.

5055_6
轟 〔 **Hung** 〕 *n.* rumbling of carriages, roaring of cannon, *v.* blast, bombard.

10-- 下台	shout one down.
12-- 烈	grand.
24-- 動	sensational, stirring.
-- 動一時	sensational.
27-- 響	thunder, boom.
57-- 擊	bombard, shell.
98-- 炸	bomb, blow up, bombard.
-- 炸機	bomber.

5060_0

由〔**Yu**〕 *n.* cause, reason, *v.* follow, let, permit, pass by, *prep.* from, by, through.

08--	於	caused by, arising from, because of, owing to, due to.
10--	正入邪	turn aside from the path of truth.
21--	此	from here, hence.
--	此可見	hence we know.
--	此往前	go from here.
24--	他去罷	let him be, let him alone.
27--	你決定	it's up to you make the decision.
33--	淺入深	from the shallow to the profound.
38--	海路	by sea.
40--	來	origin, source, cause.
60--	是	therefore.
74--	陸地	by land.

5060₁

書〔**Shu**〕 *n.* book, writing, letter, handwriting, *v.* write.

00--	亭	book pavilion.
--	商	book seller.
--	市	book fair.
--	齋	study.
--	店	bookstore, bookshop.
07--	記	secretary, clerk.
--	記官	clerk of the court.
--	記處	secretariat.
--	記長	chief secretary.
10--	面	book cover, in writing, in writing form.
--	面證明	written evidence (document, confirmation).
--	面要求	written request.
--	面通知	written notice, notice in writing.
--	面契約	writer contract.
12--	刊	books and periodicals.
20--	信	letter, epistle, correspondence.
21--	經	Historical Classic.
--	桌	desk, writing-table.
23--	獃子	bookworm.
25--	生	scholar, pedant.

27--	包	satchel, bag.
--	名	title of a book.
30--	房	study, classroom.
--	家	penman, calligrapher.
--	寫	write, inscribe.
34--	法	penmanship, script, hand writing, calligraphy.
41--	櫥	bookcase.
43--	域	building in which there are a number of book stores.
46--	架	bookshelf, bookstand.
50--	攤	bookstall, bookstand.
60--	目	book catalogues.
75--	體	calligraphic style.
88--	籤	bookmark.
--	籍	books.
90--	卷氣	one's academic qualities, bookishness.

5060₃

春〔**Chun**〕 *n.* spring, lust, *adj.* alive, living.

10--	天	spring.
--	雷	spring thunder.
20--	季	spring, primrose season.
24--	裝	spring cloth, spring fashion.
27--	假	spring vacation.
--	色	cheerful looking, delightful view.
33--	心	lustful desires, passion.
37--	汛	spring flood.
--	潮	spring tide.
44--	藥	love potion.
47--	期	puberty.
52--	播作物	spring crop.
55--	耕	spring planting.
59--	捲	spring roll.
60--	日	spring days.
77--	風	spring breeze.
80--	分	spring equinox.
88--	節	Spring Festival, Chinese New Year.
90--	光	spring scenes, lustful scenes.
95--	情	sexual desire.

5071₁

屯〔**Tun**〕*v.* assemble, collect, gather, store up, station (troops), *adj.* hard, difficult.

25--	積	store, amass.
42--	紮	quarter, encamp.
70--	駐	quarter, station at.
99--	營	billet.

5073₂

表〔**Piao**〕*n.* table, list, meter, gauge, watch, model, good example, report to the emperor, *v.* manifest, show, express, indicate, make known, *adj.* external, exterior, outer.

00--	章	memorial.
--	率	example, leader.
--	裏	outside and inside.
01--	語	predicative (in grammar).
02--	彰	blazon.
07--	記	symbol, token, signal, mark.
10--	面	*n.* surface, outside, *adj.* superficial.
--	面價值	face value.
--	示	show, manifest, exhibit, indicate, express, give sign.
--	示同意	give one's adhesion.
--	露	make plain, express, expose.
12--	列	list, catalogue.
16--	現	express, appear, exhibit, show, display.
--	現好	well-behaved.
21--	態	make known one's stand.
26--	白	express, vindicate, clear up.
28--	儀	one's majestic appearance.
33--	演	perform, exhibit, play, show.
--	演者	performer.
34--	達	express, convey.
35--	決	ballot, vote, put to vote.
--	決權	right of voting.
37--	次	tabular order.
40--	皮	epidermis, surface.
43--	式	tabular form.
45--	姊妹	cousin, female cousins.
47--	格	table, list, form.
56--	揚	praise, commend.
60--	兄弟	cousin, male cousins.
--	圖	tables and graphs.
67--	明	show, indicate, express.
77--	同情	express sympathy.
--	層	surface, layer.
--	冊	table, indexes, files.
95--	情	expression.

囊〔**Nang**〕*n.* bag, sack, purse, case, pocket, sachet.

30--	空如洗	without a penny in one's purse.

5077₇

舂〔**Chung**〕*v.* pestle, pound, ram down.

90--	米	hull rice, pound rice.

5080₆

責〔**Tse**〕*n.* duty, responsibility, *v.* blame, punish, ask for, demand, be responsible, press, reprove, demand, ask.

22--	任	duty, responsibility, liability, obligation, charge.
--	任重大	the responsibility is heavy and great.
--	任制	system of personal responsibility.
--	任保險	liability insurance.
--	任感	sense of responsibility.
--	任心	sense of responsibility.
24--	備	blame, rebuke, reprove, reproach.
40--	難	censure, find fault with.
53--	成	enjoin, instruct, charge with.
60--	罰	punish, fine, give a person beaus.
--	罵	scold, blame.
77--	問	question, ask for an explanation.
97--	怪	reprimand, lay blame on.

貴〔**Kuei**〕*adj.* noble, honorable, illustrious, dignified, high-class, valuable, precious, dear, costly, expensive.

08--	族	noble, lord, peer, nobility,

		aristocrat.
--	族政治	aristocracy.
--	族院	house of lords, house of peers.
20--	重	valuable, precious, rare.
--	重商品	valuable merchandise.
--	重貨物	valuable cargo.
--	重的	valuable, expensive, precious.
30--	客	guest of honor.
--	賓	distinguished guests.
--	賓席	seats reserved for distinguished guests.
--	賓室	VIP room, VIP lounge.
47--	婦	lady.
--	妃	highly honored woman officials, imperial concubine.
63--	賤	dear and cheap, gentle and simple.
80--	人	nobleman.
--	金屬	precious metal.

5090₀

未 〔Wei〕 adv. not, not yet, not now, never.

00--	亡人	survived wife, widow.
--	證實	unconfirmed.
04--	熟	raw.
10--	雨籌謀	take precautions beforehand, provide against the future.
12--	到貨	goods afloat.
17--	了	unfinished, not finished yet.
--	及	unable to make in time.
21--	上市股票	unlisted stock.
--	便	not convenient, improper.
23--	卜先知	foresee accurately.
24--	付	unpaid, outstanding.
--	付費用	unpaid expenses.
--	付賬目	unpaid account.
27--	免	unavoidable, inevitable.
--	免過份	being rather to presumptuous.
30--	定	uncertain, undecided.
--	完	unfinished, not completed.
--	完工程	unfinished (incomplete) construction.

33--	必	unlikely, not necessarily.
--	必如此	it is not necessarily so.
35--	決	n. suspense, adj. unsettled, undecided.
38--	遂	unaccomplished.
--	遂犯	unaccomplished offense.
40--	來	future, forthcoming, in the future.
--	有	have not, there never was, there has not been.
--	有頭緒	there is no clue yet.
42--	婚妻	fiancée.
--	婚夫	fiancé.
46--	加工	crude, raw.
53--	成	not completed.
--	成事實	not yet materialized.
--	成品	unfinished works.
--	成年者	minor.
77--	開發	undeveloped.
80--	曾	not yet, never, at no time.
--	知	unknown, uncertain.
--	知項	unknown term.
--	知數	unknown number, unknown factor.
--	知量	unknown quantity.
87--	卸貨物	goods afloat.
90--	嘗	never, not yet.

末 〔Mo〕 n. end, tip, last, final, powder, dust, adj. small, mean, insignificant, unimportant, adv. finally, at last, subsequently.

00--	座	last seat.
01--	站	terminus.
02--	端	extremity, terminal end.
20--	秀	last part of a period.
22--	後	at last, finally, subsequently.
37--	次	last time.
44--	世	last years (of a dynasty).
47--	期	last stage.
50--	日	last day of the world.
--	日將至	one's last day is soon reached.
67--	路	miserable end.
--	路窮途	reach the end of the rope.
77--	尾	end.
88--	節	minor details.

耒 〔Lei〕 *n.* handle of a plow.
57-- 耜　　　plough.

5090₂

棗 〔Tsao〕 *n.* date.
17-- 子　　　date.
-- 子糕　　　date-cake.
40-- 核　　　date-stone.
44-- 樹　　　date tree.

5090₃

素 〔Su〕 *n.* vegetable food, white silk, origin, nature, *adj.* plain, simple, pure, white, *adv.* commonly, usually, formerly.
00-- 交　　　old acquaintance.
-- 諳　　　be versed in.
-- 衣　　　plain cloth, mourning garment.
03-- 識　　　old acquaintance.
22-- 稱　　　usually called, commonly known as.
24-- 裝　　　simple dress.
27-- 色　　　plain, white.
40-- 來　　　originally, hitherto, usually, commonly.
41-- 麵　　　vegetarian noodles.
44-- 菜　　　vegetable diet, vegetable food.
50-- 事　　　funeral matter.
54-- 描　　　sketch.
71-- 願　　　long-cherished ambition.
72-- 髮　　　white hair.
-- 質　　　quality, fiber, predisposition.
77-- 服　　　white dress.
-- 聞　　　have often heard.
80-- 食　　　vegetarian food, vegetarian diet.
95-- 性　　　temperament, original nature of a person.

5090₄

秦 〔Chin〕 *n.* Chin (a family name).

5090₆

束 〔Shu〕 *n.* bundle, bunch, sheaf, *v.* control, restrain, tie in a bundle, bind with cords.

20-- 手　　　powerless, have one's hand tied.
-- 手無策　　　be helpless, be at one's wit's end.
-- 住　　　tie up, bind.
23-- 縛　　　bind, tie, control.
24-- 裝　　　pack up, bind fast.
44-- 帶　　　girdle.
71-- 腰　　　waist band or belt.

柬 〔Chien〕 *n.* visiting card, letter, note.

東 〔Tung〕 *n.* east, master, employer, *adj.* eastern.
00-- 方　　　the east, Orient.
-- 方文化　　　Oriental civilization.
-- 方人　　　Oriental.
-- 京　　　Tokyo.
10-- 西　　　east and west, things, articles.
11-- 北　　　north-east.
-- 非　　　East Africa.
21-- 經　　　east longitude.
30-- 家　　　master, employer.
31-- 江　　　East River.
36-- 邊　　　east side, on the east.
38-- 海　　　East China Sea.
-- 洋車　　　rickshaw.
-- 道主　　　host.
-- 道國　　　host country.
40-- 南　　　south-east.
-- 南亞　　　Southeast Asia.
-- 南西北　　　east, south, west and north, in all direction.
-- 奔西走　　　run about busily, be on the run.
50-- 拉西扯　　　ramble in speech or writing.
58-- 拼西湊　　　patch up from bits.
77-- 風　　　east wind.
-- 門　　　east gate.
90-- 半球　　　Eastern Hemisphere.

5101₀

扛 〔Kang〕 *v.* lift, hold up, carry on shoulder.
53-- 抬　　　carry on a pole.

扯 〔Che〕 *v.* tear, drag, pull, talk nonsense.
04-- 謊　　　lie, tell a lie.

08-- 旗　　raise a flag.
10-- 下　　take down, tear off.
-- 平　　on an average.
-- 碎　　tear to pieces, tear asunder.
14-- 破　　tear pieces.
20-- 住　　grasp firmly.
22-- 後腿　pull one back, hinder one from success.
40-- 去　　strip, rend.
-- 皮　　wrangle, dispute over trifles.
47-- 起　　hoist, lift.
77-- 毀　　tear and destroy.
-- 開　　tear open, pull apart.
78-- 脫　　break loose.

批〔**Pi**〕*n.* criticism, petition, a whole batch, *v.* comment, criticize, reply officially to a petition.
00-- 註　　*n.* comments, *v.* comment on.
01-- 評　　criticize, comment.
-- 評家　critic.
10-- 覆　　reply officially.
-- 示　　comments and instructions on an official paper.
12-- 發　　*n.* wholesale, jobbing, *v.* sell by wholesale, sell in bulk.
-- 發商　wholesaler, wholesale dealer.
-- 發店　wholesale store.
-- 發價　wholesale price.
-- 發貨　wholesale goods.
18-- 改　　correct.
30-- 准　　*n.* ratification, approval, sanction, *v.* ratify, sanction.
-- 准條約　ratify a treaty.
32-- 透　　criticize thoroughly.
37-- 深　　criticize penetratingly.
-- 次　　batch.
72-- 斥　　rebuke, reprove, reprimand.
74-- 駁　　refuse, rebut, turn down.
77-- 閱　　read and write down comments.
80-- 令　　instruction.
92-- 判　　criticize, denounce.

-- 判會　repudiation meeting, public criticism.

輒〔**Che**〕*adv.* often, consequently, always.

5101₁
排〔**Pai**〕*n.* row, line, rank, *v.* arrange, place in order, expel, exclude.
11-- 班　　fall in line, arrange turns of work.
-- 頭　　stand first in the line, file leader.
12-- 列　　*n.* arrangement, *v.* arrange, set in array.
-- 水　　*n.* drainage, *v.* drain.
-- 水溝　drainage ditch.
-- 水口　drainage outlet.
-- 水量　volume of water displacement.
-- 水管　drainpipe.
13-- 球　　volleyball.
21-- 行　　one's seniority.
-- 便　　defecation, bowel movement.
-- 版　　type-setting.
-- 行第一　number one in rank.
22-- 出　　eject.
23-- 外　　anti-foreign, exclusion.
25-- 練　　rehearsal.
27-- 解　　resolve, mediate, reconcile.
30-- 字　　set type, compose.
-- 字工　type-setter.
-- 字機　linotype.
33-- 演　　rehearse.
34-- 泄　　excretion, ejection.
-- 泄物　output, excreta, excrement.
-- 泄器官　excretory organ.
39-- 潦　　drain a waterlogged area.
44-- 華　　anti-Chinese.
46-- 場　　display of splendor.
49-- 檔　　gear (in automobile).
50-- 擠　　expel, squeeze out.
71-- 長　　platoon leader.
72-- 斥　　exclude, reprobate, expel, reject.
77-- 骨　　ribs of animals.
-- 卵　　ovulate.

-- 尿		urinate.
-- 開		spread out.
-- 印		set type and print.
78-- 除		exclude, keep out, eliminate.
-- 隊		line up.
80-- 氣管		exhaust pipe.
88-- 筆		row of brushes.

輕 〔Ching〕 n. mitigate, lessen, slight, adj. light, dissipated, unimportant, easy, simple, soft, gentle, frivolous, fickle.

00-- 率	rash, careless, unsteady, heedless.
-- 音樂	light music.
08-- 敵	underestimate the enemy, belittle the enemy.
-- 放	put down gently.
10-- 工業	light industry.
-- 而易舉	east, easily.
11-- 巧	agile, nimble.
-- 巧玲瓏	agile and elegant.
17-- 取	beat easily, win an easy victory.
20-- 重	weight, light and heavy.
-- 信	trust indiscriminately, believe lightly.
21-- 便	handy, light.
-- 便鐵路	light railing.
22-- 佻	frivolous, corky, lighthearted.
25-- 生	commit suicide.
27-- 忽	be careless, neglect, ignore.
28-- 微	slight, light, little.
-- 侮	insult, take by the beard.
-- 傷	slight wound.
32-- 浮	unsteady, light-minded.
36-- 視	despise, disregard, sneeze at, look down upon.
41-- 狂	giddy-headed, frivolous.
42-- 機槍	submachine gun.
44-- 薄	frivolous, dissipated.
-- 蔑	despise, disdain, slight off.
60-- 量級	light weight (boxing).
-- 罪	misdemeanor.
-- 易	readily, easily.

72-- 鬆	easy, relaxed, lighthearted.
74-- 騎兵	light cavalry.
77-- 舉妄動	imprudent.
80-- 金屬	light metal.
-- 氣	hydrogen.
95-- 快	agile, quick, fleeting, lightsome.
99-- 勞動	light work.

攏 〔Lung〕 v. assemble, collect, gather, close up, seize, grasp.

5101₂

扼 〔O〕 v. grasp, seize, clutch, hold, repress.

10-- 死	strangle, throttle.
-- 要	n. summary, commanding point, adv. briefly.
20-- 住	hold in check.
22-- 制	repress, keep under by force.
30-- 守	hold, guard, hold and defend.
47-- 殺	strangle, smother.
51-- 據	occupy and hold.
78-- 險	hold the key of a position.

輄 〔O〕 n. yoke, v. suffer, endure, struggle against, put up with.

44-- 苦	suffer hardship.
83-- 餓	endure hunger.

5101₄

捱 〔Ai〕 v. suffer, endure, struggle against, put up with.

10-- 不住	cannot endure any more.
37-- 過	survive.
51-- 打	be beaten.
44-- 苦	suffer hardship.
60-- 罵	be scolded.
83-- 餓	endure hunger.

5101₇

拒 〔Chu〕 v. resist, withstand, oppose, prevent, stop, reject, decline.

08-- 敵	resist enemy.
24-- 付	dishonor, refuse to pay.
-- 納	repulse.
27-- 絕	refuse, reject, deny, repel, exclude.

--絕付款	refuse payment.	
28--收	rejection, refusal to accept.	
30--守	guard, defend.	
53--捕	resist arrest.	

5102₀

打 〔Ta〕 *n.* blow, stroke, dozen, *v.* beat, hit, strike, fight, shoot, operate on.

00--磨	polish, furnish.
--雜	do odd job.
01--顫	tremble, shudder.
10--死	beat to death.
--碎	smash, dash, break in pieces.
--雷	thunderclap.
--更	keep watch.
--電話	make a telephone call, telephone.
--電報	send a telegram or cable.
--不倒	unconquerable, cannot be knocked down.
--不開	cannot be opened.
12--水	draw water.
--發	dispatch, send off.
--到底	fight to a finish.
13--球	play a ball game.
14--破	break, smash.
--破紀錄	set a new record.
--聽	enquire, detect, ascertain.
--聽消息	ask for information.
16--彈子	play billiards.
20--手	bully, ruffian.
--禾	thrash the grains.
22--倒	overthrow.
--斷	interrupt, discontinue.
24--結	knot.
25--仗	*n.* war, *v.* fight, go to war.
26--牌	play cards.
27--魚	fishing.
--包	pack, bale, bundle.
--包機	packing machine (press), sack-and-bale machine.
--包人	packer.
--翻	upset, overset, overturn.
28--傷	wounded.
29--秋千	swing.
30--字	type, typewrite.

--字紙	manifold paper, typing paper.
--字機	typewriter.
--字員	typist.
--滾	welter, wallow.
37--洞	perforate.
--退	beat back.
--通	get through, open a connecting.
--褶	plait, crease.
38--游擊	engage in guerrilla warfare.
39--消	cancel, cross off.
40--內戰	fight a civil war.
42--獵	hunting.
44--鼓	beat a drum.
--劫	rob, plunder.
--垮	crush, break down.
45--椿	drive piles.
46--架	fight.
47--靶	shoot at a target.
--靶場	range.
--穀	thrash rice.
50--中	hit.
51--擾	bother, cause trouble.
52--折扣	give a discount.
55--井	dig a well.
57--掃	sweep, clean.
--抱不平	try to redress an injustice to the weak.
--探	find out.
--擊	blow, strike, beat.
58--扮	dress up.
59--撈	salvage.
--撈工程	refloating operation.
--撈物	salvage.
--撈船	salvor.
--撈費用	salvage expenses.
--撈拖船	salvage tug.
--撈人員	salvor.
--撈公司	salvage company.
60--量	measure, size up.
--罵	beat and abuse.
--回電	wire back.
61--點滴	administer intravenous drop.
64--賭	bet, stake.
68--敗	be defeated.

71-- 長途電話	make a long distance call.
73-- 胎	artificial abortion.
77-- 屁股	*n.* spanking, *v.* flog the buttocks.
-- 開	break open, open.
-- 印	stamp.
79-- 勝	conquer, win.
80-- 入市場	market penetration.
-- 鐘	ring the bell.
-- 氣	inflate, cheer.
-- 分數	grade (student's papers).
-- 氣筒	pump.
84-- 針	*n.* injection, *v.* inject.
88-- 坐	sit in meditation.
-- 算	intend, plan, calculate.
90-- 拳	boxing.
-- 火石	flint.
-- 火機	lighter.
98-- 樣	close the store for the night.

5102_7

輛 〔Liang〕 *n.* cart, carriage, chariot.

擄 〔Lu〕 *v.* capture prisoner, seize.

44-- 獲	capture.
-- 劫	plunder, rob.
50-- 掠	plunder, carry off.

5103_2

振 〔Chen〕 *v.* rouse, arouse, move, stimulate, shake, agitate, excite, stir up, raise.

24-- 動	*n.* vibration, *v.* vibrate, rock, shake, sway, move.
-- 動器	vibrator.
28-- 作	stimulate, cheer, awake, brace up.
-- 作精神	buck up.
36-- 盪	oscillate.
40-- 奮	hearten, inspire, rouse.
53-- 威	inspire awe, extend one's prestige.
77-- 興	promote, prosper.

據 〔Chu〕 *n.* witness, evidence, proof, *v.* occupy, take possession of, *adv.* according to.

08-- 說	according to what is said, as the story goes.
16-- 理力爭	argue vigorously on the basis of reason.
17-- 了解	it is understood that......
22-- 稱	according to reports, claims, assertion.
23-- 我所知	to the best of my knowledge.
30-- 守	guard.
-- 實	in fact.
-- 實招供	tell the fact in court.
34-- 爲己有	rob it for oneself.
40-- 有	in possession of, take possession of.
47-- 報	according to reports.
61-- 點	foothold, stronghold.
78-- 險	hold a strategic pass.
95-- 情	according to circumstances.

5103_4

輭=**軟** 5708_0

5104_0

軒 〔Hsuan〕 *n.* carriage, porch, pavilion, side-room.

23-- 峻	lofty.
51-- 輕	*n.* difference in rank, *adj.* high and low.
60-- 昂	dignified, grand, high, lofty.

5104_1

攝 〔She〕 *v.* gather, collect, attract, regulate, control, take in.

04-- 護腺	prostate.
12-- 引	attract.
17-- 取	take in.
18-- 政	regency, serve as a regent.
-- 政王	Prince Regent.
-- 政者	regent.
25-- 生	sanitation.
62-- 影	photograph, take a picture (or photo).
-- 影記者	cameraman.
-- 影術	photography.
-- 影機	camera.
-- 影師	photographer.
72-- 氏表	centigrade thermometer.

5104_6

掉 〔Tiao〕 *v.* shake, fall, slip off, change, turn, substitute, move, wave.

10-- 下	fall down, drop down.
11-- 頭	turn the head.
24-- 動	move, stir, change.
27-- 色	fade.
37-- 過來	turn around, on the other hand.
47-- 期	change-over.
55-- 轉	turn around.
57-- 換	exchange, substitute.
67-- 眼淚	shed tear.
78-- 隊	fall behind.

5104_7

扳〔Pan〕v. pull.

10-- 下	pull down.
47-- 起	pull up.
84-- 鉗	spanner.

擾〔Jao〕v. disturb, annoy, agitate, annoy, confuse.

22-- 亂	disturb, violate, agitate, disquiet, make trouble.
-- 亂治安	disturb peace and order.
-- 亂人心	agitation.
24-- 動	stir, agitate.
30-- 害	disturb.
50-- 攘	disturbance, tumult.

5104_9

抨〔Peng〕v. censure, blame, attack by words.

| 57-- 擊 | attack, denounce. |

5106_0

拈〔Nien〕v. pick up, carry, handle, take with finger.

| 44-- 花 | pick a flower. |

拓〔To〕v. open, enlarge, expand, break, develop, colonize.

| 14-- 殖 | colonize. |
| 44-- 荒者 | pioneer. |

5106_1

指〔Chih〕n. finger, digit, v. pint out, indicate, denote, refer.

07-- 望	n. expectation, v. look forward to, hope for.
-- 認	identify.
10-- 正	correct.

-- 示	direct, show, indicate, denote, instruct.
16-- 環	ring.
20-- 紋	fingerprint.
-- 紋學	dactylography.
22-- 出	indicate, call attention to, point out.
25-- 使	incite, direct, instigate.
-- 使者	instigator.
27-- 向	point to, direct to.
-- 名	mention by name, name, nominate.
30-- 定	assign, appoint, designate.
32-- 派	appoint, assign.
38-- 導	direct, instruct, conduct, guide, manage.
-- 導委員會	steering committee.
-- 導員	director, instructor.
40-- 南	guide book.
-- 南針	compass.
41-- 標	indication, quota, target.
44-- 模	finger print.
48-- 教	instruct, correct, advise.
50-- 摘	find fault with, censure, denounce.
-- 責	accuse, censure, charge.
57-- 揮	n. conductor (in music), v. command, conduct, manage, administer, lead.
-- 揮刀	saber.
-- 揮棒	baton.
-- 揮官	commander, officer in command.
58-- 數	index number.
-- 數值	index value.
60-- 甲	nail.
-- 甲油	fingernail polish.
-- 甲鉗	nail clipper.
61-- 點	point out, give guidance.
67-- 明	show, express, indicate, signify, demonstrate.
80-- 令	order, instruct.
84-- 針	indicator, pointer.

搢〔Chin〕v. insert, advance, recommend.

5106_2

揩〔Kai〕v. wipe, brush, clean, rub.
10-- 面　　　wash face, wipe the face.
20-- 手巾　　napkin.
48-- 乾淨　　wipe clean.
5106_3

擂〔Lei〕v. rub, grind, drum, pound.
23-- 台　　　platform for contest in martial arts.
44-- 鼓　　　beat a drum.
87-- 錘　　　pestle.
5106_6

輻〔Fu〕n. the spoke of a wheel.
24-- 射　　　n. radiation, v. radiate.
-- 射塵　　radioactive dust, atomic fallout.
-- 射能　　radiant energy.
-- 射線　　radiant rays.
-- 射波　　radiant wave.
-- 射熱　　radiant heat.
-- 射損害　radiation damage.
-- 射體　　radiator, radiation body.
-- 射針　　radio meter.
55-- 輳　　　concentration congestion.
5109_0

抔〔Pou〕v. take up in both hand.
87-- 飲　　　drink out of the hands.
5111_0

虹〔Hung〕n. rainbow.
10-- 霓　　　rainbow and its reflection.
20-- 采　　　banner, flags.
22-- 彩　　　color of a rainbow.
42-- 橋　　　rainbow shape bridge.
67-- 吸　　　siphon.
5111_4

蛭〔Chih〕n. leech, bloodsucker.
10-- 石　　　vermiculite (mining).
5112_7

螞〔Ma〕n. ant.
54-- 蟥　　　kind of leech.
58-- 蚱　　　locust.
-- 蟻　　　ant.

蠕〔Ju〕n. crawling of a worm, v. wriggle, creep.
21-- 行　　　creep, crawl.
24-- 動　　　wriggling.

蠣〔Li〕n.oyster.
44-- 黃　　　edible part of an oyster.
5114_0

蚜〔Ya〕n. harmful insect.
50-- 虫　　　ant-cow, plant-louse, aphis.
5116_6

蝠〔Fu〕n. bat.
5119_6

螈〔Yuan〕n. lizard.
5178_6

頓〔Tun〕n. time, turn, period, meal, v. bow the head, stamp, stop, cease, arrange, regulate, adv. suddenly, immediately, at once.
58-- 挫　　　encounter failure, receive a set back.
64-- 時　　　immediately, suddenly.
77-- 腳　　　stamp the foot.
80-- 首　　　bow the head, kowtow.
88-- 筆　　　stop writing.
91-- 悟　　　understand suddenly.
5193_1

耘〔Yun〕v. weed, root up.
44-- 草　　　root up weeds.
60-- 田　　　weed a field.
5194_3

耨〔Nou〕n. hoe, v. weed, hoe.
5200_0

划〔Hua〕n. small boat, v. pole a boat, paddle, row.
20-- 手　　　oarsman.
22-- 艇　　　rowboat.
27-- 船　　　row a boat.
88-- 算　　　calculate, weight.
90-- 拳　　　finger guessing game.
5201_0

軋〔Ya〕v. crush, grind.
10-- 碎　　　crush to pieces.
28-- 傷　　　run over and injure.
37-- 澀　　　stammer.
40-- 布機　　mangle.
44-- 機　　　rolling mill.
46-- 棉機　　gin, cotton ginning machine.

-- 棉花	cotton-ginning.
48-- 姘頭	pump over the broom stock.
87-- 鋼廠	steel rolling mill.

5201₃

挑〔Tiao〕v. select, elect, choose, lift, carry on the shoulder.

10-- 不動	too heavy to carry.
12-- 水	carry water.
37-- 選	select, choose, pick.
44-- 花	embroider.
50-- 夫	porter, coolie, bearer, carrier.
52-- 撥	provoke, instigate.
53-- 挖	dredge, clear.
57-- 擔	carry a load on the shoulder.
62-- 剔	find faults.
63-- 戰	challenge, give battle, call out, pit against.
77-- 釁	pick a quarrel.
-- 開	clear out, brush aside.
84-- 錯	find fault, pick flaws.
95-- 情	arouse, make amorous advances.

5201₄

托〔To〕v. entrust, cast on, support, bear up, ask someone for help.

20-- 辭	pretend, allege, pretext, excuse.
24-- 付	entrust, cast on.
27-- 盤	tray.
28-- 收	collect, apply for collection.
31-- 福	Thanks!
-- 福測驗	TOEFL (Test of English as a Foreign Language).
37-- 運	consign for shipment, check.
48-- 故	give a pretext, make an excuse.
50-- 拉斯	trust.
57-- 賴	rely upon.
72-- 兒所	nursery.
88-- 管	trusteeship.
-- 管地	trust territory, mandated territory.
89-- 銷	consign.

捶〔Chui〕v. cudgel, beat with a staff.

44-- 鼓	beat drum.
51-- 打	beat, thump.

摧〔Tsui〕v. break, destroy, suppress, frustrate.

13-- 殘	destroy, despoil, blast.
21-- 頹	in ruins.
26-- 促	press for.
-- 壞	destroy.
52-- 折	break off.
77-- 毀	demolish, destroy, shatter.

撬〔Chiao〕v. lift.

5202₁

折〔Che〕n. discount, loss, v. snap in two, break off, fold, bend, refract, discount.

00-- 磨	ill-treat, afflict, oppress, harass, torture.
16-- 現	convert into cash.
21-- 價	n. reduced rate, v. reduce the, get a discount off a price.
-- 價票	cheap ticket.
22-- 斷	break off, break into two.
24-- 射	refract.
26-- 息	native interest.
27-- 經	crease.
44-- 舊	depreciation.
-- 枝	snag.
47-- 款	day to day loan, call money.
50-- 中	take average.
-- 本	failed in business.
-- 衷	compromise.
-- 衷主義	eclecticism.
51-- 攏	fold together.
52-- 抵	set off against.
56-- 扣	discount, rebate.
-- 扣率	discount rate.
-- 扣商店	discount store (house).
-- 扣價格	reduced price, rebate.
57-- 換	price convert.
58-- 挫	dispirit.
60-- 疊	fold.
-- 疊床	folding bed.
-- 回	turn back.
77-- 服	convince.
-- 股	stock split.

80--	兌	convert, exchange.
--	合	equivalent to.
88--	算	conversion.
--	箱	bellows.
90--	光	refraction.
--	半	reduce by half, give 50 percent discount.

斬 〔Chan〕 v. slay, kill, behead, cut off, chop.

10--	碎	mince.
22--	斷	chop off.
23--	伐	subjugate.
35--	決	carry out an execution by beheading.
42--	刈	mow down.
44--	獲	score a victory on the battlefield.
--	草除根	uproot, eliminate completely.
47--	殺	slay, kill.
77--	開	cut apart.
80--	首	behead.
--	首示眾	behead a person and display the head to the public.

撕 〔Ssu〕 v. tear, break, pluck away.

10--	下	tear off.
--	碎	tear into pieces, tatter.
--	票	kill a hostage.
14--	破	rip, rend.
40--	去	tear off, tear away.
51--	打	beat up.
77--	開	tear open, rip open.
97--	爛	tear to shreds, rip to pieces.

5202₇

揣 〔Chuai〕 v. estimate, guess.

00--	度	speculate, appraise.
32--	測	conjecture, fathom.
80--	人	arrest.

攜 〔Hsi〕 v. carry, bring, join hands, lead by hands, bring along.

20--	手	join hands, hand in hand.
--	手同來	go together hand in hand.
40--	來	bring, carry.
44--	帶	carry, bring, bear, take.
57--	抱	carry in one's arm.
77--	同	bring along.
90--	眷	carry one's family along.

轎 〔Chiao〕 n. sedan chair.

17--	子	sedan chair.
50--	車	limousine, car, sedan.
--	夫	sedan bearer.

5203₀

抓 〔Chua〕 v. scratch, tickle, grasp, claw, seize.

00--	癢	scratch an itch.
10--	碎	tear to rage.
14--	破	injure the skin by scratching.
20--	重點	grasp the essential point.
--	住	clutch, seize, grasp.
--	住機會	seize the opportunity.
22--	彩	raffle, draw lots for a lottery.
25--	生產	give all-around attention in production.
27--	綱	take firm hold of the key link.
28--	傷	injure by scratching.
30--	牢	grip, clutch.
40--	去	arrest, snatch.
44--	權	grab power.
55--	典型	grasp typical example.
61--	點	take hold of selected basic units.
77--	舉	snatch (in weight lifting).
--	緊	grasp firmly, keep a firm grasp on.
--	緊時間	lose no time.
80--	人	arrest.

5203₁

拆 〔Chai〕 v. open, break, destroy, demolish, take down, tear down.

10--	下	take down, unfix.
20--	信	open a letter.
26--	白	swindle.
--	白黨	swindler.
--	息	short-term interest.
--	線	take out stitches.
30--	空	expose.
--	穿	expose.
40--	壞	break down.
44--	封	break up a seal.

48-- 散	break away.
72-- 除	dismantle.
77-- 毀	demolish, take down.
-- 屋	pull down a house.
-- 股	dissolve partnership.
-- 閱	open and read.
-- 開	open, break down.

5203₄

揆 〔**Kuei**〕 v. consider, guess, calculate, reckon.

| 00-- 席 | premier, prime minister. |
| 32-- 測 | guess, estimate. |

撲 〔**Pu**〕 v. pat, flap, whip, flog, strike lightly, rush on.

30-- 空	come to nought.
33-- 滅	exterminate, extinguish, quench, suppress, stamp out.
40-- 克	poker.
-- 克牌	playing cards.
47-- 殺	kill.
51-- 打	beat, pat, swat.
57-- 擊	flap.

5204₀

抵 〔**Ti**〕 v. arrive, reach, oppose, withstand, resist.

00-- 充	use something for substitute.
22-- 岸	ashore.
-- 岸價格	land price.
-- 制	boycott, oppose.
-- 制外貨	economic boycott, boycott of foreign goods.
24-- 借	pledge against a loan.
25-- 債	pay a debt with goods or by labor.
26-- 觸	conflict with.
29-- 償	compensate, atone for.
34-- 港	arrival at port.
-- 達	arrive at, reach.
39-- 消	offset, cancel out each other.
50-- 抗	resist, withstand, counteract, oppose, combat.
-- 抗到底	resist to the end.

-- 抗力	power of resistance.
56-- 扣	deduct from.
-- 押	mortgage, pledge, hold in pawn (pledge).
-- 押市場	mortgage market.
-- 押經紀人	mortgage middleman.
-- 押利息	mortgage interest.
-- 押貸款	mortgage loan, loan on mortgage (security).
-- 押付款	mortgage payments.
-- 押借款	raise mortgage, give security for debt.
-- 押物	object given as a pledge.
-- 押資金	mortgage money.
-- 押者	pledger.
-- 押契據	instrument of pledge, mortgage deed.
-- 押品	mortgage, hypothecated goods, hostage, gage, pledge, security.
-- 押合同	mortgage contract.
-- 押銀行	mortgage bank.
57-- 換	substitute.
-- 賴	repudiate.
58-- 數	balance an account.
59-- 擋	resist, check, hinder, ward, keep back.
60-- 罪	bear the crime.
80-- 命	life for a life.
89-- 銷	offset, set off, elimination.

5204₁

挺 〔**Ting**〕 v. stick out, stiffen, stand upright, straighten, pull up, adj. upright, outstanding, eminent, prominent, straight.

00-- 立	stand straight up, stand stiff.
11-- 硬	very hard, stiff and stubborn.
27-- 身	straighten the body.
30-- 進	breast, thrust forward, advance.
-- 進隊	tough vanguards unit.
40-- 直	straight, upright.
47-- 好	excellent, very good.
-- 起	heave, thrust forward.
77-- 胸	thrust forward the chest.
-- 舉	clean and snatch (weighting

lifting).

| -- 緊 | pull tight. |

5204₇

授〔Shou〕*v.* give to, bestow, confer, teach, pay to.

00-- 意	intimate, hint.
06-- 課	teach.
08-- 旗	give the national flag to.
13-- 職	*n.* installation, *v.* confer the rank of.
17-- 予	award, confer, give.
20-- 位	confer a title, confer a dignity.
-- 受	give and receive.
24-- 勳	confer orders, award a decoration.
27-- 獎	give a prize.
44-- 權	empower, authorize, commission, warrant.
73-- 胎	impregnate, fecundate.
77-- 與	give to.
80-- 命	sacrifice one's life.
95-- 精	inseminate.

援〔Yuan〕*v.* assist, rescue, help, relieve, save.

12-- 引	quote, cite, lead, draw.
20-- 手	help, extend a helping hand.
22-- 例	quote a precedent.
37-- 軍	auxiliary troop.
48-- 救	relieve, rescue, save, assist, help.
51-- 據	cite as proof.
72-- 兵	reinforcement.
74-- 助	help, assist, aid, give support to.
77-- 用	invoke, quote.
80-- 入	transfer from others.

撥〔Po〕*v.* move, remove, distribute, appropriate, transfer, set apart for, detach, appoint.

00-- 充	appropriate.
-- 交	hand over to, appropriate to.
10-- 正	correct, revise.
-- 弄	toy with, stir up.
22-- 出	transfer to others.
24-- 動	move, turn.

-- 付	make payment.
27-- 款	appropriate a fund.
28-- 給	appropriate.
47-- 款	allocate funds, allotment, appropriation.
-- 款要求	requisition for money.
-- 款申請書	appropriation request.
61-- 號碼	dial a number.
72-- 兵	detach troops.
77-- 用	be appropriate to, be set apart for.
-- 開	push open.
80-- 鐘	regulate a clock.

5205₇

掙〔Cheng〕*v.* struggle, make an effort, get free from, get rid of.

22-- 斷	break by an effort.
52-- 扎	struggle hard.
78-- 脫	get rid, break away, get free from.
80-- 命	sacrifice one's life.
83-- 錢	earn money.

5206₃

輜〔Chih〕*n.* baggage, wagon.

20-- 重	baggage, supplies for troops, military supplies impediment of an army.
-- 重車	transport vehicles.
-- 重兵	commissariat soldier, transport corps.
-- 重隊	army service corps.
50-- 車	covered carriage.

5206₄

括〔Kuo〕*v.* enclose, include, contain, envelope, enforce.

10-- 要	comprehensive, compendious.
12-- 弧	parenthesis, bracket, brace.
40-- 有	consist of, contain.
61-- 號	sign of aggregation (mathematics).

5206₉

播〔Po〕*v.* sow, scatter, disperse, spread, promulgate, extent, flee, publish, make known.

00--	音	broadcast.
--	音室	studio.
--	音台	broadcasting station.
--	音機	broadcasting equipment.
--	音員	broadcaster, announcer.
08--	放	broadcast on the air.
10--	弄	mishandle, make a mess of, stir up dispute.
22--	種	sow.
--	種機	sowing machine.
--	種期	seedtime.
25--	傳	spread abroad, give currency.
38--	送	broadcast. circulation.
56--	揚	propagate and uphold.

5207₂

拙〔Cho〕 adj. stupid, awkward, clumsy, unskilled, foolish, poor.

04--	計	foolish scheme.
10--	工	poor craftsman, incompetent worker.
20--	手	poor hand.
30--	實	raw and sturdy, solidly built.
88--	笨	unskillful, unwise.
90--	劣	clumsy, bad, poor.
--	劣手段	clumsy tactics.
95--	性	n. stupidity, adj. slow-witted, clumsy.

5207₇

插〔Cha〕 v. insert, put between, stick in, pierce, thrust into, introduce, take part in.

00--	座	socket.
08--	旗	stick up a flag.
11--	班	classify.
--	頭	plug.
20--	手	interpose, meddle.
25--	秧	plant out rice shoot, rice transplanting.
--	秧機	rice transplanter.
27--	身	take part in, join in.
44--	花	arrange flowers.
--	枝	cutting.
55--	曲	interlude, episode.
60--	口	interrupt.
--	圖	illustration, figure.
61--	嘴	meddle by words, interrupt.
78--	隊	cut in, push in.
80--	入	insert, put between, stick in, interpose, interject.

5209₄

採〔Tsai〕 v. pluck, pick, collect, gather, select, choose, suck, sip, mine, pay attention to.

00--	辦	purchase, procure.
--	辦處	purchasing office.
--	訪	cover a news item, make inquiries, spy out.
--	訪主任	city editor.
--	訪新聞	cover a news item.
--	訪員	news correspondent.
10--	礦	mining.
--	礦權	mining right.
17--	取	select, choose.
--	取措施	take measures (steps).
20--	集	gather, collect.
35--	油	oil extraction.
37--	選	select, pick.
44--	花	pick flowers.
--	茶	collect tea leaves.
--	藥	gather herbs.
--	納	accept, adopt.
50--	摘	pick, gather.
65--	購	purchase, buy, go shopping.
--	購方案	procurement scheme.
--	購計劃	procurement program.
--	購部	purchasing department.
--	購項目	procurement items.
--	購價格	procurement price.
--	購協議書	purchaser's agreement.
--	購中心	shopping center.
--	購申請	procurement demand (requisition).
--	購量	purchase quantity.
--	購員	buy clerk, procurement officer (agent).
--	購團	purchase mission.
--	購合同	procurement contract.
--	購站	purchasing station.
77--	用	adopt, introduce, give in,

	take up.	
-- 桑	pick mulberry leaves.	
80-- 金	gold mining.	
-- 礦	mine.	
87-- 錄	collect and record.	
95-- 煤	mine coal.	

5210₀

蜊 〔Li〕 *n.* clam.

蚓 〔Yin〕 *n.* earthworm.

劃 〔Hua〕 *v.* divide, demarcate, carve, engrave, cut, mark off.

10-- 一	uniform, fixed.	
-- 一定價	price on a uniform basis.	
14-- 破	scratch.	
26-- 線	mark.	
-- 線支票	crossed cheque.	
27-- 歸	incorporate.	
28-- 傷	wound, deface.	
30-- 定	define, mark of.	
35-- 清	draw a clear line, make a clean distinction.	
51-- 掉	cross out.	
52-- 撥	remit-transfer.	
-- 撥款項	remit money.	
60-- 界線	draw a line between, draw a line of demarcation.	
64-- 時代	epoch-making.	
77-- 開	cut open, slash open.	
80-- 分	divide, segregation.	

5210₄

塹 〔Chian〕 *n.* the moat around a city.

40-- 壕　trench, entrenchment work.

5211₁

蚯 〔Chiu〕 *n.* earthworm.

5211₆

蠟 〔La〕 *n.* wax.

22-- 製	waxen.	
24-- 紙	wax-paper.	
26-- 線	wax-thread.	
27-- 像	wax figure, wax image.	
44-- 黃	waxen (color).	
48-- 梅	kind of plum blooming in winter.	
80-- 人	wax figure.	
88-- 筆	crayon.	

96-- 燭	candle.	
-- 燭台	candlestick.	

5212₁

蜥 〔His〕 *n.* lizard.

56-- 蜴　lizard.

5213₆

蜇 〔Che〕 *n.* jellyfish.

5213₉

蟋 〔Shi〕 *n.* cricket.

50-- 蟀　cricket.

5214₁

蜒 〔Yen〕 *n.* millipede.

蜓 〔Ting〕 *n.* dragonfly.

5215₃

蟣 〔Chi〕 *n.* nit, louse grub.

5216₉

蟠 〔Pan〕 *v.* curl up, coil around, crouch under.

43-- 桃	flat peach.	
51-- 據	occupy.	

5225₇

靜 〔Ching〕 *adj.* quiet, calm, still, tranquil, silent, peaceful, virtuous.

10-- 電	static electricity.	
-- 電復印	xerox.	
-- 電復印機	xerox printer.	
14-- 聽	listen attentively.	
21-- 止	rest, still.	
-- 態	static state.	
27-- 候	wait patiently.	
-- 物	still life, inanimate object.	
33-- 心	peaceful mind.	
60-- 思	meditate, think quietly.	
63-- 默	*n.* silence, stillness, *v.* keep silence, hold one's peace.	
72-- 脈	vein.	
-- 脈注射	intravenous injection.	
77-- 居	quiet retirement.	
80-- 美	static beauty.	
-- 養	resting, repose.	
88-- 坐	sit quietly, meditate.	
-- 坐怠工	sit-down strike.	

5260₁

誓 〔Shih〕 *n.* oath, vow, *v.* swear, vow,

take an oath.

00-- 言	oath, vow.
07-- 詞	oath, vow.
10-- 死不屈	vow to fight till oneself or the other party falls.
21-- 師	address an army.
27-- 約	oath, pledge, word of honor.
71-- 願	vow, pledge.

5260_2

哲〔Che〕*n.* philosophy, wisdom, sage, wise man.

16-- 理	philosophical principle.
77-- 學	philosophy.
-- 學系	philosophy department.
-- 學的	philosophical.
-- 學家	philosopher.
80-- 人	sage.
-- 人其萎	The wise man is dead.

暫〔Chan〕*adv.* temporarily, briefly, suddenly, for the time being.

12-- 延	adjourn temporarily.
17-- 忍	be patient for a while.
20-- 住	sojourn, pitch one's tent.
-- 停	*n.* recess, suspension, *v.* adjourn, intermit, suspend.
-- 停辦公	suspend public business.
-- 停工作	suspend work.
-- 停營業	temporary cessation of business.
21-- 行條例	provisional regulation.
22-- 緩	hold for a while.
24-- 付	payment on account.
-- 借	borrow for a short time.
26-- 息	lull.
30-- 定	tentatively set on.
64-- 時	temporarily, for the time being, for a short time.
-- 時休戰	truce.
85-- 缺	vacant for the time being.

5290_0

剌〔Tzu〕*n.* thorn, spine, sting, *v.* stab, pierce, thrust.

00-- 痛	bite, sting.
10-- 耳	jarring.
-- 死	stab to death.
17-- 刀	bayonet.
25-- 繡	embroider.
-- 繡品	fancy work.
28-- 傷	hurt, puncture.
30-- 字	brand, tattoo.
-- 客	assassin.
38-- 激	stimulate, provoke, excite.
-- 激作用	*n.* stimulation, *v.* spread effect.
-- 激物	stimulant, irritant.
-- 激熱情	stir up passion.
47-- 殺	*n.* assassination, *v.* assassinate, stab.
56-- 蝟	hedgehog.
57-- 探	probe.
80-- 入	pierce.

5291_4

耗〔Hao〕*n.* news, tidings, information, *v.* waste, spend, consume, diminish, destroy.

00-- 廢	waste.
06-- 竭	exhaust, use up.
10-- 電量	power consumption.
17-- 子	rat.
33-- 減	diminish by expending.
50-- 盡	exhaust.
55-- 費	consume, waste, squander.
56-- 損	wear, wear and tear.
64-- 時間	time-consuming.

5300_0

戈〔Ke〕*n.* spear, lance, weapon.

掛〔Kua〕*v.* hang, suspend, think of, worry.

00-- 意	mind.
08-- 旗	hoist a flag.
21-- 慮	concern, feel anxious about.
-- 上	hang up.
25-- 失	report the loss.
-- 失支票	lost check.
26-- 牌價格	listed price.
-- 牌股票	listed stock, quoted share.
-- 牌公司	listed company.
27-- 名董事	dummy (nominal) director.
-- 名合伙人	nominal partner.

-- 久	on credit.
-- 欠	on credit.
33-- 心	concern, feel anxious about.
41-- 麵	dried noodles.
-- 車	trailer (mail).
60-- 圖	scroll picture, wall map.
61-- 號	registration.
-- 號信	registered letter (mail).
-- 賬	on account.
80-- 鐘	wall clock.
-- 念=掛慮	miss, care, think of, be anxious about.
87-- 鉤	link up, be connected.

5301₁
控〔Kung〕*n.* accuse, charge, sue, impeach, suppress, control, rein in.

02-- 訴	appeal, accuse, charge, impeach, bring an action, complain.
-- 訴狀	letter of appeal.
-- 訴人	appellant, suitor.
-- 訴會	accusation meeting.
22-- 制	control, overrule, ride, rein in.
-- 制範圍	span of control.
-- 制權	domination, control.
24-- 告=控訴	
77-- 股公司	holding company, controlling company.

搾〔Cha〕*v.* crush out, squeeze out.

17-- 取	squeeze, exact.
34-- 汁機	juicer.
35-- 油	extract oil.
44-- 菜	salted vegetable root.
60-- 果汁	squeeze fruit for juice.

5301₇
挖〔Wa〕*v.* dig out, excavate, scoop.

10-- 耳	pick the ears.
14-- 破	break by scooping.
22-- 出	dig out, excavate.
30-- 空	hollow.
37-- 洞	dig a hole.
-- 泥	scoop out earth.
-- 泥機	dredger, dredging machine.
40-- 壕	entrench, dig in.
44-- 苦	ridicule.
47-- 塚	ridicule.
-- 根	uproot, root out, dig out root.
55-- 井	dig a well.
57-- 掘	excavate.
-- 掘機	excavator.

5302₁
擰〔Ning〕*v.* wring, twist, turn away.

22-- 彎	contort.
-- 斷	twist off.
77-- 開	twist off, turn on.
-- 緊	screw.

5302₇
捕〔Pu〕*n.* police, *v.* arrest, seize, catch.

27-- 鼠	catch mouse.
-- 鼠機	rat-trap.
-- 魚	fishing.
-- 魚業	fishing industry.
-- 魚限額	catch quota.
-- 魚量	fish catches.
30-- 房	police station.
44-- 獲	capture, seizure.
47-- 殺	catch and kill.
63-- 獸機	trap.
-- 賊	arrest thief.
80-- 拿	arrest, seize, catch.

捐〔Chien〕*v.* bear.

30-- 客	broker.

輔〔Fu〕*v.* assist, help, aid.

00-- 音	consonant.
38-- 導	coach, tutor.
-- 導員	coach, guide.
74-- 助	help, assist.
-- 助設備	additional equipment, service equipment, accessory equipment.
-- 助收入	subsidiary revenue (income).
-- 助報告	satellite report.
-- 助費用	auxiliary expense.
-- 助工	auxiliary worker.
98-- 幣	auxiliary coin, subsidiary coin.

5303₃
撚〔Nien〕*v.* roll up, twist with fingers.
5303₄

挨〔Ai〕 v. suffer, force in, press on, lean against, adj. near, next to, side by side.

00--	磨	delay, procrastinate.
24--	靠	lean on, depend on.
32--	近	v. approach, adj. near, close to.
37--	次	by order, in turn, from hand to hand, one by one.
44--	苦	suffer.
51--	打	be beaten.
60--	罵	be scolded.
83--	餓	be hungry, suffer from hunger.

捱〔Li〕 v. turn. adj. stubborn, obstinate, willful.

5304$_0$

拭〔Shih〕 v. wipe, rub, cleanse.

32--	淨	wipe and clean.
33--	淚	wipe tears.
40--	去	abandon, reject.

拼〔Pin〕 v. sweep, brush away, reject.

78--	除	abandon, clear away.
80--	命	desperation.

5304$_2$

搏〔Po〕 v. seize, strike with hands.

17--	取	seize, catch.
47--	殺	fight and kill.
57--	擊	attach, strike.
63--	戰	combat, battle, wrestle.
77--	鬪	wrestle, fight.

5304$_4$

按〔An〕 v. hold, grasp, press down, stop, cease, repress, place the hand on, examine, prep. according to, in accordance with.

00--	序	by order.
--	市價	at market price.
--	摩	massage.
--	摩師	masseur, masseuse.
07--	部就班	step by step.
10--	下	press down.
--	需分配	distribution according to needs, to each according to one's needs.
--	百分比	in percentage term.
16--	理	according to common practice.
--	重量計算	calculate by weight.
--	季付款	quarterly payment.
20--	住	repress, restrain.
21--	比例	pro rata, in proportion.
--	比例分配	proportional allocation, proportional distribution.
--	價值	according to one's merits.
22--	例	according to law, by law.
25--	件計工	work-print based on piece work done.
--	件計酬	pay on piece work basis.
27--	名次	according to the order of names listed.
--	條件付款	payment on term.
30--	戶推銷員	house-to-house salesman, door-to-door salesman.
--	戶檢查	house-to-house inspection.
--	戶推銷	house-to-house selling.
37--	次	according to order.
44--	著	according to.
47--	期	according to the fixed period, on schedule.
--	期舉行	convene according to the stated periods.
48--	樣訂貨	order by sample.
52--	折扣價	at discount.
53--	成本	at cost.
60--	日	hire by day.
64--	時	on time, according to the time specified.
67--	照	act according to, in accordance with.
72--	脈	feel the pulse.
77--	服	monthly, by the month, per month.
--	務需要	according to requirement of service.
80--	人口	per head, per capita.
--	合同	ex contract.
--	年	per year, yearly, annually.
88--	鈴	press on the bell, ring the bell.
--	勞計酬	pay according to work.

5304$_7$

拔〔**Pa**〕v. pull up, pluck, eradicate, uproot, extirpate, elevate.

20-- 毛	pluck out hairs.
22-- 出	extract, pull out.
27-- 身	get away.
31-- 河	tug of war.
44-- 草	weed.
-- 萃	prominent.
47-- 根	root out.
57-- 擢	promote, raise.
71-- 牙	extract a tooth.
78-- 除	uproot, extirpate.
84-- 錨	cut the anchor, lift anchor.

5305₀

找〔**Chao**〕v. find, seek, look for, return change.

00-- 齊	make equal, even up.
10-- 死	seek death, invite death.
-- 零	odd change.
-- 不到	unable to find.
11-- 頭	balance, change.
12-- 到	find, discover.
17-- 尋	find, seek, search, look for.
22-- 出	discover, search.
-- 出路	find a way out.
33-- 遍	have searched everywhere.
34-- 對象	look for a partner for marriage.
35-- 清	pay off the balance.
44-- 藉口	find an excuse.
47-- 根源	go to the root, find the cause.
50-- 事	look for job, seek employment.
57-- 換	exchange bank notes of different denominations.
80-- 人	look for someone.
-- 岔子	find fault.
83-- 錢	give change.

撼〔**Han**〕v. shake, move, excite.

24-- 動	shake, rock.
-- 動人心	move one's heart, shake one's faith.

5306₀

抬〔**Tai**〕v. carry on a pole, lift, raise.

00-- 高	raise, boost.
-- 高市價	jacking up price.
-- 高物價	boost the price.
10-- 不動	incapable of lifting.
11-- 頭	raise one's head.
-- 頭人	addressee.
40-- 走	carry away.
42-- 轎子	carry a sedan chain.
47-- 起	uphold, lift up.
77-- 舉	do a good favor.

5306₁

轄〔**Hsia**〕v. govern, rule, regulate.

10-- 下	under the command or jurisdiction.
32-- 治	govern, rule, administer.
44-- 地	dominion of a ruler.
71-- 區	area under jurisdiction.

5308₆

擯〔**Pin**〕v. reject, expel, exclude, renounce.

00-- 棄	reject.
27-- 絕	get rid of.
31-- 逐	expel, oust.
-- 逐出境	expatriate from the country.
44-- 落	suffer rejection and downfall.
62-- 黜	banish, exile.
72-- 斥	dismiss, reject, expel.
78-- 除	expel, oust.
-- 除障礙	remove obstacles.

5309₁

擦〔**Tsa**〕v. rub, brush, wipe.

00-- 亮	polish.
-- 字膠	eraser.
14-- 玻璃	wipe glass.
17-- 子	rubber, eraser.
28-- 傷	scratch.
31-- 汗	wipe off sweat or perspiration.
34-- 洗	scrub.
35-- 油	varnish, grease, rub on oil.
40-- 布	wiping rags.
-- 去	wipe out.
44-- 地板	mop the floor.
-- 鞋	polish shoes.
-- 鞋童	shoeshine boy, shoeblack.
-- 鞋油	shoe polish.

48-- 乾　　　　　wipe clean.
50-- 車　　　　　wax a car.
51-- 掉　　　　　wipe out.
77-- 臉　　　　　wash face.
90-- 火柴　　　　strike a match.

5310₀
或 〔Huo〕 *adj.* uncertain, some, *adv.* perhaps, perchance, maybe, *conj.* if, whether, either, or.

08-- 許　　　　　perhaps, may be, probable.
-- 許是　　　　　perhaps so, may be, probably, presumably.
-- 許不是　　　　perhaps not.
10-- 可　　　　　probably.
21-- 此或彼　　　either this or that.
23-- 然　　　　　probably.
-- 然性　　　　　probability.
40-- 大或小　　　either large or small.
-- 有利益　　　　contingent gain.
-- 有費用　　　　contingent charge.
-- 有損失　　　　loss contingencies.
-- 來或往　　　　either coming or going.
44-- 者　　　　　perhaps, may be, likely, it may happen.
60-- 早或遲　　　sooner or later.
-- 是　　　　　　perhaps.
77-- 問　　　　　someone may ask.

5310₇
盞 〔Chan〕 *n.* wine cup, tea cup, bowl, small cup.

5311₁
蛇 〔Shei〕 *n.* snake, serpent.

21-- 行　　　　　move like a snake.
40-- 皮　　　　　snake's skin.

5311₂
蜿 〔Wan〕 *n.* the squirming motion of a snake.

42-- 蜒　　　　　wriggle, squirm.

5312₇
蝙 〔Bian〕 *n.* bat.

51-- 蝠　　　　　bat.

5315₀
蛾 〔O〕 *n.* moth.

5320₀
戍 〔Shu〕 *n.* garrison, *v.* guard the frontier.

00-- 卒　　　　　soldier on guard.
27-- 役　　　　　garrison duty.
30-- 守　　　　　set up frontier garrison.
45-- 樓　　　　　garrison tower.

成 〔Cheng〕 *v.* finish, succeed, complete, achieve, accomplish, succeed, effect, become, make, change into, *adj.* finished, completed, settled, fixed, entire, complete full, whole, all right.

00-- 立　　　　　establish, found, accomplish, come into existence, be true, hold good.
-- 立大會　　　　inaugural meeting.
-- 文　　　　　　existing writings.
-- 文契約　　　　written contract.
-- 文憲法　　　　written constitution.
-- 文法　　　　　written law.
-- 交　　　　　　strike a bargain, consumption of a transaction, conclude a transaction, come to a deal.
-- 交價格　　　　transaction price.
-- 交額　　　　　volume of transaction (trade).
-- 交契約　　　　literal contract.
-- 交量　　　　　turnover.
-- 衣　　　　　　ready made suit.
-- 衣匠　　　　　tailor, dress maker.
-- 衣鋪　　　　　tailor's shop.
01-- 語　　　　　idiom, phrase.
03-- 就　　　　　*n.* success, completion, achievement, attainment, *v.* accomplish.
04-- 熟　　　　　ripe, mature.
06-- 親　　　　　get married.
08-- 效　　　　　result, effect.
-- 效卓著　　　　the achievement is outstanding.
-- 效管理　　　　results management.
-- 議　　　　　　come to agreement.
10-- 丁者　　　　adult.
14-- 功　　　　　*n.* success, accomplishment,

	achievement, *v.* succeed, fulfill, carry out.
-- 功立業	make one's fortune.
-- 功秘訣	secret of success.
-- 功者	successor.
18-- 群	group, herd.
-- 群結黨	from groups and cliques.
20-- 千成萬	thousands and tens of thousands.
21-- 仁取義	die to preserve one's virtue intact, die a martyr's death.
-- 行	embark on a journey.
22-- 例	established precedent.
25-- 績	result, records, achievements.
-- 績單	report card.
27-- 名	become famous.
28-- 份	element, ingredient, class status.
30-- 家立業	get married and start a career.
34-- 對	match, form a pair.
-- 法	*n.* existing law, *v.* become a law.
34-- 爲	become.
40-- 套	whole set.
-- 套設備	complete set of equipment.
-- 套軟件	software kit.
47-- 都	Chengtu.
50-- 本	cost, cost of business.
-- 本上漲	cost inflation.
-- 本稅	tax on cost.
-- 本加運費	cost and freight.
-- 本加利	cost plus.
-- 本控制	cost control.
-- 本單	cost sheet.
-- 本單價	cost unit price.
-- 本分析	cost analysis.
-- 本分攤	cost sharing (allocation).
-- 本管理	cost management.
-- 本價格	cost price.
-- 本會計	cost accounting.
-- 事	things done, bygone.
51-- 批	batches, group by group.
56-- 規	established practice, rule or regulation.
58-- 數	whole number, percentage.
60-- 日	whole day, all day.
-- 見	prejudice.
-- 品	finished product.
-- 品庫存	inventory of finished goods.
-- 品市場	outlet for finished goods.
-- 品出口國	finished product-exporting country.
-- 品檢驗	finished product inspection.
-- 品單	work completed forms.
-- 員	member.
-- 員國	member state.
-- 果	result, fruit, product.
66-- 器	become a useful person.
71-- 長	grow up.
77-- 風	become a common practice.
80-- 人	adult, manhood, mature age, full age.
-- 全	help another accomplish something.
-- 分	essence, element, component.
-- 年	come of age, reach adulthood.
-- 年累月	year after year and month after month, for a long time.
-- 年人	adults.
88-- 竹在胸	knowing what to do.
95-- 性	become habitual.

威 〔**Wei**〕 *n.* majesty, dignity, grandeur, awe, *adj.* majestic, grave, imposing.

07-- 望	prestige.
13-- 武	*n.* martial looking, brave looking, *adj.* majestic, dignified.
20-- 信	prestige.
27-- 名	prestige, reputation, awe inspiring.
28-- 儀	majesty.
31-- 逼	coerce, intimidate.
40-- 力	might, power, strength, force.
-- 士忌酒	whiskey.
-- 脅	threaten, intimidate, coerce.
44-- 勢	prestige and influence.
-- 權	absolute authority.
47-- 猛	domineering.

64--	嚇	frighten, intimidate, show one's teeth.
66--	嚴	august, majestic, stern.
71--	壓	overawe, overpower.
77--	風	dignity, awe, majesty, imposing air.
--	服	overawe, coerce.
91--	懾	overawe.

戚 〔Chi〕 n. relation, adj. sorrowful.

03--	誼	ties between relatives.
30--	容	sad look, sorrowful expression.

咸 〔Hsien〕 adj. all, adv. wholly, entirely.

20--	信	generally believed that.

盛 〔Sheng〕 adj. flourishing, abundant, grand, excellent, fine, blooming, plenteous.

00--	意	thoughtfulness, generosity.
--	產	abound in.
--	衰	the ups and downs.
10--	夏	midsummer.
21--	行	v. prevail, adj. prevailing, popular, in full swing.
24--	德	great virtue.
--	裝	n. full dress, v. dress up.
25--	傳	n. fame, v. spread some information.
27--	名	great reputation.
36--	況空前	festivity, unprecedented in grandeur.
40--	大	grand, magnificent, pompous.
44--	世	prosperous age.
47--	怒	furious, in passion, in great anger.
50--	事	grand occasion.
77--	服	in full dress.
--	開	in full bloom.
--	譽	well known, of great reputation.
80--	年	flourishing year.
--	會	great meeting, splendid meeting.
--	氣	arrogant, full of spirit.
54--	饌	feast.

95--	情	courtesy, hospitality, kindness.

感 〔Kan〕 n. sentiment, feeling, emotion, v. touch, affect, rouse, excite, feel, move, respond to feelings.

00--	應	influence, induction (in physics), response.
--	應電	induced electricity.
--	應器	induced machine.
04--	謝	thankful, grateful.
--	謝之至	be exceedingly thankful.
10--	電	electric induction, electrification.
12--	到	feel, perceive.
--	到不快	feel unhappy.
20--	受	be affected, feel.
24--	化	persuade, induce, influence, bring round.
--	化教育	reformatory education.
--	化院	reformatory.
--	化人心	reform the heart of people.
--	動	influence, inspire, touch, affect, provoke, make an impassion upon.
--	動人心	move one's heart.
--	德	be grateful for a kindness.
26--	觸	affection.
28--	傷	v. feel sad, adj. sorrowful.
--	傷主義	sentimentalism.
30--	官	senses, sense-organs.
34--	染	infect, be imbued with.
--	染力	infecting power.
38--	激	n. gratitude, adj. grateful.
--	激之至	be extremely grateful.
40--	奮	be moved to action.
44--	慕	thanks and adore.
--	舊	remember the deceased with emotion.
46--	想	feeling, impressing, one's opinion about something.
60--	恩	indebted, gratified.
--	恩圖報	feel grateful for a kind act and plan to repay it.
--	恩節	Thanksgiving Day.
--	冒	n. cold, v. catch a cold.
64--	嘆	n. exclamation, sign, v. sigh.

--	嘆詞	interjection.
--	嘆號	exclamation mark.
77--	覺	*n.* sensation, feeling, *v.* feel, sense.
--	覺器官	sensory organs.
--	覺神經	sensory nerves.
--	同身受	be grateful as if one were the object of the favor done.
80--	人	affecting, touching, moving.
--	念	remember with gratitude.
90--	光	be exposed to light.
--	光劑	sensitizer.
--	光紙	sensitized paper.
--	懷	recall with emotion.
91--	慨	feeling, emotional excitement.
95--	性	sensibility, perceptibility.
--	情	sentiment, feeling, emotion.
--	情破裂	fall out.
--	情激動	impulsive.
--	情作用	action of the emotion.
--	情用事	act according to one's sentiment.

5322₇
甫 〔Fu〕 *v.* begin, *adj.* great, large, fine, good, *adv.* just, immediately after.

5328₁
靛 〔Tien〕 *n.* indigo.
| 50-- | 青 | indigo. |

5330₀
惑 〔Huo〕 *n.* suspicion, doubt, unbelief, confusion, *v.* suspect, doubt, impose upon, befool, delude
10--	弄	delude, befool.
22--	亂	bewilder.
60--	眾	confuse the people.

5340₀
戎 〔Jung〕 *n.* weapon, arm, soldier, troops, warfare, military operation.
00--	衣	military dress.
18--	政	military affairs.
21--	行	military ranks.
24--	裝	in military dress, military uniform, clad in uniform.
42--	機	military secret.
50--	車	chariot.

戒 〔Chieh〕 *n.* warning, precaution, *v.* warn, caution, beware of, guard against, refrain from, abstain from.
24--	備	stand guard, be on the alert.
25--	律	taboo, precept.
27--	條	precept.
--	絕	forbear, abstain, do without.
31--	酒	give up wine, abstain from wine.
33--	心	alertness.
51--	指	ring.
64--	賭	abstain from gambling.
66--	嚴	proclaim martial law.
--	嚴時期	period during which martial law is in force.
--	嚴令	martial law.
78--	除	break of.
80--	食	fast, abstain from food.
96--	烟	abstain from opium smoking.

5350₃
戔 〔Chien〕 *v.* hurt, wound, *adj.* narrow, small.

5380₁
蹙 〔Tsu〕 *v.* press, impel, urge, hasten, contract, wrinkle, *adj.* grieved, troubled.
| 31-- | 額 | scowl, frown, bend one's brow, contract the eyebrows |
| 77-- | 眉 | frown. |

5400₀
抖 〔Tou〕 *v.* tremble, shake.
| 24-- | 動 | shake, tremble, vibrate. |
| 27-- | 翻 | turn up, expose. |

拊 〔Fu〕 *v.* pat, slap.
| 20-- | 手 | clap hands. |

5401₁
揕 〔Chen〕 *v.* strike.
撓 〔Nao〕 *v.* disturb, vex, twist, wrench, distort, scratch.
00--	癢	scratch itch.
11--	頭	scratch one's head.
22--	亂	disturb, vex.

52-- 折　　　　bend and break.
95-- 性　　　　flexibility.

5401₂

拋〔Pao〕v. throw away, abandon, give up, fling, cast off.

00-- 棄　　　　abandon, reject, cast aside, throw away.
13-- 球　　　　play ball.
20-- 售　　　　dump large stocks of merchandise, heavy selling.
22-- 出　　　　throw out.
27-- 物線　　　parabola.
30-- 空　　　　sell short (stock market).
48-- 散　　　　spread out, separate.
77-- 開　　　　throw off.
84-- 錨　　　　cast anchor, drop anchor, develop engine trouble on the way (said of a car).

5401₄

捵〔Chueh〕v. strike, beat, cudgel, consult with, deliberate upon.

攂=抬 5306₀

5401₆

掩〔Yen〕v. cover, screen, conceal, hide, close, shut.

01-- 襲　　　　mount a surprise attack.
04-- 護　　　　protect, shelter, screen.
-- 護部隊　　　screening force.
-- 底　　　　shelter.
10-- 耳　　　　cover one's ear.
-- 耳盜鈴　　　self-deceit, stuff the ear when stealing a bell.
-- 覆　　　　cover, muffle.
-- 面　　　　hide the face, conceal the face.
-- 不住　　　unable to cover or hide.
21-- 上　　　　shut, cover.
44-- 蓋　　　　cover up.
-- 蔽　　　　screen, shelter, conceal.
-- 藏　　　　hide.
46-- 埋　　　　bury.
77-- 門　　　　close door.
88-- 飾　　　　disguise, conceal, camouflage, palliate.

5401₇

軌〔Kuei〕n. railroad, rut, track, rule, law.

30-- 迹　　　　locus.
38-- 道　　　　railroad, track, orbit.
44-- 模　　　　pattern, rule.
61-- 距　　　　track gauge.
62-- 則　　　　rule, regulation.
88-- 範　　　　mode, rule, guide.

5402₇

拷〔Kao〕v. beat, flog, torture.

07-- 訊　　　　try by torture.
51-- 打　　　　flog, beat, torture.
77-- 問　　　　examine by torture.

5403₂

轅〔Yuan〕n. shafts of a carriage, headquarter.

5403₄

摸〔Mo〕v. touch, feel.

00-- 底　　　　investigate, probe to the bottom.
10-- 不清　　　do not understand, not quite sure.
12-- 到門路　　　have learned the ways of the trade.
22-- 彩　　　　draw lots (in a raffle game).
27-- 魚　　　　catch fish.
35-- 清　　　　have a thorough understanding.
40-- 索　　　　grope for, fumble about.

5403₈

挾〔Hsia〕v. clasp, pinch, coerce, hold as hostage, hold under the arm.

22-- 制　　　　coerce, control, intimidate.
44-- 帶　　　　carry under arms, smuggle.
-- 勢　　　　presume upon one's influence.
48-- 嫌　　　　cherish resentment.
54-- 持　　　　hold someone under duress.
97-- 恨　　　　bear grudge.

5404₁

持〔Chih〕v. hold, grasp, keep, maintain, manage, control, support.

08-- 說　　　　be of the opinion.
10-- 正　　　　upright conduct.
-- 票人　　　bearer, heavy selling, note

holder, bill holder.

24-- 續	last, continue.
-- 續增長	sustainable growth.
27-- 久	continue, endure, persist, hold.
-- 久戰	running fight, battle of attrition, protracted warfare.
-- 久戰略	Fabian tactics.
30-- 家	housekeeping.
34-- 法	enforce law.
40 --有人	bearer.
48-- 槍	hold a gun.
-- 股公司	holding corporation proprietary company.

5404₇

技 〔Chi〕 n. talent, ability, art, skill, technique, ingenuity.

10-- 工	craftsman, mechanic, skilled worker.
-- 正	senior specialist.
11-- 巧	n. artifice, skill, art, know-how, adj. skillful, clever.
21-- 能	ability, talent, technique, skill.
-- 術	craft, technique, art, craftsmanship.
-- 術高明	super techniques.
-- 術革新	technical innovation.
-- 術交流	exchange of technology, technical exchange.
-- 術設計	technical design.
-- 術效率	technical efficiency.
-- 術研討會	technical seminars.
-- 術水平	technical level.
-- 術刊物	technical publication.
-- 術進步	technical progress.
-- 術協作	technical collaboration.
-- 術落後	lay in technology.
-- 術費用	technical fee.
-- 術服務	technical service.
-- 術問題	technical matters.
-- 術人員	technical personnel (staff).
-- 術合作	technical cooperation.
-- 術顧問	technical adviser.
-- 術管理	technological management.
-- 術犯規	technical foul.
-- 術員	technician.

-- 術學校	technical school.
-- 術性	technical.
-- 術精良	be excellent in skill.
-- 師	machine, engineer, artificer.
44-- 藝	skill, art.
57-- 擊	martial art.

披 〔Pi〕 v. open, spread out, unroll, uncover.

00-- 衣	throw on clothes.
10-- 露	publish.
11-- 頭	Beetles (British vocal group).
30-- 肩	shawl, cape.
53-- 掛	wear full battle dress.
60-- 甲	wear armor.
77-- 閱	read.
90-- 卷	open a volume and read.

5406₀

描 〔Miao〕 v. draw, design, trace.

30-- 寫	describe.
-- 準	take sight, aim at.
33-- 述	describe.
44-- 花	make a flower design.
-- 摹	copy exactly.
60-- 圖	tracing.

5406₁

措 〔Tso〕 v. put, set, arrange.

00-- 意	pay attention, mind.
-- 辦	arrange, transact, furnish.
08-- 施	execute, administer.
20-- 手不及	be caught unprepared.
-- 辭	wording, diction.
60-- 置	execute, arrange, manage.

搭 〔Ta〕 v. build, add to, go aboard.

09-- 談	talk to, have conversation with.
17-- 配	match, select, go together.
20-- 住	take up one's lodging.
21-- 上	take (a bus, etc.), add, make contact.
-- 乘	travel by.
26-- 線	make contact, act as a go-between.
27-- 船	take passage in a ship.
30-- 客	passenger.
-- 賣	tied sale.

42--	橋	build a bridge.
--	機	board an airplane.
43--	載	carry.
46--	架	put up a framework.
48--	救	rescue, help.
59--	擋	*n.* partner, *v.* cooperate, work together.
89--	銷	tie-in sale.

5407₀

拑 〔**Chien**〕 *v.* pinch, nip.

| 81-- | 釘子 | pull out a nail. |

5408₁

拱 〔**Kung**〕 *n.* arch, *adj.* arched, curved.

00--	廊	cloister.
20--	手	fold one's hand in a bow.
21--	衛	guard defend.
38--	道	archway.
42--	橋	arch bridge.
57--	抱	surround, encircle with two arms.
77--	門	arch.

5408₆

攢 〔**Tsuan**〕 *v.* store, hoard, gather, bring.

17--	聚	huddle together, crowd together.
24--	動	surging.
83--	錢	put money together.

5409₄

搽 〔**Cha**〕 *v.* smear, adorn, rub on.

| 44-- | 藥 | spread a plaster. |
| 98-- | 粉 | powder the face. |

5409₆

撩 〔**Liao**〕 *v.* grasp, tease, take hold of.

22--	亂	confused, disorderly.
31--	逗	provoke, entice.
47--	起	raise, lift up.
80--	人	make one excited.
95--	情	flirt.
63--	戰	challenge to fight.

5410₀

蚪 〔**Tou**〕 *n.* tadpole.

5411₄

蝌 〔**Ko**〕 *n.* tadpole.

蛙 〔**Wa**〕 *n.* frog.

33--	泳	breast stroke (in swimming).
67--	鳴	croaks of frogs.
80--	人	frogman.

5414₃

蟒 〔**Mang**〕 *n.* serpent, python.

| 53-- | 蛇 | boa constrictor, python. |

5414₇

蠖 〔**Hua**〕 *n.* worm.

5416₀

蛄 〔**Ku**〕 *n.* mole, cricket.

5418₁

蜞 〔**Chi**〕 *n.* leech.

5419₄

蝶 〔**Tieh**〕 *n.* butterfly.

| 00-- | 衣 | wings of butterfly. |
| 33-- | 泳 | butterfly stroke (swimming). |

5492₇

耡=敊 5894₀

勑=鋤 8412₇

5500₀

井 〔**Ching**〕 *n.* well.

12--	水	well water.
23--	然	orderly.
47--	欄	curb, brim.
55--	井有條	in good order.
60--	田	system of land division.
--	田制	the nine-square system of dividing the land.
--	里	village.

5502₇

弗 〔**Fu**〕 *v.* reject, *adj.* not, no.

| 46-- | 如 | not as good as, not equal to. |

拂 〔**Fu**〕 *v.* wipe, rub off, shake off, brush away.

00--	塵子	duster.
--	衣	tidy up one's dress.
35--	袖	shake one's sleeves.
53--	拭	brush, wipe away.
60--	晨	day break, dawn.
78--	除	wipe off, brush off.

5503₀

扶 〔**Fu**〕 *v.* aid, assist, help, support, lean on, uphold, protect, defend.

| 00-- | 病 | brave sickness. |

10-- 正	right.	
-- 靈	escort a casket, serve as a pallbearer.	
20-- 手	support by hand.	
-- 手椅	armchair.	
44-- 植	foster, patronize.	
47-- 起	help up.	
48-- 梯	staircase, stairway.	
54-- 持	support, sustain, uphold, back up, take the part.	
58-- 輪會	rotary club.	
74-- 助	aid, help, assist, support, encourage, stand by, set up.	
-- 助者	supporter.	
-- 助貧窮	aid the poor and the weak.	
80-- 養	support, bring up, nourish, take care of.	
-- 貧	poverty alleviation, help the poor.	
-- 貧計劃	aid-the-poor campaign.	
-- 貧工作	aid to poor regions.	

抉〔Chueh〕v. rake, dig, pick, choose, pluck out.

56-- 擇	select, choose, pick.
-- 擇良計	select a good plan.

軼〔Yi〕v. scatter, overflow, excel, rush together, adj. scattered, dispersed, lost.

04-- 詩	scattered poems.
40-- 才	outstanding talent.
50-- 事	stories, anecdotes.
77-- 聞	anecdotes.

5503₄

轇〔Tsou〕v. concentrate, collect together.

80-- 合	converge.

5504₃

摶〔Tuan〕v. roll in balls.

轉〔Chuan〕v. turn, revolve, rotate, transmit, go back, return, turn round and round.

00-- 意	change one's mind.
-- 交	care of, transmit, hand over, forward.
-- 讓	transfer, devolve, assignor, transferor.
-- 讓權	right of alienation.
02-- 託	request through another person.
07-- 調	modulate.
11-- 頭	turn one's head.
12-- 型	transform, reshape.
20-- 手	change hands.
-- 售	resale.
22-- 變	n. transition, change, transformation, v. change, transform.
-- 彎	turn a corner.
-- 崗	transfer one's post.
24-- 動	turn, rotate.
-- 化	transform into.
-- 告	transmit, communicate, pass on.
27-- 向	turn, turn to, change direction.
-- 角	corner.
-- 租	sublease, sublet, unlease.
-- 租人	sub-lessor.
-- 身	turn the body, turn round.
-- 移	displace, divert from, turn away.
-- 移陣地	have a shift of position.
30-- 守為攻	change from defensive to the offensive.
32-- 業	change one's occupation.
-- 業軍人	demobilized soldier.
34-- 達	inform another, communicate to another.
-- 港	transit port.
35-- 速	rotational speed.
37-- 運	n. transportation, v. transfer, transport, convey.
-- 運站	junction, transfer post, transshipment station.
-- 運業	transporting business.
38-- 送	transfer, send on.
-- 道	make a detour.
40-- 去	turn and go, go back.
-- 賣	resell, resale.
-- 來轉去	walk back and forth.
42-- 機	crisis, turning point.
43-- 嫁	remarry.
-- 載	reproduce, reprint.

44--	椅	swivel chair.
47--	好	take a turn for the better.
50--	車	transfer, change trains or buses.
52--	播	relay a broadcast.
--	播站	relay station.
--	折	complication.
--	授權	sublicense.
53--	捩點	turning point.
55--	軸	axle, shaft.
57--	換	exchange, convert.
--	投資	shift in investment.
60--	口	transit.
	口港	transit port.
--	回	turn back, return.
61--	賬	transfer accounts.
62--	瞬	n. moment, v. blink, wink.
67--	眼間	in a twinkling, in a wink.
68--	敗爲勝	turn a defeat into a victory.
77--	學	transfer to another school.
--	學生	transfer student.
80--	入	turn into.
--	念	change one's mind.
--	義	trope.
91--	爐	converter.

5504₄
摟 〔**Lou**〕 v. embrace, take up in arms, pull, draw.

20--	住	embrace, hold in the arms.
57--	抱	embrace, fall on one's neck.

5504₇
搆 〔**Kou**〕 v. pull, drag.

08--	訟	enter a lawsuit.
10--	不著	unable to reach it.
26--	和	make peace.
27--	怨	incur a grudge.
37--	禍	incur misfortune.

5505₃
捧 〔**Peng**〕 v. hand up, hold up.

20--	住	hold firmly and securely.
21--	上天	overpraise someone.
46--	場	render support.

5505₆
攆 〔**Nien**〕 v. drive, expel.

40--	走	expel.

5506₀

抽 〔**Chou**〕 v. take out, pull up, draw forth, levy, exact.

12--	水	pump water.
--	水馬桶	flush toilet.
--	水管	pump.
07--	調	transfer.
10--	丁	draft able-bodied men for military service.
22--	出	abstract, draw, elicit.
27--	獎	draw a lottery.
--	象	abstract.
28--	稅	levy taxes.
30--	審	audit at random.
40--	查	test at random, test check, spot check.
44--	考	unannounced quiz.
50--	盡	exhaustion.
52--	打	lash, whip.
60--	回	revulsion.
--	回資本	revulsion of capital.
61--	點存貨	inventory testing.
77--	風	convulsions (medicine).
--	風機	exhaust fan.
--	屜	drawer.
--	緊銀根	money squeeze, tighten the money in circulation.
80--	氣機	air-pump.
88--	籤	cast lots, draw cuts.
--	筋	cramp, spasm.
96--	煙	smoke.

軸 〔**Chou**〕 n. axis, axle, roller, scroll.

17--	承	shaft bearing.
--	承廠	bearing plant.
33--	心	roller, axis.
--	心國	Axis countries, Axis powers.

5508₁
捷 〔**Chieh**〕 n. victory, v. win, gain a victory, adj. quick, swift, active, smart, clever.

21--	徑	shortcut, cross cut.
35--	速	swift, quick, prompt.
37--	運	rapid transit.
--	運系統	rapid transit system.
--	運公司	express company.
40--	克	Czechoslovakia (Czech Republic).

47-- 報　announcement of victory.
60-- 足先得　the first prize will go to the nimblest, early bird catches the worm.

5509_0
抹〔**Mo**〕 *v.* rub, wipe off, brush, dust.
40-- 去　wipe off, efface.
98-- 粉　paint the face.

5509_6
揀〔**Chien**〕 *v.* choose, select, pick out.
21-- 柴　gather firewood.
37-- 選　choose, select.
56-- 擇　choose, select.

5510_0
蚌〔**Pang**〕 *n.* oyster, clam, mussel.
15-- 珠　pearl.
47-- 殼　oyster shell.

5512_7
蜻〔**Ching**〕 *n.* dragonfly.
52-- 蜓　dragonfly.

5513_0
蚨〔**Fu**〕 *n.* marine worm.

5514_4
螻〔**Lou**〕 *n.* mole cricket, *adj.* putrid.
54-- 蛄　mole cricket.

5516_0
蚰〔**Yu**〕 *n.* millipede.

5516_5
蠐〔**Ching**〕 *n.* grub, maggot.

5517_7
彗〔**Hui**〕 *n.* broom, comet.
57-- 掃　sweep with a broom.
60-- 星　comet.

5519_0
蛛〔**Chu**〕 *n.* spider.
22-- 絲　gossamer.
-- 絲馬跡　clues, leads.
27-- 網　cobweb, spider web.

5519_4
蟭〔**Chin**〕 *n.* small cicada.

5519_6
蝀〔**Tung**〕 *n.* rainbow.

5523_2
農〔**Nung**〕 *n.* agriculture, farming, hus-bandman, farmer.
00-- 產物　agricultural products, farm produce.
07-- 郊　countryside.
10-- 工　hired farm workers.
-- 工企業　agro-business.
12-- 副業　agricultural and subsidiary production.
24-- 貨　agricultural loan, agricultural credit.
-- 科　department of agriculture.
27-- 墾區　land-reclamation area.
28-- 作物　crops, farm products.
30-- 戶　peasant family.
-- 家　farming family.
32-- 活　farm work.
-- 業　agriculture, farming.
-- 業部　Ministry of Agriculture.
-- 業部長　Minister of Agriculture.
-- 業集體化　agricultural collectivization.
-- 業稅　agricultural tax.
-- 業家　agriculturalist.
-- 業機械化　mechanization of agriculture.
-- 業技術　agro-technique.
-- 業國　agricultural nation, agrarian nation.
-- 業學校　agricultural school.
-- 業化學　agricultural chemistry.
-- 業合作化　agricultural cooperation.
44-- 地　farmland, agricultural area.
-- 藝學　agronomy.
-- 村　village, countryside, rural area.
-- 藥　insecticide, pesticide.
-- 藥廠　insecticide factory.
-- 林　agriculture and forestry.
46-- 場　farm.
47-- 奴　bondman, serf.
-- 奴主　serf-owner.
-- 婦　farmer's wife.
50-- 夫　farmer, peasant, husband-man.
-- 事　farming, husbandry.
60-- 田　farm land, crop land.
-- 田水利　irrigation and water con-

	servancy.
-- 田灌溉	irrigation farming.
64-- 時	season for farming.
71-- 曆	lunar calendar.
77-- 民	farmer, peasant.
-- 民協會	farmer's association.
-- 具	agricultural implements, farm tool.
-- 學	agriculture.
-- 學院	college of agriculture.
-- 學家	farmer, husbandman.
-- 閑	slack farming season.
80-- 舍	cottage.
-- 會	farmers' association, peasants' union.
90-- 忙	busy season for farmers.

5533_7
慧〔**Hui**〕 *n.* wisdom, intellect, *adj.* wise, bright, intelligent, clever, ingenious.

33-- 心	bright mind.
40-- 力	power of intelligence.
60-- 星	comet.
67-- 眼	eagle eye.
95-- 性	intelligence.

5550_6
輦〔**Nien**〕 *n.* car, imperial car, *v.* transport, bring by car.

10-- 下	the metropolis, the capital.
50-- 夫	porter.

5560_0
曲〔**Chou**〕 *n.* song, plays, lyrics, tune, piece of music, *adj.* crooked, bent, curved.

00-- 率	curvature.
07-- 調	melody, air.
08-- 譜	musical notation.
11-- 頸瓶	retort, flask.
17-- 子	song, tune.
21-- 徑	crooked road, winding path.
24-- 射砲	howitzer, curl-fire gun.
26-- 線	curve, curved line.
-- 線美	curve of beauty.
27-- 解	distort, misinterpret.
40-- 直	right and wrong.
-- 直不分	failing to discriminate right and wrong.

44-- 藝	ballad singing and story telling, trivial skills.
46-- 棍球	hockey.
52-- 折	winding, zigzag, tortuous, twists and turns.
-- 折性	tortuous nature, circuitous character.
77-- 尺	carpenter's square.

5560_3
替〔**Ti**〕 *v.* substitute, change, take the place of, *prep.* for, instead of, behalf of, in place of, as a substitute for.

10-- 工	take up the work temporarily, substitute worker.
11-- 班工人	spare hand.
20-- 手	substitute, standby, understudy.
-- 代	*v.* substitute, prep. instead of, in place of.
-- 代品	substitute.
27-- 身	double, understudy.
57-- 換	exchange, replace.
60-- 罪羊	scapegoat.

5560_6
曹〔**Tsao**〕 *n.* Tsao (a family name), company, class.

5580_1
典〔**Tien**〕 *n.* ceremony, rite, canon, statute, code, law, rule, *v.* pawn, mortgage, take charge of.

03-- 試	examination.
-- 試委員會	committee in charge of examination.
12-- 型	pattern, type, prototype.
-- 型人物	typical character.
27-- 物	pledge, pawn.
35-- 禮	ceremony, rite, celebration.
40-- 賣	mortgage.
43-- 獄長	warden.
48-- 故	classical allusion, episode.
56-- 押	mortgage.
57-- 契	deed of mortgage.
70-- 雅	well-bred.
72-- 質	pawn, pledge, mortgage.
83-- 鋪	pawnshop.
88-- 範	model, example.

-- 籍	books, records.	
90-- 當	pawn, hock.	
-- 當商	pawn broker (operator).	
-- 當者	hocker.	

5580₆

費〔Fei〕 *n.* expense, costs, fee, outlay, *v.* spend, use, consume, waste.

10-- 工	labor consuming.
-- 電	power consuming.
14-- 勁	labor consuming, strenuous, difficult.
27-- 解	difficult to explain, difficult to understand.
33-- 心	*v.* exhaust one's mind, take trouble, *adj.* painstaking, troublesome.
40-- 力	*v.* use effort, take trouble, *adj.* laborious, painstaking.
44-- 材料	require large quantity of material.
50-- 事	troublesome.
64-- 時	waste time, time consuming.
67-- 眼	strain the eye, waste eyesight.
77-- 用	expenditure, expense, charge, outlay.
-- 用預付	charge prepaid.
83-- 錢	expensive, costly.

5590₀

耕〔Keng〕 *v.* cultivate, plow, till, plough.

00-- 畜	draught animal.
22-- 種	farm, plow and sow.
23-- 稼	tilling and planting.
25-- 牛	ox used in farming.
28-- 作	farm, till, cultivate.
-- 牧	tilling and pasturing.
44-- 地	tillage, farm land.
-- 地面積	area under cultivation, cultivated area.
-- 者有其田	land-to-the-tiller.
50-- 事	farm work.
-- 夫	farmer.
51-- 耘	cultivation.
-- 耘機	power tiller.

60-- 田	plough the field.

5599₂

棘〔Chi〕 *n.* thorny bushes, *adj.* troublesome, difficult, thorny.

20-- 手	troublesome, difficult, thorny, ticklish.
-- 手難辦	thorny affair.
84-- 針	buckthorns.

5600₀

扣〔Kou〕 *v.* strike, hit, discount, deduct, fasten, buckle, detain, impound, hook on, link.

12-- 發	garnish.
-- 發工資	garnished wage.
17-- 子	button, buckle.
20-- 住	seize, button, pin.
21-- 上	buckle.
28-- 繳額	deductible amount.
-- 繳捐稅	tax withhold.
30-- 牢	tie securely.
33-- 減	deduct.
40-- 肉	Chinese dish of steamed meat.
44-- 薪	deduct from pay.
47-- 款	deduct money.
56-- 押	detain, put in jail, keep in custody.
-- 押資產	seizure of assets.
71-- 壓	withhold.
77-- 問	ask, inquire.
-- 留	detain, intern.
-- 留貨物	detainment of the cargo, detained goods.
78-- 除	deduct from, subtract, strike out.
87-- 鈕	button, fasten a button.

拍〔Pai〕 *v.* pat, beat, strike, clap, caress, strike with the hand.

10-- 電影	shoot a film.
-- 電報	cable, send a telegram.
13-- 球	bounce a ball, play ball.
17-- 子	rhythm.
20-- 手	clap hands.
-- 手歡迎	receive with applause.
21-- 桌子	pound the table.
22-- 紙簿	writing pad.

40-- 賣		*n.* auction, *v.* bring to hammer, sell by auction.
-- 賣行		auctioneer.
-- 賣場		auction mart, bidding block.
-- 賣人		auctioneer.
41-- 板		beat time, give the final verdict.
51-- 打		clap, swat.
67-- 照		take a picture or photo.
71-- 馬		flatter.
77-- 門		knock at the door.

捆 〔**Kun**〕 *n.* package, *v.* bind, plait, tie up.

20-- 住	tie up, bind up.
21-- 上	bind up.
23-- 縛	bind, tie up.
24-- 裝	in bundle.
27-- 包	bale packing.

摑 〔**Kuo**〕 *v.* box, slap.
5601_0

担=**擔** 5706_1

規 〔**Kuei**〕 *n.* law, rule, regulation, custom, usage, compasses, *v.* regulate, plan, advise, correct.

00-- 章	rules, regulation.
10-- 正	advise so as to correct a mistake.
25-- 律	law, rules, regularity.
-- 律性	regularity.
27-- 約	covenant, statute.
-- 條	rules.
28-- 復	return to normalcy.
30-- 避	evade, elude.
-- 定	regulate, define, fix, determine, provide for.
-- 定價格	fix the price, regulated price.
-- 定佣金	stipulate a commission rate.
-- 定期限	prescribed time-limit.
-- 定時間	official hours.
44-- 勸	*n.* advice, admonition, *v.* advise, exhort, admonish.
-- 模	scale, scope, extent.
47-- 格	standards, specifications.
50-- 畫	map out, draw up.
52-- 劃	planning, design, project, scheme.
62-- 則	regulation, code, rule.
-- 則手冊	rule book.
67-- 略	plan and operate.
81-- 矩	rule, custom, regulation, well-behaved.
88-- 範	standard, model, norm.
-- 範化	normalize, standardize.

5601_1

擺 〔**Pai**〕 *n.* pendulum, *v.* wave, swing, put, place, spread out, expose, display, exhibit, arrange, shake, move to and fro.

00-- 齊	arrange evenly.
07-- 設	arrange, display.
10-- 下	put down, arrange.
-- 平	put down something securely.
-- 弄	play with.
-- 弄是非	spread tales.
12-- 列	arrange, display, array.
20-- 手	waft, beckon, wave the hand.
24-- 動	swing, oscillate.
-- 佈	arrange, manipulate.
30-- 渡	ferry across.
46-- 架子	stand upon one's dignity, put on airs.
50-- 事實	bring out the facts.
52-- 撥	put aside, dismiss from attention.
77-- 開	spread out.
78-- 脫	get rid of, break away.
-- 脫責任	shake off responsibilities.
82-- 針	pendulum.
84-- 錘	oscillating needle.

5601_7

挹 〔**I**〕 *v.* pour out.

30-- 注	readjust.

5602_7

拐 〔**Kuai**〕 *v.* kidnap, swindle, decoy, deceive, change direction.

17-- 子	kidnapper.
22-- 彎	turn a corner.
32-- 逃	seduce, make off with.
40-- 去	kidnap, swindle.

-- 賣	kidnap and sell, engage in white slavery.
44-- 帶	seduce, decoy, kidnap.
45-- 杖	crutch.
73-- 騙	decoy away.

捐〔Chuen〕*n.* subscription, contribution, taxation, *v.* subscribe, contribute, reject, give up, put away, throw away.

00-- 棄	cast away, abandon.
21-- 軀	sacrifice one's life.
23-- 獻	donation, contribution.
27-- 血	blood donation.
28-- 稅	duty, taxation.
30-- 官	purchase an official rank.
37-- 資	donate one's property.
44-- 募	collect contribution.
47-- 款	subscription, contribution, donation.
-- 款收入	contribution receipt.
-- 款者	money donor, subscriber, contributor.
68-- 贈	*n.* donation, *v.* donate, contribute, subscribe.
-- 贈財產	donated assets (property).
74-- 助	contribute, donate.
77-- 冊	subscription book.

揭〔Chieh〕*v.* lift up, raise, uncover, disclose, publicize, make known, expose.

00-- 言	reveal the inside story.
10-- 露	uncover, unmask.
-- 示	post proclamation.
12-- 發	disclose, bring to light.
14-- 破	disclose, lay bare.
30-- 穿	expose.
40-- 榜	publish a list of successful candidates, announce the results of an examination.
44-- 蓋子	take the lid off.
-- 封	tear off the seal.
-- 幕	raise the curtain.
-- 幕禮	opening ceremony.
77-- 開	uncover, open up.

揚〔Yang〕*v.* raise, lift up, praise, applaud, spread, scatter, extend, praise.

00-- 言	exaggerate, declare in public.
08-- 旗	raise a flag.
17-- 子江	Yangtze river.
20-- 手	raise the hand.
27-- 名	make famous, spread one's name, gain distinction.
-- 名於世	become world-famous.
47-- 帆	set sail, put to sea, raise a sail.
53-- 威	show one's great authority.

暢〔Chang〕*adj.* joyful, pleasant, delightful, happy, smooth, without obstruction.

09-- 談	talk pleasantly, have a delightful talk.
30-- 流	flowing freely.
34-- 達	fluent, smooth.
37-- 通	unblocked, unimpeded.
38-- 遊	enjoy a sightseeing tour.
61-- 旺	flourishing, prosperous.
72-- 所欲言	talk without any restraint.
-- 所欲爲	do whatever one likes.
74-- 馳	full gallop.
87-- 飲	crack a bottle.
88-- 敘	converse joyfully.
89-- 銷	active demand, sell well, sell like wild fire.
-- 銷書	best seller.
-- 銷貨	articles in great demand, fast moving goods.
-- 銷品	best seller.
95-- 快	delightful, happy, pleasant, pleased, merry.

5604₁
捍〔Han〕*v.* defend, ward off.

| 21-- 衛 | ward off, defend, safeguard. |
| 27-- 禦 | ward off, guard against. |

揖〔I〕*v.* salute, make a bow.

| 00-- 讓 | abdicate, give up a position for a better man. |
| 62-- 別 | bid adieu. |

擇〔Tse〕*v.* choose, select, pick out, distinguish.

| 00-- 交 | choose friends. |

06-- 親	make marriage arrangement. choose spouse.
10-- 要	outline, digest, select the important parts.
32-- 業	choose profession.
40-- 友	choose friends.
-- 吉開張	choose an auspicious day to start a business.
44-- 地	select a site.
47-- 期	select a good time.
80-- 食	select one's food.

輯 〔Chi〕 v. compile, collect together, compose.

10-- 要	outline, summary.
87-- 錄	compile and record.

5604₄

攖 〔Ying〕 v. provoke, rush against.

80-- 人心	disturb peace of mind.

5604₇

撮 〔Tso〕 v. select from, pick up, pinch, take with fingers.

10-- 要	n. outline, summary, v. digest, make extracts.
-- 弄	make a fool of.
25-- 牛奶	milk a cow.
62-- 影	photograph.
80-- 合	bring together.

攫 〔Kuo〕 v. seize, grasp, grab, snatch, take hold of.

17-- 取	grab, seize, snatch, take by force.
-- 取暴利	take in exorbitant profits.
40-- 奪	seize, snatch.

5605₀

押 〔Ya〕 v. mortgage, pledge, detain, put in jail, escort, guard.

06-- 韻	rhyme.
24-- 貨	escort goods.
27-- 租	rent deposit.
-- 解	transfer or deport under guard.
36-- 送	escort, send under escort.
37-- 運	escort goods in transportation.
-- 運費	escort fees.
-- 運人	conveyer.
47-- 款	mortgage.
57-- 契	mortgage deed.
60-- 品	security, mortgage.
80-- 金	deposit.
90-- 當	pawn.

5608₁

捉 〔Cho〕 v. seize, arrest, catch, grasp, lay hold of.

10-- 弄	play a joke on, make fun of.
12-- 到	catch, arrest.
20-- 住	catch, seize, take hold of
27-- 魚	fish.
30-- 牢	grapple.
39-- 迷藏	hide and seek, blindman's buff.
40-- 姦	seize an adulterer.
63-- 賊	seize a thief, catch a thief.
80-- 拿	catch, arrest, apprehend.

提 〔Ti〕 v. lift, raise, carry, hold, pull up, bring up, mention, bring to mind, suggest, propose.

00-- 高	raise, lift, elevate.
-- 高效益	raise efficiency.
-- 高收入	raise income.
-- 交	deliver, hand over, present, submit.
-- 意見	criticize, give views.
02-- 訴	prosecute.
08-- 議	n. proposition, suggestion, proposal, motion, v. propose, suggest, recommend, advocate, propound.
10-- 要	outline, summary, digest, abstract.
-- 示	n. reference, suggestion, v. suggest.
-- 票	summons.
11-- 琴	violin.
-- 琴手	violinist.
12-- 到	mention, refer to.
16-- 醒	remind, hint, suggest, call attention.
17-- 取	draw, pick up, extract, re-

	cover, withdraw, collect.
-- 及	mention, speak of, suggest, bring to notice.
21-- 價	increase price, raise the price.
22-- 出	hold out, put forward, bring up.
-- 出證據	produce evidence.
-- 出訴訟	litigate, enter an action.
-- 出申訴	make a complaint.
-- 出抗議	raise one's voice, make a protest against.
24-- 升	promote.
-- 供	provide, supply, offer.
-- 供證據	present evidence, produce evidence.
-- 供資金	provide fund.
-- 供擔保	tender guarantee, furnish security.
-- 供服務	provide service.
-- 供情報人	informant.
-- 貨	take delivery, pick up goods.
-- 貨單	bill of lading, delivery order.
26-- 倡	promote, introduce.
-- 倡者	promoter, advocate.
-- 倡國貨	encourage native product.
27-- 名	nominate.
-- 綱	outline.
-- 包	handbag.
-- 條件	specify the terms.
30-- 審	bring before the court, remove the case for trial.
-- 審法	The Habeas Corpus Act.
-- 案	n. proposal, motion, v. submit a proposal.
-- 案權	initiative.
-- 案人	one who makes a proposal.
33-- 心吊膽	be scared, cautious and anxious.
35-- 神	refresh, take care, be on the alert.
47-- 款	draw money, withdraw.
-- 款單	withdrawal ticket (slip) .
-- 款人	withdrawer.
-- 桶	bucket, pail.
-- 起	mention, refer to.

-- 起公訴	indict, arraign, accuse.
53-- 拔	promote, advance, lift, elevate, bring to eminence.
-- 成	v. deduct a percentage, draw a percentage.
60-- 早	in advance, ahead of schedule.
66-- 單	bill of lading.
70-- 防	guard against, take precaution against.
77-- 舉	promote someone.
80-- 前	give precedence, ahead of time.
88-- 籃	basket.
-- 箱	suitcase.
95-- 煉	refine, purify.

5608₆

損〔Sun〕n. damage, loss, disadvantage, injure, wound, v. lose, wound, hurt, injure, spoil, destroy, damage, diminish, decrease, lessen.

25-- 失	n. damage, loss, v. lose.
-- 失賠償	compensation for damage.
-- 失慘種	suffer a great loss.
28-- 傷	wound, hurt, injure.
30-- 害	injure, harm, damage, spoil, impair.
40-- 壞	spoil, damage, cripple, wrecked, break down.
52-- 耗	n. spoilage, wastage, v. wear away.
-- 耗率	rate of waste.
80-- 人	at the expense of others.
-- 益	profit and loss, increase and decrease.
-- 益表	statement of profit and loss.

5609₄

操〔Tsao〕v. exercise, drill, hold, grasp, handle, manage.

17-- 刀	hold a knife or sword.
21-- 行	conduct, behavior.
25-- 練	drill, exercise.
28-- 作	work, manipulate, operate.
-- 作說明書	operating manual.
-- 作技巧	operative skills.
-- 作規程	operational procedures, op-

	eration rules (standard).
--作人員	operation staff.
--作粗暴	rough handling.
--縱市場	manipulate the market.
--縱	control, command, manage, manipulate.
30--守	discretion in conduct.
32--業	practice.
33--心	worry.
--演	maneuver.
35--神	worry.
46--場	parade ground, play ground, drill ground.
47--切	hasty, eager, rash.
48--槍	rifle drill.
54--持	manage, handle.
55--典	drill book.
72--兵	drill troops.
99--勞	be burdened with cares, toil.
--勞過度	overwork.

5610_0

蛔 〔Hui〕 *n.* a small white worm in the bowels, roundworm.

蜘 〔Chih〕 *n.* spider.

55--蛛	spider.
--蛛網	spider's web.
--蛛絲	gossamer.

5611_0

蜆 〔Hsien〕 *n.* a small clam, a small black insect.

5611_4

蝗 〔Hwang〕 *n.* locust.

22--災	plague of locusts.
50--虫	locust.

5612_7

蜴 〔I〕 *n.* lizard.

蝟 〔Wei〕 *n.* hedgehog, porcupine.

20--毛	spines of a hedgehog.
--集	be crowded and complicated.
23--縮	*v.* recoil, wince, shrink, *adj.* scared.
47--起	arise in large numbers.

蠋 〔Shu〕 *n.* caterpillar.

5613_4

蜈 〔Wu〕 *n.* centipede.

58--蚣	centipede.

5615_6

蟬 〔Chan〕 *n.* cicada.

12--聯	stay on a position.
17--翼	wings of the cicada.
29--紗	kind of very fine silk.
67--鳴	chirp of cicadas.

5619_3

螺 〔Lo〕 *n.* spiral, shell, conch, screw like.

08--旋	screw.
--旋形	spiral.
--旋槳	propeller, screw-propeller.
--旋鉗	wrench.
20--紋	screw-thread.
22--絲刀	screw driver.
--絲帽	screw-cap.
--絲釘	screw, male screw.
26--線	spiral (mathematics).
--線管	solenoid (physics).
71--階	spiral staircase.

5621_0

靓 〔Ching〕 *v.* powder the face.

00--衣	beautiful dress.
24--妝	full dressed and ornamented.

5692_7

耦 〔Ou〕 *n.* mate, fellow, *v.* pair, match.

00--語	whisper to each other.
55--耕	plough side by side.
58--數	even number.

5701_1

捏 〔Nieh〕 *n.* work with fingers, fabricate.

34--造	fabricate, cook up, fake.

5701_2

抱 〔Pao〕 *v.* embrace, enfold, grasp, harbor, carry in the arms.

00--病	fall sick.
10--不平	indignant at an injustice.
20--住	hold fast in the arm.
27--怨	*n.* grudge, *v.* bear malice, complain.
--負	one's ideal, one's ambition.

77-- 緊	hold tightly.
80-- 養	adopt and raise.
87-- 歎	regret, feel sorry.
93-- 憾	regret, deplore, be sorry about.
96-- 愧	feel ashamed.
97-- 恨	feel regret, cherish hatred.
-- 恨終生	regret forever.

5701₃

拯〔Cheng〕v. rescue, deliver, save.

| 48-- 救 | rescue, save. |
| 97-- 恤 | save and help. |

攙〔Chan〕v. mix, assist, help, support with hand.

00-- 雜	blend, mix, mingle.
27-- 假	adulterate.
39-- 淡	dilute.
47-- 起	help someone to stand up.
55-- 扶	support, lead (a person) by the hand.
61-- 嘴	interrupt.
80-- 合	mix, blend, mingle.

5701₄

握〔Wo〕v. grasp, hold fast.

10-- 要	grasp the essential point.
20-- 住	hold fast, grasp, catch hold of.
-- 手	shake hands.
40-- 力	grip, power of gripping.
-- 有	possess.
44-- 權	be in power, be in command.
-- 權者	the authorities.
62-- 別	say good-bye.
70-- 臂	grasp an arm.
77-- 緊	grasp, clench, hold fast.
88-- 筆	hold a pen.
90-- 拳	clinch the fist.

擢〔Cho〕v. raise, promote, select, induce, lead on.

| 24-- 升 | raise, promote. |
| 77-- 用 | pick and promote. |

5701₅

扭〔Niu〕v. wring, twist, wrench, wrest, turn round.

| 22-- 斷 | break by twisting. |

24-- 動	wriggle, twist.
28-- 傷	sprain.
48-- 乾	wring (towel) dry.
51-- 打	struggle, grapple.
55-- 轉	twist about, turn over, turn for the better, turn back.
-- 轉大局	save a critical situation.
-- 轉時勢	turn the tide.
-- 曲	twist.
57-- 捏	fidget, mince.
71-- 腰	twist the waist, sprain one's back.
77-- 毆	grapple with someone.

5701₆

挽〔Wan〕v. pull, draw, lead, restore.

20-- 手	hold hands, arm in arm.
-- 住	hold back.
48-- 救	rescue, save from disaster.
60-- 回	recover, bring back.
77-- 留	request to stay, urge to stay.

輓〔Wan〕v. pull a carriage, draw a cart, mourn.

04-- 詩	elegy, funeral ode.
12-- 聯	funeral scroll.
17-- 歌	elegy, dirge.

攪〔Chiao〕v. stir up, mix, excite, disturb, annoy, confuse.

22-- 亂	disturb, confuse, throw into disorder, make hay of.
24-- 動	mix, stir.
26-- 和	mix evenly.
36-- 混	blend, mix by stirring.
51-- 擾	disturb, trouble, annoy.
59-- 拌機	mixer.
77-- 局	spoil, disturb.

5701₇

把〔Pa〕n. handle, bundle, fagot, v. hold, guard.

11-- 頭	gang-master.
17-- 子	target.
20-- 手	handle, knob.
22-- 穩	firm, stable, steady, dependable.
23-- 戲	magic, tricks, jugglery.
-- 舵	pilot, steer.
30-- 守	guard, hold fast, watch over.

41-- 柄　handle, evidence, proof.
54-- 持　control, manage, monopolize.
-- 持力　retention.
57-- 握　*n.* confidence, *v.* grasp, take hold of, safeguard, hold fast.
77-- 風　keep watch.
-- 門　watch the door, guard the door.

5702₀

抑〔I〕*v.* restrain, repress, depress, curb, rule, control, force to, *conj.* else, otherwise, either, or.
21-- 止　restrain, check, stop.
22-- 制　restrain, repress, withhold, control, suppress.
30-- 塞　reject, give no chance to.
36-- 遏　curb, restrain, suppress.
44-- 鬱　depressed, grieved, melancholy.
56-- 揚　cadence, intonation.
58-- 挫　bring lower.
80-- 首　bend one's head.

掬〔Chu〕*v.* grasp in both hands.
12-- 水　scoop up water with the hands.

拘〔Chu〕*v.* seize, arrest, detain, restrict, stop, grasp, lay hold of.
10-- 票　warrant of arrest.
30-- 守　holding fast to.
37-- 泥　bigoted, go strictly by book.
44-- 禁　detain, imprison.
50-- 束　restraint, binding.
53-- 捕　detain, arrest.
56-- 押　imprison.
77-- 留　detain, keep in custody, arrest.
-- 留所　house of detention.

靭〔Jen〕*adj.* tough.
22-- 出來　pull out, draw out.
54-- 摸　search and feel.
55-- 井　dredge a well.
83-- 錢　take out money, spend money.

掏〔Tao〕*v.* draw out, pull out.

捫〔Meng〕*v.* touch, feel.

擱〔Ke〕*v.* lay on, place on, put down, delay, obstruct.
10-- 下　put down, put aside.
-- 不下　unable to lay down.
33-- 淺　go shore, run aground.
41-- 板　shelf.
60-- 置　shelve, put aside, delay, lay by, put away.
88-- 筆　stop writing.

攔〔Lan〕*v.* stop, hinder, block, prevent, obstruct, debar.
20-- 住　block, stop, check, obstruct.
31-- 河壩　dam.
-- 河閘　barrage, dam gate, sluice gate.
77-- 阻　hinder, obstruct, stop.

5702₂

抒〔Shu〕*v.* pour, expose, express.
00-- 意　express one's ideas.
30-- 寫　express, describe.
95-- 情　express one's feeling.
-- 情詩　lyric.

5702₇

邦〔Pang〕*n.* state, country, nation, kingdom.
00-- 交　diplomatic relation.
40-- 土　nation's territory, land of a country.
50-- 本　foundation of a nation.
60-- 國　state, nation, country.

挪〔No〕*v.* move, remove, change place of.
24-- 借　borrow money for a short time.
27-- 移　move, borrow.
77-- 用　embezzle, misappropriate, divert.
-- 用公款　embezzle public fund, misappropriation of public fund.

揶〔Yeh〕*v.* ridicule, laugh, make sport of.

掃〔Sao〕*v.* sweep, brush, clean up.
00-- 塵　sweep clean.

10--	平	put down, crush, suppress.
--	雷艇	minesweeper.
17--	帚	broom.
24--	射	*n.* sweeping fire, *v.* shoot, rake.
32--	淨	clean up.
44--	墓	sweep the tomb--pay respect to one's ancestor at his grave.
--	地	sweep the floor.
--	蕩戰	mopping warfare.
--	黃	crack down on pornography.
54--	描	scanning.
--	描儀	scanner.
60--	黑	crack down on crime.
77--	興	cast down.
78--	除	clear away, throw off, keep clear of .

搗 〔Tao〕 *v.* beat, pound, attack.

10--	碎	pound to pieces.
17--	蛋	make trouble, be mischievous, raise hell.
22--	亂	disturb.
--	亂份子	trouble makers.
26--	鬼	play trick, sow discord.
97--	爛	pound something until it become pulp.

擲 〔Chih〕 *v.* throw, fling away, cast, reject, waste, jump, cast down, let fly.

10--	下	throw down.
16--	彈筒	grenade launcher.
22--	出	throw out.
36--	還	please return (something) to me.
40--	去	fling away.
41--	標槍	javelin throw.
44--	地	throw to the ground.
60--	回	reject, return.
77--	骰子	dice.
83--	鐵球	shot put, put the shot.
--	鐵餅	discus throw.

搦 〔Ni〕 *v.* grasp, seize, lay the hand on.

63--	戰	challenge to battle.

5703₂

撾 〔Chua〕 *v.* beat (a drum), strike.

44--	鼓	beat the drum.

輾 〔Chan〕 *v.* crush, grind, roll over, turn half round.

10--	平	roll over and flatten.
55--	轉	circulate, turn over and over.
71--	壓廠	rolling mill.
--	壓機	roll.
87--	鋼	rolled steel.
98--	斃	run over by a vehicle and got kill.

5703₄

換 〔Huan〕 *v.* change, exchange, replace, alter, substitute.

00--	主	change hands.
--	衣	change clothes.
--	文	exchange of notes.
02--	新	change something for a new one.
11--	班	relieve guard, change shifts.
--	班制	relay system.
12--	發證件	renew certificate, replacement of goods.
20--	位	conversion.
--	毛	molt.
--	季	change seasons.
21--	上	make change, substitute.
24--	貨	barter, replacement of goods.
27--	血	blood exchange, transfusion.
--	句話	in other words.
44--	藥	dress a wound again.
50--	車票	transfer ticket.
53--	成	change into, transform into.
83--	錢	exchange money.
88--	算	convert.
--	算率	conversion rate.
--	算表	conversion table.

5703₆

搔 〔Sao〕 *v.* scratch.

00--	癢	scratch an itch, tickle.
11--	背	scratch the back.
24--	動	disturbance, commotion.
51--	擾	annoy, harass.
80--	首	scratch one's head.

5703₇

搥 〔Chui〕 *v.* beat.

44--	鼓	beat a drum.
51--	打	beat, pound with fists.
71--	腰	massage the waist by light

pounding.

5704₁

捀〔**Ping**〕*v.* remove.

00-- 棄	abandon, get rid of.
49-- 擋	arrange in order.
78-- 除	remove, get rid of.

5704₂

捊〔**Lieh**〕*v.* gather, scrape off.

5704₇

扱〔**Cha**〕*v.* take.

投〔**Tou**〕*v.* throw, cast, fling, toss, give to, present.

00-- 交	friendship, friendly intercourse.
-- 棄	give up, abandon.
03-- 誠	surrender.
04-- 效	volunteer.
08-- 放	throw in, put on the market.
-- 敵	defect to the enemy.
10-- 票	vote, poll, put to vote, cast a ballot.
-- 票處	voting booth, polls.
-- 票選舉	poll, vote.
-- 票權	suffrage.
-- 票表決	decide by voting.
-- 票人	voter.
-- 票箱	ballot box.
16-- 彈	bomb, bomb dropping.
-- 彈點	point of release.
20-- 手	pitcher (baseball).
-- 稿	*n.* contribution, *v.* contribute an article.
-- 稿者	one who contributes articles.
22-- 出	projection.
24-- 靠	go over and serve, seek the patronage of.
-- 射	dart.
26-- 保	cover, insure, effect insurance.
-- 保價值	insured value.
-- 保單	insurance slip, proposal form.
-- 保人	policy holder, insured.
-- 保金額	insured amount.
30-- 宿	put up for the night, check in.

-- 案	surrender oneself to justice, give oneself up to the police.
31-- 河	drown one's self.
32-- 遞	deliver, hand over.
37-- 資	*n.* investment, *v.* invest.
-- 資市場	investment market.
-- 資收入	income from investment.
-- 資者	investors.
-- 資公司	investment company.
-- 資專家	investment expert.
-- 資人	investor.
-- 軍	enlist, join the army.
41-- 標	bid in a public tender.
42-- 機	speculation, adventure.
-- 機市場	speculation market.
-- 機取巧	speculative, opportunistic.
-- 機者	speculator, profiteer.
-- 機事業	speculative enterprise.
-- 機性	speculative.
44-- 考	participate in an examination.
57-- 擲	throw, cast, dart, project.
62-- 影	project.
77-- 降	surrender, lay down arms, capitulate.
-- 降主義	capitulationism.
80-- 入	plunge, throw into.
-- 首	give oneself up.
-- 命	give one's life to.
-- 合	agree with, see eye to eye.
88-- 籃	shoot (in basketball).

掇〔**To**〕*v.* incite.

10-- 弄	stir up, handle a matter.
52-- 採	gather, select.

搜〔**Sou**〕*v.* search, seek for, inquire.

10-- 票	search warrant.
17-- 尋	search, hunt, seek, look for.
20-- 集	pile up, collect, gather.
-- 集資料	collect data.
22-- 刮	plunder, loot.
27-- 身	frisk.
40-- 查	search, examine.
-- 查證	search warrant.
-- 索	search, hunt for.
-- 索兵	searcher.

43--	求	seek, find, look for.
48--	救	search for and rescue.
--	檢	search and investigate.
52--	括	search, extort, loot, plunder.
53--	捕	round up.
60--	羅	collect, call together.
65--	購	collect for purchase.

搬〔**Pan**〕*v.* remove, move, transport.

10--	弄	fiddle with, show off.
22--	出	move out.
24--	動	move, shift.
30--	家	remove, move house.
31--	遷=搬家	
37--	運	conveyance, transportation.
--	運部	trucking department.
--	運設備	haulage equipment.
--	運貨物	cargo handling.
--	運業務	cartage service.
--	運工	stevedore, mover, porter.
--	運費	carriage, freight, moving expense.
--	運公司	moving company.
40--	去	carry away.
77--	開	move away.

輟〔**Cho**〕*v.* stop, cease, suspend, halt.

10--	工	stop work.
77--	學	suspend from school.

5705₅
拇〔**Mu**〕*n.* thumb.

51--	指	thumb.
61--	趾	big toe.
77--	印	thumbprint.

5705₆
揮〔**Hui**〕*v.* shake, wave, wag, move, wield.

08--	旗	wave a flag.
10--	霍	*v.* spend freely, *adj.* profuse, lavish.
--	霍者	spendthrift.
12--	發	evaporate, volatilize.
--	發油	benzene, gasoline.
17--	刀	wield a sword.
20--	手	wave the hand.
24--	動	wave, swing.
31--	汗	wipe off perspiration.
33--	淚	wipe away tears, shed tears.

37--	軍	march troop to war.
80--	金如土	squander money like dust.
--	舞	wave, brandish.
90--	拳	swing the fist.

5706₁
擔〔**Tan**〕*n.* burden, load, *v.* bear, undertake, sustain.

10--	憂	be anxious, worry.
12--	水	carry water.
17--	子	burden, load.
22--	任	undertake, assume.
24--	待	be lenient, be magnanimous.
26--	保	guarantee, insure, secure.
--	保物	security, pledge.
--	保人	guarantor, surety.
--	保物權	security lien.
--	保協定	guarantee agreement.
--	保權	security right.
--	保期	period of guarantee.
--	保書	warranty.
--	保抵押	guaranteed mortgage.
--	保合同	guarantee contract.
--	公司	bonding company.
27--	負	burden, responsibility.
33--	心	be anxious.
41--	杆	pole.
57--	擱	delay.
77--	風險	run a risk.
90--	當	take responsibility.
--	當不起	unable to bear the burden, cannot accept a position.

5706₂
招〔**Chao**〕*v.* invite, call, confess, recruit, entice, beckon, incur.

00--	商局	China Merchant Navigation Co.
05--	請	invitation.
07--	認	*n.* confession, *v.* confess, admit.
10--	工	recruitment of employers (workers), hands wanted.
12--	引	incur, induce.
--	延	recruit.
15--	聘	advertise for office vacancies, position vacant, recruitment.

18--	致	contract, incur, give rise to.
20--	集	call in, get together.
--	手	beckon with hand.
24--	待	entertain, treat, receive, wait on, attend.
--	待員	usher, waiter, receptionist.
--	待所	hotel, guest house.
--	待會	reception.
--	待券	complimentary ticket.
--	供	confess.
25--	生	advertise for students, enroll students.
26--	牌	sign, signboard, name plate.
27--	租	let (a house), house to be let.
28--	收	enroll, accept, admit.
38--	邀	invite, request somebody to come.
41--	標	invite to bid, call for tender (bid).
44--	惹	incur, provoke, entice.
--	募	enlist, recruit.
--	考	advertise for employees or students through competitive examination.
46--	架	resist, ward off.
57--	搖	attract undue publicity.
58--	攬	collect, gather together, solicit.
--	攬生意	bring in business, drum up business.
61--	貼	*n.* poster, *v.* bill, post.
62--	呼	call to, hail, greet.
72--	兵	enlist, recruit.
77--	股	solicit shareholder, call for capital.

摺〔Che〕*n.* document, fold, *v.* enfold, fold up, double, bend and break.

00--	痕	crease.
--	床	folding bed.
17--	子	piece of paper folded into pages.
27--	縐	wrinkle.
30--	扇	folding fan.
37--	裙	plaited skirt.
44--	椅	folding chair, camp chair.
60--	疊	double up, fold up.

77--	門	folding door.

5707₂

搖〔Yao〕*v.* shake, wave, wag, move, row.

08--	旗	wave a flag.
11--	頭	wag the head.
20--	手	wave the hand.
24--	動	shake, swing, move, wave.
27--	船	row a boat.
30--	滾樂	rock'n'roll, rock music.
40--	來搖去	swing to and fro.
44--	椅	rocking chair.
56--	擺	waddle, sway, swing.
58--	籃	cradle.
--	鈴	ring the bell.

掘〔Chueh〕*v.* excavate, dig.

22--	出	dig out.
30--	穿	dig through.
37--	洞	dig a hole.
--	鑿機	excavator, excavating machine.
40--	土機	excavator.
--	濠	entrench, dig a trench.
44--	地	dig the ground.
55--	井	dig a well.
80--	入	dig in.
--	金	dig for gold.
--	金者	gold digger, opportunist.

5708₁

擬〔Ni〕*v.* propose, intend, guess, estimate, decide.

00--	辦	intend to execute.
01--	訂	draw up, work out, map out.
08--	議	tentative decision.
20--	悉	have drawn up.
--	稿	draft, draw.
30--	定	decide.
60--	罪	sentence.

撰〔Chuan〕*v.* compose, write.

00--	文	write an essay.
20--	稿	write, prepare manuscripts.
--	稿人	writer.
26--	和	soft, gentle, kind.
33--	述	narrate, record.

5708₂

掀〔Hsien〕*v.* raise up.

24-- 動　　　raise, lift, stir up, instigate.
77-- 開　　　cause, open.

軟 〔Juan〕 adj. soft, weak, flexible, feeble.

00-- 席　　　soft (cushioned) seats.
-- 膏　　　ointment.
17-- 弱　　　weak, feeble, cowardly.
-- 弱無能　　weak and incapable.
-- 弱性　　weakness, flabbiness.
22-- 片　　　photographic film.
24-- 化　　　soften, melt.
25-- 件　　　software.
26-- 和　　　soft, gentle, kind.
33-- 心腸　　soft hearted.
40-- 木　　　cork.
-- 木塞　　cork, cork stopper.
44-- 禁　　　be placed in confinement, under house arrest.
75-- 體動物　　mollusk.
76-- 腭　　　soft palate, velum.
77-- 骨　　　cartilage.
-- 骨病　　rickets.
-- 骨頭　　weak-kneed fellow.
87-- 飲料　　soft drink.
88-- 管　　　hose.
95-- 性　　　soft, mild, bland, gentle.

撳 〔Chin〕 v. lay hand on.
5708₆

摜 〔Kuan〕 v. throw down.

00-- 交　　　wrestling.
10-- 碎　　　dash to pieces.
22-- 出　　　throw out.
5709₄

探 〔Tan〕 n. detective, spy, v. detect, search out, spy, examine, investigate, explore, test, try, visit, inquire after.

00-- 病　　　inquire after a patient.
-- 訪　　　visit, call at, make inquiries.
03-- 試　　　try.
04-- 討　　　discuss.
06-- 親　　　visit one's relative.
07-- 詢　　　inquire.
10-- 礦　　　prospect mineral deposits.
14-- 聽　　　fish for, inquire about.

17-- 取　　　draw money in advance.
-- 子　　　scout, spy, detective.
30-- 究　　　investigate, examine.
32-- 測　　　probe, survey.
36-- 視　　　visit.
38-- 海燈　　searchlight.
39-- 消息　　search news, fish for information.
40-- 友　　　visit friend.
-- 喪　　　condole.
-- 索　　　quest, search.
-- 索隊　　exploring party.
43-- 求　　　seek, explore.
44-- 勘　　　prospect.
53-- 戈　　　tango (dancing).
67-- 明　　　detect, spy out, ferret out.
-- 明燈　　searchlight.
77-- 問　　　inquire about.
78-- 險　　　explore, adventure.
-- 險家　　explorer, adventurer.
-- 險隊　　exploration party.

揉 〔Jou〕 v. make flexible.
5711₀

蛆 〔Chu〕 n. maggot, larva.
50-- 虫　　　maggot.
5711₇

蜢 〔Man〕 n. grasshopper.

蠅 〔Ying〕 n. fly.
56-- 拍　　　swatter, flapper.
5712₀

蜩 〔Tiao〕 n. cicadas.
60-- 甲　　　shell of the cicadas.

蝴 〔Hu〕 n. butterfly.
54-- 蝶　　　butterfly.
-- 蝶結　　bow-tie, rosette.
-- 蝶花　　fringed iris.
5712₇

蛹 〔Yung〕 n. pupa, chrysalis.
24-- 化　　　pupation.

蝸 〔Kua〕 n. snail.
25-- 牛　　　snail.
5714₇

蝦 〔Hsia〕 n. shrimp, prawn, lobster.
17-- 子　　　shrimps.

21-- 仁	flesh of shrimps.
27-- 醬	salty shrimp paste.
35-- 油	shrimp sauce.
72-- 鬚	barbels of a shrimp.
90-- 米	dried shrimps.

5715₄

蜂 〔**Feng**〕 *n.* bees, wasp.

10-- 王	queen bee.
17-- 羣	swarm of bees.
22-- 巢	honey comb.
30-- 蜜	honey.
-- 房	beehive.
-- 窩	honeycomb.
50-- 擁	crowd, swarm.
52-- 蠟	beeswax.

5716₁

蟾 〔**Chan**〕 *n.* toad.

26-- 魄	moon.
30-- 宮	lunar palace.
58-- 蜍	toad.
90-- 光	moonlight.

5718₀

螟 〔**Ming**〕 *n.* worm, a kind of grain insect.

50-- 虫	kind of moth.
58-- 蛉	caterpillar.
-- 蛉子	adopted son.

5718₂

蠍 〔**Hsieh**〕 *n.* scorpion.

17-- 子	scorpion.
21-- 虎	house lizard.

5743₀

契 〔**Chi**〕 *n.* contract, agreement, deed, bond, *v.* agree, be compatible.

27-- 約	contract, agreement, bond, covenant.
-- 約生效	execution of contract.
40-- 友	intimate friend.
42-- 機	turning point, critical point.
51-- 據	deed, escrow.
80-- 合	agreeable.

5750₂

挈 〔**Chieh**〕 *v.* take up, raise, assist, help.

81-- 領	make a summary, present the main points.

90-- 眷	travel with one's dependents.

擊 〔**Chi**〕 *v.* beat, strike, hit, knock, attack, kill.

10-- 碎	break in pieces.
14-- 破	break, crush, rout.
22-- 倒	knock down.
35-- 潰	disperse, smash, defeat.
37-- 退	beat back, heat away, repulse, drive back, repel.
44-- 鼓	beat a drum.
-- 鼓鳴冤	strike a drum to tell one's grievances.
-- 落	shoot down.
50-- 中	hit.
-- 中要害	touch the tender spot.
51-- 打	beat, strike.
68-- 敗	defeat, overpower.
82-- 劍	fencing.
98-- 斃	kill.

5772₇

邨=村 4490₀

5777₃

齧 〔**Yeh**〕 *v.* gnaw, bite.

5790₃

絜 〔**Chieh**〕 *v.* rule, repress, assess, measure, *adj.* pure, clean.

繫 〔**Hsi**〕 *v.* tie, bind, fasten, hold on, hang up.

20-- 辭	commentary.
22-- 戀	cherish, be reluctant to leave.
29-- 絆	bridle, hinder.
36-- 泊	moor.
60-- 累	implicate, involve.
-- 囚	be imprisoned.
71-- 馬	fasten a horse.
90-- 懷	have one's heart drawn by.

5791₇

耙 〔**Pa**〕 *n.* harrow, rake.

17-- 子	drag, harrow.
54-- 鋤	plough.

5797₇

耛 〔**Ssu**〕 *n.* plow.

5798₆

賴 〔**Lai**〕 *v.* rely on, depend on, lean

on, deny, disclaim, disavow, accuse without ground.

25--	債	repudiate one's debt.
40--	皮	rogue, person without any sense of shame.
42--	婚	break a marriage contract.
51--	掉	deny, repudiate.
61--	賬	welsh.
--	賬人	dead beat.
77--	學	play truant, evade study at school.
80--	人	impute a fault to another.
90--	光	deny all.

5800₀
扒 〔**Pa**〕 v. scratch.

20--	手	pickpocket, cut-purse.
30--	竊	steal, pick pocket.

5801₁
搓 〔**Tso**〕 v. rub between the hands.

00--	麻將	play mah-jong.
10--	弄	rub.
--	碎	rub into powder.
20--	手	rub hands.
41--	板	washboard.

5801₂
挳 〔**Peng**〕 v. touch.

60--	見	meet accidentally.

拖 〔**To**〕 v. pull, drag, tow, lead, delay, haul, tug.

12--	延	delay, protract, put off.
--	延時間	stall for time.
27--	繩	tow, towline.
--	欠	be in debt, fall in arrears.
--	網	dragnet, townet.
--	船	tug boat, towing boat.
35--	油瓶	woman's children by previous marriage.
37--	運	haulage.
44--	帶	drag along, involve, implicate.
--	鞋	slipper.
50--	車	trailer.
--	曳	pull, drag.
--	拉機	tractor.
57--	把	mop.
58--	輪	tug, tugboat.

60--	累	entangle, involve, implicate.
64--	時間	drag on, stall for time.
71--	長	lengthen.
80--	入	draw into.

5801₄
挫 〔**Tso**〕 n. adversity, v. humble.

00--	磨	ill-treatment, ill-use.
08--	敵	defeat the enemy.
52--	折	humble, depress.
68--	敗	v. fail, adj. disappointed.
71--	辱	humiliate, put to shame.

拴 〔**Shuan**〕 n. bind, fasten.

23--	縛	tie up.
50--	束	pack, tie up, restrain.
71--	馬	tie up a horse.

輇 〔**Chuan**〕 n. wheel, without spoke.

5801₆
攬 〔**Lan**〕 v. grasp, clutch, undertake, monopolize.

17--	取	get hold of.
24--	貨	monopolize the distribution.
44--	權	grasp authority, usurp power, seize all the power.
--	權專政	grasp full authority and form a despotic government.
79--	勝	enjoy scenery.

5802₁
揄 〔**Yu**〕 v. lead, draw, praise.

56--	揚	praise, admire, extol.

輸 〔**Shu**〕 v. transport, convey, send, lose, be defeated.

00--	贏	losses and gains, defeat or victory.
10--	電	power transmission.
--	電網	power transmission network.
--	電塔	power transmission tower.
16--	理	be in the wrong.
22--	出	n. exportation, v. export.
--	出稅	export duties.
--	出額	amount of export.
--	出品	exports.

-- 出港	port of export.
24-- 納	pay or submit.
27-- 血	*n.* blood transfusion, *v.* transfuse.
28-- 稅	pay taxes.
30-- 家	loser.
35-- 油管	pipeline, oil pipeline.
38-- 送	transport, convey.
-- 送系統	conveyer system.
77-- 尿管	ureter.
-- 卵管	oviduct.
80-- 入	import, introduce.
-- 入港	port of import.
-- 入品	import.
83-- 錢	lose money.
95-- 精管	sperm duct.

5802₂

轃 〔**Chen**〕 *v.* move, turn.

44-- 莫	remember with deep emotion.
90-- 懷	painful thought.
94-- 惜	mourn with deep regret, have pity on.
97-- 恤	pity deeply.

5802₇

扮 〔**Pan**〕 *v.* disguise, dress up.

24-- 裝	disguise, make up.
26-- 鬼臉	make face.
28-- 作	dress up as.
33-- 演	act the part of, play the role of.

掄 〔**Lun**〕 *v.* select.

40-- 才	select men of ability.

擒 〔**Chin**〕 *v.* capture, catch, seize, arrest.

20-- 住	succeed in capture.
52-- 斬	capture and behead.
56-- 捉	arrest, capture.
80-- 拿	seize, capture.

輪 〔**Lun**〕 *n.* wheel, *v.* turn, rotate, take turn.

00-- 廓	outline, profile.
02-- 訓	training in rotation.
07-- 調	serve at a post by turns.
11-- 班	work in rotation, work in shift.
12-- 到	be on one's turn.
21-- 齒	gear teeth.
22-- 掣	brakes.
-- 種	rotation of crops.
24-- 值	take one's turn.
-- 休	rotate holidays.
27-- 船	steamer, steamship.
-- 船公司	shipping company.
30-- 渡	ferry boat, steam ferry.
-- 流	by turn, alternate, take turns.
-- 流值班	rotating shift.
36-- 迴	transmigration.
44-- 椅	wheelchair.
55-- 轉	revolve, turn round.
-- 轉機	rotary press (printing).
-- 軸	axle, wheel shaft.
57-- 換	*n.* rotation, *v.* rotate.
60-- 暴	gang rape.
66-- 唱	troll.
73-- 胎	tire, tyre.

5803₁

撫 〔**Fu**〕 *v.* hold, touch, handle, soothe, quiet, comfort, console, pat, stroke, bring up.

00-- 育	cherish, nourish, nurture, bring up.
10-- 弄	finger, caress.
20-- 愛	love, endear.
58-- 摸	feel, touch, stroke, pat.
74-- 慰	soothe, comfort, pacify.
80-- 養	foster, rear, nurture, bring up.
-- 養津貼	dependency allowance.
97-- 恤	relieve, comfort and compensate a bereaved family.
-- 恤金	pension, compensation, survivor's pension.

5803₂

捻 〔**Nien**〕 *v.* finger.

5804₀

撇 〔**Pieh**〕 *v.* reject, abandon, desert, cast away, skim off.

00-- 棄	abandon, cast away.
10-- 下	abandon, desert.

35--	清	pretend innocence.
51--	掉	throw away, cast away.
77--	開	put aside.

撤〔**Che**〕v. withdraw, remove, send away.

00--	廢	abolish, rescind, revoke.
--	離	move away, withdraw.
--	辦	fire a delinquent official and subject him to disciplinary action.
13--	職	n. dismissal, v. dismiss from a position.
22--	任	remove from office.
26--	保	withdraw guaranty.
30--	守	withdraw, move back.
37--	退	withdraw, dismiss, evacuate.
39--	消	dismiss, cancel.
40--	去	remove, withdraw, pull out.
60--	回	withdraw, recall, take back.
72--	兵	withdraw, evacuate.
78--	除	remove.
80--	差	dismiss.
89--	銷	n. cancellation, v. annul, revoke, cancel.
--	銷訂單	cancel an order.
--	銷承兌	revocation of an acceptance.
--	銷條款	cancellation clause.
--	銷租約	cancel a lease.
--	銷投標	withdraw a bid.
--	銷日期	cancellation date.
--	銷合同	cancel a contract.
--	銷公司	liquidate a firm.

撒〔**Sa**〕v. scatter, spread, let go, relax, unleash, let go.

04--	謊	tell a lie.
08--	放	release, unleash.
20--	手	give up, let go.
22--	種	sow seeds.
27--	網	cast a net.
32--	潑	behave rudely.
42--	嬌	show pettishness.
52--	播	scatter, spread out.
57--	賴	behave like a rascal.
67--	野	v. run wild, adj. naughty.

| 77-- | 尿 | urinate, pee, piss. |
| -- | 開 | spread. |

轍〔**Che**〕n. rut, track, groove.

| 30-- | 跡 | wheel track, ruts. |

5804₆

捓=掩 5401₆

撙〔**Tsun**〕v. regulate, adjust.

| 88-- | 節 | restrain, follow rule and order. |
| 90-- | 省 | economize. |

5806₁

拾〔**Shih**〕v. pick up, collect, arrange, go up, go ascend, adj. ten.

5806₄

捨〔**She**〕v. leave, abandon, let go, part with, relinquish, give up.

00--	棄	abandon, give up.
10--	不得	reluctant to give up.
17--	己	self sacrifice, sacrifice one's life or interest.
25--	生取義	give up one's life for righteousness.
26--	得	generous.
27--	身	give up one's life.

5806₇

搶〔**Chiang**〕n. robbery, plunder, v. rob, plunder, snatch, seize away, do something haste.

20--	手貨	commodity in great demand.
22--	種	rush-plant.
24--	先	steal a march on, struggle for precedence.
27--	修	rush-repair.
28--	收	rush-harvest.
30--	渡	cross speedily.
--	案	case of robbery.
37--	運	rush-transport.
40--	奪	rob, ravish, seize, snatch.
--	去	snatch, wrest.
--	走	take away by force.
47--	劫	rob, pirate, ransack, plunder.
48--	救	rescue, save, salvage.
65--	購	shopping rush, panic buying,

rush to purchase.
77-- 風　　　　　head winds.

5808₆

撿 〔**Chien**〕 *v.* take, pick up.
47-- 起　　　　　pick up.

5810₁

整 〔**Cheng**〕 *v.* arrange, set in order, tidy, *adj.* even, uniform, regular, orderly, complete, whole, entire.
00-- 齊　　　　　uniform, regular, neat, orderly, in order.
-- 齊劃一　　　　neat and uniform.
-- 夜　　　　　the whole night.
-- 衣　　　　　adjust the dress.
02-- 訓　　　　　training and consolidation.
10-- 天　　　　　all the day, through out the day.
-- 頁　　　　　full page.
12-- 列　　　　　whole row or column.
-- 形　　　　　orthopedics.
-- 形手術　　　　plastic operation.
16-- 理　　　　　adjust, arrange, regulate, clean, make up, put in order.
23-- 然　　　　　good order.
-- 編　　　　　reorganize.
24-- 備　　　　　prepare.
-- 裝　　　　　dress up.
26-- 個　　　　　entire, whole.
27-- 修　　　　　repair, put in order.
30-- 流器　　　　rectifier, commutator.
-- 容　　　　　dress up, dress the hair.
-- 容醫生　　　　plastic surgeon.
32-- 治　　　　　set in order, adjust and repair.
37-- 潔　　　　　neat, tidy, clean.
-- 軍　　　　　renovation of the army.
40-- 套　　　　　complete set.
-- 套設備　　　　complete set of equipment.
44-- 枝　　　　　pruning.
46-- 塊　　　　　whole piece.
50-- 肅　　　　　strict, rigid, stern.
51-- 頓　　　　　fix, settle, rectify, rearrange, readjust, bring into order.
-- 批　　　　　batch, by the gross, full lot.
58-- 數　　　　　round number, whole number.

60-- 日　　　　　whole day, all day long.
75-- 體　　　　　entirely, whole.
-- 體計劃　　　　corporate planning.
77-- 風運動　　　　rectification movement.
78-- 隊　　　　　file, form neat line.
-- 除　　　　　divide exactly.
80-- 合　　　　　conformity.
-- 年　　　　　all the year, throughout the year.
88-- 飭　　　　　orderly, systematic.
90-- 黨　　　　　party consolidation.

5811₁

蚱 〔**Cha**〕 *n.* grasshopper.
57-- 蜢　　　　　grasshopper.

5811₆

蛻 〔**Tui**〕 *v.* cast off skin, shed skin, exuviate, slough.
22-- 變　　　　　decay, undergo transformation.
24-- 化　　　　　undergo transformation.
-- 化分子　　　　degenerate.
40-- 皮　　　　　exuviate, cast off the skin.

5812₀

蚧 〔**Chieh**〕 *n.* lizard.

5812₁

蝓 〔**Yu**〕 *n.* slug, snail.

5813₂

蚣 〔**Kung**〕 *n.* centipede.

5813₆

螫 〔**Che**〕 *n.* nippers (of crabs), poisonous insects, *v.* sting.

5813₇

蛉 〔**Ling**〕 *n.* dragonfly.

5814₇

蜉 〔**Yu**〕 *n.* an ephemeral insect.

蝮 〔**Fu**〕 *n.* poisonous snake, viper.

5815₃

蟻 〔**I**〕 *n.* ant.
24-- 動　　　　　move like ants.
-- 結　　　　　band together.
30-- 穴　　　　　ant's nest.
72-- 丘　　　　　ant hill.

5816₁

蛤 〔**Ko**〕 *n.* oyster, toad, clam, mussel.

52--	蜊	clam.
54--	蟆	toad.

5819_4

蜍〔Chu〕*n.* toad.

5821_4

鳌〔Li〕*n.* grain, hundredth, *v.* regulate.

10--	正	correct, rectify, reform.
30--	定	formulate.
44--	革	reform.
56--	捐	transit duty.
80--	金	li-kin, transportation tax.
90--	米	centimeter.

5824_0

敖〔Ao〕*n.* amusement.

敷〔Fu〕*v.* spread out, state, announce, lay over, explain, *adj.* enough, sufficient.

07--	設	establish, lay.
18--	政	execute administration.
21--	衍	*v.* neglect one's duty, *adj.* perfunctory.
24--	化	teach and convert.
32--	泛	diffuse.
44--	藥	salve.
48--	教	spread a religion or a culture.
60--	足	sufficient, abundant.
77--	用	enough for use.
98--	粉	powder.

5824_4

嫠〔Li〕*n.* widow.

5825_1

犛〔Li〕*n.* buffalo.

25--	牛	yak.

5832_7

驁〔Ao〕*n.* noble steed.

5833_4

熬〔Ao〕*v.* boil, simmer, distill.

00--	夜	sit up late at night.
33--	心	unhappy, annoying, vexing.
36--	湯	stew, simmer.
44--	菜	cook food.
60--	日子	go through hard time.
80--	煎	boil and fry.
95--	煉	boil and smelt.

97--	爛	boil to rags.

5843_0

獒〔Ao〕*n.* fierce dog.

5844_0

數〔Shu〕*n.* number, account, *v.* count, enumerate, tell off.

07--	詞	numeral.
10--	一數二	one of the best.
--	天	several days.
--	不清	countless, beyond count.
11--	碼	number, amount.
20--	倍	several times, manifold.
--	位	digital.
24--	值	numerical value.
25--	件	several articles.
30--	完	count up.
--	字	number, figure.
31--	額	amount, sum.
35--	清	count clearly.
37--	次	several times.
40--	十	scores, several tens.
44--	萬	tens of thousands, several myriads.
50--	盡	running out of life, days numbered.
51--	據	datum.
60--	口之家	small family.
--	日	several days.
--	目	number.
--	目字	digit.
--	量	amount, quantity.
--	罪俱發	concurrence of offences.
77--	月	several month.
--	學	mathematics.
--	學家	mathematician.
80--	人	several people.
--	年	several year.
83--	錢	count money.
84--	錯	miscount.

5880_6

贅〔Chui〕*n.* man who takes his wife's family name and live in her house, *v.* hang on, connect.

00--	疣	tumor, excrescence.
--	言	repetition, verbosity, tautology.

01-- 語　　　verbosity, reiteration.
07-- 詞　　　pleonasm, redundancy.
27-- 物　　　excrescence, superfluous thing.
33-- 述　　　repetitious statement.
5894₀

敕=勅 5492₇

5901₂

捲 〔Chuan〕 v. roll up, wrap, curl, enfold, pack up, seize, gather.

00-- 席　　　roll up the mat.
31-- 逃　　　abscond, clear up everything and run away.
33-- 心菜　　cabbage.
35-- 袖　　　roll up the sleeves.
40-- 土重來　bounce back.
47-- 起　　　roll up.
56-- 揚機　　hoisting machine.
72-- 鬚　　　tendrils.
77-- 尺　　　tape measure.
80-- 入　　　involve, be drown into.
88-- 筒　　　roll.
96-- 烟　　　cigarettes.
5902₀

抄 〔Chao〕 v. copy, transcribe, seize, take, confiscate.

01-- 襲　　　crib, imitate, copy, plagiarize.
20-- 集　　　collect by copying.
30-- 家　　　confiscate the property of an offender.
　-- 寫　　　copy, transcribe.
38-- 道　　　take a short cut.
　-- 送　　　send a copy of.
40-- 查　　　confiscate.
50-- 本　　　manuscript, transcript, copy, handwritten copy.
　-- 掠　　　rob, plunder.
　-- 書　　　plagiarize a book.
64-- 賭　　　search a place for gamblers.
79-- 謄　　　transcribe, make a copy.
80-- 拿　　　seize, grab.
87-- 錄　　　make a copy of.
5902₇

撈 〔Lao〕 v. drag out, dredge for, fish

up.
17-- 取　　　reap, grab.
27-- 魚　　　catch fish by a net.
37-- 資本　　recover the money invested.
47-- 起　　　drag out of water.
54-- 摸　　　search underwater for.
77-- 屍　　　recover the body of a drowned person.

5904₁

撐 〔Cheng〕 v. support, pole.

10-- 不住　　too weak to support.
14-- 破　　　burst.
20-- 住　　　prop up.
27-- 船　　　pole a boat.
46-- 場面　　keep up appearance.
71-- 腰　　　back up, support.
77-- 開　　　prop open.
80-- 傘　　　prop open an umbrella.
88-- 竿跳　　vault.
5905₂

撑=撐

5906₆

擋 〔Tang〕 v. impede, stop, withstand, resist, ward off.

10-- 雨　　　shelter one from the rain.
20-- 住　　　block up, stem.
37-- 泥板　　mudguard.
67-- 路　　　stop the way, stand in the way.
77-- 風　　　keep off the wind.
　-- 風玻璃　windshield.
　-- 開　　　parry.
88-- 箭牌　　shield.
5908₀

揪 〔Chiu〕 v. grasp, collect.

22-- 出　　　uncover, ferret out.
33-- 心　　　anxious, nervous, worried.
57-- 扭　　　seize by hand, grapple.
5908₉

掞 〔Shan〕 v. spread out, adj. sharp.

5911₂

蜷 〔Chuan〕 n. creeping motion of worms, wriggle.

23-- 伏　　　curl up, huddle up.

-- 縮	twisted, wriggly.
55-- 曲	n. curl, v. curl up, adj. wriggly.

5911₄
螳〔Tang〕 n. mantis.
57-- 螂　　mantis.

5912₇
蛸 〔Shao〕 n. long-legged spider.

6

6000₀
口 〔Kou〕 n. mouth, entrance, opening, hole, gorge.

00-- 音	pronunciation, accent.
01-- 語	n. colloquialism, adj. colloquial.
03-- 試	oral examination, oral test.
06-- 譯員	interpreter.
08-- 說無憑	A verbal promise isn't binding.
11-- 頭	n. conversation, talk, adj. verbal, by word of mouth.
-- 頭上	orally, in words.
-- 頭禪	conventional expression, repeated empty expression.
-- 頭報告	verbal report, oral report.
-- 頭契約	verbal contract, oral (parole) contract.
-- 頭辯論	debate orally.
-- 頭約定	verbal agreement.
-- 頭表決	pass (a motion) by acclamation, oral vote.
-- 琴	harmonica, mouth organ.
12-- 水	saliva, slaver.
20-- 舌	altercation, argument.
-- 舌之爭	contention of mouth and tongue, squabble.
-- 信傳達	transmit a verbal message.
21-- 徑	caliber.
-- 齒不清	be unclear in enunciation.
-- 齒伶俐	be fluent in speech.
-- 齒清晰	talk distinctly.
-- 紅	lipstick.
22-- 岸	port, harbor.
-- 出惡言	utter bad language.
-- 出狂言	speak arrogantly.
23-- 袋	bag, sack, pocket.
24-- 供	confession, attestation, affidavit.
-- 供不符	The deposition does not fit.
25-- 傳	hearsay.
26-- 臭	halitosis, foul breath.
27-- 角	n. quarrel, v. dispute, altercate, quarrel.
-- 角是非	wrangle about right and wrong.
30-- 實	pretext.
31-- 福不淺	have good luck in enjoying good food.
32-- 涎	spit.
33-- 述	v. tell, adj. oral.
34-- 爲禍門	A fool's mouth is his destruction.
35-- 沫	spittle, saliva.
40-- 才	eloquence.
-- 才便捷	having a ready tongue.
44-- 若懸河	glib, eloquent.
48-- 乾	thirsty.
52-- 授	dictate.
54-- 技	mimicry, vocal imitation.
60-- 罩	respirator, mouth-muffle, mask.
-- 蹄疫	(in veterinary science) foot-and-mouth disease.
-- 是心非	duplicity, hypocrisy, double-faced.
-- 口聲聲	say repeatedly.
61-- 號	watchword, password, slogan.
65-- 味	taste, flavor.
68-- 吃	stammer, stutter, falter.
69-- 哨	whistle.
71-- 脣	lip.
-- 脣膏	lipstick.
73-- 腔	mouth cavity.
80-- 令=口號	
-- 氣	tone, expression.
-- 氣太衝	too blunt in speaking.
90-- 快心直	quick in speech and straightforward in mind.
96-- 糧	provisions.

6001₄

唯〔**Wei**〕 v. answer affirmatively, yes, adj. sole, adv. only, but.

00--	意志論	voluntarism.
10--	一	only, sole, one, single.
--	一之例	solitary precedent, only example.
--	一問題	only problem.
16--	理論	rationalism.
17--	恐有變	lest the circumstances should change.
22--	利是圖	profit-grabbing, profit seeking.
23--	我論	solipsism.
--	我獨尊	I am alone to be honored, I am the most honored, overlordship.
27--	物	materialism.
--	物主義者	materialist.
--	物論	materialism, doctrine of materialism.
33--	心	idealism.
--	心主義者	idealist.
--	心論 (心主義)	idealism.
80--	命是從	do whatever is told.

睢〔**Sui**〕 v. look upwards, look at angrily.

瞳〔**Tung**〕 n. pupil, pupil of the eye, apple of the eye.

12--	孔	pupil of the eye.
80--	人	pupil, pupil of the eye.

6001₇

吭〔**Hang**〕 n. throat, v. utter.

10--	一聲	utter a sound.

喨〔**Liang**〕 n. clear note.

6002₇

嘀〔**Ti**〕

64--	嘀咕	mutter, murmur.

唷〔**Yo**〕 v. O! oh! (an exclamation of pain or surprise).

昉〔**Fang**〕 adj. just at the time.

啼〔**Ti**〕 v. howl, cry, crow, caw, scream, bewail.

47--	聲	cry.

64--	叫	scream, cry.
66--	哭	cry, weep and wail.
88--	笑皆非	between tears and laughter.

哼〔**Heng**〕 v. moan, groan, hum.

47--	哼聲	groan.
60--	哼唧唧	groan and moan.
66--	唱	hum.

6003₁

噍〔**Chiao**〕 v. chew, ruminate.

瞧〔**Chiao**〕 v. see, look at, peep.

10--	不起瞧	despise, disdain.
60--	瞧	have a look.

6003₂

眩〔**Hsuan**〕 n. vertigo, adj. confused, dizzy, dazzled, giddy.

22--	亂	dizzy.
60--	目	dazzle, dazzling.
--	暈	n. dizziness, vertigo v. dizzy, adj. dazzled.
91--	耀	dazzle.

嚎〔**Haw**〕 v. cry loudly.

62--	啕	utter a loud cry.
67--	啕大哭	cry loudly with abandon.

嚷〔**Yang**〕 v. bawl, cry, cry out, scold and bluster, clamor.

60--	嚷	bawl.
66--	罵	scold.
77--	鬧	quarrel.
--	鬥	quarrel.

6003₆

噫〔**I**〕 v. moan, sigh, interj. alas!

6004₈

咬〔**Yao**〕 v. bite, gnaw, chew, snap.

00--	文嚼字	pedantry, mince words in speech or writing.
10--	一口	bite off a mouthful.
--	死	bite to death.
--	碎	masticate.
22--	斷	bite into two, bite off.
28--	傷	bite, injure by biting, be wounded by biting.
30--	穿	bite through.
62--	嚼	chew, gnaw.
71--	牙	gnash the teeth.
--	牙切齒	gnash one's teeth in anger

or hatred.

-- 牙擦掌　gnash the teeth and rub the palms.

77-- 緊　clench (one's teeth).

-- 緊牙關　clench one's teeth in enduring pain.

唉 〔Tsui〕 v. taste.

睟 〔Tsui〕 v. look at straight.

6006_1

唁 〔Yen〕 n. condolence, v. condole, moan, sympathize.

10-- 電　message of condolence.

17-- 弔　condole.

暗 〔An〕 n. secret, clandestine, adj. dark, somber, cloudy, gloomy, dim, obscure, secret, private, hidden, stupid, ignorant, adv. secretly.

07-- 記　code mark.

10-- 示　n. hint, suggestion, v. imply, hint, give a hint, insinuate.

-- 礁　reef, hidden rock.

11-- 碼　cipher.

30-- 室　dark room.

-- 害　secret injury.

35-- 溝　ditch, underground drain.

39-- 淡　dim, dull, cold, muddy.

44-- 藏　conceal, hide.

-- 地埋伏　ambush.

47-- 殺　murder, assassinate.

50-- 中　secretly, privately.

-- 中高興　laugh in one's sleeve.

51-- 指　allude.

57-- 探　spy, detective.

61-- 號　secret cipher, secret code, watchword, secret sign.

77-- 鬥　veiled strife.

88-- 笑　laugh in one's sleeve.

-- 算　foul play, plot, intrigue.

92-- 燈　blind lantern.

6008_2

咳 〔Ko〕 v. cough, cough up.

22-- 出　cough out.

67-- 嗽　cough.

-- 嗽藥　cough-mixture.

-- 嗽糖　cough-drop.

6008_6

曠 〔Kuang〕 n. wilderness, desert, v. neglect, leave empty, adj. desolate, empty, extensive, broad, open.

06-- 課　absent from class.

10-- 工　neglect one's duty, absenteeism in work, neglect business, absent without leave, stay away from work.

13-- 職　n. delinquency, v. neglect study, neglect one's duty, be absent duty without leave.

40-- 古未有　never seen in past history.

44-- 世奇才　remarkable talent of many ages.

67-- 野　wilderness, desert, wild plain.

77-- 學　neglect study.

6009_6

晾 〔Liang〕 v. dry in the sun or in the air.

00-- 衣架　clothes-horse.

48-- 乾　dry in the air or in the sun.

77-- 開　spread out to air.

6010_0

日 〔Jih〕 n. sun, day, daytime, Japan, Japanese, adj. daily.

00-- 夜　day and night, night and day.

-- 夜商店　round-the-clock store, all-night service store, day-and-night shop.

-- 夜服務　round-the-clock service.

-- 產量　daily output.

01-- 語　Japanese language.

02-- 新月異　continuous improvement.

07-- 記　diary.

-- 記簿　diary, journal.

10-- 工　day-labor.

-- 耳曼　Germany.

11-- 班　day shift.

13-- 戳　date stamp, date mark.

17-- 子好過　live comfortably.

22-- 出　sunrise.

23-- 戲　day performance.

26-- 程表　schedule, schedule of the

		day, order schedule.
40--	校	day school.
--	内	in a few days.
--	有進步	progress constantly.
--	有起色	turn for the better steadily.
--	本貨	Japanese goods.
44--	落	sunset.
--	暮	evening, eve, fall of day.
46--	場	day show.
47--	報	daily news, daily newspaper, daily report.
--	期	date, time.
50--	本	Japan.
52--	托	day-nursery, part-time nursery.
60--	日	daily, day by day, day after day.
--	暈	solar halo.
71--	曆	calendar.
77--	間	day time.
--	月	sun and moon.
--	用	daily expenses.
--	用品	essential goods, daily necessaries, day-to-day goods, articles of daily use, daily articles.
--	用品商店	general merchandise.
--	用必需品	prime necessities.
--	用消費品	goods for everyday consumption, nondurable consumer goods.
80--	前	the other day.
--	益	more and more.
--	食(蝕)	solar eclipse.
85--	蝕	eclipse of the sun.
90--	光	sunshine, sunlight, sunbeam.
--	光浴	sunbath.
--	光燈	fluorescent lamp.
--	常	usual, ordinary, day-to-day.
--	常工作	routine work.
--	常需要	daily needs, the needs of daily, daily necessaries.
--	常供給	daily supplies.
--	常收入	current income, daily receipts.
--	常業務	daily routine, day-to-day business.
--	常檢查	daily inspection, running control.
--	常費用	current expenses, running expenses.
--	常開支	carrying (current) expense.

曰 〔Yueh〕 v. say, speak, state.

且 〔Tan〕 n. morning, dawn, daybreak, day.

27--	夕	morning and evening, morning and night, short time.
--	夕之間	in a short moment.

6010₁

目 〔Mu〕 n. eye, chief, v. look upon, regard, eye, see, look.

00--	疾	disease of the eye.
--	盲	blind.
10--	下	nowadays, at present.
27--	的	aim, object, goal, purpose, intention, end.
--	的地	destination, place of destination.
37--	次	table of contents.
38--	送	look behind.
40--	力	eyesight, vision.
41--	標	object, mark, goal, target, aim.
57--	擊	witness.
60--	瞳	pupil of the eye.
--	眩	dizzy, giddy.
61--	標	objective, target.
64--	睹	see witness by eye, witness, see personally.
80--	前	now, at present, before one's eye, for the moment.
--	無尊長	show no respect to elders and superiors.
87--	錄	catalogue, table of contents, list, contents.

6010₄

呈 〔Cheng〕 v. present, offer, show, hand in a petition.

00--	文	petition, accusation.
--	交	present, deliver to.
05--	請	apply, request.

16-- 現	present, display, appear, show.
28-- 繳	proffer, submit, hand in.
30-- 准	apply and get permission.
38-- 送	send up, submit to.
47-- 報	submit a report.
-- 報人	reporter.
77-- 閱	bring forward, submit for inspection.
-- 閱擬稿	hand in a draft for perusal.

里〔**Li**〕*n.* li (Chinese measure of distance), place of residence, village, lane, neighborhood, mile.

10-- 弄	alley, lane.
26-- 程	mileage.
-- 程碑	milestone.

星〔**Hsing**〕*n.* star, planet, any heavenly body that shines.

00-- 座	constellation.
10-- 雲	nebula.
17-- 羣	asterism.
23-- 卜	astrology.
31-- 河	milky way.
47-- 期	week.
-- 期一	Monday.
-- 期二	Tuesday.
-- 期三	Wednesday.
-- 期四	Thursday.
-- 期五	Friday.
-- 期六	Saturday.
-- 期日	Sunday.
71-- 辰	planets, stars.
77-- 際	interplanetary, interstellar.
90-- 光	starlight.

墨〔**Mo**〕*n.* ink, Chinese ink-stick, Chinese-ink, *adj.* black, dark.

10-- 西哥	Mexico.
-- 西哥的 (西哥人的)	Mexican.
-- 西哥人	Mexican.
12-- 水	ink.
-- 水點	blot.
-- 水瓶	inkpot, ink bottle, ink-stand.
23-- 台	ink-stone, ink-stand.
27-- 魚	squid, cuttlefish.
-- 綠	dark green.

30-- 守成法	adhere to the established laws.
-- 守成規	get into a rut.
34-- 汁	ink.
16-- 硯	ink-stone.
80-- 盒	ink-box.
88-- 筆	Chinese pen.

罣〔**Kua**〕*n.* obstacle, hindrance.

| 21-- 慮 | anxiety. |
| 80-- 念 | think anxiously about. |

量〔**Liang**〕*n.* capacity, measure, quantity, *v.* measure, estimate, calculate, consider, weight.

00-- 度	measure, consider.
10-- 電器	electrical measuring instrument.
17-- 子	quantum (in physics).
22-- 變	quantitative change.
27-- 角器	protractor.
-- 角規	protractor.
40-- 力而行	do what one's strength allows.
-- 布	measure cloth.
75-- 體溫	take the temperature of.
77-- 尺寸	measure, take measurements.
-- 具	measuring instrument.
90-- 米	measure out rice.

壘〔**Lei**〕*n.* fortress, rampart, castle, bulwark, base (in baseball).

| 13-- 球 | baseball (softball). |

6010₇

置〔**Chi**〕*v.* put, place, arrange, establish, constitute, buy, lay.

00-- 辦	buy, purchase.
-- 立	establish, set up.
08-- 於死地	expose someone to mortal danger, doom a person to death.
27-- 身於	place oneself.
30-- 之一笑	laugh out of court.
-- 之不理	disregard, ignore.
-- 之不顧	turn one's back upon.

疊〔**Tieh**〕*n.* stack, *v.* pile up, fold up,

duplicate, redouble.

27-- 句	repeated sentence, refrain.
37-- 次	many times, repeatedly, time after time.
47-- 起	double, fold up, pile up.

6011₁

罪 〔Tsui〕 *n.* crime, offense, trespass, sin, wrong, guilt, fault, vice, suffering, punishment, *v.* criminate, blame, charge.

02-- 證	evidence of a crime.
10-- 惡	evil, crime, sin, vice.
12-- 刑	penalty.
21-- 行	criminal act.
24-- 魁禍首	arch-criminal, ringleader.
27-- 名	guilt, crime, charge.
40-- 大惡極	heinous crime.
-- 有應得	serve you right.
47-- 犯	criminal, malefactor, prisoner.
80-- 人=罪犯	

6011₃

晁 〔Chao〕 *n.* morning, dawn.

6011₄

雖 〔Sui〕 *v.* although, even if, though.

| 23-- 然 | although, not withstanding, after all, even if, though. |

6012₃

躋 〔Chih〕 *v.* ascend, go up, rise.

6012₇

蜀 〔Shu〕 *n.* Szechwan Province, caterpillar.

蹄 〔Ti〕 *n.* hoof.

6013₀

跡 〔Chi〕 *n.* trace, track, footmark, clue, footprint.

| 27-- 象 | indication, symptom. |

6013₁

蹢 〔Chih〕 *n.* the sole of a foot, *v.* tread, step, pass in to.

6013₂

暴 〔Pao〕 *n.* cruelty, violence, sudden.

v. exhibit, show, discover, bring to light, expose, manifest, fight with bare hands, *adj.* cruel, harsh, oppressive, tyrannical, violent, fierce, merciless, atrocious, *adv.* suddenly.

00-- 主	tyrant.
10-- 露	expose, bare, show, discover, disclose, bring to light.
-- 雨	violent shower, shower, torrential rain.
-- 雨成災	A heavy shower results in a disaster.
-- 露危險	expose danger.
12-- 發	break out.
-- 烈	terrific, violent.
17-- 君	tyrant.
18-- 政	tyranny.
21-- 虐	tyrannical, cruel, hard-hearted.
-- 行	outrage, violent actions, acts of outrage, atrocities.
22-- 亂	run riot.
-- 利	quick profit, sudden huge profits, windfall profit.
24-- 動	*n.* riot, disturbance, violent conduct, uprising, insurrection, *v.* rage, turn riot.
-- 動者	rioter.
-- 徒	desperado, mobs, rioters, rebels.
30-- 富	upstart, sudden wealth.
-- 客	robber, highway man.
31-- 漲	boom, run wild, sharp up.
40-- 力	violence, naked force.
-- 力革命	violent revolution.
47-- 怒	very angry, in hot blood.
65-- 跌	drastic setback, bust, sharp fall, slump.
66-- 躁	hot-tempered, turbulent, irritable, hot-headed.
71-- 厲	severe.
77-- 風	typhoon, windstorm.
-- 風雨	storm.
-- 風雪	snowstorm.
95-- 性	violent temper.

6013₇

蹠 見 6013₁

6014₀

躕 〔 Chu 〕 v. hesitate, stagger.

6014₃

踤＝捽 5004₃

6014₇

最 〔 Tsui 〕 adj. most, superlative, adv. very, extremely, exceedingly.

00-- 高	highest, supreme.
-- 高度	maximum.
-- 高點	peak, climax, culminating point.
-- 高級	top level, superlative degree.
-- 高統帥	high command, commander in-chief, generalissimo.
-- 高法院	Supreme Court.
-- 高權	supremacy.
-- 高權力	supreme power.
-- 高年產量	peak annual output.
-- 高記錄	new high.
-- 高效率	peak efficiency.
-- 高工資	maximum wage.
-- 高價格	maximum price, peak price, record price, top price, highest price.
-- 高收入	highest income, peak yield.
-- 高額	ceiling amount, maximum amount.
-- 高薪水	ceiling on wages.
-- 高限額	ceiling, maximum amount limitations, maximum limit, top limit.
-- 高管理部門	top management.
02-- 新	latest, newest, most up-to-date.
-- 新工藝	latest techniques.
-- 新資料	up-to-date information.
-- 新消息	hot news, latest news, news update.
-- 新花色	up-to-date patterns.
-- 新款式	up-to-the-minute style.
-- 新技術	up-to-date technology.
-- 新目錄	latest catalogue.
10-- 要	most important.
-- 惡	worst.
-- 可惡	vilest, most abominable.
21-- 上	supreme, highest.
-- 優價格	best price.
22-- 低	lowest.
-- 低工資	minimum wage.
-- 低售價	lowest selling price, minimum selling price.
-- 低價	minimum price.
-- 低價格	bottom price, lowest price, ground floor price, rock bottom price, minimum price.
-- 低生活標準	minimum standard of living.
-- 低生活費	absolute standard of living, minimum cost of living.
-- 低數	minimum.
-- 低點	zero, lowest point.
-- 低限度	minimum, at least.
-- 後 (終)	finally, last, at last, in conclusion, hindmost, final, ultimate.
-- 後通牒	ultimatum.
-- 後機會	last chance.
-- 後回答	final reply.
-- 後關頭	decisive moment.
-- 後勝利	final victory, ultimate triumph.
-- 後期限	deadline.
-- 後裁決	final award.
23-- 外	outmost.
24-- 先	foremost, first of all.
-- 佳效率	optimum efficiency.
-- 佳值	optimum value.
-- 佳條件	optimal condition, optimum.
27-- 久	at the longest.
-- 終	final, ultimate.
-- 終需求	ultimate demand, final demand.
-- 多	most, at most, most of all.
-- 多數	largest majority.
32-- 近	nearest, latest, up-to date.
-- 近消息	news update, recent infor-

34-- 遠	farthermost, farthest.	
37-- 初	primary, first, initial, original.	
40-- 大	largest, greatest, biggest, maximum.	
-- 大能量	ultimate capacity.	
-- 大額	maximum.	
-- 大量	maximum.	
-- 壞	worst.	
-- 有效	most effective.	
-- 大限度	maximum, utmost, extreme limit.	
47-- 好	best.	
-- 好的	best, first-rate.	
50-- 惠國	most favored nation.	
-- 惠條件	the most favored nation clause.	
80-- 前	foremost, first.	
-- 普遍	widespread.	
-- 令人滿意的	optimal.	
90-- 少	least, at least, least of all.	
-- 小	smallest, least, minimum.	
-- 小量	minimum.	
-- 最小值	minimum value.	

6014₈

跤 〔Chiao〕 *n.* fall, stumble.
踱 〔To〕 *v.* walk, step.

6015₃

國 〔Kuo〕 *n.* country, nation, state, kingdom, empire.

00-- 慶日	national holiday, National Day, national fete.
-- 庫	treasury, national treasury, exchequer, state treasury.
-- 庫收支	national treasury receipts and payments.
-- 庫收入	public revenue, national treasury, treasury receipt.
-- 庫通貨	treasury currency.
-- 庫存款	treasury deposit.
-- 產品	domestic products, home-made goods.
-- 產的	home-made.
-- 交	diplomatic relation.
-- 立	state, national.
-- 立大學	national university.
01-- 語	Mandarin, national tongue, national language.
04-- 計民生	national economy and livelihood of the masses, national economy and people's livelihood, national welfare and people's livelihood.
08-- 旗	flag, ensign, national colors, national flag.
10-- 王	king, ruler.
13-- 恥	national disgrace.
14-- 破家亡	The country is defeated and the family destroyed.
17-- 歌	national anthem.
-- 君	sovereign, emperor, king.
-- 務	state affairs.
-- 務院	Cabinet, department of state, State Council, State Department.
-- 務卿	Secretary of State.
-- 務總理	premier, prime minister.
23-- 外	abroad, overseas.
-- 外市場	foreign market.
-- 外資產	external assets.
-- 外業務	foreign operations.
-- 外銷售	foreign sales.
-- 外投資	foreign investment, investment abroad.
-- 外部	foreign department.
-- 外代理商	overseas agent, foreign agent.
-- 外代理處	foreign agency.
-- 外代表	representative abroad.
-- 外匯款	foreign remittance.
-- 外存款	foreign deposit.
-- 外分公司	overseas affiliated firm.
24-- 貨	national products, home-made goods, domestic products.
25-- 債	public debt, state debt, national debt, government loan.
27-- 色天香	national beauty and heavenly fragrance — very beautiful woman.

28-- 稅	national tax, national tariff, central tax, general tax, state tax.
-- 徽	insignia, state emblem, national emblem.
-- 俗	national custom.
30-- 宴	state banquet.
-- 賓	state guest.
-- 寶	national treasure.
-- 定本	government-prepared text books.
-- 家	nation, state, country.
-- 家隊	national team.
-- 家工黨	national labor party.
-- 家主義	nationalism.
-- 家主權	national sovereignty.
-- 家壟斷	government monopoly, national monopoly, state monopoly.
-- 家計畫	state planning.
-- 家計畫經營	state planned economy.
-- 家預算	national budget, state budget.
-- 家政策	state policy.
-- 家利益	national interest.
-- 家儲蓄金	state reserve funds.
-- 家債券	government securities.
-- 家收入	national revenue, state income, state revenue.
-- 家補貼	public subsidies.
-- 家資本	national capital, official capital, state capital.
-- 家資源	national resources.
-- 家支出	national expenditure.
-- 家機關	state organ, state agency.
-- 家專賣	state monopoly, government monopoly, public monopoly.
-- 家財政	national finance.
-- 家財富	national wealth.
-- 家至上	national interest is above everything else.
-- 家多故	there are many troubles in the nation.
34-- 法	national law.
-- 法不容	not allowed by laws.
37-- 運昌隆	the nation is on a prosperous course.
40-- 土	land, realm, national territory.
-- 土領有權	the right of eminent domain.
-- 土發展	national development.
-- 有	state-owned.
-- 有地	state-owned land.
-- 有化	v. nationalize, n. nationalization.
-- 有制	state property, state ownership, government ownership.
-- 有財產	public property, state-owned property.
-- 有公司	government-owned corporation.
-- 有公路	state road.
-- 有銀行	state-owned bank.
-- 內	internal, domestic, civil.
-- 內外	at home and abroad, domestic and foreign.
-- 內事務	internal affairs.
-- 內市場	domestic market, home market.
-- 內商業	internal commerce.
-- 內商品	interior goods.
-- 內交通	internal traffic.
-- 內旅行	home journey.
-- 內需求	domestic demand, home demands, national demand.
-- 內電報	domestic telegrams.
-- 內政策	domestic policy.
-- 內航空	domestic air mail, domestic airmail.
-- 內價格	domestic price, national price.
-- 內製造	home manufacture.
-- 內代理人	domestic agent.
-- 內債務	internal bond, internal debts.
-- 內郵資	domestic postage.
-- 內客戶	home client.
-- 內運費	inland forwarding expenses.
-- 內運輸	domestic carriage.
-- 內資產	domestic assets.

-- 內消費	home consumption, domestic consumption.		penditure, defense outlays.
-- 內消費者	home consumer.	-- 防債券	defense bonds.
-- 內檢疫	internal quarantine.	-- 防技術	defense technology.
-- 內貿易	domestic commerce, interior trade, internal trade, domestic trade.	-- 防軍	national defense forces.
		-- 防費	expenditure on national defense.
-- 內銷售	home sales.	-- 防最高委員會	supreme national defense committee.
-- 內投資	domestic investment.	72-- 際	international.
-- 力	national power, national strength.	-- 際歌	Internationale.
-- 境	border, territory.	-- 際主義	internationalism.
-- 難	national crisis.	-- 際交誼	comity of nations.
-- 難方殷	The nation is facing great danger.	-- 際競爭	international competition.
		-- 際市場	world market, international market.
-- 境	frontier.	-- 際商務	business international, international commerce.
44-- 葬	state funeral, state burial.		
-- 勢調查	census.	-- 際商業	international business.
-- 勢垂危	The nation is in imminent danger.	-- 際商法	International Commercial Law, international trade law.
-- 基鞏固	The foundation of the state is stable.	-- 際商品	international commodity, international merchandise.
47-- 都	capital, national capital.		
48-- 教	established church, state religion.	-- 際商會	International Chamber of Commerce (ICC).
50-- 畫	Chinese traditional painting.	-- 際廣告	international advertising.
		-- 際廣告公司	international advertising agency.
-- 書	credentials.	-- 際交往	international intercourse, international transaction.
-- 史	national history.		
-- 事	state affairs.	-- 際壟斷	international monopoly.
-- 事犯	political offender, political criminal.	-- 際調解	international conciliation.
		-- 際電信	international telecommunication.
-- 事訪問	state visit.		
-- 泰民安	The state is prosperous and the people are peaceful.	-- 際水道	international waterway.
		-- 際聯盟	League of Nations.
60-- 界	frontier, boundary, national boundary.	-- 際私法	private international law, law of conflict.
70-- 防	national defense.	-- 際象棋	international chess.
-- 防訂貨	defense order.	-- 際信譽	international good faith.
-- 防工業	defense industry, industry of national defense.	-- 際信用卡	international card.
		-- 際航空線	international airway.
-- 防部	Ministry of National Defense.	-- 際航線	international airline.
-- 防預算	defense budget, national defense budget.	-- 際航道	international navigational route.
-- 防經費	defense appropriations, defense spending, defense ex-		

-- 際版權協定 International Copyright Agreement.
-- 際經濟人　international broker.
-- 際糾紛　international discord.
-- 際私法　international private law, private international law.
-- 際貨幣基金 International Monetary Fund (IMF).
-- 際仲裁　international arbitration.
-- 際危機　international crisis.
-- 際條約　international treaty.
-- 際爭端　international dispute.
-- 際包裹　international parcels.
-- 際空域　international air space.
-- 際匯率　international exchange rate.
-- 際法　law of nations, international law, internationalization.
-- 際法庭　international court of justice.
-- 際法院 (聯合國) International Court of Justice (ICJ).
-- 際法學會　Institute of International Law.
-- 際社會　world community.
-- 際通商　international commerce.
-- 際運輸　international traffic.
-- 際海域　international sea area.
-- 際標準　international standard.
-- 際機場　international airport.
-- 際裁判　international arbitration.
-- 際協定　international agreement.
-- 際地位　international status.
-- 際聲譽　international prestige.
-- 際檢疫　international quarantine.
-- 際事務　international affairs, world affairs.
-- 際專利　international patent.
-- 際援助　international aid, international assistance.
-- 際投資　international investment.
-- 際原子能機構 International Atomic Energy Agency (IAEA).
-- 際局勢　international situation.
-- 際展覽會　international exhibition, international show.
-- 際貿易　international trade, international commercial transaction.
-- 際貿易港口 international trade port.
-- 際貿易額　value of international trade.
-- 際貿易逆差 (入超) adverse balance of trade, unfavorable balance of international trade.
-- 際貿易博覽會 international trade fair.
-- 際會議　international conference.
-- 際公法　international public law, public international law.
-- 際企業　international enterprise, international firm.
-- 際合作　international cooperation.
-- 際銀行　international bank.
-- 際關係　international relation.
-- 際慣例　international practice, international usage.
-- 際勞工局　international labor organization.
75-- 體　form of the state, form of government.
-- 風　national air.
77-- 民　people of a country, citizens, people, commonwealth.
-- 民需求　national demand.
-- 民經濟　national economy.
-- 民經濟總產值 total value of production in national economy.
-- 民生產淨值　net national product (NNP).
-- 民生產力　per capita productivity.
-- 民生計　material life of the people.
-- 民健康保險 national health insurance.
-- 民總收入　gross national income.
-- 民總支出　change against gross national balance, gross national expenditure.
-- 民收入　national income, national revenue.
-- 民淨支出　net national expenditure (NNE).
-- 民支出　national expenditure.

-- 民財富	national wealth, wealth of nations.
-- 民黨	The Nationalist Party (Kuomintang, KMT).
-- 民會議	people's assembly.
-- 民政府	national government, National Government of the Republic of China before 1948.
-- 民外交	people-to-people diplomacy.
-- 民革命	national revolution.
-- 民會議	national conference.
-- 民兵役	national service.
-- 民參政會	people's political council.
-- 民革命軍	national revolutionary army.
-- 民軍	national army.
-- 民大會	national congress.
80-- 人	countryman, national.
-- 會	parliament, congress.
-- 會議員	congressman.
88-- 策	national policy, state policy.
-- 籍	nationality.
-- 籍證書	certificate of nationality.
-- 籍法	law of nationality.
-- 籍喪失	loss of nationality.
90-- 光	national glory.
-- 粹	nationality.
-- 情	the state of affairs.
98-- 幣	legal money, coin of the realm, national currency.
99-- 營	state-operated, state-owned, government-operated.
-- 營工廠	government-run factory.
-- 營經濟	state-operated economy, state-owned economy.
-- 營農場	state farm.
-- 營貿易	national trade, state trade, state trading.
-- 營企業	government-operated enterprises, national enterprise, state (owned) enterprise.
-- 營公司	government-operated firm, state corporation, state-operated corporation.

| -- 營公用事業 | national utility, government utility. |
| -- 營事業 | government undertaking. |

6016₁
踣 〔Po〕 v. kill.

6021₀
四 〔Sse〕 adj. four, fourth.

00-- 方	square, four directions, all quarters.
-- 庫全書	complete set of classical books in four divisions.
07-- 部合奏	quartet.
10-- 面	everywhere, all around, on all sides.
-- 面玲瓏	tactful or diplomatic with all sorts of people.
-- 面受敵	surrounded by the enemy on all sides.
-- 面八方	all directions.
20-- 倍	quadruple.
-- 季	four seasons.
-- 重奏	(in music) quartet.
21-- 處	everywhere.
-- 處搜尋	look for everywhere.
22-- 川	Szechuan.
31-- 顧茫然	see nothing but emptiness all around.
-- 顧無人	find nobody anywhere when looking around.
36-- 邊形	quadrilateral.
37-- 通八達	open on all sides, as a road.
38-- 海一家	The whole world is one family.
-- 海之內	all within the four seas — the world.
-- 海爲家	wander about the world.
-- 海兄弟	brothers of the four seas.
40-- 十	forty.
-- 大皆空	all is vanity, everything is unreal.
50-- 史	four books of history — Shih Chi, Book of Han, Book of Later Han, Annals of the Three Kingdoms.
-- 書五經	The Four Books and Five Classics.
60-- 足獸	quadruped.

62-- 則	four operations (in math).
-- 則算	four fundamental operations.
71-- 巨頭	big four.
74-- 肢	four limbs of the body, all fours.
77-- 月	April.
-- 周	round, all around.
-- 開本	quarto.
-- 腳朝天	fall backwards with hands and legs in the air.
80-- 分之一	quarter, one fourth.
-- 分五裂	disintegration, disintegrated.
-- 合院	quadrangle, quadrangular building.
97-- 鄰	neighborhood, neighbors.

兄〔Hsiung〕n. elder brother.

50-- 事友	treat one's friend as an elder brother.
80-- 弟	brothers.
-- 弟會	fraternity, brotherhood.
-- 弟般的	fraternal, brotherly.
-- 弟國家	fraternal countries.
-- 弟如手足	brothers are like hands and feet.

見〔Chien〕v. see, observe, find, visit, call on, appear, meet, n. opinion, view.

00-- 棄	be rejected.
02-- 證	witness, evidence.
-- 證人	eyewitness, witness.
03-- 識	knowledge and experience.
08-- 效	effective, efficacious.
10-- 面	have an interview with, interview, meet.
-- 面即付	payable at sight.
-- 不得人	too ashamed to show up in public.
17-- 習	probation, apprenticeship.
-- 習生	probationary student.
27-- 解	view, position, opinion.
44-- 地	standpoint, viewpoint, position.
-- 世面	experienced, face the world.
74-- 附表	as per list enclosed.

77-- 聞	information, experience.
88-- 笑	be laughed at.
97-- 怪	be surprised, take offense.

6021₁

罷〔Pa〕v. stop, cease, discontinue, suspend, adj. worn out, fatigued.

00-- 市	suspension of business, close all shops, stoppage of business, close up shop, cease trade, shop keeping strike.
-- 市抗議	protest by closing up shops.
06-- 課	student's strike, strike of students.
10-- 工	strike, stop, go on strike, stay out.
-- 工補助	strike benefit.
-- 工權力	right of strike.
20-- 手	cease, stop.
27-- 免	dismiss, displace, dismiss from office, remove from office, recall.
63-- 戰	truce.
72-- 斥	n. dismissal, v. dismiss.

晃〔Huang〕v. sway, flash past, adj. bright, dazzling.

67-- 眼	dazzling, glaring.

6021₆

冕見 6041₆

6022₇

罱〔Lan〕n. net for fishing or mud.

吊=弔 1752₇

囫〔Hu〕adj. round, whole, entire.

60-- 圇	complete, whole.
-- 圇吞下	swallow without chewing.

易〔I〕n. change, alteration, ease, v. change, exchange, alter, trade, adj. easy, indifferent to, negligent.

00-- 主	change owner, change hands.
08-- 於	be apt to, be easy to.
10-- 碎貨物	fragile goods.
20-- 位	transpose.
-- 手	change hands.

21-- 經　　　Book of Changes, I Ching.
22-- 變　　　changeable.
24-- 貨　　　exchange of commodities.
-- 貨交易　　barter, barter business, barter transaction, barter deal, barter trade, goods exchanging trade.
27-- 名　　　change a name.
47-- 怒　　　*n.* temper, *adj.* passionate.
60-- 見　　　obvious, easily seen.
77-- 學　　　easy to learn.
86-- 知　　　easy to understand.

禹 見 6042₇

圇 〔Lun〕*adj.* gross, whole.

胃 〔Wei〕*n.* stomach, *adj.* gastric.
00-- 病　　　stomach ailment.
-- 痛　　　stomachache.
-- 癌　　　cancer of the stomach.
17-- 弱　　　indigestion, dyspepsia.
30-- 液　　　gastric juice.
35-- 潰瘍　　gastric ulcer.
44-- 藥　　　pepsin.
60-- 口　　　appetite.
-- 口大　　greedy, gluttonous.
80-- 氣痛　　gripes in the stomach.
90-- 炎　　　gastritis.

囿 〔Yu〕*n.* park, menagerie, walled yard for animals, *v.* limit, confine.

圊 〔Pu〕*n.* garden, orchard.

圊 〔Ching〕*n.* privy.
6022₈

界 〔Chieh〕*n.* boundary, border, frontier, barrier terminus, limit, *v.* demarcate, define, border.
08-- 說　　　definition.
10-- 石　　　landmark.
26-- 線　　　boundary-line.
41-- 址　　　location.
-- 標　　　landmark.
45-- 椿　　　boundary marker, boundary stone.
77-- 尺　　　ruler (for ruling a line).
-- 限　　　limit, bounds, margin, limitation, dividing line.
-- 限作用　　marginal utility.

6023₂
眾 〔Chung〕*n.* multitude, crowd, majority, *adj.* many, much, all.
07-- 望所歸　　command public respect and support.
08-- 議　　　public opinion.
-- 議院　　House of Commons, House of Representatives.
-- 議員　　Representative.
27-- 多　　　numerous, very many.
30-- 寡不敵　　the few can't fight the many.
58-- 數　　　majority, multitude.
80-- 人　　　mankind, people, populace, crowd, public, multitude.

園 〔Yuan〕*n.* garden, park.
00-- 亭　　　garden and pavilion.
10-- 丁　　　gardener.
44-- 藝　　　gardening.
-- 藝學　　horticulture.
-- 林　　　landscape garden.
60-- 景　　　garden scenery.
74-- 陵　　　imperial tomb.

晨 〔Chen〕*n.* morning, dawn.
56-- 操　　　morning exercise.

6028₁
昃 〔Tse〕*n.* afternoon.

6030₇
囹 〔Ling〕*n.* prison, jail.

6032₇
罵 〔Ma〕*v.* scold, rail at, revile, curse, rebuke, reproach, blame.
10-- 不絕口　　curse unceasingly.
80-- 人　　　curse at somebody.
-- 人取樂　　criticize others as a pastime.

6033₀
思 〔Ssu〕*n.* meaning, *v.* think, reflect, consider, contemplate, recall, mourn.
20-- 維　　　revolve, reflect, mind, thought, thinking.
-- 維再四　　think over and over again.
21-- 慮　　　deliberation, care, concernment.
-- 慮週到　　think over thoroughly.
-- 慮過度　　worry too much.

30-- 家病	homesick.	95-- 情	affection, graciousness, grace, devotion.
37-- 潮	trend of thought.		
-- 深慮遠	think deep and far ahead.	**6033₁**	
40-- 索	consider, think, think over.	**羆** 〔Pi〕 n. brown bear.	
44-- 考	n. thinking, reflection, v. speculate, think over, reflect, meditate on.	**黑** 〔Hei〕 n. black, adj. sinister, evil, dark.	
-- 考能力	power to think.	00-- 痣	mole, mole on the skin.
46-- 想	n. thought, idea, ideology, v. think, reflect.	-- 夜	night, dark night.
-- 想家	thinker.	-- 市	black market, black house, illicit market.
-- 想意識	ideology, thinking.	-- 市商人	black marketer.
-- 想武器	ideological weapon.	-- 市行情	curb rate.
-- 想改造	ideological remolding.	-- 市價格	black prices, black market price, black rate.
-- 想開通	be advanced in thought.	-- 市匯率	black market rate.
-- 想體系	ideology.	-- 市匯兌	black market exchange.
-- 想性	ideological level or content (of a writing).	-- 市銷售	black market sale.
67-- 路	one's way of thinking.	01-- 龍江	Amur, Amur River, Heilungkiang Province.
80-- 前顧後	think carefully.	10-- 死病	plague, Black Death.
-- 前想後	ponder over.	21-- 熊	black bear.
-- 念	think of, miss, recall.	22-- 種	black race.
90-- 懷往事	recollect the past affair.	24-- 貨	opium.
恩 〔En〕 n. favor, grace, mercy, benevolence, kindness, beneficence, adj. gracious, kind, charitable.		26-- 白不分	not able to distinguish between right and wrong.
00-- 主	benefactor, patron.	-- 白片	black-and-white movie.
20-- 愛	affection (between man and woman), love.	-- 白分明	sharp contrast between black and white or right and wrong.
24-- 仇未報	have not settled old accounts.	27-- 名單	black list.
25-- 俸	pension.	-- 白廣告	black and white advertising.
27-- 將仇報	return evil for good.	33-- 心	evil-hearted.
-- 怨分明	kindness and hatred are clearly distinguished.	-- 心腸	black-hearted, diabolical.
35-- 澤	favor.	38-- 海	Black Sea.
37-- 深似海	kindness as deep as the sea.	-- 道人物	underworld figure.
-- 深意重	the spiritual debt is deep and great.	41-- 板	blackboard.
50-- 惠	mercy, benefaction favor, beneficence.	-- 板報	blackboard newspaper.
		-- 板刷	blackboard eraser.
55-- 典	kindness, bounty, imperial favor.	-- 麵包	brown bread.
66-- 賜	grant, bestow favors.	44-- 幕	black-screen — dark secret.
-- 賜主義	paternalism.	-- 幫	sinister gang, secret clique.
80-- 人=恩主		47-- 奴	Negro slave, darky.
		50-- 棗	black date.
		60-- 暗	dark.
		-- 暗面	dark aspect.
		-- 暗世界	world without justice.

522

--暗時代	dark ages.	
66--啤酒	black beer.	
80--人	Negro (輕蔑用語), black people.	
--會	sinister meeting or organization.	
83--錢	black money, backhander.	
94--煤	black coal.	

罴 見 6003₁

6033₂

愚 〔Yu〕 n. stupidity, folly, ignorance, v. deceive, befool, make fool of, fool, cheat, adj. foolish, silly, stupid, ignorant, dull, unwise.

00--妄	foolish, silly.
10--弄	fool, make sport of, make fool of, deceive.
27--魯	stupid, ignorant.
50--夫	fool, dunce.
--蠢	brainless, folly, foolish, silly, stupid, blunt witted.
52--拙	clumsy, stupid, awkward.
65--昧	n. ignorance, adj. ignorant.
77--民政策	policy to keep the people in ignorance, obscurantism.
80--人	fool, simpleton, dunce.
--人愚行	fools rush in where angels fear to tread.
--公移山	where there is a will, there is a way.
87--鈍	dull, stupid.
88--笨	stupid, foolish, clumsy, awkward.

6034₃

團 〔Tuan〕 n. sphere, globule, group, lump, body, mass, regiment, corps, v. collect, group, end, adj. united, collected, round, globular.

10--丁	militiaman, volunteer.
17--聚	unite, gather together.
21--拜	festive gathering.
24--結	n. cohesion, cooperation, union, v. league, unite closely, hang together, consolidate, adj. united, inseparated.
--結一致	solidarity, unity.
--結的	united, inseparable.
--結即力量	unity is strength.
--練	militia, volunteer home guards.
60--團圍住	completely surround.
--圓	reunion.
71--長	regimental commander.
75--體	unity, union, community, association, body, public body, corps, organization, group, team.
--體保險	group insurance.
--體賽	team event.
88--簇	crowd, cluster.

6036₁

黯 〔An〕 adj. black, dark.

23--然	dejected, depressed.
--然失色	be cast into the shade.
27--色	dead color.

6039₆

黥 〔Ching〕 v. brand the face.

6040₀

田 〔Tien〕 n. field, arable land, rice-field.

00--主	landlord of a field.
--產	estate, real estate, land property.
01--壟	ridges of a land.
20--雞	frog.
21--徑隊	track and field team.
22--岸	bank of a field.
27--租	rent, land rental.
28--稅	land tax.
30--賽	field events.
35--溝	field drains.
41--埂	path in the field.
42--獵	hunt, hunting.
44--地	field, farm.
--莊	farm house.
56--螺	vivipara, mud-snail.
57--契	land-deed.
60--園	garden, fields and gardens.
63--賦	land-tax.
67--野	cultivable land, fields.
77--鼠	mole, field mouse.

80-- 舍　　　　farm house, farmyard.

早 〔Tsao〕 *n.* morning, good morning, *adj.* early, beginning, previous, beforehand, soon, already.

00-- 產	miscarriage, premature birth.
-- 衰	early decrepitude.
-- 市	morning market, morning session.
04-- 熟	premature, precocious, ripen early.
-- 熟作物	early ripening crops.
11-- 班	dawn shift, morning shift.
12-- 到	arrive early.
17-- 已	already.
21-- 些時候	earlier, some time before.
22-- 出早歸	go out early and return home early.
-- 稻	early rice, first crop of the year.
24-- 先	previously.
-- 結帳	early closing.
27-- 餐	breakfast.
-- 盤	morning session.
30-- 安	good-morning!
34-- 達	succeed in early life.
40-- 在	as early as.
-- 來	come early.
44-- 世	die at an early age.
46-- 場	morning show.
47-- 起	early rising, get up early.
56-- 操	morning exercises or drill.
60-- 晨	morning.
62-- 睡	go to bed early.
67-- 晚	morning and evening, sooner or later.
80-- 年	some years ago.
81-- 飯	breakfast.

6040₁

旱 〔Han〕 *n.* drought, dry weather, *adj.* dry, rainless.

22-- 災	drought.
39-- 澇	drought and flood.
42-- 橋	overbridge.
44-- 地	dry land, arid land.
67-- 路	land route.

圉 〔Yu〕 *n.* stable.

睪 〔Kao〕 *v.* spy, detect.

40-- 丸　　　　testes, testicle.

6040₄

囝 〔Nieh〕 *n.* daughter, young girl.

晏 〔Yen〕 *n.* evening, *adj.* late, tardy, quiet, peaceful, clear (sky).

6040₆

罩 〔Chao〕 *n.* basket, cover, shade, mantle, cloak, *v.* catch, protect, cover over, shade, surround.

00-- 衣	cloak, overcoat, blouse.
17-- 子	cover, shade.

6040₇

曼 〔Man〕 *adj.* long, extended, prolonged, wide.

12-- 延　　　　widespread.

6041₆

冕 〔Mien〕 *n.* crown, hat, coronet.

35-- 禮　　　　coronation.

6042₇

另 〔Ling〕 *adj.* another, separate, distinct, other, besides.

00-- 立門戶	become independent.
04-- 謀生路	find another way of living.
05-- 請高明	(please) find some better person than myself.
08-- 議	discuss further.
10-- 一	another.
-- 一方	the other side, on the other hand.
-- 一碼事	(that is) another pair of shoes, (that is) another matter.
-- 一種	another kind.
17-- 娶	remarry (said of a man).
18-- 改	change.
21-- 行通知	further notice.
23-- 外	in addition, another, extra, besides, still, again.
27-- 郵	by separated mail.
28-- 作	remake.
-- 做打算	make some other plans.
30-- 定時日	make a specific date.
-- 寄	by separate post, post sep-

	arately, post under separate cover.
40-- 有	there is another, there are still some.
-- 有文章	There's another side to the picture.
-- 有要務	have other fish to fry.
-- 有企圖	have other intentions.
46-- 加	additional.
47-- 起爐竈	start all over again, start a new business.
51-- 打主意	seek some other ways.
67-- 眼看待	give special treatment.
77-- 闢蹊徑	try to find a new path or snap course.

男 〔**Nan**〕 *n.* man, male, son.

00-- 主角	chief actor.
-- 高音	tenor.
10-- 孩	boy.
17-- 子	man, male.
20-- 爵	baron.
22-- 僕	man servant, boy.
-- 低音	bass.
23-- 儐相	best man.
25-- 生	schoolboy, boy-student.
27-- 的	male.
40-- 女平等	sexual equality, equality between the sexes.
-- 女老少	men and women, old and young.
-- 女同校	coeducation.
50-- 中音	baritone.
77-- 學生	school boy.
80-- 人	man.
95-- 性	male.

禺 〔**Yu**〕 *n.* an animal resembling monkey.

6043_0

因 〔**Yin**〕 *n.* cause, reason, *v.* follow, go along with, *adv.* according to, *conj.* because, for, as, so, therefore, *prep.* for, owing to, because of, on account of.

01-- 襲	follow the conventional.
10-- 而	consequently.
-- 工負傷	work-related injury.

17-- 子	(in math) factor.
20-- 往推來	judge the future from the past.
21-- 此	therefore, on that account, for this reason, hence, thus.
-- 何	for what?
-- 何如此	why is it so?
22-- 循	follow the routine, conservative, negligence.
34-- 為	for, since, as, on account of, because, owing to, by reason of, due to, in consequence of, for the sake of.
37-- 禍得福	an affliction turns into a blessing.
44-- 其不便	from inconvenience.
50-- 素	factor, element, agent.
-- 事制宜	do what is suitable to the circumstances.
58-- 數	(in math) factor.
60-- 果	cause and effect, causality.
-- 果律	causality, law of causation.
-- 果倒置	invert cause and effect.
-- 果報應	as a man sows, so let him reap.
-- 果關係	causality, causation.
80-- 人設事	create jobs just to accommodate some people.
-- 公	on duty, on business.
-- 公死亡	lose one's life while on duty.
-- 公殉職	death in line of duty.
90-- 小失大	lose the main goal because of small gains.

6044_0

畀 〔**Pi**〕 *v.* confer, give.

昇 〔**Sheng**〕 *v.* rise, ascend, come up, *adj.* peaceful, tranquil, calm.

10-- 汞	corrosive sublimate, bichloride of mercury.
-- 平之世	age of peace.
-- 天	ascension, go to heaven.
21-- 上	ascend.
27-- 級	*n.* promotion, *v.* be promoted, rise in rank.

77-- 降	ascend and descend.	
-- 降機	elevator.	

6050_0

甲〔Chia〕*n.* the first, armor, nail, shell, cuirass, measure of land equal to 0.97 hectare, *v.* begin, excel, surpass, *adj.* first, most outstanding.

00-- 方	first party, party A.
23-- 狀腺	thyroid, thyroid gland.
27-- 魚	green turtle.
-- 級	grade A.
41-- 板	deck, deck of a ship.
47-- 殼	shell.
-- 殼動物	crustaceans.
50-- 蟲	bug, insect, beetle.
-- 冑	armors.
77-- 骨	oracle bone.
88-- 等	first class, first grade.

6050_4

畢〔Pi〕*v.* finish, close, complete, *adj.* ended, terminated, entire, all, whole, *adv.* entirely, totally, all.

00-- 竟	after all.
25-- 生	lifelong, one's lifetime, one's whole life.
-- 生事業	enterprise for life.
32-- 業	*n.* graduation, *v.* graduate.
-- 業證書	diploma.
-- 業生	graduate, alumnus or alumna.
-- 業考試	graduation examination.
-- 業典禮	graduation, commencement.
-- 業年限	term of years for graduation.

6050_6

圍〔Wei〕*n.* enclosure, surrounding, circumference, *v.* surround, invest, besiege, enclose, encircle.

13-- 殲	surround and wipe out, encircle and wipe out.
18-- 攻	*n.* siege, encirclement campaign, *v.* lay siege to, lay siege, beset.
20-- 住	encircle, surround.
24-- 牆	surrounding wall, enclosure.
-- 繞	*v.* enclose, compass, surround, *adv.* around.
37-- 裙	apron, overalls.
40-- 巾	shawl, scarf, muffler.
43-- 城	besiege a city.
44-- 棋	chess, go, Chinese draughts, Weichi.
60-- 困	*n.* siege, *v.* besiege, surround, beset.

暈〔Yun〕*n.* fainting, swoon, catalepsy, halo, mist, *v.* faint, be giddy, feel dizzy, *adj.* dizzy, giddy.

22-- 倒	fall into a swoon.
27-- 船	seasick.
60-- 眩	giddy.

6052_1

羈〔Chi〕*n.* inn, tavern, lodging house, *v.* lodge.

6052_7

羈〔Chi〕*n.* bridle, halter, *v.* restrain, control, bridle, halter, arrest, detain.

29-- 絆	tied down, fettered.
50-- 束	control.
77-- 留	keep in custody, detain.
-- 留所	lock-up.

6060_0

回〔Hui〕*n.* times, number of times, Mohammedanism, Moslems, *v.* return, go back, return to.

00-- 音	reply, answer, echo.
02-- 話	return an answer.
10-- 覆	reply, answer.
-- 手	give a blow in return.
11-- 頭	turn the head, turn about, repent.
12-- 到	return.
20-- 信	answer a letter.
21-- 拜	return a visit.
24-- 升 (復甦)	recovered.
26-- 程	return journey, return trip, round trip.
-- 程票	return ticket.
-- 程運費	back freight, home freight, homeward freight.
-- 程費用	return expenses.

27-- 歸線	tropic, tropic of Cancer or Capricorn.
-- 歸熱	relapsing fever.
-- 佣	return commission.
-- 租	lease back, sale and lease back.
28-- 收	recovery.
-- 收計畫	recycling program.
-- 收利用	recycle.
-- 收值	recover value.
-- 收期	pay-off period, pay back period.
-- 收成本	recovery cost.
30-- 家	go home, get home, return home.
-- 避	evade, shun, dodge.
31-- 顧	review, look back.
-- 顧往事	look back at the past affairs.
33-- 心	repent, reform.
37-- 祿	god of fire, fire.
-- 運	ship back.
40-- 來	return, come back.
-- 去	go back, return.
46-- 想	reflect, recall, recollect.
47-- 聲	echo.
48-- 教	Mohammedanism, Islam.
-- 教徒	Mohammedan.
-- 教寺	mosque.
50-- 本期	payback period.
55-- 轉	return.
56-- 扣	refund and rebate, rebates, sales commission, kickback.
57-- 擊	counter-attack, rebuff.
60-- 國	return to one's fatherland, return to one's own country, go home.
61-- 嘴	retort.
65-- 購	buy back, counterpurchase, repurchase.
80-- 合	round.
88-- 答	*n.* answer, reply, *v.* reply, answer, respond.
90-- 憶	*n.* recollection, *v.* remember, recollect, bring back, recall.
-- 憶錄	memoirs.

呂 〔**Lu**〕 *n.* Lu (a family name).

昌 〔**Chang**〕 *v.* prosper, thrive, *adj.* glorious, prosperous, flourishing, elegant, beautiful, bright.

00-- 言	good words.
53-- 盛	*n.* prosperity, *adj.* prosperous, abundant, flourishing, thriving.
67-- 明	bright, advanced.

冒 〔**Mao**〕 *v.* venture, risk, presume, forge, counterfeit, pretend, brave, feign, *adj.* imprudent.

00-- 充	*n.* adulteration, *v.* pretend to be, assume the identity of, adulterate.
-- 充貨	adulterated goods.
07-- 認	claim falsely.
10-- 雨	walk in the rain, brave the storm.
23-- 然闖入	butt in.
24-- 失	pert, rash.
25-- 失鬼	blunderer.
26-- 牌	*n.* imitation, counterfeit, imitation brand, mockery *v.* imitate a trademark.
-- 牌貨	adulteration, pinchbeck.
-- 牌醫生	fake doctor.
27-- 名	assume a name, assume the name of.
-- 名頂替	assume the identity of another person.
30-- 進	adventurous advance.
34-- 瀆	disturb, bring trouble to.
47-- 犯	*n.* offence, *v.* offend, affront, provoke, trespass.
-- 犯者	offender.
61-- 號	colon.
65-- 昧	rude, rash, presumptuous, headlong, take the liberty of.
-- 昧從事	do something heedlessly.
77-- 風險	run risk.
78-- 險	*n.* adventure, *v.* hazard, dare, adventure, run a risk, take a risk, *adj.* adventurous.

-- 險家　adventurer.
-- 險主義　adventurism.
-- 險事業　adventurous enterprise.

6060₁

囹 〔Yu〕 n. prison, jail, v. put in prison.
詈 〔Li〕 v. abuse, scold.

6060₄

固 〔Ku〕 n. make firm, secure, adj. strong, firm, sturdy, secure, fortified, strengthened, constant, fixed, solid, stubborn, sure, adv. certainly, originally.

23-- 然　surely.
24-- 結　solidify, coagulate, consolidate.
30-- 定　n. stability, fixing, v. fix, adj. fixed, firm, stationary, stable.
-- 定產出　fixed output.
-- 定工資　fixed salary, fixed wage, regular earnings, regular pay, set wage.
-- 定需求　fixed demand.
-- 定評價　fixed parity.
-- 定預算　fixed budget, right budget.
-- 定職工　permanent staff.
-- 定職業　permanent job, regular work.
-- 定航線　regular shipping lines.
-- 定比率　fixed ratio.
-- 定價格　certain price, firm price, fixed price.
-- 定利息　fixed interest.
-- 定債務　fixed debts.
-- 定佣金　dead commission.
-- 定收入　constant income, constant revenues, regular income, settled income.
-- 定資本　fixed capital.
-- 定匯率　constant rate of exchange, fixed rate, fixed rate of exchange.
-- 定資產　fixed assets, capital assets, passive assets, permanent assets.
-- 定報價　fixed offer, firm bid, firm tender.
-- 定成本　fixed cost, lock-in capital.
-- 定費用　fixed expenses, regular fee, standing charges.
-- 定投資　fixed investment.
-- 定財產　fixed property.
-- 定月薪　fixed monthly salary.
-- 定用戶　regular end user.
-- 守　guard carefully, persist, hold one's ground.
-- 守成規　stick to old rules.
40-- 有　natural, original, innate, intrinsic.
-- 有價值　indigenous value, intrinsic value.
-- 有色　natural color.
44-- 執　n. bigotry, v. persist, preserve, hold, hang on, adj. obstinate, perverse, persistent, bigoted, stubborn.
-- 執不移　obstinate and unaltered.
-- 執己見　self-opinioned, bigoted.
-- 執成見　obstinate of one's forgone conclusion.
-- 執的　bigoted, dogged.
75-- 體　solid.
-- 體燃料　solid fuels.

晷 〔Kuei〕 n. gnomon, sun dial.
署 〔Shu〕 n. public office, court, v. arrange, sign, write, be on a deputy.

16-- 理　administer temporarily.
27-- 名　n. sign, signature, v. sign, sign one's name.

暑 〔Shu〕 n. summer, hot weather.

10-- 天　hot weather, dog days.
27-- 假　summer vacation.
80-- 氣　heat of summer.

圖 〔Tu〕 n. picture, figure, chart, diagram, drawing, plan, map, v. scheme, plot, plan.

00-- 章　seal, stamp.
04-- 謀　plan, plot, conspire.
-- 謀不軌　engage in illegal activities, plot an uprising or rebellion.
10-- 面　plans of a house.

-- 示	diagrammatic presentation, graphic presentation.
12-- 形	figure.
21-- 版	illustration.
22-- 利	make money.
-- 利他人	with the intention to profit others.
-- 紙	blueprint, plan paper.
27-- 像	portrait.
-- 解	*n.* illustration, diagram, *v.* diagram, graph.
30-- 案	design, pattern, draft.
48-- 樣	pattern, plan, chart, plot, design.
50-- 畫	picture, illustration, drawing, painting.
-- 畫書	picture-book.
-- 畫名信片	picture postcard.
-- 書	books, charts, maps.
-- 書館	library.
-- 書館員	librarian.
-- 表	chart, table, schedule, illustration, diagram, figure, tabular presentation.
60-- 景	prospect or view (from a mountain, etc).
64-- 財害命	murder for money.
79-- 騰	totem.
81-- 釘	drawing pin, thumbtack.

6062₀

罰〔**Fa**〕*n.* penalty, punishment, fine, *v.* punish.

13-- 球	penalty (in a ball game).
47-- 款	fine, impose fines, penalty, penalty fine, pecuniary penalty, forfeit.
-- 款條款	penalty clause.
62-- 則	penal regulation.
80-- 金	fine, pecuniary penalty, forfeit.

6066₀

品〔**Pin**〕*n.* goods, rank, order, class, kind, sort, character, personality, grade, *v.* appraise, criticize.

01-- 評	criticize.
20-- 位	rank.

21-- 行	conduct, action, behavior, character.
-- 行不端	misconduct.
-- 行端正	upright in character.
22-- 種	variety, item, kind.
26-- 貌	appearance.
-- 貌端莊	respectable in one's bearing.
-- 貌不揚	not prominent in personal appearance.
27-- 級	rank, grade.
47-- 格	quality, character, personality.
-- 格高雅	noble in character.
60-- 目繁多	the names and descriptions of articles are numerous.
72-- 質	quality, character.
-- 質保證	quality guarantee.
77-- 學兼優	good both in character and in scholarship.
91-- 類不齊	not uniform in grade or kind.
95-- 性	temper, disposition.

晶〔**Ching**〕*n.* crystal, *adj.* bright, clear, pure, brilliant.

24-- 化	crystallization.
75-- 體	crystal.
99-- 瑩	bright.
-- 焱	lustrous, shining.

6071₁

昆〔**Kun**〕*n.* descendant, multitude, elder brother, *adj.* numerous, many.

25-- 仲	brothers.
50-- 蟲	insects.
-- 蟲學	entomology.

6071₂

圈〔**Chuan**〕*n.* circle, ring, coil, draw.

17-- 子	circle.
20-- 住	enclose, hem in.
40-- 套	snare, plot, trap, noose.
-- 套陳舊	the snare is old-fashioned.
-- 中人語	remarks of the persons within a circle.

囤〔**Tun**〕*n.* bin to hold grain, *v.* hoard, store up.

24-- 儲	stockpile, hoard and corner.

25-- 積　　　　*n.* speculative stockpiling, *v.* hoard, hoard for speculation, make a corner in, corner, buy up.

-- 積品　　　　hoarded goods.

-- 積居奇　　　corner, hoard, corner the market, hoarding and speculation, hoarding and profiteering, hoard goods.

30-- 戶　　　　hoarder.

44-- 藏　　　　store up, storage.

邑 〔I〕 *n.* city, town, district, county, melancholy, *adj.* sad.

30-- 宰　　　　county magistrate.

80-- 人　　　　citizen, townsfolk.

6072₇

昂 〔Ang〕 *v.* rise, elevate, increase, *adj.* grand, high, lofty, dear.

21-- 價　　　　heavy price.

50-- 貴　　　　expensive, dear, costly, cost, long price, long figure.

80-- 首　　　　raise the head.

曷 〔Ho〕 *adv.* why? why not? how?

6073₁

曇 〔Tan〕 *n.* black cloud over the sky, *adj.* cloudy, overcast.

40-- 花　　　　canna.

-- 花一現　　　temporary, short-lived, ephemeral.

6073₂

畏 〔Wei〕 *v.* fear, dread, be afraid of, revere, *adj.* fearful.

23-- 縮　　　　*v.* fear, flinch, shrink, *adj.* hesitating, timid.

-- 縮不前　　　flinch from fear.

30-- 避　　　　skulk, recoil.

40-- 難　　　　fear difficulty.

-- 難而退　　　be awed by the difficulty and stop.

50-- 妻　　　　henpecked.

60-- 罪　　　　fear punishment.

80-- 羞　　　　bashful, shy, nervous.

94-- 怯　　　　*n.* timidity, coward, *adj.* coward, fearful, timid, cowardly.

96-- 懼　　　　*v.* fear, dread, be afraid of,

adj. afraid, frightened.

99-- 勞　　　　afraid of labor.

曩 〔Nang〕 *adv.* formerly.

6080₀

只 〔Chih〕 *adv.* only, merely, simply, yet, *conj.* but.

10-- 要　　　　only, if only, as long as.

-- 不過　　　only, nothing but.

21-- 此　　　　only this.

-- 能　　　　can only, cannot but.

-- 能是　　　can be nothing but, can only be.

24-- 備具有　　be provided with, possess.

26-- 得　　　　be obliged to, cannot help.

32-- 顧　　　　care only, look after exclusively.

40-- 有　　　　only, have only.

47-- 好　　　　be forced to, have to.

60-- 是　　　　but, yet, however, nevertheless.

88-- 管　　　　not to hesitate to.

96-- 怕　　　　fear only, be merely afraid that.

囚 〔Chiu〕 *n.* captive, prisoner, criminal, prison, jail, *v.* imprison, put in prison, confine.

00-- 衣　　　　prison-garb.

24-- 徒　　　　felon.

44-- 禁　　　　*n.* imprisonment, *v.* imprison, confine.

47-- 犯　　　　prisoner, criminal, convict.

50-- 車　　　　prison van, prisoner's cart.

貝 〔Pei〕 *n.* shells, money, riches, cowries, valuable things, *adj.* precious, valuable.

17-- 子　　　　cowries.

6080₁

足 〔Tsu〕 *n.* foot, leg, locomotive organ, *v.* full, *adj.* enough, satisfied.

00-- 音　　　　step.

10-- 下　　　　sir.

13-- 球　　　　football, soccer.

-- 球隊　　　football team.

-- 球賽　　　football match.

21-- 價　　　　full price.

27-- 夠　　　　enough, satisfied, suffi-

	-- 夠應付	sufficient to meet.
60--	跡	foot step, trace, footprint, footmark.
61--	趾	toes.
77--	印	footprint.
80--	金	pure gold, solid gold.

異 〔**I**〕 v. differ, differ from, marvel, vary, vary with, separate, wonder, adj. different, wonderful, strange, rare, unusual, particular.

02--	端	superstition, heterodoxy, heresy.
08--	說	heresy.
	-- 議	objection, opposition, dissension, disagreement.
	-- 於	differ from, be different from.
17--	己	those who differ from oneself.
22--	種	heterogeneous.
24--	化	alienation.
30--	客	stranger.
33--	心	alienated heart.
48--	教	paganism.
	-- 教徒	pagan, heretic.
57--	邦	foreign country.
60--	口同聲	with one accord, with one voice, all in one voice.
	-- 日	another day.
61--	點	dissimilarity, difference.
77--	同	similarity and dissimilarity.
80--	人	strange person, extraordinary man.
90--	常	unusual, strange, abnormal, extraordinary.
95--	性	of a different nature, of the other sex.

是 〔**Shi**〕 v. to be, adj. right, correct, this, that, which, adv. yes.

10--	否	whether or not.
11--	非	right and wrong.
	-- 非不明	right or wrong is not clear.
27--	的	yes.
40--	真是假	is it true or false?

6080₆

員 〔**Yuan**〕 n. member, officer, official.

10--	工	workers and staff members.
	-- 工福利	employee welfare.

買 〔**Mai**〕 v. buy, purchase, seek, look for, win over.

00--	主	purchaser, buyer, customer.
	-- 辦	compradore, comprador, person responsible for making purchase.
	-- 方 (採購員)	buyer, purchaser.
26--	得起	can afford.
30--	空	buy a bull, buy long, going long, bull, short purchase.
	-- 空賣空	speculate, bears and bulls, cross trade, fictitious bargain, marginal transaction, speculate on the rise and fall of prices.
	-- 客	buyer.
40--	賣	trade, commerce, bargain.
	-- 賣契約	bargain.
50--	東西	go shopping.
60--	回	repurchase, redeem, buyback.

圓 〔**Yuan**〕 n. globe, ball, sphere, dollar, circle, adj. round, circular.

10--	面	round face.
12--	形	round, circular.
15--	珠筆 (子筆)	ball-pen, ball-point pen.
21--	桌會議	round-table conference, round-table discussion.
	-- 徑	diameter.
27--	盤	disk.
30--	寂	(said of a Buddhist monk or nun) to die.
33--	心	center of a circle.
34--	滿	n. perfection, satisfaction, v. complete, consummate, adj. perfect, satisfactory.
	-- 滿結束	round off.
	-- 滿解決	be settled satisfactorily.
37--	滑	accommodating, tactful.
	-- 滑手段	tactful means.

-- 通	accommodating, obliging.
40-- 柱體	cylinder.
-- 柱體的	cylindric, cylindrical.
52-- 括弧	parentheses.
56-- 規	compasses.
60-- 圈	circle, ring.
-- 柱	column, pillar.
75-- 體	sphere, round body.
77-- 周	circle, circumference, circumference of a circle.
-- 周率	circular constant.
-- 屋頂	dome, cupola, vault.
78-- 臉	moon face, full face.
80-- 錐體	cone.
-- 錐體的	conic, conical.
-- 舞曲	waltz.
87-- 鋸	circular saw.
88-- 筒	cylinder.

6081₄

賍＝**贓** 6385₀

6086₁

賠 〔**Pei**〕 *n*. compensation, *v*. compensate, recompense, pay for, lose money, offer (apology).

29-- 償	*n*. indemnity, compensation, reparation, *v*. repay, recompense, compensate, make reparation for, pay a compensation of.
-- 償金	damages, compensation payment, compensatory payment.
33-- 補	make up a deficiency of public funds.
47-- 款	*n*. indemnity, reparation, repayment, *v*. make compensation, pay an indemnity, pay reparations.
50-- 本	lose money, lose one's capital, run a business at a loss, sustain losses in business.
60-- 罪	*n*. apology, *v*. apologize.
83-- 錢	repay money.

6088₂

賅 〔**Kai**〕 *adj*. rare, uncommon, rich.

6090₃

累 〔**Lei**〕 *n*. burden, trouble, *v*. tie together, bind, pile up, accumulate, heap, involve, implicate, owe, be in debt, *adj*. tired, weary, repeated, *adv*. repeatedly, often.

04-- 計	add up, accumulative total.
-- 計盈餘	accumulated surplus.
17-- 了	tired, weary.
-- 及	implicate, involve.
-- 及無辜	make the innocent suffer.
25-- 積	*v*. accumulate, *adj*. accumulated, cumulative, accumulative.
30-- 進	progressive.
-- 進稅	progressive tax.
37-- 次	repeatedly, often.
46-- 加利息	cumulative interest.
57-- 贅	tiresome, troublesome.

纍 〔**Lei**〕 *n*. large rope, *v*. join, tie, place up, pile on, *adj*. joining together.

60-- 纍	strung together, heaps on heaps.

6090₄

呆 〔**Tai**〕 *adj*. foolish, silly, doltish, prim, dull.

01-- 語	nonsense.
11-- 頭呆腦	idiot-like.
34-- 滯	clumsy.
-- 滯市場	narrow market, sluggish market.
-- 滯的	sluggish.
-- 滯資本	dead capital.
-- 滯資產	bad assets, slow assets.
-- 滯存款 (滯商品)	dead stock.
41-- 板	prim, boring.
61-- 賬	uncollectible account, bad debts, bad accounts, doubtful accounts.
-- 賬準備	reserve for doubtful account, reserve for doubtful debts, reserve for bad debts.
-- 賬劃銷	bad debt written off.
-- 賬損失	loss from doubtful accounts.

88-- 笨　foolish, brainless.

困〔**Kun**〕*n.* distress, difficulty, poverty, *v.* confine, weary, distress, lay siege to, be confused, disturb, *adj.* confined, exhausted, fatigued, weary, tired, afflicted.

20-- 乏　weary, fatigued, worn out, insufficient, wanting, tired.

29-- 倦　fatigued, tired, weary, wearied.

30-- 窮　*n.* poverty, *adj.* very poor.

-- 窘　untoward circumstances.

40-- 難　*n.* difficulty, trouble, *adj.* difficult, troublesome, hard.

-- 境　plight, difficult situation.

44-- 苦　*v.* distress, *adj.* distressed, wearied.

60-- 累　harass.

71-- 阨　be poverty-stricken.

92-- 惱　vexation.

杲〔**Kao**〕*adj.* high, clear.

果〔**Kuo**〕*n.* fruit, seed, result, effect, *v.* fill, succeed, *adv.* really, exactly.

17-- 子　fruit.

-- 子凍　jelly.

18-- 敢　daring, courageous, brave.

22-- 醬　jelly, jam.

-- 斷　resolute, determined.

23-- 然　certainly, really.

27-- 仁　nut.

30-- 實=果子

34-- 汁　fruit juice.

35-- 決勇敢　resolute and daring.

40-- 皮　peel.

-- 核　stone.

44-- 樹　fruit-tree.

46-- 如所料　it happened exactly as expected.

47-- 報　retribution of one's deeds.

60-- 園　orchard.

78-- 腹　*n.* bellyful, *v.* fill one's stomach.

6090₆

景〔**Ching**〕scenery, sight, aspect, view, light, prospect, situation, condition, *v.* admire, *adj.* great.

27-- 仰　adore, idolize, admire.

-- 仰大名　look up to your great name.

-- 象　prospect, outlook, sight.

-- 物　spectacle, view, scenes.

-- 色　scene, prospect, landscape, scenery, view, perspective.

36-- 況　condition, circumstance.

-- 況不佳　the circumstances are not good.

50-- 泰藍　cloisonne.

80-- 氣　boom, prosperity.

6091₄

罹〔**Li**〕*n.* sorrow, grief, sadness, *v.* incur, encounter, meet with.

30-- 害　be murdered.

40-- 難　incur misfortune.

羅〔**Lo**〕*n.* light silk, silk gauze, net, snare, *v.* arrange orderly, spread out, recruit.

12-- 列　arrange in order, spread out.

18-- 致人才　gather men of talents together.

21-- 網　net, cobweb, snare.

27-- 盤　compass.

34-- 漢　enlightened disciple of the Buddha.

71-- 馬　Rome.

-- 馬字　Roman letters (or characters).

-- 馬法　Roman law.

-- 馬教　Roman Catholic.

-- 馬教皇　Pope.

-- 馬尼亞　Romania.

-- 馬人　Roman.

6101₀

毗〔**Pi**〕*v.* assist, help, join, adjoin.

35-- 連　adjoining.

呲〔**Tzu**〕*v.* scold.

6101₁

啡〔**Fei**〕*n.* sound of snoring.

眶〔**Kung**〕*n.* eye-socket, socket of the eye.

嚨〔**Lung**〕*n.* throat.

曬〔**Shai**〕*v.* dry, dry in the sun, air, sun.

00-- 衣架　　　clothes horse.
-- 衣服　　　sun clothes, dry clothes in the sun.
40-- 太陽　　　bask in the sun.
47-- 棚　　　　drying terrace, drying rack.
48-- 乾　　　　sun-dried, dry in the sun.
60-- 黑　　　　sun-burned, tan.

曨 〔Lung〕 *n.* dim light before dawn.
6101₂
呃 〔E〕 *n.* hiccup.
38-- 逆　　　　hiccup, or hiccough.
唬 〔Hu〕 *v.* intimidate.
咂 〔Tsa〕 *v.* smack, suck in.
61-- 嘴　　　　smack.
嘘 見 6101₇
6101₄
旺 〔Wang〕 *adj.* glorious, brightening, brilliant, bright, prosperous, flourishing.
00-- 市　　　　bull market.
20-- 季　　　　busy season, peak season, booming season, buy season, high season, rush season, peak selling period.
53-- 盛　　　　*v.* flourish, prosper, *adj.* prosperous.
77-- 月　　　　busy month.
80-- 年　　　　prosperous year.
89-- 銷　　　　brisk sales, sell briskly.
嘅 〔Kai〕 *n.* the sound of sighing, *v.* sigh, regret.
睚 〔Ai〕 *n.* outer corner of the eye.
60-- 目　　　　stare at.
6101₆
嘔 〔Ou〕 *v.* vomit, disgorge.
27-- 血　　　　spit blood.
-- 血致死　　　die by spitting blood.
33-- 心瀝血　　　make painstaking efforts.
64-- 吐　　　　vomit, disgorge.
暱 〔Ni〕 *adj.* intimate, familiar.
6101₇
啞 〔Ya〕 *n.* adverb describing sounds. *v.* keep silent, *adj.* dumb, mute.
09-- 謎　　　　enigma.

-- 謎猜中　　　have found out the answer to a riddle.
17-- 子　　　　dumb-man, dumb person, mute.
-- 子手語　　　A dumb person speaks with hands.
22-- 劇　　　　pantomime.
60-- 口無言　　　be silent as a dumb person.
61-- 啞學語　　　A child is learning to talk.
63-- 喧嘈雜　　　noisy sound of a crowd.
66-- 咽　　　　sound of crying of a child.
88-- 鈴　　　　dumbbell.
嘘 〔Hsu〕 *v.* breathe out, expire, exhale, blow.
47-- 聲　　　　hisses, catcalls.
80-- 氣　　　　expire, exhale.
6102₀
叮 〔Ting〕 *v.* bid, order, enjoin upon, bite, sting, reiterate.
03-- 嚀告誡　　　enjoin repeatedly.
-- 嚀吩咐　　　give advice repeatedly.
67-- 囑　　　　reiterate, enjoin repeatedly.
-- 囑再三　　　repeat an order again and again.
69-- 噹聲　　　ding-dong, chink.
盯 〔Ding〕 *v.* gaze steadily.
呵 〔He〕 *v.* scold, scold loudly, expel the breath, exhale, yawn.
27-- 欠　　　　*n.* yawning, *v.* yawn.
61-- 呵大笑　　　roar with laughter.
62-- 呵　　　　the sound of laughter.
72-- 斥　　　　scold, reproach.
80-- 氣　　　　breathe out.
啊 〔A〕 *interj.* oh! ah!
67-- 喲　　　　alas!
6102₇
嗎 〔Ma〕 *n.* particle at the end of a question, *interj.* (an interrogative sign.)
61-- 啡　　　　morphine, morphia.
嚅 〔Ju〕 *n.* hesitation.
眄 〔Mien〕 *v.* ogle, cast glances, look.
嘴 〔Tsui〕 *n.* mouth.
11-- 硬心軟　　　be tough in speech and soft

in heart.

71-- 脣　lips.

77-- 巴　mouth.

  -- 緊　tight-lipped.

78-- 臉　face, features.

87-- 饞　gluttonous.

啃 〔Ken〕 *v.* nibble, gnaw.

唡 〔Liang〕 *n.* ounce.

6103₂

啄 〔Cho〕 *v.* peck, pick up.

40-- 木鳥　woodpecker.

80-- 食　pick, eat by pecking.

90-- 米　peck rice.

噱 〔Chueh〕 *n.* hearty laugh, laughter.

11-- 頭　claptrap, gag.

6104₀

吁 〔Hsu〕 *n.* sigh, interj. alas !

呀 〔Ya〕 *n.* creaking sound, interj. particle indicating surprise — oh ! ah !

23-- 然一聲　with a creaking sound.

盱 〔Hsu〕 *v.* open the eyes, *adj.* sorry, vexed.

6104₁

囁 〔Nieh〕 *n.* hesitation.

6104₆

哽 〔Keng〕 *n.* stoppage in the throat, choking from grief, *v.* sob, choke.

66-- 咽　choking with sobs, sob.

  -- 咽哀感　be choked with grief.

6104₉

嘑 〔Hu〕 *v.* call.

6106₀

呫 〔Chan〕 *v.* whisper.

哂 〔Shen〕 *n.* smiling.

晒=曬 6101₁

6106₁

晤 〔Wu〕 *v.* meet, see.

00-- 商大計　discuss a great plan in an interview.

09-- 談　meet and talk.

10-- 面　meet, meet face to face.

27-- 解　understand, perceive.

62-- 別之時　at the time of parting.

6108₆

噸 〔Tun〕 *n.* ton

20-- 位　tonnage.

58-- 數頗巨　the tonnage is rather big.

6109₁

瞟 〔Piao〕 *v.* cast a glance, look askance.

10-- 一眼　glance at, wink at.

69-- 眇　indistinct, not reliable.

6110₀

趾 〔Chih〕 *n.* toes, digit.

60-- 甲　nail, toenail.

80-- 舞　toe dance.

90-- 尖　tip toe.

跕 〔Tieh〕 *v.* walk slowly, fall, drop, walk on tiptoe.

6111₇

距 〔Chu〕 *n.* distance, bird's spur, *v.* depart, oppose, resist.

00-- 離　distance, interval.

6112₇

踖 〔Chi〕 *v.* walk with short steps.

6113₁

躚 〔Hsien〕 *v.* wobble.

6114₀

跰 〔Chien〕 *n.* tough skin on the foot or hand.

躅 〔Chu〕 *adj.* undecided, irresolute.

6114₁

躡 〔Nieh〕 *v.* tread, tread on, step, step over, follow.

6116₀

跖 〔Chih〕 *n.* the sole of the foot.

6118₂

蹶 〔Chueh〕 *v.* tread, slip, topple, walk fast, stumble.

6121₇

號 〔Hao〕 *n.* sign, mark, name, signal, number, order, call, title, bugle, *v.* roar, scream, crow, cry, weep, shout, howl.

00-- 音　bugle call.

  -- 衣　uniform.

11-- 碼　　　　number.
-- 碼系統　　　coding system.
-- 碼牌 (執照) number plate.
17-- 召　　　　summon, urge, call.
20-- 手　　　　trumpeter, bugler.
22-- 稱　　　　call, name, reputedly, so-called.
23-- 外　　　　extra issue of a newspaper.
27-- 角　　　　bugle, horn.
47-- 聲　　　　trumpet-call.
62-- 叫　　　　yell, roar.
66-- 哭　　　　cry, wail.
72-- 兵　　　　trumpeter, bugler.
80-- 令　　　　order, command.
88-- 筒　　　　cornet, bugle, trumpet.

6128₆
顋 〔 E 〕 *n.* high check bone.

6136₀
點 〔 Tien 〕 *n.* point, pip, spot, dot, speck, drop, snacks, hours, *v.* nod, bow, point out, check, ignite, light, point at, punctuate.
00-- 交　　　　check and hand over.
11-- 頭　　　　nod.
17-- 子　　　　*n.* small trace, schemes, plots, *adj.* a little.
24-- 貨員　　　cargo checker, tally man.
27-- 名　　　　call the roll.
-- 名冊　　　roll.
-- 名簿　　　roll of names.
-- 綴　　　　embellish, adorn.
28-- 收　　　　check and receive.
30-- 滴　　　　drops, drips.
33-- 心　　　　refreshments, dessert.
44-- 菜　　　　order a dinner, order dishes at a restaurant.
58-- 數　　　　tally, check the number, count.
61-- 號　　　　period, full stop.
78-- 驗　　　　inspect.
88-- 鐘　　　　o'clock.
90-- 火　　　　fire, set fire, ignite, kindle.
92-- 燈　　　　light a lamp.
93-- 燃　　　　*n.* ignition, *v.* light, ignite.

6138₆

顊 〔 Sai 〕 *n.* jaw, jowl.
顯 〔 Hsien 〕 *v.* exhibit, display, be evident, appear, show, manifest, expose, *adj.* apparent, evident, clear, bright, glorious, prominent, conspicuous, famous, eminent.
10-- 露　　　　emerge, appear, display, come to light.
-- 示　　　　show, display, appear, manifest.
16-- 現　　　　appear.
22-- 出　　　　exhibit, reveal.
23-- 然　　　　clearly, apparently, visibly, evidently.
26-- 得　　　　appear to be.
28-- 微照片　　microfilm.
-- 微鏡　　　*n.* microscope, *adj.* microscopic.
44-- 著　　　　manifest, apparent, prominent, evident, remarkable, striking.
56-- 揚　　　　exalt.
62-- 影藥　　　developer (in photography).
67-- 明　　　　conspicuous, apparent, manifest, clear.
-- 眼　　　　showy, conspicuous, eye-catching.

6173₂
饕 〔 Tao 〕 *adj.* avaricious.
6180₁
匙 〔 She 〕 *n.* key, spoon, teaspoon.
6180₆
題 〔 Ti 〕 *n.* title, topic, forehead, sign, signal, theme, title, topic, subject, commentaries, notes, *v.* write, inscribe, sign.
00-- 序　　　　preface.
07-- 詞　　　　motto, inscription.
27-- 名　　　　write one's name.
31-- 額　　　　inscription on a tablet.
44-- 材　　　　subject matter.
60-- 目　　　　text, title, topic, subject, theme of a writing or speech.

68-- 贈　　inscribe.

6183₂

賑〔**Chen**〕v. relieve, give, supply, aid, assist.

22-- 災　　relieve the afflicted people.
-- 災濟貧　relieve famine and the poor.
30-- 濟　　relieve, give aid.
-- 濟機關　charity institute.
47-- 款　　relief funds.

賬〔**Chang**〕n. accounts, bills, debts.

10-- 面價值　book value (BV), recorded valuation.
11-- 項　　account items.
30-- 房　　accountant, counting room, bookkeeping department, cashier's department, accountant's office.
-- 戶　　account, account currents.
41-- 櫃　　counter.
47-- 款　　funds on account, credit.
60-- 目　　accounts, bills, item of an account.
-- 目不清　accounts not in order.
61-- 號　　account number (A.N).
66-- 單　　bills, account bill, statement of account.
77-- 冊　　account book, book of account.
88-- 簿　　account books, ledger.

6184₇

販〔**Fan**〕v. deal in, trade, sell.

40-- 賣　　sell, peddle.
-- 賣術　　salesmanship.
-- 賣代理人　selling agent.
-- 賣軍火　peddle munitions.
-- 賣人口　traffic in persons.
50-- 毒　　drug trafficking.
-- 毒集團　drug cartel.

6186₀

貼〔**Tieh**〕n. subsidy, aid, v. stick, stick on, paste up, supply, subsidize, adj. in touch, in contact, proper, comfortable.

00-- 膏藥　plaster.
12-- 水　　premium, exchange at pre-mium.

16-- 現　　discount, discount for cash.
21-- 上　　stick on.
22-- 出　　put up.
-- 紙條　　label, put labels on.
27-- 郵票　stick a stamp.
-- 條　　bill, poster.
32-- 近　　near, close to.
33-- 補　　subsidize, help (out) financially.
-- 補家用　help out with the family expenses.
-- 心　　intimate, close.
47-- 切　　pertinent, apposite, proper.

6198₆

顆〔**Ko**〕n. clod, a lump of earth, grain, drop, droplet.

90-- 粒　　grain, drop.

顥〔**Hao**〕adj. bright.

6200₀

喇〔**La**〕n. sound of a trumpet, v. chatter, talk fast.

60-- 嘛　　lama.
-- 嘛教　　Lamaism.
68-- 叭　　trumpet, bugle.
-- 叭手　　trumpeter.
-- 叭花　　petunia, morning glory.

唎〔**Lieh**〕v. stretch the mouth horizontally.

61-- 嘴　　grin.

6201₀

吼〔**Hou**〕n. roar, v. roar, howl.

62-- 叫　　roar, howl.

6201₃

咷〔**Tao**〕v. wail.

眺〔**Tiao**〕v. gaze at, stare at, look far away.

07-- 望　　look at, gaze at, look far away.

6201₄

唾〔**To**〕n. saliva, spittle, v. spit.

00-- 棄　　cast aside, cast off.
22-- 出　　spit.
30-- 液　　saliva, slaver.
35-- 沫　　saliva, spit, spittle.

60-- 罵　　　　spit on and revile.
64-- 吐　　　　spit.

睡 〔Shui〕 *v.* sleep, doze, nod in one's chair, nap.

00-- 衣　　　　pajamas, gown.
04-- 熟　　　　sleep soundly.
10-- 不着　　　sleepless, unable to sleep.
16-- 醒　　　　wake up, awake.
27-- 鄉　　　　the land of nod.
44-- 椅　　　　sofa.
　-- 蓮　　　　pond-lily, water-lily.
50-- 車　　　　sleeper.
64-- 時　　　　bedtime.
66-- 眠　　　　sleep, sleeping.
80-- 着　　　　fall asleep, sleeping.

6201₈

瞪 〔Teng〕 *v.* gaze at, stare at.
67-- 眼　　　　glare at, stare at angrily.

6202₁

晰 〔Hsi〕 *adj.* bright, clear, perspicuous, explicit, *v.* neigh.

嘶 〔Hsi〕 *n.* the neighing of a horse.
47-- 殺　　　　din of battle.
63-- 喊　　　　roar, cry hoarsely.

6202₇

喘 〔Chuan〕 *v.* pant, gasp, breathe hard.
26-- 息　　　　*v.* gasp, pant, *adj.* out of breath.
80-- 氣　　　　gasp, pant.

6203₀

呱 〔Ku〕 *v.* sob, wail.

吆 〔Yao〕 *v.* shout, cry.
66-- 喝　　　　*n.* outcry, *v.* roar, shout.

6203₁

曛 〔Hsun〕 *n.* twilight.

6203₄

睽 〔Kuei〕 *v.* squint, separate, gaze, stare, *adj.* separated.
62-- 睽　　　　stare.

6203₆

嗤 〔Chih〕 *v.* laugh at, jeer at, scoff.
88-- 笑　　　　*n.* sneer, *v.* scoff at, laugh at.

6203₇

眨 〔Cha〕 *v.* wink, blink.

67-- 眼　　　　wink, blink, twinkle in the eye.

6204₆

嚼 〔Chu〕 *v.* chew, crunch.

6204₇

暖 〔Nuan〕 *n.* warmth, *adj.* warm, genial.

12-- 水瓶　　　thermos bottle, vacuum bottle, vacuum flask, heater.
26-- 和　　　　*adj.* warm, *adv.* warmly.
30-- 房　　　　hothouse, greenhouse.
77-- 風　　　　warm breeze.
80-- 氣　　　　heating, warm air.
　-- 氣裝置　　radiator, central heating system, heater.

曖 〔Ai〕 *adj.* obscure, clouded, dim, dark.

65-- 昧　　　　obscure, vague.
　-- 昧行爲　　scandal.
　-- 昧之事　　affair of the dark.

6204₉

呼 〔Hu〕 *v.* call, breathe out, address, speak to, cry out, yell, exclaim, exhale.

00-- 應　　　　respond.
10-- 天搶地　　cry bitterly.
27-- 名　　　　name.
47-- 聲　　　　voice, outcry.
48-- 救　　　　cry for help.
61-- 號　　　　cry, howl.
63-- 喊　　　　*n.* shout, *v.* shout, bawl, clamor, exclaim, cry.
65-- 嘯　　　　*n.* roar, *v.* roar.
67-- 嚕　　　　snoring sound.
　-- 喚　　　　call, summon.
　-- 吸　　　　*v.* breathe, respire, *n.* breath, breathing, expiration.
　-- 吸計　　　spirometer.
　-- 吸作用　　respiration.
80-- 氣　　　　exhale, expire.
88-- 籲　　　　appeal, call for.

6205₂

瞬 〔Shun〕 *v.* blink, glance, wink, twinkle.

26-- 息　　instant, flash, wink, in a flash, in a wind, in a moment, in an instant.

77-- 間　　in an instant, in a moment.

6205₇

睜〔Cheng〕v. look at angrily, open the eyes.

67-- 眼　　open the eyes.

6207₇

咄〔To〕n. angry cry, sigh, sound of surprise, v. scold loudly.

62-- 咄　　sound showing surprise or alarm.

-- 咄怪事　what a queer story! strange matter.

6209₄

睬〔Tsai〕v. mind, observe, pay attention, look, care.

6211₃

跳〔Tiao〕v. jump, leap, flee, spring, skip.

00-- 高　　high jump.

12-- 水　　dive, springboard diving.

16-- 環　　jumping through the hoop.

17-- 蚤　　flea.

-- 蚤市場　flea market.

21-- 上　　jump up.

24-- 動　　jump, beat, throb.

34-- 遠　　broad jump, long jump.

37-- 過　　overleap, leap over.

41-- 板　　gangplank, springboard, diving board.

47-- 欄　　hurdle.

-- 欄賽跑　hurdle race.

67-- 踴　　skip.

-- 躍　　jump, leap, hop, dance, spring.

80-- 舞　　dancing, dance.

-- 舞會　　dancing party.

-- 傘　　n. parachute, v. bail out, parachute.

-- 塔　　parachute tower.

6211₄

踵〔Chung〕n. heel, v. follow, reach.

6211₆

躐〔Lieh〕v. tread, overstep.

6211₈

蹬〔Teng〕v. tread, step.

6212₇

踹〔Chuai〕v. tread, stamp, trample.

蹻〔Chiao〕n. sandals, v. lift the foot high.

蹦〔Peng〕v. skip, caper, jump, leap.

62-- 跳　　skip, leap, jump.

6213₄

蹊〔Hsi〕n. footpath, path, pathway.

21-- 徑　　footpath, pathway.

64-- 蹺　　queer, strange.

蹼〔Po〕n. web, webs on the feet of a water fowl.

60-- 足　　web feet.

6216₃

踏〔Ta〕v. stamp, tread, tread upon, trample.

30-- 實　　solid, sound.

41-- 板　　tread, treadle, pedal.

44-- 勘　　explore, survey, investigate.

77-- 腳石　stepping-stone.

6217₇

蹈〔Tao〕v. tread, trample, step on, stamp, tramp.

6218₁

蹤〔Tsung〕n. trace, footprint.

60-- 跡　　trace, track, vestige.

6218₆

躓〔Chih〕v. fall, obstruct.

6219₄

躒〔Li〕v. move, jump, step on, spring.

踩〔Tsai〕v. tramp, tread upon, trample.

12-- 水　　tread water.

6220₀

剔〔Ti〕v. reject, pick from, pick out.

22-- 出　　reject, pick out.

77-- 牙　　pick the teeth.

78-- 除　n. disallowance, rejection, v. eliminate, charge off, peck out.

6233₉

懸 〔 Hsuan 〕 v. hang, suspend, impend.

22-- 崖　precipice, overhanging cliffs.
30-- 空　suspended.
53-- 掛　hang up, suspend.
80-- 念　anxiety, concernment.

6237₂

黜 〔 Cho 〕 v. degrade, dismiss, reject, get rid of.

27-- 免　remove from office.
37-- 退　dismiss.

6240₀

別 〔 Pieh 〕 v. distinguish, separate, divide, part, leave, differ, do not, adj. other, different.

00-- 離　n. departure, parting, v. depart.
21-- 處　another place, elsewhere, everywhere.
22-- 出心裁　create something new.
-- 後　after parting.
24-- 動隊　detached unit.
25-- 生枝節　have new complications.
27-- 名　nickname, alias.
-- 墅　villa.
28-- 緻　particular, unusual.
30-- 字連篇　there are a lot of characters wrongly written.
-- 客氣　don't mention it!
40-- 有新聞　have heard of another story.
-- 有天地　different world.
-- 有依據　it is based on another source.
-- 有洞天　hidden but beautiful spot, world all its own.
-- 有風味　have a particular flavor.
-- 有用心　have an axe to grind, have

an ulterior motive.
-- 有所遇　have a lover outside.
44-- 惹麻煩　let sleeping dogs lie.
-- 樹一幟　hoist separately one's banner, become independent.
60-- 具心裁　creative.
-- 具慧心　have a special insight or understanding.
61-- 號　alias, nickname.
67-- 墅　villa.
77-- 開生面　break fresh ground, open up a fresh outlook.
80-- 無出路　have no other way out.
-- 無他法　there are no other ways.
-- 無他圖　have no ulterior motive or different plan.
-- 無所有　have no other possessions.
84-- 針　pin, safety-pin.
88-- 管它　let it alone.
-- 管閒事　don't have your finger in the pie.

6280₀

則 〔 Tse 〕 n. rule, law, regulation, pattern, model, conj. then, so, therefore.

6283₇

貶 〔 Pien 〕 v. bring down, degrade, take down, level down, demote, blame, censure, reduce, lower.

07-- 詞　expression of censure.
21-- 價　reduce, devalue.
-- 價出售　sell at a reduced price.
22-- 低　minimize, degrade, lower.
24-- 值　n. devaluation, depreciation, v. depreciate, devaluate.
57-- 抑　debase.
67-- 黜　degradation.
71-- 辱　bring down.

6292₂

影 〔 Ying 〕 n. shadow, image.

17-- 子　shadow.
-- 子內閣　shadow cabinet.
22-- 片　films, motion pictures.
23-- 戲　motion picture.

-- 戲院	cinema, movie theater.
-- 戲劇本	film play.
24-- 射	insinuate, hint at.
-- 射商標	counterfeit trademarks.
27-- 像	shadow.
-- 像藝術	art of photo-taking.
-- 響	*n.* effect, influence, *v.* affect, influence, move, have influence.
40-- 壇故事	stories of the movie circle.
77-- 印	photostat, photogravure, photocopy.
-- 印本	photocopy.
-- 印機	photocopier.

6299₃

縣〔Hsien〕*n.* district.

80-- 會	district assembly.
71-- 長	magistrate.

6301₀

吮〔Yen〕*v.* suck, lick.

22-- 乳	suck milk (or the breast).

6301₄

咤〔Cha〕*v.* hoot at, upbraid, shout with anger.

6301₆

喧〔Hsuan〕*n.* clamor, noise, uproar, brawl, *v.* brawl, clamor, *adj.* warm, genial.

60-- 嚷	*v.* clamor, make a hullabaloo, *adj.* noisy.
64-- 嘩	*n.* clamor, noisy talk, noise, *v.* din.
66-- 噪	clamorous.
77-- 鬧	quarreling, uproar, noisy quarrel.

6302₇

哺〔Pu〕*v.* feed.

00-- 育	nurture, nurse.
22-- 乳	suckle, nurse.
-- 乳動物	mammal.
-- 乳室	nursing room.
80-- 養	feed.

6303₂

咏=詠 0363₂

6303₄

吠〔Fei〕*v.* bark, yelp, cry.

甽〔Chuan〕*n.* small drain between fields.

唉〔Ai〕*interj.* ah! oh!

47-- 聲嘆氣	give deploring interjections and sighs.

6304₇

唆〔So〕*v.* incite, urge, set on.

25-- 使	incite, instigate.
-- 使犯法	instigate someone to commit an offence.
28-- 慫	enrage, provoke.
-- 慫罷工	provoke a strike.
50-- 事弄非	make mischief and play foul.

6305₀

哦〔E〕*interj.* hum ! o! oh! indeed!

喊〔Han〕*v.* cry, call, call aloud, light up the voice, shout.

00-- 高價	rule high.
22-- 低價	rule low.

眸〔Mo〕*n.* pupil, pupil of the eye.

17-- 子	pupil of the eye, eyes.

6306₁

嘻〔Hay〕*interj.* hey!

瞎〔Hsia〕*adj.* blind, reckless, rash, *adv.* blindly.

08-- 說	*n.* nonsense, *v.* lie, talk recklessly.
10-- 弄	mishandle, toy with.
17-- 子	blind man, blind person.
46-- 想	*n.* sheer delusion, *v.* daydream.
51-- 扯	talk nonsense.
60-- 買	buy a pig in a poke.
67-- 吹	puff, brag.
77-- 鬧	make nonsense, create a disturbance.

6311₄

蹴〔Tsu〕*v.* kick, stamp.

6312₇

蹁〔Pien〕*v.* walk lamely.

6313₂

跟 〔**Lang**〕 v. hop, limp.
68-- 蹌　　　stumble.

6314₇
跋 〔**Pa**〕 n. heel, postscript, v. travel, walk.
31-- 涉　　　climb and wade, travel afar, travel over land and water.
72-- 扈　　　domineering.

6315₀
戡 〔**Chi**〕 v. draw tight.

6315₃
踐 〔**Chien**〕 v. walk, step, tread on, tread upon, trample on, fulfill.
27-- 約　　　keep one's promise, fulfill one's promise.
62-- 踏　　　trample, tramp, tread upon.
66-- 言　　　confirm one's word, keep one's word, keep one's promise.

6319₁
踪=蹤 6218₁

6333₄
默 〔**Mo**〕 adj. silent, still, secret, quiet, taciturn.
00-- 哀　　　mourn in silence.
04-- 讀　　　silent reading.
07-- 認　　　n. acquiescence, tacit consent, tacit approval, v. acquiesce.
   -- 記　　　learn by heart.
08-- 許　　　n. connivance, tacit permission, tacit consent, implicit consent, v. connive, acquiesce in.
10-- 示　　　allude, imply, indicate in silence.
23-- 然　　　speechless, silent.
30-- 寫　　　n. dictation, v. write from memory.
34-- 禱　　　silent prayer.
46-- 想　　　n. meditation, v. speculate, contemplate, meditate, adj. meditative.
57-- 契　　　tacit understanding, tacit agreement, implicit agree-ment.
88-- 算　　　mental arithmetic.

6355₀
戰 〔**Chan**〕 n. war, battle, fight, v. fight, bear arms against, take arms.
10-- 死　　　death from action.
   -- 雲　　　war cloud.
14-- 功　　　military achievement.
20-- 爭　　　war, battle, hostility, fighting.
21-- 術　　　tactics, art of war.
   -- 術家　　tactician, strategist.
22-- 後　　　post-war.
   -- 後問題　post-war problem.
   -- 利品　　prize of war, spoils of war.
25-- 債　　　war bonds, war debts.
26-- 線　　　war zone, battle front, battle line.
27-- 役　　　campaign.
   -- 爭損害　war damage.
   -- 爭賠款　war indemnity, war reparation.
   -- 爭險 (兵險) war risk, war risk insurance.
28-- 艦　　　battleship, man of war.
34-- 法　　　tactical method.
35-- 神　　　war god.
40-- 士　　　warrior, fighter.
   -- 壕　　　trench, rifle pit.
44-- 地郵政　war post.
46-- 場　　　battle field, battle zone, theater of war.
50-- 車　　　chariot, tank.
   -- 史　　　military history.
   -- 事　　　warfare.
64-- 時　　　wartime.
   -- 時新聞　war news.
   -- 時配給　war rationing.
   -- 時保險　war risk insurance.
   -- 時經濟　economics of wartime.
   -- 時編制　war establishment.
   -- 時法令　laws of war.
   -- 時內閣　war cabinet.
   -- 時禁制品　contraband of war.
   -- 時公債　war loan, war bond.
   -- 時節約儲蓄券 war saving certificate.

67-- 略	stratagem.
68-- 敗	lost a battle.
71-- 區	war area.
-- 馬	charger.
77-- 鬭	*n.* war, combat, *v.* fight.
-- 鬭計劃	plan for the attack.
-- 鬭綱要	battle principle.
-- 鬭員	fighter, combatant.
-- 鬭區域	battle zone, dangerous space.
-- 鬭機	battle plane, pursuit plane.
79-- 勝	*n.* victory, *v.* gain the battle.
91-- 慄	shake, tremble, shiver.

6363₄
獸〔Shou〕*n.* animals, beasts.

00-- 疫	animal plague.
17-- 羣	herd, flock.
21-- 行	brutality, beastly act.
30-- 穴	den, lair.
40-- 力車	animal-drawn cart.
-- 皮	animal hide, animal skin.
44-- 革	hide.
77-- 醫	veterinarian.
-- 醫學	veterinary science.
87-- 慾	animal passion, animal appetite.
91-- 類	animals, beasts, brutes.
95-- 性	beastliness, brutishness, bestiality, brutality.

6380₄
吠〔Fei〕*v.* bark (said of a dog).

| 47-- 聲 | bark. |

6382₁
貯〔Chu〕*v.* store up, hoard.

12-- 水池	reservoir.
24-- 備金	reserve.
44-- 藏	*n.* storage, deposit, *v.* reserve, conserve, deposit, store up, hoard.
-- 藏所	depository, storage room.
-- 藏室	storeroom.
-- 蓄	save, lay up, store up, hoard.
-- 蓄銀行	savings bank.
96-- 糧	reserve grains.

6384₀
賦〔Fu〕*n.* land tax, natural gift, natural endowment, rhymed prose, poem. *v.* give, exact, describe, compose (poems).

04-- 詩	compose a poem.
17-- 予	give.
28-- 稅	*n.* taxes, *v.* tax, impost, charges.
-- 稅收入	tax revenue.
77-- 閒	disengaged, retired, unemployed.
95-- 性	nature, disposition.

6384₂
賻〔Fu〕*n.* funeral gift.

6385₀
賊〔Tsei〕*n.* thief, robber, bandit, rebel, burglar, *v.* harm, *adj.* cunning, crafty.

22-- 巢	nest, robbers' den.
63-- 贓	spoils, booty, stolen goods.
95-- 性	thievish propensity.

贓〔Tsang〕*n.* stolen goods, booty, spoils, bribes.

27-- 物	spoils, booty, stolen goods.
30-- 官	corrupt official.
60-- 品	plunder, loot, booty.

6385₃
賤〔Chien〕*v.* slight, *adj.* mean, low, poor, cheap, base, inexpensive.

21-- 價	low-prices, cheap.
-- 價拋售	go for a song.
24-- 貨	inferior goods, cheap goods.
40-- 內	my wife.
-- 賣 (虧本出售)	cheap sale, sacrifice, sell cheap.
80-- 人	miserable person.

6386₀
貽〔I〕*v.* give, present, hand down, bequeath.

06-- 誤	mislead, delay.
30-- 害	cause evil or injury.
88-- 笑	become a laughing stock.

6400₀
吋〔Tsuen〕*n.* inch.

叫 〔Chiao〕 v. call, shout, cry out, shriek.
16-- 醒　　　awake.
21-- 價　　　bid.
24-- 化　　　beg.
-- 化子　　　beggar.
40-- 賣　　　peddle.
44-- 苦　　　complain.
-- 苦連天　　complain a lot about hardships.
47-- 好　　　n. applause, v. applaud.
-- 聲　　　call, cry.
60-- 嚷　　　shout, raise a hue and cry.
61-- 號電話　station-to-station call.
63-- 喊　　　cry, shout.
66-- 囂　　　vociferate, clamor.
80-- 人電話　person-to-person call, personal call.

咐 〔Fu〕 v. order, instruct, bid, enjoin.
6401₀

叱 〔Chih〕 v. scold, hoot at, revile.
50-- 責　　　rate, blame, reproach.
63-- 咤風雲　lord it over the world.
66-- 喝無理　bawl at one for being rude.

吐 〔Tu〕 v. vomit, spit out, utter, spew.
00-- 痰　　　spit, spit phlegm.
10-- 露　　　utter, express, disclose, reveal, confide.
-- 露實情　reveal the fact.
22-- 出　　　spit, cast forth.
-- 絲　　　(said of a silkworm) to spin, spinning.
27-- 血　　　spit blood, vomit blood.
33-- 瀉　　　vomit and purge.
44-- 花　　　blossom.
62-- 唾沫　spit, eject saliva.
80-- 氣揚眉　breathe out the air and smooth down one's frown — feel proud.

6401₁

曉 〔Hsiao〕 n. morning, dawn, v. understand, comprehend, know, perceive, tell, explain, adj. bright, light.
26-- 得　　　understand, comprehend, know.
67-- 明　　　dawn.

6401₂

眈 〔Tan〕 v. be addicted to (pleasure), look downward.
64-- 眈　　　look fiercely.

6401₄

睦 〔Mu〕 n. in concord, adj. kind, affectionate, harmonious, amiable, friendly, conciliated.
97-- 鄰　　　be on good terms with neighbors.
-- 鄰政策　policy of promoting peace with neighboring states.

哇 〔Wa〕 n. sound of a child's crying. v. vomit.
64-- 哇大哭　cry very loudly.
-- 哇聲　　squeal, croak.
-- 哇學語　a child is learning to talk.

畦 〔Shi〕 n. division of the field, plot of land.

6401₇

瞌 〔Ko〕 v. doze off, nod, drowse.
62-- 睡　　　drowse, nod, doze off.

6401₈

噎 〔Yeh〕 n. choking, v. be choked with food, hiccough.
20-- 住　　　choked with food.

6402₁

畸 〔Chi〕 adj. odd, strange.
13-- 形　　　deformity, malformation.
-- 形發展　uneven development.

6402₇

呐 〔Na〕 v. stammer, stutter, shout.
64-- 呐　　　stammer.
67-- 喊　　　v. yell, shout, clamor, n. rattle cry.

唏 〔Hsi〕 n. lamentation.

喃 〔Nan〕 v. chatter, gabble, murmur.
64-- 喃自語　mutter, murmur to oneself.

瞞 〔Man〕 v. deceive, cheat, alarm, conceal, conceal, hoodwink, adj. dull, indistinct.
37-- 過　　　deceive successfully.
64-- 哄=瞞騙
73-- 騙　　　cheat, deceive, palm on.

80-- 着　　conceal, hoodwink.

6403₁

嚇〔Hsia〕v. threaten, scare, alarm terrify, terrify, intimidate, frighten.

08-- 詐　　extort by threats, threaten, frighten and extort.
10-- 一跳　　startle.
-- 死　　v. be frightened to death, adj. greatly terrified.
-- 不倒　　not to be cowed.
40-- 壞　　astound, shock.
-- 走　　frightened away.
60-- 呆　　be struck dumb, be stunned.
61-- 唬　　terrify, frighten, scare.
67-- 跑　　scare away, be frightened off.
72-- 昏　　frightened out of wits.
77-- 阻　　deter.
80-- 人　　threaten, terrify, take away one's breath, scare people, bluff people.

嚥〔Yen〕v. swallow, gulp.

10-- 下　　swallow down.

囈〔I〕n. talking in one's sleep.

01-- 語　　ravings, mutterings.

6403₂

矇〔Meng〕n. the dim light before down.

矇〔Meng〕adj. blind, ignorant, unlearned.

17-- 子　　blind man.

6403₄

嘆〔Tan〕v. moan, praise, applaud, sigh, regret, mourn.

07-- 詞　　interjection (in grammar).
26-- 息　　sigh, regret, moan.
80-- 羨　　admire.
-- 氣　　sigh.
90-- 賞　　admiration.
94-- 惜　　pity, regret.

6404₀

哎〔Ai〕n. interjection of surprise — oh, alas.

61-- 呀　　oh, oh! — what a surprise!

6404₁

時〔Shih〕n. time, season, hour, period, occasion, opportunity, epoch, adj. proper, timely, adv. always, constantly, often.

00-- 疫　　plague, periodical epidemics.
01-- 評　　editorial.
02-- 刻　　n. hour, adv. constantly.
08-- 效　　effectiveness for a given period of time.
10-- 而　　sometimes.
21-- 價 (市價)　　current price, market value, current ruling price, running price.
-- 價不同　　current prices vary.
23-- 代　　age, day, date, era, period, time, generation.
-- 代精神　　spirit of the age.
-- 代思潮　　current trend of thought.
24-- 裝模特　　fashion model.
28-- 鮮貨　　fresh and easily perishable goods.
37-- 運　　luck.
-- 運亨通　　be lucky.
-- 運不佳　　be at a low ebb in luck.
-- 運盛衰　　rise and fall of fortune.
42-- 機　　opportunity, chance, proper time, favorable time.
-- 機不佳　　the times are unfavorable for the enterprise.
-- 機已至　　the time has come.
-- 機成熟　　the time is propitious.
43-- 式　　mode.
44-- 勢　　state of affairs, present circumstance, situation.
47-- 期　　date, age, time, period, stage.
48-- 樣　　fashionable, stylish.
50-- 事　　current affairs, current events.
-- 事評論　　comments on current events.
-- 事問題　　problems of current events.
64-- 時　　often, always, now and then, from time to time.
71-- 辰　　hour.
-- 辰鐘　　watch.

72-- 髦 | *n.* fashion, *adj.* fashionable.
-- 髦人物 | man of fashion.
77-- 間 | time, hour, day.
-- 間表 | timetable, schedule.
-- 間匆迫 | be in a rush.
-- 間短促 | be pressed for time.
-- 間管理 | time management.
-- 局=事勢 |
-- 局平靖 | time of peace.
-- 限 | deadline, time limit, time deadline, limit of time.
80-- 差 | time difference, time differential, equation of time.
-- 令 | seasons.
-- 令風 | monsoon.
-- 鐘 | clock.
84-- 針 | hour hand of a clock or a watch.
88-- 節 | occasion, time.
-- 節來到 | the time has come.
90-- 常=時時 | frequently, often, always.
-- 光流逝 | time slips by.

6404₁

疇 〔 Chou 〕 *n.* field.

6404₇

哮 〔 Hsiao 〕 *v.* howl, bellow, scream, roar, gasp, pant.
62-- 喘 | asthma.

吱 〔 Tzu 〕 *n.* squeaky sound.
64-- 吱 | chirp.

6405₄

嘩 〔 Hua 〕 *n.* noise, clamor, tumult.
66-- 噪 | wrangle, uproar.

6406₀

咕 〔 Ku 〕 *v.* mutter, murmur, *adj.* speaking indistinctly.
65-- 噥 | mutter, utter indistinctly.

睹 〔 Tu 〕 *v.* see, look, observe, perceive, look at.
27-- 物思人 | think of a person as one sees the thing he has left behind.

瞄 〔 Miao 〕 *v.* take aim, look at.
30-- 準 | aim at, point, take aim.
-- 準點 | aiming point.

-- 準器 | gun sight.
-- 準射擊 | take aim and fire.

6406₁

嗜 〔 Shih 〕 *v.* relish, take delight in, indulge in, have an appetite, be fond of.
27-- 色 | be addicted to sensuality.
31-- 酒 | fond of wine.
-- 酒好色 | being addicted to drinking and lewdness.
47-- 好 | *n.* hobby, addiction, *v.* be fond of, be addicted of.
-- 殺 | bloody, bloodstained.
-- 殺成性 | be habitually fond of killing.
64-- 賭 | fond of gambling.
87-- 慾 | appetite, liking.

嗒 〔 Ta 〕 *adj.* disappointed, dejected, depressed.
23-- 然 | despondent.
40-- 喪 | downcast, depressed.

6406₅

嘻 〔 Hsi 〕 *n.* giggle, cackling, laugh.
40-- 皮笑臉 | giggling.
88-- 笑 | chuckle, smirk.

6408₁

哄 〔 Hung 〕 *v.* cheat, trick, deceive, tempt, beguile, make a roaring sound (said of a crowd).
02-- 誘 | tempt, beguile.
10-- 弄 | make a fool of.
24-- 動 | prevail on, delude into, stir, cause an uproar.
-- 動一時 | cause a sensation.
25-- 傳 | noise abroad.
58-- 抬 | bid up, drive up, whoop up.
-- 抬價格 | price jacking, price pushing, whoop up the price.
-- 抬物價 | push up price, jack up prices, bull the market, force up prices.
73-- 騙 | deceive, mislead, hoax, cheat.
88-- 笑 | burst into laughter.
90-- 堂大笑 | the audience roared in laughter.

嗔 〔 Chen 〕 *v.* be angry at, stare at scornfully.

嚏 〔**Ti**〕*v.* sneeze.

6408_6

噴 〔**Pen**〕*v.* puff, spurt, sneeze, snort.

10-- 霧	*n.* atomization, *v.* atomize.
-- 霧器	sprayer, atomizer.
12-- 水	jet, spurt water.
-- 水泉	fountain.
-- 水池	fountain.
20-- 香	diffuse fragrance.
22-- 出	spurt out, jet.
24-- 射	jet.
-- 射器	ejector.
-- 射飛機	jet plane.
26-- 泉	fountain, geyser.
34-- 漆	spray-paint.
40-- 壺	sprinkler, watering pot (or can).
64-- 嚏	*n.* sneeze, *v.* sneeze.
80-- 氣	snort, puff.
-- 氣發動機	turbojet, jet engine.
-- 氣式飛機	jet plane.
88-- 筒	flame thrower.

6409_0

咻 〔**Hsiu**〕*v.* jeer.

6409_1

噤 〔**Chin**〕*v.* keep the mouth shut, *adj.* silent.

6409_3

嗦 〔**Suo**〕*v.* quiver, tremble, shiver.

6409_4

喋 〔**Tieh**〕*v.* talk too much, *adj.* loquacious.

27-- 血沙場	let one's blood flow on the battlefield.
64-- 喋	*v.* babble, prate, *adj.* talktive, loquacious.
-- 喋不休	talk one's head off.

6409_6

瞭 〔**Liao**〕*n.* clearness of sight, *v.* see, be clear, overlook from a higher place, *adj.* sharp-eyed.

00-- 亮	loud and clear.
07-- 望	take a distant view, overlook, look at from afar.
-- 望台	watching tower, observation tower.
23-- 然	clearly, plainly.

6409_8

睞 〔**Lai**〕*v.* glance at, peep at.

6410_0

跗 〔**Fu**〕*n.* the top part of the foot.

6411_1

跣 〔**Hsien**〕*v.* walk with bare foot.

蹺 〔**Chao**〕*v.* raise the foot, lift the foot high.

| 64-- 蹺板 | seesaw, teeterboard. |
| 77-- 腳 | cross the legs. |

6412_7

蹣 〔**Man**〕*v.* walk lamely, pass over, get over, jump, limp,

| 64-- 跚 | walk lamely, stagger, dodder. |

跨 〔**Kua**〕*v.* bestride, ride, straddle, span, extend over.

00-- 度	span.
21-- 步	step over, straddle.
37-- 過	stride, bestride, step over.
43-- 越	bestride, pass over.
60-- 國的	transnational.
-- 國公司	transnational corporation, multinational corps, multinational enterprise.

躝 〔**Lan**〕*v.* tread, run over, ravage.

6414_1

躊 〔**Chou**〕*v.* hesitate, waver, *adj.* irresolute, hesitating.

| 64-- 躇 | hesitate. |
| -- 躇不決 | hesitate and be undecided. |

6414_7

跛 〔**Pi**〕*adj.* lame, crippled.

17-- 子	cripple.
21-- 行	limp, hobble.
60-- 足	lame foot.

6419_4

蹀 〔**Tieh**〕*v.* stamp, tread.

6432_7

黝 〔**Yu**〕*adj.* black, dark.

| 25-- 牲祀祖 | use black cattle for sacrifice |

	to ancestors.
50-- 青	bluish black.
60-- 黑	swarthy, pitchy.

6436₁

黠〔Hsia〕*adj.* clever, cunning, smart, crafty, artful.

86-- 智	clever, smart, crafty.

6438₆

黷〔Tu〕*v.* annoy, insult, defile, corrupt, tarnish, indulge in, abuse.

13-- 武	disposed on war, militant.
-- 武主義	militarism.
-- 武窮兵	abuse military power, be militaristic.

6480₀

財〔Tsai〕*n.* money, wealth, property, riches.

00-- 主	millionaire, rich person.
-- 產	property, estate, assets, fortune, havings, belongings, property, possessions.
-- 產繼承	inheritance of property.
-- 產估計	property valuation.
-- 產保險	insurance of property, property insurance.
-- 產盤存	property inventory.
-- 產淨值	net worth.
-- 產收入	property income, funded income.
-- 產稅	property tax, estate duty, tax on property.
-- 產查封	attachment of property.
-- 產共有人	tenant in common.
-- 產權	proprietary, property right.
-- 產轉讓	transfer of property.
-- 產監護人	guardian of estate.
-- 產分配	distribution of an estate, distribution of assets, distribution of property.
-- 產管理人	receiver.
-- 庫	treasury.
17-- 務	financial affairs.
-- 務官	financial agent.
-- 務主任	chief of finance, financial officer.
-- 務交易	financial transaction.
-- 務計畫	financial planning.
-- 務調查	financial investigation.
-- 務預算	financial budget.
-- 務委員會	financial committee.
-- 務比較	financial comparison.
-- 務經理	financial management, funds management.
-- 務經營	financial operation.
-- 務制度	fiscal system.
-- 務代理人	finance agent, fiscal agent.
-- 務秘書	financial secretary.
-- 務審計	financial audit.
-- 務實力	fiscal solvency.
-- 務科目	account of finance.
-- 務總經理	chief financial officer.
-- 務收支	financial revenue receipts and expenditure.
-- 務決策	financial decision.
-- 務董事	finance director.
-- 務報告	financial report, financial statement.
-- 務檢查	inspection of accounts.
-- 務費用	financial expenses, finance charge.
-- 務分析	financial analysis.
-- 務公司	finance company.
-- 務會計	financial accounting.
-- 務管理	financial management.
-- 務管理制度	financial control system.
18-- 政	finance.
-- 政家	financier.
-- 政部	Ministry of Finance.
-- 政部長	minister of finance.
-- 政政策	financial policy.
-- 政狀態	financial standing.
-- 政補貼	financial subsidies, financial allowance, grant-in-aid.
-- 政赤字	financial deficit.
-- 政措施	fiscal action, fiscal measures.
21-- 經部門	economic and financial section.
-- 經情況	pecuniary condition.
27-- 物	goods and chattels.
30-- 富	wealth, treasury, riches, money, fortune.
-- 富分配	distribution of wealth.

-- 富稅	wealth tax, worth tax.	
-- 寶	treasures, jewels.	
31-- 源	resources of wealth, financial resources, economic resources, fiscal resources, source of income, source of revenue.	
-- 源不足	shortage of financial resources.	
35-- 神	Mammon, God of wealth.	
40-- 力	financial ability, financial power, financial strength, purse, strings.	
-- 力狀況	financial status.	
44-- 權	financial power.	
60-- 團	financial group, consortium, finance corps.	
77-- 閥	plutocrat.	

6480₄
韙 〔Wei〕 *adj.* right, proper, that which is right.

6482₇
勛=勳 2432₇

賄 〔Hui〕 *n.* wealth, riches, *v.* bribe.

67-- 賂	heavy eyes, bribe, bribery, corrupt practice.
-- 賂行爲	corrupt transaction.
-- 賂金	golden key, glove money.

6486₄
賭 〔Tu〕 *v.* gamble, wager, bet, lay a wager, compete, swear.

24-- 徒	gambler.
30-- 賽	bet.
36-- 注	stakes at gambling.
43-- 博	*n.* gambling, *v.* gamble, play.
-- 博者	gambler.
46-- 場	gaming house, gambling house, house of ill fame.
-- 棍	gambler.
66-- 咒	swear.
77-- 具	gambling implements.
80-- 金	bet, stales.

6488₆
贖 〔Shu〕 *v.* ransom, redeem, pay a fine, atone for, expiate.

10-- 票	withdraw a bill, retire a bill, take up bill.
21-- 價	ransom price.
27-- 身	ransom oneself, redeem oneself.
60-- 回	*n.* retirement, redemption, *v.* call, redeem, ransom, retire.
-- 回者	redeemer.
-- 罪	*n.* atonement, redemption, *v.* expiate, redeem from sin, atone for a crime, expiate a crime.
-- 買	ransom, redeem, buy out.
66-- 單	retire documents, retire shipping documents.
80-- 金	ransom (money).
90-- 當	redeem a pledge.

6500₀
畊=耕 5590₀

6500₆
呻 〔Shen〕 *v.* moan, groan, bewail.

68-- 吟	moan, groan.

6501₇
旽 〔Tun〕 *n.* nap, doze.

67-- 眼	heavy eyes.

6502₇
睛 〔Ching〕 *n.* clear sky, *adj.* fine, fair, sunny.

10-- 天	fine day, fair day, fair weather, glorious day.
-- 雨表	barometer.
-- 雨無阻	do something rain or shine.
37-- 朗	*n.* clearness, *adj.* clear, fine.
67-- 明	bright and clear.

睛 〔Ching〕 *n.* pupil of the eye, eyeball.

嘯 〔Hsiao〕 *v.* whistle, shout in a sustained voice.

47-- 聲	whistling sound.
67-- 喚	roar.

6503₀
映 〔Yin〕 *n.* reflection, *v.* shine, reflect.

67-- 眼	*n.* dazzle, *adj.* dazzling.

6503₂

咦 〔Yi〕(an interjection of surprise) eh! oh!

6504₄

嘍 〔Lou〕 *n.* crying of a bird.

66-- 囉　minor bandits, stooges of a bandit.

6506₆

嘈 〔Tsao〕 *n.* noise, hubbub, clamor, uproar, din, continuous outcry, *adj.* noisy, clamorous.

00-- 雜　noisy and confused.
77-- 鬧　noisy, clamorous.

6507₇

嘒 〔Hui〕 *n.* little voice.

6508₁

睫 〔Chieh〕 *n.* eyelashes.

20-- 毛　eyelashes.

6508₆

嘖 〔Tse〕 *n.* noise, interjection of admiration, *v.* argue, *adj.* plenty.

40-- 有煩言　there are complaints all around.
65-- 嘖　sound of praise.

6509₀

味 〔Wei〕 *n.* taste, savor, flavor, smell, delicacy.

38-- 道　taste, odor, savor.
77-- 覺　sense of taste.
-- 覺器官　organ of taste.
-- 兒　smell, flavor, taste.
80-- 美　delicious.
--美可口　fine flavor and palatable.
95-- 精　flavor essence, gourmet powder.

眛 〔Mei〕 *adj.* color-blind.

6509₃

嗉 〔Su〕 *n.* crop of a bird.

6513₀

跌 〔Tieh〕 *v.* stumble, slip, fall, stamp.

10-- 下　fall down.

20-- 停板 (交易所) limit down.
21-- 價　*n.* fall in price, falling price, price reduction, down in price, depreciation, *v.* depreciate.
22-- 倒　tumble.
-- 後回升　rally.
44-- 落　drop down, recede, drop.
60-- 跤　stumble, fall.
77-- 風　bearish tone, sagging tendency.

6518₆

蹟=跡 6013₀

6581₇

贐 〔Chin〕 *n.* parting gift.

6584₇

購 〔Kou〕 *v.* buy, purchase.

24-- 貨　purchase merchandise, purchase commodity.
-- 貨價格　purchase price.
-- 貨代理商　purchasing agent (buyer).
-- 貨佣金　buy commission, buying commission.
-- 貨成本　purchase cost, cost of goods purchased.
-- 貨轉銷　buying for resale.
-- 貨合同　contract of purchase, purchase contract, purchase note.
27-- 物　go shopping, shopping.
-- 物中心　shopping center.
-- 物單　shopping list, order form.
28-- 併　purchase and take over an enterprise.
60-- 置價格　acquisition price.
-- 置日期　date of acquisition.
-- 買　buy, purchase.
-- 買預算　purchasing budget.
-- 買集團　purchase group.
-- 買價　buying price, purchase price, acquisition price.
-- 買力　purchasing power, purchase power, buying power, pur-

		chasing capacity.
-- 買者		purchaser.
66-- 單		buying order.
80-- 入		buying-in.
-- 入價值		purchased value.
-- 入成本		buying cost.
89-- 銷		purchase and sale, buying and selling.
94-- 料		buy material.

6600₀

咽 〔**Yen**〕*n.* throat, pharynx, gullet, *v.* swallow, gulp.

67-- 喉	gullet, throat, red lane.
-- 喉痛	angina, sore throat.

咖 〔**Ka**〕*n.* sound element.

61-- 啡	coffee.
-- 啡店	cafe, coffee house (shop).
-- 啡壺	coffee pot.
66-- 哩	curry.
-- 哩粉	curry-powder.

咱 〔**Tsa**〕*pron.* I, me.

27-- 們	we, us.

睏 〔**Kuen**〕*v.* sleep.

啪 〔**Pa**〕*n.* cracking sound.

51-- 打聲	plunk.

6601₁

呪 〔**Chou**〕*v.* curse, imprecate, swear, take an oath.

01-- 語	curses, imprecation.
60-- 罵	curse, damn, swear at.

6601₄

哩 〔**Li**〕*n.* mile, *v.* speak indistinctly.

囉 〔**Lo**〕*n.* talkative, *v.* chatter.

63-- 嗦	verbose, wordy.

6602₇

喝 〔**He**〕*v.* drink, sip, shout, call aloud.

10-- 醉	get drunk.
-- 西北風	have nothing to eat.
12-- 水	drink water.
22-- 彩	*n.* applause, *v.* cheer, applaud, acclaim.
30-- 完	drink up.
31-- 酒	drink wine.
36-- 湯	take soup.
44-- 茶	drink tea, take tea.
80-- 令	shout an order.

喟 〔**Yi**〕*n.* the mouth of a fish turning up.

喟 〔**Kuei**〕*v.* sigh.

6603₂

喂 = **餵** 8673₂

曝 〔**Pu**〕*v.* sun, rake air, expose to the sun, bask.

90-- 光	exposure (in photography).
-- 光表	photometer, exposure meter.

6603₃

嗯 〔**Ng**〕*n.* nasal sound responding to a call.

6603₄

嗅 〔**Hsiu**〕*v.* smell, nose, scent.

22-- 出	nose, smell.
65-- 味	smell, scent.
77-- 覺	olfactory, smelling sense, sense of smell.

6604₀

啤 〔**Pi**〕*n.* sound element.

31-- 酒	beer, ale.
-- 酒店	beer house.

6604₃

嗥 〔**Hao**〕*v.* howl, roar, growl.

67-- 啕大哭	bawl, wail aloud.

6605₀

呷 〔**Hsia**〕*v.* sip, drink.

31-- 酒	sip wine.

6606₀

唱 〔**Chang**〕*v.* sing, lead, go before, carol.

00-- 高調	make high sounding.
17-- 歌	*n.* singing, *v.* sing, carol.
22-- 片	phonograph record, record.
42-- 機	gramophone, phonograph.
71-- 反調	harp on a discordant tune, sing a different tune.

6606₄

曙 〔**Shu**〕*n.* dawn, daybreak, light of

the rising sun.
27-- 色　　　　light at dawn.
90-- 光　　　　twilight, light at dawn.

6609₄

噪 〔Tsao〕 *n.* chirping of birds, hubbub, din, *v.* chirp, clamor.
00-- 音　　　　unpleasant noise.

6610₀

跏 〔Chia〕 *v.* sit.

踟 〔Chih〕 *n.* hesitating, *v.* hesitate.
61-- 躕　　　　hesitating, irresolute.
-- 躕不前　　hesitate and stop advancing.

6612₇

踢 〔Ti〕 *v.* kick, make a hell, spurn.
13-- 球　　　　play football.
22-- 出去　　　kick out.
25-- 子　　　　kick the shuttlecock.
77-- 開　　　　spurn, kick out of the way.

蹋 〔Ta〕 *v.* tread on, stamp, waste, ravage.

躅 〔Chu〕 *v.* walk slowly.

6618₁

踶 〔Ti〕 *n.* the foot of a quadruped, *v.* kick, step.

6619₄

踝 〔Huai〕 *n.* ankle.
77-- 骨　　　　anklebone.

躁 〔Tsao〕 *adj.* hasty, rash, fierce, fiery, quick-tempered, restless.
47-- 急　　　　hasty, quick-tempered, impatient, passionate.

6621₄

瞿 〔Chu〕 *v.* glance at, *adj.* afraid of, alarmed.

6621₇

咒 〔Chou〕 *n.* curse, spell, *v.* imprecate, curse, swear.
60-- 罵　　　　curse, swear, damn.
01-- 語　　　　imprecation, spell.
07-- 詛　　　　*n.* curse, *v.* accuse, curse.

6624₈

嚴 〔Yen〕 *n.* father, *adj.* stern, severe, grave, strict, rigid, relentless, rigorous, majestic, dignified, *adv.* extremely, very.
00-- 辦　　　　deal with strictly (or seriously), deal with severely.
02-- 刻　　　　severe, harsh.
07-- 詞責備　read the riot act, reproach severely.
-- 詞拒絕　repudiate with stern words.
10-- 正　　　　solemn, stern, severe.
12-- 刑　　　　cruel punishment, severe punishment.
14-- 酷　　　　cruel, harsh, ruthless, grim, rigid, severe, tyrannical.
20-- 重　　　　grave, serious, crucial.
-- 重虧損　heavy losses.
-- 重過失　gross negligence, serious misconduct.
-- 重困難　serious difficulties.
-- 重抗議　lodge a strong protest.
21-- 行禁封　take stringent action in blockade.
27-- 冬　　　　cold winter.
28-- 懲　　　　punish severely.
30-- 寒　　　　severe (or bitter) cold.
-- 守秘密　keep the secret strictly.
-- 守中立　observe strict neutrality.
-- 守陣地　hold the position in a battle.
-- 究　　　　investigate closely, examine carefully, inquire strictly.
-- 究不貸　offenders will be strictly prosecuted.
-- 密　　　　close, strict, exact, meticulous.
-- 密看守　keep watch and ward.
-- 密防範　guard carefully against.
40-- 查　　　　investigate strictly.
44-- 禁　　　　prohibit stringently, place under a ban.
-- 禁賭博　prohibit gambling strictly.
46-- 加責備　haul a person over the coals.
-- 加管束　control rigorously.
47-- 格　　　　strict, rigid, austere, rigorous.
-- 格言之　speak strictly.
-- 格要求　exact, insist on.
-- 格考驗　rigorous test.

--	聲屬色	with stern tones and severe countenance.
50--	肅	*n.* austerity, severity, solemnity, *adj.* solemn, grave, austere.
--	肅整齊	serious and tidy in manner.
--	肅性	solemnity, severity, austerity.
--	責	scold, reproach severely.
60--	罰	punish severely.
67--	明	peremptory, rigid.
70--	防	take strict precaution against, beware of, take care severely, look sharp.
--	防偷漏	take severe precaution against smuggling.
--	防扒手	take strict precaution against pickpockets.
71--	厲	rigorous, strict, severe.
--	厲批評	severe criticism.
--	厲斥責	bite someone's head off.
75--	陣以待	stand ready in battle formation.
80--	父慈母	stern father and a compassionate mother.

6640₄

嬰〔**Ying**〕*n.* baby, infant, *v.* encircle.

10--	孩時期	babyhood.
--	孩時代	time when one was a baby.
77--	兒	baby, infant, babe.

6640₇

矍〔**Chueh**〕*v.* look right and left in alarm.

6642₇

嬲〔**Niao**〕*v.* bother and vex.

6643₀

哭〔**Ku**〕*v.* cry, wail, weep.

02--	訴苦情	tell one's bitter feelings in tears.
22--	斷肝腸	cry one's heart out.
30--	泣	wail, weep, sob.
40--	喪著臉	look mournful as if in bereavement.
42--	聲震天	the noise of wailing rises to heaven.
63--	喊	*v.* cry and shout, wail, *adj.* crying.
88--	笑	weep and smile.

6650₆

單〔**Tan**〕*n.* bill, check, receipt, note, list, *adj.* single, only, lonely, alone.

00--	方面	one-sided, unilateral.
--	音節詞	monosyllable.
07--	調	monotonous.
--	詞	single word.
10--	一	*n.* unity, *adj.* single, simple.
--	一產品	single product.
--	一價格	single price.
--	一責任	single liability.
--	丁之身	one alone.
--	元	unit.
11--	項工程	single project.
--	項投資	independence investment.
12--	引號	single quotation marks.
17--	子	bill, slip of paper.
20--	位	unit.
--	位面積	unit area.
--	位價值	per unit value, unit value.
--	位成本	unit cost.
--	位時間	unit time.
--	航次	single voyage.
21--	價	unit price, price per unit.
--	價表	schedule of rates.
--	行本	separate volume.
--	行詩	poem of one verse.
25--	件生產	individual piece production, individual production, single item production, single unit production.
--	件包裝	individual packing.
--	純	simple.
--	純契約	simple contract.
26--	程	one-way, single journey.
--	程交通	one way traffic.
--	程票	one way ticket, single ticket.
--	程票價	single fare.
--	程費	one way fare, one way fee.
--	程貿易	one way trade.
27--	身	*n.* bachelor, *adj.* single, unmarried.

-- 身漢　　　bachelor.
-- 向航程　　single trip.
36-- 邊出口、單邊輸出 unilateral exportation.
-- 邊(方)的　unilateral.
-- 邊貿易　　unilateral trade.
41-- 槓　　　(in sport) horizontal bar.
44-- 薄　　　thin, weak.
46-- 獨　　　single, alone, one, individual.
-- 獨行動　　unilateral act.
-- 獨成本　　individual cost.
-- 獨經營　　separate operation.
48-- 幹　　　work on one's own, go it alone.
-- 幹戶　　　go-it-aloners.
-- 槍匹馬　　single-handed.
50-- 本位　　single standard.
51-- 打　　　(in sports) singles.
-- 據　　　note, bill, receipt, document, supporting document.
-- 據不全　　the incomplete documentation.
58-- 數　　　singular number, singular in number, odd number.
60-- 思病　　one-sided lovesickness.
80-- 人床　　single bed.
-- 人房　　　single-bed room.
-- 人飛行　　solo flight.

6666₁

囂 〔Yin〕 *adj.* simple, foolish.

6666₃

器 〔Chi〕 *n.* implement, article, instrument, tool, vessel, utensil.

20-- 重　　　value, respect, have a high opinion of.
22-- 樂　　　instrumental music.
30-- 官　　　organ (in the body).
43-- 械　　　arms, weapon, apparatus, instrument.
44-- 材　　　material and equipment.
60-- 量　　　capacity.
77-- 皿　　　vessel, implement, utensil.
-- 具　　　instrument, tool, apparatus, furniture, utensil.

6666₈

囂 〔Hsiao〕 *n.* clamor, uproar, *v.* cry aloud.

11-- 張　　　blatant, clamorous, rampant.
-- 張浮誇　　excitable and pompous.
34-- 凌　　　insult.

6677₄

罌 〔Ying〕 *n.* earthen jar with a small mouth.

10-- 粟　　　opium poppy.

6681₀

貺 〔Kuang〕 *v.* give, confer, bestow.

6682₇

賜 〔Ssu〕 *v.* give, confer, bestow, grant.

17-- 予　　　bestow, confer, grant.
28-- 給　　　confer upon.
31-- 福　　　bless.
48-- 教　　　condescend to teach.

6701₀

咀 〔Chu〕 *v.* chew, chew slowly, taste, suck.

62-- 嚼　　　chew, study carefully.

6701₁

呢 〔Ni〕 *n.* woolen cloth, woolen fabrics, woolen, *v.* murmur.

23-- 絨　　　woolen textile.
47-- 帽　　　felt hat, felt cap.
64-- 喃　　　*n.* chirp of a swallow, *v.* murmur.

6701₂

咆 〔Pao〕 *v.* roar, bluster, bawl, howl.

64-- 哮　　　*n.* roar, growl, *v.* growl, howl, bawl, rage.
-- 哮如雷　　roar like thunder.

6701₄

喔 〔Wo〕 *n.* crowing, cackling, *v.* cackle, crow.

67-- 喔　　　crowing of a cock.

曜 〔Yao〕 *n.* light of the sun, *adj.* glorious, dazzling.

67-- 眼　　　dazzling the eye.

6701₆

晚 〔Wan〕 *n.* evening, night, time, sunset, *adj.* late, later, *prep.* behind.

00-- 市	afternoon market.	
04-- 熟	late maturing.	
10-- 霞	sunglow at dusk, afterglow, glow of sunset.	
11-- 輩	younger generation.	
-- 班	night shift, late shift.	
21-- 上	night, evening.	
22-- 稻	late crop of rice.	
27-- 餐	supper.	
30-- 安	good night, good evening!	
34-- 禱	vesper.	
42-- 婚	late marriage.	
47-- 報	evening paper, evening newspaper.	
60-- 景	condition in one's old age.	
77-- 間	in the evening.	
80-- 年	declining year, one's old age.	
-- 會	evening party.	
82-- 飯	supper, evening meal, dinner.	
88-- 節	integrity in one's later years.	

6702₀

叨 〔**Tao**〕 v. crave, desire, long for, receive.

51-- 擾	bother (you).
90-- 光	receive a favor (from you).

啁 〔**Chou**〕 v. chirp.

69-- 啾	chatter, chirp.

叩 〔**Kou**〕 v. knock, ask, inquire, implore, tap.

11-- 頭	kowtow.
-- 頭求赦	kowtow and beg for pardon.
24-- 告	petition.
43-- 求資助	beg for one's pecuniary assistance.
77-- 問	ask, inquire.
-- 門	knock at the door.
-- 門請見	knock at the door and ask for an interview.

吻 〔**Wen**〕 n. kiss, lips, v. kiss.

80-- 合	coincide, accord with, match, tally.

喲 〔**Yao**〕 interj. O! oh!

晌 〔**Shang**〕 n. noon, midday, period of time.

80-- 午	middy, noon.

明 〔**Ming**〕 v. know, understand, adj. bright, clear, intelligent, evident, apparent.

00-- 亮	bright, brilliant.
-- 言	speak out, avow.
-- 文	definite instrument.
-- 文規定	in black and white.
10-- 示	manifestation.
-- 天	tomorrow.
-- 天見	see you tomorrow!
14-- 確	definite, explicit, unequivocal, evident, clear.
20-- 爭暗鬥	fight overtly and covertly.
-- 信片	post card, mailing-card, postal card.
24-- 升暗降	kick upstairs.
26-- 白	v. understand, comprehend, catch the idea, know, adj. clear, plain, obvious, understood, clever, clearheaded.
-- 細表	schedule, statement.
30-- 察	discern.
34-- 達	understand perfectly.
37-- 朗	lucid, clear, open-minded.
44-- 礬	alum.
47-- 媚	charming, fascinating.
60-- 日	tomorrow.
-- 星	star.
61-- 顯	obvious, prominent, evident, striking.
62-- 晰	n. clearness, adj. distinct, clear.
63-- 眸	bright-eyed, bright eyes.
64-- 瞭	understand, comprehend.
80-- 年	next year.
86-- 智	sagacious, judicious, wise.
88-- 敏	quick-witted.
90-- 火打劫	open robbery.

嗃 〔**Tao**〕 v. cry loudly, bewail mournfully.

唰=**衙** 2122₁

唧〔Hsien〕 *v.* hold in the mouth.

唧〔Chi〕 *n.* humming, buzzing as of insects.
67-- 唧　buzz.
88-- 筒　pump.

嘲〔Chao〕 *v.* ridicule, laugh at, jest at, mock at, scorn, jeer.
10-- 弄　mock, joke, make fun of, make fool of, make game of.
60-- 罵　abuse, rail.
88-- 笑　scoff, scorn, jeer at, laugh, jest, ridicule, mock at, make fun of.

6702₇

嗚〔Wu〕 *interj.* ah！ alas！
62-- 呼　*interj.* alas！ *v.* die.
-- 呼哀哉　what a tragic loss！
66-- 咽　whimper, sob.

哆〔To〕 *v.* shiver or tremble.
64-- 嗦　tremble (with cold or fear).

哪〔Na〕 (interrogative particle) which, what, where, how, when.
00-- 裏　where.
10-- 天　what day.
26-- 個　which.
80-- 年　what year, which year.
96-- 怕　even if.

嘟〔Tu〕 *v.* mutter and grumble.
65-- 嚷　mutter, murmur, grumble.

鳴〔Ming〕 *v.* sing, sound, cry, caw.
04-- 謝　in acknowledgement of.
08-- 放　air one's views.
10-- 不平　repine.
37-- 冤　complain of unfairness or grievances.
80-- 鐘　toll.
97-- 炮　fire a gun, fire a salute.

囑〔Chu〕 *n.* will, order, *v.* bid, order, enjoin, instruct, gaze at, look at, stare at, watch.
52-- 托　entrust, charge.
60-- 目　stare at, gaze at, look at eagerly.
64-- 咐　enjoin, bid.

-- 咐再三　charge again and again.
80-- 人注意　charge one to be careful.

6703₂

喙〔Hui〕 *n.* beak, nib, bill.

眼〔Yen〕 *n.* eye, holo, tiny hole, main point.
00-- 痛　eyesore, pain in the eye.
-- 疾　disease of the eyes.
10-- 下　just now, at the moment.
13-- 球　orb.
15-- 珠 (球)　eyeballs.
20-- 毛　eyelashes.
21-- 紅　show covetous eyes, be jealous.
24-- 科　ophthalmology, ophthalmic department.
-- 科醫生　oculist, eye doctor.
26-- 線　spy, contact, informer.
27-- 色　expression of the eyes, facial expression.
30-- 窩　eye holes, eye sockets.
33-- 淚　tears.
40-- 力　eyesight.
-- 皮　eye-lid.
44-- 花　eyes blurred.
-- 藥　eyewater, eye-medicine, eyedrops.
50-- 中無人　haughty.
-- 中釘　eyesore, thorn in the flesh.
60-- 瞳　pupil of the eye.
-- 界　sight, scope, horizon, prospect, outlook, field of view.
-- 暈　dizzy, giddy.
-- 目失明　have lost one's sight.
61-- 眶　eye sockets.
65-- 睛　eyes.
77-- 眉　eyebrow.
78-- 瞼、皮　eyelids.
80-- 前　immediately, under one's nose, before one's eyes.
-- 前利益　immediate interests.
-- 鏡　glasses, spectacles, eye-glasses.
-- 鏡架　spectacle-frame.
-- 鏡蛇　cobra.
88-- 簾　iris of an eye.

90-- 尖 have sharp eyes, be quick of sight.
-- 光 eyesight, vision, insight.
-- 光遠大 farsighted.
-- 光銳利 sagacious, sharp of sight.
-- 光短小 short-sighted.

6703₃
咚 〔Tung〕 *n.* thump, sound of impact.
67-- 咚 bang.

6703₄
喚 〔Huan〕 *v.* call, name, summon.
16-- 醒 wake up, awake, awaken, waken, arouse.
22-- 出 call out.
27-- 起 rouse, provoke, call forth, stir up.
-- 起同情 awaken one's sympathy.
-- 起精神 brace oneself up, shake up.

噢 〔Yu〕 *v.* groan.

喉 〔Hou〕 *n.* throat, larynx.
00-- 痛 throat-ache, throat sore.
-- 音 gutter, guttural sound.
11-- 頭 larynx, throat.
20-- 舌 mouthpiece, spokesman.
61-- 嚨 gorge.

喫 〔Chih〕 *v.* eat, swallow.
21-- 虧 suffer loss.
44-- 苦 suffer hardship.

6703₇
呎 見 6708₇

6704₇
吸 〔Hsi〕 *v.* suck, absorb, inhale, attract, draw, breathe.
00-- 塵器 vacuum-cleaner, dust catcher, dust collector.
12-- 引 attract, draw, appeal.
-- 引力 attraction, force of attraction.
17-- 取 soak, absorb, draw, assimilate.
20-- 住 grip, attract.
27-- 血鬼 bloodsucker, vampire.
-- 盤 sucker, sucking disk.
28-- 收 *n.* absorption, *v.* absorb, assimilate.

-- 收作用 absorption, assimilation.
40-- 力 gravity, attraction, suction.
48-- 乾 suck dry.
60-- 墨紙 blotting paper.
80-- 入 inspire, inhale, imbibe.
-- 氣 breathe in, inhale.
83-- 鐵石 loadstone, magnet.
87-- 飲 sip.
88-- 管 sucker, siphon.
90-- 菸 smoke.
-- 菸室 smoking room.
96-- 烟 smoke.

眠 〔Mien〕 *v.* sleep, lie sown, close the eyes, slumber.
24-- 牀 couch, bed.

暇 〔Hsia〕 *n.* leisure, vacant time, vacant hours, free time, *adj.* free, leisurely.
37-- 逸 easy going.
60-- 日 leisure day.

啜 〔Cho〕 *v.* drink, taste, suck.
30-- 泣 weep, sob.
61-- 嘴 kiss.
87-- 飲 drink, sip.

6705₆
暉 〔Hui〕 *adj.* bright, splendid, radiant.

6705₇
咿 〔I〕 *n.* smirking, sound.
61-- 啞 babble.

6706₁
瞻 〔Chen〕 *v.* look up, look at, reverence.
07-- 望 look forward to.
27-- 仰 admire, look up at, regard with respect.
-- 仰遺容 pay respects to the remains.
31-- 顧 behold.
36-- 視 look at.
80-- 前顧後 look before and behind, look forward and backward.

6706₂
昭 〔Chao〕 *v.* show, illuminate, disclose, *adj.* bright, splendid, luminous, manifest, clear.
02-- 彰 manifested, plainly shown.

10-- 雪　　　　　　prove the innocence.
44-- 著　　　　　　evident, plain, clear.
67-- 明　　　　　　bright.

6706₃

嚕〔**Lu**〕 *v.* talk too much, *adj.* talkative, wordy.
64-- 嘛　　　　　　*v.* nag, *adj.* talkative.

6706₄

略〔**Lueh**〕 *n.* summary, outline, sketch, plan, scheme, *v.* capture, seize, define, mark out, diminish, slight, invade, gain, omit, *adj.* simple, slight.
01-- 語　　　　　　abbreviation.
08-- 說　　　　　　say briefly.
17-- 取　　　　　　take by force.
22-- 變　　　　　　modify.
27-- 多　　　　　　a little more.
33-- 述　　　　　　outline, state briefly.
40-- 有　　　　　　only a few, there are only a few, there is only a little.
-- 有所聞　　　　have heard something.
-- 有門徑　　　　have some rough understanding of a subject.
-- 去　　　　　　omit, leave out.
60-- 圖　　　　　　sketch.
80-- 知　　　　　　understand a little.

咯〔**Luoh**〕 *v.* cough and spit.
00-- 痰　　　　　　spit.
27-- 血　　　　　　spit blood.
67-- 咯聲　　　　　cackle of a hen.

6708₀

瞑〔**Ming**〕 *v.* close the eyes, shut the eyes.
60-- 目而逝　　　　close one's eyes and pass away.
67-- 冥　　　　　　indistinct, dark.

6708₂

吹〔**Chui**〕 *v.* blow, puff, blast, brag, boast.
20-- 毛求疵　　　　nag, find fault with.
22-- 倒　　　　　　blow down.
25-- 牛　　　　　　brag, boast.
27-- 過　　　　　　blow over.
33-- 滅　　　　　　blow out.
40-- 去　　　　　　blow away.
44-- 落　　　　　　blow off.

-- 鼓手　　　　　buglers and drummers.
48-- 散　　　　　　blow over.
55-- 捧　　　　　　extol, lavish praise on.
60-- 口哨　　　　　whistle.
61-- 噓　　　　　　recommend, advertise oneself, boast oneself of.
62-- 喇叭　　　　　trumpet, wind a trumpet.
72-- 陰風　　　　　stir up a malicious wind.
88-- 簫　　　　　　pipe.
-- 笛　　　　　　flute, play the flute.
-- 管　　　　　　blowpipe.
96-- 熄　　　　　　blow out.

嗽〔**Sou**〕 *v.* cough, hack, clear the throat.
60-- 口　　　　　　rinse the mouth.

6708₇

呎〔**Chih**〕 *n.* foot (in English measure).

6709₄

嗓〔**Sang**〕 *n.* throat, one's voice.
00-- 音　　　　　　one's voice.
17-- 子　　　　　　larynx, throat, one's voice.
-- 子痛　　　　　sore throat.

6710₄

墅〔**Shu**〕 *n.* villa, cottage.

6710₇

盟〔**Meng**〕 *n.* alliance, compact, oath, league, *v.* swear, vow.
00-- 主　　　　　　lord of covenants.
27-- 約　　　　　　pact, treaty.
-- 約條件　　　　terms of an allied treaty.
40-- 友　　　　　　allied friend, comrades, allies, sworn friends.
52-- 誓　　　　　　*n.* oath, *v.* take an oath.
60-- 國　　　　　　allied nations.
-- 國軍隊　　　　troops of the allied states.
65-- 兄弟　　　　　sworn brothers.

6711₂

跑〔**Pao**〕 *n.* running, *v.* run, gallop, trot, run away, escape.
12-- 到　　　　　　run (up) to.
21-- 步　　　　　　run fast, double march, at a run.
-- 街　　　　　　drummer, solicitor.
-- 街經紀　　　　curb-stone, broker.
38-- 道　　　　　　racetrack, runway.

44-- 鞋   track shoes, spiked shoes.
51-- 掉   run away, flee.
71-- 馬   horse-race.
  -- 馬場   turf, racetrack.
90-- 堂   restaurant waiter.

跪〔Kuei〕v. kneel, fall upon one's knees.

6711₄

躍〔Yao〕v. jump, leap, spring, skip.
30-- 進   leap forward.
67-- 躍欲試   itch for, eager to try.

6711₇

跪〔Kuei〕v. kneel.
10-- 下   kneel down, fall on one's knees.

6712₂

野〔Ye〕n. wilderness, limit, borderline, masses, adj. wild, savage, rustic, rude, impolite.
13-- 球比賽   baseball contest.
17-- 砲   field gun.
20-- 雞   pheasant.
22-- 蠻   n. barbarism, brutality, adj. barbarous, wild, brutal, brutish, fierce, savage, barbarous.
  -- 蠻人   savage, barbarian.
  -- 蠻行爲   barbarity, barbarous acts.
  -- 蠻民族   barbarous race.
23-- 外演習   field exercise.
  -- 外旅行   take an excursion in an open country.
  -- 外考察   field work.
25-- 生   wild, growing in the wild.
  -- 生植物   wild plant.
27-- 餐   picnic, junket.
  -- 兔   hare.
30-- 宿   camping.
33-- 心   ambition, aggressive designs, wild desire.
  -- 心家   careerist, man of ambition.
44-- 貓   wild cat.
  -- 草   weeds.
  -- 豬   wild boar.
  -- 花   wild flowers.
  -- 菜   wild vegetables.

63-- 戰   field gun.
  -- 戰砲   field artillery.
  -- 戰軍   field army, army of operations, combat troops.
  -- 戰醫院   ambulance, field hospital.
  -- 獸   wild beast.
65-- 味   game as food.
67-- 鴨   wild duck.
80-- 合   illicit sexual intercourse.
90-- 火   prairie fire.
95-- 性   wild disposition.
99-- 營   camp, camping.

6712₇

踊〔Yung〕v. jump.

跼〔Chu〕adj. bent, crooked.

躑〔Chih〕v. stop, cease, come to a standstill, falter, hesitate.
66-- 躅   ramble, wander, stroll, falter.

踴〔Yung〕v. leap, jump.
67-- 躍   v. jump, leap, adj. enthusiastic, zealous.

6713₂

跟〔Ken〕n. heel, v. follow, imitate, conj. and.
10-- 不上   fall behind.
11-- 班   servant, waiter.
21-- 上   keep abreast of, catch up with.
68-- 蹤   trace, tail.
  -- 蹤調查   follow-up survey.
74-- 隨   follow, accompany.
80-- 着   follow, in the wake of.

踐〔Chan〕v. stamp, tread.

6714₂

蹡〔Chiang〕v. walk.

6714₅

跚〔Shan〕v. limp.

6716₄

路〔Lu〕n. road, path, way, route.
00-- 旁(邊)   wayside, roadside.
10-- 面   road surface.
21-- 逕   route, path, way.
26-- 線   direction, line, route.
  -- 牌   guideboard.

	--程	journey.
32--	透電	Reuter telegram.
	--透社	Reuters.
	--透消息	Reuter message.
37--	過	pass by.
41--	標	guidepost, road sign.
	--基	roadbed.
48--	警	railway police, policemen patrolling highways.
50--	攤	roadside market.
55--	費	traveling expenses.
60--	口	entrance to a road, intersection.
80--	人	passerby, men in the street.
92--	燈	street lamp (light).

踞〔Chu〕*v.* crouch, sit on, squat, occupy.

88--	坐	squat.

6719₄

蹂〔Jou〕*v.* tread, trample on.

64--	躪	ravage, trample, devastate.

跢〔To〕*v.* stamp.

77--	腳	stamp one's feet.

6722₀

嗣〔Sse〕*n.* heir, offspring, descendant. *v.* inherit, adopt, continue.

17--	子	adopted son, heir.
22--	後	hereafter.
34--	續	succeed.

6722₇

鄂〔O〕*n.* boundary, border, limit.
鴞〔Hsiao〕*n.* owl.
鵑〔Chuan〕*n.* cuckoo.
鶚〔E〕*n.* fish eagle.

6732₇

鷺〔Lu〕*n.* egret, padding bird.

22--	鷥	egret.

6733₂

煦〔Hsu〕*n.* favors, kindness, *v.* heat, *adj.* kind, gracious, warm.

6733₆

照〔Chao〕*n.* sunshine, photograph, license, *v.* shine on, enlighten, illuminate, follow, light, compare, collate, photograph, take a picture, look after, notify.

00--	亮	illuminate, light.
	--章	according to regulations.
	--章辦理	handle a matter according to regulations.
	--辦	act accordingly.
	--應	look after, take care of.
08--	說	say so.
11--	碼對折	offer a 50 percent discount on the tagged prices.
21--	此類推	draw analogous conclusions.
	--價收買	buy according to the price declared by the owner.
22--	片	photo, photograph, picture.
	--例	as usual, according to usage, customary.
24--	付	meet (honor, pay)draft.
30--	準	aim at.
	--實道來	state the facts as they are.
31--	顧	take care of, look after.
44--	舊	still, as before.
46--	相	photograph, take a picture.
	--相機	camera.
	--相館	photo studio.
	--相簿	album.
48--	樣	follow suit, as before.
	--樣做	follow the pattern, do the same.
50--	本出售	sell at cost price.
53--	成本	on cost.
59--	抄	make a copy.
67--	明	*n.* illumination, lighting, *v.* illuminate, light.
	--明彈	flare bomb, illuminating shell.
80--	會	*n.* license, communique, note, *v.* notify.
	--鏡子	look in a mirror (or glass).
88--	算	reckon accordingly.
90--	常	as usual.
	--常營業	business as usual.
94--	料=照應	
97--	耀	*v.* shine, lighten, brighten, illumine, *adj.* bright, brilliant, shining.

6742₇

鸚 〔Ying〕 *n.* parrot, cockatoo.

17-- 鵡	parrot, cockatoo.

6752₇

鴨 〔Ya〕 *n.* duck.

17-- 蛋	duck egg, zero.
23-- 絨	duck down.
61-- 嘴獸	duckbill.
62-- 叫	quack, quacks of a duck.
75-- 肫	duck gizzard.
90-- 掌	duck web.

6762₇

鄙 〔Pi〕 *n.* remote area, suburbs, *v.* despise, *adj.* rustic, low, mean.

00-- 吝	mean, stingy, miserly.
-- 吝者	miser.
36-- 視	despise, hold in contempt.
44-- 薄	*v.* despise, *adj.* mean, base.
71-- 陋	mean, base, lowly.
90-- 劣	worthless.

6778₂

歇 〔Hsieh〕 *v.* rest, halt, desist, stop.

10-- 工	stop work, cease work.
22-- 市	close market.
26-- 息	*n.* rest, repose, *v.* stop, rest.
30-- 宿	stay overnight.
32-- 業	close business, give up a business, close door, put up the shutters, retire from practice, shut up a business.

6786₁

贍 〔Shan〕 *v.* help with money, support, provide, supply, *adj.* plenty, abundance.

80-- 養	support, supply with food and clothing.
-- 養費	alimony, family allowance.

6786₄

賂 〔Lu〕 *v.* bribe.

6792₇

夥 〔Huo〕 *n.* company, party, band, partner, colleague, group, *adj.* numerous, many.

04-- 計	counter jumper, clerk.
29-- 伴	partner, partner in business, companion.
37-- 盜	bandits, fellow thieves.
73-- 騙	cheat together.

6800₀

叭 〔Pa〕 *n.* trumpet.

6801₁

昨 〔Tso〕 *n.* yesterday, *adj.* past, *adv.* formerly.

00-- 夜	last night.
10-- 天	yesterday.
60-- 日	yesterday.
67-- 晚	yesterday evening.

6801₂

嗟 〔Chueh〕 *v.* sigh, lament, mourn. *interj.* alas ！

50-- 夫	alas.

6801₇

吃 〔Chih〕 *v.* eat, stammer, take, have.

00-- 齋	be a vegetarian, fast.
-- 言	lose one's promise.
10-- 豆腐	eat bean curd, make advances to a woman without serious intentions.
-- 不消	intolerable.
12-- 水	draft.
-- 水重量	draft weight.
-- 水線	load line, line of flotation, waterline.
-- 水深度	deep draught.
14-- 醋	be jealous.
21-- 虧	list ground, incur, loss, suffer a loss.
30-- 空缺	pad a payroll.
-- 這行飯	live by this profession.
40-- 力	laborious, hard to do.
-- 力不討好	thankless job.
44-- 老本	live off one's past glory.
-- 苦	suffer hardship, bear hardships.
-- 藥	take medicine.
48-- 驚	*v.* be frightened, have a fright, *adj.* astonished, surprised, amazed, frightened.
50-- 盡苦頭	have been in the wars.
57-- 軟不吃硬	yielding to soft approach

		but rejecting force.
61--	點心	take refreshments.
66--	喝	eat and drink.
--	喝嫖賭	be dissipated and dissolute.
67--	眼前虧	suffer a loss under one's nose.
77--	閒飯	lead an idle life.
--	緊	critical.
81--	飯	take a meal.
90--	光	eat up.
91--	煙	smoke.

6801₈

噬〔Shih〕 v. gnaw.

6802₁

喻 〔Yu〕 n. illustration, example, allegory, v. understand, explain.

00--	言	figure of speech.
--	言的	figurative.
28--	以利害	explain the advantages and disadvantages.

咋 〔Cha〕 n. loud noise, v. bite, gnaw.

20--	舌	be regretful or terrified.

6802₂

畛 〔Chen〕 n. border, dykes, footpath between fields.

43--	域	boundary, scope.

6802₇

吟 〔Yin〕 v. hum, ponder, moan, chant, mutter, recite, sigh.

03--	詠	chant.
04--	詩	hum a verse, recite poems.
07--	誦	chant.

吩 〔Fen〕 v. direct, order, bid, look, long for, hope.

07--	望	hope, expect, long for.
64--	咐	command, tell.

盼 〔Pan〕 v. gaze at, glance at, long for.

07--	望	expect, lay one's account with.

6803₂

唸 〔Nien〕 v. read, chant.

50--	書	read.

6803₄

嗾 〔Sou〕 v. give order to a dog, instigate,

		incite, stir up, goad.
25--	使	incite, instigate.

6804₀

畋 〔Tien〕 v. cultivate, hunt.

42--	獵	hunt.

瞰 〔Kan〕 v. look at, spy, watch.

27--	伺	peep, watch.

6805₃

曦 〔Hsi〕 n. light of the sun, sunlight, sunshine.

6805₇

晦 〔Hui〕 n. night, evening, last day of every moon in the lunar calendar, adj. obscure, dark, dull, dim, misty, unlucky.

37--	冥	dark.
80--	氣	ill luck, bad luck.

嗨 〔Hai〕 interj. heigh!

64--	喲	heigh-ho!

6806₁

哈 〔Ha〕 interj. ha ! sound of laughter.

68--	哈	ha! ha!
--	哈大笑	roar with laughter.
77--	巴狗	pug, lapdog.

6806₄

啥 〔Sha〕 what, which, who, why.

6806₇

嗆 〔Chiang〕 n. cough.

6811₁

蹉 〔Tso〕 v. miss, fall, tumble.

6812₁

踰=逾 3830₂

踰 〔Yu〕 v. exceed, pass over.

77--	限	overpass the limit.

6814₆

蹲 〔Tsun〕 v. crouch, squat.

6816₇

蹌 〔Chiang〕 v. move.

6832₇

黔 〔Chien〕 adj. black.

6883₇

賺 〔Chuan〕 v. make money, gain, earn.

40-- 大錢　　　*n.* killing, *v.* make a killing, earn good money, make one's jack.
83-- 錢　　　earn, gain.
-- 錢生意　　good bargain, good business.

6884₀
敗 〔 **Pai** 〕 *v.* defeat, destroy, ruin, spoil, knock, in the head.
02-- 訴　　　lose an action.
-- 訴一方　　losing party.
11-- 北　　　defeat.
24-- 德　　　depravity.
37-- 退　　　lose the field.
40-- 壞　　　spoil, corrupt, destroy.
72-- 兵　　　defeated soldier.

6886₆
贈 〔 **Tseng** 〕 *v.* present, give, bestow.
10-- 言　　　give an advice.
38-- 送　　　give present.
47-- 款　　　grant, outright grant.
60-- 品　　　present, extra gift.
62-- 別　　　give a parting gift.
77-- 與　　　*n.* gift, donation, *v.* give, bestow.
90-- 券　　　gift cheque, gift coupon.

6889₁
賒 〔 **She** 〕 *v.* borrow, buy on credit.
27-- 欠　　　buy on credit.
61-- 賬　　　on credit.

6901₄
瞠 〔 **Tang** 〕 *v.* gaze, stare, open the eyes wide.

6902₀
吵 〔 **Chao** 〕 *v.* quarrel, wrangle, disturb, annoy.
47-- 聲　　　noise.
77-- 鬧　　　brawl, uproar.
眇 〔 **Miao** 〕 *adj.* blind in one eye.

6902₇
哨 〔 **Shao** 〕 *n.* outpost, guard station, *v.* whistle, patrol.
72-- 兵　　　watchman, guard.

6905₀
畔 〔 **Pan** 〕 *n.* land mark, side walk, bank.

6908₀
啾 〔 **Chiu** 〕 *v.* twitter.

6908₉
啖 〔 **Tan** 〕 *v.* eat.

6909₄
咪 〔 **Mi** 〕 *n.* meter.

7

7010₃
璧 〔 **Pi** 〕 *n.* jade, jade badge of office.
04-- 謝　　　return with thanks.
36-- 還原主　　return the jewel to the owner.

7010₄
壁 〔 **Pi** 〕 *n.* wall, walls of a room, fortress, defense, screen.
00-- 立　　　stand upright.
-- 立千仞　　high cliff.
21-- 虎　　　lizard.
41-- 櫥　　　closet, wall chest.
47-- 報　　　wall newspaper, wall poster.
50-- 畫　　　mural, wall-painting, fresco.
60-- 壘　　　rampart, fortress, barrier.
-- 壘森嚴　　well-guarded stronghold, a strict demarcation of opposing parties.
80-- 龕　　　niche.
91-- 爐　　　fireplace.

7011₄
睢 〔 **Tsu** 〕 *n.* marine bird.

7021₄
雅 〔 **Ya** 〕 *n.* crow, *adj.* elegant, refined, graceful, gentle, usual, your, *adv.* exactly, very much.
00-- 意　　　your ideas.
10-- 爾達會議　Yalta Conference.
07-- 望　　　your good reputation
22-- 片　　　opium.
28-- 緻　　　elegant, refined, graceful.
50-- 典　　　Athens.
81-- 人　　　man of taste.
雕 〔 **Tiao** 〕 *n.* kite, vulture, *v.* cut, carve,

engrave.

02-- 刻	*n.* sculpture, engraving. *v.* carve, engrave, sculpture.
-- 刻品	carving, carved work.
-- 刻家	sculptor.
10-- 工	engraver, carved work.
11-- 琢	chisel and polish.
17-- 刀	graver, carving tool.
27-- 像	statue, carved statue.
30-- 字	carve letters.
44-- 花	engrave figures.
87-- 塑	sculpture.
-- 塑家	statuary, sculptor.

臃 〔Yung〕*v.* swell, *adj.* fat and clumsy.
72-- 腫　　*n.* swelling, adj. fat and clumsy.

7021₇
阬 〔Keng〕*n.* pit.
骯 〔Ang〕*adj.* fat, fleshy, dirty, filthy.
74-- 髒　　dirty, filthy.

7022₃
臍 〔Chi〕*n.* navel.
44-- 帶　　umbilical cord.

7022₇
防 〔Fang〕*n.* bank, dyke, defense, protection, *v.* defend, protect, protect from, guard against, provide against, ward off, prepare for.

00-- 疫	anti-epidemic.
-- 疫站	epidemic-prevention station.
-- 疫所	quarantine office.
-- 疫隔離	*n.* quarantine, *v.* quarantine.
-- 腐	antisepsis, preservation, preservation from decay.
-- 腐劑	preservative, antiseptic.
04-- 護	defence.
-- 護衣	protective cloth.
12-- 水	water proof, anti-flood.
-- 水油漆	water repellent paint.
16-- 彈	bullet-proof, bomb-proof.
-- 彈車	bullet-proof car.
21-- 止	prevent, prohibit, protect against (or from).
-- 止假冒	beware of counterfeiting.
-- 止浪費	avoid waste.
-- 止偷竊	avoid theft.
-- 止損失	*n.* prevention of loss, *v.* stop loss.
-- 止損壞	avoid damage.
-- 衛	defend, guard.
22-- 災	guard against calamity, prevention of disaster.
24-- 備	prepare for, provide against, guard against, take precautions against.
26-- 線	defense line.
27-- 禦=防衛	*n.* defense *v.* defend.
-- 禦工程	defense.
-- 禦工事	entrenchment, defense fortifications.
-- 禦地位	on the defensive.
-- 禦物	bulwark.
-- 禦戰	defensive war, defensive battle.
-- 修	prevent revisionism (in Red China).
30-- 空	air-raid defense, air defense.
-- 空司令	air defense command.
-- 空洞	air-raid shelter, bomb shelter.
-- 空壕	dugout.
-- 空監視所	signal station.
-- 空氣球網	balloon barrage.
-- 守	guard, defend.
-- 寨	barricade.
34-- 波堤	pier, breakwater.
-- 洪	flood-control.
37-- 盜	guard against robbery or theft.
-- 漏	against leakage, leakage-proof.
46-- 坦克	anti-tank.
50-- 毒	anti-gas defense.
-- 毒門	air lock.
-- 毒室	gas-proof shelter.
-- 毒面具	respirator, gas mask.
-- 蛀	moth proof.
66-- 噪聲設備	soundproof devices.
-- 噪聲的	soundproof.
77-- 風林	windbreak.

82-- 鏽的	antirust, rustproof.	
90--火	*n.* fire prevention, fire re-sistance, *v.* guard against fire, *adj.* fireproof.	
-- 火設備	fire equipment.	
-- 火建築	fire proof construction.	
-- 火安全措施	fire security measures.	
-- 火牆	fire wall (masonry), firewall (computer).	
-- 火材料	fireproof material.	

肪〔Fang〕*n.* fat, grease.

肺〔Fei〕*n.* lung.

00-- 癌	cancer of the lung.
--病	tuberculosis.
12-- 形草	lung-wort.
24-- 結核	tuberculosis, consumption.
32-- 活量	vital capacity.
-- 活量計	spirometer.
44-- 葉	lobes of the lungs.
74-- 膜	pleura.
90-- 炎	pneumonia.

膀〔Pang〕*n.* bladder, upper arms.

17-- 子	arm.
79-- 胱	bladder.
-- 胱炎	cystitis, inflammation of the bladder.

劈〔Pi〕*n.* wedge, *v.* cut open, split, split open, rive, rend.

14-- 破	split out.
21-- 柴	chop wood for fuel.
52-- 刺	bayonet fighting.
77-- 開	cut, cleave, split open, wedge.

臂〔Pi〕*n.* arm.

00-- 章	chevron, arm badge, arm band.
57-- 挽臂	arm in arm.

7023₆

臆〔I〕*n.* breast, bosom, one's views, thoughts, feelings.

00-- 度=臆測	
08-- 說	assume, assumption.
32-- 測	guess, surmise, speculate
-- 測不中	guess wide.
46-- 想	surmise, conjecture.

7024₀

腑〔Fu〕*n.* bowels, viscera.

74-- 臟	entrails.

7024₁

辟見 7064₁

7024₆

障〔Chang〕*n.* obstruction, embankment, barricade, protection, defence, obstacle, barrier, hindrance, *v.* screen, embank, separate, divide.

17-- 礙	*n.* obstacle, block, barrier, *v.* hinder, prevent, block.
-- 礙物	obstacles, obstruction, barricade, entanglement, hindrance, handicap.
-- 礙賽跑	obstacle-race.

7024₇

腋〔Yeh〕*n.* armpit.

10--下	armpits.
26-- 臭	tetter of armpit.

7026₁

陪〔Pei〕*v.* accompany, assist, second, attend on, *adj.* secondary, subordinate.

29-- 伴	accompany, bear company.
30--客	receive guests.
--審員	jury, juryman, juror, assessor.
36--襯	contrast, prop.
47--都	the secondary capital.
60--罪	apologize.
77--同	accompany, attend.

7028₂

陔〔Kai〕*n.* step.

骸〔Hai〕*n.* bone, skeleton, shinbone.

77-- 骨	skeleton.

7031₄

駐〔Chu〕*v.* halt, stay, sojourn, stop at, station.

23-- 外使節	mission, diplomatic representative.
30-- 守	occupy.
37-- 軍	station troops, garrison. troops, garrison.
42-- 紮	quarter, encamp, station.

44--	地	station, garrison.
50--	屯軍	army of occupation.
70--	防	garrison.
--	防邊疆	be garrisoned at the frontier.
99--	營	encampment.

7033_2
驤　〔Hsiang〕 *adj.* plunge, prance.

7038_2
駭　〔Hai〕 *v.* frighten, strike dumb. *adj.* frightened, frightening, horrible, alarmed, surprised, amazing, marvelous, terrible.

33--	浪	fearful billows.
60--	異	astonishment.
80--	人聽聞	terrifying, astounding, shocking.
96--	怕	frighten, surprise.
--	愕萬分	be amazed to the greatest degree.

7040_4
變　〔Pi〕 *adj.* lecherous.

7050_2
擘　〔Po〕 *n.* thumb, *v.* split, tear, tear apart, break apart, open.

50--	畫	contrive, plan.
--	畫經營	create and execute plans for a project or an institution.
--	畫精詳	devise thoroughly.

7060_1
譬　〔Pi〕 *n.* comparison, metaphor, illustration, *v.* punish, kill, avoid, compare, illustrate, liken.

46--	如	for example, for instance.
48--	喻	analogy, metaphor.

7064_1
辟　〔Pi〕 *v.* punish, kill, avoid.

7071_7
鐾　〔Pi〕 *n.* jar.

7073_2
襞　〔Pi〕 *v.* fold cloth.

7110_4
壓　見 7121_4

7110_6

瞀　〔Chi〕 *v.* reach, *conj.* and, as well as, *prep.* together with.

7110_7
盔　〔Kuei〕 *n.* helmet, headpiece.

60--	甲	helmet and armor.

7113_6
蠶　〔Tsan〕 *n.* silkworm.

10--	豆	horse bean, broad bean.
22--	絲	natural silk.
44--	繭	cocoon, silkworm cocoon.
50--	虫	silkworm.
53--	蛾	silkworm moth.
80--	食	*n.* aggression, encroachment. *v.* nibble, eat away, invade, encroach upon.

7120_0
厂　〔Han〕 *n.* projecting cliff.

7121_1
阮　〔Yuan〕 *n.* Yuan (a family name.).

歷　〔Li〕 *n.* past, *v.* pass over, pass through, go through, undergo, *adj.* orderly, *adv.* clearly.

23--	代	generation, from age to age, generation after generation.
27--	久	for a long time.
--	久不衰	long lasting.
37--	次	successive, in the past.
40--	來	hitherto.
50--	史	history.
--	史家	historian.
--	史學家	historian.
--	史上	historically.
--	史劇	historical play.
--	史的真實性	historicity.
--	史唯物主義	historical materialism.
--	盡辛苦	have gone through many hardships.
--	盡甘苦	have experienced all sweet and bitter.
80--	年	year after year, for years.

脛　〔Ching〕 *n.* shank, shin, calf.

77--	骨	shinbone.

腓　〔Fei〕 *n.* fleshy part of the shank.

77--	骨	fibula.

隴　〔Lung〕 *n.* grave, bank, dike.

朧〔Lung〕*n.* rising moon.
7121₂

厄〔E〕*n.* distress, in distress, *adj.* distressed, cramped.
00--難　calamity, disaster.
37--運　miserable condition, bad luck.

尨〔Mang〕*adj.* great, confused.

阰〔E〕*n.* strategic point (position), narrow road, hindrance, obstruction, distress, difficulty, *v.* distress, impede, hinder.
40--難　distressed.

肛〔Gang〕*n.* anus.
77--門　anus.

陋〔Lou〕*adj.* of bad quality, low, rustic, rude, vulgar, ugly, narrow, mean, shallow.
17--習　bad habit.
30--室　humble abode, hut.
44--巷　narrow dirty lane.
90--劣　vile, base, vulgar.
7121₃

魘〔Yen〕*n.* nightmare.
7121₄

雁〔Yen〕*n.* wild geese.

厘＝釐 5821₄

陛〔Pi〕*n.* steps heading to the throne, platform on which the throne stands.
10--下　His (or Your, Her) Majesty.

壓〔Ya〕*v.* press, repress, oppress, suppress, crush, overthrow.
10--死　crush to death.
--碎　crush, squash.
--平　flatten.
--下去　subdue, suppress.
--不垮　cannot be subdued.
16--迫　oppress, press, coerce.
--迫者　oppressor.
20--住　weigh down, hold down.
22--倒　excel, whelm, overbear, prevail over.
--倒一切　all-conquering, overriding.
--制　oppress, strangle, suppress, control, put down, subdue.
--制批評　suppress criticism.
--彎　bend.
--低　depress.
23--縮　compress, condense, reduce, cut down.
30--害百姓　oppress the masses.
36--迫　*n.* oppression, *v.* oppress, coerce, crush, repress, subdue.
--迫者　oppressor.
--迫輿論　oppress public opinions.
40--力　pressure, stress.
43--搾　squeeze, oppress and exploit.
53--成肉餅　crush into a hamburger.
57--抑　depress, suppress, curb.
67--路機　road roller.
77--服　bear down, bring under, overpower, beat down.
--緊　*n.* compression, *v.* compress.
7121₆

颭〔Chan〕*v.* waft, be moved by the wind.
7121₇

臚〔Lu〕*n.* belly, *v.* arrange orderly, spread out.
12--列　make out a list.
7121₉

胚〔Pei〕*n.* embryo, fetus.
17--子　germ.
44--芽　embryo, sprout.
73--胎　embryo, fetus, pregnant womb.
--胎學　embryology.
7122₀

阿〔Ah〕*n.* high ridge, river bank, initial particle used before a name, word used in transliterations, *v.* favor, toady, discharge, rely on.
07--諛　flatter, toady.
11--彌陀佛　Amitabha (in Buddhism), the Buddha of infinite life and infinite light.
17--司匹靈　aspirin.
30--富汗　Afghanistan.

45-- 姨　　　　　aunt (mother's sister).
50-- 拉伯　　　　Arabia.

7122₁

陞〔Chih〕v. go up, promote, mount, ascend, proceed.

7122₇

隔〔Ko〕v. obstruct, divide, separate, interpose, adj. apart, separated, obstructed.

00--離　　　　separate, isolate, keep apart.
　--離室　　　　isolation ward.
　--夜　　　　overnight, last night.
22--斷　　　　cut off, block up.
27--絕　　　　preclude.
44--熱　　　　keep away from heat.
60--日　　　　every other day, on alternate days.
70--壁　　　　neighbor, next door.
74--膜　　　　diaphragm.
　--膜重重　　a lot of misunderstandings.
77--開　　　　separate, partition.
　--閡　　　　alienation, misunderstanding.
　--月　　　　every other month.

脣〔Chun〕n. lip.

00-- 膏　　　　lipstick.
　-- 音　　　　labial.
85-- 缺　　　　hare-lip.

厲〔Li〕n. whetstone, v. whet, adj. severe, harsh, cruel, stern.

21-- 行禁令　　carry out the law strictly.
　-- 行節約　　practice rigid economy.
27-- 色　　　　gruff look, stern. countenance.
　-- 色正言　　speak with stern countenance.
30-- 害　　　　severe, serious, cruel.
47-- 聲　　　　speak sternly.
　-- 聲而言　　talk in a harsh voice.
　-- 聲斥責　　scold in an irritating voice.
60-- 目而視　　look with a stern glare.
77-- 風　　　　severe air.

膈〔Ko〕n. diaphragm, midriff.

74-- 膜　　　　diaphragm.

7123₂

辰〔Chen〕n. 7:00 — 9:00 in the morning, time, hour, luck, stars.

豚〔Tun〕n. porker, sucking pig, young pig.

脹〔Chang〕v. swell, puff, n. swelling of the stomach.

40-- 大　　　　n. inflation, v. swell, inflate.
80-- 氣　　　　flatulence.
87-- 飽　　　　full, glutted.

7123₄

厭〔Yen〕v. dislike, hate, be tired of, loathe, adj. satiated.

00-- 棄　　　　reject, discard, have a distaste for.
10-- 惡　　　　n. aversion, abomination, antipathy, v. hate, loathe, dislike, detest, adj. wearisome.
29-- 倦　　　　tired of, weary of.
　-- 倦人世　　be weary of life.
44-- 世派　　　pessimist.
　-- 世主義　　pessimism.
48-- 故喜新　　dislike the old and take a delight in the new.
63-- 戰　　　　weary of war, war-weariness, war fatigue.
77-- 悶　　　　sorrow.
91-- 煩　　　　troublesome, be tired of.
　-- 煩瑣碎　　feel great hatred for trifles.

7123₆

蜃〔Shen〕n. large clam.

45-- 樓　　　　mirage.

7124₀

牙〔Ya〕n. tooth, tusks.

00-- 痛　　　　toothache.
　-- 膏　　　　toothpaste.
　-- 疳　　　　gumboil.
12-- 齒　　　　tooth.
24-- 科　　　　dentistry.
　-- 床　　　　jaw, teethridge, gum.
27-- 齦　　　　gum.
47-- 根　　　　root of a tooth.
70-- 雕　　　　ivory carving.
72-- 刷　　　　tooth brush.

77-- 醫	dentist.
88-- 籤	toothpick.
98-- 粉	tooth powder.

肝〔**Kan**〕*n.* liver.

00-- 病	liver complaint, liver ailment.
-- 癌	cancer of the liver.
11-- 硬化	liver cirrhosis.
77-- 膽	bravery, courage, liver and gall.
90-- 炎	hepatitis.

廚＝厨 0024_0

7124_4

腰〔**Yao**〕*n.* waist, loin, kidneys.

00-- 痛	lumbago.
07-- 部	waist.
17-- 子	kidneys.
27-- 身	waist size.
44-- 帶	girdle, sash.
-- 鼓	hip drum.
60-- 圍	apron.

7124_7

反〔**Fan**〕*n.* repetition, revolt, *v.* turn back, turn over, reverse, oppose, return, turn, send back, rebel, revolt, *adj.* contrary, opposite.

00-- 帝	anti-imperialism, oppose imperialism.
-- 應	*n.* reaction, response, *v.* respond, react.
-- 應爐	reactor.
02-- 證	counterevidence, disproof, negative evidence.
-- 訴	cross action.
04-- 結	cross examination.
08-- 效用	negative utility.
10-- 正	anyway, in any case, after all.
-- 而	on the contrary.
-- 面	reverse, opposite (or negative) side.
-- 面教材	lesson of negative example.
-- 面人物	negative character.
-- 面無情	turn the cold shoulder to a friend.
-- 覆	*n.* repetition, reversal, *adj.* repeated.
-- 覆思量	think over and over again.
-- 覆無常	capricious, inconstant.
18-- 攻	counterattack.
21-- 比例	inverse proportion, reciprocal proportion, reciprocal ratio.
-- 傾銷	anti-dumping.
22-- 側不安	toss about in bed unable to sleep.
24-- 動	reaction, reactionary.
-- 動派	reaction, reactionary.
-- 動性	reactionary nature.
-- 動論點	reactionary viewpoint.
-- 動透頂	ultra-reactionary.
-- 動分子	reactionist, reactionary.
-- 射	*n.* reflection, *v.* reflect.
-- 供	give counterevidence.
-- 告	countercharge.
-- 科學	in opposition to science.
27-- 芻	*n.* rumination, *v.* ruminate, chew the cud.
-- 響	*n.* echo, response, *v.* re-echo, reverberate.
-- 包圍	counter-encirclement.
-- 修	*n.* anti-revisionism, *v.* oppose revisionism.
28-- 復	*n.* repetition, *v.* repeat, reiterate.
-- 作用	counteraction, reaction.
30-- 之	on the contrary, on the other hand.
-- 流	reflux.
-- 宣傳	counterpropaganda.
-- 突擊	counter-assault.
32-- 派角色	role of a villain.
33-- 浪費	be against waste.
34-- 對	*n.* objection, *v.* be against, go against, object to, oppose, counter, deprecate, be in opposition to.
-- 對票	negative vote, opposite lot.
-- 對者	opposite.
-- 對派	opposition faction (or party).
-- 對黨	opposition, opposite party.
-- 對倒退	oppose retrogression.
-- 對霸權主義	oppose hegemonism.

37--	潮流	go against the tide.
--	過來	vice versa.
--	通貨膨脹	*n.* anti-inflation, disinflation, *v.* counter inflation, fight against inflation.
40--	右傾	fight against right deviation (rightist).
--	索賠	counterclaim.
43--	求諸己	make self-examination.
44--	封建	anti-feudalism.
--	革命	anti-revolution, counter-revolution.
--	革命政變	counter-revolutionary coup d'etat.
--	老還童	turn back to youthfulness, rejuvenate.
50--	抗	*n.* opposition, *v.* resist, oppose, defy oppose, set against.
53--	撲	counterattack.
--	感	repugnance, ill feeling, antipathy.
--	控制	resist someone's control.
--	戈起義	rebel and start an uprising.
55--	轉	reverse.
57--	擊	rebuff, repel.
60--	罵	retort.
--	圍攻	counter-encirclement.
--	口	retract, disown.
--	口無信	deny and go back on one's words.
--	目不顧	turn away the eyes.
63--	戰公約	peace pact.
65--	映	reflect.
68--	敗爲勝	turn defeat into victory.
71--	反覆覆	again and again.
74--	駁	retort, refute, disprove.
--	射作用	reflex action.
77--	問	cross examination.
--	邪歸正	return to orthodoxy.
--	間諜	counterespionage.
80--	人民	anti-popular, turn against the people.
--	貪污	anti-corruption.
88--	坐	retaliation.
90--	光	reflection of light.
--	光攝影機	reflex camera.

--	常	out of ordinary, eccentricity, abnormality.
--	省	*n.* reflection, self-examination, *v.* reflect, collect one's thought.
--	省檢討	introspection and self-examination.
--	省哲學	reflection philosophy.
91--	叛	*n.* rebellion, *v.* rebel, revolt, bear arms against.
--	叛的	mutinous.
--	判者	rebel, insurgent.
95--	情報	counter intelligence.
98--	悔	*n.* repentance, *v.* regret, repent.
--	悔已遲	too late to repent.

7124₈

厰 = 廠 0024₈

阪 〔**Pan**〕*n.* hillside.

厚 〔**Hou**〕*adj.* thick, dense, sincere, faithful, rich, generous, deep.

00--	度	thickness.
01--	顏	shameless, brazen-faced.
--	顏無恥	brazen, shameless.
21--	此薄彼	be liberal to one and stingy to another.
22--	利多銷	large profits and quick turnover.
24--	德	great virtue.
36--	遇	hospitality.
38--	道	generous, kind-hearted.
40--	皮	thick-skinned.
68--	贈	bestow liberally.
95--	情	deep friendship, deep affection.
--	情難卻	kind feelings are hard to refuse.

7126₀

阽 〔**Yen or Tien**〕*adj.* dangerous.

陌 〔**Mo**〕*n.* market street, road, path between fields, street.

25--	生	strange, new, unacquainted, unfamiliar.
--	生人	stranger.

7126₁

脂 〔**Chih**〕*n.* fat, grease, lard, gum,

sap, cosmetics.

70--	肪	fat, tallow.
98--	粉	cosmetics.

7126_2

階 〔Chieh〕 *n.* step, stair, degree, rank, grade.

27--	級	class, degree, grade, rank, steps.
--	級性	class character.
--	級鬪爭	class strife, class war, class struggle.
--	級本性	class nature.
--	級感情	class feeling.
--	級覺悟	class consciousness.
--	級分析	class analysis.
48--	梯	ladder, flight of steps, flight of stairs.
77--	層	stratum.
--	段	stage, phase.

7127_9

曆 〔Li〕 *n.* calendar, almanac, *v.* calculate.

34--	法	system of determining the seasons and solar terms of a year.
50--	本	calendar, almanac.
--	書	calendar.
58--	數	heaven's will, astrological fates.

7128_0

仄 〔Tse〕 *n.* oblique, consonant, one of the three tones other than the even tone (in Chinese phonology).

47--	聲	oblique tones, tones other than the even tone.
71--	陋之人	mean fellow.
77--	聞人言	hear indirectly from a person.

7128_2

厥 〔Chueh〕 *pron.* he, she, it, this, that, *v.* be choked, faint, *adj.* third-person possessive.

14--	功甚偉	great are his services to the country.

22--	倒	faint, swoon.

7128_6

頎 〔Chi〕 *adj.* tall, long.

願 〔Yuan〕 *n.* will, wish, vow, desire, *v.* wish, desire, hope, want.

00--	意	will, please.
07--	望	hope, will, expectation, intention.

7128_9

灰,灰 〔Hui〕 *n.* ash, cinder, dust, lime, *adj.* grey.

00--	塵	dust.
27--	色	grey, ash-color.
--	色收入	income from moonlighting.
33--	心	discouraged, dejected, disappointed, disheartened.
77--	肥	ash fertilizer.
--	鼠	grey squirrel.
80--	領工人	grey collar.
95--	爐	ashes.

7129_1

膘 〔Piao〕 *adj.* fat.

7129_6

原 〔Yuan〕 *n.* origin, source, beginning, plain, open ground, level field, *v.* forgive, *adj.* originally, primarily.

00--	意	original idea, original intention.
--	文	text, original text.
--	諒	*n.* forgiveness, *v.* excuse, pardon, forgive.
--	主	original proprietor, rightful owner, original owner, proprietor.
--	產地	country of origin, place of origin.
12--	型	prototype.
--	形	prototype, one's colors, original form.
--	形質	protoplasm.
--	形畢露	completely unmasked or exposed.
16--	理	theory, principle.
17--	子	atom.
--	子彈	atomic bomb, atom bomb.

-- 子能	atomic energy.	
-- 子能工業	atomic energy industry.	
-- 子堆	atomic pile.	
-- 子核	atomic nucleus.	
-- 子塵	atomic fallout.	
-- 子量	atomic weight.	
-- 子論	atomic theory.	
-- 子武器	A-weapons, atomic weapons.	
-- 子時代	atomic age.	
-- 子核物理學	nucleonics.	
-- 子核對裂	nuclear fission.	
20-- 稿	manuscript, original copy, protocol.	
-- 委	circumstances of a case.	
21-- 價	prime cost, original price, cost price.	
24-- 告	plaintiff, accuser, appellant.	
-- 告敗訴	the plaintiff lost the case.	
-- 動力	prime mover (or power).	
-- 先	at first, primarily, originally.	
-- 裝貨	real thing.	
27-- 色	primary color.	
-- 物寄回	the original goods were mailed back.	
30-- 定	originally decided.	
-- 宥其罪	forgive his offense.	
35-- 油	crude oil, raw oil.	
40-- 木	timber.	
-- 來	originally, primarily.	
-- 來如此	it was as it is now, so, that is what you mean.	
43-- 始	primitive, elemental, original.	
-- 始者	originator.	
-- 始人	primitive man.	
-- 始森林	virgin forest.	
-- 始時代	primitive ages.	
44-- 著	original work.	
-- 封不動	keep intact.	
-- 材料	materials, raw and processed material, primary materials.	
46-- 棉	raw cotton.	
47-- 報價	original offer.	
48-- 樣	original sample.	
50-- 本	origin, source.	

-- 素	element.	
-- 由	cause.	
60-- 因	cause, reason.	
62-- 則	principle, law, axiom.	
-- 則上	in principle.	
-- 則性	principle.	
-- 則問題	matters of principle.	
67-- 野	moorland, wild, wilderness.	
71-- 原本本	from the very beginning to the end.	
72-- 質	element.	
80-- 氣	vitality.	
88-- 籍	one's native place, birthplace.	
92-- 判取消	the original judgment was cancelled.	
94-- 料	material, raw material, raw produce.	
-- 料缺乏	material shortage.	

7131₁

驪〔Li〕n. black horse.

7131₆

驅〔Chu〕v. drive away, expel, urge, compel, force.

22-- 出	expel.	
25-- 使	drive, urge on by force.	
31-- 逐	drive out, drive away, chase, expel, oust.	
-- 逐出境	n. deportation, v. deport, banish, banish abroad.	
-- 逐艦	destroyer.	
-- 逐機	pursuit plane, chaser.	
48-- 散	scatter, dispel, disperse.	
78-- 除	get rid of, drive out.	
-- 除禍患	drive out the weight of woes.	
88-- 策	urge.	

7131₇

驢〔Lu〕n. donkey, mule, ass.

17-- 子	ass, donkey.	

7132₇

馬〔Ma〕n. horse.

00-- 廄	stable.	
12-- 到成功	immediate success upon arrival.	
-- 列主義	Marxism-Leninism.	

11-- 背	horseback.	
21-- 上	soon, at once.	
23-- 弁	orderly messenger.	
-- 戲	circus.	
-- 戲團	circus.	
30-- 房	livery.	
-- 褲	riding breeches.	
33-- 褂	riding jacket.	
34-- 達	motor.	
40-- 力	horse power (h.p.).	
-- 奇諾防線	Maginot Line.	
-- 克思主義	Marxism.	
41-- 鞭	horse whip.	
43-- 鞍	saddle.	
-- 鞍形	U-shape, U-shaped.	
44-- 靴	boot, riding boots.	
45-- 韁	reins.	
47-- 棚	stable.	
-- 桶	stool, chamber stool, night stool.	
50-- 車	cart, coach, carriage.	
-- 夫	groom, hostler.	
-- 拉松賽跑	Marathon, Marathon race.	
54-- 蝗	horseleech.	
60-- 口鐵	galvanized iron, tin plate.	
-- 蹄	horse hoof, hoof of a horse.	
-- 蹄鐵	staple.	
62-- 嘶	neigh.	
67-- 鳴	n. neigh, v. neigh.	
-- 路	road.	
53-- 賊	mounted bandit.	
72-- 鬃	horsehair, mare.	
77-- 醫	horse doctor.	
-- 尾	horsetail.	
78-- 隊	cavalry.	
82-- 鐙	stirrup.	
88-- 鈴薯	potato.	
99-- 糞紙	cardboard, strawboard.	

7133₁

懇〔Te〕v. do evil.

7133₉

愿〔Yuen〕adj. sincere, honest, pure, faithful, respectful, virtuous.

7134₃

辱〔Ju〕v. insult, dishonor, disgrace, put

to shame, defile.

60-- 罵	insult, abuse, call hard name, revile, vilify.	

7138₁

驥〔Chi〕n. fine horse.

7139₁

驃〔Piao〕n. cream-colored horse, adj. brave.

7160₃

唇〔Chun〕n. lips.

00-- 膏	lipstick.	
21-- 齒	lips and teeth.	
87-- 缺者	harelipped person.	

7171₁

匹〔Pi〕n. pair, mate, numerary particle for horses, bolt of cloth, v. match, compare, adj. equal, common.

08-- 敵	n. match, rival v. be a match for.	
26-- 偶	mate.	
50-- 夫	individual, common man.	
-- 夫匹婦	common people, common man and woman.	
-- 夫之勇	animal courage.	
-- 夫有責	every common man has his obligation.	
71-- 馬單槍	(go to battle) single-handed.	

匡〔Kuang〕adj. right, regular, correct.

10-- 正	correct.	

匯〔Hui〕n. remittance, exchange, v. remit, remit money, collect, converge.

00-- 率	rate of exchange, exchange rate.	
10-- 票	draft, bill, bill of exchange, money order (M.O.), remittance draft, remittance bill, bill of exchange (B/E).	
12-- 水	charge for remittances, charges for transfers, remittance fee.	
20-- 集一隅	gather in one corner.	
-- 往國外	remit abroad.	
22-- 出額	remitting amount.	
21-- 價	rate of exchange, conversion rate, exchange quotation.	

24-- 付（匯寄）　*n.* remittance, money remittance, *v.* remit, remit money, make remittance.
30-- 流　conflux.
47-- 款　*n.* remittance, money remittance, remit, *v.* remit money, make remittance.
-- 款收款人　beneficiary of remittance.
-- 款接濟　remit money to relieve.
-- 款單　remittance bill, money order, cash remittance.
-- 款人　remitter.
-- 報格式　reporting formula.
-- 報表格　reporting form.
55-- 費　remittance fee, charge for remittances, remittance charge.
80-- 合　merge with, combine with
-- 兌　exchange, currency exchange, remittance.
-- 兌率　rate of exchange, course of exchange.
-- 兌變動　fluctuation in exchange.
-- 兌政策　exchange policy.
-- 兌銀行　exchange bank.

匪〔Fei〕*n.* bandit, rebel, rascal, robber, vagabond, *adj.* not.
24-- 徒　vagabond, rascal, villain, outlaw, blackguard, bandit, robber.
-- 特　enemy agent.
44-- 幫　gang of bandits.
47-- 禍　bandit scourge.
50-- 夷所思　unthinkable.
80-- 首　chieftain of the bandit gang.
-- 首伏法　the rebel leader was executed.

7171₂

匝〔Tsa〕*n.* revolution, circuit, *v.* go round.

匠〔Chiang〕*n.* worker, workman, artificer, maker, smith, craftsman.
33-- 心經營　manage with creativity.

匾〔Pien〕*n.* tablet, plaque, signboard.
31-- 額高懸　a horizontal tablet hangs high.

7171₄

既〔Chi〕*v.* finish, exhaust, *adv.* already, entirely, *conj.* since.
10-- 而　then, not long afterwards.
20-- 往　past, gone.
23-- 然　in so much, since, now that.
-- 然如此　since it is so.
26-- 得權　acquired right.
-- 得利益　vested interests.
-- 得權利　acquired right, established right.
30-- 定價值　given value.
-- 定原則　settled principle.
38-- 遂犯　consummated crime.
53-- 成事實　accomplished fact.

7171₅

匣〔Hsia〕*n.* box, chest, trunk, case.
17-- 子　box, case.

7171₆

匿〔Ni〕*v.* hide, conceal, keep out of sight.
27-- 名　anonymous.
-- 名信　anonymous letter.
30-- 迹消聲　be in complete hiding.

區〔Chu〕*n.* district, canton, section, zone, *v.* distinguish.
20-- 委　District Party Committee.
43-- 域　region, area, district, realm.
-- 域性　regional significance.
52-- 劃　compartment.
62-- 別　*n.* discrimination, distinction, *v.* discriminate, distinguish, make a distinction between, *adj.* distinct.
71-- 區　trifling, petty, small.
-- 區之心　one's tiny heart, my heart.
-- 區之數　petty amount.
77-- 間車　local train, local bus, shuttle, shuttle bus.
78-- 隊　district contingent.
80-- 分　differentiate, partition.

回〔Po〕*adj.* unable, *adv.* quite, very, so, therefore.
20-- 信之人　untrustworthy man.
32-- 測　unfathomable, unexpected.

鼯〔Wu〕*n.* flying squirrel.
7171₇

巨〔Chu〕*adj.* big, large, vast, enormous, gigantic.
11--頭	magnate, national leader, giant.
12--型	giant, mammoth, colossal.
17--砲	heavy gun.
22--災	catastrophe.
27--物	monster.
28--纜	cable.
31--額	large number, big amount, big sum, huge sum, long figure.
33--浪	billow.
37--禍臨頭	a great calamity is drawing near.
40--大	big, huge, immense, great, large, stupendous, gigantic.
--大貢獻	substantial contribution.
--大風險	great risk.
--大企業	business giant.
70--擘	thumb, great man.
47--劫	catastrophe.
80--人	giant.

臣〔Chen〕*n.* minister, courtier, official, subject, vassal, term for "I" used by officials when addressing the emperor.
77--民	subject.
--服	be conquered.

甌〔Ou〕*n.* bowl, glass.
7171₈

匱〔Kuei〕*n.* big case, *v.* lack.
20--乏	lack, be short of.

7173₂

長〔Chang〕*n.* senior, head, chief, an elder, the eldest, *v.* grow, develop, increase, look, appear, *adj.* long, distant, far, older, elder, good, *adv.* often, regularly.
00--方形	rectangular, rectangle, oblong.
--度	length, dimension.
--衣	long gown.
10--工	farm hand.
--元音	long vowel.
11--輩	elder.
12--凳	bench.
17--子	first son, eldest son.
20--統靴	high boots.
21--處	strong side, strong point, merit.
--征	Long March (of the Chinese Communists), expedition.
25--生	long life.
--生果	peanut.
--生不老	perpetual rejuvenation.
--生之訣	secret of immortality.
27--久	long, long time, for long.
--久之計	permanent arrangement.
30--官	superior, senior.
--進	make progress.
31--江三角洲	Yangtze River Delta.
32--衫	long gown.
34--波	long wave.
--襪	stockings.
35--袜	hose.
37--江	Yangtze River.
38--途	long distance.
--途電話	long distance telephone.
--途電話通話	toll call.
--途飛行	long distance flight.
40--女	eldest daughter.
--大	grow up.
--壽	longevity, long-lived.
--志氣	heighten or raise one's morale.
42--欓	form, bench.
--機	pilot plane, command plane.
43--城	Great Wall.
44--者（輩）	senior, one's senior, elder.
--老	elder.
--老會	presbytery, presbyterian church.
47--期	long period, long-term, over a long period of time.
--期方案	long-term project.
--期許可證	standing permit.
--期儲蓄	permanent saving.

-- 期計畫　　　long range plan.
-- 期調整　　　long run adjustment.
-- 期平均成本　long run average cost.
-- 期預算　　　long range budget, long term budget.
-- 期研究　　　long range research.
-- 期發展　　　long run development, secular development.
-- 期承包工程　long-term construction contracts.
-- 期停滯　　　secular stagnation.
-- 期信託　　　long-term trust.
-- 期信用　　　long credit, standing credit.
-- 期經濟計畫　long-term economic plan, long range business plan.
-- 期出差　　　long-term business trip.
-- 期出租　　　long lease.
-- 期利率　　　long-term interest rate, secular rate.
-- 期利潤率　　long-term yield.
-- 期利益　　　long-term benefit.
-- 期貸款　　　fixed loan, loan.
-- 期動向　　　long-term trend.
-- 期失業　　　long-term unemployment.
-- 期債務　　　long-term debt.
-- 期債券　　　long bonds, long-term bonds.
-- 期保險　　　long-term insurance.
-- 期負債 (長期借款) long-term debt, long-term liability.
-- 期租約　　　long-term lease.
-- 期穩定　　　secular stability.
-- 期收益　　　income over the long-term.
-- 期收入　　　permanent income.
-- 期波動　　　long wave.
-- 期決策　　　long range decision, long run decision.
-- 期資產　　　long-lived assets, long-term assets, funded property.
-- 期資本　　　long-capital.
-- 期資金　　　long-term funds.
-- 期消費　　　permanent consumption.
-- 期抵押　　　long-term mortgage.
-- 期投資　　　long range investment, permanent investment.
-- 期居住　　　long-term stay.
-- 期發展計畫　long range developmental program.
-- 期貿易　　　long-term trade.
-- 期合同　　　long-term agreement, long-term contract, period contract.
-- 期押金　　　long-term annuity.
-- 期公債　　　long-term government bond, long-term public bond.
-- 期繁榮　　　secular exhilaration.
-- 期性　　　　protracted nature.
53-- 成　　　　grown up, grow into.
71-- 驅直入　　drive straight in.
79-- 胖　　　　grow fat, gain weight.
80-- 命百歲　　may you live a hundred years!
-- 命富貴　　　long life of abundance and respectability.
81-- 短　　　　length.
88-- 笛　　　　flute.
-- 篇大論　　　lengthy speech or writing.
-- 篇小說　　　novel.

7173₂
鬟 〔Yen〕 v. satisfy.

7178₆
頤 〔I〕 n. chin, cheeks, v. nourish, rear.
26-- 和園　　　Summer Palace.
28-- 養　　　　nourish, maintain.

7198₆
顙 〔Sang〕 n. forehead.

7210₀
劉 〔Liu〕 n. Liu (a family name), a kind of weapon, v. kill.
38-- 海　　　　fringe of hair.

7210₁
丘 〔Chiu〕 n. hill, mound, height, hill.
00-- 疹　　　　pimple.
44-- 墓　　　　grave, tomb.
74-- 陵　　　　mound, hillock.

7211₁
髭 〔Tzu〕 n. mustaches.

7212₁
斲 〔Cho〕 v. chop, hack.

7220₀
刷 〔Shua〕 n. brush, cleanse, v. brush,

scrub, rub, wipe out.

00--	衣服	brush clothes.
02--	新	*n.* renovation, *v.* rub down, renovate.
13--	恥雪恨	wipe out a disgrace and avenge a hatred.
17--	子	brush.
26--	白	whitewash.
34--	洗	scrub.
40--	去	brush off.
44--	鞋	brush shoes.
71--	牙	brush the teeth.

剛 〔**Kang**〕*adj.* hard, firm, steady, stiff, strong, unyielding, *adv.* just now.

07--	毅	*n.* fortitude, bravery, *adj.* resolute, unyielding.
--	毅果決	resolute and daring.
10--	正	upright.
11--	硬	hard, stubborn.
--	巧	just in time, incidentally.
14--	勁有力	vigorous and forcible.
16--	強	tough, strong.
--	強正直	indomitable and upright.
--	強果斷	indomitable and resolute.
17--	勇	*n.* courage, manhood, valor, *adj.* valorous.
--	柔	hard and soft, toughness and gentleness.
40--	才	just, just now.
--	志	iron will.
--	直	inflexible, upright.
--	去	just gone.
--	來	just come.
47--	猛	tough and daring.
--	好	exactly, just, just right.
95--	性	rigidity.
--	性憲法	rigid constitution.
98--	愎	obstinate, stubborn.

7221_1

乒 〔**Ping**〕*n.* a sound element.

72--	乓 (球)	ping-pong, table tennis.
--	乓拍	bat.

7221_4

陲 〔**Chui**〕*n.* frontier.

腫 〔**Chung**〕*n.* boil, swelling, *v.* swell, tumefy, *adj.* swollen, bloated.

00--	瘤	tumor.
47--	起	swell up, tumefy.
71--	脹	tumefaction, swelling.

7221_6

臘 〔**La**〕*n.* winter sacrifice, sacrifice to the gods offered three days after the winter solstice.

40--	肉	salted meat, cured meat, dried meat.
70--	腑	viscera.
76--	腸	sausage.
77--	月	twelfth lunar month.

7222_1

斤 〔**Chin**〕*n.* catty, hatchet.

所 〔**Suo**〕*n.* office, bureau, *conj.* as, then, therefore.

06--	謂	so-called.
26--	得	revenue, income, earnings, gains.
--	得稅	income tax, tax on income.
--	得額	amount of income.
27--	向無敵	all-conquering, invincible.
28--	以	therefore, henceforth.
40--	有	possess, own.
--	有產	chose in possession.
--	有地	manor.
--	有者	owner.
--	有權	ownership, possession, property, title of possession, proprietary, proprietary right, right of ownership, proprietorship.
--	有物	property, possession.
--	在地點	location, seat, place.
--	有權證	title of ownership, certificate of title.
--	有人	owner.
71--	長	director of a bureau.
81--	短	one's shortcoming.

7222_2

彫 〔**Tiao**〕*v.* carve.

02--	刻	carve.

膨 〔**Peng**〕*v.* swell, puff out, expand, *adj.* swollen, bloated, fat.

71-- 漲　　bloat, swell, blow up, expand, puff.

-- 脹　　dilate, expand, inflate.

7223₀

爪〔Chao〕*n.* claw, talon, nail.

64-- 哇　　Java.

-- 哇人　　Javanese.

77-- 牙　　lackeys, accomplices.

瓜〔Kua〕*n.* melons, gourds, cucumbers.

02-- 瓤　　melon pulp.

17-- 子　　melon seeds.

44-- 藤　　melon vines.

-- 葛　　melon vines, complication, connection.

60-- 田　　melon field.

-- 果　　melons and fruits.

80-- 分　　divide, separate, partition, dismember.

7223₁

斥〔Chih〕*v.* reprimand, blame, reproach, reject, expel, dismiss.

37-- 退　　*n.* dismissal, discharge, *v.* discharge, dismiss.

50-- 責　　denounce, rebuke, reproach.

7223₂

脈〔Mo〕*n.* pulse, vein, veins and arteries.

05-- 訣　　secret of the pulse.

21-- 衝　　(in electrics) impulse.

27-- 絡　　veins and arteries, system of related things.

53-- 搏　　pulse.

88-- 管　　arteries.

7223₇

隱〔Yin〕*n.* riddle, pains, suffering, *v.* hide, conceal, retire, pity, withdraw, *adj.* obscure, not evident, poor.

01-- 語　　slang.

23-- 伏　　skulk, lie concealed.

27-- 身　　hide oneself.

-- 約　　indistinct, obscure.

-- 名合夥　　dormant partnership, slee-

ping partnership.

-- 名合夥人　　dormant partner.

40-- 士　　hermit, anchorite.

44-- 藏　　hide, conceal.

-- 蔽　　shelter, cover, conceal.

-- 蔽所　　shelter.

-- 蔽活動　　work under cover.

50-- 患　　hidden danger.

64-- 瞞　　conceal, cover up.

68-- 喻　　metaphor.

71-- 匿　　disguise, cloak, conceal.

77-- 居　　*n.* seclusion, privacy, *v.* retire, live a hermit's life.

7224₀

阡〔Chien〕*n.* footpath between fields, paths on a plantation, path leading to a grave.

71-- 陌　　criss-cross foot-paths between fields.

胝〔Chih〕*n.* callosity, thickening of skin on hands or feet.

7224₇

孵見 7274₇

7226₁

后〔Hou〕*n.* queen, empress, ruler.

7226₂

腦〔Nao〕*n.* brain.

17-- 子　　brain, mental power.

23-- 袋　　head.

35-- 神經　　cranial nerves.

38-- 溢血　　haemorrhage of the brain.

40-- 力　　mental power, brains.

-- 力勞動　　mental labor.

47-- 殼　　skull.

74-- 膜炎　　meningitis.

80-- 貧血　　cerebral anaemia.

88-- 筋靈敏　　keen and sharp in thinking.

-- 筋簡單　　simple-minded.

90-- 炎　　encephalitis, inflammation of the brain.

7226₄

盾〔Tun〕*n.* shield.

26-- 牌　　shield.

7228_6
鬚 〔Hsu〕 n. beard, whisker.
7230_0
馴 〔Hsun〕 v. tame, adj. tame, mild, docile, well-bred.
00-- 鹿	reindeer.
21-- 順	docile, tame.
26-- 和	gentle, yielding.
30-- 良	docile, tame, mild, tractable.
63-- 獸者	animal tamer.
71-- 馬	break horse.
77-- 服	v. tame, subdue, adj. subdued.
80-- 養	v. tame, raise, domesticate, adj. domestic.

7232_7
驕 〔Chiao〕 n. big, strong horse. adj. proud, haughty, self-important, conceited, harsh, intense, severe.
17-- 子	spoilt child, proud favorite.
21-- 態	swaggering gait.
28-- 傲	n. pride, arrogance, adj. proud, haughty, arrogant.
40-- 奢	extravagant.
44-- 橫	insolence, overbearing, arrogant.
-- 者必敗	pride goes before a fall.
80-- 氣	arrogant airs.

7240_0
刪 〔Shan〕 v. cut, cancel, delete.
18-- 改	revise.
33-- 減	abridge.
-- 減冗文	abridge lengthy writings.
37-- 潤詞句	revise and polish phrases and sentences.
40-- 去	delete, cut off, expunge, cross out.
78-- 除	efface, blot, cancel.
88-- 簡	condense.
-- 繁就簡	condense and simplify.

7242_2
彤 〔Tung〕 adj. red, rosy, scarlet.
| 10-- 雲 | red clouds. |

7244_7
髮 〔Fa〕 n. hair.
00-- 辮	cue, tress, plait of hair.
27-- 網	hair net.
35-- 油	hair oil.
40-- 夾	hairpin, hair grip.
43-- 式	hair style.
44-- 帶	fillet, hair lace.
52-- 指	hair-raising.
59-- 捲	puff.
72-- 刷	hair brush.

7252_7
髴 〔Fu〕 adj. resembling.
7255_7
髯 〔Jan〕 n. whiskers, beard.
| 72-- 鬚如霜 | grey whiskers and beard. |

7260_1
髻 〔Chi〕 n. tress, coiffure with a top-knot, tuft, bun.
7260_4
昏 〔Hun〕 n. evening, dusk, twilight, in disorder, adj. dark, obscure, dim, gloomy, unconscious, senseless, dull, confused.
17-- 君	despot.
22-- 亂	confused, disordered.
-- 倒	faint.
39-- 迷	stupefied, unconscious.
-- 迷不醒	unconscious and unawakened.
-- 迷狀態	unconscious state.
44-- 暮	evening.
60-- 暈	faint.
-- 眩	dizzy, giddy.
-- 暗	dim, dark, gloomy.
72-- 昏欲睡	drowsy.

7262_7
鬍 〔Hu〕 n. beard.
| 72-- 鬚(子) | beard. |

7271_2
鬈 〔Chuan〕 n. curly hair.
| 72-- 髮 | curly hair, frizzled hair. |

7271_4
髦 〔Mao〕 n. infant's tuff.

7271₆
鬣〔Lieh〕*n.* beard or whiskers, crest, mane, fins.

7274₀
氏〔Shih〕*n.* family, clan, person, surname.
08-- 族　　　clan, family.
-- 族制度　　clan system.

7274₇
孵〔Fu〕*v.* hatch, incubate.
24-- 化　　　hatch, incubate.
-- 化期　　　hatching stage.
77-- 卵　　　brood.
-- 卵器　　　incubator.
90-- 小雞　　hatch chickens.

7277₂
岳〔Yueh〕*n.* lofty mountain, wife's parent.
77-- 母　　　mother-in-law.
80-- 父　　　father-in-law.

7280₁
兵〔Ping〕*n.* soldier, fighter, man in the ranks, weapons.
00-- 卒　　　soldier.
01-- 站　　　military station, army service station.
10-- 工廠　　arsenal, armory.
-- 不由將　　disobedient soldiers, troops that do not obey orders.
22-- 變　　　revolt, mutiny.
-- 種　　　classification of military units.
27-- 役　　　military service.
-- 役法　　　conscription law.
-- 役署　　　conscription department.
-- 役年齡　　military age.
30-- 家常事　commonplace in military operations.
33-- 強馬壯　well-equipped and well-trained troops with high morale.
34-- 法　　　tactics, military tactics, strategy.
-- 法家　　　strategist, tactician.
37-- 禍連年　successive years of military disaster.
40-- 士　　　soldier, enlisted man.
-- 力　　　military force.
-- 力不足　　the military strength is insufficient.
44-- 權　　　military authority.
-- 荒馬亂　　in a disorder caused by continuous military operations.
50-- 事　　　warfare.
-- 貴乎精　　trained soldiers are of more value than untrained ones.
53-- 戎相見　meet on the battle ground.
55-- 曹　　　sergeant, petty officer.
56-- 操　　　drill.
60-- 團　　　army corps.
66-- 器　　　weapon, arm.
78-- 艦　　　warship, battleship.
-- 隊　　　troop, range and life.
-- 臨城下　　the army is at the city gate.
-- 險　　　war risk, insurance.
87-- 餉　　　ration, soldier's pay.
96-- 糧　　　provision.
99-- 營　　　camp, barrack.

7280₆
質〔Chih〕*n.* substance, stuff, matter, nature, one's disposition, quality, *v.* examine, cross, confront, mortgage, question, pawn, pledge, *adj.* simple, natural.
07-- 詢　　　ask for an explanation.
17-- 子　　　(in physics) proton.
22-- 變　　　qualitative change, change in quality, quality change.
27-- 疑　　　ask for an explanation.
42-- 樸　　　plain, simple, homely.
44-- 地　　　quality, material.
-- 權　　　pledge.
56-- 押　　　pledge, hypothecate.
60-- 量　　　mass, quality.
-- 量保證　　quality assurance, quality guarantee.
-- 量檢查　　check up for quality, quality check, quality inspection, quality review, quality test.
-- 量差　　　poor quality.
-- 量分析　　quality analysis.

-- 量管理	quality control, quality management.
61-- 點	particle.
77-- 問	question, inquire, ask, query.
94-- 料	material, quality.

鬢 〔Pin〕 *n.* curl, tress, hair on the temples.

27-- 角	temples.
72-- 髮	hair on the temples.
77-- 腳	side-whiskers.

7290₁

鬃 〔Tsung〕 *n.* mane of a horse, topknot of headdress, horse hair, bristles.

20-- 毛	mane.

7293₀

鬆 〔Sung〕 *v.* relax, let go, loosen, *adj.* loose, slack, easy, lax.

14-- 勁	slack, loose strength.
-- 弛	*n.* laxity, *adj.* lax, loose.
20-- 手	leave hold of, let go.
40-- 爽	elated, refreshed.
-- 土	loosen the soil.
48-- 散	loose, incompact.
57-- 軟	spongy, loose and soft.
77-- 脆	crispy, brittle.
-- 緊帶	elastic braid.
97-- 懈	slacken.

7321₁

陀 〔To〕 *n.* steep bank, rugged place.

56-- 螺	top (toy).

院 〔Yuan〕 *n.* yard, courtyard, hall, college, asylum, walled enclosure, site.

17-- 子	yard, court, courtyard.
30-- 宅	residence.
40-- 士	academician.
44-- 落	courtyard.
71-- 長	dean, director, president, superintendent.

脘 〔Kuan〕 *n.* esophagus.

7321₂

腔 〔Chiang〕 *n.* breast, tune, note, cavity in the chest or thorax, accent.

07-- 調	tone, tune, accent.

腕 〔Wan〕 *n.* wrist.

40-- 力	strength of the wrist.
77-- 骨	wrist bone.
82-- 釧	bracelet.

7321₆

颱 〔Tai〕 *n.* typhoon.

77-- 風	typhoon.

7322₇

脯 〔Fu〕 *n.* dried meat, dried fruit, flesh in the general area of breast or chest.

7324₀

膩 〔Ni〕 *adj.* greasy, fat, smooth, glossy, dirty, tired, fatty, oily, close, intimate.

34-- 滯	indigestion.
91-- 煩	be sick of, be tired with.

7324₁

膊 〔Po〕 *n.* shoulder, upper arms.

7326₀

胎 〔Tai〕 *n.* womb, embryo, fetus.

00-- 衣	placenta.
25-- 生	viviparous.
27-- 盤	placenta.
48-- 教	antenatal training.
77-- 兒	fetus, child in the womb.

7328₆

臏 〔Pin〕 *n.* kneepan, bone of the leg.

7331₁

駝 〔To〕 *n.* camel, *adj.* hunchbacked.

11-- 背	humpback, camel back.
17-- 子	humpback.
20-- 毛	camel's hair.
22-- 峰	hump of a camel.
27-- 鳥	ostrich.

7332₂

驂 〔Tsan〕 *n.* team of three horses.

7332₇

騙 〔Pien〕 *n.* deceive, cheat, swindle, palm off, impose on, get by fraud.

10-- 不了	not to be deceived.
17-- 子	deceiver, crook, swindler.
-- 取	defraud, obtain by fraud, get by fraud.
28-- 稅	tax fraud, tax evasion.
77-- 局	fraud, trickery, deception.
80-- 人	swindle, be phony, be de-

ceitful.

7333₄

駃〔**Ai**〕*n.* animal walking.

7334₇

駿〔**Chun**〕*n.* noble steed, good horse, fine horse, outstanding man, *adj.* fleet, fast, great, speedy.

73-- 馬	thoroughbred, fine horse.

7336₀

駘〔**Tai**〕*n.* inferior horse.

7370₀

臥〔**Wo**〕*v.* sleep, lie down, rest, repose.

00-- 病	be ill abed, take to one's bed.
-- 床	lie on bed.
22-- 倒	lie down.
24-- 射	prone fire.
26-- 息	rest.
30-- 室	bedroom, chamber.
50-- 車	sleeper, pullman.
77-- 具	bedding.
83-- 舖	sleeping berth.

7410₄

墮〔**To**〕*n.* fall down, sink, let fall, destroy, ruin, *v.* fall, descend, sink, let fall.

10-- 下	fall down.
22-- 後	fall behind.
44-- 落	*n.* demoralization, downfall, *v.* fall down, sink, degrade, degenerate, run awry, debauch.
73-- 胎	*n.* abortion, miscarriage, *v.* cast young, miscarry.
80-- 入	fall into, sink into.
-- 入圈套	be caught in a trap.

7412₇

助〔**Chu**〕*v.* help, aid, assist, second, co-operate.

00-- 產士	midwife.
16-- 理	*n.* assistant, *v.* help.
-- 理員	staff, assistant.
-- 理工程師	assistant engineer.
20-- 手	assistant, helper, helping hand.
24-- 動字	auxiliary verb.
-- 動詞	auxiliary verb.
34-- 法	auxiliary law.
48-- 教	assistant, assistant teacher.
-- 教生	monitor.
53-- 成其事	help to finish a business.
56-- 捐	subscribe, contribute.
71-- 長	abet, encourage.
77-- 學金	student subsidies, scholarship, studies grant.
80-- 人爲快樂之本	service begets happiness.

7420₀

附〔**Fu**〕*n.* supplement, appendix, *v.* subjoin, aid, enclose, be near to, add, increase, attach, join, fit, rely on, match, adhere, *adj.* near.

00-- 庸	vassal state.
-- 庸國	subordinate state.
-- 言（又及）	postscript.
08-- 議	second a motion.
10-- 頁（附件）	attached sheet.
-- 函	accompanying letter, enclosed letter.
25-- 件	annex, enclosure, accessory, appended documents, accompanying documents, accompanying papers, appendix, attached paper, attachment.
26-- 和	*n.* partisan, second, *v.* echo, fallow.
30-- 注	notes.
32-- 近	in the vicinity, in the neighborhood, near, nearby, *adj.* neighboring.
40-- 有	be accompanied by.
44-- 帶	accessory, supplementary.
-- 帶請求	accessory claim.
-- 帶條件	provisory condition, collateral condition.
46-- 加	*v.* add to, annex to, *adj.* supplementary.
-- 加稅	surtax, additional tax.
-- 加條款	rider (in a document).
48-- 樣	the enclosed sample.
50-- 表	attached list, schedule, sta-

	tements, addendum.
62-- 則	by-law, supplementary rule, supplementary provisions.
66-- 單	coupon, attached list.
77-- 屬	*n.* dependant, accessory, subsidiary, *adj.* affiliated, subordinate, attached.
-- 屬物	appendix, attachment, accessory.
-- 屬機構	auxiliary body, secondary organ, subsidiary, subsidiary body, subsidiary organ.
-- 屬國	dependent state, vassal stat.
-- 屬公司	fellow subsidiaries, subsidiary, auxiliary.
80-- 入	*v.* enclose, *adj.* enclosed, attached.
87-- 錄	appendix, supplement, annex.

肘 〔**Chou**〕 *n.* elbow.

| 17-- 子 | elbow. |
| 77-- 關節 | elbow-joint. |

尉 〔**Wei**〕 *n.* military officer of the third class, military rank, company-grade officer, junior officer.

7421₀

肚 〔**Tu**〕 *n.* stomach, belly, abdomen.

00-- 痛	belly-ache, stomach-ache.
17-- 子	belly.
70-- 臍	navel.
-- 臍眼	navel.
71-- 脹	dropsy.
77-- 兜	stomacher.

7421₄

陞 〔**Sheng**〕 *v.* advance, ascend, mount, go up.

| 00-- 座 | ascend a dais. |
| 77-- 降 | promotion and degradation. |

陸 〔**Lu**〕 *n.* land, continent.

21-- 上	ashore, overland.
24-- 續	in succession, one after another.
30-- 空聯運	train-air-truck.
37-- 運	land-carriage, land transportation.
-- 軍	army.

-- 軍部	ministry of the army.
-- 軍部長	minister of war.
-- 軍上將	full general.
-- 軍上校	colonel.
-- 軍上尉	captain.
-- 軍中將	lieutenant general.
-- 軍中校	lieutenant colonel.
-- 軍中尉	lieutenant.
-- 軍少將	major general.
-- 軍少校	major.
-- 軍少尉	second lieutenant.
-- 軍編制	military organization.
-- 軍大學	military staff college.
-- 軍學校	military academy, military school.
-- 軍監獄	detention barracks.
-- 軍供應隊	army service forces.
-- 軍地面部隊	army ground forces.
44-- 地	land.
63-- 戰	land operation.
-- 戰隊	landing party.
67-- 路	land journey, overland route, by land.

7421₆

腌 〔**Yen**〕 *v.* salt.

| 27-- 魚 | salted fish. |
| 40-- 肉 | salted meat. |

7422₇

肋 〔**Lei**〕 *n.* rib, sides.

| 77-- 骨 | ribs. |

肭 〔**Na**〕 *adj.* very fat.

胯 〔**Kua**〕 *n.* crotch between legs.

隋 〔**Sui**〕 *n.* Sui dynasty.

腩 〔**Nan**〕 *n.* dried meat.

勵 〔**Li**〕 *v.* stimulate, incite, encourage.

21-- 行改革	press on with reformation.
40-- 志社	Moral Endeavour Association.
-- 志實行	be determined to carry out.

7423₁

肶 〔**Chu**〕 *v.* open, go away from.

7423₂

肱 〔**Kung**〕 *n.* arm.

膝 〔**Hsi**〕 *n.* knee.

44-- 蓋　　　　　knee-cap.
-- 蓋骨　　　　kneecap, kneepan.

隨 〔**Sui**〕 *v.* follow, obey, comply with, accompany, wait on, come after.
00-- 意　　　　at will, at pleasure.
-- 意請用　　please help yourself.
-- 意契約　　contract of discretion.
20-- 手關門　shut the door as you pass by.
21-- 便　　　　at will, at random, hit or miss.
-- 處　　　　everywhere.
22-- 後　　　　afterwards, in due course.
24-- 付　　　　accompanied with.
27-- 即　　　　at once.
-- 你　　　　as you please.
-- 身攜帶　carry about with one.
28-- 從　　　　*n.* attendants, entourage, *v.* attend, follow, succeed.
33-- 心所欲　at one's will, as one likes.
37-- 軍記者　war correspondent.
40-- 大流　　go with the tide.
42-- 機應變　decide according to the changing situation, use one's discretion.
44-- 帶　　　　bring along.
-- 地吐痰　spit everywhere.
60-- 員　　　　attach, retinue, suite.
-- 口亂說　be free with one's tongue.
-- 口答應　promise at once without hesitation.
62-- 叫隨到　be available anytime, be at one's beck and call.
64-- 時　　　　anytime, at once, whenever, at any moment.
77-- 同　　　　accompany.
-- 即　　　　forthwith, immediately, at once.
-- 風倒　　veer with the wind.
80-- 人安排　be shoved about by others.
-- 着　　　　along with.
88-- 筆　　　　memoir, essay, sketch.

朦 〔**Meng**〕 *adj.* dim, obscure, hazy.
71-- 朧　　　　obscure, gloomy, dim, hazy.
-- 朧不清　not bright and not clear.

髓 〔**Sui**〕 *n.* marrow in a bone, pith, essence.

7423₄

膜 〔**Mo**〕 *n.* membrane, thin membrane, fiber, *v.* kneel and worship.
21-- 拜　　　　kneel and make a prostration.

7423₈

陝 〔**Shan**〕 *n.* Shanhsi province.

7424₁

髒 〔**Tsang**〕 *adj.* dirty, dusty, filthy.
80-- 東西　　foul thing, rubbish, filth.

7424₇

陂 〔**Po**〕 *n.* hillside, slope, *adj.* uneven.

肢 〔**Chih**〕 *n.* limb.
27-- 解　　　　dismember, amputate.
75-- 體　　　　trunk and limbs, body.

脖 〔**Po**〕 *n.* neck.

陵 〔**Ling**〕 *n.* tomb, tomb mound, high mount, mausoleum, *v.* offend, insult.
44-- 墓　　　　tomb, grave.

7424₈

膵 〔**Tsui**〕 *n.* pancreas.

7425₃

臟 〔**Tsang**〕 *n.* entrails, viscera, *adv.* inwards.

7426₀

骷 〔**Ku**〕 *n.* skeleton, human skeleton, bones of the body.
75-- 髏　　　　human skeleton.

7426₁

腊 〔**La**〕 *n.* dried meat.

7428₁

陡 〔**Tou**〕 *adj.* steep, high, *adv.* suddenly, abruptly.
23-- 然　　　　suddenly, abruptly.
-- 峻　　　　precipitous.
44-- 坡　　　　steep slope.

7430₀

駙 〔**Fu**〕 *n.* an extra horse alongside of the team.
71-- 馬　　　　son-in-law of an emperor.

7431₁

驍 〔**Hsiao**〕 *n.* noble steed, *adj.* brave.
27-- 將　　　　brave general.

7431₂
馳 〔**Chih**〕 v. gallop, run, run fast, speed, fleet, spread.

21-- 往	go quickly.
27-- 名	famous, well-known, celebrated, noted.
-- 名商標	well-known brand.
-- 名的	famous, well-known.
67-- 躍	running, jumping.
71-- 馬	gallop.
-- 驅	trot, ride.

7432₁
騎 〔**Chi**〕 v. mount, ride on, sit astride on.

20-- 手	horseman.
21-- 術	horsemanship, equitation.
-- 師	jockey.
24-- 牆	be on the fence, sit on the fence.
-- 牆派	fence-sitters, neutral people, people who take no side.
40-- 士	knight, cavalier.
71-- 馬	n. riding, v. ride, ride a horse.
72-- 兵	horseman, cavalier, cavalry, mounted troops.
-- 兵隊	cavalry.

7433₀
馱 〔**To**〕 n. burden, load, v. bear, carry on back.

17-- 子	pack.
43-- 載	carry on the back.
63-- 獸	pack animal, beast of burden.

慰 〔**Wei**〕 v. condole, console, comfort, soothe.

60-- 唁	condole.
77-- 問	comfort, console, give compliment to, send one's regards to.
-- 問信	consolatory letter.
-- 問團	delegation of consolation.
-- 問傷兵	inquire after the wounded soldiers.
99-- 勞	comfort.

-- 勞品	comfort present.
-- 勞金	gratuity.
-- 勞災民	console the refugees with kind words and material gifts.

7434₀
駁 〔**Po**〕 v. dispute, rebut, criticize, refute, argue against, put down, adj. parti-colored, mixed.

00-- 辯	n. rebuttal, v. refute, argue.
10-- 不倒	irrefutable.
21-- 倒	n. confutation, v. confute.
24-- 貨	transship goods.
27-- 船	lighter, barge, cargo boat, craft.
37-- 運	lighter.
40-- 殼槍	automatic pistol.
60-- 回	reject, turn down.
-- 回上訴	dismiss an appeal.
72-- 斥	refute, repudiate.

7438₁
騏 〔**Chi**〕 n. horse of grey and black color.

7480₉
熨 〔**Yun**〕 v. iron, settle (matters).

34-- 斗	flat iron, box iron.
61-- 貼	well-done, settled.

7520₀
阱 〔**Ching**〕 n. pitfall, hole, v. fall into a hole.

7520₆
陣 〔**Chen**〕 n. battalion, array, array of troops in battle, battle, moment, a little while, v. battle.

00-- 痛	labor in childbirth, sudden sharp pain.
-- 亡	die in battle, bite the dust.
10-- 雨	shower, rainfall.
26-- 線	front, battle array, battle line.
30-- 容	line-up, battle array.
-- 容整齊	flawless deployment, everyone is a top choice.
34-- 法奇巧	ingenious in the plan of a campaign.

44-- 地　battle field, military position.

　-- 地戰　positional warfare.

　-- 勢　battle order, disposition of forces.

50-- 中勤務　field service.

77-- 風　gust of wind.

99-- 營　camp, barrack.

7521₇

肫〔Chun〕*n.* gizzard, gizzard of a fowl, *adj.* earnest, sincere.

7521₈

體〔Ti〕*n.* body, substance, limbs, form, shape, style, system, entity, essence, principle, *v.* put into practice.

00-- 育　physical education, athletics, physical culture, gymnastic.

　-- 育家　sportsman, athletics.

　-- 育館　gymnasium.

　-- 育場　stadium, athletic field.

　-- 育精神　sportsmanship.

　-- 育運動　sports.

　-- 諒　*n.* delicacy, *v.* allow for.

10-- 面　honor, reputation.

12-- 刑　corporeal punishment.

16-- 現　materialize.

17-- 弱　weak.

20-- 重　body weight.

　-- 重計　weighing machine.

　-- 系　system.

　-- 統　decorum, propriety in conduct.

22-- 例　form, general form of a writing.

　-- 制　system, frame, framework, mechanism, system of organization.

　-- 制條例　system and regulations.

25-- 健　strong, healthy, in good healthy.

　-- 積　volume, mass, bulk.

36-- 溫　temperature, body temperature, animal heat, blood heat.

　-- 溫表　clinic thermometer.

40-- 力　force, strength, physical strength.

　-- 力勞動　physical labor, manual labor.

　-- 力工作　manual work.

43-- 裁　form or style of writing.

47-- 格　physique, frame, body.

　-- 格檢查　physical examination, medical examination.

50-- 素　tissue.

56-- 操　gymnastics, physical exercise, physical drill.

60-- 罰　corporal punishment.

　-- 量　size.

61-- 貼　sympathize with.

72-- 質　physique, constitution (of the body).

78-- 驗　experience.

80-- 會　comprehend, understand.

97-- 恤　pity, regard, sympathize with, take into consideration, be compassionate.

7523₂

胰〔I〕*n.* pancreas, soap.

17-- 子　soap.

27-- 島素　insulin, pancreatin.

76-- 腺　pancreas.

膿〔Nung〕*n.* pus, purulence.

00-- 疱　festering sore, abscess.

　-- 瘡　pimple, fester, abscess, boil.

12-- 水　pus.

27-- 血　bloody pus, pus and blood.

72-- 腫　boil, abscess, purulent swelling.

7523₄

腠〔Tsou〕*n.* under the skin.

7524₀

腱〔Chien〕*n.* tendon.

7524₄

髏〔Lou〕*n.* skull.

7528₁

腆〔Tien〕*n.* protruding, *v.* blush, *adj.* fat, rich, thick, liberal, worthy, *proper,* good, beautiful, bashful.

7529₆
陳 〔Chen〕 *n.* Chen (a family name.), *v.* tell, show, arrange, set in order, spread out, state, narrate, *adj.* old, stale, out of state.

00-- 腐	stale, musty, obsolete, out of fashion.
07-- 設	*n.* arrangement, *v.* arrange.
08-- 說	narrate, mention.
12-- 列	*n.* on display, *v.* show, exhibit, display, expose, demonstrate.
-- 列品	exhibit, articles on display.
-- 列所	museum.
-- 列室	exhibition room, showroom, gallery.
-- 列展覽術	showmanship.
-- 列館	pavilion, show house.
24-- 貨	old stock, shopworn goods.
33-- 述	*n.* statement, mention, *v.* state, tell, give detail, give an account of, represent.
-- 述單	representation letter, letter of representation.
44-- 舊	*n.* secondhand goods, obsolescence, *adj.* old-fashioned, old, stale.
-- 舊設備	obsolete equipment.
-- 舊存貨	obsolete stock.
72-- 兵	mass troops.
80-- 年老酒	aged wine.

7530₀
駛 〔Shih〕 *v.* drive, sail, steer, run, gallop, move fast, *adj.* fast.

21-- 行	drive, sail.
27-- 向	drive to, be bound for.
80-- 入	sail into.

7532₇
騁 〔Cheng〕 *v.* hasten on, run away.

7570₄
肆 〔Ssu〕 *n.* shop, store, warehouse, marketplace, *v.* expand, extend, spread out, arrange, hold (a pen), *adj.* four, reckless, outrageous, *adv.* excessively.

00-- 意	wanton, rampant.
17-- 習	practice, get skillful.
21-- 行劫掠	indulge in looting.
-- 行無忌	act disorderly and care for nobody.
32-- 業	study, learn a profession.

7571₆
鼬 〔Yu〕 *n.* weasel.

77-- 鼠	weasel, stoat.

7578₆
隤 〔Tse〕 *n.* abstruseness.

7620₀
胭 〔Yen〕 *n.* throat, rouge, cosmetics.

71-- 脂	rouge.
-- 脂虎	termagant, virago.

7621₄
隍 〔Huang〕 *n.* empty pool.

腥 〔Hsing〕 *n.* raw flesh, *adj.* rank, stinking, rancid.

26-- 臭	*n.* stink, *adj.* stinking, noisome.
65-- 味	bad flavor, offensive smell of fish, meat, etc.
80-- 羶	unpleasant smell of goat.
-- 氣	offensive smell of fish or meat.

7622₇
隅 〔Yu〕 *n.* corner, nook, angle, cove.

陽 〔Yang〕 *n.* sun, male, solar, *adj.* bright, sunny, light, brilliant, masculine, positive, strong.

10-- 電	positive electricity.
23-- 台	balcony, veranda.
71-- 曆	solar calendar.
80-- 傘	parasol, umbrella.

腸 〔Chang〕 *n.* intestine, gut, entrails, bowels.

00-- 衣	casing.
17-- 子	bowels, intestines.
22-- 斷魂銷	heartbroken.
24-- 結核	consumption of the bowels.
44-- 熱症	typhoid fever.
60-- 胃病	stomach disease.
90-- 炎	enteritis, intestinal catarrh.

髑〔Tu〕*n.* skull.

7623₀

腮〔Sai〕*n.* cheeks.

| 76-- 腺 | parotid gland. |
| -- 腺炎 | parotitis. |

7623₂

隈〔Wei〕*n.* bend, cove, winding, corner.

腺〔Hsien〕*n.* gland.

| 26-- 細胞 | gland cell. |

7623₃

隰〔Hsi〕*n.* low marshy land.

7624₀

陴〔Pi〕*n.* parapet on a wall.

脾〔Pi〕*n.* spleen, temper, temperament.

60-- 胃	spleen and stomach, appetite.
74-- 臟	spleen.
80-- 氣	humor, temper, disposition.
-- 氣惡劣	bitterness of temper.

髀〔Pi〕*n.* thigh.

7625₀

胛〔Chia〕*n.* scapula.

7628₁

隄〔Ti〕*n.* bank, dike.

| 70-- 防洪水 | guard against the flood. |

7628₆

隕〔Yun〕*v.* fall, drop, roll down.

10-- 石	meteorite.
44-- 落	fall, drop.
60-- 星	meteor.

7629₄

臊〔Sao〕*adj.* fetid, rancid, rank, smelling bad, bashful, shy.

髁〔Ko〕*n.* thigh bone.

7630₀

駟〔Ssu〕*n.* team of four horses.

駰〔I〕*n.* post horse.

7633₀

驄〔Tsung〕*n.* black and white horse.

7634₁

驛〔I〕*n.* post, stage, post horse, courier station.

00-- 亭	post house.
01-- 站	stage, post.
25-- 使	courier.
37-- 運	transport by horse.
71-- 馬	post horse.

7639₃

騾〔Lo〕*n.* mule.

17-- 子	mule.
50-- 車	mule cart.
-- 夫	muleteer.

7680₈

咫〔Chih〕*n.* a short foot of 8 inches, measure of eight inches.

| 77-- 尺 | very near, not far away, closely. |
| -- 尺之間 | within a foot, very near. |

7710₀

皿〔Min〕*n.* vessel, dish, plate.

且〔Chieh〕*adv.* temporarily, in addition, moreover, besides, furthermore, still, yet, also.

08-- 說	by the way.
21-- 行且作	do something at a run.
30-- 泣且訴	sob out something.
63-- 戰且走	fight a retreat back, fight while falling back.

7710₄

堅〔Chien〕*adj.* strong, firm, stable, hard, durable, lasting, solid.

07-- 毅	constancy.
10-- 不吐實	obstinately refuse to speak up.
11-- 硬	rigid, hard, inflexible.
-- 硬如石	as solid as stone.
16-- 強	strong, vigorous.
17-- 忍	*n.* fortitude, patience, perseverance, *v.* persevere, *adj.* persevering.
20-- 信	convince, believe firmly.
-- 信不移	firmly believe in.
21-- 貞不屈	stand firmly.
27-- 穩的	steady.

30-- 守	maintain, keep to, keep firmly.
-- 守陣地	stand one's ground.
-- 實	firm, solid, durable.
-- 定	firm, resolute, steadfast.
-- 定性	steadfastness.
-- 定不移	inflexible, unswerving.
-- 定的支持	staunch support.
35-- 決	v. resolve, adj. resolute, determined.
-- 決支持	back solidly.
44-- 執	v. hold on to, adj. obstinate.
-- 苦卓絕	endure hardships to the utmost.
46-- 如磐石	as firm as a rock.
47-- 韌	hard, firm, tough, persistent, resilient.
51-- 拒	offer a strong resistance.
52-- 挺	firmness.
54-- 持	n. persistence, v. insist, persist, hold on, preserve, assert, hang on, maintain.
-- 持主張	stick to one's opinion.
-- 持立場	stick to one's guns.
-- 持不懈	persistently, consistently.
-- 持到底	stand out a crisis.
-- 持己見	be firm in one's view.
-- 持原則	adhere to principle.
-- 持原價	sit on price quotations.
60-- 固	solid, strong, firm, hard, tough, durable.
-- 果	nut.

閏〔Jen〕n. intercalary, intercalary month.
60-- 日	intercalary day.
77-- 月	intercalary month.
80-- 年	leap year, intercalary year.

閨〔Kuei〕n. boudoir, women's apartment.
| 40-- 女 | virgin, spinster, maid, maiden, daughter. |
| 77-- 閣 | ladies' apartment. |

7710₇

閂〔Shuan〕n. bar, crossbar, bolt or latch of a door.

20-- 住	bolt.
21-- 上	bar, bolt.
77-- 門	bar a door.

鹽〔Kuan〕v. wash, wash hands.
34-- 洗	wash, bathe.
-- 洗室	lavatory, washroom, toilet.
80-- 盆	wash basin.

闔〔He〕n. leaf of door, v. shut, adj. whole, entire.
| 30-- 家 | whole family. |

7710₈

豎〔Shu〕v. erect, establish, set up, put up, adj. vertical, upright.
00-- 立	stand, stand up, erect.
11-- 琴	harp.
40-- 直	perpendicular, set up-right.
-- 坑	pit, shaft.
47-- 起	set up, erect.
55-- 井	(in mining) vertical shaft.
-- 井礦	shaft mine.

7711₄

鬥〔Dow〕v. fight, struggle, contest, compete.
20-- 爭	struggle, fight.
-- 爭性	fighting spirit.
22-- 倒	refute, strike down.
25-- 牛	bullfight.
27-- 臭	discredit.
40-- 力	wrestling.
-- 志	fighting will, fighting spirit.
44-- 垮	overthrow.
51-- 批（改）	struggle-criticism-transformation (in Red China).
77-- 毆	fight, brawl.
86-- 智	battle of wits.
90-- 拳	boxing.

7712₇

邱〔Chiu〕n. Chiu (a family name.).

翳〔I〕n. feather fan, film, screen, v. screen, shade, film over the eye,

7713₆

蚤〔Tsao〕n. flea.
| 17-- 虱 | fleas and lice. |

閩〔Min〕n. the province of Fukien.

7714₇

毀 〔Hui〕 *v.* destroy, break, ruin, spoil, injure, break to pieces, damage, defame, slander.

00--	謗	slander, defame.
12--	形	deform.
28--	傷	injure, hurt.
33--	滅	*n.* destruction, *v.* destroy, demolish, smash, ravage, kill, exterminate, ruin.
40--	壞	destroy, spoil, ruin, damage.
--	壞信用	injury of credit.
47--	約	break one's promise, scrap a contract or treaty.
56--	損	wreck, spoil, harm.
80--	人名譽	cast a slur on one's reputation.

7716₄

闊 〔Kuo〕 *n.* width, *adj.* wide, broad, open, rich, extravagant.

00--	度	width.
21--	步	stride, walk in strides.
22--	綽	wealthy, rich.
62--	別	long separated.
80--	氣	extravagant.

7721₀

几 〔Chi〕 *n.* desk, table.

凡 〔Fan〕 *adj.* all, every, common, ordinary, usual, whatever, general, worldly.

00--	庸	ordinary.
10--	爾賽協約	Versailles Treaty.
22--	例	general rules.
27--	物	everything.
28--	俗	vulgar, worldly.
40--	士林	Vaseline.
50--	事	everything.
--	事須忍耐	what can't be cured must be endured.
--	事皆有始	everything must have a beginning.
80--	人	common man, mortals.

夙 〔Su〕 *n.* dawn, morning, *adj.* early, old, former.

00--	夜	morning and night, day and night.
20--	愛	predilection.
24--	仇	old enemy.
44--	世冤家	enemy of former life.

肌 〔Chi〕 *n.* flesh, flesh under the skin, muscle.

21--	膚	skin.
40--	肉	muscle.

阻 〔Tsu〕 *v.* hinder, prevent, stop, obstruct, oppose, put down, impede.

17--	礙	interrupt, retard, hinder, obstruct, impede, hamper.
--	礙物	obstruction, obstacle.
21--	止	stop, check, prevent, obstruct.
22--	斷	obstruct, block up.
30--	塞	obstruct, stop, block up, barricade.
34--	滯	retard.
36--	遏	inhibit.
40--	力	resistance.
54--	撓	obstruct, thwart, check.
57--	擊	*n.* interception, *v.* intercept.
59--	擋	resist, hinder, block.
71--	膈	*n.* separation, *v.* separate.
77--	留	detain.

凰 〔Huang〕 *n.* female phoenix.

鳳 〔Feng〕 *n.* male phoenix.

22--	仙花	balsam.
--	梨	pineapple.
77--	凰	Chinese phoenix.

風 〔Feng〕 *n.* wind, gale, air, education, influence, customs, style, folk songs, news, information, kind of ailment.

00--	度	appearance, bearing, demeanor.
06--	韻猶存	look still attractive.
10--	雪	snowdrift.
--	雨	storm, wind and rain, storm of wind and rain.
--	雨表	barometer.
--	雨無阻	do something or go somewhere regardless of weather

	changes.	
-- 平浪靜	calm at sea.	
-- 雲人物	celebrity.	
11-- 琴	organ (musical instrument).	
-- 頭主義	showiness.	
21-- 行	prevalent.	
-- 行一時	become a fad of the time.	
22-- 災	hurricane havoc, be hit by windstorm, disaster caused by windstorm.	
27-- 向	windward, way the wind blows.	
-- 向標	vane, weathercock.	
-- 紀	public morality, discipline.	
28-- 俗	custom, manner, usage, practices.	
30-- 涼	n. sarcastic remarks, adj. cool and breezy.	
-- 扇	electric fan.	
-- 流	gallant, refined, elegant.	
-- 流才子	romantic scholar, refined and cultured man.	
-- 流人物	romantic person.	
33-- 浪	waves, crises.	
34-- 波	disturbances.	
36-- 濕	rheumatism.	
-- 濕病	rheumatism.	
37-- 潮	disturbance, campaign, storm.	
39-- 沙	sandstorm.	
40-- 土	climate, social practices, customs.	
-- 土人情	local customs and practices.	
-- 力	wind power, wind force.	
-- 力計	windgauge.	
41-- 趣	humorous, interesting.	
47-- 格	taste, style, manner.	
50-- 車	windmill.	
60-- 暴	storm, tempest, windstorm.	
-- 暴損傷	damage by storm.	
-- 景	scene, scenery, landscape picture, view, prospect.	
-- 景區	scenic spot.	
-- 景畫	landscape painting.	
65-- 味	taste, flavor, savor.	
70-- 雅	elegant, refined.	
77-- 聞	hearsay.	

78-- 險	risk.	
-- 險預防	prevention of risk.	
-- 險估價	valuation of risk.	
-- 險額	amount at risk.	
-- 險分析	risk analysis.	
-- 險分擔	allocation of risk, risk sharing.	
-- 險管理	risk management.	
80-- 氣	fashion, custom.	
88-- 箏	kite.	
-- 範	model, paragon.	
-- 箱	bellows.	
90-- 光	scenery, scene, good reputation.	
-- 尚	customs, practices.	
95-- 情	romantic feelings.	

7721₁

尼〔**Ni**〕n. nun.

00-- 庵	nunnery.	
01-- 龍	nylon.	
40-- 古丁	nicotine.	
44-- 菴	nunnery, convent.	
-- 姑	nun, sister.	

屁〔**Pi**〕n. flatulence, fart, hip. v. break wind.

77-- 股	hip, buttock, posteriors.	

隉〔**Nieh**〕n. dangerous.

7721₂

屍〔**Shih**〕n. corpse, carcass.

25-- 體	corpse, carcass.	

胞〔**Pao**〕n. cell, bladder, womb, placenta.

00-- 衣	placenta.	
17-- 子	(in botany) spore.	
60-- 兄	elder brother.	

脆〔**Tsui**〕adj. brittle, crisp, fragile, frail.

17-- 弱	weak, frail, fragile.	
-- 弱點	vulnerable point.	
20-- 香可口	crisp, fragrant and pleasant to taste.	
90-- 性	fragility.	
94-- 怯無能	weak and timid, without ability.	

甩〔**Shuai**〕v. fling off, cast away.

20-- 手榴彈	throw (or cast) the grenade.	

51-- 掉	throw away.
77-- 開	tear oneself away from.

7721₄

尾 〔**Wei**〕 *n.* tail, end, extremity, *v.* follow.

47-- 聲	epilogue, conclusion, end.
58-- 數	arrears of a payment, remainder.
74-- 隨	follow.
77-- 巴	tail of an animal.

屋 〔**Wu**〕 *n.* house, room, building.

00-- 主	landlord.
10-- 瓦	tile.
11-- 脊	ridge, ridge of a house.
-- 頂	roof, roof of a house.
-- 頂窗	dormer window.
-- 頂花園	roof garden.
17-- 子	room, apartment, house.
27-- 租	house rent.
30-- 宇	building.
40-- 內	indoor, inside the house.
41-- 址	address.
57-- 契	title deed.
88-- 簷	eaves.

隆 〔**Lung**〕 *n.* prosperity, *adj.* high, eminent, prosperous, opulent, rich, lofty, generous, rumbling.

20-- 重	*v.* honor, *adj.* very beneficent, solemn, ceremonious.
27-- 冬	depth of winter.
-- 冬時候	at the time of bitter winter.
47-- 起	protrude, swell up.
95-- 情	great favor, great kindness.
-- 情盛意	your great favors.
-- 情厚誼	your great kindness, hospitality and friendship.

颼 〔**Sou**〕 *n.* wind, whiz, *v.* whiz, sough.

7721₆

閱 〔**Yueh**〕 *v.* look at, inspect, review, go over, examine, read, see.

04-- 讀	*n.* reading, *v.* read.
71-- 歷	*n.* experience, *v.* experience.
72-- 兵	review, review troops, military review, parade.
-- 兵式	military review.
78-- 覽	read, review.
-- 覽室	reading room.
90-- 卷	grade examination papers.

覺 〔**Chiao**〕 *v.* understand, feel, perceive, convince, instruct, wake up, awaken.

16-- 醒	wake up, awaken.
26-- 得	feel, perceive.
30-- 察	perceive, find.
91-- 悟	awaken, be awakened, be aroused, be aware of, realize.

7721₇

兒 〔**Er**〕 *n.* son, boy, child, infant.

00-- 童	boy, child, lad, children.
-- 童節	Children's Day.
-- 童文學	children's literature.
-- 童演員	child actor.
-- 童醫院	children's hospital.
12-- 孫	children and grandchildren.
17-- 子	son.
23-- 戲	boy's play, trifling matter, child's play.
26-- 皇帝	vassal-king, puppet emperor.
40-- 女	children, sons and daughters.
-- 女情長	long is the love between man and woman.
46-- 媳	daughter-in-law.

兕 〔**Ssu**〕 *n.* rhinoceros.

屜 〔**Ti**〕 *n.* drawer.

肥 〔**Fei**〕 *adj.* fat, plump, stout, fleshy, oily, rich, fertile, fruitful.

00-- 瘦	fat and lean.
14-- 豬	fat pig.
24-- 壯	stout and strong.
26-- 皂	soap.
-- 皂水	suds.
-- 皂盒	soap box.
-- 皂沫	lather.

--皂泡沫	lather, soap-bubbles.
32--沃	fertile, rich.
34--滿	fatness.
40--力	fertility.
--土	rich soil.
--大	brawny, plump, obese, fat and big.
--肉	fat of the flesh, fat, fat meat.
60--田粉	fertilizer powder.
73--膩	greasy.
79--胖	fat, corpulent, obese.
--胖病	obesity.
82--矮	stout.
85--缺	fat job.
94--料	fertilizer, manure.
--料廠	fertilizer plant.

兜〔Tou〕n. helmet, head-covering, small pocket, v. encircle, walk around, solicit, peddle.

10--一轉	spin, take a stroll around.
22--剿土匪	surround and extirpate the brigands.
27--翻老底	dig up one's personal stories and discredit him.
--穿而過	thread one's way through a crowd.
37--過來	come round.
54--搭婦女	seduce women.
58--攬生意	solicit business.
60--圈子	take a stroll.
77--風逛逛	take a ride for joy.
--兜	helmet.

7721₈

颮〔Chu〕n. typhoon, storm, hurricane, cyclone.

77--風	hurricane, cyclone.

7722₀

月〔Yueh〕n. moon, month.

00--亮、球	moon.
10--下老人	matchmaker.
12--刊	monthly, monthly publication.
13--球火箭	moon rocket.
20--季票	season ticket.
21--經	menstruation, menses.
23--台	platform (of a train station).
--台票	platform ticket, station ticket.
27--色	moonlight.
28--份	month.
35--津貼	monthly allowance.
37--初	at the beginning of the month.
40--吉	first day of the lunar month.
44--老	matchmaker.
--桂樹	laurel.
47--報	monthly report.
60--暈	lunar halo, halo of the moon.
80--食	lunar eclipse, eclipse of the moon.
85--蝕=月食	
88--餅	moon cake.
90--光	moonlight, moonshine, moonbeam.

用〔Yung〕n. effect, function, finances, expenditure, expense, v. apply, use, spend, employ, utilize, make use, put in practice.

00--度	outlay, expenditure.
--意	purpose, intention.
04--計	contrive, scheme.
10--工	v. work hard, adj. diligent.
--不完	inexhaustible.
--不着	needless, no need.
11--非所學	be engaged in an occupation not related to one's training.
13--武	use violence.
--武力	n. by force, v. use force.
14--功	n. diligence, v. study hard.
20--手	by hand.
21--處	use, service, purpose.
30--戶	subscriber, consumer, user.
--戶服務	user service.
--完（盡）	work up, finish, exhaust, use up.
33--心	n. attentiveness, v. take

care, give attention, pay attention, study carefully.

34-- 法	direction, direction for use, way to use.	
38-- 途	use, application, purpose.	
40-- 力	*n.* with force, *v.* use strength, make an effort, exert oneself.	
-- 力過度	make too strenuous efforts.	
50-- 盡	exhaust, use up, play out.	
-- 盡方法	use every possible means.	
-- 盡心力	exhaust one's abilities.	
55-- 費	expenditure, expenses.	
60-- 量	dose, dosage.	
-- 具	instrument, tools, implements.	
72-- 腦筋	use one's brains, give oneself trouble about something.	
80-- 人	*n.* personnel management, *v.* employ people.	
-- 人失當	employ a person wrongly.	
81-- 飯	take a meal.	
83-- 錢	*n.* commission, brokerage, *v.* spend money.	

岡 〔Kang〕 *n.* hill, peak, mountain ridge.

巴 見 6060₀

同 〔Tung〕 *v.* unite, harmonize, share in, assemble, *adj.* same, equal, similar, identical, united, *adv.* alike, altogether, in common, together with, *conj.* and, as well as, *prep.* with, in company with.

00-- 意	*n.* agreement, concord, accord, consent, harmony, *v.* agree, consent, assent, accord, accept.	
-- 音字	homophone.	
-- 病相憐	fellow sufferers have mutual sympathy.	
-- 文同種	the same language and the same race.	
-- 音異義字	homophone, homonym.	

04-- 謀	*n.* accomplice, *v.* conspire, conspire with, form a conspiracy.	
-- 謀者	conspirator.	
07-- 調	in concert.	
08-- 族	akin, allied.	
10-- 一	identical.	
-- 一性	identity.	
-- 工同酬	reward the same work with the same pay, equal pay for equal work, equal pay for equal job.	
11-- 班	classmate.	
-- 班同學	classmate.	
-- 輩	associate, compeer, peer, of the same generation.	
12-- 列一等	be listed in the same class.	
20-- 位	apposition.	
-- 位素	isotope.	
-- 儕=同輩		
21-- 價	par.	
-- 行	partner, fellow traveler, fellow-trader, people of the same trade, *v.* keep accompany with, go with.	
-- 歲	of the same age.	
-- 上（同前）	ditto, the same as above.	
22-- 種	the same race.	
24-- 化	assimilate.	
-- 化作用	assimilation, anabolism.	
-- 僚	colleague, associate.	
-- 仇敵愾	share hatred of the same enemy.	
25-- 生共死	live and die together.	
27-- 級生	classmate.	
-- 鄉	fellow countryman, fellow townsman, countryman.	
-- 名	name sake, of the same name.	
-- 歸於盡	come to an end together, destroy each other.	
-- 舟共濟	be all in the same boat.	
29-- 伴	companion, mate.	
-- 伴協心	companions are of one	

	mind.
30-- 宗	clansmen.
-- 窗、學	schoolmate.
-- 流合污	follow the current bad practices.
-- 濟會	Kiwanis club.
32-- 業	fellow profession, the same calling, the same trade or business.
-- 業公會	association of fellow profession, guild, trade association, trade council.
33-- 心協力	unite all efforts for a common purpose.
-- 心同德	be of one mind.
-- 心合意	with the same heart and the same purpose.
36-- 溫	stratosphere.
-- 溫層	stratosphere.
38-- 道中人	men of the same path.
40-- 志	comrade, fraternity, companion.
44-- 甘共苦	for better or for worse, stick through thick and thin.
47-- 聲	in concert.
-- 聲一哭	share the same feeling of loss.
-- 聲相應	echo the same call, support the same cause.
48-- 樣	alike, same, similar, equal.
50-- 事	colleague, associate, partner.
53-- 感	n. fellow feeling, v. have the same feeling.
60-- 罪	of same guilt.
64-- 時	meantime, meanwhile, in the same breath, at the same time.
-- 時的	concurrent.
67-- 盟	alliance, federation, league, union, ally.
-- 盟國	ally, allied nations.
-- 盟軍	allied forces.
-- 盟條約	alliance treaty.
-- 盟罷工	be on strike together.
-- 路人	fellow-traveler.
77-- 胞	brethren, fellow-countryman, countryman, compatriot.
-- 胞兄弟	own brother, full brother.
-- 居	n. fellow-lodger, cohabitation, concubine, v. live with, lie with, cohabit, live together.
-- 學	schoolmate, school fellow.
80-- 義	synonymous, of the same meaning.
-- 義字	synonym.
-- 義詞	synonym.
88-- 等	n. equality, adj. equal, equivalent, of the same class, (rank, status), on an equal basis (footing).
-- 等價值	equal value.
-- 等對待	make no discrimination.
90-- 黨相爭	quarrel within the same group or party.
91-- 類	kindred, akin, of the same kind, of the same class of things.
-- 類相殘	kill one's own kind.
95-- 性戀愛	homosexuality.
-- 性戀者	gay, homosexual.
-- 情	n. sympathy, compassion, fellow feeling, v. sympathize.
-- 情心	pity.
-- 情的	sympathetic.

罔 〔Wang〕 n. net, v. deceive, cheat, adj. no, not any, pron. none.

周 〔Chou〕 n. Chou (a family name), surrounding, environment, circumference, week, curve, bend, circle, circuit, v. surround, adj. perfect, complete, considerate, thoughtful, thorough.

00-- 率	frequency (in electricity).
08-- 旋	treat politely.

-- 旋到底	fight to the end .
12-- 到	thorough, thoughtful, considerate.
21-- 行	revolve.
27-- 身	whole body, all over the body.
30-- 密	well-considered, minutely-planned.
-- 濟	relieve, give alms, bestow, assist.
-- 濟難民	relieve the refugees.
34-- 波	cycle (in electricity).
38-- 游	tour, travel around, make a circuit.
-- 游列國	tour the various countries.
47-- 期	cycle.
52-- 折	trouble, difficulty, complication.
55-- 轉	business turnover.
-- 轉率	turnover rate.
-- 轉量	traffic mileage.
-- 轉金	revolving fund.
60-- 圍	surrounding, circuit, circumference, environment.
-- 圍情況	environment, circumstances.
71-- 長	perimeter.
80-- 年	anniversary.
-- 年紀念	anniversary.
-- 全	complete, perfect.
-- 全之計	perfect plan.
86-- 知	make known to the public.

胸〔Hsiung〕n. bosom, breast, chest, mind.

00-- 衣	waist.
27-- 像	bust.
34-- 襟	the mind.
60-- 口（脯）	breast, chest.
71-- 膈	thorax, breast.
73-- 腔	thorax, chest.
77-- 肌	pectoral muscles.
-- 骨	breast bone, sternum.
79-- 膛	breast, bosom, chest.
80-- 針	chest pin.

90-- 懷	feeling, mind.

陶〔Tao〕n. earthenware, pottery, v. feel happy, teach and transform a person.

10-- 工	potter.
-- 醉	intoxicated, highly pleased.
33-- 冶	cultivate, shape, mold or smelt.
37-- 瓷	earthenware and porcelain.
-- 瓷工業	ceramic industry.
-- 瓷藝術品	ceramic.
-- 瓷專家 (陶瓷藝術家)	ceramist.
40-- 土	potter's clay.
66-- 器	earthenware, pottery.
-- 器廠	pottery.
95-- 情	relieve one's feelings.

朋〔Peng〕n. friend, acquaintance, companion, clique.

40-- 友	friend, comrade, fellow, acquaintance.
90-- 黨	party, clique, group.

腳〔Chiao〕n. foot or feet, leg.

00-- 癬	athlete's foot.
-- 註	footnote.
11-- 背	instep.
20-- 手架	scaffolding.
30-- 注	footnote.
21-- 步	footstep.
50-- 夫	porter, coolie.
60-- 跡	trace.
61-- 趾	toe.
62-- 踏	step on.
-- 踏板	pedal.
-- 踏車	bicycle, bike.
-- 踏實地	down-to-earth.
66-- 踝	ankle.
67-- 跟	heel.
77-- 印	footprint.
80-- 氣	beriberi.
83-- 錢	porterage.
84-- 鐐	fetter, shackle.
90-- 尖	tiptoe.
-- 尖舞	toe dance, tap dance.

7722₂

膠〔Chiao〕*n.* glue, gum, resin, sap, anything sticky, *v.* glue, cohere, be obstinate, adhere, *adj.* sticky, glutinous.

12--	水	glue.
20--	住	stuck fast.
21--	黏	glue, stick.
--	版	jelly graph.
32--	州	Kiaochow.
34--	漆	glue and varnish, very much in love.
40--	布	adhesive plaster, plastic cloth.
41--	樹	gum tree.
44--	鞋	galoshes, rubber shoes.
50--	囊	medical capsule.
72--	質	*n.* glue, gum, *adj.* gluey, gelatinous.
80--	合板	plywood.
90--	卷	film.

7722₇

邪〔Hsieh〕*adj.* perverse, vicious, deflected, depraved, corrupt, evil, magical.

08--	說	heterodoxy.
10--	惡	*n.* evil, vice, naughty, wicked, corrupt.
--	不勝正	the evil will not triumph over the virtuous.
21--	術	black art, black magic.
48--	教	superstition, heresy, wrong doctrine.
80--	氣	noxious influence.

局〔Chu〕*n.* bureau, board, office, game, inning, circumstances.

07--	部	*n.* part, *adj.* partial, local.
--	部化	localize.
--	部性	partial in nature.
10--	面	appearance, state of affairs.
--	面一新	enter upon a new phase.
23--	外	neutrality.
--	外人	man in the street, outsider.
45--	勢	condition, condition of things, situation, circumstances.
--	勢危迫	the situation is critical.

71--	長	director of a bureau, chief of a bureau, bureau head.
77--	限	limited.
--	限性	limitation.

屑〔Hsieh〕*n.* fragment, trifle, crumbs, bits, *v.* care, belittle.

90--	粒	fragments, bits.

隖〔Wu〕*n.* bank, wall.

骨〔Ku〕*n.* bone, frame, framework.

00--	痛	osteocope, bone-ache.
11--	頭	bone.
17--	子裏	in the bone, inside, at heart.
22--	斷	fracture of bone.
27--	盤	pelvis.
40--	肉	in one's own flesh and blood, bone and flesh, blood relations.
46--	架	frame work, skeleton.
--	相學	phrenology.
48--	幹	core, mainstay, diaphysis.
52--	折	fracture of bone.
71--	灰	bone ashes.
74--	髓	marrow.
77--	骼	skeleton.
--	學	osteology.
80--	盆	pelvis.
88--	節	joint, bone-joints.
98--	粉	bone dust.

鴉〔Ya〕*n.* crow, raven.

22--	片	opium.
--	片癮	opium habit.
--	片戰爭	The Opium War — Anglo-Sino War of 1840-1842.

腎〔Shen〕*n.* kidney, testicles.

00--	痛	nephralgia.
10--	石	kidney-stone.
74--	臟	kidneys.
90--	炎	nephritis.

鬧〔Nao〕*n.* disturbance, bustle, noise, uproar, tumult, noise, *v.* disturb, trouble, experience, *adj.* noisy, clamorous.

00--	市	busy market, downtown area.
--	意氣	pick a quarrel.

22-- 劇	farce.
40-- 大風潮	cause a great trouble.
47-- 聲	noise.
50-- 事	cause trouble, create disturbances.
80-- 鐘	alarm clock.
95-- 情緒	lose one's temper, be out of temper.

閒 〔Hsien〕 *n.* leisure, idleness.

00-- 言	idle talk, gossip.
09-- 談	chat, gossip.
13-- 職	sinecure.
38-- 游	stroll.
44-- 蕩	dally.
67-- 暇	leisure, spare moment.
77-- 民	the unemployed.
80-- 人	bystander.
-- 人免進	no admittance (except on business).

鵰 〔Tiao〕 *n.* eagle, hawk, large bird of prey.

臀 〔Tun〕 *n.* buttock, rump, hip, breech

77-- 骨	rump-bone.

鵬 〔Peng〕 *n.* roc.

26-- 程萬里	rise to unknown heights.

屬 〔Shu〕 *n.* class, kind, category, genus, group, *v.* connect, gather, compose, instruct, focus one's attention, belong to, *adj.* belonging to, attached to, related to, connected to.

00-- 意	pay attention to.
08-- 於	belong to, concern, pertain to.
44-- 地	dependency, colonial state, territory.
60-- 目而視	stare, gaze, give much attention to.
95-- 性	attribute.

釁 〔Hsin〕 *n.* defect, flaw, crevice, rift, quarrel, *v.* anoint.

02-- 端	cause of a quarrel.

冪 〔Mi〕 *n.* power (in mathematics).

00-- 方	involution (in mathematics).
37-- 次	power (in mathematics).
58-- 數	exponent (in mathematics).

7723₁

爬 〔Pa〕 *v.* climb, crawl, creep, scratch.

10-- 不起來	unable to get up.
21-- 上	climb up.
-- 行	*n.* reptile, *v.* creep, crawl.
-- 行動物	reptiles.
22-- 山	climb up a hill, climb up a mountain.
-- 山越嶺	over hills and mountains.
44-- 樹	climb up a tree.
47-- 起來	get up, pick oneself up.
50-- 虫	reptile, creepers.

7723₂

尿 〔Niao〕 *n.* urine, *v.* urinate.

38-- 道	urethra, urinary canal.
40-- 布	diaper.
50-- 素	urea.

展 〔Chan〕 *v.* open out, spread, expand, unroll, look into, dilate, prolong.

07-- 望	*n.* prospect, outlook, *v.* look forward.
08-- 放	open, unfold.
22-- 出	*n.* on display, on show, *v.* display.
47-- 期	*n.* postponement, extension, *v.* postpone, hold over, renew.
-- 期日	rollover date.
77-- 開	open, open out, expand, outspread, spread, unfold.
78-- 覽	show, expose, exhibit.
-- 覽室	show room.
-- 覽櫥窗	exhibition case.
-- 覽中心	exhibition center.
-- 覽品	exhibit, things on display, show piece.
-- 覽會	exhibition, show.
-- 覽館	exhibition hall.
89-- 銷店 (陳列商品店)	show shop, exhibition shop.
-- 銷會	trade fair.

限 〔Hsien〕 *n.* limit, boundary, *v.* limit, restrict, confine, fix, specify, appoint.

00-- 度	restriction, limit, bounds, restricted measure.
08-- 於	be confined to.
21-- 價	price-limit, price control.
22-- 制	*n.* limitation, *v.* restrict, confine, qualify, limit.
30-- 定	*n.* restriction, *v.* fix, restrict, determine, set out.
-- 定時日	fix a time limit.
31-- 額	quota, quota norm, maximum number or amount, restrained limit.
-- 額分配	ration.
47-- 期	limit of time, net period.
60-- 日	appointed day.
64-- 時	appointed time, limit of time.

7723₃

腿 〔Tui〕 *n.* thigh, leg.

74-- 肚	calf of the leg.
77-- 骨	bones of the legs.
88-- 筋	hamstring.

閼 〔O〕 *v.* shut, stop.

7723₇

腴 〔Yu〕 *n.* the fat on the belly, *adj.* fat and soft, rich, fertile.

7724₀

陬 〔Tsou〕 *n.* corner.

7724₁

屏 〔Ping〕 *n.* defense, screen, shelter, shield, *v.* reject, dismiss, screen, cover, exclude, shield.

00-- 棄	reject, dismiss, expel.
21-- 衛	protect.
26-- 息	hold one's breath, catch one's breath.
27-- 絕	get rid of.
46-- 慢	screen.
70-- 障	*n.* shelter, barrier, *v.* shield.
77-- 風	curtain, screen, folding-screen.

7724₄

屢 〔Lu〕 *adv.* frequently, often, repeatedly, time after time, again and again.

15-- 建奇功	make repeated wonderful achievements.
21-- 經挫折	repeatedly meet with setbacks.
24-- 告不聽	wouldn't listen to repeated advice.
37-- 次	frequently, often, repeatedly, often times, once and again.
63-- 戰屢敗	fight and lose repeatedly.
-- 戰屢勝	fight and win repeatedly.
68-- 敗屢戰	fight repeatedly after being defeated.
80-- 年	for series of years.

屨 〔Chu〕 *n.* hempen sandals.

7724₇

屐 〔Chi〕 *n.* sabot, wooden shoes.

服 〔Fu〕 *n.* clothes, dress, garment, mourning clothes, *v.* dress, submit, wear, put on, obey, wait on, serve, yield, take (medicine).

00-- 膺	wear on the breast, lay to heart.
16-- 理	listen to reason, be open to conviction.
17-- 務	*n.* service, *v.* serve.
-- 務站	public service station.
-- 務台	information.
-- 務員	waiter, steward.
-- 務設施	service facility.
-- 務部門	service department.
-- 務系統	service system.
-- 務上門	door-to-door service.
-- 務能力	service capacity.
-- 務台	service desk.
-- 務協議	service agreement.
-- 務時間	hour of service.
-- 務事業	service business.
-- 務成本	service cost.
-- 務費用	service fee.
-- 務單位	service unit.
-- 務質量	quality of service.
-- 務周到	provide good service.
-- 務合同	contract of service.
-- 務性公司	service company.
24-- 侍	serve, wait on.

-- 裝	dress, clothes, costume, dressing.
-- 裝廠	garment factory.
-- 裝工業	clothing industry.
-- 裝貿易	garment trade.
-- 裝公司	garment corporation.
-- 裝式樣	style, fashion.
27-- 役	serve, be in military service.
28-- 從	*n.* obedience, *v.* obey, follow, give in, submit to, *adj.* obedient.
-- 從法律	abide by the law.
44-- 藥	take medicine.
50-- 事	wait on, serve.
-- 毒	take poison.
80-- 氣	be willing to submit.
-- 人之心	make people accept at heart.

股〔Ku〕*n.* thigh, share, portion, stock.

10-- 票	*n.* stock, share, *v.* share certificates.
-- 票上漲	rise of stock.
-- 票市場	stock market.
-- 票交易	stock deals, buying and selling stocks.
-- 票交易所	stock exchange.
-- 票證券	share certificate.
-- 票票面價值	face value of stock (share).
-- 票發行	capital issue, stock issue, stock issuance.
-- 票發行價格	issue price of shares (stocks).
-- 票發行額	capital stock issued.
-- 票價格	share price, stock price.
-- 票行市	share price.
-- 票行情指數	share price index.
-- 票行情看漲	bullish.
-- 票行情表	share list, stock list.
-- 票紅利	stock dividends.
-- 票經紀人	stockbroker, stockjobber.
-- 票值	share worth.
-- 票過戶	stock transfer, share transfer.
-- 票權期	stock option.
-- 票增值	stock appreciation.
-- 票轉手	stock transfer, stock-turn.
-- 票投資	investment in stocks.

-- 票投機	speculation in stocks.
-- 票跌價	fall in stock.
-- 票所有權	stock ownership.
-- 票分割	stock split-up.
-- 票管理	regulation of stock.
26-- 息	dividends.
-- 息分配	dividend distribution.
28-- 份	stock, share.
-- 份公司	stock company.
-- 份兩合公司	joint share company.
-- 份有限公司	limited stock company.
44-- 權	stock, stock ownership, stock right, stockholdings, stockholder's right.
-- 權所有人	stock owner.
50-- 本	stock, subscribed capital.
-- 東	stockholder, shareholder.
-- 東會	meeting of shareholders.
63-- 戰	trembling with fear.
91-- 慄	shuddering with fear.

閉〔Pi〕*v.* close, shut, obstruct, stop, block up.

00-- 庭	dismiss the court.
-- 店	close the shop.
-- 市	close.
21-- 經	amenorrhea.
30-- 塞	choke, block up, stop.
34-- 港	closure of port.
44-- 幕	the curtain falls. close, conclude.
60-- 口	shut one's mouth, shut up.
-- 目	close one's eye.
67-- 路電視	closed circuit TV.
77-- 關	break of foreign intercourse, isolate.
-- 關政策	*n.* policy of exclusion, break of foreign intercourse, isolation policy, *v.* isolate.
-- 關時代	period of isolationism.
-- 關自守	seclusion, self-seclusion, cut oneself off from the outside world, close the door to the outside world.
-- 門	shut the door.

-- 會	conclude a meeting.
殿	〔Tien〕*n.* palace, temple, rear guard.
10-- 下	Your Highness, Your (or His, Her) Royal Highness.
22-- 後	rearward, be the rear guard.
27-- 軍	rear guard.
履	〔Li〕*n.* leather shoes, *v.* walk, tread, act, perform.
21-- 行	*n.* implement, implementation, performance, *v.* perform, act, give effect, fulfill.
-- 行諾言	keep one's promise, fulfill one's promise, keep one's word.
-- 行契約	meet one's engagements.
71-- 歷	record, experience, personal autobiography, personal details.
孱	〔Chan〕*adj.* humble, weak, frail, feeble.
17-- 弱	week, feeble.
-- 弱體質	enfeebled constitution.
50-- 夫	coward.
骰	〔Sai〕*n.* dice.

7725₃

犀	〔Hsi〕*n.* rhinoceros.
22-- 利	sharpened.
25-- 牛	rhinoceros.
27-- 角	rhinoceros horn.
閥	〔Fu〕*n.* linage, clique, valve.
77-- 門	valve.
-- 門廠	valve plant.

7725₄

降	〔Chiang〕*v.* submit, subjugate, surrender, give in, fall, drop, descend, come down, lower, degrade, deign, condescend.
10-- 雨	rain.
-- 雨量	rainfall, precipitation.
-- 下	fall down, descend.
11-- 班	degradation.
21-- 價	*n.* price abatement, reduction of price, *v.* abate a price, reduce (decrease) price, scale down price, squeeze down prices.
22-- 低	fall, abate, descend, lower, drop, knock down, reduce, depress.
-- 低利率	reduction of interest.
-- 低成本	*n.* reduction of cost, *v.* reduce the cost.
27-- 級	degrade, demote, reduce to a lower rank.
36-- 溫	reduce the temperature.
44-- 落	land, descend, bale out.
-- 落傘	parachute.
-- 落傘部隊	paratroop.
77-- 服	surrender, lay down arms, yield.
78-- 臨	advent, coming down.

7726₁

膽	〔Tan〕*n.* gall, bladder, courage, inner part of something.
03-- 識	intelligence, foresight.
10-- 石	gall stone.
18-- 敢	dare, presume, venture, be audacious enough to.
34-- 汁	bile, choler.
40-- 大	bold, brave, courageous.
-- 大妄爲	act in foolhardy manner.
-- 大包天	extremely audacious.
-- 大心細	brave but not reckless.
50-- 囊	gall bladder.
60-- 量	courage, bravery.
63-- 戰	tremble.
-- 戰心驚	tremble with fear.
67-- 略	bravery and resourcefulness.
90-- 小	timid, craven, cowardly, chickenhearted.
-- 小鬼	coward.
-- 小卑怯	chickenhearted, timid.
94-- 怯	timid, nervous, faint-hearted, cowardly.

7726₂

脗	〔Wen〕*v.* fit, match.
80-- 合	fit exactly.

7726₄

居	〔Chu〕*n.* residence, dwelling, abode, *v.* live, dwell, reside, inhabit, stay.

14--功　　　　claim credit for oneself.
20--住　　　　dwell, lodge, live, inhabit, abide, reside.
　--住者　　　resident.
　--住期限　　term of stay.
21--處　　　　residence (of colonists), abode.
23--然　　　　unexpectedly.
30--室　　　　room, residence.
33--心　　　　intention.
　--心不良　　ill-disposed, having ill intentions.
50--中　　　　come between.
　--中調停　　mediate between two parties in a dispute.
77--民　　　　inhabitant, citizen, resident, dweller.
　--民點　　　residential center.
　--間　　　　go between, between two parties.
　--間人　　　intermediary.
　--留　　　　stay, sojourn, reside, residence.
　--留證　　　residence permit.
　--留地　　　settlement.
　--間人　　　broker.
80--首　　　　lead.

屠〔Tu〕 v. butcher, slaughter.
17--刀　　　　cleaver, butcher knife.
30--宰　　　　butcher, slaughter.
　--宰場　　　slaughterhouse, abattoir.
47--殺　　　　slaughter, massacre.
50--夫　　　　butcher.

骼〔Ko〕 n. skeleton, dry bones.
胳〔Ko〕 n. arms.
73--膊　　　　arms.
74--肢窩　　　armpits.

7726₆

層〔Tseng〕 n. layer, bed, course, story, floor.
22--出不窮　　appear again and again.
37--次　　　　order, series, degree, gradation.
　--次分明　　distinct in the order (of importance).
60--疊　　　　overlapping.

7726₇

眉〔Mei〕 n. eye-brow, brow.
20--毛　　　　eye-brow.
40--壽　　　　long life.
51--批　　　　marginal notes.
60--目　　　　outline, general appearance, sequence of things.
　--目傳情　　make sheep's eye.

7727₀

尸〔Shih〕 n. corpse, dead body.

7727₂

屈〔Chu〕 n. injustice, wrong, v. bend, bow, stoop, subject, crook, stoop, bow.
23--伏　　　　keep under, subject.
27--身　　　　stoop.
28--從　　　　submit oneself to, yield to.
51--打成招　　beat a man in order to extort a confession.
　--指可數　　countable on the fingers of a hand.
52--折　　　　refraction.
55--曲　　　　crooked, bent.
71--辱　　　　humiliation, disgrace.
74--膝　　　　bend the knees.
77--服　　　　yield, bow, go under, keep under, surrender.
　--服權勢　　submit to those in power.

屆〔Chieh〕 n. limit, time, term, periodic term, v. reach, arrive.
64--時　　　　at the appointed time.
47--期　　　　at the appointed time, in due time, in due course.

7727₇

陷〔Hsien〕 n. pit, trap, fault, flaw, v. fall, sink, descend, capture, pillage, sack, drop into, entrap, crush, occupy.
08--於詭計　　be entangled in a plot.
　--於死地　　be driven to desperation.
　--於重圍　　be closely hemmed in by the enemy.
　--於絕境　　have no hope for escape or recovery.
　--於困境　　get into hot water.
　--於賊中　　fall among thieves.

10-- 下	collapse, sink.	
30-- 害	entrap, betray, ensnare.	
37-- 沒	sink, fall down, be captured.	
44-- 落	capture, occupy.	
75-- 阱	pit, snare, trap, pitfall.	
80-- 入	cave in, fall (or sink) into, get involved.	
-- 入僵局	come to a standstill.	
-- 入泥沼	bog down.	
-- 入網羅	fall into a snare.	
-- 入危機	be bogged down in a crisis.	

7728₀
閡 〔Ai〕 *n.* obstacle.

7728₁
屣 〔Hsi〕 *n.* straw sandal.

7728₂
欣 〔Hsin〕 *n.* joy, delight, gladness, happiness, *adj.* delighted, joyful, happy, jolly, merry, cheerful.

23-- 然	merrily, joyfully, happily, with a light heart.
-- 然應承	jump at an offer.
-- 然承諾	happily agree to the proposal.
-- 然爲之	do something with joy.
40-- 喜	happy, glad, joyful, delighted.
-- 喜若狂	*n.* in raptures, *v.* be beside oneself with joy, *adj.* exulted, rejoiced.
74-- 慰	*v.* gladden, *adj.* solaced, satisfied, gladdened.
77-- 欣自得	proud and self-satisfied.
-- 欣向榮	prosperous, thriving, flourishing.
90-- 賞	*n.* appreciation, *v.* enjoy, admire, appreciate.
-- 賞自然	enjoy nature.
94-- 悅	happy.

7729₁
際 〔Chi〕 *n.* border, limit, side, edge, *prep.* between, among, during, *adv.* when.

77-- 遇	opportunity, occasion.

7729₄
屎 〔Shih〕 *n.* excrement, feces, filth, ordure, dung.

40-- 坑	privy.

7730₄
闥 〔Ta〕 *n.* door, inner door.

7731₀
駔 〔Tsang〕 *n.* strong horse.

7732₀
駒 〔Chu〕 *n.* colt.

7732₇
騶 〔Tsou〕 *n.* groom.

闖 〔Chung〕 *v.* thrust out, burst in, bolt in, rush in, intrude into, come across, experience the ways of the world, cause.

14-- 勁	spirit of a pathbreaker.
27-- 將	pathbreaker.
30-- 進	break into.
37-- 禍	induce calamity, cause a disaster.
80-- 入	burst, intrude, obtrude, break into.

7733₁
熙 〔Hsi〕 *adj.* light, bright, extensive, ample, splendid, glorious, vast, expansive, peaceful and happy, *v.* flourish, prosper.

77-- 熙攘攘	hustle and bustle.

7733₂
驟 〔Chou〕 *v.* trot, gallop, *adv.* suddenly, quickly, frequently.

10-- 雨	shower, rain shower.
-- 雨狂風	rainstorm.
23-- 然	suddenly.
46-- 想	at first blush.

7733₆
騷 〔Sao〕 *n.* grief, sorrow, sadness, grievance, worry, poetry, stink, *v.* disturb, agitate, *adj.* mournful, disturbed, agitated, disquieted, amorous, erotic.

22-- 亂	disturb, trouble, confuse.
24-- 動	*n.* agitation, riot, commotion, *v.* excite, stir up, riot, agitate.
-- 動不安	agitated, disturbed, in com-

motion.

51-- 擾　　　annoy, trouble, disturb, riot.
-- 擾治安　　disturb public security.

7733₇

悶 〔 Men 〕 *adj.* sad, depressed, grieved, melancholy, unhappy, suffocating, oppressive, quiet, inactive.

10-- 死　　　suffocate, be suffocated to death, be stifled to death.
11-- 頭兒　　diligently but quietly.
40-- 在心裏　keep in mind and unsaid.
44-- 熱　　　sultry, sweltering.
47-- 聲不響　remain quiet.
-- 悶不樂　　be in low spirits.

閟 〔 Pi 〕 *v.* shut the door, keep secret.

7734₀

馭 〔 Yu 〕 *v.* drive, drive a horse, control, manage, govern.

50-- 車　　　drive a carriage.
71-- 馬　　　control a horse.

7734₇

駸 〔 Chin 〕 *n.* galloping fast.

7736₂

驑 〔 Liu 〕 *n.* noble steed.

7736₄

駱 〔 Lo 〕 *n.* white horse with black mane, camel.

73-- 駝　　　camel.
-- 駝毛　　　camel's hair.

7740₀

又 〔 Yu 〕 *adv.* again, more, also, further, moreover, besides, further more, too. *conj.* and, while, *prep.* in addition to.

48-- 驚又喜　surprised and happy at the same, time.
60-- 是老調　it's the same old tune again.
66-- 哭又笑　cry and laugh at the same time.
87-- 飢又渴　both hungry and thirsty.

叉 見 4000₀

閔 〔 Min 〕 *n.* evil, misfortune, *v.* pity, commiserate.

7740₁

聞 〔 Wen 〕 *n.* fame, news, knowledge, information, *v.* hear, inform, report, smell, convey, make known.

07-- 訊　　　hear of the news.
27-- 名　　　well-known, famous, reputed.
47-- 聲　　　hear the sound.
60-- 見　　　experience.
72-- 所未聞　unheard of.
77-- 聞看　　smell at.
80-- 人　　　celebrity, man of note, famous person.

7740₇

叟 〔 Sou 〕 *n.* elder, senior, old man.

學 〔 Hsueh 〕 *n.* school, study, science, *v.* learn, study, practice.

03-- 識　　　knowledge, scholarship.
08-- 說　　　doctrine, theory, tenet.
10-- 工　　　learn industrial production.
-- 而不厭　　learn with indefatigable zeal.
-- 而知之　　obtain knowledge by studies.
11-- 非所用　one does not do that which one has learned.
16-- 理　　　theory, principle.
17-- 習　　　practice, study, learn.
20-- 位　　　degree, academic degree.
21-- 術　　　learning, art, techniques, scholarship.
-- 術界　　　academic circles, academic world.
-- 術性　　　technicality.
-- 術討論會　symposium, seminar.
-- 行俱佳　　excellent in both scholarship and character.
-- 銜　　　　academic title.
22-- 制　　　educational system, school system.
-- 制改革　　reform in the school system.
24-- 徒　　　apprentice.
-- 科　　　　course of study, curriculum, subject of study.
-- 先進　　　learn from the advanced.
25-- 生　　　student, pupil.
27-- 級　　　class, grade.
28-- 齡　　　school age.

-- 以致用	learn in order to practice, use what one has learned.
30-- 究	pedant.
32-- 派	school, school of thought.
-- 業	education, studies.
37-- 軍	learn military affairs.
40-- 士	bachelor, bachelor degree, B.A.(or B.S.).
-- 校	school, college, academy.
-- 校教育	schooling.
-- 友	schoolmate.
-- 力根深	one's scholarship is deeply rooted.
-- 有專長	have acquired a specialty from study.
44-- 者	scholar.
47-- 報	academic journal.
-- 期	school term, term, semester.
55-- 費	school fees, tuition.
-- 農	learn agricultural production.
56-- 規	school regulation.
60-- 界	educational circle.
-- 界泰斗	prominent figure in the academic circles, good moral cultivation.
72-- 兵團	cadet corps.
73-- 院	institute, college, academy.
77-- 問	learning, knowledge, scholarship.
-- 問淵博	wide and profound in learning.
-- 問無捷徑	there is no royal road to learning.
-- 風	spirit of a school, style of study.
-- 閥	scholar-tyrant, educational autocrat.
-- 貫古今	well-versed in the learning of both ancient and modern times.
78-- 監	proctor.
80-- 人	scholar.
-- 年	academic year.
-- 會	society, academy, institute.
-- 舍	school house.
-- 分	credit.

-- 無止境	learning is endless.
-- 無老少	in scholarship there is no difference of age.
90-- 堂=學校	

7742₇

舅 〔Chiu〕 n. uncle, mother's brother, brother-in-law, maternal uncle, wife's brother.

| 77-- 母 | aunt, maternal aunt (mother's brother's wife). |
| 80-- 父 | uncle, maternal uncle. |

7743₀

闋 〔Chueh〕 v. close the door, stop, rest.

7743₂

閎 〔Hung〕 n. entrance, gate, adj. large.

7743₇

臾 〔Yu〕 n. moment, very short time, little while.

7744₀

丹 〔Tan〕 n. red, red color, powder, cinnabar, sophisticated decoction, adj. red, sincere, loyal.

03-- 誠	pure-hearted.
11-- 頂鶴	crane.
19-- 砂	cinnabar.
27-- 色	cinnabar color.
33-- 心	sincere-hearted, sincere heart.
40-- 丸	pill.
-- 麥	Denmark.
47-- 楹刻桷	red pillars and carved rafters.
50-- 毒	erysipelas, rose.
60-- 田	lower part of the abdomen.

冊 〔Tse〕 n. volume, copy, book, order to confer a title of nobility.

| 00-- 立皇后 | be appointed as the queen. |
| 44-- 封 | confer titles of nobility on the emperor's wives or princes. |

7744₁

開 〔Kai〕 v. open, enfold, disclose, explain, reveal, teach, guide, begin, drive, develop, list, write down, discover, eliminate, divide into, found, establish.

00-- 市	open the market.
-- 庭	hold a court, open the hearing, open a court session, call the court to order.
-- 庭審理	try a case, deal with a case of the matter.
-- 店	keep a shop, set up a shop.
-- 方	(in math) evolution.
-- 夜車	work at night, burn the midnight oil.
-- 辦	begin, start, set up, open.
-- 辦費	establishment charges, formation expenses, initial expenditure, opening expenses, organization expense, promotion expense.
02-- 端	beginning.
03-- 誠佈公	be sincere and just.
-- 誠相見	heart-to-heart.
07-- 設	establish, set up.
08-- 放	throw open, open, liberalize, open-door, open to public use.
-- 放經濟	open economy.
09-- 設	open, establish.
10-- 礦	mine.
-- 工	set to work, start work, ground-breaking, start operation.
-- 工典禮	ground-breaking ceremony.
11-- 頭	at the start, in the beginning.
-- 玩笑	joke, make fun.
12-- 發	n. development, exploitation, v. develop, exploit.
-- 發市場	exploit market.
-- 發票	invoice.
-- 發資源	develop resources, development resource, exploit natural resources, tap natural resources.
-- 發資金	initial fund.
-- 發成本	organization cost.
-- 發公司	development corporation.
-- 水	boiled water.
13-- 球	n. serve v. serve (in a ball game).
17-- 刀	operate.
-- 司米	Cashmere, Kashmir.
20-- 航	sailing, departure.
21-- 價	initial price, quote, make a quotation, starting price, state a price.
-- 紅燈	give the red light to.
24-- 化	civilize.
22-- 倒車	turn back the clock, retrograde.
-- 後門	have backdoor dealings.
27-- 墾	exploit, reclaim, break ground, cultivate wasteland.
-- 船	set sail, sail out.
-- 船日期	date of departure.
-- 盤價	opening price, opening quotation.
-- 綠燈	give the green light to.
-- 獎	draw a lottery.
31-- 渠	build an irrigation canal.
-- 源節流	increase revenues (income) and reduce expenditure.
32-- 業	enter upon business, start a business, set up a business, open business.
33-- 演	raise, raise the curtain, begin to perform, start a show.
-- 心	exhilaration, happy.
35-- 溝	ditch, gutter.
-- 凍	thaw.
38-- 導	enlighten, offer advice to.
40-- 支	expense, outgo, out-going, expenditures, spending.
41-- 標	opening of tender, open tender.
42-- 機器	run a machine.
43-- 始	begin, commence, originate, enter, initiate, bring on, start.
-- 始生效 (開始實行)	come into effect, come into force, go into operation.
44-- 動	operate, start working.
-- 荒	reclaim wasteland.
-- 花	bloom, flower.

-- 藥方	prescribe.	
-- 幕	inaugurate, draw the curtain, open the hall.	
-- 幕禮	inauguration.	
-- 幕詞	opening speech, opening address.	
46-- 場白	prologue.	
48-- 槍	open fire, fire a shot.	
50-- 車	drive a car.	
-- 本	format of a book.	
51-- 拓	exploit, open up.	
-- 拓市場	develop new market.	
52-- 採	exploit, mine, extract.	
60-- 罪	offend.	
-- 胃	relish, appetizing.	
-- 口	speak, open one's mouth.	
63-- 戰	n. outbreak of war, v. go into action, wage war.	
67-- 路	make way, give exit, open a door to, clear the way, build a road.	
-- 路先鋒	pioneer, vanguard.	
-- 眼界	widen one's field of vision, see something new.	
77-- 闢	open up, start, build.	
-- 闢市場	dig market for...	
-- 闊	spacious.	
-- 展	develop.	
-- 學	school opens.	
-- 門	open the door.	
-- 關	switch.	
-- 關廠	switch factory.	
-- 闢者	pioneer.	
78-- 脫	whitewash oneself.	
-- 除	dismiss, dismiss from school or work.	
80-- 會	n. meeting, v. hold a meeting, attend a meeting.	
82-- 創	establish, found.	
84-- 罐刀	tin opener.	
88-- 鎗	fire.	
89-- 銷=開支		
-- 鎖	unlock.	
90-- 火	open fire.	
-- 燈	switch on the light.	
-- 小差	desert, escape.	

7744₇

段 〔Tuan〕 *n.* portion, piece, section, part, paragraph.

44-- 落	section, passage, segment, paragraph.

舁 〔Yu〕 *v.* lift up, raise.

7748₂

闕 〔Chueh〕 *n.* city gate, imperial palace.

7750₀

母 〔Mu〕 *n.* mother, mama, female.

00-- 音	vowel.
06-- 親	mother, mama.
17-- 子之情	love between mother and son.
20-- 雞	hen.
-- 愛	maternal love.
-- 系	distaff side.
-- 系制度	matriarchy.
25-- 牛	cow.
40-- 校	mother school, Alma Mater.
42-- 機	machine-tool.
44-- 豬	sow.
48-- 教	mother's instruction.
60-- 國	mother country.
71-- 馬	mare.
72-- 后	queen mother.
73-- 胎	mother's womb.
77-- 舅	maternal uncle.
80-- 羊	ewe.
-- 公司	parent company, parent corporation, parent firm.
95-- 性	maternity.

7750₆

閘 〔Cha〕 *n.* water gate, flood gate, lock, sluice, dam, break on a car, switch.

20-- 住	stem.
41-- 板	sluice, flash-board.
60-- 口	sluice.
77-- 門	lock gate, sluice gate.

闈 〔Wei〕 *n.* side door of the palace.

闡 〔Shan〕 *v.* open, expose, disclose, enlighten, explain, expound.

67-- 明	clear up, decipher, explain, clarify, elucidate.

7750₈

舉 〔Chu〕 v. lift up, uphold, raise, hold up, elect, recommend, adj. entire, whole, all.

00--	辦	conduct, sponsor, organize, hold.
02--	證	testimony, proof.
--	證責任	burden of proof.
20--	止	behavior, deportment, demeanor.
--	重	weight lifting.
--	手	lift up hand, raise the hand, hands up!
--	手表決	vote by raising hands.
21--	步	step.
--	行	hold, sponsor.
--	行典禮	hold a ceremony.
22--	出	enumerate, raise.
--	例	for example, for instance.
--	例說明	cite an example by way of explanation.
24--	動	action, behavior, conduct.
25--	債	float a loan, contract a loan to, borrow.
41--	杯	drink a toast.
44--	世震驚	strike the world with.
--	世聞名	all the world knows, world-famous.
--	世無匹	without a match in the world.
--	棋不定	v. hesitate, adj. indecisive.
47--	起	lift up, hold up, raise, elevate, hoist.
60--	國	whole country.
--	足輕重	pivotal, very important.

7755₀

毋 〔Wu〕 adj. not, do not.

00--	庸說明	the thing tells its own tale.
--	庸詳述	no need to go into the details.
--	庸贅述	no need to repeat it.
--	忘在莒	do not forget the national humiliation in time of peace and security.
06--	誤前途	don't hurt your career.
26--	自菲薄	do not belittle yourself.
--	自辱焉	do not disgrace yourself.
44--	藐視人	do not hold anyone cheap.

7760₁

譽 〔Ku〕 n. quick information.

誾 〔Yin〕 n. admonish, reprove mildly.

闇 〔An〕 n. evening, adj. dark, dim.

譽 〔Yu〕 n. reputation, fame, v. praise, extol.

醫 〔I〕 n. doctor, physician, v. cure, treat, heal.

00--	病	cure diseases.
--	療	cure, treat, remedy, medical treatment.
--	療站	medical station.
--	療保險	hospitalization insurance, insurance for medical care, medical insurance.
--	療保健費	health expenditure.
--	療機構	medical establishment.
--	療設備	medical equipment.
--	療費	medical and dental expenses.
--	療服務	medical service.
17--	務	medical affairs, medical service.
--	務所	clinic, dispensary.
21--	術	physic, medicine, medical skill.
24--	科	medical department, medicine department (in a university).
25--	生	doctor, physician, surgeon.
32--	業	medical profession.
33--	治	cure, heal, treat.
44--	藥	medicine, drugs.
--	藥費	medical fee.
--	藥顧問	consulting physician.
50--	書	medical book.
73--	院	hospital.
77--	學	medicine, medical science.
--	學生	medical student.
--	學院	medical college.
--	學院長	dean of medical college.

7760₂

留 〔Liu〕 v. detain, retain, remain, stay, delay, leave, save, keep, reserve.

00-- 意	pay attention, attend to, give heed to, be careful, be attentive.
-- 言	leave word.
-- 言簿	visitors' book.
10-- 下	leave behind, stay.
-- 下印象	impress.
13-- 職停薪	leave without pay.
20-- 住	keep, stay, detain.
21-- 步	stop going on.
22-- 戀	unwilling to leave, hanker after.
-- 任	retain in office, remain in office.
24-- 待	remain.
27-- 級	degrade.
-- 名千古	leave a good reputation for ages.
30-- 宿	lodge.
-- 客	keep a guest.
-- 空	leave a blank, leave a space in writing.
33-- 心	take care, note, bear in mind.
35-- 神	be cautious, take care.
40-- 存盈餘	retained earnings, retained surplus.
-- 有餘地	allow some leeway, make allowance for unexpected needs.
47-- 聲機	phonograph, gramophone.
60-- 置	retention.
-- 置權	lien.
-- 置權人	lien holder.
62-- 別	keepsake.
-- 別紀念	souvenir or keepsake.
77-- 學	study abroad.
-- 學生	student studying abroad.
-- 學考試	examination for studying abroad.
95-- 情	have mercy, relent.

7760₄

閣 〔Ko〕 n. chamber, pavilion, loft, cabinet, screen, upper story of a building.

10-- 下	Your Excellency.
45-- 樓	garret.
60-- 員	cabinet minister.

閽 〔Hun〕 n. door keeper.

7760₆

閭 〔Lu〕 n. habitation, gate of a village.

閶 〔Chang〕 n. gate of heaven.

7760₇

問 〔Wen〕 v. question, inquire, ask, examine.

07-- 訊處	inquiry office, information desk.
27-- 候	n. regards, greetings, v. greet, regard, remember.
-- 句	interrogative sentence.
33-- 心有愧	have something on one's conscience.
-- 心無愧	be conscious of having done right.
44-- 世	burst into life, come into being.
47-- 好	greet.
50-- 事處	information office.
-- 東問西	ask all sorts of questions.
60-- 罪	bring to account.
61-- 號	question mark, interrogation mark.
-- 題	question, problem, enquiry.
-- 題解決	solving problem.
67-- 路	ask the way.
-- 明原委	find out the origin of an affair.
71-- 長問短	ask many questions about other people's affairs.
88-- 答	conversation, dialogue, questions and answers.
-- 答教學法	catechism.

間 〔Chien〕 n. space, interval, room, crevice, v. substitute, change, divide, block up, prep. between, among.

04-- 謀	spy.

-- 諜	spy.
-- 諜活動	espionage.
22-- 斷	interrupt, discontinue.
-- 種	inter-planting.
44-- 苗	thin out young shoots.
53-- 或	occasionally.
56-- 接	*adj.* indirect, *adv.* indirectly.
-- 接稅	indirect tax.
-- 接原因	indirect cause.
-- 接競爭	indirect competition.
-- 接證據	indirect evidence, circumstantial evidence.
-- 接需求	indirect demand.
-- 接收益	indirect yield.
-- 接消耗	indirect consumption.
-- 接成本	indirect cost, burden cost.
-- 接費用	overhead, overhead expense, overhead charges, indirect expense.
-- 接損害	consequential damage, indirect damage, remote damages.
-- 接開支	indirect expenditure, overhead expenditure.
-- 接管理費	management indirect costs.
67-- 歇	*n.* intermittence, *adj.* intermittent.
70-- 壁	partition.
71-- 隔	compartment.
79-- 隙	gap, crevice, interval.

閫 〔**Kun**〕 *n.* threshold.
7764₁

闢 〔**Pi**〕 *v.* rid, open, refute, develop, burst forth.

07-- 謠	dispute a rumor, repudiate a rumor, deny a rumor.

7771₆

閹 〔**Yen**〕 *n.* eunuch, *v.* geld, castrate.

20-- 雞	capon.
30-- 宦	eunuch.
32-- 割	castrate.
44-- 豬	castrate a boar.
80-- 人	eunuch.

7771₇

巳 〔**Szu**〕 *n.* sixth of the twelve branches.

巴 〔**Pa**〕 *n.* large serpent, ancient state in Eastern Szechwan.

07-- 望	expect.
10-- 豆	croton.
-- 西	Brazil.
-- 西人	Brazilian.
-- 不得	if only, would that.
21-- 比倫	Babylonia.
24-- 結	flatter, curry favor with, scrape acquaintance with.
34-- 達維亞	Batavia.
27-- 黎	Paris.
-- 黎公社	Paris Commune.
77-- 兒狗	lapdog, pug.
80-- 拿馬	Panama.
90-- 掌	palm of a hand.

黽 〔**Min**〕 *n.* frog, *v.* endeavor, strive, exert.

鼠 〔**Shu**〕 *n.* rat, mouse, rodent.

00-- 疫	plague, pestilence, bubonic plague.
30-- 竄	dash away, flee like rats.
-- 竊	pilfer.
-- 竊狗偷	petty thieves.
-- 穴	mouse-hole.
40-- 夾	mouse-trap.
60-- 目寸光	short-sighted.
62-- 蹊	groin.
71-- 牙雀角	litigation over trifles.

7772₀

卯 〔**Mao**〕 *n.* fourth period of the twelve divisions of the day.

卵 〔**Luan**〕 *n.* egg, ovum, testicles.

12-- 形	ovum, oval.
17-- 子	egg, ovum.
-- 翼之下	under the protection of.
22-- 巢	ovary.
25-- 生	oviparous, egg-born.
26-- 白	albumen, egg white.
-- 細胞	ovum.
44-- 黃	yolk.

印 〔**Yin**〕 *n.* stamp, mark, spot, stain, trace, seal, *v.* print, impress, seal, stamp.

00--	章	seal, stamp.
--	度人	Indian.
--	度的	Indian.
--	度洋	Indian Ocean.
07--	記	impression, imprint, mark.
21--	行	print.
22--	出	run off, print, come out in print.
27--	象	impression.
--	象派	impressionism.
--	象主義	impressionism.
34--	染	printing and dyeing.
--	染廠	printing and dyeing works.
44--	花	stamp, fiscal stamp, tax stamp, revenue stamp printing.
--	花布	printed cloth (or cotton).
--	花稅	stamp duty, stamp duties.
--	花稅法	law of stamp duty.
50--	書	printing, print books.
57--	把子	official seal, government position.
72--	刷	print, put to press.
--	刷術	art of printing, typography, printing.
--	刷物	printed matter.
--	刷機	press machine, printing machine, printing press.
--	刷所	printer, press, print shop.
--	刷品	printed matter.
--	刷廠	printing house.
--	刷工人	printer, pressman.
--	刷油墨	printing ink.
78--	鑒卡	signature card.

即 〔 **Chi** 〕 v. approach, come to, go, be, adv. now, immediately, presently, instantly, at once, conj. even, though, even if.

00--	交貨	immediate delivery.
--	席議決	decide on the spot.
02--	刻	immediately, at once, presently, as soon as.
08--	說即做	no sooner said than done.
10--	可使用	usable at once.
20--	位	enthrone, come to throne.
21--	此	only this, thus.

24--	付	pay in sight, pay on demand, at sight.
--	付匯票	a sight bill.
27--	將	on the verge of.
--	將來到	forthcoming, approaching.
35--	使	though, even though, even if, supposing that.
--	速	quickly, speedily.
40--	來	come at once.
47--	期	at sight, delivery on spot, on demand.
--	期交貨	prompt delivery, delivery on spot, immediate delivery, ready delivery.
--	期票據	demand note.
--	期付款 (即付)	immediate payment, payment at sight, payment on demand, cash down.
--	期資金	immediate funds.
--	期存款	demand deposit.
--	期銷售	prompt sale, sales for current term.
60--	日	today, this day, at the same day.
--	回信	reply by return mail.
64--	時處理	immediate processing.
--	時出售	prompt sale.
--	時付現	immediate cash payment, prompt cash payment.
--	時付款	immediate payment.
--	時訂貨單	immediate order.

卿 〔 **Ching** 〕 n. high official, minister.
7772₇

邸 〔 **Ti** 〕 n. mansion, lodging place.

88--	第	mansion.

鴟 〔 **Chih** 〕 n. owl, kite.

鷗 〔 **Ou** 〕 n. sea gull, gull.
7773₂

艮 〔 **Ken** 〕 n. limit, bound.

閬 〔 **Lang** 〕 n. high door.
7774₇

民 〔 **Min** 〕 n. people, populace, subject, citizen, the public.

00-- 主	*n.* democracy, *adj.* democratic.
-- 主國	democratic country, republic.
-- 主主義	democracy.
-- 主人士	democrat.
-- 主政府	democracy.
-- 主主義者	democrat.
-- 主集中制	democratic centralism.
-- 主政體	democratic government.
-- 主黨	democratic party.
-- 主潮流	tide of democracy.
-- 意	public opinion, the will of the people, popular opinions.
-- 意測驗	test of public opinion, public opinion survey, poll.
-- 意代表	people's representatives.
-- 意機關	people's representative body.
07-- 謠	ballad, folk songs.
08-- 族	race, nation, nationality.
-- 族主義	nationalism, Principle of Nationalism.
-- 族復興	national renaissance.
-- 族至上	nation above all.
-- 族運動	national movement.
-- 族革命	national revolution.
-- 族英雄	national hero.
-- 族自決	national self-determination.
-- 族自覺	national consciousness.
-- 族資產階級	national bourgeoisie.
10-- 工	civilian worker.
-- 不聊生	the people find it hard to live on.
17-- 歌	ballad, folk songs.
18-- 政	civil administration.
20-- 航	civil aviation.
25-- 生	livelihood, people's livelihood.
-- 生主義	livelihood, Principle of the People's Livelihood.
-- 生問題	problem of the people's livelihood.
-- 約論	social compact.
28-- 俗	people's custom.
34-- 法	civil law, civil code.

37-- 選	popular election.
-- 軍	militia, volunteer.
44-- 權	popular rights, civil rights.
-- 權主義	democracy, Principle of the People's Rights.
50-- 事訴訟	civil action, civil suit.
-- 事裁判	civil judgment.
-- 事責任	civil liability.
-- 事訴訟法	Code of Civil procedure.
60-- 團=民軍	
-- 眾	mass, masses, commonwealth, people, populace.
-- 眾教育	education of the masses.
-- 眾團體	civic organization.
-- 風	popular custom.
72-- 兵	militia, militiaman.
-- 兵師	contingent of the people's militia.
77-- 用	civil.
-- 用機場	civil airport.
-- 間舞	folk dance.
-- 間文學	popular literature.
-- 間音樂	folk music.
-- 間藝術	folk art.
-- 間故事	folk-tales.
94-- 憤	indignation among the people.
95-- 情	popular feeling, condition of the people.

毆 〔**Ou**〕 *v.* beat, strike, fight.

28-- 傷	wound by beating, beat black and blue.
51-- 打	*n.* assault and battery, *v.* beat, fight, strike, manhandle, fall foul of.
77-- 鬥	fight with the fist, have fisticuffs.
98-- 斃	beat to death.

7777₀

凹 〔**Ao**〕 *adj.* concave, hollow, curved.

00-- 痕	pit, dent.
21-- 版	intaglio.
-- 處	concave.
27-- 的	concave
37-- 渦	hollow.

72-- 彫刻	intaglio.
77-- 凸	concave and convex.
80-- 鏡	concave lens, concave mirror.

臼 〔**Chiu**〕 *n.* mortar (of stone), bowl, dish, socket at a bone joint.

21-- 齒	molars (teeth).

7777_2

關 〔**Kuan**〕 *n.* frontier, frontier pass, gate, pass, custom house, customs barrier, key point, *v.* shut, close, fasten, connect, involve, catch, concern, draw (pay).

08-- 於	in connection with, with regard to, with reference to, with relation to, with respect to concerning, in respect of, regarding, relating to.
11-- 頭	crucial moment.
12-- 聯	correlation.
21-- 卡	customs.
22-- 係	relation, relationship, connection, bearing.
-- 係惡化	deterioration of relations.
-- 係人	affiliated person.
-- 係企業	affiliated enterprise.
28-- 稅 (進口稅)	impost, customs, customs duty, tariff, tariff duty.
-- 稅率	tariff rate.
-- 稅談判	tariff negotiation.
-- 稅改革	tariff reform.
-- 稅征收	collection of customs duty.
-- 稅制度	tariff system.
-- 稅特惠	tariff preference.
-- 稅保護	tariff protection.
-- 稅條約	tariff treaty.
-- 稅減免	Deduction and Exemption of Customs Duty.
-- 稅協定	customs convention, tariff agreement, tariff compact.
-- 稅戰爭	tariff war.
-- 稅局	Bureau of Customs, Tariff Bureau.

-- 稅自主	tariff autonomy.
-- 稅同盟	customs union, customs cartel, tariff alliance, tariff union.
-- 稅降低	tariff reduction.
-- 稅壁壘	tariff wall.
-- 稅報復	tariff retaliation.
33-- 心	take care, be concerned, be concerned about, feel interested in, be interested in, show concern.
35-- 連	*n.* correlation, *v.* involve.
40-- 境 (關稅國境)	customs frontier, customs boundary.
57-- 押	take into custody.
60-- 口	pass, frontier pass.
67-- 照	notify, inform.
77-- 閉	*n.* closure, *v.* shut, close, close down.
-- 門	shut a door.
-- 門主義	exclusionism.
85-- 鍵	key, crux.
88-- 節	joints.
89-- 節炎	arthritis.
92-- 燈	switch off the light.
94-- 懷=關心	

7777_7

凸 〔**Tu**〕 *adj.* convex, projecting, jutting.

10-- 面	convex surface.
22-- 出	*n.* projection, *v.* jut, project, swell up.
27-- 的	convex, projecting.
32-- 透鏡	convex lens, convex mirror.
77-- 凹不平	rough and uneven in surface.
80-- 鏡	convex lens.

門 〔**Men**〕 *n.* door, gate, gateway, entrance, family, clan, school of thought, key, main point.

00-- 廊	porch, vestibule.
-- 市部	sales department, retail sales department, sales room, selling retail department.
08-- 診部	out patients' department.

10--	丁	doorkeeper.
--	面	style of a shop, shop front.
--	票	admission ticket.
16--	環	knocker.
23--	外	outdoor.
--	外漢	layman.
24--	徒	disciple, pupil.
25--	生=門徒	
26--	牌	doorplate, house number (plate).
30--	帘	door screen.
--	房	doorkeeper.
--	戶	doors.
--	戶開放	open door, open-door policy.
--	戶開放主義	open door principle.
--	戶開放政策	open door policy.
32--	派	sect.
41--	板	door plank.
47--	楣	lintel.
48--	警	doorkeeper, porter.
--	檻	threshold.
60--	口	doorway, entry, gate, entrance.
--	口台階	door step.
--	羅主義	Monroe Doctrine.
71--	牙	front tooth.
--	階	door step.
--	閂	bar, latch.
--	限=門檻	
80--	人	disciples.
88--	鈴	door bell.
--	第	birth.
--	簾	door screen.
89--	鎖	door lock.

閭〔**Yen**〕*n.* gate of a village.

10--	王	Pluto, ruler of Hell.

7778₂

歐〔**Ou**〕*n.* Europe, European, *v.* vomit.

10--	亞	Eurasia.
24--	化	European civilization.
32--	洲	Europe, European.
--	洲人	European.
--	洲復興方案	European Recovery program.
63--	戰	European war.
80--	人	European.

7780₁

具〔**Chu**〕*n.* tool, utensil, *v.* prepare, furnish, arrange, supply, *adj.* prepared, ready, every, all.

00--	文	dead letter.
24--	備	have, be equipped with.
40--	有	have, possess.
75--	體	concrete.
--	體化	incarnate, substantiate.
--	體表現	embody.
75--	體計畫	concrete plan.
--	體任務	specific target.

與〔**Yu**〕*v.* give, commit, transfer, allow, agree, take part in, participate, *conj.* and, as well as, *prep.* with.

44--	世無爭	be in harmony with the rest of the world.
50--	事不符	not in accordance with facts.
60--	日俱增	grow with each passing day.
64--	時並進	keep pace with the times.
80--	會	attend a meeting.
--	會國	participating countries.

巽〔**Hsun**〕*adj.* mild, bland.

鬨〔**Hung**〕*n.* noise of fighting, clamor, uproar, *v.* fight, wrangle, *adj.* boisterous.

40--	走	hoot away.
77--	鬧	*n.* clamor, uproar *v.* make riot, be clamorous.

興〔**Hsing**〕*n.* joy, happiness, interest, enthusiasm, *v.* arise, rise, get up, prosper, start, found, thrive, happen, occur, *adj.* prosperous, flourishing, cheerful, happy, merry.

00--	高采烈	full of beans.
--	衰	prosperity and adversity.
--	亡	rise or fall, prosperous and declining.
10--	工	commence work, start construction work.
40--	奮	*n.* exhilaration, excitement, rapture, *v.* stimulate, intoxicate, *adj.* exhilarated, ex-

		cited.
--	奮劑	stimulant.
41--	趣	interest, pleasure.
47--	起	arise, get up.
53--	盛	v. flourish, be in the ascendant, adj. prosperous, flourishing.
61--	旺=興盛	
77--	隆	prosper, flourish.

興 〔 Yu 〕 n. chariot, carriage, sedan chair, vehicle, land, territory, v. bear, hold, sustain, carry, adj. public.

08--	論	public opinion.
60--	圖	map, atlas.
95--	情	public feelings.

7780₆

貿 〔 Mao 〕 n. buy, exchange, trade, v. barter, trade, traffic, adj. mixed, confused.

23--	然	without due consideration.
60--	易	trade, commerce, traffic, commercial transaction.
--	易部	board of trade.
--	易中心	commercial center.
--	易糾紛	trade dispute.
--	易逆差	adverse balance, adverse trade balance, passive balance of trade, trade deficit, unfavorable trade balance.
--	易中心	trade center.
--	易量	trade volume.
--	易戰	trade war.
--	易區	trade area.
--	易公司	trading corporation.

貫 〔 Kuan 〕 n. thread to string up holed coins, v. connect, string, run through, penetrate, go through, understand thoroughly.

28--	徹	carry...through, carry out.
--	徹到底	do a thorough job to something.
30--	穿	pass through, perforate, penetrate.
50--	串	connect, string up.
70--	通	understand thoroughly.

80--	入	penetrate.

賢 〔 Hsien 〕 n. able and virtuous person, v. respect, adj. moral, worthy, virtuous, able, talented, good.

21--	能	superior ability.
24--	德	n. exalted virtue, virtue, adj. virtuous.
44--	者	able and virtuous man.
50--	妻	worthy wife.
55--	慧	virtuous and wise.
67--	明	wise, judicious.
80--	人	sage, person of virtue and talent.
99--	勞	laborious, hardworking.

7780₇

尺 〔 Chih 〕 n. foot (unit in Chinese linear measurement), ruler, foot ruler.

00--	度	size, measurement.
--	度相同	same scale.
24--	牘	letters, letter-writing, correspondence.
--	牘大全	complete guide to correspondence styles.
40--	寸	size, measurement, dimension.
--	寸不足	short size.
--	寸不合格	off size.
--	寸不符	different size.
--	寸過大	oversize.
--	寸過小	undersize.
44--	地寸土	tiny pieces of land.

閃 〔 Shan 〕 n. flash, v. flash, dodge, lose, twist, avoid, evade.

10--	亮	shining.
--	電	lightning.
--	電戰	blitzkrieg, lighting war.
24--	動	flare.
--	避	avoid, dodge.
37--	過	avoid.
67--	眼	flashing.
90--	光	v. glitter, flash, adj. sparkling.
--	光燈	flashlight.
--	耀	flicker, flare, shine.
97--	燦	flash, glimmer.

7788₂

歟〔Yu〕*interj.* ah！alas！

7790₃

緊〔Chin〕*v.* bind tight, *adj.* tense, tight, fast, important, pressing, urgent.

10-- 要	*n.* importance, *adj.* important, momentous.
-- 要關頭	crisis.
11-- 張	*n.* tension, *adj.* tense.
-- 張局勢	tension, tense situation.
-- 縮	*n.* austerity, contraction, retrenchment, *v.* reduce, retrench, tighten.
-- 縮計畫	austerity plan.
-- 縮措施	austerity measures, retrenchment measures, contraction measures.
--縮開支	curtail expenditure, curtailing expenditure, cut down expenses, retrench expenditure.
--縮銀根	tighten money.
24-- 結	fasten.
27-- 急	*n.* urgency, emergency, *adj.* urgent, critical, emergent.
-- 急處理	emergency treatment.
-- 急狀態	state of emergency.
-- 急救濟	urgent relief.
-- 急事項	matter of urgency.
-- 急申請	last-minute application.
-- 急措施	emergency measure.
-- 急命令	urgent order, emergent order.
-- 急任務	urgent task.
-- 急動議	urgent or emergent motion, motion of urgent necessity.
-- 急警報	urgent alarm, air raid alarm sounded when enemy planes are near or already overhead.
29-- 俏貨	articles in great demand.
30-- 密	tight, fast, compact, close together, inseparable.
35-- 湊	tightly packed and arranged.

36-- 迫	pressing.
-- 迫需求	pressing demands.
50-- 接	come after.
-- 接着	close behind.
57-- 握	cling, embrace, cuddle, grasp, press, grip, clench.
-- 抱	cling, embrace, cuddle.
61-- 貼	tight.

7790₄

朵〔To〕*n.* cluster, bud, *v.* move, shake.

桑〔Sang〕*n.* mulberry, mulberry tree.

17-- 子	mulberry seed.
44-- 葚	mulberry.
-- 葉	mulberry leaves.
60-- 園	mulberry orchard.

閑〔Hsien〕*n.* leisure, spare time, *v.* guard, defend, restrain, *adj.* idle, dilatory, quiet, calm.

02-- 話	chit-chat, idle talk.
09-- 談	gossip, chat.
31-- 逛	saunter, stroll, ramble.
44-- 蕩	wander.
48-- 散	idle, unoccupied.
50-- 事	impertinent matter.
60-- 置	idle.
-- 置不用	shelve, put aside.
67-- 暇	leisure, spare time.
-- 暇時間	spare time.
80-- 人	idler.
-- 人免進	admittance to staff only, no admittance except on business.

7790₆

闌〔Lan〕*n.* balustrade, door curtain, *v.* block up, cut off, *adj.* end of, late, weakened, withered.

10-- 干	railing, rails.
77-- 尾	appendix.
-- 尾炎	appendicitis.

7810₄

墜〔Chui〕*v.* fall down, sink, collapse, crumble, decline.

10-- 下	fall down.
44-- 落	depress, fall down.
60-- 圈套中	fall into someone's trap.
65-- 跌	topple over.

71-- 馬 fall off a horse.
73-- 胎 miscarriage.
77-- 毀 crash.
80-- 入 fall into.

7810₇
監〔**Chien**〕*n.* prison, custody, jail, *v.* examine carefully, oversee, supervise, inspect, confine, imprison.

04-- 護 guardianship, chaperon.
-- 護人 governor, guardian.
-- 護權 guardianship.
10-- 工 *n.* supervisor of construction work, overseer, supervisor, factory superintendent, superintendent of work, *v.* oversee work, supervise work.
-- 工費 supervising expenses.
27-- 督 *n.* director, supervisor, superintendent, supervision, boss, overseer, *v.* direct, supervise, superintend.
-- 督委員會 watchdog committee.
-- 督經理 monitor manager.
-- 督制度 inspecting system.
-- 督權 supervisory authority.
-- 督人 supervisor.
-- 督管理 management by personal supervision.
30-- 牢 prison, jail.
-- 守 custody.
-- 察 control, supervise, inspect.
-- 察院 Control Yuan.
-- 察人 supervisor.
-- 察員 inspector.
-- 察委員 member of the Supervisory Committee, member of Control Yuan.
36-- 視 guard, oversee, superintend, look after, watch.
-- 視所 lookout post.
40-- 查人 auditor.
43-- 獄 prison, jail.
44-- 禁 *n.* imprisonment, custody, *v.* imprison.
47-- 犯 prisoner.
53-- 控器 monitor.

77-- 學 school superintendent.
89-- 銷 supervising sale.

鹽〔**Yen**〕*n.* salt.
10-- 礦 salt mine.
12-- 水 saline water.
13-- 酸 hydrochloric acid.
-- 碱地 alkaline land, saline soil.
17-- 蛋 salted egg.
-- 湖 salt lake.
28-- 份 salinity.
44-- 基 base (in chemistry).
46-- 場 salt pan, salt field.
55-- 井 salt well.
60-- 田 salt pond.
65-- 味 saline taste.
74-- 腌 *v.* salt, *adj.* salted.

7810₉
鑒〔**Chien**〕*n.* metal mirror, example, *v.* reflect, examine.
08-- 於 since, in view of.
30-- 定 *n.* expert evidence, appraisement, appraisal cost, surveyor's fee, *v.* appraise, identify.
-- 定報告 survey report.
-- 定人 surveyor, appraiser.
40-- 核 examine, look into.
62-- 別 distinguish, judge.
-- 別力 power of discrimination.
90-- 賞 appreciate, appraise.

7821₁
胙〔**Tso**〕*n.* sacrificial meat.

7821₄
脞〔**Tso**〕*adj.* trifling.

7821₆
脫〔**To**〕*v.* strip, omit, take escape, take off, evade, escape from, drop of, cast away, cast off, get out of, undress, leave.
00-- 衣 disrobe, undress, take off one's clothes.
-- 產 be disengaged from work.
-- 離 break away from, separate oneself from, separate from, be divorced from, get away

	from, escape, free, leave, set off, throw off, get rid of, get clear of.
10-- 下	take off.
12-- 水	n. dehydration, v. dehydrate.
20-- 手	disengage one's hand, dispose of, sell.
21-- 價	out-of-the market.
27-- 身	disengage oneself, escape, slip away.
-- 色	decolorize.
32-- 逃	escape, desert.
40-- 去	take off.
-- 皮	slough, ecdyses.
-- 帽	uncover.
44-- 落	fall off.
47-- 殼	slough, cast the shell.
71-- 脂乳	skim milk.
-- 脂棉	absorbent cotton.
73-- 胎	produced from, originated from.
78-- 險	be out of danger.
87-- 卸	unload.
88-- 節	disjointed, out of keeping with.
89-- 銷	have a drain on supplies, run out of supplies, sell out, shortage, goods were sold out, out of stock.
90-- 黨	apostasy.
-- 粒	husk, shell.
-- 粒機	sheller.

覽〔Lan〕v. view, look at, look around, observe, inspect, read over.

7821₇

隘〔Ai〕n. pass, defile, adj. narrow, confined, obstructed.

30-- 害	strategic point.
44-- 巷	narrow lane.
60-- 口	entrance to a pass.

7822₂

朕〔Chen〕n. gizzard of a fowl.

7823₁

陰〔Yin〕n. shadow, shade, female, adj. dark, cloudy, gloomy, cold, somber, obscure, negative, crafty, cunning.

04-- 謀	n. plot, close design, intrigue, conspiracy, v. plan secretly, conspire.
-- 謀家	conspirator, plotter.
-- 謀詭計	intrigues and plots.
07-- 部	vagina, genital, private part.
10-- 天	dark cloudy day, cloudy weather, overcast day.
-- 電	negative electricity.
20-- 毛	pubes, hairs at the private part.
24-- 德	secret and kind acts.
30-- 戶	vagina.
-- 涼	cool, shady.
35-- 溝	drain, sewer.
37-- 沉	gloomy, dark, somber.
38-- 冷	raw, cold.
40-- 森	somber, gloomy.
41-- 極	cathode, negative pole.
44-- 莖	penis.
50-- 事洩漏	the secret affair was disclosed.
60-- 暗	somber, obscure, dark, gloomy.
-- 暗面	dark side, seamy side.
62-- 影	shadow, shade.
71-- 曆	lunar calendar.
76-- 陽家	necromancer.
77-- 間	hades, hell, underworld.
78-- 險	sinister, insidious, cunning.
95-- 性	female, feminine, feminine gender, adj. negative.

7823₂

隊〔Tui〕n. group, company, team, gang, army, squadron, brigade, squad, band, contingent of troops.

00-- 商	caravan.
12-- 形	formation, formation of troops.
21-- 伍	army, troop, troops in ranks and files.
60-- 員	team member.
71-- 長	captain, captain of a sports team, team leader, head of

a production team.

7823₃

隧 〔**Sui**〕*n.* path to a tomb, bypath, tunnel, subway.

| 38-- 道 | subway, tunnel. |

7823₄

朕 〔**Chen**〕*pron.* I, me (used by an emperor only), omen.

| 32-- 兆 | symptom, omen. |

7824₁

胼 〔**Pien**〕*n.* thickening of skin, calluses.

| 72-- 胝 | *n.* callosity, calluses, *adj.* callous. |

7824₇

腹 〔**Fu**〕*n.* belly, abdomen, stomach, middle of something, front part.

00-- 痛	bellyache, stomachache.
07-- 部	abdomen.
11-- 背	front and rear.
33-- 洩	flux, diarrhea.
44-- 地	interior, inland.
71-- 脹	dropsy.
73-- 腔	abdominal cavity.
74-- 膜	peritoneum.
-- 膜炎	peritonitis.

7826₅

膳 〔**Shan**〕*n.* food, fare, meal, board

00-- 廳	dining hall.
30-- 宿	food and lodging, board and lodging, room and board.
-- 宿所	boarding house.
-- 宿費	board and lodging, meals and lodging expenses.
55-- 費	fee for food, charge for board.
80-- 食	meal.

7826₆

膾 〔**Kuai**〕*n.* fine minced meat.

| 27-- 炙 | hash up meat and bake it. |
| -- 炙一時 | very pleasant to eat or hear at one time. |

-- 炙人口   very popular.

7828₆

險 〔**Hsien**〕*n.* danger, obstacle, defile, strategic pass, risky matter, *adj.* dangerous, evil, cunning, vicious, *adv.* almost, nearly.

00-- 症	dangerous disease, severe illness.
08-- 詐	treacherous, knavish.
10-- 惡	malicious, evil.
-- 要	*n.* strategic point, *adj.* strategically important.
-- 要堅守	guard the strategic post securely.
-- 死環生	have narrowly escaped death.
21-- 處	dangerous place.
23-- 峻	abrupt, precipitous.
35-- 遭不測	barely escaped a fatal accident, was nearly killed.
40-- 境	dangerous situation.
44-- 地	dangerous place.
47-- 猾	treacherous.
77-- 阻	hilly, iron-bound, in difficulties.
-- 阻艱難	obstructed by all sorts of difficulties.

臉 〔**Lean**〕*n.* face, check.

21-- 紅	redden, blush.
-- 紅耳赤	flush red in the face.
40-- 皮	face.
-- 皮厚	shameless, brazen.
71-- 厚	shameless.
80-- 盆	washing basin.

7829₄

除 〔**Chu**〕*v.* deduct, divide, take away, wipe out, get rid of, remove, exclude, be appointed to a new post, *conj.* but, only, *prep.* with the exception of, besides, in addition of.

00-- 病良方	best remedy for a malady.
11-- 非	unless, except.
17-- 了	expect, except for.
21-- 此而外	moreover, besides.

23-- 外		except, apart from, exclude.
27-- 夕		New Year's Eve.
-- 名		strike one's name off, strike out the name.
30-- 害		remove evil.
34-- 法		*n*. division, *v*. (in math) divide.
37-- 淨		ex-all.
40-- 去		remove, take away, clear away, get rid of, do away with.
44-- 草機		mower, mowing machine.
-- 草藥		weed killer.
47-- 根		root out, uproot, eradicate.
58-- 數		(in math) divisor, constant divisor.
60-- 暴安良		weed out the wicked and let the law-abiding.
77-- 開		*v*. count out, exclude, *prep*. apart from.

7834₁

駢〔 Pien 〕*n*. two horses going abreast.

7838₆

驗〔 Yen 〕*n*. examine, prove, verify, come true, test, be effective.

00-- 疫		health inspection.
02-- 證		experimental verification.
08-- 訖放行		let goods pass after they are examined.
24-- 貨		inspect goods, examine goods.
-- 貨員		examiner.
27-- 血		blood test.
28-- 傷		examine an injury.
-- 收		*n*. inspection and receipt, *v*. examine and accept, acceptance check, examine and receive, check and receive, check before acceptance.
30-- 究原因		examine the cause.
40-- 查		examine, inspect.
-- 大便		stool test.
67-- 明		verify, examine clearly.
-- 明正身		make a positive identification of a criminal before execution.

77-- 關		customs examination inspection, customs examination, customs inspection.
-- 尿		urine test.
-- 屍		post-mortem examination.
-- 屍所		mortuary.

7870₄

臥見 7370₀

7876₆

臨〔 Lin 〕*v*. approach, attend, visit, copy, imitate, look down from above, reach, come to, *prep*. near to, during, *adv*. on the point of, at the time of.

00-- 夜		at nightfall.
-- 產		be brought to bed, at the time of childbirth.
-- 症		examine a disease.
-- 床		clinical.
-- 床經驗		clinical experience.
17-- 了		at last.
12-- 到		on arriving.
21-- 行		on leaving, on the point of departure.
27-- 終、死		about to die, at the point of death, on one's deathbed.
-- 終之言		dying advice or instructions.
-- 終時候		before one expires.
32-- 近		on arriving, on approaching.
40-- 去		before going.
42-- 機應變		presence of mind.
44-- 摹		copy or imitate (in calligraphy or painting).
60-- 界點		(in physics) critical point.
62-- 睡		before going to bed.
-- 別		on the point of departure.
-- 別贈言		valediction, parting words.
64-- 時		*adj*. temporary, provisional, *adv*. temporarily, for the occasion.
-- 時主席		temporary chairman.
-- 時議程		provisional agenda.
-- 時工		jobber, odd-jobber, casual laborer, casual labor, odd-jobbers, seasonal workers.

-- 時工程 temporary work.
-- 時工作 odd job.
-- 時建築 temporary buildings.
-- 時收據 teller receipt, interim receipt, temporary receipt.
-- 時雇工 temporary employment.
-- 時通融 temporary accommodation.
-- 時措施 interim measures, provisional measures, stopgap measure.
-- 時費用 casual expenses, interim charges, interim expenses, non-recurrent cost, non-recurring expenses.
-- 時開支 interim charges.
-- 時政府 provisional government.
-- 時事故 accident.
-- 時動議 extraordinary motion.
-- 時簽署 initial.
-- 時住所 provisional domicile.
-- 時生活費 subsistence money.
-- 時警察 special constable.
75-- 陣 enter into action, be on service, take the field, go into battle, at the front.

7921_1
胱〔**Kuang**〕 *n.* bladder.

7921_4
勝〔**Sheng**〕 *n.* scenic spot, *v.* sin, conquer, triumph over, win.
02-- 訴 obtain satisfaction of a claim, win a lawsuit, win an action.
-- 訴人 suit winner.
22-- 任 adequate to the post, qualified for the office.
-- 利 victory, triumph.
-- 利凱旋 have won a victory and returned in triumph.
27-- 負難分 it is difficult to tell who will win.
-- 負難料 it is hard to predict victory or defeat.
-- 負未卜 the result of the contest cannot be predicted yet.
37-- 過 out strip, transcend, run before, prevail over, excel, surpass.
68-- 敗 victories and defeats.
-- 敗未分 to win or to lose is still doubtful.
88-- 算可操 victory is within grasp.

騰〔**Teng**〕 *v.* leap on, mount, ascend gallop, run, prance, ascend, rise, soar, transfer.
22-- 出 *n.* evacuation, *v.* evacuate, vacate, clear out.
30-- 空 leave empty, soar.
67-- 躍 leap, gallop, prance, soar.

膅〔**Tang**〕 *n.* breast, chest, chamber of a firearm.

7923_2
縢〔**Teng**〕 *n.* Teng (a family name.)

7925_0
胖〔**Pang**〕 *adj.* fat, stout, fleshy, plump.
17-- 子 *n.* fat fellow, fat person, stout man, *adj.* fatty.

7926_1
謄〔**Teng**〕 *v.* copy, transcribe.
30-- 寫 copy, transcribe.
-- 寫者 copyist, copier.
35-- 清 copy clearly, make a fair copy.
50-- 本 transcript.

7928_6
賸〔**Sheng**〕 *v.* leave over, increase.
88-- 餘 surplus, remainder.

7929_6
隙〔**Hsi**〕 *n.* fissure, crack, chick, interval, breach, gap, cleft, crevice, grudge.
27-- 縫 aperture, crack, crevice.
44-- 地 open space.

8

8000_0
八〔**Pa**〕 *adj.* eight, eighth.
00-- 方風雨 wind and rain from eight (all) directions.
10-- 面玲瓏 be a perfect mixer in any company.

-- 面周全	satisfactory in every detail.
-- 面威風	awe-inspiring reputation extending in eight directions.
-- 百羅漢	eight hundred Buddhist Saints.
22-- 仙	eight immortals in Taoism.
-- 仙桌子	square dinner table seating eight.
24-- 紘一宇	unite the whole world under one sovereign by force of arms.
27-- 角形	octagon.
-- 級工資制	eight-grade wage system.
30-- 字	horoscope.
-- 字腳	splay-foot.
34-- 斗之才	man of great talent.
40-- 十	eighty, fourscore.
43-- 卦	eight divine diagrams in the Book of Changes.
52-- 折	twenty percent discount.
53-- 成	eighty percent.
60-- 國聯軍	The Allied Forces of the Eight Powers.
67-- 路軍	Eighth Route Army.
77-- 月	August.
-- 股文	stereotyped writing.
-- 股文章	stereotyped writing.
-- 開本	octavo (8 vo).
80-- 分之一	one eighth.
90-- 小時工作制	eight hour day, eight hour shift, eight working hour day, eight hour system of labor.

人 〔Jen〕 n. man, person, people, others, mortal being, living soul, human being.

00-- 言可畏	people will talk.
-- 文	human knowledge.
02-- 證	personal testimony, testimony of a witness.
10-- 工	n. human labor, manual work, art, artificial product, adj. artificial, man-made.
-- 工呼吸	artificial respiration.
-- 工成本	labor cost.
-- 工製品	manufactured article.
-- 死留名	a man should leave a name behind him.
-- 面獸心	wolf in a sheep's skin.
-- 丁冊	poll.
11-- 頭稅	poll tax, head money, head tax.
17-- 羣	crowd, flock.
20-- 手不足	underhanded.
21-- 行道	sidewalk, pavement.
22-- 稱	person (in grammar).
-- 種	race, tribe.
-- 種學	ethnology.
-- 山人海	big crowd.
23-- 蔘	ginseng.
25-- 生	human life.
-- 生觀	life-view, outlook on life.
-- 生如夢	life is but a dream.
27-- 物	great man, figure, personage, personality.
-- 物畫	portrait.
-- 們	folks, people.
-- 像	portrait.
-- 的	personal, human.
28-- 倫	human relationship.
30-- 家	household, others.
-- 之常情	it's only human.
33-- 心	public opinion.
-- 心惶惶	jittery or panicky.
-- 心大快	the public is satisfied.
34-- 爲	artificial.
-- 爲淘汰	artificial selection.
-- 造	artificial, synthetic.
-- 造絲	rayon, artificial silk, rayon filament yarn, rayon staple.
-- 造黃油	margarine.
-- 造汽油	synthetic gasoline.
-- 造衛星	man-made satellite, artificial satellite.
-- 造纖維	artificial fibers.
-- 造纖維品	rayon.
37-- 次	person/times.
38-- 道	humanity, sexual intercourse.
-- 道主義	humanism.
-- 海戰術	human wave tactics.
40-- 力	human strength, manpower,

	labor power.
-- 力車	rickshaw, jinrikisha.
-- 力發展	manpower development.
-- 才	talent, a person of ability.
-- 才輩出	every generation produces its men of ability.
-- 才外流	brain drain, brain power drain, drain of brain.
-- 才回歸	return of talents.
-- 才濟濟	large gathering of men of talents.
-- 肉市場	sex market.
-- 壽保險	life insurance.
-- 壽保險公司	life-insurance company.
-- 壽保險單	life policy (L/P), life insurance policy (L.I.P).
44-- 猿	ape, anthropoid.
-- 權	personal right.
-- 地生疏	in an unfamiliar place.
-- 老珠黃	(said of a woman) in old age.
46-- 相學	physiognomy.
47-- 格	personality, character.
-- 格化	personification.
-- 均收入	per capita income.
50-- 事	personal, human affairs, personnel, human resources.
-- 事處	office of personnel affairs, personnel department, personnel division.
-- 事科	personnel section (or department).
-- 事檔案	personal records, personnel records.
-- 事費	personnel expenses, staff cost.
-- 事關係	human relations.
-- 事管理	personal management, manpower management, personnel administration.
58-- 數	population, number of people.
60-- 品	character of a person.
-- 員	personnel, staff.
-- 口	population.
-- 口計劃	population program.
-- 口調查	demographic census.
-- 口登記	national register.
-- 口論	principle of population.
-- 口統計	demographic statistics, population statistics, statistics of population, vital statistics.
-- 口稅	external taxes.
-- 口稠密	populous.
-- 口密度	population concentration, population density.
-- 口過剩	overpopulation.
-- 口控制	birth control, population control.
-- 口出生率	birth rate.
-- 口普查	population census, census.
-- 口普查員	census taker.
62-- 影	figure, person's shadow.
72-- 質	hostage.
75-- 體	human body.
-- 體解剖	human anatomy.
77-- 民	people, subject, public folk.
-- 民幣	Renminbi (RMB).
-- 民公社	people's commune.
-- 民戰爭	people's war.
-- 民陣線	popular front.
-- 民代表	people's representative.
-- 民權利書	bill of rights.
-- 民代表大會	People's Congress.
-- 民民主專政	people's democratic dictatorship.
-- 間	in the world, human world.
-- 間天堂	heaven on earth.
-- 間地獄	veritable hell on earth.
80-- 人	everybody, everyman, everyone.
-- 人自危	everyone feels insecure.
-- 命	human life.
86-- 智	human understanding.
87-- 慾橫流	human desires run riot.
91-- 類	mankind, human being, human race.
-- 類學	anthropology.
91-- 煙稠密	crowded, populous.
95-- 性	personality, humanity, human nature.
-- 性論	theory of the human nature.

-- 情	human feeling, human nature, human relationships.	
-- 情味	human touch.	
96-- 烟稠密	densely populated.	

入 〔**Ju**〕 *n.* entry, income earning, *v.* enter, go into, step in, fall in.

00-- 座	take a chair.
-- 庫單	godown entry, warehousing entry.
-- 不敷出	live beyond one's income, income falls short of the expenditure, run behind one's expenses.
20-- 手	*n.* beginning, *v.* begin with, *adj.* elementary.
21-- 伍	be enlisted.
-- 伍當兵	be enlisted and be a soldier.
26-- 息	income, earning.
27-- 侵	invade.
-- 鄉隨俗	in Rome do as the Romans do.
30-- 寇	invader.
-- 官	confiscate.
-- 官見妒	encounter jealousy in the palace.
-- 室升堂	enter the room and proceed to the hall (to get the core of a doctrine).
37-- 選	be placed upon the selection list.
39-- 迷	be captivated, be fascinated.
40-- 境	*n.* entry, *v.* enter the country.
-- 境辦事處	office of entry.
-- 境手續	entry procedures, immigration procedure.
-- 境權	passport.
-- 境問俗	inquire about the custom on entering a country.
-- 境簽證	entrance visé, entry visa.
-- 土爲安	be laid to rest.
-- 木三分	expressed in a forceful style.
-- 幕之賓	serve as adviser to someone.
-- 其圈中	fall into the trap.
46-- 場	*n.* admission, entry, entrance, *v.* enter a meeting place.
-- 場票	ticket, pass, permit, admission ticket.
-- 場費	admission fee, entrance fee, door money, gate money.
-- 場券	admission ticket, entrance ticket.
47-- 超	adverse trade balance, excess of imports, imbalance in trade, import excess, import surplus, unfavorable balance of trade, unfavorable trade.
60-- 口	importation, entrance, import, entry.
-- 口貨	import.
61-- 賬	entering books, enter an item in an account, enter into the account.
62-- 睡	go to bed, fall asleep.
77-- 學	enter a school.
-- 學試驗	entrance examination.
-- 學考試	entrance examination.
-- 學登記	register, matriculate.
-- 閣大臣	cabinet minister.
-- 門	*n.* beginning, primer, *v.* be initiated.
-- 門問諱	learn about the taboos on going to a friend's house.
-- 股	buy a share, become a shareholder, admission.
78-- 隊	fall into ranks.
80-- 會	enroll.
-- 會費	initiation fee.
88-- 籍	naturalization.
90-- 黨	take side, join a party.
-- 情入理	be very reasonable.
99-- 營式	induction.

8010₁

仝＝**同** 7722₀

企 〔**Chi**〕 *v.* hope, expect, long, long for, stand on tiptoe and look for.

00-- 立	stand erect.
07-- 望	expect, hope, look up to, be on tiptoe.

-- 望回音	await your reply.	
27-- 鵝	penguin.	
-- 候回音	await your reply eagerly.	
32-- 業	enterprise, undertaking, establishment, business.	
-- 業自由	freedom of enterprise.	
-- 業家	entrepreneur, businessman, industrialist, enterpriser, business executive.	
-- 業界	business circles, business community.	
-- 業管理	business administration, business management, enterprise management.	
60-- 圖	*n.* attempt, intention, endeavor, *v.* intend, seek, attempt, propose, contemplate.	

8010₂

並 〔**Ping**〕 *adv.* together, side by side, moreover, *adj.* and, and also, as well as.

00-- 立	stand side by side.
10-- 不	not at all, in no respect, in no way, by no means.
-- 不至此	not really so bad.
11-- 非	not, by no means, not by any means.
-- 非誇口	without boasting.
-- 非如此	really not so.
-- 非無因	not without a cause.
12-- 列	coordinate, put close together.
21-- 行	*v.* parallel, walk together, *adj.* collateral.
-- 行線	parallel lines.
30-- 肩	shoulder to shoulder, side by side.
-- 肩而行	walk abreast.
-- 肩作戰	fight shoulder by shoulder.
44-- 世無雙	unparalleled in the same generation.
46-- 駕齊驅	be equal to, match with, keep pace with.
51-- 排	alongside, side by side.
77-- 且	moreover, besides, further,

	furthermore.
-- 舉	promote simultaneously.
80-- 無	not a bit.
-- 無怨言	have no complaint.
-- 無差錯	nothing is wrong.
88-- 坐	sit together, sit side by side.

8010₄

全 〔**Chuan**〕 *v.* keep, *adj.* whole, complete, entire, perfect, all, total, *adv.* totally, wholly, fully, entirely, altogether.

00-- 市	whole city.
-- 文	full text.
-- 夜	throughout the night.
02-- 新	brand-new, absolutely new.
07-- 部	full, entire, total, all, whole.
-- 部付訖	paid in full, payment in full.
-- 部成本	complete cost.
-- 部財產	total assets.
10-- 不	not at all.
-- 不用心	totally careless.
-- 不瞅睬	not to pay any attention.
-- 面	all-round, overall.
-- 面攻擊	all-out offensive.
11-- 班	whole class.
12-- 副武裝	be armed to the teeth.
13-- 球	globe, whole world.
-- 殲	complete annihilation, wipe out thoroughly.
20-- 集	complete works.
-- 受全歸	live a perfect life.
21-- 能	almighty, omnipotent.
-- 行業	whole trade.
23-- 然	altogether, outright.
-- 然不知	not to know beans, know nothing about.
26-- 貌	entire outlook.
-- 程	all along, whole journey, whole course.
27-- 身	whole body, neck and heels.
-- 身像	full-length portrait.
-- 身武裝	be armed to the teeth.
-- 盤計劃	overall program or plan.
-- 盤托出	make a clean breast.
-- 盤着眼	holistic approach.
-- 般罪惡	gamut of crimes.

30--	家	whole family.
33--	心全意	whole-hearted, whole-heartedly, heart and soul.
35--	神貫注	be completely concentrated.
37--	軍	whole army.
--	軍覆沒	the whole army was annihilated.
40--	力	in full strength.
--	力應付	meet with all the strength.
--	力以赴	spare no efforts, all out.
--	套	full suit, whole set, full set, complete set.
--	校	whole school.
43--	始全終	perfect beginning and ending.
44--	薪	full pay.
--	權	n. full powers, full authority, adj. plenipotentiary.
--	權代表	plenipotentiary, envoy plenipotentiary.
--	權大使	plenipotentiary ambassador, ambassador plenipotentiary.
--	世界	whole world, universe.
--	公使	minister plenipotentiary.
52--	托	full-time nursery.
53--	盛	be in full flush.
--	盛時代	golden age, heyday.
58--	數	in full, total number, whole amount.
60--	國	whole country, all over the country, throughout the country, whole nation.
--	國鼎沸	the whole country is like a boiling caldron.
--	國代表大會	national congress.
--	景	panorama.
--	日工	full-timers.
--	日制	full-time.
--	日營業	full business day session, open business all day.
68--	敗	perdition.
71--	長	overall length.
75--	體	in a body, without exception, all hands, general, all, entire, whole.
--	體人員	whole personnel, all the personnel.
--	體出席	all are present at the meeting.
--	體會議	plenary session.
77--	局	situation as a whole.
--	民皆兵	all the people are soldiers.
80--	年	whole year, all the year round.
--	人類	mankind.
--	無意思	totally uninterested.
--	無章法	utterly without a literary style.
--	無頭緒	make neither head nor tail of it.
85--	蝕	total eclipse.
86--	智全能	omniscient and omnipotent.
95--	性保真	keep one's original nature.
99--	勞力	full labor power.

8010₇

盆 〔**Pen**〕 n. basin, tub, basin tub, bowl, dish, case, casket.

44--	地	basin (in geology).
60--	口	brim.
--	景	potted plant.

益 〔**I**〕 n. advantage, profit, benefit, utility, v. increase, enrich, help, adj. useful, advantageous, adv. increasingly.

21--	處	advantage, benefit.
27--	鳥	useful bird.
40--	友	mentor, beneficial friend.
44--	世	benefit the world.

盒 〔**Ho**〕 n. box, case, casket, small box.

17--	子	small box, box, case.
--	子砲	Thompson gun, sub-machine gun.
43--	式錄像帶	video tape cassette, videotape.
44--	蓋	lid of a box, cover of a box.
88--	箱	cartons and crates.

8010₉

金 〔**Chin**〕 n. gold, money, metal, arms, weapons, golden color, adj. golden, solid, durable, precious, valuable.

00--	庫	treasury, national treasury,

	state treasury.
10-- 礦	gold mine.
-- 元	golden dollar.
-- 霉素	aureomycin.
-- 石學	mineralogy.
15-- 融	circulation of money, money, finance, currency.
-- 融市場	money market, finance market, monetary market.
-- 融改革	banking reform.
-- 融外交	financial diplomacy.
-- 融家	financier.
-- 融顧問 (財政顧問) financial adviser (advisor).
-- 融機關	banking organ.
-- 融中心	financial center, banking center.
-- 融投機	monetary speculation.
-- 融界 (財政界) financial circle, financial community, financial interests, financial quarters, financial world.
-- 融財富	financial wealth.
-- 融財團	financial syndicate.
-- 融巨頭	financial magnate.
-- 融危機	financial crisis.
-- 融公司	finance company, finance corporation, finance house, financial company.
-- 融管制 (財政監督) monetary control, fiscal control.
20-- 雞納霜	quinine.
21-- 價	gold value.
27-- 魚	goldfish.
-- 色	golden, golden color.
-- 條	golden bar, gold bar.
30-- 字塔	pyramid.
-- 字招牌	first-class, most reliable, well established.
31-- 額	sum, amount, amount or sum of money.
39-- 沙	gold dust.
42-- 婚	golden wedding.
50-- 本位	gold standard.
53-- 戒子	gold ring.

60-- 星	planet Venus.
71-- 匠	gold smith.
72-- 剛鑽	diamond.
-- 髮女郎	blonde.
77-- 屬	metal.
-- 屬礦	metallic ore.
-- 屬元素	metallic element.
-- 屬結構	metal structure.
-- 屬製品	metal goods.
80-- 礦	gold mine.
83-- 錢	money, wealth.
-- 錠	gold bar.
90-- 雀	goldfinch.
98-- 幣	gold coin, gold currency, gold piece.

釜 〔**Fu**〕 n. pan, cauldron, boiler, rice-boiler.

| 50-- 中魚 | fish in a kettle — doomed. |

8011₃

銃 〔**Chung**〕 n. pistol.

8011₄

錐 〔**Chui**〕 n. awl, broach, borer, drill, v. pierce.

| 12-- 形 | cone. |
| 17-- 子 | awl, drill. |

鏟 〔**Chan**〕 n. spade, shovel, scoop, v. pare, shovel, dig, smooth off.

17-- 子	spade, shovel.
40-- 土機	earth-scraper.
78-- 除	uproot, eradicate, clear off.

鐘 〔**Chung**〕 n. clock, bell, time piece.

12-- 形	bell-shaped.
-- 鼎文	inscriptions on bronze bells or tripods.
-- 乳石	stalactite.
45-- 樓	bell tower, clock tower.
47-- 聲	bell, toll, toll of a bell.
56-- 擺	pendulum.
61-- 點	hours, time.
85-- 錶	clocks and watches.
-- 錶店	watchmaker's shop.
-- 錶裝置	clockwork.

8011₆

鏡 〔**Ching**〕 n. mirror, glass, looking-glass, lens, spectacle.

11-- 頭　　　　lens, scene.
41-- 框　　　　picture frame.

8011₇

氯〔**Lu**〕 n. chlorine.
10-- 霉素　　　chloromycetin.
24-- 化物　　　chloride.
　-- 化鈉　　　sodium chloride.
80-- 氣　　　　chlorine.

氫〔**Ching**〕 n. hydrogen.
13-- 武器　　　hydrogen weapons.
16-- 彈　　　　hydrogen-bomb, H-bomb.
80-- 氣　　　　hydrogen.
　-- 氧化物　　hydrate, hydroxide.

氬〔**Ya**〕 n. argon.

8011₉

鑫=**興** 7780₁

8012₇

翁〔**Weng**〕 n. old man, father, father-in-law.

爺〔**Ye**〕 n. father, master, sir.
43-- 娘　　　　parents.
80-- 爺　　　　grandfather, grandpa.

翕〔**Shih**〕 v. close, shut, collect, unite.

翦〔**Chien**〕 n. scissors, clippers, shears, v. shear, clip down, cut with scissors.
17-- 子　　　　shears, clippers, scissors.
22-- 斷　　　　cut.

鎊〔**Pang**〕 n. pound, pound sterling.

鏑〔**Ti**〕 n. arrowhead, barb of an arrow, sharp point of an arrow, dysprosium muskets, guns, spears.

鎬〔**Hao**〕 n. heating vessel, pick, kind of hoe.

鏞〔**Yung**〕 n. large bell.

鑹〔**Chuan**〕 v. carve, engrave.

8013₁

鏢〔**Piao**〕 n. javelin.

8013₂

鑲〔**Hsiang**〕 v. inlay, inset, encase, border, hem.

10-- 玉指環　　ring inlaid with a gem.
　-- 工　　　　inlayer.
22-- 嵌　　　　inlay, set.
　-- 嵌工　　　inlayer.
36-- 邊　　　　border, hem.
77-- 牙　　　　fill in an artificial tooth, fill a tooth.

銥〔**Yi**〕 n. iridium.

8013₇

鐮〔**Lian**〕 n. sickle, scythe.
17-- 刀　　　　sickle, scythe.

8014₁

鋅〔**Hsin**〕 n. zinc.
10-- 礦　　　　zinc ore.
21-- 版　　　　zinc plate, zinc type, zincograph.

8014₇

鍍〔**Tu**〕 v. gild, overlay, plate.
80-- 金　　　　gild, gild with gold, win some fame abroad.
　-- 鋅　　　　n. zinc-plating, v. galvanize.
86-- 錫　　　　tin-plating.
　-- 鎳　　　　nickel, nickel-plating.
87-- 銀　　　　n. silver-plating, v. silver.

8014₈

鉸〔**Chiao**〕 n. shears, hinges, clamps, scissors.
17-- 刀　　　　shears, scissors.
85-- 鏈　　　　hinges.

8018₂

羨〔**Hsien**〕 n. admire, praise, desire.
44-- 慕　　　　admire, long for.

8018₆

鑛〔**Kuang**〕 n. mine, ore.
00-- 工　　　　miner.
　-- 石　　　　ore.
21-- 師　　　　mining engineer.
26-- 泉　　　　mining spring.
27-- 物　　　　mineral.
72-- 脈　　　　mining vein.

8020₀

个=**個** 2620₀

8020₇

丫〔**Ya**〕 n. fork, crotch.

11-- 頭　　　　girl, slave girl, young slave girl, maid.

44-- 枝　　　　branch.

47-- 杈　　　　crotch.

今〔Chin〕*adj.* present, modern, *adv.* now, at present.

00-- 夜　　　　tonight.

10-- 天　　　　today.

11-- 非昔比　　the present cannot compare with past.

17-- 已作古　　already dead now.

22-- 後　　　　hence, hereafter, from now on.

40-- 古奇談　　modern and ancient strange tales.

44-- 昔之感　　feeling that time has changed, that the situation is not what it used to be.

60-- 日　　　　today.

 -- 早　　　　this morning.

 -- 是昨非　　the present is right and the past is wrong (one is to do right from now on).

67-- 晚　　　　tonight.

80-- 年　　　　this year.

兮〔Hsi〕*interj.* alas !

爹〔Tieh〕*n.* father, dad, daddy, papa.

43-- 娘　　　　parents, father and mother.

80-- 爹　　　　father, dad.

8021₁

乍〔Cha〕*adj.* sudden, *adv.* abruptly, suddenly.

20-- 看　　　　at first sight, at a glance.

23-- 然　　　　suddenly.

 -- 然相逢　　meet unexpectedly.

38-- 冷乍熱　　by fits and starts; now cold, now hot.

44-- 著膽子　　summon up courage.

48-- 驚　　　　taken back.

65-- 晴乍雨　　now shine now rain (changeable weather).

羌〔Chiang〕*n.* the Chiang tribe.

差〔Cha〕*n.* service, errand, differences, mistakes, *v.* send, commission,

mistake, err, *adj.* unequal, uneven, irregular, *adv.* nearly, almost.

06-- 誤　　　　err, mistake.

08-- 旅津貼　　travel allowance.

 -- 旅費　　　travel charge, travel expense, traveling expense on official business.

 -- 旅招待費　travel and entertainment expenses.

10-- 不多　　　nearly, almost.

21-- 價　　　　price differential, rate difference.

25-- 使　　　　errand, engagement, business.

26-- 得遠　　　not by a long sight.

31-- 額　　　　balance — difference between two sums, difference, margin.

35-- 遣　　　　*n.* errand *v.* dispatch, send, commission.

41-- 幅　　　　spread.

50-- 事　　　　engagement, commission.

60-- 異　　　　*n.* variation, variance, discrepancy, *adj.* various, different.

 -- 量成本　　differential cost.

61-- 距　　　　gap, difference, discrepancy.

62-- 別　　　　*n.* difference, distinction, dissimilarity, *v.* differ.

 -- 別工資　　differential pay, differential wages.

 -- 別成本　　differential cost.

84-- 錯　　　　mistake, error.

龕〔Kan〕*n.* niche, shrine.

8021₅

羞〔Hsiu〕*v.* blush, feel ashamed, disgrace, insult, shame, *adj.* ashamed, bashful, blushing, shy.

13-- 恥　　　　shame, mortification.

60-- 口難開　　too embarrassed to speak.

71-- 辱　　　　*v.* insult, disgrace, cause shame.

95-- 怯　　　　shy, bashful, timid.

96-- 愧　　　　feel ashamed, feel cheap.

8021₆

兌〔Tui〕*v.* exchange, convert.
16-- 現　　　　*n.* redemption, *v.* cash, realize, cash a check, pay cash, cash in, honor, fulfill.
-- 現支票　　cash a check.
24-- 付　　　cash (a check, etc.)
53-- 成現金　cashing.
57-- 換　　　*n.* conversion, *v.* exchange, change, convert.
-- 換率　　　convertible rate, rate of conversion.
-- 換現金　　turn into cash.
-- 換處　　　exchange office.
-- 換佣金　　exchange commission.
-- 換所　　　bourse, exchange.
-- 換券　　　banknote.
-- 換率　　　rate of exchange.
8021₇
氣〔Fen〕*n.* vapor, gas, air.
氖〔Nai〕*n.* neon.
90-- 光燈　　neon light (or lamp).
氰〔Ching〕*n.* cyanogen.
24-- 化物　　cyanide.
8022₀
介〔Chieh〕*n.* scale, shelled water animal, *v.* lie between, border on, assist, introduce, *adj.* upright.
00-- 立　　　stand alone.
-- 意　　　care, mind.
07-- 詞　　　preposition.
08-- 於　　　between.
-- 於生死　　between life and death.
20-- 系字　　preposition.
27-- 紹　　　introduce, recommend, present.
-- 紹信　　　letter of introduction, letter of recommendation, recommendation.
-- 紹費　　　middleman fee, procuration.
-- 紹人　　　go-between.
80-- 入　　　*n.* intervention, *v.* intervene, involve, get involved.
94-- 懷　　　take to heart.
8022₁

斧〔Fu〕*n.* axe, hatchet, *v.* cut
兪〔Yu〕*v.* assent.
前〔Chien〕*n.* front, future, *v.* advance, proceed, go forward, *adj.* previous, former, past, forward, *prep.* in front of, *adv.* formerly, previously, ahead.
00-- 方　　　*n.* front, *adj.* forward.
-- 言　　　foreword, preface.
08-- 敵　　　enemy in the front.
10-- 天　　　day before yesterday.
-- 面　　　ahead, front, in front, before, anterior.
-- 頁　　　preceding page.
11-- 輩　　　elder, senior.
12-- 列　　　front.
14-- 功盡棄　all the previous efforts have been in vain.
20-- 往　　　proceed to, advance, go forward, leave for.
21-- 行=前往
-- 衛　　　advance guard.
-- 衛要塞　bastion.
22-- 任　　　predecessor.
-- 後　　　to and fro, before or after, back and forth.
-- 後矛盾　inconsistency.
-- 後受敵　be attacked by the enemy in the front and in the rear.
23-- 仆後繼　one stepping into the breach as another falls.
26-- 線　　　the front.
-- 程　　　the future.
-- 程萬里　have a very bright future.
27-- 夕　　　eve.
30-- 定　　　*v.* destine, *adj.* preordained.
-- 進　　　march, proceed, advance, progress, go ahead, set forward.
-- 進曲　　marching song.
31-- 額　　　brow.
-- 述　　　above mentioned.
-- 述詞　　antecedent.
37-- 次　　　last time.
38-- 途　　　future prospect.
-- 途有望　the goose hangs high.
-- 途茫茫　one's future is indefinite.

44-- 者	formerly, previously, the former.
50-- 奏曲	prelude.
-- 事	antecedent.
-- 車之鑑	lesson from the failure of one's predecessor.
56-- 提	premise, prerequisite.
60-- 日	the other day, day before yesterday.
-- 置詞	preposition.
-- 足	forefoot.
-- 景	fore ground, prospect, out-look.
-- 思後想	think about repeatedly.
-- 因後果	cause and effect in human life.
69-- 哨	advanced post, outpost.
-- 哨站	outpost battle.
70-- 臂	forearm.
71-- 驅	forerunner.
72-- 所未有	unprecedented, unparal-leled.
-- 所未見	have never seen before.
-- 所未聞	never heard of before.
77-- 門	front door.
-- 月	month before last.
80-- 人	people of the past.
-- 年	year before last.
-- 前後後	from front to rear.
-- 無古人	have no predecessors.
86-- 知	prophecy.
87-- 鋒	vanguard, forward.

8022₇

分 〔Fen〕 *n.* cent, minute, branch, divide, separate, share, part, apportion, scatter, role played by a person in life, part or portion of the whole, *v.* divide, separate, sever, give, distribute, disperse.

00-- 離	*n.* parting, separation, *v.* separate, detach, divorce.
-- 售處	branch, agent.
-- 店(行)	branch, sub-branch, branch firm.
-- 毫	in the least.
-- 毫不差	not the least portion is wrong, exactly right.
-- 廠	branch factory.
-- 享	share, have a share in.
-- 享利益	share in the profits.
-- 文不取	not to take a penny.
-- 辨	explain.
-- 辨是非	distinguish right and wrong.
07-- 詞	participle (in grammar).
-- 部	portion, sub-department.
-- 部經理	division manager, section manager.
10-- 工	*n.* division of labor, division of work, *v.* divide the work.
-- 工合作	divide labor and join in work.
-- 不開	inseparable.
11-- 班	*v.* divide into classes, *adv.* by turns.
-- 裂	divide, split, part.
-- 頭	separately.
-- 頭進行	proceed separately.
-- 項	sub-items.
12-- 發	distribute, hand out.
-- 列表	spread sheet.
-- 裂	*n.* split, *v.* split, rend, tear asunder, divide, part.
-- 水嶺	watershed.
17-- 子	molecule, member, element, numerator.
-- 子式	molecular formula.
-- 子量	molecular weight.
-- 配	*n.* distribution, allocation, appropriation, partition, *v.* distribute, deal, share out, parcel out, allocate.
-- 配利潤	split the profit.
-- 配表	schedule of apportionment.
-- 配成本	allocation cost.
-- 配費用	distribution cost.
-- 配量	distribution.
20-- 手	part company, separate.
-- 利	dividend.
-- 售處	retail sales office.
21-- 紅	receive dividends, distribute a bonus (dividend), share profit, draw dividends.
-- 行	branch bank, agency bank.

-- 行經理	branch manager.
-- 批出售	sell by lots.
23-- 外	*adj.* extra, undue, *adv.* excessively, beyond bounds.
-- 外之物	undue gain.
24-- 內	of one's own duty.
-- 內之事	matter within one's duties.
-- 歧	*n.* divergence, difference, *v.* diverge.
-- 化	*n.* differentiation, *v.* disintegrate, sow discord.
-- 化政策	wrecking policy, policy of differentiation.
-- 化瓦解	collapse.
-- 佈	spread, distribute.
26-- 保	reassure, reinsurance.
27-- 包	subcontract, sub-contracting.
-- 身	get away.
-- 解	*n.* decomposition, *v.* decompose, analyze, disintegrate.
-- 級	classify, grade, rate.
-- 組	divide into sections, divide into groups.
-- 租	sublet, sublease.
28-- 給	distribute, divide among.
29-- 秒必爭	every minute counts.
30-- 家	divide family property.
32-- 割	partition, cut.
-- 派	distribute, disperse, ration, allot, apportion.
-- 派贓物	distribute the loot.
33-- 心	distract, call away the attention.
-- 泌	*n.* secretion, *v.* secrete.
-- 泌作用	secretion.
35-- 清	distinguish, draw a distinction.
-- 遣	dispatch.
-- 遣隊	detachment.
38-- 道揚鑣	go separate ways.
40-- 支	branch.
-- 支店	branch store.
-- 支的	affiliated.
-- 布=分佈	
42-- 析	*n.* analysis, *v.* analyze, break down.
-- 析法	analytical approach, analytic method.
-- 析者	analyst.
-- 析表	analysis sheet.
-- 析化學	analytic chemistry.
44-- 枝	*n.* ramification, *v.* ramify.
-- 甘共苦	share and share alike.
47-- 娩	*n.* childbirth, childbearing, lying-in, *v.* travail, be confined, lie in, labor with child.
-- 期	installment.
-- 期交貨	installment delivery.
-- 期貸款	installment credit.
-- 期付清	pay by installment.
-- 期付款	easy payment, installment buying, installment payment, progressive payment.
-- 期付款制	installment plan.
-- 期付款條件	installment term.
-- 期付款銷售	installment sale.
-- 期償還 (攤提)	amortization.
-- 期支付	installment, payable by installment.
-- 期購買	installment purchase.
48-- 散	*n.* dispersion, *v.* scatter, disband, disperse, sweep away, decentralize.
-- 散定貨	split order.
-- 散投資	decentralized investment.
50-- 攤	*n.* allocation, contribution, *v.* split the cost, share, allot.
-- 批生產	batch production, job production.
53-- 成	divide into.
57-- 擔	share (work, burden etc.).
58-- 數	weight, fraction.
60-- 田	land distribution.
-- 量	weight, quantity.
-- 界	*n.* borderline, *v.* delimit.
-- 界線	borderline, dividing line, demarcation line.
61-- 號	semicolon.
62-- 別	separate, differentiate, dis-

tinguish, discriminate.

-- 別地   respectively.

63-- 贓   divide up the loots or bribes.

67-- 野   division, borderline.

-- 明   clear, evident.

-- 路   go by different road.

71-- 隔   separated.

-- 區   sub-region.

72-- 兵   *n.* divided forces, *v.* detach some troops.

-- 所應爲   act in accord with one's own capacity.

77-- 母   denominator.

-- 局   branch bureau, suboffice.

-- 股   distributes share.

-- 段   paragraph.

-- 叉   fork.

-- 開   *n.* separation, *v.* part, divide, separate, branch, cut, draw apart.

-- 層   stratify.

-- 層負責   delegation of the right authority to the right level of officials.

-- 門別類   sort out into categories, classify.

-- 銷處   retail sales office, sale agency, subagency.

-- 銷公司   sub-underwriter.

79-- 勝負   decide the issue.

80-- 會   branch, affiliated society, sub-committee.

-- 公司   constituent company, branch office, branch company, constituent corporation.

90-- 光器   spectroscope.

91-- 類   *n.* sorting, classification, *v.* classify, range, assort, sort.

-- 類廣告   classified advertisement.

-- 類器   sorter.

8022₇

侖 〔**Lun**〕 *n.* Kun-lun (name of a mountain.).

弟 〔**Ti**〕 *n.* younger brother.

17-- 子   pupil, disciple.

45-- 妹   younger brother and youn-

ger sister.

46-- 媳   wife of a younger brother.

60-- 兄   brothers.

剪 〔**Chien**〕 *v.* shear, clip.

10-- 碎   cut into pieces.

17-- 刀   scissors.

22-- 紙   paper-cutting.

-- 綵   cut the ribbon.

43-- 裁   cut, tailor.

44-- 草除根   mow the grass and pull out the roots, exterminate.

47-- 報   clippings.

48-- 樣   sample cutting.

56-- 輯   cut and edit.

72-- 髮   have the hair cut.

-- 髮軋   hair clippers.

81-- 短   clip.

8023₂

汆 〔**Tun**〕 *v.* boil food, float, push an object on water, *adj.* floating.

8024₇

夔 〔**Kuei**〕 *n.* one-legged monster, *adj.* respectful.

8025₁

舞 〔**Wu**〕 *n.* dancing, *v.* dance, make posture, brandish, wave.

22-- 劇   ballet, dance drama.

23-- 台   stage, arena.

-- 台說明   stage-directions.

-- 台裝置   stage-setting.

24-- 動   brandish, flourish.

40-- 女   dancer, dancing girl, cabaret girl.

46-- 場   dance, hall.

55-- 曲   dance music.

62-- 蹈   *n.* dancing, *v.* dance, shake a leg.

-- 蹈家   dancer.

80-- 會   ball, dancing party.

82-- 劍   *n.* swordplay, *v.* exhibit swordplay.

98-- 弊   corruption, embezzlement, fraud, fraudulent practices.

8025₃

羲 〔**Hsi**〕 *n.* vapour, air.

8030₇

令〔Ling〕*n.* order, law, rule, instruction, ream, *v.* order, command, cause, make, *adj.* good, fine.

08-- 旗	banner as a sign of authority.
23-- 狀	writ.
27-- 名	honor, reputation, good reputation.
80-- 人心痛	cut one to the heart, distressing.
-- 人發怒	make one angry.
-- 人垂涎	make one's mouth water.
-- 人失望	disappointing, discouraging.
-- 人淚下	bring tears to one's eyes.
-- 人滿意	warm the cockles of one's heart.
-- 人深省	make one ponder.
-- 人難忘	impressive.
-- 人切齒	make one gnash the teeth.
-- 人髮指	make one's blood boil.
-- 人欽佩	praiseworthy, admirable.

8033₁

無〔Wu〕*adj.* no, wanting, *adv.* not, *pron.* none, *prep.* without.

00-- 言	silent.
-- 言可答	have nothing to say in reply
-- 主物	ownerless thing.
-- 意	*v.* show no intention, *adj.* unintentional.
-- 意識	*n.* unconsciousness, nonsense, *adj.* unconscious.
-- 意義	*n.* nonsense, *adj.* meaningless, senseless.
-- 意犯	unintentional crime.
-- 意進行	not interested in proceeding further.
-- 庸費心	no need to waste your thought.
-- 底深淵	a pit having no bottom, abyss.
-- 疵可尋	be above reproach.
-- 病而死	die without any illness.
-- 病呻吟	groan when there is no physical pain.

-- 產階級	proletariat, proletarian classes.
-- 產階級文化大革命	Great Proletarian Cultural Revolution .
01-- 顏見人	fly from the face of men.
02-- 端生有	making trouble out of nothing.
-- 話可說	have nothing to say.
-- 話可駁	have nothing to refute.
03-- 識	ignorance.
-- 誠意	insincere.
04-- 計可施	at a loss as to what to do.
06-- 誤	no mistake, correct.
-- 謂	no significance.
-- 謂犧牲	useless sacrifice.
-- 謂開銷	unprofitable expenses.
-- 謂舉動	foolish act.
07-- 望	hopeless.
-- 記名	unnamed.
-- 記名股	unregistered shares, bearer-shares.
-- 記名背書	endorsement in blank.
-- 記名支票	check to bearer.
-- 記名投票	secret ballot.
-- 記名票據	bearer instrument, bearer paper.
08-- 敵	matchless, invincible.
-- 敵艦隊	dreadnaught squadron.
-- 效	ineffective, ineffectual, invalid, of no effect, resultless, null and void.
-- 效行爲	void action.
-- 論	whatever, however, no matter, regardless of.
-- 論如何	however, anyhow, anyway, no matter how, in any case, at any rate.
-- 論何時	whenever, anytime.
-- 論何人	whoever, anybody.
-- 論甚麼	whatever, anything.
-- 論哪裏	wherever, anywhere.
10-- 需	unnecessary, no need.
-- 需說明	it needs no explanation.
-- 一	none, not a bit, not a button.
-- 一不能	be able to handle everything, good at everything.

-- 一不備	everything is available.		nonsense, fiddle-faddle, cheerless.
-- 一不通	extremely versatile.	-- 聊之極	extremely boring.
-- 一不曉	know everything.	18-- 政府	anarchy.
-- 一不精	be an expert in everything.	-- 政府主義	anarchism.
-- 惡不作	stop at nothing.	-- 政府狀態	anarchy.
-- 憂無慮	without a worry or care in the world, completely carefree.	20-- 雙	unequaled, incomparable.
		-- 往不勝	invincible.
-- 可疵議	up to the knocker.	-- 往不利	lucky in every endeavor.
-- 可辯解	admit of no excuse.	-- 依無靠	friendless and helpless.
-- 可諱言	undeniable.	-- 千無萬	thousands and tens of thousands.
-- 可非議	irrefutable, unimpeachable.	21-- 上	topmost, highest, supreme
-- 可爭辯	indisputable, incontestable.	-- 上光榮	highest honor.
-- 可比擬	incomparable.	-- 能	n. disability, loss of wits adj. incompetent, incapable.
-- 可稽考	it cannot be examined.		
-- 可寬恕	unpardonable.	-- 能爲力	incapable, powerless, cannot do anything about it.
-- 可奈何	helpless, hopeless.		
-- 可救藥	past hope.	-- 處	nowhere.
-- 可推諉	admit of no excuse.	-- 處安頓	nowhere to settle down.
-- 可抵賴	undeniable.	-- 虞失敗	no fear of a failure.
-- 可挽回	the die is cast.	-- 須驚恐	need not be scared.
-- 可置疑	beyond doubt.	-- 須答辯	no need to answer.
-- 可置答	admit of no reply.	-- 價	above price.
-- 可厚非	beyond reproach.	-- 價值	worthless.
-- 可匹敵	be without a rival.	-- 價寶	priceless treasure.
-- 可勝數	innumerable.	-- 價之寶	n. priceless treasure, priceless thing, adj. invaluable, inestimable.
-- 可饒恕	unpardonable.		
-- 不贊成	everyone approves.		
-- 不如意	have everything going one's way.	-- 比	incomparable, matchless, without a parallel, unparalleled.
-- 不周知	be known to everybody.		
11-- 疆	boundless.	-- 師自通	self-taught, learned without a teacher.
-- 非是	nothing but.		
-- 頭無尾	without beginning or end, without clues, in disorder.	22-- 私	selfless, disinterested.
		-- 任歡迎	most welcome.
12-- 形	invisible, formless, intangible.	-- 任感激	feel most grateful.
		-- 後顧憂	no worry in looking back — no worry about one's family.
-- 孔不入	all-pervasive.		
13-- 恥	shameless, brazen.		
-- 恥之徒	shameless fellow.	-- 利可圖	profitless.
16-- 理	unreasonable.	-- 例外	without exception.
-- 理取鬧	mischief-making, make trouble for no reason.	23-- 稽	nonsense.
		-- 稽之談	fiction, fabrication, nonsense talk.
17-- 瑕	without blemish.		
-- 瑕可謫	flawless.	24-- 貨	be out of stock.
-- 聊	time hangs heavy, listless,		

-- 告	poor, penniless.
-- 告窮民	helpless people.
-- 結果	without result, in vain.
26-- 保留	unreserved.
-- 線通訊	wireless communications.
-- 線電	wireless, radio.
-- 線電報	radiogram, radio telegram, wireless, wireless message.
-- 線電務員	radio operator.
-- 線電話	wireless telephone.
-- 線電台	radio station.
-- 線電傳真	radio photo.
-- 線電視	radio television.
-- 線電通訊	radio message.
-- 線電操縱	wireless control.
-- 線電廣播	radio broadcasting.
-- 線電收音機	wireless, radio.
-- 線電波探測法	radiolocation.
27-- 條件	unconditional, without reservation, unreserved.
-- 條件投降	unconditional surrender.
-- 條件投誠	unconditional surrender.
-- 疑	*adj.* undoubted, no doubt, *adv.* certainly, doubtless.
-- 名	nameless.
-- 名英雄	unknown hero, unsung hero.
-- 名氏	anonymous.
-- 名指	ring finger.
-- 名小卒	nobody.
-- 紀律	undisciplined, disorderly.
28-- 給職	service without payment.
-- 從說起	don't know where to begin telling a story.
-- 從探究	there is no way to make a thorough investigation.
-- 從置喙	admit of no criticism.
-- 從答辯	admit of no reply.
-- 從知道	unable to find out.
-- 稅的	tax-free.
-- 以復加	last word, best, to the utmost.
-- 以爲生	have nothing to live on.
-- 以爲對	do not know how to reply.
-- 以爲報	be unable to repay (a favor).
-- 傷大雅	it doesn't matter.

-- 微不至	meticulous, very considerate.
29-- 償	no consideration, free of expense, gratis, gratuitous.
-- 償行爲	act without consideration.
-- 償契約	gratuitous contract.
-- 償取得	acquisition without consideration.
30-- 定	indefinite, uncertain.
-- 害	harmless.
-- 害於	harmless to.
-- 窮	inexhaustible, indefinite, endless.
-- 窮大	infinite.
-- 濟於事	of no help to the matter.
-- 家可歸	homeless.
-- 容置疑	allow of no doubt.
-- 案可稽	no records can be investigated.
-- 實彈射擊	dry shoot.
31-- 涯	boundless.
32-- 業遊民	wanderer with no job, vagrant, hobo.
33-- 心	*adj.* unintentional, *adv.* unintentionally.
-- 心管事	have no intention to attend to business.
-- 心之錯	unintentional mistake.
-- 補大局	be of no help, don't help matters.
34-- 遠見	lack foresight.
-- 法	cannot be helped, not having a leg to stand on, no way, impossible.
-- 法可施	unable to do anything about it.
-- 法可治	there is no way cure it, incurable.
-- 法可想	helpless.
-- 法形容	*v.* despair of description, *adj.* indescribable.
-- 法解脫	inextricable.
-- 法挽回	irretrievable, irrevocable.
-- 法阻擋	irresistible, overpowering.
-- 法分身	have one's hands full.
-- 法無天	completely lawless and Godless, licentious.

35-- 禮	*n.* impoliteness, audacity, *adj.* impolite, discourteous, audacious.
-- 神論	atheism.
36-- 視	in defiance of, *v.* disregard, ignore.
37-- 資力	insolvency.
40-- 趣	uninteresting, dry.
-- 辜	innocent, guiltless.
-- 力	*n.* weakness, inability, *adj.* impotent, unable, weak.
-- 奇不有	nothing is too strange in the world.
42-- 機物	inorganic matter.
-- 機鹽	mineral salt.
-- 機化學	inorganic chemistry.
44-- 花果	fig.
-- 地自容	no place to hide, extremely embarrassed or ashamed.
-- 地容身	nowhere to live, ashamed to show one's face.
-- 甚趣味	of little interest.
-- 權過問	have no right to inquire into.
47-- 聲	noiseless, silent.
-- 根據	groundless, unfounded, ungrounded.
-- 期	indefinite time.
-- 期徒刑	penal servitude for life.
-- 期徒刑者	life timer.
48-- 故	gratuitous, causeless, with no reason.
-- 故延誤	unreasonable delay.
-- 故生有	making trouble out of nothing.
-- 赦	without mercy.
-- 機體	inorganic body.
50-- 事	without employment, at leisure, not busy.
-- 事生非	make the fur fly.
-- 事自擾	tempest in a teapot.
-- 中生有	groundless, unfounded.
52-- 抵抗主義	non-resistance.
53-- 感覺	insensible, unfeeling.
54-- 軌電車	trolley tram, trolley bus, trolley car.
57-- 賴	rogue, vagrant, vagabond, rascal.

-- 賴之徒	worthless fellow who cannot be trusted, a vagabond, bad scamp.
-- 拘無束	without any restraint, carefree.
58-- 數	countless, numberless, innumerable, incalculable.
60-- 目的	aimless.
-- 國籍	denationalization.
-- 異	as good as.
-- 罪	innocence.
-- 日忘之	never forget it for one day.
-- 因契約	abstract contract.
-- 畏精神	fearless spirit, undauntedness.
-- 足輕重	insignificant, unimportant.
-- 異投降	tantamount to surrender.
64-- 時無地	every minute and everywhere.
65-- 味	tasteless.
67-- 暇	no leisure, busy.
-- 路可走	at the end of one's rope.
-- 路求生	there is no way to earn a living.
71-- 原則	unprincipled.
72-- 所謂	it does not matter.
-- 所不至	do everything to help.
-- 所不能	capable of doing anything.
-- 所不備	there is nothing that is unprepared.
-- 所不包	nothing is left out.
-- 所不爲	stop at nothing.
-- 所不在	omnipresent.
-- 所不有	have all.
-- 所不會	can do anything.
-- 所不知	know everything.
-- 所依據	have nothing to prove, groundless.
-- 所依靠	have nothing to depend upon.
-- 所顧忌	*adj.* unscrupulous, fearless *adv.* unscrupulously.
-- 所適從	don't know whose suggestion to follow.
-- 所措手	do not know what to do.
-- 所事事	do nothing all day.
-- 所畏忌	stop at nothing.

-- 所畏懼	fearless, daring, bold.	
-- 所反顧	never to look back, set on a determined course.	
75-- 體物	things incorporeal.	
77-- 關	have nothing to do with, have no connection with.	
-- 關大局	insignificant, unimportant.	
-- 關緊要	unimportant.	
-- 用	useless, of no avail, good for nothing, futile, inefficacious.	
-- 用之才	useless person.	
-- 限	infinite, immeasurable, unlimited, boundless, limitless, boundless.	
-- 限小	infinitesimal.	
-- 限制	without limit, zero restriction.	
-- 限公司	unlimited company, ordinary partnership.	
-- 限責任	unlimited liability, unlimited liability account.	
-- 限責任股東	partner with unlimited liability.	
-- 風起浪	start a big trouble out of nothing.	
78-- 監視考試	honor system.	
79-- 隙可乘	be armed at all points, invulnerable.	
80-- 人	nobody, deserted.	
-- 人不適	there is no one who does not feel comfortable.	
-- 人不曉	everybody knows.	
-- 人過問	unwanted, unclaimed, uncared for.	
-- 人拒絕	no one declines.	
-- 益	of no avail, of no benefit.	
-- 恙	healthy, well, in good health.	
83-- 錢	poor, out of pocket.	
86-- 知	foolish, ignorant.	
90-- 恆	inconstancy.	
-- 常	inconstant, impermanent.	
-- 黨派	non-partisan.	
-- 黨派人士	non-partisan people.	
-- 米之炊	cook a meal without rice.	
95-- 情	cold-hearted, relentless, ruthless, pitiless.	
-- 精打采	dispirited, disheartened.	
96-- 愧於	worthy of.	
-- 烟煤	anthracite.	
97-- 怪	no wonder.	
-- 懈可擊	invulnerable, flawless.	

8033₁

怎〔Tsen〕 adv. how？ why？ what？
00-- 麼	how? what? how is it?
-- 麼得了	there is no telling the serious consequences.
-- 麼搞的	how did it happen?
48-- 樣	how, what.

恙〔Yang〕 n. illness, sickness, complaint.

羔〔Kao〕 n. lamb, kid.
17-- 子（羊）	lamb, kid.
40-- 皮	lambskin.

8033₂

忿〔Fen〕 n. anger, wrath, rage, indignation, hatred, resentment, adj. angry, wrathful.
00-- 言怨詞	angry and spiteful words.
38-- 激	n. zeal and eagerness, adj. excited, enraged.
47-- 怒	n. resentment, indignation, adj. angry, wrathful.
80-- 忿	indignant, resentful.
-- 忿不平	indignant and disturbed.
97-- 恨	n. hatred, malice, v. hate bitterly.
-- 恨在心	harbor hatred in the heart.

念〔Nien〕 n. thought, reflection, v. reflect, ponder over, remember, think of, consider, chant, recite, read, adj. thoughtful, twenty.
04-- 熟	learn by heart.
07-- 誦	recite, repeat.
11-- 頭	idea, thought.
15-- 珠	rosary.
21-- 經	chant prayer.
25-- 佛修行	repeat the name of the Buddha as a way of religious discipline.
50-- 書	read, study, peruse.

80-- 念不忘　　　keep in mind always, un-
　　　　　　　　forgettable.

愈〔Yu〕v. get well, recover, surpass,
excel, overcome, recover from illness, adv. more, further.

27-- 多愈好　　　the more the better.
40-- 來愈多　　　more and more are coming.
44-- 甚　　　　　further, much more.
46-- 加　　　　　further, much more.
47-- 好　　　　　better, still better.
95-- 快愈好　　　the sooner the better.

煎〔Chien〕v. boil, decoct, fry.

17-- 蛋　　　　　n. fried eggs, v. fry eggs.
27-- 魚　　　　　n. fried fish, v. fry fish.
44-- 藥　　　　　decoct medicine.
46-- 乾　　　　　boil away.
88-- 餅　　　　　fry cakes.
99-- 炒　　　　　fry.

8033₃

慈〔Tzu〕n. kindness, mercy, love,
profound love, mother, adj. kind,
gentle, merciful, humane, softhear-
ted, loving, benevolent, maternal.

11-- 悲　　　　　merciful, gracious, com-
　　　　　　　　passionate, kind and com-
　　　　　　　　passionate.
-- 悲爲本　　　　kindness and compassion
　　　　　　　　is the principle of life.
-- 悲好善　　　　merciful and benevolent.
-- 悲人士　　　　men of commiseration.
20-- 愛　　　　　n. affection, adj. affection-
　　　　　　　　ate, loving, tender, v. love
　　　　　　　　tenderly.
33-- 心對人　　　treat another with a kind
　　　　　　　　heart.
38-- 祥　　　　　kind, benign, lenient.
44-- 姑　　　　　arrowhead, kind mother-
　　　　　　　　in-law.
50-- 惠　　　　　beneficent.
77-- 母嚴父　　　kind mother and a stern fa-
　　　　　　　　ther.
80-- 善　　　　　n. charity, benevolence, be-
　　　　　　　　neficence, adj. charitable,
　　　　　　　　kind, beneficent, merciful,
　　　　　　　　philanthropic, benevolent.

-- 善信託　　　　charitable trust.
-- 善家　　　　　philanthropist.
-- 善機關　　　　charity, charity institution,
　　　　　　　　charity organization.
-- 善跳舞會　　　charity ball.
-- 善學校　　　　charity school.
-- 善醫院　　　　charity hospital.
-- 善事業　　　　charitable affairs, charity
　　　　　　　　work, charity.

8033₇

兼〔Chien〕v. unite in one, absorb, annex, exhaust, complete, adj. both,
additional, adv. together, moreover,
also, conj. and.

10-- 而有之　　　have both.
13-- 職　　　　　by-work, sideline, side job,
　　　　　　　　part-time job, v. take double
　　　　　　　　duties, hold two or more
　　　　　　　　posts concurrently.
-- 職工作　　　　part-time job.
-- 職的　　　　　part-time.
17-- 司他職　　　also in charge of other duti-
　　　　　　　　es.
20-- 愛　　　　　love without distinction.
22-- 任　　　　　serve concurrently as.
-- 任教授　　　　part time professor.
26-- 程而往　　　travel by long stages.
-- 程而進　　　　advance twice as quickly
　　　　　　　　as usual.
28-- 併　　　　　n. annexation, merger, mer-
　　　　　　　　ger into a joint stock part-
　　　　　　　　nership, v. annex.
-- 併者　　　　　merger.
30-- 容並包　　　be all-inclusive, be open-
　　　　　　　　minded.
31-- 顧　　　　　give attention to both...
　　　　　　　　and...
70-- 用　　　　　double use.
80-- 管　　　　　be in charge of both.
-- 人之量　　　　have the capacity of two
　　　　　　　　persons combined, be tol-
　　　　　　　　erant.
-- 善天下　　　　benefit all the people in the
　　　　　　　　world.

8034₆

尊〔Tsun〕v. honor, dignify, adore, respect, revere, *adj.* honorable, noble, respectable, esteemed.

06-- 親屬	ascendant.
20-- 重	respect, esteem, honor, regard.
-- 重事實	have respect for facts.
-- 重民權	respect civil rights.
21-- 師重道	honor teachers and esteem truth.
26-- 程拜訪	make a special trip to call on someone.
48-- 敬	*n.* reverence, estimation, *v.* respect, revere, venerate, honor, adore, do honor, hold in esteem, esteem.
50-- 貴	noble.
66-- 嚴	dignity, solemnity, majesty.
-- 嚴神氣	air of dignity.
80-- 命是從	your commands are to be followed accordingly.
99-- 榮	glorious.

8040_0
父〔**Fu**〕*n.* father, daddy, sire, papa, male elders, *v.* do what a father should do.

06-- 親	father, daddy, papa.
-- 親節	Father's Day.
17-- 子	father and son.
-- 子相傳	passed down through generations from fathers to sons.
20-- 系	paternity.
40-- 女	father and daughter.
44-- 老	senior, city elders.
-- 權	paternal power.
60-- 兄	father and elder brother.
77-- 母	parents.
-- 母之喪	bereavement.
-- 母雙全	with both parents living.
80-- 慈子孝	the father is affectionate and the son is dutiful.

午〔**Wu**〕*n.* noon, midday, seventh of the twelve stems.

00-- 夜	midnight.
22-- 後	afternoon.
24-- 休	midday rest, noon-time rest.

27-- 餐櫃檯	canteen.
-- 餐券	lunch voucher.
62-- 睡	noontide nap, siesta.
64-- 時	noon, noontide, midday.
78-- 膳	dinner, lunch.
80-- 前	forenoon.
81-- 飯（餐）	lunch, tiffin.

8040_4
傘〔**San**〕*n.* umbrella, parasol, parachute.

| 72-- 兵 | parachute troop, paratroopers. |

姜〔**Chiang**〕*n.* Chiang (a family name).

8040_7
孳〔**Tzu**〕*n.* produce and suckle, *v.* bear, reproduce, breed, work with sustained diligence.

25-- 生	propagate, breed.
26-- 息	fruits.
44-- 孳	work diligently without end.

8041_4
雉〔**Chih**〕*n.* pheasant.

8041_7
氨〔**An**〕*n.* ammonia.

| 12-- 水 | ammonia water. |
| 80-- 氮 | ammonia nitrogen. |

8042_7
禽〔**Chin**〕*n.* birds, fowl.

| 44-- 獲 | capture. |
| 63-- 獸 | animal, bird and beast. |

8043_0
矢〔**Shih**〕*n.* arrow, dart, dung, excrement. *v.* vow, display, carry out, *adj.* straight forward.

| 00-- 言 | oath, vow. |
| 52-- 誓 | take an oath. |

美〔**Mei**〕*adj.* beautiful, pretty, fine, handsome, good, nice, delicious, excellent.

| 11-- 麗 | *n.* beauty, *adj.* beautiful, handsome, pretty, fair, bonny. |
| 21-- 術 | fine arts. |

-- 術家	artist.
-- 術的	artistic.
-- 術品	works of art.
-- 術館	art gallery.
-- 術展覽會	exhibition of fine arts.
24-- 德	virtue, perfection.
26-- 貌	*n.* handsome looking, beauty, good looks, good-looking.
27-- 物	beauty.
30-- 容術	facial culture.
-- 容院	beauty parlor.
32-- 洲	Americas.
34-- 滿	satisfactory, satisfied, perfect, happy.
40-- 女	pretty girl, belle.
44-- 夢	fond dream, beautiful dream.
46-- 觀	*v.* look fine, *adj.* beautiful, handsome.
47-- 好	fine, fair, nice, good.
49-- 妙	wonderful, marvelous.
50-- 中不足	beautiful yet incomplete.
60-- 國	the United States of America.
-- 國人	American.
-- 國的	American.
-- 景	fine scenery, fine view, beauty spot.
65-- 味	*n.* delicacy, relish, *adj.* delicious, delicate.
77-- 學	aesthetics.
80-- 人	beauty, belle.
-- 食	good fare, good food.
89-- 鈔	American bill, greenback.
90-- 少年	beau.

奠〔Tien〕*v.* settle, fix, determine, put down, place, lay foundation, offer a libation.

30-- 定	*v.* establish, make firm, *adj.* settled, well governed.
-- 定大局	quiet the general situation.
44-- 基	lay the cornerstone (or foundation).
-- 基人	founder.

羹〔Keng〕*n.* soup, spoon, broth, thick soup.

61-- 匙	spoon, ladle.

8044_1
幷〔Ping〕*v.* unite, combine.

8044_6
弇〔Yen〕*v.* cover.

8050_0
年〔Nien〕*n.* year, age, one's age, *adj.* annual.

00-- 高	aged.
-- 高望重	aged and in high standing.
-- 高老邁	reach a venerable age.
-- 產量	annual production, annual output, yearly capacity, yearly production.
-- 度	*n.* year, *adj.* yearly, annual.
-- 度結算	annual closing, annual accounting, annual report.
-- 度報告	annual report, annual bulletin.
12-- 刊	annual.
21-- 紅燈	neon light.
22-- 利	annual interest.
23-- 代	generation, age.
24-- 幼	young.
-- 幼無知	ignorant for being young of age.
25-- 俸	annual salary.
26-- 息	annual interest, interest annually, interest per annum.
27-- 級	class, grade.
-- 紀	age.
-- 假	new year vacation.
-- 終	at the end of the year.
-- 終獎金	December bonus.
-- 久失修	worn down by the years without repair.
28-- 收入	annual income.
-- 齡=年紀	
30-- 富力強	virile, sappy, in the prime of life.
34-- 邁力衰	aged and feeble.
37-- 深日久	after a long lapse of time.
-- 初	beginning of the year (BOY).
-- 資	seniority.

44--	老	old, aged, advanced in age.
--	薪	annual pay.
47--	報	annual report.
50--	畫	new year picture.
51--	輕人	youth, youngster.
58--	輪	annual ring.
75--	陳日久	in the course of time.
77--	限	limit of time.
--	月日	date.
--	關在即	the end of the year is fast approaching.
80--	年	annually, yearly, year after year.
--	年不斷	year in year out.
--	年歲歲	year after year.
--	年有餘	having more than enough every year.
--	年如意	New Year greetings.
--	金	annuity.
--	前	before the end of the year.
--	會	annual conference, annual session.
88--	鑑	year book, annals.
90--	少氣盛	young and impetuous.
98--	糕	new year cake.

8050₁

羊〔Yang〕*n.* sheep, goat, lamb, ewe.

00--	癇	epilepsy.
--	瘋	epilepsy.
20--	毛	wool, fleece.
--	毛商	wool stapler.
--	毛工業	woolen industry.
--	毛衫	woolen cloth, woolen sweater.
23--	絨	fine wool.
27--	角風	whirlwind, epilepsy.
40--	肉	mutton.
--	皮	sheepskin.
--	皮紙	parchment, parchment paper.
47--	欄	sheep fold.
60--	圈	sheep fold.
62--	叫	*n.* bleat, bleating, *v.* bleat.
71--	脂	suet.
76--	腸線	absorbable surgical suture.
--	腸小徑	winding pass.

80--	羔	lamb.

8050₂

拿〔Na〕*v.* take, bring, seize, arrest, grasp.

20--	手	expert, dexterous.
--	住	grasp, seize.
30--	究	arrest.
40--	去	take away.
--	來	bring to.
57--	捏	manipulate.
63--	賊	arrest a thief.

8050₇

每〔Mei〕*adj.* every, each, *adv.* usually, commonly, constantly, always.

00--	夜	every night.
10--	一	every one.
11--	班	per shift.
21--	處	everywhere.
26--	個	everyone, apiece, each, every.
--	個角落	every nook and cranny.
37--	次	every time.
--	逢佳節	on every festival.
50--	事	everything.
60--	日	everyday, day by day, daily, each day, per diem (per day).
--	日費用	per diem expenses.
66--	單位	per unit.
71--	隔	at intervals of.
--	隔一天	every two days, every second day.
77--	月	monthly, every month.
--	周	weekly, every week.
80--	人	everybody, one and all, per capita.
--	年	every year, yearly, annual.
--	每成功	always successful.
--	每推故	often to make some excuse.
90--	小時	per hour.

8051₃

毓〔Yu〕*v.* nurture, nurse, educate, rear, bring, up.

8051₆

羶〔Shan〕n. rank odor of sheep, rank odor, *adj.* rancid.

65-- 味   rank odor, odor of a sheep or goat.

8051_7

氧 〔Yang〕 *n.* oxygen.

24-- 化   oxidize.
-- 化物   oxide.
-- 化劑   oxidizer, oxidizing agent.
-- 化鋁   aluminum oxide.
-- 化銅   copper oxide, cupric oxide.

8051_7

氟 〔Fu〕 *n.* fluorine.

8055_3

義 〔I〕 *n.* meaning, sense, signification, equity, justice, righteousness, *adj.* right, just, *proper.* loyal, patriotic, dutiful, faithful, righteous, artificial, false.

04-- 塾   charity school.
08-- 旗   banner of righteousness.
10-- 不容辭   act from a strong sense of duty.
17-- 子   adopted son.
-- 勇隊   volunteer corps, volunteer army, militia.
-- 務   duty, obligation, commitment.
-- 務教育   compulsory education.
21-- 行   righteous act.
26-- 和團   Boxing Rebels, Boxers.
40-- 賣   charity sale, sale of goods for charity.
44-- 地   public ground.
47-- 塚   public burial ground.
56-- 捐   donation.
77-- 舉   righteous act.
80-- 氣   moral courage, chivalry, self-sacrificing spirit.
-- 父   god-father, foster father.
-- 金量   gold content.
87-- 鉛汽油   leaded gasoline.
94-- 憤   justified indignation, righteous indignation.

8060_1

合 〔Ho〕 *v.* shut, close, fold up, join, unite, match, pair, collect, convene, meet, combine, fit, *adj.* agreeable, accordant, suitable, whole.

00-- 意   agreeable.
-- 辦項目   joint project.
-- 辦企業   joint enterprise.
-- 併公司   merged company.
01-- 訂本   bound volume.
04-- 計   sum, sum up, add up, add up to ..., total, total up, total up to ..., aggregate.
-- 謀   conspire, plot together.
08-- 於   accord with, agree with.
-- 議制   council system.
10-- 一   unite, concur.
-- 而爲一   be united as one.
16-- 理   reasonable, rational.
-- 理意見   just opinion.
-- 理辦法   reasonable approach.
-- 理調整   rational readjustment.
-- 理工資   fair wage, just wage.
-- 理建議   rational suggestion.
-- 理配置   rational distribution.
-- 理價格   right price, reasonable price, justified price.
-- 理制度   rational system.
-- 理化   rationalization.
-- 理利潤   reasonable profit.
-- 理解釋   reasonable excuse.
-- 理的價格   reasonable price.
-- 理作價   fair pricing and square dealing.
-- 理索賠   legitimate claim.
-- 理報酬   fair return, just reward turn clause.
-- 理時間   reasonable time.
-- 理風險   reasonable risk.
-- 理性   rationality.
20-- 乎   accord with.
-- 乎需要的   desirable.
-- 乎條件   fill the bill, meet the requirements.
-- 乎實際的   realistic.
-- 乎道理   in accord with reason.
-- 乎規格   meet the specifications.
27-- 身   fit (said of clothes).
-- 股者   co-partner.
28-- 作   *n.* team work, cooperation

		v. cooperate, collaborate.
-- 作商店		cooperative store.
-- 作可能性		potential cooperation.
-- 作經營		contractual joint venture, cooperative business operation, cooperative management, joint business operation.
-- 作生產		cooperative production.
-- 作化		collectivization.
-- 作的		cooperative.
-- 作社		cooperative society, cooperative.
-- 作連鎖店		cooperative chain.
-- 作協定		cooperative agreement.
-- 作者		cooperator.
-- 作農場		cooperative farm.
-- 作發展		joint development, cooperative exploitation.
-- 作銀行		cooperative bank.
-- 作黨		co-operative party.
-- 併		*n.* annexation, combination, merger, consolidation, *v.* annex, embody, combine, amalgamate, consolidate, *adj.* consolidated.
-- 併集團		consolidated group.
-- 併成本		combined cost.
-- 併賬目		consolidated account.
29-- 伙		partnership.
-- 伙經營		deed of partnership, partnership agreement.
-- 伙解散		termination of partnership.
-- 伙收入		partnership income.
-- 伙者		business partner.
-- 伙投資		joint venture investment.
-- 伙投機		joint speculation.
-- 伙契約		article of cooperation, deed of partnership, partnership agreement, partnership deed.
-- 伙人		partner, copartner.
30-- 宜		suitable, proper, decent, appropriate.
-- 適=合宜		
34-- 法		legal, right, lawful, legitimate.
-- 法要求		legitimate claim, lawful.

-- 法手段		legal means.
-- 法行爲		lawful act.
-- 法經營		lawful operation.
-- 法繼承人		inheritance at law.
-- 法代表		legal representative.
-- 法收入		lawfully-earned income, legitimate income.
-- 法權力		lawful authority.
-- 法權利		just title, legal title.
-- 法投資		legal investment.
-- 法財產		lawful property.
-- 法當局		lawful authorities.
35-- 禮		*n.* decency, *adj.* decent.
37-- 資		joint capital, joint adventure.
-- 資公司		joint stock company.
-- 資經營企業		joint venture.
-- 資伙伴		joint-venture partnership.
-- 資協議		joint venture agreement.
-- 資合同		joint venture contract.
40-- 力		join force, cooperate, concur, hold together.
-- 力管理		cooperative control.
44-- 著		joint authorship.
47-- 格		qualified, competent, up to the standard, up to the mark, come up to standard.
-- 格產品		acceptable product, accepted product, qualified products, satisfactory product.
-- 格證書		certificate of proficiency, certificate of soundness, certificate of conformity.
-- 格工人		qualified worker.
-- 格健康證明書		clean bill of health.
-- 格條件		acceptable condition, acceptance condition.
-- 格檢驗		acceptance inspection.
-- 格技術人員		qualified technicians.
-- 格品		acceptable quality level, good unit, quality products.
-- 格質量		acceptable quality.
50-- 奏		chorus.
53-- 成		*n.* synthesis, *v.* compose, *adj.* synthetic.
-- 成產品		synthetic product.

-- 成石油	synthetic oil.
-- 成氨	synthetic ammonia.
-- 成纖維	synthetic fiber.
-- 成紙	synthetic paper.
-- 成橡膠	synthetic rubber.
56-- 拍	keep time.
60-- 眾國	united state.
-- 眾社	united press.
66-- 唱	*n.* chorus, *v.* sing in chorus.
-- 唱團	chorus troupe.
67-- 夥	partnership.
-- 夥者	partner.
77-- 同	agreement, contract, compact, contractual agreement.
-- 同訂立	conclusion of the contract.
-- 同效力	validity of treaty.
-- 同談判	contract negotiation.
-- 同工	contract laborer, indenture labor, indentured worker.
-- 同要求	contract requirement.
-- 同價格	contract price.
-- 同保證金	contract deposit, contract money.
-- 同終止	contract termination, termination of contract.
-- 同解除	rescission of the contract.
-- 同修訂	contract modification (alteration).
-- 同條件	contract terms, treaty conditions.
-- 同法	contractual law, law of contract.
-- 同內容	contract contents, treaty contents.
-- 同有效期	duration of contract, life of contract.
-- 同有效截止日期	expiration date of contract.
-- 同有效期限	contract life.
-- 同草案	draft agreement.
-- 同期滿	contract expires, expiration of the contract period.
-- 同期限	contract period, period of contract, term of contract.
-- 同格式	contract form.

-- 同摘要	treaty particulars.
-- 同措施	contract wording.
-- 同轉讓	contractual transfer.
-- 同規定	contractual obligation, contract provisions, contract stipulations.
-- 同風險	contractual risks.
-- 同履行	implementation of a contract, performance of the contract.
-- 同關係	contractual relationship.
-- 同義務	contract obligations.
-- 同範圍	scope of contract.
-- 同簽訂日期	contract award date, date of contract.
-- 同慣例	contractual practice.
-- 用	useful, fit for use.
-- 股	enter into partnership joint stock, pool capital, form a partnership, joint stock.
-- 股公司	joint stock company.
-- 股投資公司	mutual investment company.
80-- 金	alloy.
-- 金鋼	alloy steel.
-- 掌	clasp the hands.
88-- 算	economical, profitable.
-- 算交易	real bargains.
-- 算買賣	good buy.
95-- 情合理	reasonable.
99-- 營	run a business in partnership, jointly owned, jointly operated.
-- 營者	joint venturer.
-- 營企業	joint venture, joint enterprise.
-- 營公司	joint venture corporation.

首 〔**Shou**〕 *n.* head, chief, leader, beginning, first.

00-- 席	chief, first place, seat of honor.
-- 席代表	chief delegate.
10-- 要	primary, of first importance.
20-- 位	place of honor, primary, first one.
21-- 肯	nod assent, agree.

24--	先	first, first and foremost.
26--	倡	pioneer.
--	倡大義	initiate the sense of right.
37--	次演出	premiere (of a movie).
46--	相	premier, prime minister.
47--	都	capital, capital city.
--	期付款	initial payment.
71--	長	leader, commander, leading cadre.
72--	腦	head, leader.
--	腦人物	leading personages.
77--	尾	beginning and end, head and tail.
--	屈一指	second to none, best.
81--	領	leader, chief, captain, head.
82--	創	*n.* originality, *v.* originate, start, found.
88--	飾	headdress, ornaments, jewel, jewelry.
90--	當其衝	first to bear the brunt of.

酋〔Chiu〕*n.* headman, chief, chieftain.

71--	長	chieftain, leader, chief.

普〔Pu〕*adj.* general, universal, all, common.

10--	天之下	in all the world.
--	天同慶	day for universal or national celebration.
17--	及	*v.* popularize, *adj.* prevailing, widespread, popular.
--	及教育	popular education.
25--	傳天下	proclaim to the world.
27--	魯士	Prussia.
--	魯士人	Prussian.
33--	遍=普及	
--	遍性	generality, universality.
--	遍的	universal, general, widespread.
--	遍真理	universal truth.
--	遍宣傳	publicize.
--	遍規律	universal law.
37--	通	common, ordinary, in general, general.
--	通話	common Chinese language.
--	通名詞	common noun.
--	通習慣	common usage.
--	通盈利	general surplus.
--	通制服	service dress.
--	通貨物	general cargo, general fright.
--	通法	general law, common law.
--	通車	local car.
--	通護照	ordinary passport.
--	通基金	general fund.
--	通知識	general knowledge.
--	通勞動者	ordinary laborer.
--	選	general election.
--	選制	system of universal suffrage.
40--	查	general investigation.

着〔Cho〕*n.* move in chess, *v.* place, wear, put on, order, apply, get, catch (cold), catch (fire), touch.

00--	衣	wear clothes.
20--	重	emphasize, stress.
--	重點	stressed point.
--	手	start, begin, set to, engage in, undertake, set hand to, take in hand.
--	手調查	institute (initiate) an inquiry.
27--	色	color, paint, paint with color.
--	急	anxious, in hot haste, impatient.
38--	冷	catch cold.
39--	迷	be intoxicated, be fascinated.
44--	落	whereabouts, result.
--	棋	play chess.
46--	想	for the sake of.
48--	驚	be frightened.
64--	陸場	landing ground (or field).
67--	眼點	point of view, vital point.
74--	陸	*v.* land, *adv.* ashore.
90--	火	*n.* burning, inflammation, *v.* catch fire.
94--	慌	be scared, be startled, be in a fluster.

8060₄

舍〔She〕*n.* lodge, cottage, hut, residence, house, giving, *v.* abandon, give up, give.

17--	己爲人	sacrifice oneself for others.
27--	身報國	give up one's life for the country.
78--	監	director of dormitory.

8060_5

善 〔**Shan**〕 v. be good at, adj. good, virtuous, wise, clever, skillful, kind, gentle.

00--	忘	come in at one ear and go out at the other, amnesia.
--	意	n. friendliness, good will, good faith, bona fides, good intention, adj. intentioned, well-meant.
--	意的中立	benevolent neutrality.
--	言相勸	advise with good words.
08--	於	be skilled in, be adept at.
--	於變通	be flexible.
--	於自處	acquit oneself well.
--	於適應	be good in accommodating oneself to circumstances.
10--	惡	good and evil.
--	惡不分	unable to tell the good from the evil.
18--	政	good government.
21--	行	benevolence.
22--	後	rehabilitation(after a disaster, a tragedy, etc).
--	後救濟	relief measures for rehabilitation.
--	後事宜	rehabilitation measures to be taken after a natural disaster.
--	後會議	rehabilitation conference.
24--	德	virtues.
--	待他人	treat others well.
27--	終	peaceful death.
30--	良	good, virtuous, kind.
--	良風俗	good morals.
33--	心	kind heart.
34--	爲利用	make the best of.
--	爲保管	take good care of it.
40--	有善報	those who do good will receive good rewards.
46--	加利用	make a good use of.
50--	事	charitable work.
--	書	carry a good quill.
60--	男信女	good men and believing women — religious devotees.
77--	用	make a good use of.
--	舉	virtuous act, good acts.
80--	人	honest man, good fellow.

8060_6

曾 〔**Tseng**〕 n. Tseng (a family name), order or younger by three generations, adv. already, still, ever, once.

12--	孫	great grandson.
21--	經	already done, having been, once, ever.
22--	幾何時	not long since, not long ago.
37--	祖	great-grandfather.
--	祖母	great-grandmother.

會 〔**Hui**〕 n. association, society, club, union, party, meeting, v. meet, collect, join, associate, can, be able to, gather, know, understand, add, compute, adj. able, capable.

00--	商	consult, consult together, talk together, confer.
--	意	catch the idea, get the hint.
--	章	society regulation.
02--	話	n. conversation, discourse, colloquy, v. converse.
04--	計	accountant, treasurer, cashier, accounting.
--	計主任 (會計長) chief accountant.
--	計方針 (會計政策) accounting policy.
--	計師	professional accountant.
--	計制度	account system, system of account (accounting).
--	計處	accountant department.
--	計室	accountant's office, accounting department, accounting office.
--	計法	accountancy law, accounting law, financial law, fiscal law, law of accounting.
--	計員	accountant.

-- 計原理 (會計原則) accounting principle.
-- 計學　　　accounting.
-- 計人員　　accounting personnel, accountable person.
-- 計年度　　fiscal year, account year, accounting year, fiscal accounting year.
-- 計公司 (會計事務所) accountant's firm.
-- 計管理 (會計統計) accounting control.
08-- 議　　　conference, meeting, council, convention.
-- 議室　　　chamber.
-- 議廳　　　conference hall.
-- 議紀錄　　proceedings, minutes, agenda paper.
-- 議事項　　agenda.
-- 診　　　　medical consultation.
09-- 談　　　interview, converse, talk, negotiation.
10-- 面　　　meet.
20-- 集　　　collect, assemble, gather.
30-- 客　　　meet a guest, meet a visitor.
-- 客室　　　parlor, drawing room, reception room, sitting-room.
-- 審　　　　make a joint check-up.
33-- 演　　　festival.
34-- 社　　　society, association.
35-- 費　　　membership fee, club dues.
44-- 考　　　mass examination.
46-- 場　　　meeting place, assembly room, meeting house, hall.
47-- 期　　　session.
55-- 費　　　fee, membership fee.
56-- 操　　　mass drill.
60-- 見　　　interview, meet.
-- 員　　　　member, member of an association.
-- 員證書　　membership certificate, certificate of membership.
-- 員資格　　membership qualification.
-- 員會費　　membership fee.
63-- 戰　　　n. battle, general engagement, v. encounter, meet in battle.
71-- 長　　　chairman, president, president or chairman of an association, president of a so-

ciety.
-- 師　　　　join forces.
80-- 合　　　join, meet, gather together.
83-- 館　　　guild.
88-- 簽　　　countersign, joint signature.

8060₇

含 〔Han〕 v. contain, embrace, hold in the mouth.
00-- 意　　　implication.
17-- 忍　　　bear, endure, tolerate.
27-- 血噴人　make false accusations against others.
30-- 冤　　　feel a grievance.
33-- 淚　　　restrain tear, with tears in one's eyes.
36-- 混　　　confused, indistinct.
40-- 有　　　contain, include.
44-- 蓄　　　v. imply, adj. implicit.
47-- 怒　　　cherish anger.
80-- 羞　　　n. pudency, adj. bashful, shy.
-- 含糊糊　　befuddled or uncertain.
88-- 笑　　　smile, chuckle.
97-- 恨　　　cherish resentment.
-- 糊　　　　muttering, not clear, ambiguous, vague.
-- 糊了事　　settle a case carelessly.
-- 糊不明　　muddled and unclear.
-- 糊其詞　　be vague and ambiguous in speech.

倉 〔Tsang〕 n. granary, storehouse, bin, barn.
00-- 庫　　　　warehouse, storehouse, godown, goods storage, depository.
-- 庫面積　　storage space.
-- 庫理貨員　godown tally.
-- 庫保管員　storekeeper.
-- 庫存貨　　warehouse stock.
-- 庫式商店　warehouse store.
-- 庫費　　　storage charge.
-- 庫服務費　warehouse service charge.
-- 卒主人　　be a host on the spur of the moment.
-- 卒之間　　in a hurried moment.
24-- 儲　　　　warehousing.

-- 儲費	fee for warehousing, go-down charges, warehouse charges.
-- 儲號碼	warehousing port.
-- 儲極豐	the stored grains are plentiful.
-- 儲合同	warehousing contract.
26-- 皇	v. hurry, in a hurry, adj. hurried.
-- 皇就道	take leave hurriedly.
-- 皇而去	go in a hurry.
-- 皇失挫	be in panic, not knowing what to do.
27-- 租	godown charges, storages charge.
66-- 單	godown warrant, warehouse certificate, warehouse receipt, warehouse warrant (W/W).

8060₈

谷 〔**Gu**〕 n. valley, vale, ravine, gorge, difficulty, poverty.

00-- 底	bottom of a gorge.
30-- 穴	hollow behind the ankle.
44-- 樹	paper mulberry, from the bark of which paper is made.
60-- 口	outlet of a gorge.
77-- 風	east wind, up-draft in a valley.

8062₇

命 〔**Ming**〕 n. life, vitality, order, command, decree, fate, lot, luck, v. order, command.

27-- 名	name, designate, christen, denominate.
30-- 定	destined.
-- 案	case of murder, case of homicide.
37-- 運	luck, fortune, fate, destiny, doom.
-- 運不好	ill-fated, unlucky.
40-- 在旦夕	death may come any minute.
47-- 根子	lifeline, most beloved one.
50-- 中	hit one's mark, hit the target, score a hit.
-- 中點	impact point.
-- 中注定	be decreed by fate, predestined.
-- 中目的	hit the mark.
61-- 題	proposition, thesis.
71-- 長	long life.
72-- 脈	life-blood.
77-- 門	vitals.
80-- 令	n. order, command, decree, v. order, command, dictate, direct, mandate.
81-- 短	short life.

8071₇

乞 〔**Chi**〕 v. beg, entreat, ask alms.

10-- 丐	beggar.
-- 靈藥石	seek help from medicine.
24-- 休告老	request resignation or retirement.
27-- 假返家	ask for leave and go home.
43-- 求	beg, sue, entreat.
52-- 援	call in one's aid.
-- 援於	seek help from.
66-- 賜垂聽	please give me a hearing.
80-- 食	bet one's bread.
-- 食以終	die in a ditch.
99-- 憐	beg for mercy.

爸 〔**Pa**〕 n. papa, father, dad, daddy.

8073₂

公 〔**Kung**〕 n. duke, lord, gentleman, male, office, adj. public, common, general, open, just, fair, equitable, unselfish, official.

00-- 主	princess.
-- 立	established by the public.
-- 立小學	public elementary.
-- 產	public property.
-- 庭	court.
-- 庫	public treasury.
-- 文	official letter (note), public document.
-- 文副本	office-copy.
-- 言	profess.
-- 章	official seal.
-- 文	document.
02-- 證	n. attestation, v. notarize.

-- 證證書	notarial deed.
-- 證單	certificate issued by public notary.
-- 證費	notarial charges.
-- 證員	notary public.
-- 證人	notary, notary public, public notary, surveyor.
-- 證人簽證 (公證人證明)	attestation of notary public, notarial certificate.
-- 證會計師	chartered public accountant.
-- 訴	public prosecution.
04-- 諸同好	let others with the same taste share (something or some experience).
-- 諸於世	blaze abroad.
07-- 認	public approval, general compact, generally accepted (or acknowledged).
-- 認的	generally accepted, generally acknowledged, established, recognized.
-- 認原理	acceptable principle.
-- 論	public opinion.
-- 敵	public enemy, common enemy.
-- 議	public discussion.
10-- 元	Anno Domini (A.D.).
-- 元前	before Christ (B.C.).
-- 正	n. justice, adj. right, just, righteous, impartial, fair.
-- 正人	referee.
-- 正的仲裁人	unbiased arbitrator.
-- 正友好解決	just and amicable settlement.
-- 正持平	fair and just.
-- 平	fair, just, equitable, impartial, in a fair, reasonable, comprehensive and balanced manner.
--平交易	fair transaction, fair deal, fair trade, even bargain, even dealing, fair bargain, square deal.
-- 平交換	even exchange.
-- 平市價	fair market price.
-- 平競爭	fair competition.
-- 平就業	fair employment.
-- 平工資	fair wage.
-- 平價格	just price, moderate price.
-- 平解決	equitable settlement.
-- 平稅	equity tax.
-- 平誠實	play the game.
-- 平安排	fair shake.
-- 平治理	rule with an even hand.
-- 平對待	n. fair game, square treatment, v. do justice to.
-- 平報價	fair offer.
-- 平報酬	fair return.
-- 平分配	equitable distribution.
-- 平無私	fair and unselfish.
-- 而忘私	forget oneself in the interests of the public.
-- 示催告	public summons.
-- 示送達	delivery by public notice.
13-- 職	public duty.
16-- 理	axiom, universal principle.
17-- 函	official letter.
-- 務	public service, public affairs (duties).
-- 務員	officer, official, civil servant, civil service, public officers, public servant.
-- 子王孫	sons of the rich or powerful.
-- 子	master.
-- 司	company, corporation, firm.
-- 司高級職員	company officer.
-- 司商譽 (公司形象)	company image.
-- 司章程	articles of association, association articles, memorandum of association.
-- 司證書 (公司註冊證)	corporation charter.
-- 司證券	corporation securities.
-- 司政策	company policy.
-- 司集團	consortium of corporations.
-- 司虧損	corporate deficit.
-- 司債	debentures.
-- 司債券	corporate bonds, corporation bond, debenture stock.
-- 司總裁	president of a company.

-- 司條例	articles of incorporation, company's act, company ordinance.
-- 司名稱	trading name.
-- 司的創立	formation of a company.
-- 司收益	company earning.
-- 司稅	corporation tax.
-- 司註冊地	place of incorporation.
-- 司實績	company performance.
-- 司法	company law, corporation law, law of partnership.
-- 司法律顧問	corporation attorney, corporation lawyer.
-- 司資產	corporate assets.
-- 司內幕	inside story of a firm.
-- 司董事	company director.
-- 司執照(公司章程)	articles of association, corporate charter.
-- 司股票	corporation stock.
-- 司所得稅	company income tax, corporate income tax.
-- 司印章	corporate seal, seal of company.
-- 司合併	amalgamation of business, corporate combination.
-- 司會計	corporation accounting.
-- 司會議	company meeting.
-- 司公章	company seal, corporate seal.
-- 司創辦人(公司發起人)	company founder, company promoter.
-- 司管理	company management.
20-- 倍數	common multiple.
-- 爵	duke.
-- 爵夫人	duchess.
-- 雞	cock.
21-- 頃	hectare.
22-- 制	metric system.
-- 斷	arbitrate.
-- 斷人	arbitrator.
-- 斷處決	settle by arbitration.
-- 私	public and private.
-- 私兩便	advantageous to both public and private interests.
-- 私不分	make no distinction between public and private interests.

-- 私分明	be scrupulous in separating public from private interests.
-- 私合營	state and private joint ownership, jointly operated by government and private individuals, public-private operation, joint state-private management.
-- 私關係	relation between the state and private sectors of the economy.
-- 私兼顧	take both pubic and private interests into account.
-- 出	absence on duty.
23-- 然	openly, in public, in open, publicly.
-- 然侮辱	open insult.
-- 然竊取	take a sheet off a hedge.
-- 然反抗	give open resistance to the authority.
-- 僕	public servant.
24-- 德	public spirit, public virtue.
-- 升	liter, litre.
-- 佈	n. publication, v. publish, make known.
-- 告	announcement, notification.
-- 告牌	bulletin board.
-- 告天下	public notification to all under heaven.
25-- 牛	bull.
-- 使	minister (in diplomacy), envoy.
-- 使館	legation.
-- 債	public loan, government bonds, state loan, national bonds, public debts.
-- 債券	bond, government bond certificate, public bond, public stock.
-- 積金	reserve fund, public reserve funds, accumulated fund, common reserve fund, public accumulated fund.
27-- 役	public servant.
-- 約	pact, convention.

-- 約數	common factor, common divisor.	
30-- 安	public safety, public welfare, public security.	
-- 安部門	department of public security.	
-- 安人員	police.	
-- 寓	apartment, apartment house.	
-- 害	public nuisance, public hazard.	
-- 害病 (污染病)	pollution-related disease.	
-- 審	public trial, open trial.	
-- 定價格	official price, public price.	
34-- 社	commune.	
-- 法	public law, public act.	
-- 法人	public juristic person.	
38-- 海	open sea, high seas, international waters.	
-- 海自由	freedom of high sea.	
-- 道	n. justice, adj. fair, just.	
-- 道價格	equitable price, fair price, just price, reasonable price.	
40-- 有	in common, publicly owned.	
-- 有制	public ownership.	
-- 有土地	nationalized land, public domain.	
-- 有事業 (公共機關)	public institution.	
-- 有財產	government properties.	
-- 布	n. announcement, v. proclaim, publish, bring forth, announce, make known, promulgate, publicize.	
-- 布價	published price.	
-- 寸	decimeter.	
-- 賣	public auction, government sale, public sale.	
43-- 式	formula.	
-- 式化	n. formulation, v. formularize.	
-- 式主義	formulism.	
44-- 豬	boar.	
-- 共	common, public.	
-- 共部門	public sector.	
-- 共設施	public facility, public utilities.	

-- 共工程	public works.
-- 共工程費	public works expenses.
-- 共需求	public wants.
-- 共預算	public budget.
-- 共建築物	public building.
-- 共信用	public credit.
-- 共價值	public value.
-- 共衛生	public health.
-- 共機關	public institution.
-- 共秩序 (公共準則)	public order, public policy.
-- 共秩序法律	rules of public order.
-- 共保健事業	public health service.
-- 共綠地	public open space.
-- 共租界	international settlement.
-- 共收入	public receipt.
-- 共福利	general welfare, public welfare.
-- 共補助金	public aid.
-- 共消費	public consumption.
-- 共汽車	bus, omnibus.
-- 共基金	public fund.
-- 共支出	public expenditure.
-- 共事業	public services and facilities, public utilities.
-- 共車輛	public-service vehicle.
-- 共費用	public spending.
-- 共投資	public investment.
-- 共團體	public body.
-- 共廁所	public lavatory, public convenience, comfort station.
-- 共道德	public morals.
-- 共汽車站	bus stop.
-- 共財物	public goods.
-- 共喉舌	throats and tongues of the public.
-- 共圖書館	public library.
-- 共開支	public expense.
-- 共關係	public relations.
-- 共倉庫	public warehouse.
-- 共會計師	public accountant.
-- 權	civil right.
47-- 報	bulletin, gazette, communique, official report, official journal, public report.

-- 款	public fund, public money.
-- 款賬	public account.
50-- 事	public affairs, public business, official business.
-- 事公辦	business is business.
55-- 費	public expenditure, public expense, at the public expense.
-- 費醫療	free medical care, free medical treatment(service).
-- 費醫療制	socialized medicine.
-- 費生	student supported by public funds.
57-- 擔	quintal.
60-- 里	kilometer.
-- 園	park, garden, public garden.
-- 國	dukedom.
-- 署	public office.
-- 量	weight, conditioned weight.
-- 眾	the puble, community, common people.
-- 眾衛生	public health.
-- 眾利益	public interest.
-- 眾事務	public affairs.
-- 眾捐款	public contribution.
61-- 噸	metric ton (M/T).
67-- 路	highway, public road.
-- 路交通	road traffic.
-- 路運輸	carriage by road, highway transportation, road transit, road transportation.
-- 路運輸網	road transport system.
-- 路網	highway network.
71-- 馬	stallion.
72-- 斤	kilogram (kg).
-- 所	guild.
75-- 休假日	public holiday.
77-- 民	n. citizen, adj. civil.
-- 民權	civil rights.
-- 尺	metre.
-- 用	public, public utility, for public use.
-- 用電話亭	phone-box, telephone booth.
-- 用電話間	call-box.
-- 用事業	public use, public utilities, public utility services, public welfare establishments.
-- 學	public school.
-- 開	n. publicity, public opening, adv. publicly, openly.
-- 開競爭	open competition.
-- 開市場	market overt, open market, public market.
-- 開履行	public issue.
-- 開上市	go public.
-- 開信	open letter.
-- 開秘密	open secret.
-- 開股份有限公司	public limited company.
-- 開展覽	public exhibition.
-- 開法庭	open court.
-- 開讚揚	sing someone's praise.
-- 開標售市場	attrition market.
-- 開報價	public offer.
-- 開費率	published rate.
-- 開拍賣	public auction.
-- 開投資公司	open-end company.
-- 開投標 (公開招標)	competitive tender, general bid, open bid, public bidding, public tender system, advertised bidding .
-- 開招標	public tender.
-- 開原則	principle of publicity.
-- 開貿易	public trading.
-- 開公司	open corporation.
-- 關	public relations (PR).
-- 關小姐	public relations girl.
-- 民	citizen.
-- 民自由	civil liberty.
-- 民資格	citizenship.
-- 民大會	mass meeting.
-- 民權	citizen right.
-- 門桃李	pears and plums of your excellency's residence — your students.
80-- 羊	ram.
-- 益	common good, public benefit, public welfare, public interest.
-- 益服務	public service.
-- 益金	public welfare funds, public benefit.
-- 益社團	association for promoting

	public welfare.
--分	centimeter, gram.
--會	guild.
--差	public errand, tolerance, common difference.
83--館	mansion.
88--餘之暇	leisure after official duties.
90--判	pubic trial.
--堂	court.
96--糧	public grains, grain tax.
99--營	publicly-owned, publicly-operated.
--營農場	public farm.
--營(國營)企業	public enterprise, government business enterprise, government-operated business.
--營性質	public nature.

8073₂

衾 〔Chin〕 n. coverlet, quilt, bedclothes.

食 〔Shih〕 n. food, meal, diet, v. eat, take food.

00--言	eat one's words, break promise, go back on one's word, retract one's promise.
08--譜	recipe, collection of recipes.
27--物(品)	food, nourishment, diet, provisions, eatables, victuals.
30--宿	board and lodging, bed and board.
--宿費	board and lodging expenses.
38--道	gullet, esophagus.
--道癌	cancer of the esophagus.
40--肉動物	carnivore.
50--盡	eat up.
51--指	forefinger.
60--品=食物	
--品廠	bakery, confectionary.
--品商	grocer.
--品店	food shop.
--量	capacity for eating.
77--具	table wares, eating utensils, kitchen utensils.

--用	edible, for food.
78--鹽	table salt.
87--慾	appetite.
90--堂	dining hall, mess hall.
--料	food stuff.
--糧=食料	

兹 〔Tzu〕 n. coarse mat, adj. this, adv. at present, now.

| 02--證明 | we hereby certify that..., this is to certify that... |
| 40--有 | there is, there is now. |

養 〔Yang〕 v. bear, nourish, bring up, give birth, support, keep, feed, rear, raise, nurse, educate, cultivate.

00--病	give cure to one's disease, undergo a period of recuperation.
--病所	hospital, sanatorium.
--育	nourish, breed, rear, foster, bring up.
--育之恩	parental love and care received since childhood.
--育成人	bring up to manhood.
14--殖	cultivation.
17--子	adopted son, foster child, foster son.
20--雞鴨	poultry raising.
25--生要素	essential elements of keeping good health.
--生之道	way of keeping good health.
27--魚業	fish breeding.
30--家	support a family.
40--女	adopted daughter, foster daughter.
44--豬	pig breeding.
--老院	home for the aged, nursing home.
--老金	pension, old age pension, pension allowance, annuity, endowment annuity.
--老年金	annuity for the aged.
--老保險	endowment insurance.
53--成	train up.
57--蜂	bee-keeping.
67--路	maintenance of roads.
--路費	highway users tax, road

charges, road maintenance costs, road toll.

71-- 蠶　silkworm breeding, sericulture.

77-- 母　foster mother.

80-- 父　foster father.

94-- 料　food, nourishment, nutrition.

8074₈

餃〔Chiao〕*n.* meat dumpling, stuffed dumpling, ravioli.

17-- 子　ravioli, stuffed dumpling.

8076₄

饝〔Mo〕*n.* bread.

8077₂

岔〔Cha〕*n.* divergent road, branch, *v.* branch off.

17-- 子　accident, trouble.

67-- 路　diverging road.

77-- 開　shunt, distract, branch off.

缶〔Fou〕*n.* earthenware.

8080₆

貧〔Pin〕*n.* poverty, destitution, *adj.* poor, impoverished, destitute, insufficient, deficient, lacking.

00-- 瘠　arid, barren.

-- 病相連　poverty and sickness are closely connected.

20-- 乏　*n.* beggary, meager, adj. poor, wanting, destitute, scanty.

23-- 僱農　poor peasants and farm laborers (in Communist China).

27-- 血　anaemia.

30-- 窮　*n.* poverty, destitution, *adj.* poor, hard up, in bad circumstance.

-- 窮潦倒　down-and-out.

-- 富　poor and rich, high and low.

-- 富不均　disparity between rich and poor, unequal distribution of wealth.

44-- 苦　poor and miserable, poor, poverty-stricken.

55-- 農　poor peasants.

60-- 困　privation, poverty.

-- 困地區　poverty-stricken zone.

77-- 民　paupers, poor people.

-- 民窟　slum.

-- 民院　poorhouse.

-- 民學校　ragged school.

80-- 人　poor man, empty pocket.

貪〔Tan〕*v.* covet, desire, be greedy for, *adj.* avaricious, greedy.

11-- 玩　fond of play, fond of playing.

22-- 利　greedy for gain.

-- 戀　hanker after, be enamored of.

27-- 色　fond of woman, be addicted to women.

31-- 污　*n.* corruption, *v.* graft, take graft, peculate, *adj.* corrupted.

-- 污腐化　graft and corruption.

-- 污者　grafter.

33-- 心　*n.* greed, avarice, *adj.* greedy, avaricious.

44-- 婪　greedy, covetous, rapacious, avaricious.

60-- 圖　be greedy for, long for.

63-- 贓　take bribe, practice graft.

64-- 財　covetousness, greedy of money *v.* covet riches.

80-- 食　*n.* gorge, glut, *adj.* voracious.

87-- 慾　greed, lust.

8081₇

氮〔Tan〕*n.* nitrogen.

77-- 肥　nitrogenous fertilizer.

8088₆

僉〔Chien〕*adj.* all, unanimous.

8090₄

余〔Yu〕*pron.* I, me.

8091₇

氣〔Chi〕*n.* air, vapor, gas, steam, atmosphere, mist, breath, spirit, character, manner, smell, anger, *v.* anger.

12-- 孔　gas pore.

-- 水　distilled water, soda water.

13-- 球　balloon.

26-- 息　breath.

-- 魄	vitality, spirit, courage.	
27-- 候	weather, climate.	
-- 候圖	climate chart.	
-- 候學	climatology.	
-- 絕	v. die, adj. breathless, dead.	
-- 色	complexion, one's appearance.	
-- 船	steam boat.	
-- 象	weather, climate.	
-- 象學	meteorology.	
-- 象台	weather station, meteorological observatory.	
-- 象衛星	weather satellite.	
-- 象萬千	things change in countless ways.	
-- 象報告	weather forecast.	
29-- 燄	bluster, overweening arrogance.	
30-- 流	air-current.	
-- 窗	transom, air window, ventilating window.	
36-- 溫	temperature.	
37-- 泡	bubble.	
40-- 力	strength, vigor, energy.	
41-- 慨	spirit, manner, looks.	
45-- 墊船	hovercraft.	
60-- 量	forbearance, tolerance.	
-- 味	odor, smell.	
62-- 喘	n. gasp, asthma, panting, v. pant, adj. breathless.	
-- 喘病	asthma.	
65-- 味	smell, odor.	
-- 味難聞	stink awfully.	
-- 味相投	be congenial to each other.	
71-- 壓	atmospheric pressure.	
72-- 質	temperament, character.	
75-- 體	gas.	
80-- 氛	atmosphere, air.	
82-- 餒	n. discouragement, v. become downhearted.	
88-- 管	trachea, windpipe.	
-- 鎗	air gun.	
-- 節	lofty moral integrity.	
92-- 惱	angry, be annoyed.	

8111₀

釭 〔 Kung 〕 n. iron band on the nave of a wheel.

8111₁

鉦 〔 Cheng 〕 n. a kind of bell.

8111₃

鈺 〔 Yu 〕 n. strong metal.

8111₇

鉅 〔 Chu 〕 adj. great, large, huge, gigantic.

30-- 富	millionaire, as rich as a Jew.	
47-- 款	large sum of money.	
55-- 費	great expenses.	

鋂 〔 Ya 〕 n. ammonium.

鑪 〔 Lu 〕 n. stove.

8112₀

釘 〔 Ting 〕 n. nail, peg, v. nail.

17-- 子	nail.	
20-- 住	nail on.	
27-- 鎚	tack hammer.	
44-- 鞋	shoes with spikes, track shoes, running shoes.	
50-- 書機	sewing-press, stapler.	
80-- 入	drive a nail home.	

8112₇

鑷 〔 Nieh 〕 n. pincers, forceps, nipper, v. nip, pull out.

17-- 子	tweezers, forceps.	

8112₇

鈣 〔 Kai 〕 n. calcium.

24-- 化	n. calcification, v. calcify.	

鎘 〔 Ko 〕 n. cadmium.

8113₂

釬 〔 Han 〕 v. solder metal.

8116₃

鐳 〔 Lei 〕 n. radium.

83-- 錠療法	radium therapy.	

8119₁

鏢 〔 Piao 〕 n. javelin.

8128₆

頒 〔 Pan 〕 n. publish, proclaim, bestow, donate, v. promulgate, confer on.

07-- 詔	proclaim an edict.	
12-- 發	distribute, issue, bestow.	
-- 發許可證	issue of license.	

24-- 佈	promulgate.	
28-- 給	confer on.	
40-- 布	publish, make known.	
66-- 賜勳章	confer medals upon.	

8138₆

領 〔Ling〕 *n.* neck, collar, leader, *v.* lead, direct, command, receive, guide, understand.

00-- 章	collar badge, collar insignia.
11-- 頭	leader, be at the head of.
-- 班	gang boss, shift foreman, gang foreman, head of shift, section foreman.
12-- 水	territorial waters, island waters.
17-- 取	accept, receive, draw.
-- 子	collar.
20-- 航	*n.* navigation, *v.* navigate, pilot.
-- 航員	navigator, pilot.
-- 受	*n.* acknowledge, receipt, *v.* accept, receive.
24-- 先	precede, take the lead, lead, be in the lead
-- 結	bow tie.
30-- 空	territorial air, territorial space, air domain.
-- 進	usher into.
34-- 港	*n.* pilot (in a port), *v.* pilot, pilot a ship into or out of a harbor.
-- 港費	pilot dues, pilotage.
35-- 袖	leader, head.
38-- 海	territorial sea, territorial waters.
-- 海權	territorial sea rights.
-- 海主權	sovereign right of the territorial sea.
-- 導	*n.* leader, leadership, *v.* direct, lead.
-- 導權	leadership.
-- 導幹部	leading cadre.
-- 導地位	leadership.
40-- 土	territory, dominion.
-- 土權	sovereign right over terri-

	tory, territorial sovereignty.
-- 土野心	territorial ambition.
-- 巾	scarf.
43-- 域	field, domain, realm.
-- 域廣大	the domain is vast.
44-- 帶	necktie, tie.
50-- 事	consul.
-- 事官員	consular officers.
-- 事裁判權	consular jurisdiction.
-- 事團	consular corps.
-- 事館	consulate.
80-- 會	*n.* comprehension, *v.* understand, perceive, comprehend, make out.
83-- 錢	receive money.
91-- 悟=領會	

8141₇

瓶 〔Ping〕 *n.* bottle, jar, vase, flask, jug.

17-- 子	bottle, jar.
24-- 裝	in bottles, bottling.
30-- 塞	cork, stopper, bottle stopper.
44-- 蓋	lid of a bottle.
46-- 架	pedestal.

矩 〔Chu〕 *n.* carpenter's square, law, rule, pattern, usage, custom.

12-- 形	rectangle.
-- 形的	rectangular.
77-- 尺	carpenter's square.

8141₈

短 〔Tuan〕 *n.* be short of, be in debt to, faults, shortcomings, *adj.* short, brief, contracted, lacking, wanting, needing, deficient.

00-- 衣	jacket.
-- 文	short essay.
-- 交	short delivery, shortage in delivery.
10-- 工	day labor, seasonal laborer.
20-- 統靴	buskins.
21-- 處	defect, weak-side, weak point, shortcoming.
22-- 片	short film.
24-- 貨	short shipment.
26-- 促	transient.
30-- 褲	breeches, shorts, short pan-

	ts.
33-- 褂	jacket.
34-- 波	short wave.
-- 襪	sock.
36-- 視	short-sighted.
38-- 途	short journey.
47-- 期	short time, short period, short-term, short date.
-- 期計劃	short-range plan.
-- 期放款	short-term loan, money at call, money on call.
-- 期工作	short-run job.
-- 期職員	short-term staff.
-- 期信貸	short-term credit.
-- 期變動	short-time fluctuation.
-- 期出租	short lease.
-- 期貸款	loan for a short time, short-term loan, street loan, teller loan, way-and-means advances.
-- 期借款	short loan, short-term borrowing.
-- 期的供應	short-run supply.
-- 期負債	short-term obligations.
-- 期淨益	net short-term gain.
-- 期存款	short-term deposits.
-- 期墊款	teller advance, temporary advance.
-- 期投資	short-range investment, short-term investment, teller investment, temporary investments.
-- 期居住	short-term stay.
-- 期學習班	short-term courses.
-- 期合同	short contract.
60-- 量	shortage, loss of quantity, short in weight.
67-- 跑	dash, sprint.
-- 跑健將	short-distance runner, sprinter.
72-- 髮	bob, bobbed hair.
-- 兵相接	hand-to-hand fighting
80-- 命	short-lived.
82-- 劍	dirk, sword.
85-- 缺	n. deficiency, defect, adj. deficient, wanting.

88-- 鎗	musket.
-- 笛	piccolo.
90-- 少	lacking, wanting, deficient.
-- 小	small, short.
-- 小精悍	small but efficient.

8168₆

頷 〔Han〕 n. jaw.

8171₀

缸 〔Gang〕 n. jar, urn.

8174₀

餌 〔Erh〕 n. bait, food, allurement, v. lure, entice, allure.

50-- 蟲	lugworm.

8174₇

飯 〔Fan〕 n. food, meal, cooked rice.

00-- 廳	dining hall, dinning room.
-- 店	restaurant, hotel.
-- 店服務	hotel service.
10-- 票	meal coupon, husband.
13-- 碗	rice bowl, job.
21-- 桌	dining table.
22-- 後	after meal.
47-- 桶	rice-bucket, good-for-nothing.
60-- 量	appetite.
80-- 食	n. food, v. eat.
-- 盒子	mess tin, lunch box.
83-- 館=飯店	
87-- 鍋	rice pot.

8174₉

罅 〔Hsia〕 n. split, crack, chink, fissure, leak, gap, cleft.

79-- 隙	fissure, gap, crack, flaw.

8178₆

頌 〔Sung〕 n. eulogy, encomium, hymn, v. praise, extol, admire.

04-- 讚	commend, eulogize, panegyrize.
07-- 詞	eulogy, panegyric, tribute.
17-- 歌	song of praise, hymn.
54-- 揚	praise, eulogize.
56-- 播	extol.
77-- 賦	laud.

8194₇

敍 〔Hsu〕 n. order, series, preface, interview, meeting, v. describe, state out, narrate, meet, rate or evaluate, gather, tell.

00-- 文　preface.

09-- 談　chat, gossip, talk.

14-- 功行賞　go over the records and decide on awards.

33-- 述　n. description, v. narrate, relate.

44-- 舊　talk about old times.

50-- 事　statement, description, narration.

-- 事詩　epic, narrative poem.

8210₀

剉〔Tso〕v. file, cut.

10-- 平　smooth, even.

17-- 子　file.

52-- 折　harassment.

90-- 完　polish.

釧〔Chuan〕n. armlet, bracelet.

鍘〔Jar〕n. lever-knife, v. cut, chop.

17-- 刀　grass cutter, chaff chopper.

44-- 草　cut grass.

-- 草機　straw cutter.

8211₄

錘〔Chui〕n. hammer, weight, weight on a steelyard, v. hammer, pound.

95-- 煉　hammer and forge, train, discipline.

鍾〔Chung〕n. cup, goblet, wine cup, v. concentrate, converge.

20-- 愛　love, love deeply, show deep affection for.

95-- 情　fall in love, lose one's heart to.

8211₈

鎧〔Kai〕n. armor, stirrup.

60-- 甲　armor, coat of fence.

77-- 骨　stirrup bone.

鐙〔Teng〕n. stirrup.

8212₇

銹〔Hsiu〕n. rust, v. become rusty.

85-- 蝕　corrosion.

8214₁

鋋〔Ting〕n. iron ore.

8214₇

鎈〔Huan〕n. ring.

8215₇

錚〔Cheng〕n. jingling of metal.

8216₃

鎦〔Tzu〕n. a small unit of weight.

8216₄

銛〔Hsien〕adj. sharp.

8219₄

鑠〔Shuo〕v. melt, fuse, adj. bright, shining, lustrous.

80-- 金　fuse metal.

8220₀

剃〔Ti〕n. shave, v. shave.

11-- 頭　shave, cut hair, have a haircut.

-- 頭店　barber's shop.

-- 頭匠　barber.

17-- 刀　razor.

72-- 鬚　shave the beard.

-- 鬍子　shave.

8242₇

矯〔Chiao〕v. correct, rectify, feign, stimulate, straighten, raise high, pretend, fake, adj. strong, robust.

10-- 正　rectify, correct, right, set right, mend, straighten.

25-- 健　vigorous, strong.

88-- 飾　pretend.

8244₄

矮〔Ai〕n. dwarf, adj. short, low.

12-- 凳　stool.

17-- 子　dwarf, short person.

42-- 櫈　low stool.

44-- 樹　bush wood.

-- 樹叢　bush.

90-- 小　n. dwarf, adj. undersized, dwarfish.

8260₀

劄〔Jar〕n. document, diary, dispatch, v. prick, stab.

05-- 請　request by writing.

07--	記	*n.* record *v.* give an account of.
--	詢	write to inquire.
10--	覆	reply to an inferior official.
17--	子	dispatch from a superior.

創〔Chuang〕*n.*wound, *v.* begin, start, commence, create, punish.

00--	立	establish, set up, found.
--	立會	inaugural meeting.
--	立實業	open up industries.
--	辦	found, initiate, institute, establish, promote, set up.
--	辦資本	initial capital.
--	辦成本	initial cost, organization cost.
--	辦費用	promotion expense.
--	辦時期	initial stage.
--	辦人	promoter, founder, floater, organizer, originator.
--	辦企業	found a business.
--	辦公司	float a company, floatation of a firm.
--	痍滿目	ruins and debris meet the eye everything.
07--	設=創立	
12--	刊號	initial issue.
22--	制權	initiative, right of initiative.
27--	紀錄	break the record.
28--	作	*n.* literature and artistic works, *v.* invent, originate, create.
--	傷	wound.
--	收	income-reaping, make profits, increase income.
32--	業	start a business, found an enterprise.
--	業利潤	promotional profit.
--	業費	initial expense, formation expenses.
34--	造	*n.* creation, *v.* create.
--	造行銷	creative marketing.
--	造力	creative power.
--	造性	creativeness.
43--	始	*v.* begin, start, initiate, *adj.* initiative.
--	始費用	initial outlay.

--	始投入	initial input.
--	始日期	initiation date.
--	始人	founder, author.
44--	世紀	genesis.
--	世以來	from the beginning of time until the present.
60--	見	original view.
77--	舉	unprecedented act, innovation.
81--	鉅痛深	greatly damaged and deeply pained.

剏〔Kuai〕*v.* cut apart, amputate, execute.

17--	子手	executioner, hatchet man.

8271₄
飪〔Jen〕*v.* cook.
8373₄
飫〔Yu〕*v.* satisfy, bestow, eat to repletion.
8274₄
餒〔Nei〕*n.* hunger, decay, *adj.* hungry, famished, putrid, dejected, discouraged.
餧〔Wei〕*v.* feed.
8275₃
饑〔Chi〕*n.* hunger, famine, dearth.

30--	寒	hunger and cold.
--	寒交迫	suffer from both cold and hunger.
44--	荒	starvation, famine.
--	荒流年	year of famine.
77--	民	victims of famine, starving masses.
83--	餓	*n.* hunger, starvation, *v.* starve.
--	餓遊行 (失業者)	hunger march.
84--	饉	famine, dearth.

8280₀
劍〔Chien〕*n.* sword, lance.

21--	術	fence, swordsmanship.
43--	鞘	scabbard.
53--	拔弩張	sabre rattling, ready to fight.
60--	口	blade.

80-- 舞   sword-dance.

8310_0

鉍 〔**Bi**〕*n.* bismuth.

8312_7

鋪 〔**Pu**〕*v.* spread, spread out, arrange, lay, lay over, pave, arrange.

07-- 設   lay, arrange, build.

10-- 石子   gravel.

11-- 張   paint in bright colors, display, show, overdo, overpraise, be pompous.

24-- 牀   make bed.

44-- 蓋   bedding.

67-- 路   pave a road.

77-- 開   spread out.

8313_2

鑭 〔**Lang**〕*n.* lanthanum.

8313_3

鏹 〔**Chiang**〕*n.* metal, cash.

8314_3

鏄 〔**Po**〕*n.* bell.

8314_4

銨 〔**An**〕*n.* ammonium.

鈸 〔**Bar**〕*n.* cymbals.

8315_0

鉞 〔**Yueh**〕*n.* large axe.

鍼 〔**Chen**〕*n.* needle.

鐵 〔**Tieh**〕*n.* iron, *adj.* ferrous, strong, cruel, durable, firm, unyielding, ferrous.

00-- 廠   ironworks, iron-smelting plant.

02-- 證   ironclad proof, strong proof.

10-- 礦   iron ore, iron mine.

-- 工   blacksmith, ironworker.

-- 石心腸   iron-hearted, unfeeling.

-- 面無私   unmoved by personal appeals, without fear or favor.

12-- 水   molten iron.

-- 砧   anvil.

21-- 衛團   iron guard.

22-- 絲   iron wire, wire.

-- 絲網   wire entanglement, barbed-wire entanglements.

24-- 牀   iron bed.

27-- 血   blood and iron.

-- 條   iron bar, bar-iron.

34-- 漢   determined man, strong man.

38-- 道   railway.

-- 道部   Ministry of Railways.

-- 道兵   railway corps, railway unit.

41-- 板   iron plate, sheet iron.

44-- 幕   iron curtain.

54-- 軌   iron rails.

60-- 蹄   iron hoofs.

-- 甲   armor.

-- 甲車   tank, land battleship, armored car.

-- 甲巡洋艦   armored cruiser.

66-- 器   iron ware.

-- 器時代   iron age.

67-- 路＝鐵道   railway, railroad.

-- 路局   Railway Administration.

-- 路網   railway network.

-- 路運輸   railway transportation.

-- 路局長   director of the Railway Administration.

70-- 肺   iron lung.

71-- 匠   blacksmith, knight of the hammer.

-- 匠店   smithy.

77-- 屑   iron filings, iron dross.

80-- 人   iron man.

-- 鏟   spade, shovel.

81-- 釘   iron nails.

-- 飯碗   iron-rice bowl.

82-- 銹   iron rust.

84-- 鉗   tongs.

-- 罐   iron flask.

85-- 鏈   iron chain.

87-- 鎚   iron hammer.

-- 鉤   grapping iron.

88-- 箱   safe.

89-- 鍬   spade.

90-- 拳   iron fist.

8315_3

錢 〔**Chien**〕 *n.* money, copper, cash, coin, one tenth of a tael.

10-- 票	paper money, bank notes.
23-- 袋	purse.
27-- 包	purse, wallet.
30-- 滾錢	money begets money.
44-- 莊	money exchanger, banking house.
-- 莊票子	bank notes issued by a bank.
64-- 財	wealth, money, treasure.
77-- 局	mint.
88-- 箱	till, cash-box.
98-- 幣	coin, money, coinage, currency.
-- 幣學	numismatics.

8316₈

鎔 〔**Jung**〕 *n.* mold, *v.* melt, fuse.

27-- 解	melt, fuse.
91-- 爐	smelting furnace.

8318₁

錠 〔**Ting**〕 *n.* slab, cake, spindle, ingot of gold or silver, tablet (of medicine).

17-- 子	spindle.

8355₀

羢 〔**Jung**〕 *n.* fine wool.

8362₇

舖 〔**Pu**〕 *n.* shop, store, bed.

17-- 子	shop, store.
26-- 保	tradesman's guarantee.
44-- 蓋	bedclothes, bedding.

8363₄

猷 〔**Yu**〕 *n.* plan, scheme, merit.

8372₇

餔 〔**Pu**〕 *n.* supper, *v.* feed.

8375₀

餓 〔**O**〕 *n.* hunger, starvation, *adj.* hungry, starved.

10-- 死	starve, famish, be starved to death, die of famine.
12-- 殍	bodies of the dead famished people.
22-- 倒	fall down from hunger.
26-- 鬼	hungry devil.

8375₃

餞 〔**Chien**〕 *n.* sweetmeats, *v.* entertain a departing friend, give a farewell feast, send off, give a farewell party.

21-- 行	entertain a friend going on a journey.

8376₀

飴 〔**I**〕 *n.* malt sugar, syrup, *v.* feed, *adj.* very sweet.

8377₇

館 〔**Kuan**〕 *n.* inn, hotel, lodging place, institute, hall, chamber.

17-- 子	restaurant.
71-- 長	director.

8410₀

釵 〔**Chai**〕 *n.* hairpin.

針 〔**Chen**〕 *n.* pin, sting, needle.

23-- 織廠	knit goods mill, knitwear mill.
-- 織品	knit goods, knitwear.
26-- 線	sewing, needlework, needle and thread.
-- 線包	sewing kit.
-- 線活	needlework.
27-- 灸	acupuncture and moxibustion.
34-- 對	direct at, point at, aim at.
44-- 藥	injection.
-- 葉樹	needle-leaved tree, conifer.
52-- 刺法	acupuncture.
67-- 眼	needle's eye.
77-- 腳	stitch.
84-- 尖	needle-point.
88-- 箍	thimble.

8411₀

鋩 〔**Mang**〕 *n.* edge of a sword.

8411₁

銑 〔**Hsien**〕 *n.* shiny metal, pig iron, *adj.* bright, burnished.

10-- 工	milling work, milling attendant (or worker).
17-- 刀	milling tool, milling cutter.
24-- 牀	milling machine.
83-- 鐵	pig iron.
鐃 〔Nau〕 n. cymbals.	
83-- 鈸	cymbals.
8411_4	
鑵 〔Kuan〕 n. water jar.	
8412_7	
鈉 〔Na〕 n. natrium, sodium.	
銬 〔Kao〕 n. handcuffs, manacles.	
鋤 〔Chu〕 n. spade, hoe, v. hoe, dig.	
11-- 頭	hoe.
44-- 草	weed.
60-- 田	hoe the field.
8413_0	
鈦 〔Tai〕 n. titanium.	
8413_8	
鋏 〔Chia〕 n. pincer, sword, hilt.	
84-- 鉗	pincers.
8414_1	
鑄 〔Chu〕 v. fuse, cast, found, make.	
10-- 工	caster, founder, foundry worker.
25-- 件	casting .
34-- 造	strike, cast, found, make.
-- 造廠	foundry.
44-- 模	mold.
53-- 成品	cast articles.
-- 成大錯	make a great mistake.
83-- 鐵	cast iron.
87-- 鋼	cast steel.
98-- 幣	coin, coinage, coined money, mint coins, specie.
-- 幣廠	mint.
8414_7	
鑊 〔Huo〕 n. pan, caldron.	
00-- 烹	punishment of boiling the criminal alive in a caldron.
8416_0	
錨 〔Mao〕 n. anchor.	

28-- 纜	hawser.
41-- 標	anchor buoy.
85-- 鏈	chain cable.
鈷 〔Gu〕 n. cobalt.	
10-- 礦	cobalt ore.
8416_1	
錯 〔Tso〕 n. wrong, mistake, error, whetstone, v. make a mistake, be wrong, grind, cross, adj. wrong, erroneous, irregular, disorderly.	
00-- 雜	confused.
06-- 誤	mistake, error, fault.
-- 誤百出	full of mistakes.
-- 誤估計	miscalculate, misjudge.
-- 誤條件	wrong judgment of the situation.
07-- 認	mistake for.
20-- 愛	misplace.
22-- 亂	in disorder, in confusion, out of order, confused.
23-- 綜	complicate.
-- 綜複雜	complicated, intricate.
25-- 失良機	have missed good opportunity.
30-- 字	erratum.
37-- 過	miss, cross.
-- 過機會	miss the bus.
62-- 別字	erroneous character.
77-- 覺	phantasm, illusion, misapprehension.
-- 用	misuse, abuse.
80-- 入歧途	fall into a wrong path.
88-- 算	n.miscalculation, v. miscalculate.
8417_0	
鉗 〔Chien〕 n. pincer, forceps, tweezers, v. pinch, hold with pincers.	
10-- 工	fitter.
17-- 子	pincers, tongs.
20-- 住	clamp tight.
21-- 行運動	pincers movement.
22-- 制	pin down.
8418_1	

鎮 〔Jen〕 *n.* town, weight for pressing, *v.* repress, press, pierce, quell.

00-- 痙劑	antispasmodic.
-- 痛劑	anodyne, painkiller.
22-- 紙	paper-weight.
30-- 定	*v.* allay, keep presence of mind, calm, tranquillize, soothe, *adj.* cool, composed.
-- 定神經	quiet one's nerves or mental excitement .
-- 守	guard, defend.
31-- 江	Chenkiang.
52-- 靜	*v.* quiet, compose, tranquillize, *adj.* calm, tranquil, composed.
-- 靜劑	sedative.
71-- 壓	repress, suppress, overbear, quell.
77-- 民	townsman.

8418_6

鑽 〔Tsuan〕 *n.* borer, drill, awl, auger, *v.* bore, pierce, dig, drill, go through.

10-- 石	diamond.
11-- 研	delve, study, research.
-- 頭	drilling bit.
12-- 孔	bore, perforate, punch, drill.
-- 孔機	drill, boring machine.
17-- 子	bore, auger, drill.
24-- 牀	drilling machine.
30-- 進	bore into, go into.
-- 進去	drill into, worm into.
-- 空子	avail oneself of loopholes.
37-- 通	drill through.
55-- 井	well-boring.
-- 井機	boring machine for sinking wells.
57-- 探	explore, prospect.
-- 探機	drilling machine, boring machine.
-- 探隊	surveying and drilling group.
80-- 入	bore into.
99-- 營	seek profits for oneself.

8419_6

鐐 〔Liao〕 *n.* fetters, fetter handcuffs, shackles, silver of the purest kind.

84-- 銬	fetters and manacles.

8471_1

饒 〔Jao〕 *v.* forgive, pardon, release, be lenient, set free, be merciful, excuse, spare, *adj.* rich, plenty, abundant, plentiful.

20-- 舌	*v.* chatter, blab, *adj.* talkative, chattering, loquacious.
46-- 恕	pardon, excuse, forgive.
48-- 赦	forgive, pardon.
80-- 命	spare one's life.

8471_4

饉 〔Chin〕 *n.* famine.

罐 〔Guan〕 *n.* can, pot, jug, kettle, container, jar.

11-- 頭	can, tin, canned goods, tinned goods.
-- 頭食物	canned goods.
-- 頭工廠	cannery.
-- 頭工業	canning industry.
-- 頭貨物	canned goods.
-- 頭肉	canned meat.
-- 頭蔬菜	canned vegetable.
-- 頭食品	canned foods.
-- 頭食品廠	cannery.
24-- 裝啤酒	canned beer.
77-- 兒	can, jar.

8471_7

饁 〔Yeh〕 *v.* carry food to field laborers.

8471_8

饠 〔I〕 *n.* cooked rice that has turned sour.

8472_7

餚 〔Yau〕 *v.* feed, provide food, *n.* food, dishes and foods.

8474_7

餑 〔Po〕 *n.* cake, biscuit.

8490_0

斜 〔Hsieh〕 *adj.* slant, inclined, sloping,

oblique, distorted, slanting.

00-- 度	obliquity, inclination, gradient.
-- 方形	rhombus.
10-- 面	slanting surface, sloping, oblique, distorted, inclined plane.
20-- 紋	slanting stripes.
-- 紋布	twill, drill.
21-- 傾	aslant, obliquely.
24-- 射	oblique fire.
-- 倚	recline.
26-- 線	slope, oblique line.
27-- 角	oblique angle.
36-- 視	v. leer, look askance, adj. squint, cross-eyed.
44-- 坡	slope, declivity.
67-- 路	oblique way.
75-- 體字	italics.

8511₇
鈍 〔Tun〕 adj. n. blunt, obtuse, stupid, dull.

17-- 刀	blunt knife, dull knife.
27-- 角	obtuse angle.

8512₇
鏽 〔Hsiu〕 n. rust.

8513₀
鈇 〔Fu〕 n. axe.

鉢 〔Po〕 n. priest's alms bowl, pot, bowl.

鏈 〔Lien〕 n. chain.

17-- 子	chain.
27-- 條	chain.
28-- 黴素	streptomycin.
40-- 索	chain, cable chain.
89-- 鎖	padlock.

8513₂
錶 〔Biao〕 n. watch.

44-- 帶	watchband.

8514₀
鍵 〔Chien〕 n. lock, key.

27-- 盤	keyboard.

8514₄

鏤 〔Lou〕 n. steel, v. carve, engrave.

02-- 刻	engrave, carve.

8516₀
鈾 〔Yu〕 n. uranium.

10-- 礦	uranium ore.

8519₀
銖 〔Chu〕 n. an ancient unit of weight.

8519₆
鍊 〔Lien〕 n. chain, v. refine, smelt, smelt ore.

80-- 金	fuse gold, refine gold.
-- 金術	alchemy.
83-- 鐵	refine iron.
87-- 鋼廠	steel refinery.

8571₇
飩 〔Tun〕 n. dumplings.

8573₀
缺 〔Chueh〕 n. blemish, shortness, shortage, deficiency, defect, vacancy, post, v. lack, want, adj. deficient, short, wanting.

00-- 席	n. absence, adj. absent.
-- 席者	absentee.
-- 席判決	decision given in the absence of one party.
06-- 課	absence (or absent) from school.
13-- 殘	ruined, broken.
20-- 乏	needing, lacking, wanting, scanty, short.
-- 乏人才	be short of talents.
21-- 虧	deficit, loss.
-- 處	breach, break.
24-- 貨	be in short supply, be out of stock.
31-- 額	vacancy, vacant position.
56-- 損	damage, damaged.
60-- 口	gap, breach.
61-- 點	defect, deficiency, imperfection, blemish, weak side, shortcoming.
-- 嘴唇	harelip.
77-- 陷	n. defect, imperfection,

drawback, *adj.* deficient, imperfect.

90-- 少=缺乏　*n.* shortage, deficiency, *v.* lack, want.

93-- 憾　defect, flaw.

96-- 糧　grain deficit.

-- 糧戶　grain-short household.

8573_6

蝕 〔Shih〕 *n.* eclipse, erosion, *v.* eclipse, erode, corrode.

50-- 本　lose money in business, fail in business, loss capital.

-- 本生意　business that causes a loss of capital.

8578_6

饋 〔Kuei〕 *n.* present, gift, *v.* give, present.

8579_6

餗 〔Su〕 *n.* food.

8610_0

釦 〔Kou〕 *n.* button, clasps.

17-- 子　buttons, clasps.

鉑 〔Bo〕 *n.* platinum.

鈿 〔Tien〕 *n.* hair-pin, filigree.

錮 〔Ku〕 *n.* restrain, fetter.

8611_4

鑼 〔Luo〕 *n.* gong.

44-- 鼓　gongs and drums.

8612_7

錦 〔Chin〕 *n.* brocade, embroidered work, *adj.* brilliant, colorful.

21-- 上添花　be blessed with a double portion of good fortune, win honors one after another in quick succession.

25-- 繡　*n.* embroidery, *adj.* splendid, majestic.

-- 繡河山　beautiful landscape, land of splendor.

27-- 緞　brocade, damask silk.

41-- 標　champion, championship, trophy.

-- 標賽　sports tournament.

50-- 囊　embroidered purse.

錫 〔Hsi〕 *n.* tin, pewter, *v.* bestow.

10-- 礦　tin mine.

44-- 蘭　Ceylon.

71-- 匠　tinman.

88-- 箔　pewter foils.

鐲 〔Cho〕 *n.* bracelet, wristlet.

17-- 子　bracelet, wristlet.

鐫 〔Chuan〕 *n.* abolish, annul, free.

鍔 〔O〕 *n.* sharp edge of a sword.

8613_0

鍶 〔So〕 *n.* strontium.

8613_2

鐶 〔Wan〕 *n.* ring.

8614_1

鐸 〔To〕 *n.* large bell.

銲=焊 9684_1

8615_0

鉀 〔Kai〕 *n.* kalium, potassium.

77-- 肥　potassium fertilizer.

8616_0

鋁 〔Lu〕 *n.* aluminum.

8618_0

鋇 〔Bei〕 *n.* barium.

8619_4

鎳 〔Nieh〕 *n.* nickel.

98-- 幣　nickel coin.

8621_0

覦 〔Yu〕 *v.* desire, long for.

8640_0

知 〔Chih〕 *n.* knowledge, wisdom, learning, friendship, friend, *v.* know, recognize, distinguish, comprehend, understand, be aware of, acquaint, befriend, control, take charge of, wait on.

00-- 交　bosom friend, intimacy.

03-- 識　knowledge, information.

-- 識產業　brain industry, knowledge industry.

-- 識階級	intellectual class.
-- 識傳播	knowledge dissemination.
-- 識青年	educated youth.
-- 識份子	intellectuals, intelligentsia.
10-- 更鳥	robin.
13-- 恥	shame, feel ashamed, have a sense of shame.
17-- 了	cicada.
-- 己	confidant, bosom friend.
-- 己友人	bosom friend.
-- 己知彼	know one's own and the enemy's situation or strength.
20-- 悉	know, perceive, be aware of.
27-- 名	well-known.
-- 名人士	celebrities, well-known people.
33-- 心	intimate friend, intimacy.
38-- 道	know, recognize, understand.
40-- 難而退	withdraw in the face of difficulties.
-- 難行易	it's easier to do a thing than to know the why.
50-- 事	magistrate.
60-- 足	contented, satisfied.
67-- 照	inform.
77-- 覺	perception, consciousness, sense, sensation.
95-- 情	know the fact.
-- 情人	insiders, those in the know.

8652₇

羯 〔Chieh〕 *n.* wether, gelded goat.

8660₀

智 〔Chi〕 *n.* wisdom, knowledge, intellect, cleverness, wit, *adj.* bright, wise, intelligent.

00-- 育	intellectual culture, mental education.
04-- 謀	shrewdness, strategy.
11-- 巧	ingenuity.
17-- 取	outwit, win by strategy rather than by force.

-- 勇雙全	combine wisdom with courage.
21-- 能	wit, intellect, intelligence.
22-- 利	Chile.
-- 利人	Chilean.
30-- 窮力竭	be at one's wit's end and exhausted.
40-- 力	mind, intellect, wit, intelligence.
-- 力產品	intellectual products.
-- 力測驗	intelligence test.
50-- 囊	brain trust.
-- 囊團	brain trust, think tank.
55-- 慧	intelligence, brightness, wisdom, wit.

8671₁

餛 〔Hun〕 *n.* dumpling, delicate stuffed dumplings.

85-- 飩	delicate stuffed dumplings.

8671₃

餽 〔Kuei〕 *v.* offer, give.

88-- 贈	*n.* gift, present, *v.* present as a gift.

8673₂

餵 〔Wei〕 *v.* feed, fodder.

47-- 奶	suckle, give a child the breast.
71-- 馬	feed a horse.
80-- 養	feed, raise.
87-- 飽	cram, feed to the fill.

8674₇

饅 〔Man〕 *n.* pie, bread, steamed dumpling, stuffed or unstuffed dumpling.

11-- 頭	bread, steamed dumpling, steamed bread.

8710₄

塑 〔Su〕 *n.* plastics, *v.* model, model in clay, make a statue, make an idol.

27-- 像	statue.
34-- 造	create, model.
40-- 土爲像	mould an idol in clay.

70-- 膠袋	plastic bag.	
71-- 壓	plastic compression.	
77-- 膠	plastic.	
94-- 料=塑膠		
-- 料廠	plastics plant.	
-- 料工業	plastics industry.	
-- 料袋	plastic bag, polybag.	

8711_0
鉏 〔Chu〕 n. hoe.

8711_2
鉋 〔Pao〕 n. plane (for carpentry), curry comb, v. plane.

00-- 床	planer, planning-machine.
10-- 工	planer, planning-work.
-- 平	plane away.
44-- 花	shavings.
90-- 光	plane smooth.

8711_4
鏗 〔Keng〕 n. ringing of metal.

8711_5
鈕 〔Niu〕 n. button, knob, handle.

77-- 門	hole.
86-- 釦	button (on a garment).

8711_7
鈀 〔Pa〕 n. rake, harrow, palladium.
錳 〔Man〕 n. manganese.

30-- 之游子	ions of manganese.
87-- 鋼	manganese steel.

8712_0
釣 〔Tiao〕 n. fish, bait, fishhook, v. fish, angle.

27-- 魚	n. fishing, adj. fish, angle.
-- 魚鈎	fishhook.
77-- 譽	fish for praise or fame.
88-- 竿	fishing rod, fishing pole.

卸 〔Hsieh〕 v. lay aside, get rid of, put off, give up, unload, discharge, remove, resign.

17-- 職	relief of a post.
22-- 任回里	resign office and leave for home.

-- 岸	unloading ashore.	
24-- 貨	unload, unload cargoes, break bulk, discharge, discharge goods, clear a ship, land.	
-- 貨機	unloader, unloading mechanisms.	
30-- 肩	rest the shoulders, lay down the responsibility.	
40-- 去	discharge, lay aside.	
47-- 卻擔負	lay down a burden.	
50-- 責	release one's duty.	
-- 車	unload a car.	

鈎 〔Gou〕 n. hook.
鈞 〔Chun〕 n. weight of thirty catties, ancient unit of weight — thirty catties.
鈎 〔Gou〕 n. hook, scythe, clasp, v. hook, seduce, lure.

11-- 引	ensnare, entice.
17-- 子	clasp, hook.
20-- 住	clasp, hook.
26-- 鼻	hooked nose.
33-- 心鬥角	maneuver for positions against one's rivals.
50-- 蟲	hookworm.

鋼 〔Kang〕 n. steel, adj. hard, strong.

11-- 琴	piano.
-- 琴家	pianist.
12-- 水	molten steel.
22-- 絲	steel wire.
-- 絲牀	spring bed.
-- 絲繩	steel cable.
-- 絲布	wire-cloth.
-- 絲刷	steel-brush.
-- 製品	steel.
27-- 條	steel bar.
34-- 渣	steel slag.
40-- 盔	helmet, steel helmet.
41-- 板	steel plate, steel sheets and plates.
44-- 材	steel materials, steel products, steels.

60-- 甲	steel armor.
77-- 骨	steel rods.
83-- 錠	steel ingot, steel slab.
-- 鐵	iron and steel.
-- 鐵廠	steelworks, iron and steel plant.
-- 鐵工業	iron and steel industry.
-- 鐵漢	man of steel, iron man.
84-- 鑄件	steel-casting.
87-- 鋸	hacksaw.
88-- 管	steel tube, steel pipe.
-- 管廠	steel tubing plant.
-- 筋	reinforced steel bar, steel rod.
-- 筋混凝土	ferro-concrete.
-- 筆	pen, fountain pen.
-- 筆畫	pen drawing.

銅 〔Tong〕 *n.* copper, brass, bronze.

10-- 礦	copper ore.
21-- 版	copper plate.
22-- 絲	copper wire.
27-- 像	bronze statue.
-- 綠	verdigris.
40-- 壺	copper kettle.
41-- 板	copper plate.
44-- 鼓	copper drum.
60-- 器	copper utensil.
71-- 匠	coppersmith.
83-- 錢	copper coin.
86-- 鑼	brass gong.
98-- 幣	copper coin.

8712_7

鎢 〔Wu〕 *n.* tungsten, wolfram.

| 22-- 絲 | tungsten filament. |
| 87--鋼 | tungsten steel. |

鍋 〔Guo〕 *n.* pan, pot, cooking pot, boiler.

17-- 子	pan.
91-- 爐	boiler.
-- 爐廠	boiler factory.
-- 爐房	boiler room.

8713_2

錄 〔Lu〕 *n.* record, register, *v.* record, copy, write down.

00-- 音	*n.* sound-recording, *v.* record.
-- 音帶	recording tape.
-- 音機	recorder, tape-recorder.
10-- 下	write down, take down.
17-- 取	accept (applicants).
27-- 像磁帶	video tape.
50-- 事	junior clerk.
77-- 用	employ, accept, hire.

銀 〔Yin〕 *n.* silver, *adj.* silvery.

00-- 庫	treasury.
10-- 礦	silver ore or mine.
-- 元	silver dollar.
-- 票	bank note, bank bill, money order, silver certificate.
17-- 子	silver.
21-- 行	bank.
-- 行學	banking.
-- 行匯兌	bank bill.
-- 行信貸	bank credit.
-- 行利息	bank interest.
-- 行貸款	bank loan, bank advances loan, bank lending.
-- 行收款員	receiving teller.
-- 行保管箱	safe deposit box.
-- 行透支	bank of overdraft, bank overdraft, overdrafts with banks.
-- 行法	bank law.
-- 行存摺	bankbook, passbook.
-- 行存款	cash in bank, cash on bank, cash in deposit, bank currency, money in bank.
-- 行存款單	deposit receipt, deposit certificate.
-- 行本票	bank check, cashier's cheque, cashier's check, cashier's order.
-- 行界	banking circles.
22-- 紙=銀票	
27-- 魚	whitebait, silverfish.
-- 色世界	screen world.
-- 條	silver bar.
31-- 河	Milky Way.
40-- 杏	gingko, ginkgo.

42-- 婚　　　　silver wedding.
-- 婚紀念　　　25th anniversary of one's wedding.
44-- 幕　　　　screen, screen for motion pictures, silver screen.
47-- 根　　　　money market, money.
-- 根緊　　　　stringent cash, hard up for money, monetary stress and strain, monetary stringency, money to be tight, stringency, tighten, tight money, dear money.
-- 根短絀　　　deficiency of currency, shortage of money.
50-- 本位　　　silver standard.
60-- 圓　　　　dollar.
-- 圓本位　　　silver standard.
66-- 器　　　　silver ware.
71-- 匠　　　　silversmith.
77-- 鼠　　　　ermine.
83-- 錢　　　　money, wealth.
88-- 箱　　　　safe.
98-- 幣　　　　silver coin.

8713_4
鍥 〔Chieh〕 v. cut, engrave.

8713_7
鎚 〔Chui〕 n. hammer, v. hammer.
17-- 子　　　　hammer.
51-- 打　　　　hammer.
57-- 擊=鎚打

8714_2
鏘 〔Chiang〕 n. ringing of metal.

8714_7
鍛 〔Tuan〕 n. forge, forge metal, refine, smelt.
10-- 工　　　　blacksmith, metal worker.
71-- 壓機　　　forging press.
83-- 鐵　　　　wrought-iron.
85-- 鍊　　　　n. training, v. forge, train, smelt, temper.
-- 鍊身體　　　n. physical training, v. train oneself physically.
87-- 鋼　　　　forged steel.

8715_4
鋒 〔Feng〕 n. spear, adj. sharp.
22-- 利　　　　acute, sharp.

8716_0
銘 〔Ming〕 n. book of precepts, inscriptions, v. carve, engrave, inscribe.
00-- 文　　　　inscription.
02-- 刻　　　　impress, engrave.
07-- 記　　　　bear in mind.
-- 記心頭　　　be engraved on one's mind.
53-- 感不忘　　remember with gratitude always.

8716_1
鉛 〔Chien〕 n. lead (metal).
10-- 礦　　　　lead ore.
21-- 版　　　　stereotype.
27-- 條　　　　lead bar.
30-- 字　　　　type, lead type (in printing).
44-- 黃　　　　proofreading.
50-- 中毒　　　plumbism.
71-- 匠　　　　plumber.
88-- 筆　　　　pencil.
-- 筆心　　　　lead of a pencil.
-- 筆畫　　　　pencil sketch.
-- 筆盒　　　　pencil box.
98-- 粉　　　　ceruse, white lead.

8716_4
鋸 〔Chu〕 n. saw, v. saw.
21-- 齒　　　　teeth of a saw.
22-- 斷　　　　saw off.
24-- 牀　　　　sawing machine.
27-- 條　　　　saw blade.
40-- 木　　　　saw wood.
-- 木廠　　　　saw mill.
42-- 木機　　　slasher (machine).
51-- 掉　　　　saw up.
77-- 屑　　　　dust, sawdust.
-- 開　　　　　saw asunder.

鉻 〔Ko〕 n. chromium, chrome.

8718_2
欽 〔Chin〕 n. term of address to the emperor, v. respect, revere, adj. respectful, imperial.

27-- 仰　respect, look up.

-- 佩　n. respect, admiration, capital, v. admire, respect.

80-- 差　imperial envoy.

-- 命　imperial order.

8732_0

翎 [Ling] n. plume, feather.

20-- 毛　long feather.

8732_7

鴒 [Ling] n. wagtail.

鸚 [Chien] n. spoonbill.

8733_8

慾 [Yu] n. passion, appetite, desire, lust, greed.

07-- 望　expectation, want, desire, craving.

08-- 念　appetite, carnal thoughts.

95-- 情　passion, desire, appetite, lust.

8738_2

歉 [Chien] adj. sorry, regretful, discontented, deficient, scanty, lacking.

28-- 收　bad harvest.

71-- 仄實深　with deepest regret.

8742_0

朔 [Shuo] n. the first day of the moon, beginning, north.

77-- 風　north wind.

8742_7

鄭 [Cheng] n. Jeng (a family name), name of an ancient state, adj. solemn, formal.

20-- 重　v. emphasize, adj. serious, solemn, earnest, adv. seriously.

-- 重其事　act with due care and respect.

-- 重聲明　declare solemnly.

8752_0

翔 [Hsiang] v. soar, fly, hover.

8762_0

卻 [Chueh] v. decline, reject, deny, retire, refuse, retreat, adv. still. conj. but.

10-- 不提防　one's surprise.

21-- 步而行　walk stepping backwards, retreat.

30-- 之不恭　it is impolite to decline it.

60-- 是　nevertheless.

8762_2

舒 [Shu] v. spread, spread out, expand, open, stretch out, unfold, relax, adj. comfortable, slow, leisurely.

30-- 適　comfortable, pleasant.

64-- 暢　pleasant, cheerful, in good spirits.

77-- 服　v. comfort, adj. comfortable, easy, cozy.

8762_7

鴿 [Ko] n. pigeon, dove.

17-- 子　dove, pigeon.

30-- 房　dovecote, pigeon house.

8768_2

欲 [Yu] n. desire, wish, lust, passion, v. wish, hope, desire, expect, long for.

07-- 望　desire, lush, wish, want.

10-- 不可縱　desire must be put under rein.

35-- 速則不達　more haste, less speed.

8771_0

飢 [Chi] n. hunger, famine.

44-- 荒　famine, dearth.

93-- 餓　hungry.

-- 餓工資　starvation wages.

-- 餓點　starvation point.

8771_2

飽 [Pao] v. eat to the full, adj. satiated, full of food, gratified.

20-- 受　suffer enough from.

-- 受虛驚　suffer from nervous fears.

21-- 經世故　well-experienced in the ways of the world.

26-- 和　n. saturation, adj. saturated.

-- 和度　saturated ratio.

-- 和量　saturation capacity.

-- 和點　saturation point.

62-- 暖　be in good keep.

77-- 學　very learned.

80-- 食	eat heartily, eat one's fill.
-- 入私囊	embezzle public funds.

8771_3
饞〔Chan〕 adj. greedy, gluttonous, voracious.

32-- 涎	drool over.

8772_0
餉〔Hsiang〕 n. pay, ration, taxes, provisions.

飼〔Ssu〕 v. feed, nourish, raise.

80-- 養	raise, rear, breed, nourish.
-- 養員	feeder.
94-- 料	fodder, forage, feed, feed grains, provender.

餬〔Hu〕 n. congee, gruel, porridge, paste.

60-- 口	make a living.

8774_7
餿〔Sou〕 v. decay and turn smelly, adj. sour, frowzy.

8776_2
餾〔Liu〕 v. distill.

8777_7
餡〔Hsien〕 n. stuffing of a pie or dumpling.

88-- 餅	pie.

8778_1
饌〔Chuan〕 v. feed, provide food.

8778_2
飲〔Yin〕 n. drinks, v. drink, suck, be hit.

10-- 醉	get drunk.
12-- 水思源	drink water and think of its source — be grateful.
30-- 泣	weep mournfully.
31-- 酒	drink wine.
44-- 茶	drink tea.
48-- 乾	drink up.
77-- 用水	drinking water.
80-- 食	food, diet, food and drink.
-- 食店	restaurant, cafe.
-- 食費	food and beverage expenses.
94-- 料	drinks, beverages.

8781_0

俎〔Tsu〕 n. sacrificial bowl.

8790_4
槊〔Shuo〕 n. lance.

8791_4
糴〔Ti〕 v. buy rice, purchase grains.

8794_0
叙=敍 8194_7

8810_1
竺〔Chu〕 n. bamboo.

8810_4
坐〔Tso〕 n. seat, v. sit.

00-- 立	sitting and standing.
-- 立不安	sit on pins and needles.
-- 享其利	enjoy the profit without working.
10-- 下	sit down.
20-- 位	seat, chair.
24-- 待時機	quietly wait for an opportunity.
25-- 失良機	watch a golden chance slip by, lose an opportunity.
27-- 船	go by boat.
28-- 以待旦	quietly wait for the day to dawn.
-- 以待斃	resign oneself to death.
31-- 褥	cushion.
36-- 視	keep oneself aloof from, watch with indifference.
-- 視不救	watch without giving a helping hand.
40-- 支	unauthorized outlays, out of receipts.
44-- 落	be situated (or located) in.
50-- 車	ride on a car.
68-- 吃山空	do nothing but sit and eat and wear away a mountain of wealth, sit at home eating away one's fortune.
78-- 臥不寧	not peaceful in both sitting and lying, restless.
80-- 等	sit idly waiting for.
-- 食	idle bread.
-- 食山空	sit idly and eat up a hill of food-live without a source of income.

笙 〔Sheng〕 *n.* pipe, reed organ.
8810₇

籃 〔Lan〕 *n.* basket, hamper.
13-- 球   basketball.
17-- 子   basket.
46-- 球場   basketball ground.
8810₈

笠 〔Li〕 *n.* hamper, open basket.

筮 〔Shih〕 *v.* divine.
8811₄

銓 〔Chuan〕 *v.* measure, weight, estimate.

銼 〔Tso〕 *n.* file, iron pan, *v.* file, scrape.
10-- 平   file smooth.
17-- 刀   file.
8811₆

銳 〔Jui〕 *adj.* sharp, keen, acute, quick-witted, strong, energetic.
22-- 利   keen, sharp, acute, cutting, pointed.
27-- 角   acute angle.
33-- 減   sharp reduction.
40-- 志   keen will.
55-- 感   sensibility.
72-- 兵   well-trained troops.
80-- 氣   ardor, arduous spirit, ardent spirit.
-- 氣正盛   the ardent spirit is just in its height.
8811₇

筑 〔Chu〕 *n.* a kind of musical instrument, the Kweichow Province.

鑑 〔Chien〕 *n.* example, precedent, precept, *v.* reflect.
30-- 定   judge.
-- 定書   written expert testimony.
8812₇

銻 〔Ti〕 *n.* antimony.
10-- 礦   antimony ore.

鑰 〔Yao〕 *n.* lock, key.
12-- 孔   keyhole.
24-- 牡   key.
61-- 匙   key.
-- 匙眼   keyhole.
-- 匙圈   key ring.

鎂 〔Mei〕 *n.* magnesium.
8813₄
90-- 光   magnesium light.
-- 光燈   flash lamp, flash light.

鏃 〔Tsu〕 *n.* head of an arrow, arrowhead.
8813₇

鈴 〔Ling〕 *n.* bell.
47-- 聲   ring of a bell.
8814₂

簿 〔Pu〕 *n.* book, tablet, account book, register, memorandum book.
07-- 記   book-keeping.
-- 計制度   book keeping system.
-- 記員   book-keeper.
8815₃

籤 〔Chien〕 *n.* lot, lottery, label, slip of bamboo used in divination or gambling, *adj.* sharp.
01-- 語   oracle, response of lot.
08-- 譜   book on divination by lot.
27-- 條   label, tag.
88-- 筒   tube for holding lots.
8816₂

箔 〔Pa〕 *n.* leaf, sheet, foil, gilt.
8816₇

鎗 〔Chiang〕 *n.* gun, pistol, rifle, firearms.
16-- 彈   bullet.
17-- 砲   firearms.
20-- 手   gunner.
28-- 傷   bullet wound.
34-- 法   marksmanship.
47-- 聲   pop, sound of a gunshot.
52-- 托   stock or butt of a gun.
-- 刺   bayonet.
60-- 口   muzzle, muzzle of a gun.
97-- 炮手   gunner.
98-- 斃   shoot to death, execute by shooting.
8817₇

篲 〔Hei〕 *n.* broom.
8818₁

鏇 〔Hsuan〕 *n.* wine heater, copper tray, *v.* cut with a lathe.

00-- 床	lathe, turning lathe.

8821₁

簏 〔Lu〕 *n.* basket.
籠 〔Lung〕 *n.* basket, cage.
17-- 子　　cage.
20-- 統　　indiscriminately, in general terms.
27-- 絡　　entice, entangle, ensnare.
60-- 罩　　cover, close in.

8822₀

竹 〔Chu〕 *n.* bamboo.
17-- 子　　bamboo.
30-- 帘　　bamboo-screen.
44-- 林　　bamboo grove, bamboo plantation.
46-- 榻　　bamboo couch.
60-- 園　　bamboo garden.
66-- 器　　bamboo ware.
88-- 籃　　bamboo basket.
-- 籬　　bamboo fence.
-- 筒　　bamboo tube.
-- 竿　　bamboo pole, bamboo cane.
-- 箬　　sheath of the bamboo.
-- 筍　　bamboo shoot.
-- 節　　bamboo-joint.

8822₁

箭 〔Chien〕 *v.* arrow.
11-- 頭　　arrowhead.
46-- 桿　　shaft.
50-- 囊　　quiver.
88-- 筒　　quiver.

8822₇

笏 〔Fu〕 *n.* tablet.
筲 〔Shau〕 *n.* bamboo basket.
88-- 箕　　bamboo basket.

籌＝帚 1722₇

第 〔Ti〕 *n.* series, order, class, sequence, degree, rank, mansion, residence, *adv.* only, merely.
10-- 一　　first, number one.
-- 一課　　first lesson, lesson one.
-- 一手　　first-hand.
-- 一等　　first-class.
-- 一線　　front, front line.
-- 一名　　first, first place.

-- 一流	first-class, ace.

-- 一流質量　tip-top quality.
-- 一流的商行 first-class business house (firm).
-- 一版　　front page.
-- 一次　　first time.
-- 一抵押權　first mortgage.
-- 一炮　　opening shot.
-- 一類郵件　first-class mail.
-- 二　　second, number two.
-- 二班　　second shift.
-- 二抵押權　second mortgage.
-- 二線　　second line.
-- 三　　third, number three.
-- 三方　　third party.
-- 三者　　third party.
-- 三黨　　The third party.
-- 三帝國　third empire.
-- 三國際　Comintern.
-- 三世界　Third World.
-- 五縱隊　fifth column.

筒 〔Tung〕 *n.* pipe, tube, case, cylinder.
筋 〔Chin〕 *n.* muscle, tendon, sinews.
00-- 疲力盡　be completely exhausted, have used up all energy.
13-- 強力壯　hale and hearty, ablebodied.
34-- 斗　　somersault.
40-- 肉　　muscle.
-- 力　　vigor, energy, strength.
77-- 骨　　sinews and bones, the build of one's body.

篇 〔Pien〕 *n.* chapter, book, section.
00-- 章　　chapter, section.
41-- 幅　　pages, length or space of a printed writing.
60-- 目　　heading.

篙 〔Kao〕 *n.* bamboo pole.
17-- 子　　boat pole.

簫 〔Hsiao〕 *n.* pipe, bamboo pipe, flute.
簡 〔Chien〕 *n.* document, note, letter, slip of bamboo for writing, *v.* arrange, appoint, neglect, choose, select, slight, treat coolly, *adj.* simple, brief, easy.
00-- 言　　in a few words.
08-- 譜　　simple musical notation.
10-- 要　　brief and to the point.

-- 要報告	briefing.
21-- 便	convenient, handy.
22-- 稱	short form of a name.
24-- 化	simplify.
30-- 寫	abbreviation.
33-- 述	summarize.
37-- 潔	succinct, compact, laconic.
40-- 直	virtually, literally, simply.
42-- 樸	austere.
47-- 報	brief report, bulletin.
52-- 活	in a few words, in a small compass, concise.
55-- 捷法	short-cut method.
60-- 易	*n.* simplicity, *adj.* easy.
-- 易程序	summary procedure.
66-- 單	simple, easy.
67-- 略	compact, abridged, compendious, summary.
-- 明	concise, terse.
-- 明小傳	profile.
71-- 陋	simple and crude.
75-- 體字	simplified Chinese characters.
81-- 短	*n.* brevity, *adj.* brief, short.
96-- 慢	slight, treat coolly.

8823₂
篆 〔**Chuan**〕*n.* seal-character, seal type of Chinese characters, (your) name.

33-- 字	seal-character.

籐 〔**Teng**〕*n.* cane, vine, rattan.

8823₄
笨 〔**Pen**〕*adj.* stupid, foolish, awkward, dull, clumsy.

11-- 頭笨腦	stupid, muddle-headed.
20-- 重	ponderous, cumbersome, bulky and clumsy.
-- 手笨腳	clumsy-handed.
28-- 伯	fat-head.
34-- 漢	booby, fool.
52-- 拙	awkward, clumsy.
80-- 人	silly person, stupid fellow.

簇 〔**Tsu**〕*n.* arrow head, bunch, cluster, foliage.

02-- 新	brand-new.
50-- 擁	crowd about, attend.

8823₇

簾 〔**Lien**〕*n.* screen, curtain, sun blind.

17-- 子	curtain, screen.

8824₃
符 〔**Fu**〕*n.* amulet, sear, charm, spell, tally for identification, tag, omen, *v.* agree, correspond, coincide, match.

61-- 號	symbol, sign, notation, tag, label, mark.
66-- 咒	charm, amulet, spell.
80-- 合	suit, fit, agree with, correspond, coincide, harmonize, be in conformity with, accord with, in agreement with, in line with.
-- 合市價	in line with the market.
-- 合證明	certificate of compliance.
-- 合規定	up to specifications.

8824₇
笈 〔**Chi**〕*n.* book case.

8824₈
筱 〔**Hsiao**〕*n.* young bamboo.

8825₃
筏 〔**Fa**〕*n.* raft.
箴 〔**Chen**〕*v.* warn, exhort.

00-- 言	admonition.

篾 〔**Mieh**〕*n.* bamboo splint.

00-- 席	bamboo mat.
50-- 青	bamboo-splint.

8826₁
簷 〔**Yen**〕*v.* eaves, eaves of a house.

10-- 下	under the eaves.

8828₆
籲 〔**Yu**〕*v.* pray, invoke, implore, appeal, entreat.

05-- 請	appeal, petition, request humbly.
43-- 求	implore.

8829₄
篠 〔**Hsiao**〕*n.* young bamboo.

8830₄
篷 〔**Peng**〕*n.* sail, covering, awning.

40-- 布	canvas.
47-- 帆	sail.

8832₇
篤 〔**Tu**〕*adj.* sincere, earnest, true,

serious, dangerous, deep, profound, much.

20-- 信　　　　*n.* earnest belief, *v.* have deep faith in, *adj.* faithful, honest.

8833₆
鰵〔**Min**〕*n.* perch.
27-- 魚肝油　　cod-liver oil.

8834₁
等〔**Teng**〕*n.* class, sort, rank, order, grade, *v.* wait, wait for, await, *adj.* equal to, same, same as, similar to.
08-- 於　　　　be equal to, be equivalent to, amount to.
10-- 一等　　　wait a moment (or minute).
12-- 到　　　　wait until.
20-- 重貨　　　heavy cargo, bulky cargo, measurement cargo.
21-- 價　　　　equivalence, equal in value.
　-- 價的　　　equivalent.
　-- 價物　　　equivalent.
24-- 待　　　　await.
　-- 待時間　　waiting time.
　-- 值報酬　　parity return.
　-- 候　　　　wait for, hold on.
　-- 候期　　　waiting period.
27-- 級　　　　grade, rank, class, degree, rate.
　-- 級制度　　ranking system.
　-- 級品　　　graded product.
36-- 邊　　　　equilateral.
43-- 式　　　　equation.
60-- 量　　　　equivalent.
61-- 號　　　　sign of equation.
　-- 距離　　　*n.* equal distance, *adj.* equidistant.
77-- 閑　　　　common, ordinary, usual, indifferent, negligent.
88-- 等　　　　et cetera (etc.), and so on, and so forth, so forth, so and so.

8840₁
竿〔**Kan**〕*n.* pole, rod, or cane, bamboo, bamboo pole, stick.
筵〔**Yen**〕*n.* feast, banquet.
00-- 席　　　　feast, banquet.
　-- 席稅　　　feast tax.

8840₄
簍〔**Lou**〕*n.* bamboo basket, basket, hamper.

8840₆
簟〔**Tien**〕*n.* mat.

8841₄
籬〔**Li**〕*n.* hedge, bamboo fence.
88-- 笆　　　　fence, hedge.

8843₀
笑〔**Hsiao**〕*v.* smile, laugh, ridicule, deride, make oneself merry.
02-- 話　　　　jest, joke, pleasantry, laughable mistake, nonsense!
09-- 談　　　　amusing conversation.
10-- 面虎　　　treacherous person, smiling tiger.
41-- 柄　　　　laughing-stock.
47-- 聲　　　　sound of laughter.
66-- 罵　　　　blaspheme, ridicule and revile.
78-- 臉　　　　smiling face.
80-- 着　　　　laughingly, with a laugh.
　-- 氣　　　　laughing gas.

8843₈
筴〔**Chia**〕*n.* plan, slip.

8844₁
筓〔**Chi**〕*n.* hair-pin.

8844₆
算〔**Suan**〕*v.* calculate, estimate, reckon, count, compute, plan, contrive, foretell, guess, regard, consider.
21-- 上　　　　take into account.
　-- 術　　　　arithmetic.
27-- 盤　　　　abacus, counting-frame.
43-- 式　　　　formula (in math).
58-- 數　　　　be valid.
61-- 賬　　　　do accounts, work out accounts, balance the books, make up accounts, settle account.
77-- 學　　　　mathematics.
　-- 學家　　　mathematician.
80-- 命　　　　fortune-telling.
84-- 錯　　　　miscalculate.

8844₇

籌〔**Gou**〕*n.* bamboo basket.
90-- 火狐鳴　　　rumors to mislead people.
8846₀

筘〔**Chia**〕*n.* bugle.
8850₃

箋〔**Chien**〕*n.* letter, written document, notes, writing paper, notepaper.
8850₄

篳〔**Pi**〕*n.* wicker.
8850₆

簞〔**Tan**〕*n.* bamboo basket.
8850₇

箏〔**Cheng**〕*n.* kite.

筆〔**Pi**〕*n.* pen, pencil, writing brush, *v.* write.
00-- 店　　　　　pen-shop.
03-- 試　　　　　written examination.
06-- 誤　　　　　slip of the pen, clerical error.
07-- 記　　　　　*n.* note, *v.* take note.
-- 記簿　　　　　notebook.
-- 記本　　　　　notebook.
11-- 頭　　　　　pen-nib.
27-- 名　　　　　pen name.
34-- 法　　　　　penmanship, style of writing, pen craft.
40-- 直　　　　　upright, straight.
-- 套　　　　　　pen-cap.
46-- 架　　　　　pen-stand.
-- 桿　　　　　　pen-holder.
50-- 畫　　　　　stroke, stroke in handwriting.
52-- 據　　　　　written proof.
60-- 墨難言　　　beyond description.
-- 跡　　　　　　handwriting.
71-- 匠　　　　　pen-maker.
87-- 錄　　　　　record.
88-- 管　　　　　pen-holder.
-- 算　　　　　　manual computation.
90-- 尖　　　　　tip of the pen, pen nib.
8851₂

篐〔**Ku**〕*n.* hoop, *v.* hoop, band, belt, draw tight.
47-- 桶　　　　　hoop a bucket.

範〔**Fan**〕*n.* pattern, model, standard, usage, rule, law, example, scope, range.
22-- 例　　　　　pattern, example.
50-- 本　　　　　model, pattern, copybook.
60-- 圍　　　　　limit, sphere, extent, scope, bound.
64-- 疇　　　　　category, range, scope.
8853₇

羚〔**Ling**〕*n.* antelope.
80-- 羊　　　　　antelope.
-- 羊角　　　　　antelope's horn.
8854₆

敏〔**Min**〕*adj.* active, quick, clever, sharp, skilled in, prompt, speedy, intelligent, diligent, hard-working.
08-- 於學習　　　be keen to learn.
28-- 以求之　　　work hard to get it.
40-- 力爲之　　　do it energetically.
51-- 捷　　　　　active, facile, agile.
53-- 感　　　　　*n.* sensitivity, *adj.* sensitive, allergic.
-- 感性　　　　　sensibility.
55-- 慧　　　　　intelligent, sagacious.
-- 捷　　　　　　nimble, quick-witted, alert, prompt, smart.
-- 捷機智　　　　quick-witted and sagacious.
80-- 銳　　　　　acute, keen, sharp.
-- 銳見解　　　　sagacious perception.
8857₅

箝〔**Chien**〕*n.* nipper, pincers, pliers, tweezers, *v.* fasten, clasp, lock, gag, forbid, pinch.
01-- 語　　　　　stop free speech, gag people's mouths.
17-- 子　　　　　nippers.
22-- 制　　　　　force submission.
60-- 口　　　　　shut up, reduce to silence.
77-- 緊　　　　　clasp tight.
8860₁

答〔**Ta**〕*n.* reply, answer, *v.* reply, answer, respond, recompense.
00-- 訪　　　　　return a call.
-- 辯　　　　　　plead, rebut, plea, speak in self-defence.
-- 應　　　　　　promise, respond, rejoin.
04-- 謝　　　　　convey one's thanks.
-- 謝宴會　　　　return banquet.
10-- 覆　　　　　reply, answer.

16-- 理	take notice of, pay attention to.
30-- 案	key, answer.
34-- 對如流	answer questions fluently.
35-- 禮	return the compliment.
58-- 數	result (in math).
77-- 問	answer a question.

簪 〔Tsang〕 *n*. hairpin, cap-clasp, *v*. stick in the hair, wear.

| 17-- 子 | hairpin. |

8860₂

笤 〔Tiao〕 *n*. bamboo broom.

| 17-- 帚 | bamboo broom. |

8860₃

答 〔Chih〕 *n*. scourge, *v*. flog, beat, whip.

笛 〔Di〕 *n*. fife, flute, whistle.

| 17-- 子 | fife, flute. |

8860₄

箸 〔Ju〕 *n*. chopstick.

8862₇

筍 〔Sun〕 *n*. bamboo shoot.

| 48-- 乾 | dried bamboo shoots. |

8864₁

籌 〔Chou〕 *n*. ticket, lot, chip or tally, *v*. devise, plan, plot, deliberate, raise money.

11-- 碼	counter, tally, medium of exchange.
15-- 建費	expenses for preparatory work.
20-- 委會	preparatory committee.
-- 集資金	fund, raise fund, raise capital funds.
24-- 備	prepare, plan, prepare beforehand.
-- 備處	preparation office.
-- 備成本	starting-lead cost, starting-load cost.
-- 備費	start-up cost, preliminary expenditure.
37-- 資方法	ways and means.
-- 資工具	financial vehicle.
-- 資制度	funding system.
-- 資活動	fund raising activity, fund raising campaign.

-- 資業務	financing operation.
-- 資決策	financing decision.
-- 資協定	replenishment agreement.
-- 資成本	cost of procuring money, cost of raising funds, financing cost.
-- 資目標	financing objective.
-- 資開辦人	floater.
47-- 款	raise money (or funds), procure money.
50-- 畫	devise, plan.
52-- 劃	deliberate, arrange.
54-- 措資金	finance, financing, money raising.
60-- 思	deliberate, consider.
88-- 算	compute.
-- 策	plan, scheme.

8871₁

筐 〔Kuang〕 *n*. basket, bamboo chest.

| 17-- 子 | bamboo chest. |

篦 〔Pi〕 *n*. comb, fine-toothed comb.

8871₃

篋 〔Chieh〕 *n*. trunk, chest, case.

8871₇

饈 〔Hsiu〕 *n*. meal.

笆 〔Pa〕 *n*. fence, hedge.

8872₇

飭 〔Chih〕 *v*. order, instruct, prepare, *adj*. careful, orderly, respectful.

飾 〔Shih〕 *n*. ornaments, clothing, dresses, decoration, *v*. ornament, paint, adorn, pretend, decorate.

| 07-- 詞 | *n*. pretence, ornamental words, *v*. trump up a story. |
| 27-- 物 | ornaments. |

節 〔Chieh〕 *n*. knock, joint, chapter, section, purity, chastity, paragraph, passage, node, knob, festival, season, integrity, *v*. restrain, restrict, limit, save, economize.

00-- 育	birth control.
22-- 制	*n*. temperance, moderation, *v*. control, restrain, regulate.
27-- 約	save, practice economy.
28-- 儉	*n*. frugality, economy, *v*. economize, *adj*. thrifty,

		economical, frugal.
30--	流開源	try to increase income and reduce expense.
47--	期	festival, feast.
50--	本	abridged edition.
--	奏	rhythm.
56--	拍	beat, rhythm.
60--	日	holiday, festival.
--	目	section, paragraph, program.
67--	略	abridgment, memorandum.
77--	用	economize, husband.
80--	氣	seasonal periods.
81--	短	curtail.
90--	省	spare, cut, restrain, save, frugal, practice economy, practice frugality, stint, economize.
--	省消費	retrenchment in consumption.
--	省勞力	save one's pains.
--	省費用	cut down expenses.
--	省時間	save time.
97--	慾	temperance.

篩 〔Shai〕 n. strainer, v. sift.
8873₂

簑 〔Suo〕 n. coir raincoat.
8873₃

篡 〔Tsuan〕 v. rebel, usurp, seize.

18--	政	usurp government power.
--	改	change a writing with an evil intent.
20--	位	usurp the throne.
37--	軍	usurp military power.
40--	奪	usurp, seize.
43--	弒	murder the sovereign.

8874₁

餅 〔Bing〕 n. cake, biscuits, pastry.

48--	乾	biscuit.
77--	肥	bean-cake fertilizer.

8874₆

罇=樽 4894₆
8876₁

饍 〔Shan〕 n. meal, v. eat.
8877₇

管 〔Kuan〕 n. tube, pipe, reed, flute,

		v. rule, control, govern, manage, take care of, meddle with.
10--	弦樂	orchestral music.
--	弦樂隊	orchestra.
16--	理	n. management, administration, management practice, v. dominate, govern, conduct, manage, administer, direct, control, care for, take charge of.
--	理方法	managerial approach, management process.
--	理方針	managerial policies.
--	理計劃	administrative planning.
--	理部門	management.
--	理效果	managerial effectiveness.
--	理不善	ill-management, maladministration.
--	理研究	management review.
--	理職能	management function.
--	理委員會	management council.
--	理手段	ladder of management.
--	理系統	supervisory system.
--	理集團	managerial body.
--	理能力	dynamics of management.
--	理科目	administration account.
--	理失當	misadministration, mismanagement.
--	理程序	managerial process, management procedure.
--	理制度	management system, managerial system, regulatory regime, system of management.
--	理顧問	management consultant.
--	理決策	administrative decision, management decision, managerial decision.
--	理過程	process of management.
--	理才能	management talent.
--	理概念	management concept.
--	理權	authority, right of management.
--	理機構	administrative structure, setup for economic administration.
--	理報告	management report, mana-

	gerial report.
-- 理專門化	management specialization.
-- 理成效	management performance.
-- 理成本	administration cost, handling cost, managed cost.
-- 理技能	managerial expertise.
-- 理技術	management techniques, management technology, managerial technique, soft technology.
-- 理費	administration expense, management expenses, management fee, managing expenses.
-- 理目標	management objectives.
-- 理財產	administration of property.
-- 理員	superintendent.
-- 理局	administration bureau, bureau of administration.
-- 理學	management engineer.
-- 理監督	managerial control.
-- 理人	manager, superman, administrator.
-- 理人員	managerial staff, managerial personnel, operating personnel, executives, administrative staff.
-- 理人員培訓	management training.
-- 理企業	manage (conduct) an enterprise.
-- 理公司	management company.
-- 理領導人員	management leadership.
-- 理策略	management game, management strategy.
-- 理等級	managerial class.
-- 理當局	administering authority.
17-- 子	pipe, tube.
22-- 制	control, under public surveillance, regulate.
-- 制市場	regulated market, controlled market.
-- 制商品	regulated commodity, controlled commodity.
-- 制價格	administered price, controlled price.
-- 樂	wind music.
-- 樂器	pipe, wind instrument.

30-- 家	n. steward, butler, v. keep house.
-- 家婦	housewife.
38-- 道	pipeline, channel, piping.
-- 道運輸	transportation by pipelines.
41-- 帳	accountant, treasurer.
48-- 教	teach, instruct, supervise.
50-- 管	n. manager, v. administer.
-- 束	restrain, control, restrict.
53-- 轄	n. jurisdiction, v. govern, rule over.
-- 轄權	jurisdiction.
-- 轄區域	jurisdiction.
56-- 押	keep in custody.

8879₄

餘〔**Yu**〕 n. remainder, remnant, surplus, the rest, spare time, balance, adv. after.

20-- 孽	left-over evils.
22-- 利	profit.
-- 剩	surplus.
31-- 額	balance, remaining sum, excesses of earnings, balance of earning, residual amount.
44-- 地	vacant ground.
47-- 款	spare cash.
58-- 數	remainder, margin of profit.
67-- 暇	time to spare, spare time, leisure.
77-- 閒	leisure.
96-- 糧	surplus grains.

8880₁

箕〔**Chi**〕 n. dust pan, winnower.

8880₆

簧〔**Huang**〕 n. flute, spring, spring or catch of a lock, reed (in a musical instrument).

| 00-- 言 | lie. |
| 88-- 管 | reed-pipe. |

簣〔**Kuei**〕 n. bamboo basket, wicker hod.

8884₀

斂〔**Lien**〕 v. collect, gather, shrink, contract, amass.

| 60-- 跡 | give up evil ways. |

83-- 錢	collect money, hoard money.	

8884_7

簸 〔**Bo**〕 *n.* winnow, winnowing fan, *v.* winnow.

47-- 殼	winnow grains.
56-- 揚	winnow.
88-- 箕	dust-pan, winnowing-pan.

8888_6

簽 〔**Chien**〕 *n.* lot, label, signature, *v.* sign, write one's name.

00-- 註意見	put down one's comments on a document or official correspondence.
01-- 訂	sign, conclude (treaty), conclude and sign.
-- 訂合同	sign a contract, award a contract, enter into a contract.
-- 訂日期	date of signing.
02-- 證	visa.
-- 證延期	extend a visa.
-- 證費	visa fee.
12-- 到簿	attendance book.
-- 發	issue.
-- 發地點	place of issue.
27-- 名	*n.* signature, *v.* sign, subscribe.
-- 名人	signer, subscriber.
-- 約國	signatory, signatory country, signatory power.
-- 約人	parties to a contract.
28-- 收	sign a receipt, sign in, endorse, sign after receiving something.
30-- 字	*n.* signature, *v.* sign.
-- 字樣本	signature book.
-- 字國	signatory, signatory country.
60-- 署	*n.* signature, *v.* subscribe, endorse, sign.

8890_2

策 〔**Tse**〕 *n.* plan, whip, scheme, expository writing on government affairs, *v.* whip, urge, spur.

24-- 動	instigate, incite.
30-- 進	urge.
31-- 源地	source or cradle of something.
52-- 劃	contrive, plot, plan.
67-- 略	policy, device, tactics, strategy, stratagem.
-- 略顧問	strategic consultant.
-- 略管理	strategic management.

8888_3

繁 〔**Fan**〕 *adj.* many, much, numerous, abundant, complex, complicated, manifold.

00-- 雜	complex, intricate, complicated.
14-- 殖	*n.* multiplication, *v.* propagate, breed, multiply.
19-- 瑣手續	red tape.
20-- 重	heavy, cumbersome.
27-- 多	numerous, plenty, multitudinous.
40-- 難	troublesome.
44-- 茂	luxuriant, flourishing.
-- 華	pompous, prosperous, flourishing.
53-- 盛	*v.* flourish, *adj.* abundant, blooming, prosperous.
88-- 簡	complex and simple.
90-- 忙運輸	heavy traffic.
99-- 榮	*n.* pomp, prosperity, briskness, boom, *v.* flourish, prosper.
-- 榮時期	boom period, good time.

纂 〔**Tsuan**〕 *v.* edit, compose, compile, collect, glean.

01-- 訂	revise and prepare for publication.
-- 訂工作	work of collecting and revising.
27-- 修	compile, edit.
33-- 述詞典	compile and edit a dictionary of phrases.

8890_4

築 〔**Chu**〕 *v.* build, construct, raise, erect.

41-- 壩	build a dam.
46-- 堤	build a dam, build an em-

	bankment, embank.
67-- 路	build a road, pave a road.
83-- 鐵路	build a railway.

8891_4
籮〔Lo〕*n.* basket, crate, hamper.

8893_4
筷〔Kuai〕*n.* chopstick.

| 17-- 子 | chopsticks. |
| 88-- 筒 | case for chopsticks. |

8894_0
敘＝敍 8194_7

8896_1
籍〔Chi〕*n.* record, list, register, book, one's native place.

| 77-- 貫 | birthplace, native place, one's birthplace, one's native place. |

8896_2
箱〔Hsiang〕*n.* box, trunk, chest, casket, case, container.

17-- 子	chest, box, case.
24-- 箱	in cases.
41-- 框	box frame.
44-- 蓋	lid of a box.

8898_6
籟〔Lai〕*n.* pipe, whistling.

8911_1
銧〔Guang〕*n.* radium.

8911_4
鎲〔Tang〕*n.* noise of a drum or ball, small gong.

8912_0
鈔〔Chao〕*n.* paper money, bank note.

| 10-- 票 | bank note, paper, billpaper money. |
| -- 票發行 | bank note issue. |

8912_7
銷〔Hsiao〕*v.* fuse, melt, sell, dispel, eliminate, cancel, exhaust.

16-- 魂	rapture.
20-- 售	*n.* for sale, sale, market, sell.
-- 售稅	sales tax, tax on sales.
24-- 貨	merchandise sales.
-- 貨員	salesman.
-- 貨清單	bill of sales.

30-- 案	close a case.
47-- 聲匿跡	draw in one's horns, live in seclusion.
52-- 耗	*n.* consumption, *v.* consume, waste, spend.
-- 耗浩大	cost a great deal.
60-- 暑地方	summer resort.
61-- 賬	cross off accounts, cancel a debt, cancel from an account, write off, remove from an account.
67-- 路	circulation, market demand, sale, sales outlet, market, outlet.
-- 路好	be in great demand.
77-- 毀	destroy, destroy by melting or burning, ruin, melt down.
78-- 除	*n.* elimination, *v.* eliminate.

8913_0
鍬〔Chiao〕*n.* spade, shovel.

8916_6
鐺〔Tang〕*n.* heater.

8918_6
鎖〔So〕*n.* lock, chain, fetter, *v.* lock.

20-- 住	lock up.
61-- 匙	key.
67-- 眼	keyhole.
71-- 匠	locksmith.
77-- 骨	collarbone.
-- 門	lock the door.
85-- 鏈	shackles, chains.

9

9000_0
小〔Hsiao〕*v.* belittle, *adj.* small, little, tiny, petty, slight, minute, young, trifling, narrow.

00-- 病	indisposition, slight illness.
-- 產	abortion, premature birth, miscarriage.
-- 康	well to do, in easy circumstance.
-- 商品	petty commodities.
-- 商人	small trader.
-- 廣播	gossip, hearsay.

-- 意思	token of one's appreciation.
-- 計	subtotal.
07-- 調	ballad, ditty.
08-- 說	fiction, novel, story, romance.
-- 說家	story writer, novelist.
10-- 孩	lad, urchin, child.
-- 雨	dribble, drizzle.
-- 工	coolie.
11-- 巧玲瓏	delicate and fragile.
12-- 孔	slot.
-- 型	miniature.
16-- 聰明	sharp-witted but petty-minded.
17-- 丑	buffoon, clown, jester.
-- 刀	knife.
21-- 便	n. urine, v. urinate, pass water.
-- 便處	urinal.
22-- 片	scrap, small piece.
-- 山	hill.
25-- 牛	calf.
-- 生意	petty trading.
-- 生產	small-scale production.
27-- 船	small boat.
-- 雞	chicken.
-- 島	islet.
-- 包	packet.
-- 包郵件	small packet.
-- 組	group, section, squad.
-- 組會	group meeting.
28-- 偷	pilferer, shoplifter, thief.
29-- 伙子	youth, lad, young man.
30-- 室	cabinet.
-- 窗	wicket.
-- 寫	small letter.
31-- 河	creek, rivulet.
32-- 溪	brooklet, creek.
-- 灣	creek.
-- 業主	small proprietor, small owner.
33-- 心	v. take care, beware, look out, adj. careful, regardful, cautious.
-- 心輕放	handle with care.
-- 心眼	petty-minded.
-- 心應付	handle with kid gloves.

-- 心行動	look before you leap.
-- 心火燭	caution against fire, beware of fire.
34-- 池	pool.
37-- 過	petty fault.
-- 資產階級	petty bourgeoisie.
38-- 汽船	motor boat.
-- 汽車	cycle-car, mini-car.
-- 洋	small money.
40-- 皮夾	wallet.
-- 麥	wheat, rye.
-- 賣部	canteen, buffet.
-- 才大用	man of little ability in high capacity.
41-- 帳	tip.
-- 標題	sub-heading.
44-- 鼓	snare drum.
-- 坡	hillside.
-- 村	hamlet.
-- 豬	pigling, piggy, piglet.
47-- 姐	miss.
-- 桶	keg.
-- 狗	puppy.
50-- 事	trifle, incident, trifling matter.
-- 本商人	small dealer.
-- 本經營	run or operated with a small capacity.
-- 本生意	small business.
51-- 批	small lot.
-- 批生產	job lot production, limited production.
52-- 轎車	car, sedan.
55-- 曲	ballad.
-- 費	tips, gratuity.
56-- 規模	small scale.
-- 提琴	violin.
-- 提琴家	violinist.
-- 提箱	suitcase.
58-- 輪船	steam launch, steam ship.
-- 數	decimal, decimal fraction.
-- 數點	decimal point.
60-- 星	concubine.
-- 口徑	small-caliber.
-- 品文	essay.
-- 圈子	small circle.
-- 團體	small clique, small group.

-- 團體主義	cliquism.
-- 量	small quantity.
61-- 販	vender, peddler, hawker, small trader.
-- 賬＝小費	
-- 點	dot.
-- 號	trumpet.
-- 題大做	making a molehill into a mountain.
62-- 睡	nap.
64-- 時	hour.
-- 時工資	hourly pay, per-hour wage.
67-- 路	footpath, lane.
68-- 吃部	refreshment room.
71-- 馬	colt, pony.
72-- 腦	cerebellum.
75-- 肆	stall.
76-- 腸	small intestines.
77-- 風	breeze.
-- 屋	cabin, lodge.
-- 腿	calf, shank, lower leg.
-- 冊子	pamphlet.
-- 學	elementary school, primary school.
-- 學生	pupil, elementary school student.
-- 學校	elementary school.
-- 學校長	schoolmaster.
-- 兒科	pediatrics.
-- 兒麻痺症	infantile paralysis.
-- 兒科醫生	pediatrician.
78-- 隊	squad, team.
80-- 羊	lamb.
-- 企業	small business, small concern.
-- 食	lunch.
-- 食堂	grill.
-- 氣	petty, mean, stingy, narrow-minded.
-- 人物	small man, small figure.
-- 分隊	contingent, detachment.
87-- 鋼砲	taming gun.
83-- 箱	casket.
90-- 米	millet.
-- 米加步槍	millet plus rifles.

9001_0

忙 〔Mang〕 *adj.* busy, occupied, hurried, bustling, stirring.

00-- 裏偷閒	take a breathing spell in the midst of pressing affairs.
08-- 於	be busy with, be occupied with.
10-- 不過來	have more work than one can handle properly.
17-- 碌	busy, engaged, occupied, in a bustle.
22-- 亂	in hurry and confusion, in a bustle.
26-- 得很	very busy.
50-- 中有錯	haste makes waste.
90-- 忙碌碌	fully occupied.

9001_4

惟 〔Wei〕 *v.* consider, plan, scheme, think, think of, *adv.* only, merely, simply, *conj.* but, however, only that.

10-- 一	only one.
-- 一無二	only one and second to none.
17-- 恐做錯	be afraid of making mistakes.
-- 恐失敗	fear that it may fail.
-- 恐人知	be afraid that somebody may know it.
22-- 利是圖	be interested only in material gains.
23-- 我論	solipsism.
-- 我獨尊	no one is noble but me — haughty.
27-- 物論	materialism.
-- 你是問	you are wholly responsible for it.
33-- 心論	idealism.
40-- 有	only, there is only.
-- 有一人	there is only one person.
46-- 獨	only, but.
49-- 妙惟肖	so skillfully imitated as to be indistinguishable from the original.
80-- 命是從	receive one's instruction.

憧 〔Chung〕 *v.* imagine, *adj.* irresolute, indecisive.

96-- 憬	hanker after, aspire to, imagine with yearning.

9002₇

慵 〔Yung〕 adj. indolent, lazy, idle.
94-- 惰成性　indolence has become one's second nature.

9003₀

忭 〔Pien〕 adj. delighted, joyous.

9003₁

憔 〔Chiao〕 adj. grieving, depressed, melancholy, distressed, haggard, worn-out (in one's appearance).
90-- 悴　v. languish, fade, look haggard adj. haggard.

9003₂

慷 〔Kang〕 adj. firm, generous, impassioned, bountiful, open-handed.
91-- 慨　n. generosity, liberality, adj. generous, liberal, heroic.
-- 慨言之　speak with arousing feeling.
-- 慨就義　sacrifice one's life heroically for a cause, belief, or principle.
-- 慨解囊　make generous contributions.
-- 慨激昂　impassioned.
-- 慨成仁　sacrifice one's life heroically for justice.

懷 〔Huai〕 n. bosom, breast, heart, v. hold, harbor, long for, think of.
00-- 裏　in the bosom.
17-- 孕　n. pregnancy, v. conceive, become pregnant, adj. pregnant.
27-- 疑　n. suspicion, discredit, v. doubt, distrust, suspect.
-- 疑論　skepticism.
-- 疑論者　skeptic.
42-- 妊　with child.
46-- 想　remember, think of.
57-- 抱　embrace, cherish, nestle.
80-- 念　remember, long for.
-- 着惡意　malicious, with ill intent.
-- 着好意　with good intent, have good will.
97-- 恨　cherish resentment, bear ill will, bear grudge.

9003₆

9003₇ (right column)

憶 〔I〕 v. reflect, recall, recollect, remember, think, call to mind, bear in mind.
44-- 昔之時　think of olden times.
-- 苦思甜　recall past miseries and think of present happiness.
46-- 想　remember, think about.
47-- 起　recall, call up, call to mind.
-- 起往事　recall past events.

9004₇

惇 〔Tun〕 adj. kind, generous.

9004₈

悴 〔Tsui〕 n. grief, sorrow, adj. sad, downcast.

9006₁

恬 〔Tian〕 v. remember, think of.
07-- 記　be concerned about, miss.
80-- 念往事　reflect on the past event.
90-- 懷前途　think of the road ahead.

愔 〔Yin〕 adj. quiet, still.

9009₁

懍 〔Lin〕 n. respect, inspiring awe, adj. awe-stricken.
23-- 然　awe-struck, awe-inspiring.

9010₄

堂 〔Tang〕 n. hall, mansion, court, adj. stately, lofty.
26-- 皇　proud, magnificent.
45-- 姊妹　cousin, female cousin on the father's side.
60-- 兄弟　cousin, male cousin on the father's side.
90-- 堂大國　great, powerful nation.
-- 堂皇皇　magnificent, in open view.
-- 堂正正　honorable and upright.
-- 皇大方　dignified and liberal.
-- 堂大丈夫　upright, dignified gentleman.

9020₀

少 〔Shao〕 v. lack, lose, adj. few, little, rare, scarce, seldom, young, scanty, junior, juvenile.
08-- 說閒話　save one's breath.
-- 說廢話　stop chattering!
-- 許　a little, a bit.

10-- 不得　　　*adj.* indispensable, *adv.* in-
　　　　　　　dispensably.
17-- 君　　　　master.
24-- 壯　　　　young and strong.
-- 待片刻　　　please wait a little while.
27-- 候　　　　wait a while.
-- 將　　　　　major general, rear admiral.
40-- 有　　　　*adj.* rare, scarce, seldom,
　　　　　　　adv. rarely, scarcely.
-- 女　　　　　girl, lass, young woman.
-- 校　　　　　major.
47-- 報　　　　underreport.
53-- 找錢　　　shortchange.
58-- 數　　　　*n.* minority, *adj.* a few.
-- 數民族　　　national minority.
60-- 量　　　　suspicion, pittance, sprinkle,
　　　　　　　small quantity.
-- 見多怪　　　inexperienced and easily
　　　　　　　surprised.
74-- 尉　　　　second-lieutenant.
77-- 留片刻　　please stay for a little while.
80-- 年　　　　youth, youngster, lad.
-- 年工　　　　juvenile labor.
-- 年犯　　　　juvenile delinquent.
-- 年老成　　　old head on young shoul-
　　　　　　　ders.
-- 年時代　　　boyhood, girlhood, youth.
85-- 缺　　　　insufficient, lacking.
88-- 管閒事　　don't put your finger in the
　　　　　　　pie.

9021₁

光 〔**Kuang**〕*n.* light, luster, shine, hon-
　　or, glory, *adj.* glorious, brilliant, bright,
　　glossy.
00-- 度　　　　intensity of light, light in-
　　　　　　　tensity.
-- 亮　　　　　bright, radiate.
08-- 譜　　　　spectrum.
-- 說不做　　　all talk and no deed.
10-- 天化日　　in broad daylight.
11-- 頭　　　　bareheaded, baldhead, bald.
20-- 手而來　　come with bare hands.
22-- 彩　　　　*n.* splendor, radiance, bril-
　　　　　　　liance, *adj.* shining.
-- 彩奪目　　　dazzlingly lustrous.
26-- 線　　　　light, ray, beam.
28-- 復　　　　*n.* restoration, *v.* restore.

-- 復失地　　　regain possession of the
　　　　　　　lost territory.
-- 復城池　　　restore the city.
30--宗耀祖　　glorify one's ancestors.
31-- 顧　　　　patronize.
-- 源　　　　　source of light.
34-- 被四表　　your benefits are spread in
　　　　　　　the four directions.
36-- 澤　　　　*n.* gloss, luster, *adj.* lu-
　　　　　　　strous.
37-- 潔　　　　smooth, refined.
-- 輝　　　　　*n.* brilliancy, *adj.* splendid,
　　　　　　　brilliant.
-- 滑　　　　　smooth, polished, glossy.
-- 滑如鏡　　　bright and smooth as a mir-
　　　　　　　ror.
40-- 大門楣　　do honor to one's family.
44-- 帶　　　　spectrum.
-- 芒　　　　　ray.
-- 芒萬丈　　　shining far and wide, bril-
　　　　　　　liant, radiant.
-- 芒四射　　　flash of light radiating in
　　　　　　　all directions.
46-- 棍　　　　bad egg, scoundrel, villain,
　　　　　　　single man.
-- 棍兒生活　　life of a single man.
60-- 景　　　　outlook, prospect, circum-
　　　　　　　stances.
-- 景甚佳　　　one's circumstance is rather
　　　　　　　good.
-- 圈　　　　　aperture of a camera.
67-- 明　　　　*n.* brightness, light, *adj.*
　　　　　　　bright.
-- 明正大　　　above-board, open and abo-
　　　　　　　ve-board.
-- 明磊落　　　frank, open.
77-- 學　　　　optics.
-- 學儀器　　　optical apparatus.
-- 學檢測　　　optical detection.
-- 學家　　　　optician.
-- 腳　　　　　barefooted.
78-- 陰　　　　time.
-- 陰倏過　　　the hours run rapidly by.
-- 陰似箭　　　time flies like an arrow.
-- 陰如流水　　time passes like flowing
　　　　　　　water.
-- 臨　　　　　arrive, come over.

-- 臨舍下   your arrival at my house.
80-- 年   light-year.
-- 合作用   photosynthesis.
97-- 怪陸離   strange looking.
-- 耀門楣   bring honor to the family
                 name.
-- 輝   splendor, blaze.
-- 輝燦爛   glorious and lustrous, bril-
                 liant.
99-- 榮   glory, honor, splendor.
-- 榮榜   board of honor, roll of hon-
                 or.
-- 榮傳統   glorious tradition.

9021₄
雀 〔**Chiao**〕 n. small bird, sparrow,
small birds like sparrows.
11-- 斑   freckle.
22-- 巢   sparrow's nest.
67-- 躍   dance for joy.
-- 躍歡呼   jump and cheer.

9022₇
肖 〔**Hsiao**〕 v. resemble, be like, adj.
like, similar.
27-- 像   portrait, image, semblance,
                 snapshot.
28-- 似   v. resemble, adj. alike.

尚 〔**Shang**〕 v. honor, respect, esteem,
uphold, adv. however, nevertheless,
still, yet.
05-- 請教正   Please give me some ad-
                 vice.
10-- 可   still possible, passable.
13-- 武精神   militarism, warlike spirit,
                 martial spirit.
24-- 待證明   remain to be seen.
40-- 有   there are still some.
-- 有可爲   still retrievable.
-- 有他事   have other fish to fry, have
                 something else to do.
-- 來得及   there is still time to do it.
50-- 未   not yet.
-- 未確定   be all in the air.
77--且   still, even.
80-- 無不可   permissible.

券 〔**Chuan**〕 n. ticket, note, bond.

常 〔**Chang**〕 adv. always, frequently,
often, usually, constantly.
03-- 識   common sense.
07-- 設委員會   permanent committee.
-- 設機構   permanent establishment.
09-- 談   common talk.
17-- 務委員   member of standing com-
                 mittee.
-- 務   day-to-day business, rou-
                 tine.
-- 務董事   standing director, managing
                 director.
-- 務委員會   standing committee, work-
                 ing committee, executive
                 committee, regular com-
                 mittee.
20-- 住工程師   resident engineer.
-- 住人口   permanent population.
21-- 態   normal.
-- 衡制   avoirdupois system.
22-- 任審計員   standing auditor.
24-- 備庫存   running stock.
-- 備軍   regular troop, standing
                 army.
40-- 去   resort, go often.
50-- 事   usual thing.
56-- 規   routine.
-- 規工作   routine job.
-- 規檢查   routine inspection.
70-- 駐辦事處   resident office.
-- 駐代理商   resident agent.
-- 駐代表   resident representative.
-- 駐專家   resident expert.
-- 駐公司   resident company.
80-- 人   common being.
-- 年雇用   year-round employment.
-- 年定單   standing order.
-- 年展覽   perennial exhibition.
-- 年客戶   regular client (customer).
90-- 常   always, often, frequently.

9023₂
豢 〔**Cheng**〕 v. feed, feed animals with
grains, support.
80-- 養   rear, feed.

9024₁
弮 〔**Shen**〕 v. support.

9033₁

黨 〔Tang〕 *n.* party, league, clique, faction, relatives, friends, *v.* take sides.

00-- 章	party constitution.
08-- 旗	party banner.
17-- 羽	followers, adherents.
20-- 委	party committee.
-- 爭	factional squabble.
24-- 徒	follower, adherent.
26-- 總支	general party branch.
27-- 綱	party policy, party program, platform.
-- 的建設	party-building.
28-- 齡	party standing.
32-- 派	party, faction, party groupings, cliques.
40-- 校	party school.
-- 支部	party branch.
44-- 權	party power.
50-- 中央	Central Committee of the Party.
55-- 費	membership dues.
60-- 國	party and state.
-- 員	party member, partisan.
62-- 則	party rules.
74-- 魁	leader of a party, cock of the roost.
77-- 風	style in the party's internal and external relations.
-- 閥	factional leaders.
80-- 八股	stereotyped party writing.
90-- 小組	party groups, basic units of the party.
95-- 性	party spirit.

9042₇

劣 〔Lieh〕 *adj.* bad, inferior, ill, mean.

31-- 行	misconduct, ill behavior.
24-- 貨	low-grade goods, cheap stuff, faulty goods.
44-- 勢	inferiority, unfavorable situation.
60-- 跡	bad reputation, infamous behavior.
72-- 質	poor, bad, of inferior quality.
88-- 等	inferior grade, low grade.
-- 等貨	substandard goods, low-grade goods, seconds.
95-- 紳	evil (or vicious) gentry, depraved gentry.
97-- 根性	bad characteristics, depraved character.

9043₀

尖 〔Chien〕 *n.* tip or point of something, top, *adj.* sharp, pointed, keen.

02-- 端	tip, top, point, acme.
-- 端產品	highly sophisticated products.
-- 端技術	sophisticated technique.
-- 端科學	sophisticated science.
11-- 頂	peak, spire, apex.
17-- 子	ace.
-- 刀	sharp-pointed knife.
-- 刀班	Dagger Squad.
21-- 齒	jag.
42-- 刺	prick.
60-- 圓形	conical.
72-- 兵	vanguard.
88-- 銳	sharp, acute.
-- 銳化	intensify.

9050₀

半 〔Pan〕 *n.* half, *v.* divide, halve.

00-- 夜	midnight.
-- 夜三更	midnight and third watch.
02-- 新不舊	half-new.
08-- 旗	flag at half-mast.
10-- 工半讀	work one's way through school, part work part study.
-- 死不活	half-dying.
-- 票	half-price ticket, half-fare.
13-- 球	hemisphere.
14-- 殖民地	semi-colony.
20-- 信半疑	be half-believing and half-doubting.
21-- 價	half-price.
-- 價出售	sell at a half price.
-- 徑	radius.
25-- 生不死	half-dead.
-- 生半死	half alive, half dead.
26-- 自動化	semi-automation.
27-- 島	peninsula.
-- 身像	bust.
-- 身不遂	hemiplegia.
30-- 官方	semi-official.

32-- 透明	translucent.	
33-- 心半意	half-hearted.	
36-- 途	midway, halfway.	
37-- 通不通	know or understand only a little.	
38-- 導體	semiconductor, transistor.	
-- 導體收音機	transistor radio.	
-- 途而廢	give up halfway.	
40-- 賣半送	sell goods at rock bottom prices.	
42-- 機械化	semi-mechanization.	
44-- 封建	semi-feudal.	
-- 薪	half-pay.	
47-- 期	half life.	
50-- 推半就	with half-refusal and half consent.	
53-- 成品	semi-finished product, partly finished product.	
58-- 數	half, half quantity.	
-- 輪明月	a radiant half-moon.	
60-- 圓	semicircle.	
-- 日	half a day.	
-- 日學校	half-day school.	
-- 吊子	shallow person.	
62-- 睡半醒	somnolence.	
67-- 路	halfway.	
-- 路出家	without solid foundation or training, start midway.	
-- 明半暗	half-bright and half-shadowy.	
-- 晌不語	be silent for a moment.	
70-- 壁江山	half of the national territory.	
72-- 斤八兩	not much to choose between the two.	
77-- 月	half a month.	
-- 月刊	semimonthly.	
-- 月形	crescent-shaped.	
-- 學年	semester.	
-- 開半掩	half-opened, half-closed.	
78-- 鋼	semi steel.	
80-- 年	half a year.	

9050_2

拳 〔Chuan〕 *n.* fist, boxing, *v.* clasp, grasp.

11-- 頭	fist.
21-- 術	boxing, the manly art.
51-- 打	strike with the fist.

71-- 師	boxer.

掌 〔Chang〕 *n.* palm, sole, *v.* grasp, slap with the hand.

41-- 櫃	accountant, teller.
57-- 握	grasp.

9060_1

嘗 〔Chang〕 *v.* taste, test, try, *adv.* ever, already.

03-- 試	try, attempt, endeavor.
-- 試法	trial and error procedure.
65-- 味	taste.

9060_2

省 〔Sheng〕 *n.* province, *v.* visit, examine, examine oneself, enquire, perceive, feel, abbreviate, save, economize, spare, reserve, awake to, test.

06-- 親	visit one's parents.
08-- 議會	provincial assembly.
18-- 政府	provincial government.
20-- 委	Provincial Party Committee.
27-- 約	abridge.
28-- 儉	frugal, thrifty, economical.
33-- 減	reduce, economize.
40-- 力	labor-saving.
-- 去	omit.
47-- 城=省會	
-- 卻	spare, avoid.
50-- 事	avoid trouble.
64-- 時	save time.
67-- 略	save, omit, jump over, abridge.
-- 略號	ellipsis.
71-- 長	governor.
80-- 會	provincial capital.
-- 分	province.
83-- 錢	save money.
88-- 筆	abbreviation.
90-- 黨部	provincial party headquarters.
91-- 悟	*v.* awake, realize, *adj.* convinced.

9060_3

眷 〔Chuan〕 *n.* family, relative, dependents, *v.* love, be fond of, care for, look after, long for.

77--	屬	one's family, one's dependents.
80--	念	care for, regard with affection.

9060₆

當 〔Dang〕 *n.* trap, *v.* be, become, ought to, be in charge of, accept, deserve, face, match, equal, happen, pawn, pledge, regard as, take as, *adj.* suitable, proper, equal, *conj.* when, as soon as, while, *prep.* during.

10--	下	just now, presently.
--	票	pawn-ticket.
--	天	today, that day, at the same day, during that day.
--	面	face to face, in the presence of.
--	面言明	state clearly in one's presence.
11--	班	be on duty.
17--	務之急	business or task of the greatest urgency at present.
20--	受	deserve.
23--	然	of course, by all means, naturally, certainly.
--	代	contemporary, present age.
--	代豪傑	hero of the present age.
28--	作	take as.
30--	家	*n.* housekeeper, head of a household, *v.* keep up a household.
--	之無愧	deserve.
33--	心	beware, take care.
--	心破碎	fragile.
--	心扒手	watch out for pickpockets!
37--	選	be elected.
--	選人	elected person.
--	初	originally, at first, in the beginning, at the beginning.
40--	真	be serious, be in earnest.
44--	地	local.
--	地價格	local price.
--	地存貨	local stocks.
--	地公司	local company.
--	權	*n.* authorities, *v.* be in power, keep in power.

--	權派	clique in power.
--	機立斷	decide promptly.
46--	場	on the spot.
--	場交貨	spot delivery.
--	場付款	prompt cash, sharp cash.
--	場決定	on-the-spot decision.
--	場出醜	suffer embarrassment right before a crowd.
50--	中	among, in the midst.
--	事人	party concerned, person concerned.
60--	日	today, nowadays.
--	眾	in the presence of all, before the public, in public.
--	眾宣布	announce publicly.
--	眾拍賣	public auction.
64--	時	then, meanwhile, at that time.
--	時市價	current market value.
72--	兵	join the army, become a serviceman.
77--	局	authorities.
80--	差	take charge.
--	今	at present.
--	前	present, current.
--	前市況	the ruling market.
--	前形勢	prevailing situation.
--	令	seasonable.
--	年	that year, in former years.
83--	鋪	pawnshop.

9071₂

卷 〔Chuan〕 *n.* volume, copy, roll, scroll, book, examination paper, *v.* roll up, *adj.* curved, curled.

10--	一	first volume, volume I .
17--	子	examination papers.
22--	紙=卷子	
30--	宗	archives, filed documents.
45--	帙浩繁	books are numerous.
96--	煙工業	tobacco industry.

9073₂

裳 〔Shang〕 *n.* garment, skirt, petticoat, clothes.

9080₀

火 〔Huo〕 *n.* fire, flame, fever, firearms, *v.* burn, get angry, *adj.* red, fire-like, urgent, speedy.

10-- 石	flint.	
-- 電站	thermal power station.	
20-- 雞	turkey.	
21-- 上加油	set the heater on fire.	
-- 柴	match.	
-- 柴桿	matchwood.	
-- 柴匣	matchbox.	
22-- 山	volcano.	
-- 種	tinder, ember.	
-- 災	fire, calamity of fire, conflagration.	
-- 災保險	fire insurance.	
-- 災保險費	fire insurance premium.	
-- 災保險單	fire insurance policy, fire policy.	
-- 災危險	fire peril.	
-- 災損失	fire losses.	
27-- 網	barrage, cross fire.	
-- 急	urgent, very urgent.	
28-- 傷	burned.	
29-- 燄	flame.	
31-- 酒	alcohol.	
35-- 速	extra urgent.	
-- 速送到	deliver immediately.	
-- 油	kerosene, kerosene oil.	
36-- 邊	fireside.	
38-- 海戰術	tactics featuring intensive firepower to counter human-wave tactics.	
40-- 力	combustive force, fire power, thermal.	
-- 力集中	concentration of fire.	
44-- 花	sparks.	
-- 藥	gunpowder, ammunition.	
-- 藥味	smell of gunpowder.	
-- 藥庫	magazine.	
-- 葬	n. cremation, v. cremate.	
-- 葬場	crematory.	
45-- 棒	poker.	
48-- 警	fire alarm.	
50-- 夫	fireman.	
-- 車	train.	
-- 車站	railway station.	
-- 車站站長	station master.	
-- 車票	railway ticket.	
-- 車頭	locomotive, engine, iron house.	

-- 車渡輪	train-ferry.	
-- 車車廂	carriage.	
-- 車時刻表	railway timetable.	
56-- 損	fire damage.	
57-- 把（炬）	torch, firebrand, torchlight.	
60-- 星	planet Mars.	
77-- 腿	ham, Chinese ham.	
-- 腿蛋	ham and egg.	
78-- 險	fire insurance, fire risk.	
-- 險保險商	fire underwriter.	
-- 險合同	fire insurance contract.	
-- 險公司	fire insurance company.	
79-- 燄	flames.	
80-- 氣	hot temper, anger.	
-- 盆	brazier.	
84-- 鉗	tongs.	
88-- 箭	rocket, missile.	
-- 箭筒	rocket launcher.	
-- 箭技術	rocketry.	
90-- 光	fire-light.	
91-- 爐	stove, fire.	
-- 炬	torch.	
92-- 焰	blaze, flame.	
96-- 線	firing line.	
97-- 炮	cannon, gun.	

9080₁

糞〔**Fen**〕n. ordure, dung, feces, muck, manure, night soil.

34-- 斗	tumbrel.	
40-- 坑	manure pit, cesspit, cesspool.	
47-- 桶	dung tub, night-soil tub.	
50-- 車	dung-cart, night-cart.	
-- 夫	night-soil man.	
77-- 肥	muck, manure.	
88-- 箕	dustpan.	

9080₆

賞〔**Shang**〕n. rewards, prize, v. reward, bestow, confer, grant, appreciate, enjoy.

03-- 識	n. appreciation, v. appreciate, recognize a person's virtues.	
11-- 玩	enjoy.	
26-- 牌	prize, medal.	
60-- 罰	reward and punishment.	
66-- 賜	guerdon, gift from a su-	

perior.
80-- 金　　　reward.

9080₉

炎 〔Yen〕 n. flame, blaze, v. flame, blaze, adj. brilliant, glorious, hot, burning.
00-- 症　　　inflammation.
10-- 夏　　　hot summer.
44-- 熱　　　blazing heat, very hot.
60-- 日　　　burning sun.

9081₄

炷 〔Chu〕 n. wick.

9081₇

炕 〔Keng〕 n. dry, brick bed warmed by a fire underneath, v. dry.
24-- 牀　　　hot bed.

9082₇

熇 〔Kao〕 v. dry by fire.

9083₂

炫 〔Hsuan〕 v. dazzle, lighten, shine, show off, adj. luminous, shining, dazzling.
60-- 目　　　dazzle the eves.
97-- 耀　　　n. bravery. v. showoff, display, adj. dazzling, shining.
-- 耀於人　　show off before others.

9084₈

焠=淬 3014₈

9086₁

焙 〔Pei〕 v. bake, dry, scorch.
48-- 乾　　　dry by fire.
98-- 粉　　　caking-powder, baking-powder.

9090₄

米 〔Mi〕 n. rice, food, husked and uncooked rice, meter.
00-- 店　　　rice shop.
27-- 色　　　rice color.
30-- 突　　　meter or metre.
36-- 湯　　　rice soup.
81-- 飯　　　cooked rice.
90-- 糠　　　rice husk, rice bran.
98-- 粉　　　rice flour.
-- 糕　　　rice cake.

棠 〔Tang〕 n. begonia.

9091₄

粧 〔Chuang〕 v. dress up, ornament, adorn, adorn or doll up.
58-- 扮　　　dress up, adorn.

9091₈

粒 〔Li〕 n. grain, kernel, granule, pill.
17-- 子　　　grain, pill.
23-- 狀　　　granular.

9093₂

糠 〔Kang〕 n. bran, husk, chaff.
44-- 皮　　　chaff, rice bran.

9094₈

粹 〔Sui〕 adj. pure, unmixed.

9096₇

糖 〔Tang〕 n. sugar, honey, candy.
00-- 廠　　　sugar refinery.
12-- 水　　　molasses, syrup.
16-- 彈　　　sugar-coated bullet, sugar-coated poison.
22-- 醬　　　jam.
27-- 漿　　　syrup, molasses, jam.
31-- 酒　　　rum.
60-- 果　　　candy, sweetmeat, sweets, confection.
-- 果店　　　confectionery, candy store.
77-- 尿病　　diabetes.
95-- 精　　　saccharin.

9101₁

怔 〔Cheng〕 adj. fearful, afraid.
恇 〔Kuang〕 adj. timid.

9101₃

愜 〔Chieh〕 adj. satisfied, contented, pleased, cheerful, joyful.
00-- 意　　　pleased, satisfied, contented.
33-- 心　　　satisfied, pleased, contented.
95-- 情愜意　　satisfied and pleased.

9101₄

慨 〔Kai〕 n. generous, generous feeling, v. sigh emotionally, adj. noble-minded, generous.
23-- 允　　　consent readily.
-- 然　　　generously.
-- 然允諾　　consent generously.

64-- 嘆　　　sigh mournfully.

9101₆

恒〔Heng〕*adj*. constant, regular, perpetual, permanent.

00-- 產　　　immovable property, real estate.

27-- 久　　　perpetual, permanent, for a long time.

30-- 定　　　constant.

33-- 心　　　constancy, stableness, perseverance.

36-- 溫　　　constant temperature.

60-- 星　　　fixed star.

88-- 等式　　(in math) identity, identical equation.

90--常　　　permanent, constant.

慪〔Ou〕*v*. annoy.

80-- 氣　　　*v*. annoy, exasperate, *adj*. exasperated.

9101₇

恆=恒 9101₆

9102₇

懦〔No〕*adj*. timid, weak, cowardly, feeble, infirm.

17-- 弱　　　weak, feeble, cowardly, feeble-minded, weak-spirited.

50-- 夫　　　coward.

9103₂

悵〔Chang〕*adj*. despaired, disappointed, frustrated, discontented.

23-- 然　　　disappointedly.

-- 然於懷　　be dissatisfied in one's bosom.

97-- 惘　　　dispirited, depressed.

9103₄

懨〔Yen〕*adj*. sickish.

9104₁

懾〔Che〕*v*. fear, subdue, influence, bring under, *adj*. afraid, agitated.

08-- 於權勢　　be awed by one's authority.

77-- 服　　　yield because of fear.

9104₆

悼〔Tao〕*v*. grieve for, pity, lament, bewail, mourn, *adj*. sad, mournful, sorrowful.

07-- 詞　　　memorial speech.

80-- 念　　　mourn for.

94-- 惜　　　feel great sorrow for.

9104₉

怦〔Peng〕*adj*. impulsive, earnest, eager.

9106₁

悟〔Wu〕*n*. enlightenment, *v*. awake, become aware of, understand, apprehend, realize, (in Buddhism) be enlightened.

95-- 性　　　ability to understand.

-- 性不佳　　be dull of comprehension.

-- 性極好　　be excellent in the power of comprehension.

9106₆

愢〔Pi〕*adj*. honest, sincere.

9108₉

恢〔Hui〕*v*. enlarge, magnify, recover, restore, *adj*. liberal, great, extensive.

28-- 復　　　*n*. restoration, *v*. restore, recover, make good.

-- 復健康　　recover from illness, recuperate.

-- 復生產　　resumption of production.

-- 復原狀　　revert to the original condition, reinstate.

9109₁

慄〔Li〕*adj*. afraid, frightened, fearful.

9148₆

類〔Lei〕*n*. class, category, species, kind, sort, race, *adj*. similar, like, resembling, alike.

12-- 型　　　type, pattern.

21-- 此　　　like this.

28-- 似　　　*v*. resemble, be similar, *adj*. similar, like, resembling.

50-- 推　　　analogize, by analogy.

60-- 目　　　category.

62-- 別　　　category, classification, sort, class.

9154₇

叛〔Pan〕*v*. rebel, revolt.

22-- 亂　　　*n*. insurrection, rebellion, revolt, *v*. rebel, revolt.

-- 變　　　*n*. rebellion, insurrection, mutiny, *v*. rebel, revolt.

24-- 徒 traitor, renegade, rebel, mutineer.

38-- 逆 *v.* rebel, *adj.* traitorous.

-- 逆罪 treason.

60-- 國 sedition, treason.

-- 國罪 high treason, treason felony.

-- 國分子 traitor.

71-- 匪 rebel, bandit.

90-- 黨 *n.* rebellious party, *v.* turn against the party.

9181₄

煙 〔Yen〕 *n.* smoke, vapor, mist tobacco.

00-- 塵 smoke and dust.

26-- 囪 funnel, chimney.

34-- 斗 pipe.

44-- 草 tobacco.

-- 幕 smoke screen.

-- 幕彈 smoke bomb.

83-- 館 opium dens.

90-- 火 firework.

94-- 煤 softcoal.

9181₇

炬 〔Chu〕 *n.* torch, torchlight, firebrand.

爐 〔Lu〕 *n.* stove, oven, fireplace, furnace.

17-- 子 stove, furnace.

-- 子間 furnace room.

36-- 邊 fireside.

-- 邊談話 fireside chat.

9182₀

灯=**燈** 9281₈

9182₇

炳 〔Bing〕 *adj.* bright, brilliant.

9186₆

煏 〔Bi〕 *v.* dry.

9188₆

煩 〔Fan〕 *n.* annoyance, trouble, vexation, *v.* vex, annoy, trouble, *adj.* troublesome, annoyed, perplexed.

00-- 交 care of.

19-- 瑣 trivial, troublesome.

-- 瑣不堪 unbearably troublesome.

-- 瑣哲學 scholasticism.

22-- 亂 discomposed, bothered.

33-- 心 weight on one's mind.

35-- 神 vexatious, troublesome.

40-- 難 burdensome, troublesome, arduous.

51-- 擾 harass, trouble, annoy, bother, disturb.

66-- 躁 fretful, ill-tempered.

-- 躁不安 have the fidgets.

77-- 悶 annoyed, vexed, depressed, perplexed, grieved.

92-- 惱 *v.* worry, vex, *adj.* annoyed, vexatious, vexed, perplexed.

9191₄

糎 〔Li〕 *n.* centimeter.

9192₇

糯 〔No〕 *n.* glutinous rice.

90-- 米 glutinous rice.

糲 〔Li〕 *n.* coarse grain, uncleaned rice.

9194₆

粳 〔Keng〕 *n.* nonglutinous rice.

90-- 米 round-shaped nonglutinous rice.

9196₀

粘=**黏** 2116₀

9200₀

惻 〔Tse〕 *v.* pity, sympathize.

72-- 隱 natural sympathies.

9201₈

愷 〔Kai〕 *adj.* joyful, cheerful, contented, satisfied, gentle.

9202₁

忻=**欣** 7728₀

慚 〔Tsan〕 *adj.* ashamed, shy.

96-- 愧 shame, shameful, ashamed.

9202₇

惴 〔Chui〕 *adj.* sorrowful, afraid, anxious, uneasy.

92-- 惴不安 worried, afraid, anxious.

9204₇

悸 〔Chi〕 *v.* palpitate, pant, *adj.* uneasy, perturbed, hanging.

24-- 動 pant, throb, palpitate.

9206₂

惱 〔Nao〕 n. vexation, irritation, anger, v. anger, annoy, adj. angered, vexed, annoyed.

47--	怒	vexed, angry.
80--	人	irritating, annoying.
--	羞成怒	become angry from embarrassment.
97--	恨	hate, detest.

9206_4

恬 〔Tien〕 adj. calm, quiet, still, peaceful, undisturbed, tranquil.

10--	不知恥	shameless, unblushing.
23--	然	undisturbed.
52--	靜	quiet, tranquil.

惛 〔Hun〕 adj. stupid, dull, confused in mind.

9220_0

削 〔Hsiao〕 v. cut, shave, sharpen, pare off, scrape off, strike out.

10--	平	level, raze, out raze.
13--	球	cut the ball.
17--	弱	weaken, diminish.
21--	價	price-cut, lower the price.
33--	減	curtail, retrench, cut down.
40--	皮	rind, scrape off.
--	去	pare off, deduct, take away.
70--	壁	cliff.
78--	除	cut off.
87--	鉛筆	sharpen a pencil.
90--	尖	sharpen.

9250_2

判 〔Pan〕 n. decision, verdict, v. judge, decide, distinguish, separate, halve, sentence.

01--	語	sentence, judgment.
--	語正當	a judgment is justified.
07--	詞	sentence.
22--	斷	n. judgment, v. judge, give judgment.
--	斷力	judgment.
--	斷錯誤	back the wrong horse.
30--	定	judge, decide.
--	官	judge.
35--	決	n. verdict, sentence, decision, determination, v. sentence, judge, decree.
--	袂以來	ever since we parted.

44--	若兩人	become as different as if one weren't the same person.
--	若天淵	the difference is as between the heavens and depths.
--	若鴻溝	the difference is far reaching.
60--	罪	n. conviction, v. condemn.

9280_0

剡 〔Yen〕 adj. sharp.

9281_8

燈 〔Teng〕 n. lamp, light, lantern.

11--	頭	electric light socket.
33--	心	wick.
--	心絨	corduroy.
37--	泡	electric bulb, lightbulb.
44--	臺	lamp stand.
--	塔	lighthouse, beacon.
--	塔船	lightship.
--	芯	lamp wick.
46--	架	lamp stand, lamp holder.
60--	罩	lamp shade.
88--	籠	lantern.
--	籠褲	knickers, knickerbockers, plus-fours.
--	節	lantern festival.
90--	光（火）	lamplight.
--	光廣告	illuminated advertising (signs).
--	火管制	blackouts.
--	火輝煌	brilliant lights.

9283_1

燻＝燻 2033_1

9284_6

爝 〔Chueh〕 n. torch.

9284_7

煖 〔Nuan〕 adj. warm, genial, soft.

87--	鍋	copper heater, table pan.

9286_9

燔 〔Fan〕 v. roast.

40--	肉	steak.

9289_4

爍 〔Shuo〕 v. melt, smelt, adj. bright, brilliant, flaring, sparkling.

9301_1

悾〔**Kung**〕*adj.* ignorant.
9301₂

悗〔**Wan**〕*v.* be surprised, be startled, be alarmed, sigh, regret, *adj.* alarmed, surprised, annoyed, vexed.

94-- 惜	regret, feel sorry for.
-- 惜嗟歎	grieve and heave a sigh.

9302₂

慘〔**Tsan**〕*adj.* sorrowful, grieved, sad, miserable, cruel, tragical, ruthless, brutal, dark, dull.

00-- 痛	distressing, painful.
10-- 死	die distressingly.
-- 不忍睹	tragic that one cannot bear to look at it.
12-- 刑	torture, cruel punishment.
14-- 酷	cruel.
20-- 重	disastrous, calamitous.
22-- 劇	tragedy.
23-- 狀	sadness, wretchedness.
27-- 絕人寰	so miserable that it can hardly be found in the human world.
35-- 遭橫禍	meet a tragic accident.
37-- 禍	dire calamity.
-- 澹經營	take pains on the undertaking.
65-- 跌	sharp fall, sharp drop.
68-- 敗	bitter defeat, disastrous defeat.
80-- 無天日	so dark, or full of suffering, that it is as if the sun were not in the sky.
-- 無人道	inhuman, brutal.

9304₇

悛〔**Chuan**〕*v.* change, alter, repent, reform.

9305₀

憾〔**Han**〕*n.* vexation, regret, hatred, enmity, remorse, *adj.* regretful, regrettable.

50-- 事	regrettable matter, matter of regret.
97-- 恨	deep regret.
98-- 悔已遲	it is too late to regret now.

懺〔**Chan**〕*v.* regret, repent, feel sorry for, confess one's sins.

78-- 除罪障	repent and to remit sin and retribution.
98-- 悔	*n.* repentance, *v.* repent, regret.
-- 悔改過	repent and reform oneself.
-- 悔自新	repent and to reform oneself.

9306₀

怡〔**I**〕*n.* concord, *adj.* harmonious, pleasant, delightful, pleased.

01-- 顏悅色	cheerful and pleasant look.
23-- 然自得	happy and satisfied.
47-- 聲下氣	with a subdued and soft voice.
98-- 悅	rejoice, be delightful, pleased at.

9309₄

怵〔**Shu**〕*adj.* afraid, fearful.
9381₆

煊〔**Shun**〕*adj.* shining, bright.
9382₇

煽〔**Shan**〕*v.* excite, stir up, blaze, fan, flame, instigate.

22-- 亂	sedition.
24-- 動	*n.* agitation, incitement, *v.* instigate, incite, agitate, stir, blow upon.
-- 動者	instigator, agitator.
53-- 惑人心	undermine popular morale by spreading unfounded rumors.

9383₃

燃〔**Jan**〕*v.* burn, light, fire, ignite, kindle.

47-- 起	ignite.
77-- 屑	ember.
-- 眉之急	as urgent as if the eyebrows were burning, extremely urgent.
94-- 燒	*n.* combustion, *v.* burn, fire.
-- 燒彈	incendiary bomb, incendiary shell.
-- 燒物	combustibles.
-- 料	fuel.
-- 料庫	fuel storage, fuel depot.

9385₀

熾 〔 Chih 〕 *n.* flame, glare, blaze, *v.* burn, blaze up, illumine, *adj.* flourishing, raging.

44-- 熱　　　　intense heat.
53-- 盛之時　　at the time of abundance.
9386₈

熔 〔 Jung 〕 *v.* melt.
9392₂

糝 〔 San 〕 *n.* grain.
9393₂

粮=糧 9691₄
9399₁

粽=糉 9294₇
9400₀

忖 〔 Tsun 〕 *v.* guess, suppose, conjecture, ponder, calculate, imagine, surmise.

00-- 度　　　　consider, conjecture, guess, suppose, presume, ponder.
-- 度人心　　　conjecture at another's mind.
32-- 測不差　　The guess is not wrong.
9401₁

慌 〔 Huang 〕 *v.* be alarmed, apprehend, be nervous, be afraid, lose self-possession, *adj.* agitated, excited, hurried, alarmed, nervous, startled.

11-- 張　　　　abashed, alarmed.
22-- 亂　　　　hurried and confused, in disorder, confused.
28-- 作一團　　panic-stricken, fall into a flutter.
90-- 忙　　　　in a hurry, hurried.
94-- 慌張張　　be in a hurry-scurry.
9401₂

忱 〔 Shen 〕 *n.* heart, *adj.* sincere.
9401₄

懂 〔 Tung 〕 *v.* understand, perceive, know.

18-- 政策　　have a grasp of policy, understand the policy.
26-- 得　　　know, comprehend, be familiar with.

懽=歡 4728₀

9402₇

怖 〔 Pu 〕 *v.* frighten, *adj.* afraid, frightened, terrified.

96-- 懼鬼神　　be scared of spiritual beings.

惰 〔 To 〕 *n.* laziness, idleness, indolence, *adj.* lazy, idle, indolent.

23-- 怠　　　lazy, idle.
38-- 遊　　　loaf about.
95-- 性　　　inertia.

慟 〔 Tung 〕 *n.* extreme grief, deep sorrow, *v.* bewail, lament.

66-- 哭　　　lament, mourn, wail.
-- 哭不已　　crying from sorrow incessantly.
9403₁

怯 〔 Chueh 〕 *v.* be afraid, lose heart, *adj.* shy, timid, afraid, fearful, timorous, cowardly.

46-- 場　　　stage-fright.
80-- 羞　　　bashful, shy.
91-- 懦　　　*n.* cowardice, timidity, *adj.* timid, cowardly.
-- 懦無能　　cowardly and incompetent.
9404₁

恃 〔 Shih 〕 *v.* trust, depend upon, rely upon, turn to, presume upon.

40-- 力　　　rely on one's strength.
44-- 勢　　　presume on one's power.
-- 勢凌人　　presume upon one's power and bully others.
64-- 財　　　presume upon one's wealth.

悻 〔 Hsing 〕 *adj.* angry, indignant.

94-- 悻　　　angrily, sullenly.
-- 悻然　　　enraged.
9404₇

忮 〔 Chih 〕 *v.* envy, be jealous, *adj.* stubborn.

43-- 求　　　jealous and covetous.

悖 〔 Pei 〕 *adj.* unreasonable, disobedient.

38-- 逆　　　rebellious.
9406₀

怙 〔 Hu 〕 *n.* one's father, *v.* depend on,

rely on.

10-- 惡凌人　intimidate and oppress others.

27-- 終不改　persist in one's ways.

9406₁
惜〔Hsi〕v. spare, pity, compassionate, regret, love.

27-- 物　careful of things, no wasteful.

78-- 陰　be careful of one's time.

83-- 錢　save money.

9406₂
懵〔Meng〕adj. stupid, ignorant, dull, confused, muddle-headed.

94-- 懂　muddle-headed.

9408₁
慎〔Shen〕n. carefulness, prudence, adj. cautious, careful, attentive, prudent.

00-- 言　be careful in speaking.

-- 言慎行　exercise caution in speech and conduct.

20-- 重　prudent, discreet, cautious, attentive.

-- 重過度　be over-prudent.

-- 重其事　be very careful, handle the matter with care.

30-- 之又慎　make assurance doubly sure.

60-- 思　think carefully.

-- 思而後行　look before you leap.

70-- 防錯誤　guard against error.

9408₆
憤〔Fen〕n. ardor, zeal, anger, exasperation, indignation.

00-- 言　with an angry tone.

10-- 不欲生　tire of life at the extremity of indignation, be angered to death.

38-- 激之詞　words uttered with indignation.

41-- 慨　resentment.

47-- 怒　n. indignation, adj. angry, indignant, v. filled with anger and vexation.

94-- 憤不平　be resentful or indignant because of injustice.

97-- 恨　hatred, resentment.

9481₀
灶=**竈** 3071₇

9481₁
燒〔Shao〕n. fever, v. burn, light, set on fire, roast, cook.

10-- 死　burn to death.

15-- 磚　burn bricks.

20-- 焦　scorch, sear.

28-- 傷　n. burn, v. burn.

30-- 完　burn out.

-- 窯　n. kiln, v. build a fire in a kiln.

40-- 肉　grill.

44-- 盡　burn away.

-- 菜　cook food.

53-- 成灰燼　incinerate.

77-- 毀　burn out, burn down.

81-- 飯　cook rice, cook meals.

88-- 餅　baked cake.

90-- 光　burn up, burn down.

-- 火　build a fire, set a fire.

94-- 烤　bake and roast, broil.

97-- 燉　burn out, be burnt down.

9482₇
烤〔Kao〕v. roast, bake, toast, warm by a fire.

40-- 肉　n. roasted meat, v. roast meat.

41-- 麵包　toast, bake bread.

67-- 鴨　roast a duck.

90-- 火　warm oneself at a fire.

96-- 烟　cured tobacco.

9485₆
煒〔Wei〕adj. glowing red.

9488₁
烘〔Hung〕v. bake, toast, roast, scorch, dry near a fire.

48-- 乾　dry by the fire, dry, parch.

91-- 爐　stove.

94-- 烤　roast, grill, bake.

9489₄
煤〔Mei〕n. coal.

10-- 礦　coal mine, collier.

-- 礦工人　coal miner.

13-- 球	briquet, coal ball.
20-- 焦油	coal tar.
24-- 牀	coal-bed.
34-- 渣	coal cinders, cinder.
35-- 油	kerosene, petroleum, coal oil.
-- 油燈	kerosene lamp, oil lamp.
40-- 坑	coal-pit.
44-- 藏量	coal reserve.
60-- 田	coal-field.
77-- 屑	coal-dust.
-- 層	coal-seam.
80-- 倉	coal-bunker.
-- 氣	gas, coal-gas.
-- 氣表	gas meter.
-- 氣灶	gas range.
-- 氣燈	gaslight.
96-- 烟	soot.

9489₆

燎 〔Liao〕v. burn, blaze, singe.

| 71-- 原 | start a prairie fire. |
| -- 原之火 | great prairie fire. |

9490₀

料 〔Liao〕n. material, stuff, v. estimate, reckon, calculate, consider, foresee, manage, take care of.

16-- 理	n. management, v. manage, arrange.
-- 理後事	make arrangements for the funeral.
17-- 子	material.
46-- 想	expect, guess, foresee, suppose, consider, reckon.
50-- 事如神	foresee with divine accuracy.

9491₆

糙 〔Tsao〕adj. coarse, rough, rash.

| 90-- 米 | coarse rice. |

9500₆

忡 〔Chung〕adj. sorrowful, worried, uneasy.

| 95-- 忡 | uneasy, worried. |

9501₄

性 〔Hsing〕n. sex, gender, disposition, temper, nature, quality.

00-- 交	sexual intercourse.
-- 病	sexual disease, venereal diseases.
12-- 烈如火	fiery-tempered.
21-- 能	function, properties, performance.
-- 能良好	excellent performance.
27-- 急	n. impatience, adj. impatient, impetuous, hasty, quick-tempered.
47-- 格	temperament, character, nature, tendency.
-- 格不合	incompatibility of temperament.
52-- 靜情逸	have a quiet and easy disposition.
62-- 別	sex.
72-- 質	quality, nature, property, character.
77-- 學	sexual studies.
80-- 命	life.
-- 命干連	it's a serious matter involving life and death.
-- 命攸關	matter of life and death.
87-- 慾	sexual appetite, sexual desire.
-- 慾主義	sensualism.
95-- 情	temper, spirit, humor, instinct, disposition.
-- 情相合	be born under the same star, be on good terms with each other.

9502₇

情 〔Ching〕n. passion, emotion, feeling, desire, affection, love, romance, sentiment, fact, detail, condition, situation.

00-- 意濃濃	intimate affection.
02-- 話	bill and coo.
03-- 誼	friendship, affection.
-- 誼深厚	be on very good terms with each other.
10-- 面	favor, good graces, influence, regard for others.
-- 面難卻	hard to refuse or decline for the sake of friendship

	or face.
-- 不自禁	be seized with an impulse, cannot but, cannot help.
-- 至義盡	have done one's best morally.
12-- 形	condition, circumstance, state, state of affairs, situation.
16-- 理	reason.
-- 理之外	beyond all considerations, unreasonable.
-- 理難容	contrary to reason or common sense.
20-- 愛	affection, love between man and woman.
22-- 絲	silken tie.
23-- 狀	condition.
24-- 緒	emotion, passion, feelings, sentiment.
27-- 急	urgent.
-- 急生智	good ideas come at times of crisis.
36-- 況	condition, circumstance, case.
-- 況不明	situation unknown.
37-- 郎	gallant, beau, lover.
-- 深似海	the love (of parents) is as deep as the sea.
40-- 有可原	pardonable, under mitigating and extenuating circumstances.
44-- 勢	status.
-- 勢危急	the situation is critical.
-- 勢如何	what is the situation?
46-- 場失意	frustrated in love.
47-- 婦	mistress, one's best girl.
-- 報	information, message, intelligence.
-- 報部	intelligence department, ministry of information.
-- 報網	information system.
-- 報機關	intelligence agency.
-- 報資料	intelligence data.
-- 報員	intelligence officer, secret agent.
-- 報局	intelligence bureau.
50-- 事	love affair, romance.

-- 書	love letter.
53-- 感	feeling, emotion, sentiment.
-- 感衝動	be under an emotional impulse.
56-- 操	sentiment.
71-- 願	be willing, will.
-- 長紙短	the paper is too short to contain what I have to say.
80-- 人	sweetheart, mistress, lover.
87-- 慾	passion, lust, carnal desire.
88-- 節	plot, circumstances.
-- 節重大	be of a serious nature.
-- 節曲折	the plot is intricate.

9503₀

快 [Kuai] v. be happy, be pleased, *adj.* quick, swift, fast, rapid, sharp, keen, honest, straight forward.

17-- 刀	sharp knife.
18-- 攻	(in basketball) fast break.
20-- 信	express letter.
-- 手快腳	nimble of hands and fast of feet — do things quickly.
21-- 步	trot.
22-- 樂	*n.* happiness, pleasure, *adj.* gay, happy, joyful, glad, merry, in high spirit, pleasant.
-- 樂主義	hedonism.
-- 艇	speed boat.
25-- 件	express.
27-- 郵	by express post.
-- 船	clipper.
-- 餐	fast foods, quick lunch, short order.
-- 餐部	snack bar department.
-- 餐館	fast food restaurant.
32-- 遞	express delivery.
35-- 速	high-speed, quick, prompt.
41-- 板	ballad, quick tempo.
50-- 車	express train.
-- 車道	speedway.
55-- 捷	hasty, speedy.
-- 捷妥當	quick and proper.
61-- 嘴	loquacious, talkative.
-- 嘴快舌	prone to talk rashly.
67-- 跑	run fast.

71-- 馬加鞭	proceed at high speed.
-- 匯	express.
77-- 門	camera shutter.
80-- 人快語	straight talk from an honest man.
-- 人快事	pleasant deed performed by a straightforward man.

快〔Yang〕*adj.* discontented, dissatisfied, displeased, sad.

| 00-- 意 | glad, gleeful, jovial. |
| 95-- 快不樂 | discontented and unhappy. |

9504₄

悽〔Chi〕*adj.* grieved, sorrowful, afflicted, suffering.

44-- 楚	miserable, desolate.
92-- 慘	melancholy, sorrowful, miserable, tragic, pathetic.
-- 惋	sad, plaintive.
95-- 悽	pathetic, pitiful.
96-- 惶	sad, sick at heart, distressed.
98-- 愴	pathetic, deplorable, desolate.

9508₆

憒〔Kui〕*adj.* troubled, vexed.

9509₆

悚〔Sung〕*adj.* fearful, terrified, frightened, alarmed, agitated.

| 23-- 然而懼 | be terrified. |
| 95-- 悚驚魂 | soul trembling with fear. |

9581₇

爐〔Chin〕*n.* ash, ember, snuff.

9589₆

煉〔Lien〕*v.* refine, melt, smelt, condense.

20-- 焦	make coke.
-- 焦廠	coke oven plant.
-- 焦爐	coke oven.
-- 焦煤	coking coal.
22-- 乳	condensed milk.
-- 製廠	refinery.
35-- 油廠	oil refinery.
83-- 鐵	*n.* iron-smelting, *v.* refine iron.
-- 鐵廠	iron-smelting plant.
-- 鐵爐	iron-smelting furnace.

87-- 鋼	steel-making, steel-smelting.
-- 鋼廠	steel works, steel plant.
-- 鋼爐	steel-smelting furnace, steel-making furnace.
-- 鋼工人	steel-worker.
90-- 糖廠	sugar-refinery.

9592₇

精〔Ching〕*n.* essence, spirit, extract, purest part of a thing, ghosts, spirits, sperm, semen, mental force, *v.* be expert at, *adj.* refined, delicate, bare, sharp, keen, *adv.* extremely, very.

00-- 度	measure of precision.
04-- 讀	*n.* perusal, *v.* peruse.
06-- 竭	exhausted.
10-- 工	fine workmanship.
-- 要	essence, sum and substance.
11-- 巧	cleverness, skill, dexterity, *adj.* dexterous, skillful.
14-- 確	exact, accurate, precise.
17-- 子	sperm.
20-- 采百出	have hundreds of highlights
22-- 製	*v.* refine, *adj.* refined, well-made.
23-- 彩	excellent.
24-- 裝本	deluxe edition.
26-- 細	fine, refined.
28-- 緻	*n.* fineness, *adj.* delicate, exquisite, fine.
30-- 密	elaborate, exact, accurate, with accuracy.
-- 密儀器	precision apparatus (instruments).
-- 密機械	precision machine.
-- 良	excellent, well-made.
33-- 心	elaborately worked out.
35-- 神	spirit, energy, soul, life, one's mental force.
-- 神病	mental disease, psychosis.
-- 神文明	spiritual civilization.
-- 神失常	be out of one's mind.
-- 神食糧	mental food.
-- 神病院	mad house.
-- 神教育	moral education.
-- 神勝利	moral victory.
-- 神錯亂	delirious, insanity aberra-

tion.

-- 神飽滿	vigorous, in high spirits.
37-- 選	*n.* choice, *v.* pick the best *adj.* hand-picked.
-- 選品	selected quality.
-- 通	*v.* master, be proficient in, have a good command of, *adj.* proficient, conversant.
40-- 力	spirit and energy, strength, psychic force, vigor.
44-- 華	flower, marrow, essence, pick.
48-- 幹	intelligent and capable.
50-- 蟲	sperm, semen.
51-- 打細算	operate within a tight budget.
60-- 品店	boutique.
67-- 明	clever, bright, shrewd, sharp, astute, keen, intelligent.
72-- 兵	picked soldiers.
74-- 髓	quintessence.
77-- 闢	incisive.
80-- 美	excellent, fine, exquisite.
85-- 鍊	refine.
86-- 銳	picked, accurate.
-- 銳部隊	crack troops, elite troops.
87-- 飼料	concentrated feed.
88-- 簡	reduce, cut down, simplify.
95-- 煉	*v.* refine, *adj.* refined.
97-- 怪	demons, monsters.

9596₆

糟 〔Tsao〕 *n.* sediment, dreg, lees, *v.* become a mess, *adj.* rotten, spoiled, lousy.

17-- 了	bad luck, deuce, damn it!
27-- 魚	fish cured in grains.
66-- 蹋	waste, ravage, spoil.
96-- 粕	dregs, slag, scum, residue, rubbish.
98-- 糕	awful, too bad, what a mess!

9600₀

怕 〔Pa〕 *v.* fear, dread, be afraid of.

| 10-- 死 | afraid of death. |
| 88-- 羞 | shy, bashful. |

悃 〔Kun〕 *n.* sincerity.

9601₀

怳 〔Huang〕 *adj.* delirious, disappointed.

怛 〔Ta〕 *adj.* shocked, alarmed, distressed.

9601₃

愧 〔Kuei〕 *adj.* ashamed, abashed, bashful.

| 10-- 不敢當 | be embarrassed by an undeserved praise or gift. |
| 33-- 心之事 | conscience-stricken affair. |

9601₄

悝 〔Kuei〕 *adj.* sorrowful, grieved.

惺 〔Hsing〕 *v.* awake, *adj.* tranquil, wavering

| 48-- 忪 | clear, wavering. |

惶 〔Huang〕 *n.* fear, terror, dread, *adj.* frightened, fearful, scared, agitated, hurried.

17-- 恐	alarmed, frightened.
-- 恐之至	very fearful.
53-- 惑	doubtful, hesitating, in doubt.
96-- 惶	fearful, hurried.

懼 〔Chu〕 *v.* fear, be afraid of, dread.

| 40-- 內 | hen-pecked, fear one's wife. |
| 94-- 怯 | timid, cowardly. |

9601₇

慍 〔Yun〕 *n.* anger, wrath, *adj.* indignant, wrathy, angry, irritated.

| 27-- 色 | angry appearance. |
| 47-- 怒 | angry, irritated, sulky, indignant. |

悒 〔I〕 *n.* anxiety, sorrow, *adj.* sorrowful, sad, gloomy, dejected.

| 96-- 悒 | sorrowful, sad. |
| -- 悒不樂 | depressed and unhappy. |

9602₇

悁 〔Chuan〕 *adj.* angry, irritated, distressed.

惕 〔Ti〕 *adj.* respectful, fearful, cautious, watchful.

愒 〔Chieh〕 *v.* rest, stop.

愕〔O〕*v.* be astonished, be startled, be amazed, be alarmed, *adj.* astonished.

23-- 然　in surprise, in amazement, amazed, startled, astonished.

-- 然相視　glance at each other in amazement.

愣〔Leng〕*adj.* dumbfounded, stupefied, stupid.

20-- 住　be struck dumb .

9604₁

悍〔Han〕*adj.* fierce, cruel, violent, brave, strong, stubborn.

23-- 然　outrageously, stubbornly.

-- 然不顧　ignore outrageously.

47-- 婦　shrew, termagant.

9604₇

慢〔Man〕*adj.* slow, indifferent, remiss, late, sluggish, negligent, haughty, rude, *adv.* slowly.

10-- 工出細活　working slowly produces fine goods.

20-- 手慢腳　slow in doing things.

21-- 步　*n.* slow walk, *v.* walk leisurely.

50-- 車　slow train.

-- 車道　slow-traffic lane.

95-- 性　chronic.

-- 性病　chronic disease.

96-- 慢吞吞　very slowly.

懱〔Chueh〕*adj.* respectful.

9605₆

憚〔Tan〕*v.* dread, fear, dislike.

10-- 不敢言　being afraid, one dare not speak.

91-- 煩不幹　quit, for fear of the trouble of the matter.

9609₆

憬〔Ching〕*v.* wake up, perceive, realize.

91-- 悟前非　realize one's former errors.

9680₀

烟〔Yen〕*n.* smoke, fumes, tobacco, cigarette, opium, mist.

00-- 癮　opium or tobacco addiction.

10-- 霧　vapor, mist.

26-- 囱　chimney, smokestack, funnel.

31-- 酒稅　wine and tobacco tax.

-- 酒專賣　state monopoly of sales of tobacco and alcoholic drinks.

34-- 斗　pipe.

40-- 灰盤　ash-tray.

44-- 草　tobacco.

-- 草商　tobacconist.

-- 草稅　tobacco tax.

-- 葉　tobacco leaves.

-- 幕　smokescreen, smoke cloud.

-- 幕彈　smoke-bomb.

-- 花巷　zone of brothels.

77-- 具　smoking set.

80-- 盆　cigarette case.

90-- 卷　cigarette.

-- 火　fireworks, kitchen smoke, cooked food, beacon.

94-- 煤　bituminous coal, soft coal.

9681₄

煌〔Huang〕*adj.* blazing, bright.

9681₈

煜〔Yu〕*adj.* bright, glorious.

9682₇

煬〔Yang〕*v.* fuse, melt, smelt.

燭〔Chu〕*n.* candle, light, *v.* shine upon.

23-- 台　candle-stand, candlestick.

33-- 心　wick.

44-- 芯　candle-wick.

90-- 光　candle-light, candle power.

9683₀

熄〔Hsi〕*v.* quash, blaze out, obliterate, put out.

33-- 滅　extinguish.

92-- 燈號　taps.

9683₂

煨〔Wei〕*v.* roast, bake, simmer, stew.

22-- 山薯　bake sweet potato the loving care a mother gives to her child.

40-- 肉　　　　　　stew meat.

爆〔Pao〕 *n.* explosion, *v.* crack, burst, crackle, explode, pop.

12-- 發　　　　　　*n.* explosion, outbreak, outburst, eruption, *v.* break out, erupt.

-- 裂　　　　　　blow up, blaze, crack, pop open, burst.

-- 裂聲　　　　　crackle.

88-- 竹　　　　　　cracker, firecracker.

90-- 火　　　　　　crackling fire.

98-- 炸　　　　　　*n.* outbreak, burst, *v.* explode, burst, bomb, blow up.

-- 炸品　　　　　exploder, explosive.

9684₁
焊〔銲〕〔Han〕 *v.* weld, solder.

10-- 工　　　　　　welder, welding worker.

27-- 條　　　　　　welding rod.

50-- 接　　　　　　weld, solder.

9689₄
燥〔Tsao〕 *adj.* dry, scorched, arid, restless.

12-- 烈　　　　　　fierce.

44-- 熱　　　　　　dry and hot.

9690₀
粕〔Po〕 *n.* sediment of liquor.

糰〔Tuan〕 *n.* rice dumplings, dough.

17-- 子　　　　　　dumplings.

9691₄
糧〔Liang〕 *n.* grain, food, provisions.

00-- 店　　　　　　grain shop, provisions store.

10-- 票　　　　　　provisions coupon.

25-- 秣　　　　　　food and forage, military food supplies.

44-- 荒　　　　　　food shortage.

80-- 食　　　　　　provisions, food.

-- 食部　　　　　Ministry of Food.

-- 食袋　　　　　feed bag.

-- 倉　　　　　　granary.

9701₀
恤〔Hsu〕 *n.* compassion, pity, sympathy.

44-- 老扶弱　　　　pity the aged and support the young.

47-- 款　　　　　　compensation, indemnity.

9701₁
怩〔Ni〕 *adj.* shy, blushing.

9701₄
怪〔Kuai〕 *v.* blame, *adj.* strange, curious, supernatural, weird.

00-- 癖　　　　　　peculiarity, eccentricity, idiosyncrasy.

02-- 話　　　　　　absurdity, odd expression.

-- 誕　　　　　　antic, grotesque.

-- 誕離奇　　　　weird and unheard of.

10-- 不得　　　　　no wonder.

16-- 現象　　　　　strange phenomenon.

27-- 物　　　　　　monster, apparition, hobgoblin.

44-- 模怪樣　　　　ugly, queer appearance and manners.

46-- 想　　　　　　whim, whimsy.

47-- 聲怪氣　　　　speak in an unpleasant falsetto.

50-- 事　　　　　　strange affair, strange matter.

60-- 異　　　　　　*n.* whimsicality, *adj.* strange, whimsical.

80-- 人　　　　　　odd fish, strange person.

90-- 性　　　　　　eccentricity.

慳〔Chien〕 *adj.* sparing, stingy.

9701₅
忸〔Niu〕 *adj.* shy, blushing, ashamed.

97-- 怩　　　　　　*v.* feel shy, *adj.* blushing, shy, timid.

-- 怩不安　　　　blush with shame and be uncomfortable.

9702₀
忉〔Tao〕 *adj.* grieved, sorrowful.

恟〔Hsiung〕 *adj.* timorous.

恫〔Tung〕 *n.* pain, *v.* threaten, frighten, *adj.* painful.

64-- 嚇　　　　　　threaten, intimidate.

恂〔Hsun〕 *adj.* refined, sincere.

惘〔Wang〕 *adj.* disappointed, depressed, dejected.

23-- 然　　　　　　disappointedly, at a loss.

惆〔Chou〕 *adj.* distressed, disappoin-

ted, vexed, annoyed, sad, dejected, regretful.

91-- 悵　　　　sad, disappointed, regretful.

憫〔Min〕*n.* grief, sorrow, pity, compassion, sympathy, *v.* mourn, pity, sympathize, be compassionate to.

92-- 惻　　　　pity, sympathize.
97-- 恤　　　　pity and help.
-- 恤民生　　pity and help the masses.

9703_3

惚〔Hu〕*adj.* confused, indistinct.

恨〔Hen〕*n.* hatred, dislike, regret, indignation. *v.* hate, dislike, resent, regret.

10-- 不得　　would that, wish that one could.
27-- 怨　　　　hate, abhor.
30-- 之入骨　deepest hatred.
41-- 極　　　　hate bitterly.

9703_4

懊〔Ao〕*v.* regret, feel remorse, *adj.* vexed, angry, regretful.

40-- 喪　　　　vexed, disappointed, downcast.
92-- 惱　　　　irritated, vexed, annoyed, harassed.
97-- 恨　　　　hate.
98-- 悔　　　　*v.* regret, repent, *adj.* regretful.

9705_2

懈〔Hsieh〕*adj.* idle, lazy, remiss, slack, negligent.

23-- 怠　　　　negligent, idle, sluggish.

9706_4

恪〔Ko〕*adj.* respectful, faithful, reverent.

30-- 守　　　　adhere faithfully.
-- 守法規　　reverently observe the law.

9708_6

慣〔Kuan〕*v.* spoil, *adj.* accustomed, used, familiar to, lazy, idle, indolent, habitual, usual.

08-- 於　　　　be accustomed, used to.
17-- 習　　　　custom, habit.

22-- 例　　　　usage, custom, convention.
-- 例價格　　conventional price.
-- 例折扣　　customary discount.
30-- 竊　　　　confirmed thief.
47-- 犯　　　　habitual criminal.
48-- 散　　　　*n.* sloven, *adj.* sluggish.
77-- 骨頭　　lazybones, lazy fellow.
-- 用法　　　common usage.
95-- 性　　　　inertia.

懶〔Lan〕*adj.* lazy, listless, idle, indolent.

34-- 漢　　　　sluggard, idler.
80-- 人漢　　idler, sluggard, lazy fellow.
94-- 惰　　　　lazy, idle, indolent.
-- 惰成性　　have laziness as one's second nature.

9721_4

耀〔Yao〕*n.* light, brilliance, *v.* illumine, shine on, glorify, bluff, *adj.* glorious, brilliant.

13-- 武揚威　bluff and bluster, put on airs.
67-- 眼　　　　daze, dazzle the eye.

9722_7

鄰〔Lin〕*n.* neighbor, *adj.* near, close by, contiguous, adjacent.

03-- 誼　　　　neighborhood.
32-- 近　　　　near, close by, neighboring.
60-- 里　　　　vicinity, neighborhood.
-- 國、邦　　neighboring country.
77-- 居　　　　neighbor.
80-- 人　　　　neighbor.

9725_6

輝〔Hui〕*adj.* bright, brilliant, glorious, shining.

96-- 煌　　　　brilliant, magnificent.

9781_2

炮〔Pao〕*n.* cannon, gun, big gun, rocket, *v.* bake, roast, burn.

16-- 彈　　　　shell, cannon-ball.
18-- 攻　　　　bomb.
20-- 手　　　　gunner, artilleryman, cannoneer.
22-- 製　　　　decoct, refine.
23-- 台　　　　fort.

28-- 艦	gunboat.	
45-- 樓	gun turret.	
47-- 聲	report of a gun.	
50-- 轟	*n.* bombardment, *v.* bombard.	
63-- 戰	artillery warfare.	
67-- 眼	embrasure, dynamite hole, bore hole.	
72-- 兵	artillery.	
78-- 隊	artillery corps.	
88-- 筒	gun-barrel.	
90-- 火	artillery fire, gunfire.	

9782₀
灼 〔 **Cho** 〕 *v.* burn, singe, sear, *adj.* clear, distinct, blooming (flowers).

44-- 熱	intense heat, red-hot.
47-- 灼	bright, sparkling, flowers in bloom.
60-- 見	clear view.

炯 〔 **Chiung** 〕 *adj.* bright, shining.

97-- 炯	bright, shining, discerning.

燜 〔 **Men** 〕 *v.* steam, cook in a closed vessel.

爛 〔 **Lan** 〕 *v.* tear, overcook, *adj.* broken, smashed, ruined, torn, overcooked, well cooked, rotten, bright, brilliant, shinging.

04-- 熟	overripe, cooked soft.
10-- 醉	dead drunk.
32-- 透	rotten to the core, well cooked.
37-- 泥	mud, mire.
50-- 攤子	rotten legacy, mess.
51-- 掉	putrid, rotten, ruined.

9783₄
煥 〔 **Huan** 〕 *adj.* bright, brilliant, lustrous.

12-- 發	glowing, shining.
-- 然一新	brand new, completely renovated.

9784₇
燬 〔 **Hui** 〕 *v.* destroy, burn.

9785₄
烽 〔 **Feng** 〕 *n.* beacon, beacon fire, signal fire.

90-- 火	beacon fire, signal fire, balefire.
-- 火台	ancient beacon tower.
-- 火連年	continuous wars.
91-- 煙四起	land beset by war.

9786₂
炤 〔 **Chao** 〕 *adj.* bright, shining.

9786₄
烙 〔 **Lao** 〕 *v.* burn, bake, iron, brand.

77-- 印	*n.* brand, *v.* brand.
83-- 鐵	iron.
88-- 餅	pancake, flapjack.

9788₂
炊 〔 **Chui** 〕 *v.* cook, steam.

50-- 事員	cook.
-- 事班	cooking squad.
77-- 具	cooking utensils.
82-- 飯	steamed rice.

9789₄
燦 〔 **Tsan** 〕 *adj.* bright, resplendent, brilliant, glittering.

97-- 爛	*n.* splendor, brightness, brilliancy, *adj.* brilliant, splendid.

9791₀
粗 〔 **Tsu** 〕 *adj.* thick, coarse, crude, gross, rough, harsh, rude, rash, big, vulgar, sketchy.

02-- 話	vile talk.
22-- 製	roughcast.
-- 製品	rough quality, crude goods.
24-- 估	rough estimation.
-- 貨	rough cargo.
27-- 魯	rude, rough.
-- 的	harsh, crude, coarse.
28-- 俗	rustic, vulgar.
40-- 布	sackcloth.
-- 大	thick, bulky.
60-- 暴	rough, violent.
67-- 略	roughly.
-- 野	vulgar.
-- 鄙	brute, rude.
71-- 陋	crude.
80-- 人	boor, rustic.
-- 食	simple diet.

88--	笨	rough, artless.
90--	劣	of poor quality.
--	糖	crude sugar, raw sugar.
91--	糧	coarse grain.
94--	糙	coarse, rough.
96--	細	coarse and fine.

9792_0
糊 〔Hu〕 n. paste, v. paste, stick, adj. sticky, blurred, obscure, confused.

08--	說	talk nonsense.
24--	牆	paper a wall.
--	牆紙	wallpaper.
27--	漿	paste.
30--	窗	paper a window.
38--	塗	muddled, doltish, reckless, stupid, confused.
--	塗蟲	muddle-headed fellow.

9794_0
籽 〔Tzu〕 n. seeds of plants.

46--	棉	raw cotton, unpinned cotton.

9798_7
粎 〔Che〕 n. meter.

9799_4
糅 〔Jou〕 v. mix, adj. mixed

80--	合	blend, intermix.

9801_1
怍 〔Tso〕 v. be ashamed, adj. ashamed.

23--	然變色	feeling ashamed, one changes color.

9801_6
悅 〔Yueh〕 v. please, rejoice, delight, adj. pleased, delighted, contented, agreeable, delightful, pleasant, joyous.

00--	意	agreeable, amusing, pleasing, pleasant.
10--	耳	pleasant to the ear.
--	耳之言	words that please the ear.
60--	目	charming, pleasant to the eye.
77--	服	concede happily.

9801_7
愾 〔Hsi〕 n. auger, v. sigh.

9802_1
愉 〔Yu〕 adj. happy, pleased, glad, joyful.

95--	快	pleased, delighted, happy.
--	快勝任	discharge one's duty happily and efficiently.

9802_7
悌 〔Ti〕 adj. respectful.

9804_0
忤 〔Wu〕 v. displease, adj. obstinate, perverse.

38--	逆	disobedient.

9804_7
愎 〔Pi〕 adj. perverse, self-willed.

9805_6
悔 〔Hui〕 v. regret, repent.

10--	不當初	regret a previous mistake.
18--	改	n. repentance, v. reform, repent.
--	改自新	repent and reform oneself.
30--	之已晚	it is too late to repent or regret.
37--	過	n. penitence, v. repent, feel remorse.
60--	罪	n. penance, v. do penance, show repentance.
91--	悟	n. penitence, adj. penitent.
97--	恨	n. remorse, v. sorrow, repent, feel remorse for.

9806_1
恰 〔Chia〕 adj. proper, suitable, adv. just, exactly.

10--	到好處	just right.
11--	巧	luckily, fortunately, by chance.
47--	好	just, precisely, just right.
--	好時機	proper time, right time.
80--	合	fit exactly.
90--	當	fit, suitable.
--	當時令	in season, proper time.

9806_6
憎 〔Tseng〕 v. hate, dislike, abhor.

10--	惡	hate, detest, abhor, loathe, dislike.

-- 惡惡人	hate an evil man.
40-- 嫉不容	be jealous and intolerant.
97-- 恨	hate, abominate.
-- 恨仇敵	hate an enemy.

9806_7

憎 〔Chuang〕 *adj.* sad, sick at heart.

9821_2

斃 〔Pi〕 *v.* die, kill, bite the dust, *adj.* dead.

80-- 命	die, meet one's death.

9822_7

幣 〔Pi〕 *n.* money, coin, currency, present.

22-- 制	currency, currency system.
24-- 值	currency value, value of money.
-- 值改革	currency reform.
-- 值穩定	monetary stability.
-- 值升降	currency depreciation and appreciation.

9824_0

敝 〔Pi〕 *adj.* worn-out, poor, ragged, broken, exhausted, tired, *pron.* my, our.

敞 〔Chang〕 *adj.* open, lofty, spacious.

88-- 篷車	open car, convertible.

9833_4

憋 〔Pieh〕 *v.* suppress one's feeling with efforts.

77-- 悶	bored, depressed.
80-- 氣	feel oppressed, feel suffocated, hold one's breath.

9844_4

弊 〔Pi〕 *n.* fraud, corruption, abuses, defect, *adj.* corrupt, vicious.

00-- 病	fraud, abuse, viciousness.
02-- 端	corruption, abuse.
-- 端百出	trouble after trouble comes up.

9860_4

瞥 〔Pieh〕 *v.* glimpse, glance at, catch a glimpse of.

24-- 他一眼	give him a glance.
60-- 見	peep, catch a glimpse of, glance, glimpse.

9871_4

氅 〔Chang〕 *n.* woolen coat.

9871_7

鼈 〔Pieh〕 *n.* turtle, fresh-water turtle

9880_1

瞥 〔Pieh〕 *adj.* lame, crippled.

77-- 腳	lame, dejected.

9881_1

炸 〔Cha〕 *v.* fry, fry in oil, explode, bomb, burst, get angry, disperse noisily.

14-- 破	blast.
16-- 彈	bomb, bombshell.
27-- 魚	fried fish.
40-- 肉丸	fried meat balls.
44-- 藥	explosive, dynamite, gunpowder.
-- 藥包	dynamite charge, package of explosives.
77-- 毀	dynamite, destroy.
-- 開（掉）	blow up.
97-- 燬	destroy, dynamite.

9883_3

燧 〔Sui〕 *n.* flint, beacon, torch.

10-- 石	flint.

9884_0

燉 〔Tun〕 *v.* stew, boil, simmer.

17-- 蛋	stewed eggs.
27-- 雞	stewed chicken.
40-- 肉	stewed meat.

9885_1

烊 〔Yang〕 *v.* assay, fuse, melt.

9892_7

粉 〔Fen〕 *n.* flour, powder, *v.* paint, adorn, whitewash, make up, doll up.

10-- 碎	smashed to pieces, pulverize, smash, crush up.
21-- 紅色	pink.
27-- 身碎骨	utterly crushed.
50-- 末	powder.
52-- 撲	puff, powder-puff.
-- 刺	pimples.
72-- 刷	plaster, whitewash.

88-- 飾	n. adornment, v. whitewash, gloss over, adorn, dress up.
-- 筆	chalk.
90-- 粒	grain.

9893_1

糕〔Kao〕n. cake, pastry, pudding.

60-- 團	cakes and dumplings.
88-- 餅	cakes and biscuits.

9901_1

恍〔Huang〕adj. indistinct, absent-minded.

23-- 然	suddenly.
-- 然大悟	sudden revelation, be suddenly enlightened.
-- 然若失	feel like having lost one's bearings.
46-- 如隔世	so different that it is as if a generation had passed.
97-- 惚	n. languor, v.absent-minded.

9902_7

悄〔Chiao〕adj. sad, grieved, sorrowful, quiet, calm.

23-- 然而去	leave very quietly.
99-- 悄	quietly, gently, softly.
-- 悄地說	whisper.

9905_9

憐〔Lien〕v. pity, sympathize, commiserate, love, be fond of.

20-- 愛	love, be fond of.
94-- 惜	be compassionate to.
97-- 憫	commiserate, pity.
-- 恤老弱	manifest pity for the aged and the weak.

9910_3

瑩〔Ying〕n. stone with the luster of a gem, adj. pure, brilliant, shining, clear, transparent.

37-- 潔	pure and clear.

9913_6

螢〔Ying〕n. firefly, glowworm.

90-- 光	fluorescence.
-- 火蟲	firefly, glowworm.

9932_7

鶯〔Ying〕n. oriole, greenfinch, nightingale.

9940_7

燮〔Hsieh〕v. regulate.

9942_7

勞〔Lao〕v. labor, toil, work, trouble, tire, entertain.

10-- 工	labor, laborer, worker.
-- 工組織	labor organization.
-- 工神聖	the dignity of labor.
-- 工階級	laboring class.
-- 而無功	labor in vain.
17-- 務	service.
-- 務出資	service contribution.
18-- 改	reform through labor.
24-- 動	work, labor, toil.
-- 動力	labor power, labor force, work force, manpower.
-- 動效率	efficiency of labor.
-- 動者	laborer, worker, workman.
-- 動節	Labor day, May Day.
-- 動法	labor law.
-- 動黨	Labor Party.
-- 動組合	labor union.
-- 動協約	collective agreement.
26-- 保	labor insurance.
27-- 役	labor service, manual labor.
-- 多工少	labor hard to little avail.
33-- 心	tax the mind.
35-- 神	bother, be bothered, worried.
37-- 逸	work and leisure, labor and rest.
-- 軍	cheer troops.
-- 資	capital and labor.
-- 資關係	industrial relations.
-- 資爭議	labor disputes.
-- 資糾紛	trouble between labor and management, labor dispute.
40-- 力所得	income from labor.
-- 力	labor.
44-- 苦	toil, travail, hardship, pains.
-- 苦的	toilsome, arduous.
-- 苦工高	with toilsome services and great achievements.
46-- 駕	excuse me, may I trouble

you?
99-- 勞碌碌　weary, toiling.

9960₆

營〔Ying〕n. camp, battalion, military barracks, v. manage, administer to work, scheme, plan, confuse, disturb.
00-- 商　deal in, trade.
04-- 謀　seek, scheme.
22-- 利　profit-making.
　-- 利目的　object of profit-making.
　-- 私　on one's own account.
　-- 私舞弊　embezzlement, malpractice.
30-- 房　barracks, quarters.
32-- 業　n. business, trade, v. trade, manage a business.
　-- 業主任　sale manager.
　-- 業證　business license, certificate of business.
　-- 業部　sales department, business department.
　-- 業利潤　operating profit, business profit.
　-- 業收入　income from business, operating income (revenue).
　-- 業地點　place of business.
　-- 業費用　business expenses.
　-- 業資本　working capital.
　-- 業日　business day.
　-- 業稅　business tax, transaction tax, sales tax.
　-- 業額　turnover in business, business volume.
　-- 業報告　business report.
　-- 業時間　hours of business.
　-- 業年度　business year.
　-- 業範圍　scope of business.
34-- 造　n. construction, v. construct, build.
41-- 帳　camp.
44-- 地　camp, camp site, camping ground.
　-- 幕　tent.
48-- 救　rescue, save.
60-- 壘　camp.
71-- 長　battalion commander.
80-- 養　nutrition, nourishment.
　-- 養物　nutriment, nutrient.
　-- 養不足　malnutrition.
　-- 養不良　malnutrition, undernourishment.
　-- 養價值　nutritiousness, nutritive value.

9980₉

熒〔Ying〕adj. sparkling, twinkling, bright, brilliant.
90-- 光屏　fluorescent (or television) screen.
　-- 光鏡　fluoroscope.
　-- 光燈　fluorescent lamp.

9982₀

炒〔Chao〕v. fry, roast, parch, broil.
10-- 豆　parched beans.
17-- 蛋　omelet, scrambled egg.
30-- 家　scalper.
38-- 冷飯　rehash.
41-- 麵　fried noodles.
77-- 股　speculate in the stock market.

9985₉

燐=磷 1965₉
燐〔Lin〕n. phosphorus.

9990₃

縈〔Ying〕v. wind, twine, coil around.
16-- 廻　go round and round.
24-- 繞　surround.
90-- 懷　worry oneself.

9990₄

榮〔Jung〕n. glory, honor, splendor, excellency, adj. glorious, honorable, prosperous, splendid, lush, luxuriant.
30-- 宗耀祖　bring glory to one's family and ancestors.
40-- 幸　have the honor.
44-- 華富貴　splendor, wealth and honor.
71-- 辱　honor and disgrace.
77-- 譽　reputation, honor, dignity, glory.
　-- 譽軍人　honorable soldier.
　-- 歸故里　return to one's native place with honor.
90-- 光　splendor.
97-- 耀　n. glory, splendor, adj. glorious, splendid.

一　畫

部	字	四角	頁碼
一	一	1000_0	58
乙	乙	1771_0	138

二　畫

部	字	四角	頁碼
一	丁	1020_0	73
	七	4071_0	374
	乃	1722_7	131
乙	九	4001_7	353
丨	了	1720_7	130
二	二	1010_0	63
人	人	8000_0	621
入	入	8000_0	623
八	八	8000_0	620
几	几	7721_0	589
刀	刀	1722_0	131
	刁	1712_0	129
力	力	4002_7	353
十	十	4000_0	352
七	匕	2171_0	172
卜	卜	2300_0	190
厂	厂	7120_0	565
又	叉	7740_0	603

三　畫

部	字	四角	頁碼
一	丈	5000_0	444
	三	1010_1	67
	上	2110_0	160
	下	1023_0	76
丨	丫	8020_7	627
丶	丸	4001_7	353
丿	久	2780_0	254

部	字	四角	頁碼
乙	乞	8071_7	648
	也	4471_2	411
二	于	1040_0	81
亠	亡	0071_0	29
儿	兀	1021_0	73
几	凡	7721_0	589
刀	刃	1732_0	133
勹	勺	2732_0	246
十	千	2040_0	148
又	叉	4000_0	352
口	口	6000_0	507
土	土	4010_0	359
士	士	4010_0	360
夕	夕	2720_0	239
大	大	4003_0	354
女	女	4040_0	369
子	子	1740_7	134
	孑	1740_7	134
寸	寸	4030_0	368
小	小	9000_0	681
尸	尸	7727_0	601
山	山	2277_0	184
川	川	2200_0	176
工	工	1010_0	63
己	己	1771_7	138
	已	1771_7	138
	巳	7771_7	609
巾	巾	4022_7	363
干	干	1040_0	81
弓	弓	1720_7	131
手	才	4020_0	362

四　畫

部	字	四角	頁碼
一	不	1090_0	94

部	字	四　角	頁　碼	部	字	四　角	頁　碼
欠	欠	2780_2	254		全	8010_1	623
止	止	2110_0	162		代	2324_0	194
歹	歹	1020_7	73		令	8030_7	633
毋	毋	7755_0	607		以	2810_0	259
比	比	2171_0	172	几	兄	6021_0	519
毛	毛	2071_4	156	冂	回	7722_0	593
氏	氏	7274_0	579		甩	7721_2	590
水	水	1223_0	109		冊	7744_0	604
火	火	9080_0	689		冉	5044_7	455
爪	爪	7223_0	577	冫	冬	2730_3	246
父	父	8040_0	639	凵	凸	7777_7	612
爻	爻	4040_0	369		凹	7777_0	611
片	片	2202_1	176		出	2277_2	184
牙	牙	7124_0	567	刀	刊	1240_0	114
牛	牛	2500_0	216	力	功	1412_7	120
犬	犬	4303_0	386		加	4600_0	420
玉	王	1010_4	69	勹	包	2771_2	252

五　畫

部	字	四　角	頁　碼	部	字	四　角	頁　碼
一	且	7710_0	587	匕	北	1111_0	101
	互	1010_7	70	匚	匝	7171_2	573
	丕	1010_9	72		匡	7171_6	573
	世	4471_7	411	十	半	9050_0	687
	丘	7210_1	575	卜	占	2160_0	172
	丙	1022_7	74		卡	2123_1	168
丶	主	0010_4	1	卩	卯	7772_0	609
丿	乍	8021_1	628	厶	去	4073_1	374
	乏	2030_7	148	口	古	4060_0	372
人	仔	2724_7	243		叭	6800_0	560
	仕	2421_0	202		句	2762_0	252
	他	2421_2	203		另	6042_7	523
	仗	2520_0	220		叨	6702_0	554
	付	2420_0	201		叩	6702_0	554
	仙	2227_0	182		只	6080_0	529
					叫	6400_0	543
					召	1760_2	135
					叮	6102_0	533

部	字	四角	頁碼	部	字	四角	頁碼
	可	1062_0	88		札	4291_0	385
	台	2360_0	197		木	4090_0	376
	叱	6401_0	543	止	正	1010_1	68
	史	5000_6	446	毋	母	7750_0	606
	右	4060_0	372	氏	民	7774_7	610
	司	1762_0	136	水	永	3023_2	276
口	囚	6080_0	529		氾	3711_2	328
	四	6021_0	518		汀	3112_0	291
夕	外	2320_0	191		汁	3410_0	308
大	央	5003_0	449	犬	犯	4721_2	428
	失	2503_0	217	玄	玄	0073_2	30
女	奴	4744_0	431	玉	玉	1010_3	69
	奶	4742_7	430	瓜	瓜	7223_0	577
子	孕	1740_7	134	瓦	瓦	1071_7	93
宀	它	3071_4	286	甘	甘	4477_0	412
尸	尼	7721_1	590	生	生	2510_0	218
工	左	4001_1	352	用	用	7722_0	592
	巧	1112_7	103	田	田	6040_0	522
	巨	7171_7	574		由	5060_0	452
巾	市	0022_7	12		甲	6050_0	525
	布	4022_7	364		申	5000_6	446
干	平	1040_9	82	疋	疋	1780_1	138
幺	幼	2472_7	211	白	白	2600_0	225
廾	弁	2344_0	197	皮	皮	4024_7	366
弓	弗	5502_7	482	皿	皿	7710_0	587
	弘	1320_2	118	目	目	6010_1	510
心	必	3300_0	303	矛	矛	1722_2	131
	叨	9702_0	703	矢	矢	8043_0	639
手	扒	5800_0	501	石	石	1060_0	86
	打	5102_0	62	示	示	1090_1	101
斤	斥	7223_1	577	禾	禾	2090_4	157
日	旦	6010_0	510	穴	穴	3080_2	288
木	未	5090_0	458	立	立	0010_8	2
	末	5090_0	458				
	本	5023_0	452		六　畫		

部	字	四　角	頁　碼	部	字	四　角	頁　碼
一	丞	1710_3	128		划	5200_0	465
	丟	2073_1	156		列	1220_0	110
丿	乒	7221_1	576	力	劣	9042_7	687
二	互	1010_7	70	勹	匈	2772_0	254
亠	交	0040_8	24	匚	匠	7171_2	573
	亦	0033_0	21		匡	7171_1	572
人	仰	2722_0	241	卩	印	7772_0	609
	仲	2520_6	220		危	2721_2	240
	仵	2824_0	261	口	呼	6104_0	534
	件	2520_0	220		吃	6801_7	560
	任	2221_4	178		各	2760_4	251
	份	2822_7	260		吆	6203_0	537
	仿	2022_7	145		合	8060_1	642
	企	8010_1	623		吉	4060_1	372
	伉	2021_7	144		吊	6022_7	519
	伊	2725_7	245		吋	6400_0	542
	伎	2424_7	206		同	7722_0	593
	伍	2121_7	164		名	2760_0	251
	伏	2323_4	194		后	7226_1	577
	伐	2325_0	195		吏	5000_6	446
	休	2429_0	208		吐	6401_0	543
	伙	2928_0	268		向	2722_0	241
几	兇	2221_7	179	囗	回	6060_0	525
	兆	3211_3	296		因	6043_0	524
	充	0021_3	9		囡	6040_4	523
	光	9021_1	685	土	在	4021_4	363
	先	2421_1	203		圭	4010_4	360
入	全	8010_4	624		圮	4711_7	427
八	共	4480_1	413		圩	4114_0	379
	并	8044_1	640		地	4411_2	393
冂	再	1044_7	85	夕	夙	7721_0	589
	兩	1022_7	75		多	2720_7	240
冫	冰	3213_0	297	大	夷	5003_2	449
刀	刎	2220_0	177		夸	4020_7	363
	刑	1240_0	114	女	她	4441_2	404

部	字	四　角	頁　碼	部	字	四　角	頁　碼
	奸	4144_0	380	木	朱	2590_0	223
	好	4744_7	431		朵	7790_4	615
	妁	4742_0	430		朽	4192_7	382
	如	4640_0	424	欠	次	3718_2	331
	妃	4741_7	430	止	此	2111_0	162
	妄	0040_4	23	歹	死	1021_2	74
子	字	3040_7	282	水	汐	3712_0	328
	存	4024_7	367		汕	3217_0	299
宀	宅	3071_4	286		汗	3114_0	292
	字	3040_1	281		汙	3114_0	292
	守	3034_2	280		汛	3711_0	327
	安	3040_4	281		汎	3711_0	327
寸	寺	4034_1	368		汝	3414_0	312
小	尖	9043_0	687		江	3111_0	290
山	屹	2871_7	265		池	3411_2	310
川	州	3200_0	295		氽	8023_2	632
巾	帆	4721_0	428	火	灯	9182_0	693
干	年	8050_0	640		灰	7128_9	570
弋	式	4310_0	387	牛	牝	2451_0	209
弓	弛	1421_2	122		牟	2350_0	197
心	忖	9400_0	696	白	百	1060_0	87
	忙	9001_0	683	竹	竹	8822_0	673
戈	成	5320_0	476	米	米	9090_4	691
	戎	5340_0	479	糸	糸	2290_3	187
手	托	5201_4	466	缶	缶	8077_2	654
	扛	5101_0	459	羊	羊	8050_1	641
	扣	5600_0	487	羽	羽	1712_0	129
攴	收	2874_0	265	老	老	4471_1	410
日	旨	2160_1	172		考	4420_7	396
	早	6040_0	523	而	而	1022_7	75
	旬	2762_0	252	耒	耒	5090_0	459
	旭	4601_0	421	耳	耳	1040_0	81
曰	曲	5560_0	486	聿	聿	5000_7	447
	曳	5000_6	446	肉	肉	4022_7	364
月	有	4022_7	365		肋	7422_7	582

部	字	四角	頁碼	部	字	四角	頁碼
	肌	7721_0	589		佐	2421_1	203
臣	臣	7171_7	574		佑	2426_0	206
自	自	2600_0	226		佔	2126_0	170
至	至	1010_4	69		何	2122_0	165
臼	臼	7777_0	612		余	8090_4	654
舌	舌	2060_4	154		佚	2523_0	221
舟	舟	2744_0	249		佛	2522_7	221
艮	艮	7773_2	610		作	2821_1	259
色	色	2771_7	253		倭	2024_4	146
艸	艾	4440_0	403	儿	克	4021_6	363
皿	血	2710_0	237		兌	8021_5	629
行	行	2122_1	165		免	2741_5	248
衣	衣	0073_2	29	八	兵	7280_1	579
西	西	1060_0	87	冫	冶	3316_0	305
阜	阝	7224_0	577		冷	3813_7	344

七　畫

部	字	四角	頁碼	部	字	四角	頁碼
				刀	初	3722_0	333
丨	串	5000_6	446		刪	7240_0	578
冫	況	3611_0	323		判	9250_2	694
亠	亭	0020_1	8		別	6240_0	539
人	伯	2620_0	229		刮	4270_0	384
	估	2426_0	206		刼	4772_0	434
	你	2729_2	246		刨	2270_0	183
	伴	2925_0	268		利	2290_0	187
	伸	2520_6	220	力	助	7412_7	581
	伺	2722_0	239		努	4742_7	431
	似	2820_0	259		劫	4472_7	412
	佃	2620_0	229	匚	匣	7171_5	573
	但	2621_0	229	卩	即	7772_0	610
	佇	2322_1	193		卵	7772_0	609
	佈	2422_7	204	口	君	1760_7	136
	位	2021_8	144		客	0060_4	28
	低	2224_0	179		吞	2060_3	154
	住	2021_4	144		吟	6802_7	561
					吠	6303_4	540
					吩	6802_7	561

部	字	四　角	頁　碼	部	字	四　角	頁　碼
	含	8060_7	647	女	妒	4347_7	389
	吱	6404_7	545		妓	4444_7	406
	吳	2643_0	233		妖	4243_4	384
	吭	6001_7	508		妙	4942_0	444
	吮	6301_0	540		妝	2424_0	205
	呈	6010_4	510		妣	4141_0	380
	吵	6902_0	562		妊	4241_4	384
	呐	6402_7	543		妥	2040_4	148
	吸	6704_7	556		妨	4042_7	370
	吹	6708_2	557	子	孜	1844_0	141
	吻	6702_0	554	宀	宋	3090_4	290
	吼	6201_0	536		完	3021_1	274
	吾	1060_1	88		宏	3043_0	283
	告	2460_1	211	尢	尬	4801_2	438
	呀	6104_0	534	尸	尾	7721_4	591
	呂	6060_0	526		尿	7723_2	597
	呃	6101_2	533		局	7722_7	596
	呆	6090_4	531		屄	7721_1	590
	呎	6708_7	557	山	岐	2474_7	213
口	囤	6071_2	528		岔	8077_2	654
	圂	2600_0	226	巛	巡	3230_3	300
	囮	6022_7	519	工	巫	1010_8	72
	困	6090_4	532	巾	希	4022_7	365
土	圻	4212_1	383	广	庇	0021_1	8
	坂	4714_7	428		序	0022_2	11
	坍	4714_0	428	廴	延	1240_1	115
	址	4111_0	379		廷	1240_1	114
	坂	4114_7	379	廾	弄	1044_1	85
	均	4712_0	427	弓	弟	8022_7	632
	坊	4012_7	362	彡	形	1242_2	115
	坎	4718_2	428		彤	7242_2	578
	坐	8810_4	671	彳	彷	2022_2	145
	坑	4011_7	361		役	2724_7	243
士	壯	2421_0	202	心	忌	1733_1	133
大	夾	4003_8	359		忍	1733_2	133

部	字	四　角	頁　碼	部	字	四　角	頁　碼
	弍	4330_0	388		折	5202_1	466
	志	4033_1	368		扙	5004_0	450
	忘	0033_1	21		扳	5104_7	464
	忡	9500_6	698	气	氖	8021_7	629
	忤	9804_0	706	文	攸	2824_0	261
	快	9503_0	699		改	1874_0	141
	忭	9003_0	684		攻	1814_0	139
	忮	9404_7	696	日	旱	6040_1	523
	忱	9401_2	696	田	更	1050_6	86
	忸	9701_5	703	木	杉	4292_2	385
	忻	9202_1	693		李	4040_7	370
	忑	1033_3	81		杏	4060_9	373
戈	成	5320_0	476		材	4490_0	414
	我	2355_0	197		村	4490_0	414
	戒	5340_0	479		杖	4590_0	419
手	扭	5701_5	493		杜	4491_0	416
	扮	5802_7	502		杞	4791_7	436
	扯	5101_0	459		束	5090_6	459
	扱	5704_7	496		杓	4792_0	436
	扶	5503_0	482		杠	4191_0	381
	批	5101_0	460	止	步	2120_1	163
	抵	5204_0	468	毋	每	8050_7	641
	扼	5101_2	461	水	求	4313_2	387
	找	5305_0	475		永	1023_2	78
	技	5404_7	481		汪	3111_4	291
	抄	5902_0	506		汰	3413_0	311
	抉	5503_0	483		汲	3714_7	330
	把	5701_7	493		汴	3013_0	273
	抑	5702_0	494		汶	3014_0	273
	抒	5702_2	494		決	3513_0	318
	抓	5203_0	467		汽	3811_7	343
	抔	5109_0	465		汾	3812_7	343
	投	5704_7	496		沃	3213_4	297
	抖	5400_0	479		沅	3111_1	290
	抗	5001_7	449		沈	3411_2	309

部	字	四角	頁碼
	沌	3511_7	317
	沐	3419_0	313
	沒	3714_7	330
	沖	3510_6	317
	沙	3912_0	350
	沂	3212_1	296
火	灶	9481_0	697
	灸	2780_9	255
	灼	9782_0	705
	災	2280_9	186
牛	牡	2451_0	209
	牢	3050_2	283
疒	疔	0012_1	4
犬	狄	4928_0	444
玉	玖	1718_0	130
用	甫	5322_7	479
	甬	1722_7	131
田	男	6042_7	524
	甸	2762_0	252
禾	禿	2021_7	144
	秀	2022_7	145
	私	2293_0	188
穴	究	3041_7	282
糸	系	2090_3	156
网	罕	3740	340
肉	肖	9022_7	686
	肘	7420_0	582
	肚	7421_0	582
	肛	7121_2	566
	肝	7124_0	568
艮	良	3073_2	286
艸	芋	4440	403
	芒	4471_0	410
	芭	4471_7	411
見	見	6021_0	519

部	字	四角	頁碼
角	角	2722_7	242
言	言	0060_1	26
谷	谷	8060_8	648
豆	豆	1010_8	72
豕	豕	1023_2	78
貝	貝	6080_0	529
赤	赤	4033_1	368
走	走	4080_1	375
足	足	6080_1	529
身	身	2740_0	248
車	車	5000_6	447
辛	辛	0040_1	23
辰	辰	7123_2	567
辵	迂	3130_4	294
	迄	3830_1	345
	迅	3730_1	334
邑	邑	6071_2	529
	那	1752_7	135
	邦	5702_7	494
	邪	7722_7	596
	邨	5772_7	500
里	里	6010_4	511
阜	陁	7121_2	566
	阪	7124_7	569
	阮	7021_7	563
	阢	7121_1	565
	附	7520_0	584
	防	7022_7	563

八畫

部	字	四角	頁碼
一	並	8010_2	624
丿	乖	2011_1	143
乙	乳	2241_0	182
亅	事	5000_7	447

部	字	四　角	頁　碼	部	字	四　角	頁　碼
二	亞	1010_7	71		剄	4220_0	383
	亟	1010_4	70		剁	1290_0	117
	些	2110_1	162		制	2220_0	177
亠	享	0040_7	23		刷	7220_0	575
	京	0090_6	31		刺	5290_0	472
人	佩	2721_0	240		刻	0220_0	35
	來	4090_8	376		券	9022_7	686
	佯	2825_1	263	力	効	0442_7	41
	佳	2421_4	204		劲	0422_7	40
	使	2520_6	220	十	卑	2640_0	233
	侈	2722_7	242		卒	0040_8	25
	例	2220_0	177		卓	2140_6	172
	侍	2424_1	205		協	4402_7	390
	侏	2529_0	223	卩	卷	9071_2	689
	併	2824_1	262		卸	8712_0	667
	侔	2325_0	196		卹	2712_0	238
	侖	8022_7	632	又	叔	2794_0	259
	供	2428_1	207		取	1714_0	129
	依	2023_2	145		受	2040_7	149
	侃	2621_0	229	口	呢	6701_1	553
	侚	2722_0	242		哐	6101_2	533
	佬	2421_1	203		咒	6621_7	551
儿	兒	7721_7	591		周	7722_0	594
	兔	1741_3	134		呪	6601_0	550
	兕	7721_7	591		呫	6106_0	534
入	兩	1022_7	75		呱	6203_0	537
八	其	4480_1	413		哎	6404_0	544
	具	7780_1	613		咚	6703_3	556
	典	5580_1	486		味	6509_0	549
冫	冽	3210_0	295		呵	6102_0	533
几	凭	2221_7	179		呷	6605_0	550
凵	函	1077_2	94		呻	6500_6	548
刀	刮	2260_0	183		呼	6204_9	537
	到	1210_0	107		命	8062_7	648
	刹	4290_0	384		咀	6701_0	553

部	字	四角	頁碼	部	字	四角	頁碼
	咆	6701_2	553	子	孟	1710_7	128
	咋	6802_1	561		季	2040_7	150
	和	2690_0	234		孤	1243_0	116
	咎	2860_4	265	宀	宗	3090_1	289
	咖	6600_0	550		官	3077_7	287
	咐	6400_0	543		宙	3060_5	284
	咕	6406_0	545		定	3080_1	287
口	圂	6030_7	520		宛	3021_2	274
	固	6060_4	527		宜	3010_7	271
土	坡	4414_7	395	小	尚	9022_7	686
	坤	4510_6	419	尸	居	7726_4	600
	坦	4611_0	421		屆	7727_2	601
	坳	4412_7	394		屈	7727_2	601
	坏	4111_9	379	山	岡	7722_0	593
	坪	4114_9	379		岳	7277_2	579
	坼	4213_1	383		岸	2224_1	180
	垂	2010_4	142		岬	2675_0	234
	垃	4011_8	361	巾	帕	4620_0	422
夕	夜	0024_7	17		帖	4126_0	380
大	奄	4071_6	374		帚	1722_7	131
	奇	4062_1	373		帛	2622_7	230
	奈	4090_1	376	干	幸	4040_1	369
	奉	5050_3	455	广	底	0024_2	17
女	妮	4741_1	430		庖	0021_7	11
	妹	4549_0	419		店	0026_1	19
	妻	5040_4	455		庚	0023_7	17
	妾	0040_4	23		府	0024_0	17
	姆	4745_5	432	弓	弦	1023_2	78
	姊	4542_7	419		弧	1223_0	112
	始	4346_0	388		弩	4720_7	428
	姍	4744_5	431	彳	彼	2424_7	206
	姐	4741_0	430		往	2021_4	144
	姑	4446_0	406		彿	2522_7	221
	姓	4541_0	419		征	2121_1	163
	委	2040_4	149		徂	2721_0	240

部	字	四　角	頁　碼	部	字	四　角	頁　碼
心	忠	5033_6	453		抽	5506_0	484
	念	8033_2	637		拑	5407_0	482
	忽	2733_2	247		拂	5502_7	482
	忿	8033_2	637		拆	5203_1	467
	怍	9801_1	706		拇	5705_5	497
	快	9503_0	700		拈	5106_0	464
	怔	9101_1	691		担	5601_0	488
	怕	9600_0	701		拉	5001_8	449
	怖	9402_7	696		拊	5400_0	479
	怙	9406_0	696		抛	5401_2	480
	怛	9601_0	701		拍	5600_0	487
	怡	9306_0	695		拐	5602_7	488
	怦	9104_9	692		拒	5101_7	461
	性	9501_4	698		拓	5106_0	464
	怩	9701_1	703		拔	5304_7	475
	怪	9701_4	703		拖	5801_2	501
	怯	9403_1	696		拘	5702_0	494
	怳	9601_0	701		拙	5207_2	470
	怵	9309_4	695		拚	5304_0	474
戈	戔	5350_3	479		招	5706_2	497
	戕	2325_0	196	攴	放	0824_0	53
	或	5310_0	476		政	1814_0	139
爪	爬	7723_1	597	斤	斧	8022_1	629
戶	戽	3024_7	277	方	於	0823_3	53
	戾	3023_4	277	日	旺	6101_4	533
	房	3022_7	275		昂	6072_7	529
	所	7222_1	576		昃	6028_1	520
手	承	1723_2	131		昆	6071_1	528
	抨	5104_9	464		昇	6044_0	524
	披	5404_7	481		昉	6002_7	508
	抬	5306_0	475		昌	6060_0	526
	抱	5701_2	492		明	6702_0	554
	抵	5204_0	468		昏	7260_4	578
	抹	5509_0	485		易	6022_7	519
	押	5605_0	490		昔	4460_1	408

部	字	四　角	頁　碼	部	字	四　角	頁　碼
月	朋	7722_0	595		沸	3512_7	317
	服	7724_7	598		油	3516_0	319
予	矜	1822_7	140		治	3316_0	305
木	杭	4091_7	377		沼	3716_2	331
	柿	4092_7	377		沽	3416_0	313
	杯	4199_0	382		沿	3716_1	331
	杳	4060_9	373		泄	3411_7	310
	杵	4894_0	443		泗	3610_0	323
	杷	4791_7	436		污	3112_7	291
	柕	4792_2	436		泓	3310_0	303
	松	4893_2	442		況	3611_0	323
	板	4194_7	382		泊	3610_0	323
	枇	4191_0	381		泌	3310_0	303
	枉	4191_4	381		法	3413_1	311
	析	4292_1	385		泛	3213_7	297
	枕	4491_2	416		沾	3116_0	292
	林	4499_0	419		泡	3711_2	328
	枚	4894_0	443		波	3414_7	312
	果	6090_4	532		泣	3011_8	272
	枝	4494_7	418		泥	3711_1	327
	杲	6090_4	532		注	3011_4	272
	枸	4791_2	436		泮	3915_0	351
欠	欣	7728_2	602		泯	3714_7	330
止	武	1314_0	118		泳	3313_2	303
	歧	2414_7	201	父	爸	8071_7	648
歹	殁	1724_7	133	火	炊	9788_2	705
	殀	1223_4	112		炎	9080_9	691
毋	毒	5050_5	455		炒	9982_0	709
氏	氓	0774_7	52		炕	9081_7	691
气	氛	8021_7	629		炙	2780_9	255
水	沫	3519_0	320	爪	爬	7723_1	597
	沮	3711_0	327		爭	2050_7	153
	沛	3012_7	272	爿	牀	2429_0	209
	沱	3311_1	303	片	版	2104_7	160
	河	3112_0	291	牛	牧	2854_1	264

部	字	四角	頁碼	部	字	四角	頁碼
犬	物	2752_0	250		肪	7022_7	564
	狀	2323_4	194		胚	7521_7	585
	狃	4625_6	423		胕	7422_7	582
	狐	4223_0	383		肯	2122_7	167
	狗	4722_0	428		肱	7423_2	582
	狙	4721_0	428		育	0022_7	13
	狒	4522_7	419		肴	4022_7	366
玉	玩	1111_1	102	臣	臥	7370_0	581
	玟	1814_0	139	臼	臾	7743_7	604
田	畀	6044_0	524	艸	芙	4453_0	407
疒	疝	0017_2	7		芝	4430_7	401
	疚	0018_7	8		芨	4440_7	404
白	的	2762_0	252		芥	4422_8	399
皿	盂	1010_7	71		芬	4422_7	398
目	盱	6104_0	534		芭	4471_7	411
	盲	0060_1	27		花	4421_4	397
	直	4010_7	360		芳	4422_7	398
曰	沓	1269_3	117		芸	4473_1	412
石	矴	1762_0	137		芹	4422_1	398
矢	知	8640_0	665		韭	4410_1	391
示	社	3421_0	313		芽	4424_1	400
	祀	3721_7	333	虍	虎	2121_7	164
	祁	3722_7	334	虫	虱	1711_0	129
禾	秉	2090_7	158	車	軋	5201_0	465
穴	穹	3020_7	274	辵	迎	3730_2	334
	空	3010_1	269		近	3230_2	300
竹	竺	8810_1	671		迓	3130_4	294
糸	糾	2290_0	187		返	3130_4	294
舌	舍	8060_4	645	邑	邱	7712_7	588
网	罔	7722_0	594		邸	7772_7	610
羊	羌	8021_1	628	采	采	2090_4	157
肉	股	7724_7	599	金	金	8010_9	625
	肢	7424_7	583	長	長	7173_2	574
	肥	7721_7	591	門	門	7777_7	612
	肩	3022_7	275	阜	阜	2740_7	248

部	字	四　角	頁　碼	部	字	四　角	頁　碼
	阻	7721_0	589		俠	2423_8	205
	阽	7126_0	569		信	2026_1	147
	阿	7122_0	566	冂	冒	6060_0	526
	陀	7321_1	580	冖	冠	3721_4	333
	陂	7424_7	583	刀	剃	8220_0	658
	附	7420_0	581		到	1210_0	107
隹	隹	2021_4	144		則	6280_0	539
雨	雨	1022_7	75		剉	8210_0	658
青	青	5022_7	452		削	9220_0	694
非	非	1111_1	101		剄	4221_0	383
					刺	5290_0	472

九畫

部	字	四　角	頁　碼	部	字	四　角	頁　碼
					前	8022_1	629
亠	亭	0020_1	8	力	勁	1412_7	121
	亮	0021_7	11		勃	4442_7	405
人	侮	2825_7	263		敇	5492_7	482
	侯	2723_4	243		勇	1742_7	134
	侵	2724_7	243		勉	2441_2	209
	侶	2626_0	230	勹	匍	2722_0	241
	偏	2722_7	242		麃	4721_2	428
	便	2124_6	169	十	南	4022_7	366
	係	2229_3	182	卩	卻	8762_0	670
	怱	2723_2	242	厂	厔	7121_2	566
	促	2628_1	231		厘	7121_4	566
	俄	2325_0	195		厚	7124_8	569
	俊	2324_7	195	又	叛	9154_7	692
	俎	8781_0	671	口	咤	6301_4	540
	俏	2922_7	268		咦	6503_2	549
	俐	2220_0	177		咱	6600_0	550
	俗	2826_8	263		哆	6702_7	555
	俘	2224_7	181		哪	6702_7	555
	俚	2621_4	230		咯	6706_4	557
	保	2629_4	231		呲	6101_0	532
	俞	8022_1	629		咧	6200_0	536
	侲	2323_4	194		咨	3760_8	341
					咪	6909_4	562

部	字	四角	頁碼	部	字	四角	頁碼
	咡	7680_8	587		姻	4640_0	425
	咬	6004_8	508		姿	3740_4	340
	咳	6008_2	509		威	5320_0	477
	咷	6201_3	536		娃	4441_4	404
	咸	5320_0	478	子	孩	1048_2	86
	咻	6409_0	546	宀	客	3060_4	284
	咽	6600_0	550		宣	3010_6	270
	哀	0073_2	30		室	3010_4	270
	品	6066_0	528		宥	3022_7	275
	哂	6106_0	534		宦	3071_7	286
	哄	6408_1	545	寸	封	4410_0	391
	咿	6705_7	556	尸	屋	7721_4	591
	哇	6401_4	543		屏	7724_1	598
	哈	6806_1	561		屍	7721_2	590
口	囿	6022_7	520		屎	7729_4	602
土	型	1210_4	108	山	峙	2474_1	213
	垓	4018_2	362	己	巷	4471_2	411
	垢	4216_1	383	巾	帝	0022_7	12
	垣	4111_6	379		帥	2472_7	212
大	奎	4010_4	360	幺	幽	2277_0	184
	奏	5043_0	455	广	度	0024_7	18
	契	5743_0	500	廴	建	1540_0	124
	奔	4044_4	370	廾	弇	8044_6	640
	奐	2743_0	249	弓	弭	1124_0	105
女	姚	4241_2	384	彐	彖	2723_2	242
	姜	8040_4	639	彡	形	1242_2	115
	姝	4549_0	419	彳	待	2424_1	205
	姣	4044_8	371		徇	2722_0	242
	姥	4441_1	404		很	2723_2	243
	姦	4044_4	370		徊	2620_0	229
	姨	4543_2	419		徉	2825_1	263
	姹	4341_4	388		律	2520_7	221
	姪	4141_4	380		後	2224_7	180
	姬	4141_6	380	心	怎	8033_1	637
	妍	4144_0	380		怒	4733_4	429

部	字	四　角	頁　碼	部	字	四　角	頁　碼
	思	6033_0	520		映	6503_0	548
	怠	2333_6	196		昧	6509_0	549
	急	2733_7	247		春	5060_3	456
	怨	2733_1	247		昭	6706_2	556
	恆	9101_7	692		是	6080_1	530
	恂	9702_0	703		昶	3623_0	325
	恃	9404_1	696	曰	曷	6072_7	529
	恒	9101_6	692	木	枯	4496_0	418
	恍	9901_1	708		柏	4396_0	390
	恟	9702_0	703		枴	4692_7	427
	恢	9108_9	692		柔	1790_4	138
	恤	9701_0	703		架	4690_4	427
	恪	9706_4	704		枷	4690_0	425
	恫	9702_0	703		柄	4192_7	382
	恬	9206_4	694		柏	4690_0	425
	恓	9101_1	691		某	4490_4	416
	恰	9806_1	706		柑	4497_0	418
戶	扁	3022_7	275		柒	3490_4	316
手	拜	2155_0	172		染	3490_4	316
	括	5206_4	469		柘	4196_0	382
	拭	5304_0	474		柚	4596_0	420
	拯	5701_3	493		柢	4294_0	385
	拱	5408_1	482		查	4010_6	360
	拴	5801_4	501		樞	4191_8	382
	拷	5402_7	480		柬	5090_6	459
	拾	5806_1	503		柯	4192_0	382
	持	5404_1	480		柱	4091_4	377
	指	5106_1	464		柜	4191_7	382
	按	5304_4	474		柳	4792_0	436
	挑	5201_3	466		柴	2190_4	173
	挖	5301_7	473		柵	4794_5	437
攴	故	4864_0	442	止	歪	1010_1	69
斤	斫	1262_1	117	歹	殂	1721_0	131
方	施	0821_2	52		殃	1523_0	124
日	星	6010_4	511		殆	1326_0	120

部	字	四角	頁碼
殳	段	7744_7	606
气	氟	8051_7	642
水	泉	2623_2	230
	洋	3815_1	345
	酒	3116_0	292
	洗	3411_1	309
	洛	3716_4	331
	洞	3712_0	328
	流	3011_3	271
	洩	3510_6	317
	洪	3418_1	313
	洲	3210_0	295
	洵	3712_0	328
	洶	3712_0	328
	活	3216_4	298
	洽	3816_1	347
	派	3213_2	297
	洫	3711_0	327
	洮	3211_3	296
火	炫	9083_2	691
	炬	9181_7	693
	炭	2228_9	182
	炮	9781_2	704
	炯	9782_0	705
	炳	9182_7	693
	炷	9081_4	691
	炸	9881_1	707
	炤	9786_2	705
	為	3402_7	307
牛	牲	2551_0	223
犬	狠	4723_2	429
	狡	4024_8	368
	狩	4324_2	388
玉	玲	1813_7	139
	玷	1116_0	103
	玻	1414_7	121
	珀	1610_0	125
	珊	1714_5	130
	珍	1812_2	139
	珂	1112_0	103
甘	甚	4471_1	411
田	畋	6804_0	561
	毗	6101_0	532
	界	6022_8	520
	畎	6303_4	540
	畏	6073_2	529
	畍	6500_0	548
疒	疤	0011_7	4
	疥	0012_8	6
	疫	0014_7	7
白	皆	2160_2	172
	皇	2610_4	228
皿	盅	5010_7	451
	盆	8010_7	625
	盈	1710_7	128
目	相	4690_0	425
	盹	6501_7	548
	盼	6802_7	561
	盾	7226_4	577
	省	9060_2	688
	眄	6102_7	533
	眇	6902_0	562
	眈	6401_2	543
	眉	7726_7	601
	看	2060_4	154
石	砂	1962_0	142
	研	1164_0	107
	砍	1768_2	137
	砒	1161_0	106
	研	1164_0	107

部	字	四角	頁碼	部	字	四角	頁碼
	砌	1762_0	137		胚	7121_9	566
示	祇	3224_0	299		胝	7224_0	577
	祈	3222_1	299		胞	7721_2	590
	祉	3121_0	293		胡	4762_0	433
内	禹	6042_7	524		胥	1722_7	131
禾	秋	2998_0	269		胅	7423_1	582
	科	2490_0	214	至	致	1814_0	140
	秒	2992_0	269	舟	舡	2247_0	183
穴	穿	3024_1	277	艸	茲	8073_2	653
	窀	3055_8	283		苑	4421_2	397
	突	3043_0	283		苓	4430_7	401
竹	竿	8840_1	675		苔	4460_3	408
米	籽	9794_0	706		苗	4460_0	408
	籵	9798_7	706		苛	4462_1	409
糸	紀	2791_7	256		芋	4420_1	396
	約	2792_0	257		茅	4422_2	398
	紅	2191_0	174		茗	4460_2	408
	紇	2891_7	267		苯	4423_4	400
	納	2491_7	215		茉	4490_4	416
	紉	2792_0	257		苣	4410_8	392
缶	缸	8171_0	657		苦	4460_4	408
羊	美	8043_0	639		苴	4477_2	412
老	者	4460_0	408		苞	4471_2	411
而	耍	1040_4	81		苟	4462_7	410
	耐	1420_0	122		苦	4460_4	408
耳	耶	1712_7	129		英	4453_0	407
肉	胃	6022_7	520		茂	4425_3	400
	胄	5022_7	452		茄	4446_0	406
	背	1122_7	104		茉	4490_4	416
	胎	7326_0	580	虍	虐	2121_1	164
	胖	7925_0	620	虫	虹	5111_0	465
	胙	7821_1	616	行	衍	2122_1	166
	胗	7822_2	617	臼	舁	7744_7	606
	胂	7625_0	587	衣	表	5073_2	457
	肺	7022_7	564		衫	3222_2	299

部	字	四角	頁碼	部	字	四角	頁碼
西	要	1040_4	81	頁	頁	1080_6	94
角	觔	2422_7	205	風	風	7721_0	589
言	訂	0162_0	33	飛	飛	1241_3	115
	訃	0360_0	39	食	食	8073_2	653
	計	0460_0	41	首	首	8060_1	644
貝	貞	2180_6	173	香	香	2060_9	155
	負	1780_6	138				

十畫

部	字	四角	頁碼
走	赳	4280_0	384
	赴	4380_0	389
車	軌	5401_7	480
	軍	3760_6	340
辵	迢	3730_6	338
	迥	3730_2	335
	迫	3330_6	307
	迪	3530_6	322
	迹	3030_3	279
	迤	3830_1	348
	迫	3630_0	325
	迭	3530_3	322
	述	3330_9	307
邑	郊	0742_7	48
酉	酋	8060_1	645
里	重	2010_4	142
門	閂	7710_7	588
阜	陋	7121_2	566
	郁	4722_7	429
	陌	7126_0	569
	降	7725_4	600
	胝	7224_0	577
	限	7723_2	597
	陔	7028_2	564
面	面	1060_0	87
革	革	4450_6	407
韋	韋	4050_6	371
音	音	0060_1	27

部	字	四角	頁碼
亠	毫	0071_4	29
人	修	2722_2	242
	俯	2024_0	146
	俱	2728_1	246
	俸	2525_3	222
	俺	2421_6	204
	俾	2624_0	230
	併	2824_1	262
	倆	2122_7	167
	倉	8060_7	647
	個	2620_0	229
	倍	2026_1	147
	倏	2723_4	243
	們	2722_0	242
	倒	2220_0	177
	倔	2727_2	246
	倬	2424_1	206
	倘	2922_7	268
	候	2723_4	243
	倚	2422_1	204
	借	2426_1	207
	倡	2626_0	230
	傲	2824_0	261
	值	2421_7	204
	倦	2921_2	268
	倨	2726_4	246

部	字	四　角	頁　碼	部	字	四　角	頁　碼
	倩	2522_7	221		唉	6303_4	540
	倫	2822_7	260		唏	6402_7	543
	倭	2224_4	180		唐	0026_7	20
	侳	2321_1	193	口	圃	6022_7	520
八	兼	8033_7	638		圄	6060_1	527
冖	冢	3723_2	334	土	埃	4313_4	387
	冤	3741_3	340		埋	4611_4	421
	冥	3780_0	342		城	4315_0	387
冫	准	3011_4	272	夂	夏	1024_7	78
	凋	3712_0	328	大	套	4073_1	374
	凌	3414_7	313	女	娉	4542_7	419
	凍	3519_6	320		娌	4641_4	425
刀	剔	6220_0	538		娓	4741_4	430
	剖	0260_0	35		娘	4343_2	388
	剛	7220_0	576		娛	4643_4	425
	剝	2210_0	176		娟	4642_7	425
	剡	9280_0	694		娠	4143_2	380
匕	乘	2090_1	156		娥	4345_0	388
匚	匪	7171_1	573		嫂	4744_7	432
厂	原	7129_6	570		娩	4741_6	430
又	叟	7740_7	603		婀	4142_0	380
口	員	6080_6	530		娜	4742_7	431
	哥	1062_1	90	子	孫	1249_3	116
	哦	6305_0	540	宀	寇	3021_4	275
	哨	6902_7	562		宮	3060_6	284
	哩	6601_4	550		宰	3040_1	281
	哭	6643_0	552		害	3060_1	283
	哮	6404_7	545		宴	3040_4	282
	哲	5260_2	472		宵	3022_7	275
	哺	6302_7	540		家	3023_2	276
	哼	6002_7	508		容	3060_8	285
	哽	6104_6	534	寸	射	2420_0	202
	唁	6006_1	509	尸	展	7724_7	598
	唆	6304_7	540		屑	7722_7	596
	唇	7126_3	570		展	7723_2	597

部	字	四　角	頁　碼	部	字	四　角	頁　碼
山	峨	2375_0	197		悝	9601_4	701
	峭	2972_7	269		悟	9106_1	692
	峯	2250_4	183		悁	9602_7	701
	島	2772_7	254	戶	扇	3022_7	276
	峻	2374_7	197	手	拳	9050_2	688
	峽	2473_8	212		挈	5750_2	500
工	差	8021_1	628		拿	8050_2	641
巾	師	2172_7	173		捋	5704_2	496
广	席	0022_7	13		挨	5303_4	474
	座	0021_4	9		挪	5702_7	494
	庫	0025_6	19		挫	5801_4	501
	庭	0024_1	17		振	5103_2	463
弓	弱	1712_7	129		挹	5601_7	488
彳	徐	2829_4	264		挺	5204_1	468
	徑	2121_1	163		挽	5701_6	493
	徒	2428_1	208		挾	5403_8	480
心	恐	1733_1	133		捆	5600_0	488
	恕	4633_0	424		捉	5608_1	490
	恙	8033_1	637		捍	5604_1	489
	恣	3733_8	340		捏	5701_1	492
	恥	1310_0	117		捐	5602_7	489
	恩	6033_0	521		捕	5302_7	473
	恭	4433_8	403	攴	效	0844_0	54
	息	2633_0	233	斗	料	9490_0	698
	悄	9602_7	701	方	旁	0022_7	13
	悃	9600_0	701		旅	0823_2	52
	悄	9902_7	708		旃	0821_4	52
	悅	9801_6	706	日	晃	6011_3	512
	悌	9802_7	706		晁	6021_3	519
	悍	9604_1	702		晒	6106_0	534
	悒	9601_7	701		晌	6702_0	554
	悔	9805_6	706		時	6404_1	544
	悖	9404_7	696		晉	1060_1	88
	悚	9509_6	700		晏	6040_4	523
	悛	9304_7	695	曰	書	5060_1	456

部	字	四角	頁碼	部	字	四角	頁碼
月	朔	8742_0	670		浣	3311_1	303
	胨	7823_4	618		浦	3312_7	303
木	栓	4891_4	442		浩	3416_1	313
	栖	4196_0	382		浪	3313_2	303
	栗	1090_4	101		浮	3214_7	298
	校	4094_8	378		浴	3816_8	347
	株	4599_0	420		海	3815_7	345
	核	4098_2	378		浸	3714_7	331
	根	4793_2	436		浬	3611_4	323
	格	4796_4	438		涂	3819_4	347
	栽	4395_0	390		涇	3111_1	290
	桀	2590_4	223		消	3912_7	350
	柞	4891_1	442		涉	3112_1	291
	桂	4491_4	416		涌	3712_7	329
	桃	4291_3	385		涎	3214_1	297
	桅	4791_2	436		涓	3612_7	324
	框	4191_1	381		涕	3812_7	343
	案	3090_4	290	火	烟	9680_0	702
	桌	2190_4	173		烈	1233_0	114
	桎	4191_4	381		烊	9885_1	707
	桐	4792_0	436		烏	2732_7	246
	桑	7790_4	615		烘	9488_1	697
	桓	4191_6	382		烙	9786_4	705
	桔	4496_1	418		烤	9482_7	697
	桁	4192_1	382	父	爹	8020_7	628
歹	殉	1722_0	131	牛	特	2454_1	209
	殊	1529_0	124	犬	狷	4622_7	422
殳	殷	2724_7	244		狸	4621_4	422
气	氣	8091_7	654		狳	4829_4	440
	氧	8051_7	642		狹	4423_8	400
	氨	8041_7	639		狼	4323_2	388
水	泰	5013_2	452		狽	4628_0	423
	浙	3212_1	296	玉	珠	1519_0	124
	浚	3314_7	304		班	1111_4	102
	浜	3218_7	299	田	留	7760_2	608

部	字	四　角	頁　碼	部	字	四　角	頁　碼
	畛	6802_2	561		秤	2194_9	176
	畜	0060_3	27		秦	5090_4	459
	畝	0768_0	52		秧	2593_0	224
	畔	6905_0	562		秩	2593_0	224
疒	疲	0014_7	7	穴	窅	3021_1	274
	疳	0017_5	7		窈	3072_7	286
	疵	0011_1	4	立	站	0116_1	32
	疹	0012_2	4		竛	0312_1	38
	疼	0013_3	6	竹	笆	8871_7	677
	疾	0013_4	6		笈	8824_7	674
	病	0012_7	4		笋	8850_7	676
	症	0011_1	3		笏	8822_7	673
皿	益	8010_7	625		笑	8843_0	675
	盌	2710_7	238	米	粉	9892_7	707
	盎	5010_7	451	糸	紊	0090_3	31
目	真	4080_1	375		紋	2094_0	160
	眠	6704_7	556		納	2492_7	215
	眨	6203_7	537		紐	2791_5	256
	眩	6003_2	508		紘	2493_0	215
矢	短	8141_8	656		紓	2792_2	257
石	砝	1463_1	123		純	2591_7	223
	砥	1264_0	117		紗	2992_0	269
	砰	1164_9	107		紙	2294_0	189
	砧	1166_0	107		級	2794_7	259
	破	1464_7	123		紛	2892_7	267
	砲	1761_2	136		素	5090_3	459
示	祐	3426_0	314		紡	2092_7	159
	祖	3721_0	333		索	4090_3	376
	祝	3621_0	325	缶	缺	8573_0	664
	神	3520_6	320	羽	翁	8012_7	627
	祕	3320_0	306		翅	4740_2	430
	祠	3722_0	331	老	耆	4460_1	408
禾	秘	2390_0	198	耒	耕	5590_0	487
	租	2791_0	255		耗	5291_4	472
	秣	2599_0	225		耘	5193_1	465

部	字	四　角	頁　碼	部	字	四　角	頁　碼
	耙	5791_7	500		荏	4421_4	398
耳	耽	1411_2	120		茱	4490_4	416
	耿	1918_0	142	羊	羔	8033_1	637
肉	朐	7620_0	586	虍	虔	2124_0	168
	胯	7422_7	582	虫	蚊	5014_0	452
	胱	7921_1	620		蚪	5410_0	482
	胼	7824_1	618		蚌	5510_0	485
	脆	7721_2	590		蚓	5210_0	471
	胰	7523_2	585		蚜	5114_0	465
	胸	7722_0	595		蚣	5813_2	504
	能	2121_1	164		蚤	7713_6	588
	胳	7726_4	601		蚧	5812_0	504
	脂	7126_1	569		蚨	5513_0	485
	脅	4022_7	366	衣	衰	0073_2	30
	脈	7223_2	577		衷	0073_2	30
	脊	1122_7	105		衽	3221_4	299
自	臭	2643_0	233		袤	8073_2	653
舌	舐	2264_0	183		袁	4073_2	374
舟	航	2041_7	151	言	訐	0164_0	34
	舫	2042_7	152		訊	0761_1	48
艸	芻	2742_7	249		訌	0161_0	33
	茗	4460_7	409		討	0460_0	42
	荔	4442_7	405		訓	0260_0	36
	茜	4460_1	408		訕	0267_0	37
	茫	4411_0	393		訖	0861_7	56
	茯	4423_4	400		託	0261_4	36
	茴	4460_0	408		記	0761_7	49
	茵	4460_0	408	豆	豈	2210_8	176
	茶	4490_4	415		豇	1111_2	102
	茸	4440_1	403	豸	豹	2722_0	241
	茹	4446_0	406		豺	2420_0	202
	荀	4462_7	410	貝	財	6480_0	547
	荆	4240_0	384		貢	1080_6	94
	草	4440_6	403	走	赶	4180_4	381
	荒	4421_1	397		起	4780_1	434

部	字	四　角	頁　碼
身	躬	2722_7	242
車	軒	5104_0	463
	軔	5702_0	494
辰	辱	7134_3	572
辵	迷	3930_9	352
	迹	3030_3	279
	追	3730_7	338
	退	3730_3	337
	送	3830_3	348
	逃	3230_1	299
	逆	3830_4	349
	迴	3630_0	325
邑	郎	3772_7	342
	郡	1762_7	137
酉	酌	1762_0	137
	配	1761_7	136
	酒	3116_0	292
金	釘	8112_0	655
	釜	8010_9	626
	針	8410_0	661
門	閃	7780_7	614
阜	陡	7121_4	566
	陝	7423_8	583
	陸	7421_4	582
	陟	7122_1	567
	陛	7428_1	583
	院	7321_1	580
	陣	7520_6	584
	除	7829_4	618
隹	隻	2040_7	150
食	飡	3813_2	344
馬	馬	7132_7	571
骨	骨	7722_7	596
高	高	0022_7	14
鬥	鬥	7711_4	588

部	字	四　角	頁　碼
鬼	鬼	2621_3	229

十一畫

部	字	四　角	頁　碼
乙	乾	4841_7	440
人	假	2724_7	244
	偉	2425_6	206
	偏	2322_7	193
	偕	2126_2	170
	做	2824_0	261
	停	2022_1	144
	健	2524_0	221
	偌	2426_4	207
	側	2220_0	177
	偵	2128_6	170
	偶	2622_7	230
	偷	2822_7	260
	偽	2422_7	204
几	兜	7721_7	592
冂	冕	6041_6	523
冫	凑	3513_4	319
几	凰	7721_0	589
刀	剩	2290_0	187
	副	1260_0	116
	剪	8022_7	632
	勒	4452_7	407
	動	2412_7	200
	勘	4472_7	412
	務	1722_7	131
勹	匐	2762_0	252
匕	匙	6180_1	535
匚	匭	7171_2	573
	匩	7171_6	573
	區	7171_6	573
厶	參	2320_2	192

部	字	四　角	頁　碼	部	字	四　角	頁　碼
口	售	2060_1	154		堅	7710_4	587
	唯	6001_4	508		堆	4011_4	361
	唾	6201_4	536		埧	4718_1	428
	啡	6101_1	532	女	娑	1740_4	134
	啤	6604_0	550		姘	4844_1	441
	啄	6103_2	534		婆	3440_4	316
	啇	0022_7	13		婉	4341_2	388
	問	7760_7	608		婚	4246_1	384
	啊	6102_0	533		婊	4543_2	419
	啕	6702_0	554		婢	4644_0	425
	啐	6004_8	509		婦	4742_7	431
	啓	3860_4	349		婁	4440_4	403
	啖	6908_9	562		娼	4646_0	425
	啜	6704_7	456	子	孰	0441_7	41
	啞	6101_7	533	宀	宿	3026_1	278
	唎	6702_0	554		寂	3094_7	290
	啥	6806_4	561		寇	3021_4	275
	唱	6606_0	550		冤	3041_3	282
	啁	6702_0	554		寄	3062_1	285
	唷	6002_7	508		密	3077_2	286
	唸	6803_2	561	寸	將	2724_0	243
	唬	6101_1	533		專	5034_3	454
	啃	6102_7	534	尸	屜	7721_7	591
	啊	6102_7	534		尉	7420_0	582
囗	圇	6022_7	520	山	峻	2474_7	213
	圈	6071_2	528		崇	2290_1	187
	圉	6040_1	523		崎	2472_1	211
	國	6015_3	514		崑	2271_1	183
	圍	6022_7	520		崖	2221_4	179
土	域	4315_0	388		崗	2222_7	179
	埠	4714_7	428		崛	2777_2	254
	執	4441_7	404		崩	2222_7	179
	培	4016_1	362	巛	巢	2290_4	187
	基	4410_4	391	巾	帳	4123_2	379
	堂	9010_4	684		帶	4422_7	398

部	字	四　角	頁　碼	部	字	四　角	頁　碼
攴	敘	8194_7	657		梳	4091_3	377
	敏	8854_6	676		梵	4421_7	398
	救	4814_0	438		椚	4792_7	436
	敕	5894_0	506	欠	欲	8768_2	670
	敖	5824_0	505	气	氫	8011_7	627
	敗	6884_0	562	水	涯	3111_4	291
文	斌	0344_0	38		淒	3514_4	319
斗	斜	8490_0	663		梁	3390_4	307
斤	斬	5202_1	467		清	3512_7	317
方	旋	0828_1	54		淋	3419_0	313
	旌	0821_4	52		液	3014_7	273
	族	0823_4	53		涵	3117_2	293
无	既	7171_4	573		涸	3610_0	323
日	晚	6701_6	553		涼	3019_6	273
	晝	5010_6	451		涿	3113_2	291
	晤	6106_1	534		淛	3212_1	296
	晦	6805_7	561		淑	3714_0	330
	晨	6023_2	520		淘	3712_0	328
	曹	5560_6	486		淚	3313_4	304
	曼	6040_7	523		淩	3414_7	313
月	朗	3772_0	342		淯	3412_7	311
	望	0710_4	48		淹	3411_6	310
木	桶	4792_7	436		淞	3813_0	343
	梧	4196_1	382		淡	3918_9	351
	梅	4895_5	443		淤	3813_3	344
	梏	4496_1	418		淨	3215_7	298
	梓	4094_1	378		淪	3812_7	343
	梗	4194_6	382		淫	3211_4	296
	條	2729_4	246		淮	3011_4	272
	梟	2790_1	255		深	3719_4	332
	梢	4992_7	444		淳	3014_7	273
	梨	2290_4	187		淵	3210_0	296
	桿	4694_1	427		混	3611_0	323
	梯	4892_7	442		淺	3315_3	305
	械	4395_0	390		添	3213_3	297

部	字	四　角	頁　碼	部	字	四　角	頁　碼
	淀	3318_1	305		眸	6305_0	540
	淬	3014_8	273		眺	6201_3	536
	淖	3114_6	292		眼	6703_2	555
火	烹	0033_2	21	石	硃	1569_0	125
	焉	1032_7	80		砲	1660_0	128
	焊	9604_1	703		研	1164_0	107
	烽	9785_4	705	示	祥	3825_1	347
爻	爽	4003_4	358		票	1090_1	101
牛	牽	0050_2	26		祭	2790_1	255
	犀	7725_3	600	禾	移	2792_7	257
犬	猖	4626_0	423	穴	窒	3010_4	270
	猙	4225_7	383		窕	3011_3	271
	猛	4721_7	428	立	竟	0021_6	10
	猜	4522_7	419		章	0040_6	23
	猝	4024_8	368	竹	笙	8810_4	672
玄	率	0040_3	23		笛	8860_3	677
玉	現	1611_0	125		答	8860_3	677
	理	1611_4	126		笠	8810_3	672
	琉	1011_3	72		符	8824_3	674
	球	1313_2	118		笨	8823_4	674
瓦	瓷	3771_7	342		笤	8860_2	677
	瓶	8141_7	656		第	8822_7	673
甘	甜	2467_0	211		笳	8846_0	676
生	產	0021_4	9	米	粒	9091_8	691
田	畢	6050_4	525		粕	9690_0	703
	略	6706_4	557		粗	9791_0	705
	畦	6401_4	543		粘	9196_0	693
疒	痊	0011_4	4	糸	紫	2190_3	173
	痔	0014_1	7		累	6090_3	531
	痕	0013_2	6		細	2690_0	234
白	皎	2064_8	156		紳	2590_6	223
皿	盒	8010_7	625		終	2793_3	258
	盔	7110_7	565		絃	2093_2	160
目	眶	6101_1	532		組	2791_0	255
	眷	9060_3	688		絆	2995_0	269

部	字	四 角	頁 碼	部	字	四 角	頁 碼
网	罣	6010_4	511		蚱	5811_1	504
羊	羚	8853_7	676		蚯	5011_4	451
	羞	8021_5	628		蛄	5416_0	482
羽	翌	1710_8	129		蛆	5711_0	499
	翌	1760_2	135		蛇	5311_1	476
耳	聊	1712_0	129		蛉	5813_7	504
肉	腌	7726_2	600		蛋	1713_6	129
	腕	7321_2	580	耒	耜	5797_7	500
	脛	7121_1	565	衣	袈	4673_2	425
	脡	7821_4	616		袋	2373_2	197
	脣	7122_7	567		袍	3721_2	333
	脖	7424_7	583		袒	3621_0	325
	腳	7722_0	595		袖	3526_0	321
	脫	7821_6	616		袚	3324_4	307
	脯	7322_7	580		袜	3529_0	321
	脘	7321_1	580		被	3424_7	314
臼	舂	5077_7	457	見	規	5601_0	488
舟	舵	2341_1	196		覓	2021_6	144
	舶	2640_0	233	言	訝	0164_0	34
	舷	2043_2	152		訟	0863_2	56
	船	2746_1	250		訴	0262_1	36
艸	荳	4410_8	392		訣	0563_0	45
	荷	4422_1	398		訥	0462_7	43
	莧	4421_6	398		訛	0267_0	37
	莉	4492_0	417		訬	0461_0	42
	莊	4421_4	398		訪	0062_7	28
	莎	4412_9	395		設	0764_7	51
	莖	4410_1	391		許	0864_0	56
	莘	4440_1	403	豆	豉	1414_7	121
	莠	4422_7	398	豕	豚	7123_2	567
	莢	4443_8	406	貝	貧	8080_6	654
	莫	4443_6	406		貨	2480_6	213
虍	處	2124_1	168		販	6184_7	536
虫	蚯	5211_1	471		貪	8080_6	654
	蚰	5516_0	485		貫	7780_6	614

部	字	四　角	頁　碼	部	字	四　角	頁　碼
	創	8260_0	659		喬	2022_7	145
几	凱	2711_0	238		單	6650_6	552
力	勝	7921_4	620	口	圍	6050_6	525
	勞	9942_7	708	土	堡	2610_4	228
	勛	6482_7	548		堤	4618_1	422
十	博	4304_2	387		堪	4411_1	393
卩	卿	7772_0	610		堯	4021_1	363
厂	厥	7128_2	570		堝	4712_7	427
	廚	7124_0	568		報	4744_7	432
口	啼	6002_7	508		場	4612_7	422
	啾	6908_0	562		堵	4416_0	395
	喎	6602_7	550	士	壹	4010_8	361
	喂	6603_2	550		壺	4010_7	361
	喃	6402_7	543		堉	4712_7	427
	善	8060_5	646		堰	4111_4	379
	喇	6200_0	536	大	奠	8043_0	640
	喉	6703_4	556		奢	4060_4	373
	喊	6305_0	540	女	婷	4042_1	370
	喋	6409_4	546		嫣	4442_1	405
	嗒	6406_1	545		媒	4449_4	406
	喔	6701_4	553		媚	4746_7	432
	喘	6202_7	537		媛	4244_7	384
	喙	6703_2	555		嫂	4744_7	432
	喚	6703_4	556		媧	4742_7	431
	喜	4060_5	373	子	孱	7724_7	600
	喝	6602_7	550	宀	富	3060_6	284
	喇	6702_0	554		寐	3029_4	278
	唧	6702_0	554		寒	3030_3	279
	喞	6702_0	555		寓	3042_7	283
	喟	6602_7	550	寸	尊	8034_6	638
	喧	6301_6	540		尋	1734_1	133
	嘵	6001_7	508	尢	就	0391_4	40
	喻	6802_1	561	尸	屠	7726_4	601
	喪	4073_2	374	山	嵌	2278_2	186
	喫	6703_4	556	己	異	7780_1	613

部	字	四　角	頁　碼	部	字	四　角	頁　碼
巾	幀	4128_6	380	戶	扉	3021_1	274
	幃	4425_6	401	手	掌	9050_2	688
	幄	4721_4	428		掣	2250_2	183
	帽	4626_0	423		揶	5702_7	494
	幅	4126_6	380		揀	5509_6	485
幺	幾	2245_3	183		揆	5203_4	468
广	廁	0022_0	11		揉	5709_4	499
	廂	0026_0	19		描	5406_1	481
弋	弑	4394_0	390		提	5608_1	490
彡	彭	4212_2	383		揕	5401_1	479
彳	徧	2322_7	194		插	5207_7	470
	徨	2621_4	230		揖	5604_1	489
	復	2824_7	262		揚	5602_7	489
	循	2226_4	182		換	5703_4	495
心	悲	1133_1	106		揜	5804_6	503
	悶	7733_7	603		握	5701_4	493
	惑	5330_0	479		揄	5802_1	501
	惠	5033_3	453		摒	5704_1	496
	惡	1033_1	80		揣	5202_7	467
	惰	9402_7	696		揩	5106_2	465
	惱	9206_2	694		揪	5908_0	506
	惴	9202_7	693		揭	5602_1	489
	愎	9804_7	706		揮	5705_6	497
	愒	9602_7	701		援	5204_7	469
	惶	9601_4	701	攴	敞	9824_0	707
	惺	9601_4	701		敝	9824_0	707
	惻	9200_0	693		敢	1814_0	140
	愊	9106_6	692		散	4824_0	439
	愉	9802_1	706		敦	0844_0	55
	惝	9006_1	684	文	斑	1111_4	102
	愕	9602_7	702		斐	1140_0	106
	愜	9101_3	691	斤	斯	4282_1	384
	愣	9602_7	702	日	普	8060_1	645
	惦	9006_1	684		景	6090_6	532
戈	戟	4345_0	388		晰	6202_1	537

部	字	四　角	頁　碼	部	字	四　角	頁　碼
	晳	4260_2	384	欠	欺	4788_2	435
	冕	6041_6	523		欽	8718_2	669
	晴	6502_7	548		款	4798_2	438
	晶	6066_0	528	歹	殖	1421_7	122
	晷	6060_4	527		殘	1325_3	119
	智	8660_0	666	殳	殼	4724_7	429
	曾	8060_6	646	毛	毯	2971_8	268
	替	5560_3	486	气	氮	8081_7	654
	晾	6009_6	509		氛	8021_7	629
曰	最	6014_7	513		氲	8021_7	629
	曾	8060_6	646	水	滅	3315_0	304
月	朝	4742_0	430		渝	3812_1	343
	期	4782_0	435		渠	3190_4	295
木	棄	0090_4	31		渡	3014_7	373
	棉	4692_7	427		溫	3611_7	323
	棋	4498_1	418		湛	3411_8	310
	棍	4691_1	427		涅	3711_1	328
	棒	4595_3	420		渣	3411_6	310
	棠	9090_4	691		渦	3712_7	329
	棗	5090_2	459		渙	3713_4	330
	棘	5599_2	487		渥	3711_4	328
	棚	4792_0	436		測	3210_0	295
	棟	4599_6	420		港	3411_7	310
	棣	4593_2	420		渴	3612_7	324
	棕	4399_1	390		游	3814_7	345
	棧	4395_3	390		渺	3912_0	350
	森	4099_4	378		渾	3715_6	331
	棱	4494_7	418		湍	3212_7	297
	樓	4594_4	420		湖	3712_0	328
	棹	4194_6	382		湘	3610_0	323
	棺	4397_7	390		湧	3712_7	329
	椅	4492_1	417		湮	3111_4	291
	椎	4091_4	377		湯	3612_7	324
	椒	4794_0	437	火	焙	9086_1	691
	椏	4191_7	382		無	8033_1	633

部	字	四　角	頁　碼	部	字	四　角	頁　碼
	焚	4480_9	414		盜	3710_7	327
	焦	2033_1	148	目	睏	6600_0	550
	然	2333_2	196	矢	短	8141_8	656
片	牌	2604_0	228	石	硝	1962_7	142
	牋	2305_3	191		硫	1061_3	88
牙	掌	9024_1	686		硬	1164_6	107
牛	犂	2750_2	250		硯	1661_0	128
犬	貓	4426_0	401	用	甯	3022_7	275
	猢	4722_0	428	禾	稀	2492_7	215
	猥	4623_2	423		稅	2891_6	266
	猪	4426_0	401		稈	2694_1	237
	猩	4621_4	422		程	2691_4	235
	猴	4723_4	429		稍	2992_7	269
	猶	4826_1	439	穴	窖	3060_1	283
	猱	4729_4	429		窗	3060_2	284
	猬	4622_7	422		窘	3060_7	284
	猠	4629_4	423	立	竣	0314_7	38
玉	琛	1719_4	130		竦	0519_6	45
	琢	1113_2	103		童	0010_4	2
	琦	1412_1	120	竹	筍	8862_7	677
	琴	1120_7	104		筆	8850_7	676
	琵	1171_1	107		筏	8825_3	674
生	甥	2612_7	229		筐	8871_1	677
田	畫	5010_6	451		筑	8811_7	672
	異	6080_1	530		筒	8822_7	673
疋	疏	1011_3	72		筋	8822_7	673
疒	痘	0011_8	4		筅	8844_1	675
	痙	0011_1	3		答	8860_1	676
	痛	0012_7	5		策	8890_2	680
	痢	0012_0	4	米	粟	1090_4	101
	痣	0013_1	6		粵	2620_7	229
癶	登	1210_8	108		粥	1722_7	131
	發	1224_7	112		粧	9091_4	691
白	皓	2466_1	211	糸	結	2496_1	215
皿	盛	5320_0	478		絕	2791_7	256

部	字	四角	頁碼	部	字	四角	頁碼
	絞	2094_8	160		菱	4424_7	400
	絡	2796_4	259		菲	4411_1	393
	綑	2590_6	223		菴	4471_6	411
	絜	5790_3	500		菸	4423_3	400
	給	2896_1	267		萃	4440_8	404
	絨	2395_0	198		萄	4472_7	412
	絮	4690_3	426		萊	4490_8	416
	統	2091_3	158		萌	4462_7	410
	絲	2299_3	190		萍	4414_9	395
羊	羢	8355_0	661		菱	4440_4	403
	翔	8752_0	670	虍	虛	2121_7	164
羽	翁	8012_7	627	虫	蛙	5411_4	482
肉	脹	7123_2	567		蛔	5610_0	492
	脾	7624_0	587		蛛	5519_0	485
	腆	7528_1	585		蛟	5014_8	452
	腊	7426_1	583		蛤	5816_1	504
	腋	7024_7	564	行	街	2122_1	166
	腌	7421_6	582	衣	袱	3323_4	307
	腎	7722_7	596		袴	3422_7	314
	腑	7024_0	564		裁	4375_0	389
	腓	7121_1	565		裂	1273_2	117
	腔	7321_2	580		袖	3620_0	324
	腕	7321_2	580	見	視	3621_0	325
舌	舒	8762_2	670	言	訴	0263_1	36
艸	着	8060_1	645		詄	0563_0	45
	菁	4422_7	399		訶	0162_0	34
	菇	4446_4	406		診	0862_2	56
	菊	4492_7	417		註	0061_4	28
	菌	4460_0	408		証	0161_1	33
	菓	4490_4	416		詁	0466_0	44
	莽	4444_5	406		詆	0264_0	37
	菜	4490_4	415		詈	6060_1	527
	菠	4414_7	395		詠	0363_2	39
	菩	4460_1	408		詎	0161_7	33
	華	4450_4	406		詐	0861_1	55

部	字	四　角	頁　碼	部	字	四　角	頁　碼
	詒	0366_0	40	車	輊	5802_2	502
	詔	0766_2	51		軸	5506_0	484
	評	0164_9	34		軼	5503_0	483
	詖	0464_7	43	辵	逮	3530_3	322
	詛	0761_0	48		週	3730_2	336
	詞	0762_0	49		進	3030_1	278
豕	象	2723_2	242		逵	3430_1	315
豸	貂	2726_2	245		逸	3730_1	334
貝	貯	6382_1	542	邑	都	4762_7	433
	貳	4380_0	389		鄂	6722_7	559
	貴	5080_6	457	酉	酣	1467_0	123
	貶	6283_7	539		酥	1269_4	117
	買	6080_6	530	里	量	6010_4	511
	貸	2380_6	197	金	鈀	8711_7	667
	覘	6681_0	553		鈇	8513_0	664
	費	5580_6	487		鈦	8413_0	662
	貼	6186_0	536		鈎	8712_0	667
	貽	6386_0	542		鈉	8412_7	662
	貿	7780_6	614		鈍	8511_7	664
	賀	4680_6	425		鈔	8912_0	681
	賁	4080_6	375		鈕	8711_5	667
赤	赦	4734_7	429		鈞	8712_0	667
辛	辜	4040_1	369		鈣	8112_7	655
走	趁	4880_2	442	門	開	7744_1	604
	超	4780_6	435		間	7760_7	608
	越	4380_5	389		閔	7743_2	604
足	跋	6314_7	541		閏	7710_4	588
	跗	6410_0	546		閑	7790_4	615
	跌	6513_0	549		開	7722_7	597
	跏	6610_0	551		閔	7740_0	603
	跑	6711_2	557	阜	陽	7622_7	586
	距	6116_0	534		隄	7628_1	587
	跚	6714_5	558		隅	7622_7	586
	跋	6414_7	546		隆	7721_4	591
	距	6111_7	534		隊	7823_2	617

部	字	四　角	頁　碼
	隋	7422_7	582
	隍	7621_4	586
	階	7126_2	570
	陽	7721_1	590
	限	7623_2	587
隹	雁	7121_4	566
	雄	4001_4	353
	雅	7021_4	562
	雇	3021_4	275
	集	2090_4	157
雨	雲	1073_1	93
韋	韌	4752_0	433
頁	項	1118_6	103
	順	2108_6	160
	須	2128_6	170
馬	馭	7734_0	603
	馮	3112_7	291
黃	黃	4480_6	414
黍	黍	2013_2	143
黑	黑	6033_1	521

十三畫

部	字	四　角	頁　碼
乙	亂	2221_0	178
人	催	2221_4	178
	傭	2022_7	145
	傲	2824_0	261
	傳	2524_3	221
	債	2528_6	223
	傷	2822_7	260
	傻	2624_7	230
	傾	2128_6	170
	僂	2524_4	222
	僉	8088_6	654
	傴	2121_6	164

部	字	四　角	頁　碼
刀	劏	0220_0	35
	剿	2290_0	187
	剽	1290_0	117
力	募	3022_7	276
	勢	4442_7	405
	勤	4412_7	394
匚	匯	7171_1	572
口	嗅	6603_4	550
	嗆	6806_7	561
	嗨	6805_7	561
	嘟	6702_7	555
	嗯	6603_3	550
	嗇	4060_1	372
	嗓	6709_4	557
	嗔	6408_1	545
	鳴	6702_7	555
	嗜	6406_1	545
	嗟	6801_2	560
	嗣	6722_0	559
	嗤	6203_6	537
	嗦	6409_3	546
	嗒	6306_1	540
	嗦	6509_3	549
	園	6023_2	520
	圓	6080_6	530
土	塊	4611_3	421
	塢	4712_7	427
	塌	4612_7	422
	塚	4713_2	427
	塑	8710_4	666
	塔	4416_1	395
	塗	3810_4	342
	塘	4016_7	362
	塞	3010_4	270
	填	4418_1	396

部	字	四　角	頁　碼	部	字	四　角	頁　碼
士	壺	4010_7	361		愫	9801_7	706
大	奧	2743_0	249		慄	9109_1	692
山	嵯	2871_0	265		慌	9401_1	696
女	媳	4643_0	425		慍	9601_7	701
	媪	4641_7	425		愴	9806_7	707
	媽	4142_7	380	戈	戡	6315_0	541
	媾	4544_7	419	手	搆	5504_7	484
	嫁	4343_2	388		推	5401_4	480
	嫉	4043_4	370		損	5608_6	491
	嫋	4742_7	431		搏	5304_2	474
	嫌	4843_7	440		搓	5801_1	501
	媲	4741_1	430		搔	5703_6	495
子	孳	8040_7	639		搗	5702_7	495
	孵	7274_7	579		搖	5707_2	498
尢	尵	4801_3	438		搜	5704_7	496
巾	幌	4621_1	422		搢	5106_1	464
干	幹	4844_1	441		搶	5703_7	495
广	鷹	0022_7	13		搦	5702_7	495
	廈	0024_7	18		搬	5704_7	497
	廉	0023_7	17		搭	5406_7	481
	廓	0022_7	16		搶	5806_7	503
尸	屢	7724_4	598		搾	5301_1	473
弓	彀	4724_7	429		搽	5409_4	482
彳	微	2824_0	260	斗	斟	4470_0	410
心	想	4633_0	424	支	敬	4864_0	442
	惹	4433_6	403	斤	新	0292_1	37
	愁	2933_8	268	日	暇	6704_7	556
	愈	8033_2	638		暈	6050_6	525
	意	0033_6	21		暉	6705_6	556
	愚	6033_2	522		暑	6060_4	527
	愛	2024_7	146		暖	6204_7	537
	感	5320_0	478		暗	6006_1	509
	愧	9601_3	701	木	椰	4792_7	436
	愷	9201_8	693		榱	4294_7	385
	慎	9408_1	697		椽	4793_2	436

部	字	四　角	頁　碼	部	字	四　角	頁　碼
	椿	4596_3	420		溺	3712_7	330
	楊	4692_7	427		漼	3111_4	291
	楓	4791_0	436		湃	3114_3	292
	楔	4793_4	437		滂	3012_7	272
	楚	4480_1	414		滄	3816_7	347
	榆	4892_1	442		滅	3315_0	304
	楣	4796_7	438		滋	3813_2	344
	楫	4694_1	427		滌	3719_4	332
	業	3290_4	301		溏	3016_7	273
	極	4191_4	381		滑	3712_7	329
	楷	4196_2	382		滓	3314_1	304
	楹	4791_7	436		滔	3217_7	299
	椹	4491_1	416	火	煴	9186_6	693
	楂	4491_6	417		煊	9381_6	695
	榔	4792_7	436		煉	9589_6	700
欠	歇	6778_2	560		煌	9681_4	702
止	歲	2125_3	170		煎	8033_2	638
殳	殿	7724_7	600		煮	4433_6	403
	毀	7714_7	589		煒	9485_6	697
毛	毽	2571_4	223		熙	7733_1	602
气	氳	8011_7	627		煖	9284_7	694
水	溫	3611_7	323		煜	9681_8	702
	溜	3716_2	331		煤	9489_4	697
	源	3119_6	296		煥	9783_4	705
	準	3040_1	281		煦	6733_2	559
	溝	3515_5	319		照	6733_6	559
	溟	3718_0	331		煨	9683_2	702
	溢	3811_7	343		煩	9188_6	693
	溥	3314_2	304		煬	9682_7	702
	滙	3111_1	290	父	爺	8012_7	627
	溴	3613_4	324	犬	獃	8363_4	661
	溧	3119_4	293		猻	4229_3	384
	溪	3213_4	297		猾	4722_7	429
	溯	3712_0	328		猿	4423_2	400
	溶	3316_8	305		獅	4122_7	379

部	字	四 角	頁 碼	部	字	四 角	頁 碼
玉	瑁	1616_0	127		稠	2792_0	257
	瑕	1714_7	130		稚	2091_4	158
	瑛	1413_4	121		稜	2494_7	215
	瑞	1212_7	109		稟	0090_4	31
	瑟	1133_1	106	穴	窟	3027_2	278
田	當	9060_6	689		窠	3090_4	290
	畸	6402_1	543	竹	筮	8810_8	672
疒	瘓	0018_9	8		筲	8822_7	673
白	皙	4260_2	384		筱	8824_8	674
皿	盞	5310_7	476		筴	8843_8	675
	盟	6710_7	557		筵	8840_1	675
目	睛	6502_7	548		筷	8893_4	681
	睜	6205_7	538	米	粮	9393_2	696
	睡	6101_4	533		粱	3390_4	307
	睢	6001_4	508		粲	2790_1	255
	督	2760_4	252		粳	9194_6	693
	睦	6401_4	543	糸	絹	2692_7	235
	睫	6508_1	549		綁	2792_7	258
	䁖	6209_4	538		綆	2494_7	215
	睟	6004_8	509		綃	2992_7	269
	睞	6409_8	546		綏	2294_4	190
矢	矮	8244_4	658		經	2191_1	174
石	碇	1368_1	120	网	罩	6040_6	523
	碉	1762_0	137		罪	6011_1	512
	硼	1762_0	137		置	6010_7	511
	碌	1763_2	137	羊	羣	1750_1	135
	碎	1064_8	90		羨	8018_2	627
	碑	1664_4	128		義	8055_3	642
	碗	1361_2	120	耒	耡	5492_7	482
示	祺	3428_1	315	耳	聖	1610_4	125
	禁	4490_1	415		聘	1512_7	124
	祿	3723_2	334	聿	肄	2540_0	223
禸	禽	8042_7	639		肅	5022_7	452
禾	稔	2893_2	267		肆	7570_4	586
	稗	2694_0	237	肉	腮	7623_0	587

部	字	四　角	頁　碼	部	字	四　角	頁　碼
	媵	7523_4	585		葷	4450_6	407
	腥	7621_4	586		蒂	4422_7	398
	腳	7722_0	595	虍	虞	2123_4	168
	腦	7226_2	577		虜	2122_7	167
	腩	7422_7	582		號	6121_7	534
	腫	7221_4	576	虫	蛸	5912_7	507
	腰	7124_0	568		蛹	5712_7	499
	腱	7524_0	585		蛻	5811_6	504
	腴	7723_7	598		蛾	5315_0	476
	腸	7622_7	586		蜃	7123_6	567
	腹	7824_7	618		蛋	5213_6	471
	腺	7623_2	586		蜀	6012_7	512
臼	舅	7742_7	604		蜂	5715_4	500
	輿	7780_1	614		蜆	5611_0	492
舟	艇	2244_1	183		蜈	5613_4	492
艸	萬	4442_7	405		蜓	5214_1	471
	蒿	4422_7	399		蜒	5214_1	471
	尊	4420_7	397		蛉	5819_4	505
	落	4416_4	396	行	衙	2122_1	166
	葉	4490_4	416	衣	裏	0073_2	31
	著	4460_4	409		裔	0022_7	15
	葛	4472_7	412		裕	3826_8	347
	葵	4443_1	405		裘	4373_2	389
	葫	4462_7	410		裙	3726_7	334
	葡	4422_7	399		補	3322_7	306
	董	4410_4	392		裝	2473_2	212
	葦	4450_6	407		裟	3973_7	352
	葩	4461_7	409	角	解	2725_2	244
	萌	4462_7	410	言	詡	0762_0	49
	葬	4444_1	406		詢	0762_0	49
	萱	4410_6	392		詣	0166_1	34
	葆	4429_4	401		試	0364_0	39
	葬	4444_1	406		詩	0464_1	43
	葯	4492_7	417		詫	0361_4	39
	葱	4433_2	402		詬	0266_1	37

部	字	四　角	頁　碼	部	字	四　角	頁　碼
	詮	0861_4	55	辵	逼	3130_6	295
	詰	0466_1	44		逾	3830_2	348
	話	0266_1	37		遁	3230_6	301
	該	0068_2	29		遂	3830_3	348
	詳	0865_1	56		遇	3630_2	326
	詹	2726_1	245		遊	3830_4	348
	詠	0168_9	34		運	3730_5	338
	誄	0569_0	46		遍	3330_2	307
	誅	0569_0	46		過	3730_2	336
	誇	0462_7	43		遏	3630_2	326
聿	肆	7570_4	586		退	3730_4	337
豕	豢	9023_2	686		遑	3630_1	326
豸	貉	2726_4	245		道	3830_6	349
	貂	2726_2	245		達	3430_4	315
貝	賂	6786_4	560		違	3430_4	315
	賃	2280_6	186		遄	3230_2	300
	賄	6482_7	548	邑	鄒	2742_7	249
	賅	6088_2	531		鄉	2772_7	254
	資	3780_6	342	酉	酪	1766_4	137
	賈	1080_6	93		酬	1260_0	116
	賊	6385_0	542	金	鈴	8813_7	672
	賍	6081_4	531		鈿	8610_0	665
足	跟	6713_2	558		鉀	8615_0	665
	踩	6719_4	559		鈸	8314_4	660
	跡	6013_0	512		鉅	8111_7	655
	跣	6411_1	546		鉆	8416_0	662
	跨	6412_7	546		鈾	8516_0	664
	跪	6711_7	558		鉍	8310_0	660
	路	6716_4	558		鉋	8711_2	667
	跳	6211_3	538		鉏	8711_0	667
車	較	5004_8	450		鉑	8610_0	665
	軽	5801_4	501		鉗	8417_0	662
	載	4355_0	389		鉛	8716_1	669
辛	辟	7064_1	565		鉞	8315_0	660
辰	農	5523_2	485		鉢	8513_0	664

部	字	四角	頁碼
	鉤	8712_0	667
	鈺	8111_3	655
	鉦	8111_1	655
門	閘	7750_6	606
	鬧	7722_7	596
	閣	7733_7	603
阜	隔	7122_7	567
	隕	7628_6	587
	隖	7722_7	596
	隘	7821_7	617
	隙	7929_6	620
隹	雉	8041_4	639
	雌	2011_4	143
	雍	0071_4	29
	睢	7011_4	562
雨	零	1030_7	79
	雷	1060_3	88
	電	1071_6	91
	雹	1071_2	91
青	靖	0512_7	45
革	靳	4252_1	384
	靴	4451_0	407
	靶	4751_7	433
音	歆	0768_2	52
頁	頌	8178_6	657
	頎	7128_6	570
	預	1128_6	105
	頑	1128_6	106
	頒	8128_6	655
	頓	5178_6	465
食	飩	8571_7	664
	飪	8271_4	659
	飭	8872_7	677
	飲	8778_2	671
	飫	8273_4	659

部	字	四角	頁碼
	飯	8174_7	657
瓦	甄	1111_7	103
馬	馱	7433_0	584
	馳	7431_2	584
	馴	7230_0	578
鳥	鳩	4702_7	427
	鳧	2721_7	241
黽	黽	7771_7	609
鼎	鼎	2222_1	179
鼓	鼓	4414_7	395
鼠	鼠	7771_7	609

十四畫

部	字	四角	頁碼
人	像	2723_2	243
	僑	2222_7	179
	僕	2223_4	179
	僚	2429_6	209
	僥	2421_1	203
	僧	2826_6	263
	僭	2126_1	170
	僖	2426_5	207
	僮	2021_4	144
	僱	2321_4	193
	僬	2023_1	145
儿	兢	4421_6	398
几	凳	1221_7	110
刀	劃	5210_0	471
匚	匱	7171_8	574
厂	厭	7123_4	567
口	嗽	6708_2	557
	嗾	6803_4	561
	嘅	6101_4	533
	嘆	6403_4	544
	嘈	6506_6	549

部	字	四角	頁碼	部	字	四角	頁碼
	嘉	4046_5	371		瘧	3026_1	278
	嘍	6504_4	549		寤	3040_4	282
	嘷	6104_9	534		實	3080_6	288
	嘻	6507_7	549		寧	3020_1	273
	嘔	6101_6	533		寨	3090_4	290
	噴	6508_6	549	尸	屨	7728_1	602
	嘗	9060_1	688	寸	對	3410_0	308
口	圖	6060_4	527	山	嶂	2074_6	156
	團	6034_3	522		嶇	2171_6	173
子	孵	7274_7	579	巾	幔	4624_7	423
土	塵	0021_4	10		幕	4422_7	399
	塹	5210_4	471		幗	4620_0	422
	塾	0410_4	40	广	廕	0023_1	16
	境	4011_6	361	彡	彰	0242_2	35
	墅	6710_4	557	心	愨	2733_4	247
	墊	4410_4	392		慈	8033_3	638
	墓	4410_4	392		態	2133_1	172
士	壽	4064_1	374		愿	7133_9	572
夕	夢	4420_7	397		慪	9101_6	692
	夥	6792_7	560		慘	9302_2	695
大	奩	4071_6	374		慟	9402_7	696
	奪	4034_1	368		慣	9708_6	704
	獎	2743_0	249		慨	9101_4	691
女	嫖	4149_1	380		慳	9701_4	703
	嫗	4141_6	380		慚	9202_1	693
	嫠	5824_4	505		慵	9002_7	684
	嫡	4042_7	370		慷	9003_2	684
	嫣	4142_7	380	戈	截	4325_0	388
	嫦	4942_7	444	手	摑	5600_0	488
	嫩	4844_0	441		摜	5708_6	499
宀	寞	3043_0	283		摔	5004_3	450
	察	3090_1	290		摘	5002_7	449
	寡	3022_7	276		摟	5504_4	484
	寥	3020_2	274		摧	5201_4	466
	寢	3024_7	277		摭	5003_1	449

部	字	四角	頁碼	部	字	四角	頁碼
	搏	5504_3	483		漆	3413_2	312
	摸	5403_4	480		漏	3712_7	329
	摺	5706_2	498		漑	3111_4	291
支	敲	0124_7	32		演	3318_6	305
斤	斲	7212_1	575		漚	3111_6	291
方	旗	0828_1	54		漠	3413_4	312
	旖	0822_1	52		漢	3413_4	312
日	暨	7110_6	565		漩	3818_1	347
	暢	5602_7	489		漫	3614_7	324
木	榛	4599_4	420		漲	3113_2	291
	榷	4491_4	417		漸	3212_1	296
	榜	4092_7	377		漾	3813_2	344
	榨	4391_1	390		漥	3311_4	303
	榮	9990_4	709		滯	3412_7	311
	榻	4692_7	427		漣	3513_0	318
	榴	4796_2	437		漕	3516_6	319
	槁	4092_7	377		滾	3013_2	273
	榕	4396_8	390		漱	3718_2	332
	槃	8790_4	671	火	煬	9382_7	695
	構	4594_7	420		熄	9683_0	702
	槌	4793_7	437		熇	9082_7	691
	槍	4896_7	443		熊	2133_1	172
	槐	4691_3	427		熏	2033_1	148
	槓	4198_6	382		熒	9980_9	709
欠	歉	8738_2	670		熔	9386_8	696
	歌	1768_2	137	爻	爾	1022_7	76
歹	殞	1628_6	128	犬	獃	2313_4	191
母	毓	8051_3	641		獄	4323_4	388
水	滬	3311_7	303	玉	瑣	1918_6	142
	滲	3312_2	303		瑤	1717_2	130
	滴	3012_7	273		瑰	1611_3	126
	滷	3116_0	292		瑪	1112_7	103
	滿	3412_7	310	疋	疑	2748_1	250
	漁	3713_6	330	疒	瘋	0011_7	4
	漂	3119_1	293		瘍	0012_7	6

部	字	四　角	頁　碼	部	字	四　角	頁　碼
皿	盡	5010_7	451		緒	2496_0	215
	監	7810_7	616		縮	2397_7	199
目	瞑	6203_4	537		綣	2791_6	256
	睹	6406_0	545		綢	2792_0	257
	睪	2640_1	233		綦	4490_3	415
石	碟	1469_4	124		維	2091_4	158
	碧	1660_1	128		綱	2792_0	257
	碩	1168_6	107		網	2792_0	257
	碳	1268_9	117		綴	2794_7	259
示	禍	3722_7	334		綸	2892_7	267
	禎	3128_6	293		綫	2395_3	199
	福	3126_6	293		綺	2492_1	215
	祿	3723_2	334		綻	2398_1	199
衣	裨	3624_0	325		綽	2194_6	175
	裸	3629_4	325		綾	2494_7	215
禾	種	2291_4	188		綿	2692_7	235
	稱	2194_7	176		緊	7790_3	615
穴	窩	3022_7	276	网	罰	6062_0	528
	窪	3011_4	272		署	6060_4	527
立	竭	0612_7	46	羽	翠	1740_8	134
	端	0212_7	35		翡	1112_7	103
竹	箋	8850_3	676	耳	聚	1723_2	132
	箍	8851_2	676		聞	7740_1	603
	箏	8850_7	676	聿	肇	3850_7	349
	箔	8816_2	672	肉	腐	0022_7	13
	箕	8880_1	679		腿	7723_3	598
	算	8844_6	675		膀	7022_7	564
	劄	8260_0	658		膂	0822_7	52
	箱	8857_5	676		腰	7124_0	568
	管	8877_7	678		膊	7324_1	580
米	粹	9094_8	691		膏	0022_7	16
	粽	9399_1	696	臣	臧	2325_0	196
	精	9592_7	700	至	臺	4010_4	360
糸	綜	2399_1	199	舛	舞	8025_1	632
	綠	2793_2	258	艸	蒙	4423_2	400

部	字	四　角	頁　碼	部	字	四　角	頁　碼
	蒜	4499_1	419	言	誌	0463_1	43
	蒔	4422_7	399		認	0763_2	51
	蒲	4412_7	394		誑	0161_4	33
	蒸	4433_1	401		誓	5260_1	471
	蒞	4411_8	394		誕	0264_1	37
	蒔	4464_1	410		誘	0262_7	36
	蒼	4460_7	409		誚	0962_7	57
	蒸	4449_3	406		語	0166_1	34
	蓄	4460_3	408		誠	0365_0	39
	蓉	4460_8	409		誠	0365_0	40
	蓋	4410_7	392		誣	0161_8	33
	蓓	4416_1	396		誤	0663_4	46
	蔭	4423_1	400		誥	0466_1	44
	蓁	4490_4	416		誦	0762_7	51
	蓢	4442_7	405		誨	0865_7	57
虫	蜘	5610_0	492		說	0861_6	55
	蜜	3013_6	273	豕	豪	0023_2	16
	蜞	5418_1	482	豸	貌	2721_7	241
	蜢	5711_7	499		貍	2621_4	230
	蜥	5212_1	471	貝	賑	6183_2	536
	蜩	5712_0	499		賒	6889_1	562
	蝎	5612_7	492		賓	3080_6	288
	蜻	5512_7	485	赤	赫	4433_1	401
	蜷	5911_2	506	走	趙	4980_2	444
	蜿	5311_2	476		趕	4680_4	425
	蜚	1113_6	103	足	踞	6712_7	558
	蜾	5519_6	485		跟	6313_2	541
衣	裳	9073_2	689		踴	6712_7	558
	裴	1173_2	107	車	輒	5101_0	460
	裹	0073_2	31		輓	5701_6	493
	製	2273_2	184		輔	5302_7	473
	褂	3320_0	306		輕	5101_7	461
	裱	3523_2	321	辛	辣	0549_6	45
	褐	3622_7	325	辵	遙	3730_7	339
角	觫	2529_6	223		遜	3230_9	301

部	字	四　角	頁　碼
	遞	3230_{1}	300
	遣	3530_{7}	322
	遛	3730_{6}	338
	違	3430_{4}	315
邑	鄙	6762_{7}	560
酉	酵	1464_{7}	123
	酷	1466_{1}	123
	酸	1364_{7}	120
金	鉻	8716_{4}	669
	銨	8314_{4}	660
	銥	8013_{2}	627
	鉸	8014_{8}	627
	銀	8713_{2}	668
	銃	8011_{3}	626
	銅	8712_{0}	668
	銑	8411_{1}	661
	銓	8811_{4}	672
	銖	8519_{0}	664
	銘	8716_{0}	669
	銧	8911_{1}	681
	銛	8216_{4}	658
	銹	8412_{7}	662
門	閡	7728_{0}	602
	閣	7760_{4}	608
	閥	7725_{3}	600
	閨	7710_{4}	588
	閩	7713_{6}	588
	閧	7780_{1}	613
阜	際	7729_{1}	602
	障	7024_{6}	564
雨	需	1022_{7}	76
革	靼	4651_{0}	425
	鞅	4553_{0}	419
頁	頗	4128_{6}	380
	領	8138_{6}	656
風	颯	0711_{0}	48
	颭	7121_{6}	566
	颱	7321_{6}	580
食	飴	8376_{0}	661
	飼	8772_{0}	671
	飽	8771_{2}	670
	飾	8872_{7}	677
馬	駁	7434_{0}	584
	駟	7630_{0}	587
骨	骯	7021_{7}	563
	骰	7724_{7}	600
髟	髯	7255_{7}	578
	髦	7271_{4}	578
鬼	魁	2421_{0}	203
	魂	1671_{3}	128
鳥	鳳	7721_{0}	589
	鳴	6702_{7}	555
	鳶	4332_{7}	388
麻	麼	0023_{9}	17
音	韶	0766_{2}	51
鼻	鼻	2644_{6}	233
齊	齊	0022_{3}	11

十五畫

部	字	四　角	頁　碼
人	僵	2121_{6}	164
	儆	2824_{0}	262
	價	2128_{6}	170
	僻	2024_{1}	146
	儀	2825_{3}	263
	億	2023_{6}	146
	儈	2826_{6}	263
	儉	2828_{6}	264
巾	冪	7722_{7}	597
刀	劇	2220_{0}	177

部	字	四角	頁碼	部	字	四角	頁碼
	劈	7022_7	564		幣	9822_7	702
	劉	7210_0	575	广	廚	0024_0	17
	劊	8260_0	659		厮	0022_1	11
	劍	8280_0	659		廟	0022_7	16
厂	厲	7122_7	567		廠	0024_8	19
口	嘯	6502_7	548		廡	0023_1	16
	嘲	6702_0	555		廢	0024_7	18
	嘴	6102_7	533		廣	0028_6	20
	嘶	6202_1	537	廾	弊	9844_4	707
	嘻	6406_5	545	弓	彈	1625_6	127
	噍	6003_1	508	彡	影	6292_2	539
	噎	6401_8	543	彳	徹	2824_0	262
	嘘	6101_7	533		徵	2824_0	262
	嘩	6604_3	550		德	2423_1	205
	嘩	6405_4	545	心	慕	4433_3	402
土	墜	7810_4	615		慝	7133_1	572
	增	4816_6	439		慧	5533_7	486
	墟	4111_7	379		慮	2123_6	168
	墨	6010_4	511		慰	7433_0	584
	墩	4814_0	439		慶	0024_7	18
	墮	7410_4	581		慾	8733_8	670
	墳	4418_6	396		憂	1024_7	79
女	嬉	4446_5	406		憎	9806_8	706
	嬌	4442_7	405		憐	9905_6	708
	嬋	4645_6	425		憬	9609_6	702
	嬌	4242_7	384		憔	9003_1	684
	嫻	4742_0	430		憚	9605_6	702
宀	審	3060_9	285		憤	9408_6	697
	寫	3032_7	280		憧	9001_4	683
	寬	3021_3	274		憫	9702_0	704
	寮	3090_6	290		憒	9508_6	700
尸	層	7726_6	601		憋	9833_4	707
	履	7724_7	600	歹	殤	1822_7	140
巾	幟	4325_0	388	戈	戮	1325_0	119
	幡	4226_9	384	手	摩	0025_2	19

部	字	四　角	頁　碼	部	字	四　角	頁　碼
	撥	5204_7	469		標	4199_1	382
	摯	4450_2	406		樑	4399_4	390
	摹	4450_2	406		樓	4594_4	420
	撇	5804_0	502		樞	4191_6	382
	撈	5902_7	506		樟	4094_6	378
	撐	5904_1	506		模	4493_4	417
	撒	5804_0	503		樣	4893_2	443
	撓	5401_1	479	欠	歟	4758_2	433
	撕	5202_1	467		歐	7778_2	613
	撙	5804_6	503	殳	毅	0724_7	48
	撚	5303_3	473		毆	7774_7	611
	撞	5001_4	448	水	漿	2723_2	243
	撤	5804_0	503		潑	3214_7	298
	撩	5409_6	482		潔	3719_3	332
	撫	5803_1	502		潘	3216_9	299
	播	5206_9	469		潛	3116_1	292
	撮	5604_7	490		潤	3712_0	328
	撰	5708_1	498		潦	3419_6	313
	撲	5203_4	468		滕	7923_2	620
	撑	5905_2	506		潭	3114_6	292
	撅	5708_2	499		潮	3712_0	329
	撬	5201_4	466		潼	3011_4	272
攴	敵	0824_0	54		潤	3712_0	329
	敷	5824_0	505		潲	3912_7	351
	數	5844_0	505		澎	3212_2	296
日	暫	5260_2	472		潯	3714_1	330
	暮	4460_3	408		潰	3518_6	319
	暸	6101_6	533		潺	3714_7	331
	暴	6013_2	512		澄	3211_8	296
木	概	4191_4	381		澆	3411_1	309
	槳	2790_4	255		澈	3814_0	345
	槽	4596_6	420	火	熟	0433_1	40
	椿	4597_7	420		熨	7480_9	584
	樂	2290_4	187		熬	5833_4	505
	樊	4443_0	405		熱	4433_1	402

部	字	四　角	頁　碼	部	字	四　角	頁　碼
	窯	3033_1	280	竹	箭	8822_1	673
牛	犛	5825_1	505		箱	8896_2	681
犬	獒	5843_0	505		箴	8825_3	674
	獗	4128_2	380		箸	8860_4	677
玉	瑩	9910_3	704		節	8872_7	677
	璃	1012_7	72		範	8851_2	676
	璋	1014_6	72		箍	8851_2	676
疒	瘤	0016_2	7		篆	8823_2	674
	瘟	0011_7	4		篇	8822_7	673
	瘠	0012_7	6		篋	8871_3	677
	瘡	0016_7	7	米	糊	9792_0	706
	瘦	0014_7	7		粿	9191_4	693
	瘴	0011_1	4	糸	緒	2496_0	215
皮	皺	2444_7	209		線	2693_2	237
目	瞇	6401_7	543		緝	2694_1	237
	瞌	6306_1	540		緞	2794_7	259
	瞄	6406_0	445		締	2092_7	159
	瞑	6708_0	557		緣	2793_2	258
石	碼	1162_7	107		編	2392_7	198
	碾	1763_2	137		緘	2395_0	199
	確	1461_4	122		緩	2294_7	190
	磁	1863_2	141		緯	2495_6	215
	磅	1062_7	90		練	2599_6	225
	磊	1066_1	91		緊	7790_3	615
	磋	1861_1	141	网	罵	6032_7	520
	磕	1461_7	122	羊	羯	8652_7	666
示	褉	3221_7	299	羽	翥	8012_7	627
禾	稷	2694_7	237		翩	3722_0	334
	稻	2297_7	190	耒	耦	5692_7	492
	穀	4794_7	437	肉	膚	2122_7	167
	稽	2396_1	199		膜	7423_4	583
	稼	2393_2	198		膝	7423_2	582
	稿	2092_7	159		膠	7722_2	596
穴	窮	3022_7	276		膡	7424_8	583
皿	盤	2710_7	238		臁	7129_1	570

部	字	四　角	頁　碼	部	字	四　角	頁　碼
舌	舖	8362_7	661		誼	0361_7	39
艸	蓬	4430_5	401		調	0762_0	50
	蓮	4430_5	401		諂	0767_7	52
	蔗	4423_7	400		諄	0064_7	28
	蔑	4425_3	400		談	0968_9	57
	蔓	4440_6	404		諉	0264_4	37
	萄	4462_7	410		請	0562_7	45
	蔡	4490_1	415		諍	0265_7	37
	蔣	4424_7	400		詠	0163_2	34
	蔟	4423_4	400		諒	0069_6	29
	蔬	4411_3	394		論	0862_1	56
	蔭	4423_1	400	豆	豌	1311_2	118
虫	蝌	5411_4	482		豎	7710_8	588
	蝓	5812_1	504	貝	賜	6682_7	553
	蝕	8573_6	665		賞	9080_6	690
	蝗	5611_4	492		賠	6086_1	531
	蝙	5312_7	476		賣	4080_6	375
	蝟	5612_7	492		賤	6385_3	542
	蝠	5116_6	465		賦	6384_0	542
	蟒	5814_7	504		質	7280_6	579
	蝦	5714_7	499		賬	6183_3	536
	蝨	1713_6	129		賢	7780_6	614
	蝮	5814_7	504	走	趣	4780_4	434
	蝴	5712_0	499		趙	4980_2	444
	蝶	5419_4	482	足	踐	6315_3	541
衣	複	3824_7	347		踝	6619_4	551
	褊	3322_7	307		踞	6716_4	559
	襃	0073_2	31		踏	6216_3	538
	褐	3622_7	325		踩	6219_4	538
	褓	3629_4	325		踢	6612_7	551
	褚	3426_0	314		蹈	6016_1	518
言	誰	0061_4	28		踟	6610_0	551
	課	0669_4	47		踪	6319_1	541
	諄	0064_8	29	身	躬	2922_7	268
	誹	0161_1	33	車	輛	5102_7	463

部	字	四角	頁碼	部	字	四角	頁碼
	輻	5206_3	469		闆	7760_1	607
	輝	9725_6	704		闉	7773_2	610
	轂	5704_7	497	雨	霄	1022_7	76
	輦	5550_6	486		霖	1019_4	73
	輩	1150_6	106		霆	1040_1	81
	輪	5802_7	502		震	1023_2	78
辵	遨	3830_4	348		需	1012_7	72
	適	3030_2	279		霉	1050_7	86
	遭	3530_6	322	青	靚	5621_0	492
	遮	3030_3	279	非	靠	2411_1	200
	遲	3730_5	338	革	鞋	4451_4	407
邑	鄭	8742_7	670		鞍	4354_4	389
	鄰	9722_7	704		鞏	1750_6	135
酉	醃	1461_6	122	頁	頤	7178_6	575
	醉	1064_8	90		頰	4108_6	379
	醋	1466_1	123	食	餅	8874_1	678
	醇	1064_7	90		餃	8074_8	654
金	銳	8811_6	72		餉	8772_0	671
	銹	8212_7	658		養	8073_2	653
	銷	8912_7	681		餌	8174_0	657
	銼	8811_4	672	馬	駐	7031_4	564
	銻	8812_7	672		駕	4632_7	423
	鋁	8616_0	665		駒	7732_0	602
	鋅	8014_1	627		駙	7430_0	583
	鋌	8214_1	658		駛	7530_0	586
	鋏	8413_8	662		駝	7331_1	580
	鋒	8715_4	669		駉	7630_0	587
	鋇	8618_0	665		駘	7336_0	581
	鋤	8412_7	662		駔	7731_0	602
	鋙	8411_0	661	骨	骷	7426_0	583
	鋪	8312_7	660	髟	髭	7211_1	575
	銀	8313_2	660		髮	7244_7	578
門	闈	7760_7	609		髯	7255_7	578
	閣	7760_6	608		髫	7252_7	578
	閱	7721_6	591	鬥	鬧	7722_7	596

部	字	四　角	頁　碼
鬼	魄	2661_3	233
	魅	2521_9	221
魚	鮋	2531_7	223
	魯	2760_3	251
鳥	鴉	7722_7	596
	鴒	2742_7	249
麻	麾	0021_4	10
黍	黎	2713_2	239
齒	齒	2177_2	173

十六畫

部	字	四　角	頁　碼
人	儒	2122_7	167
	償	2328_6	196
	儔	2424_1	206
	儘	2521_7	221
八	冀	1180_1	107
冫	凝	3718_1	331
刀	劑	0220_0	35
力	勳	2432_0	209
口	噢	6703_4	556
	噤	6409_1	546
	器	6666_3	553
	噪	6609_4	551
	噫	6003_6	508
	噬	6801_8	561
	嘻	6103_2	534
	噸	6108_6	534
土	墾	2710_4	238
	甕	0010_4	2
	壁	7010_4	562
	壇	4011_6	361
大	奮	4060_1	372
女	變	7040_4	565
子	學	7740_7	603

部	字	四　角	頁　碼
宀	寰	3073_2	286
寸	導	3834_3	349
	幫	4422_7	399
广	廩	0029_4	21
彳	徼	2824_0	262
心	懍	2433_2	209
	憑	3133_2	295
	憶	9003_6	684
	憾	9305_0	695
	懂	9401_4	696
	懈	9705_2	704
	懊	9703_4	704
	憨	1833_4	140
	懷	9009_1	684
戈	戰	6355_0	541
手	撼	5305_0	475
	撾	5703_2	495
	擁	5001_4	448
	播	5106_3	465
	擄	5102_7	463
	擅	5001_6	448
	擇	5604_1	489
	擋	5906_6	506
	操	5609_4	491
	擒	5802_7	502
	擔	5706_1	497
	據	5103_2	463
	擗	5004_1	450
	撿	5808_6	504
攴	整	5810_1	504
日	暹	3630_1	326
	曆	7127_9	570
	曡	6073_1	529
	曉	6401_1	543
木	樵	4093_1	377

部	字	四　角	頁　碼	部	字	四　角	頁　碼
	樸	4293_4	385		燙	3680_9	327
	樺	4495_4	418		燜	9782_0	705
	樽	4794_1	437	犬	獨	4622_7	422
	樹	4490_0	414		獪	4826_6	440
	橄	4894_0	443	瓦	甌	7171_7	574
	橇	4291_4	385	疒	瘴	0014_6	7
	橋	4292_7	385	皿	盥	7710_7	588
	橘	4792_7	436	目	瞞	6402_7	543
	橈	4491_1	416		瞠	6901_4	562
	橙	4291_8	385	石	磧	1568_6	125
	機	4295_3	385		磨	0026_1	19
	橡	4793_2	437		磚	1564_3	125
	橢	4492_7	417		磬	4760_1	433
	橫	4498_6	418	示	禦	2790_1	255
止	歷	7121_1	565	禾	穆	2692_2	235
歹	殫	1625_6	127		積	2598_6	224
毛	氅	9871_4	707	穴	窺	3051_6	283
水	澡	3619_4	324	竹	築	8890_4	680
	澤	3614_1	324		篙	8822_7	673
	澱	3714_7	334		篡	8873_3	678
	澳	3713_4	330		篤	8832_7	674
	澹	3716_1	331		篩	8872_7	678
	激	3814_0	344		篝	8844_7	676
	濁	3612_7	324		篦	8871_1	677
	濃	3513_2	318		簑	8873_2	678
火	熹	4033_6	368	米	糕	9893_1	708
	燃	9383_3	695		糖	9096_7	691
	熾	9385_0	696	糸	繪	2891_7	267
	燈	9281_8	694		縐	2792_7	258
	燉	9884_0	707		縛	2394_2	198
	燐	9985_9	709		緻	2894_0	267
	燎	9489_6	698		縞	2092_7	159
	燒	9481_1	697		縣	6299_3	540
	燔	9286_9	694		縈	9990_3	709
	燕	4433_1	402	网	罹	6091_4	532

部	字	四　角	頁　碼	部	字	四　角	頁　碼
羽	翰	4842_7	440	言	論	0862_1	56
耒	耨	5194_3	465		謔	0264_7	37
肉	膨	7222_2	576		諄	0064_7	28
	膩	7324_0	580		諛	0763_2	51
	膳	7826_5	618		諜	0469_4	45
臼	興	7780_1	613		諞	0362_7	39
舟	艘	2744_7	249		諢	0765_6	51
	艙	2846_7	264		諤	0662_7	46
艸	蔽	4424_8	400		諦	0062_7	28
	蕃	4460_9	409		諟	0668_1	47
	蕉	4433_1	402		諧	0166_2	34
	蕈	4440_6	404		諫	0569_6	46
	蕊	4433_3	402		諮	0766_8	52
	蕎	4422_7	399		諱	0465_6	44
	蕙	4433_3	402		諳	0066_1	29
	蕩	4412_7	394		諶	0461_1	42
	蕪	4433_1	402		諷	0761_0	48
	蕭	4422_7	399		諸	0466_0	44
虫	螃	5012_7	452		諼	0062_2	28
	融	1523_6	124		諾	0466_4	44
	螓	5519_4	485		謀	0469_4	44
	螞	5112_7	465		謁	0662_7	46
	螟	5718_0	500		謂	0662_7	46
	螢	9913_6	708	豕	豫	1723_2	132
行	衛	2122_1	167		豬	1426_0	122
	衡	2122_1	166	豸	貓	2426_0	206
衣	褥	3124_3	293		貌	2721_7	241
	褪	3723_3	334	貝	賭	6486_4	548
	褫	3221_7	299		賴	5798_6	500
	褲	3025_0	277	赤	赬	4138_6	380
見	觀	8621_0	665		赭	4436_0	403
	覩	4661_0	425	足	踦	6812_1	561
	親	0691_0	47		踱	6014_8	514
	覽	7821_6	617		踵	6211_4	538
至	臻	1519_4	124		踹	6212_7	538

60 十六畫 筆畫索引

部	字	四 角	頁 碼	部	字	四 角	頁 碼
	蹀	6419_4	546		錫	8612_7	665
	蹂	6719_4	559		鋼	8610_0	665
	蹄	6012_7	512		錯	8416_1	662
	踴	6712_7	558		錳	8711_7	667
	蹁	6312_7	540		鍊	8519_6	664
	蹉	6618_1	551	革	鞘	4952_7	444
車	輮	5103_4	463	門	闆	7771_6	609
	輯	5604_1	490		閣	7777_7	613
	輳	5503_4	483		闕	7723_3	598
	輸	5802_1	501		閶	7760_6	608
	輻	5106_6	465		閣	7760_4	608
	轂	4724_7	429	阜	隧	7823_3	618
辛	辦	0044_1	26		隨	7423_2	583
	辨	0044_1	25		險	7828_6	618
辵	遵	3830_4	348	隸	隸	4593_2	420
	遷	3130_1	294	隹	雕	7021_4	562
	選	3730_8	339	雨	霍	1021_4	74
	遺	3530_8	322		霎	1040_4	82
	遼	3430_9	316		霏	1011_1	72
	遙	3730_2	337		霓	1021_7	74
	遴	3930_5	351		霖	1099_4	101
	遵	3430_1	315	青	靛	5328_1	479
酉	醒	1661_4	128		靜	5225_7	471
金	鋸	8716_4	669	頁	頭	1118_6	103
	鋼	8712_0	667		煩	4108_6	379
	錄	8713_2	668		頜	8168_6	657
	錐	8011_4	626		頸	1118_6	103
	錶	8513_2	664		頰	2128_6	171
	錘	8211_4	658		頻	2128_6	171
	錙	8216_3	658	食	餐	2773_2	254
	錚	8215_7	658		餚	8474_7	663
	錠	8318_1	661		餗	8579_6	665
	錏	8111_7	655		餃	8274_4	659
	錢	8315_3	661		餓	8375_0	661
	錦	8612_7	665		舖	8372_7	661

部	字	四角	頁碼	部	字	四角	頁碼
	餘	8879_4	679		孀	6642_7	552
馬	駭	7038_2	565		嬪	4348_6	389
	騈	7834_1	619	子	孺	1142_7	106
骨	骸	7028_2	564	尸	屨	7724_4	598
	骼	7726_4	601	山	嶺	2238_6	182
髟	髻	7260_1	578		嶼	2778_1	254
鬥	鬨	7780_1	613		嶽	2223_4	179
魚	鮑	2731_2	246	巾	幫	4422_7	399
鳥	鴿	8732_7	670	弓	彌	1122_7	104
	鴕	2331_1	196	彳	徽	2824_0	261
	鴛	2732_7	246	心	懇	2733_3	247
	鴉	6722_7	559		應	0023_1	16
	鴟	7772_7	610		懋	4433_9	403
	鴣	4762_7	433		懦	9102_7	692
	鴦	5032_7	453		懨	9103_4	692
	鴨	6752_7	560	戈	戲	2325_0	196
黑	黔	6832_7	561	手	擊	5750_2	500
	默	6333_4	541		擎	4850_2	441
龍	龍	0121_1	32		擘	7050_2	565
龜	龜	2711_7	238		擠	5002_3	449

十七畫

部	字	四角	頁碼	部	字	四角	頁碼
					擅	5401_4	480
					擢	5701_4	493
人	償	2928_6	268		擦	5309_1	475
	儡	2626_0	230		擬	5708_1	498
	優	2124_7	169		擯	5308_6	475
力	勵	7422_7	582		擰	5302_1	473
口	嚎	6003_2	508		擱	5702_0	494
	嚅	6102_7	533	攴	斂	8884_0	679
	嚇	6403_1	544	日	暧	6204_7	537
	嚏	6408_1	546	木	檀	4091_6	377
土	墼	2710_4	238		檄	4894_0	443
	壓	7121_5	566		檔	4996_6	444
	壕	4013_2	362		檜	4796_1	437
					檢	4898_6	443
女	嬰	6640_4	552	歹	殭	1121_6	104

62 十七畫 筆畫索引

部	字	四　角	頁　碼	部	字	四　角	頁　碼
	殮	1828_6	140	石	磷	1965_9	142
毛	氈	0211_4	35		礁	1063_1	90
水	濕	3613_3	324		磺	1468_6	124
	濘	3312_1	303	示	禧	3426_5	314
	濟	3012_3	272	禾	穗	2593_3	224
	濠	3013_2	273	穴	窿	3021_4	275
	濡	3112_7	291	皿	盪	3610_7	323
	澀	3711_1	328	竹	篳	8850_4	676
	濤	3414_1	312		篷	8830_4	674
	濫	3811_7	343		簏	8821_1	673
	濯	3711_4	328		簀	8880_6	679
	濱	3318_6	306		簇	8823_4	674
火	營	9960_6	709		簍	8840_4	675
	燥	9689_4	703		篠	8829_4	674
	燦	9789_4	705		篝	8817_7	672
	燧	9883_3	707		篾	8825_3	674
	燬	9784_7	705	米	糙	9491_6	698
	燭	9682_7	702		糝	9392_2	696
	燮	9940_7	708		糞	9080_1	690
爿	牆	2426_1	207		糟	9596_6	701
犬	獰	4322_1	388		糠	9093_2	691
	獲	4424_7	400	糸	縫	2793_4	258
玉	璨	1719_4	130		繃	2792_0	257
	環	1613_2	127		繂	2095_3	160
疒	療	0019_6	8		縮	2396_1	199
	癆	0012_7	5		縱	2898_1	267
	癌	0017_2	7		縲	2699_3	237
目	瞥	9860_4	707		縵	2694_7	237
	瞧	6003_1	508		縷	2594_4	224
	瞪	6201_8	537		總	2693_0	235
	瞬	6205_2	537		績	2598_6	225
	瞭	6409_6	546		繁	8890_3	680
	瞰	6804_0	561		繆	2792_2	257
	瞳	6001_4	508	缶	罅	8174_9	657
矢	矯	8242_7	658	羊	羲	8025_3	632

部	字	四　角	頁　碼	部	字	四　角	頁　碼
辵	避	3030_4	279	革	鞠	4752_0	433
	邀	3830_4	348	韋	韓	4445_6	406
	邁	4430_2	401	頁	顆	6198_6	536
	還	3630_3	326	瓜	瓢	1293_0	117
	邂	3730_4	337	風	颺	7721_8	592
	邃	3130_3	294	食	餚	8472_7	663
酉	醜	1661_3	128		餡	8777_7	671
	醞	1661_7	128		餛	8671_1	666
金	錨	8416_0	662		餞	8375_3	661
	鍊	8519_6	664		餒	8274_4	659
	鍋	8712_7	668		館	8377_7	661
	鍍	8014_7	627	馬	駿	7334_7	581
	鍔	8612_7	665		騁	7532_7	586
	鍛	8714_7	669		駸	7333_4	581
	鍥	8713_4	669		駿	7734_7	603
	鍾	8211_4	656	魚	鮮	2835_1	264
	鍶	8613_0	665		鮫	2034_8	148
	鍰	8214_7	658	鳥	鴻	3712_7	330
	鍼	8315_0	660		鴿	8762_7	670
	鐘	8011_4	626	黍	黏	2116_0	163
	鎂	8813_4	672	黑	黛	2333_1	196
	鍘	8210_0	658		黜	6237_2	539
	鍵	8514_0	664		黝	6432_7	546
	鍬	8913_0	681		點	6136_0	535
門	闈	7760_1	607	鼻	鼾	2144_0	172
	闐	7750_6	606	齊	齋	0022_3	11
	闊	7716_4	589				
	關	7743_0	604		**十八畫**		
	闌	7790_6	615	部	字	四　角	頁　碼
阜	隰	7623_3	587	人	儲	2426_0	206
	隱	7223_3	577	又	叢	3214_7	298
隶	隸	4593_2	420	口	嚕	6706_3	557
隹	雛	6011_4	512		嚚	6666_8	553
雨	霜	1096_3	101	土	壘	6010_4	511
	霞	1024_7	79	女	嬸	4346_9	389

部	字	四　角	頁　碼	部	字	四　角	頁　碼
戈	戳	1325_0	119	石	礎	1468_1	124
	戴	4385_0	390	疒	癒	0013_2	6
手	擲	5702_7	495		癖	0014_1	6
	擴	5008_6	450		癘	0012_7	6
	擺	5601_1	488	目	瞻	6706_1	556
	擾	5104_7	464		瞽	4460_4	409
	撞	5505_6	484		瞿	6621_4	551
支	斃	9821_2	707	示	禮	3521_8	320
斤	斷	2272_1	183	禾	穡	2496_1	216
日	曙	6606_4	550		穢	2195_3	176
	曜	6701_4	553	穴	竄	3071_7	286
	曚	6403_2	544		竅	3024_8	277
	曛	6203_1	537	竹	簞	8850_6	676
木	檬	4493_2	417		簟	8840_6	675
	橢	4291_1	385		簡	8822_7	673
	櫃	4191_8	382		簣	8880_6	679
	檀	4491_4	417		簧	8880_6	679
	檳	4398_6	390		簪	8860_1	677
	檸	4392_1	390		簫	8822_7	673
欠	歟	7788_2	615	米	糧	9691_4	703
止	歸	2712_7	239	糸	繕	2896_5	267
歹	殯	1328_6	120		繡	2592_7	224
水	濺	3315_3	305	缶	罈	8874_6	678
	濾	3113_6	292	羽	翹	4721_2	428
	瀉	3312_7	303		翻	2762_0	252
	瀋	3316_9	305		翼	1780_1	138
	瀆	3418_6	313	耳	職	1315_0	118
	瀅	3911_3	350		聶	1014_1	72
	瀏	3210_0	296	肉	臍	7022_3	563
	瀑	3613_2	324		朦	7423_2	583
火	燼	9581_7	700		臏	7328_6	580
爪	爵	2074_6	156	艸	舊	4477_7	412
犬	獵	4221_6	383		薯	4460_4	409
玉	璧	7010_3	562		薰	4433_1	402
瓦	甓	7071_7	565		藉	4496_1	418

部	字	四　角	頁　碼	部	字	四　角	頁　碼
	藍	4410_7	392		鎮	8918_6	681
	藏	4425_3	401		鎗	8816_7	672
	藐	4421_7	398		鎚	8713_7	669
虫	蟒	5414_3	482		鎧	8211_8	658
	蟠	5216_9	471		鎢	8712_7	668
	蟬	5615_6	492		鎬	8012_7	627
	蟲	5013_6	452		鎖	8418_1	663
	蟻	5215_3	471		鎳	8619_4	665
西	覆	1024_7	79		鎘	8112_7	655
見	觀	4611_0	421	韋	韙	6480_4	548
角	觴	2822_7	261	門	闔	7710_7	588
言	謨	0463_4	43		闕	7748_2	606
	謫	0062_7	28		闖	7732_7	602
	謬	0762_2	50	隹	雙	2040_7	150
	謳	0161_6	33		雛	2041_4	151
	謹	0461_4	42		雜	0091_4	32
	謾	0664_7	47		雞	2041_4	151
	譸	0164_9	34	革	鞦	4958_0	444
豆	豐	2210_8	176		鞭	4154_6	380
貝	贅	4480_6	414		鞣	4759_4	433
	贄	5880_6	505	香	馥	2864_7	265
足	蹙	5380_1	479	頁	顋	6138_6	535
	蹤	6818_1	561		題	6180_6	535
	蹠	6013_7	513		額	3168_6	295
	蹣	6412_7	546		顎	6128_6	535
	蹯	6714_2	558		顏	0128_6	33
身	軀	2121_6	164	風	颺	7721_4	591
車	轆	5001_1	448	食	餬	8772_0	671
	轉	5504_3	483		餧	8673_2	666
酉	醫	7760_1	607	馬	騈	7834_1	619
	醬	2760_1	251		騎	7432_1	584
辵	邇	3130_2	294		騏	7438_1	584
里	釐	5821_4	505		鶩	1832_7	140
金	鏘	8012_7	627	骨	髀	7624_0	587
	鎔	8316_8	661		髁	7629_4	587

部	字	四　角	頁　碼	部	字	四　角	頁　碼
彡	鬆	7293_0	580	歹	殯	1325_0	119
	鬈	7271_2	578	水	瀕	3118_6	293
	鬃	7290_1	580		瀘	3111_7	291
鬼	魏	2641_3	233		瀛	3011_7	272
魚	鯉	2631_4	233		瀝	3111_1	290
	鯊	3933_6	352		瀟	3412_7	311
鳥	鵑	6722_7	559		瀨	3718_6	332
	鵝	2752_7	251	火	爆	9683_2	703
	鵠	2762_7	252		爍	9289_4	694
	鵡	1712_7	129	片	牘	2408_6	200
黑	點	6436_1	547	牛	犢	2458_6	211
鼠	鼬	7571_6	586	犬	獸	6363_4	542

十九畫

部	字	四　角	頁　碼	部	字	四　角	頁　碼
				犬	獺	4728_6	429
口	嚥	6403_1	544	玉	瓊	1714_7	130
	嚨	6101_1	532		璽	1010_3	69
土	壞	4013_2	362	瓜	瓣	0044_1	26
	壟	0110_4	32	田	疆	1111_6	103
宀	寵	3021_1	274		疇	6404_1	545
广	廬	0021_7	11	疒	癡	0018_1	7
心	懲	2833_4	264	目	矇	6403_2	544
	懺	9305_0	695	石	礙	1768_1	137
	懵	9406_2	697	禾	穩	2293_7	189
	懶	9708_6	704		穫	2494_7	215
	懷	9003_2	684	竹	簷	8826_1	674
手	攀	4450_2	406		簸	8884_7	680
	攏	5101_1	461		簽	8888_6	680
日	曝	6603_2	550		簾	8823_7	674
	曠	6008_6	509		簿	8814_2	672
木	櫥	4094_0	377	糸	繩	2791_7	257
	櫛	4892_7	442		繪	2896_6	267
	櫓	4796_3	437		繮	2693_2	237
	櫧	4496_0	418		繫	5790_3	500
	櫟	4299_4	386		繭	4422_7	399
					繳	2894_0	267
					繹	2694_1	237

部	字	四　角	頁　碼	部	字	四　角	頁　碼
	繮	2191_6	175		贊	2480_6	214
网	羅	6091_4	532	足	躄	9880_1	707
	罷	6033_1	521		蹲	6814_6	561
羊	羶	8051_6	641		蹬	6211_8	538
	羸	0021_7	11		蹴	6311_4	540
	羹	8043_0	640		蹶	6118_2	534
肉	臘	7221_6	576		蹺	6411_4	546
艸	藕	4492_7	417		蹻	6212_7	538
	藜	4413_2	395		蹼	6213_4	538
	藝	4473_1	412	車	轍	5804_0	503
	藤	4423_2	400		轎	5202_7	467
	藥	4490_4	417	辛	辭	2024_1	146
	藩	4416_9	396	辵	邊	3630_2	326
虫	蟹	2713_6	239	金	鏃	8813_4	672
	蟻	5815_3	504		鏈	8513_0	664
	蟾	5716_1	500		鏑	8012_7	627
	蠅	5711_7	499		鏗	8711_4	667
	蠋	5612_7	492		鏄	8314_3	660
	蠍	5718_2	500		鏉	8313_3	660
衣	襖	3723_4	334		鏘	8714_2	669
	襄	7073_2	565		鏇	8818_1	672
	襠	3926_6	351		鏜	8911_4	681
	襟	3429_1	315		鏞	8012_7	627
示	禱	3424_1	314		鏟	8011_4	626
言	譁	0465_4	43		鏡	8011_6	626
	譆	0761_1	48		鏢	8119_1	655
	證	0261_8	36		鏤	8514_4	664
	譎	0762_7	51	門	關	7777_2	612
	譜	0866_1	57	阜	隴	7121_1	565
	譏	0265_3	37	隹	離	0041_4	25
	譖	0166_1	34		難	4051_4	371
	識	0365_0	40	雨	霧	1022_7	76
	譙	0063_1	28	麻	靡	0021_1	8
	譚	0164_6	34	音	韻	0668_6	47
貝	贈	6886_6	562	頁	願	7128_6	570

部	字	四　角	頁　碼
玉	璨	1013_2	72
石	礄	1064_8	91
米	糲	9192_7	693
糸	續	2498_6	216
	纍	6090_3	531
	纏	2091_4	159
艸	蘚	4435_1	403
	蘭	4422_7	399
虫	蠟	5211_6	471
	蠹	5013_6	452
	蠣	5112_7	465
衣	襪	3425_3	314
言	譴	0563_7	45
	謹	0461_4	43
	籌	0464_1	43
	讎	2021_4	144
	護	0464_7	43
	辯	0044_1	26
貝	贐	6581_7	549
	賦	6385_0	542
足	躊	6414_1	546
	躋	6012_3	512
	躍	6711_4	558
車	轟	5055_6	455
金	鐫	8012_7	627
	鐮	8013_7	627
	鐲	8612_7	665
	鐵	8315_0	660
	鐶	8613_2	665
	鐸	8614_1	665
	鐺	8916_6	681
	鐳	8116_3	655
門	闥	7764_1	609
	闡	7730_4	602
雨	霸	1052_7	86
	霹	1064_1	90
酉	醴	1263_1	117
頁	顧	3128_6	293
	顥	6198_6	536
食	饋	8578_6	665
	饌	8778_1	671
	饁	8471_8	663
	饞	8275_3	659
	饒	8471_1	663
馬	驟	7639_3	587
	驁	4432_7	401
	驃	7139_1	572
	驅	7131_1	571
	驂	7332_2	580
	驄	7633_0	587
骨	髏	7524_4	585
鬼	魔	0021_3	9
魚	鰶	2633_3	233
	鰭	2436_1	209
鳥	鷟	9932_7	708
	鶴	4722_7	429
	鷉	2742_7	249
	鶺	2772_7	254
	鷞	8732_7	670
鹿	麝	0024_1	17
黑	黯	6036_1	522
鼓	鼙	4440_6	404
齒	齧	5777_3	500

二十二畫

部	字	四　角	頁　碼
人	儷	2923_1	268
	儼	2624_8	230
口	囉	6601_4	550
	嚇	6403_1	544

部	字	四　角	頁　碼	部	字	四　角	頁　碼
	囊	5073_2	457	雨	霽	1021_4	74
子	孿	2240_7	182	革	韃	4151_6	380
山	巔	2288_6	186	音	響	2760_1	251
弓	彎	2220_7	178	頁	顫	0118_6	32
心	戀	4713_8	428	食	饕	6173_2	535
手	攢	5408_6	482		饗	2773_2	254
	攤	5001_4	448	馬	驍	7431_1	583
木	權	4491_4	417		驕	7232_7	578
欠	歡	4728_2	429	彡	鬚	7228_6	578
水	灑	3111_1	290	魚	鱉	8833_6	675
	灘	3011_4	272	鳥	鷗	0722_7	48
犬	玀	4621_4	422		鷗	7772_7	610
广	癬	0015_1	7	龍	龕	8021_1	628
穴	竊	3092_7	290				

二十三畫

部	字	四　角	頁　碼	部	字	四　角	頁　碼
竹	籟	8898_6	681	山	巖	2224_8	182
	籠	8821_1	673	心	戀	2233_9	182
米	糴	8791_4	671		懞	9604_6	702
网	羇	6052_1	525	田	疊	6010_7	511
耳	聽	1413_1	121	手	攬	5701_6	493
	聾	0140_1	33	日	曬	6101_1	532
肉	臟	7425_3	583	竹	籤	8815_3	672
衣	襯	3621_0	325	糸	纓	2694_4	237
	襲	0173_2	35		纖	2395_0	199
見	覽	7821_6	617	艸	蘿	4491_4	417
言	讀	0468_6	44		蘸	4441_4	404
貝	贖	6488_6	548		蠱	5010_7	451
足	躐	6211_6	538	虫	蠲	8612_7	665
	躑	6712_7	558	言	變	2224_7	181
	躒	6219_4	538		讌	0463_1	43
	躊	6014_0	513	足	躚	6113_1	534
	躓	6218_6	538	辵	邐	3630_1	326
金	鑄	8414_1	662	金	鑛	8018_6	627
	鏤	8414_7	662		鑠	8219_4	658
	鑑	8811_7	672				
	鑒	7810_9	616				

部	字	四　角	頁　碼
糸	纘	2891_6	267
言	讜	0963_1	57
	讞	0363_4	39
足	躪	6412_7	546
金	钁	8611_4	665
	鑽	8418_6	663
	鑿	3710_9	327
頁	顴	4128_6	380
馬	驤	7033_2	565
	驦	7138_1	572
魚	鱷	2131_6	171
黑	黷	6438_6	547

二十八畫

部	字	四　角	頁　碼
豆	豔	2411_7	200
鳥	鸚	6742_7	560
	鸛	4722_7	429

二十九畫

部	字	四　角	頁　碼
馬	驪	7131_1	571
鬯	鬱	4472_2	412

三十畫

部	字	四　角	頁　碼
鳥	鸞	2233_7	182

三十二畫

部	字	四　角	頁　碼
竹	籲	8828_6	674

注 音	字	四 角	頁 碼
ㄅㄧˋ	壁	7010_3	562
ㄅㄧˋ	髀	7624_0	587
ㄅㄧˋ	襞	7073_2	565
ㄅㄧㄝ	憋	9833_4	707
ㄅㄧㄝ	鱉	9871_7	707
ㄅㄧㄝˊ	別	6240_0	539
ㄅㄧㄝˊ	蹩	9880_1	707
ㄅㄧㄠ	標	4199_1	382
ㄅㄧㄠ	膘	7129_1	570
ㄅㄧㄠ	鏢	8119_1	655
ㄅㄧㄠ	鑣	8013_1	627
ㄅㄧㄠˇ	表	5073_2	457
ㄅㄧㄠˇ	婊	4543_2	419
ㄅㄧㄠˇ	錶	8513_2	664
ㄅㄧㄠˇ	褾	3523_2	321
ㄅㄧㄢ	邊	3630_1	326
ㄅㄧㄢ	編	2392_7	198
ㄅㄧㄢ	鞭	4154_6	380
ㄅㄧㄢ	蝙	5312_7	476
ㄅㄧㄢˇ	扁	3022_7	275
ㄅㄧㄢˇ	貶	6283_7	539
ㄅㄧㄢˇ	匾	7171_2	573
ㄅㄧㄢˇ	褊	3322_7	307
ㄅㄧㄢˋ	卞	0023_0	016
ㄅㄧㄢˋ	徧	2322_7	194
ㄅㄧㄢˋ	弁	2344_0	197
ㄅㄧㄢˋ	汴	3013_0	273
ㄅㄧㄢˋ	忭	9003_0	684
ㄅㄧㄢˋ	便	2124_6	169
ㄅㄧㄢˋ	遍	3330_2	307
ㄅㄧㄢˋ	辨	0044_1	025
ㄅㄧㄢˋ	辮	0044_1	026
ㄅㄧㄢˋ	辯	0044_1	026
ㄅㄧㄢˋ	變	2224_7	181
ㄅㄧㄣ	浜	3218_7	299

ㄅ

注 音	字	四 角	頁 碼
ㄅㄧ	逼	3130_6	295
ㄅㄧˊ	鼻	2644_6	233
ㄅㄧˇ	匕	2171_0	172
ㄅㄧˇ	比	2171_0	172
ㄅㄧˇ	彼	2424_7	206
ㄅㄧˇ	筆	8850_7	676
ㄅㄧˇ	鄙	6762_7	560
ㄅㄧˇ	妣	4141_0	380
ㄅㄧˋ	必	3300_0	303
ㄅㄧˋ	庇	0021_1	008
ㄅㄧˋ	畀	6044_0	524
ㄅㄧˋ	陛	7121_4	566
ㄅㄧˋ	畢	6050_4	525
ㄅㄧˋ	閉	7724_7	599
ㄅㄧˋ	詖	0464_7	043
ㄅㄧˋ	婢	4644_0	425
ㄅㄧˋ	愊	9106_6	692
ㄅㄧˋ	愎	9804_7	706
ㄅㄧˋ	敝	9824_0	707
ㄅㄧˋ	閟	7733_7	603
ㄅㄧˋ	鉍	8280_0	660
ㄅㄧˋ	煏	9186_6	693
ㄅㄧˋ	碧	1660_1	128
ㄅㄧˋ	裨	3624_0	325
ㄅㄧˋ	弊	9844_4	707
ㄅㄧˋ	幣	9822_7	707
ㄅㄧˋ	蔽	4424_8	400
ㄅㄧˋ	壁	7010_4	562
ㄅㄧˋ	變	7040_4	565
ㄅㄧˋ	篦	8871_1	677
ㄅㄧˋ	避	3030_4	279
ㄅㄧˋ	箅	8850_4	676
ㄅㄧˋ	斃	9821_2	707

注 音	字	四 角	頁 碼	注 音	字	四 角	頁 碼
ㄅㄛˊ	博	4304$_2$	387	ㄅㄟˋ	臂	7022$_7$	564
ㄅㄛˊ	鉑	8610$_0$	665	ㄅㄠ	包	2771$_2$	252
ㄅㄛˊ	薄	4414$_2$	395	ㄅㄠ	苞	4471$_2$	411
ㄅㄛˊ	鎛	8314$_3$	660	ㄅㄠ	枹	4791$_2$	436
ㄅㄛˊ	膊	7324$_1$	580	ㄅㄠ	胞	7721$_2$	590
ㄅㄛˊ	駁	7434$_0$	584	ㄅㄠ	襃	0073$_2$	031
ㄅㄛˊ	箔	8816$_2$	672	ㄅㄠˊ	雹	1071$_2$	091
ㄅㄛˇ	跛	6414$_7$	546	ㄅㄠˇ	保	2629$_4$	231
ㄅㄛˇ	簸	8884$_7$	680	ㄅㄠˇ	堡	2610$_4$	228
ㄅㄛˋ	播	5206$_9$	469	ㄅㄠˇ	葆	4429$_4$	401
ㄅㄛˋ	擘	7050$_2$	565	ㄅㄠˇ	褓	3629$_4$	325
ㄅㄛ˙	蔔	4462$_7$	410	ㄅㄠˇ	飽	8771$_2$	670
ㄅㄞˊ	白	2600$_0$	225	ㄅㄠˇ	寶	3080$_6$	289
ㄅㄞˇ	百	1060$_0$	087	ㄅㄠˇ	鴇	2742$_7$	249
ㄅㄞˇ	擺	5601$_1$	488	ㄅㄠˋ	抱	5701$_2$	492
ㄅㄞˋ	拜	2155$_0$	172	ㄅㄠˋ	豹	2722$_0$	241
ㄅㄞˋ	敗	6884$_0$	562	ㄅㄠˋ	鉋	8711$_2$	667
ㄅㄞˋ	稗	2694$_0$	237	ㄅㄠˋ	報	4744$_7$	432
ㄅㄟ	卑	2640$_0$	233	ㄅㄠˋ	暴	6013$_2$	512
ㄅㄟ	杯	4199$_0$	382	ㄅㄠˋ	鮑	2731$_2$	246
ㄅㄟ	俾	2624$_0$	230	ㄅㄠˋ	爆	9683$_2$	703
ㄅㄟ	悲	1133$_1$	106	ㄅㄢ	扳	5104$_7$	464
ㄅㄟ	碑	1664$_4$	128	ㄅㄢ	班	1111$_4$	102
ㄅㄟˇ	北	1111$_0$	101	ㄅㄢ	般	2744$_7$	249
ㄅㄟˋ	貝	6080$_0$	529	ㄅㄢ	斑	1111$_4$	102
ㄅㄟˋ	背	1122$_7$	104	ㄅㄢ	編	0342$_7$	038
ㄅㄟˋ	倍	2026$_1$	147	ㄅㄢ	搬	5704$_7$	497
ㄅㄟˋ	被	3424$_7$	314	ㄅㄢ	頒	8128$_6$	655
ㄅㄟˋ	狽	4628$_0$	423	ㄅㄢˇ	坂	4114$_7$	379
ㄅㄟˋ	輩	1150$_6$	106	ㄅㄢˇ	阪	7124$_8$	569
ㄅㄟˋ	蓓	4416$_1$	396	ㄅㄢˇ	板	4194$_7$	382
ㄅㄟˋ	備	2422$_7$	205	ㄅㄢˇ	版	2104$_7$	160
ㄅㄟˋ	悖	9404$_7$	696	ㄅㄢˋ	半	9050$_0$	687
ㄅㄟˋ	鋇	8618$_0$	665	ㄅㄢˋ	伴	2925$_0$	268
ㄅㄟˋ	憊	2433$_2$	209	ㄅㄢˋ	扮	5802$_7$	502

注 音	字	四 角	頁 碼	注 音	字	四 角	頁 碼
ㄅㄢˋ	絆	2995_0	269	ㄆㄧˊ	毗	6101_0	532
ㄅㄢˋ	辦	0044_1	026	ㄆㄧˊ	貔	2621_1	229
ㄅㄢˋ	瓣	0044_1	026	ㄆㄧˊ	啤	6604_0	550
ㄅㄣ	奔	4044_4	370	ㄆㄧˊ	陴	7624_0	587
ㄅㄣ	賁	4080_6	375	ㄆㄧˊ	疲	0014_7	007
ㄅㄣˇ	本	5023_0	452	ㄆㄧˊ	皮	4024_7	366
ㄅㄣˇ	苯	4423_4	400	ㄆㄧˊ	脾	7624_0	587
ㄅㄣˋ	笨	8823_4	674	ㄆㄧˊ	鼙	4440_6	404
ㄅㄤ	邦	2752_7	251	ㄆㄧˇ	疋	1780_1	138
ㄅㄤ	邦	5702_7	494	ㄆㄧˇ	圮	4711_7	427
ㄅㄤ	幫	4422_7	399	ㄆㄧˋ	屁	7721_1	590
ㄅㄤˇ	綁	2792_7	258	ㄆㄧˋ	辟	7064_1	565
ㄅㄤˇ	榜	4092_7	377	ㄆㄧˋ	媲	4741_1	430
ㄅㄤˇ	膀	7022_7	564	ㄆㄧˋ	僻	2024_1	146
ㄅㄤˋ	謗	0062_7	028	ㄆㄧˋ	擗	5004_1	450
ㄅㄤˋ	蚌	5510_0	485	ㄆㄧˋ	甓	7071_7	565
ㄅㄤˋ	棒	4595_3	420	ㄆㄧˋ	癖	0014_1	006
ㄅㄤˋ	鎊	8012_7	627	ㄆㄧˋ	譬	7060_1	565
ㄅㄤˋ	磅	1062_7	090	ㄆㄧˋ	闢	7764_1	609
ㄅㄥ	崩	2222_7	179	ㄆㄧㄝ	瞥	9860_4	707
ㄅㄥ	繃	2792_0	257	ㄆㄧㄝˇ	撇	5804_0	502
ㄅㄥˋ	蹦	6212_7	538	ㄆㄧㄠ	飄	1791_0	138
	ㄆ			ㄆㄧㄠˊ	嫖	4149_1	380
				ㄆㄧㄠˊ	瓢	1293_0	117
注 音	字	四 角	頁 碼	ㄆㄧㄠˇ	瞟	6109_1	534
ㄆㄧ	丕	1010_9	072	ㄆㄧㄠˋ	漂	3119_1	293
ㄆㄧ	匹	7171_1	572	ㄆㄧㄠˋ	票	1090_1	101
ㄆㄧ	坯	4111_9	379	ㄆㄧㄠˋ	剽	1290_0	117
ㄆㄧ	批	5101_0	460	ㄆㄧㄠˋ	驃	7139_1	572
ㄆㄧ	披	5404_7	481	ㄆㄧㄢ	偏	2322_7	193
ㄆㄧ	砒	1161_0	106	ㄆㄧㄢ	篇	8822_7	673
ㄆㄧ	劈	7022_7	564	ㄆㄧㄢ	翩	3722_0	334
ㄆㄧ	霹	1064_1	090	ㄆㄧㄢˊ	便	2124_6	169
ㄆㄧˊ	琵	1171_1	107	ㄆㄧㄢˊ	胼	7824_1	618
ㄆㄧˊ	枇	4191_0	381	ㄆㄧㄢˊ	論	0362_7	039

注 音	字	四 角	頁 碼	注 音	字	四 角	頁 碼
ㄆㄧㄢˊ	蹁	6312$_7$	540	ㄆㄨˇ	普	8060$_1$	645
ㄆㄧㄢˊ	駢	7834$_1$	619	ㄆㄨˇ	譜	0865$_7$	057
ㄆㄧㄢˋ	片	2202$_1$	176	ㄆㄨˇ	溥	3314$_2$	304
ㄆㄧㄢˋ	騙	7332$_7$	580	ㄆㄨˋ	舖	8362$_7$	661
ㄆㄧㄣ	姘	4844$_1$	441	ㄆㄨˋ	瀑	3613$_2$	324
ㄆㄧㄣ	拚	5304$_0$	474	ㄆㄨˋ	曝	6603$_2$	550
ㄆㄧㄣˊ	嬪	4348$_6$	389	ㄆㄚˊ	扒	5800$_0$	501
ㄆㄧㄣˊ	貧	8080$_6$	654	ㄆㄚˊ	杷	4791$_7$	436
ㄆㄧㄣˊ	頻	2128$_6$	171	ㄆㄚˊ	爬	7723$_1$	597
ㄆㄧㄣˇ	品	6066$_0$	528	ㄆㄚˊ	耙	5791$_7$	500
ㄆㄧㄣˋ	牝	2451$_0$	209	ㄆㄚˇ	葩	4461$_7$	409
ㄆㄧㄣˋ	聘	1512$_7$	124	ㄆㄚˋ	帕	4620$_0$	422
ㄆㄧㄥ	乒	7221$_1$	576	ㄆㄚˋ	怕	9600$_0$	701
ㄆㄧㄥ	娉	4542$_7$	419	ㄆㄛ	波	3414$_7$	312
ㄆㄧㄥˊ	平	1040$_9$	082	ㄆㄛ	坡	4414$_7$	395
ㄆㄧㄥˊ	憑	2221$_7$	179	ㄆㄛ	陂	7424$_7$	583
ㄆㄧㄥˊ	坪	4114$_9$	379	ㄆㄛ	潑	3214$_7$	298
ㄆㄧㄥˊ	屏	7724$_1$	598	ㄆㄛˊ	婆	3440$_4$	316
ㄆㄧㄥˊ	瓶	8141$_7$	656	ㄆㄛˇ	叵	7171$_6$	573
ㄆㄧㄥˊ	評	0164$_9$	034	ㄆㄛˇ	剖	0260$_0$	035
ㄆㄧㄥˊ	萍	4414$_9$	395	ㄆㄛˇ	頗	4128$_6$	380
ㄆㄧㄥˊ	憑	3133$_2$	295	ㄆㄛˋ	珀	1610$_0$	125
ㄆㄧㄥˊ	蘋	4428$_6$	401	ㄆㄛˋ	迫	3630$_0$	325
ㄆㄨ	仆	2320$_0$	191	ㄆㄛˋ	破	1464$_7$	123
ㄆㄨ	撲	5203$_4$	468	ㄆㄛˋ	粕	9690$_0$	703
ㄆㄨ	鋪	8312$_7$	660	ㄆㄛˋ	魄	2661$_3$	234
ㄆㄨˊ	匍	2722$_0$	241	ㄆㄞ	拍	5600$_0$	487
ㄆㄨˊ	僕	2223$_4$	179	ㄆㄞ	啪	6600$_0$	550
ㄆㄨˊ	菩	4460$_1$	408	ㄆㄞˊ	排	5101$_0$	460
ㄆㄨˊ	葡	4422$_7$	399	ㄆㄞˊ	牌	2604$_0$	228
ㄆㄨˊ	樸	4293$_4$	385	ㄆㄞˊ	徘	2121$_1$	163
ㄆㄨˊ	蒲	4412$_7$	394	ㄆㄞˋ	派	3213$_2$	297
ㄆㄨˊ	蹼	6213$_4$	538	ㄆㄟ	胚	7121$_9$	566
ㄆㄨˇ	浦	3312$_7$	303	ㄆㄟˊ	培	4016$_1$	362
ㄆㄨˇ	圃	6022$_7$	520	ㄆㄟˊ	焙	9086$_1$	691

注 音	字	四 角	頁 碼	注 音	字	四 角	頁 碼
ㄆㄟˊ	陪	7026_1	564	ㄆㄤˊ	螃	5012_7	452
ㄆㄟˊ	裴	1173_2	107	ㄆㄤˊ	龐	0021_1	008
ㄆㄟˊ	賠	6086_1	531	ㄆㄤˋ	胖	7925_0	620
ㄆㄟˋ	配	1761_7	136	ㄆㄥ	砰	1164_9	107
ㄆㄟˋ	佩	2721_0	240	ㄆㄥ	抨	5104_9	464
ㄆㄟˋ	沛	3012_7	272	ㄆㄥ	怦	9104_9	692
ㄆㄟˋ	霈	1012_7	072	ㄆㄥ	烹	0033_2	021
ㄆㄠ	抛	5401_2	480	ㄆㄥˊ	彭	4212_2	383
ㄆㄠˊ	袍	3721_2	333	ㄆㄥˊ	朋	7722_0	595
ㄆㄠˊ	刨	2270_0	183	ㄆㄥˊ	棚	4792_0	436
ㄆㄠˊ	咆	6701_2	553	ㄆㄥˊ	硼	1762_0	137
ㄆㄠˊ	庖	0021_2	008	ㄆㄥˊ	澎	3212_2	296
ㄆㄠˇ	跑	6711_2	557	ㄆㄥˊ	蓬	4430_5	401
ㄆㄠˋ	炮	9781_2	704	ㄆㄥˊ	膨	7222_2	576
ㄆㄠˋ	泡	3711_2	328	ㄆㄥˊ	篷	8830_4	674
ㄆㄠˋ	礮	1064_8	091	ㄆㄥˊ	鵬	7722_7	597
ㄆㄠˋ	砲	1761_2	136	ㄆㄥˇ	捧	5505_3	484
ㄆㄠˋ	皰	4721_2	428	ㄆㄥˋ	椪	5801_2	501
ㄆㄡˊ	抔	5109_0	465				
ㄆㄢ	潘	3216_9	299			ㄇ	
ㄆㄢ	攀	4450_2	406	注 音	字	四 角	頁 碼
ㄆㄢˊ	盤	2710_7	238	ㄇㄧ	咪	6909_4	562
ㄆㄢˊ	蟠	5216_9	471	ㄇㄧˊ	迷	3930_9	352
ㄆㄢˋ	判	9250_2	694	ㄇㄧˊ	謎	0968_9	057
ㄆㄢˋ	盼	6802_7	561	ㄇㄧˊ	彌	1122_7	104
ㄆㄢˋ	叛	9154_7	692	ㄇㄧˊ	麋	0021_1	008
ㄆㄢˋ	畔	6905_0	562	ㄇㄧˊ	獼	4122_7	379
ㄆㄢˋ	泮	3915_0	351	ㄇㄧˇ	米	9090_4	691
ㄆㄣ	噴	6408_6	546	ㄇㄧˇ	瀰	3112_7	291
ㄆㄣˊ	盆	8010_7	625	ㄇㄧˇ	弭	1124_0	105
ㄆㄤ	滂	3012_7	272	ㄇㄧˋ	糸	2290_3	187
ㄆㄤˊ	旁	0022_7	013	ㄇㄧˋ	祕	3320_0	306
ㄆㄤˊ	逢	3730_4	337	ㄇㄧˋ	秘	2390_0	198
ㄆㄤˊ	厖	7121_2	566	ㄇㄧˋ	泌	3310_0	303
ㄆㄤˊ	傍	2022_7	145	ㄇㄧˋ	密	3077_2	286

注音	字	四角	頁碼	注音	字	四角	頁碼
ㄇㄧˋ	蜜	3013_6	273	ㄇㄧㄣˇ	泯	3714_7	330
ㄇㄧˋ	覓	2021_6	144	ㄇㄧㄣˇ	黽	7771_7	609
ㄇㄧㄝˋ	滅	3315_0	304	ㄇㄧㄣˇ	繁	8833_6	675
ㄇㄧㄝˋ	蔑	4425_3	400	ㄇㄧㄥˊ	名	2760_0	251
ㄇㄧㄝˋ	篾	8825_3	674	ㄇㄧㄥˊ	明	6702_0	554
ㄇㄧㄠˊ	苗	4460_0	408	ㄇㄧㄥˊ	冥	3780_0	342
ㄇㄧㄠˊ	描	5406_0	481	ㄇㄧㄥˊ	茗	4460_7	409
ㄇㄧㄠˊ	瞄	6406_0	545	ㄇㄧㄥˊ	酩	1766_4	137
ㄇㄧㄠˇ	秒	2992_0	269	ㄇㄧㄥˊ	銘	8716_0	669
ㄇㄧㄠˇ	杳	4060_9	373	ㄇㄧㄥˊ	溟	3718_0	331
ㄇㄧㄠˇ	渺	3912_0	350	ㄇㄧㄥˊ	鳴	6702_7	555
ㄇㄧㄠˇ	藐	4421_7	398	ㄇㄧㄥˊ	瞑	6708_0	557
ㄇㄧㄠˇ	眇	6902_0	562	ㄇㄧㄥˊ	螟	5718_0	500
ㄇㄧㄠˋ	妙	4942_0	444	ㄇㄧㄥˋ	命	8062_7	648
ㄇㄧㄠˋ	廟	0022_7	016	ㄇㄨˇ	姆	4745_5	432
ㄇㄧㄡˋ	謬	0762_2	050	ㄇㄨˇ	母	7750_0	606
ㄇㄧㄡˋ	繆	2792_2	257	ㄇㄨˇ	牡	2451_0	209
ㄇㄧㄢˊ	棉	4692_7	427	ㄇㄨˇ	畝	0768_0	052
ㄇㄧㄢˊ	眠	6704_7	556	ㄇㄨˇ	拇	5705_5	497
ㄇㄧㄢˊ	綿	2692_7	235	ㄇㄨˋ	木	4090_0	376
ㄇㄧㄢˇ	免	2741_5	248	ㄇㄨˋ	目	6010_1	510
ㄇㄧㄢˇ	勉	2441_2	209	ㄇㄨˋ	牧	2854_1	264
ㄇㄧㄢˇ	娩	4741_6	430	ㄇㄨˋ	幕	4422_7	399
ㄇㄧㄢˇ	冕	6041_6	523	ㄇㄨˋ	沐	3419_0	313
ㄇㄧㄢˇ	靦	1661_0	128	ㄇㄨˋ	穆	2692_2	235
ㄇㄧㄢˇ	眄	6102_7	533	ㄇㄨˋ	睦	6401_4	543
ㄇㄧㄢˇ	緬	2791_6	256	ㄇㄨˋ	慕	4433_3	402
ㄇㄧㄢˋ	面	1060_0	087	ㄇㄨˋ	募	4442_7	405
ㄇㄧㄢˋ	麵	4124_2	379	ㄇㄨˋ	墓	4410_4	392
ㄇㄧㄣˊ	民	7774_7	610	ㄇㄨˋ	霖	1019_4	073
ㄇㄧㄣˇ	敏	8854_6	676	ㄇㄨˋ	暮	4460_3	408
ㄇㄧㄣˇ	憫	9702_0	704	ㄇㄨˋ	冪	7722_7	597
ㄇㄧㄣˇ	閩	7713_6	588	ㄇㄚ	媽	4142_7	380
ㄇㄧㄣˇ	閔	7740_0	603	ㄇㄚˊ	麻	0029_4	020
ㄇㄧㄣˇ	皿	7710_0	587	ㄇㄚˊ	痲	0019_4	008

注　音	字	四　角	頁　碼	注　音	字	四　角	頁　碼
ㄇㄚˇ	馬	7132_7	571	ㄇㄞˋ	麥	4020_7	362
ㄇㄚˇ	碼	1162_7	107	ㄇㄞˋ	邁	3430_2	315
ㄇㄚˇ	瑪	1112_7	103	ㄇㄞˋ	勱	4442_7	405
ㄇㄚˇ	螞	5112_7	465	ㄇㄟˊ	枚	4894_0	443
ㄇㄚˋ	罵	6032_7	520	ㄇㄟˊ	楣	4796_7	438
ㄇㄚ・	嗎	6102_7	533	ㄇㄟˊ	玫	1814_0	139
ㄇㄛ	摸	5403_4	480	ㄇㄟˊ	梅	4895_5	443
ㄇㄛˊ	摩	0025_2	019	ㄇㄟˊ	眉	7726_7	601
ㄇㄛˊ	魔	0021_3	009	ㄇㄟˊ	湄	3716_7	331
ㄇㄛˊ	模	4493_4	417	ㄇㄟˊ	煤	9489_4	697
ㄇㄛˊ	膜	7423_4	583	ㄇㄟˊ	霉	1050_7	086
ㄇㄛˊ	磨	0026_1	019	ㄇㄟˊ	媒	4449_4	406
ㄇㄛˊ	謨	0463_4	043	ㄇㄟˇ	每	8050_7	641
ㄇㄛˊ	摹	4450_2	406	ㄇㄟˇ	美	8043_0	639
ㄇㄛˊ	饝	8076_4	654	ㄇㄟˇ	鎂	8813_4	672
ㄇㄛˇ	抹	5509_0	485	ㄇㄟˋ	妹	4549_0	419
ㄇㄛˋ	末	5090_0	458	ㄇㄟˋ	媚	4746_7	432
ㄇㄛˋ	沒	3714_7	330	ㄇㄟˋ	寐	3029_4	278
ㄇㄛˋ	沫	3519_0	320	ㄇㄟˋ	魅	2521_9	221
ㄇㄛˋ	漠	3413_4	312	ㄇㄟˋ	昧	6509_0	549
ㄇㄛˋ	默	6333_4	541	ㄇㄠ	貓	2426_0	206
ㄇㄛˋ	墨	6010_4	511	ㄇㄠ	猫	4426_0	401
ㄇㄛˋ	陌	7126_0	569	ㄇㄠˊ	毛	2071_4	156
ㄇㄛˋ	寞	3043_6	283	ㄇㄠˊ	矛	1722_2	131
ㄇㄛˋ	歿	1724_7	133	ㄇㄠˊ	茅	4422_2	398
ㄇㄛˋ	莫	4443_6	406	ㄇㄠˊ	旄	0821_4	052
ㄇㄛˋ	茉	4490_4	416	ㄇㄠˊ	錨	8416_0	662
ㄇㄛˋ	秣	2599_0	225	ㄇㄠˊ	髦	7271_4	578
ㄇㄛˋ	驀	4432_7	401	ㄇㄠˇ	卯	7772_0	609
ㄇㄛ・	麼	0023_9	017	ㄇㄠˋ	茂	4425_3	400
ㄇㄞˊ	埋	4611_4	421	ㄇㄠˋ	貿	7780_6	614
ㄇㄞˊ	霾	1021_4	074	ㄇㄠˋ	冒	6060_0	526
ㄇㄞˇ	買	6080_6	530	ㄇㄠˋ	帽	4626_0	423
ㄇㄞˋ	賣	4080_6	375	ㄇㄠˋ	懋	4433_9	403
ㄇㄞˋ	脈	7223_2	577	ㄇㄠˋ	貌	2721_7	241

注　音	字	四　角	頁　碼	注　音	字	四　角	頁　碼
ㄇㄠˋ	瑁	1616_0	127	ㄇㄥˊ	曚	6403_2	544
ㄇㄡˊ	謀	0469_4	044	ㄇㄥˊ	朦	7423_2	583
ㄇㄡˊ	牟	2350_0	197	ㄇㄥˊ	矇	6403_2	544
ㄇㄡˊ	侔	2325_0	196	ㄇㄥˊ	懜	9406_2	697
ㄇㄡˊ	眸	6305_0	540	ㄇㄥˇ	猛	4721_7	428
ㄇㄡˇ	某	4490_4	416	ㄇㄥˇ	蜢	5711_7	499
ㄇㄢˊ	瞞	6402_7	543	ㄇㄥˇ	錳	8711_7	667
ㄇㄢˊ	蠻	2213_6	177	ㄇㄥˋ	孟	1710_7	128
ㄇㄢˊ	蹣	6412_7	546	ㄇㄥˋ	夢	4420_7	397
ㄇㄢˊ	饅	8674_7	666				
ㄇㄢˇ	滿	3412_7	310			ㄈ	
ㄇㄢˋ	曼	6040_7	523	注　音	字	四　角	頁　碼
ㄇㄢˋ	蔓	4440_7	404	ㄈㄨ	夫	5003_0	449
ㄇㄢˋ	漫	3614_7	324	ㄈㄨ	枹	4791_2	436
ㄇㄢˋ	慢	9604_7	702	ㄈㄨ	孵	7274_7	579
ㄇㄢˋ	幔	4624_7	423	ㄈㄨ	膚	2122_7	167
ㄇㄢˋ	縵	2694_7	237	ㄈㄨ	敷	5824_0	505
ㄇㄢˋ	謾	0664_7	047	ㄈㄨ	跗	6410_0	546
ㄇㄣ	悶	7733_7	603	ㄈㄨ	鈇	8513_0	664
ㄇㄣˊ	門	7777_7	612	ㄈㄨˊ	芙	4453_0	407
ㄇㄣˊ	捫	5702_0	494	ㄈㄨˊ	扶	5503_0	482
ㄇㄣˋ	燜	9782_0	705	ㄈㄨˊ	拂	5502_7	482
ㄇㄣ・	們	2722_0	242	ㄈㄨˊ	弗	5502_7	482
ㄇㄤˊ	忙	9001_0	683	ㄈㄨˊ	彿	2522_7	221
ㄇㄤˊ	芒	4471_0	410	ㄈㄨˊ	浮	3214_7	298
ㄇㄤˊ	氓	0774_7	052	ㄈㄨˊ	氟	8051_7	642
ㄇㄤˊ	盲	0060_1	027	ㄈㄨˊ	伏	2323_4	194
ㄇㄤˊ	茫	4411_0	393	ㄈㄨˊ	服	7724_7	598
ㄇㄤˊ	鋩	8411_0	661	ㄈㄨˊ	匐	2762_0	252
ㄇㄤˇ	莽	4444_5	406	ㄈㄨˊ	福	3126_6	293
ㄇㄤˇ	蟒	5414_3	482	ㄈㄨˊ	髴	7252_7	578
ㄇㄥˊ	萌	4462_7	410	ㄈㄨˊ	縛	2394_2	197
ㄇㄥˊ	盟	6710_7	557	ㄈㄨˊ	俘	2224_7	181
ㄇㄥˊ	蒙	4423_2	400	ㄈㄨˊ	幅	4126_6	380
ㄇㄥˊ	檬	4493_2	417	ㄈㄨˊ	符	8824_3	674

注音	字	四角	頁碼	注音	字	四角	頁碼
ㄈㄨˊ	輻	5106_6	465	ㄈㄨˋ	負	1780_6	138
ㄈㄨˊ	茯	4423_4	400	ㄈㄨˋ	阜	2740_7	248
ㄈㄨˊ	袱	3323_4	307	ㄈㄨˋ	赴	4380_0	389
ㄈㄨˊ	蝠	5116_6	465	ㄈㄨˋ	婦	4742_7	431
ㄈㄨˊ	綍	2494_7	215	ㄈㄨˋ	賦	6384_0	542
ㄈㄨˊ	蚨	5513_0	485	ㄈㄚ	發	1224_7	112
ㄈㄨˊ	被	3324_4	307	ㄈㄚˊ	伐	2325_0	195
ㄈㄨˊ	凫	2721_7	241	ㄈㄚˊ	閥	7725_3	600
ㄈㄨˇ	府	0024_0	017	ㄈㄚˊ	筏	8825_3	674
ㄈㄨˇ	俯	2024_0	146	ㄈㄚˊ	砝	1463_1	123
ㄈㄨˇ	拊	5400_0	479	ㄈㄚˊ	乏	2030_7	148
ㄈㄨˇ	腑	7024_0	564	ㄈㄚˊ	罰	6062_0	528
ㄈㄨˇ	腐	0022_7	013	ㄈㄚˇ	法	3413_1	311
ㄈㄨˇ	甫	5322_7	479	ㄈㄚˇ	髮	7244_7	578
ㄈㄨˇ	輔	5302_7	473	ㄈㄚˋ	琺	1413_1	121
ㄈㄨˇ	脯	7322_7	580	ㄈㄛˊ	佛	2522_7	221
ㄈㄨˇ	斧	8022_1	629	ㄈㄟ	非	1111_1	101
ㄈㄨˇ	釜	8010_9	626	ㄈㄟ	霏	1011_1	072
ㄈㄨˇ	撫	5803_1	502	ㄈㄟ	扉	3021_1	274
ㄈㄨˋ	付	2420_0	201	ㄈㄟ	菲	4411_1	393
ㄈㄨˋ	附	7420_0	581	ㄈㄟ	啡	6101_1	532
ㄈㄨˋ	咐	6400_0	543	ㄈㄟ	飛	1241_3	115
ㄈㄨˋ	駙	7430_0	583	ㄈㄟ	妃	4741_7	430
ㄈㄨˋ	復	2824_7	262	ㄈㄟ	腓	7121_1	565
ㄈㄨˋ	父	8040_0	639	ㄈㄟˊ	肥	7721_7	591
ㄈㄨˋ	覆	1024_7	079	ㄈㄟˇ	誹	0161_1	033
ㄈㄨˋ	馥	2864_7	265	ㄈㄟˇ	翡	1112_7	103
ㄈㄨˋ	複	3824_7	347	ㄈㄟˇ	蜚	1113_6	103
ㄈㄨˋ	蝮	5814_7	504	ㄈㄟˇ	斐	1140_0	106
ㄈㄨˋ	腹	7824_7	618	ㄈㄟˇ	匪	7171_1	573
ㄈㄨˋ	傅	2324_2	195	ㄈㄟˋ	吠	6303_4	540
ㄈㄨˋ	賻	6384_2	542	ㄈㄟˋ	沸	3512_7	317
ㄈㄨˋ	副	1260_0	116	ㄈㄟˋ	狒	4522_7	419
ㄈㄨˋ	富	3060_6	284	ㄈㄟˋ	廢	0024_7	018
ㄈㄨˋ	訃	0360_0	039	ㄈㄟˋ	癈	0014_8	007

注 音	字	四 角	頁 碼	注 音	字	四 角	頁 碼
ㄈㄟˋ	費	5580_6	487	ㄈㄣˊ	焚	4480_9	414
ㄈㄟˋ	肺	7022_7	564	ㄈㄣˇ	粉	9892_7	707
ㄈㄡˇ	否	1060_9	088	ㄈㄣˋ	份	2822_7	260
ㄈㄡˇ	缶	8077_2	654	ㄈㄣˋ	忿	8033_2	637
ㄈㄢ	番	2060_9	155	ㄈㄣˋ	奮	4060_1	372
ㄈㄢ	繙	2296_9	190	ㄈㄣˋ	糞	9080_1	690
ㄈㄢ	翻	2762_0	252	ㄈㄣˋ	憤	9408_6	697
ㄈㄢ	幡	4226_9	384	ㄈㄤ	方	0022_7	011
ㄈㄢ	蕃	4460_9	409	ㄈㄤ	坊	4012_7	362
ㄈㄢˊ	凡	7721_0	589	ㄈㄤ	芳	4422_7	398
ㄈㄢˊ	帆	4721_0	428	ㄈㄤˊ	房	3022_7	275
ㄈㄢˊ	藩	4416_9	396	ㄈㄤˊ	妨	4042_7	370
ㄈㄢˊ	燔	9286_9	694	ㄈㄤˊ	防	7022_7	563
ㄈㄢˊ	樊	4443_0	405	ㄈㄤˊ	肪	7022_7	564
ㄈㄢˊ	礬	4460_1	408	ㄈㄤˇ	訪	0062_7	028
ㄈㄢˊ	繁	8890_3	680	ㄈㄤˇ	仿	2022_7	145
ㄈㄢˊ	煩	9188_6	693	ㄈㄤˇ	彷	2022_7	145
ㄈㄢˇ	反	7124_7	568	ㄈㄤˇ	舫	2042_7	152
ㄈㄢˇ	返	3130_4	294	ㄈㄤˇ	紡	2092_7	159
ㄈㄢˋ	氾	3711_2	328	ㄈㄤˇ	倣	2823_7	261
ㄈㄢˋ	范	4411_2	394	ㄈㄤˇ	昉	6002_7	508
ㄈㄢˋ	犯	4721_2	428	ㄈㄤˋ	放	0824_0	053
ㄈㄢˋ	範	8851_2	676	ㄈㄥ	丰	5000_6	447
ㄈㄢˋ	販	6184_7	536	ㄈㄥ	峯	2250_4	183
ㄈㄢˋ	飯	8174_7	657	ㄈㄥ	蜂	5715_4	500
ㄈㄢˋ	汎	3711_0	327	ㄈㄥ	鋒	8715_4	669
ㄈㄢˋ	梵	4421_7	398	ㄈㄥ	烽	9785_4	705
ㄈㄢˋ	泛	3213_7	297	ㄈㄥ	風	7721_0	589
ㄈㄣ	分	8022_7	630	ㄈㄥ	瘋	0011_7	004
ㄈㄣ	紛	2892_7	267	ㄈㄥ	楓	4791_0	436
ㄈㄣ	芬	4422_7	398	ㄈㄥ	豐	2210_8	176
ㄈㄣ	吩	6802_7	561	ㄈㄥ	封	4410_0	391
ㄈㄣ	氛	8021_7	629	ㄈㄥˊ	縫	2793_4	258
ㄈㄣˊ	墳	4418_6	396	ㄈㄥˊ	逢	3730_4	337
ㄈㄣˊ	汾	3812_7	343	ㄈㄥˊ	馮	3112_7	291

注音	字	四角	頁碼	注音	字	四角	頁碼
ㄈㄥˋ	奉	5050_3	455	ㄅ一ㄝ	爹	8020_7	628
ㄈㄥˋ	俸	2525_3	222	ㄅ一ㄝˊ	諜	0469_4	045
ㄈㄥˋ	諷	0761_0	048	ㄅ一ㄝˊ	碟	1469_4	124
ㄈㄥˋ	鳳	7721_0	589	ㄅ一ㄝˊ	牒	2409_4	200

ㄅ

注音	字	四角	頁碼	注音	字	四角	頁碼
				ㄅ一ㄝˊ	蝶	5419_4	482
				ㄅ一ㄝˊ	喋	6409_4	546
ㄅ一	低	2224_0	179	ㄅ一ㄝˊ	蹀	6419_4	546
ㄅ一	滴	3012_7	273	ㄅ一ㄝˊ	迭	3530_3	322
ㄅ一ˊ	敵	0824_0	054	ㄅ一ㄝˊ	跌	6513_0	549
ㄅ一ˊ	嫡	4042_7	370	ㄅ一ㄝˊ	疊	6010_7	511
ㄅ一ˊ	嘀	6002_7	508	ㄅ一ㄝˊ	絰	0563_0	045
ㄅ一ˊ	鏑	8012_7	627	ㄅ一ㄝˊ	跕	6111_0	534
ㄅ一ˊ	迪	3530_6	322	ㄅ一ㄠ	碉	1762_0	137
ㄅ一ˊ	笛	8860_3	677	ㄅ一ㄠ	凋	3712_0	328
ㄅ一ˊ	滌	3719_4	332	ㄅ一ㄠ	雕	7021_4	562
ㄅ一ˊ	狄	4928_0	444	ㄅ一ㄠ	彫	7222_2	576
ㄅ一ˊ	翟	8791_4	671	ㄅ一ㄠ	刁	1712_0	129
ㄅ一ˇ	底	0024_2	017	ㄅ一ㄠ	鵰	7722_7	597
ㄅ一ˇ	詆	0264_0	037	ㄅ一ㄠ	貂	2726_2	245
ㄅ一ˇ	砥	1264_0	117	ㄅ一ㄠˋ	調	0762_0	050
ㄅ一ˇ	柢	4294_0	385	ㄅ一ㄠˋ	弔	1752_7	135
ㄅ一ˇ	抵	5204_0	468	ㄅ一ㄠˋ	吊	6022_7	519
ㄅ一ˇ	邸	7772_7	610	ㄅ一ㄠˋ	掉	5104_6	463
ㄅ一ˋ	帝	0022_7	012	ㄅ一ㄠˋ	釣	8712_0	667
ㄅ一ˋ	諦	0062_7	028	ㄅ一ㄡ	丟	2073_1	156
ㄅ一ˋ	締	2092_7	159	ㄅ一ㄢ	巔	0018_6	008
ㄅ一ˋ	蒂	4422_7	398	ㄅ一ㄢ	顛	4188_6	381
ㄅ一ˋ	弟	8022_7	632	ㄅ一ㄢ	巓	2288_6	186
ㄅ一ˋ	第	8822_7	673	ㄅ一ㄢˇ	典	5580_1	486
ㄅ一ˋ	的	2762_0	252	ㄅ一ㄢˇ	點	6136_0	535
ㄅ一ˋ	遞	3230_1	300	ㄅ一ㄢˇ	碘	1568_1	125
ㄅ一ˋ	地	4411_2	393	ㄅ一ㄢˋ	玷	1116_0	103
ㄅ一ˋ	棣	4593_2	420	ㄅ一ㄢˋ	店	0026_1	019
ㄅ一ˋ	踶	6618_1	551	ㄅ一ㄢˋ	阽	7126_0	569
				ㄅ一ㄢˋ	恬	9006_1	684

注 音	字	四 角	頁 碼	注 音	字	四 角	頁 碼
ㄉㄧㄢˋ	佃	2620_0	229	ㄉㄨˇ	睹	6406_0	545
ㄉㄧㄢˋ	甸	2762_0	252	ㄉㄨˇ	賭	6486_4	548
ㄉㄧㄢˋ	鈿	8610_0	665	ㄉㄨˇ	篤	8832_7	674
ㄉㄧㄢˋ	殿	7724_7	600	ㄉㄨˋ	度	0024_7	018
ㄉㄧㄢˋ	澱	3714_7	331	ㄉㄨˋ	渡	3014_7	273
ㄉㄧㄢˋ	淀	3318_1	305	ㄉㄨˋ	鍍	8014_7	627
ㄉㄧㄢˋ	靛	5328_1	479	ㄉㄨˋ	杜	4491_0	416
ㄉㄧㄢˋ	電	1071_6	091	ㄉㄨˋ	肚	7421_0	582
ㄉㄧㄢˋ	墊	4410_4	392	ㄉㄨˋ	妒	4347_7	389
ㄉㄧㄢˋ	奠	8043_0	640	ㄉㄨㄛ	多	2720_7	240
ㄉㄧㄢˋ	簟	8840_6	675	ㄉㄨㄛ	哆	6702_7	555
ㄉㄧㄥ	丁	1020_0	073	ㄉㄨㄛˊ	奪	4034_1	368
ㄉㄧㄥ	疔	0012_1	004	ㄉㄨㄛˊ	鐸	8614_1	665
ㄉㄧㄥ	叮	6102_0	533	ㄉㄨㄛˊ	掇	5704_7	496
ㄉㄧㄥ	町	6102_0	533	ㄉㄨㄛˇ	躲	2729_4	246
ㄉㄧㄥ	釘	8112_0	655	ㄉㄨㄛˇ	朵	7990_4	615
ㄉㄧㄥˇ	頂	1128_6	105	ㄉㄨㄛˋ	剁	1290_0	117
ㄉㄧㄥˇ	鼎	2222_1	179	ㄉㄨㄛˋ	跺	6719_4	559
ㄉㄧㄥˋ	定	3080_1	287	ㄉㄨㄛˋ	墮	7410_4	581
ㄉㄧㄥˋ	訂	0162_0	033	ㄉㄨㄛˋ	惰	9402_7	696
ㄉㄧㄥˋ	碇	1368_1	120	ㄉㄨㄛˋ	舵	2341_1	196
ㄉㄧㄥˋ	錠	8318_1	661	ㄉㄨㄛˋ	踱	6014_8	514
ㄉㄨ	都	4762_7	433	ㄉㄨㄛˋ	咄	6207_7	538
ㄉㄨ	嘟	6702_7	555	ㄉㄨㄟ	堆	4011_4	361
ㄉㄨ	督	2760_4	252	ㄉㄨㄟˋ	對	3410_0	308
ㄉㄨˊ	讀	0468_6	044	ㄉㄨㄟˋ	隊	7823_2	617
ㄉㄨˊ	牘	2408_6	200	ㄉㄨㄟˋ	兌	8021_6	629
ㄉㄨˊ	犢	2458_6	211	ㄉㄨㄢ	端	0212_7	035
ㄉㄨˊ	瀆	3418_6	313	ㄉㄨㄢˇ	短	8141_8	656
ㄉㄨˊ	黷	6438_6	547	ㄉㄨㄢˋ	段	7744_7	606
ㄉㄨˊ	獨	4622_7	422	ㄉㄨㄢˋ	緞	2794_7	259
ㄉㄨˊ	髑	7622_7	587	ㄉㄨㄢˋ	鍛	8714_7	669
ㄉㄨˊ	毒	5050_5	455	ㄉㄨㄢˋ	斷	2272_1	183
ㄉㄨˇ	堵	4416_0	395	ㄉㄨㄣ	敦	0844_0	055
ㄉㄨˇ	覩	4661_0	425	ㄉㄨㄣ	惇	9004_7	684

注　音	字	四　角	頁　碼	注　音	字	四　角	頁　碼
ㄅㄨㄣ	墩	4814_0	439	ㄅㄞˇ	歹	1020_7	073
ㄅㄨㄣ	蹲	6814_6	561	ㄅㄞˋ	代	2324_0	194
ㄅㄨㄣˇ	躉	4480_1	414	ㄅㄞˋ	玳	1314_0	118
ㄅㄨㄣˋ	沌	3511_7	317	ㄅㄞˋ	黛	2333_1	196
ㄅㄨㄣˋ	盹	6501_7	548	ㄅㄞˋ	袋	2373_2	197
ㄅㄨㄣˋ	鈍	8511_7	664	ㄅㄞˋ	殆	1326_0	120
ㄅㄨㄣˋ	飩	8571_7	664	ㄅㄞˋ	怠	2333_6	196
ㄅㄨㄣˋ	頓	5178_6	465	ㄅㄞˋ	迨	3330_6	307
ㄅㄨㄣˋ	遁	6108_6	534	ㄅㄞˋ	貸	2380_6	197
ㄅㄨㄣˋ	盾	7226_4	577	ㄅㄞˋ	待	2424_1	205
ㄅㄨㄣˋ	遁	3230_6	301	ㄅㄞˋ	戴	4385_0	390
ㄅㄨㄣˋ	燉	9884_0	707	ㄅㄞˋ	帶	4422_7	398
ㄅㄨㄥ	東	5090_6	459	ㄅㄠ	刀	1722_0	131
ㄅㄨㄥ	冬	2730_3	246	ㄅㄠ	叨	6702_0	554
ㄅㄨㄥ	咚	6703_3	556	ㄅㄠ	忉	9702_0	703
ㄅㄨㄥ	蝀	5519_6	485	ㄅㄠˇ	島	2772_7	254
ㄅㄨㄥˇ	董	4410_4	392	ㄅㄠˇ	搗	5702_7	495
ㄅㄨㄥˇ	懂	9401_4	696	ㄅㄠˇ	導	3834_3	349
ㄅㄨㄥˋ	動	2412_7	200	ㄅㄠˇ	倒	2220_0	177
ㄅㄨㄥˋ	洞	3712_0	328	ㄅㄠˇ	禱	3424_1	314
ㄅㄨㄥˋ	恫	9702_0	703	ㄅㄠˋ	稻	2297_7	190
ㄅㄨㄥˋ	凍	3519_6	320	ㄅㄠˋ	蹈	6217_7	538
ㄅㄨㄥˋ	棟	4599_6	420	ㄅㄠˋ	到	1210_0	107
ㄅㄚ	搭	5406_1	481	ㄅㄠˋ	盜	3710_7	327
ㄅㄚˊ	答	8860_1	676	ㄅㄠˋ	道	3830_6	349
ㄅㄚˊ	達	3430_4	315	ㄅㄠˋ	悼	9104_6	692
ㄅㄚˊ	怛	9601_0	701	ㄅㄡ	都	4762_7	433
ㄅㄚˊ	靼	4651_0	425	ㄅㄡ	兜	7721_7	592
ㄅㄚˇ	打	5102_0	462	ㄅㄡˇ	斗	3400_0	307
ㄅㄚˋ	大	4003_0	354	ㄅㄡˇ	抖	5400_0	479
ㄅㄜˊ	得	2624_1	230	ㄅㄡˇ	蚪	5410_0	482
ㄅㄜˊ	德	2423_1	205	ㄅㄡˇ	陡	7428_1	583
ㄅㄞ	呆	6090_4	531	ㄅㄡˋ	豆	1010_8	072
ㄅㄞ	獃	2313_4	191	ㄅㄡˋ	痘	0011_8	004
ㄅㄞˇ	逮	3530_3	322	ㄅㄡˋ	逗	3130_1	294

注 音	字	四 角	頁 碼	注 音	字	四 角	頁 碼
ㄅㄡˋ	荳	4410_8	392	ㄅㄥˋ	凳	1221_7	110
ㄅㄡˋ	鬥	7711_4	588	ㄅㄥˋ	櫈	4291_1	385
ㄅㄢ	耽	1411_2	120	ㄅㄥˋ	瞪	6201_8	537
ㄅㄢ	眈	6401_2	543	ㄅㄥˋ	鐙	8211_8	658
ㄅㄢ	躭	2421_2	203	ㄅㄥˋ	蹬	6211_8	538
ㄅㄢ	擔	5706_1	497				
ㄅㄢ	担	5601_0	488		**ㄊ**		
ㄅㄢ	單	6650_6	552	注 音	字	四 角	頁 碼
ㄅㄢ	簞	8850_6	676	ㄊㄧ	踢	6612_7	551
ㄅㄢ	丹	7744_0	604	ㄊㄧ	梯	4892_7	442
ㄅㄢˇ	膽	7726_1	600	ㄊㄧˊ	堤	4618_1	422
ㄅㄢˋ	旦	6010_0	510	ㄊㄧˊ	提	5608_1	490
ㄅㄢˋ	但	2621_0	229	ㄊㄧˊ	題	6180_6	535
ㄅㄢˋ	淡	3918_9	351	ㄊㄧˊ	隄	7628_1	587
ㄅㄢˋ	啖	6908_9	562	ㄊㄧˊ	啼	6002_7	508
ㄅㄢˋ	氮	8081_7	654	ㄊㄧˊ	蹄	6012_7	512
ㄅㄢˋ	彈	1625_6	127	ㄊㄧˇ	體	7521_8	585
ㄅㄢˋ	殫	1625_6	127	ㄊㄧˋ	涕	3812_7	343
ㄅㄢˋ	憚	9605_6	702	ㄊㄧˋ	剃	8220_0	658
ㄅㄢˋ	誕	0264_1	037	ㄊㄧˋ	銻	8812_7	672
ㄅㄢˋ	蛋	1713_6	129	ㄊㄧˋ	悌	9802_7	706
ㄅㄢˋ	澹	3716_1	331	ㄊㄧˋ	剔	6220_0	538
ㄅㄤ	當	9060_6	689	ㄊㄧˋ	惕	9602_7	701
ㄅㄤ	襠	3926_6	351	ㄊㄧˋ	替	5560_3	486
ㄅㄤ	鐺	8916_6	681	ㄊㄧˋ	嚏	6408_1	546
ㄅㄤˇ	黨	9033_1	687	ㄊㄧˋ	雁	7721_7	591
ㄅㄤˇ	讜	0963_1	057	ㄊㄧㄝ	貼	6186_0	536
ㄅㄤˇ	檔	4996_6	444	ㄊㄧㄝˇ	鐵	8315_0	660
ㄅㄤˇ	擋	5906_6	506	ㄊㄧㄝˇ	帖	4126_0	380
ㄅㄤˋ	蕩	4412_7	394	ㄊㄧㄠ	挑	5201_3	466
ㄅㄤˋ	盪	3610_7	323	ㄊㄧㄠˊ	條	2729_4	246
ㄅㄥ	登	1210_8	108	ㄊㄧㄠˊ	迢	3730_6	338
ㄅㄥ	燈	9281_8	694	ㄊㄧㄠˊ	苕	4460_2	408
ㄅㄥ	灯	9182_0	693	ㄊㄧㄠˊ	笤	9960_2	677
ㄅㄥˇ	等	8834_1	675	ㄊㄧㄠˊ	蜩	5712_0	499

注音	字	四角	頁碼	注音	字	四角	頁碼
ㄊㄧㄠˇ	窕	3011_3	271	ㄊㄨˋ	吐	6401_0	543
ㄊㄧㄠˋ	跳	6211_3	538	ㄊㄨㄛ	託	0261_4	036
ㄊㄧㄠˋ	眺	6201_3	536	ㄊㄨㄛ	托	5201_4	466
ㄊㄧㄢ	天	1043_0	083	ㄊㄨㄛ	拖	5801_2	501
ㄊㄧㄢ	添	3213_3	297	ㄊㄨㄛ	脫	7821_6	616
ㄊㄧㄢˊ	田	6040_0	522	ㄊㄨㄛˊ	沱	3311_1	303
ㄊㄧㄢˊ	甜	2467_0	211	ㄊㄨㄛˊ	陀	7321_1	580
ㄊㄧㄢˊ	恬	9206_4	694	ㄊㄨㄛˊ	鴕	2331_1	196
ㄊㄧㄢˊ	填	4418_1	396	ㄊㄨㄛˊ	駝	7331_1	580
ㄊㄧㄢˊ	畋	6804_0	561	ㄊㄨㄛˊ	馱	7433_0	584
ㄊㄧㄢˇ	腆	7528_1	585	ㄊㄨㄛˇ	妥	2040_4	148
ㄊㄧㄥ	聽	1413_1	121	ㄊㄨㄛˇ	橢	4492_7	417
ㄊㄧㄥ	廳	0023_1	016	ㄊㄨㄛˋ	拓	5106_0	464
ㄊㄧㄥ	汀	3112_0	291	ㄊㄨㄛˋ	唾	6201_4	536
ㄊㄧㄥˊ	廷	1240_1	114	ㄊㄨㄟ	推	5001_4	448
ㄊㄧㄥˊ	庭	0024_1	017	ㄊㄨㄟˊ	頹	2128_6	171
ㄊㄧㄥˊ	霆	1040_1	081	ㄊㄨㄟˇ	腿	7723_3	598
ㄊㄧㄥˊ	蜓	5214_1	471	ㄊㄨㄟˋ	退	3730_3	337
ㄊㄧㄥˊ	亭	0020_1	008	ㄊㄨㄟˋ	蛻	5811_6	504
ㄊㄧㄥˊ	停	2022_1	144	ㄊㄨㄢ	湍	3212_7	297
ㄊㄧㄥˊ	婷	4042_1	370	ㄊㄨㄢˊ	團	6034_3	522
ㄊㄧㄥˇ	艇	2244_1	183	ㄊㄨㄢˊ	糰	9690_0	703
ㄊㄧㄥˇ	挺	5204_1	468	ㄊㄨㄢˊ	摶	5504_3	483
ㄊㄧㄥˇ	鋌	8214_1	658	ㄊㄨㄢˋ	彖	2723_2	242
ㄊㄨ	禿	2021_7	144	ㄊㄨㄣ	吞	2060_3	154
ㄊㄨˊ	塗	3810_4	342	ㄊㄨㄣˊ	屯	5071_1	457
ㄊㄨˊ	涂	3819_4	347	ㄊㄨㄣˊ	魨	2531_7	223
ㄊㄨˊ	途	3830_9	349	ㄊㄨㄣˊ	囤	6071_2	528
ㄊㄨˊ	徒	2428_1	208	ㄊㄨㄣˊ	豚	7123_2	567
ㄊㄨˊ	突	3043_0	283	ㄊㄨㄣˊ	臀	7722_7	597
ㄊㄨˊ	圖	6060_4	527	ㄊㄨㄣˊ	邨	5772_7	500
ㄊㄨˊ	屠	7726_4	601	ㄊㄨㄣˇ	氽	8023_2	632
ㄊㄨˊ	凸	7777_7	612	ㄊㄨㄣˋ	褪	3723_3	334
ㄊㄨˇ	土	4010_0	359	ㄊㄨㄥ	通	3730_2	335
ㄊㄨˋ	兔	1741_3	134	ㄊㄨㄥˊ	童	0010_4	002

注音	字	四角	頁碼	注音	字	四角	頁碼
ㄊㄨㄥˊ	僮	2021_4	144	ㄊㄞˊ	駘	7336_0	581
ㄊㄨㄥˊ	潼	3011_4	272	ㄊㄞˊ	臺	4010_4	360
ㄊㄨㄥˊ	瞳	6001_4	508	ㄊㄞˊ	抬	5306_0	475
ㄊㄨㄥˊ	桐	4792_0	436	ㄊㄞˊ	擡	5401_4	480
ㄊㄨㄥˊ	銅	8712_0	668	ㄊㄞˋ	太	4003_0	358
ㄊㄨㄥˊ	筒	8822_7	673	ㄊㄞˋ	汰	3413_0	311
ㄊㄨㄥˊ	彤	7242_2	578	ㄊㄞˋ	鈦	8413_0	662
ㄊㄨㄥˊ	仝	8010_1	623	ㄊㄞˋ	態	2133_1	172
ㄊㄨㄥˊ	同	7722_0	593	ㄊㄞˋ	泰	5013_2	452
ㄊㄨㄥˇ	統	2091_3	158	ㄊㄠ	掏	5702_0	494
ㄊㄨㄥˇ	桶	4792_7	436	ㄊㄠ	滔	3217_7	299
ㄊㄨㄥˋ	痛	0012_7	005	ㄊㄠ	饕	6173_2	535
ㄊㄨㄥˋ	慟	9402_7	696	ㄊㄠˊ	洮	3211_2	296
ㄊㄚ	他	2421_2	203	ㄊㄠˊ	逃	3230_1	299
ㄊㄚ	它	3071_4	286	ㄊㄠˊ	桃	4291_3	385
ㄊㄚ	她	4441_2	404	ㄊㄠˊ	咷	6201_3	536
ㄊㄚ	塌	4612_7	422	ㄊㄠˊ	萄	4472_7	412
ㄊㄚˇ	塔	4416_1	395	ㄊㄠˊ	啕	6702_0	554
ㄊㄚˋ	踏	6216_3	538	ㄊㄠˊ	淘	3712_0	328
ㄊㄚˋ	杳	1269_3	117	ㄊㄠˊ	陶	7722_0	595
ㄊㄚˋ	榻	4692_7	427	ㄊㄠˊ	濤	3414_1	312
ㄊㄚˋ	蹋	6612_7	551	ㄊㄠˇ	討	0460_0	042
ㄊㄚˋ	獺	4728_6	429	ㄊㄠˋ	套	4073_1	374
ㄊㄚˋ	嗒	6406_1	545	ㄊㄡ	偷	2822_7	260
ㄊㄚˋ	闥	7730_4	602	ㄊㄡˊ	投	5704_7	496
ㄊㄜˋ	忑	1033_3	081	ㄊㄡˊ	頭	1118_6	103
ㄊㄜˋ	特	2454_1	209	ㄊㄡˋ	透	3230_2	300
ㄊㄜˋ	忒	4330_0	388	ㄊㄢ	攤	5001_4	448
ㄊㄜˋ	慝	7133_1	572	ㄊㄢ	貪	8080_6	654
ㄊㄞ	胎	7326_0	580	ㄊㄢ	灘	3011_4	272
ㄊㄞˊ	台	2360_0	197	ㄊㄢ	坍	4714_0	428
ㄊㄞˊ	檯	4491_4	417	ㄊㄢ	癱	0011_4	004
ㄊㄞˊ	枱	4396_0	390	ㄊㄢˊ	談	0968_9	057
ㄊㄞˊ	苔	4460_3	408	ㄊㄢˊ	譚	0164_6	034
ㄊㄞˊ	颱	7321_6	580	ㄊㄢˊ	潭	3114_6	292

注　音	字	四　角	頁　碼
ㄊㄢˊ	檀	4091_6	377
ㄊㄢˊ	壇	4011_6	361
ㄊㄢˊ	彈	1625_6	127
ㄊㄢˊ	痰	0018_9	008
ㄊㄢˊ	曇	6073_1	529
ㄊㄢˇ	坦	4611_0	421
ㄊㄢˇ	袒	3621_0	325
ㄊㄢˇ	毯	2971_8	268
ㄊㄢˋ	探	5709_4	499
ㄊㄢˋ	嘆	6403_4	544
ㄊㄢˋ	碳	1268_9	117
ㄊㄢˋ	炭	2228_9	182
ㄊㄢˋ	歎	4758_2	433
ㄊㄤ	湯	3612_7	324
ㄊㄤˊ	唐	0026_7	020
ㄊㄤˊ	溏	3016_7	273
ㄊㄤˊ	塘	4016_7	362
ㄊㄤˊ	螳	5911_4	507
ㄊㄤˊ	糖	9096_7	691
ㄊㄤˊ	堂	9010_4	684
ㄊㄤˊ	膛	7921_4	620
ㄊㄤˊ	鏜	8911_4	681
ㄊㄤˊ	棠	9090_4	691
ㄊㄤˇ	躺	2922_7	268
ㄊㄤˇ	倘	2922_7	268
ㄊㄤˇ	淌	3912_7	351
ㄊㄤˇ	儻	2923_1	268
ㄊㄤˋ	趟	4980_2	444
ㄊㄤˋ	燙	3680_9	327
ㄊㄥˊ	藤	4423_2	400
ㄊㄥˊ	騰	7921_4	620
ㄊㄥˊ	謄	7926_1	620
ㄊㄥˊ	滕	7923_2	620
ㄊㄥˊ	籐	8823_2	674
ㄊㄥˊ	疼	0013_3	006

ㄋ

注　音	字	四　角	頁　碼
ㄋㄧˊ	尼	7721_1	590
ㄋㄧˊ	泥	3711_1	327
ㄋㄧˊ	妮	4741_1	430
ㄋㄧˊ	呢	6701_1	553
ㄋㄧˊ	怩	9701_1	703
ㄋㄧˊ	霓	1021_7	074
ㄋㄧˇ	你	2729_2	246
ㄋㄧˇ	擬	5708_1	498
ㄋㄧˋ	匿	7171_6	573
ㄋㄧˋ	暱	6101_6	533
ㄋㄧˋ	溺	3712_7	330
ㄋㄧˋ	逆	3830_4	349
ㄋㄧˊ	膩	7324_0	580
ㄋㄧㄝ	捏	5701_1	492
ㄋㄧㄝˋ	聶	1014_1	072
ㄋㄧㄝˋ	囁	6104_1	534
ㄋㄧㄝˋ	躡	6114_1	534
ㄋㄧㄝˋ	鑷	8112_7	655
ㄋㄧㄝˋ	涅	3711_1	328
ㄋㄧㄝˋ	陧	7721_1	590
ㄋㄧㄝˋ	孽	4440_7	404
ㄋㄧㄝˋ	齧	5777_3	500
ㄋㄧㄝˋ	鎳	8619_4	665
ㄋㄧㄠˇ	鳥	2732_7	246
ㄋㄧㄠˇ	嫋	4742_7	431
ㄋㄧㄠˇ	嬲	6642_7	552
ㄋㄧㄠˋ	尿	7723_2	597
ㄋㄧㄡˊ	牛	2500_0	216
ㄋㄧㄡˇ	紐	2791_5	256
ㄋㄧㄡˇ	扭	5701_5	493
ㄋㄧㄡˇ	鈕	8711_5	667
ㄋㄧㄡˇ	忸	9701_5	703
ㄋㄧㄢˊ	黏	2116_0	163

注　音	字	四　角	頁　碼	注　音	字	四　角	頁　碼
ㄋㄧㄢˊ	粘	9196_0	693	ㄋㄨㄥˋ	弄	1044_1	085
ㄋㄧㄢˊ	年	8050_0	640	ㄋㄩˇ	女	4040_0	369
ㄋㄧㄢˇ	輦	5550_6	486	ㄋㄩㄝˋ	虐	2121_1	164
ㄋㄧㄢˇ	撵	5505_6	484	ㄋㄩㄝˋ	謔	0161_1	033
ㄋㄧㄢˇ	跕	5106_0	464	ㄋㄩㄝˋ	瘧	0011_1	004
ㄋㄧㄢˇ	撚	5303_3	473	ㄋㄚˊ	拿	8050_2	641
ㄋㄧㄢˇ	捻	5803_2	502	ㄋㄚˇ	哪	6702_7	555
ㄋㄧㄢˇ	碾	1763_2	137	ㄋㄚˋ	納	2492_7	215
ㄋㄧㄢˋ	廿	4477_0	412	ㄋㄚˋ	吶	6402_7	543
ㄋㄧㄢˋ	念	8033_2	637	ㄋㄚˋ	肭	7422_7	582
ㄋㄧㄢˋ	唸	6803_2	561	ㄋㄚˋ	鈉	8412_7	662
ㄋㄧㄤˊ	娘	4343_2	388	ㄋㄚˋ	那	1752_7	135
ㄋㄧㄤˋ	釀	1063_2	090	ㄋㄚˋ	娜	4742_7	431
ㄋㄧㄥˊ	寧	3020_1	273	ㄋㄜˋ	訥	0462_7	043
ㄋㄧㄥˊ	獰	4322_1	388	ㄋㄞˇ	乃	1722_7	131
ㄋㄧㄥˊ	檸	4392_1	390	ㄋㄞˇ	奶	4742_7	430
ㄋㄧㄥˊ	擰	5302_1	473	ㄋㄞˇ	氖	8021_7	629
ㄋㄧㄥˊ	甯	3022_7	276	ㄋㄞˋ	奈	4090_1	376
ㄋㄧㄥˊ	凝	3718_1	331	ㄋㄞˋ	耐	1420_0	122
ㄋㄧㄥˋ	佞	2024_4	146	ㄋㄟˇ	餒	8274_4	659
ㄋㄧㄥˋ	濘	3312_1	303	ㄋㄟˋ	內	4022_7	363
ㄋㄨˊ	奴	4744_0	431	ㄋㄠˊ	猱	4729_4	429
ㄋㄨˇ	努	4742_7	431	ㄋㄠˊ	硇	1660_0	128
ㄋㄨˇ	弩	4720_7	428	ㄋㄠˊ	橈	4491_1	416
ㄋㄨˋ	怒	4733_4	429	ㄋㄠˊ	撓	5401_1	479
ㄋㄨㄛˊ	挪	5702_7	494	ㄋㄠˊ	鐃	8411_1	662
ㄋㄨㄛˋ	懦	9102_7	692	ㄋㄠˇ	腦	7226_2	577
ㄋㄨㄛˋ	糯	9192_7	693	ㄋㄠˇ	惱	9206_2	694
ㄋㄨㄛˋ	諾	0466_4	044	ㄋㄠˋ	鬧	7722_7	596
ㄋㄨㄛˋ	搦	5702_7	495	ㄋㄠˋ	淖	3114_6	292
ㄋㄨㄢˇ	暖	6204_7	537	ㄋㄡˋ	耨	5194_3	465
ㄋㄨㄢˇ	煖	9284_7	694	ㄋㄢ	囝	6040_4	523
ㄋㄨㄥˊ	農	5523_2	485	ㄋㄢˊ	南	4022_7	366
ㄋㄨㄥˊ	濃	3513_2	318	ㄋㄢˊ	喃	6402_7	543
ㄋㄨㄥˊ	膿	7523_2	585	ㄋㄢˊ	男	6042_7	524

注　音	字	四　角	頁　碼	注　音	字	四　角	頁　碼
ㄋㄢˊ	難	4051_4	371	ㄌㄧˇ	禮	3521_8	320
ㄋㄢˇ	赧	4734_7	429	ㄌㄧˇ	娌	4641_4	425
ㄋㄢˇ	㝹	6022_7	519	ㄌㄧˇ	糎	9191_4	693
ㄋㄢˇ	腩	7422_7	582	ㄌㄧˋ	利	2290_0	187
ㄋㄣˋ	嫩	4844_0	441	ㄌㄧˋ	痢	0012_0	004
ㄋㄤˊ	囊	5073_2	457	ㄌㄧˋ	俐	2220_0	177
ㄋㄤˇ	曩	6073_2	529	ㄌㄧˋ	莉	4492_0	417
ㄋㄥˊ	能	2121_1	164	ㄌㄧˋ	厲	7122_7	567
				ㄌㄧˋ	癘	0012_7	006
	ㄌ			ㄌㄧˋ	勵	7422_7	582

注　音	字	四　角	頁　碼	注　音	字	四　角	頁　碼
ㄌㄧˊ	狸	4621_4	422	ㄌㄧˋ	立	0010_8	002
ㄌㄧˊ	貍	2621_4	230	ㄌㄧˋ	曆	7127_9	570
ㄌㄧˊ	釐	5821_4	505	ㄌㄧˋ	笠	8810_8	672
ㄌㄧˊ	厘	7121_4	566	ㄌㄧˋ	麗	1121_1	104
ㄌㄧˊ	璃	1012_7	072	ㄌㄧˋ	礫	1269_4	117
ㄌㄧˊ	離	0041_4	025	ㄌㄧˋ	歷	7121_1	565
ㄌㄧˊ	籬	8841_4	675	ㄌㄧˋ	例	2220_0	177
ㄌㄧˊ	梨	2290_4	187	ㄌㄧˋ	栗	1090_4	101
ㄌㄧˊ	犁	2750_2	250	ㄌㄧˋ	隸	4593_2	420
ㄌㄧˊ	黎	2713_2	239	ㄌㄧˋ	戾	3023_4	277
ㄌㄧˊ	藜	4413_2	395	ㄌㄧˋ	荔	4442_7	405
ㄌㄧˊ	罹	6091_4	532	ㄌㄧˋ	力	4002_7	353
ㄌㄧˊ	驪	7131_1	571	ㄌㄧˋ	吏	5000_6	446
ㄌㄧˊ	蘺	4441_4	404	ㄌㄧˋ	粒	9091_8	691
ㄌㄧˊ	嫠	5824_4	505	ㄌㄧˋ	慄	9109_1	692
ㄌㄧˊ	犛	5825_1	505	ㄌㄧˋ	溧	3119_4	293
ㄌㄧˊ	蜊	5210_0	471	ㄌㄧˋ	躒	6219_4	538
ㄌㄧˇ	李	4040_7	370	ㄌㄧˋ	茘	4411_8	394
ㄌㄧˇ	里	6010_4	511	ㄌㄧˋ	詈	6060_1	527
ㄌㄧˇ	理	1611_4	126	ㄌㄧˋ	櫟	4299_4	386
ㄌㄧˇ	俚	2621_4	230	ㄌㄧˋ	蠣	5112_7	465
ㄌㄧˇ	鯉	2631_4	233	ㄌㄧˋ	瀝	3111_1	290
ㄌㄧˇ	浬	3611_4	323	ㄌㄧˋ	糲	9192_7	693
ㄌㄧˇ	裏	0073_2	031	ㄌㄧˋ	靂	1021_1	074
				ㄌㄧ˙	哩	6601_4	550

注 音	字	四 角	頁 碼	注 音	字	四 角	頁 碼
ㄌㄧㄝ	咧	6200_0	536	ㄌㄧㄡˇ	柳	4792_0	436
ㄌㄧㄝˋ	列	1220_0	110	ㄌㄧㄡˋ	六	0073_2	031
ㄌㄧㄝˋ	烈	1233_0	114	ㄌㄧㄡˋ	餾	8776_2	671
ㄌㄧㄝˋ	裂	1273_2	117	ㄌㄧㄢˊ	連	3530_0	321
ㄌㄧㄝˋ	冽	3210_0	295	ㄌㄧㄢˊ	聯	1217_2	109
ㄌㄧㄝˋ	獵	4221_6	383	ㄌㄧㄢˊ	憐	9905_9	708
ㄌㄧㄝˋ	躐	6211_6	538	ㄌㄧㄢˊ	廉	0023_7	017
ㄌㄧㄝˋ	捩	5303_4	474	ㄌㄧㄢˊ	蓮	4430_5	401
ㄌㄧㄝˋ	劣	9042_7	687	ㄌㄧㄢˊ	漣	3513_0	318
ㄌㄧㄝˋ	鬣	7271_6	579	ㄌㄧㄢˊ	簾	8823_7	674
ㄌㄧㄠˊ	聊	1712_0	129	ㄌㄧㄢˊ	鐮	8013_7	627
ㄌㄧㄠˊ	燎	9489_6	698	ㄌㄧㄢˊ	奩	4071_6	374
ㄌㄧㄠˊ	療	0019_6	008	ㄌㄧㄢˇ	臉	7828_6	618
ㄌㄧㄠˊ	僚	2429_6	209	ㄌㄧㄢˋ	練	2599_6	225
ㄌㄧㄠˊ	撩	5409_6	482	ㄌㄧㄢˋ	戀	2233_9	182
ㄌㄧㄠˊ	寥	3020_2	274	ㄌㄧㄢˋ	煉	9589_6	700
ㄌㄧㄠˊ	寮	3090_6	290	ㄌㄧㄢˋ	鏈	8513_0	664
ㄌㄧㄠˊ	遼	3430_9	316	ㄌㄧㄢˋ	斂	8884_0	679
ㄌㄧㄠˊ	潦	3419_6	313	ㄌㄧㄢˋ	鍊	8519_6	664
ㄌㄧㄠˊ	獠	4429_6	401	ㄌㄧㄢˋ	殮	1828_6	140
ㄌㄧㄠˊ	鐐	8419_6	663	ㄌㄧㄣˊ	林	4499_0	419
ㄌㄧㄠˇ	了	1720_7	130	ㄌㄧㄣˊ	鄰	9722_7	704
ㄌㄧㄠˇ	瞭	6409_6	546	ㄌㄧㄣˊ	臨	7876_6	619
ㄌㄧㄠˋ	料	9490_0	698	ㄌㄧㄣˊ	霖	1099_4	101
ㄌㄧㄡ	溜	3716_2	331	ㄌㄧㄣˊ	麟	0925_2	057
ㄌㄧㄡˊ	劉	7210_0	575	ㄌㄧㄣˊ	琳	1419_0	121
ㄌㄧㄡˊ	流	3011_3	271	ㄌㄧㄣˊ	淋	3419_0	313
ㄌㄧㄡˊ	留	7760_2	608	ㄌㄧㄣˊ	磷	1965_9	142
ㄌㄧㄡˊ	榴	4796_2	437	ㄌㄧㄣˊ	燐	9985_9	709
ㄌㄧㄡˊ	瘤	0016_2	007	ㄌㄧㄣˊ	遴	3930_5	351
ㄌㄧㄡˊ	琉	1011_3	072	ㄌㄧㄣˊ	鱗	2935_9	268
ㄌㄧㄡˊ	硫	1061_3	088	ㄌㄧㄣˇ	凜	3019_4	273
ㄌㄧㄡˊ	瀏	3210_0	296	ㄌㄧㄣˇ	廩	0029_4	021
ㄌㄧㄡˊ	騮	7736_2	603	ㄌㄧㄣˇ	懍	9009_1	684
ㄌㄧㄡˊ	遛	3730_6	338	ㄌㄧㄣˋ	吝	0060_4	028

注　音	字	四　角	頁　碼	注　音	字	四　角	頁　碼
ㄌㄧㄣˋ	蹦	6412₇	546	ㄌㄧㄥˇ	嶺	2238₆	182
ㄌㄧㄤˊ	良	3073₂	286	ㄌㄧㄥˋ	另	6042₇	523
ㄌㄧㄤˊ	梁	3390₄	307	ㄌㄧㄥˋ	令	8030₇	633
ㄌㄧㄤˊ	粱	3390₄	307	ㄌㄨ	嚕	6706₃	557
ㄌㄧㄤˊ	樑	4399₄	390	ㄌㄨˊ	盧	0021₇	011
ㄌㄧㄤˊ	糧	9691₄	703	ㄌㄨˊ	爐	9181₇	693
ㄌㄧㄤˊ	涼	3019₆	273	ㄌㄨˊ	瀘	3111₇	291
ㄌㄧㄤˊ	量	6010₄	511	ㄌㄨˊ	蘆	4421₇	398
ㄌㄧㄤˇ	兩	1022₇	075	ㄌㄨˊ	臚	7121₇	566
ㄌㄧㄤˇ	倆	2122₇	167	ㄌㄨˊ	鑢	8111₇	655
ㄌㄧㄤˋ	輛	5102₇	463	ㄌㄨˇ	魯	2760₃	251
ㄌㄧㄤˋ	亮	0021₇	011	ㄌㄨˇ	擄	5102₇	463
ㄌㄧㄤˋ	諒	0069₀	029	ㄌㄨˇ	虜	2122₇	167
ㄌㄧㄤˋ	晾	6009₆	509	ㄌㄨˇ	櫓	4796₃	437
ㄌㄧㄤˋ	喨	6001₇	508	ㄌㄨˇ	滷	3116₀	292
ㄌㄧㄤˋ	啢	6102₇	534	ㄌㄨˇ	鹵	2160₀	172
ㄌㄧㄥˊ	零	1030₇	079	ㄌㄨˋ	路	6716₄	558
ㄌㄧㄥˊ	玲	1813₇	139	ㄌㄨˋ	陸	7421₄	582
ㄌㄧㄥˊ	齡	2873₇	265	ㄌㄨˋ	鹿	0021₁	008
ㄌㄧㄥˊ	靈	1010₈	072	ㄌㄨˋ	露	1016₄	072
ㄌㄧㄥˊ	苓	4430₇	401	ㄌㄨˋ	祿	3723₂	334
ㄌㄧㄥˊ	鈴	8813₇	672	ㄌㄨˋ	碌	1763₂	137
ㄌㄧㄥˊ	菱	4424₇	400	ㄌㄨˋ	轆	5001₁	448
ㄌㄧㄥˊ	陵	7424₇	583	ㄌㄨˋ	錄	8713₂	668
ㄌㄧㄥˊ	伶	2823₇	261	ㄌㄨˋ	戮	1325₀	119
ㄌㄧㄥˊ	囹	6030₇	520	ㄌㄨˋ	簏	8821₁	673
ㄌㄧㄥˊ	凌	3414₇	313	ㄌㄨˋ	麓	4421₁	397
ㄌㄧㄥˊ	翎	8732₀	670	ㄌㄨˋ	鷺	6732₇	559
ㄌㄧㄥˊ	羚	8853₇	676	ㄌㄨˋ	賂	6786₄	560
ㄌㄧㄥˊ	凌	3414₇	313	ㄌㄨㄛˊ	羅	6091₄	532
ㄌㄧㄥˊ	鴒	8732₇	670	ㄌㄨㄛˊ	鑼	8611₄	665
ㄌㄧㄥˊ	聆	1813₇	139	ㄌㄨㄛˊ	螺	5619₃	492
ㄌㄧㄥˊ	綾	2494₇	215	ㄌㄨㄛˊ	囉	6601₄	550
ㄌㄧㄥˊ	蛉	5813₇	504	ㄌㄨㄛˊ	騾	7639₃	587
ㄌㄧㄥˇ	領	8138₆	656	ㄌㄨㄛˊ	籮	8891₄	681

注 音	字	四 角	頁 碼	注 音	字	四 角	頁 碼
ㄌㄨㄛˊ	蘿	4491_4	417	ㄌㄩˊ	閭	7760_6	608
ㄌㄨㄛˊ	玀	4621_4	422	ㄌㄩˇ	旅	0823_2	052
ㄌㄨㄛˊ	邏	3630_1	326	ㄌㄩˇ	呂	6060_0	526
ㄌㄨㄛˇ	裸	3629_4	325	ㄌㄩˇ	屢	7724_4	598
ㄌㄨㄛˋ	洛	3716_4	331	ㄌㄩˇ	鋁	8616_0	665
ㄌㄨㄛˋ	烙	9786_4	705	ㄌㄩˇ	履	7724_7	600
ㄌㄨㄛˋ	絡	2796_4	259	ㄌㄩˇ	侶	2626_0	230
ㄌㄨㄛˋ	酪	1766_4	137	ㄌㄩˇ	縷	2594_4	224
ㄌㄨㄛˋ	落	4416_4	396	ㄌㄩˇ	褸	3524_4	321
ㄌㄨㄛˋ	駱	7736_4	603	ㄌㄩˇ	膂	0822_7	052
ㄌㄨㄢˊ	鸞	2232_7	182	ㄌㄩˋ	律	2520_7	221
ㄌㄨㄢˊ	欒	2290_4	187	ㄌㄩˋ	綠	2793_2	258
ㄌㄨㄢˇ	卵	7772_0	609	ㄌㄩˋ	慮	2123_6	168
ㄌㄨㄢˋ	亂	2221_0	178	ㄌㄩˋ	濾	3113_6	292
ㄌㄨㄣˊ	輪	5802_7	502	ㄌㄩˋ	氯	8011_7	627
ㄌㄨㄣˊ	倫	2822_7	260	ㄌㄩㄝˋ	略	6706_4	557
ㄌㄨㄣˊ	淪	3812_7	343	ㄌㄩㄝˋ	掠	5009_6	451
ㄌㄨㄣˊ	侖	8022_7	632	ㄌㄩㄢˊ	攣	2240_7	182
ㄌㄨㄣˊ	綸	2892_7	267	ㄌㄚ	拉	5001_8	449
ㄌㄨㄣˊ	掄	5802_7	502	ㄌㄚˇ	喇	6200_0	536
ㄌㄨㄣˊ	論	0862_7	056	ㄌㄚˋ	辣	0549_6	045
ㄌㄨㄣˊ	圇	6022_7	520	ㄌㄚˋ	臘	7221_6	576
ㄌㄨㄥˊ	龍	0121_1	032	ㄌㄚˋ	蠟	5211_6	471
ㄌㄨㄥˊ	隆	7721_4	591	ㄌㄚˋ	臘	7426_1	583
ㄌㄨㄥˊ	籠	8821_1	673	ㄌㄜˋ	樂	2290_4	187
ㄌㄨㄥˊ	聾	0140_1	033	ㄌㄜˋ	勒	4452_7	407
ㄌㄨㄥˊ	嚨	6101_1	532	ㄌㄜˋ	肋	7422_7	582
ㄌㄨㄥˊ	朧	7121_1	566	ㄌㄜˋ	垃	4011_8	361
ㄌㄨㄥˊ	瓏	0160_1	033	ㄌㄜˋ	扐	5704_2	496
ㄌㄨㄥˊ	窿	3021_4	275	ㄌㄞˊ	來	4090_8	376
ㄌㄨㄥˊ	曨	6101_1	533	ㄌㄞˊ	萊	4490_8	416
ㄌㄨㄥˇ	攏	5101_1	461	ㄌㄞˋ	賴	5798_6	500
ㄌㄨㄥˇ	隴	7121_1	565	ㄌㄞˋ	瀨	3718_6	332
ㄌㄨㄥˇ	壟	0110_4	032	ㄌㄞˋ	籟	8898_6	681
ㄌㄩˊ	驢	7131_7	571	ㄌㄞˋ	癩	0018_6	007

注音	字	四　角	頁碼	注音	字	四　角	頁碼
ㄌㄞˋ	睞	6409_8	546	ㄌㄢˊ	欄	4792_0	436
ㄌㄟˊ	雷	1060_3	088	ㄌㄢˊ	籃	8810_7	672
ㄌㄟˊ	擂	5106_3	465	ㄌㄢˊ	闌	7790_6	615
ㄌㄟˊ	縲	2699_3	237	ㄌㄢˊ	瀾	3712_0	329
ㄌㄟˊ	鐳	8116_3	655	ㄌㄢˊ	攔	5702_0	494
ㄌㄟˊ	羸	0021_7	011	ㄌㄢˊ	婪	4440_4	403
ㄌㄟˇ	壘	6010_4	511	ㄌㄢˊ	襤	3821_7	347
ㄌㄟˇ	磊	1066_1	091	ㄌㄢˊ	讕	0762_0	049
ㄌㄟˇ	儡	2626_0	230	ㄌㄢˇ	纜	2891_6	267
ㄌㄟˇ	累	6090_3	531	ㄌㄢˇ	覽	7821_6	617
ㄌㄟˇ	耒	5090_0	459	ㄌㄢˇ	懶	9708_6	704
ㄌㄟˇ	蕾	6090_3	531	ㄌㄢˇ	攬	5801_6	501
ㄌㄟˇ	誄	0569_0	046	ㄌㄢˋ	濫	3811_7	343
ㄌㄟˋ	類	9148_6	692	ㄌㄢˋ	爛	9782_0	705
ㄌㄟˋ	淚	3313_4	304	ㄌㄤˊ	郎	3772_7	342
ㄌㄠ	撈	5902_7	506	ㄌㄤˊ	狼	4323_2	388
ㄌㄠˊ	勞	9942_7	708	ㄌㄤˊ	廊	0022_7	014
ㄌㄠˊ	牢	3050_2	283	ㄌㄤˊ	榔	4792_7	436
ㄌㄠˊ	嶗	3712_7	351	ㄌㄤˊ	踉	6313_2	541
ㄌㄠˊ	癆	0012_7	005	ㄌㄤˊ	鋃	8613_2	660
ㄌㄠˇ	老	4471_1	410	ㄌㄤˇ	閬	7773_2	610
ㄌㄠˇ	佬	2421_1	203	ㄌㄤˇ	朗	3772_0	342
ㄌㄠˇ	姥	4441_1	404	ㄌㄤˋ	浪	3313_2	303
ㄌㄡˊ	樓	4594_4	420	ㄌㄥˊ	稜	2494_7	215
ㄌㄡˊ	嘍	6504_4	549	ㄌㄥˊ	棱	4494_7	418
ㄌㄡˊ	僂	2524_4	222	ㄌㄥˊ	崚	2474_7	213
ㄌㄡˊ	螻	5514_4	485	ㄌㄥˇ	冷	3813_7	344
ㄌㄡˊ	髏	7524_4	585	ㄌㄥˋ	愣	9602_7	702
ㄌㄡˇ	簍	8840_4	675				
ㄌㄡˇ	摟	5504_4	484	**ㄍ**			
ㄌㄡˋ	漏	3712_7	329	注音	字	四　角	頁碼
ㄌㄡˋ	鏤	8514_4	664	ㄍㄨ	估	2426_0	206
ㄌㄡˋ	陋	7121_2	566	ㄍㄨ	沽	3416_0	313
ㄌㄢˊ	蘭	4422_7	399	ㄍㄨ	鴣	4762_7	433
ㄌㄢˊ	藍	4410_7	392	ㄍㄨ	蛄	5416_0	482

注音	字	四角	頁碼	注音	字	四角	頁碼
ㄍㄨ	咕	6406_0	545	ㄍㄨㄛ	鍋	8712_7	668
ㄍㄨ	鈷	8416_0	662	ㄍㄨㄛˊ	國	6015_3	514
ㄍㄨ	姑	4446_0	406	ㄍㄨㄛˊ	幗	4620_0	422
ㄍㄨ	菇	4446_4	406	ㄍㄨㄛˊ	摑	5600_0	488
ㄍㄨ	孤	1243_0	116	ㄍㄨㄛˇ	果	6090_4	532
ㄍㄨ	辜	4040_1	369	ㄍㄨㄛˇ	菓	4490_4	416
ㄍㄨ	箍	8851_2	676	ㄍㄨㄛˇ	猓	4629_4	423
ㄍㄨˇ	古	4060_0	372	ㄍㄨㄛˇ	裹	0073_2	031
ㄍㄨˇ	詁	0466_0	044	ㄍㄨㄛˋ	過	3730_2	336
ㄍㄨˇ	鼓	4414_7	395	ㄍㄨㄞ	乖	2011_1	143
ㄍㄨˇ	瞽	4460_4	409	ㄍㄨㄞˊ	枴	4692_7	427
ㄍㄨˇ	賈	1080_6	094	ㄍㄨㄞˇ	拐	5602_7	488
ㄍㄨˇ	穀	4794_7	437	ㄍㄨㄞˋ	怪	9701_4	703
ㄍㄨˇ	蠱	5010_7	451	ㄍㄨㄟ	圭	4010_4	360
ㄍㄨˇ	骨	7722_7	596	ㄍㄨㄟ	閨	7710_4	588
ㄍㄨˇ	股	7724_7	599	ㄍㄨㄟ	瑰	1611_3	126
ㄍㄨˇ	谷	8060_8	648	ㄍㄨㄟ	龜	2711_7	238
ㄍㄨˋ	僱	2321_4	193	ㄍㄨㄟ	歸	2712_7	239
ㄍㄨˋ	雇	3021_4	275	ㄍㄨㄟ	規	5601_0	488
ㄍㄨˋ	顧	3128_6	293	ㄍㄨㄟˇ	軌	5401_7	480
ㄍㄨˋ	固	6060_4	527	ㄍㄨㄟˇ	鬼	2621_3	229
ㄍㄨˋ	錮	8610_0	665	ㄍㄨㄟˇ	詭	0761_2	048
ㄍㄨˋ	梏	4496_1	418	ㄍㄨㄟˇ	晷	6060_4	527
ㄍㄨˋ	故	4864_0	442	ㄍㄨㄟˋ	貴	5080_6	457
ㄍㄨㄚ	瓜	7223_0	577	ㄍㄨㄟˋ	櫃	4191_8	382
ㄍㄨㄚ	呱	6203_0	537	ㄍㄨㄟˋ	桂	4491_4	416
ㄍㄨㄚ	刮	2260_0	183	ㄍㄨㄟˋ	跪	6711_7	558
ㄍㄨㄚ	括	5206_4	469	ㄍㄨㄟˋ	媿	4442_7	405
ㄍㄨㄚ	蝸	5712_7	499	ㄍㄨㄢ	關	7777_2	612
ㄍㄨㄚˇ	寡	3022_7	276	ㄍㄨㄢ	官	3077_7	287
ㄍㄨㄚˋ	褂	3320_0	306	ㄍㄨㄢ	觀	4621_0	422
ㄍㄨㄚˋ	掛	5300_0	472	ㄍㄨㄢ	棺	4397_7	390
ㄍㄨㄚˋ	罣	6010_4	511	ㄍㄨㄢ	鰥	2633_3	233
ㄍㄨㄛ	郭	0742_7	048	ㄍㄨㄢˇ	管	8877_7	678
ㄍㄨㄛ	堝	4712_7	427	ㄍㄨㄢˇ	館	8377_7	661

注　音	字	四　角	頁　碼	注　音	字	四　角	頁　碼
《ㄨㄢˇ	脘	7321_1	580	《ㄨㄥˋ	貢	1080_6	094
《ㄨㄢˋ	冠	3721_4	333	《ㄚˊ	軋	5201_0	465
《ㄨㄢˋ	灌	3411_4	310	《ㄚˋ	尬	4801_2	438
《ㄨㄢˋ	罐	8471_4	663	《ㄜ	哥	1062_1	090
《ㄨㄢˋ	慣	9708_6	704	《ㄜ	歌	1768_2	137
《ㄨㄢˋ	貫	7780_6	614	《ㄜ	戈	5300_0	472
《ㄨㄢˋ	摜	5708_6	499	《ㄜ	割	3260_0	301
《ㄨㄢˋ	鸛	4722_7	429	《ㄜ	擱	5702_0	494
《ㄨㄢˋ	鑵	8411_4	662	《ㄜ	鴿	8762_7	670
《ㄨㄢˋ	盥	7710_7	588	《ㄜ	胳	7726_4	601
《ㄨㄣˇ	滾	3013_2	273	《ㄜˊ	格	4796_4	438
《ㄨㄣˋ	棍	4691_1	427	《ㄜˊ	閣	7760_4	608
《ㄨㄤ	光	9021_1	685	《ㄜˊ	鎘	8112_7	655
《ㄨㄤ	洸	3911_1	350	《ㄜˊ	革	4450_6	407
《ㄨㄤ	銧	8911_1	681	《ㄜˊ	隔	7122_7	567
《ㄨㄤ	胱	7921_1	620	《ㄜˊ	咯	6706_4	557
《ㄨㄤˇ	廣	0028_6	020	《ㄜˊ	膈	7122_7	567
《ㄨㄤˋ	逛	3130_1	294	《ㄜˊ	骼	7726_4	601
《ㄨㄥ	供	2428_1	207	《ㄜˇ	葛	4472_7	412
《ㄨㄥ	公	8073_2	648	《ㄜˋ	各	2760_4	251
《ㄨㄥ	宮	3060_6	284	《ㄜˋ	個	2620_0	229
《ㄨㄥ	功	1412_7	120	《ㄜˋ	个	8020_0	627
《ㄨㄥ	弓	1720_7	131	《ㄜˋ	鉻	8716_4	669
《ㄨㄥ	攻	1814_0	139	《ㄞ	該	0068_2	029
《ㄨㄥ	恭	4433_8	403	《ㄞ	賅	6088_2	531
《ㄨㄥ	躬	2722_7	242	《ㄞ	垓	4018_2	362
《ㄨㄥ	工	1010_0	063	《ㄞ	陔	7028_2	564
《ㄨㄥ	肱	7423_2	582	《ㄞˇ	改	1874_0	141
《ㄨㄥ	蚣	5813_2	504	《ㄞˋ	蓋	4410_7	392
《ㄨㄥˇ	鞏	1750_6	135	《ㄞˋ	概	4191_4	381
《ㄨㄥˇ	拱	5408_1	482	《ㄞˋ	鈣	8112_7	655
《ㄨㄥˇ	汞	1023_2	078	《ㄞˋ	丐	1020_7	073
《ㄨㄥˇ	廾	4400_0	390	《ㄞˋ	溉	3111_4	291
《ㄨㄥˋ	共	4480_1	413	《ㄟˇ	給	2896_1	267
《ㄨㄥˋ	供	2428_1	207	《ㄠ	高	0022_7	014

注音	字	四角	頁碼	注音	字	四角	頁碼
‹‹ㄠ	糕	9893_1	708	‹‹ㄢ	疳	0017_5	007
‹‹ㄠ	羔	8033_1	637	‹‹ㄢˇ	趕	4680_4	425
‹‹ㄠ	膏	0022_7	016	‹‹ㄢˇ	感	5320_0	478
‹‹ㄠ	篙	8822_7	673	‹‹ㄢˇ	桿	4694_1	427
‹‹ㄠˇ	稿	2092_7	159	‹‹ㄢˇ	橄	4894_0	443
‹‹ㄠˇ	杲	6090_4	532	‹‹ㄢˇ	敢	1814_0	140
‹‹ㄠˇ	睪	2640_1	233	‹‹ㄢˇ	稈	2694_1	237
‹‹ㄠˇ	睪	6040_1	523	‹‹ㄢˇ	趕	4180_4	381
‹‹ㄠˇ	槁	4092_7	377	‹‹ㄢˋ	幹	4844_1	441
‹‹ㄠˇ	縞	2092_7	159	‹‹ㄣ	跟	6713_2	558
‹‹ㄠˇ	藁	4490_4	416	‹‹ㄣ	根	4793_2	436
‹‹ㄠˋ	誥	0466_1	044	‹‹ㄣˇ	艮	7773_2	610
‹‹ㄠˋ	告	2460_1	211	‹‹ㄣˋ	亙	1010_7	070
‹‹ㄡ	勾	2772_0	253	‹‹ㄤ	剛	7220_0	576
‹‹ㄡ	鉤	8712_0	667	‹‹ㄤ	鋼	8712_0	667
‹‹ㄡ	溝	3515_5	319	‹‹ㄤ	岡	7722_0	593
‹‹ㄡ	鈎	8712_0	667	‹‹ㄤ	崗	2222_7	179
‹‹ㄡ	篝	8844_7	676	‹‹ㄤ	綱	2792_0	257
‹‹ㄡˇ	狗	4722_0	428	‹‹ㄤ	缸	8171_0	657
‹‹ㄡˇ	苟	4462_7	410	‹‹ㄤ	肛	7121_2	566
‹‹ㄡˋ	垢	4216_1	383	‹‹ㄤ	杠	4191_0	381
‹‹ㄡˋ	構	4594_7	420	‹‹ㄤ	釭	8111_0	655
‹‹ㄡˋ	搆	5504_7	484	‹‹ㄤˇ	港	3411_7	310
‹‹ㄡˋ	購	6584_7	549	‹‹ㄤˋ	槓	4198_6	382
‹‹ㄡˋ	夠	2722_0	241	‹‹ㄥ	耕	5590_0	487
‹‹ㄡˋ	彀	4724_7	429	‹‹ㄥ	畊	6500_0	548
‹‹ㄡˋ	媾	4544_7	419	‹‹ㄥ	庚	0023_7	017
‹‹ㄡˋ	詬	0266_1	037	‹‹ㄥ	羹	8043_0	640
‹‹ㄢ	甘	4477_0	412	‹‹ㄥ	粳	9194_6	693
‹‹ㄢ	乾	4841_7	440	‹‹ㄥˇ	耿	1918_0	142
‹‹ㄢ	竿	8840_1	675	‹‹ㄥˇ	梗	4194_6	382
‹‹ㄢ	干	1040_0	081	‹‹ㄥˇ	哽	6104_6	534
‹‹ㄢ	柑	4497_0	418	‹‹ㄥˋ	更	1050_6	086
‹‹ㄢ	肝	7124_0	568				
‹‹ㄢ	尷	1821_1	140				

ㄎ

注　音	字	四　角	頁　碼	注　音	字	四　角	頁　碼
ㄎㄨ	哭	6643_0	552	ㄎㄨㄟˊ	夔	8024_7	632
ㄎㄨ	枯	4496_0	418	ㄎㄨㄟˊ	暌	6203_4	537
ㄎㄨ	窟	3027_2	278	ㄎㄨㄟˇ	傀	2621_3	229
ㄎㄨ	刳	4220_0	383	ㄎㄨㄟˋ	潰	3518_6	319
ㄎㄨ	骷	7426_0	583	ㄎㄨㄟˋ	愧	9601_3	701
ㄎㄨˇ	苦	4460_4	408	ㄎㄨㄟˋ	匱	7171_8	574
ㄎㄨˋ	庫	0025_6	019	ㄎㄨㄟˋ	憒	9508_6	700
ㄎㄨˋ	褲	3025_0	277	ㄎㄨㄟˋ	喟	6602_7	550
ㄎㄨˋ	酷	1466_1	123	ㄎㄨㄟˋ	餽	8671_3	666
ㄎㄨˋ	嚳	7760_1	607	ㄎㄨㄟˋ	饋	8578_6	665
ㄎㄨˋ	袴	3422_7	314	ㄎㄨㄟˋ	簣	8880_6	679
ㄎㄨㄚ	誇	0462_7	043	ㄎㄨㄢ	寬	3021_3	274
ㄎㄨㄚ	夸	4020_7	363	ㄎㄨㄢˇ	款	4798_2	438
ㄎㄨㄚˋ	跨	6412_7	546	ㄎㄨㄣ	坤	4510_6	419
ㄎㄨㄚˋ	胯	7422_7	582	ㄎㄨㄣ	昆	6071_1	528
ㄎㄨㄛ	闊	7716_4	589	ㄎㄨㄣ	崑	2271_1	183
ㄎㄨㄛ	廓	0022_7	016	ㄎㄨㄣˇ	悃	9600_0	701
ㄎㄨㄛˋ	擴	5008_6	450	ㄎㄨㄣˇ	捆	5600_0	488
ㄎㄨㄞˋ	快	9503_0	699	ㄎㄨㄣˇ	閫	7760_7	609
ㄎㄨㄞˋ	塊	4611_3	421	ㄎㄨㄣˋ	困	6090_4	532
ㄎㄨㄞˋ	會	8060_6	646	ㄎㄨㄣˋ	睏	6600_0	550
ㄎㄨㄞˋ	儈	2826_6	263	ㄎㄨㄤ	框	4191_1	381
ㄎㄨㄞˋ	劊	8260_0	659	ㄎㄨㄤ	匡	7171_1	572
ㄎㄨㄞˋ	筷	8893_4	681	ㄎㄨㄤ	筐	8871_1	677
ㄎㄨㄞˋ	膾	7826_6	618	ㄎㄨㄤ	誆	0161_1	033
ㄎㄨㄞˋ	獪	4826_6	440	ㄎㄨㄤ	恇	9101_1	691
ㄎㄨㄟ	窺	3051_6	283	ㄎㄨㄤˊ	狂	4121_4	379
ㄎㄨㄟ	虧	2122_7	167	ㄎㄨㄤˊ	誑	0161_4	033
ㄎㄨㄟ	悝	9601_4	701	ㄎㄨㄤˋ	曠	6008_6	509
ㄎㄨㄟ	盔	7110_7	565	ㄎㄨㄤˋ	眶	6101_1	532
ㄎㄨㄟˊ	魁	2421_0	203	ㄎㄨㄤˋ	礦	1068_6	091
ㄎㄨㄟˊ	奎	4010_4	360	ㄎㄨㄤˋ	況	3611_0	323
ㄎㄨㄟˊ	揆	5203_4	468	ㄎㄨㄤˋ	貺	6681_0	553
ㄎㄨㄟˊ	葵	4443_1	405	ㄎㄨㄤˋ	鑛	8018_6	627
ㄎㄨㄟˊ	達	3430_1	315	ㄎㄨㄥ	空	3010_1	269

注　音	字	四　角	頁　碼	注　音	字	四　角	頁　碼
ㄎㄨㄥ	倥	2321_1	193	ㄎㄞˋ	嘅	6101_4	533
ㄎㄨㄥ	悾	9301_1	695	ㄎㄞˋ	愾	9801_7	706
ㄎㄨㄥˇ	孔	1241_0	115	ㄎㄞˋ	愒	9602_7	701
ㄎㄨㄥˇ	恐	1733_1	133	ㄎㄠˇ	考	4420_7	396
ㄎㄨㄥˋ	控	5301_1	473	ㄎㄠˇ	烤	9482_7	697
ㄎㄚ	咖	6600_0	550	ㄎㄠˇ	拷	5402_7	480
ㄎㄚˇ	卡	2123_1	168	ㄎㄠˋ	靠	2411_1	200
ㄎㄜ	窠	3090_4	290	ㄎㄠˋ	銬	8412_7	662
ㄎㄜ	棵	4699_4	427	ㄎㄡˇ	口	6000_0	507
ㄎㄜ	科	2490_0	214	ㄎㄡˋ	扣	5600_0	487
ㄎㄜ	顆	6198_6	536	ㄎㄡˋ	寇	3021_4	275
ㄎㄜ	柯	4192_0	382	ㄎㄡˋ	叩	6702_0	554
ㄎㄜ	珂	1112_0	103	ㄎㄡˋ	釦	8610_0	665
ㄎㄜ	苛	4462_1	409	ㄎㄢ	刊	1240_0	114
ㄎㄜ	磕	1461_7	122	ㄎㄢ	堪	4411_1	393
ㄎㄜ	瞌	6401_7	543	ㄎㄢ	勘	4472_7	412
ㄎㄜ	蝌	5411_4	482	ㄎㄢ	龕	8021_1	628
ㄎㄜˊ	殼	4724_7	429	ㄎㄢˇ	坎	4718_2	428
ㄎㄜˊ	咳	6008_2	509	ㄎㄢˇ	砍	1768_2	137
ㄎㄜˇ	可	1062_0	088	ㄎㄢˇ	侃	2621_0	229
ㄎㄜˇ	渴	3612_7	324	ㄎㄢˋ	看	2060_4	154
ㄎㄜˋ	克	4021_6	363	ㄎㄢˋ	瞰	6804_0	561
ㄎㄜˋ	客	3060_4	284	ㄎㄣˇ	肯	2122_7	167
ㄎㄜˋ	課	0669_4	047	ㄎㄣˇ	啃	6102_7	534
ㄎㄜˋ	恪	9706_4	704	ㄎㄣˇ	墾	2710_4	238
ㄎㄜˋ	剋	4221_0	383	ㄎㄣˇ	懇	2733_3	247
ㄎㄜˋ	刻	0220_0	035	ㄎㄤ	康	0023_2	016
ㄎㄜˋ	髁	7629_4	587	ㄎㄤ	慷	9003_2	684
ㄎㄞ	開	7744_1	604	ㄎㄤ	糠	9093_2	691
ㄎㄞ	揩	5106_2	465	ㄎㄤˊ	扛	5101_0	459
ㄎㄞˇ	凱	2711_0	238	ㄎㄤˋ	抗	5001_7	449
ㄎㄞˇ	楷	4196_2	382	ㄎㄤˋ	亢	0021_7	011
ㄎㄞˇ	愷	9201_8	693	ㄎㄤˋ	伉	2021_7	144
ㄎㄞˇ	慨	9101_4	691	ㄎㄤˋ	炕	9081_7	691
ㄎㄞˇ	鎧	8211_8	658	ㄎㄥ	坑	4011_7	361

注音	字	四角	頁碼	注音	字	四角	頁碼
ㄎㄥ	吭	6001_7	508	ㄏㄨㄚ	花	4421_4	397
ㄎㄥ	鏗	8711_4	667	ㄏㄨㄚˊ	華	4450_4	406
ㄎㄥ	阬	7021_7	563	ㄏㄨㄚˊ	滑	3712_7	329
				ㄏㄨㄚˊ	划	5200_0	465
		ㄏ		ㄏㄨㄚˊ	樺	4495_4	418
注音	字	四角	頁碼	ㄏㄨㄚˊ	譁	0465_4	043
ㄏㄨ	忽	2733_2	247	ㄏㄨㄚˊ	嘩	6405_4	545
ㄏㄨ	惚	9703_3	704	ㄏㄨㄚˊ	猾	4722_7	429
ㄏㄨ	謼	0164_9	034	ㄏㄨㄚˋ	話	0266_1	037
ㄏㄨ	呼	6204_9	537	ㄏㄨㄚˋ	化	2421_0	202
ㄏㄨ	嘑	6104_9	534	ㄏㄨㄚˋ	劃	5210_0	471
ㄏㄨˊ	湖	3712_0	328	ㄏㄨㄚˋ	畫	5010_6	451
ㄏㄨˊ	蝴	5712_0	499	ㄏㄨㄛˊ	活	3216_4	298
ㄏㄨˊ	壺	4010_7	361	ㄏㄨㄛˇ	火	9080_0	689
ㄏㄨˊ	弧	1223_0	112	ㄏㄨㄛˇ	伙	2928_0	268
ㄏㄨˊ	狐	4223_0	383	ㄏㄨㄛˇ	夥	6792_7	560
ㄏㄨˊ	糊	9792_0	706	ㄏㄨㄛˋ	或	5310_0	476
ㄏㄨˊ	鬍	7262_7	578	ㄏㄨㄛˋ	獲	4424_7	400
ㄏㄨˊ	鵠	2762_7	252	ㄏㄨㄛˋ	惑	5330_0	479
ㄏㄨˊ	囫	6022_7	519	ㄏㄨㄛˋ	貨	2480_6	213
ㄏㄨˊ	胡	4762_0	433	ㄏㄨㄛˋ	霍	1021_4	074
ㄏㄨˊ	猢	4722_0	428	ㄏㄨㄛˋ	禍	3722_7	334
ㄏㄨˊ	葫	4462_7	410	ㄏㄨㄛˋ	豁	3866_8	350
ㄏㄨˊ	餬	8772_0	671	ㄏㄨㄛˋ	壑	2710_4	238
ㄏㄨˇ	虎	2121_7	164	ㄏㄨㄛˋ	穫	2494_7	215
ㄏㄨˇ	唬	6101_2	533	ㄏㄨㄛˋ	蠖	5414_7	482
ㄏㄨˇ	琥	1111_7	103	ㄏㄨㄛˋ	鑊	8414_7	662
ㄏㄨˋ	互	1010_7	070	ㄏㄨㄞˊ	懷	9003_2	684
ㄏㄨˋ	怙	9406_0	696	ㄏㄨㄞˊ	淮	3011_4	272
ㄏㄨˋ	護	0464_7	043	ㄏㄨㄞˊ	槐	4691_3	427
ㄏㄨˋ	滬	3311_7	303	ㄏㄨㄞˊ	踝	6619_4	551
ㄏㄨˋ	戶	3027_7	278	ㄏㄨㄞˊ	徊	2620_0	229
ㄏㄨˋ	祜	3426_0	314	ㄏㄨㄞˋ	壞	4013_2	362
ㄏㄨˋ	戽	3024_7	277	ㄏㄨㄟ	輝	9725_6	704
ㄏㄨˋ	笏	8822_7	673	ㄏㄨㄟ	揮	5705_6	497

注　音	字	四　角	頁　碼	注　音	字	四　角	頁　碼
ㄏㄨㄟ	暉	6705_6	556	ㄏㄨㄢˊ	環	1613_2	127
ㄏㄨㄟ	灰	7128_9	570	ㄏㄨㄢˊ	寰	3073_2	286
ㄏㄨㄟ	恢	9108_9	692	ㄏㄨㄢˊ	桓	4191_6	382
ㄏㄨㄟ	徽	2824_0	261	ㄏㄨㄢˊ	還	3630_3	326
ㄏㄨㄟ	詼	0168_9	034	ㄏㄨㄢˊ	繯	2693_2	237
ㄏㄨㄟ	麾	0021_4	010	ㄏㄨㄢˊ	鐶	8613_2	665
ㄏㄨㄟˊ	回	6060_0	525	ㄏㄨㄢˊ	鍰	8214_7	658
ㄏㄨㄟˊ	迴	3630_0	325	ㄏㄨㄢˇ	緩	2294_7	190
ㄏㄨㄟˊ	廻	7722_0	593	ㄏㄨㄢˋ	換	5703_4	495
ㄏㄨㄟˊ	茴	4460_0	408	ㄏㄨㄢˋ	患	5033_6	454
ㄏㄨㄟˊ	蛔	5610_0	492	ㄏㄨㄢˋ	煥	9783_4	705
ㄏㄨㄟˇ	毀	7714_7	589	ㄏㄨㄢˋ	喚	6703_4	556
ㄏㄨㄟˇ	悔	9805_6	706	ㄏㄨㄢˋ	奐	2743_0	249
ㄏㄨㄟˇ	燬	9784_7	705	ㄏㄨㄢˋ	幻	2772_0	254
ㄏㄨㄟˇ	海	0865_7	057	ㄏㄨㄢˋ	宦	3071_7	286
ㄏㄨㄟˋ	會	8060_6	646	ㄏㄨㄢˋ	渙	3712_7	330
ㄏㄨㄟˋ	惠	5033_3	453	ㄏㄨㄢˋ	豢	9023_2	686
ㄏㄨㄟˋ	滙	3111_1	290	ㄏㄨㄣ	婚	4246_1	384
ㄏㄨㄟˋ	匯	7171_1	572	ㄏㄨㄣ	昏	7260_4	578
ㄏㄨㄟˋ	慧	5533_7	486	ㄏㄨㄣ	葷	4450_6	407
ㄏㄨㄟˋ	賄	6482_7	548	ㄏㄨㄣ	惛	9206_4	694
ㄏㄨㄟˋ	繪	2896_6	267	ㄏㄨㄣ	閽	7760_4	608
ㄏㄨㄟˋ	卉	4044_0	370	ㄏㄨㄣˊ	渾	3715_6	331
ㄏㄨㄟˋ	喙	6703_2	555	ㄏㄨㄣˊ	魂	1644_8	128
ㄏㄨㄟˋ	晦	6805_7	561	ㄏㄨㄣˊ	餛	8671_1	666
ㄏㄨㄟˋ	彗	5517_7	485	ㄏㄨㄣˋ	混	3611_1	323
ㄏㄨㄟˋ	蕙	4433_3	402	ㄏㄨㄣˋ	諢	0765_6	051
ㄏㄨㄟˋ	穢	2195_3	176	ㄏㄨㄤ	荒	4421_1	397
ㄏㄨㄟˋ	諱	0465_6	044	ㄏㄨㄤ	慌	9401_1	696
ㄏㄨㄟˋ	嘒	6507_7	549	ㄏㄨㄤˊ	黃	4480_6	414
ㄏㄨㄟˋ	篲	8817_7	672	ㄏㄨㄤˊ	煌	9681_4	702
ㄏㄨㄢ	歡	4728_2	429	ㄏㄨㄤˊ	皇	2610_4	228
ㄏㄨㄢ	讙	0461_4	043	ㄏㄨㄤˊ	磺	1468_6	124
ㄏㄨㄢ	懽	9401_4	696	ㄏㄨㄤˊ	蝗	5611_4	492
ㄏㄨㄢ	獾	4421_4	398	ㄏㄨㄤˊ	凰	7721_0	589

注音	字	四角	頁碼	注音	字	四角	頁碼
ㄏㄨㄤˊ	徨	2621_4	230	ㄏㄜˊ	和	2690_0	234
ㄏㄨㄤˊ	簧	8880_6	679	ㄏㄜˊ	涸	3610_0	323
ㄏㄨㄤˊ	遑	3630_1	326	ㄏㄜˊ	禾	2090_4	157
ㄏㄨㄤˊ	隍	7621_4	586	ㄏㄜˊ	曷	6072_7	529
ㄏㄨㄤˊ	惶	9601_4	701	ㄏㄜˊ	闔	7710_7	588
ㄏㄨㄤˇ	恍	9901_1	708	ㄏㄜˊ	褐	3622_7	325
ㄏㄨㄤˇ	悦	9601_0	701	ㄏㄜˊ	貉	2726_4	245
ㄏㄨㄤˇ	謊	0461_1	042	ㄏㄜˊ	劾	0422_7	040
ㄏㄨㄤˇ	幌	4621_1	422	ㄏㄜˊ	紇	2891_7	267
ㄏㄨㄤˇ	晃	6021_6	519	ㄏㄜˊ	闔	7728_0	602
ㄏㄨㄥ	烘	9488_1	697	ㄏㄜˋ	赫	4433_1	401
ㄏㄨㄥ	哄	6408_1	545	ㄏㄜˋ	嚇	6403_1	544
ㄏㄨㄥ	轟	5255_6	455	ㄏㄜˋ	喝	6602_7	550
ㄏㄨㄥ	籺	9798_7	706	ㄏㄜˋ	鶴	4722_7	429
ㄏㄨㄥˊ	紅	2191_0	174	ㄏㄜˋ	賀	4680_6	425
ㄏㄨㄥˊ	宏	3043_0	283	ㄏㄜˋ	熇	9082_7	691
ㄏㄨㄥˊ	虹	5111_0	465	ㄏㄞ	嗨	6805_7	561
ㄏㄨㄥˊ	鴻	3712_7	330	ㄏㄞˊ	孩	1048_2	086
ㄏㄨㄥˊ	泓	3310_0	303	ㄏㄞˊ	骸	7028_2	564
ㄏㄨㄥˊ	訌	0161_0	033	ㄏㄞˇ	海	3815_7	345
ㄏㄨㄥˊ	弘	1320_2	118	ㄏㄞˋ	害	3060_1	283
ㄏㄨㄥˊ	紘	2493_0	215	ㄏㄞˋ	駭	7038_2	565
ㄏㄨㄥˊ	洪	3418_1	313	ㄏㄞˋ	嗐	6306_1	540
ㄏㄨㄥˊ	閎	7743_2	604	ㄏㄟ	黑	6033_1	521
ㄏㄨㄥˋ	鬨	7780_1	613	ㄏㄠ	蒿	4422_7	399
ㄏㄚ	哈	6806_1	561	ㄏㄠˊ	豪	0023_2	016
ㄏㄚˊ	蛤	5816_1	504	ㄏㄠˊ	毫	0071_4	029
ㄏㄜ	訶	0162_0	034	ㄏㄠˊ	嚎	6003_2	508
ㄏㄜ	呵	6102_0	533	ㄏㄠˊ	壕	4013_2	362
ㄏㄜˊ	何	2122_0	165	ㄏㄠˊ	濠	3013_2	273
ㄏㄜˊ	合	8060_1	642	ㄏㄠˊ	蠔	5013_2	452
ㄏㄜˊ	核	4098_2	378	ㄏㄠˊ	嗥	6604_3	550
ㄏㄜˊ	河	3112_0	291	ㄏㄠˇ	好	4744_7	431
ㄏㄜˊ	盒	8010_7	625	ㄏㄠˋ	號	6121_7	534
ㄏㄜˊ	荷	4422_1	398	ㄏㄠˋ	浩	3416_1	313

注音	字	四角	頁碼	注音	字	四角	頁碼
ㄏㄠˋ	耗	5291_4	472	ㄏㄢˋ	頷	8168_6	657
ㄏㄠˋ	皓	2466_1	211	ㄏㄣˊ	痕	0013_2	006
ㄏㄠˋ	鎬	8012_7	627	ㄏㄣˇ	很	2723_2	243
ㄏㄠˋ	顥	6198_6	536	ㄏㄣˇ	狠	4723_2	429
ㄏㄡˊ	侯	2723_4	243	ㄏㄣˋ	恨	9703_3	704
ㄏㄡˊ	喉	6703_4	556	ㄏㄤˊ	航	2041_7	151
ㄏㄡˊ	猴	4723_4	429	ㄏㄤˊ	杭	4091_7	377
ㄏㄡˇ	吼	6201_0	536	ㄏㄥ	哼	6002_7	508
ㄏㄡˋ	後	2224_7	180	ㄏㄥˊ	衡	2122_1	166
ㄏㄡˋ	后	7226_1	577	ㄏㄥˊ	橫	4498_6	418
ㄏㄡˋ	候	2723_4	243	ㄏㄥˊ	恒	9101_6	692
ㄏㄡˋ	厚	7124_8	569	ㄏㄥˊ	恆	9101_7	692
ㄏㄢ	酣	1467_0	123	ㄏㄥˊ	桁	4792_1	382
ㄏㄢ	憨	1833_4	140				
ㄏㄢ	鼾	2144_0	172			ㄐ	
ㄏㄢˊ	函	1077_2	094	注音	字	四角	頁碼
ㄏㄢˊ	含	8060_7	647	ㄐㄧ	機	4295_3	385
ㄏㄢˊ	涵	3117_2	293	ㄐㄧ	基	4410_4	391
ㄏㄢˊ	寒	3030_3	279	ㄐㄧ	績	2598_6	225
ㄏㄢˊ	韓	4445_6	406	ㄐㄧ	雞	2041_4	151
ㄏㄢˇ	喊	6305_0	540	ㄐㄧ	積	2598_6	224
ㄏㄢˇ	罕	3740_1	340	ㄐㄧ	几	7721_0	589
ㄏㄢˇ	厂	7120_0	565	ㄐㄧ	羈	6052_7	525
ㄏㄢˋ	汗	3114_0	292	ㄐㄧ	姬	4141_6	380
ㄏㄢˋ	旱	6040_1	523	ㄐㄧ	跡	6013_0	512
ㄏㄢˋ	悍	9604_1	702	ㄐㄧ	飢	8771_0	670
ㄏㄢˋ	焊	9684_1	703	ㄐㄧ	奇	4062_1	373
ㄏㄢˋ	銲	8614_1	665	ㄐㄧ	畸	6402_1	543
ㄏㄢˋ	猂	4624_1	423	ㄐㄧ	蹟	6518_6	549
ㄏㄢˋ	捍	5604_1	489	ㄐㄧ	箕	8880_1	679
ㄏㄢˋ	漢	3413_4	312	ㄐㄧ	譏	0265_3	037
ㄏㄢˋ	憾	9305_0	695	ㄐㄧ	饑	8275_3	659
ㄏㄢˋ	撼	5305_0	475	ㄐㄧ	稽	2396_1	199
ㄏㄢˋ	翰	4842_7	440	ㄐㄧ	笄	8844_1	675
ㄏㄢˋ	釬	8113_2	655	ㄐㄧ	躋	6012_3	512

注 音	字	四 角	頁 碼	注 音	字	四 角	頁 碼
ㄐㄧㄚˊ	莢	4443_8	406	ㄐㄧㄝˊ	孑	1740_7	134
ㄐㄧㄚˊ	鋏	8413_8	662	ㄐㄧㄝˊ	櫛	4892_7	442
ㄐㄧㄚˇ	假	2724_7	244	ㄐㄧㄝˇ	解	2725_2	244
ㄐㄧㄚˇ	甲	6050_0	525	ㄐㄧㄝˇ	姐	4741_0	430
ㄐㄧㄚˇ	岬	2675_0	234	ㄐㄧㄝˇ	姊	4542_7	419
ㄐㄧㄚˇ	胛	7625_0	587	ㄐㄧㄝˋ	界	6022_8	520
ㄐㄧㄚˇ	鉀	8615_0	665	ㄐㄧㄝˋ	屆	7727_2	601
ㄐㄧㄚˋ	價	2128_6	171	ㄐㄧㄝˋ	介	8022_0	629
ㄐㄧㄚˋ	架	4690_4	427	ㄐㄧㄝˋ	借	2426_1	207
ㄐㄧㄚˋ	嫁	4343_2	388	ㄐㄧㄝˋ	藉	4496_1	418
ㄐㄧㄚˋ	駕	4632_7	423	ㄐㄧㄝˋ	芥	4422_8	399
ㄐㄧㄚˋ	稼	2393_2	198	ㄐㄧㄝˋ	戒	5340_0	479
ㄐㄧㄝ	接	5004_4	450	ㄐㄧㄝˋ	疥	0012_8	006
ㄐㄧㄝ	街	2122_1	166	ㄐㄧㄝˋ	誡	0365_0	040
ㄐㄧㄝ	皆	2160_2	172	ㄐㄧㄝˋ	蚧	5812_0	504
ㄐㄧㄝ	揭	5602_7	489	ㄐㄧㄠ	嬌	4242_7	384
ㄐㄧㄝ	階	7126_2	570	ㄐㄧㄠ	膠	7722_2	596
ㄐㄧㄝ	嗟	6801_2	560	ㄐㄧㄠ	教	4844_0	440
ㄐㄧㄝˊ	潔	3719_3	332	ㄐㄧㄠ	澆	3411_1	309
ㄐㄧㄝˊ	傑	2529_4	223	ㄐㄧㄠ	礁	1063_1	090
ㄐㄧㄝˊ	節	8872_7	677	ㄐㄧㄠ	蕉	4433_1	402
ㄐㄧㄝˊ	結	2496_1	215	ㄐㄧㄠ	郊	0742_7	048
ㄐㄧㄝˊ	捷	5508_1	484	ㄐㄧㄠ	焦	2033_1	148
ㄐㄧㄝˊ	刦	4270_0	384	ㄐㄧㄠ	僬	2824_0	262
ㄐㄧㄝˊ	劫	4472_7	412	ㄐㄧㄠ	椒	4794_0	437
ㄐㄧㄝˊ	刧	4772_0	434	ㄐㄧㄠ	交	0040_8	024
ㄐㄧㄝˊ	桔	4496_1	418	ㄐㄧㄠ	蛟	5014_8	452
ㄐㄧㄝˊ	截	4325_0	388	ㄐㄧㄠ	跤	6014_8	514
ㄐㄧㄝˊ	訐	0164_0	034	ㄐㄧㄠ	驕	7232_7	578
ㄐㄧㄝˊ	詰	0466_1	044	ㄐㄧㄠ	僬	2023_1	145
ㄐㄧㄝˊ	竭	0612_7	046	ㄐㄧㄠ	鮫	2034_8	148
ㄐㄧㄝˊ	桀	2590_4	223	ㄐㄧㄠ	噍	6003_1	508
ㄐㄧㄝˊ	絜	5790_3	500	ㄐㄧㄠ	姣	4044_8	371
ㄐㄧㄝˊ	睫	6508_1	549	ㄐㄧㄠˇ	繳	2894_0	267
ㄐㄧㄝˊ	羯	8652_7	666	ㄐㄧㄠˇ	角	2722_7	242

注　音	字	四　角	頁　碼	注　音	字	四　角	頁　碼
ㄐㄧㄠˇ	腳	7722_0	595	ㄐㄧㄡˋ	鷲	0332_7	038
ㄐㄧㄠˇ	攪	5701_6	493	ㄐㄧㄡˋ	舅	7742_7	604
ㄐㄧㄠˇ	狡	4024_8	368	ㄐㄧㄡˋ	柩	4191_8	382
ㄐㄧㄠˇ	僥	2421_0	203	ㄐㄧㄢ	間	7760_7	608
ㄐㄧㄠˇ	矯	8242_7	658	ㄐㄧㄢ	兼	8033_7	638
ㄐㄧㄠˇ	剿	2290_0	187	ㄐㄧㄢ	堅	7710_4	587
ㄐㄧㄠˇ	皎	2064_8	156	ㄐㄧㄢ	肩	3022_7	275
ㄐㄧㄠˇ	絞	2094_8	160	ㄐㄧㄢ	尖	9043_0	687
ㄐㄧㄠˇ	餃	8074_8	654	ㄐㄧㄢ	箋	8850_3	676
ㄐㄧㄠˇ	鉸	8014_8	627	ㄐㄧㄢ	姦	4044_4	370
ㄐㄧㄠˋ	較	5004_8	450	ㄐㄧㄢ	煎	8033_2	638
ㄐㄧㄠˋ	叫	6400_0	543	ㄐㄧㄢ	艱	4753_2	433
ㄐㄧㄠˋ	窖	3060_1	283	ㄐㄧㄢ	殲	1325_0	119
ㄐㄧㄠˋ	校	4094_8	378	ㄐㄧㄢ	緘	2395_0	199
ㄐㄧㄠˋ	轎	5202_7	467	ㄐㄧㄢ	監	7810_7	616
ㄐㄧㄠˋ	徼	2824_0	262	ㄐㄧㄢ	戔	5350_3	479
ㄐㄧㄡ	糾	2290_0	187	ㄐㄧㄢ	牋	2305_3	191
ㄐㄧㄡ	鳩	4702_7	427	ㄐㄧㄢ	奸	4144_0	380
ㄐㄧㄡ	揪	5908_0	506	ㄐㄧㄢ	械	4395_0	390
ㄐㄧㄡ	啾	6908_0	562	ㄐㄧㄢ	鶼	8732_7	670
ㄐㄧㄡˇ	九	4001_7	353	ㄐㄧㄢ	鷹	0022_7	013
ㄐㄧㄡˇ	久	2780_0	254	ㄐㄧㄢ	櫼	4801_3	438
ㄐㄧㄡˇ	酒	3116_0	292	ㄐㄧㄢˇ	檢	4898_6	443
ㄐㄧㄡˇ	灸	2780_9	255	ㄐㄧㄢˇ	儉	2828_6	264
ㄐㄧㄡˇ	玖	1718_0	130	ㄐㄧㄢˇ	撿	5808_6	504
ㄐㄧㄡˇ	韭	1110_1	101	ㄐㄧㄢˇ	減	3315_0	304
ㄐㄧㄡˇ	韮	4410_1	391	ㄐㄧㄢˇ	剪	8022_7	632
ㄐㄧㄡˇ	赳	4280_0	384	ㄐㄧㄢˇ	簡	8822_7	673
ㄐㄧㄡˋ	舊	4477_7	412	ㄐㄧㄢˇ	柬	5090_6	459
ㄐㄧㄡˋ	救	4814_0	438	ㄐㄧㄢˇ	繭	4422_7	399
ㄐㄧㄡˋ	究	3041_7	282	ㄐㄧㄢˇ	翦	8012_7	627
ㄐㄧㄡˋ	就	0391_4	040	ㄐㄧㄢˇ	揀	5509_6	485
ㄐㄧㄡˋ	咎	2860_4	265	ㄐㄧㄢˇ	鹸	2868_6	265
ㄐㄧㄡˋ	疚	0018_7	008	ㄐㄧㄢˋ	趼	6114_0	534
ㄐㄧㄡˋ	臼	7777_0	612	ㄐㄧㄢˋ	建	1540_0	124

注音	字	四角	頁碼	注音	字	四角	頁碼
ㄐㄧㄢˋ	見	6021_0	519	ㄐㄧㄣˋ	進	3030_1	278
ㄐㄧㄢˋ	健	2524_0	221	ㄐㄧㄣˋ	勁	1412_7	121
ㄐㄧㄢˋ	鑑	8811_7	672	ㄐㄧㄣˋ	禁	4490_1	415
ㄐㄧㄢˋ	件	2520_0	220	ㄐㄧㄣˋ	儘	2521_7	221
ㄐㄧㄢˋ	艦	2841_7	264	ㄐㄧㄣˋ	盡	5010_7	451
ㄐㄧㄢˋ	劍	8280_0	659	ㄐㄧㄣˋ	晉	1060_1	088
ㄐㄧㄢˋ	箭	8822_1	673	ㄐㄧㄣˋ	燼	9581_7	700
ㄐㄧㄢˋ	濺	3315_3	305	ㄐㄧㄣˋ	浸	3714_7	331
ㄐㄧㄢˋ	鍵	8514_0	664	ㄐㄧㄣˋ	噤	6409_1	546
ㄐㄧㄢˋ	腱	7524_0	585	ㄐㄧㄣˋ	覲	4611_0	421
ㄐㄧㄢˋ	間	7760_7	608	ㄐㄧㄣˋ	近	3230_2	300
ㄐㄧㄢˋ	漸	3212_1	296	ㄐㄧㄣˋ	靳	4252_1	384
ㄐㄧㄢˋ	僭	2126_1	170	ㄐㄧㄣˋ	贐	6581_7	549
ㄐㄧㄢˋ	諫	0569_6	046	ㄐㄧㄣˋ	搢	5106_1	464
ㄐㄧㄢˋ	建	2571_4	223	ㄐㄧㄤ	將	2724_0	243
ㄐㄧㄢˋ	薦	4422_7	399	ㄐㄧㄤ	江	3111_0	290
ㄐㄧㄢˋ	鑒	7810_9	616	ㄐㄧㄤ	姜	8040_4	639
ㄐㄧㄢˋ	餞	8375_3	661	ㄐㄧㄤ	疆	1111_6	103
ㄐㄧㄢˋ	檻	4891_7	442	ㄐㄧㄤ	漿	2723_2	243
ㄐㄧㄢˋ	賤	6385_3	542	ㄐㄧㄤ	僵	2121_6	164
ㄐㄧㄢˋ	踐	6315_3	541	ㄐㄧㄤ	薑	4410_6	392
ㄐㄧㄣ	金	8010_9	625	ㄐㄧㄤ	殭	1121_6	104
ㄐㄧㄣ	巾	4022_7	363	ㄐㄧㄤ	韁	4151_6	380
ㄐㄧㄣ	今	8020_7	628	ㄐㄧㄤ	繮	2191_6	175
ㄐㄧㄣ	津	3510_7	317	ㄐㄧㄤ	豇	1111_2	102
ㄐㄧㄣ	斤	7222_1	576	ㄐㄧㄤˇ	獎	2743_0	249
ㄐㄧㄣ	筋	8822_7	673	ㄐㄧㄤˇ	蔣	4424_7	400
ㄐㄧㄣ	襟	3429_1	315	ㄐㄧㄤˇ	講	0564_5	045
ㄐㄧㄣ	矜	1822_7	140	ㄐㄧㄤˇ	槳	2790_4	255
ㄐㄧㄣ	觔	2422_7	205	ㄐㄧㄤˋ	降	7725_4	600
ㄐㄧㄣˇ	緊	7790_3	615	ㄐㄧㄤˋ	匠	7171_2	573
ㄐㄧㄣˇ	謹	0461_4	042	ㄐㄧㄤˋ	醬	2760_1	251
ㄐㄧㄣˇ	僅	2421_4	204	ㄐㄧㄥ	精	9592_7	700
ㄐㄧㄣˇ	錦	8612_7	665	ㄐㄧㄥ	京	0090_6	031
ㄐㄧㄣˇ	饉	8471_4	663	ㄐㄧㄥ	經	2191_1	174

注音	字	四角	頁碼	注音	字	四角	頁碼
ㄐㄧㄥ	鯨	2039_6	148	ㄐㄩ	狙	4721_0	428
ㄐㄧㄥ	驚	4832_7	440	ㄐㄩ	雎	7011_4	562
ㄐㄧㄥ	晶	6066_0	528	ㄐㄩˊ	局	7722_7	596
ㄐㄧㄥ	菁	4422_7	399	ㄐㄩˊ	鞠	4752_0	433
ㄐㄧㄥ	荊	4240_0	384	ㄐㄩˊ	菊	4492_7	417
ㄐㄧㄥ	莖	4410_1	391	ㄐㄩˊ	橘	4792_7	436
ㄐㄧㄥ	兢	4421_6	398	ㄐㄩˊ	侷	2722_7	242
ㄐㄧㄥ	睛	6502_7	548	ㄐㄩˊ	掬	5702_0	494
ㄐㄧㄥ	涇	3111_1	290	ㄐㄩˊ	跼	6712_7	558
ㄐㄧㄥ	旌	0821_4	052	ㄐㄩˇ	舉	7750_8	607
ㄐㄧㄥˇ	警	4860_1	441	ㄐㄩˇ	矩	8141_7	656
ㄐㄧㄥˇ	景	6090_6	532	ㄐㄩˇ	沮	3711_0	327
ㄐㄧㄥˇ	井	5500_0	482	ㄐㄩˇ	咀	6701_0	553
ㄐㄧㄥˇ	憬	9609_6	702	ㄐㄩˇ	櫃	4191_7	382
ㄐㄧㄥˇ	頸	1118_6	103	ㄐㄩˋ	巨	7171_7	574
ㄐㄧㄥˇ	阱	7500_0	584	ㄐㄩˋ	具	7780_1	613
ㄐㄧㄥˇ	穽	3055_8	283	ㄐㄩˋ	據	5103_2	463
ㄐㄧㄥˇ	剄	1210_0	107	ㄐㄩˋ	劇	2220_0	177
ㄐㄧㄥˇ	儆	2824_0	262	ㄐㄩˋ	俱	2728_1	246
ㄐㄧㄥˋ	境	4011_6	361	ㄐㄩˋ	懼	9601_4	701
ㄐㄧㄥˋ	靜	5225_7	471	ㄐㄩˋ	聚	1723_2	132
ㄐㄧㄥˋ	竟	0021_6	010	ㄐㄩˋ	拒	5101_7	461
ㄐㄧㄥˋ	淨	3215_7	298	ㄐㄩˋ	句	2762_0	252
ㄐㄧㄥˋ	競	0021_6	010	ㄐㄩˋ	距	6111_7	534
ㄐㄧㄥˋ	敬	4864_0	442	ㄐㄩˋ	鉅	8111_7	655
ㄐㄧㄥˋ	鏡	8011_6	626	ㄐㄩˋ	遽	3130_3	294
ㄐㄧㄥˋ	靖	0512_7	045	ㄐㄩˋ	鋸	8716_4	669
ㄐㄧㄥˋ	逕	3130_1	294	ㄐㄩˋ	倨	2726_4	246
ㄐㄧㄥˋ	徑	2121_1	163	ㄐㄩˋ	詎	0161_7	033
ㄐㄧㄥˋ	靚	5621_0	492	ㄐㄩˋ	埧	4718_1	428
ㄐㄧㄥˋ	痙	0011_1	003	ㄐㄩˋ	炬	9181_7	693
ㄐㄧㄥˋ	脛	7121_1	565	ㄐㄩˋ	踞	6716_4	559
ㄐㄩ	居	7726_4	600	ㄐㄩˋ	颶	7721_8	592
ㄐㄩ	駒	7732_0	602	ㄐㄩˋ	窶	3040_4	282
ㄐㄩ	拘	5702_0	494	ㄐㄩˋ	屨	7724_4	598

注　音	字	四　角	頁　碼	注　音	字	四　角	頁　碼
ㄐㄩㄝˊ	絕	2791_7	256	ㄐㄩㄣ	君	1760_7	136
ㄐㄩㄝˊ	攫	5604_7	490	ㄐㄩㄣˋ	俊	2324_7	195
ㄐㄩㄝˊ	覺	7721_6	591	ㄐㄩㄣˋ	峻	2374_7	197
ㄐㄩㄝˊ	決	3513_0	318	ㄐㄩㄣˋ	菌	4460_0	408
ㄐㄩㄝˊ	戄	9604_7	702	ㄐㄩㄣˋ	郡	1762_7	137
ㄐㄩㄝˊ	厥	7128_2	570	ㄐㄩㄣˋ	浚	3314_7	304
ㄐㄩㄝˊ	掘	5707_2	498	ㄐㄩㄣˋ	竣	0314_7	038
ㄐㄩㄝˊ	爵	2074_6	156	ㄐㄩㄣˋ	駿	7334_7	581
ㄐㄩㄝˊ	譎	0762_7	051	ㄐㄩㄥˇ	炯	9782_0	705
ㄐㄩㄝˊ	矍	6640_7	552	ㄐㄩㄥˇ	窘	3060_7	284
ㄐㄩㄝˊ	訣	0563_0	045	ㄐㄩㄥˇ	迥	3730_2	335
ㄐㄩㄝˊ	蹶	6118_2	534				
ㄐㄩㄝˊ	嚼	6204_6	537	<center>**ㄑ**</center>			
ㄐㄩㄝˊ	橛	4792_7	436	注　音	字	四　角	頁　碼
ㄐㄩㄝˊ	抉	5503_0	483	ㄑㄧ	妻	5040_4	455
ㄐㄩㄝˊ	崛	2777_2	254	ㄑㄧ	淒	3514_4	319
ㄐㄩㄝˊ	爝	9284_6	694	ㄑㄧ	棲	4594_4	420
ㄐㄩㄝˊ	獗	4128_2	380	ㄑㄧ	悽	9504_4	700
ㄐㄩㄝˋ	倔	2727_2	246	ㄑㄧ	戚	5320_0	478
ㄐㄩㄢ	捐	5602_7	489	ㄑㄧ	漆	3413_2	312
ㄐㄩㄢ	娟	4642_7	425	ㄑㄧ	柒	3490_4	316
ㄐㄩㄢ	涓	3612_7	324	ㄑㄧ	七	4071_0	374
ㄐㄩㄢ	鵑	6722_7	559	ㄑㄧ	欺	4788_2	435
ㄐㄩㄢ	鐫	8012_7	627	ㄑㄧ	沏	3712_0	329
ㄐㄩㄢ	蠲	8612_7	665	ㄑㄧ	栖	4196_0	382
ㄐㄩㄢˇ	卷	9071_2	689	ㄑㄧˊ	其	4480_1	413
ㄐㄩㄢˋ	眷	9060_3	688	ㄑㄧˊ	麒	0428_1	040
ㄐㄩㄢˋ	倦	2921_2	268	ㄑㄧˊ	旗	0828_1	054
ㄐㄩㄢˋ	絹	2692_7	235	ㄑㄧˊ	祺	3428_1	315
ㄐㄩㄢˋ	雋	2022_7	145	ㄑㄧˊ	綦	4490_3	415
ㄐㄩㄢˋ	悁	9602_7	701	ㄑㄧˊ	期	4782_0	435
ㄐㄩㄢˋ	狷	4622_7	422	ㄑㄧˊ	棋	4498_1	418
ㄐㄩㄣ	均	4712_0	427	ㄑㄧˊ	蜞	5418_1	482
ㄐㄩㄣ	鈞	8712_0	667	ㄑㄧˊ	騏	7438_1	584
ㄐㄩㄣ	軍	3750_6	340	ㄑㄧˊ	奇	4062_1	373

注　音	字	四　角	頁　碼	注　音	字	四　角	頁　碼
〈一ˊ	琦	1412_1	120	〈一ㄝˊ	伽	2620_0	229
〈一ˊ	崎	2472_1	211	〈一ㄝˊ	茄	4446_0	406
〈一ˊ	騎	7432_1	584	〈一ㄝˇ	且	7710_0	587
〈一ˊ	歧	2414_7	201	〈一ㄝˋ	竊	3092_7	290
〈一ˊ	岐	2474_7	213	〈一ㄝˋ	篋	8871_3	677
〈一ˊ	祈	3222_1	299	〈一ㄝˋ	愜	9101_3	691
〈一ˊ	圻	4212_1	383	〈一ㄝˋ	妾	0040_4	023
〈一ˊ	頎	7128_6	570	〈一ㄝˋ	挈	5750_2	500
〈一ˊ	齊	0022_3	011	〈一ㄝˋ	鍥	8713_4	669
〈一ˊ	臍	7022_3	563	〈一ㄠ	敲	0124_7	032
〈一ˊ	耆	4460_1	408	〈一ㄠ	橇	4291_4	385
〈一ˊ	鰭	2436_1	209	〈一ㄠ	蹺	6212_7	538
〈一ˊ	祁	3722_7	334	〈一ㄠ	鍬	8913_0	681
〈一ˊ	畦	6401_4	543	〈一ㄠ	蹻	6411_1	546
〈一ˇ	起	4780_1	434	〈一ㄠˊ	嘺	6003_1	508
〈一ˇ	杞	4791_7	436	〈一ㄠˊ	瞧	6003_1	508
〈一ˇ	豈	2210_8	176	〈一ㄠˊ	瞧	6033_1	522
〈一ˇ	綺	2492_1	215	〈一ㄠˊ	譙	0063_1	028
〈一ˇ	啓	3860_4	349	〈一ㄠˊ	樵	4093_1	377
〈一ˇ	乞	8071_7	648	〈一ㄠˊ	憔	9003_1	684
〈一ˋ	企	8010_1	623	〈一ㄠˊ	喬	2022_2	145
〈一ˋ	訖	0861_7	056	〈一ㄠˊ	僑	2222_7	179
〈一ˋ	汽	3811_7	343	〈一ㄠˊ	橋	4292_7	385
〈一ˋ	迄	3830_1	348	〈一ㄠˊ	蕎	4422_7	399
〈一ˋ	砌	1762_0	137	〈一ㄠˊ	翹	4721_2	428
〈一ˋ	棄	0090_4	031	〈一ㄠˇ	巧	1112_7	103
〈一ˋ	磧	1568_6	125	〈一ㄠˇ	悄	9902_7	708
〈一ˋ	緝	2694_1	237	〈一ㄠˋ	誚	0962_7	057
〈一ˋ	泣	3011_8	272	〈一ㄠˋ	俏	2922_7	268
〈一ˋ	契	5743_0	500	〈一ㄠˋ	峭	2972_7	269
〈一ˋ	器	6666_3	553	〈一ㄠˋ	鞘	4952_7	444
〈一ˋ	氣	8091_7	654	〈一ㄠˋ	竅	3024_8	277
〈一ㄚˋ	洽	3816_1	347	〈一ㄠˋ	撬	5201_4	466
〈一ㄚˋ	恰	9806_1	706	〈一ㄡ	秋	2998_0	269
〈一ㄝ	切	4772_0	433	〈一ㄡ	鞦	4958_0	444

注　音	字	四　角	頁　碼	注　音	字	四　角	頁　碼
ㄑㄧㄡ	丘	7210_1	575	ㄑㄧㄢˋ	倩	2522_7	221
ㄑㄧㄡ	蚯	5211_1	471	ㄑㄧㄢˋ	蒨	4422_7	399
ㄑㄧㄡ	邱	7712_7	588	ㄑㄧㄢˋ	欠	2780_2	254
ㄑㄧㄡˊ	求	4313_2	387	ㄑㄧㄢˋ	歉	8738_2	670
ㄑㄧㄡˊ	球	1313_2	118	ㄑㄧㄢˋ	縴	2095_3	160
ㄑㄧㄡˊ	裘	4373_2	389	ㄑㄧㄢˋ	茜	4460_1	408
ㄑㄧㄡˊ	囚	6080_0	529	ㄑㄧㄢˋ	塹	5210_4	471
ㄑㄧㄡˊ	泅	3610_0	323	ㄑㄧㄣ	親	0691_0	047
ㄑㄧㄡˊ	犰	4421_7	398	ㄑㄧㄣ	侵	2724_7	243
ㄑㄧㄡˊ	酋	8060_1	645	ㄑㄧㄣ	駸	7734_7	603
ㄑㄧㄢ	千	2040_0	148	ㄑㄧㄣ	衾	8073_2	653
ㄑㄧㄢ	阡	7224_0	577	ㄑㄧㄣ	欽	8718_2	669
ㄑㄧㄢ	僉	8088_6	654	ㄑㄧㄣˊ	秦	5090_4	459
ㄑㄧㄢ	簽	8888_6	680	ㄑㄧㄣˊ	蠄	5519_4	485
ㄑㄧㄢ	遷	3130_1	294	ㄑㄧㄣˊ	禽	8042_7	639
ㄑㄧㄢ	韆	4153_1	380	ㄑㄧㄣˊ	擒	5802_7	502
ㄑㄧㄢ	牽	0050_2	026	ㄑㄧㄣˊ	琴	1120_7	104
ㄑㄧㄢ	謙	0863_7	056	ㄑㄧㄣˊ	勤	4412_7	394
ㄑㄧㄢ	嵌	2278_2	186	ㄑㄧㄣˊ	芹	4422_1	398
ㄑㄧㄢ	騫	3032_7	280	ㄑㄧㄣˇ	寢	3024_7	277
ㄑㄧㄢ	鉛	8716_1	669	ㄑㄧㄣˋ	沁	3310_0	303
ㄑㄧㄢ	籤	8815_3	672	ㄑㄧㄣˋ	撳	5708_2	499
ㄑㄧㄢ	慳	9701_4	703	ㄑㄧㄤ	鏹	8714_2	669
ㄑㄧㄢˊ	拑	5407_0	482	ㄑㄧㄤ	蹡	6714_2	558
ㄑㄧㄢˊ	鉗	8417_0	662	ㄑㄧㄤ	槍	4896_7	443
ㄑㄧㄢˊ	箝	8857_5	676	ㄑㄧㄤ	鎗	8816_7	672
ㄑㄧㄢˊ	虔	2124_0	168	ㄑㄧㄤ	腔	7321_2	580
ㄑㄧㄢˊ	潛	3116_1	292	ㄑㄧㄤ	羌	8021_1	628
ㄑㄧㄢˊ	掮	5302_7	473	ㄑㄧㄤˊ	牆	2426_1	207
ㄑㄧㄢˊ	黔	6832_7	561	ㄑㄧㄤˊ	薔	4460_1	408
ㄑㄧㄢˊ	前	8022_1	629	ㄑㄧㄤˊ	強	1323_6	119
ㄑㄧㄢˊ	錢	8315_3	661	ㄑㄧㄤˊ	戕	2325_0	196
ㄑㄧㄢˇ	譴	0563_7	045	ㄑㄧㄤˇ	襁	3323_6	307
ㄑㄧㄢˇ	遣	3530_8	322	ㄑㄧㄤˇ	鏹	8313_3	660
ㄑㄧㄢˇ	淺	3315_3	305	ㄑㄧㄤˇ	搶	5806_7	503

注音	字	四角	頁碼	注音	字	四角	頁碼
〈一尢ˋ	嗆	6806_7	561	〈ㄩˋ	趣	4780_4	434
〈一尢ˋ	蹌	6816_7	561	〈ㄩㄝ	缺	8573_0	664
〈一ㄥ	青	5022_7	452	〈ㄩㄝˋ	確	1461_4	122
〈一ㄥ	鯖	2532_2	223	〈ㄩㄝˋ	榷	4491_4	417
〈一ㄥ	清	3512_7	317	〈ㄩㄝˋ	摧	5401_4	480
〈一ㄥ	蜻	5512_7	485	〈ㄩㄝˋ	関	7743_0	604
〈一ㄥ	圊	6022_7	520	〈ㄩㄝˋ	闋	7748_2	606
〈一ㄥ	氫	8011_7	627	〈ㄩㄝˋ	鵲	4762_7	433
〈一ㄥ	氰	8021_7	629	〈ㄩㄝˋ	卻	8762_0	670
〈一ㄥ	傾	2128_6	170	〈ㄩㄝˋ	雀	9021_4	686
〈一ㄥ	卿	7772_0	610	〈ㄩㄝˋ	怯	9403_1	696
〈一ㄥ	輕	5101_1	461	〈ㄩㄢ	圈	6071_2	528
〈一ㄥˊ	晴	6502_7	548	〈ㄩㄢ	悛	9304_7	695
〈一ㄥˊ	情	9502_7	698	〈ㄩㄢˊ	全	8010_4	624
〈一ㄥˊ	擎	4850_2	441	〈ㄩㄢˊ	痊	0011_4	004
〈一ㄥˊ	黥	6039_6	522	〈ㄩㄢˊ	詮	0861_4	055
〈一ㄥˇ	請	0549_6	045	〈ㄩㄢˊ	輇	5801_4	501
〈一ㄥˇ	頃	2178_6	173	〈ㄩㄢˊ	銓	8811_4	672
〈一ㄥˋ	磬	4760_1	433	〈ㄩㄢˊ	顴	4128_6	380
〈一ㄥˋ	罄	4777_4	434	〈ㄩㄢˊ	權	4491_4	417
〈一ㄥˋ	慶	0024_7	018	〈ㄩㄢˊ	泉	2623_2	230
〈ㄩ	區	7171_6	573	〈ㄩㄢˊ	鬈	7271_2	578
〈ㄩ	驅	2121_6	164	〈ㄩㄢˊ	拳	9050_2	688
〈ㄩ	嶇	2171_6	173	〈ㄩㄢˊ	蜷	5911_2	506
〈ㄩ	驅	7131_6	571	〈ㄩㄢˇ	犬	4303_0	386
〈ㄩ	趨	4780_2	434	〈ㄩㄢˇ	畎	6303_4	540
〈ㄩ	蛆	5711_0	499	〈ㄩㄢˋ	勸	4422_7	399
〈ㄩ	胠	7423_1	582	〈ㄩㄢˋ	券	9022_7	686
〈ㄩ	屈	7727_2	601	〈ㄩㄣˊ	裙	3726_7	334
〈ㄩˊ	渠	3190_4	295	〈ㄩㄣˊ	羣	1750_1	135
〈ㄩˊ	瞿	6621_4	551	〈ㄩㄥˊ	穹	3020_7	274
〈ㄩˇ	取	1714_0	129	〈ㄩㄥˊ	窮	3022_7	276
〈ㄩˇ	娶	1740_4	134	〈ㄩㄥˊ	瓊	1714_7	130
〈ㄩˇ	曲	5560_0	486				
〈ㄩˋ	去	4073_1	374				

ㄒ

注 音	字	四 角	頁 碼	注 音	字	四 角	頁 碼
ㄒㄧ	僖	2426_5	207	ㄒㄧˊ	蓆	4422_7	399
ㄒㄧ	淅	3212_1	296	ㄒㄧˊ	襲	0173_2	035
ㄒㄧ	嬉	4446_5	406	ㄒㄧˊ	習	1760_2	135
ㄒㄧ	熹	4033_6	368	ㄒㄧˊ	檄	4894_0	443
ㄒㄧ	嘻	6406_5	545	ㄒㄧˊ	隰	7623_3	587
ㄒㄧ	析	4292_1	385	ㄒㄧˊ	錫	8612_7	665
ㄒㄧ	晳	4260_2	384	ㄒㄧˇ	喜	4060_5	373
ㄒㄧ	皙	4260_2	384	ㄒㄧˇ	禧	3426_5	314
ㄒㄧ	蜥	5212_1	471	ㄒㄧˇ	徙	2128_1	170
ㄒㄧ	晰	6202_1	537	ㄒㄧˇ	屣	7728_1	602
ㄒㄧ	希	4022_7	365	ㄒㄧˇ	璽	1010_3	069
ㄒㄧ	稀	2492_7	215	ㄒㄧˇ	洗	3411_1	309
ㄒㄧ	唏	6402_7	543	ㄒㄧˋ	系	2090_3	156
ㄒㄧ	谿	2846_8	264	ㄒㄧˋ	係	2229_3	182
ㄒㄧ	溪	3213_4	297	ㄒㄧˋ	翕	8012_7	627
ㄒㄧ	蹊	6213_4	538	ㄒㄧˋ	繫	5790_3	500
ㄒㄧ	羲	8025_3	632	ㄒㄧˋ	夕	2720_0	239
ㄒㄧ	犧	2855_3	265	ㄒㄧˋ	矽	1762_0	137
ㄒㄧ	曦	6805_3	561	ㄒㄧˋ	汐	3712_0	328
ㄒㄧ	扱	5704_7	496	ㄒㄧˋ	戲	2325_0	196
ㄒㄧ	吸	6704_7	556	ㄒㄧˋ	細	2690_0	234
ㄒㄧ	西	1060_0	087	ㄒㄧˋ	隙	7929_6	620
ㄒㄧ	悉	2033_9	148	ㄒㄧㄚ	蝦	5714_7	499
ㄒㄧ	蟋	5213_9	471	ㄒㄧㄚ	瞎	6306_1	540
ㄒㄧ	攜	5202_7	467	ㄒㄧㄚˊ	瑕	1714_7	130
ㄒㄧ	膝	7423_2	582	ㄒㄧㄚˊ	遐	3730_4	337
ㄒㄧ	犀	7725_3	600	ㄒㄧㄚˊ	暇	6704_7	556
ㄒㄧ	熙	7733_1	602	ㄒㄧㄚˊ	俠	2423_8	205
ㄒㄧ	兮	8020_7	628	ㄒㄧㄚˊ	峽	2473_8	212
ㄒㄧˊ	息	2633_0	233	ㄒㄧㄚˊ	狹	4423_8	400
ㄒㄧˊ	媳	4643_0	425	ㄒㄧㄚˊ	挾	5403_8	480
ㄒㄧˊ	熄	9683_0	702	ㄒㄧㄚˊ	狎	4625_6	423
ㄒㄧˊ	昔	4460_1	408	ㄒㄧㄚˊ	匣	7171_5	573
ㄒㄧˊ	惜	9406_1	697	ㄒㄧㄚˊ	霞	1024_7	079
ㄒㄧˊ	席	0022_7	013	ㄒㄧㄚˊ	轄	5306_1	475

注 音	字	四　角	頁　碼	注 音	字	四　角	頁　碼
ㄒㄧㄚˊ	呷	6605_0	550	ㄒㄧㄠ	綃	2992_7	269
ㄒㄧㄚˊ	黠	6436_1	547	ㄒㄧㄠ	宵	3022_7	275
ㄒㄧㄚˋ	夏	1024_7	078	ㄒㄧㄠ	消	3912_7	350
ㄒㄧㄚˋ	廈	0024_7	018	ㄒㄧㄠ	逍	3930_2	351
ㄒㄧㄚˋ	下	1023_0	076	ㄒㄧㄠ	蛸	5912_7	507
ㄒㄧㄚˋ	嚇	6403_1	544	ㄒㄧㄠ	銷	8912_7	681
ㄒㄧㄚˋ	罅	8174_9	657	ㄒㄧㄠ	削	9220_0	694
ㄒㄧㄝ	歇	6778_2	560	ㄒㄧㄠ	蕭	4422_7	399
ㄒㄧㄝ	蠍	5718_2	500	ㄒㄧㄠ	瀟	3412_7	311
ㄒㄧㄝ	些	2110_1	162	ㄒㄧㄠ	簫	8822_7	673
ㄒㄧㄝˊ	諧	0166_2	034	ㄒㄧㄠ	驍	7431_1	583
ㄒㄧㄝˊ	偕	2126_2	170	ㄒㄧㄠ	梟	2790_4	255
ㄒㄧㄝˊ	脅	4022_7	366	ㄒㄧㄠ	鴞	6722_7	559
ㄒㄧㄝˊ	協	4402_7	390	ㄒㄧㄠ	嚻	6666_8	553
ㄒㄧㄝˊ	鞋	4451_4	407	ㄒㄧㄠ	哮	6404_7	545
ㄒㄧㄝˊ	邪	7722_7	596	ㄒㄧㄠˇ	筱	8824_8	674
ㄒㄧㄝˊ	斜	8490_0	663	ㄒㄧㄠˇ	篠	8829_4	674
ㄒㄧㄝˇ	血	2710_0	237	ㄒㄧㄠˇ	小	9000_0	681
ㄒㄧㄝˇ	寫	3032_7	280	ㄒㄧㄠˇ	曉	6401_1	543
ㄒㄧㄝˋ	蟹	2713_6	239	ㄒㄧㄠˋ	孝	4440_7	404
ㄒㄧㄝˋ	邂	3730_4	337	ㄒㄧㄠˋ	酵	1464_7	123
ㄒㄧㄝˋ	懈	9705_2	704	ㄒㄧㄠˋ	效	0844_0	055
ㄒㄧㄝˋ	瀉	3312_7	303	ㄒㄧㄠˋ	傚	2824_0	261
ㄒㄧㄝˋ	泄	3411_7	310	ㄒㄧㄠˋ	校	4094_8	378
ㄒㄧㄝˋ	洩	3510_6	317	ㄒㄧㄠˋ	効	0442_7	041
ㄒㄧㄝˋ	械	4395_0	390	ㄒㄧㄠˋ	嘯	6502_7	548
ㄒㄧㄝˋ	楔	4793_4	437	ㄒㄧㄠˋ	笑	8843_0	675
ㄒㄧㄝˋ	褻	0073_2	031	ㄒㄧㄠˋ	肖	9022_7	686
ㄒㄧㄝˋ	謝	0460_0	042	ㄒㄧㄡ	休	2429_0	208
ㄒㄧㄝˋ	屑	7722_7	596	ㄒㄧㄡ	咻	6409_0	546
ㄒㄧㄝˋ	卸	8712_0	667	ㄒㄧㄡ	羞	8021_5	628
ㄒㄧㄝˋ	爕	9940_7	708	ㄒㄧㄡ	饈	8871_7	677
ㄒㄧㄝˋ	緤	2590_6	223	ㄒㄧㄡ	修	2722_2	242
ㄒㄧㄠ	霄	1022_7	076	ㄒㄧㄡˇ	朽	4192_7	382
ㄒㄧㄠ	硝	1962_7	142	ㄒㄧㄡˋ	漠	3613_4	324

注　音	字	四　角	頁　碼	注　音	字	四　角	頁　碼
ㄒㄧㄡˋ	嗅	6603_4	550	ㄒㄧㄢˋ	現	1611_0	125
ㄒㄧㄡˋ	秀	2022_7	145	ㄒㄧㄢˋ	綫	2395_3	199
ㄒㄧㄡˋ	銹	8212_7	658	ㄒㄧㄢˋ	莧	4421_6	398
ㄒㄧㄡˋ	繡	2592_7	224	ㄒㄧㄢˋ	陷	7727_7	601
ㄒㄧㄡˋ	鏽	8512_7	664	ㄒㄧㄢˋ	餡	8777_7	671
ㄒㄧㄡˋ	袖	3526_0	321	ㄒㄧㄢˋ	霰	1024_8	079
ㄒㄧㄢ	仙	2227_0	182	ㄒㄧㄢˋ	獻	2323_4	194
ㄒㄧㄢ	纖	2395_0	199	ㄒㄧㄢˋ	線	2693_2	237
ㄒㄧㄢ	先	2421_1	203	ㄒㄧㄢˋ	憲	3033_6	280
ㄒㄧㄢ	鮮	2835_1	264	ㄒㄧㄢˋ	縣	6299_3	540
ㄒㄧㄢ	暹	3630_1	326	ㄒㄧㄢˋ	腺	7623_2	587
ㄒㄧㄢ	銛	8216_4	658	ㄒㄧㄢˋ	限	7723_2	597
ㄒㄧㄢ	掀	5708_2	498	ㄒㄧㄢˋ	羨	8018_2	627
ㄒㄧㄢ	躚	6113_1	534	ㄒㄧㄣ	辛	0040_1	023
ㄒㄧㄢˊ	弦	1023_2	078	ㄒㄧㄣ	莘	4440_1	403
ㄒㄧㄢˊ	舷	2043_2	152	ㄒㄧㄣ	鋅	8014_1	627
ㄒㄧㄢˊ	絃	2093_2	160	ㄒㄧㄣ	新	0292_1	037
ㄒㄧㄢˊ	澗	3712_0	328	ㄒㄧㄣ	薪	4492_1	417
ㄒㄧㄢˊ	閒	7722_7	597	ㄒㄧㄣ	訢	0262_1	036
ㄒㄧㄢˊ	嫻	4742_0	430	ㄒㄧㄣ	忻	9202_1	693
ㄒㄧㄢˊ	啣	6702_0	555	ㄒㄧㄣ	歆	0768_2	052
ㄒㄧㄢˊ	咸	5320_0	478	ㄒㄧㄣ	欣	7728_2	602
ㄒㄧㄢˊ	鹹	2365_0	197	ㄒㄧㄣ	心	3300_0	301
ㄒㄧㄢˊ	銜	2122_1	166	ㄒㄧㄣ	鑫	8011_9	627
ㄒㄧㄢˊ	涎	3214_1	297	ㄒㄧㄣ	馨	4760_9	433
ㄒㄧㄢˊ	嫌	4843_7	440	ㄒㄧㄣˋ	信	2026_1	147
ㄒㄧㄢˊ	賢	7780_6	614	ㄒㄧㄣˋ	釁	7722_7	597
ㄒㄧㄢˊ	閑	7790_4	615	ㄒㄧㄤ	相	4690_0	425
ㄒㄧㄢˇ	跣	6411_1	546	ㄒㄧㄤ	廂	0026_0	019
ㄒㄧㄢˇ	銑	8411_1	661	ㄒㄧㄤ	湘	3610_0	323
ㄒㄧㄢˇ	癬	0015_1	007	ㄒㄧㄤ	箱	8896_2	681
ㄒㄧㄢˇ	蘚	4435_1	403	ㄒㄧㄤ	襄	0073_2	031
ㄒㄧㄢˇ	顯	6138_6	535	ㄒㄧㄤ	瓖	1013_2	072
ㄒㄧㄢˇ	險	7828_6	618	ㄒㄧㄤ	驤	7033_2	565
ㄒㄧㄢˇ	蜆	5611_0	492	ㄒㄧㄤ	鑲	8013_2	627

注　音	字	四　角	頁　碼	注　音	字	四　角	頁　碼
ㄒㄧㄤ	香	2060_9	155	ㄒㄩ	墟	4111_7	379
ㄒㄧㄤ	鄉	2772_7	254	ㄒㄩ	噓	6101_7	533
ㄒㄧㄤˊ	詳	0865_1	056	ㄒㄩ	吁	6104_0	534
ㄒㄧㄤˊ	祥	3825_1	347	ㄒㄩ	盱	6104_0	534
ㄒㄧㄤˊ	翔	8752_0	670	ㄒㄩ	須	2128_6	170
ㄒㄧㄤˊ	降	7725_4	600	ㄒㄩ	鬚	7228_6	578
ㄒㄧㄤˇ	響	2760_1	251	ㄒㄩ	需	1022_7	076
ㄒㄧㄤˇ	饗	2773_2	254	ㄒㄩ	胥	1722_7	131
ㄒㄧㄤˇ	享	0040_7	023	ㄒㄩˊ	徐	2829_4	264
ㄒㄧㄤˇ	想	4633_0	424	ㄒㄩˇ	詡	0762_0	049
ㄒㄧㄤˇ	餉	8772_0	671	ㄒㄩˇ	許	0864_0	056
ㄒㄧㄤˋ	象	2723_2	242	ㄒㄩˇ	煦	6733_2	559
ㄒㄧㄤˋ	像	2723_2	243	ㄒㄩˇ	卹	2712_0	238
ㄒㄧㄤˋ	橡	4793_2	437	ㄒㄩˋ	洫	3711_0	327
ㄒㄧㄤˋ	項	1118_6	103	ㄒㄩˋ	恤	9701_0	703
ㄒㄧㄤˋ	向	2722_0	241	ㄒㄩˋ	敘	8894_0	681
ㄒㄧㄤˋ	巷	4471_2	411	ㄒㄩˋ	敍	8194_7	657
ㄒㄧㄤˋ	相	4690_0	425	ㄒㄩˋ	叙	8794_0	671
ㄒㄧㄥ	星	6010_4	511	ㄒㄩˋ	緒	2496_0	215
ㄒㄧㄥ	猩	4621_4	422	ㄒㄩˋ	續	2498_6	216
ㄒㄧㄥ	腥	7621_4	586	ㄒㄩˋ	序	0022_2	011
ㄒㄧㄥ	惺	9601_4	701	ㄒㄩˋ	酗	1267_0	117
ㄒㄧㄥ	興	7780_1	613	ㄒㄩˋ	蓄	4460_3	408
ㄒㄧㄥˊ	型	1210_4	108	ㄒㄩˋ	旭	4601_0	421
ㄒㄧㄥˊ	刑	1240_0	114	ㄒㄩˋ	絮	4690_3	426
ㄒㄧㄥˊ	形	1242_2	115	ㄒㄩˋ	壻	4712_7	427
ㄒㄧㄥˊ	行	2122_1	165	ㄒㄩㄝ	靴	4451_0	407
ㄒㄧㄥˇ	醒	1661_4	128	ㄒㄩㄝ	薛	4474_1	412
ㄒㄧㄥˋ	幸	4040_1	369	ㄒㄩㄝ	噱	6103_2	534
ㄒㄧㄥˋ	倖	2424_1	206	ㄒㄩㄝˊ	學	7740_7	603
ㄒㄧㄥˋ	悻	9404_1	696	ㄒㄩㄝˇ	雪	1017_7	073
ㄒㄧㄥˋ	姓	4541_0	419	ㄒㄩㄝˋ	謞	0062_7	028
ㄒㄧㄥˋ	性	9501_4	698	ㄒㄩㄝˋ	穴	3080_2	288
ㄒㄧㄥˋ	杏	4060_9	373	ㄒㄩㄢ	宣	3010_6	270
ㄒㄩ	虛	2121_7	164	ㄒㄩㄢ	諠	0361_7	039

注　音	字	四　角	頁　碼	注　音	字	四　角	頁　碼
ㄒㄩㄢ	萱	4410_6	392	ㄒㄩㄣˋ	汛	3711_0	327
ㄒㄩㄢ	喧	6301_6	540	ㄒㄩㄣˋ	迅	3730_1	334
ㄒㄩㄢ	煊	9381_6	695	ㄒㄩㄣˋ	訓	0260_0	036
ㄒㄩㄢ	諼	0264_7	037	ㄒㄩㄣˋ	殉	1722_0	131
ㄒㄩㄢ	軒	5104_0	463	ㄒㄩㄣˋ	遜	3230_9	301
ㄒㄩㄢˊ	旋	0828_1	054	ㄒㄩㄣˋ	蕈	4440_6	404
ㄒㄩㄢˊ	漩	3818_1	347	ㄒㄩㄣˋ	巽	7780_1	613
ㄒㄩㄢˊ	玄	0073_2	030	ㄒㄩㄥ	凶	2277_0	184
ㄒㄩㄢˊ	懸	6233_9	539	ㄒㄩㄥ	訩	0267_0	037
ㄒㄩㄢˇ	選	3730_8	339	ㄒㄩㄥ	匈	2772_0	254
ㄒㄩㄢˋ	眩	6003_2	508	ㄒㄩㄥ	兇	2221_7	179
ㄒㄩㄢˋ	炫	9083_2	691	ㄒㄩㄥ	洶	3712_0	328
ㄒㄩㄢˋ	鏇	8818_1	672	ㄒㄩㄥ	胸	7722_0	595
ㄒㄩㄣ	熏	2033_1	148	ㄒㄩㄥ	恟	9702_0	703
ㄒㄩㄣ	醺	1263_1	117	ㄒㄩㄥ	兄	6021_0	519
ㄒㄩㄣ	勳	2432_0	209	ㄒㄩㄥˊ	熊	2133_1	172
ㄒㄩㄣ	薰	4433_1	402	ㄒㄩㄥˊ	雄	4001_4	353
ㄒㄩㄣ	曛	6203_1	537				
ㄒㄩㄣ	燻	9283_1	694				

ㄓ

注　音	字	四　角	頁　碼
ㄒㄩㄣ	勛	6482_7	548

注　音	字	四　角	頁　碼
ㄒㄩㄣˊ	旬	2762_0	252
ㄒㄩㄣˊ	詢	0762_0	049
ㄒㄩㄣˊ	徇	2722_0	242
ㄒㄩㄣˊ	洵	3712_0	328
ㄒㄩㄣˊ	荀	4462_7	410
ㄒㄩㄣˊ	恂	9702_0	703
ㄒㄩㄣˊ	尋	1734_1	133
ㄒㄩㄣˊ	鱘	2734_1	248
ㄒㄩㄣˊ	潯	3714_1	330
ㄒㄩㄣˊ	樳	4794_1	437
ㄒㄩㄣˊ	循	2226_4	182
ㄒㄩㄣˊ	巡	3230_2	300
ㄒㄩㄣˊ	馴	7230_0	578
ㄒㄩㄣˋ	徇	2722_0	242
ㄒㄩㄣˋ	訊	0761_0	048

注　音	字	四　角	頁　碼
ㄓ	支	4040_7	369
ㄓ	枝	4494_7	418
ㄓ	肢	7424_7	583
ㄓ	胝	7224_0	577
ㄓ	知	8640_0	665
ㄓ	蜘	5610_0	492
ㄓ	之	3030_7	280
ㄓ	芝	4430_7	401
ㄓ	隻	2040_7	150
ㄓ	織	2395_0	199
ㄓ	汁	3410_0	308
ㄓ	脂	7126_1	569
ㄓˊ	直	4010_7	360
ㄓˊ	殖	1421_7	122
ㄓˊ	值	2421_7	204

注 音	字	四 角	頁 碼	注 音	字	四 角	頁 碼
ㄓˊ	植	4491_7	417	ㄓˋ	峙	2474_1	213
ㄓˊ	擲	5702_7	495	ㄓˋ	摯	4450_2	406
ㄓˊ	躑	6712_7	558	ㄓˋ	贄	4480_6	414
ㄓˊ	摭	5003_1	449	ㄓˋ	秩	2593_0	224
ㄓˊ	蹠	6013_7	513	ㄓˋ	炙	2780_9	255
ㄓˊ	職	1315_0	118	ㄓˋ	治	3316_0	305
ㄓˊ	姪	4141_4	380	ㄓˋ	滯	3412_7	311
ㄓˊ	執	4441_7	404	ㄓˋ	幟	4325_0	388
ㄓˊ	跖	6116_0	534	ㄓˋ	置	6010_7	511
ㄓˊ	質	7280_6	579	ㄓˋ	陟	7122_1	567
ㄓˇ	止	2110_0	162	ㄓˋ	智	8660_0	666
ㄓˇ	祉	3121_0	293	ㄓˋ	忮	9404_7	696
ㄓˇ	址	4111_0	379	ㄓㄨ	朱	2590_0	223
ㄓˇ	趾	6111_0	534	ㄓㄨ	讀	0568_6	046
ㄓˇ	旨	2160_1	172	ㄓㄨ	誅	0569_0	046
ㄓˇ	指	5106_1	464	ㄓㄨ	侏	2529_0	223
ㄓˇ	紙	2294_0	189	ㄓㄨ	硃	1569_0	125
ㄓˇ	祇	3224_0	299	ㄓㄨ	珠	1519_0	124
ㄓˇ	咫	7680_8	587	ㄓㄨ	茱	4490_4	416
ㄓˇ	只	6080_0	529	ㄓㄨ	株	4599_0	420
ㄓˋ	至	1010_4	069	ㄓㄨ	蛛	5519_0	485
ㄓˋ	致	1814_0	140	ㄓㄨ	銖	8519_0	664
ㄓˋ	緻	2894_0	267	ㄓㄨ	豬	1426_0	122
ㄓˋ	窒	3010_4	270	ㄓㄨ	猪	4426_0	401
ㄓˋ	桎	4191_4	381	ㄓㄨ	諸	0466_0	044
ㄓˋ	蛭	5111_4	465	ㄓㄨ	櫧	4496_0	418
ㄓˋ	志	4033_1	368	ㄓㄨˊ	竹	8822_0	673
ㄓˋ	痣	0013_1	006	ㄓㄨˊ	竺	8810_1	671
ㄓˋ	誌	0463_1	043	ㄓㄨˊ	筑	8811_7	672
ㄓˋ	制	2220_0	177	ㄓㄨˊ	築	8890_4	680
ㄓˋ	製	2273_2	184	ㄓㄨˊ	蠋	5612_7	492
ㄓˋ	稚	2091_4	158	ㄓㄨˊ	躅	6612_7	551
ㄓˋ	躓	6218_6	538	ㄓㄨˊ	燭	9682_7	702
ㄓˋ	雉	8041_4	639	ㄓㄨˊ	逐	3130_3	294
ㄓˋ	痔	0014_1	007	ㄓㄨˇ	主	0010_4	001

注　音	字	四　角	頁　碼	注　音	字	四　角	頁　碼
ㄓㄨˇ	煮	4433_6	403	ㄓㄨㄛˊ	鐲	8612_7	665
ㄓㄨˇ	貯	6382_1	542	ㄓㄨㄛˊ	斫	1262_1	117
ㄓㄨˇ	囑	6702_7	555	ㄓㄨㄛˊ	斲	7212_1	575
ㄓㄨˋ	住	2021_4	144	ㄓㄨㄛˊ	卓	2140_6	172
ㄓㄨˋ	註	0061_4	028	ㄓㄨㄛˊ	著	4460_4	409
ㄓㄨˋ	注	3011_4	272	ㄓㄨㄟ	隹	2021_4	144
ㄓㄨˋ	柱	4091_4	377	ㄓㄨㄟ	追	3730_7	338
ㄓㄨˋ	蛀	5011_4	451	ㄓㄨㄟ	椎	4091_4	377
ㄓㄨˋ	駐	7031_4	564	ㄓㄨㄟ	錐	8011_4	626
ㄓㄨˋ	炷	9081_4	691	ㄓㄨㄟˋ	綴	2794_7	259
ㄓㄨˋ	苎	0312_1	038	ㄓㄨㄟˋ	贅	5880_6	505
ㄓㄨˋ	佇	2322_1	193	ㄓㄨㄟˋ	墜	7810_4	615
ㄓㄨˋ	竚	4420_1	396	ㄓㄨㄟˋ	惴	9202_7	693
ㄓㄨˋ	著	4460_4	409	ㄓㄨㄢ	專	5034_3	454
ㄓㄨˋ	箸	8860_4	677	ㄓㄨㄢ	磚	1564_3	125
ㄓㄨˋ	祝	3621_0	325	ㄓㄨㄢˇ	轉	5504_3	483
ㄓㄨˋ	杼	4792_2	436	ㄓㄨㄢˋ	撰	5708_1	498
ㄓㄨˋ	助	7412_7	581	ㄓㄨㄢˋ	饌	8778_1	671
ㄓㄨˋ	鑄	8414_1	662	ㄓㄨㄢˋ	賺	6883_7	561
ㄓㄨㄚ	抓	5203_0	467	ㄓㄨㄢˋ	篆	8823_2	674
ㄓㄨㄚ	撾	5703_2	495	ㄓㄨㄣ	諄	0064_7	028
ㄓㄨㄚˇ	爪	7223_0	577	ㄓㄨㄣ	肫	7521_7	585
ㄓㄨㄛ	桌	2190_4	173	ㄓㄨㄣˇ	准	3011_4	272
ㄓㄨㄛ	涿	3113_2	291	ㄓㄨㄣˇ	準	3040_1	281
ㄓㄨㄛ	捉	5608_1	490	ㄓㄨㄤ	裝	2473_2	212
ㄓㄨㄛ	諑	0163_2	034	ㄓㄨㄤ	莊	4421_4	398
ㄓㄨㄛˊ	琢	1113_2	103	ㄓㄨㄤ	妝	2424_0	205
ㄓㄨㄛˊ	啄	6103_2	534	ㄓㄨㄤ	粧	9091_4	691
ㄓㄨㄛˊ	酌	1762_0	137	ㄓㄨㄤ	樁	4597_7	420
ㄓㄨㄛˊ	灼	9782_0	705	ㄓㄨㄤˋ	狀	2323_4	194
ㄓㄨㄛˊ	茁	4477_2	412	ㄓㄨㄤˋ	壯	2421_0	202
ㄓㄨㄛˊ	拙	5207_2	470	ㄓㄨㄤˋ	撞	5001_4	448
ㄓㄨㄛˊ	濯	3711_4	328	ㄓㄨㄥ	中	5000_6	444
ㄓㄨㄛˊ	擢	5701_4	493	ㄓㄨㄥ	盅	5010_7	451
ㄓㄨㄛˊ	濁	3612_7	324	ㄓㄨㄥ	忠	5033_6	453

注音	字	四角	頁碼	注音	字	四角	頁碼
ㄓㄨㄥ	鐘	8011_4	626	ㄓㄜˊ	摺	5706_2	498
ㄓㄨㄥ	鍾	8211_4	658	ㄓㄜˊ	謫	0062_7	028
ㄓㄨㄥ	衷	0073_2	030	ㄓㄜˊ	輒	5101_0	460
ㄓㄨㄥ	終	2793_3	258	ㄓㄜˊ	慴	9104_1	692
ㄓㄨㄥˇ	種	2291_4	188	ㄓㄜˇ	者	4460_0	408
ㄓㄨㄥˇ	踵	6211_4	538	ㄓㄜˇ	赭	4436_0	403
ㄓㄨㄥˇ	腫	7221_4	576	ㄓㄜˋ	蔗	4423_7	400
ㄓㄨㄥˇ	冢	3723_2	334	ㄓㄜˋ	鷓	0722_7	048
ㄓㄨㄥˇ	塚	4713_2	427	ㄓㄜˋ	這	3030_6	280
ㄓㄨㄥˋ	重	2010_4	142	ㄓㄜˋ	浙	3212_1	296
ㄓㄨㄥˋ	種	2291_4	188	ㄓㄜˋ	柘	4196_0	382
ㄓㄨㄥˋ	仲	2520_6	220	ㄓㄞ	齋	0022_3	011
ㄓㄨㄥˋ	眾	6023_2	520	ㄓㄞ	摘	5002_7	449
ㄓㄚ	渣	3411_6	310	ㄓㄞˊ	宅	3071_4	286
ㄓㄚ	楂	4491_6	417	ㄓㄞˇ	窄	3021_1	274
ㄓㄚˊ	札	4291_0	385	ㄓㄞˋ	債	2528_6	223
ㄓㄚˊ	閘	7750_6	606	ㄓㄞˋ	寨	3090_4	290
ㄓㄚˊ	鍘	8210_0	658	ㄓㄠ	召	1760_2	135
ㄓㄚˊ	劄	8260_0	658	ㄓㄠ	招	5706_2	497
ㄓㄚˇ	眨	6203_7	537	ㄓㄠ	昭	6706_2	556
ㄓㄚˋ	乍	8021_1	628	ㄓㄠ	朝	4742_0	430
ㄓㄚˋ	炸	9881_1	707	ㄓㄠˊ	着	8060_1	645
ㄓㄚˋ	詐	0861_1	055	ㄓㄠˇ	沼	3716_2	331
ㄓㄚˋ	榨	4391_1	390	ㄓㄠˇ	找	5305_0	475
ㄓㄚˋ	搾	5301_1	473	ㄓㄠˋ	兆	3211_3	296
ㄓㄚˋ	蚱	5811_1	504	ㄓㄠˋ	晁	6011_3	512
ㄓㄚˋ	咋	6802_1	561	ㄓㄠˋ	詔	0766_2	051
ㄓㄚˋ	柵	4794_5	437	ㄓㄠˋ	照	6733_6	559
ㄓㄚˋ	咤	6301_4	540	ㄓㄠˋ	焯	9786_2	705
ㄓㄜ	遮	3030_3	279	ㄓㄠˋ	棹	4194_6	382
ㄓㄜ	螫	5813_6	504	ㄓㄠˋ	罩	6040_6	523
ㄓㄜˊ	折	5202_1	466	ㄓㄠˋ	肇	3850_7	349
ㄓㄜˊ	蜇	5213_6	471	ㄓㄠˋ	趙	4980_2	444
ㄓㄜˊ	哲	5260_2	472	ㄓㄡ	洲	3210_0	295
ㄓㄜˊ	褶	3726_2	334	ㄓㄡ	周	7722_0	594

注 音	字	四 角	頁 碼	注 音	字	四 角	頁 碼
ㄓㄡ	喌	6702_0	554	ㄓㄢˋ	湛	3411_8	310
ㄓㄡ	週	3730_2	336	ㄓㄢˋ	棧	4395_3	390
ㄓㄡ	擣	0464_1	043	ㄓㄢˋ	暫	5260_2	472
ㄓㄡ	粥	1722_7	131	ㄓㄢˋ	戰	6355_0	541
ㄓㄡ	舟	2744_0	249	ㄓㄣ	貞	2180_6	173
ㄓㄡ	州	3200_0	295	ㄓㄣ	偵	2128_6	170
ㄓㄡˊ	軸	5506_0	484	ㄓㄣ	禎	3128_6	293
ㄓㄡˇ	帚	1722_7	131	ㄓㄣ	臻	1519_4	124
ㄓㄡˇ	箒	8822_7	673	ㄓㄣ	溱	4490_4	416
ㄓㄡˇ	肘	7420_0	582	ㄓㄣ	榛	4599_4	420
ㄓㄡˋ	皺	2444_7	209	ㄓㄣ	箴	8825_3	674
ㄓㄡˋ	縐	2792_7	258	ㄓㄣ	鍼	8315_0	660
ㄓㄡˋ	呪	6601_1	550	ㄓㄣ	甄	1111_7	103
ㄓㄡˋ	咒	6621_7	551	ㄓㄣ	砧	1166_0	107
ㄓㄡˋ	宙	3060_5	284	ㄓㄣ	珍	1812_2	139
ㄓㄡˋ	晝	5010_6	451	ㄓㄣ	真	4080_1	375
ㄓㄡˋ	冑	5022_7	452	ㄓㄣ	斟	4470_0	410
ㄓㄢ	占	2160_0	172	ㄓㄣ	針	8410_0	661
ㄓㄢ	沾	3116_0	292	ㄓㄣ	胗	7822_2	617
ㄓㄢ	佔	6106_0	534	ㄓㄣˇ	疹	0012_2	004
ㄓㄢ	詹	2726_1	245	ㄓㄣˇ	診	0862_2	056
ㄓㄢ	譫	0766_1	051	ㄓㄣˇ	軫	5802_2	502
ㄓㄢ	瞻	6706_1	556	ㄓㄣˇ	畛	6802_2	561
ㄓㄢ	氈	0211_4	035	ㄓㄣˇ	枕	4491_2	416
ㄓㄢˇ	展	7723_2	597	ㄓㄣˋ	震	1023_2	078
ㄓㄢˇ	輾	5703_2	495	ㄓㄣˋ	振	5103_2	463
ㄓㄢˇ	蹍	6713_2	558	ㄓㄣˋ	賑	6183_2	536
ㄓㄢˇ	斬	5202_1	467	ㄓㄣˋ	酖	1461_2	122
ㄓㄢˇ	盞	5310_7	476	ㄓㄣˋ	摵	5401_1	479
ㄓㄢˇ	颭	7121_6	566	ㄓㄣˋ	陣	7520_6	584
ㄓㄢˋ	占	2160_0	172	ㄓㄣˋ	鎮	8418_1	663
ㄓㄢˋ	站	0116_1	032	ㄓㄣˋ	朕	7823_4	618
ㄓㄢˋ	佔	2126_0	170	ㄓㄤ	章	0040_6	023
ㄓㄢˋ	顫	0118_6	032	ㄓㄤ	彰	0242_2	035
ㄓㄢˋ	綻	2398_1	199	ㄓㄤ	璋	1014_6	072

注 音	字	四　角	頁　碼	注 音	字	四　角	頁　碼
ㄓㄤ	樟	4094_6	378	ㄓㄥˋ	掙	5205_7	469
ㄓㄤ	蟑	5014_6	452	ㄓㄥˋ	鄭	8742_7	670
ㄓㄤ	張	1123_2	105				
ㄓㄤˇ	掌	9050_2	688			**ㄔ**	
ㄓㄤˋ	漲	3113_2	291	注 音	字	四　角	頁　碼
ㄓㄤˋ	帳	4123_2	379	ㄔ	癡	0018_1	007
ㄓㄤˋ	賬	6183_2	536	ㄔ	嗤	6203_6	537
ㄓㄤˋ	脹	7123_2	567	ㄔ	喫	6703_4	556
ㄓㄤˋ	瘴	0014_6	007	ㄔ	吃	6801_7	560
ㄓㄤˋ	嶂	2074_6	156	ㄔ	鴟	7772_7	610
ㄓㄤˋ	幛	4024_6	366	ㄔ	答	8860_3	677
ㄓㄤˋ	障	7024_6	564	ㄔˊ	弛	1421_2	122
ㄓㄤˋ	丈	5000_0	444	ㄔˊ	池	3411_2	310
ㄓㄤˋ	仗	2520_0	220	ㄔˊ	遲	3730_4	338
ㄓㄤˋ	杖	4590_0	419	ㄔˊ	馳	7431_2	584
ㄓㄥ	爭	2050_7	153	ㄔˊ	持	5404_1	480
ㄓㄥ	諍	0265_7	037	ㄔˊ	踟	6610_0	551
ㄓㄥ	猙	4225_7	383	ㄔˇ	尺	7780_7	614
ㄓㄥ	睜	6205_7	538	ㄔˇ	呎	6708_7	557
ㄓㄥ	錚	8215_7	658	ㄔˇ	恥	1310_0	117
ㄓㄥ	箏	8850_7	676	ㄔˇ	齒	2177_2	173
ㄓㄥ	征	2121_1	163	ㄔˇ	侈	2722_7	242
ㄓㄥ	鉦	8111_1	655	ㄔˇ	褫	3221_7	299
ㄓㄥ	怔	9101_1	691	ㄔˋ	斥	7223_1	577
ㄓㄥ	徵	2824_0	262	ㄔˋ	赤	4033_1	368
ㄓㄥ	癥	0014_8	007	ㄔˋ	翅	4740_2	430
ㄓㄥ	蒸	4433_1	401	ㄔˋ	勅	5492_7	482
ㄓㄥˇ	整	5810_1	504	ㄔˋ	敕	5894_0	506
ㄓㄥˇ	拯	5701_3	493	ㄔˋ	叱	6401_0	543
ㄓㄥˋ	正	1010_1	068	ㄔˋ	飭	8872_7	677
ㄓㄥˋ	症	0011_1	003	ㄔˋ	熾	9385_0	696
ㄓㄥˋ	証	0161_1	033	ㄔㄨ	出	2277_2	184
ㄓㄥˋ	政	1814_0	139	ㄔㄨ	初	3722_0	333
ㄓㄥˋ	證	0261_8	036	ㄔㄨˊ	廚	0024_0	017
ㄓㄥˋ	幀	4128_6	380	ㄔㄨˊ	厨	7124_0	568

注 音	字	四 角	頁 碼	注 音	字	四 角	頁 碼
彳ㄨˊ	櫥	4094_0	377	彳ㄨㄟˊ	槌	4793_7	437
彳ㄨˊ	蹰	6014_0	513	彳ㄨㄟˊ	搥	5703_7	495
彳ㄨˊ	躕	6114_0	534	彳ㄨㄟˊ	鎚	8713_7	669
彳ㄨˊ	蒭	2742_7	249	彳ㄨㄢ	川	2200_0	176
彳ㄨˊ	雛	2041_4	151	彳ㄨㄢ	釧	8210_0	658
彳ㄨˊ	鶵	2742_7	249	彳ㄨㄢ	穿	3024_1	277
彳ㄨˊ	蜍	5819_4	505	彳ㄨㄢˊ	傳	2524_3	221
彳ㄨˊ	除	7829_4	618	彳ㄨㄢˊ	船	2746_1	250
彳ㄨˊ	耡	5492_7	482	彳ㄨㄢˊ	遄	3230_2	300
彳ㄨˊ	鋤	8412_7	662	彳ㄨㄢˊ	椽	4793_2	436
彳ㄨˊ	儲	2426_0	206	彳ㄨㄢˇ	喘	6202_7	537
彳ㄨˊ	鉏	8711_0	667	彳ㄨㄢˋ	串	5000_6	446
彳ㄨˇ	楚	4480_1	414	彳ㄨㄣ	春	5060_3	456
彳ㄨˇ	礎	1468_1	124	彳ㄨㄣ	椿	4596_3	420
彳ㄨˇ	處	2124_1	168	彳ㄨㄣˊ	醇	1064_7	090
彳ㄨˇ	褚	3426_0	314	彳ㄨㄣˊ	鶉	0742_7	048
彳ㄨˇ	杵	4894_0	443	彳ㄨㄣˊ	淳	3014_7	273
彳ㄨˋ	畜	0060_3	027	彳ㄨㄣˊ	唇	7160_3	572
彳ㄨˋ	處	2124_1	168	彳ㄨㄣˊ	脣	7122_7	567
彳ㄨˋ	觸	2622_7	230	彳ㄨㄣˊ	純	2591_7	223
彳ㄨˋ	矗	4011_7	361	彳ㄨㄣˇ	蠢	5013_6	452
彳ㄨˋ	黜	6237_2	539	彳ㄨㄤ	瘡	0016_7	007
彳ㄨˋ	怵	9309_4	695	彳ㄨㄤ	窗	3060_2	284
彳ㄨㄛ	戳	1325_0	119	彳ㄨㄤˊ	牀	2429_0	209
彳ㄨㄛˋ	綽	2194_6	175	彳ㄨㄤˇ	闖	7732_7	602
彳ㄨㄛˋ	輟	5704_7	497	彳ㄨㄤˋ	創	8260_0	659
彳ㄨㄛˋ	啜	6704_7	556	彳ㄨㄤˋ	愴	9806_7	707
彳ㄨㄞˇ	揣	5202_7	467	彳ㄨㄥ	充	0021_3	009
彳ㄨㄞˋ	踹	6212_7	538	彳ㄨㄥ	沖	3510_6	317
彳ㄨㄟ	吹	6708_2	557	彳ㄨㄥ	仲	9500_6	698
彳ㄨㄟ	炊	9788_2	705	彳ㄨㄥ	衝	2122_1	167
彳ㄨㄟˊ	垂	2010_4	142	彳ㄨㄥ	舂	5077_7	457
彳ㄨㄟˊ	捶	5201_4	466	彳ㄨㄥ	憧	9001_4	683
彳ㄨㄟˊ	陲	7221_4	576	彳ㄨㄥˊ	重	2010_4	142
彳ㄨㄟˊ	錘	8211_4	658	彳ㄨㄥˊ	崇	2290_1	187

注音	字	四角	頁碼	注音	字	四角	頁碼
彳ㄨㄥˊ	蟲	5013_6	452	彳ㄡˊ	疇	6404_1	545
彳ㄨㄥˇ	寵	3021_1	274	彳ㄡˊ	躊	6414_1	546
彳ㄨㄥˋ	銃	8011_3	626	彳ㄡˊ	籌	8864_1	677
彳ㄚ	叉	4000_0	352	彳ㄡˊ	綢	2792_0	257
彳ㄚ	插	5207_7	470	彳ㄡˊ	稠	2792_0	257
彳ㄚ	差	8021_1	628	彳ㄡˊ	惆	9702_0	703
彳ㄚˊ	察	3090_1	290	彳ㄡˊ	酬	1260_0	116
彳ㄚˊ	查	4010_6	360	彳ㄡˊ	讎	2021_4	144
彳ㄚˊ	茶	4490_4	415	彳ㄡˊ	仇	2421_7	204
彳ㄚˋ	詫	0361_4	039	彳ㄡˊ	愁	2933_8	268
彳ㄚˋ	姹	4341_4	388	彳ㄡˇ	醜	1661_3	128
彳ㄚˋ	岔	8077_2	654	彳ㄡˇ	丑	1710_5	128
彳ㄜ	車	5000_6	447	彳ㄡˋ	臭	2643_0	233
彳ㄜˇ	扯	5101_0	459	彳ㄢ	攙	5701_3	493
彳ㄜˋ	徹	2824_0	262	彳ㄢˊ	嬋	4645_6	425
彳ㄜˋ	澈	3814_0	345	彳ㄢˊ	蟬	5615_6	492
彳ㄜˋ	撤	5804_0	503	彳ㄢˊ	讒	0761_2	049
彳ㄜˋ	轍	5804_0	503	彳ㄢˊ	饞	8771_3	671
彳ㄜˋ	掣	2250_2	183	彳ㄢˊ	孱	7724_7	600
彳ㄜˋ	坼	4213_1	383	彳ㄢˊ	潺	3714_7	331
彳ㄞ	拆	5203_1	467	彳ㄢˊ	纏	2091_4	159
彳ㄞ	釵	8410_0	661	彳ㄢˊ	蟾	5716_1	500
彳ㄞˊ	柴	2190_4	173	彳ㄢˇ	產	0021_4	009
彳ㄞˊ	豺	2420_0	202	彳ㄢˇ	剷	0220	035
彳ㄠ	超	4780_6	435	彳ㄢˇ	鏟	8011_4	626
彳ㄠ	抄	5902_0	506	彳ㄢˇ	諂	0267_7	037
彳ㄠ	鈔	8912_0	681	彳ㄢˇ	諂	0767_7	052
彳ㄠˊ	潮	3712_0	329	彳ㄢˇ	闡	7750_6	606
彳ㄠˊ	朝	4742_0	430	彳ㄢˋ	懺	9305_0	695
彳ㄠˊ	嘲	6702_0	555	彳ㄣ	嗔	6408_1	545
彳ㄠˊ	巢	2290_4	187	彳ㄣ	琛	1719_4	130
彳ㄠˇ	吵	6902_0	562	彳ㄣˊ	塵	0021_4	010
彳ㄠˇ	炒	9982_0	709	彳ㄣˊ	辰	7123_2	567
彳ㄡ	抽	5506_0	484	彳ㄣˊ	晨	6023_2	520
彳ㄡˊ	儔	2424_1	206	彳ㄣˊ	娠	4143_2	380

注 音	字	四 角	頁 碼	注 音	字	四 角	頁 碼
ㄔㄣˊ	沈	3411_2	309	ㄔㄥˊ	誠	0365_0	039
ㄔㄣˊ	忱	9401_2	696	ㄔㄥˊ	城	4315_0	387
ㄔㄣˊ	諶	0461_1	042	ㄔㄥˊ	澄	3211_8	296
ㄔㄣˊ	臣	7171_7	574	ㄔㄥˊ	橙	4291_8	385
ㄔㄣˊ	陳	7529_6	586	ㄔㄥˊ	呈	6010_4	510
ㄔㄣˋ	讖	0365_0	040	ㄔㄥˊ	程	2691_4	235
ㄔㄣˋ	襯	3621_0	325	ㄔㄥˊ	丞	1710_3	128
ㄔㄣˋ	趁	4880_2	442	ㄔㄥˊ	承	1723_2	131
ㄔㄤ	昌	6060_0	526	ㄔㄥˊ	乘	2090_1	156
ㄔㄤ	猖	4626_0	423	ㄔㄥˊ	懲	2833_4	264
ㄔㄤ	娼	4646_0	425	ㄔㄥˇ	逞	3630_1	326
ㄔㄤ	閶	7760_6	608	ㄔㄥˇ	騁	7532_7	586
ㄔㄤˊ	常	9022_7	686	ㄔㄥˋ	秤	2194_9	176
ㄔㄤˊ	嫦	4942_7	444				
ㄔㄤˊ	償	2928_6	268				

ㄕ

注 音	字	四 角	頁 碼
ㄔㄤˊ	長	7173_2	574
ㄔㄤˊ	腸	7622_7	586
ㄔㄤˊ	嘗	9060_1	688
ㄔㄤˇ	敞	9824_0	707
ㄔㄤˇ	廠	0024_8	019
ㄔㄤˇ	厰	7124_8	569
ㄔㄤˇ	氅	9871_4	707
ㄔㄤˇ	昶	3623_0	325
ㄔㄤˇ	場	4612_7	422
ㄔㄤˋ	倡	2626_0	230
ㄔㄤˋ	唱	6606_0	550
ㄔㄤˋ	暢	5602_7	489
ㄔㄤˋ	悵	9103_2	692
ㄔㄥ	撐	5904_1	506
ㄔㄥ	撑	5905_2	506
ㄔㄥ	瞠	6901_4	562
ㄔㄥ	掌	9024_1	686
ㄔㄥ	稱	2194_5	176
ㄔㄥ	禎	4138_6	390
ㄔㄥˊ	成	5320_0	476

注 音	字	四 角	頁 碼
ㄕ	失	2503_0	217
ㄕ	施	0821_2	052
ㄕ	師	2172_7	173
ㄕ	獅	4122_7	379
ㄕ	屍	7721_2	590
ㄕ	詩	0464_1	043
ㄕ	濕	3613_3	324
ㄕ	溼	3613_3	291
ㄕ	尸	7727_0	601
ㄕ	虱	1711_0	129
ㄕ	蝨	1713_6	129
ㄕˊ	十	4000_0	352
ㄕˊ	時	6404_1	544
ㄕˊ	實	3080_6	288
ㄕˊ	石	1060_0	086
ㄕˊ	拾	5806_1	503
ㄕˊ	蝕	8573_6	665
ㄕˊ	食	8073_2	653
ㄕˊ	蒔	4464_1	410

注 音	字	四 角	頁 碼	注 音	字	四 角	頁 碼
ㄕˊ	什	2420_0	201	ㄕˋ	舐	2264_0	183
ㄕˇ	使	2520_6	220	ㄕˋ	諟	0668_1	047
ㄕˇ	始	4346_0	388	ㄕˋ	飾	8872_7	677
ㄕˇ	矢	8043_0	639	ㄕ·	匙	6180_1	535
ㄕˇ	駛	7530_0	586	ㄕㄨ	書	5060_1	456
ㄕˇ	屎	7729_4	602	ㄕㄨ	輸	5802_1	501
ㄕˇ	豕	1023_2	078	ㄕㄨ	疏	1011_3	072
ㄕˇ	史	5000_6	446	ㄕㄨ	舒	8762_2	670
ㄕˋ	式	4310_0	387	ㄕㄨ	抒	5702_2	494
ㄕˋ	市	0022_7	012	ㄕㄨ	梳	4091_3	377
ㄕˋ	是	6080_1	530	ㄕㄨ	殊	1529_0	124
ㄕˋ	試	0364_0	039	ㄕㄨ	姝	4549_0	419
ㄕˋ	士	4010_0	360	ㄕㄨ	蔬	4411_3	394
ㄕˋ	室	3010_4	270	ㄕㄨ	樞	4191_6	382
ㄕˋ	釋	2694_1	237	ㄕㄨ	紓	2792_2	257
ㄕˋ	氏	7274_0	579	ㄕㄨˊ	淑	3714_0	330
ㄕˋ	勢	4442_7	405	ㄕㄨˊ	叔	2794_0	259
ㄕˋ	世	4471_7	411	ㄕㄨˊ	孰	0441_7	041
ㄕˋ	適	3030_2	279	ㄕㄨˊ	塾	0410_4	040
ㄕˋ	示	1090_1	101	ㄕㄨˊ	贖	6488_6	548
ㄕˋ	誓	5260_1	471	ㄕㄨˇ	署	6060_4	527
ㄕˋ	事	5000_7	447	ㄕㄨˇ	屬	7722_7	597
ㄕˋ	視	3621_0	325	ㄕㄨˇ	數	5844_0	505
ㄕˋ	識	0365_0	040	ㄕㄨˇ	暑	6060_4	527
ㄕˋ	嗜	6406_1	545	ㄕㄨˇ	鼠	7771_7	609
ㄕˋ	逝	3230_2	300	ㄕㄨˇ	薯	4460_4	409
ㄕˋ	恃	9404_1	696	ㄕㄨˇ	蜀	6012_7	512
ㄕˋ	仕	2421_0	202	ㄕㄨˇ	黍	2013_2	143
ㄕˋ	侍	2424_1	205	ㄕㄨˋ	恕	4633_0	424
ㄕˋ	柿	4092_7	377	ㄕㄨˋ	束	5090_6	459
ㄕˋ	弒	4394_0	390	ㄕㄨˋ	樹	4490_0	414
ㄕˋ	噬	6801_8	561	ㄕㄨˋ	墅	6710_4	557
ㄕˋ	拭	5304_0	474	ㄕㄨˋ	術	2122_1	166
ㄕˋ	簉	8810_8	672	ㄕㄨˋ	述	3330_9	307
ㄕˋ	跂	1414_7	121	ㄕㄨˋ	數	5844_0	505

注　音	字	四　角	頁　碼	注　音	字	四　角	頁　碼
ㄕㄨˋ	曙	6606_4	550	ㄕㄚ	殺	4794_7	437
ㄕㄨˋ	倏	2723_4	243	ㄕㄚ	沙	3912_0	350
ㄕㄨˋ	庶	0023_1	016	ㄕㄚ	裟	3973_7	352
ㄕㄨˋ	漱	3718_2	332	ㄕㄚ	莎	4412_9	395
ㄕㄨˋ	豎	7710_8	588	ㄕㄚ	砂	1962_0	142
ㄕㄨˋ	戍	5320_0	476	ㄕㄚ	紗	2992_0	269
ㄕㄨㄚ	刷	7220_0	575	ㄕㄚ	鯊	3933_6	352
ㄕㄨㄚˇ	耍	1040_4	081	ㄕㄚ	痧	0012_9	006
ㄕㄨㄛ	說	0861_6	055	ㄕㄚˊ	啥	6806_4	561
ㄕㄨㄛˋ	蒴	4442_7	405	ㄕㄚˇ	傻	2624_7	230
ㄕㄨㄛˋ	碩	1168_6	107	ㄕㄚˋ	煞	2833_4	264
ㄕㄨㄛˋ	朔	8742_0	670	ㄕㄚˋ	剎	4290_0	384
ㄕㄨㄛˋ	爍	9289_4	694	ㄕㄚˋ	霎	1040_4	082
ㄕㄨㄛˋ	鑠	8219_4	658	ㄕㄜ	賒	6889_1	562
ㄕㄨㄛˋ	妁	4742_0	430	ㄕㄜ	奢	4060_4	373
ㄕㄨㄛˋ	槊	8790_4	671	ㄕㄜˊ	蛇	5311_1	476
ㄕㄨㄞ	摔	5004_3	450	ㄕㄜˊ	什	2420_0	201
ㄕㄨㄞ	衰	0073_2	030	ㄕㄜˊ	舌	2060_4	154
ㄕㄨㄞˇ	甩	7721_2	590	ㄕㄜˇ	捨	5806_4	503
ㄕㄨㄞˋ	率	0040_3	023	ㄕㄜˋ	設	0764_7	051
ㄕㄨㄞˋ	帥	2472_7	212	ㄕㄜˋ	社	3421_0	313
ㄕㄨㄞˋ	蟀	5014_3	452	ㄕㄜˋ	涉	3112_1	291
ㄕㄨㄟˇ	水	1223_0	110	ㄕㄜˋ	射	2420_0	202
ㄕㄨㄟˋ	稅	2891_6	266	ㄕㄜˋ	舍	8060_4	645
ㄕㄨㄟˋ	睡	6201_4	537	ㄕㄜˋ	攝	5104_1	463
ㄕㄨㄢ	栓	4891_4	442	ㄕㄜˋ	赦	4834_0	440
ㄕㄨㄢ	拴	5801_4	501	ㄕㄜˋ	麝	0024_1	017
ㄕㄨㄢ	閂	7710_7	588	ㄕㄞ	篩	8872_7	678
ㄕㄨㄣˇ	吮	6301_0	540	ㄕㄞˇ	骰	7724_7	600
ㄕㄨㄣˋ	順	2108_6	160	ㄕㄞˋ	曬	6101_1	532
ㄕㄨㄣˋ	瞬	6205_2	537	ㄕㄞˋ	晒	6106_0	534
ㄕㄨㄤ	雙	2040_7	150	ㄕㄟˊ	誰	0061_4	028
ㄕㄨㄤ	霜	1096_3	101	ㄕㄠ	稍	2992_7	269
ㄕㄨㄤ	孀	4146_3	380	ㄕㄠ	燒	9481_1	697
ㄕㄨㄤˇ	爽	4003_4	358	ㄕㄠ	梢	4992_7	444

注　音	字	四　角	頁　碼	注　音	字	四　角	頁　碼
ㄕㄠ	箵	8822_7	673	ㄕㄢˋ	汕	3217_0	299
ㄕㄠˊ	杓	4792_0	436	ㄕㄢˋ	繕	2896_5	267
ㄕㄠˊ	勺	2732_0	246	ㄕㄢˋ	膳	7826_5	618
ㄕㄠˊ	芍	4432_7	401	ㄕㄢˋ	訕	0267_0	037
ㄕㄠˊ	韶	0766_2	052	ㄕㄢˋ	贍	6786_1	560
ㄕㄠˇ	少	9020_0	684	ㄕㄢˋ	謆	0362_7	039
ㄕㄠˋ	哨	6902_7	562	ㄕㄢˋ	饍	8876_1	678
ㄕㄡ	收	2874_0	265	ㄕㄢˋ	鱔	2836_1	264
ㄕㄡˊ	熟	0433_1	040	ㄕㄢˋ	疝	0017_2	007
ㄕㄡˇ	手	2050_0	152	ㄕㄢˋ	掞	5908_9	506
ㄕㄡˇ	首	8060_1	644	ㄕㄣ	身	2740_0	248
ㄕㄡˇ	守	3034_2	280	ㄕㄣ	深	3719_4	332
ㄕㄡˋ	受	2040_7	149	ㄕㄣ	申	5000_6	446
ㄕㄡˋ	售	2060_1	154	ㄕㄣ	伸	2520_6	220
ㄕㄡˋ	壽	4064_1	374	ㄕㄣ	紳	2590_6	223
ㄕㄡˋ	授	5204_7	469	ㄕㄣ	砷	1560_0	125
ㄕㄡˋ	瘦	0014_7	007	ㄕㄣ	呻	6500_6	548
ㄕㄡˋ	獸	6363_4	542	ㄕㄣ	詵	0461_1	042
ㄕㄡˋ	狩	4324_2	388	ㄕㄣˊ	神	3520_6	320
ㄕㄢ	山	2277_0	184	ㄕㄣˇ	審	3060_9	285
ㄕㄢ	杉	4292_2	385	ㄕㄣˇ	嬸	4346_9	389
ㄕㄢ	删	7240_0	578	ㄕㄣˇ	哂	6106_0	534
ㄕㄢ	姍	4744_5	431	ㄕㄣˇ	瀋	3316_9	305
ㄕㄢ	衫	3222_2	299	ㄕㄣˋ	甚	4471_1	411
ㄕㄢ	跚	6714_5	558	ㄕㄣˋ	慎	9408_1	697
ㄕㄢ	煽	9382_7	695	ㄕㄣˋ	腎	7722_7	596
ㄕㄢ	珊	1714_5	130	ㄕㄣˋ	滲	3312_2	303
ㄕㄢ	舢	2247_0	183	ㄕㄣˋ	椹	4491_1	416
ㄕㄢ	羶	8051_6	641	ㄕㄣˋ	蜃	7123_6	567
ㄕㄢ	苫	4440_7	404	ㄕㄤ	商	0022_7	013
ㄕㄢˇ	閃	7780_7	614	ㄕㄤ	傷	2822_7	260
ㄕㄢˇ	陝	7423_8	583	ㄕㄤ	殤	1822_7	140
ㄕㄢˋ	善	8060_5	646	ㄕㄤ	觴	2822_7	261
ㄕㄢˋ	扇	3022_7	276	ㄕㄤˇ	賞	9080_6	690
ㄕㄢˋ	擅	5001_6	448	ㄕㄤˇ	晌	6702_0	554

注　音	字	四　角	頁　碼	注　音	字	四　角	頁　碼
ㄕㄤˋ	上	2110_0	160	ㄖㄨˋ	褥	3124_3	293
ㄕㄤˋ	尙	9022_7	686	ㄖㄨˋ	蓐	4424_3	400
ㄕㄤ•	裳	9073_2	689	ㄖㄨㄛˋ	若	4460_4	408
ㄕㄥ	生	2510_0	218	ㄖㄨㄛˋ	弱	1712_7	129
ㄕㄥ	聲	4740_1	429	ㄖㄨㄛˋ	偌	2426_4	207
ㄕㄥ	甥	2612_7	229	ㄖㄨㄟˇ	蕊	4433_3	402
ㄕㄥ	牲	2551_0	223	ㄖㄨㄟˋ	瑞	1212_7	109
ㄕㄥ	昇	6044_0	524	ㄖㄨㄟˋ	銳	8811_6	672
ㄕㄥ	笙	8810_4	672	ㄖㄨㄢˇ	阮	7121_1	565
ㄕㄥ	升	2440_0	209	ㄖㄨㄢˇ	軟	5708_2	499
ㄕㄥ	陞	7421_4	582	ㄖㄨㄢˇ	輭	5103_4	463
ㄕㄥˊ	繩	2791_7	257	ㄖㄨㄢˇ	蝡	5112_7	465
ㄕㄥˇ	省	9060_2	688	ㄖㄨㄣˋ	潤	3712_0	329
ㄕㄥˋ	盛	5320_0	478	ㄖㄨㄣˋ	閏	7710_4	588
ㄕㄥˋ	剩	2290_0	187	ㄖㄨㄥˊ	榮	9990_4	709
ㄕㄥˋ	乘	2090_1	156	ㄖㄨㄥˊ	容	3060_8	285
ㄕㄥˋ	勝	7921_4	620	ㄖㄨㄥˊ	蓉	4460_8	409
ㄕㄥˋ	賸	7928_6	620	ㄖㄨㄥˊ	鎔	8316_8	661
ㄕㄥˋ	聖	1610_4	125	ㄖㄨㄥˊ	融	1523_6	124
				ㄖㄨㄥˊ	戎	5340_0	479
				ㄖㄨㄥˊ	榕	4396_8	390

ㄖ

注　音	字	四　角	頁　碼	注　音	字	四　角	頁　碼
ㄖˋ	日	6010_0	509	ㄖㄨㄥˊ	溶	3316_8	305
ㄖˋ	馹	7630_0	587	ㄖㄨㄥˊ	絨	2395_0	198
ㄖㄨˊ	如	4640_0	424	ㄖㄨㄥˊ	熔	9386_8	696
ㄖㄨˊ	茹	4446_0	406	ㄖㄨㄥˊ	茸	4440_1	403
ㄖㄨˊ	儒	2122_7	167	ㄖㄨㄥˊ	羢	8355_0	661
ㄖㄨˊ	孺	1142_7	106	ㄖㄨㄥˇ	冗	3721_7	333
ㄖㄨˊ	濡	3112_7	291	ㄖㄜˇ	惹	4433_6	403
ㄖㄨˊ	嚅	6102_7	533	ㄖㄜˋ	熱	4433_1	402
ㄖㄨˇ	汝	3414_0	312	ㄖㄠˊ	饒	8471_1	663
ㄖㄨˇ	乳	2241_0	182	ㄖㄠˇ	擾	5104_7	464
ㄖㄨˋ	辱	7134_3	572	ㄖㄠˋ	繞	2491_1	214
ㄖㄨˋ	入	8000_0	623	ㄖㄠˋ	遶	3430_1	315
ㄖㄨˋ	溽	3114_3	292	ㄖㄡˊ	柔	1790_4	138
				ㄖㄡˊ	揉	5709_4	499

注音	字	四角	頁碼	注音	字	四角	頁碼
ㄖㄡˊ	鞣	4759_4	433	ㄗ	咨	3760_8	341
ㄖㄡˊ	蹂	6719_4	559	ㄗ	茲	8073_2	653
ㄖㄡˇ	糅	9799_4	706	ㄗ	諮	0766_8	052
ㄖㄡˋ	肉	4022_7	364	ㄗ	孜	1844_0	141
ㄖㄢˊ	然	2333_2	196	ㄗ	輜	5206_3	469
ㄖㄢˊ	燃	9383_3	695	ㄗ	錙	8216_3	658
ㄖㄢˊ	髯	7255_7	578	ㄗ	吱	6404_7	545
ㄖㄢˇ	染	3490_4	316	ㄗ	孳	8040_7	639
ㄖㄢˇ	冉	5044_7	455	ㄗ	髭	7211_1	575
ㄖㄣˊ	仁	2121_0	163	ㄗˇ	子	1740_7	134
ㄖㄣˊ	人	8000_0	621	ㄗˇ	仔	2724_7	243
ㄖㄣˇ	忍	1733_2	133	ㄗˇ	紫	2190_3	173
ㄖㄣˇ	稔	2893_2	267	ㄗˇ	梓	4094_1	378
ㄖㄣˇ	荏	4421_4	398	ㄗˇ	籽	9794_0	706
ㄖㄣˋ	任	2221_4	178	ㄗˇ	滓	3314_1	304
ㄖㄣˋ	軔	4752_0	433	ㄗˋ	自	2600_0	226
ㄖㄣˋ	認	0763_2	051	ㄗˋ	字	3040_7	282
ㄖㄣˋ	刃	1732_0	133	ㄗˋ	恣	3733_8	340
ㄖㄣˋ	賃	2280_6	186	ㄗˋ	漬	3518_6	320
ㄖㄣˋ	紉	2792_0	257	ㄗㄨ	租	2791_0	255
ㄖㄣˋ	妊	4241_4	384	ㄗㄨˊ	族	0823_4	053
ㄖㄣˋ	衽	3221_4	299	ㄗㄨˊ	足	6080_1	529
ㄖㄣˋ	軔	5702_0	494	ㄗㄨˊ	卒	0040_8	025
ㄖㄣˋ	餁	8271_4	659	ㄗㄨˊ	捽	5004_8	450
ㄖㄤˇ	壤	4013_2	362	ㄗㄨˊ	踤	6014_3	513
ㄖㄤˇ	嚷	6003_2	508	ㄗㄨˇ	組	2791_0	255
ㄖㄤˇ	攘	5003_2	450	ㄗㄨˇ	祖	3721_0	333
ㄖㄤˋ	讓	0063_2	028	ㄗㄨˇ	阻	7721_0	589
ㄖㄥˊ	仍	2722_7	242	ㄗㄨˇ	俎	8781_0	671

ㄗ

注音	字	四角	頁碼	注音	字	四角	頁碼
				ㄗㄨˇ	詛	0761_0	048
				ㄗㄨㄛˊ	昨	6801_1	560
ㄗ	姿	3740_4	340	ㄗㄨㄛˇ	左	4001_1	352
ㄗ	資	3780_6	342	ㄗㄨㄛˇ	佐	2421_1	203
ㄗ	滋	3813_2	344	ㄗㄨㄛˋ	怍	9801_1	706
				ㄗㄨㄛˋ	作	2821_1	259

注　音	字	四　角	頁　碼	注　音	字	四　角	頁　碼
ㄗㄨㄛˋ	做	2824_0	261	ㄗㄜˊ	嘖	6508_6	549
ㄗㄨㄛˋ	座	0021_4	009	ㄗㄜˊ	賾	7578_6	586
ㄗㄨㄛˋ	坐	8810_4	671	ㄗㄜˋ	昃	6028_1	520
ㄗㄨㄛˋ	柞	4891_1	442	ㄗㄜˋ	仄	7128_0	570
ㄗㄨㄛˋ	胙	7821_1	616	ㄗㄞ	災	2280_9	186
ㄗㄨㄟˇ	嘴	6102_7	533	ㄗㄞ	栽	4395_0	390
ㄗㄨㄟˋ	最	6014_7	513	ㄗㄞˇ	宰	3040_1	281
ㄗㄨㄟˋ	醉	1064_8	090	ㄗㄞˋ	在	4021_4	363
ㄗㄨㄟˋ	罪	6011_1	512	ㄗㄞˋ	再	1044_7	085
ㄗㄨㄢ	鑽	8418_6	663	ㄗㄞˋ	載	4355_0	389
ㄗㄨㄢˇ	纂	8890_3	680	ㄗㄟˊ	賊	6385_0	542
ㄗㄨㄣ	尊	8034_6	638	ㄗㄠ	遭	3530_6	322
ㄗㄨㄣ	遵	3830_4	348	ㄗㄠ	糟	9596_6	701
ㄗㄨㄣ	鐏	8874_6	678	ㄗㄠˊ	鑿	3710_9	327
ㄗㄨㄣˇ	撙	5804_6	503	ㄗㄠˇ	早	6040_0	523
ㄗㄨㄥ	宗	3090_1	289	ㄗㄠˇ	澡	3619_4	324
ㄗㄨㄥ	棕	4399_1	390	ㄗㄠˇ	棗	5090_2	459
ㄗㄨㄥ	蹤	6218_1	538	ㄗㄠˇ	蚤	7713_6	588
ㄗㄨㄥ	踪	6319_1	541	ㄗㄠˇ	藻	4419_4	396
ㄗㄨㄥ	鬃	7290_1	580	ㄗㄠˋ	躁	6619_4	551
ㄗㄨㄥ	椶	4294_7	385	ㄗㄠˋ	噪	6609_4	551
ㄗㄨㄥˇ	總	2693_0	235	ㄗㄠˋ	竈	3071_7	286
ㄗㄨㄥˇ	偬	2723_2	242	ㄗㄠˋ	灶	9481_0	697
ㄗㄨㄥˋ	縱	2898_1	268	ㄗㄠˋ	燥	9689_4	703
ㄗㄨㄥˋ	綜	2399_1	199	ㄗㄠˋ	譟	0669_4	047
ㄗㄨㄥˋ	粽	9399_1	696	ㄗㄠˋ	造	3430_6	316
ㄗㄚ	紮	4290_3	385	ㄗㄡ	鄒	2742_7	249
ㄗㄚ	匝	7171_2	573	ㄗㄡ	諏	0762_7	051
ㄗㄚ	咂	6101_2	533	ㄗㄡ	騶	7732_7	602
ㄗㄚˊ	雜	0091_4	032	ㄗㄡ	陬	7724_0	598
ㄗㄚˊ	砸	1161_2	106	ㄗㄡˇ	走	4080_1	375
ㄗㄜˊ	則	6280_0	539	ㄗㄡˋ	奏	5043_0	455
ㄗㄜˊ	澤	3614_1	324	ㄗㄡˋ	驟	7733_2	602
ㄗㄜˊ	擇	5604_1	489	ㄗㄢ	簪	8860_1	677
ㄗㄜˊ	責	5080_6	457	ㄗㄢˊ	咱	6600_0	550

注音	字	四角	頁碼
ㄗㄢˇ	攢	5408_6	482
ㄗㄢˋ	讚	0468_6	044
ㄗㄢˋ	贊	2480_6	214
ㄗㄣˇ	怎	8033_1	637
ㄗㄣˋ	譖	0166_1	034
ㄗㄤ	臟	6385_0	542
ㄗㄤ	賍	6081_4	531
ㄗㄤ	髒	7424_1	583
ㄗㄤ	臧	2325_0	196
ㄗㄤˇ	駔	7731_0	602
ㄗㄤˋ	葬	4444_1	406
ㄗㄤˋ	臟	7425_3	583
ㄗㄥ	增	4816_6	439
ㄗㄥ	憎	9806_6	706
ㄗㄥˋ	贈	6886_6	562

ㄘ

注音	字	四角	頁碼
ㄘ	疵	0011_1	004
ㄘˊ	辭	2024_1	146
ㄘˊ	詞	0762_0	049
ㄘˊ	慈	8033_3	638
ㄘˊ	磁	1863_2	141
ㄘˊ	瓷	3771_7	342
ㄘˊ	祠	3722_0	334
ㄘˊ	雌	2011_4	143
ㄘˊ	呲	6101_0	532
ㄘˇ	此	2111_0	162
ㄘˋ	次	3718_2	331
ㄘˋ	刺	5290_0	472
ㄘˋ	賜	6682_7	553
ㄘㄨ	粗	9791_0	705
ㄘㄨˊ	殂	1721_0	131
ㄘㄨˊ	徂	2721_0	240
ㄘㄨˋ	促	2628_1	231

注音	字	四角	頁碼
ㄘㄨˋ	簇	8823_4	674
ㄘㄨˋ	猝	4024_8	368
ㄘㄨˋ	蹴	6311_4	540
ㄘㄨˋ	醋	1466_1	123
ㄘㄨˋ	蹙	5380_1	479
ㄘㄨˋ	蔟	4423_4	400
ㄘㄨˋ	鏃	8813_4	672
ㄘㄨㄛ	搓	5801_1	501
ㄘㄨㄛ	蹉	6811_1	561
ㄘㄨㄛ	磋	1861_1	141
ㄘㄨㄛˊ	嵯	2871_0	265
ㄘㄨㄛˇ	脞	7821_4	616
ㄘㄨㄛˋ	錯	8416_1	662
ㄘㄨㄛˋ	挫	5801_4	501
ㄘㄨㄛˋ	措	5406_1	481
ㄘㄨㄛˋ	撮	5604_7	490
ㄘㄨㄛˋ	剉	8210_0	658
ㄘㄨㄛˋ	銼	8811_4	672
ㄘㄨㄟ	催	2221_4	178
ㄘㄨㄟ	摧	5201_4	466
ㄘㄨㄟˋ	翠	1740_8	134
ㄘㄨㄟˋ	脆	7721_2	590
ㄘㄨㄟˋ	粹	9094_8	691
ㄘㄨㄟˋ	萃	4440_8	404
ㄘㄨㄟˋ	淬	3014_8	273
ㄘㄨㄟˋ	焠	9084_8	691
ㄘㄨㄟˋ	啐	6004_8	509
ㄘㄨㄟˋ	膵	7424_8	583
ㄘㄨㄟˋ	悴	9004_8	684
ㄘㄨㄢ	竄	3071_7	286
ㄘㄨㄢ	篡	8873_3	678
ㄘㄨㄣ	村	4490_0	414
ㄘㄨㄣˊ	存	4024_7	367
ㄘㄨㄣˇ	忖	9400_0	696
ㄘㄨㄣˋ	吋	6400_0	542

注 音	字	四 角	頁 碼	注 音	字	四 角	頁 碼
ち ㄨ ㄣ ㄟ	寸	4030_0	368	ち ㄡ ㄟ	湊	3513_4	319
ち ㄨ ㄥ	聰	1613_0	127	ち ㄡ ㄟ	輳	5503_4	483
ち ㄨ ㄥ	蔥	4433_2	402	ち ㄡ ㄟ	腠	7523_4	585
ち ㄨ ㄥ	囪	2600_0	226	ち ㄢ	參	2320_2	192
ち ㄨ ㄥ	驄	7633_0	587	ち ㄢ	餐	2773_2	254
ち ㄨ ㄥ ／	從	2828_1	263	ち ㄢ	驂	7332_2	580
ち ㄨ ㄥ ／	叢	3214_7	298	ち ㄢ	澹	3813_2	344
ち ㄚ	擦	5309_1	475	ち ㄢ ／	殘	1325_3	119
ち ㄚ	搽	5409_4	482	ち ㄢ ／	慚	9202_1	693
ち ㄜ ㄟ	廁	0022_0	011	ち ㄢ ／	蠶	7113_6	565
ち ㄜ ㄟ	測	3210_0	295	ち ㄢ ㄧ	慘	9302_0	695
ち ㄜ ㄟ	冊	7744_0	604	ち ㄢ ㄟ	燦	9789_4	705
ち ㄜ ㄟ	側	2220_0	177	ち ㄢ ㄟ	璨	1719_4	130
ち ㄜ ㄟ	策	8890_2	680	ち ㄢ ㄟ	粲	2790_4	255
ち ㄜ ㄟ	惻	9200_0	693	ち ㄤ	倉	8060_7	647
ち ㄞ	猜	4522_7	419	ち ㄤ	滄	3816_7	347
ち ㄞ ／	財	6480_0	547	ち ㄤ	蒼	4460_7	409
ち ㄞ ／	裁	4375_0	389	ち ㄤ	艙	2846_7	264
ち ㄞ ／	才	4020_0	362	ち ㄤ	傖	2826_7	263
ち ㄞ ／	材	4490_0	414	ち ㄤ ／	藏	4425_3	401
ち ㄞ ㄧ	採	5209_4	470	ち ㄥ	曾	8060_6	646
ち ㄞ ㄧ	彩	2292_2	188	ち ㄥ ／	層	7726_6	601
ち ㄞ ㄧ	采	2090_4	157				
ち ㄞ ㄧ	踩	6219_4	538	厶			
ち ㄞ ㄧ	睬	6209_4	538	注 音	字	四 角	頁 碼
ち ㄞ ㄟ	蔡	4490_1	415	厶	廝	0022_1	011
ち ㄞ ㄟ	菜	4490_4	415	厶	司	1762_0	136
ち ㄠ	操	5609_4	491	厶	私	2293_0	188
ち ㄠ	糙	9491_6	698	厶	思	6033_0	520
ち ㄠ ／	曹	5560_6	486	厶	嘶	6202_1	537
ち ㄠ ／	槽	4596_6	420	厶	撕	5202_1	467
ち ㄠ ／	漕	3516_6	319	厶	絲	2299_3	190
ち ㄠ ／	嘈	6506_6	549	厶	鍶	8613_0	665
ち ㄠ ／	螬	5516_5	485	厶	斯	4282_1	384
ち ㄠ ㄧ	草	4440_6	403	厶 ㄧ	死	1021_2	074

注音	字	四角	頁碼	注音	字	四角	頁碼
ㄙˋ	四	6021_0	518	ㄙㄨㄛˇ	瑣	1918_6	142
ㄙˋ	似	2820_0	259	ㄙㄨㄛ˙	嗦	6409_3	546
ㄙˋ	寺	4034_1	368	ㄙㄨㄟ	雖	6011_4	512
ㄙˋ	俟	2323_4	194	ㄙㄨㄟ	綏	2294_4	190
ㄙˋ	肆	7570_4	586	ㄙㄨㄟ	睢	6001_4	508
ㄙˋ	嗣	6722_0	559	ㄙㄨㄟˊ	隨	7423_2	583
ㄙˋ	祀	3721_7	333	ㄙㄨㄟˊ	隋	7422_7	582
ㄙˋ	飼	8772_0	671	ㄙㄨㄟˇ	髓	7423_2	583
ㄙˋ	伺	2722_0	241	ㄙㄨㄟˋ	遂	3830_3	348
ㄙˋ	駟	7630_0	587	ㄙㄨㄟˋ	歲	2125_3	170
ㄙˋ	耜	5797_7	500	ㄙㄨㄟˋ	燧	9883_3	707
ㄙˋ	兕	7721_7	591	ㄙㄨㄟˋ	碎	1064_8	090
ㄙˋ	巳	7771_7	609	ㄙㄨㄟˋ	穗	2593_3	224
ㄙㄨ	蘇	4439_4	403	ㄙㄨㄟˋ	隧	7823_3	618
ㄙㄨ	酥	1269_4	117	ㄙㄨㄟˋ	誶	0064_8	029
ㄙㄨˊ	俗	2826_8	263	ㄙㄨㄟˋ	晬	6004_8	509
ㄙㄨˋ	訴	0263_1	036	ㄙㄨㄢ	酸	1364_7	120
ㄙㄨˋ	速	3530_9	323	ㄙㄨㄢˋ	算	8844_6	675
ㄙㄨˋ	素	5090_3	459	ㄙㄨㄢˋ	蒜	4499_1	419
ㄙㄨˋ	嗉	6509_3	549	ㄙㄨㄣ	孫	1249_3	116
ㄙㄨˋ	肅	5022_7	452	ㄙㄨㄣ	蓀	4449_3	406
ㄙㄨˋ	宿	3026_1	278	ㄙㄨㄣ	猻	4229_3	384
ㄙㄨˋ	溯	3712_0	328	ㄙㄨㄣˇ	損	5608_6	491
ㄙㄨˋ	塑	8710_4	666	ㄙㄨㄣˇ	筍	8862_7	677
ㄙㄨˋ	夙	7721_0	589	ㄙㄨㄥ	松	4893_2	442
ㄙㄨˋ	粟	1090_4	101	ㄙㄨㄥ	鬆	7293_0	580
ㄙㄨˋ	餗	8579_6	665	ㄙㄨㄥ	淞	3813_0	343
ㄙㄨˋ	觫	2529_6	223	ㄙㄨㄥˇ	聳	2840_1	264
ㄙㄨㄛ	縮	2396_1	199	ㄙㄨㄥˇ	悚	9509_6	700
ㄙㄨㄛ	嗦	6509_3	546	ㄙㄨㄥˇ	竦	0519_6	045
ㄙㄨㄛ	唆	6304_7	540	ㄙㄨㄥˋ	送	3830_3	348
ㄙㄨㄛ	簑	8873_2	678	ㄙㄨㄥˋ	宋	3090_4	290
ㄙㄨㄛˇ	所	7722_1	576	ㄙㄨㄥˋ	頌	8178_6	657
ㄙㄨㄛˇ	鎖	8918_6	681	ㄙㄨㄥˋ	誦	0762_7	051
ㄙㄨㄛˇ	索	4090_3	376	ㄙㄨㄥˋ	訟	0863_2	056

注音	字	四角	頁碼	注音	字	四角	頁碼
ㄙㄚ	撒	5804_0	503	ㄙㄤˇ	嗓	6709_4	557
ㄙㄚˇ	灑	3111_1	290	ㄙㄤˇ	顙	7198_6	575
ㄙㄚˇ	洒	3116_0	292	ㄙㄤˋ	喪	4073_2	374
ㄙㄚˋ	卅	4400_5	390	ㄙㄥ	僧	2826_6	263
ㄙㄚˋ	颯	0711_0	048				
ㄙㄜˋ	色	2771_7	253				

一

注音	字	四角	頁碼
ㄧ	一	1000_0	058
ㄧ	依	2023_2	145
ㄧ	衣	0073_2	029
ㄧ	伊	2725_7	245
ㄧ	醫	7760_1	607
ㄧ	壹	4010_8	361
ㄧ	咿	6705_7	556
ㄧ	揖	5604_1	489
ㄧ	噫	6003_6	508
ㄧ	銥	8013_2	627
ㄧ	漪	3412_1	310
ㄧˊ	怡	9306_0	695
ㄧˊ	飴	8376_0	661
ㄧˊ	誼	0361_7	039
ㄧˊ	宜	3010_7	271
ㄧˊ	疑	2748_1	250
ㄧˊ	移	2792_7	257
ㄧˊ	儀	2825_3	263
ㄧˊ	咦	6503_2	549
ㄧˊ	沂	3212_1	296
ㄧˊ	夷	5003_2	449
ㄧˊ	遺	3530_8	322
ㄧˊ	姨	4543_3	419
ㄧˊ	貽	6386_0	542
ㄧˊ	胰	7523_2	585
ㄧˊ	頤	7178_6	575
ㄧˊ	迤	3830_1	348
ㄧˊ	詒	0366_0	040

(續左欄)

注音	字	四角	頁碼
ㄙㄜˋ	瑟	1133_1	106
ㄙㄜˋ	澀	3711_1	328
ㄙㄜˋ	嗇	4060_1	372
ㄙㄜˋ	圾	4714_7	428
ㄙㄜˋ	穡	2496_1	216
ㄙㄜˋ	譅	0761_1	048
ㄙㄞ	塞	3010_4	270
ㄙㄞ	腮	7623_0	587
ㄙㄞ	鰓	2633_0	233
ㄙㄞ	顋	6138_6	535
ㄙㄞˋ	賽	3080_6	289
ㄙㄠ	搔	5703_6	495
ㄙㄠ	騷	7733_6	602
ㄙㄠ	艘	2744_7	249
ㄙㄠˇ	掃	5702_7	494
ㄙㄠˇ	嫂	4744_7	432
ㄙㄠˋ	臊	7629_4	587
ㄙㄡ	搜	5704_7	496
ㄙㄡ	颼	7721_4	591
ㄙㄡ	餿	8774_7	671
ㄙㄡˇ	叟	7740_7	603
ㄙㄡˇ	嗾	6803_4	561
ㄙㄡˋ	嗽	6708_2	557
ㄙㄢ	三	1010_1	067
ㄙㄢˇ	傘	8040_4	639
ㄙㄢˇ	糝	9392_2	696
ㄙㄢˋ	散	4824_0	439
ㄙㄣ	森	4099_4	378
ㄙㄤ	桑	7790_4	615

注　音	字	四　角	頁　碼	注　音	字	四　角	頁　碼
一ˇ	以	2810_0	259	一ˋ	屹	2871_7	265
一ˇ	已	1771_7	138	一ˋ	役	2724_7	243
一ˇ	乙	1771_0	138	一ˋ	詣	0166_1	034
一ˇ	倚	2422_1	204	一ˋ	繹	2694_1	237
一ˇ	椅	4492_1	417	一ˋ	億	2023_6	146
一ˇ	旖	0822_1	052	一ˋ	驛	7634_1	587
一ˇ	蟻	5815_3	504	一ˋ	嚙	6403_1	544
一ˋ	逸	3730_1	334	一ˋ	刈	4200_0	383
一ˋ	掖	5004_7	450	一ˋ	悒	9601_7	701
一ˋ	藝	4473_1	412	一ˋ	翳	7712_7	588
一ˋ	疫	0014_7	007	一ˋ	蜴	5612_7	492
一ˋ	裔	0022_7	015	一ˋ	軼	5503_0	483
一ˋ	挹	5601_7	488	一ˋ	饐	8471_8	663
一ˋ	翌	1710_8	129	一ㄚ	押	5605_0	490
一ˋ	毅	0724_7	048	一ㄚ	壓	7121_4	566
一ˋ	義	8055_3	642	一ㄚ	丫	8020_7	627
一ˋ	譯	0664_1	047	一ㄚ	鴨	6752_7	560
一ˋ	益	8010_7	625	一ㄚ	鴉	7722_7	596
一ˋ	議	0865_3	057	一ㄚ	椏	4191_7	382
一ˋ	抑	5702_0	494	一ㄚˊ	牙	7124_0	567
一ˋ	意	0033_6	021	一ㄚˊ	芽	4424_1	400
一ˋ	液	3014_7	273	一ㄚˊ	衙	2122_1	166
一ˋ	曳	5000_6	446	一ㄚˊ	蚜	5114_0	465
一ˋ	溢	3811_7	343	一ㄚˊ	涯	3111_4	291
一ˋ	異	6080_1	530	一ㄚˇ	亞	1010_7	071
一ˋ	翼	1780_1	138	一ㄚˇ	雅	7021_4	562
一ˋ	懿	4713_8	428	一ㄚˇ	啞	6101_7	533
一ˋ	佚	2523_0	221	一ㄚˋ	訝	0164_0	034
一ˋ	邑	6071_2	529	一ㄚˋ	氩	8011_7	627
一ˋ	易	6022_7	519	一ㄚˋ	錏	8111_7	655
一ˋ	臆	7023_6	564	一ㄚˋ	砑	1164_0	107
一ˋ	亦	0033_0	021	一ㄚˋ	迓	3130_4	294
一ˋ	縊	2891_7	267	一ㄚ˙	呀	6104_0	534
一ˋ	肄	2540_0	223	一ㄛ	唷	6002_7	508
一ˋ	憶	9003_6	684	一ㄝ	耶	1712_7	129

注　音	字	四　角	頁　碼	注　音	字	四　角	頁　碼
一ㄝ	噎	6401_8	543	一ㄠ∨	殀	1223_4	112
一ㄝ／	爺	8012_7	627	一ㄠ＼	要	1040_4	081
一ㄝ／	椰	4792_7	436	一ㄠ＼	耀	9721_4	704
一ㄝ／	揶	5702_7	494	一ㄠ＼	藥	4490_4	416
一ㄝ∨	也	4471_2	411	一ㄠ＼	葯	4492_7	417
一ㄝ∨	野	6712_2	558	一ㄠ＼	曜	6701_4	553
一ㄝ∨	冶	3316_0	305	一ㄠ＼	鑰	8812_7	672
一ㄝ＼	業	3290_4	301	一ㄠ＼	鷂	2772_7	254
一ㄝ＼	葉	4490_4	416	一ㄡ	優	2124_7	169
一ㄝ＼	頁	1080_6	094	一ㄡ	憂	1024_7	079
一ㄝ＼	夜	0024_7	017	一ㄡ	攸	2824_0	261
一ㄝ＼	腋	7024_7	564	一ㄡ	幽	2277_0	184
一ㄝ＼	饁	8471_7	663	一ㄡ	悠	2833_4	264
一ㄝ＼	謁	0662_7	046	一ㄡ	喲	6702_0	554
一ㄝ＼	謁	0462_7	043	一ㄡ／	疣	0011_4	004
一ㄞ／	崖	2221_4	179	一ㄡ／	由	5060_0	456
一ㄞ／	睚	6101_4	533	一ㄡ／	油	3516_0	319
一ㄠ	邀	3830_4	348	一ㄡ／	游	3814_7	345
一ㄠ	腰	7124_4	564	一ㄡ／	郵	2712_7	238
一ㄠ	妖	4243_4	384	一ㄡ／	尤	4301_0	386
一ㄠ	吆	6203_0	537	一ㄡ／	遊	3830_4	348
一ㄠ	夭	2043_0	152	一ㄡ／	猶	4826_1	439
一ㄠ／	遙	3730_7	339	一ㄡ／	猷	8363_4	661
一ㄠ／	肴	4022_7	366	一ㄡ／	蝣	5814_7	504
一ㄠ／	搖	5707_2	498	一ㄡ／	蚰	5516_0	485
一ㄠ／	淆	3412_7	311	一ㄡ∨	有	4022_7	365
一ㄠ／	堯	4021_1	363	一ㄡ∨	友	4004_7	359
一ㄠ／	謠	0767_2	052	一ㄡ∨	黝	6432_7	546
一ㄠ／	姚	4241_2	384	一ㄡ∨	莠	4422_7	398
一ㄠ／	爻	4040_0	369	一ㄡ＼	又	7740_0	603
一ㄠ／	瑤	1717_2	130	一ㄡ＼	右	4060_0	372
一ㄠ／	餚	8472_7	663	一ㄡ＼	佑	2426_0	206
一ㄠ／	窯	3033_1	280	一ㄡ＼	幼	2472_7	211
一ㄠ∨	咬	6004_8	508	一ㄡ＼	誘	0262_7	036
一ㄠ∨	窈	3072_7	286	一ㄡ＼	囿	6022_7	520

注音	字	四角	頁碼	注音	字	四角	頁碼
一ㄡˋ	柚	4596_0	420	一ㄢˇ	衍	2122_1	166
一ㄡˋ	宥	3022_7	275	一ㄢˇ	儼	2624_8	230
一ㄡˋ	鈾	8516_0	664	一ㄢˇ	掩	5401_6	480
一ㄡˋ	鼬	7571_6	586	一ㄢˇ	揜	5804_6	503
一ㄢ	煙	9181_4	693	一ㄢˇ	剡	9280_0	694
一ㄢ	烟	9680_0	702	一ㄢˇ	魘	7121_3	566
一ㄢ	菸	4423_3	400	一ㄢˇ	扊	8044_6	640
一ㄢ	淹	3411_6	310	一ㄢˋ	堰	4111_4	379
一ㄢ	焉	1032_7	080	一ㄢˋ	燕	4433_1	402
一ㄢ	醃	1461_6	122	一ㄢˋ	驗	7838_6	619
一ㄢ	闍	7771_6	609	一ㄢˋ	宴	3040_4	282
一ㄢ	咽	6600_0	550	一ㄢˋ	豔	2411_7	200
一ㄢ	奄	4071_6	374	一ㄢˋ	嚥	6403_1	544
一ㄢ	湮	3111_4	291	一ㄢˋ	硯	1661_0	128
一ㄢ	嫣	4142_7	380	一ㄢˋ	唁	6006_1	509
一ㄢ	胭	7620_0	586	一ㄢˋ	雁	7121_4	566
一ㄢˊ	言	0060_1	026	一ㄢˋ	懨	9103_4	692
一ㄢˊ	顏	0128_6	033	一ㄢˋ	靨	7173_2	575
一ㄢˊ	研	1164_0	107	一ㄢˋ	厭	7123_4	567
一ㄢˊ	延	1240_1	115	一ㄢˋ	讞	0363_4	039
一ㄢˊ	炎	9080_9	691	一ㄢˋ	諺	0062_2	028
一ㄢˊ	鹽	7810_7	616	一ㄢˋ	晏	6040_4	523
一ㄢˊ	沿	3716_1	331	一ㄢˋ	嚥	6403_1	544
一ㄢˊ	癌	0017_2	007	一ㄢˋ	讌	0463_1	043
一ㄢˊ	巖	2224_8	182	一ㄣ	因	6043_0	524
一ㄢˊ	簷	8826_1	674	一ㄣ	音	0060_1	027
一ㄢˊ	妍	4144_0	380	一ㄣ	殷	2724_7	244
一ㄢˊ	閻	7777_7	613	一ㄣ	瘖	0016_1	007
一ㄢˊ	檐	4796_1	437	一ㄣ	茵	4460_0	408
一ㄢˊ	筵	8840_1	675	一ㄣ	陰	7823_1	617
一ㄢˊ	蜒	5214_1	471	一ㄣ	姻	4640_0	425
一ㄢˊ	嚴	6621_7	551	一ㄣ	愔	9006_1	684
一ㄢˊ	礦	1664_8	128	一ㄣ	慇	2733_4	247
一ㄢˇ	演	3318_6	305	一ㄣ	裀	3620_0	325
一ㄢˇ	眼	6703_2	555	一ㄣˊ	銀	8713_2	668

注　音	字	四　角	頁　碼
ㄧㄣˊ	吟	6802_7	561
ㄧㄣˊ	淫	3211_4	296
ㄧㄣˊ	垠	4713_2	427
ㄧㄣˊ	誾	7760_1	607
ㄧㄣˊ	嚚	6666_1	553
ㄧㄣˇ	引	1220_0	110
ㄧㄣˇ	飲	8778_2	671
ㄧㄣˇ	隱	7223_7	577
ㄧㄣˇ	癮	0013_7	006
ㄧㄣˇ	蚓	5210_0	471
ㄧㄣˋ	印	7772_0	609
ㄧㄣˋ	蔭	4423_1	400
ㄧㄣˋ	廕	0023_1	016
ㄧㄤ	秧	2593_0	224
ㄧㄤ	央	5003_0	449
ㄧㄤ	鞅	4553_0	419
ㄧㄤ	鴦	5032_7	453
ㄧㄤ	殃	1523_0	124
ㄧㄤˊ	楊	4692_7	427
ㄧㄤˊ	陽	7622_7	786
ㄧㄤˊ	揚	5602_7	489
ㄧㄤˊ	洋	3815_1	345
ㄧㄤˊ	羊	8050_1	641
ㄧㄤˊ	煬	9682_7	702
ㄧㄤˊ	烊	9885_1	707
ㄧㄤˊ	佯	2825_1	263
ㄧㄤˊ	瘍	0012_7	006
ㄧㄤˊ	徉	2825_1	263
ㄧㄤˇ	養	8073_2	653
ㄧㄤˇ	仰	2722_0	241
ㄧㄤˇ	氧	8051_7	642
ㄧㄤˇ	癢	0013_2	006
ㄧㄤˋ	樣	4893_2	443
ㄧㄤˋ	怏	9503_0	700
ㄧㄤˋ	恙	8033_1	637
ㄧㄤˋ	漾	3813_2	344
ㄧㄥ	鷹	0032_7	021
ㄧㄥ	鶯	9932_7	708
ㄧㄥ	嬰	6640_4	552
ㄧㄥ	瑛	1413_1	121
ㄧㄥ	櫻	4694_4	427
ㄧㄥ	英	4453_0	407
ㄧㄥ	鸚	6742_7	560
ㄧㄥ	纓	2694_4	237
ㄧㄥ	罌	6677_4	553
ㄧㄥ	攖	5604_4	490
ㄧㄥ	膺	0022_7	016
ㄧㄥˊ	贏	0021_7	011
ㄧㄥˊ	迎	3730_2	334
ㄧㄥˊ	盈	1710_7	128
ㄧㄥˊ	瑩	9910_3	708
ㄧㄥˊ	瀛	3011_7	272
ㄧㄥˊ	縈	9990_3	709
ㄧㄥˊ	蠅	5711_7	499
ㄧㄥˊ	螢	9913_6	708
ㄧㄥˊ	瀅	3911_3	350
ㄧㄥˊ	楹	4791_7	436
ㄧㄥˊ	營	9960_6	709
ㄧㄥˊ	熒	9980_9	709
ㄧㄥˇ	影	6292_2	539
ㄧㄥˋ	應	0023_1	016
ㄧㄥˋ	映	6503_0	548
ㄧㄥˋ	硬	1164_6	107

ㄨ

注　音	字	四　角	頁　碼
ㄨ	巫	1010_8	072
ㄨ	污	3112_7	291
ㄨ	汙	3114_0	292
ㄨ	誣	0161_8	033

注　音	字	四　角	頁　碼	注　音	字	四　角	頁　碼
ㄨ	嗚	6702_7	555	ㄨㄚ	哇	6401_4	543
ㄨ	屋	7721_4	591	ㄨㄚ	窪	3011_4	272
ㄨ	烏	2732_7	246	ㄨㄚ	漥	3311_4	303
ㄨ	鎢	8712_7	668	ㄨㄚ	蛙	5411_4	482
ㄨˊ	無	8033_1	633	ㄨㄚ	媧	4742_7	431
ㄨˊ	吳	2643_0	233	ㄨㄚˊ	娃	4441_4	404
ㄨˊ	吾	1060_1	088	ㄨㄚˇ	瓦	1071_7	093
ㄨˊ	梧	4196_1	382	ㄨㄚˋ	襪	3425_3	314
ㄨˊ	蕪	4433_1	402	ㄨㄚˋ	袜	3529_0	321
ㄨˊ	蜈	5613_4	492	ㄨㄚ・	哇	6401_4	543
ㄨˊ	鼯	7171_6	574	ㄨㄛ	窩	3022_7	276
ㄨˊ	毋	7755_0	607	ㄨㄛ	渦	3712_7	329
ㄨˇ	午	8040_0	639	ㄨㄛ	倭	2224_4	180
ㄨˇ	五	1010_7	070	ㄨㄛˇ	我	2355_0	197
ㄨˇ	武	1314_0	118	ㄨㄛˋ	臥	7370_0	581
ㄨˇ	舞	8025_1	632	ㄨㄛˋ	握	5701_4	493
ㄨˇ	伍	2121_7	164	ㄨㄛˋ	幄	4721_4	428
ㄨˇ	忤	9804_0	706	ㄨㄛˋ	沃	3213_4	297
ㄨˇ	侮	2825_7	263	ㄨㄛˋ	渥	3711_4	328
ㄨˇ	鵡	1712_7	129	ㄨㄛˋ	齷	2771_4	253
ㄨˇ	仵	2824_0	261	ㄨㄞ	歪	1010_1	069
ㄨˇ	廡	0023_1	016	ㄨㄞˋ	外	2320_0	191
ㄨˋ	物	2852_0	250	ㄨㄟ	威	5320_0	477
ㄨˋ	誤	0663_4	046	ㄨㄟ	煨	9683_2	702
ㄨˋ	塢	4712_7	427	ㄨㄟ	隈	7623_2	587
ㄨˋ	隖	7727_7	596	ㄨㄟˊ	危	2721_2	240
ㄨˋ	勿	2722_0	241	ㄨㄟˊ	惟	9001_4	683
ㄨˋ	霧	1022_7	076	ㄨㄟˊ	微	2824_0	261
ㄨˋ	務	1722_7	131	ㄨㄟˊ	圍	6050_6	525
ㄨˋ	兀	1021_0	073	ㄨㄟˊ	違	3430_4	315
ㄨˋ	悟	9106_1	692	ㄨㄟˊ	唯	6001_4	508
ㄨˋ	晤	6106_1	534	ㄨㄟˊ	維	2091_4	158
ㄨˋ	寤	3026_1	278	ㄨㄟˊ	桅	4791_2	436
ㄨˋ	鶩	1832_7	140	ㄨㄟˊ	帷	4021_4	363
ㄨㄚ	挖	5301_7	473	ㄨㄟˊ	闈	7750_6	606

注音	字	四角	頁碼	注音	字	四角	頁碼
ㄨㄟˊ	幃	4425_6	401	ㄨㄢ	豌	1311_2	118
ㄨㄟˊ	韋	4050_6	371	ㄨㄢˊ	完	3021_1	274
ㄨㄟˇ	委	2040_4	149	ㄨㄢˊ	玩	1111_1	102
ㄨㄟˇ	尾	7721_4	591	ㄨㄢˊ	丸	4001_7	353
ㄨㄟˇ	緯	2495_6	215	ㄨㄢˊ	頑	1128_6	106
ㄨㄟˇ	煒	9485_6	697	ㄨㄢˊ	紈	2491_7	215
ㄨㄟˇ	娓	4741_4	430	ㄨㄢˇ	晚	6701_6	553
ㄨㄟˇ	諉	0264_4	037	ㄨㄢˇ	婉	4341_2	388
ㄨㄟˇ	葦	4450_6	407	ㄨㄢˇ	挽	5701_6	493
ㄨㄟˇ	萎	4440_4	403	ㄨㄢˇ	碗	1361_2	120
ㄨㄟˇ	偉	2425_6	206	ㄨㄢˇ	浣	3311_1	303
ㄨㄟˇ	猥	4623_2	423	ㄨㄢˇ	宛	3021_2	274
ㄨㄟˇ	韙	6480_4	548	ㄨㄢˇ	腕	7321_2	580
ㄨㄟˋ	蔚	4424_0	400	ㄨㄢˇ	綰	2397_7	199
ㄨㄟˋ	為	3402_7	307	ㄨㄢˇ	輓	5701_6	493
ㄨㄟˋ	未	5090_0	458	ㄨㄢˇ	盌	2710_7	238
ㄨㄟˋ	位	2021_8	144	ㄨㄢˋ	萬	4442_7	405
ㄨㄟˋ	味	6509_0	549	ㄨㄢˋ	惋	9301_2	695
ㄨㄟˋ	衛	2122_1	167	ㄨㄣ	溫	3611_7	323
ㄨㄟˋ	慰	7433_0	584	ㄨㄣ	瘟	0011_7	004
ㄨㄟˋ	胃	6022_7	520	ㄨㄣˊ	文	0040_0	022
ㄨㄟˋ	魏	2641_3	233	ㄨㄣˊ	聞	7740_1	603
ㄨㄟˋ	尉	7420_0	582	ㄨㄣˊ	蚊	5014_0	452
ㄨㄟˋ	畏	6073_2	529	ㄨㄣˊ	紋	2094_0	160
ㄨㄟˋ	僞	2422_7	204	ㄨㄣˊ	穩	2293_7	189
ㄨㄟˋ	謂	0662_7	046	ㄨㄣˇ	吻	6702_0	554
ㄨㄟˋ	餵	8673_2	666	ㄨㄣˇ	刎	2220_0	177
ㄨㄟˋ	喂	6603_2	550	ㄨㄣˇ	脗	7726_2	600
ㄨㄟˋ	猬	4622_7	422	ㄨㄣˋ	問	7760_7	608
ㄨㄟˋ	蝟	5612_7	492	ㄨㄣˋ	汶	3014_0	273
ㄨㄟˋ	餧	8274_4	659	ㄨㄣˋ	抆	5004_0	450
ㄨㄢ	灣	3212_7	297	ㄨㄣˋ	紊	0090_3	031
ㄨㄢ	彎	2220_7	178	ㄨㄤ	汪	3111_4	291
ㄨㄢ	蜿	5311_2	476	ㄨㄤˊ	王	1010_4	069
ㄨㄢ	剜	3220_0	299	ㄨㄤˊ	亡	0071_0	029

注 音	字	四 角	頁 碼	注 音	字	四 角	頁 碼
ㄨㄤˇ	網	2792_0	257	ㄩˊ	腴	7723_7	598
ㄨㄤˇ	往	2021_4	144	ㄩˊ	娛	4643_4	425
ㄨㄤˇ	惘	9702_0	703	ㄩˊ	禺	6022_7	520
ㄨㄤˇ	枉	4191_4	381	ㄩˊ	於	0823_3	053
ㄨㄤˇ	罔	7722_0	594	ㄩˊ	隅	7622_7	586
ㄨㄤˋ	望	0710_4	048	ㄩˊ	輿	7780_1	614
ㄨㄤˋ	旺	6101_4	533	ㄩˊ	虞	2123_4	168
ㄨㄤˋ	忘	0033_1	021	ㄩˊ	臾	7743_7	604
ㄨㄤˋ	妄	0040_4	023	ㄩˊ	圩	4114_0	379
ㄨㄥ	翁	8012_7	627	ㄩˊ	歟	7788_2	615
ㄨㄥˋ	甕	0071_7	029	ㄩˊ	舁	7744_7	606
				ㄩˇ	與	7780_1	613

ㄩ

注 音	字	四 角	頁 碼	注 音	字	四 角	頁 碼
				ㄩˇ	雨	1022_7	075
ㄩ	淤	3813_3	344	ㄩˇ	宇	3040_1	281
ㄩ	迂	3130_4	294	ㄩˇ	語	0166_1	034
ㄩˊ	于	1040_0	081	ㄩˇ	羽	1712_0	129
ㄩˊ	俞	8022_1	629	ㄩˇ	嶼	2778_1	254
ㄩˊ	逾	3830_2	348	ㄩˇ	圄	6060_1	527
ㄩˊ	狳	4829_4	440	ㄩˇ	圉	6040_1	523
ㄩˊ	踰	6812_1	561	ㄩˇ	傴	2121_6	164
ㄩˊ	愉	9802_1	706	ㄩˋ	御	2722_0	241
ㄩˊ	渝	3812_1	343	ㄩˋ	郁	4722_7	429
ㄩˊ	榆	4892_1	442	ㄩˋ	域	4315_0	388
ㄩˊ	覦	8621_0	665	ㄩˋ	獄	4323_4	388
ㄩˊ	蝓	5812_1	504	ㄩˋ	嫗	4141_6	380
ㄩˊ	魚	2733_6	247	ㄩˋ	芋	4440_1	403
ㄩˊ	漁	3713_6	330	ㄩˋ	禦	2790_1	255
ㄩˊ	予	1720_2	130	ㄩˋ	鬱	4472_2	412
ㄩˊ	盂	1010_7	071	ㄩˋ	慾	8733_8	670
ㄩˊ	余	8090_4	654	ㄩˋ	毓	8051_3	641
ㄩˊ	餘	8879_4	679	ㄩˋ	譽	7760_1	607
ㄩˊ	愚	6033_2	522	ㄩˋ	浴	3816_8	347
ㄩˊ	揄	5802_1	501	ㄩˋ	育	0022_7	013
ㄩˊ	諛	0763_7	051	ㄩˋ	預	1128_6	105
				ㄩˋ	寓	3042_7	283

注 音	字	四 角	頁 碼	注 音	字	四 角	頁 碼
ㄩˋ	豫	1723_2	132	ㄩㄢˊ	園	6023_2	520
ㄩˋ	煜	9681_8	702	ㄩㄢˊ	原	7129_6	570
ㄩˋ	欲	8768_2	670	ㄩㄢˊ	源	3119_6	293
ㄩˋ	玉	1010_3	069	ㄩㄢˊ	員	6080_6	530
ㄩˋ	鈺	8111_3	655	ㄩㄢˊ	援	5204_7	469
ㄩˋ	癒	0013_1	006	ㄩㄢˊ	圓	6080_6	530
ㄩˋ	喻	6802_1	561	ㄩㄢˊ	緣	2793_2	258
ㄩˋ	遇	3630_2	326	ㄩㄢˊ	袁	4073_2	374
ㄩˋ	籲	8828_6	674	ㄩㄢˊ	媛	4244_7	384
ㄩˋ	馭	7734_0	603	ㄩㄢˊ	沅	3111_1	290
ㄩˋ	禺	6042_7	524	ㄩㄢˊ	垣	4111_6	379
ㄩˋ	諭	0862_1	056	ㄩㄢˊ	猿	4423_2	400
ㄩˋ	聿	5000_7	447	ㄩㄢˊ	螈	5119_6	465
ㄩˋ	裕	3826_8	347	ㄩㄢˊ	轅	5403_2	480
ㄩˋ	鷸	1722_7	131	ㄩㄢˇ	遠	3430_3	315
ㄩˋ	愈	8033_2	638	ㄩㄢˋ	院	7321_1	580
ㄩˋ	遹	3730_2	337	ㄩㄢˋ	怨	2733_1	247
ㄩˋ	飫	8373_4	659	ㄩㄢˋ	願	7128_6	570
ㄩㄝ	約	2792_0	257	ㄩㄢˋ	愿	7133_9	572
ㄩㄝ	曰	6010_0	510	ㄩㄢˋ	苑	4421_2	397
ㄩㄝˋ	月	7722_0	592	ㄩㄣ	暈	6050_6	525
ㄩㄝˋ	岳	7277_2	579	ㄩㄣˊ	雲	1073_1	093
ㄩㄝˋ	越	4380_5	389	ㄩㄣˊ	勻	2712_0	238
ㄩㄝˋ	閱	7721_6	591	ㄩㄣˊ	云	1073_1	093
ㄩㄝˋ	躍	6711_4	558	ㄩㄣˊ	芸	4473_1	412
ㄩㄝˋ	悅	9801_6	706	ㄩㄣˊ	耘	5193_1	465
ㄩㄝˋ	嶽	2223_4	179	ㄩㄣˇ	允	2321_0	193
ㄩㄝˋ	粵	2620_7	229	ㄩㄣˇ	隕	7628_6	587
ㄩㄝˋ	鉞	8315_0	660	ㄩㄣˇ	殞	1628_6	128
ㄩㄢ	冤	3041_3	282	ㄩㄣˋ	運	3730_4	338
ㄩㄢ	淵	3210_0	296	ㄩㄣˋ	慍	9601_7	701
ㄩㄢ	冤	3741_3	340	ㄩㄣˋ	韻	0668_6	047
ㄩㄢ	鴛	2732_7	247	ㄩㄣˋ	孕	1740_7	134
ㄩㄢ	鳶	4332_7	388	ㄩㄣˋ	蘊	4491_7	417
ㄩㄢˊ	元	1021_1	073	ㄩㄣˋ	熨	7480_9	584

注 音	字	四 角	頁 碼
ㄩㄣˋ	醞	1661_7	128
ㄩㄥ	傭	2022_7	145
ㄩㄥ	庸	0022_7	015
ㄩㄥ	壅	0010_7	002
ㄩㄥ	鏞	8012_7	627
ㄩㄥ	慵	9002_7	684
ㄩㄥ	雍	0021_4	009
ㄩㄥ	雝	0071_4	029
ㄩㄥˊ	喁	6602_7	550
ㄩㄥˇ	永	3023_2	276
ㄩㄥˇ	泳	3313_2	303
ㄩㄥˇ	詠	0363_2	039
ㄩㄥˇ	咏	6303_2	540
ㄩㄥˇ	勇	1742_7	134
ㄩㄥˇ	擁	5001_4	448
ㄩㄥˇ	甫	1722_7	131
ㄩㄥˇ	涌	3712_7	329
ㄩㄥˇ	臃	7021_4	563
ㄩㄥˇ	湧	3712_7	329
ㄩㄥˇ	蛹	5712_7	499
ㄩㄥˇ	踴	6712_7	558
ㄩㄥˇ	踊	6712_7	558
ㄩㄥˋ	用	7722_0	592
ㄩㄥˋ	佣	2722_0	241

ㄚ

注 音	字	四 角	頁 碼
ㄚ	阿	7122_0	566
ㄚ·	啊	6102_0	533

ㆤ

注 音	字	四 角	頁 碼
ㆤ	喔	6701_4	553
ㆤˊ	哦	6305_0	540

ㄜ

注 音	字	四 角	頁 碼
ㄜ	婀	4142_0	380
ㄜˊ	額	3168_6	295
ㄜˊ	蛾	5315_0	476
ㄜˊ	娥	4345_0	388
ㄜˊ	峨	2375_0	197
ㄜˊ	鵝	2752_7	251
ㄜˊ	訛	0461_0	042
ㄜˊ	硪	1365_0	120
ㄜˋ	惡	1033_1	080
ㄜˋ	厄	7121_2	566
ㄜˋ	愕	9602_7	702
ㄜˋ	扼	5101_2	461
ㄜˋ	顎	6128_6	535
ㄜˋ	餓	8375_0	661
ㄜˋ	呃	6101_2	533
ㄜˋ	尊	4420_7	397
ㄜˋ	鄂	6722_7	559
ㄜˋ	鶚	6722_7	559
ㄜˋ	諤	0662_7	046
ㄜˋ	阨	7121_2	566
ㄜˋ	遏	3630_2	326
ㄜˋ	鱷	2131_6	172
ㄜˋ	俄	2325_0	196
ㄜˋ	鍔	8612_7	665
ㄜˋ	軛	5101_2	461
ㄜˋ	閼	7723_3	598

ㄞ

注 音	字	四 角	頁 碼
ㄞ	哀	0073_2	030
ㄞ	埃	4313_4	387
ㄞ	哎	6404_0	544
ㄞ	挨	5303_4	474

注　音	字	四　角	頁　碼
ㄞˊ	捱	5101_4	461
ㄞˊ	騃	7333_4	581
ㄞˇ	矮	8244_4	658
ㄞˇ	靄	1062_7	090
ㄞˇ	藹	4462_7	410
ㄞˋ	愛	2024_7	146
ㄞˋ	艾	4440_0	403
ㄞˋ	礙	1768_1	137
ㄞˋ	隘	7821_7	617
ㄞˋ	曖	6204_7	537
ㄞ·	唉	6303_4	540

ㄠ

注　音	字	四　角	頁　碼
ㄠ	凹	7777_0	611
ㄠ	坳	4412_7	394
ㄠˊ	敖	5824_0	505
ㄠˊ	熬	5833_4	505
ㄠˊ	獒	5843_0	505
ㄠˊ	遨	3830_4	348
ㄠˊ	驁	5832_7	505
ㄠˇ	媼	4641_7	425
ㄠˇ	襖	3723_4	334
ㄠˋ	奧	2743_0	249
ㄠˋ	澳	3712_7	330
ㄠˋ	懊	9703_4	704
ㄠˋ	噢	6703_4	556
ㄠˋ	傲	2824_0	261

ㄡ

注　音	字	四　角	頁　碼
ㄡ	歐	7778_2	613
ㄡ	毆	7774_7	611
ㄡ	甌	7171_7	574
ㄡ	慪	9101_6	692

注　音	字	四　角	頁　碼
ㄡ	謳	0161_6	033
ㄡ	鷗	7772_7	610
ㄡˇ	偶	2622_7	230
ㄡˇ	嘔	6101_6	533
ㄡˇ	耦	5692_7	492
ㄡˇ	藕	4492_7	417
ㄡˋ	漚	3111_6	291

ㄢ

注　音	字	四　角	頁　碼
ㄢ	庵	0021_6	010
ㄢ	諳	0066_1	029
ㄢ	安	3040_4	281
ㄢ	氨	8041_7	639
ㄢ	菴	4471_6	411
ㄢ	銨	8314_4	660
ㄢ	鞍	4354_4	389
ㄢ	鵪	4772_7	434
ㄢˇ	俺	2421_6	204
ㄢˋ	案	3090_4	290
ㄢˋ	按	5304_4	474
ㄢˋ	岸	2224_1	180
ㄢˋ	暗	6006_1	509
ㄢˋ	黯	6036_1	522
ㄢˋ	闇	7760_1	607

ㄣ

注　音	字	四　角	頁　碼
ㄣ	恩	6033_0	521
ㄣ	嗯	6603_3	550

ㄤ

注　音	字	四　角	頁　碼
ㄤ	肮	7021_7	563
ㄤ	腤	7421_6	582

注　音	字	四　角	頁　碼
ㄤˊ	昂	6072_7	529
ㄤˋ	盎	5010_7	451

ㄦ

注　音	字	四　角	頁　碼
ㄦˊ	而	1022_7	075
ㄦˊ	兒	7721_7	591
ㄦˇ	爾	1022_7	076
ㄦˇ	耳	1040_0	081
ㄦˇ	餌	8174_0	657
ㄦˇ	邇	3130_2	294
ㄦˋ	二	1010_0	063
ㄦˋ	貳	4380_0	389

現代漢英詞典

原校訂者◆王雲五

編者◆王學哲

發行人◆王學哲

總編輯◆方鵬程

校閱◆方文鴻

編校◆趙佩芳　侯儀玲　陳惠文

校對◆葉幗英　徐意涵　吳素慧

美術設計◆江美芳

出版發行：臺灣商務印書館股份有限公司

台北市重慶南路一段三十七號

電話：(02)2371-3712

讀者服務專線：0800056196

郵撥：0000165-1

網路書店：www. cptw. com. tw

E-mail：cptw@cptw. com. tw

網址：www. cptw. com. tw

局版北市業字第 993 號

初版一刷：2006 年 11 月

定價：新台幣 650 元

ISBN 978-957-05-2109-2

現代漢英詞典 ／王學哲編著 . -- 初版 . -- 臺北市：
臺灣商務，2006[民95]
　面：　　公分 --
參考書目；面
ISBN 978-957-05-2109-2（精裝）

1.中國語言－字典，辭典－英國語言

805.133　　　　　　　　　　　95018858

讀者回函卡

感謝您對本館的支持，為加強對您的服務，請填妥此卡，免付郵資寄回，可隨時收到本館最新出版訊息，及享受各種優惠。

姓名：＿＿＿＿＿＿＿＿＿＿＿＿＿＿＿ 性別：□男 □女

出生日期：＿＿＿年＿＿＿月＿＿＿日

職業：□學生 □公務（含軍警） □家管 □服務 □金融 □製造
　　　□資訊 □大眾傳播 □自由業 □農漁牧 □退休 □其他

學歷：□高中以下（含高中） □大專 □研究所（含以上）

地址：□□□＿＿＿＿＿＿＿＿＿＿＿＿＿＿＿＿＿
＿＿＿＿＿＿＿＿＿＿＿＿＿＿＿＿＿＿＿＿＿＿＿

電話：（H）＿＿＿＿＿＿＿＿＿ （O）＿＿＿＿＿＿＿

E-mail:
＿＿＿＿＿＿＿＿＿＿＿＿＿＿＿＿＿＿＿＿＿＿＿

購買書名：＿＿＿＿＿＿＿＿＿＿＿＿＿＿＿＿

您從何處得知本書？

　　□書店 □報紙廣告 □報紙專欄 □雜誌廣告 □DM廣告
　　□傳單 □親友介紹 □電視廣播 □其他

您對本書的意見？（A/滿意 B/尚可 C/需改進）

　　內容＿＿＿編輯＿＿＿校對＿＿＿翻譯＿＿＿
　　封面設計＿＿＿價格＿＿＿其他＿＿＿＿＿＿＿

您的建議：＿＿＿＿＿＿＿＿＿＿＿＿＿＿＿＿＿
＿＿＿＿＿＿＿＿＿＿＿＿＿＿＿＿＿＿＿＿＿＿＿
＿＿＿＿＿＿＿＿＿＿＿＿＿＿＿＿＿＿＿＿＿＿＿

臺灣商務印書館

台北市重慶南路一段三十七號　電話：（02）23713712轉分機50～57
讀者服務專線：0800056196　傳真：（02）23710274．23701091
郵撥：0000165-1號　E-mail：cptw@cptw.com.tw
網址：www.cptw.com.tw

100臺北市重慶南路一段37號

臺灣商務印書館　收

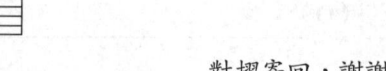

對摺寄回，謝謝！

傳統現代　並翼而翔

Flying with the wings of tradition and modernity.